Books by
Carole Cummings

The Wolf's-Own Series:
Wolf Ascendant
Raven Inconjunct

Sonata Form

Blue on Black

The Aisling Trilogy:
Guardian
Dream
Beloved Son

Don't Fear the (Not Really Grim) Reaper

The Queen's Librarian

WOLF ASCENDANT

WOLF'S-OWN – PART ONE

CAROLE CUMMINGS

Forest Path Books

COPYRIGHT INFORMATION

"But I also have to say, for the umpty-umpth time, that life isn't fair. It's just fairer than death, that's all."

— William Goldman, ***The Princess Bride***

WOLF ASCENDANT

WOLF'S-OWN — PART ONE

- Book One -

GHOST

1

It was, Malick decided, the braid. Snaking between the blades of shoulders set just wide enough, and sweeping down the pleasing taper of the torso. Capricious flickers of smoking oil lamps wove a roseate gleam through sleek chestnut plaits, and…just. Yeah.

The bound tail nearly swept the ground. Malick had never seen one so long. Those who wore them generally didn't live long enough to grow them to such a length.

This one must be close to twenty—ancient for a Ghost.

A messy, tangled fringe every now and then fell over the man's brow, obscuring his eyes. Incongruous enough to the otherwise neat picture he presented to make Malick squint through the gloom of the Girou's public floor, calculating.

Pretty, this Ghost. Not-quite-olive skin and angular face. The pleasingly masculine build set a nice contrast to the more delicate composition of high cheekbones, sharp nose, and jutting chin. Relaxed pose. Hands open and at his sides. Clearly trying to look approachable for the whores who were disposed to ignoring the braid in favor of offered koin. It wasn't quite working.

Probably it was the glower. And possibly the don't fuck with me attitude that practically oozed from it.

Malick smiled. "Heart's in his eyes, this one." That's why he hides behind that fringe.

"What's that, love?"

Malick spared a short glance for the chippy on his knee.

Her dark eyes were poppy-soft and kohl-lined. A languid smile tipped at her plump lips as she slicked small, warm fingers through the hair at Malick's nape, and took a delicate sip of gooseberry wine. She batted her lashes over the rim of her cup.

Damn, and Malick had already paid for her, too.

He returned the girl's smile with sincere regret. "Nothing, um…" He paused. What was her name again? Some kind of fruit or flower—

Cherry? Blossom? Cherry-blossom? Didn't matter. "Sorry, love, but we'll have to continue another time. Something more important just came up."

With a cheeky pat to the girl's hip—eh, too skinny anyway—Malick shifted his legs just enough to compel her to gain her feet. Her soft eyes hardened. Malick forestalled what was sure to be some scathing commentary with a charming grin before he drained his cup.

"Keep your fee, m'dear." He chucked his cards facedown on the table with a nod to the other players, and stood. "Your company alone this evening has been worth every koin." He collected his small pile of winnings, dropping an extra bit of silver into the kitty and then another for the dealer. With a flourish that was entirely unnecessary but pleasingly theatrical—at least to him—Malick swept gentle fingers through the raven curls at the girl's temple, behind her ear, and came up with another bit of silver; he held it between his fingers in front of her nose. "Next time, eh?"

He waited only long enough for her to snatch the koin with a glare before he sauntered away, eyes already narrowed through the gloom, fixed on his target. His heart was thumping a little more quickly than it should do. It was definitely the braid. Well, the braid was a good part of it, anyway. The face and build certainly didn't hurt. And with that heart-hungry look in his eyes, the man was a walking wet dream come to glorious life.

Untouchable or no, Malick couldn't help wondering what all that thick hair would look like unbound and spread across fine linen sheets. A smile curled at his mouth. It didn't count as slavering if it didn't actually dribble out, right?

A jostle to his ribs brought Malick back, and he suppressed a growl. Game Night at the Girou had brought the crowds, as usual. The smell of sweat and tobacco curled in his nostrils, the thick brume of poppy smoke enough by itself to turn him stupid, if he stayed too long. Good for business, Umeia would tell him. Kept the riffraff in line and the spenders spending.

No doujoun in the motley mix, though; Malick had paid quite a lot to make sure none of the city's guard would interfere tonight. Even so, most of the Girou's patrons gave the Ghost his own bubble of space. Only looking quickly enough to track his place in the room, his proximity to them, then glancing away. Speaking only when he spoke to them, and that was limited to the small clutch of prostitutes who didn't mind taking their chances.

Blank-faced, the Ghost skulked the edges of whores and customers and players and drinkers, not even bothering to try to look like he belonged—and what would be the point? The braid marked him Untouchable more clearly than a missing hand would mark a thief.

Malick angled through scattered tables and bodies, and toward the low couches and mounds of cushions at the back of the room, where the shadows shirred more thickly into the corners. Where the views and paths to the doors were clear and unobstructed, if one didn't mind the gyrating lumps of those who didn't bother to take themselves to a place more private, or didn't have the koin. Where a man could put his back to the wall and watch his quarry without risk of discovery too soon.

Unsurprisingly, Samin had already beaten Malick there and cleared them a spot. From the nasty looks he was getting and the dishabille of cushions and bodies scattered to either side of him, it appeared as though he'd not been terribly polite about it. Blue eyes, sharp and avid in a wide, granite face, focused on Malick as he approached. Malick gave Samin a subtle nod, and leaned hip-shot against the wall, close enough to talk without being overheard, but far enough they could always say they weren't together if one got caught and the other got away. Not that they needed to worry about that here. It was just habit.

"It's him." Samin surely meant it to be a whisper, but it emerged more as a gruff growl.

Malick shot him a look replete with *No shit, genius.*

How many Untouchables, after all, ventured into a place like this? How many of them lived long enough to be of age to enter? Not that "of age" really mattered, when it came to the laws of Untouchables.

Samin narrowed his eyes across the room, tilting his head like a curious pup. "He doesn't *look* mental."

Malick's eyebrows rose as he pulled his focus back to the Ghost. With the want clenching in Malick's gut—well, more precisely, in his trousers—"mental" was rather beside the point, but Samin was right. Calm and calculating, not wild and desperate like the few Untouchables Malick had seen before. And fit, too, where the others had been thin and fragile, rickety with ill health, and too pale. This one's color was full and hearty, his eyes alive with intelligence. He was obviously well fed, and all that hair plaited down his back looked thick and lustrous. Even as they watched, the braid swung heavily over the man's shoulder, the end brushing against the slight bulge in his boot.

"Knives," Malick said quietly.

Samin's mouth pinched. "Shouldn't be allowed." Clearly disapproving, and when he noted Malick's quizzical look, he shook his head. "They're dangerous enough as it is. An Untouchable oughtn't be allowed a weapon any more than a child."

"You don't think they should be allowed to defend themselves?" Malick posed the question with genuine interest. If anyone had an informed opinion on the matter, it would be Samin.

"Defend themselves against what? They're called 'Untouchable' for a reason." A weird mix of sympathy and disgust twisted Samin's hard face.

"I've seen enough of them, starved and raving. Their own kin won't touch them, not even to help."

Malick peered at Samin closely. "Would you ever interfere?"

"Isn't that why we're here?"

"You're a funny man, Samin."

"I'm a practical man, Mal."

Malick politely refrained from giving Samin a sharp thwack to his big, giant head. "You know what I mean."

Samin huffed, annoyed, and shot a careful glance to all sides before lowering his voice. "The laws are there for a reason." His narrow blue gaze followed the Ghost, watched him pause to speak to one of the boys, before Samin turned to look at Malick squarely. "But the laws are still locked in fear. The Ancestors have been sending their Untouchables insane for too long, and something needs to be done. If I ever came across some poor, mad soul who couldn't keep enough sense in his head to know he was hungry, or even remember how to eat, if I was alone and unobserved, yeah, I'd interfere."

"Huh." Malick looked back at the Ghost. "I suppose the real worry is the ones who've gone completely off the jump, and decide they need to take a few others with them."

He'd seen it once, when he'd had a commission in one of the camps: a young girl, perhaps thirteen or so, with that telltale braid, wild-eyed and snarling insanity, stoning a middle-aged woman who'd done nothing but stand there and scream, taking it. A crowd of onlookers merely stood watching, eyes full of horror and sorrow, but Malick hadn't been able to tell for whom either was meant. And when a man Malick guessed was the woman's husband attempted halfheartedly to lay hands on the girl, pull his wife away, the crowd stepped in and beat him. Malick didn't know if it was to death—he hadn't waited around to find out.

A far cry from what the Untouchables used to be. Catalysts once, now they were merely Ghosts, haunted by the laws once meant to set them apart, almost revere them, but now only dragged out an inevitably ugly end.

Touching an Untouchable—for good or ill—with the intent to alter his course, was death. No excuses, no explanations, no quarter. One of the few laws the Jin had been allowed to keep when they were overridden and conquered by Ada. Even the Adan held to it, though it had never really been tested, and Malick would be surprised if an Adan were ever put to death for the sake of a Jin. At any rate, no Untouchable he'd heard of had ventured into the city for a very long time, let alone a whorehouse, and that after the gates had already closed for the night.

Malick wondered idly if this anomaly of a Ghost planned to stay the night in one of Umeia's rooms, and then wondered—a little less idly—if Malick would be able to talk Umeia into telling him which one. Though, he supposed, if things worked out, the pretty Untouchable might even tell Malick himself.

"So, if he pulls one of them knives on me," Samin ventured slowly, "I'm not supposed to be allowed to turn it back on him."

Malick shrugged. "Not supposed to." He smirked. "But if no one's around to see a thing, does it really happen?"

Samin heaved a sour snort. "Can't make shit like this up."

"Sure you could. But who'd want to?"

They were quiet for a moment, watching the Ghost watching the crowd and trying to look like he wasn't, searching. "He's pretty, though," Samin finally put in, thoughtful.

Malick grinned. "That's why we're going to take him in the bath."

"Save me, Mal, is your mind always on—?"

"No, sometimes it's on food and liquor. But I was thinking more along the lines of not having to deal with those knives. The potential view is merely a bonus."

"You can't use magic. It doesn't work on them."

Malick waggled his eyebrows. "That's what makes it fun."

"That's what makes it stupid and riskier than it needs to be, and you a bloody idiot."

"Aw, stop, I'll blush." Malick nodded toward the eastern door that led to the baths, where the Ghost was being escorted by his chosen whore. "Look, he's picked one."

A dark-haired boy—*boy*, Malick's libido pointed out gleefully—with fair skin and a pleasant blankness to his expression that spoke to a willingness for just about anything that involved the proper amount of koin. The choice wasn't terribly surprising; Madi was a ready favorite of many whose purses likely weighed heavier than this Untouchable's. Too bad for said Untouchable he wasn't going to get the chance to find out why.

"Go tell Umeia we need twenty minutes."

Samin glared. "*You* go tell Umeia. Last time we brought our business here she threatened to castrate me. *Me*—like it isn't you as gives the orders."

"I only relay them, friend, I don't give them." That responsibility Malick happily laid squarely on the shoulders of the phantom he knew only as the Mage. And he had no interest in learning any more than the scant bits he already knew. "Go on, then, before he slips through. We'll never hear the end of it if Shig and Yori get him."

He didn't wait for Samin to stop sputtering. With just a touch of magic to veil him, Malick slid away from the wall, merging into the anonymity of the patronage, and sauntered to the other end of the public floor. He dropped the veil before heading down the lamp-lit stone stairway to the baths.

The Ghost was already availing himself of one of the shower-boxes, rinsing off with a couple of buckets behind a screen of woven rushes. *Naked*, Malick's libido put in helpfully, and he couldn't help wondering if all that hair was unbound, and what it would look like wet and stuck to sinewy arms and rippled torso. Just how long would it be, untethered?—down to ankles, at least, surely. *Yum.* All sorts of delightful possibilities swept through the little brain, and Malick forced the big brain to put them reluctantly but firmly aside. Business first. Though he did manage a bit of a leer when Madi slipped silently past him and back out the door with a conspiratory wink.

The coals in the corner hob glowed red and hot, the scented pot of water hanging above burbling quietly. The metallic sting of minerals hung in the close cavern, weighted heavily with sulfur. Malick sucked a breath through his nose, clearing his senses of the less pleasing residue of the Girou. Granite tiles looped the uneven rim of the great steaming pool, kept naturally hot by springs flowing beneath half the city. Malick checked the shadows creased into the rough-hewn stone of the walls, the steady *drip-drip-drip* of condensation rhythmic beneath the sporadic splashing coming from the lone occupied shower-box. No one else lurked, not that Malick could see.

Umeia must have been several steps ahead of him, as usual, and cleared everyone out when she spied their quarry. With the exception of Samin, likely now keeping watch outside the door, no one would stumble in and interrupt.

The black, high-collared tunic the man had been wearing, along with boots and belts and trousers, lay safely out of reach on the stone bench meant for disrobing. Malick almost tsked at the carelessness, thought about searching the bundle—just out of idle curiosity, to see how many knives the Ghost carried, and what sorts he favored—but decided to err on caution's side, for once. Samin would be so proud.

"Why are you watching me?"

Malick did not clutch at his chest like a startled auntie. Damn it all, *how—?*

You know what? Didn't matter.

Keeping his reaction to a lift of eyebrows, Malick propped his shoulder to the wall, and casually crossed one leg over the other, draping his lanky self artistically, and adding a brash grin. For good measure—and better effect—he brushed the long skirt of his duster back to expose the small knife at his belt, propped elbow to hipbone and made a show of inspecting his fingernails. A damned tempting picture he made, if he did say so.

He completed the effect with a lazily drawled "Well, good evening to you too."

The screen jittered then rattled aside. Clad in nothing but a bathsheet and attitude, the Ghost pinned Malick with a glare from behind the half cover of the flimsy screen.

The hair was still disappointingly bound, but the wild fringe had come loose again to hang frayed and dripping over the eyes; Malick was surprised the fierce, furious stare didn't singe the ends. Lamp-tawny water droplets slipped over abrasions, bruises, and scars—apparent evidence of close wet-work—mottled unevenly but for a heavy swath of thin, silvery stripes on the left bicep. Not defensive wounds. And not the irregular, incidental strips along the outer bones of the forearms that spoke to the reverse grip style the man apparently favored with his knives, and a clear need for vambraces. These were neat and straight, as though they'd been put there apurpose.

Threat assessment complete, Malick let his eyes rove unfettered, taking in every line and swell, lingering too long for manners on the way the sheet bunched in a tight-knuckled grip between the man's groin and the tantalizing wing of his left hip. Gaze skidding upward, Malick took careful note that he couldn't see the right hand behind the screen, and by the way the pectoral on that side quivered tense, the Ghost likely had something very unfriendly clutched in his fist. Malick was ridiculously pleased that the carelessness at which he'd earlier curled his lip was a figment of his own assumptions, and warned himself not to indulge them again. He would likely not live to regret underestimating this Untouchable.

"*Why* are you *watching* me?" Bitten out through teeth clenched tight. Such pretty white little teeth, straight and even. Malick wondered if they'd draw blood when they nipped… wondered if he'd like it. Of course, if those full lips were to follow along, soothe the hurt…

Oh, fuck me. I really think I want this one.

Malick's shrug was deliberately insouciant. "And why wouldn't I be?"

"What do you want?"

Malick nearly snorted. What did he want? The possibilities nearly made his eyes cross.

"Don't ask questions to which you don't want an answer, little Ghost."

The man's eyes darkened, and his nostrils flared. "If you know what I am, then you know what the penalty is for interfering."

His accent was… odd. Malick had a good ear for them, but he couldn't place this one, and it certainly didn't have the twangy Jin sound to it. More like it was from everywhere and nowhere at once, no distinct characteristic to classify it, and yet hints of every one Malick had ever heard. Odd.

Malick put it away for later. "Funny, a friend and I were just discussing that. Seems the consensus is that a thing can't actually be said to have happened, if no one was there to see it."

The man's gaze flickered over to the door with the mention of "a friend," and Malick's smirk broadened. Not only pretty but clever too, and if there was any madness behind that glare, it was the kind that was born of rage and… betrayal, most likely. After all, didn't it usually come down to that?

A lethal combination, rage and betrayal, the best combination with the highest potential. It didn't generally take much to harness those emotions, point them, use them. The Mage had been right again.

"Here we are, all alone." Malick pushed away from the wall to meander idly around the edges of the pool, boots clocking softly on wet stone, eyes locked to the Ghost's. "No one to disturb us. No one to interrupt."

Muscles beneath bare skin tightened and jumped ever so slightly as Malick neared. Malick never would've seen it, had he not been looking for it. Fuck, but the man was good, all calm restraint.

Wary, Malick kept a loose perimeter, lingering at the periphery of the man's personal space like a prowling tom. It was probably a bit reckless to lean lightly into the screen, but that was what Malick did anyway, all too aware the sharp point of a knife was no doubt just on the other side, aimed directly at his gut. No, his heart—this one would go for the sure, immediate kill.

Malick turned his wrist in his sleeve to feel the garrote reassuringly coiled around his forearm. He kept his gaze geared toward seduction as he lifted it, peered into…

Bloody damn, those *eyes*. Dark-rimmed gray, shot through with shards of gilt-amber, glaring back with a flat look of loathing and a disappointing lack of awe for Malick's enticing self.

Perhaps Malick should've unlaced his shirt an eyelet or two.

"You," Malick murmured through his smile, "have been a very naughty boy."

"Step. Away." Low and full of venomous intent.

Not *What are you talking about?* not a question at all, in fact. The man merely stood his ground, glaring death at Malick. Cornered, bare but for a single bathsheet and whatever weapon he had in his hand behind that screen, and still his breath came steady and even.

Fuck, I don't even think I care if he guts me—I've got *to have this one.*

It was the braid, had to be, the novelty of it or… something. Or all that not-quite-olive skin and the solid curves of muscle beneath it. Surely it couldn't be the glare, the dark look of menace that too closely resembled the part of a map that warned *Here be monsters.*

Malick sighed theatrically and shook his head with overdone regret. "Even if I wanted to, I'm afraid I can't." He let his smile crimp and shrugged. "Orders."

That got a narrowing of the eyes. Reluctant interest.

"I'm afraid you've gone and called attention to yourself, little Ghost." Daring, Malick reached out slowly, swiped a fingertip down the damp, smooth lumps of the plait hanging over a thew-molded shoulder. Malick wasn't sure if the tiny hiss of breath was a reaction to the name or the liberty. "Don't worry, I haven't come to kill you—"

A deliberate snort, a very clear *as if you could*, so Malick ignored it.

"—nor have I come to blackmail you, or any of the ten thousand other possibilities that are likely blooming in your twisted little mind this second." Malick let his fingers slip around the braid, and stepped in closer. "Although, I could be talked into a quick go against the wall if you're—"

He'd been wrong. The knife hadn't been behind the screen in the man's right hand, it had been twisted into the bathsheet in his left. Now its tip rested just below Malick's chin, and he couldn't even care, because the grip on the sheet had been forsaken for the advantage and now lay puddled at the man's ankles.

Malick didn't even reach for his own knife, didn't slip his fingers through the loop of the garrote, didn't try to step back or attack. He merely stared, raked his gaze up and down, and tightened his grip on the braid. Fizzy little bubbles went *pop-pop-pop* in his brain when his gaze instinctively hitched and hung between the man's legs—*gah, yum*—before he forced it on.

The same sort of scars as on the arm striped the man's right thigh—thin and tight, most of them silvered, but a few still pink and newish. One wound was still scabbed and not yet scarred over. Odd. Ritualistic, almost, and clearly self-inflicted. Some Jin tradition Malick didn't know about?

"Let. *Go.*"

So much control in that command, such intensity beneath it.

"Can't, sorry." Malick couldn't help the sigh, the regret sincere this time. It was looking less and less likely that the Untouchable was going to let Malick touch. "You assassinated the wrong prefect this time, and you're— Ah-ah, watch it." The knife had jerked, and Malick adjusted his stance to accommodate, though he didn't draw back. "Don't kill me just yet, or your exit from here will be a bit more difficult and attract a lot more attention than I've no doubt you'd prefer."

"It's a little damp in here," the man said through his teeth. "My fingers are a bit slick, and you never know when my grip might… *slip*." He stepped up, chest flush to the screen—well, what do you know, he *did* have a blade in his right hand, too, now poking just as firmly at Malick's gut as the other was beneath his chin. "Perhaps it would be best if you got to the point."

Bad dog. Sit.

Malick had to grin. "I'm rather *on* the point, don't you think? Two of them, in fact."

Apparently, the man was not as amused with Malick as Malick was with himself. The tips of both knives pressed harder, one drawing a tiny warm trickle of blood down Malick's throat and one threatening to slip right through the layers of leather and thin mail under his tunic. Fuck, his trousers were actually getting a bit painful. Umeia always said Malick's brain lived in his pants, and now here was proof.

"All right, all right." Malick took a small step back but didn't release his hold on the braid. "To put it bluntly, you've been recruited. You're no longer an independent agent. You're no longer to be left to your own devices or discretion."

The impassive mask, if possible, grew even stonier. "I don't know what you're talking about."

"Of course you don't. And so you won't know exactly what's happening the next time you go after a prefect or a curate or a lord, and we're there waiting for you." The man's gaze once again shot quickly to the door and back. Malick sighed. "Look, what's your name?"

Cold silence and a slow blink were all he got for an answer.

Malick rolled his eyes. "If you don't give me a name to call you, I'm going to have to keep calling you 'Ghost.'"

Still with the blinking. And the unfortunate continued lack of awe.

Malick's jaw tightened. Definitely should've unlaced his shirt. Maybe tousled his hair a bit too.

"Fine, *Ghost*. You're causing too much trouble, *Ghost*. You're making it all too risky for the rest of us, and your kills aren't even making a difference."

"Us." A pause. A tilt of the head. "A difference to whom?"

"Ah, not going to tell you that just yet. We've not yet reached the part where I decide whether to let you dress and come outside with me, or just kill you right here and pay the extra koin for the mess."

Dark eyebrows rose and the man's gaze went half-lidded. Malick could hear the *You really think you can?* as clearly as though the man had spoken it aloud, instead of merely standing there, no outward reaction but a long, slow blink.

Seriously—no man needed lashes that long and lush.

And anyway, fuck it. Malick was tired of this game. Mostly because he clearly wasn't winning it. Time to change the rules.

Reckless, Malick knocked the blade away from his chin, dodged a quick parry that almost got his throat cut for him, and snagged the dirk from his belt. The braid was pinned to the wooden frame of the screen before the man could lunge at Malick through it.

Good thing Malick had stepped back, because there was now a long, clean slice in the rushes of the screen, though the knife that did it had moved so fast he hadn't even seen it.

Malick grinned, backing off with his hands held palms out. "Unless you'd prefer to prove your superiority in a more pleasant fashion?" He waggled his eyebrows. "I usually prefer top, but I've been known to make an exception now and again."

The loathing in the man's glare was almost a live thing. And still no awe. Bloody stone, the man was.

Malick huffed, impatient now. "Look, Ghost, we can have ourselves a little pissing contest in here, where one of us will surely end up very messily dead, or you can come with me and we'll go somewhere we can talk about it like very much alive grownups. The customers will be clamoring for the baths soon, and we can't faff about much longer. What'll it be?"

Not only that, but Umeia was going to have Malick's head if he cost her much more money tonight. Those screens were cheap, but Umeia wouldn't see it that way, and this little exploit was already holding up the custom for the baths and so therefore the whores.

The man twirled a knife. "Why should I?"

Ah, finally, an intelligent question. "Because you've been given a choice, if you can call it that—join us and live to see whatever vengeance it is you're looking for, or the hunter becomes the hunted. My patron does not share the Adan's generosity, and believes quite firmly that *no one* is Untouchable."

The man's control was slipping: his jaw tightened, and his eyes took on a very slight shimmer in the soft light. Malick couldn't help but wonder what he would look like with all of that control puddled about his feet like that forgotten bathsheet.

"What d'you know about any of it?" Nearly a whisper this time, and toneless, hardly a question at all.

"Nothing but what I know about myself." Malick made his tone kind. "Except you've been promised that the man you want will one day twitch at the end of your blade—*if* you join us. If not..."

He stepped back over and retrieved his knife with a last, lingering caress of the shiny braid. He purposefully turned his eyes to the small knife and watched the lamplight scud over its honed edge and now slightly blunted tip. Offering an opportunity to attack, but avidly on watch for it.

The Ghost didn't take the opening.

Intrigued, Malick slid the dirk into its sheath. "I like you. You're pretty, even if you are a bit of an ass." He flashed a grin. "I don't want to kill you. And I certainly don't want you to kill me. Do us both a favor—get dressed and come outside."

The man stared, eyes narrowed beneath the obscuring fringe.

Malick stared back, kept his own gaze and mien blank, and his hands very still. The urge to smirk was twitching at him, and he fought it down. Those knives were still out and looked very sharp.

"You go first," the man finally said. "I'll want privacy to dress. I'll follow."

Malick's eyebrows rose, and his gaze dipped inexorably down the sleek, bare skin, resting on the bathsheet still crumpled on the floor.

Privacy. Sure.

"You're joking, right?"

Another of those slow blinks was all he got for an answer.

"What's to stop you from just skiving off?"

The man shrugged, casually lifted the knife in his left hand and wound it through his fingers—blade-hilt-blade-hilt—like another would weave a koin. "I should imagine you've all the exits covered."

Too bloody right. And somehow, this Untouchable didn't seem terribly worried about it.

Why did Malick suddenly feel like a cat toy being batted about between a couple of deceptively clawless paws?

Malick allowed the smirk to bloom, and dipped his head: challenge accepted. "You'll be there, then? I've your word?"

"Oh, I'll be there."

There was no way to know if the promise meant a thing, and that bland tone could have implied anything at all. Malick was absurdly hooked by the prospect of finding out what it *could* mean.

He stepped back with hands raised. "I'll wait for you outside, and we'll go somewhere to talk where we won't be overheard. Who knows? P'raps you'll even allow me to make up for ruining your, um… plans for the evening."

Malick didn't wait for an answer, merely winked, cocky, and deliberately turned his back on the Ghost as he sauntered to the door. Those gray eyes might be glaring daggers into Malick's back, but no actual daggers were coming for him, he could feel it. Somehow, Malick was absurdly certain that if he took a blade from this Untouchable, it wouldn't be in the back. He didn't even flick a glance over his shoulder to make sure as he opened the door and stepped through.

Samin was, of course, waiting on the other side. The scowl on his face said he'd been listening carefully, and wasn't happy about what he'd heard.

"Why'd you leave him *alone*? Have you completely lost your small mind?"

Malick decided that was a clear possibility. He shrugged. "Manners."

Samin produced a fair twin to the slow blink Malick had been getting for the past fifteen minutes. "Manners."

"What, I have some!"

"Mal, I'm being serious."

"So am I!"

"Yeah, but I've met you."

"Just." Malick huffed. "I gave him a chance to come quietly. It seemed… I dunno—fair."

"You kill people for a living. When has 'fair' ever meant a damn?"

"I kill *bad* people for a living, Samin." Malick's voice had frosted over. "And so do you. Remember it."

Samin chewed on that for a moment, somewhat chastened. "Will he come quietly?"

Malick grimaced, and led the way up the stone stairs. "Not a chance." He jerked his head toward the back doors of the Girou. "Go give Shig and Yori a heads-up, then follow the Ghost and don't lose sight of him. I'll be in the alley behind the kitchens waiting for the inevitable escape attempt."

It was the braid, Malick grumbled at himself as he made his way through the crowd and arrowed through the kitchen, retrieved his belts and kit from one of the lads then pounded down the steps and to the alley. He didn't pause but merely strapped on his gear as he stalked, the long tails of his duster flapping behind him. That damned *bloody* braid.

⛩

Samin rolled his eyes as he watched Malick go. Best tactical mind Samin knew, that lad, but in some things, Malick was purely and simply a blazing bloody idiot. Not enough blood to the big brain, because it was forever rushing down to the little one, that was Samin's opinion.

Mouth tight, Samin shoved his way toward the gaming tables where Umeia was busy keeping the losers from starting trouble and the winners playing. At least until she'd made sure the House had won back whatever the players thought they were going home with. Since Umeia was the House, she gave it her full attention.

Samin didn't bother to try to catch her glance. One eye on the stairs to the baths, watching for their quarry to emerge, he instead waved down Lex, Umeia's right hand, and if Samin wasn't seriously mistaken, her toy when she was in the mood. Not that Lex seemed to mind. Nor would Samin, in truth. Umeia was gorgeous. And bloody well stunningly stacked.

"I need you for a moment," Samin said as he grabbed hold of Lex's arm.

Lex made a woebegone effort to extract himself. "Haven't got one."

"Make one. Or I'll be sure to tell Malick he got a knife in the ribs because you couldn't find the time to go tell his backup they're needed outside."

"Aren't you his backup?"

Samin graciously refrained from knocking Lex cold. "*Now.*"

"Right, fine." Lex sighed, all put-upon and self-sacrificing. "But you owe me."

Um, no, really not how it worked. But Samin was happy to let Lex think it, if it got his ass moving.

"Shig's watching the front, and Yori's at the stairway up to the rooms. Tell them Mal's on his way to the alley behind the kitchens, and tell them to move quick."

"Done with the baths, then?"

"By the time you tell Shig and Yori, we will be. The sooner you're back, the sooner Umeia's purse swells."

That seemed to convince Lex. Samin would swear the man could throttle silver and make it cough up gold just as ably as Umeia could.

Not quite as annoyed now, Samin returned his full attention to the stairs to the baths, squinting through the gloom that gathered at the landing. He congratulated himself for not stepping on any of the writhing bodies on the cushions near his feet as he sank into the shadows against the wall.

Leave it to bloody Malick to risk making this errand twice as dangerous as it needed to be, merely because he was a soft touch for a pretty face. As if Malick didn't get his wick dipped enough as it was. Asking for a knife in the back or a cut throat, that boy was, letting his prick lead him like he did.

Annoyed all over again, Samin gave the man accidentally humping his shin a swift kick, and stepped away.

The Ghost was taking too long. There was only the one way in and out of the baths, so no escape there. Drowning himself out of fear? He didn't seem the type. Even if he did, it was no skin off Samin's nose. Samin didn't think they really needed a fifth, and it would likely make his life a bit easier if this ended tonight with the pretty Ghost dead.

Samin rubbed at his eyes. The poppy fumes were starting to get to him. The shadows thickened and blurred deeper for a moment, the greasy lamplight shifting and sputtering in the stir of a draft. Samin blinked, narrowed his eyes, a spurt of adrenaline flowing through his heart and spangling up his backbone. Was that...?

No, couldn't be. It wasn't that dark, and even a man head to toe in black would've been obvious. No stealthy Ghost could get by, no matter how good he was, and Malick had said this Ghost was supposed to be very good. Took out an Adan prefect, of all people, and in his own office, with his guard right outside the door, or so Malick had said. These things always grew in the telling, so who knew, really? Still, it wouldn't hurt to be careful. Damned poppy; it always softened the senses, and Samin would be too stoned to be of any use at all soon enough, if he didn't hurry things along.

Anyway, waiting wasn't one of the things Samin did well.

Fuck manners. And fuck "fair."

Samin pushed away from the wall and made his way quietly down the stairs. With all the stealth he could gather, which wasn't much—he was built for brute force, not slinking—he pushed the heavy door open far enough to peer cautiously inside. And frowned. Could be right behind the door, waiting for him, and Samin knew Malick hadn't disarmed the fellow. Idiot. Samin could see a little of the small chamber from this angle—the far side of the pool, and one shower-box—and it all appeared clear, but there was an awful lot he *couldn't* see, and there was still the small fact that he couldn't see through the door.

"Lad?" Samin wasn't really expecting an answer, which was good because he didn't get one. He thought about craning his neck to get a look behind the door, but all that might have done was hand over a good opportunity to break Samin's neck—no fuss, no muss—and Samin would deserve it, if he did something that stupid. "I'm not here to fight, just to hie you along a little, yeah? Haven't got all night."

Still nothing.

Already-stretched patience at its limit, Samin figured fuck it, he'd given fair warning, so he threw his weight into the door. If the Ghost was waiting behind it, he'd be squashed like a very stroppy little bug, and Samin would merely shrug at Malick and find a good place to dispose of the body. Easier for everyone all around.

There was only the heavy *thunk* of wood against stone as Samin shot his gaze to every shadowed corner and recessed cranny. Benches, shower-boxes, linen cupboard, pool—all empty.

Gone. The little son of a bitch. How the hell...? Samin had been watching almost every bloody second, he *couldn't* have missed—

Shit.

Untouchables didn't have magic, and magic didn't work on them. So how had the damned Ghost got by him?

More to the point—now what? Besides the fact that Malick was going to be exquisitely pissed when he...

Actually, Malick was going to be exquisitely pissed only if he got the opportunity. He was, after all, waiting by himself down in that alley, and who knew if Lex had bothered to hurry fetching Shig and Yori. And Malick had paid the Doujou to stay away tonight.

"Oh, fucking hell!"

Not even sparing the two seconds it would take to kick his own ass, Samin spun, and raced up the stairs.

ᛗ

It was pure chance Malick looked up when he did. Pure chance he'd been growing bored and a little edgy, and a child's song about Wolf and Raven and Bear had flitted through his head. Pure chance he'd peered up to check which phases they happened to be in. Pure chance Wolf was gibbous tonight, and backlit the creeping figure on the second floor's terrace roof as though it had been limned in silver.

"Oh, that's…"

That was all Malick managed as he watched the Ghost swirl down from the sagging eaves, and glide to the ground with an ease Malick wouldn't have credited had he not seen it himself. Long knives glittered in the moonlight, almost forming a tangled orbit around the Ghost as he advanced on Malick. It was like watching a silent, twisting storm. Too economical for grace. Too efficient for artistry. A perfect tempest of ice and fire, and all Malick could do was watch it come.

"Well, would you look at that."

Oh, yeah. He wanted this one.

Instinct had taken Malick's hands to the belts crisscrossed over his hips, one drawing his dagger and the other drawing a short sword. He'd already shifted into a defensive stance. Adrenaline made a welcome—if a bit belated—entrance as Malick swirled the blade of the short sword down and around his forearm, then brought it back up to rest at an angle in front of him. He shot a quick glance out the corner of his eye

Yori's slim figure was hugging the shadowed brick of the building, at least a dozen paces behind the man and to his left, her bow nocked and drawn. Shig must be around here somewhere too, then. Both of them waited for Malick's signal.

"You don't have to do this." Malick's gaze was even, playtime over now. "You're safer with us. Think about it. You're wanted. They're looking for you."

"They're looking for a phantom."

"And look at this—I've gone and found one." Malick shook his head. "You're good, but you're not invincible. How long d'you think it'll be before they hunt you down?"

"You didn't find anything—your 'patron' did. He won't find me again. I don't need a pimp."

Frosty and contemptuous. Clearly unwilling to hear reason, let alone see it. There was no point in arguing. Malick had known that from the moment he'd stepped into the baths. The Ghost wanted a fight—Malick would have to give him one. He'd rather tender another way to work out aggressions, but it seemed the stony little prick was also an uncooperative stony little prick. Who clearly didn't recognize a good offer when he saw one—witness his repeated failure to succumb to awe.

Footsteps pounded down from the kitchen stairs behind Malick, a heavy tread that could only belong to Samin. Malick stopped him with a short whistle.

"Stay back. I've got this." The Ghost's eyes narrowed to slits; Malick couldn't help the smile. "All right, Ghost." He firmed his stance. "C'mon, love, at least give us your name, then. We'll want to know who we're burning incense for."

The man twirled a knife, then flipped it up by the tip, and caught it neatly by its wirebound hilt. "Fuck you."

"Promise?"

Malick parried when the first strike drew sparks from steel.

Then he grinned.

Change-month, Year 1299, Cycle of the Raven

In the old days, Qiri fumed to herself—back when the Ancestors spoke sanity and sense to their Untouchables, and didn't send them mad in the speaking—she would have been a lot happier to have been called to the more affluent part of the village on the cusp of the New Cycle, and in weather such as this. Though, "village," she thought with a cynical snort, was putting it kindly these days, and getting less apposite with each Turning. Camp, more like, but they weren't allowed to call it that.

A sideways glare crept over to the man who stepped along beside her, though she yanked it back again before he caught her at it. Still, it wasn't as though he wouldn't know anyway, if he chose to, so what did it matter?

Qiri bunched her bony shoulders beneath her cloak, sank deeper into the scraggy fox pelt of the hood, and blinked against the chill rain. She risked another sideways glance, let it linger this time, but still the man didn't look back, had hardly acknowledged her existence at all since he'd come pounding on the door of her hut to inform her Fen-onna's time had come 'round and Qiri was to collect her kit and accompany him to the birth. Telling Qiri her own business, that was what he'd been about. As though she'd needed anyone to do that, having been about it smartly enough herself for nearly half the Raven Cycle. And looking to be about it well into the Wolf Cycle, too, if the Adan didn't one day tire of taking Jin lives away a hair at a time and simply decide to go for the whole head and have done with it.

And this Adan—this Adan *seer*, as if Qiri didn't know—looked to be as full of himself as the rest of them, with his high ways and ill manners. What he wanted with poor Fen-onna, Qiri hardly dared speculate. Had he imposed himself to prevent or help along?

Would he do the deed himself, or just stand there and make sure Qiri did? Or would he simply take the babes from between their mother's legs and Disappear them, like so many others? Qiri had never heard of them taking such tiny ones before. And she'd never heard of an Adan seer imposing himself on an actual birth. To what purpose, after all? No child manifested before their Change. What use would infants be to these people?

"She is unstable, this Fen-onna?"

Qiri's eyebrows rose—they were the first words the man had spoken to her since they'd left her dooryard. She slid a quick look through the weak, dusky light thrown by globed gas lamps lining the muddy walk between shacks and huts and the occasional more respectable cottage. Class meant nothing anymore. Possessions were no longer truly their own. But some families had managed to keep more than others after the invasion. And the Adan hadn't yet got 'round to taking what little wealth was left among those once well-off and influential.

"She is… delicate," Qiri answered carefully.

Too delicate to risk keeping the last set of twins and hiding their magic. Qiri's price for silence had been a mere pittance then, out of deference to Fen-onna's hysteria and Fen-seyh's honest grief for both his wife and lost children. More than a year ago, that was, but for Fen-onna, it might as well have been yesterday. Poor thing had always been precarious, from the moment Qiri had pulled her from her mother's womb, all blue and brittle, and singing with the Blood as its strength poured into Qiri's hands.

Frailty turned to fragile beauty, back when Fen-onna had been little Marika, Changed and full with the spirits, and just beginning to catch the eye of young Fen Olanne. Not all could allow the spirits into their hearts and still keep their minds, and Qiri had continued to be surprised as each year passed and pretty little Marika somehow maintained the balance. Ripe with the Blood but without magic himself, Fen Olanne had been fascinated. They'd barely waited the proper six months before the binding, and it was barely another fortnight before the Adan had tightened their noose, increased their raids, and the rumors of the Disappeared had crept through the camps.

Brilliant with life and stunningly bold once, Fen Marika, but always with that tenuous grip on the sane side of madness. The poor girl's eyes, when Qiri had felt her full belly and told her it was twins again. The blood and pain when Qiri tried to end the pregnancy and couldn't.

A shiver racked up Qiri's spine and out through her creaking bones.

"You have known the family long?"

The man's tone was much too casual and disinterested. It made Qiri more suspicious than she already was.

The first thing the Adan had done upon the occupation—after they'd commandeered the ports and usurped all trade—was to outlaw Jin magic and put to death any who had it. Except for the midwives; they were "useful" to the Adan in a way that turned Qiri's stomach, but she'd done her best over the years to be of as little use to them as possible. She'd helped many a desperate mother since the occupation took its newest, cruelest turn. And if the Ancestors had something to say about the blood on her hands when she finally faced them, she'd have a thing or two to say herself about their decided lack of help for their faithful.

Certainly, Qiri had taken koin from the Adan for carrying out her repugnant duties, and she'd taken koin from the Jin for pretending to. But more Jin families were intact because of her, and more magic was hidden in their folds than the Adan might suspect, regardless of their constant efforts to wipe it out or take it all for themselves. In Qiri's own considered opinion, she'd done more to protect the Jin in the last few decades than the Ancestors had done since before the Binding Wars. And look how that had turned out.

"Being as ancient as I," Qiri replied, her tone even, "I have known all the families in the… village all their lives." She shot a bold glare sideways. "All that are and all that were. There are considerably fewer to keep track of these days."

"Indeed." Dispassionate.

Qiri could've happily cut his throat.

The huts and shacks were dwindling behind them, more cottages and the rare house along the street now, and the walkway slowly turned from mud to rocky cart ruts. Meager, oily light flickered through slat-bound shutters, rain and shadow reeking of the tangy stench of animal fat cooked over coal fires. It coiled heavy through Qiri's nose and clenched with a warning burn at her bowels as they neared what was once the farm of Fen Olanne and his wife, Marika, and was now little more than ruined earth and scrag-strewn rows of wheat and rye. Verdant fields and pastureland, when Qiri was a girl, and before Fen Olanne was even a gleam in the corner of his father's eye. Now it lay nearly as bald and blasted as Qiri felt.

This Cycle would not end well for any of them.

She paused at the end of the muddy path that led up to their destination, reluctant to continue, but all too aware she had no choice. Already, she could hear the cries of labor, the high-pitched shrieking of driven panic and pre-emptive grief. A woman in the throes of insanity, grinding through beatific agony to birth children already dead, or better so. Tears scorched Qiri's eyes, and she was, for once this terrible evening, glad for the rain.

The man—the Adan prophet, damn him—merely stood silent, mud up to the ankles of his fine boots and dragging heavy on the hem of his thick, fur-lined cloak. Waiting.

Qiri led the way to the door, chin up and eyes straight ahead. How could she do else? She kept her expression calm when Fen-seyh shoved the door open, his demeanor moving quicksilver from relief to confusion to alarm and then, finally, knowing grief. He'd been good-looking and close to strapping once. Now he was thin and sallow, his lank hair hanging in amber-shot gray eyes gone dull—just another man defeated. He stared, Fen-onna's moans and nonsensical jabber leaking all around him and out into the oppressive night, turning it near unbearably heavy, before defeat slumped his shoulders, grayed his face. After a long, gravid moment, he merely cast his heavy gaze to the ground.

He stepped aside.

It went harder this time, mostly because Qiri could not—no matter what she said or threatened—compel Fen-onna to cooperate, to push, to tilt her hips… to stop her bloody pitiful weeping before Qiri lost her damned mind. The presence of the seer only seemed to drive Fen-onna closer to the edge, though Qiri had insisted that he keep himself out of sight.

The first emerged red and squalling, announcing his arrival with all the ill grace of a hearty set of newborn lungs.

"He's beautiful," Qiri said, to no one in particular; Fen-seyh had withdrawn directly after showing them to the bedchamber, and Fen-onna refused to look.

Earthbound this one, just like Fen-onna's firstborn, rest him. Qiri could feel the tremble of it in her fingertips, and she closed her eyes, bowed her head. She nearly snapped the little thing's neck right there.

"I'm so sorry." She kissed the babe's scrunched brow. "I don't know what waits for you, but I wish I could say I didn't suspect." The tremble moved right up her arms, swirled along her backbone and into her chest. Her heart took several painful lurches behind her breastbone, and she stubbornly choked back a small sob.

Strong enough to move continents, this one might one day be.

Qiri shot a look to the Adan man outside the door, then, on inexplicable impulse held the child up so he could see. Perhaps, if he could see the babe for the radiant new life it was…

The man merely tipped a curt nod, said, "So ends the Raven Cycle," and turned his gaze back to Fen-onna, expectant.

The second came quickly, almost too quickly for Qiri to clean the mouth and nose of the first and settle him in linens, even as his twin was crowning. Fen-onna was shrieking again, refusing to push, so Qiri had to actually reach in and pull the child from her body in a rush of blood and viscid waters.

"Thus, the Cycle of the Wolf is born," the seer intoned, and stepped into the room.

Qiri expected Fen-onna to go into hysterics, but she merely lay there, panting and weeping softly, and stared blankly at the ceiling.

Quiet, this second-born, blinking his father's eyes in his wrinkly little face, placid and puckered and altogether as exquisite as his brother. Qiri's hands went numb this time, as though the child held within them had sucked all the feeling away, and she nearly dropped him, even though she'd half-expected it. This time, the sob escaped before she could stop it.

"Give him to me."

Qiri lifted a heavy gaze from the babe to the seer as the child's brother continued to wail robust displeasure. She shook her head.

She'd never told Fen-onna, nor Fen-seyh, what sort of magic was in those first two little souls Qiri had put to rest last year. Not only because they'd never asked and Qiri had thought it best they didn't torture themselves more than they already would, but because to admit what the second child had been, and that Qiri had known, would be to speak her own death. With the Ancestors, she'd lift her chin defiantly and defend her actions with the sense they seemed to have forgotten in their collective insanity; with her own people, sense and justice and mercy would mean nothing.

"Let me see to him." Qiri's tone was low, only for the Adan prophet, and baldly pleading. "He is Untouchable. You don't understand the sort of life—"

"Give him to me." Harsh. Formidable.

As with everything since she'd opened the door of her hut that evening, Qiri had no choice. She wiped the child's mouth, pinched then dabbed at the tiny nose, then wrapped him in clean linens. With another whispered apology, she held the bundle out to the seer.

The man took the child up with avid eyes, a small smile curling his stern mouth, and genuine care in the delicacy of his hold and the way he rocked the child in his cupped palms. He stared for quite a while.

Qiri could swear she saw a world of futures unfolding behind the man's lively, dark gaze—whole universes opening up. She was nearly spellbound.

"The first of the Wolf Cycle." The seer sounded... awed. "True perfection; true potential."

Qiri had no idea what to make of it. "Seyh." She paused, cleared her throat, because her voice sounded shaky and small, and that simply wouldn't do. "He is Untouchable. I felt it. He is as doomed as any sent to Ada's Courts. You must know—"

"And yet with more of a chance than his two elder brothers, no?"

Qiri's throat closed up.

The man's smile turned cold as he cut his sharp glance from the boy. "You merely alerted me to Fate with your 'good deed', Qiri-onna, you did not change it, and for that, your own fate may be kind." He turned back to the child. "So much to do, this one, and his chance to do it taken away by one who meant so well." He shook his head, still enrapt with the puckered mouth and wrinkled brow.

Qiri slumped. She'd known. Somehow she'd known as soon as she held the first twin in her hands and felt the strength of the earth shiver through her limbs, and even when she'd held the second, she hadn't really admitted it.

"They are…?" She couldn't finish.

"They are the same. I would have known when he reached his Change, had you not… interceded, but his first death cried out to me." The man slipped his little finger into the babe's soft, creased palm. A smile curled wide and genuine when the child's tiny fingers wrapped 'round and gripped. "It is better this way. Better that he is born under Wolf's eye. He was never meant for Raven." The man stepped slowly over toward the bed. "Go and fetch the father."

And even though it would mean leaving poor Fen-onna—still weeping quietly, and whispering desperate prayers to the ceiling—alone with the man, Qiri merely stood, pushing through the sharp aches in her joints, and did as the man said.

When she returned with a red-eyed Fen-seyh in tow, she found the seer bent over the bed, draping a soiled sheet over Fen-onna's legs, speaking to her in a quiet, soothing voice. He paused once to stroke her damp brow with a gentle hand and—Qiri was shocked to note—what appeared to be honest care. Both babes were now swaddled, and even as Qiri watched, Fen-onna placed the firstborn to her breast, coaxing him to suckle. The room fell silent immediately when he latched on, the cries and mewls that had become so much background noise in the moments since his birth turning abruptly to soft sucking sounds and tiny grunts of effort.

"I don't understand." Qiri couldn't even get Fen-onna to look at her children only moments ago.

The rain wept *tap-tap-tap* on the clay tiles of the roof, and the silence of the din was nearly as full of madness as this strung-out moment of thwarted destiny.

Fen-seyh seemed just as stunned as Qiri. "What is this?" It came out more confusion than command, though it was clear and bold and aimed at the seer.

"He says we may keep them," Fen-onna whispered, beatific. There was still madness in her eyes, frailty, but it had softened with the apparent reprieve. "They have no magic."

Qiri sucked in her breath. She'd felt it, she *knew*—they were twins; everyone knew. Twins meant magic, always. What was this seer about, and how could he be so cruel to a woman already so fragile?

The seer turned his gaze from the babe to the mother then to the father. "This is the beginning of the end."

"We've been blessed, Olanne." Fen-onna's eyes were shining. "He says we will have more children—another son and a daughter—and that they will not have magic. That they'll be safe—*safe*, Olanne. Our children shall outlive us, all of them. He's promised it."

The seer stepped over toward Fen-seyh, and curled his voice low. "Your firstborn shall one day move the earth at his will. It is yours to teach him control and stealth. You will tell no one. You will keep any—even your own, even his mother—from discovery, and if any should guess the truth of him, even suspect, you will deal death swiftly and quietly. Fen-onna will believe it because she wants to. It is yours to divine a way to convince your people." He paused, leaned in, looming and intent. "He *must not* be found out. There is no torture you can imagine that will be worse than what you will actually suffer, should harm come to him while in your care."

Fen-seyh was speechless, clearly trying to work it through. His shocked gaze turned thoughtful, wary.

"And what is an Adan's price for this boon to a Jin?"

The seer's smile was sardonic this time. He stepped back over to the bed, gently lifting the other babe from the crook of his mother's arm. Fen-onna only smiled up at him, all weary contentment and open trust. He carried the child back over to his father, held him out like an offering, and stood silent until Fen-seyh took him up.

"He is to be called Fen Jacin-rei."

"*Rei.*" Fen-seyh's mouth curled down in an angry frown. "You would have me name my son 'ghost'?"

"He is Untouchable, Fen-seyh," Qiri told him quietly. "Ghost" was putting it all too gently.

Fen-seyh jolted, pained revulsion flaring at his sallow face, and he unconsciously held the child away from him. So very predictable, so very poignant, but Qiri couldn't find blame in it.

"You will see to his needs until I come for him." It was a clear admonishment as the seer narrowed his eyes at Fen-seyh's reaction.

"Come for him?" Fen-seyh whispered, dazed.

"The child is mine upon his Change. This is my price."

Qiri jolted, daring to touch the seer's sleeve. "If you mean to take the child, why not take him now? No one needs to know what he is, not if he is among the Adan. You must know what awaits him if he is—"

"You will see to his needs." The man's dark gaze was hard on Fen-seyh, not even so much as a flick in Qiri's direction. "He will wear the plait and learn what it means to be what he is. You will feed him and clothe him, educate and guide him until his Change, as is permitted by your traditions."

"But..." Fen-seyh was too obviously reeling, and no wonder—for months, he'd been resigned to the murder of two more sons, and tonight he'd been given them back, only to be told he might love only one of them. "But I may not prevent him from doing harm. What if...?" He paused, still staring at the babe, lying peaceful in his hands, small fists jammed tight in the seeking mouth. "His brother." Fen-seyh's voice quavered. "You say his brother must not come to harm. What if this one—?"

"He will not." The seer's firm gaze turned threatening. "You will not keep him from his brother."

Fen-seyh swallowed, his dazed stare drifting to the bed, and the child quiescent at his mother's breast. Eyes soft with confusion but going harder, already pulling away from the son he still held in an easy grip, Fen-seyh's shoulders slumped with a long sigh that sounded like it came from well-deep in his soul. He shook his head.

"I will not, seyh."

With one last stroke to the babe's soft cheek, the seer nodded, pulled his cloak tight to his throat, and turned to leave.

"I will come for him when he comes to his Change."

"But how will you know?" Fen-seyh frowned at the seer. "I don't know who you are—how shall I send for you?"

The man didn't answer, merely smiled, almost pitying, and strode to the door.

"Why do you do this?" Fen-seyh called after him. "What are we to you?"

The man stopped, furrowed his brow, but didn't turn. "You are nothing to me. The Ghost is everything. My reasons are my own."

And he was gone.

Qiri stared after him for only a moment before Fen-seyh wordlessly pushed the child at her, looked at her with clear grief and regret, then, with one tender glance toward his wife and the son that still belonged to him, slowly quit the room.

Still reeling, Qiri allowed another moment to gather her wits then placed the boy at the foot of the bed and set about the last of this evening's business. It only took a moment of kneading to encourage the afterbirth, and then this horrible night was nearly done.

"Where is my son?" Fen-onna asked hazily as Qiri began to wash the blood from her thighs and set clean linens beneath her. Even now, Fen-onna clutched the other babe to her, as though afraid he would be snatched away.

"He is here, *misin*. I'll have him cleaned up anon, and you may have him while I bathe the other."

"No, give him to me now, clean him later."

Only a tinge of panic in Fen-onna's voice, but what could Qiri expect, really? She sighed, dropped the soiled linens to the floor and took the boy to his mother.

Hesitated. "The boy is…" Faltered. Damn the men for cowards, both of them, leaving Qiri this task. "He is Untouchable, *misin*," she told Fen-onna as gently as she could.

Fen-onna stared, hazel eyes stark and swimming, that too-familiar madness crouching at her edges. And then her jaw tightened, her gaze hardened, and she held out her arm, crooking her fingers.

"No child is Untouchable to his mother."

The rain had only come harder by the time Qiri escaped into the bleak small hours of the morning. The dawn of the New Cycle, she reminded herself, the Cycle of the Wolf, though she couldn't see him through the murky clouds.

Typical.

Wolf only showed his face every hundred and fifty years, and that for only just over three decades, so his coming was rather ominous… or fortuitous. It depended upon how one looked at it, Qiri supposed. An age of reason and conflict, of division and union. Dichotomy, old Wolf. Six cycles in a Turning—one for each moon; one moon for each god— and the last, the Wolf Cycle, had always been the most tumultuous, its coming the most portentous. Still, Qiri would have liked to see him as he dawned for the first time in a century and a half.

She shook her head. She had just as much faith in the Cycles these days as she did in the Ancestors. And what she'd seen tonight had done nothing toward changing her opinion. As for the gods…

The gods could go hang.

The Jin were a cowed people now, their numbers and power dwindling with each Turning. There was the occasional riot still, and the last one had given her hope all too cruel, but it hadn't succeeded in the end. They never did. Even when the Jin dared use the little magic left to them, the Adan still had more thirst in their bloodthirst, more intent in their murderous intent, and all wielding magic did was ferret out those Jin who still had it for the Courts. The Jin had been demi-divine warriors once, centuries ago, but peace and complacency had muted it. Now, it had been beaten out of them entirely.

The rain drummed a soft *pit-pit-pat* on the hood of Qiri's cloak, and though the fox fur around the collar was ancient and smelled of must and dry rot, she was still grateful to have it. She'd never seen a more dismal start to a new Cycle. Then again, she'd never seen one at all, so she'd just rather mooted her own grievance. Pointless natter. Still, better to let her mind blather on about nonsense than allow it to dwell on what she'd seen tonight, what she'd allowed to happen… what she'd conspired in. Because who knew what would come of it?

The man had suffered children of the full-Blood to live, one as powerful as he whose delicate neck bones had crunched beneath Qiri's own strong fingers only little more than a year ago. And though a part of Qiri wanted desperately to believe it benevolence—not all Adan thought the Jin less than people; not all of them approved of the Courts or the camps—the man was still Adan. Who but he could guess his purpose?

Qiri and the new family would be safe in exchange for their silence.

Of that much Qiri could be sure, at least. The seer risked death himself, if any of his own were to discover what he'd done tonight—what he'd seen and what he'd permitted; that he could *see* at all. And though the Courts were harsh and terrible for the Jin, the Adan did not suffer traitors amongst their own. If the seer was found out, his death would be as long and cruel as any Jin's. He risked much in ensuring those children lived.

But to what purpose?

"And to what purpose do you wonder, old woman?" Qiri muttered to herself. Best this night was forgotten altogether.

She'd neglected to collect her fee, either from the seer or Fen-seyh, too caught up in the insanity of the evening. She somehow didn't care. Surely it was enough that there was no blood on her hands to end the old Cycle and begin the new. Surely she would suffer for any atrocity in which she'd colluded tonight another time. Not tonight, not this minute.

Tonight, she would get her sorry self home, dry off in front of the fire, and get her throbbing bones to bed. Swaddle herself in the sheets she could still imagine smelled of her Syuu, though he'd been gone near to ten years now. Qiri still missed him sometimes with a pain that was new and raw. Tonight was one of those times.

Not even halfway there yet, and already burning knives were sticking at Qiri's knees, the gnawing, fiery ache working its predictable way into her hips and spine. Sighing against the self-pity that encroached when she considered the rest of her long walk home and the hobbled body with which she'd have to do it, Qiri hunched into her cloak and plodded on. When she'd limped her way to a lone stretch of nothing—a swath of sandy mud that used to be a barley field and was now merely an ugly fracture between one cluster of shanties and the next—somehow she wasn't at all surprised to see the hooded figure waiting for her.

The seer stood tall and straight, limned in rain and shadow. He tipped a polite nod to her as she approached.

Qiri nodded back, wondering why she wasn't afraid in the face of this man who looked so much like the etchings of Death that used to frighten her so—back when she was a girl and still knew what happiness and freedom meant. Though she hadn't appreciated them then, not until the Adan decided almost-freedom was too much freedom, and so took away even the illusion of it. Of course, by then, Death had begun to look more like friend than foe.

"What would you give, Qiri-onna?" The man's voice was gentle, almost affectionate.

It sent a cold chill up Qiri's spine, but still, she wasn't afraid. "I don't know what you mean, seyh." Though she thought maybe she did.

He turned his face up to the rain. "It is a question I do not think many would ask themselves, but... I think you have done. Perhaps not in so many words, but in the small ways you can affect yourself." He pushed the hood from his head, turning so he was looking Qiri in the eye. "If I understand your traditions aright—and I assure you, I do—your soul was forfeit when you killed him the first time. Never to return to Raven to await a new Cycle, but instead a fiery death for your soul in the penury of the suns. Never to be reborn. And yet, you were prepared to do it again a second time."

He tilted his head, avid interest in his dark gaze, and waited for a reply.

Qiri didn't think she had one.

The beliefs of the Jin, perhaps, but they hadn't been Qiri's for a very long time. Someone like her couldn't afford to keep them, not without forsaking the very last of her compassion. If she was here for a reason, as all were said to be, it wasn't to watch idly while the Ancestors dragged children she'd helped birth into their insanity. And it certainly wasn't to keep feeding souls into the hungry bellies of weak gods who hadn't lifted a finger for her people in… well, ever, as far as Qiri had witnessed.

It decided her.

"Yes. I was prepared to do so again."

And she wished with everything in her that he'd let her.

The seer nodded, unsurprised. "So, I would like to know—what would you do, if you knew your action or inaction would save countless of those for whom you tell yourself you care so much?" He leaned in, pierced her with those strange oracle-eyes. "Would you give yourself for them, Qiri-onna? Would you give yourself for just one?"

The child, of course—the Untouchable. It seemed the man had more prices than just the one. No wonder Qiri hadn't feared him. He truly was Death after all. And she was but a mote in his eye.

"Yes." Qiri's voice was little more than a whisper this time, though she'd spoken honestly. After all, she'd done it once already, had sealed her fate a year ago with her own ruthless compassion. She swallowed, but didn't cow or back away. "But, seyh… I would not tell."

"You would not mean to." The man opened a hand, as if in apology. "A delirium, in your sickbed."

Qiri nearly rolled her eyes at the irony. She almost never got sick.

Miles away, but she could swear she smelled the fishy-salt scent of the sea. Too dark and murky, but she *knew* she could see the stark, black shape of Mount Subie, home and chosen grave of the Ancestors, bracketing the man in cold outline, could feel the low grumble of its bowels in her chest. She closed her eyes, sighed.

Strangely placid. Resigned.

Shifting her weight from one sore hip to the other, she opened her eyes, tipped her face up into the rain as he had done, borrowed the sky's tears, since she had none of her own. She would've liked to see Wolf dawn, at least once, but the damnable clouds…

Ah, well.

A long, somewhat wistful sigh she refused to rue slid from her throat, then Qiri firmed her neck, straightened her shoulders. She looked at the man evenly.

"You said my fate might be kind."

"And so it shall be." The seer smiled, gentle and strangely benign. He reached out and placed two fingers to Qiri's temple.

It didn't hurt as much as Qiri had thought it would.

And then, it didn't hurt at all.

2

Malick dodged yet *another* of those damned little throwing knives that seemed to grow right out of the man's fingers. *How did he manage to throw the things and keep a grip on the long knife* at the same time?

Cursing, Malick willed the sweat not to run into his eyes and queer his focus. He hadn't had such a workout in… well, a while now, and he'd *never* enjoyed a challenge like this before.

You're a sick, sick man, Kamen Malick.

He lunged to his right, sliding into a forward recovery that gained him a little ground and moved him just a half step farther away from the wall. Until now, he hadn't thought allowing himself to be cornered and losing the advantage such a terrible thing, really—he wasn't playing for blood, after all. A contest of skill, Malick had assumed, feints pulled at the last second and attacks blunted, limited to injury versus actual death.

Ha-fucking-ha.

The Ghost had other ideas, apparently. And a seemingly limitless supply of bloody throwing knives. The way things were going, this wasn't going to end until one of them was dead. Which would defeat Malick's purposes, at best—hurt a lot, at worst.

Malick clenched his teeth, pressed in with the sword, then thrust up with the knife as he spun. The parry was predictable, but still something to see, all twirling limbs and spinning blades, glinting moonlight in an eddy of refracted, straightforward elegance. Hard, sinewy muscle clamped directly to the bone. Tall, dark, and oh so fuckable.

Gah.

If Malick didn't need every last fiber of his concentration, he'd be sporting a rather embarrassing erection, which… no, he didn't have the focus to spare on everything that was wrong with that. At the moment, thankfully, he didn't have the time for it. The Ghost apparently didn't believe in playing for points. Either that, or he'd stopped his training right after the fight-to-the-death part and, of course, that *would* be the part that stuck.

"Nice move." Malick spun, swept the sword down on a forward feint then followed with a cross with the knife for a compound attack.

The Ghost didn't answer, didn't even seem to hear, merely whirled back in a counter-defense, and whipped one of those cursed little knives. Advanced again, flipped the long knife from a reverse grip to a hammer grip so fast it was a mere flash in the moonlight that preceded a sweeping cut that nearly took Malick's nose off as he whirled out of his dodge of another damned throwing knife.

Little shit was really trying to kill him.

"You're—" Malick ducked under a press with the long knife, feinted to his right, watching for another of the little knives to come whistling at his head. "You're very skilled." He just managed to keep a wheeze out of it.

Again, the Ghost was silent, concentrating, entirely focused on what his body was doing and what Malick's was doing in response.

Focus, purpose—all smooth economy and lethal drive, this pretty man with the hard glare and soft braid.

Too focused, perhaps, *too* driven. Fast and seamless, but foreseeable, if one paid attention. No personal little flourishes to the moves, no stepping outside the lines of that perfection of skill. Malick could almost count out the steps himself, trace the shapes of the positions in his own head just before the man made them. As though the Ghost was performing for a trainer, or reciting the instructions in his head as he followed the steps. The technique was nearly faultless, every move in perfect form, every parry and advance styled and structured. A flawless copy.

"Let's see what you do with this." Malick lunged in with the knife and followed with an indirect attack with the sword. The knife was smoothly parried and the sword deflected with a forward press.

Malick smirked.

Control—that was the key. Malick had never seen a body so completely under the control of the mind that inhabited it. Control was generally a good thing. Except when it equaled predictability.

No surprises from this man, none but for the deadly drive behind his attacks and the apparent conviction that the only way this could end was with one of their corpses cooling on the damp, dirty stone of the alley. He could beat Malick with his speed and determination—he was more skilled, and more focused in his attention to it—but Malick had to wonder what would happen if the rules were changed.

Grinning now, Malick lunged again, forced an opening when the man parried, and caught him in a spinning counterattack with a hard shove of his boot to the solar-plexus. A thin *whoof* huffed from the man's chest, and his eyes went wide before they narrowed down to slits, nostrils flaring and lips pressing tight. Malick could almost hear the, *Hey, that's cheating!* that was all too obvious in the man's indignant glower.

Malick broadened his grin, waggled his eyebrows. With a deep breath he was all too aware might be his last, Malick turned to his right, left himself open—clear invitation—then swept the sword under his arm. He caught the man in the momentum of his own spin to turn the offensive, putting them in positions opposite of where they'd been just a second ago. Lunged in again with a sideswipe of his foot toward the backs of the man's knees. Turned it into a spinning kick to the thigh when the man dodged backward. Malick drove in right up close at the resulting stumble, one long knife tangled with Malick's sword, the other grinding at the hilt of Malick's knife.

The man glared, right up close. "Figures you'd fight dirty." Like it was the lowest form of insult he could imagine.

Malick's brain went a little wobbly.

Almonds. He smells of almonds.

Sweat and leather and metal polish, too, but mostly almonds.

Right. And so does cyanide.

Pressing in close, so close they were chest-to-chest for a heady half second, Malick backed the man another two steps toward the wall of the building. Brick to his back and his left, Samin to his right and Malick in front of him. Two more steps and the Ghost would be neatly cornered.

"C'mon, love." Malick kept his smile and let his eyelids droop halfway. "Everyone likes it dirty now and again."

The man growled and shoved him away. Malick laughed, swiped away the expected chop with the blunt of his sword and a strangely harmonic screech of metal on metal. Dodged in again, dipping between the extension and attack. Sliced a carved button off the man's tunic and tweaked the braid with the same sweep before he spun back again. Mimed a kiss.

And the man… blinked. Stymied. Only for a breath of a millisecond, but for that breath, he was stunned still. As if Malick had just yanked the ground from underneath him. Outrage, affront, and wonderful, beautiful shock.

Untouchable. He wasn't used to people challenging him, let alone following through. And young too—too old for what he was, but too young for the ruthless assassin he was trying to be.

It was too easy then—Malick *knew*. The Ghost had learned by the book, classically trained by someone who'd clearly been a very skilled teacher, had studied all the moves, all the counterattacks and how to defend against them. And he'd practiced them. Perfected them. Made himself lethal with the use of them. But he'd never learned anything beyond them.

And he'd never expected to have to actually use them.

A damned good assassin—at least from what Malick knew—but still, an assassin who did his bloody work through stealth and surprise.

Aiming for all the points on the body that counted, but unable to handle a defense unless it was letter-perfect and rote. The man had sparred endlessly, Malick could tell just by the precision of the forms and the muscle tone he'd seen down in the bath, but this Ghost had never had an opponent who didn't follow the rules. And it shocked him. Two lords, a judge, and a prefect to this man's tally, and those were only the ones Malick knew about. Who among them would have given a Ghost a real fight?

Heh. Gotcha.

"I've just won." Malick held up a hand. "We can stop this now and call it a draw, or we can keep going, but I warn you—you're beaten. You just don't know it yet."

"Maybe. In your self-important dreams."

It only made Malick sigh. Malick was actually the lesser-skilled between them, and they both knew it—the knowledge blared out from a hate-filled glare—but Malick was the better fighter. Too bad this stubborn, angry, pretty Untouchable wasn't going to believe it until he was bleeding out on his back in the alley.

Malick didn't want to see that. He certainly didn't want to be the cause of it. And he wasn't about to waste magic on preventing it. It was time to end this.

"Yori?"

A soft snort huffed out of the dark. "As soon as you get your fat head out of the way."

Malick smirked. No respect.

"Not unless he kills me."

Malick was still talking as he drove in low. He took the body with his shoulder, dropped his own weapons and reached for the man's wrists as Malick shoved them both back another step toward the brick wall.

Said, "Now, *this* is dirty," and gave the Ghost a swift, brutal knee to the stones.

Malick had a brief moment of sympathetic victory at the man's strained gasp and wheezy little, "Fucking... *fuck!*" but that was all he allowed before he swept his foot behind the man's knees and tripped him back against the wall, pressing him flat.

"There." Malick inhaled deeply the scent of almonds, right up close as he was, and only just kept himself from nipping at an earlobe. "*Now* we can talk."

ᛗ

Samin let the knot in his lungs unwind, mildly disgusted and thoroughly disgruntled. Bloody Malick and his bloody games. And he'd nearly lost this one. Grinning and chattering like a magpie as he dodged very clear attempts to kill him. Didn't he know this silent Ghost wasn't even close to sane, and would do nothing more than walk away and clean Malick's guts off his blade if it had ended the other way 'round?

"Have fun, Mal?" Samin couldn't help the sarcastic bite to it.

"Take his right side, Samin, and don't let his hand free—he's got knives bloody everywhere."

"You're enjoying this a little too much."

"I'm enjoying it exactly the proper amount."

Samin rolled his eyes as he took hold and reluctantly wedged up against their... captive, potential associate, whatever the Ghost was supposed to be. There was a surge and strain as Samin got into position, but Samin managed to contain it and follow suit as Malick began patting the Ghost down and relieving him of the... save them all, how many knives did the man *have*? Strapped to his forearms, secured in sheaths and belts around waist and thighs, secreted in the tops of tall boots. And Malick bloody *snorted*, every time he found another.

And you know what? Fuck Malick for taking such chances with himself and then having the audacity to be happy about it. Didn't he know there were people depending on him? Didn't he care that this pretty Ghost, against whom he was now so conveniently plastered, wanted him dead and likely wouldn't stop trying?

The *silence*, that was what had got to Samin. Juxtaposed to Malick's endless prattle while they'd fought, it had been unnerving.

Malick chucked yet another of those bloody little throwing knives to the growing pile on the stone of the alley, frowning as he peered at the Ghost. "Aw, don't cry, love, it isn't so bad, I promise."

Samin nearly punched him. Instead, he took his anger out on the object of both his ire and Malick's temporary affections, tightened his grip on the Ghost's wrist, and ground bone into brick and mortar.

He got a low gasp out of it that was completely unsatisfactory, but it at least seemed to snap the Ghost somewhat to the reality of his situation: he sucked in a wavery breath, glaring between them.

"What are you?"

Finally, actual words, though they were snapped out in a manner not much different from the snarls. The question still curled something in Samin's gut. "*What* are you?" not "*Who* are you?" There was a distinction, and the thin line of it made Samin narrow his eyes.

"I believe I've already introduced myself." Malick's tone was friendly, almost gentle, the idiot. Clearly not taking it seriously. "But perhaps you weren't listening. I'm Malick. This is Samin."

The Ghost whipped his whole body into a hard jolt that shouldn't have surprised Samin, but it did. He nearly lost his grip.

"*Damn* it." He rammed the Ghost's wrist into the brick and ground down harder. "Will you keep *still* for half a second?"

"All right, Samin, don't damage him. This was all for a reason, y'know. Anyway, I doubt you'd be very still if you were in this position."

"I'd like to see the punter who could *get* me in this position." Still, Samin relaxed his grip.

Until the Ghost jolted again, tried to twist loose. It was too much, this writhing little Ghost's silence and snarls and dangerous question, and Malick's nonreaction to it all.

Samin ground his teeth, shoved "*Still*, I tell you" from between them, and landed a cathartic gut punch. It made the Ghost gag on a gasp and try to curl in, which only pissed Samin off more, for some reason, and he couldn't help but crush the Ghost harder into the wall.

"*Samin.*"

Malick's voice was harsh now, clear reprimand. It snapped through Samin like a cold dash of water.

Pity—that was Samin's problem. He was feeling sorry for the Ghost, and it pissed him off. Because mental or no, the lad was pinned to a wall, hopeless and helpless, and *still fighting*. Samin almost had to respect that. And he didn't want to feel pity for someone who could be so potentially dangerous to all of them. He was paid to be pitiless, after all.

"C'mon, Ghost, settle down and tell me your name." Malick tossed another of the small knives to the pile with a bit of a clang, then shifted sideways to strengthen the restraint. He offered up a smile soft enough to give Samin some real worry. "You know mine, you know Samin's— you'll meet Shig and Yori in just a bit—so it's only fair."

The Ghost clenched his teeth against more gasping, shut his eyes tight. For a moment, Samin thought they weren't going to get an answer.

All at once, the Ghost sagged, tense muscles going looser, defeated. "Fen." He forced it out like victory spoils, like he was actually giving something up.

Samin wasn't fooled. A consolation prize, maybe, or perhaps an attempt at delay and distraction.

"Fen, eh?" Malick waited for a beat, lifted an eyebrow. "That it?"

The Fen-Ghost only wheezed out a weak growl.

Malick shrugged. "All right, have it your way, Fen. Got it all, Samin?"

"If he's got more, he's got 'em stuck in places I'm not going." Samin chucked another three knives to the ridiculously deep pile. Stars above, how did the man not jingle when he walked?

Malick gave the Fen-Ghost an assessing look. "Can I trust you not to run, if we let go?"

The Fen-Ghost didn't even acknowledge the question. "What are you?" he asked again, narrow stare nailed to Malick. "What kind of magic is this?"

Bloody hell, was Malick trying to use his magic on the Untouchable?

Even when he knew magic didn't work on them, because Samin had bloody well made sure to remind him? And how was it the Untouchable could feel it?

Damn it, Samin had known this one was all kinds of trouble. Why hadn't Malick?

Malick darted a sharp glance to Samin, index finger of his free hand tapping idly against brick. Samin could almost see Malick's mind gearing up, calculating.

"That's a very dangerous question," Malick said slowly. "You shouldn't go about asking it. You'll get people in trouble or worse." He leaned in. "Why d'you want to know?"

The Fen-Ghost ground his teeth, tensing again, like he deserved something better to a question like that than the nonanswer he'd got. Anger was very clearly battling a need to know before the Fen-Ghost looked away, sank his gaze down to the ground.

"It… it's gone quiet."

This time, it was Samin who lifted an eyebrow, peering at Malick with an expression that was likely blaring *I told you so*, but he was too pissy and off-center to care. Pots clanging through the open door of the kitchen upstairs, shouting and laughing and the slide of the bodhaison and flute drifting down from the Girou, dogs yarking somewhere a few streets over, not to mention all the normal city noises. *Quiet*. The man was mental. And they were supposed to just take him in and trust him at their backs?

Samin looked over at Yori, who'd been quietly watching and listening from her rearguard position toward the mouth of the alley; he caught her frown and grimaced in agreement. Shig had sidled up to her sister while Samin hadn't been paying attention. Now she stood beside Yori, nodding her bizarre multicolored head, staring at this Fen with sympathy, like she knew exactly what he was talking about and agreed. Samin rolled his eyes. Shig had always been a bit off.

"Quiet." Malick was still narrow-eyed, measuring. "Right." He thumped the Fen-Ghost lightly on the breastbone. "That'll happen when you're a violent, closed-mouthed little pain in the ass who'd rather skewer a person than bloody *talk* to him."

It was the first thing Malick had said all night with which Samin completely agreed. "Mental," he huffed.

The Fen-Ghost snapped the glare over at Samin, deepened it. "Fuck you."

"No thanks. I like mine with a little more tit and a lot less snarl."

As if to vindicate every thought in Samin's head, the Fen-Ghost snarled again.

"All right, now that we've established that you're both five years old." Malick was getting impatient.

Welcome to my world, Samin thought, snide.

Malick directed a lift of eyebrows at the Ghost. "P'raps we could move this along a little?"

The Fen-Ghost ignored it, merely held Samin's stony stare. Clearly challenging, as though he were in any position for it. And then had the audacity to curl his lip—bloody *sneering* at Samin, like he had the right—before shifting a dark look over to Malick. He said nothing, only glowered, jaw clamped tight.

Malick rolled his eyes. "We're going upstairs now." Slow and enunciated very clearly, as though speaking to a halfwit or a child. Which didn't seem altogether off the mark. "You'll come quietly this time, won't you."

Not a question, and Samin could tell the Fen-Ghost knew it. Though he apparently had no intention of giving them an answer anyway. He merely stared some more then deliberately turned his gaze up to the sky, rested his head back against the wall, and set his jaw. Like he was digging in for the night, hanging there against the wall, completely willing to wait them out, and not giving an inch more than he'd already been forced to.

"Oh, for the love of—" It was all Samin could do not to wallop him again. "Are you bloody *kidding* me?"

"Samin," Malick said tiredly, "will you just shut it for five seconds? You're not exactly the most pleas—"

"No, Mal, this is getting absurd." Samin was really pissed now. He was crossing lines all over the place, but someone had to say it. What did they need this little shit for, anyway? Sure, he was good, but they all were—even Shig, for all her oddities—they didn't actually need him, and Samin was *bloody* tired of this *bloody* alley and bone-weary of being growled at by this, this… *reprobate*. "I say we just slit his fool throat and have done with it. What are you going to do—drag him out and *make* him kill people for you? What good is he, if he doesn't even want to know what you're about?"

And how dangerous would he be when he found out? *Damn it, Mal, think with something other than your cock for five seconds!*

Malick turned a flat look on Samin. "Don't you have a flesh-eating maijin to go taunt or something?"

"Why should I go looking for one?" Samin jerked his chin at the Fen-Ghost. "There's a handy one right here."

"*Bloody*—" Malick grumbled the rest of the curse under his breath then shot a tight look at Samin. "I'm not wasting a perfectly good opportunity and a promising asset because you've got your crooked nose out of joint."

"He isn't even that good!" A lie, but Samin wasn't about to sing the crazy Ghost's praises. "You managed to beat him, didn't you?"

"Not without a hell of a lot of effort, and—wait, what's that supposed to bloody mean, anyway, 'I managed to beat him,' like I'm not—" Malick sputtered to a stop and clamped his jaw. "Why am I even arguing with you about this? Who hands you your purse every week, Samin? If I say he's worth it then he's damn well worth it!"

When Malick pulled rank, he really pulled it.

Samin's anger was further piqued by the flush he could feel spreading over his face. "That isn't fair, Mal, and you bloody know it. How many times have I had your back?" He nodded at the Fen-Ghost. "Are you going to trust him in my place? I'm well worth my purse, so are Yori and Shig. So why are we wasting time on this menace, and why is he worth risking us all to get him when he'd just as soon rip out all our throats as look at us? No one could be worth—"

"He'll come along."

Shig's soft voice carried strangely down the alley. It stopped Samin in mid-insult.

Propped against the wall now, staring up at the sky as the Fen-Ghost had been doing, Shig's blonde hair shone close to platinum in the silvery moonlight, dyed streaks of red and blue turned black—the effect was altogether too close to an inverted skunk. An incongruously pretty picture in the light of the moons, though, Samin had always thought so, with her elegantly angled face and snubbed nose, a sedate, dreamy look that softened her bearing and made her age hard to guess to any who didn't know her.

She turned her head, looked at the Ghost with a placid quirk of her mouth. "Just keep a hold on him." A friendly singsong. "He'll stay as long as it's quiet." She broadened her smile, turned to Yori. "I don't like it when it's loud, either."

Malick peered over his shoulder at Shig, his gaze focused.

Samin sighed. All the woman had to do was open her nonsensical pseudo-oracle of a mouth and Malick came over all attentive disciple.

"And you *know* this, Shig?" Malick's tone was cautious but not disbelieving.

Shig merely snorted, rolled her eyes at the Ghost like they shared some kind of private joke, then turned her gaze back up to the sky. Samin stared, frowning, but Shig didn't say anything else, and she didn't look at him again.

"Well, there you have it." Malick sighed, the smirk back in his voice, if not actually on his face. "Shig says so."

And then he merely stepped back—kept a light grip on the Ghost's elbow. Samin had no choice but to do the same, at least not when Malick glowered at him like that. Samin stepped back too, grudgingly held onto a wire-tense arm when breath abruptly filled the Fen-Ghost's starved lungs and he stumbled with the sudden lack of restraint.

Hunched in, guarded, the Fen-Ghost peered around, gaze lingering a little too long on the pile of weapons that lay on the damp alley floor. Samin watched warily, strangely pleased when the Fen-Ghost quickly but carefully scanned over all the angles, marking Yori with her bow down the alley, the dead end at his back, Samin to his right and Malick to his left. Malick had retrieved his sword, but all Samin really needed was his fists. A last almost desperate glance upward, like the Ghost was hoping for an escape from the heavens, then he clamped his mouth tight, curled his hands into empty fists. And just stood there. Silent.

It was bloody unnerving.

"Malick," Samin said evenly, quietly, "just… let me."

He didn't have to elaborate. Samin had made no secret of what he wanted here.

And he'd apparently finally run to the end of Malick's patience with his protests. Malick gave Samin a glare that rivaled the Fen-Ghost's, hard and cold and utterly devoid of the past five years of friendship and mutual survival.

"When you question me, Samin, you question our patron." All cool detachment. Malick paused, waited through Samin's twitch and helplessly indrawn breath. "Is that your intention?"

Maybe it was. Their patron, after all, was the one who'd put them all here. And though Samin had never questioned those bland orders in their block letters on parchment before, this one… he knew where it would lead, he could see it in those blank-bitter eyes of this Fen-creature and the lamps gone bright in Malick's.

And Samin hadn't a right to say any of it. Not if he didn't want his own name to show up in those hateful block letters. He didn't really fear death. He just didn't want to have to watch Malick bring it.

"Fine." Samin tried very hard to keep the disgust out of his tone, and something he wouldn't admit was fear, but he wasn't very good at pretense. "You've got what you want, it seems, O Master. You don't need me anymore, I trust?"

He'd been dancing the edge of real insubordination all evening. He might have just crossed over.

Malick eyed him with two parts chagrin and eight parts cold anger. "No. I don't expect I do."

And just fuck it, Samin wanted out of here, and away from the Ghost of a man who fought with death in his eyes and spoke with cold nothing in his voice, when he chose to speak at all. Samin knew crazy when he saw it, and this Fen-Ghost might as well be carrying its banner and banging its drum.

Why couldn't Malick see it, when he saw everything else so clearly? What was it about this Ghost that lit that light behind Malick's eyes and killed all the sense in him?

"We'll see you tomorrow, then?" Strange and scary Shig might be, but she always managed to cut to the heart of things in her ruthless-passive way.

Samin looked from Shig to the Ghost then, a little hesitant, to Malick. He nodded, cleared his throat. "Tomorrow." Then waited.

Save him, but Malick could have a cruel stare when you found yourself on the wrong side of him. Samin had almost forgotten that—it had been so long since he'd had to notice.

Eventually, Malick sighed like Samin—*Samin!*—was just too exhausting, said, "Tomorrow, then," tightened his hold on the Ghost's arm, and steered him to the kitchen's steps.

Samin didn't sag in relief, just waited until the shadows swallowed Malick and his new pet Ghost. Waited for Yori to follow. Waited for Shig—making a sack of the apron of her tunic and collecting the Ghost's weapons then flipping Samin a cheerful wave and a smile—to trail after.

When he was finally alone, Samin took a deep, long breath, and leaned against the wall until his heart slowed down.

He'd had to say it, every word of it. This Ghost was dangerous, more than Malick would see, because Malick would occasionally look past what the Mage told them was their purpose, but he wouldn't look past what he wanted.

What Samin needed was to watch that lad and perhaps quietly take him out himself, if it became necessary—fuck the braid and fuck "Untouchable." It would likely be a mercy, anyway.

What Samin needed was to do it all without Malick or Umeia noticing, and hope the Mage wasn't in turn watching Samin, deadly pen in hand and just waiting for a slip-up.

What Samin needed…

Samin sighed, rubbed at his neck.

What Samin needed was a very large drink.

ｍ

Umeia hadn't expected to see Malick back so soon, but there he was, leading his surly objective through the crowded public floor and up toward the rooms. She wasn't entirely sure she'd expected to see the Untouchable again at all. Umeia didn't approve of the addition, didn't want anyone new to look after—certainly not a Jin Untouchable—and Malick didn't generally have patience for anything that didn't lead to a bed. Then again, considering their direction…

No. Not with that cold look of general animosity on the Untouchable's face.

Umeia shook her head. "Lex!" She waited until Lex's hopeful brown eyes found hers then motioned him over impatiently. She might fulfill that hope later, but right now, there were bigger issues. "Take over."

Shig and Yori were following after Malick and their new charge. Shig had that faraway look of concentration and that scary little smile that told Umeia exactly what she was doing. And even though it was a good and useful thing and had saved them trouble on many occasions, it still made Umeia's mouth tighten. Because Shig shouldn't be the one doing it. And where the hell was Samin?

Umeia gave Lex a nudge. "And get Suli over to fourteen to watch that redhead. He's cheating, but I can't tell how."

She wouldn't have bothered to worry about it or interfere, if he'd been smart enough to join a table of independent players. Umeia would get her percentage of the winnings one way or the other, regardless of who won. But the fool had been arrogant enough to try his "skill" with a House-dealt table. They could cheat each other, cut each other's throats for all Umeia cared, but she'd be damned if they cheated her.

"Where are you going?" Lex was following as Umeia snagged the elbow of one of her best girls and instructed her to go distract the redhead until Suli could figure out how he was cheating. And to do it before he decided to give the Chance tables a go—if the bastard was using magic, they'd never catch him there, not unless Umeia had Malick come and—

No. Damn.

"Umeia? Love, c'mon, then."

Umeia blew a frizz of brass-blonde out of her eye. "You know, Lex, it's a damned good thing I admire a little impudence in my men." She did, actually. The wavy brown hair, soulful eyes, amazing stamina, and relative youth didn't hurt, either. Her mouth tightened when Lex grinned smugly and he slipped a familiar hand to Umeia's hip. "Then again, I've found my tastes tend to change as I get older."

Satisfied when Lex's handsome face fell at the warning—so satisfied she didn't even chide herself for implying she *could* get older—Umeia knocked Lex's hand away with a bump of her hip. She swayed away, following after Malick, fully confident that Lex's eyes watched her ass until she was out of sight. She smirked as she stepped lightly up the stairs. A little money, a firm hand, and a whole lot of sex appeal—she didn't need any spells or charms. And to think she'd actually had to talk Malick into this life.

She took her time walking the halls of the rooms. The closed doors outnumbered the open ones at least three to one, which meant good things for the coffers, but there were still too many of them open by her calculation. Perhaps merely a delay, since Malick's stunt with the baths earlier had set business back an hour at least. Umeia would have to check in with her lads and ladies when she got back downstairs, make sure they weren't slacking. That new boy, Haru, didn't seem to be backing up his proclaimed work ethic with actual work—maybe a few days of being assigned to the floor instead of the rooms would change his tune. Or maybe Umeia would dump him in the kitchens for a week and set Ragi loose on him. Ragi could turn even the smallest, most innocuous piece of kitchen equipment into a cudgel when so moved.

A passing maid tipped Umeia a timid smile. Umeia rewarded her by giving her a good chiding for turning the lamps in the sconces too high. A waste of oil, damn it. Honestly, she couldn't take her eyes off the smallest detail for a bloody second.

She was still shaking her head as she took the turn for the attic floor and climbed the last set of stairs to where her ducklings lived. Just being here made annoyance turn to something softer.

Not the motherly sort, Umeia, but she had her moments, and she'd developed some real affection for her little flock. She'd had no choice with Malick—he'd grown up under her eye, and if she had her way, would remain there—but Shig and Yori had been a conscious choice. Umeia hadn't been able to help herself. So lost and heartsore, the both of them, and she'd taken one look at Shig and melted.

Malick was the head and backbone, but the girls were the heart and spirit.

And Samin was… another story altogether.

They did good work, her ducklings, and Umeia had done good work in steering them along. If she'd done nothing else in this incarnation, she'd helped set at least three people on the right path and made sure they could get along on their own, if they ever had to. Malick, on the other hand…

Umeia sighed.

She wondered what this new one would be, and grimaced. If she'd known what the damned orders had been, she might've burned them instead of handing them over to Malick. But she'd never quite dared to break the anonymous wax seal when they appeared. Malick would tell her if she needed to know, and not bother her with it if she didn't. She'd needed to know this time, and her dismay over the money lost on the delay in custom tonight was nothing to her anger at the reason. An *Untouchable*, of all things. There was enough risk already just running the Girou and keeping all those in it out from under the notice of the Adan. She really didn't need this.

Stepping just loud enough to let them know she was coming, Umeia cleared the last riser to the attic floor and turned down toward Malick's rooms. Shig and Yori were hovering outside the open door, Yori peering in intently, listening, and Shig dreamily dragging on one of those awful cherry smokes she liked and Umeia thought smelled like singed, cherry-scented horseshit. Shig's multihued head rested against the wall, faraway gaze staring up through the smoke at the ceiling like she was watching the heavens move through it.

Shig smiled vaguely at Umeia. "He's very noisy." She blew a smoke ring, watching with uncharacteristic focus as it scattered apart halfway up to the ceiling. "Buzz, buzz, buzzzzz."

Yori rolled her eyes. "She can't read him. Says there are voices holding his spirit."

"Noooooo." Shig huffed but didn't shift her glance. "I said there are spirits inside him, drowning out his own." She frowned, closed one eye, concentrating. "He's in there. He just can't hear himself. I can probably hear him better than he can, but..." She blew another smoke ring, pouting when this one too wobbled then dissolved. "He doesn't like his voice, and he hates the others. The pain's the only thing he can stand. And the hate. So much hate. *Rage.*" Her expression turned pensive. "Almost the same thing, I guess." She waved her smoke about, shrugged, as if to say, *What can you do?* then fell silent.

Yori glanced up at Umeia, obviously gauging her reaction; when Umeia didn't have one—she'd got used to Shig very quickly—Yori merely nodded at the open doorway.

"They haven't got far. He may be 'noisy,' but he doesn't seem to actually talk much."

Umeia hmphed, scowled, and stepped past Yori and into the room. They'd just see about that.

🜊

Planting-month, Year 1312, Cycle of the Wolf

"Joori! Joori! Hey!"

Joori rolled his eyes. Very little could grate on him like Morin's voice—and the little shithead knew it, delighted in it, was careful to make himself as annoying as he possibly could because of it.

Mouth tight, Joori hunched in over the lump of wood he'd been trying to carve into some semblance of a bird, but his hands never seemed to do what he wanted them to. Jacin could carve just about anything with his nimble fingers—fingers that looked exactly like Joori's—so why couldn't Joori? It just wasn't fair.

"Stupid dull knife," Joori decided as he brushed shavings off his leg and into the grass, then shifted around to watch his brother bounce toward him through the early jasmine buds, bright sun turning Morin's fair hair gold as riven wheat. Joori resigned himself to a moment of torture until Morin deigned to tell him what he'd come all the way out here for. Or maybe he hadn't come for anything but the torture. Joori slipped the abysmal failure of a carving into his tunic—no sense in giving the little prick ammunition.

Morin jagged his way through vine and branch, bare feet squelching in the spring-soggy grass as he slipped and slid, his grin far too wide for his errand to be anything good. Either that or he'd just come from tormenting Jacin—that always put Morin in a good mood. The little troll. Panting through a grin, Morin pulled up short, toes just barely brushing the knees of Joori's grass-wet trousers.

Joori sighed. "What d'you want?"

Morin shrugged with cheerful disregard, kicking idly at Joori's knee with the tip of his muddy big toe. "What'll you give me if I tell you?"

Joori thought about that carefully. There were so many delightful ways he could answer. He settled for scowling as fiercely as he was able, and making a show of curling his hand around the little carving knife.

"How about I *won't* give you a knee to the stones or a broken face?"

Morin's reason for coming must be a really good one—his smile didn't even twitch.

"Jacin-rei sent me." Morin's grin skimmed up into an evil little smirk as he slid his hands behind his back, bobbing up on the balls of his feet for a second then bouncing back down to his heels.

Joori hated him. Absolutely *despised* him. Hated that "rei" and hated Morin for making it a point to say it. Hated their father for his harsh rebukes for anyone who "forgot" it in his hearing. Hated his father for making a Ghost of his own son before the time actually came. Which maybe it wouldn't. Joori had hit a Change he hadn't even known was coming months ago, with all the terror that had involved. And blamed Morin for a lot of how it happened, even if he knew it was stupid to do so. Still, Morin had been there, he'd started it. Made Joori so *angry* at him, though Joori couldn't even remember now why, but angry enough to think—even just for a fleeting moment—that he wouldn't mind it if Morin just... well. Maybe not *died*, exactly, but at least wasn't there anymore. It would make everyone's lives so much more pleasant.

He hadn't even noticed the earth sliding beneath his feet at first, all his rage rising with it, inside it, rumbling like a belch in the belly of a sleeping beast. Making Joori one with it, like a perversion of a twin, only this twin was awful and destructive, and somehow *inside*.

It had been Jacin then as it was Jacin always—slapping Joori back to sense, calming him until the earth calmed with him, and then giving chase when Morin bolted, terrified. The subsequent pursuit-and-tackle had left Morin with a broken wrist and a bitter hatred for his Ghost-brother. But he'd kept his bloody mouth *shut*, and that was what mattered.

Jacin was showing no signs of the terrible clutch of insanity that came with "Catalyst." So, maybe they'd been wrong. Maybe Jacin wasn't meant to be Untouchable after all. Maybe the Ancestors had... died or something, or just gone away, or decided to hear Joori's prayers and leave his brother alone. Maybe Joori could one day take that "rei" and shove it right down their father's throat. And Morin's.

"And what did Jacin send you for?" Joori was a little too pleased when Morin's eyes narrowed at the purposeful abbreviation.

Morin shrugged, gave Joori an imperious sneer, and lifted his chin. "She's doing it again."

Joori was on his feet before Morin had finished the sentence, already running toward home as he tucked the knife into his belt and shot back, "You little shit!" over his shoulder.

Only Morin the Miscreant could take pleasure in relaying that message. He had just as much fun tormenting their mother as he did their brother. Caidi seemed to be the only one safe from Morin's too-imaginative harassments, so far, but Joori figured that would end once Caidi was past the easily broken stage of toddlerhood. Mother said Morin would grow out of it someday, but Joori knew better. Morin might look like his dam, but he was his sire's get in every other way possible.

Feet pounding just as hard as his heart, Joori reached the scrubby path that wound through new-awakened red maples, varying from knee- to chest-high. Vivid contrast to the otherwise barren 'scape on which their sorry excuse for a "farm" rested. The backdoor clattered as Joori shoved it aside and bounded into the house, barreling through the kitchen then the common bower where their mats sat in rolled lumps against the wall. He reached his parents' room with almost no breath left, scalp tingling with sweat and limbs shaky.

His mother lay curled on her bed—unusual for the middle of the day, but growing less unexpected just lately. Her gaze was more alert than Joori had thought it would be, and achingly wary. Jacin sat on the pallet in the corner, staring at the door with anxious regard, his gray eyes wide and his back rigid, until he saw Joori and slumped in relief.

Joori could see the last ten minutes or so like he'd been there to witness them himself, because he had been too many times now. Jacin had been sitting with her, comforting her, touching her, talking her down from her bout with possession. And Jacin had expected Joori to be their father, coming in to catch him at it and take his frustrations out on... anyone other than the Untouchable son he refused to touch.

It wasn't so much the careful disregard from Father that plagued Jacin, nor was it Father's insistence on treating Jacin like what he was meant to become, rather than what he was. It wasn't even Father's insistence that everyone else do the same—even Mother, who'd carried the Untouchable in her womb for all those long months; even Joori, who'd shared it with him.

It was the fear. It was the lack of anything else in Father's eyes when he looked at his second son—not even hatred.

Jacin gave Joori a worried look. "Morin came to get me first."

Good. That meant Father was still safely sowing cabbages and far enough away in the north field to have not heard Mother's racket, or seen Jacin's sprint when he came for her. Perhaps Morin had a tiny little heart after all.

Sighing, Joori dropped to the edge of the thin mattress, heedless of the state of his trousers and what they might do to the linens.

"Hey." Joori kept it low, nearly a whisper.

Mother didn't answer, though she put on a weak smile. Joori tried to return it as he reached out, sinking his fingers into lank flax, dismayed that it seemed to suck in the spray of sunlight through the gap in the curtains rather than refract it with its usual luster. She was getting worse.

At least Father had missed this one.

"It's happening more now," Jacin said softly.

"I know." Mother's smile dipped down, turned rueful. "The spirits are restive. Ever since that day Morin broke his wrist."

Joori shot a nervous tic of a glance at Jacin, and then mouthed, *Don't*, at the look of guilt and regret that flushed Jacin's face. It had been an accident. Jacin never would have touched Morin had Morin not been running away, Joori's very life at stake if Morin blabbered. Anyway, it hadn't caused any permanent damage.

Jacin merely gave Joori a remorseful shrug, looked down, and ground his palm into his trouser leg, then into his left eye, like he had an itch that wouldn't go away. He was too pale today, Joori noted belatedly, a light sheen of sweat on his upper lip that couldn't be explained away by the cool spring air. And he was trembling.

Joori frowned, but Mother reached over, took Joori's hand, and held out her other toward Jacin. Jacin only hesitated a second before he pulled himself up from the pallet where they'd all spent their sick days and nights, and made his way over to the bed. A light stumble made Joori frown again, but Jacin smiled at their mother as he took her hand and sat on the other side of the bed.

"The one who is there." Mother squeezed both their hands. "That's the one who will be there, the one who will refuse to abandon you, even if they should." She spoke to both of them, but her foggy hazel eyes stayed steady on Jacin. "No laws will bind them, no laws will thwart them. The one whose face hovers over yours when you wake from your death-sleep—that will be the one."

Joori sent an asking glance at Jacin—*Is she saying what I think she's saying?*—but Jacin only ducked his head and clenched his jaw.

Mother turned to Joori. "Deliver the key into the hands of the Null— all things come to Zero in the end, even the Catalyst."

Joori started, almost wrenched his hand away. "What...?"

Catalyst—leave them to their fates, for those fates intersected the fates of the world in ways mortals couldn't see. Let the Untouchables wander in their madness, starving and stumbling, touch them not—to help or hinder—because one wisp of a touch might alter their course, change Fate. Shackle them with the braid so all would know, all could see plainly.

Joori hated the braid almost as much as he hated the words. Almost as much as he hated the Ancestors.

Mother never said the word, never. "Catalyst" rotted in her mouth before she could spit it out, the same with "rei." Their father had drilled it into them—*Catalyst, Ghost, Untouchable*—intent that Jacin knew what he was to be, intent that Joori knew his brother wasn't his to keep, and trying to pry them apart since they'd emerged from the womb. But their mother...

Joori shook his head, angry now. "Mother, what—?"

"Joori." Soft and shaky.

Joori snapped his glance up to Jacin, knowing and not wanting to, but Jacin's grip on Mother's hand had gone bone-white. Sweat was slicking tendrils of chestnut to his face, the frays of the hated braid clinging to his neck like grasping vines. Joori almost didn't notice Mother squeeze his hand again.

"The Ancestors won't be deceived." Her voice was shaky and thin. "My Blood won't contain them. My spirit is too small to hold them all."

"Mother, what—?" Except Joori *knew*.

She'd tried to trick them. Spiritbound, she'd tried to bind the Ancestors to herself and spare her son.

Joori had no idea if he loved her for trying or hated her for failing.

"*Joori.*" Jacin wrenched blind from their mother's grip, hands flying up to his head, clutching and tearing, and feet stumbling over nothing as he caromed into the wall at his back. "It's... I can't..." And then he stopped, stared like a statue—*screamed*, high-pitched and desperate. Went to his knees for a heart-stopping moment before he was up again, bolting haphazardly for the doorway. He missed it, careened into the wall before he finally wobbled through it.

Joori was still staring at the spot where Jacin had been, struck numb and paralyzed, when he heard the chickens in the yard squawking protest, then another of those piercing shrieks. It shook him into motion.

He tore after Jacin, following the sobs and eerie, frightened howls. Bursting back out the door and into the yard, Joori pulled up short, could do nothing but stare at the huddled figure of his brother for a moment before he gathered the courage to go to him. The screeches crawled right up Joori's backbone. Jacin was facedown, twisting in the dirt of the weedy yard like he was trying to press himself through it, covering his ears and tearing at his hair by turns. It was... heartbreaking. And hideously unnerving.

Insanity made flesh. Jacin was every Untouchable Joori had ever seen, telling himself as he skirted around them, obedient to tradition, that his brother would never look like that. Not Jacin. Not the boy who dragged his mat right up close in the middle of the night and then back again before their father rose at dawn. Not the boy who bore their father's refusal to love him, rather than risk the slightest touch of pain when he lost him.

Not the boy who was the other half of Joori. Who'd saved him when a Change he hadn't even known was coming had hit Joori in ways for which he couldn't possibly have been prepared, not even if he had known.

This writhing mass of tears and tremors, shrieks and shivers, trying to mindlessly bury itself in scrapped earth and tear the ears from its head—this was *not* Joori's brother.

Joori clenched his jaw, crouched down, and made himself move his hand, lay it to Jacin's back, rigid and quaking through the linen of his sweat-heavy tunic.

"Jacin." It came out a little raspy and shaky, so Joori cleared his throat, said it again, "*Jacin,*" louder and with a firm shake to Jacin's shoulder.

A cringe and more muffled screaming was all he got, so Joori dragged Jacin up to his knees, shook him, screamed it, right in his face, "*Jacin!*" and slapped him. It didn't have nearly the effect it had had on Joori when Jacin had done it to him to stop the earth from shattering beneath them. Joori tried it again, only he curled his fist this time, turned the blow into a great wallop that came right from his shoulder. "*JACIN!*"

It got through, at least a little bit. The sobs and shrieks wound down to lunatic babbling that was almost worse, things coming out his intelligent, articulate brother's mouth that made no sense, no sense at all, and tripping over themselves in their haste to wobble off his tongue.

"Balk batter baffle them all crushed and craven Wolf will *not* be thwarted he sees the Eye and calls the Prime to his own leers through a veil of burning skies to Raven's duplicity—"

"Jacin, stop it!" Joori thumped Jacin again with a hard fist, right to the temple, dazed him.

And *still*, it wouldn't *stop*.

"—the gods speak no more silent silent dead and quiet ours now our boy light the lamps of the sky and burn—"

Joori couldn't take it, knew Jacin couldn't, either—his eyes had gone glazed and hectic, madness pushing out whatever it was inside them that made him Jacin. Joori knew his brother well enough to know Jacin would rather die than live like this, knew him well enough to know he'd never ask it and damn Joori's soul to the suns. Staring into that face so like his own, those eyes—the only part of their father Joori loved anymore—it was a forfeit he was willing to offer. Somewhere, even when he'd convinced himself it would never happen, Joori had known it would come to this.

He took the small carving knife from his belt, gripped it in a tight fist.

"—too many voices everything and everything wordswordswords... Joori—"

Drew his arm back, small blade glinting in sunlight that burned bright-hot on the crown of Joori's head, yet chilled him to the bone. Watched the flare catch Jacin's crazed stare—

"—please, I can't… it won't… *stop*, make it stop makeitstop*makeitstop*—"

—swept the blade down, and… pulled it shy. Aimed for Jacin's throat and glanced his chest instead. Tried to end the misery of the heart of his heart. And *couldn't*.

"Oh, no. Jacin." Joori blinked, wretched sobs catching blunt in his throat as he watched bright scarlet bloom into the slashed weave of Jacin's tunic. "Jacin, please, I'm sorry." Weeping, shaking, Joori lunged in and clamped his arms around Jacin's neck, sobbing his treachery into the despised braid that smelled of linseed soap and sweat. "Sorry, sorry, I'm so sorry, I couldn't, can't…"

Sobbed harder when he felt shaking arms slide around his ribs. Harder still when he listened through his own babbling and realized Jacin had gone silent. Joori pushed away, just a little, just so he could see Jacin's eyes.

Almost sanity. *Almost* comprehension.

"It's… better." Jacin's voice was hoarse but even, rational, and his eyes were frightened and a little bit cloudy, but he was in them. Jacin pushed Joori back a little more, looked down, ran his fingers over the blood-stained tunic, dipping them mercilessly into the wound beneath it. He hissed, but merely pressed harder. Joori could almost see the pain in Jacin's eyes crowding out the delirium.

"Gone?" Joori asked, throttling the threat of exhilarated hope.

"Not gone." Jacin shook his head, stared at his fingertips, bright with blood. "Quieter."

⛩

"You won't!" Joori watched with intense satisfaction as his father's eyes went wide in surprise. It was only a second before they narrowed with blind resolve, but that second was almost euphoric. "He's your son just as much as I am. You *will not* turn him out like a dog to fend for himself."

"He is Untouchable." Blunt. Flat. Father turned away from the door and calmly sat down on his accustomed mat at the table.

"And what's he to do? Survive on the moldy bread of halfhearted shrines? Eat the scattered seeds left for the ghosts? He's your son! He's my *brother*!"

"*No!*" Father pounded his hand flat to the table hard enough to make Joori jump. "No one's son, no one's brother, no one's father, no one's lover. He is Untouchable! It is his *fate*!"

"*Fuck* Fate!"

It was weirdly satisfying to see Father startle and stare like he had no idea who Joori was, because he didn't, not really. Not if he thought Joori could just stand there and watch Jacin cast out to wander, pretend he didn't even know his own brother, his twin, pretend the insane babble that had come from Jacin's mouth had even meant anything. *None* of it ever meant *anything.* Why did they keep *doing* this, keep believing? Perhaps the Jin had deserved what they got from the Adan.

Joori took a long breath, tried to snag some composure, approach it all like Jacin would've done. He could feel the tremble in his gut, threatening, wanting to wind into earth and take Joori with it. Joori dug his fingernails into his palm to drive it away, bit down hard on the inside of his cheek.

Calmer. Clearer.

"Father." Joori kept it low, even. "He is your son. He has *always* been your *son.* Look at me. I have the same face, the same eyes—they're *your* eyes, Father, he's *yours.* How can you just…" His hands were aching, they were clenched so tight. "All we'd have to do is cut off the braid, take him to the—"

"*Sacrilege!*" A roar, shocked and full of wrath.

And Joori knew—by the single-minded determination, the fervent conviction. He'd never hated his father so profoundly in his life.

"Yes." Joori's voice was hoarse with dull, impotent fury. "It is." And he didn't care if he burned for it.

And what would you do if I told you what I am, Father-mine? Betray me to the Courts? Pretend I never existed after I've Disappeared? Or hide me, like you do for her—a captive to "love" in my own home, like she's been since the Adan?

He shook his head, sad-eyed and full of a disturbing mix of hatred and mourning.

And what would you do if they finally came for her? Give them me instead? You've already sacrificed one son to your useless gods and their cruel traditions—what's one more?

"What will you tell Mother?"

Father was silent for too long, staring at his callused hands on the table, then: "You ask as though you don't know what she did—for *him.*" He looked up, looked Joori in the eye. The sadness and beaten loss in his gaze might have affected Joori a moment ago, but not now. "Your mother… my Marika…" Father bowed his head, shoulders slumping. "She has never been well. I no longer know my wife, and you will not know your mother. She is not behind her own eyes."

"How would you know?" Joori stared his father down. "You refuse to see what's right in front of you." He shouldered his pack and Jacin's. "You're a coward, Father. You always have been. You don't see your wife or your son because you won't *look.*"

Done now, more than done—with Father, with all of it—Joori stormed out into the yard, punting one of the chickens out of the way when it strutted in front of him. The ruckus sent the rest squawking away in a flurry of brown feathers and indignant clucks.

"You know you can't come with me." Jacin was toying with the tender buds of one of the little maples and staring tiredly up at the sky, watching Wolf slide his bloated way across clots of stars. He'd lit an incense stick on the shrine. Joori wondered who it was for but wouldn't ask. Jacin's voice was heavier than normal, deeper, like he'd aged a hundred years just since this morning. His eyes had a faraway look they'd never had before, a wariness and a narrow, eerie haze that was nothing like him, like he was listening to—

Joori's teeth clenched.

—like he was listening to a thousand voices in his head.

Joori pushed it away, because it was exactly what Jacin was doing, and Joori didn't want to think about it. Jacin was in there, damn it, and now they knew how to keep him in there.

"You can't go by yourself, Jacin. And I can't stay here by myself, not with him."

"He's only what he is, Joori. And now I'm… what I am." Jacin paused, gaze drifting to Joori like he was moving inside a dream. "You can't leave her alone with him."

All the rage Joori had felt toward his father a moment ago came boiling back up. Not at Jacin, really, but… because of him. For him. The bruises on Jacin's face in the shape of Joori's own hand shone near-black in the gloom, and it only notched the fury up from Joori's gut to the middle of his chest.

"That isn't fair, and you know it. You can't make me choose, you can't—"

"I'm not making you choose. *I'm* choosing."

Joori set his jaw. "That isn't your right. You need me. You can't do this by yourself, no one can, you've seen it. You'll live a year, maybe two. Jacin." Joori stepped in, took hold of Jacin's shoulders, shook him until the gaze that met Joori's was brighter and more… more *Jacin*. "You've seen, you know. You can't expect me to—"

"If you came with me and someone caught you, they'd kill you, Joori."

"Don't you think I'm smarter than that? I've got it all figured. All we have to do is get out of the camp. There are houses on the coast, just sitting there empty. Dozens of them. Even that hairy gate guard says so."

"Because their Jin owners were killed by the Adan." Jacin sighed, leaned in, and pressed their foreheads together. "You'd be no safer there than—"

"We're not worrying about me right now, damn it! *You're* the one—"

"*I'm* worried about you!"

"Well, stop it and let me be the one to worry for once! 'No laws will bind them, no laws will thwart them,'—that's what Mother just said this morning." Joori firmed his hold on Jacin's shoulders, shook again, harder, refusing to think about the fact that now he could be stoned for something like this. It only made him tighten his grip. "Jacin, it hasn't gone away, just… quieted. What if it gets too loud again? And where are you going to find food? Shelter? No one will touch you; they'll watch you die in the street rather than help you, and they'll think the gods are up there smiling at them and patting them on the head for doing it. Well, *fuck* the gods, I'm not going to let—"

"Your concern for your brother is both touching and admirable, young Fen-seyh, but unnecessary now."

Joori jolted, let go of Jacin's arms, and stepped in front of him. "Who the hell are you?"

Dark-cloaked and dark-cowled, the man stepped through the weak, slatted light striping through the shutters of the kitchen window. He moved like an elegant phantom, gliding to a stop as he turned down the hood of his cloak, eyes gone black in the moonlight and looking right past Joori to lock onto Jacin.

"I am Asai." The man's deep voice hummed through the dark like a soft-struck bell. "Please go and fetch your father. Tell him I have come to collect my fee."

3

"For the love of the gods, Malick, where are your manners?" Umeia had stopped so suddenly that Yori almost sailed into her back and Shig into Yori's. "What is that man doing on the floor?"

"Hey, don't look at me." Malick's tone was defensive, which was a bit of a change from the annoyed-cajoling-aggrieved notes it had been reaching while Yori and Shig had been lingering in the hall. "I offered him the couch."

Yori bobbed up on her toes and peered around Umeia's shoulder, took in the arrangement, and raised her eyebrows. The Ghost was kneeling on the floor beneath the window, fists planted on knees and head bowed, that long braid flopped over his shoulder and coiled like a snake on the floor. His eyes were shut tight, and his jaw was clenched so hard Yori could see the muscles ticcing beneath the skin.

Meditating. Yori had seen Shig do it often enough, even tried it herself a few times, but she didn't have the patience or concentration for it. It wasn't a terribly odd thing to do, Yori supposed, but... right now? After what had just happened in the alley? Even Shig had never done something so... All right, yes, she had. But Shig was Shig, and this man was... well. Not Shig.

"Huh," Yori blurted before she could stop herself, inadvertently catching Malick's eye, but he only gave her a quick glance—neither welcoming nor forbidding—before shifting his gaze again, chagrined, to the man on the floor.

Shig breathed a happy little, "Ah!" behind Yori then elbowed her out of the way, squeezing past Umeia and into the room. Smiling at the Ghost like an old friend, Shig knelt in front of him, almost knee to knee, and mirrored his pose, dipped her head and breathed in deep, then went still and silent.

Malick's eyebrows jumped up his forehead like two startled caterpillars. He shared a dubious look with Umeia, then waved her and

Yori in. Umeia took the couch that had apparently been shunned by the Ghost, her expression thoughtful. Yori took a spot against the wall near the window—not that she thought anything would happen, exactly, but she didn't trust the Ghost and she wanted to be close and able to keep an eye on Shig. Just in case.

"Well, then." Umeia turned to Malick. "Is this… normal?"

"How the fuck am I supposed to know?"

"Watch your mouth, you insufferable reprobate."

Yori nearly burst a lung trying not to laugh. Umeia was the only one who dared to chastise Malick, and it was always amusing to see him grimace aggrievedly and do as he was told.

"…to his wrist?" Umeia was asking when Yori stopped snorting into her collar and started paying attention again.

Malick grimaced. "Samin got a little… enthusiastic when we were confiscating the mountain of weapons our little Ghost tried to kill me with. Now that you mention it, he may need some ice for… someplace else. I had to, um… well, I had to get him down quickly, and…"

Umeia gave Malick a sour look and shook her head, but unconsciously crossed her legs when she did it. Funny, the way women reacted almost as vigorously as men to the thought—even Yori winced in sympathy, and she didn't even have stones, though she sometimes wondered if Umeia did. Great big brass ones, at that.

Maybe it was the instant pity that had overtaken Yori at the Ghost's look of profound agony and white-faced blank shock when it had happened, the instant flight of anything from his angry eyes but stunned, mindless animal pain. Or maybe it was merely Yori's surprise that Malick had stooped to such a low blow. He wasn't usually the sort. Then again, people tended to change their "sort" in the blink of an eye, if it suited them. And Malick was nothing if not changeable.

"…like that," Malick was protesting heatedly to whatever censure Umeia had just lobbed at him. "Ask Yori, she saw it. He wasn't going to quit until one of us was dead, and I'd prefer it if neither of us wound up that way, thank you. Apparently, not everyone is thrilled when told they've been chosen as one of our own."

Yori nodded in support, but didn't say anything, just watched with increasing disquiet as Shig began to quietly plait braids through her motley hair, whispering to the Ghost in a sympathetic croon. Umeia and Malick were still sniping familiarly at each other, but Shig had apparently tuned them out, concentrating instead on the Ghost, who just knelt there, stiff, and as unresponsive as he'd seemed since they'd walked through the door. Except now that Shig had set herself in front of him, he appeared to be wound a little tighter, fists white-knuckled on his knees and pressing into his legs hard enough to gather and bunch the heavy fabric of his trousers. There were deep creases around eyes squeezed tight-shut, and a thin trickle of blood running down his chin.

Yori frowned, took a step in. "Mal?"

"...the fu—deuce else was I *supposed* to do?" Malick huffed, all put-upon. "He stomped in here, planted himself, and hasn't moved or spoken since. I don't even know if he can hear me."

"It's no excuse for not tending to him properly." Umeia looked angry. And disappointed. "Especially after kneeing him like that. I'm actually a little embarrassed for you. I know you were taught better."

"Oh, bullshit, Umeia, you're the dirtiest fighter I know. You'd've taken the chance if it had been you who—"

"I would *not* have—"

"I'm not bloody arguing about it! He's alive, isn't he? And so am I, because I *stooped*—I know how you so worry."

"Mal?" Yori was watching the little runlet drip in tiny splashes from the corner of the Ghost's mouth down to the wood flooring, a small pool of scarlet already gathered and seeping into the weave of rush mats covering the floorboards. She could hear Shig now, nearly chanting at the man, clear entreaty.

"He can help you, noisy Ghost. Don't you love the quiet?" Shig reached out, a languid sweep of her hand near the side of the man's face, but she didn't touch. "Sometimes I could crawl inside it and sleep forever." Shig's hand moved to hover over the Ghost's heart, but still, it was as though she didn't dare actually make contact. "A hard man, you are. You'll choose your angry pain over the quiet every time, won't you?"

It was very subtle, but Yori marked it uneasily: the man hunched in the slightest bit, and his breathing picked up pace.

"Mal?"

"...supposed to be one of us now." Somewhere along the line, though Yori had missed it completely, Umeia had come up with her medicinal kit and a cloth she waved around while chiding Malick at the same time. "Probably didn't even offer him tea. No wonder he's ignoring you."

"He didn't give me a bloody *chance* to—"

"If I have to tell you one more time to watch that mouth, I'll—"

"*Malick!*"

Finally, they both stopped their bickering and turned to Yori, Umeia still with her finger pointed accusingly at Malick, and Malick with something that looked suspiciously like annoyed relief.

Yori looked between them, then pointed at the Ghost. "He's bleeding."

Shig was still whispering to him: "...can teach you how to make sense of it, but fighting it will only hurt more, and you've enough scars, I'm thinking."

Something about it made gooseflesh bloom up Yori's arms.

Malick had gone still, narrow-eyed, the way he always did when Shig wandered into semicoherency. Umeia dove into her satchel, quickly and brusquely, but Malick held up a staying hand and brushed slowly past her, stepping softly over to Shig, deep in her one-sided conversation with this strange Untouchable.

"Can you 'hear' him, Shig?" Malick kept his voice gentle and dulcet, as he did with no one else.

Shig smirked up at him, sly. "You'd have me listen to one of our own?"

Malick's mouth tightened. It was the one thing he'd demanded of Shig, not to "eavesdrop," and it had been an easy promise for her, really, because she couldn't, not with them, not with Malick around, or at least when he was paying attention. Still, Malick was apparently not pleased to be reminded of something he knew very well, and mildly chided for it besides.

"He isn't one of 'our own' yet, is he, then?"

"Isn't he?" Shig merely shrugged at Malick's light growl, toying with the new braids tangled in her hair—an attempted kinship, no doubt, which Yori abruptly decided she didn't like at all. Shig shook her head. "He can't even hear himself. And there's *so much* to hear."

Again, she reached out, like she wanted to stroke the Ghost's cheek, but she refrained from actually touching him. Nevertheless, even with his eyes squeezed tight, the Ghost bared his teeth.

Shig pouted. "The pain isn't the only thing with a voice, prickly Ghost. It won't help you recover what you've lost." Her fingers crept toward the braid curled on the floor between them; instead of touching it, Shig ran her fingertips through the small puddle of blood, rubbed them together, then… licked them. "What have you lost, angry Ghost?"

Something walked up Yori's spine, and she suppressed a shudder.

"Get her away from me."

It was tight and thin, the first words the Ghost had spoken since the alley.

Somehow, it made Yori breathe a little easier.

"Yori."

Yori peered over at the gentle command implicit in Malick's tone. Calmly, she crouched down and laid a hand on Shig's shoulder.

"C'mon, love, let's let Malick and Umeia have at him for a bit, yeah?"

Shig turned to Yori with a sad smile, then returned her mercurial attention to the Ghost. "We'll help you get them. Isn't that what you want? It's what we do, y'know."

It got a reaction where nothing before had done: the Ghost's eyes sprang open, narrowed and homed in on Shig in a way that made Yori want to drag Shig back and away and out of the room entirely.

The lethal stare didn't affect Shig in the least. "Ah, *that's* got 'im." She snickered with a pleased look at Malick. "Promise to find what the

Ghost has lost, promise to crucify the one who took it…" Shig turned back, leaned in, lowered her voice. "He can, y'know." She bobbed a nod toward Malick. "There's a promise from me to you." She winked at the Ghost's suspicious look, then leaned back, grinning up at Yori. "Promise him, Yori."

Yori rather suspected her eyebrows were doing the same surprised-caterpillar thing Malick's were doing again. She stared at Shig, turning a questioning look to Umeia first, then Malick. Malick merely shifted a faint shrug and then a nod. With a bemused frown, Yori met the Ghost's—

No, he was one of their own now, Shig had said so, and he had a name.

—met Fen's wary distrust with an open look. "Your goals are ours, or so I've been told. I'm already oathbound."

Fen stared at her for so long Yori had to concentrate on not squirming. It wasn't any outward threat that tightened her chest and her nerves, or even an inward one, really—she couldn't see inside people the way Shig or even Malick could do. It was the intensity inside the stare, the way it came at her like a verbal shout, and yet she had no idea what it was saying.

Until Fen tilted his head, eyes glittering little slits. "Goals."

The tension that had built itself into the silence broke effectively with that single word. Malick stepped in closer, crouching down on Shig's other side, Umeia edging up right behind him.

"I've been trying to tell you, but you don't listen very well. We want the same things. All of us." Malick gave Yori a quick look of silent apology, then went on, "Yori and Shig are both half-Blood, sold by their Kente mother to an Adan sharper for Blood-magic. Show him, Shig."

Shig agreeably reached for the cuff of her sleeve, but Yori stopped her before she could draw it up.

"Mal." Yori had no doubt her tone was lousy with warning. She'd meant it to be.

Malick only gave Yori a level stare, unmoved. "Show him," he repeated to Shig, his gaze firm on Yori.

Yori could only slump and let go of Shig's arm. Malick didn't often pull rank, but when he did, it was all in. Damn him.

Shig gave Yori's hand a light pat for comfort then rolled up her sleeve without even a slight hesitation and no hint of the wince that Yori knew shadowed her own face.

Scar upon scar. There were times when the skin was so thin and fragile Yori had feared it would never knit together again. The rage still took her, every time her glance accidentally lit on Shig's arms, but it never seemed to bother Shig, and when it did, it was only because she knew it bothered Yori.

When Yori looked up, Fen's narrow stare was not leveled on Shig's scars, but Yori's face, and the things inside his severe gaze…

Ah. All right, then. This, Yori could recognize. Now she half-understood the strange kinship with Fen toward which Shig had been leaning. Yori felt it herself this time, caught up in amber-shot gray, looking back at her with watchful and mutual understanding. Perhaps she couldn't see into others with the clarity with which her sister had been cursed, but Yori knew common misery when she saw it.

This Fen was theirs now. He just didn't know it yet.

"Samin was a doujoun once," Malick said, "then retired and took a job as an Adan lord's minder."

Fen's gaze snapped up, slanting dangerously toward malice again, the tension in his body renewed and ratcheting up near to levels that made Yori blink and stiffen up herself.

"He hadn't known." Malick shrugged. "No one does, not really, except those who are doing it. It takes a lot to sicken a man like Samin to the point where he'd turn on his leash, but what he saw, what that lord was doing, what he was demanding Samin do *for* him..." He opened his hands, met Fen's hostile gaze with a direct one of his own. "He doesn't look it, but he's got a heart under that scowl."

Shig interjected with a soft snort. "Samin's got a great, squishy center." Her ingenuous grin turned toward Malick. "Like a cream comfit!"

Malick smirked, fond, brushing his knuckles along Shig's cheek with a tenderness they didn't see very often. Well, except for when he was on the make, which hardly counted.

"A great big squishy one, at that. 'Some things should not be borne, and some people should never have been born at all,' that's what Samin says, and he..." Malick paused, thoughtful, his smile slowly losing to a more serious expression. "It isn't telling tales, I suppose—Samin enjoys fixing the mistakes of the gods, and executing those he says should never have been born. He likes what he does. Says it's his calling. And I feel better having him at my back than aiming for it."

It was almost like he was justifying Samin to Fen, and Yori had to frown, disapproving. It didn't seem... fair, somehow. Samin didn't need justification—he was theirs.

There was a pause, gravid, while Fen and Malick stared at each other, measuring.

"Adan?" Fen finally asked, suspicious. Remembering, no doubt, Samin's protests and threats in the alley.

Malick merely nodded, no apologies or rationalizations this time. "You'll find they're not all alike, if you bother to look."

Fen's mouth flattened, though Yori couldn't tell if it was anger at the implied reprimand, disbelief, or even agreement. His gaze kept flicking to Shig, hanging there, before he willfully pulled it away—pointing it at the floor, the ceiling, his own hands—then, finally, allowing it to meet and settle once again on Malick.

"And you?"

Malick smiled, a rare soft one, like Fen had just handed him some kind of compliment. "I—"

"Malick has his reasons." Umeia gave Malick a quelling look.

Yori thought for a moment Malick would ignore it. He shot a narrow glance up at Umeia, clearly annoyed. Some secret almost spilled, maybe? If it was, Umeia seemed to care more about keeping it than Malick apparently did. When Umeia held her warning glare and tightened her mouth, Malick only sighed and shook his head. Whether it was or it wasn't, Umeia seemed to take it as concordance.

Yori almost slumped, strangely disappointed. If this Fen was to be one of their own, shouldn't their secrets be his? Especially if they were supposed to be prying his out of him. And anyway, Yori kinda wanted to know too.

"Back to Zero and start again." Shig threw herself forward, slapped her hands to the floor so hard and quick on either side of Fen's thighs she made Fen startle back into the wall with a vicious snarl and reach for weapons he didn't have. "Go ahead." Shig's grin was cajoling, completely unaffected. "Let him touch you. You'll see." She grinned over at Malick, a clump of messy, motley braids falling down over her face, obscuring her eyes. "Right, Mal?"

Malick only stared back, for once seeming completely at a loss for words. He shifted a questioning lift of an eyebrow at Yori. Yori could only shake her head. Sometimes she could serve as interpreter, but sometimes Shig was too obscure for even Yori to understand. And sometimes the things that spilled out of Shig's mouth really were, plain and simple, nonsense, spoken aloud purely for her own amusement.

Strangely, though, the little outburst had Fen peering at Shig like he knew what she meant and was waiting for more, and not at all sure he actually wanted it. Perhaps he did know; Shig seemed to see him as some sort of kindred, after all.

Yori gently took hold of Shig's shoulder, urging her back, which in turn seemed to loosen something in Fen. He breathed a touch easier, eyes losing some of their malice and wariness, and he no longer looked like he was trying to back himself through the wall.

Umeia hmphed, satisfied, and kicked at Malick's thigh with the toe of her pointy shoe until he rose to his feet and backed away, allowing Umeia to take his place. She crouched down in front of Fen with the damp cloth in her hand.

"What've you done to yourself, lad?" She ignored the flinch back and fiery glare she got when she came at Fen's face with the cloth. Lips pursing in annoyance, Umeia disregarded Fen's obvious discomfort and took hold of his chin. "Keep still, then." Her chiding tone was that famil-iar mix of vexation and comfort that had, over the last years, come to be inextricably tangled up with the word "home" in Yori's consciousness. "What's your name, then? Malick hasn't got any manners—"

"Hey!"

"—so, we'd best not wait for him to make introductions." Umeia cut Malick a challenging look; Malick returned it, which only made Umeia smirk. "You've met Shig and Yori, yeah? I'm Umeia." She stared at Fen, expectant, all the while cleaning the blood from his chin, when he clearly wanted to be anywhere but on the receiving end of her steel-limned concern. His mouth only tightened when she finished with his face and moved on to his wrist.

Grudgingly, he finally muttered, "Fen," fingers reflexively curling in and arm trying to jerk away, but Umeia never let go and gave no quarter. "Fen Jacin-rei."

Yori very nearly blurted out an inappropriate guffaw at Malick's look of betrayed chagrin. Umeia had, after all, bullied more out of Fen with two sentences than Malick had managed all evening.

Shig merely hummed to herself, absurdly happy. "Buzz, buzz, *buzzzz*."

Umeia gave Shig an annoyed grimace, but otherwise paid no heed. "Jacin-rei, eh? *Rei*." She grunted, brow scrunching, but her hands kept hold and kept soothing the hurts. "Does that mean what I think it means? Someone actually named you 'Ghost'?"

Clearly, that was the wrong question. Whatever softness had been leaching into Fen's expression, even through the discomfort, hardened immediately. He didn't answer, just yanked his hand away from Umeia with a finality that even she didn't protest, curled it into his chest, and looked down at his knees. Went silent. Again.

Umeia only sighed, not even looking annoyed this time. She shook her head and looked up at Malick.

"No one can know he's here. We can't have it get 'round that we're harboring an Untouchable."

"I've thought about that." Malick didn't even appear put out that Umeia was telling him his business. "We could always say he just showed up and took a room for his own, and we could hardly get in his way, could we?" He shrugged with a grimace to show his dislike of the idea.

"How many saw him come through?"

"Not many," Yori put in. "And Shig tweaked any who did."

Maybe that was why Shig was so flighty tonight. Having to adjust the memories of so many people at once had perhaps sent her outside herself for too long.

Malick eyed Fen critically. "We could cover the braid with a hood, or something, I suppose."

Yori frowned. "I thought that wasn't allowed."

"There's that too." Malick sighed, hands on hips. "To be precise, none of this is allowed, so one more transgression won't matter in the end, though any one of them could get us caught, so it's best to limit them. But I think it shouldn't get about at all. Not only would we have people coming to gawk, but I think the fact that you're—pardon me, Jacin-rei, don't take this the wrong way—but the fact that you're not some—"

"*Fen.*" Sharp and bitten out from between clenched teeth.

Malick paused. "Sorry?"

Shig shook her head, eyes rolling in disapproval as she frowned up at Malick, reproachful. Umeia gave both Shig and Fen a dubious look, but she didn't try to resume her fussing.

Fen didn't answer, just knelt there with his head bowed, because it was clear what he was saying. Yori understood it, so Malick had to. The question was some sort of bait, Yori had no doubt, or a test, to see what would happen. It was just the sort of thing Malick did. He agitated, because it was useful. And sometimes, it was just because it entertained him. Yori thought this time it was the former.

Malick stared down, eyebrows beetling. "The fact that *Fen* is not some wild-eyed lunatic would draw too much attention." He paused again, waiting, though Fen still refused to look up, still glaring at his knees with his jaw locked just as tight as his fists. Malick huffed. "Our patron has instructed us to acquire you and facilitate you. Two things I've no doubt you're aware could get us all hanged. And not only us, but every soul who happens to be patronizing the House at the time if we're discovered." Malick shot a weary look at Umeia. "We'll figure out later how we're to go about keeping it a secret.

"In return," he went on, looking back at Fen, "he asks only that you repay his generosity by keeping our secrets as if they were your own, and assisting us in our work. I've seen what you can do. I think you can be an asset, if you so choose. But Samin is right: I can't make you. I can tell you, though—you're in a position I don't envy, and I know I've put you there, but it doesn't change the fact that if you don't accept the offer, I'll have no choice in the matter anymore. I'll give it until tomorrow before your name shows up on an order in my patron's hand, and I follow his orders without question."

Shig groaned, making a great show of falling back against Yori with a theatrical roll of her eyes. "For pity's sake, will you just *promise?*"

Yori shoved Shig off her lap, trying to keep a surprised snort from breaking loose. "Promise what, love?"

"Yeah." Malick scowled at Shig. "Promise what?"

Shig sighed at Fen. "Words, words, words." Her sympathetic expression split into a grin. "We get paid, though!" She turned to Umeia. "Malick's still stuck on the touching part. *You* promise."

Umeia twitched a lopsided smile, apparently bemused but still more than willing to seize the opening. "You will be paid for your contributions, of course. Two hundred a week, room and board, plus discretionary bonuses at the completion of each commission. The discretion is, of course, your patron's."

Yori noted the wording—"*your* patron" and not "*our* patron". She often wondered about the relationship, or lack thereof, between Umeia and the Mage, but it wasn't a subject Yori had ever felt welcome to broach, and neither Malick nor Umeia ever gave any clue.

Umeia leaned in again, reached out as only Umeia would dare to do, and slipped her fingers, gently but firmly, beneath Fen's chin. Fen glared as expected, but he met her gaze, and there was no growling or snapping of teeth this time.

"Your… causes coincide." Umeia was as somber and sincere as she ever got, except for when it involved her coffers. "I can't promise you'll get back whatever it is Shig says you've lost, but I *can* promise you will have the one you seek. And you'll have the others there behind you to make sure you do. The Mage keeps his promises. Dubious choice or no, it's a good offer. If I were you, I'd take it."

"There!" Shig slumped down, happily relieved. "*Finally.*"

Fen only stared at Shig's gaudy braids, frowning, more in question now than anger. It should have made Yori less uneasy, but it didn't. Fen's harsh gaze moved to Umeia, hung there for a while, then flitted quickly to and away from Yori. Finally, it settled on Malick. Stayed there. Hard as granite. Even Umeia reaching again for his wrist didn't move him.

Shig peered up at Malick through her hair. "He's waiting for you to promise." Yori swallowed a snigger at the stage-whisper. Shig turned to eye her with reproach. "'S not funny, Yori."

If Shig sometimes reminded Yori of a child, this was not one of those times. Her jade-green gaze was just as hard and cold as Fen's, and sharper than usual, strange worlds swirling within of which Yori could only sometimes catch a glimpse. It lumped something in Yori's chest, dried up all her precarious good humor.

Yori nodded—more like a respectful bow of her head—and patted Shig's arm. "I'm sorry, sweetie."

As if to directly negate everything Yori had just been thinking, Shig grinned, wide and lovely, then turned back to Malick, all bright-eyed and expectant.

Malick was still staring at her, chewing his lip, his brow bunched tight. Finally, he blew out a long breath and ran a hand through his hair. He turned to Fen.

"Exactly who are you looking for?"

"I don't know."

"You don't know." Malick cocked his head, expression doubtful. "Do you know where this mystery person lives? Works? What he looks like?"

Fen only stared. Then he blinked. Slowly.

"Right." Malick sighed. "A Ghost looking for a phantom. Brilliant." He rubbed at the back of his neck. "Why d'you want him?"

Fen thought about that for a moment before answering, "He's stolen something from me." It was flat, somewhat thick, and he swallowed heavily, obviously not wanting to answer even that much.

Malick was relentless. Because that was just Malick. "What's he stolen?"

Fen's gaze made the rounds again—from Umeia to Yori, then finally pausing on Shig—as though gauging, calculating. He looked back up at Malick.

"He… he murdered my father and took…" He paused, set his jaw. "Took my mother."

Malick went instantly from intense and nearly cruel to all soft understanding. "And your mother is—"

"She is spiritbound." It was shoved out between clenched teeth, like it hurt to let go of it. "Of the full-Blood."

Yori's stomach dropped. No wonder Shig's scars had so plainly affected Fen. Yori knew what most of these people did with their "property," and she knew Shig had been relatively lucky, so to speak. The man who'd bought them hadn't had the money or the connections to do what had likely happened to Fen's mother, but it had only been a matter of time before Shig's "help" enabled their keeper to acquire both. The brief touch of empathy Yori had felt before closed her in a tight fist this time. Thinking back to how she'd behaved when Umeia had taken them in—all bold posturing and prickly fake pride—Yori thought perhaps this snarling, snapping Untouchable wasn't so incomprehensible after all. No wonder Shig took to him.

Malick nodded slowly, eyes narrowed. "We need to talk in private.

🇹

Malick waited until Umeia had finished her fluttering and shoved the bloody cloth at him—"Just in case," she'd said, but with stern instructions not to do anything that might require it again and a severe look to go along with it. She didn't, Malick noticed with a sour curl of his lip, demand the same from Fen. Instead, she informed him she'd bring him some salve later and bandage his wrist for him. Fen, predictably, didn't answer.

Shig and Yori wandered out behind Umeia. Malick didn't think he'd ever been so pleased before to see the back of that multicolored head. He liked Shig, even loved her in his way, and for all her outward nonsensical jabber, she usually fit quite a few gems of wisdom in between the streams of twaddle. Still, she'd unnerved him tonight, several times. That whole "promise" business was asking quite a lot, and she'd demanded it for someone who refused to demand for himself. Shig could be as bitchy as she could be sweet, but Malick couldn't remember her ever actually demanding anything before. And while he thought he had a good idea what all the talk about "quiet" was, he didn't like Shig making promises for him. Certainly not about something he might be able to use as leverage.

"I'm sorry," Malick said after the door had closed behind Yori.

He waited, but when Fen just sat there, like he'd been for almost an hour now, kneeling on the floor in his meditative pose, head bowed, Malick went on, "About your mother, I mean."

No reaction, not even a nod in acknowledgement. And Malick had been sincere too, damn it. What did a man have to do to get one little concession?

"Listen, F... can I call you Jacin-rei?"

"No."

Malick's mouth went tight, but he let the slight pass. "All right, Fen it is, then. I want to give you that promise, I really do, but you must see the difficulty. You're going to have to pry open that mouth of yours and give me some more information."

"I thought your *patron* knew it all." Sneered this time. "Twitch at the end of my blade—isn't that what you said before?"

It was. And it was close enough to the truth, but a thing like this... Malick didn't think "patience" was going to be a word Fen wanted to hear. And if Fen's mother had dropped into the same nowhere hole most of the Disappeared had gone, the promise of the Mage was perhaps not one Malick felt inclined to offer himself.

"My patron tends to do things in his own time. I'm thinking this is something you want right now, yeah?" As expected, Fen only glared at him, but Malick took it for a yes. "Right. And I'm thinking you plan to make my life absurdly difficult unless you get what you want right now?" Still with the glare. Malick was beginning to think it was a language all its own. "Uh-huh. Then I'll offer you this: join us and I'll help you find her."

And he would. Just probably not in the way Fen clearly wanted. Definitely not in the way Fen wanted. And not nearly as quickly as was probably necessary, but even Malick had limits.

Fen's eyes narrowed in warning.

Malick huffed. "All right, I'll do my best to help you find her." There— that should cover his ass. Or at least give him enough time to get familiar with Fen's. "Look, I'm very good at what I do, and this is what I do. However, I'll admit that the detective work is usually done for me, and you're going to have to cooperate by giving me the information I need. What you want is next to impossible, just so we're clear"—well, probably— "but as long as it doesn't interfere with our orders, I see no reason why I can't spend my spare time helping you."

He wouldn't mention that it would afford all kinds of opportunities to be near the Untouchable enigma, who was, after tonight, just a tiny bit less enigmatic. Who knew what Malick might find out, or what might happen in the time spent working toward a goal so close to Fen's black little heart?

"That's a promise over and above the one you get from the others and the Mage. And certainly not one I've ever offered before. Take Umeia's advice and accept it."

Fen dragged his gaze away, and pointed it once more to the floor. "Why me?"

Malick thought about that. "First, tell me what made you come here tonight."

No games this time—Malick really had been wondering about that, and how the Mage had known, and why he'd set them on the Untouchable at all, considering the very real risks. Their patron tended to know quite a lot of things no one could know, and Malick rarely ever questioned their assignments, but that didn't mean he wasn't wary. Fen's answer might help Malick give Fen one in return. Maybe even one Malick wouldn't mind giving.

Fen didn't answer for a while, but gravid pauses seemed to be the rule for him, so Malick waited him out. Then, finally: "The boy's name was on a note in Lord Hende's chambers, with the address of the Girou."

Malick's eyebrows shot up. "*You* did Lord Hende?" He hadn't been told about that one, but he remembered the talk last week when it happened. "They said he'd hanged himself."

"Well, they would, wouldn't they?"

Fair. These men would be getting more careful with what details they turned loose in public. Between Fen working alone and Malick's little bunch, quite a few wealthy, important men had been picked off just lately, and it made sense that they'd close ranks around each other and try to handle it between themselves and their personal, feudal armies. After all, what they were doing was not only ghastly, but highly illegal, and it wasn't surprising they wouldn't want the Doujou to get too interested. Malick had noticed with concern the increased number of guards and minders around their targets the last few weeks, which was one reason he'd been so keen to do the Mage's bidding in acquiring Fen.

But none of it answered Malick's original question. Lord Hende, Fen's latest victim, had been a new admirer of Madi's, so it wasn't terribly surprising that the boy's name had been found somewhere in Hende's effects, and it wasn't terribly surprising that Fen would seize on it as a breadcrumb on the way to finding his mother. It still wasn't something anyone other than Hende or Fen would have known, so the Mage seemed to be living up to his name. A little too well.

It smelled like a setup. Malick just didn't know from which side it was coming.

"So, you found Madi's name on a piece of paper, and you came here to… what? Beat some information out of him?" Malick paused, lifted an eyebrow. "Kill him?"

That would be a shame. Malick didn't really know the boy, but had seen him around. Madi seemed the soft, pleasant sort. Only half-Jin, no magic, but he had that Jin prettiness.

Fen's hands clenched tighter, and he looked down again. "I expect it would've depended."

On what, Malick didn't think he wanted to know.

And why did the thought of Fen killing the pretty, pleasant-enough boy sit better with Malick than Fen fucking him? Or being fucked by him? Malick caught the thought before it took his mind down into places it shouldn't be going right now.

"I'm afraid I can't really answer your question. I don't know why the Mage chose you." Malick held a hand out when Fen's head snapped up. "I would if I could, but I honestly don't know. The Mage has his reasons, and I don't generally disagree with them, since they usually turn out right in the end. He said, 'Get the Untouchable,' told us when you'd come, and we did it. I can't guess why he wanted you, except that p'raps you're meant for more than being Untouchable."

Malick paused, thoughtful. The Mage hadn't said *Untouchable*, actually, he'd said *Catalyst*, which was what had raised Malick's suspicions and made him wonder about these orders more than he'd usually wondered about the others. He had his own deal with the Mage, after all, and he was going to be extraordinarily pissed off if this was the first stage in the breaking of it—angry, pretty Fen-the-Untouchable or no.

"I don't know." Malick shrugged and tried to make it less uneasy than it was. "Maybe he just wants the one who took your mother, and you're his best chance of getting him. The Mage does not explain himself to me, and it's the best guess I've got."

Malick could live with that, he supposed—as long as Fen was the one doing the getting, if the mother was where Malick thought she might be.

He hadn't realized what he'd just said would have an effect like nothing else he'd said all night: Fen's gaze went from fierce to pensive between one slow blink and the next. Perhaps because it was likely very close to what he wanted to hear. Actually, it was probably exactly what he wanted to hear. He'd mown through four—no, five, including Hende now—victims in as many weeks, and had still got nowhere. That was a long time to be imagining all the horrible things that could be happening to one's mother. And now, Malick was offering probably the first bit of hope Fen had had, and backing it up with ready-made allies and an anonymous magician.

Fen was theirs, Malick had him, he could nearly taste it. All Fen had to do was say the words. Malick could actually see him wanting to. Still, something held him back.

Fen tilted his head. "Who is this Mage?"

Damn. He wasn't going to like this answer.

"I don't know."

"You don't know."

"I don't know. No one does." Malick waved, casually dismissive. "I get my orders, I follow them, he pays me. Very well. Since those I'm paid to eliminate are generally those who deserve it, I don't ask questions."

"And if you were paid to murder a Jin farmer's wife? Son? Daughter?"

So, you're from farming stock. Did you mean to give that away, or was it an accident?

Malick couldn't give an honest answer to this one. Right now, Fen wanted very specific answers, and would believe them only because they were what he wanted to hear. And he wouldn't want to hear Malick's honest answer.

So Malick said, "Then I may have cause for the very rare occasion of questioning my orders."

It might be at least halfway true. Then again, Malick might do it without question. He used to do his own digging when he got a name and the scant information necessary to doing his job—mostly out of his own curiosity, and because he didn't trust someone he'd never met face to face, just on principle. Once he'd recognized the common goal to the varied assignments, investigating the targets beforehand for anything other than determining their routines and weaknesses seemed like a waste of time. He'd twigged to the Mage's pattern right away, and by lucky chance, agreed with it.

Malick had no problem assuaging any demons that might come to call with the justification that those he took money to kill were best got off the skin of the world anyway. Wolf would approve; Malick killed no one he was forbidden to kill, so he was actually doing good deeds. No different from Samin, when you got right down to it. Except Samin sincerely believed it. Samin had lines he wouldn't cross. There was really no telling if Malick did. Even Malick didn't know.

"I need some time." Fen dipped his head in what another might take for submission, but Malick thought it was more like avoidance. "I have… things I need to take care of."

It gave Malick a suspicious prickle. What could an Untouchable have to take care of? No home, no kin, no connections—wasn't that how it was supposed to work? Wander about, influence others by mere presence, and whatever the Catalyst chose to do or not do was a command from the Ancestors and would affect the world in the way they so chose. At least that was the idea. It had rather changed since the Ancestors had gone stridently insane nearly a century and a half ago. What loose ends could this man possibly have to tie up?

Then again, why was this Fen not a babbling madman? Why was there a missing mother about whom he apparently cared deeply enough to leave a swath of corpses behind him on his hunt for her? Why was he well clothed and well fed? He certainly didn't have the look of one taking his chances in the elements, so he obviously had a home of some sort.

Damn it, why had Malick not looked into this one before? He'd received the orders almost a week ago, he'd had plenty of time. Perhaps he'd gone lazy over the years.

"What things?" Malick knew he wasn't going to get an answer. He waited for a moment anyway, taking in the deceptively submissive pose: a man on his knees, head bowed, long, glistening braid snaking on the floor beside him. Gah. Malick really needed to stick to business tonight. He sighed. "And do you plan to return?"

You accept, we both know you do, just say the words.

"Have I a choice?"

Malick rolled his eyes. "Not a very good one, no. Fine. Go take care of your *things.* I'll expect you back for breakfast. Can I trust you to not let anyone follow you back?" Shig would be pissed if Malick dragged her out of bed before dawn to take care of any inconvenient strangers' memories.

Fen's head came up, his full mouth twisted sideways, but he locked his gaze to the wall behind Malick, rather than on Malick himself. "I'll manage."

"I expect you will."

And Malick had every intention of finding out how. There was no way in the world he was going to let Fen wander about, not with all the deadly information he now possessed. And Malick knew Fen was not going to allow him to invite himself along. If Malick forced his presence on Fen, those "things" Fen wanted to take care of would simply wait for a time when he'd be out from under Malick's eye. Not that Malick would allow that to happen anytime soon. Fen-the-Untouchable had been dangerous before, but now he was a potential risk to them all.

"All right, then. I'll expect you back at sunup. If you're not here..." Malick opened a hand, let the threat hang.

Fen said nothing, just got to his feet, somehow doing it without a single grunt or apparent twinge, considering he'd been kneeling in the same position, rod-rigid, for nearly an hour. Malick expected Fen to breeze past him without another word, perhaps even a disdainful scowl for a "goodbye," but he didn't. He paused right next to Malick, stood stock-still for half a breath, then, without even an obvious shift, his hand snapped up and latched onto Malick's. Malick had to stop himself from a flinch, but this wasn't an attack.

Head up, harsh gray gaze fastened to Malick's surprised one, and a grip like bound wire. Fen stared, eyes going just a touch wider, breath indrawn quick and silent, like a throttled gasp.

It's... it's gone quiet.

Malick almost—*almost*—smirked but managed to keep his face blank.

Go ahead, little Ghost, ask me again what I am. I might just answer you this time.

Fen didn't ask, though. Wouldn't. Like he couldn't make himself, when he too obviously wanted to.

Malick gave him a purposeful hint of a smile. "Breakfast, then. Have a lovely evening, little Ghost."

Chew on that.

Fen's mouth tightened; so did his grip for half a second, then he abruptly let go, took a step back. Stared. With the tiniest curl of his lip, Fen lifted his chin, looked down his straight nose the half inch he had on Malick. Made a great show of looking Malick's wide-wiry build over thoroughly and then his own.

"Who d'you keep calling *little*?"

Malick only smirked, watched Fen irritably quit the room, and gave him to the count of thirty before he followed.

⼗

Planting-month, Year 1312, Cycle of the Wolf

Jacin only stood there like a crack-brained fool while Joori threatened and snarled at the strange man. Then again, Jacin supposed he rather was a crack-brained fool now, and whatever sanity was still ramming about the edges of the chaos would sink inside it soon enough. He'd best use it while he still could.

If he could.

The horrible new whining white buzz droning in the back of his mind every now and then ramped up and took to screaming, and it was all he could do not to scream along with it. If any of it made sense, if he could latch on to a string of words and bend them into sanity, maybe it wouldn't twist his mind so. It wasn't quite so merciful. Now he thought he had a much better idea of why Untouchables lost themselves inside it all so quickly. He supposed he was lucky he could still follow a conversation if he concentrated.

He hadn't really expected better for himself than the fates suffered by others, but... he'd caught Joori's hope by accident like some kind of contagious infection.

"What fee?" Joori was all too bold and daringly angry in the face of this Adan. "What do you want from my father?"

The man chuckled, strangely not angered by Joori's impudence. "I assure you, young Fen-seyh, I want nothing from your father he did not willingly—indeed, gladly—agree to give me." His dark eyes shifted over to Jacin again, warm and purposefully looking right at him, not shifting away like others always did when they caught sight of the braid—like Father always did. The man dipped his head in what couldn't be a respectful nod but nevertheless was. "Jacin-rei, I am pleased to make your acquaintance once again."

Jacin only kept staring. All the words made sense, but they kept getting tangled up with the confusion, and surely he couldn't have heard what he thought he'd just heard.

But perhaps he had, because Joori had been struck abruptly mute, his fingers digging into Jacin's arm in a way that would have hurt this morning but now gave Jacin a teetering little center on which to latch his mind.

"Once again." Joori's tone was cautious. "What does that mean?"

The man's gaze slid over to Joori, a little cooler than before. "I see you have come well through your Change, Fen…Joori, is it?" He cocked his head. "And how does your mother fare with the spirits that so test her?"

Jacin's gut tumbled down to the ground. This man knew. An *Adan* knew. He could snap his fingers and rain fire on both Joori and Mother, and there was nothing they could do to stop him.

Everything notched up in volume, scrabbled inside Jacin's mind like greedy fingers, tearing and splitting a wide, gaping hole in his sanity. He could do nothing but flounder on its edges, tracking what was going on around him only vaguely, but he held to it with wild desperation—

boy our boy must listen only say it once miss the sense miss the chance

"You son of a—" Joori would have leapt at the man's throat, had Jacin not taken hold of him, dragged him back. The knife was flailing about, catching Wolf's grinning face and refracting it at the Adan's calm one. "Let me *go*, Jacin, didn't you hear what—?"

"Joori." Only a breath, all Jacin could manage, all he could say, all he could think, because Joori brought the sense with him somehow, opened up Jacin's balance and forced it still with the singing sweetness of brilliant pain and—

dying magic Catalyst slides to Zero our twice-born listenlistenlisten the day comes the Null veils the Eye a cloak of night our boy clinging to corpses

—Joori, only Joori—*too much, too much, help me*—made the insanity take a step back and quiet down, let Jacin's own thoughts through, and ah, fuck, he couldn't listen to it for another second.

"Joori!" The one word that made sense to him amidst all the mad raving. "Sound the vaults of Raven cast acid to the sky they don't see like

Owl won't hear mockery it's all gone sour worm-ridden carcass of faith and hope the gods won't save them they've all gone home clinging to corpses too loud please our boy wandering both edges gutted on the spit of—"

It was everywhere—in Jacin's head, in his mouth, in his ears, crawling all over his mind like spiky-legged spiders. Whispering to him, screaming at him, couldn't tease them apart, couldn't make sense of more than two at a time. *Zero* bled into *Catalyst* blurred into *WolfRaven-WolfRaven*, then slurred all together and tried to spill out his mouth, over and over again.

It drove into his skull like saw-toothed static, whining and buzzing so loud it nearly set his teeth gnashing and his hand reaching, *reaching*, and oh, save him, *Joori*—

"It's all right, Jacin, it'll be all right, just calm down, *listen* to me, concentrate on me"—a quick shake—"on this, Jacin, *listen to me!*"

Ignoring the strange man who watched them, who knew them, ignoring the braid and what it meant, because Joori always had—

"Hold on, listen to my voice."

—Joori took his little knife and cut across Jacin's—

Jacin, I've always been Jacin to him, no "rei," not from Joori.

—cut across Jacin's palm, dug deep with the tip until the sharp burn brushed along the edges of the noise. Cut him again and then himself, gripped Jacin's hand and bled with him until the pain laid a fuzzy layer of despair over the din. Sat with him—fuck, Jacin had gone to his knees, weeping and babbling in the dirt in front of this stranger who knew them—and rocked him until Jacin stopped weeping and shaking.

Jacin didn't lift his head away from Joori's chest, didn't want to see. Couldn't bear for *him* to see. No one should be witness to a Ghost's humiliation, his degradation, it wasn't fair, unacceptable, unbearable, he hadn't given his permission, not to Joori, Joori shouldn't have to—

"How very… interesting," the Adan murmured.

Joori's arms stiffened around Jacin's ribs, like he'd forgotten the man was there just as thoroughly as Jacin had. "We have to run." Soft and low in Jacin's ear. "We've no choice now. I've just touched an Untouchable in front of an Adan."

The horrible sense of it got through where even the pain had left gaping holes. Jacin had just doomed Joori with his delirious begging.

"You mustn't try to run." The man's deep voice held clear warning, as though he'd heard. "I promise you, you will both end badly, if you do. On the other hand…" Dangled there, like a bright, shiny lure in murky depths, but he didn't finish the apparent snare. Instead, there was a pause, a shift of boots in the weedy spring growth as the man stepped slowly closer. "It's a shame your father did not warn you. Tonight would be so much easier." A heavy sigh. "Fear not, Fen Joori. Death does not follow my steps tonight. I have not come to Disappear you or your mother. I have, in fact, done my very best over the years to make sure you are not discovered."

Joori pushed away from Jacin slowly but kept a firm hold on his hand, squeezing every few seconds to renew the sharp bite in Jacin's palm. "Why?"

"Your father has not told you anything at all, has he? How terrible your Change must have been, unprepared as you were." The man tilted his head, mouth tight—a thin line of anger Jacin couldn't fathom. "Tell me— how did you manage to keep undiscovered before? Twins, after all."

Because there were no twins anymore—twins meant magic, and if a woman managed to birth them to term, no one ever saw them after. One way or another. Except for Joori and Jacin, but Jacin didn't count, wasn't half of a Self, but a void at his brother's side.

"Our father didn't know." Joori said it grudgingly. "The midwife told our parents that Jacin…" He paused, turned a guilty glance on Jacin then a defiant one back up to the Adan. "She said perhaps I had magic once, before we were born, but the *Untouchable*"—he spat the word—"nulled it in the womb."

"Hm." The man twitched his dark eyebrows. "I expect all that matters is that it was effective." He seemed to speak mostly to himself, then shook his head in disapproval. He turned a sharp glance on Jacin. "And your Change?"

"What Change?" Joori snapped, insolent. "There's nothing wrong with him."

Jacin tightened his grip on Joori's hand, slippery with their blood, hissed, "*Joori*," more alarmed by the second by the chances his brother was taking with this stranger who could be the end of him so easily. And what did it matter? *What Change?* Like the man didn't already know. Like anyone couldn't tell just by looking.

The man merely chuckled again, no condescension or derision in the pleasant surge of it. "Have it your way, Fen Joori. You are and remain undiscovered, and I am content." His dark gaze turned serious. "You must keep undiscovered—a redundant warning, I am sure, but one worth wasting breath on. Fate has a use for you. It always does."

"You're a seer." Joori's tone this time was accusing. "And how have *you* remained undiscovered?"

The man laughed, full and rich from his throat.

It was such a lovely counterpoint to the noise blundering about in Jacin's head. Jacin was nearly mesmerized. What a beautiful man, with his dark eyes and dark hair, that melodic laugh sliding up through his chest and winding all around Jacin in symphonic tones of calm, wordless reassurance. It managed to soothe him where all of Joori's bravado and selfless shielding had not.

"It helps that Fate's voice is not quite so obvious as trembling earth," the man told Joori. "I have remained undiscovered simply because I do not wish to be discovered, and am careful to prevent it."

Joori's frowned. "Would they Disappear you too, if they found you?" His tone was less harsh than a moment ago—interest, rather than blatant testing of boundaries.

The Adan shrugged, unconcerned. "I expect that would depend on who discovered me. Some would keep quiet for a price, others would bleed me just as dry as any Jin, though my blood would do them little good. I have no Jin in me. They might perhaps manage a shadow charm or two, maybe even a weak healing serum, if they're skilled enough, but nothing worth the time and expense to those who seek profit in such things."

"And the Courts?"

"The Courts would put an end to me quite thoroughly and painfully, I expect. Yet more painfully, if it were discovered that I have deliberately hidden Jin magic from them."

"Then why—?"

"And that is all I have time for, young Fen-seyh. The moons ripen, and I cannot linger. Please—go and fetch your father. There is still the matter of my fee."

"Fee for *what?*" Joori stood, dragging Jacin to his feet with a crushing wrench to his hand, pulling together the thoughts threatening to scatter apart. "What does my father owe you?"

"I think…" The man shook his head. "That is a question I leave to your father to answer. But I will thank you now for the care of your brother, and warn you once more—keep your magic cloaked deep, and watch over your mother. I do not see that she will be your inadvertent betrayal, but even Fate is changeable and one must take no chances."

Joori stared, incredulous. "Who the hell are *you* to thank *me* for caring for my own brother? What are we to you, and why are you—?"

"Your father, Fen Joori." Snapped out this time, stern and cool, where a moment ago it had been warm and friendly. "I will not ask again."

Joori scowled, distrustful, but he reached for Jacin and tugged him to a stumbling step behind him.

"Leave your brother. I would speak with Fen Jacin-rei."

"It's *Jacin.*"

The man's small smile bent cryptic. "Such a useful thing, hope."

Playing with them, but… not. It gave Jacin a strange, exhilarated little shiver, before the drone fuzzed out whatever sense he'd been trying to make of it. Joori. Right. Protect Joori from his own tongue.

"Go." Jacin gave Joori a little shove. "Before your mouth manages to slit your own throat."

"Jacin, you—" Joori peered from the man to Jacin again, then stepped in close. "I don't trust him. He's not here to protect us. He wants something. And the gods only know what Father promised him, or why. Don't say—"

"I'll be careful." Jacin shrugged at his Joori's dubious look, because right, sure, how was Jacin supposed to be careful when things came spewing from his mouth he couldn't even remember? He closed his fingers over his torn palm, dipped the tips mercilessly into the gash, sighing a little at the soothing bite of clarity. "I'll be careful," he repeated, his bloody fist held between them so Joori would see, would know Jacin meant it. "He seems..." Jacin shot a quick look at the Adan prophet. "He could've killed us already, or brought the Doujou down on us, if that's what he wanted. He seems all right."

Not entirely, but mostly, and he *looked* at Jacin, like only Joori and Mother did. Caidi too, but she was only little. It was only a matter of time before she began averting her eyes and treating Jacin like the Ghost he was now. But this man, this Adan, knew exactly what Jacin was, and met his eyes like he mattered. It was too novel not to explore.

Joori grunted unhappily, curling Jacin's fist tighter with a significant look, then hurried into the house. Jacin rhythmically poked his fingers—*one, two, three, four, Adan's knocking on your door*—into the wound, ignoring the slippery-slick ooze of blood dripping through his knuckles. He stared at the ground, silent. Waiting and hoping for something, though he had no idea what.

"I am sorry I could not be here to help you when the Ancestors called."

And that was it, what Jacin had hoped for all unknowing—words spoken directly to him, not at and around him, like Morin did, not oblique messages through Joori like Father insisted on. Not sudden silence at the bartering stalls or on the streets, people dipping their heads and looking away, pretending they didn't see Jacin at all, pretending he couldn't see them, making a Ghost of him before he was even dead or Changed. And here he was, noise in his head that shook his sanity every second while he hopelessly tried to build up dams and little mazes through it and anchor the pathways to pain. Now he *was* a Ghost, Untouchable, ragged braid hanging heavy over his shoulder.

And still, this man spoke to him.

Jacin was instantly besotted, tears leaking out from the corners of his eyes, and he didn't care. A warm hand landed on his shoulder, and Jacin slid from besotted to dangerously infatuated with a single squeeze of long fingers.

"I had foreseen that your brother would be the one to find a way for you, and I see that he has." The man took Jacin's hand, and pried open his fingers. Assessing, the man poked cautiously at the wound... tilted his head and did it again with less caution and more intent. He smiled when Jacin sucked in a quick breath and tightened his teeth. "Very good." The man curled Jacin's fingers over again and patted his fist. "It will make things easier."

What things? Jacin wanted to know, *Easier how? What am I to you? Why have you come? Why have you hidden my mother and my brother?*

And what does my father owe you for it?

Jacin didn't ask any of it, not entirely sure he cared. Instead, he asked, "Who are you?"

Another of those warm smiles lit the man's dark eyes and turned him ageless. "Ah, yes, I expect perhaps you didn't hear me when I introduced myself." He stepped back, swept Jacin a mystifying bow—an *Adan* bowing to a *Jin*—and squeezed Jacin's hand again. "I am Asai. I have come—"

"—cowardly son of a *bitch*!" Joori came barreling through the kitchen door, followed closely by their father, slumped and defeated, where Joori was very nearly on fire with seething malice. Joori ran toward Jacin, eyes intent on Jacin's hand in Asai's, and didn't stop 'til he'd nearly tackled Jacin away. "He sold you! The son of a bitch *sold* you—to *him*!" Joori's arm snapped out, finger pointed accusingly at Asai as he jerked Jacin away and behind him.

"Sold…?" Jacin shook his head, unable to make sense of the statement. Sold him for what? Who would pay even a skipping stone for a Ghost?

And would it be so bad?

Joori was weeping now, anger and outrage all over his dirty, tear-stained face. "To keep me and Mother hidden—that was his fee, Jacin. He *knew*, he *saw*, and he's come to take you away as his *fee*. Father knew and he's going to *let* him!"

And again, that single question—Would it be so bad?—turned inside Jacin's head like a faceted gem, and he had a moment of brilliant, crystal-sharp clarity.

Joori loved Jacin, was enraged on his behalf, was terrified of losing him. But Joori had never allowed himself to believe in Jacin's fate, had sometimes even half-convinced Jacin to hope against it himself. Had refused to even tack the "rei" onto Jacin's name when he could get away with it; made it a point to try to get away with it every time, even though their father never failed to make an equal point to force Joori to say it. And it *was* forced—bitten out through anger swathed like a prickly mantle over their entire lives. Willing to turn his back on the beliefs and traditions of a dying people and abscond with the Untouchable, against every law and all reason. Willing to sacrifice their mother—because oh, yes, Jacin had understood the things Joori wouldn't say—for the vague hope that he could keep the voices from untethering Jacin's mind and save his spirit from following after. Denying all the while that it was likely hopeless in the end. Jacin *would* slip one day, and the Ancestors *would* have their useless oracle-sacrifice.

And all because Joori loved the Jacin that had been this morning.

If this man, this Asai, had not shown up tonight, Joori would have merely waited until Jacin was overcome again, unable to argue with him, and dragged him off to keep him safe. Would look after him, do everything he could to help Jacin keep his sanity, would likely even cut off the braid and damn himself just as surely as that aborted attempt to put Jacin out of his misery could've done. And would one day get himself killed for a boy who didn't even exist anymore, whose life had always been counted in stolen hours until Fate and the ghosts of long-dead magicians finally caught him out.

Joori likely could love Jacin-rei-the-Untouchable, because that was just the way Joori was—all great big heart and ready fury—but he'd never let go of Fen Jacin enough to give him room. The boy Jacin had been this morning was just as much a ghost as... as he was now.

"It's you."

Jacin peered up to watch Mother come slowly across the yard, sidestepping Father like she didn't even see him, and stop in front of Asai. She absently adjusted Caidi in her arms, wobbled a half-choked sob.

"You've come back."

That was it, then, confirmation, final and solid, in his mother's ingenuous greeting.

Sold. Traded as a safeguard. Used.

Strangely, it curled a smile at Jacin's mouth. It was the only time his father had ever acknowledged overtly that his Ghost-son actually existed.

"Mother." Joori shook his head, betrayed and distraught. "Say you didn't know."

Jacin hadn't realized that Joori had taken up his hand again, compulsively squeezing it, keeping him *here*. It comforted Jacin and made him bitterly sad, all at the same time.

Mother turned slowly from Asai to Joori. "I didn't." Her eyes were saner than they'd been the last time Jacin had seen her, and her voice was steady. "But... Joori." She clenched her teeth, set Caidi down. Caidi's smile was bright and open as she latched onto the leg of Jacin's trousers and beamed up at him. "He saved you once. Perhaps...?" Mother's gaze went back to Asai, hopeful now. "Perhaps he has come again to save Jacin?"

"Jacin-rei," Father put in automatically.

Joori growled under his breath, but Jacin merely ignored it, stooping down to pull Caidi into a hug. She dipped in willingly, chubby little arms curling around Jacin's neck as Jacin closed his eyes, pressed his face into her golden curls, and breathed in her clean baby scent. Morin was hovering just outside the back door, watching—alternately frightened and smug—and Jacin thought that, oddly, he'd miss Morin too.

He wasn't surprised when Caidi was wrenched from his grip so hard she started to wail, and the chickens started up their edgy prattle again. He wasn't surprised to see it was Father dragging Caidi away.

Joori nearly let go of Jacin's hand, but he didn't, only glared at Father and bared his teeth. "You bloody hypocrite! All our lives, you've treated him like a Ghost because you said you believed your traditions, and now you're going to piss in the faces of the gods and hand him over like a piece of property. You're no better than an Adan, you awful, cowardly *fuck!*"

"Joori." Mother stepped slowly over to her sons, and took their bloodied joined hands in both of her own. "Fate does with us what it will. This man…" She peered over at Asai, tried to smile, but it turned confused, and she shuddered but then lifted her chin. "They will meet again." Oddly defiant, but too murky around the edges for the confidence she was trying to force.

Joori's grip on Jacin tightened, trying to yank their hands away, but Mother wouldn't let go. "Mother, don't. Don't let him. *Please.*" He stared at her, beseeching. "Say you didn't know." Like he hadn't believed her the first time. He probably hadn't; perhaps wouldn't ever, no matter how many times he asked the question and she answered it.

She turned back to them, her smile sad. "I did not." With a quiver of her chin, she tucked a hank of Joori's tangled hair behind his ear. "But I would have agreed, nonetheless. He is Wolf's. Wolf made sure of it." She shot a near-hostile gaze toward Asai, then shook her head and turned back to Joori. "There is little choice. A hard road your brother must walk, but he must be what he must be. He cannot be that here."

The clutch of Joori's hand on Jacin's had gone past the point of comfort and slid steadily into nothing but pain. "You can't mean—"

"Fen Jacin-rei," Asai said quietly, only for Jacin's ears, while Joori raved and Mother tried to soothe him. "He will listen to none but you, and he will hear untruths, if you speak them. This can go hard, if it is not what you want, but Fate has blazed your path. Even your mother, who loves you when she shouldn't, agrees."

So, then. This man was going to take Jacin, whether Jacin wanted it or not, payment for some morbid bargain made with their father upon their births—save one son and forfeit the one already forfeit. Not a bad deal, in truth. Jacin would've encouraged him to take it himself, if he'd been able, and if his father would ever hear anything from a Ghost's mouth in the first place but for prophecies he pretended to heed and believe. Jacin would give up anything to save Joori, even if Joori didn't think he needed saving.

Funny—Jacin hadn't even asked what Asai wanted with him. He didn't even think he cared. What difference did it make? He'd be well beyond worrying about what became of him soon enough. The constant white din was already crowding out his ability to follow one thought to another, link them together in a chain of reason.

No one should have to watch that.

"With me, there is a chance." Asai's low voice was somehow getting through the whispers in Jacin's head, and the shouts going on all around him. "I offer you a life with meaning, and not one wandering, alone and soul-starved, until the Ancestors' insanity has used you up. Under my guardianship, your mother and your brother will be overlooked, their Blood safe in their veins."

Jacin tore his gaze away from the deep-dark depths of Asai's and turned to Joori, still pleading with their mother and growling at their father every time he thought to insert himself.

Gently, Jacin pulled his hand from Joori's. "I'm going with him."

Joori only stared for an interminable moment, face going from stunned to confused to betrayed. "You don't mean that. Jacin... you don't know what you're saying."

"Right now, I'm making more sense than you are." It snapped out of Jacin, strangely angry and then even more strangely unmoved by Joori's flinch. Like Jacin's corpse was already growing cold, and death stiffness setting in.

"Jacin." Joori's voice was hoarse and small. "It's not your debt."

"Isn't it?" Jacin reached for Joori, warmed and grateful when Joori reached back. He leaned in until they were brow to brow. "Don't you know I'd pay any debt for you?"

"Don't *say* that!" Joori was weeping openly now, shaking. "Not for me, please, Jacin. This isn't for me, none of it is, and I won't have it done in my name!"

"In mine, then?" Jacin hugged Joori tight. "He offers what you want for me, what I want, and with no price to you, or to Mother. Any debt in your name has already been cleared. I would do this for myself. Let me."

Willingly discard tradition, the Ancestors, the gods, and thumb his nose at everything his father had ever said he was meant for. And what did it matter? Hadn't Father done the same from the moment Jacin had been born? If Jacin's soul was cast to burn in the suns... well, at least he'd have company.

Joori pushed Jacin back, stared at him long and hard, distraught face limned silver-blue in Wolf's heavy mantle. "Is it what you really want, Jacin?"

Joori would hear a lie, Asai had said, and Jacin knew it to be the truth. They'd breathed each other's breath, thought each other's thoughts, and losing that—and Jacin would, one way or another, no matter what he chose—was like its own death. So what did anything else matter, really? Being handed the choice to lift that away from Joori was a gift for which Jacin had never dared hope, and he would have paid any debt, any price at all for it.

"It is." Jacin hoped nothing shone in his eyes right now but calm conviction and whatever sanity he had left.

Joori yanked Jacin in again, tears flowing harder. Jacin could feel the heavy sobs locked in Joori's chest through his own breastbone. Strange—Jacin hadn't realized he was weeping too. He was unaccountably relieved.

"Who'll braid your hair?" Thin and small, not at all Joori's voice.

It lumped a chuckle in Jacin's throat, and made his tears flow hard and painful. "I will. And it will be messy and crooked, because I never was as good at it as you are."

Joori tried to snort, choked instead, and held on tighter. "Will I see you again?"

Jacin shifted his blurry gaze to Asai, waited for an answer, not entirely sure which one he wanted. Perhaps it would be better for Joori if—

"That will depend on Jacin-rei," Asai said quietly.

Jacin didn't know what that meant, but Mother had said they would, and she just knew things like that sometimes, so Jacin answered, "Yes," firmly and without the uncertainty of only a half second ago. If he was sane enough to think straight, to remember Joori, Jacin would want to see him and would do whatever this man demanded to have it so. "Yes," Jacin repeated, and he held Joori tighter, ignored Caidi tugging at his trouser leg, ignored Father's mulish insistence that Joori unhand the Untouchable, even ignored the soft touch of Mother's hand on the crown of his head. "Yes," Jacin swore, teeth set firm and arms clamped tight about Joori's neck. "I *will* see you again, brother. I swear it."

"I'll always be the one, Jacin." Nearly voiceless, the warm susurrus stirring the wispy hairs at Jacin's nape as Joori clutched him tight, sending a pleasant shiver sprawling down Jacin's backbone. "The one who will be there. All right? Keep that, if you lose everything else. *All right?*"

It made Jacin smile, though he couldn't believe his face had actually made the shape. "You've always been the one, Joori." He snuffled into Joori's shoulder, and then he broke away gently, smiling again, though wobbly, when Joori pushed the little knife into Jacin's hand with a pained grimace.

Silent, subdued, Jacin tucked it into his belt, following slowly after as Asai swept off into the gloom. They didn't take the road, where the dip and rise of the land would obscure Jacin's view after twenty or so paces. They went through his father's fields, fresh-turned earth that should've smelled sweet and new, but only smelled like dirt.

"There is a cart waiting for us at the gate of the camp," Asai told Jacin, matter-of-fact and even. No sneers at Jacin's runaway emotions, no sympathetic commentary attempting to smooth over his losses.

Jacin snuffled again, swallowed the chunks of grief locked tight in his throat. "How will we get by the Doujou?"

Asai only smiled, laid his warm hand to Jacin's shoulder, and squeezed. "You will find, my boy, that all things are possible. With the proper... motivation."

4

"Oh, you sneaky little bastard." Malick squinted against the dark and watched the shadows spiral out from the charm Fen had drawn from inside his high collar. Sinuous and sleek, just like Fen, and insubstantial until they folded in and smudged in imperceptible gradients, made him one of them.

He hardly even glanced aside or behind as he strolled past the Doujou, and boosted himself to the vertical struts of the closed gate, then braced on the iron pickets. Quick and agile as a tree-monkey, he levered up the near two-story climb until he breached the top, perched there for quite some time, just looking up at the sky, like he wasn't quite literally in the process of penetrating a city gate in plain view of its minders. Well, in plain view were it not for that charm.

Malick had wondered how one with no magic might manage to slip in and out unseen by either prey or sentinel. No surprise there were whispers of a wraith. Fen had said he'd found Madi's name on a paper in Lord Hende's *chambers*, for pity's sake. Why hadn't that clicked before? Hende was said to have been in his nightclothes, his wife and two daughters asleep in their beds, when he'd "hanged himself." The mysterious fire that had leveled the estate's garden shed had been a mere footnote, passed along as one more bit of not-terribly-juicy gossip, a strange coincidence of no real import, considering, and then dropped from the later tellings of the story altogether. Now, Malick had to wonder.

Magic didn't work on an Untouchable, but Malick hadn't even thought about whether or not it might work *for* one. And the lean figure biding at the top of the gate, wrapped in conjured shadows and communing with the moons, seemed to answer a question Malick had never thought to ask.

"Clever, clever Ghost." Malick pushed a soft whistle through his teeth, peering at the ten wardens stationed at the gate. All of them were alert and doing their jobs, none of them were slacking or not paying attention, so Malick had to assume the charm was a rather potent one. Blood-magic, though, which made Malick raise his eyebrows. Not many contributed their Blood voluntarily, and those who did set the price steep. Selling it, after all, was just as illegal as having it running through one's veins. And a charm of that strength had to be made from full-Blood.

A Ghost wrapped in enigma shrouded by mystery. This could be the most fun Malick'd had in a very long time. Or it could send him insane with frustration.

Helpless to his own fascination, Malick made his own way through the gate—unheard and unseen, though no charms for Malick—and waited, still watching. Fen was still staring up at the sky, and though his pose wasn't even close to the meditative one into which he'd drawn himself back in Malick's sitting room, it was even more obviously contemplative.

Propped against a spiked spire, legs crossed at the ankle and hands tucked into the small of his back, head atilt and angular face lit by moons and stars. Fen looked more like a sculpture than he did a person, chiseled out of marble stolen from the hills of Tougei, where the *Temshiel* once carved the altars for the gods and the shrines for the dead. Like Hitsuke, sent away from the sight of the gods because they couldn't bear a beauty more striking than their own, and ever after gazing up at his former purlieu, wondering why he'd been cursed so and cast out.

If one believed the romanticized legends, anyway. The reality of Hitsuke's fate had been quite a bit different, and not nearly as pleasant. Then again, Malick didn't think any Incendiary that had ever existed managed a pleasant fate.

Whatever introspection in which Fen was engaged had apparently ended, and he shook himself to examine his surroundings. For a moment, his gilt-gray gaze caromed right into Malick's, seemed to glitter for a breath or two, then moved on, unseeing, merely scanning for threats or a good spot to land. There was no good reason for Malick's heart to have stopped—Fen couldn't see him, no one could see him but the nattering spirits, not unless Malick wanted them to. But for a moment it had almost seemed—

No. Impossible.

Anyway, with Fen clearly bracing for a leap from the top of the gate, there were more interesting things to consider just now.

It was almost the same as when Fen had swirled down from the roof, only this time, Malick got to see the preparation, the skill and concentration that went into it. It had merely been a pretty thing before, something dangerous and pleasing to watch, something clever and novel. Now, it was something else altogether: bottom lip held between white teeth; eyes narrowed and marking a landing spot; limbs extending then contracting then extending again, their placement *just so*; long, deep breaths then *shortshortshort*; the timing of it all counted out in almost visible beats of the heart. No glittering knives this time to distract the eye, and Malick almost regretted not having given Fen's weapons back before, sending him out unarmed, but between the shadow magic and this… Weapons almost seemed redundant.

Focused, all efficient elegance and sinewy poise, Fen twirled down like a contained little dervish then lit with a startling little flip-and-turn. He came to a stop just fifteen paces from Malick, took another look around, not even breathing hard. As though he'd just breached a barrier no more challenging than a wide puddle.

Sparing a dark glance and a curl of his lip for the pikes and crows' cages, Fen straightened his tunic then turned himself west, away from the city.

Malick couldn't have stopped himself from following if he'd cut off his own legs.

Wolf had reached his apogee by the time Malick followed Fen into a small village, slightly alarmed to realize they were venturing onto Asai's lands now. Malick had done his very best since arriving in Ada to keep himself and Umeia—Shig and Yori and Samin, later—cloaked from the seer's sight while Malick had bided and watched. A misstep here could cost him the advantage, should he ever need it. And with what he was almost sure was going on in Yakuli's lands just west of Asai's, Malick wanted to preserve any slim advantage he could. So far, he'd not gone beyond keeping a sharp eye on Asai and his ostensibly completely legal and innocuous doings, but tripping up and letting the arrogant "lord" know one of Malick's kind was here could be… problematic.

The salt-air scent of the sea was stronger here than it was in Ikata, where the tanneries and smelters obliterated the scent with their own reek. Fen's path had taken them through the city's outskirts, quiet and dark, then on through sparser hamlets and lone estates. Oblate groves were abundant here, the sandy soil not good for much else besides sage, and Fen seemed to have no problem with helping himself to several oblates and tying them into his tunic.

The open-air, white-columned hummock of the Shrine of the Moons rose out of the dark, bone-white and cragged like a broken plate. Malick hadn't been expecting the seemingly purposeful stop and, fascinated, he watched Fen quietly pillage the marble altar for a thin balsa tile and paint, then hang his wish from the bare bough of one of the surrounding hackberry trees. Tight-lipped, Fen stood and stared up through the branches, gazing once again at the moons, his face set strangely defiant for a supplicant at a shrine. Almost glaring. He didn't linger to pray, only flipped a koin into the offering fountain and took a perfunctory sip of the clear, streaming water from the ladle. Having done what he'd apparently come to do, Fen bobbed his head with a fist over his breastbone, thumped once, and moved off again.

Malick wasn't really surprised when he pulled down the branch to read what Fen had not-quite-prayed for. The wish tile merely read: *Justice*. Oblique and cryptic, even when calling upon the gods. Fen's plea—more like a demand—was painted in tight, controlled characters. Naturally.

Fen was moving fast, nearly quick-stepping, so Malick couldn't pause to pay brief respect. Wolf would understand. Wolf would approve. And Malick didn't want to miss anything.

He was learning an awful lot about how a Ghost went about surviving, when the laws made it extraordinarily difficult to even exist. Once, places were set at every table for the Ancestors' Voice, meals served and reserved, in case an Untouchable came to call. And if the place remained empty at the end of the meal, the offering untouched and gone cold, the plate was set on the family's private shrine. Jin and Adan alike. Even the Kente had absorbed the tradition, back when the Jin were revered and not feared, before magic was turned against those who had none, and the Ancestors—poor, pious, well-intentioned fools—were driven to shrieking. Before their Untouchables became no better than pitiable Ghosts that none would dare put out of their misery.

Shrines were as rare now as a sane Untouchable, and those that existed were more guilty charity than real belief. Who, after all, really wanted an Untouchable to come calling now, considering what they'd become? Malick supposed the shrines were likely more common in the camps—the Jin held tightly to the letter of their traditions, if not the spirit, even if they'd forgotten why—but some Adan still took their chances, though their offerings were just as rote and equally lacking the beliefs behind them. Crusts of bread gone moldy, or rancid vegetables even a starving beggar would stop and think about. Seeds scattered in rings around dwellings to form a picket of hungry spirits to keep them feeding and discourage the Untouchables from stumbling past them, looking for an empty place that was no longer left empty and waiting.

Fen apparently knew where to look, bypassing dozens of dwellings altogether without so much as a glance or curious look before he'd turn into a yard, make his way to whatever offering was placed in the hollowed bole of a tree or beneath an overgrown arbor, inspect the tender then either take it or toss it away.

Malick was beginning to feel rather small, chiding himself for not feeding Fen before—Umeia had been right: Malick hadn't even offered Fen tea, and Fen had, at least in theory, been a guest—but he apparently wasn't ravenous. He didn't eat any of the loot he collected. Instead, he slipped it into pockets or, in the case where the offering was what looked like a decent-sized loaf of black bread, tucked it under his arm and moved on. Efficient, like always, no time wasted, and he continued to move west at a good clip, despite the infrequent intervals at the shrines, clad in his shadows the whole way. Not even dogs or dark-dwelling scrub beasts sensed him.

Malick really wanted a look at that charm.

Everything about Fen was delightfully mystifying, and every little detail Malick learned seemed to lead to a thousand more questions. The puzzle of how Fen kept himself clad in better than the rags more familiar to his kind seemed to solve itself when Fen helped himself to a pair of gloves from the closed shop of a leathersmith, picking the lock with a small knife both Malick and Samin had somehow missed when they'd searched him and taken his weapons. He apparently had some sort of scruples when it came to things not freely offered in shrines, though: he left several koins on the tanner's bench in payment. Whether that included the fleshing knife he also liberated and tucked into his boot, Malick didn't know.

The pauses were easier to figure out, those times when Fen would stop dead, stand in whatever spot he'd been, and cock his head to the side, as though listening. Sometimes for a few seconds, one stretch for so long Malick debated revealing himself and shaking Fen to see if he'd died on his feet. Each time, though, like a ritual, Fen's shoulders would sag, his head would shake, and he'd growl, curse quite colorfully, then move on. Malick was fairly certain he knew what it was about, but still, like everything else about Fen, it was intriguing. Maybe if Malick could hear the things Fen heard, if he could make sense of it...

By the set of the stars, midnight had come and gone when Fen angled into a copse of kentsha. Dense and quiet as death, it opened out onto a stretch of scruffland just off the strand of an inlet cut by seawater into a bed of basalt. Nothing more than a gorge striated through with glimmering veins of obsidian—ancient evidence of Subie's erratic temper and indifferent wrath. They were close to the coast now. Malick could feel the salt breeze on his skin. If he climbed one of the trees, he'd likely be able to see the ocean.

A tiny cottage—no more than an abandoned grover's hut—stood ramshackle and battered, grayed by the sea air and years standing beneath the heat of the suns in paintless skin. Its one window stood unshuttered and dark: an empty eye socket staring out into what used to be. Overgrown with scrub and kuuh vines, the "yard" attested to years untrod, but a thin ribbon of bent growth led through from the copse and right to the crooked door of the shack.

Fen made his steady way along the primitive path before he hitched up at the door, pausing with his hand on the cracked, rotting wood, head bent, eyes closed. With one long, deep breath, he gave himself a little shake then silently pushed open the door and slid inside.

Malick frowned.

Not a target, surely. Any with the wealth to do what the men Fen had been hunting were able to do wouldn't be holing up in a place like this. And surely Fen wouldn't go into a potentially hostile hideaway without even having checked through the window first, and clutching nothing more lethal than a loaf of bread.

Before Malick could even form a theory, Fen came back through the door, just as silently as he'd gone in, shadows gathered 'round him like smoky skin. He carefully shut the door, hands notably empty—he'd left the bread at least behind—but with a small beaten leather rucksack over one shoulder. Face set, Fen paused for a moment, head bowed and hand to the door like before, as though reaching for a connection through it, then he merely straightened his shoulders and went back the way he'd come.

For the first time, Malick was torn. Follow after Fen, or risk losing him and have himself a look inside that hut? Curiosity got him; it always did. Just as silently as Fen, Malick made his way through the wild growth then into the little shack... and stopped short.

This... was not what he'd expected.

Four mats—three occupied, another made up, expectant, but empty. Two fair heads and one chestnut rested on the occupied mats, the faces of their owners soft in sleep. The two fair-haired children held Malick's attention just long enough for him to determine they were young: one a boy of about thirteen or so, and the other a girl who couldn't be ten yet. The other was the one who caught and held his eye.

Fen... but not. The hair was shorter, and no braid, but there was no mistaking the resemblance. Had to be a twin, except there were no twins anymore, not Jin twins, anyway, but the similitude was too damned close to be anything else. Although, Malick doubted Fen's face ever looked so unguarded and still, not even in sleep. A person couldn't have so much rage knocking about inside his chest without it one way or another etching itself into his face, and this sleeping young man was... what? A cleaner version of Fen? More... innocent? Not that one could tell much about a person when they were sleeping, no matter what the romantic twaddle of the day would have one believe, but this one... Malick frowned. Not as compelling, somehow, and maybe that was simply because Malick couldn't see the young man's eyes, but he didn't think so. This copy of Fen didn't have the... harshness, the intrigue, the...

Malick shook his head. He'd grown so used to having Shig around, knowing everything he wanted to about a person, by her sight or his own touch, that he seemed to be trying to make up for it by inventing his own versions. Curious, though, Malick reached out, touched a fingertip to the sleeping face... frowned and drew it back. When he'd touched Fen, he'd felt, for the first time in a very long time, not a single thing but the corporeal tremors of a living body. This one, though.

Of the full-Blood, and earthbound. And apparently hiding on Asai's lands. And Asai was seemingly, inexplicably, unaware. Malick knew Asai's connections too well, and no way would he let this much power just sit here, untapped. Terrifyingly strong, this one, and untrained, so far as Malick could tell. The power was there and writhing, but clamped down tight and buried. That ability alone, to leash such straining might, was testament to the young man's power.

The source of the Blood for the amulet, perhaps? Had Fen and his apparent twin dabbled in spellmaking? No, couldn't be—an earthbound couldn't make shadows.

How had the mother been taken away and not this one? Buried or not, that kind of power should have been blaring out to any hunter who happened to train their talent in this young man's direction. And Adan hunters had their sights set on the camps almost continually.

More interesting—and possibly alarming—*how* was Asai missing this? On his *own lands*. Only the veil of another like Malick himself could have hidden an earthbound so thoroughly from Asai's sight, and none of those—

"Bloody—" Malick only just barely kept it a subvocal whisper.

Teeth set tight, he reached out again, really focusing this time. Touched. Tested.

And wanted to punch something.

Definitely a veil. *Shit.*

Rip it away? Deconstruct it and figure out to whom it belonged? No. He ruffled at it, but that was all he dared. It was dense and secure, too tightly woven, and if he did rip it away, or even messed with it too much, he risked exposing not only himself but also what appeared to be the remnants of Fen's family to Asai.

Bloody hell. This had damn well better not turn out to be what Malick was beginning to suspect it was.

He was abruptly very interested himself now in finding out who had taken away Fen's mother and how it was they'd missed her much more powerful son. Perhaps that promise Malick had handed out so casually earlier was not as ill-conceived as he'd feared it might be. Then again, it could be just as dangerous as he was only now beginning to imagine. With that one touch to a sleeping stranger's face, the stakes had risen.

Malick considered for a moment contacting the Mage and demanding to know whether or not he'd known about this little hut on the outskirts of Asai's own freeholds, and its occupants, but he knew he wouldn't. As attractive as answers might be, he wasn't about to tip his hand until he was sure. If Malick's suspicions were even close to reality, the Mage might well be the one person Malick *didn't* want to ask. And if he did and got an answer, Malick might have to kill his mysterious employer. He might have to kill Fen.

Damn it. Malick had been hoping for more pleasant ways to get his hands on that braid.

Still… the prospect of getting one over on Asai…

Smirking, Malick checked the other two, as well, further bemused and interest inescapably piqued when he found no power waiting to erupt from either of them. Only the Blood singing, full and biding. Pensive, he turned back to the not-Fen.

So, if this was Fen's twin brother—and really, what else could he be?—the others were likely related, as well. So, how had Fen got them out of the camp? *Had* he got them out? And how long ago? And what about that unoccupied mat? Was it waiting for Fen? Were *they* waiting for Fen? Thwarting all their laws and traditions by keeping company with an Untouchable?

Malick had a look around, noted mounds of what had to be clothes and blankets that appeared to be in good repair, cast his eye farther and saw a respectable pile of foodstuffs on a long board nailed to the wall to form a crude table. Not unexpectedly, that loaf of black bread to which Fen had been clinging lay prominent among the rest of it, along with the mound of oblates and other edible offerings he'd managed to scoop up along the way.

Small and dingy and run-down the shack might be, but these children had clothes, a place to sleep, and food, and seemed as safe as renegade Jin could be. The kills the Mage had said belonged to Fen had begun about five weeks ago, and if Fen was to be believed—and Malick had believed him tonight, every reluctant word wrung from his stubborn mouth—his father had been killed and his mother taken some time prior to Fen beginning his personal blood grudge those five weeks ago. Which coincided a little too neatly with the rumor of a botched raid in the east camp that none of Malick's more reliable contacts would talk about. And the presence of what appeared to be the rest of Fen's family here, and the hut's rather lived-in look, told Malick that Fen was the one who'd been providing for them since the loss of their parents.

And really—*how* had they ended up on Asai's lands, with Asai apparently completely oblivious? More importantly, how had they ended up protected by a *Temshiel's* veil? Did Fen know? If he did, how was it he hadn't moved them from Asai's reach? Did Fen have any clue what sort of man owned the lands on which he'd chosen to stash his family?

Possible, Malick thought, but not likely. Fen might be on the unstable side, but he too-obviously wasn't stupid. Either he knew about the veil and about Asai and had his own plots and machinations going, or he knew neither and there were bigger fingers in this Untouchable's metaphorical pie than Malick had guessed. Malick was betting on the latter; now that he was paying attention, the signs of mystical manipulation were just too plain to think otherwise. Which meant someone other than a servant of Wolf was interfering with Wolf's Catalyst.

Clearly there was a lot more to Fen that Malick and the others hadn't even touched tonight. The rage was just the surface, frozen over and protecting the rest of it. Perhaps extracting Fen from whatever sticky web in which he'd become enmeshed, helping him to avenge himself and the family he obviously cared about—maybe it could be the first step in putting a fissure in that ice. And once Malick got Fen to a point of trust, once Fen confessed to this little hut and those who dwelt here, Malick would help Fen get them out—send them to… Thesia, maybe, or even Heldesan. Malick had both the money and the resources to swoop in at just the right moment, turn himself from Fen's antagonist to Fen's hero. And then…

Malick couldn't help the grin.

He caught up with Fen on the road, heading back the way he'd come. Malick spent his time thinking, planning, paying more attention to the world inside his head than the one outside. So it took him a moment too long to notice that something was… off.

One of those pauses again, that listening thing Fen did, but something wasn't right this time. Fen was breathing heavily, face clamped down into an expression of… Malick couldn't tell, but it didn't look good. He'd seen Fen's shoulders slump, seen the pack slip down his arm, so he was expecting it when Fen dropped it to the ground like he'd lost all strength to hold it. He hadn't been expecting Fen to sway, though, to fold to one knee in the middle of the dirt road like his strings had been cut. Or for Fen to bend like a man in agonized penitence, wrench in several gasping breaths, painful-sounding and harsh, and crook his elbow over his eyes.

Alarmed, Malick slipped in tight and knelt in front of Fen as he wept, silent and alone in the road in the middle of the night, vibrating like an overwound harp. Malick used every bit of will he owned not to reach out, and… He didn't know. He rather thought any hand extended in sympathy or comfort to this man would get bitten off, so Malick had no idea what he could do, even if he were to discard his veil and reveal himself. His hand went out nonetheless, hovering, uncertain, just over Fen's nape where the braid began its twisting descent down his—

Fen's head snapped up.

With a thankfully inward curse, Malick snatched his hand back.

Cagey, Fen squinted past his shadows, out into the dark, gaze narrowed and wary, flitting everywhere at once, before he frowned, shook his head dismissively, and irritably swiped at his eyes. His glance went to the sky again, tracking Wolf in his heavy-bellied descent, then drifted down again, settled… on Malick. And again, like it had been at the gate, Malick almost thought Fen could see him, looked right at him and *perceived* him. But the gray eyes only focused on Malick for a slip of a moment and then drifted off over his shoulder.

Malick didn't know what had him reeling more—the rush of adrenaline that was dragging ropes of lightning all through him, or the passing glimpse of stricken despair in Fen's unguarded gaze.

And then it was gone, from frown to scowl, smothered once again by that all too familiar resentment and rage. It built for a moment, Malick could see the rising pressure in the clench of Fen's jaw, before Fen dropped his head back, sucked in a long breath, and let it out in a furious, wordless roar at the sky. Piercing, and not just for the decibel levels. Hollow wrath, from way down deep. If he'd not been cloaked by his shadows, dogs would be baying for leagues. Fists clenched tight, nails digging into palms, voice a helpless blade of directionless fury.

It stopped as suddenly as it had begun, silence collapsing all around in a smothering shroud. Malick could hear every night rodent and insect in the brush lining the road, even through the empty ringing in his ears.

Fen's head was tilted to the side again, gaze angled inward...listening. He blinked, narrowed his eyes. His lip curled, teeth tightened, and he loosed a sharp snarl, snatched up the rucksack then snapped to his feet so fast Malick had to break quickly sideways. Back straight and shoulders squared, Fen aimed an obscene gesture first at the moons and then at the distant shadow of Subie before moving on again. Like none of it had happened. Or like it didn't matter that it had.

Malick had to catch his breath.

Oh, hell—he really is mental.

...Except.

There was so much here. Mysteries Malick really wanted to solve, and that hadn't happened in... a long, long time.

In all Malick's years, there had never been a puzzle so compelling as Fen Jacin-rei.

Despite the apparent misery in the object of his fascination, Malick was perversely cheered. He nearly whistled as he followed, watching the braid sway down Fen's back, remembering the feel of it in his hand. Even those times Fen stopped to commune with his gibbering phantoms, Malick merely stopped, too, and waited patiently, almost hoping Fen wasn't just on his way back to the Girou to fulfill his promise. Perhaps one more stop would hand Malick another bit of mystery to add to the growing cache.

The hope lasted until he got his wish.

This time, when Fen's steps took them farther in toward the city but then angled southwest, Malick had a sinking feeling where Fen might be headed. And when Fen bypassed one of the wealthier villages and instead headed up to the hilltop that overlooked it, Malick knew.

The estate was sprawling, the mere size of it a brazen telltale of the wealth that had built it a century ago and managed to keep hold of it since. Oceans of tree cover—cypress, maple, and white pine—ringed the holding, giving it picturesque privacy and natural defense all at once. Manicured and lush, autumn flowers grew fat and healthy, lining the walk and curling vined ringlets over trellises and low stone walls that anchored the slate path around a sedate little pond. The house was grand, even by the standards of the most prosperous lords. Four stories, a wealth of windows—light still glowing in two of them on the ground floor, despite the hour—and each of them with actual glass panes. Stonework and masonry and real clay roof tiles, rather than the more modest wood- and mud- and rush-roofed standard of Adan society. Outbuildings, a gatehouse, even, and guards set around the iron-fenced perimeter, walking the watch in the moonlight led by ken-ken on their leashes.

Malick paused on the path, uncertain what he should do as he watched Fen conceal his pack in some brush in the trees then clear the gate and stroll unseen between two guards passing each other on their circuits. Fen was obviously intent on the house.

The Mage's orders had been very clear—Fen was not to be allowed to take out whomever he pleased. Assassinating a wealthy, influential "lord" like Asai could have some very serious repercussions, especially since the privileged circles in which they were all hunting were beginning to draw in on themselves and build up defenses. Not to mention the stir it would cause in the Courts.

Then again, Malick really didn't care much about any of that. Malick had wanted Asai dead for a long, long time. Maybe Fen had some reason to want the same. Maybe Fen knew what a threat Asai posed to his family and intended to eliminate it. This amazingly still-sane Untouchable, with all his lethal skill, could very well be an answer to the problem of Asai, now that Malick thought about it. Perhaps even an answer to the problem of the Disappeared. It would all depend on what Fen was doing here.

Except, when Fen abruptly dropped his shadows and actually bloody *knocked* on the front door, Malick... paused. Because most assassins— and Malick knew more than most people—didn't actually knock on the doors of their intended victims. At least not smart ones. And even if Malick—and certainly Samin—had doubts about Fen's sanity, there were none whatsoever about his intelligence. Or his skill. So, Malick merely watched while Fen stood there and waited politely on the porch, hands tucked to the small of his back and feet planted apart, chin up. Kept watching when, not a servant as expected, but Asai himself threw open the door half a moment later, gaze at first eager then relieved when he saw who it was.

"I hoped you'd come." Asai's greeting looked completely sincere.

Fen only tilted his head, his face impassive. "Didn't you know... *Beishin?*" His tone was mild, but hostility curled on that last word, just as unease curled in Malick's gut upon hearing it.

Asai's smile crimped immediately, turned bitter, and then fell altogether. He stared at Fen, measuring, cooler than his greeting had been, but when he apparently couldn't read anything in Fen's inscrutable face, Asai grimaced. With a quick look around—placing the guards, no doubt—Asai sighed, stepped back, and swung the door wide. Waited.

Fen stared blankly at him for another moment before he pointed his gaze straight ahead and entered without a word.

Malick stayed where he was. Thinking. His gut churned lightly as all the possibilities, all the implications slowly surfaced. He closed his eyes, dipped his head. This could turn out very, very badly.

A full-Blood earthbound asleep in a shack out on Asai's own lands, an Untouchable with attachments he shouldn't have and sanity he shouldn't own, Asai's apparent involvement—it changed everything. Samin, Yori and Shig—even Umeia and everyone at the Girou—were all Malick's responsibility, and this had just taken a turn onto more dangerous paths than Malick had suspected. And Fen's mere presence in their lives could prove the most dangerous of all.

"Oh, little Ghost." Malick scrubbed at his face, abruptly exhausted. "What have you got yourself into?"

⋔

Asai paced. Over to the window, peer out, pretend to be looking at something, then turn back again. Cross the room to the fireplace, glare at the flames for not needing to be stirred and therefore not giving him something to do with his hands, then back again to the window. Pause once or twice to pick up a book, raise his eyebrows as though he'd forgotten he'd left it on the tea table, put it back down. Examine a small figurine of a raven carved from obsidian and another of a wolf carved from marble on his next circuit, swipe a finger over the bear and the dragon. Try not to care that it practically blared his discomfort to the boy standing silent against the wall, shoulder propped to the bookshelf, watching him.

Boy—*ha*. Young man, now, had been for some time, and too knowing, too observant, too...

Damn it. It was Asai's own mistake. He should have taken the boy the night he slipped from his mother's womb as the midwife had practically begged him to do. Asai would've had more influence over it all, would've been able to mold the Catalyst into what he—

No use railing against Fate for not bending to Asai's own preferences. There were blank spots in his sight, naturally, but most of the things he'd foreseen were still in futures-possible and not changed entirely. He'd done right to take the boy, even if it now appeared it hadn't been soon enough, so perhaps it wasn't yet unsalvageable.

"Here you are, seyh."

A little too much relief flooded Asai when Vonshi appeared, sleep-tousled and somewhat bleary, but carrying a tray of tea and the cakes Asai knew Jacin-rei preferred. Vonshi blinked at Asai, inquiring, but Asai merely shook his head; he'd serve it himself. He didn't think he'd want anyone overhearing what Jacin-rei had come to say, whatever it might be. Vonshi merely dipped his head, shot a sideways glance over at Jacin-rei, then quietly left the room, sliding the double doors shut behind him. Asai sat on the couch and made himself busy with pouring tea.

"Well, it appears Vonshi sends you his greetings in his way." He said it lightly, angling his chin toward the plate. "He's brought you the sweet bean-paste squares you like. Don't know why he still makes them. You're the only one who eats them. And now that you've..." Asai held up a bowl, sweeping his hand toward the opposite couch. "Come. Sit."

Jacin-rei merely blinked at him and didn't move. Unreadable, but then, he'd been that for a long while now, and Asai had only himself to hold responsible.

"I've worried about you, you know." Asai was sincere, and tried to make that plain in both his voice and his expression.

"Why?" Flat. Emotionless.

"Because I care what happens to you." Asai set Jacin-rei's bowl down on the table and took his time pouring his own. "I care what happens to your brothers and your sister." He took a sip, peered over the rim of the bowl, and met the cold stare squarely. "If you'll tell me where they are, I can—"

A snort, derisive and... yes, angry. Jacin-rei pushed away from the wall, walked slowly to the end table by the chair, picked up the little wolf figurine and carelessly tumbled it into his palm.

"I'm not going to tell you. Don't ask me again." Jacin-rei tilted his head, eyes narrowed. "Why don't you know?"

Asai scowled—he couldn't help it. Giving away his thoughts all over his face, when Jacin-rei was careful to give away none, and yet it was a contest Asai knew he wouldn't win. He needed his Ghost.

"They have been gone from my sight since—" Asai cut himself off, but not quickly enough.

"Since when?" Jacin-rei's gaze went deadly-dark. "Since before or after she was taken?" He set down the marble wolf carefully, picked up the raven. "You're going to tell me you didn't see it?" He gave Asai a slow blink, baiting. "You're going to tell me it wasn't you who gave them up?"

Asai's stomach turned over. He'd been wondering exactly what Jacin-rei had heard that night.

"Why would I do that? It was I who kept them safe all these years, Jacin-rei. You've no right to question me now."

"I've no right to be alive, either, to be speaking intelligibly, to think for myself, or even feel, but..." A shrug.

"My work. My teachings."

"Oh, yes." A small twist of a smile set Jacin-rei's face into lines Asai didn't recognize. Jacin-rei set the raven next to the wolf. "And I've got the scars to prove it."

Not fair. Asai had merely used the tool Fate handed him—what Jacin-rei's own brother had so naively and unintentionally shown him. There had been no other way. And everything Jacin-rei was now was because of that tool.

"You're upset." Asai set his tea down. "You know that everything I did was necessary. Everything I did, I did for you. I would never—"

"*Don't*—" Jacin-rei clenched his teeth, shut his eyes tight; it was the most emotion he'd shown Asai in... years. "Do not pretend for a second that anything you did was for me. Fate is your god, and you will sacrifice anyone on its altar, even those you pretend to love and trick into lov—" He cut himself off, but they both knew what he almost said.

It heartened Asai. It was the first useable thing that had come his way in weeks. "I never gave you false hope, Jacin-rei. Perhaps... perhaps if—"

"I want a name." Cold as a glacier. "Give me one and I'll go. I'll even let you live." Jacin-rei lifted his head, crimped a cruel little smile. "For old times' sake."

Old times' sake. Indeed. The one thing for which Asai rightfully held fault. The one mistake he'd made in all his careful stepping through sight and visions and the machinations of Fate and the gods. The one time he'd let his own discipline falter.

Jacin-rei's almost-slip before was the only thing that kept Asai's fear away. He knew what Jacin-rei could do. But he also knew what lay at Jacin-rei's core.

"I can't give you a name." Asai sat back and spread his arms to his sides, opening himself in a pose of trust.

"You can't or you won't?"

"Does it matter?"

"*Yes!*" Jacin-rei set fisted hands to the table, as though he needed the support, and dipped his head so Asai couldn't see his face. He was breathing heavily, jaw ticcing with the effort of controlling himself. "It *matters* to those of us who can't see and don't necessarily care that our misery pleases Fate, or that we have a part to play in it, whether we want it or not. It *matters*, Beishin, and if I ever mattered to you, you will *give me a name!*"

Asai sighed. There was no one in the world who mattered more to him right now, but it couldn't be in the way Jacin-rei wanted it to be. Too much hinged on him, too many futures depended on him being what Asai had built him to be, and right now, the idealized, unrequited facet of Jacin's-rei's love for his beishin was the only thing keeping him from doing something irreparable. This break of emotion wasn't necessarily what Asai had wanted—despite what Jacin-rei thought, Asai did have a heart—but it was at least something he could work with. Jacin-rei wanted an explanation, something he could believe, and it didn't necessarily matter if it was plausible—Jacin-rei would believe it anyway, because he needed to believe in *something*.

"You mattered to me, Jacin." The abbreviation was calculated, and it had the desired effect: Jacin-rei's posture tightened, and his jaw clamped hard enough to break teeth. "You matter to me still, as do those you love. I cannot give you a name—I will not, not until the time is exactly right. If you choose to turn your knife on me for it..." Asai leaned forward. "Bring the children to me, Jacin. I can protect them better than you can, I can—"

"I saw your 'guests' that night, Beishin." It was low, breathed out on a hiss between clenched teeth. "I... I *heard*. They'd all be dead, had I not disobeyed you and gone to them." Jacin-rei lifted his head. His hate-filled glare was almost a weapon by itself. "And now you want me to believe you saw *nothing*. You gave him *amulets!*" He paused, as though the words were knives that cut him on the way out, before he gathered it all into muzzled wrath. "I would slit my own stomach and pull out my entrails for a jump rope before I would entrust them to you again."

And the worst part about it was that he was completely serious. Jacin-rei only had so much focus to spare, and all of it right now was narrowed on what remained of his family—even the one who might as well be his father reborn. And Asai's "betrayal" would not be justified or forgiven, not even when Fate stepped in to validate his actions. *If* Fate stepped in—Asai just didn't know anymore.

"I cannot see you, Jacin-rei. I never could, you know that. Your nature prevents it. I see you only in the moments when your fate intersects another's. And your family went from my sight weeks ago." Asai pursed his mouth, frustrated. "It's like a conjurer has draped a shroud over their places in Fate, and I can only now and then catch glimpses of them enough to know our purpose is not lost."

"*Your* purpose."

That made Asai pause, discomfited. "It was ours, once."

"So were other things. Or so I... imagined." Jacin-rei straightened and turned to face Asai squarely. "I come from a race of people who have forgotten what they are so completely they can't even see how they've brought their fortunes on themselves. I am, apparently, more like them than I'd ever thought, and I no longer have a wish to save those who don't know they need saving."

Asai sat back, shocked. "You don't mean that. You're just upset. Your own brother—"

"*Do not* think to use my brother to persuade me again to your cause.

You bought me once, and now you've sold him, but he is out of your reach now, and if what you say is true, out of your sight. Don't seek to regain your hold over me through him."

"There was never any *hold*." Asai was angry now, and somewhat stung. "I never forced you to anything, *Ghost*. I only ever gave you a choice. Everything between us was always by *your choice*."

It only made the glare go colder. "Anything that once might have been 'between us' is no more. I see now it never was. Any debt I may have owed you was forfeit the night you let those men leave your house, handed them what they needed to destroy my family. Any love I may once have had for you, Beishin, died when they took my mother."

"You mean when you were too late to save her." Asai couldn't help the mix of satisfaction and regret when Jacin-rei flinched. "You didn't wait, Jacin-rei. You've no idea what my orders that night might've been, how we might have saved them all—together." Asai paused, leaned in. "What if that night was all a part of the design, the impetus that would start the wheels of Fate turning, save your family, save the Jin, and you ruined it because you wouldn't listen to your beishin?" Asai's mouth wanted to curl up on a satisfied smile, watching Jacin-rei trying not to believe it. "*Your* failure, little Ghost."

And Jacin-rei... sagged. Only the slightest bend in the rigid posture, but a show of weakness, however subtle.

As unreadable as he'd grown to be, Asai remembered the boy Jacin-rei had been, remembered what mattered to him, what had always hit him at his core. And that boy still lived inside Jacin-rei, beneath all the control, all the fury, all the hatred that Asai himself had carefully cultivated.

Despair. Guilt. Loneliness.

The trinity of Fen Jacin-rei's very being. It was why it had been so easy to mold him into the killer Asai needed him to be, why he'd pulled at Asai's heart in ways Asai never should have allowed. Why Jacin-rei would leave this house without giving Asai the answers he needed, but would nonetheless leave him alive so he could perhaps find them. And despite whatever he believed Asai's part had been in his family's destruction, Jacin-rei would not betray Asai and leave him vulnerable to the Courts. Not even if Jacin-rei's own life were forfeit. Although, if the lives of his family were in the balance...

Asai shook that away until the time when his sight might tell him it was a real possibility. No sense in fretting blind. Hard not to, though, when everything that had been so clear mere weeks ago now wavered in his inner vista, distorted but not yet obliterated.

Perhaps Asai truly had been wrong about the brother, about the lure that would drag Jacin-rei to do his part. And if Asai hadn't been altogether wrong, the actions of Jacin-rei, which Asai hadn't seen or been able to predict, might have altered things to a point where all futures were now possible, for good or ill. Perhaps Asai's suspicions about the void that hovered over all the potentials, the same suspicions that had prompted him to slog through a muddy Jin camp in the rain more than twenty years ago, were more right than he wanted to know and there was an influence over the Untouchable Asai couldn't foresee or control.

There was only one kind of being that could hold such influence. Only one kind who could purposefully cloud Asai's sight. He didn't know if that exhilarated or terrified him.

"Jacin-rei." Asai said the name softly, with as much seduction in it as he dared, just enough to remind the man of what the boy had craved. "Tell me where you've been. I have heard… rumors." Eight men dead, all of them dealing in magic, all of them known to Asai, and all of them assassinated in the ruthless style of this Untouchable. Asai should know. "I fear you are testing Fate, and she is a cruel mistress. These men are not those you were trained to destroy. You don't know what you might alter, and you won't find what you're looking for by—"

"I am a Catalyst, no?" Jacin-rei arched an eyebrow, control and composure once again wrapped around him like a suit of armor. "What-ever influence I impose on Fate is my right and my purpose." He smiled, spiteful and tight, head atilt. "And you know all about purpose, don't you, *Beishin?*"

He kept saying the word like it was a curse.

Asai wanted to hit something. "And the Ancestors gave you leave to kill those men?"

"They didn't tell me not to."

Damn it, the boy had always been too intelligent, and now he was using that intelligence to actually think. Blind devotion was gone, categorical loyalty denied. Asai couldn't have it. Couldn't stop it, either. Fate had been set into motion. A dangerous thing, this deadly Catalyst he'd made, but Asai had not foreseen the danger Jacin-rei's mind might be to Asai himself. *Why* had he not foreseen it? Why had he not foreseen *any* of this?

"I won't be back." Jacin-rei shrugged, all of a sudden blasé. "I have… new matters I am compelled to attend."

"New matters." The beat of Asai's heart picked up pace. Whatever the influence now hovering over the future, threatening it, it had every-thing to do with these "new matters." It had to. There was no other explanation. "Where are you going? What are these 'new matters'?" Asai paused, trying very hard not to look as eager as he felt. "Jacin-rei… who have you been—?"

"I'm not going to tell you that. And if I ever see you again, I will return one of your knives to you in a way you won't like." Jacin-rei stepped swiftly up to Asai, leaned in until Asai was compelled to push back into the couch cushions so he could meet the cold glare. "Hear me, Beishin—I will find him and I will find the one who pulls his strings. If those strings lead back to you, I will garrote you with them, then cut your heart from your chest and make you watch it beat its last while you choke on them." Flames had bloomed behind Jacin-rei's eyes, their tongues licking out to lash at Asai with every word shoved through teeth clenched tight. "You are no longer my beishin, you no longer have a voice in what I choose to do or not do. You are dead to me."

Asai forced himself to breathe evenly. As with everything else Jacin-rei said, he meant it. Whatever control Asai might have had over any futures or fates through the Untouchable was now in very serious jeopardy. He would have to seek other ways. And two of them were finding out what these "new matters" were and where Jacin-rei had hidden his siblings.

"You won't kill me now, then?" Asai delivered the question with a cavalier composure he hadn't truly had for weeks, not since Jacin-rei had dropped from his sight like the Ghost he was.

"If I ever see you again..." Jacin-rei straightened his back slowly, toying with a long, curved knife Asai didn't recognize and hadn't seen him draw. "Yes. I will kill you. And what's more, Beishin—I'll *enjoy* it."

Blinking slowly, eyes steady on Asai, Jacin-rei spun the knife through his fingers, too fast for Asai to follow the movement, then turned sharply and stalked to the door, threw it open and was gone.

No more key to futures-possible, no more relaxing back on the comfortable surety of What Will Be, but only squinting into the blurry future and interpreting vague signs of What Might Be. Asai's pet Ghost had shaken his leash and turned his bite on his owner. Which was never what Jacin-rei had been to Asai, but he *could* have been; Asai could have been so much crueler, if he were a different man, one with no heart, as Jacin-rei clearly thought, one who didn't truly care for anything or anyone. But if that were true, if that were what Asai really was, his chest wouldn't be so tight, and his comfortable sitting room wouldn't now feel so empty for its lack of a Ghost.

Asai shook his head, collapsed back into the couch, all at once exhausted, and closed his eyes with a long sigh that came from—

The abrupt, deafening crash of shattering stone had him jolting up, his heart thundering in his chest as the report echoed from the fireplace. Asai snapped to his feet, stared, momentarily uncomprehending, at the broken figurines littering the hearthstone. Raven, Dragon, Bear, Owl, and Snake—all of them in pieces on the smooth granite. All but Wolf, tongue lolling from his marble mouth, leering at Asai from his place in the center of the table where they'd all rested only a moment ago.

"Who's there?" Asai's voice was thinner than it should have been, but he couldn't keep it steady. "Who are you?" He threw his glance all around the room, but there was no one there, not even shadows, but still he called, "Jacin-rei?"

No one answered, nothing else went flying about, no movement or sound at all but that of the logs burning bright and crackling dispassionately. Asai turned his gaze back to the table, to the carved figure that seemed to glare back.

"So, then. You've come after all." One of Wolf's. Perfect. The smile that quirked Asai's mouth was a little shaky but no less sincere. He dipped his head, placed a hand over his breastbone. "*Temshiel*."

Somehow, he wasn't surprised when the wolf came whistling at his head. Things were going to plan after all.

⋔

Planting-month, Year 1312, Cycle of the Wolf

Jacin held it together for a little while, following Asai through yards and fields, the night sounds swaying with then bleeding into the whining buzz that turned everything around him to the barest shadow of reality. He could tell when he should lift his feet more to clear clods of dirt or hop the occasional streambed, when he should step faster because the dark cloak he was following was flapping too far ahead of him.

He couldn't remember where he was going exactly, who wore that cloak, why the fog in his mind was so disconcerting—

ourboylistenlistenlistenmustn'tmissyourchance

—why his hand was sore and sticky, nor why clenching it into a fist, poking his fingers down deep, was a good thing. Until bright-hot pain seared through the porridge of his mind like a warm knife, quelling the noise, letting real thoughts through it like water through a sluice gate—

Joori, Joori gave me this, thank you, I'm sorry

—and then a different sort of pain weltered in, this one squeezing Jacin's heart too tight. Tears blurred his vision, but he kept sight of that cloak, following like an obedient pup, and every once in a while, if he stumbled or lagged too far, that steady hand would come back, clamp down on his shoulder, and give him something else on which to ground himself.

Chosen, he'd *chosen* this, *his* choice, to walk away from his brother—

Joori, I'm sorry, I didn't mean... didn't mean to make you cry, Mother, I only wanted... I don't know what I wanted, just... something else

—and into the sway of this stranger with the beautiful dark eyes and handsome face and warm hand that tingled at Jacin's skin even through his shirt.

"...hear me, Jacin-rei?"

There was shaking, words, all strung together and muffled, until a ruthless blow landed on the side of Jacin's face. White spots flashed through Jacin's wobbly vision; a high-pitched ring shrilled out the noise.

Through it, Asai's voice came to him, clear and solid: "You must listen to me now, Jacin-rei. Can you do that? Are you able?"

Jacin blinked away the sparkles, focusing on the throbbing over his cheekbone and temple, and Asai's deep-dark eyes. "I hear you."

"Good." Asai squeezed Jacin's arms, keeping tight hold. "Now, I've a cart waiting. Do you remember I told you that?"

Cart. Right. A cart at the gate. Jacin nodded.

"Good lad. The Doujou won't stop you going through the gate. They'll more likely pretend they don't even see you. Just make sure they see the braid before they stop you. Here." Asai pulled the braid around and draped it over Jacin's shoulder. "They won't stop you, but I cannot be seen taking you away with me. Do you understand?"

An Adan lord making off with an Untouchable. No, Asai couldn't be seen taking Jacin away.

Jacin breathed out slow, and as even as he could. "They can't know."

Roll him up and stuff him in a carpet, a rucksack, hide him in a cellar...

touch the Untouchable control the Catalyst belong everywhere and nowhere no one's boy the grace of the Ghost our boy

"You're doing very well, Jacin-rei. I need you to concentrate for a little while longer, all right? Once we've got you to the cart, we'll be safe, but we need to get you there first, and without getting me hanged for it."

Hanged.

No. Asai arrested and hanged, or... No.

"What d'you want me to do?"

Asai smiled, so warm and rife with approval that everything inside Jacin sparked and popped, and he smiled back. Asai's warm hand covered the place where it had slapped before; it was all Jacin could do not to close his eyes and turn his face into it.

"I want you to focus on this." Asai closed his hand over Jacin's bloody fist, squeezed it tight, apparently satisfied when Jacin hissed out a tight breath. "I want you to keep your wits until we are both through the gate, hold to them—hold to the pain—with everything you are. Can you do that?"

"I can. I will."

"All right. I shall go first. You will stay here and watch while I check out with the Doujou and drive away in the cart."

Drive...? Wait.

"Drive away?" Bright panic shot through Jacin. Even the reflexive squeeze of Asai's hand over his didn't dull it. What...? No. *Drive away?*

Another slap, this one sharper, and no warm caress to dull the sting this time.

"—not leaving you. You *must* listen to me."

Not leaving you.

Not. Leaving.

Notleavingnotleavingnotleaving—

"I—" Jacin had to clench his teeth. "I'm listening."

"Tell me what I said."

"You'll go first, check out with the Doujou, drive aw-way..." Jacin swallowed then made himself speak the rest: "I'll s-stay here and w-watch."

"You will watch, Jacin-rei, and then, after I've driven away, you will go out the gate too."

Jacin frowned. "The Doujou—"

Asai gave the braid a sharp yank, so hard it rocked Jacin's head to the side. "The Doujou will not stop you. You are Untouchable, you are meant to wander; the Doujou have no authority to stop you. Do you understand?"

"Yes, seyh. I... yes."

Asai gave the braid another tug. "Talk to yourself as you go by. Stagger. Weep. Do anything you like, but do not allow the voices to overwhelm you. Can you do that?"

Jacin scowled. "You want me to act insane?"

As soon as it came out his mouth, he knew how stupid it was. What was he, after all? Hanging onto sanity by one fingernail and a mutilated palm.

Jacin firmed his jaw, clamping his fingers down tighter. "I can do it."

"I know you can, Jacin-rei. Watch which way the cart goes, then get you through the gate and follow after. Keep your wits and do not stray from the road. I shall be waiting less than fifty paces away, where the road takes a bend out of sight of the sentries. Repeat it back to me."

"Watch which way—"

"From the beginning, Jacin-rei."

Jacin bit his lip, shut his eyes tight. Forced a stanchion through the roaring susurrus of empty chatter, made a dam of it, and pushed sense through the gap.

"Stay here until you've gone through the gate. Watch which way the cart goes, then follow after. Make sure they see the braid and try to act crazy. Stay on the road. You'll be waiting with the cart just 'round the bend."

Jacin went through it all in his head again, nodded, then opened his eyes and grinned.

Asai smiled back. "Very good, my boy. *Very* good." He took up Jacin's curled fist again and held it between them. "Keep sharp. Whatever you have to do, keep sharp. Do everything I've told you, *as* I've told you, and you will leave behind the doom of an Untouchable this night. There is a better life with me, Jacin-rei. But you cannot have any of it unless you do this now. Understand?"

Oh, yes. Jacin understood. Hadn't he just walked away from—?

The tears threatened for the…he'd lost count of how many times he'd wept tonight. Had he ever stopped?

"Will I see him again?"

Asai sighed, straightened, and threw a glance around the small copse of scraggy pines where they stood, just short of the bare stretch of dirt and lingering bruises in the land where houses used to be, razed so the Doujou had a clear view of the road. His smile this time was uneasy.

"It will depend on you, Jacin-rei."

"I…I understand." Or at least Jacin thought he did. "I can do it."

"I know you can. I shall see you when you are free of this camp and the life of an Untouchable."

Then, in a swirl of dark fabric and a flash of his warm smile, Asai turned away and left Jacin standing amidst sharp-smelling pine, trying to cling to the absurd promise, his groundless faith in it and the man who'd handed it to him. Jacin drew the little knife his brother had given him, closed it into his palm, squeezed. Watched Asai stroll confidently up to the gate, converse politely with the doujoun who guarded it, wait patiently while they checked his papers, asked him questions Jacin couldn't hear, then passed him on. Asai didn't hesitate or look back, only took his time walking to his…

That was no cart, that was a *carriage*. Drawn by a *horse*.

Jacin blinked, more mystified now than he had been when Asai had first sauntered into their scrubby dooryard. Who was this lord-prophet who had bargained for an Untouchable all those years ago then come for him in a swirl of rich fabric and warm, dark eyes? A bloody *horse*, for pity's sake. No one owned horses—too rare, too costly, too impractical for any but those with wealth beyond… well, beyond Jacin's imagining, anyway.

Jacin's hand pulsed steadily as he goggled, rhythmically curling his fingers and goring his palm as he watched Asai climb into the back of the carriage, signal to the waiting driver, and start off. The thin shrill of panic still speared through Jacin—

Don't leave me, I'll be good, I promise, please, I won't go crazy

—but he pushed it back with a faith too blind to be sane.

Sane.

Jacin snickered. He ran his fingers over the messy plait that had been smooth and shiny this morning, when Joori had woven it for him, choked back a watery little sob and willed away fresh tears. Clenched his fist tighter and bit down on the inside of his cheek besides.

As steadily as he could, Jacin took a long, deep breath and headed for the gate.

It was so easy. The hard part was not letting himself get lost in the babble coming out his own mouth. Not stopping in shock when one of the doujoun slipped out a surprised little cry and reached out as Jacin tottered by, muttering and yanking at his braid to be sure they saw it.

"Don't touch him, Syl!"

The guard blinked at the man who'd snapped the order. "But surely you can't… he's bleeding, seyh."

"And he'll bleed more, poor lad." The other guard put a hand on his comrade's arm and drew him back, inconceivable sympathy in his eyes as he looked down at Jacin. Jacin had to remind himself to renew his stream of babble. "Let him go, Syl. The law says we can't touch 'em, so we can't touch 'em."

And that was it. They got out of Jacin's way and let him wander right past them. Jacin could feel their gazes on his back as he made a point of staggering to the road, paused like he didn't know what to do with himself next, then followed the way the carriage had gone.

He kept expecting a shout behind him, a sharp command to stop, but it never came. Only night sounds, and white whispers in his head, and those compassionate gazes watching the mad Untouchable wander into the night.

Sympathy. *Sympathy*. It was… not what Jacin had expected. He'd encountered Adan before Asai. Jacin had more than once skirted the perimeter of the various gates and boundaries keeping the Jin in their places, and he'd seen the doujoun walking their watches, blank-faced but vigilant, keeping a sideways eye on him lest he make a rush for it. He'd witnessed two raids. One where the Adan hunters had killed a man outright and taken his wife to face the Courts for conspiracy, as well as carted off one girl and three boys, weeping and shrieking, all of them. One where the hunters left empty-handed and angry for it. And each time, Jacin had seen the guards' impassive faces as they carried out their bloody orders with emotionless efficiency. Jacin had come to think perhaps the Adan had no emotions at all. Perhaps they couldn't have them, in order to do their work.

Except now there was Asai, and these Adan doujoun who pitied an Untouchable. Jacin didn't know what to think anymore.

And then he didn't think at all.

Asai was waiting, right where he'd said he'd be. The rush of relief that swamped Jacin almost made him go down to his knees in the road. He hadn't realized how terrified he'd been that he'd dreamed it all, or imagined it, or… It didn't matter—Asai was there, waiting, offering a new life. Jacin staggered to the waiting carriage with something knotted high in his chest that had the frightening feel of hope.

"You have done well, Jacin-rei." With a smile, Asai uncurled Jacin's fingers, placed a clean cloth over the mess of blood and mangled tissue that was Jacin's palm, and pushed him down on the seat, covering him with a blanket. "Your work for now is done, my boy. Rest, if you can. We've a long night ahead of us."

Jacin didn't care. And probably couldn't rest, not with all the noise ramping itself back up again. *Our boy*, it nattered at him, and Jacin shut his eyes tight, clamped his jaw, and shook his head. *No*, he snapped back, *his*, and he let his mind slip down into the clamor, absurdly sure that Asai would bring him back.

╥

The night lasted for days—weeks, years, ages. Long stripes of reality veined through with disarray and a constant grasping at sense. A great house that was obviously a dream, and Asai leading Jacin to it, talking at him—*Vonshi will show you where you are to sleep. You will address me as Beishin.* Jacin frowned, dull alarm and confusion—*Have you bought me, then?* He thought he remembered Asai answering back—*No, my boy, I have merely bought a future for you*—but Jacin didn't exactly care, and it was all a dream anyway, so what did it matter?

"We'll just put your things… lad? Lad, can you hear me?"

He was raving in a corner of the dooryard, scaring the chickens, wanting to be let back in, but his father pretended he didn't see him, and wouldn't let anyone else see, and that was all right. Jacin didn't really want them to see him anyway.

Or maybe Joori had taken him away, refusing to believe, refusing to speak his Untouchable brother's name in full, dragging him drooling to a freedom that didn't exist, just a brutal death for Joori and a continuous hell for Jacin, and then Joori would go to Raven to await rebirth, and Jacin would go to Wolf, and they wouldn't meet again for a thousand years. Except Joori would go to the suns, because he'd dared touch the Untouchable, and Jacin wanted to go there with him, because anything would be better than having no room for himself in his own mind.

the one the only one ours now our boy listen always listenlistenlisten our boy we've chosen seek the Null

"I don't know, Beishin. I don't think he can hear me."

"He can hear you, Vonshi. He just needs help finding his way to reason."

He wept, he knew he wept, and he tried to count the tears, but got caught up in the prismed shards, resenting the delight they took in their beauty as they shattered from his eyes and broke his mind with each deafening *drip-drip-drop*. He screamed, he knew he screamed, because he had to, he had no choice, he had to get them *out* somehow before they pulverized his brain, he could feel it liquefying, all hot and steaming inside his head, and he couldn't remember anymore how to make them stop or quiet or at least make *sense*.

"I need you to watch, Vonshi. You may need to do it yourself."

back to Zero and start again Wolf will not forsake the Catalyst Raven would pick the corpses clean

And then Asai—wonderful, blessed Asai, Beishin, Master, savior—ripping away the bandage on Jacin's palm, the sharp-hot slap of leather and the bright sting of sanity.

Asai was kneeling where Jacin had curled on the floor, rich voice calm, confident: "I know it looks brutal, but right now it's the only way. We'll come up with better as soon as he's well enough to train." Asai peered up from Jacin's hand to Jacin's eyes, a wary smile curving his mouth. "Better now?"

Jacin could barely see, could barely breathe. His nose was clotted with snot, his face was swollen and flaming, and his chest was caught in midsob; he let it go on a gasp, sucked in a long, wet breath, and splayed his hand flat.

"Another."

"Seyh," said a voice, cragged and dry with years, "surely there must be—"

"Just watch, Vonshi," Asai ordered.

Jacin waited for it, didn't flinch when it came, only latched on to the pain of it, sighed, and started the business of piecing his mind back together again.

Asai. A carriage ride. A manor on a hill. A future.

"Thank you, Beishin." Jacin opened his eyes, and smiled at his master.

5

Harvest-month, Year 1322, Cycle of the Wolf

Storming off the way Samin had done—well, perhaps it had been more like slinking, but still—had been all well and good for making a point. Up until the time he'd got to the end of the alley and realized he had nowhere to go.

He wasn't exactly *wanted* for what he'd done years ago. No alerts filed with the Doujou, at least as far as he or Malick had ever been able to dig up. Nor had any suspicions been directed his way when Lord Mizin—Samin paused and spat—went missing. In truth, no one had missed the bastard. Well, no one but those who had an eye toward appropriating his estate, but *they* were hardly going to launch a search or investigation.

Still, Samin had spent the past five years keeping more or less to himself, to the Girou, and to his job. There were still some he'd known in the Doujou, and besides the few he used as contacts when Malick needed information otherwise not easily got, well. It was just best that Samin fade from the memories of those doujoun who might remember him.

So when he'd decided for the first time in… probably ever to make a dramatic exit, it had lost all its drama before he'd taken ten steps. Bloody typical.

City streets at night were unique. Quiet stretches where the only things moving or breathing were yourself and the rats, interspersed with splotches of drunkards or prostitutes or revelers, or all of them together. Cutthroats and cutpurses with narrowed, calculating eyes, staring out from the shadows of alleys or doorways. The occasional loner, just trying to make it from one place to another without running into any of the former.

All of them gave Samin a wide berth. They always had.

He fetched up hours later, right back where he'd started, leaning against the brick wall by the kitchen doors in the alley. Tired now but still not tired enough, he watched the moons for a while. Made himself useful scaring away the occasional mutt that came looking for the heaps of waste the kitchen lads came to dump.

"Have you got a light, seyh?"

Speaking of. Samin couldn't remember the lad's name, but he'd always been a pleasant sort, taking care to save for "Malick-seyh's people" a bit of whatever special was being served that night. He held an unlit smoke between his fingers, peering at Samin hopefully. His companion—another boy Samin had probably seen before but didn't remember—hovered by the kitchen doors, staring as though afraid Samin might eat him.

Samin gave them a light then listened to them chatter for a while. Complaints about Ragi and the tyrannical way he ran the kitchens. Lewd speculation about whomever had crossed their sight this evening. More complaints about how much there was left to do before they could go home and do... whatever it was boys like this did when they weren't working.

When the braver one offered a smoke, Samin accepted. He wished he remembered the lad's name. He wished he were the sort of person who cared enough to bother.

To be fair, it wasn't that Samin *didn't* care, because he did. Just not about people who could bloody well take care of themselves. That was at least something. He'd had to be shocked into it, but it still mattered, and what he did about it all now mattered too. Stopping men from doing the things Mizin had been doing, the things Mizin had arrogantly expected Samin to *help* him do...

Perhaps that was why Samin's moral compass was all askew with the Fen-Ghost. Samin had done his turn in the Doujou. Had believed in what he was doing. Magic was a frightening proposition, and no one could be trusted with it, at least as far as Samin had been concerned back then. When he'd been young and stupid. That kind of unchecked power had already proven deadly to those who didn't have it, so Samin had been taught, and he'd had no problem with collecting those who did have it when he was told to. Though, he'd had yet to meet anyone like Malick before then, or even Shig.

Samin did have to admit to too many uneasy nights, wondering what might have happened to those he'd arrested and presented to the Court, though in truth, that hadn't come 'til much later—not until Samin had begun to hear the rumors. After that, Samin spent his rotations in the camps watching. Silently questioning. Hoping this rotation wouldn't coincide with a raid.

The smoke had burned down to singe his fingers without him noticing it. With a muttered curse, Samin crushed the rest of it beneath his bootheel. The boys had gone on their way, and he hadn't noticed that, either. Not until the nightly exodus of evening staff who didn't live in-house began slouching their way through the door. Samin nodded politely when necessary, saying goodnights and offering smiles when they were turned on him.

"A trade for a bit of your luck, seyh, and the gods' blessing."

Absently sucking on his scorched fingers, Samin hooked a glance sideways. One of the…cooks, maybe? The young man's grin was proud, though shy, his stance perhaps a touch wary. Samin admired the bravery of the approach. People didn't generally talk to Samin if they didn't have to.

He slid his gaze down to the fresh rice cake in the young man's hand, a touch of fragrant steam wafting from it in the cool of the not-yet-morning, a poppy blossom set in its center. The young man held a basket full of the little cakes, obviously having just baked them in Umeia's kitchen to help him celebrate his good fortune.

Samin fished a koin out of his pocket to exchange for the cake. "The blessings of the gods on you and your babe to come." He nodded at the man and then the little group behind him. "This your first?"

The young man's grin widened. "The first of many, seyh, if the gods will it and the poppies do their job."

Samin held back a sigh. "Congratulations, seyh."

The young man rejoined his cheery little group and led the way out of the alley, presumably to accost everyone he saw along the way and politely strongarm good luck and koins out of strangers in exchange for cakes. The blessings of the gods, indeed.

Samin had seen what "blessings" the gods bestowed on the mortals who worshipped them, even on those who were supposed to be their most favored. He'd seen the futile, doomed lives swelling in Jin bellies like the one that young man was celebrating now. And then, one turn of the midwife's hand…

Samin grimaced and chucked the cake into the rubbish bin.

He almost wished he could blame the Jin for his turn in sentiment, back when the Doujou had made so much sense to him and then suddenly hadn't anymore. After all, if they didn't try to hide the children, if they'd just pluck them out—quick and clean—at birth, like they were supposed to, they wouldn't grow so attached, and the children wouldn't be the ones who ended up having to pay for their parents' crimes. Samin had held to that one for years, until it occurred to him to wonder if he'd be able to hold a squalling infant in his big hands and snuff its life so blithely. And he didn't even really *like* children.

Perhaps that was why this Fen seemed to affect Samin the way he did, with this strange mix of pity and anger. Fen had come from the camps, obviously, and what did Samin know about him, really?—perhaps someone the lad loved had been done to like that little girl in Mizin's cellars had been done to. Fen had fought Malick bitterly, and that little girl had never had the chance to do the same. For more than five years now Samin had been dealing out vengeance for her, and he couldn't even do it in her name because he didn't know it. Hadn't known *her.* He couldn't deny that perhaps the Jin Untouchable had more of a right than Samin did.

It was nearing dawn, the sky just taking on that hazy indigo that softened the stars into blurry puffs. It had gone quiet, the sounds of the living underbelly of the city grinding down into weary silence, when the familiar lazy gait sounded, bootheels clocking on cobbles with an unmistakable scuff-drag on each step—like their owner couldn't be bothered with lifting his feet all the way.

Samin's mouth drew up into a fond smirk when Malick came into view, sauntered to the kitchen door, paused and leaned against it.

"Evening."

"Morning."

Malick rolled his eyes.

And that was it, done. Whatever had gone wrong between them had been either forgiven or forgotten. It unknotted the low hum of tension that had been vibrating in Samin's chest all night, exhausting him and making him jittery all at the same time.

Still, all was not right with Malick. Stress wound around him in an almost visible fist, stretching his lazy smile a bit hectic and making his eyes glitter with… something. Something simmering, something dangerous.

Samin only sighed on the inside. "Where's the… Fen?" It was too much to hope that Malick had killed him and was only just getting back from burying the ashes.

The tension lines around Malick's mouth went deeper and his eyes went harder, and somehow, his face did all of that without changing the easy expression.

"Up on the roof."

"The roof?" Samin's eyebrows rose. "So… he's staying?"

"He's staying." Malick's gaze slid sideways, appraising. "Problem?"

None you'll want to hear.

Samin only shook his head. "I just don't think I expected…"

…both of you to still be alive.

Malick snorted, dropped his head back to the door, and closed his eyes. "I don't expect you did."

Samin turned his gaze up to the fading stars. "So… he's got a story, then?"

"He's Jin, Samin. They've all got a story." Malick huffed tiredly and with a touch of anger in it that seemed… off, somehow. "Bloody Untouchable who's somehow managed to hang onto his sanity by means I'm not sure I want to know. Well… most of it, at least. But if you're asking if he's been entertaining himself with his knives for a reason, the answer is yes."

The resulting pause was weighted. Samin turned his gaze once again to Malick and took a good look. Not just tired but exhausted, boots and the cuffs of his trousers layered in dust he hadn't picked up in the Girou, certainly. Just where had Malick been tonight? And why had he come back so out of sorts?

Malick rubbed at his eyes. "Dead father, Disappeared mother, and—" He stopped, shook his head. "And that's enough to be getting on with. He's ours now, that's all that matters at the moment."

Samin turned his gaze to the toes of his boots. "His mother, eh?" He shook his head, rubbing at his chin to keep his hands from fisting. "Well, then."

He had nothing else to say. It was reason enough for him.

Reason enough back when he'd retired from the Doujou to take what had looked like a comfortable position: getting paid a damned lot of money for guarding the lily ass of Mizin. Reason enough when he'd been shown down to the cellars in his second week, when he'd seen the blank... thing that used to be a pretty Jin girl of about fifteen, and listened to Mizin explain in his supercilious tones exactly what he wanted Samin to do.

Samin shuddered, rubbing at his stubbled jaw. He'd been as gentle as he could when he'd put the girl out of her horrible, mindless misery. He hadn't been quite so gentle with Mizin. At any rate, Samin had made sure no one found the bodies—a proper pyre for the girl; mud and pond slime for Mizin—and by that time, it was all anyone could do.

Malick's eyes slid open and turned to Samin, too knowing. But he was Malick, and Malick didn't pick at your sore places, not if he cared about you, and if he didn't... well, he'd make you some.

"You good for maybe another hour or so?"

Now that Malick had gone and mentioned it, Samin's body was feeling heavier, his eyes starting to burn and blink too much, but. "I expect I could last for a bit longer."

"Good." It was heartfelt and grateful. "I gave him 'til breakfast. I expect he'll roost up there until then. He doesn't know I know he's there. When he shows up, feed him, show him the room between yours and mine, and tell him he's not to go about without Shig with him, at least until I figure out how to keep him a secret without keeping him a prisoner."

"Babysitting, eh?" Samin frowned. "You going somewhere?"

"I need to talk to Umeia for a bit." It was angry. Malick shoved away from the door, laying a grip to the handle. "And then I'll be in Madi's room." He said that last with the tiniest bit of venom.

It made Samin's eyebrows rise again. The same lad the Fen-Ghost had chosen when all this started. Some kind of retribution, maybe? Rubbing Fen's face in his complete lack of power over his own situation? Trying to prove something to... someone?

This once, just for now, Samin didn't want to know.

"I'll see to our new accomplice." Samin kept it purposefully amiable, then, more somberly, "You see to yourself, Mal. We need you, y'know."

Malick didn't answer, only nodded, and let himself through the door.

Samin listened to his plodding steps on the stairway to the kitchens until the door drifted shut again. Then he listened to nothing at all, not even whatever bungled through his own head.

Somehow, ignoring it didn't take away that small coal of fear in Samin's guts, that strangely clear knowledge that the determination and anger Samin almost had to admire in Fen were also the things that were going to make Fen dangerous—to all of them, but especially to Malick. Because Malick had a way of making himself everyone's hero, but he didn't actually care about many. It was what kept him safe, kept them all safe. But Malick cared about this Fen, right from the moment the initial attraction had warped into fascination. Samin had never seen that light go bright in Malick's eyes before, but he'd recognized it right away nonetheless, and it was—

None of Samin's business, in the end. Malick had made that more than clear. Samin wouldn't forget it, but he'd be watching.

Renewed noise from the kitchens alerted him to the change of night to day, the daytime crew getting down to the more sedate business of beginning the baking and preparing breakfast for the staff and those who'd stayed the night. The day staff had it so much easier than their counterparts—less rushing about, fewer demands, less work in general.

When the first hint of rose touched the sky and one of the lads came out to burn the rubbish, Samin made his way up the four flights to the roof. He approached with as much caution and stealth as he was able, turning the rusted knob that would let him out onto the stretch of gangly herbs and pungent wild spices laid out in pots and shallow beds, and which Umeia insisted upon calling her "garden."

Fen was on the other side of the flat roof, where it was kept open for training. Though Malick himself hardly ever came up here, except perhaps once or twice a year when he'd drag a sulking Shig up for sword practice.

Sparring. The Fen-Ghost was bloody *sparring*. Slicing at shadows at bloody-ridiculous-in-the-morning on the roof of the place he'd been ordered to make his new home, whether he liked it or not. And Malick had judged Fen mostly sane.

He flowed through the steps like the ghost he was—severe and silent—lean shape a dark silhouette against the silvered ashes-of-roses of false dawn. *Parry, thrust, feint, advance.* Dealing out death to nothing more than night's lingering shadows. The glint of a knife swirled at the end of Fen's hand, and Samin could only heave an internal sigh. Malick hadn't told him the Fen-Ghost was armed again. He made a mental note to clock Malick for that one, and just hoped Malick hadn't given Fen all those damned little throwing knives back.

The lad could move, Samin had to give him that. Fast as the wind, Samin had thought when he'd watched Fen fight Malick. And his forms were almost immaculate—no wasted steps, every move carried out with intense concentration, even when his opponent was imaginary. Samin had lied when he'd told Malick that Fen wasn't that good—Fen was likely the best Samin had ever seen, and Malick had been lucky he'd walked away from it with his insides where they belonged.

Only Fen's profile was visible, and that only dimly, but his jaw was set hard, like it had been when he and Malick had fought. His long braid flew as he whirled beneath an imaginary lunge then feinted and counterattacked with an upward sweep. A soft grunt sounded as he speared in with his left hand then flicked his right, as though throwing...

Samin's mouth fell open, gaze intent as he marked every move, counted them... recognized them. "I'll be damned." Samin squinted. "Is he...?"

The Fen-Ghost was going through the paces of the fight again, repeating each step, defending against Malick's remembered attacks, driving into the echoes of his own. Trying to figure out where he'd gone wrong. How he'd lost.

There was something horribly poignant about it. And Samin didn't want to watch it anymore.

He made a business of rattling the door, cursing at the rusty knob, eyes keeping watch out the corners. For whatever reason, he didn't want Fen to know he'd been watching, and he also didn't want to surprise Fen into throwing that knife. By the time Samin had finished his feigned argument with the door, Fen was crouched at the far end of the roof, down on one knee on the wide, raised ledge, and hunched over, body tense and eyes riveted on Samin over his shoulder. He wasn't even breathing hard; only a light sheen of sweat glistening at his lip and brow testified to what he'd been doing.

He didn't relax when he recognized Samin, but Samin didn't suppose that was so strange, considering how things had turned out in the alley. Still, Samin did his best to smile and look pleasant, even though Umeia had told him once that even his best, most sincere smile looked like a jackal's grin.

"I've come to fetch you for breakfast."

Fen stared—no malice, no interest, nothing remarkable at all, really—crouching there on the edge of the roof like some kind of judgmental gargoyle. He didn't, however, whip out one of his knives and chuck it at Samin's head.

Samin took that as invitation. He let the door close behind him, ambling slowly through a tangle of brown-leafed mint and scraggly talapo, struggling, like they always did, to survive the cooler, drier weather of the autumn, when Umeia tended to get bored with nursing them.

"You were a doujoun."

The way it came at him—all deep and flat, and yet still somehow accusing—stopped Samin some ten paces away. "For twenty years."

Fen tilted his head, brow kinking. "Did you know a man named Syl?"

Samin blinked. He hadn't really been expecting conversation, and certainly not voluntary conversation. Somehow, he hadn't imagined the Ghost capable of small talk.

"No. Why do you ask?"

Fen only stared some more, and though his expression couldn't exactly be called "pleasant," Samin didn't feel the weight of hatred in it this time. Plenty of wariness, loads of discontent, but no malice.

Eventually, Fen just turned away again, gaze fixed out over the city and Subie beyond.

Dismissed. Ignored. It didn't necessarily piss Samin off, but it didn't endear Fen to him, either.

Samin cleared his throat. "Listen, little Ghost, you—"

"*Fen.*"

Not snarled this time, merely pushed out on a wave of impatience.

And. Well. Fair enough.

"Fen. Your pardon." Samin bobbed a small nod at Fen's back. "Fen, you'll do well enough here if you remember a few things. Number one is to have the courtesy to look at someone when he's talking to you." He waited, watched Fen's shoulders slump, listened to the weary sigh, satisfied when Fen finally made a conciliatory half turn on knee and bootheel and craned his neck around to meet Samin's gaze. Samin smiled, quite sincere, pleased with this small effort at progress. "Number two is that we're a family here, or as close to one as I've ever had. We look out for each other. Which means we're all looking out for you now."

He watched Fen's mouth turn down in annoyance, could almost hear the *I didn't ask you to.* Samin nodded, because, well, that was true.

"You didn't ask for this." Samin shrugged. "And I feel for your… situation. Only remember that we didn't ask for it, either, and it's *our* situation now. Like it or not, we're in it together. You back us up and we'll all back you up. And you fuck with my family, I'll happily kill you."

Fen eyed him dubiously, unimpressed, then merely turned again to his vigil over the city, eyes on the bruise of Subie overlooking it.

Samin watched Fen's profile, wondering if he should drag him downstairs and feed him, like Malick had asked, or just leave him to his stubborn solitude up here. Fen wasn't to be locked in his room, more was the pity, nor tied to a chair. Apparently, he was to have the run of his freedom, so long as he toted Shig along wherever he went so she could make sure he remained unremarkable to any who might remark him.

So Samin merely waited him out, though he was getting closer and closer to just growling and stomping away—he'd tried, after all—when Fen's head finally cocked to the side, and he went utterly still, gaze drifting distant. Even his breath paused.

It was almost the same look Shig got when she went "wandering," though this Fen looked... blanker? No—on the contrary: more intent. The "blankness" was merely the face of a man whose mind whirled faster than the outside could keep up with. Whatever was going on in there, Fen was devoting his full attention to it, and simply hadn't any left to spare. Half a moment later, Fen loosed a growl, sharp, and shook it away, hand fisting on his knee.

"You're Samin, right?"

Again, it caught Samin off-guard, and he found himself nodding, compelled to answer a question from a man who apparently had no reciprocal compulsion to answer his own.

"Kel Saminil, to be exact, though I've not gone by that since... for a long while."

Fen stood slowly, hopped off the ledge, and turned to face Samin squarely, then, to Samin's bemusement, he placed a fist over his breast-bone and dipped his head in formal greeting.

"Kel-seyh."

Then just stood there again, staring at Samin, waiting. Nothing further was offered, not even the rest of his name, but somehow, Samin got the feeling that something like this from this man was likely a pretty big concession.

Thoroughly swottled now, Samin placed a fist over his own breast and bowed his head as well. "Fen-seyh." He straightened his neck. "Please call me Samin and forget the rest, and I'll be grateful."

Fen jerked a nod, said, "Fen," like Samin didn't already know it, and again, that was all. He only stood there, staring and waiting, with the suns beginning to crest over his shoulder, splaying one side of his face in rosy gold and arranging the other in murky planes of alternating shadow. Subie was a backlit smudge behind him, silhouetting him, and Samin had the sudden, absurdly poetic notion that it was all too fitting that the Ancestors' Voice seemed overshadowed and overwhelmed by the Ancestors' grave.

Samin shifted uncomfortably. "Right, then, Fen. It's been a long night. Come along and I'll show you around. I imagine a meal and a bed would sit well about now?"

A slow blink was all he got for answer, but it wasn't a snarl or a sneer. All things considered, it was a step forward.

Samin turned and led the way across the roof and to the door to the stairs. Paused halfway there and turned again. Sudden inspiration from a place he couldn't fathom, but no less compelling.

He gestured to where Fen had just sparred with Malick's phantom. "I noticed you could do with some work on your hand-to-hand."

Fen gave him another slow blink.

For some reason, Samin hastened to soothe any offense, even though none was apparent. "I admire your skill with the knives—so does Malick. I've not seen anyone move like that before. You're very good. But you can't allow someone to get in so close to you the way Malick did. I thought you might like to spar."

Fen's brow crinkled. "Spar."

"I could show you some tactics in hand-to-hand, and perhaps you could help me improve my knife work."

"You've skill?"

"Um, well, no, not really. I used to do well with a broadsword, but I've gone out of practice. Not much call for it, anyway—Mal usually takes the close work and Yori and Shig take backup. I'm mainly for scaring the shit out of targets, sometimes beating the shit out of them, if we need them to talk."

Fen tilted his head. "And Shig does…?"

"Shig does things I'd best let Shig explain." Because Samin didn't think he could.

The dark look of appraisal was back, Fen's eyes half glimmering in the budding light at his back, then he nodded, said, "Thank you," and went silent again.

Samin supposed the offer had been accepted. And had no idea how he felt about that.

⚏

Umeia kept her face set in lingering outrage as she watched Malick pace, though in truth, her heart wasn't in it. Too busy hammering away at her ribcage while her mind raced, wondering what had got Malick in a state ill-tempered enough he'd actually stormed into Umeia's private chambers, literally thrown Lex out without ceremony or even a robe, and then took to pacing in obvious agitation. Malick didn't *get* agitated.

"How old is he, Umeia?"

The question came at Umeia from a seething mass of… damn it, she couldn't tell. Anger? Outrage? Fear?

"How old is who, Kamen?" Umeia made sure her voice was steady, the address a reminder and a warning both.

Malick stopped short, turned on her with eyes gone dark and dangerous. "Let's not forget," he said slowly, "exactly who works for whom."

Umeia felt herself pale, but kept her gaze locked to Malick's. He could be cold and terrifying when he wanted to be, but if Umeia showed one hint of fear or retreat, Malick would eat her alive, and their shared history wouldn't stop him.

She lifted her chin. "He looks about twenty or so to me."

A blaze lit behind Malick's eyes. His teeth were bared when he came at Umeia from across the room.

"You know *damn well* what I mean."

It took everything Umeia had not to look away. "Lives uncounted." She set her jaw. "He's the mark of Raven in him, but he's Wolf's creature now."

Most of her—the prideful part—was pleased when Malick jerked back, eyes narrowed and jaw ticcing. The other part—the part that had sense and healthy caution, the part that knew how clever Malick was— wobbled on the verge of real fear. Because Malick was surprised. *Malick* was surprised.

"Where did you go tonight, Kamen?" Umeia put every bit of matronly command she owned into the tone. "What happened?"

She hadn't realized how tight the tension had wound until Malick stopped staring her down. She didn't dare sigh in relief, not yet.

Distant now, Malick moved slowly over to the window. "I went for a walk."

The unease in Malick and the crawling dread in Umeia were doing unwise things to her temper. "*What*," she asked, slowly and through her teeth, "*happened?*"

Malick was silent, staring out into nascent dawn, the thin gold light of Umeia's night lamp scudding over his fine, handsome face. He sighed, long and deep, then fisted his hands, pressed them to the sill, and leaned his forehead to the chill glass.

"Asai knows." It was all but a snarl.

Honestly, though, Umeia was abstractly surprised it hadn't come out an actual roaring growl. Damn it, they'd been so *careful*.

"Knows?"

"Fen went there tonight." Malick's tone was calmer now. "If I'm not very much mistaken, Asai has been harboring him, teaching him. And I can't prove it yet, but I'm certain he's why Fen's mother's been Disappeared. I think she might be the connection between Asai and Yakuli I've been looking for."

Somehow, Umeia managed to make it over to the bed and settle on the rumpled sheets without her knees giving on her. "And Fen didn't kill him?"

"He wanted to. I could see it all over him. But he wasn't sure—I don't think he *wanted* to be sure." Malick paused, tightened his jaw. "I think there's… something between them."

"Then you have to get rid of Fen. Right now." When Malick didn't agree, didn't do anything, Umeia clenched her fists. "Malick, don't… whatever it is you're thinking, *don't*. Asai is pledged to Wolf, but he's still Raven's, and he's always had his own agenda. He doesn't even follow the gods' orders unless there's something in it for him, and you don't believe any more than I do that defecting from Raven will change that. Laws or no laws, he'll kill you if he can. And if he's made this Fen his pawn, then it's better for—"

"Then it's my duty to find out why and try to save Fen from himself."

Umeia had to stop herself from laughing outright. "*Duty*." All the gods save her. "Stop thinking with your prick, for once, Kamen Malick. When's the last time duty meant a damn to you?"

Malick turned slowly, gaze level and hard as diamonds. "I have never *stopped* doing my duty." Low and deadly quiet. "If you've got a problem with how I do it…" He tipped his head toward the door. "You've always the option of severing our tie. I've never kept you oathbound—Kamen Umeia."

A reminder, just as much as hers had been. It put a blush to Umeia's cheek that she resented with appalling embarrassment. Still, she nodded, conceding the point. Because if they were being blunt—

"And how convenient for you, little brother." It might as well have had icicles dripping from it. "A lack of oaths between us allows so many cracks in honor between which dishonesty can slip through unnoticed." Umeia lifted an eyebrow. "Tell me, Malick: does your wish to save your new pet Untouchable have as much to do with his pretty face as it does your hatred of Asai? Do you actually care about the Disappeared, or are you merely building your case against an old enemy? Or is this all vengeance for—"

"If it was vengeance," Malick grated, tight and blistering, "it would be my *right*."

Umeia held his furious gaze for quite a while, made herself see the pain behind it, the grief. Finally, she sighed.

"I have never denied that, little brother. And if we were not what we are, I would help you get it, oathbound or no. As it is, I will help you get what you can—within the limits of our laws. But you've pulled other souls into your orbit now, and you endanger them all. To them, I *am* oathbound, and I won't watch you go against the laws and risk the suns for a Catalyst who likely won't live out the month." And Umeia would be damned if she'd allow her headstrong little brother to lead her ducklings all unknowing into an impulsive pursuit for vengeance that would get them all killed. "Malick." Thick with warning. "You can't touch Asai. And you can't touch Yakuli."

"I *know*, Umeia! Did you think I forgot?"

"No. But I think you might, for a pair of tragic gray eyes and a pretty face." Umeia rose, stepping over to Malick and laying a gentle hand to his arm. "We have traveled long together, you and I, seen many places and many things, and you're right—everywhere you go, you do your duty to the spirit of Wolf's law, if not exactly the letter.

"But I've watched you languish in your relentless pleasure-seeking, watched you care less about yourself and your obligations with every drink and tumble. You've hidden away in cavalier desires for too long, and you've forgotten it was your heart that made you Wolf's creature in the beginning. And yet now that it's been prodded awake, you've gone and pointed it in a direction that risks everything."

"My heart." Malick closed his eyes and took hold of Umeia's hand, squeezed. "Umeia..." Small and hoarse. "It's too close. He's doing the *same damned thing* he did with..." He trailed off, swallowing like he was trying not to choke. "Is it... is Fen...?"

Umeia tried not to make her sigh as sad as she felt. This again. Still.

"He is not." She said it gently. "He couldn't be, Malick, you must know that. I felt it when Skel went to the suns. So did you."

Skel would never be reborn, and certainly not as a Jin Untouchable. Skel was as gone as the tears Umeia had wept for him when his soul cried out as the suns swallowed it. As gone as Malick's sense when he'd all but challenged the gods in the wake of the unfairness of the punishment and then retreated from them, if not entirely spurned their laws.

Umeia blinked back the burning in her eyes. "Please tell me we've not traveled, all these years and all these leagues, only to end up right back where we started and looking for one who cannot be found."

"No. But... Umeia—"

"Perhaps looking for one who might take his place?" Umeia shook her head. "If you mean to mold the boy into what you want him to be, Kamen Malick, it would be cleaner and more merciful to just kill him now. He's enough pulling his spirit apart already. Ask Shig. Add one more voice to the din, and it may scatter him to ash."

"I don't want to..." Malick pulled away. "I don't know how to explain it. There's something... *there*, something... something more than want. I won't kill him. He's important, and now with Asai up to his old tricks, I'm sure of it. And if Fen's mother is where I think she might be..." His jaw tightened. "Fen Jacin-rei, more than anyone I've ever met before, *needs* saving, and isn't *that* my duty? It's nothing to do with Skel."

Umeai huffed. "Lie to yourself, Malick, but don't—"

"Yes, fine, I want Fen, but that's not all of it, and if he doesn't want me, I can live with it. But if he *does* want me, if I can *get* him to want me, you're damn right I'll take him."

And not only take him, Umeia knew, because she heard what Malick didn't say, what he might not even know himself: *I'll take him away from Asai.* Because Malick might have a heart he refused to believe was as soft as it was, but he also had more pride than he'd admit to. Bloody hell, for Fen to come to them straight from Asai, of all people…

Damn it, how had they not seen this? How had *Malick* not seen it? He'd been watching, for pity's sake.

"To your bed or to your heart, Malick?"

The question was crucial, and the answer imperative.

But Malick was Malick, and he only snorted. "I've no heart to speak of anymore."

Umeia shut her eyes. Malick might believe that—indeed, did everything he could to prove it—but he was horribly, terribly wrong.

Oathbound or no, Umeia couldn't leave him to this, not on his own. He likely wouldn't listen to her—his practiced blindness was quite stunning sometimes—but it seemed the habit of looking after Malick was not an easy one to break.

"And how d'you think to save him, then? Through the power of your Almighty Cock? It isn't a magic wand, y'know."

Malick stopped and turned a heavy glare on her. "Crude, sister dear."

But all too true, Umeia didn't retort. Arguing with Malick was like shouting into a vacuum, and she had no breath left.

Umeia merely shook her head and changed the subject. "How d'you know Asai knows?"

Strangely, Malick reddened. "He called me *Temshiel*."

Umeia's shoulders drooped. "So, he knows who you are, then." Damn it, she *liked* it here. And now they were going to have to—

"No." Malick's tone was confident. "I was veiled. He didn't see me. He knows I'm here, but he doesn't know who I am or where. I think that's why he's involved a Catalyst—either trying to set Fen up to expose me or draw me out so I expose myself. Asai has moved from Raven to Wolf, interfered with a Catalyst of Wolf I didn't even know existed—I'll wager no one knew—and now he's all but waving a flag for a *Temshiel* of Wolf to come challenge him for it." He huffed a growl, short and sharp. "I don't know *why*.

"He hid an Untouchable somehow, or at least someone did. How? Why? He must've known he was being watched, but damned if I know how—I've been so bloody *careful*. Maybe too careful. I should have seen this, damn it! How did I miss an Untouchable?—*Wolf's* Untouchable." He paused, thoughtful, before flicking a hard look at Umeia. "Who d'you think the Mage is?"

Umeia's eyebrows rose. She'd done her best over the years to try not to even hazard a guess.

"I don't know. But whoever he is, he's at least a seer." Now that she'd said it, Umeia's gut gave an alarming little roll. "You're not thinking Asai—?"

"*No*." Malick snorted, as though the mere thought was too incredible to even consider. "I'm thinking much bigger than Asai."

…Oh.

Oh.

Umeia sat back down. Her knees were being far too indecisive tonight. "Malick, you don't really think—"

"I think it's very strange that the Mage's 'deal' came right around the time I was getting bored with hunting down the dregs in Kent and thinking about finding a ship to take us across to Tambalon to look into their *banpair* problem. I think it's very strange that he insisted on the heart of Ada, where Wolf's favored Jin have been so long oppressed, and that we just happened to stumble upon Asai's reek when we got here."

And yet refusing had never once occurred to Malick, not even when Umeia had pointed out—rather stridently, if she remembered right—that the gods had made their decision, and defying them would only get Malick damned. Altogether too eager for intrigue and risk, Umeia's little brother. Vengeance, more like. Malick had bided and watched Asai with more patience over the past years than Umeia had ever seen him do with anything else. Ever.

"I also think it's very strange," Malick went on more slowly, "that an Untouchable was apparently seized from Raven, and drawn under Wolf's own purview, and I never even felt a tremor."

Yes. Very strange, indeed. Malick *should* have felt something like that. And the fact that he hadn't suggested something covert and deliberate. There weren't many who could pull something like that over on Malick—not now, not when they were in Wolf's Cycle. In fact, Umeia couldn't think of a single one who had that kind of power but for the gods themselves.

Then again, if Malick had been paying attention to something other than Asai and his own libido, maybe he would have seen this coming.

Umeia frowned, pensive. If it was some kind of setup, it seemed rather unnecessarily elaborate—there were other, more direct ways to piss Malick off enough to draw him out. With his temper, it was all too easy, if one hit on just the right sore spot.

"I want this sent to the Mage." Malick pushed a folded piece of parchment it into Umeia's hand. "First thing in the morning."

"It *is* first thing in the morning," Umeia grumbled, opening the note, and when Malick didn't stop her, she read what it said. She shut her eyes. "Malick—"

"First thing in the morning." He slipped his fingers beneath Umeia's chin and waited until she opened her eyes. He gave her a grin. She could have killed him. "It'll be all right, sister dear. Do as I ask, and it'll be all right." With a light squeeze to Umeia's shoulder, Malick turned and quit the room.

Umeia only sat for a while, staring at the slow flicker of the lamp's flame until her eyes started to water, then determinedly thought about nothing at all. Almost against her will, she unfolded the note, blinked until the bold lettering slid into focus:

Meet. Now.

Well, then. Fine. But it was going to wait until she found where Lex had taken himself. She damn well needed the distraction.

⋔

Malick woke with a light hangover, the suns far too bright through the half-open curtains of… Where the hell was he? He squinted, made note of the dark hair on the pillow next to him, thought back…

Ah. Madi. Because he'd really wanted Fen, and Madi was the closest Malick was going to get right now. And Madi had been eager to make Malick forget. Malick could see why Madi would be the fast favorite of reprehensible lords—so driven to please and not afraid to show his own pleasure, to be commanded and possessed. Madi liked what he did, and he threw his affections freely at any who shared his contentment.

Malick peered blearily at Madi's sleeping face, noted the sharp angles that didn't tilt exactly into the slopes Malick wanted them to. The hair that was neither chestnut nor braided in a long plait but loose and dark as sealskin. The complexion that was pale and unblemished, not olive-toned and scarred in deliberate lines that both fascinated and horrified. Madi mumbled something thick and drowsy into the pillow then burrowed down deeper under the covers, brow scrunching adorably at the thin stream of daylight that blundered across the bridge of his nose.

The smile that tipped at Malick's mouth faded quickly.

Not Fen, and now it seemed there was an obstacle to Fen's affections Malick would never have guessed in a million years. Fucking *Asai*. How could *anyone* be in love with fucking *Asai*? It made Malick's heart pound with… anger, mostly, and yes, there was jealousy—that Asai had control over something Malick wanted, that Asai had ever *touched*—

Malick pushed that away, because it was making him growl, and he didn't want to wake Madi.

It wasn't the braid, he decided. It was that unruly fringe that hung in contrast—a bit of untamed rebellion to counteract the too-tame adherence to law and tradition. The passion that escaped, even when bound down all neat and tidy. The wildness that defied the control. Malick had seen some of it last night—in the baths, in the alley, with *bloody* Asai… on the road, echoing in that useless raging at the moons.

He wanted to see it all, unbound and laid out completely bare, for him alone.

And it bloody *infuriated* him that Asai had apparently got there first. And might still be there. Malick was almost sure the passion Fen had directed at Asai last night had been hatred, or at least bordered on it, but passion cut both ways, and love was the other side of that blade.

Fuck.

Umeia was wrong, about this one thing, at least: Malick might well be a little mournful and sullen that Madi was not Fen, but he wasn't trying to make Fen into Skel. Malick wasn't that stupid. He might have had a moment or two of blind hope, but he'd known the second the halting question stumbled from his mouth that it was impossible. Had known for a lot longer that his grief was more guilt and regret than any idealistic lost love. Skel had been Malick's friend and his occasional bedmate, but he hadn't been any more to Malick than Malick had been to him. Malick would bring Skel back in a second, if he could, but not for the reasons Umeia had always assumed.

Malick hadn't been pining all these years—he'd been *seething.*

And yes, all right, perhaps Malick did tend to try banking the coals of it by chasing blank-minded amnesty in every vice he could fathom. Xari called him "Eremite," and a reprobate, and she wasn't entirely wrong.

Still, to Malick's mind, he had a right. And so long as he abided by his nature, carried out his duties and kept the Balance, he could do as he damn well pleased.

And it pleased him to pursue Fen, with his tragic eyes and angry snarls. His Disappeared mother and his earthbound brother. Fen had told Malick about the mother, but only because he'd had to. He'd withheld the brother. Half trust, and Malick didn't suppose he could blame Fen, but Malick wanted all of it. And oddly, he thought he would have been disappointed if it had just been handed to him. He sort of looked forward to winning it.

Except… this thing with Asai…

If there was any similarity at all between Fen and Skel, it was the influence of Asai, and Malick *would not* watch it all happen again. The gods had made it impossible for Malick to claim vengeance for Skel; perhaps Fen could do it for him. *If* Fen wasn't already fully Asai's creature. Malick supposed that would be the first piece of information he'd have to force out of Fen before the shit got too deep.

Fully awake now, Malick carefully pushed back the covers and slipped from Madi's bed, laying an overabundance of koin on the clothespress in gratitude as he dressed. Umeia didn't allow Malick to indulge in the help for free—had told him once with a typical roll of her eyes that she'd have to close down, because they'd all be too exhausted to service paying customers—but he didn't begrudge it with Madi. Madi had given Malick everything he'd asked for. It wasn't Madi's fault it hadn't been enough.

Boots clutched in his hand and shirt unlaced, Malick stole from the room, and made his way down the hallway toward the attic stairs. Low noise clattered up from the kitchens, and several maids were busy rousting Umeia's "lads and ladies" so they could freshen their rooms for this evening, giving the occasional leftover customer the boot in the process. Malick greeted and grinned his way by. He didn't stop to chat and flirt as he'd normally do, just kept dodging any attempted conversation or proposition with a quick gait and cheerful shrugs and promises of later.

A bath first, when he didn't have to worry about customers intruding, then he'd see if an answer had come to his query—well, all right, demand—to the Mage. And then, perhaps, he'd seek out Fen, draw him out under the pretense of seeing that he was settling in, find out just what exactly he had to do with Asai and whether or not they'd been—

No. That answer would have to come with trust. That answer Malick would have to earn. It was the existence of the siblings he'd drag out of Fen, cooperation or not.

With a bit more energy than he'd had a moment ago, Malick reached the top of the steps and rounded the bend in the hall just in time to see Fen and Samin emerging from the stairway to the roof down at the other end. Malick's eyebrows jumped up into his hairline, surprised both at the fact that Fen was still here and apparently hadn't attempted to slink off, as well as the fact that he was just coming down from where Malick had left him… hours ago. Surely, Samin couldn't just now be dragging Fen down from his brooding?

Startled, Malick caught Fen's eye, bemused as Fen's hard gaze traveled Malick up and down, taking in his trousers slung too low, his wide-open shirt, his boots in his hand. Saw the notice, the appraisal, the… What did that slight flicker of Fen's glance *mean*, damn it? Before Malick could be sure he'd interpreted it correctly, it was gone, and Fen was looking once again at Samin.

It took Malick a moment, but he managed to note Samin's ruddy color and the sweat on his brow, a light bruise blooming along Fen's cheekbone and temple… Samin's hand laid to Fen's shoulder in a way that seemed more friendly than commanding, and Fen's failure to twitch it off. Fen's face didn't give anything away, but Malick hadn't really expected it to. It didn't stop Malick from boggling. And then Samin completely scragged Malick's tottering mind when he gave Malick what passed for a pleasant grin on his stone-cut face, and tipped a nod in salute.

"G'mornin', boss." Samin's tone held a note of cheerful sarcasm. "Up with the suns, I see."

He gave Fen a little nudge forward, ignoring the tiny growl, and led him over to Malick. Now that they were closer, Malick noted they were both barefoot, and neither of them were wearing the clothes they'd had on the night before. Both sported splotches of dust on knees and elbows; Fen had a smear of it all along the entire left side of his body.

A thwarted escape attempt? A challenge and resulting brawl?

"You've missed lunch. And you've missed the entertainment." Samin slapped Fen on the back almost hard enough to send him careening into

Malick's chest. Fen growled; Samin ignored it. "Had ourselves a bit of a session up on the roof. Yori and Shig are still up there wrestling." Samin gestured at the bruise on Fen's face, sheepish. "I'm afraid I didn't pull a punch in time, but he got me back when we worked with the knives." Samin lifted his tunic, showing off the long stripe of crusted blood that ran just under his ribs, grinning like a proud father. "He's bloody *fast*, Mal. He'll do well on the job, mark that. And if he'd only learn to use actual words when he teaches, he might improve my knife work."

Fen gusted a small snort, rolled his eyes, and… smiled. Just a tiny thing, a flash of a tic at the corner of his mouth, and you really had to look for it, but it was there. A real smile. From *Fen*.

Had Malick woken in an alternate universe? Was he stoned and didn't know it? Last night, Samin had done nothing but growl antipathy to and about "the Fen-Ghost," and Fen had been… well, Fen. Now Samin was clapping Fen on the back, and Fen was bloody *smiling*. Smiling at bloody *Samin*.

It wasn't fair.

"Sparring." Malick rubbed at his eyes. "Already?"

He'd meant "already" in the sense that it seemed a little early for Samin to be trusting Fen coming at him with knives, but Samin answered to the more obvious implication:

"It's early afternoon, Mal."

And far too soon after Malick had woken from a night of pretending he was fucking Fen, and with a hangover to boot, to be dealing with the ludicrously improbable.

Malick pinched at the bridge of his nose. "Whatever." He dropped his hand and gave Samin a look. "Give us a minute, would you?"

Samin's eyebrows rose, annoying Malick beyond sense when he peered at Fen, as though asking if it was all right with him, before shrugging and sauntering away.

"I'll be ready for another go after supper, if you're game." Samin seemed to take the slight tightening of Fen's mouth for an affirmative, because he grinned again—all chipper amusement—and let himself into his rooms.

Malick stared after him for a long, fuzzy moment before he shook himself, nodded sharply at the door to what was now Fen's room, and lifted an eyebrow. Fen's mouth tightened again—somehow, it didn't seem as friendly as it had when it had been aimed at Samin—but he merely breathed a little sigh, turned, and allowed Malick to follow him into his new quarters. Malick dropped his boots out in the hallway then shut the door behind him, ignoring how Fen's eyes narrowed at the liberty, and had himself a look around.

With the exception of the empty beaten pack now hanging off the footpost of the bed's iron frame, it looked exactly the same. The bed didn't even look slept in. Malick didn't know why it gave him a turn of irritation; it wasn't like Fen could've really made himself at home already, right? Except… Samin.

Malick shook it off. "Shig gave you back your knives, I see." He was going to have to have a little chat with Shig about taking that kind of decision for herself—Malick certainly hadn't given her the say-so to rearm the lethal little Ghost.

Naturally, Fen didn't answer, just stared. Well, glared, actually, but it was almost the same thing with Fen, Malick decided.

It made Malick's jaw want to clench, but he didn't let it. "Are you finding your way around all right?"

Fen leaned his back to the far wall beside the window, looked Malick over thoroughly, then merely nodded.

And why did Malick sense scorn beneath the blank expression? "You slept well? Eaten?"

Again, a nod.

And it was pissing Malick off. Samin had got a bloody *smile* from the little prick, and all Malick seemed to rate was silent derision and an invisible sneer.

"And you've been told you're not to go about without Shig, to—"

"I've been briefed. What d'you want?"

…All right. Fine. If that was the way Fen chose to play it, they'd just see who came out the winner. There was more than one way, after all, to get something coveted. Malick was very good at getting. And he was almost certain he knew what had been in Fen's eyes in that momentary glimpse Malick had seen out in the hallway.

Malick smiled, all sultry sin. "You keep asking me that." He reached up, slow and as graceful as he got, and ran a hand through his hair; Fen's eyes followed the movement, so Malick slid his hand slowly down to tease at the flaps of his shirt. "I'd think it would be obvious."

No response but a narrow stare and three slow blinks.

"We didn't get to, um… talk much last night." Malick took a step away from the door and toward Fen, keeping his voice low and silky. "I want to know what you've not told me. I want to know where you went last night and what you did."

Blink. Blink. Blink.

Damn the little prick.

Funny thing, though—Malick already knew what threw Fen. And disconcertion seemed to be the only thing so far that loosened Fen's tongue. So Malick moved in close, hovered there. Loose-limbed. Relaxed. Demonstrably interested and just this side of predatory.

Predictably, tension wound through Fen's stance, curled tight. His breathing picked up pace, but it wasn't all anger and outrage this time.

Malick knew what he looked like, sauntering in here looking rumpled and just-fucked. And he knew a reaction when he saw one. He'd seen the beginnings of it out in the hall, and here it was again. It seemed the little Ghost wasn't made entirely of stone after all.

Malick dropped his eyelids to half-mast. "I want to know why you're here, and why you stayed."

Fen's glare was sharp as his blades. "You said you'd help—"

"Oh, I will." Malick ran his finger along the shiny plait hanging heavy over Fen's shoulder. "But tell me, Fen…"

He drifted a hair closer, letting the tip of his index finger sweep up and over the bruise on Fen's cheek, pleased by the little gasp it provoked.

It's gone quiet.

Ruthless, Malick withdrew the touch, satisfied when Fen shut his eyes as though in pain.

"What else d'you think I might find, when I find your mother, hmm?" Malick was near enough now to align his front to Fen's side, but he purposefully didn't touch. He dipped his mouth to Fen's ear. "Who else are you hiding, little Ghost?"

Malick whipped his hand down, catching Fen's wrist before Fen could do anything more threatening with the knife abruptly in his hand. Malick didn't hold on, though, very much aware of what his touch did to this Untouchable. In fact, he was counting on it when he let go but didn't back off. Malick had something Fen wanted now, and if it helped Malick get his answers, he was prepared to use it with all coldblooded intent.

"Step away." To Fen's credit, it came out steady.

Malick slid an obvious glance all up and down Fen's body. "I don't think you really want me to."

"Since when has it mattered to you what I want?"

"Since I decided that what you want is me."

"*You.*" Fen curled his lip. "You reek of stale liquor and day-old sex."

"Would it be better if the sex was fresher?"

"It would be better if it was *out of my face.* I don't want *you,* and I don't want you *touching* me. Step. *Away.*"

Malick let a slow grin bloom as he breathed in—sweat and leather and almonds—and ran a fingertip over the knuckles of Fen's hand still clutched tight around the hilt of the knife. He only allowed the touch to stay for a second before he drew it back, then, slowly, watching closely, leaned in. And in. And *in.*

And Fen… stilled. Even his breath stopped.

For a moment, Malick was torn—if he closed the distance, Fen would let him kiss him, Malick could feel it. Not just the tiny seed of want Malick could detect in Fen's reluctant reactions, but the need for the silence Malick's touch could give him.

Fen was on the edge. Fen had got beaten up in an alley last night and was now following one of the men who'd done it around like a puppy.

Fen had walked away from what was left of his family without even saying goodbye, then wept alone in the road in the middle of the night. Fen had been unequivocally rejected only a little while later, and still couldn't bring himself to murder for it. Fen was in love with a man who didn't love him back, and if Asai had given him the smallest encouragement last night, Fen would have believed him and stayed, Malick had seen it. Fen was desperate for contact, but wouldn't allow himself to have it. Fen was desperate for love, but didn't think he deserved it, rejection more easily accepted than offering.

Fen was willing to sell his soul for a moment of quiet, and he knew Malick could give it to him.

"I don't want you." There was no strength in Fen's tone, no attempt to draw away, but no attempt to move closer, either.

So tempting to seal the deal. But not why Malick was here.

"Liar."

Malick was watching, so he really should've seen it coming, but he didn't. Fen's fist caught him just beneath the chin, sent his teeth jarring together and his ears ringing. The angle had been off, and it didn't have the right force behind it, what with how close Malick was pressed in, but damn—it *hurt*. Malick didn't back off, though; he merely flexed his jaw, dabbed at his lip and checked his fingers for blood, and when there wasn't any, he grinned. He turned and put out his arms, bracing himself so he had Fen caged between them, back to the wall. The knife had come to rest at Fen's hip, but Fen's grip on it was flexed and ready.

"You like it when I touch you." Malick slid the tip of his nose along Fen's temple. "But you've grown so used to thinking around the noise, you don't know how anymore when the noise isn't there."

"Shut up."

"Mm, I don't think so." Malick kept a sideways eye on the knife, drew back from direct contact again, and hovered at its edges. It was cruel, and he didn't care. "If I shut up every time you wanted me to, I wouldn't even know your name."

"How are you doing this?"

Malick set a hand to Fen's arm, the vibrations sliding up beneath Malick's skin and down his backbone. Fen's unwilling gasp at the contact went right to Malick's groin.

"Tell me who sent you."

Surprise flitted over Fen's face, consternation then indignation. "No one *sent* me. *You're* the one—"

"No one?" Malick's grip tightened. "No one tied you up in a pretty bow, sent you along to catch my eye?"

Fen's arm jerked in Malick's grip, but it seemed halfhearted, like Fen didn't really want Malick to let go, but couldn't stop himself from trying.

"I wouldn't think it terribly difficult to catch *your* eye. I wasn't *sent*, I was *caught*." Fen snatched hold of Malick's tunic, dragged him in until they were pressed together, chest to hip. "Is *this* what you want? If I give it to you, will you stop... stop *mocking* me?"

A tiny part of Malick's brain was elated by the offer. The larger part plunged directly into discomfiture.

Someone who would interpret Malick's overtures as mockery was not someone playing coy and unattainable. This was someone who thought he wasn't worth the attention and couldn't fathom any other reason it would be paid to him. Which meant all of this was merely torture for torture's sake, taunting a man whose mind was filled with noise, dangling silence in front of his nose, then nicking it away.

Asai hadn't sent Fen, nor had anyone else but perhaps the gods. And if the Mage had seen Fen coming and seized the opportunity, that was all it had been, at least from Fen's side.

Malick slumped, his breath going out of him in a hollow hiss, shame teasing at its edges.

Bad dog. Sit. No Fen for you.

"I'm sorry." Malick kept his hand where it was, but relaxed his grip, giving Fen the option of keeping the contact or drawing away. "Fen." On impulse, Malick reached up, swept the messy fringe from Fen's eyes. Fen flinched, as if the soft touch had been a slap, as if tenderness burned. Or maybe just tenderness offered by Malick. "I'm sorry. I had to be sure."

"And are you?"

"No. Not of anything right now. But I don't think... what I was thinking. I'm sorry, Fen. I've got a lot at stake. I had to be sure."

Fen stared, measuring, but he still didn't shake loose from Malick's light grip. "And you'll still... help?"

He said the word like he didn't really know how to use it. Didn't expect an answer when he did.

"I'll help." Malick kept his gaze level with Fen's. "We'll find her." He'd worry about consequences when he got there. "Fen... you realize... I mean, she won't be—"

"I know what she'll be." The softness of Fen's voice masked... probably hundreds of things Malick would never see.

Malick merely nodded. "I take it we're on a hunt for a proper pyre, then." When Fen said nothing, Malick tilted his head. "Is that what the fire at Hende's was about?"

Fen looked away. Which, oddly, rather answered the question. Fen had taken care of Hende, then taken care of his victims, lit them a pyre and sent them to the gods. For all Malick knew, Fen even painted the prayers on their brows and spoke the rites, burned incense for them; somehow, it was all too believable.

"All right." Malick set his hand to Fen's shoulder. "We can start now, if you like."

And if the search ended where Malick thought it might? Well. The laws might prevent Malick from killing Yakuli himself, but he didn't think it would take much to get Fen to do it. And if Malick was very lucky, Asai would make himself a very convenient blockade to that path, and Fen could take care of him too. All Malick had to do was make sure Asai was the one pulling the strings of the Puppet Master. And that Fen knew it.

Fen kept staring at the floor, but he nodded. Clearly reluctant, he tucked the knife in his belt and stepped away from the wall, angling out from Malick's touch. Malick let his hand linger, fingers gliding along the braid as Fen moved away. Back straight, shoulders squared, Fen made his way to the door then paused.

"Who did you think sent me?"

Malick rubbed his fingers together, already missing the silky feel of the braid between them. "No one."

Fen was silent, staring at his hand on the door, before he ventured haltingly, "How can you… what are—?"

"I can't tell you that yet. I'm sorry."

Fen couldn't have liked the answer, but he showed no reaction, just jerked a sharp nod then threw open the door and turned back to face Malick. He crossed his arms over his chest and glared.

"Take a bath first. You reek."

ᛗ

Tides-month, Year 1315, Cycle of the Wolf

The thing about Dani, Jacin thought as he stood in the shadows and watched Dani whirl, watched his knives flash in a glittering corona around his sleek-sinewed body—the thing about Dani was that Jacin had wanted him right away. From the first moment Jacin had seen him, he'd wanted Dani, even though Jacin knew it was… perhaps not a betrayal to Asai, but…

Disrespectful, maybe?

Except Jacin couldn't have Asai, had to be satisfied with the distant love of a tutor, a foster father; Asai had made that clear in his careful disregard of hints and clumsy overtures. Not outright rejection, Asai was too kind for that, but it was all the same in the end.

Jacin couldn't have Asai. Asai would never have Jacin. The end.

Resentment was wrong. Jacin had no right to it. He had plenty for which to be eternally grateful. But he'd be sixteen on the next Turn, and he was still a virgin. He wasn't dead and he wasn't insane—well, mostly— and if he perfected his new forms by the end of the month, he'd been promised he would see Joori for his birthday.

And Asai had given him Dani.

Where Asai was mentor and tutor, Dani was trainer, had come just when Jacin had begun to despair that he'd ever manage to get his mind under control without flaying every inch of skin off his bones. When he'd begun to wonder if Asai wouldn't give up on him after all, and when Vonshi had finally begun to balk at the only method of maintaining relative quiet. A deferential old man, acquiescent to all of Beishin's commands, except when it came to strapping a boy to stop him babbling.

"It is wrong, seyh. The boy is Untouchable. You do enough damage just by taking him in, but I will not beat him at your pleasure, though he might beg for it. He must listen, it is what he *is*, and he cannot hear if you take it away."

Jacin had wept, apologized, pleaded, because if Vonshi wouldn't help him, Asai might decide the Ghost was too much trouble after all, and then...

Jacin didn't even want to think about "and then."

"You said you would begin training." Vonshi quieted the blather with a bony hand to Jacin's shoulder. "You cannot wait for perfection in concentration to begin it. Surely the concentration necessary to it, and the"—Vonshi had paused, lips pursed—"the incidental injuries?"

It had sparked something in Asai, and then there'd been Dani.

Handsome, ruthless, grinning Dani, who'd relentlessly beaten the shit out of Jacin for months before the sense of the instructions with each blow had begun to sink in. Almost immediately, Dani's voice had become louder than the noise in Jacin's head, almost as loud to him as Asai's could be sometimes.

Block your right side when you attack from the left, don't let me get under— good! Exactly like that. Now go back to the beginning, perfect the form. Your wrist is all wrong, Jacin-rei, control, control, control.

Control and perfection, because those were the things Asai expected Jacin to learn, and the things he expected Dani to teach. They both wanted to please Asai, and Jacin wanted to please Dani.

Dani, who lived in the rooms just three doors down the massive hallway from Jacin's; who let Jacin come to chatter at him sometimes; who was patient when Jacin stopped to listen and never looked at him askance for it and never tattled on him to Beishin; who called him Jacin-rei but never Ghost. Dani, who'd managed to corner Jacin only weeks ago as he taught him a new drill, got Jacin's back to the wall, and when their bodies had pressed together, all sweat and slick and heat coming at Jacin from every direction...

Jacin's hormones had shoved his body up more firmly, and Dani's eyes had gone wide. Now Dani looked at Jacin with more than a trainer's eyes, pretty blue gaze almost smoldering at him. Jacin met it all with tension-exhilaration-anticipation-fear.

He didn't love Dani, he loved Asai, but he wanted, *needed*, and Asai didn't, and Jacin had no right to want in the first place, he was what he was—*no one's son, no one's brother, no one's father, no one's lover*—but Dani… Dani might let Jacin *have*.

Heart fluttering and alternately climbing up into his throat then plummeting to his stomach, Jacin stepped out of the shadows against the wall of the oversized hall Asai had given them for an exercise room. He had his long knives gripped in each fist. He was shirtless, because he'd filled out just lately, widened, and he'd seen Dani looking.

Determined, Jacin stood in the slope of the last of the evening sun glinting mote-thin gold through the high windows. Waited.

He knew Dani saw him. Dani saw everything, he never missed anything, except for the one time they'd sparred while Jacin wore the shadow charm, and Jacin had managed to blood him more than usual. Dani had still beaten him in the end.

Jacin could feel Dani watching him now, even though Dani's eyes were half-lidded, staring inward as he swept through his forms. Knives atwirl, muscles rippling sleek beneath the sweat-shiny skin of his bared torso, toffee-colored hair sticking to brow and cheeks.

Dani didn't shift his gaze, didn't falter in his rhythm, but he smiled. And Jacin *needed*.

He drove in, lunging into an attack from the right that was smoothly countered with a block and quick parry. Jacin managed to gain temporary advantage only because he was willing to allow Dani's knife to graze his chest as he pushed in and forced Dani to back up a pace. Dani counterattacked with an upward thrust at Jacin's throat and a block down low, forcing Jacin to give back the ground he'd gained only a second ago.

Dani grinned. "Your advantage is that you don't fear pain." He flicked his gaze down to the shallow slice that ran along Jacin's pectoral from collarbone to sternum. "Mine is that you still fear death." He lunged in again with another lethal sweep at Jacin's throat from which Jacin only just barely managed to jerk away and still maintain equilibrium while keeping his guard up to block and not lose ground.

Concentration. Winnowing out everything but the flash of knives and the flex of muscle over bone. Focusing one part of his mind on Dani's motions and his own in answer, and forcing the rest of it into a low hum beneath it all. Marking how Dani's skin took on a cast of burnt-gold umber as the light faded, how his shape should have been getting dimmer in the quick-falling gloaming, and yet it only set the lines and angles of him more stark against the gloom.

It seemed like hours. Gliding through each other's moves, steel clashing and scraping between them, Jacin meeting Dani's constant grin with a hard stare. Jacin's voices had gone lower, if not entirely quiet, but there was enough pain in maintaining the perfection of skill, twisting himself into the proper shapes, to keep them to a minimal shriek. Time lost, and lust a hot, heavy thing in his gut. Muscles screaming and drowning out everything but his need and that alluring blue gaze locked to his. Knives scraping, bodies pressing, gyrating in brief concert for stunted, sensual moments, then flying apart again.

Perfection of form. Perfection of control. Dani had it and Jacin wanted it. It was a clean ache in his chest, a not-so-clean ache in his groin, hotter and more intense.

Because Jacin *needed*.

He gave ground with an unconvincing performance of chagrin as he allowed himself to be backed to the wall, allowed Dani's right hand to disarm his left, allowed his left to pin Jacin's right... Allowed his head to lift, baring his throat—submission—as Dani leaned in, narrowed his blue gaze on Jacin's, that grin still there, but a little more feral now.

"I've caught myself a Ghost."

Though the heat of it slithered right through Jacin's bones, he still couldn't help the flinch at the name.

Dani didn't seem to notice, only tightened his grip on Jacin's wrist, slid his mouth lightly along Jacin's throat. "Whatever shall I do with him?"

Jacin butted his brow into Dani's until Dani drew back and looked Jacin in the eye.

"Don't."

Dani's grin broadened. "Don't what?"

Jacin meant to say *Don't call me that*, but Dani slipped his free hand down Jacin's chest, smearing a trail of blood down his torso, then flattened his palm over the front of Jacin's loose exercise trousers.

"Don't do this?" Dani gripped Jacin's erection through the fabric, set a light nibble to the lobe of Jacin's ear.

Jacin's knees almost buckled. *Oh, yes, do that, do that, please.* Opened his mouth to say as much, the vague niggle of *Ghost* still teasing at the back of his mind, flaring a touch of resentment, but oh, the *hand*.

"I don't... oh, fuck." Jacin shook his head, leaned in and nipped at Dani's bottom lip. "Don't... want you... uhn..."

He couldn't get his mouth to work properly. All he seemed able to do with it was suck on Dani's lip, his throat, and breathe little curses and moans into Dani's skin.

Dani rubbed his thumb all up and down the length of Jacin's erection, traced his shape with deliberate care, grinned at Jacin's glazed eyes.

"Liar."

Divine touch, searing contact. Wide swaths of pleasure striped Jacin's skin from his thighs and on up his backbone.

Jacin whined, let his head drop back, opened his mouth when Dani's descended on it. Dani's hand felt nothing like his own, doing things to

Jacin's body that wound into his head and chest and made him feel like nothing so much as a quivering mess of loose nerves. Aching, Jacin let his hand drift up, latched onto slick pectoral then down the sensual ridges of Dani's chiseled torso, hesitating on that last dip before plunging down into Dani's trousers. Rigid and hot and thick, and oh, Jacin could *smell* it, breathing it in, flaring his nostrils and pushing in tight, hips flexing now with not even a pretense at control as sweat and spit and arousal whirled together in a spicy cocktail that turned him light-headed. Sensation tore an open gap of bliss right down the middle of him as Dani's hand dipped down in return.

Existence was narrowed down to heat and motion—no voices, no thoughts, no sense at all, only shifting hips and building tension fisting Jacin's spine, a widening swath of ecstasy that unfurled in his chest and shattered all through him. Dani pressed in tight, crushing Jacin's hand between his erection and Jacin's hip, shifting them clumsily so Jacin could reciprocate. Hot breath gusted over Jacin's shoulder, and salt-sweet skin rippled against his lips; Jacin wanted to taste it, so he licked a slant from Dani's throat to his jawbone, delighted by the groan it pulled from Dani's chest.

"*Fuck*." Dani shoved against Jacin harder, as though trying to turn him into a vaguely Jacin-shaped smear on the wall, then tightened his grip, moved his hand faster. Sank his teeth into Jacin's shoulder and bit down hard, heightening pleasure with a sharp contrast of pain.

And holy fucking *shit*.

Hot, buzzing white flashed all through Jacin, blanked his mind, tripped him into a pleasure so intense he lost everything else. Relentless, it dragged his orgasm from him in wavering cries, liquefied his bones, introduced new colors to him in blinding surges of bright-white sensation, complete and devastating transcendence. He couldn't breathe. He couldn't see. He was going to die, and he just didn't care.

Holy. Fucking. *Shit*.

The pleasure he'd managed to dredge from his own hand had never been anything like this.

Amazing.

Brilliant.

Silence. Not real silence, it was all still back there, waiting, but *fuck*, it was close.

Almost—*almost*—perfection.

Dani's shaky little "Oh" came from worlds away, muffled into Jacin's shoulder.

They'd slithered to the floor in a sweaty heap while Jacin had been caught in rapture. Limbs tangled in loose knots, bare skin sticking together, trousers pushed down in messy bunches around their hips. It was… actually a bit absurd.

Jacin had to snort.

"What?" Dani feigned offense as he twitched back enough he could slant that sly grin at Jacin. "You didn't like it?"

Delightfully dizzy, Jacin gave Dani a light bop on the forehead. "And what will you do if I didn't?"

He was hoping Dani would say, *Why, do it again until I get it right, of course.*

Instead, Dani flashed his teeth. "Whatever I please." He leaned in and nuzzled Jacin's shoulder, tugging at the braid. "You're *my* Ghost, I caught you, I can do what I like with you."

It was meant lightly, even affectionately, Jacin knew that, but still. It was somehow unbearable, coming from Dani. The buzz in Jacin's head reawakened, or perhaps he was just noticing it again—it didn't matter.

He shouldered Dani off him, shoved him away. "Don't call me that."

Dani reared back, blinking, grin falling, but still there. "All right. I meant no—"

"Jacin-rei."

It was soft—not angry, not even upset—just quiet and firm.

Still, it made all the blood in Jacin's body skitter down to his gut, made heat flare at his cheeks and the voices ramp up in incoherent mocking. Slowly, Jacin lifted his head and peered over Dani's shoulder.

Asai stood inside the double doors, a harsh flare of light at his fingertips momentarily blinding the eye. Jacin only sat there, stunned, blinking as Asai lit the sconce beside the door, then Jacin was peering into dark eyes that all but gored him, drilling into him with… nothing. No rebuke, which would have at least given Jacin something to latch onto, and no anger or jealousy, which would have given him a seed of hope he thought perhaps he'd kill for.

I wanted him because I couldn't have you!

Jacin wanted to hurl the words like throwing knives. Except Asai wouldn't care. And even if Asai did care, he still wouldn't… wouldn't *do.*

"Beishin?" Jacin's throat was so dry it barely made a sound.

Dani stood up, adjusting his trousers as he did it, leaving Jacin exposed in a disheveled heap on the floor. "Seyh." Dani bobbed his head in an apologetic bow.

Asai didn't even look at him. "Out."

With a single diffident glance down at Jacin, Dani obeyed.

Jacin watched him go, kept his eyes riveted to the broad back until Dani was out the door and Jacin had nowhere else to look but Asai.

Asai's blank-steady gaze was still pinning Jacin in place. "Cover yourself."

Cheeks flaming, Jacin did, then stood, feet planted apart, hands at the small of his back, head bowed. Waiting.

The silence lurched like a great lumbering beast, rolling Jacin under, crushing him slowly, grinding him down as he stood there and waited for Asai to punish him. Beat him, repudiate him, sneer at him, anything.

The voices had renewed their striving, impatient chatter, but for once, the outward quiet pounded at Jacin with more force. A small eternity ago, he'd felt like flying, felt good, felt... almost normal. Body pressed in close to another's, hips moving in the motion for which they'd been meant, mindless pleasure soaking through every bit of him, right down to his fingertips.

Now, he was the Ghost again. He was Untouchable. And he'd let himself be touched. By someone other than Asai. And he'd liked it.

Jacin couldn't stand it anymore. Asai's silence was killing him, letting the voices take him over, whispering to him of his failure. He hadn't been listening, damn it, he'd let everything else drown them out, and what if they'd said something important and he'd missed it?

Everything in him writhing, unfocused begging, Jacin tentatively lifted his chin, cast a shrinking glance at the door...

Empty.

He frowned, shut his eyes tight, shook his head, and opened them again.

Gone.

No rebuke. No lecture. No reminders of his lack of perfection, his abysmal control.

Nothing. As though he wasn't even worth the breath it would waste to chide him. As though Jacin didn't matter at all.

Numb, Jacin stared at the door until it blurred out of focus. Shook his head slowly in denial of... What? He couldn't remember, couldn't *think—*

seek the Null only say it once light the lamps of the sky and burn the heavens whet your blades with the rites of vengeance will not thwart Wolf

—and shit, he was saying it out loud, gabbling their nonsense because he hadn't had a hold on it, he'd forgotten. How could he forget?

He'd gone down to his knees, the same spot where Dani had made him feel like he was a person, where he'd forgotten to wish Dani were Asai. Jacin could only crouch there, down on the padded floor, hands clutching his head, staring blindly at a small indent in the padding where Dani's knee had pressed a divot, and whimpering—bloody *whimpering,* damn it—between snatches of insane blather. It came right out of the calm that was there just a minute ago, filling his head, spilling out his mouth, stoppering his ears, except he couldn't stopper his mind, and it bloody *hurt* in ways that had nothing to do with pain. Everywhere and everything. Words, words, words, always, words in all the right shapes, but none of them locking together, and yet he couldn't stop *listening* as they bled all together and poured out his mouth.

It hadn't hit him this hard since the first time. He couldn't move.

Hand shaking, Jacin forced his arm to reach, stretch out until his fingertips blundered onto the knife he'd dropped somewhere between Dani cornering him and Dani kissing him, closed his fist around it. The heart, he kept thinking, better than the throat, faster, no chance of missing—

survive endure no rest not yet Wolf comes blaze the path back to Zero and start again not yours to spill

—except his hand wouldn't do it, obeying *their* voices instead of his own.

He snarled—how dare they, how *dare* they—and swiped the blade through the air in a savage arc, wild and furious, slashing at nothing, slashing at everything, slashing at them, because they didn't have the decency to die and stay dead, didn't have the mercy to leave him the fuck *alone*, didn't have the sanity or wisdom to make the least bit of fucking *sense*.

And now they didn't have the courtesy to let him die.

What could they possibly want him for? What could *anyone* want him for? They never *said* anything, and how could Asai just walk away, just *walk away*—

Searing heat slashed through the winding madness, a hot band of pure, perfect pain radiating from Jacin's upper arm. It settled atop the chaos, gave him a place to focus. He blinked his blurry gaze, watched the blood ooze from the long, perfect stripe in sluggish rivulets.

"Not mine to spill." He swiped at his face with the crook of his elbow. "Fuck you," he muttered, threw the knife, and then screamed it—"*Fuck you!*"—before his eyes rolled back and he let it all slip away.

ⵝ

"He is gone, Jacin-rei." Vonshi handed over a pot of salve and watched to make sure Jacin got all of the swollen gash with it before winding a bandage around it.

He'd found Jacin passed out in the exercise room this morning, roused him and chivvied him upstairs and asked no uncomfortable questions, helped to brush out Jacin's hair until Jacin grabbed at a knife. Vonshi stopped him from cutting off all his hair with hands stronger than they should have been and gentle care inside stern rebuke.

"You would doom your soul for something so ordinary?" He tsked.

Except Dani hadn't been ordinary. Dani had made it *this close* to quiet. And it hadn't hurt.

When Jacin finally calmed enough that Vonshi could let him go, Vonshi shook his head at the hank of yards-long hair Jacin had managed to slice away. Gaze disappointed but not cruel, he arranged the messy fringe that was left just over Jacin's eyes like it belonged there.

"If you're determined to risk yourself, boy, be sure of the cost beforehand. And be sure it's a price you can pay." Vonshi fluffed at Jacin's fringe, mouth pursed. "You cannot hide this from Beishin. Do not try. It will only make it worse."

Jacin didn't care. "Where did he go?"

Vonshi seemed to know exactly who Jacin was talking about. He was quiet as he set about plaiting the hated braid, tsking again at the ragged lengths over Jacin's brow. He didn't speak again until he was through with Jacin's hair and reaching for the bandaging around Jacin's arm.

"He left no word. He was simply gone when the house woke this morning. Beishin says it's for the best."

Jacin didn't say anything, just let Vonshi fix the mess Jacin had made of the bandage then gave him a small smile in thanks as Vonshi quietly left Jacin's room. He waited until Vonshi's steps receded down the hallway before Jacin slipped out himself, made his way down to Dani's room, and tested the door. Not locked. Jacin let himself in and shut the door behind him.

It looked remarkably the same. The linen quilt still lay on the bed, creased on the right side, as though Dani had perhaps sat there to dress. The loose trousers Dani had worn yesterday down to the exercise room were in a crumpled ball in the corner next to the basket that held the rest of his laundry, along with his indoor slippers. Jacin ventured farther into the room, quietly opened the top drawer of the clothespress. Tunics and trousers folded neatly and lined up like little soldiers. Everything was still here—Dani's books and papers, his clothes, his shaving kit, his robe—

Jacin frowned.

—a purse, filled with a goodly collection of koin.

Dani didn't seem the sort to run away, not even from Asai. And anyway, Asai hated Jacin for what happened, not Dani.

…No. Asai didn't bother to hate Jacin, didn't bother to care enough to bother.

Which wasn't the point.

Asai obviously hadn't blamed Dani for what had happened last night. So, there had been no reason for Dani to steal away in the dead of night for something his employer wasn't even blaming him for. And certainly not without at least his clothes, or the money to buy some new ones.

Not without at least telling Jacin goodbye. Not Dani.

It didn't make sense.

Beishin says it's for the best.

Perhaps Asai had forced Dani out without allowing him to collect his belongings. Perhaps Asai was angry with Dani, after all. Dani had touched the Untouchable. He'd touched Jacin. And Asai hadn't liked it.

A tiny, dubious smile tilted at Jacin's mouth, wilting almost immediately when he took another look around. It was like looking at the private quarters of someone who'd suddenly passed away.

Jacin shook his head—denial. Because it was absurd. Except...

Beishin says it's for the best.

Dani was gone. Dani with his toffee-colored hair and his blue eyes and his bright grin. Dani with his ruthless drills and his constant insistence on perfection and control. Dani with his hot mouth and long, clever fingers.

Jacin had thought Dani perfect. Asai had apparently thought him not perfect enough.

Dani had touched the Untouchable.

And Asai hadn't liked it.

Beishin says it's for the best.

Jacin jerked a sharp little nod, stepped over to the bed and straightened the quilt. Quickly, efficiently, he picked up the trousers in the corner and placed them in the basket, then tucked the slippers beneath the bed, savoring the twinges in his arm as he moved it. Last, he straightened the books into a neat stack, lined them up with the corner of the press, then tucked the papers into an orderly pile and lined them up too.

He stepped back, scanned the room with a critical eye.

Perfect.

Because if Dani wasn't here anymore to teach Jacin perfection, Jacin would have to do it himself. And if Jacin managed it... well.

Maybe there'd never be a reason for someone else to someday look on Jacin's empty room and wonder what had become of him.

Mouth tight, Jacin paced back over to the press and retrieved the purse. Then he turned his back and quit the room.

After that, Asai took over Jacin's training himself. Jacin sparred alone.

6

Harvest-month, Year 1322, Cycle of the Wolf

You could learn a lot about a person in a few days.

Malick had learned everything he needed to know about Samin in two hours. The Mage had given Malick Samin's name, and all Malick had to do was approach him, tell him what he wanted, tell him he'd appreciate a demonstration of skill—with no actual loss of life, if he could help it—then Malick sat back and watched Samin pick a fight with a rowdy group of five in the Girou. After Samin had won, quite handily and without even drawing a weapon, Malick had made him an offer and Samin had accepted it. End of story.

Yori and Shig took perhaps two days, but that was mostly because Malick had to wait for Shig to come down from whatever she'd been on and for Yori to stop hissing and spitting before she'd tell Umeia—not Malick, not at first—their story. Elder sister used and abused for her blood, younger sister who had plenty of opportunity to get herself loose but hadn't because she wouldn't leave the elder. End of story.

Fen didn't have an end to his story. Fen didn't have a beginning to his story. Fen wouldn't *tell* his story.

"All right, so tell me about your family."

Fen stared as though wondering if Malick had been dropped on his head as a child. "My father is dead and my mother is Disappeared."

"Well, I know *that*, don't I?" Malick rolled his eyes. "Are there any others I should know about?"

A blank stare was all Malick got. Slow blinking. And then a clipped, hostile "No."

Teeth only slightly clenched, Malick changed direction. "What's your mother's name?"

"Fen Marika."

All right. Answered immediately and succinctly. Apparently, Fen viewed it as information pertinent to finding her, and so had provided it without hesitation, though still with a bit of a snarl. It was like he couldn't help himself.

It took almost an hour more, Malick carefully wording questions, stumbling through trial and error of phrasing, before he got... not necessarily the answer he wanted but the one he needed. He *wanted* Fen to tell him about his family; he *got* Fen to give him something else altogether.

"This is getting us nowhere." Malick huffed irritably, sloshing the cold tea around in his bowl and smacking the porcelain a little too firmly to the tea table in his little sitting room, glaring at Fen, who sat stiffly across from him in the one chair, scowling back. "For a man who wants blood and vengeance, you're not being terribly helpful. 'A Jin farmer's wife taken from the east camp five weeks ago,' could be bloody anyone. And it's not like we're going to find her by going door to door through Ikata and asking if anyone in the house happens to have a spiritbound in their cellar."

Malick only saw Fen's minute flinch because he was watching closely. It took a moment for Malick to realize what he'd said, and when he did...

"Um. Shit. I'm sorry, that was crass and unnecessary. But you have to understand—I need more than what you're giving me. I need somewhere to *start.*"

"Why can't we start at the camp?"

"Because no one at the camp is going to talk to us." Except for the guard Malick paid a little too well, but Malick didn't think anyone in the Doujou actually knew the name he was after. The name he didn't really want. "Every poor bastard in those camps either has someone they're trying to hide themselves or knows someone who is, if they're not informing on their neighbors to keep their own family safe."

"They don't."

"Don't they?"

Fen only scowled. Perhaps he really didn't know.

Malick knew otherwise for a fact, but he saw no reason to wander off into arguments over the supposed righteousness of the Jin.

"I'm not Jin and you're Untouchable. They see us coming, and we'll be lucky to even get a glimpse of them before they hide away in their huts, let alone actually giving us information we can use. Plus, I doubt we'd get past the Doujou."

Which certainly wasn't true for Malick, and obviously not for Fen, but damned if Malick would even hint at his own capabilities for either bribery or stealth before Fen confessed about that handy little shadow charm. And why an Untouchable no one would dare stop or question would even feel the need for one.

Malick slumped back, toying with the fraying fabric on the arm of the couch. "Anyway, it isn't a good idea for you to be traipsing about, speaking coherently."

Fen's mouth twisted sourly, but he didn't add anything.

It spurred the questions Malick really wanted to ask, set them at the front of his mind like gristly bones, ripe for gnawing.

How had Fen managed not to cause even a whisper of a stir all this time?

How many knew about him?

Had Asai kept Fen locked up and hidden on his grand estate all this time? And how was it Fen could apparently show up at Asai's door in the middle of the night, threaten to gut him, and Asai hadn't appeared to even consider calling to one of his guards? Fen was suspicious enough of Asai to have done what he'd done, said what he'd said, and Malick had seen that Fen meant it, even though he'd also seen that Fen loved Asai, or at least had once, if not still—so why wouldn't Fen just *say* it?

Malick's eyebrows rose, that last question pinging at a nerve at the base of his skull.

Fen's answers weren't actually evasive—they were just extremely precise. If he didn't want to answer a question, he simply shut his mouth and stared. The answers he did give focused on particular points of the questions Malick addressed to him, not the broad meaning. Fen didn't respond to nuance; Fen only responded to directness. Perhaps that was why he tolerated Samin so well—Samin was one of the most direct people Malick knew.

Clarity bloomed.

Malick propped his elbow on the arm of the couch and rested his chin in his palm, eyes narrowed. "You've been going after very specific men. Men known to each other, traveling in the same circles. You're taking out those who you know are Disappearing people, and that's not something easy to find out, so you obviously had a way of figuring where to start. You must have some idea of how your mother was discovered. I need a name."

Fen frowned, genuine confusion. "Fen Marika." Again, it was as though he was doubting Malick's mental capacity.

Malick kept his teeth from clenching. "*Her* name doesn't help." Malick didn't add *because the men who do such things don't concern themselves with names*. Fen would know that. "I need the name of the one who took her."

Fen's fists curled tight. "I don't *know* who took her. If I knew, I'd—"

"D'you know how she was found out?"

"No." Fen paused, opened his mouth like he might go on, but then he just closed it and looked at the floor.

Malick leaned in—almost there, *almost*. "Do you suspect?"

"Yes." Whisper-thin but laced tight with anger.

"And who d'you suspect?"

Fen's dark eyelashes swept down, laid dense smudges like thick scatters of coal ash across high cheekbones. "Lord Asai."

No hesitation. It had taken an hour of aggravating, frustrating questioning, and yet when the right question had been asked plainly, the answer came just as plainly.

Malick knew then: Fen might have been Asai's creature, might have trusted Asai and loved him and been willing to do anything for him, even seek out *Temshiel* for him and risk the suns, but not now. Whatever Asai had been to Fen—teacher, very likely; protector, almost definitely; lover, quite probably—it was over now. Even if Asai hadn't betrayed Fen's family, Fen believed him capable of it, and Fen's love for the woman who was no longer his mother, and the brothers and sister he still chose not to disclose, far outweighed anything he might feel for Asai.

It was, in every sense, an excellent place to start.

"All right." Malick tried very hard to keep the delight out of his voice. "I have a few sources. I'll go and see what I can find out tonight, and tomorrow—"

"*You?*"

"Well, you can't be seen, can you? I show up with you, and my sources will never give me another bit of information again."

Fen's mouth twisted, and he stared down at his hands, curling them into fists then flexing them flat. Thinking. Until, finally—

"And if they can't see me?"

Malick was only dancing a little victory jig on the inside. "I didn't think Untouchables were also invisible."

He got a scowl this time, a scornful curl of the lip. But he also got Fen to reach into the high neck of his tunic and pull out the shadow charm.

As soon as Malick touched it, he knew. He had to stop himself from flying off the couch, heading straight for Asai and tearing his throat out. Had to stop himself from plowing through Fen first on his way. He clenched his teeth, held the amulet tight in his fist for a long, painful moment, then let it drop on its bit of leather, held it back out to Fen. Amazingly, Malick's hand didn't shake. Good thing, too, because he needed his reflexes when it came to Fen, and he definitely needed surprise.

The moment Fen reached to retrieve the charm, Malick snapped a hard grip around Fen's wrist, lurched up from the couch and dragged Fen toward him until Fen was teetering over the tea table, off balance. With a sharp downward jerk to Fen's arm, Malick kicked the table out from between then, snagged Fen's other hand, and twisted it up behind his back. Fast learner, Fen—his knee came up, tried Malick's own trick on him, but Malick merely trapped Fen's leg between his thighs, pressed in tight and leaned in until he had Fen bent backward, taking away his leverage, along with his balance.

"Where did you get it?"

"Get *off*!" Fen twisted and tried to get his arms free.

Malick only wrenched the one behind Fen's back up harder. "Not this time. Who gave it to you?"

Fen was panting—with anger, surprise, the strain of the position—but Malick knew what the shock of silence did to him too. All of it seemed to combine to stagger an answer out of him more quickly than he would've done otherwise.

"My... my patron."

"*Patron*." Malick tightened his grip until he was sure he was inflicting pain, though Fen wasn't showing it. "And when your *patron* hands you charms made of stolen Blood, you just take them and say, 'Thank you, Beishin'?"

Fen stopped fighting, glared, flecked gray ringed in indigo flaring with indignation at first, then disbelief. "*Lie*." Hoarse, and thin as a garrote wire. Pain came next, the ache of uncertainty, lashing out for all of half a second then shuttered back tight. "Asai made them. With his *own* blood. He studied alchemy, he made the spells himself, he wouldn't... he... he *wouldn't*, not..." Fen trailed off, like he'd run out of words and no longer believed the ones he'd just spoken. He stared as though he was hoping Malick was going to give them veracity, put his world back on its axis.

Malick stared back, all the anger in him colliding with doubt. "How could you not have *known*? D'you know what they use those things for?" Malick had softened his voice, but not his hold. "Have you ever wondered how it is the Adan hunters can manage to trot into a house where one of its occupants can wield fire or move the earth or even explode a man's skull, and yet they not only remain untouched and unharmed, but take them away in chains?"

"They... the—"

"It's the *amulets*, Fen. Made with the same Blood as your shadow charm, but with different spells. And believe me—the Blood did *not* come from Asai."

"It... *No*." Fen's chin quivered, then he tightened his jaw. "He... Asai said..."

The rage leaked out of Malick as he watched the hope leak out of Fen. All that was left was a seething sort of frustrated sorrow.

Asai. Fucking *Asai*. Bloody history repeating itself. Fen was a setup, he just didn't know it. And whatever Asai was up to this time, Malick would be damned if he'd sit back and watch.

"*Fuck*, Fen." Malick shook his head, bowed it 'til his brow pressed Fen's. "You really did love him, didn't you?"

A sharp jolt against him abruptly reminded Malick of their positions, the press of the hard, lean body solid to his, the heat he honestly hadn't noticed until the certainty that Fen really hadn't known set itself firmly in Malick's bones. And, fuck, now all he could smell was almonds.

Slowly, Malick straightened, pulling Fen up with him, and loosened his grip on both wrists, but only let go of one. More gently this time, he took the hand he had twisted behind Fen, settled it against the small of Fen's back, shifting them into more of an embrace than a hold, thick, silky plait knocking lightly against the backs of Malick's knuckles. Without letting himself think it through, Malick laid a hand to the side of Fen's face.

"You've no idea in the world what he is, have you?"

Surprisingly, Fen didn't fight against him, just submitted to Malick's maneuvering with a poignant look of dull shock. "He was…" His eyes went bright; he blinked it away. "He said he was going to save… save the Jin."

Malick couldn't even find the rage for Asai the lie should have risen in him. All he could feel was an odd removed regret at shattering more of Fen's illusions. He released Fen entirely, took him by the shoulders and pushed him gently back. Again, Fen merely let him, stood and watched as Malick righted the table and collected the books and papers that had scattered, stacking them atop it.

Fen only stood there, spine straight and shoulders back, as though he didn't know how to be any other way but inflexible—control of the body, when his mind was so obviously reeling. He looked like he might stand there all day, staring blankly wherever Malick wasn't.

Unsettled himself, Malick cautiously took Fen by the arm and guided him back to the chair, then took his own seat across from Fen on the couch.

Right back where they'd started.

Well… not quite.

Without a word, Fen stood again, looked at the door, staring like he was thinking of just walking through it and not coming back, then he shut his eyes and bowed his head. The messy fringe hung down, covering most of his face; all Malick could see was the line of his straight nose and a quivering chin. Fen shook his head, a sharp jerk back and forth, then took a long breath and came to sit silently beside Malick on the couch, his knee touching Malick's thigh. Just sat there. Back straight, head bowed, hands clenched into tight fists in his lap. Trembling, just enough for Malick to notice. Wound so tight he might fly apart at any second.

Not surrender, but… something else.

Malick could have him. Right now. All he'd have to do was make one move, whisper one innuendo, make one offer, and it wouldn't matter this time how crude it was.

Confused. Betrayed. On the edge. Misplaced devotion and all illusions shattered with one revelation. Ripe for any kind of acknowledgment and from anyone at all. Fen would probably have Samin right now, if he was here and asked nicely. And if he could give Fen silence.

Malick almost reached out and set a hand on Fen's knee in invitation, but stopped himself. It wasn't enough. He wanted Fen to want *more* than silence.

"All right." Malick sat back but let the touch stay. "I think it's time you told me everything."

⚕

"Come on, then lads, show some backbone." Umeia's voice came from halfway up the stairs, impatient and just edging into exasperated.

Yori poked her head out the door and peered down the hallway, though at the moment, only the crown of Umeia's brass-blonde head was visible over the top riser.

"Van, that thing goes bouncing down the steps, and your head bounces after it."

A grunt and a wavery "Yes, *misin*" was all Yori heard in response.

She frowned. "Umeia?"

Umeia peered up over the top step to smile ruefully at Yori. "Ah! Hullo, love." She beckoned Yori over. "For the common room down the end." Umeia met Yori at the top of the steps, nodding at the shabby couch two of the bouncers were trying to angle up the stairwell.

Yori blinked. "We have a common room?" She'd lived here for several years; she was pretty sure she would have noticed one, and "down the end" was only a strangely angled empty space where the roof stairs connected askew to the hallway.

"You will." Umeia's mouth pinched tight, eyes on the wobbling couch. She went back down a couple of steps. "Van, I swear, if you can't—"

"What the hell is this?" Malick sauntered up behind Yori, leaning over her shoulder and taking in Umeia, the men, and the couch with a twist of his eyebrows. "Umeia, what are Van and Bone doing up here? You can't let—"

"I know." Umeia waved it away. "And they're not up here quite yet, are they?"

"Damn it, Umeia, you know what I—"

"We can't have—" Umeia cut herself off, checked the progress of the men and the couch, then hurried back up the last several steps to Malick and Yori. "Our little Ghost has to eat, and yet we can't have him coming down to the kitchens. The girls brought him up trays for breakfast and lunch and said they were for you, but then you went down and annoyed 'another' lunch out of Ragi. I've heard about it, the kitchen staff's heard about it, everyone within six blocks probably heard about it. So, I had to come up with something more practical."

Umeia looked over her shoulder again, rolling her eyes when she noted Van and Bone had managed to get the couch stuck at an angle between the fold of a riser and the ceiling.

She turned back to Malick and Yori. "I'm putting in a common room for you. After the idiot twins get the couch up, there's another to come and a table and chairs. The kitchens will send your meals up here from now on." Umeia smirked. "You can all sit down together like a family. Samin will be the dad, which I expect makes you the—"

"*Don't* say it." Malick scrubbed at his hair. "It's a fine idea, Umeia, but…" He shot a look at the stairs, where the men had managed to get the couch unstuck, but now Van was scowling at Bone and griping about how unfair it was that he was the one ended up having to navigate backward. Malick gripped Yori's shoulder as he leaned in toward Umeia, lowering his voice. "You have to warn us when someone's coming. In fact." He gave Yori a squeeze. "Go to my rooms and make sure Fen doesn't poke his head out, yeah?"

Yori hated to miss Umeia bullying the bouncers—it was always great fun to watch her cow men twice her size—and especially Bone, on whom, as Yori had only just learned a few days ago, Shig happened to have her eye, and whom Yori had immediately decided she no longer liked in the least. But she hadn't really thought about them seeing Fen, and gossip did get around the Girou rather quickly.

"Oh, *fine*." Yori heaved a disappointed sigh and angled out from under Malick's grip.

If Yori had been thinking a little more practically, if she'd been in her "job" mindset, she never would have just opened the door and let herself in without a bit more caution. But she was at *home*, and her mind was occupied with the still-new idea of Bone and her sister and how much Yori hated it. So the hand that shot out from beside the door and flung her up against it, and then the knife suddenly at her throat, rather took Yori off her guard.

Evasion tactics and Samin's years of instruction on how to break a hold and a few bones in the process ran through her mind in the space of half a second. Yori had already braced herself for her first counterattack before she registered the wary gray eyes glaring into hers from an inch away, and understood what had happened: thumping racket out in the hall, unfamiliar voices, and Malick had likely said nothing more than "Stay here" before he'd left Fen in his rooms to go and see what the disturbance was about.

This wasn't a safe place for Fen, not yet, not like it was for Yori. Home for her, but he'd only just got here.

Yori deliberately relaxed, put on an easy smile, and raised her hands slowly. "Just me." All sunny good cheer.

Fen frowned, dark eyebrows drawing together, no recognition, and for a moment, Yori worried that "just me" would mean nothing to him. Perhaps he didn't even know who Yori was, despite the fact that she and Shig had made it a point to bring their own meals up at breakfast and lunch and drag Fen in to join them on the floor of their room to eat.

Perhaps he didn't remember; he hadn't said a word, all through either meal, after all, and Yori had no idea what Fen actually kenned through all his "voices" Shig was always on about. Damn, Yori hoped not. Malick would be *really* pissed if Yori had to kill Fen. Then again, considering her current position…

"…Sorry." Fen finally lowered the knife, sheathing it as he stepped away. That was apparently all Yori was going to get, because Fen stood there and stared.

Yori almost snorted and made a crack, but paused when Fen's head tilted to the side and his eyes went a bit distant. Doing that listening thing he did, which still disconcerted Yori but which Samin ignored. Shig always went quiet when Fen did, trying to listen in, too, though she said she only ever heard indecipherable noise.

Yori waited until Fen's head untilted, waited for the little under-the-breath growl. She cleared her throat, nudged Fen away from the door.

"That won't happen in the middle of a job, will it?"

Fen twitched at her touch, but didn't jerk away. "It might."

Oh, terrific. Yori wondered if Fen had thought to mention that to Malick. Probably not, so she'd better do it.

"Umeia's having some furniture brought up." Yori trailed behind Fen into Malick's sitting room where he and Malick had apparently been doing… whatever it was they'd been doing. Knowing Malick, and noting the city registries and papers lying about, not at all what Malick would prefer they'd been doing. "That's what the noise is about. She's got some of the lads making us a common room so you don't have to sit on the floor in our room anymore. Malick said I should come tell you to keep out of sight until they've done."

Fen sat down in the awful chair—ugly and uncomfortable—and merely watched Yori as she flopped on the couch across from him, propped her bare feet atop a small stack of bound books on the tea table, and gave him a smile.

"We usually eat down in the kitchens." Yori wrinkled her nose. "Kinda noisy and Ragi gets pissy if we come in the middle of a supper rush, so this'll be nice, I think."

Fen just kept looking at her—no hostility that Yori could detect, but no amity, either.

"Nobody here would hurt you or get in your way. But people do talk, and we can't have them talking about you, can we?" Yori paused, but… nothing. "We've done it before. Hidden people, I mean. Nobody usually comes up here but us and Umeia, so it's not too risky. Once, we had two little—" She stopped.

Once, we had two little Jin children up here, because their uncle meant to betray them to the Adan hunters. Bastard was pissed that his brother's wife wouldn't have him, so he decided he wasn't as interested in keeping his family safe as he thought he was. Malick took care of the uncle while we went in and took the children then hid them up here in what's now your room until the Thesian caravans came through for the Festivals, and no one was the wiser.

Yori never did find out if the parents knew their children were safe. Come to think of it, she didn't even know if the parents were even still alive.

It wasn't her business, so she dismissed it. "We had two people up here for nearly two whole months, and nobody twigged."

She left it there. Fen was theirs now, certainly, but it still wasn't up to Yori to blather *all* their secrets at him.

It got his attention, though. Fen's gaze went fixed and canny.

"You've hidden refugees?"

"Uh-huh." Yori shrugged. "We don't kill *everyone* we meet, y'know."

"Did they pay you?"

"Who?"

"The refugees."

Yori paused. That was an odd question. "Um… dunno, actually. Don't think so, but Malick doesn't tell me everything. But, y'know, me and Shig were refugees once, and we never paid anything."

Fen's eyebrows rose, but that was all.

Yori wondered why she felt such a distinct compulsion to go on, explain herself to a man who seemed to think he owed no explanations to anyone.

"Our mother sold us." Yori kept her tone casual, but a frisson still moved up her spine when she said it out loud. "For Shig's Blood." She gestured at her own wrist, and kept her mouth shut about what she herself had been sold for. "You know—the scars."

Fen nodded, gaze still narrow, intent. "How old?"

Yori shifted, not uncomfortable, really, but… confused. Hadn't she been asking the questions a second ago?

"Young."

She'd been… what, twelve?—when Umeia had found them hiding from the caravan of the minor argent who'd bought them, hungry and terrified and willing to face almost any indignity but the one they'd been running from. If Yori'd had to comfort her sister through one more session with the chance stones, one more terrifying bleeding, she might have lost her own grip, and then she'd be no good at all to Shig. Fucking for money hadn't seemed such a terrible thing when Yori had found herself begging from the kitchens in the back alley of the Girou. She'd been fucked almost every night for two years for nothing more than one meal a day and the assurance that her sister would stay alive through another night, so this could only be better, right? And she was pretty, so she'd been told—not as pretty as Shig, who'd only seemed to grow even more comely once her Change hit her, though what Shig had gained in beauty, she seemed to have lost in reality. But a decent bath and some clothes that didn't reek could have had Yori ready for at least the public floor of Umeia's House, if not one of the rooms.

"Bloody hell." A soft snort whiffled out of Yori's nose before she could help it.

Fen was still watching her, paying very close attention, but he stayed silent.

Just as well. Yori didn't think she wanted Fen's opinion on whether or not he thought people might have paid her for what she'd given away for free for years.

Well… not given. And certainly not free. Getting paid for it would have been a step up, in Yori's considered opinion.

Malick had seen something else in her, though—in Yori and Shig both. He'd gone out to ensure no one in the caravan would ever come looking for them, had Umeia clean Shig and Yori up, feed them, give them a room, and then Malick set to coaching Yori with a bow. He'd tried to teach Shig sword work, but it had never really taken, though Shig could swing one about efficiently enough to defend herself for a few minutes, if she had to. Shig didn't have to. Once the argent's various spells and drugs had worn off, and she was as much herself as she would ever be, they'd discovered another, more effective means of self-defense. And an offense that made even Yori shiver sometimes when she had to watch it. If only they'd known when their mother had exchanged them for an insultingly small bag of silver.

Somehow, Malick had known they were coming, had been watching for them. Malick didn't use his magic very often, and Yori never asked him about it—it was safer not knowing—but he'd seen things for Shig and Yori they never would have seen for themselves. Things that suited Yori a hell of a lot better than whoring. And though some might think spending your life on your back was better than taking the lives of others, Yori knew what darkness lived in people, had seen it up close. She'd much rather put an arrow through a man's eye than accept koin to let him groan atop her for an hour and leave his spunk inside her, like a mark of his power over her.

The Girou was their home now, Umeia and Malick and Samin their family; even the Mage was like a weird kind of invisible uncle or something. Killing people who would take it all away from them, who would use others like Shig had been used, wasn't even the price Yori paid to keep it—it was a bonus. Yori would do it for free, but she certainly didn't complain that she was well paid for it.

"So." Fen cleared his throat, eyes sober in his blank face. "You were fugitives."

That made it sound so… brave. "You could call it that."

"And there have been others."

"Uh-huh."

That was the second time Fen had asked that question, and from someone who hardly even spoke, it had to be significant. Samin said that sometimes the questions a person asked could be more telling than the answers they chose to give or not give.

Damn, Yori wished Malick was here.

"Why?" She kept her expression neutral. "Know someone who—?"

"Who is the Mage?"

Yori blinked. "Don't know, don't care. He pays me and makes it possible for me to kill Blood thieves. I don't ask."

"Who's Ragi?"

Yori hesitated as she tried to adjust to the sudden twists. Perhaps Fen simply couldn't concentrate on any one subject for too long. His turns in conversation were a bit jerkier and more noticeable than Shig's, but no more peculiar.

"Ragi is in charge of the kitchens. You're lucky you won't have to meet him. I don't think the man's ever smiled in his life, and if he did, his face would likely split in half. He only let us eat in the kitchens because Umeia made him, and no one argues with Umeia, not if they want to live for long." Yori grinned. "And now we don't have to eat in the kitchens anymore."

It would certainly make mealtimes more pleasant, and less stressful for Shig. Shig didn't like to be around Ragi if she didn't have to be. She got headaches if he came too close to her.

"And this way, we can all eat together. Like a family. Umeia was teasing Malick, saying that would make Samin the father and him the mother. Malick didn't think it was very funny."

That got a slight flick of the eyebrows.

A heavy thump came from out in the hall, followed by Umeia shrilling epithets and, if Yori didn't miss her guess, some rather colorful insults, but she couldn't hear words, only volume and cadence. Still, she snickered, caught Fen's eye, and thought she saw a tiny quirk at the corner of his mouth. Yori was absurdly encouraged.

"Bet she's got Malick humping furniture now too." Yori paused when Fen's eyebrows twitched, realized what she'd said and burst out laughing. "Oh!" She had to catch her breath. "What a mental picture. And if he wasn't so damned pretty, probably not too far off. I swear, the man would fuck anything that—" She caught herself, took her snorts down to low chuckles and changed the subject. "So, what d'you think so far?"

Fen's eyebrows didn't crawl all over his forehead like Malick's did, but they were expressive nonetheless with their subtle shifts and twitches. This time, they quirked up, questioning.

"You know." Yori rolled her hand. "What d'you think about being here? About us? Think we can grow on you?"

Fen frowned, looked down at his hands, clenched tight in his lap. "It's... acceptable."

"Meaning we're all right for a bunch of assassins who hijacked you and made you live in the attic of a whorehouse, yeah?"

That tiny quirk of the mouth again, and Fen shrugged. Maybe it was because he was so quiet, so undemonstrative except when he was pissed off, but those miniscule twitches heartened Yori like they were helpless guffaws.

She leaned in, conspiratory. "Shig's quite taken with you."

That was putting it lightly. Shig had practically begged Fen to let her braid his hair this afternoon when Samin had given him the key to the baths downstairs after they'd sparred. Fen hadn't said anything, just sort of stared at Shig like he had no idea what to make of her. Shig had been in their room since she'd stomped back up after accompanying Fen downstairs, and griped to Yori that he'd made it clear she was not to come into the empty baths with him and then had come out with his hair already braided. Shig had taken it as a personal insult, and was still determinedly sulking about it.

Though now that Yori thought about it, Bone's presence out in the hallway might manage to coax Shig out of it, if she was paying attention enough to realize he was out there. The thought gave Yori feelings that were an annoying mix of sourness and optimism.

"Shig's never known anyone else who might... understand. That's why, I think. She..." Yori paused, thought about what she wanted to say. "You've noticed the braids?" She waited until Fen cut her a quick look through his fringe and jerked a slight nod. "I think she wants to be like you. It wouldn't—"

"*No*. She really doesn't."

Yori decided not to be offended by the forceful interruption, because she agreed wholeheartedly. She didn't want her sister to be anything like this man—the small similarities were bad enough.

"Well, Shig says Malick can help with that."

That got a bit of a twitch and a sharp look.

Yori shrugged. "Don't know how, but sometimes he lets her crawl into bed with him so he can—" She caught the slight pinch of lips and shook her head with a grin. "Not anything like that, Mal would never... well, I suppose you can't ever say 'never' with Malick, but not with Shig. Or me, I expect. For all Umeia's joking, and for all Malick would deny it, I think he's not so much a father as a big brother. Not that *I'd* mind, understand— he's quite fit and he's *not* my brother, after all." Yori waggled her eyebrows just to see if it would make Fen scowl; it did. "Anyway, Shig dreams a lot, and sometimes they're... bad ones. She says Malick makes it quiet for her. He helps her. Maybe you could let him help you too."

"...I should sleep with him?"

The question, so serious and wary, made Yori laugh again. "Well, that's not for me to say, is it?" Teasing. "And Mal would likely give me a raise, did I tell you 'yes'." She quirked a sly look at Fen. "You can tell he's got it bad for you, can't you?" He didn't need to answer—the daggers in his gaze did it for him. Yori snorted. "Sleep with him, don't sleep with him, *I* don't care. I'm only saying he helps Shig, and she says he can help you. How you take it is up to you."

It seemed Yori couldn't avoid unintentional innuendo today. She held back the laugh this time.

Fen's eyes went narrow. "How?"

"How what?"

"How does he help?"

"Well, he makes it quiet, of course. Didn't I say?"

"No, how does he make it quiet?"

"Ah." Yori shrugged. "Don't know. And he doesn't say. I don't care much, really. He is what he is, whatever he is, and he helps Shig. How he does it matters much less than that he does." Because, oh, sometimes Shig needed it badly. "You should let her braid your hair for you. It must be very difficult to get it so neat and perfect, and she..." Yori sighed. "Shig likes you. And she really does want to help. And... and it would make her happy."

Fen didn't answer, but he didn't refuse, though what did that mean, really? And why should he care about making Shig happy? Not everyone loved Shig like Yori did. In fact, Shig made most people uncomfortable, and some actively disliked her. Like Ragi, for instance. Yori often thought Ragi gave Shig headaches because of all the silent animosity he drove at her whenever he laid eyes on her.

It seemed to kill conversation for a while, though what conversation there was had been fairly one-sided. Still, Yori thought perhaps this Fen wasn't so hard to get along with as she'd thought he might be. He didn't snap and snarl when you weren't actively trying to kidnap him, and if Yori paid attention, she could interpret the silences and flickers of expression easily enough, and most of them were... well, not friendly, but not hostile, either.

They listened to the continued bustle out in the hallway for a while, Yori grinning when she heard Samin's distinct unhappy muttering, then turning thoughtful when she realized she was actually rather content with the silence in the room, which wasn't strained or heavy—just there. She didn't have to stay, really; could have, in fact, left directly after she'd told Fen to keep himself hidden away in here until Malick came to tell him all was clear again. Somehow, either getting dragooned into helping move furniture, or hiding in her own room and watching Shig sulk, was less appealing than keeping Fen company. Surprisingly, Fen didn't seem to particularly mind that Yori kept not leaving—he just didn't seem to know what to do about it.

"Have you found out anything helpful?" Yori jerked her chin at the stacks of registries and directories on the table and aimed a lift of her eyebrows at Fen.

He followed her gaze, lips flattening. "No."

Yori had never encountered someone who could pack so much frustrated fury into one small word. She decided she'd best not push that topic.

"Have you got any brothers or sisters?" Yori didn't know much about Untouchables. They didn't have them in Kente. She knew her father had been Jin, somehow escaped from Ada and dead before Yori had turned a year, but she'd never known him and their mother wasn't exactly the religious sort. All Yori knew was what she'd heard from Umeia and Malick, and it sounded to her like the whole idea was that Untouchables had no attachments, since the point was for them to wander about at the gods' will. It stood to reason that family ties would curb one's wandering.

Still, Fen obviously hadn't sprung whole from Subie, since there was a missing mother out there somewhere. And it seemed Fen was an unusual Untouchable, anyway. It didn't seem unreasonable to think he might have siblings.

Perhaps not unreasonable to Yori, but… maybe to Fen, because he'd gone stiff and closed up again, eyes narrowed down to little slits and mouth tight. "Why d'you ask that?"

"…Um. Well. I mean, it's rather a normal question, isn't it?"

Perhaps he just didn't know how it worked. Shig wasn't terribly good at social graces, either, at least not since her Change. Maybe Fen simply took it the wrong way. Yori couldn't quite figure how it *could* be taken the wrong way, but she was used to dealing with her sister—who was right this moment moping because she hadn't been allowed to braid a relative stranger's hair.

"Sort of a 'getting to know you' thing when you meet new people." Yori scooped back the hair that had come loose from the tail at her nape and refastened it, making everything about her demeanor calm and casual, just new acquaintances shooting the shit. Because, whether Fen was aware of how things normally worked or not, the question had clearly thrown him. And Yori wanted to know why. "That's pretty much how these things go, y'know? I ask you something, you answer, and then we have a conversation about it." Yori made it a point to smile. "So, do you?"

Fen was staring again. Uncertain this time, Yori could tell—his face was set in a frown, but his eyes weren't blazing at her. He wasn't so hard to read, if you paid attention to the eyes.

"I—"

"Sorry, sorry." Malick rushed through the door and shut it firmly behind him, likely escaping Umeia before she found something else for him to move. "Didn't mean to be gone so long." There was still noise out in the hall, but not as loud and busy as it had been. Malick was swiping at his tunic as he came in, but he paused and lifted his eyebrows when he saw Yori lounging on his couch, and shot a quick glance to Fen. "Everything all right?"

Yes, Yori thought, then, *No*, because she was sure she'd been getting somewhere with Fen before Malick and his crap timing showed up.

Unconsciously—Yori was positive it was unconscious—Malick ran his fingers through his hair, fluffed it up, as he looked between them, as though he couldn't decide if he should be considering Yori a rival and slathering on the charm for a quick one-up.

Yori only just managed not to roll her eyes. She couldn't hold back the sigh, though.

"Well, that's me done." Yori stood and made her way to the door, giving Malick a pat to his puffed-out chest as she passed him. "See you at supper."

She shook her head as she stepped into the hall and shut the door behind her, both amused and annoyed, because she really did feel as though she'd been on the verge of something, and Malick had just bollixed it, but whatever. Getting somewhere with Fen wasn't Yori's job anyway.

╥

She shouldn't have taken her eyes off it, damn it. At the least, she should have dragged Malick's ass down to the main floor to watch. Or given Bone and Van their orders and trusted them to—

Umeia rolled her eyes. Right. Those two had definitely been busy comparing biceps when the gods were handing out brains.

She stood outside Malick's door, listening to Yori harassing Shig from down the hall, obviously wasting no time in getting used to their new common room. Despite Umeia's unease and the sweaty grip she had on the damned paper, she had to smile when Samin's voice chimed in with… agreement, sounded like. Both of them advising Shig to keep away from Bone—Bone? Seriously?—and Shig just giggling lightly at them both. Umeia could see her in her mind's eye, lounging on one of the couches, smiling softly to herself, staring at the ceiling and playing with her braids.

For a moment, it was all Umeia could do not to turn away from Malick's door and toward the voices, join her ducklings for a while, and leave Malick and Trouble to themselves. Whatever was written on this piece of paper, no good would come of it, Umeia had known it before she'd even read Malick's demand—hell, before he'd even handed it to her.

She'd checked the crock this morning, saw Malick's message was still there, just as she'd left it, and had kept an eye on it since. Not really wanting to see who came for it, or how, but everything had changed just since yesterday. Now she *had* to know. She'd given her oath to those three down the hall, and no strange little Ghost—whether sent by Asai, the Mage, or Wolf himself—was going to get in her way of keeping it. And *someone* had to keep Malick's head on straight.

Mouth tightening, Umeia knocked once before pushing Malick's door open and stepping briskly into his rooms. Malick was sitting on the couch, but Fen was standing stiffly, eyes narrowed at Umeia, arm crossed over his waist and hand on the hilt of the knife strapped there. Lucky for Umeia, Malick's hand was clamped over Fen's, restraining.

Right, so, apparently Umeia would have to be more careful about abrupt entrances until the Ghost settled in more securely. If he ever did. Umeia wasn't quite sure she wanted that. She wasn't quite sure she wanted the Ghost here at all.

She waved the paper at Malick, wordless.

"Already?"

Malick stood, giving an absent pat to Fen's hand as he made his way past him and around the couch, eyes intent on the parchment in Umeia's hand. He didn't look like his stomach was dipping down to his toes like Umeia's had done when she'd seen it—he looked pleased. Surprised but pleased.

Umeia could've smacked him.

Keen, Malick cracked the seal and folded it open. He peered at it for all of two seconds before his jaw clamped and his eyes narrowed down to slits

"Bloody fucking *bastard*." He mashed the parchment in his fist, then ran a hand through his hair. "A job." He gave Umeia a look that was altogether indignant. "I ask him for a meeting and he sends me a fucking *job*."

Relief flooded Umeia, but she wouldn't dare show as much to Malick. "For when?"

"Turn of the month." Malick had one hand clamped to the back of his neck, the other still balled around the message.

Umeia frowned. "That's only a week away." She couldn't help how her gaze flicked over at Fen, couldn't help the worry or hide it.

Malick clearly caught the look, because he gave Umeia a flat-eyed stare. "We'll be ready." Not quite threatening, but aggressive, at least. "If I even agree to take it."

"Malick, you can't—"

"I can do anything I damn well please. And especially if this is turning out to be what I think it is."

Damn him and his quick temper, his singular sense of justice, and his complete inability to turn away someone he thought needed rescuing. Especially if the someone happened to look like his new favorite Untouchable. Bloody Malick—any damsel would do.

"Maybe there just wasn't time?" It made perfect sense as soon as Umeia said it, so she pushed. "We don't even know who picks up and leaves the messages. And yours was still there this morning when I checked. Maybe the Mage just hasn't got it yet."

It made Malick pause, at least, though he was still wound pretty tight. He growled, drew back his arm like he meant to hurl the balled-up parchment, but only lowered it when Fen caught his eye.

Fen had just been standing there, watching silently as usual, gaze shunting back and forth between Umeia and Malick. Now, he seemed to retreat from both their glances. He looked away and quietly sat in the ugly, uncomfortable chair Malick kept not throwing out on the midden heap.

Malick slumped, as though he was… disappointed, maybe. He waved Umeia over to the couch.

Umeia took a seat with an eye on the stacks of registries and directories on the tea table. She lifted a questioning gaze to Malick.

"Fen and I have been…" Malick shot a glance over at Fen then back to Umeia, before he settled back into the cushions with a casual sprawl. "We've been going over some names, people who I know have been associated in some way with Asai, to see if Fen recognizes any of them."

It made Umeia startle. They were "discussing" Asai? Had Fen brought up the name, or had Malick? It would matter.

"And does he?"

"Not so far. At least—" Malick flattened out the crumpled parchment in his hand, and held it out to Fen.

Fen took it with a questioning frown, but had himself a look. "Pon is a prefect under Lord Sonji." He handed the paper back to Malick. "Or was. Sonji controlled the lands to the west of Asai's cherry orchards before his sudden death about three weeks ago, and Pon was a frequent guest of Asai's. Asai was always most intent on keeping Pon an ally. Or, at least, intent that Pon thought Asai one."

Umeia's eyebrows shot up. It was the most she'd ever heard Fen say all at once.

"Huh." Malick was grinning. "You spied. You must've done."

Fen said nothing, just flattened his mouth down to a thin, tight line.

Malick was looking at Fen as though Fen had hung the moons. "Go on, then."

Fen shrugged, irritated, but Umeia couldn't tell at what. "I recognized the name when the criers started calling the news of Sonji's stroke. Pon has laid a claim to the lands and to Sonji's wife. It seemed… convenient."

Malick's eyes were nearly sparkling, all knowing approval. "So why isn't Pon dead yet?"

Again, the irritation. Fen glared, but Umeia didn't think it was for Malick.

"He's not been to his own estate since then. I'd been watching before…" Fen's mouth twisted, and he waved between Umeia and Malick, the *before you hijacked me* all too clear. "I've kept an eye on Sonji-onna as well, but Pon hasn't been to see her—he hasn't been anywhere, and there was nothing—" He stopped, frowning suspiciously at Umeia.

"It's all right." Malick propped his feet on the tea table. "You can talk in front of her."

Fen looked away. "If Pon's getting his good luck through magic, he's got the source with him, wherever he is. I looked."

"I'll bet you did." Malick turned to Umeia, noted her stunned surprise at the revelations—and from *this* man—and grinned. "I'm afraid we haven't got far in pursuing Fen's own hunt, but he's enlightened me on a few things I think will interest you. Get someone to get us some tea, would you? Then we'll fill you in."

Umeia did. And then Malick did. Told her what Fen had told him. How Asai had taken Fen from the camp and harbored him, trained him, told him his skills would be needed one day to save the Jin, but wouldn't tell him how. Fen bided through it all silently, sitting stiffly in the uncomfortable chair, holding his bowl of tea in both hands and staring down into it, head tilted slightly to the side.

"He's listening," Malick said quietly when he caught Umeia staring with a question on her face. "Asai apparently tried to beat it out of him, but there was a steward who Fen said helped him learn to split his concentration."

Umeia eyed Fen skeptically. "That doesn't look split to me."

"Seems to work for him."

"Can't you make it…?" Umeia shifted uncomfortably. "Can't you make it go away?"

"If he wants me to." Malick sounded so… relaxed, so bloody pleased with himself.

Umeia's hands fisted until her knuckles cracked. "He doesn't want you to?"

"Sometimes."

Umeia hit him—just a smart smack to his thigh, to wipe that look of unperturbed satisfaction off his face, pleased when it twisted into surprise and pique.

"*Ow*, Umeia, what the hell?"

"What if he does that on a job?"

"Then I expect," Fen put in, quiet but cross, "I'll have to devote more attention to one thing than the other." He paused, peering at Umeia with a flat look of challenge. "I *can* hear, y'know. And I *have* done this before."

"Not with *my* ducklings, you haven't." Umeia stood, tried for *looming* but suspected she only got *hovering*. "Trouble, that's what you are. Be all the trouble you like with him"—she pointed behind her at Malick—"he can take care of himself, and generally deserves what he gets. But you do anything to endanger the others, and you'll have me to deal with."

Fen's face had closed down, expression gone cool and blank, which only stoked Umeia's anger. She sucked in a breath, readying more, when Malick tapped her on the shoulder, dangled a charm in front of her face. Reflexively, Umeia grabbed at it, gasped like Malick had just punched her in the stomach when she touched it. Her hand closed around the charm, and she turned to Malick, mouth hanging open, stunned speechless, thoughtless.

Oh, Skel. Oh, shit.

"Asai gave it to him." Malick's voice was too quiet, too calm, considering what was all but wailing in Umeia's clenched fist. "Told him he'd made it with his own blood. Told him he'd need it for his 'work'." He turned a soft look on Fen. "Told him anything he wanted to hear to get him to do what he wanted." He paused, looked back at Umeia, intent. "Sound familiar?"

⛩

They left together, Umeia and Fen, Umeia with more distressing things on her mind than she'd had in… a long, long time. Thoughts occupied with a past that seemed determined to repeat itself. And there she'd been, all ready—in fact, resolved—to dislike the little Ghost, and now look. Bloody Asai and his bloody grandiose opinion of himself, his endless scheming and his willingness to use anyone and anything to bring about the changes he wanted. And damn all gods to the suns for letting him.

She stood out in the hallway for some time after she'd closed Malick's door behind her, staring down at the toes of her shoes, brooding, before she realized Fen hadn't taken the opportunity to relieve himself of her presence. Even after the hostility Umeia couldn't quite help, and the accusations to which she had no right, Fen was still there.

He dipped his head when Umeia finally noticed him, placed a fist over his breastbone.

"Umeia-onna, I understand… I've heard…" He clenched his teeth, irritated, apparently with himself, then firmed his jaw. He lifted his head and looked Umeia in the eye. "How much to harbor a refugee?"

…What?

Umeia blinked, paused for a moment to let it sink in, make sure she'd heard correctly.

She still wasn't sure. "Sorry?"

"I…" Fen hesitated, staring wide-eyed with abrupt trepidation. Umeia tried to wipe whatever forbidding expression might be on her face off it, but too late; Fen's face paled as he backed away from her, shaking his head. "Nothing." He dipped her another of those odd, formal bows. "I beg your pardon, Umeia-onna." He couldn't seem to move fast enough when he turned quickly up the hallway and escaped into his room.

Umeia pushed out a long, slow breath, said, "Oh, bloody *hell*," then turned around and shoved open Malick's door again.

⟁

Hallows-month, Year 1315, Cycle of the Wolf

"I'll need you to wear this today, Jacin-rei."

Asai held the shadow charm out on its fine chain. Jacin watched it spin slowly in front of his nose, the afternoon sun through the window catching the chain and flaring tiny shards of gold on the walls.

Jacin let Asai drop it into his upturned hand. "Guests, Beishin?"

Asai smiled and patted Jacin's shoulder. Jacin slipped the chain over his neck, Asai's touch sending a warm thrill through his belly.

"We need allies, if we're to save your people."

"Yes, Beishin."

Jacin went back to the manuscript Asai had set him to this morning. A history of the Jin through the centuries, thick and crammed full of more detail than Jacin thought even his mother likely knew. Different viewpoints on familiar tales than Jacin had heard before too. If this volume was to be believed, it was shocking the Adan had overtaken the Jin. Shocking anyone had overtaken the Jin. Of course it *was* to be believed— Asai had written it, after all, and to doubt the book was to doubt the man.

"Beishin..." Jacin peered curiously at Asai. "It says in here that the Adan feared the Jin, and that's why they invaded. That the Jin had offended the gods and the gods set the *Temshiel* on them. But..." He paused, trying to come up with wording that didn't imply doubt, wouldn't offend. "The Adan and the Jin were almost one for centuries. The Adan even abandoned their one god for the moons. Our traditions are very nearly the same. We honor the same gods. Why—?"

"Why would the Adan suddenly turn on the Jin?" Asai smiled sadly and sat across from Jacin. "Why would the gods?" He waited until Jacin nodded. "Magic is a frightening concept to those who do not have it." Asai's voice slipped into the smooth lecture tones that Jacin found almost hypnotic. It was amazing, the information he retained, when Asai spoke to him in this voice. "The Jin have always had a strict tradition, so far as breeding—the full-Blood was to remain pure."

"So, the Jin weren't allowed to bind outside?" Jacin frowned. "But my mother said—"

"Laws were... set aside for a period." Asai shrugged, apparently unperturbed by Jacin's questions and willing to discuss the subject with him like Jacin was an actual thinking adult. "As you say, the two peoples were almost one, for a time. Traditions and laws were... not so much annulled as unobserved. It was not long after bindings between those of the Blood and those not of the Blood had become more or less open secrets that the Jin began to realize their magic was being diluted. The Ancestors instructed their Voices to proclaim an end to such bindings, and so the laws were once again enforced." Asai lifted an eyebrow at Jacin. "Can you speculate as to what the repercussions of that decision might have been, from the Adan's perspective?"

Jacin thought about the implications, concentrated on the political thread alone, and followed it. "The Adan would begin to suspect the Jin were merely trying to keep the magic to themselves."

"Very good, Jacin-rei, very good." Asai was beaming. It warmed Jacin right through. "The Ancestors were descendants of the *Temshiel*, and learned at their knees. They left many teachings before they bound their magic to their people and their lands and gave themselves to Subie. The laws concerning the protection of their lines were quite clear. And when the Untouchables began to go mad, the Jin understood it as punishment for diluting the Blood."

It was said matter-of-factly, no judgment, not even a critical flick of an eye, but Jacin couldn't help how his stomach turned over and his cheeks warmed. Untouchables. *Mad.*

Except he also couldn't help noting that the timeline was very different from the one he'd been taught—according to everything he'd ever heard, the Untouchables hadn't begun to go mad until well into the Binding War itself, when the land to which the Ancestors had bound themselves was razed by the Jin to drive away the *Temshiel* and maijin who'd interfered on behalf of the gods. He'd never heard the Untouchables had been a factor in starting it.

"The *Temshiel*," Asai went on, "fought on the side of the Adan, while maijin fought for the Jin." He sat back and waved a hand, his expression sad. "A hard betrayal by the *Temshiel*, for they'd always before been the… I suppose you would say guardians to the Jin, though it was the place of the maijin to be such advocates to mortals, and thus unprecedented." He smirked. "*Temshiel* are ever the obedient hands of their gods." His mien sobered, and he looked at Jacin closely. "When the gods instructed the *Temshiel* to subdue the Jin, the *Temshiel* obeyed. Many of the Jin's troubles can be laid directly at the feet of the *Temshiel*. The maijin assisted your people and advocated as they could, but in the end, it simply was not enough."

Jacin frowned again. According to Vonshi's tutoring, it wasn't as though either *Temshiel* or maijin had much of a choice. They weren't allowed to defy orders from their gods, not like mortals could. And Jacin had a bit of a difficult time believing that maijin—whose main roles seemed to be as troublemakers and bogeys to frighten children—could actually be considered champions for the Jin. And if they were, what did that make the Jin?

"So…" Jacin's voice was too soft, Asai would not approve, so he cleared his throat. "It would seem just, I suppose. The Ancestors gave themselves so their wisdom would not be lost, so they could speak through the Untouchables, and when the Jin abandoned their decree, their Voices were lost. The Jin are being punished."

Asai's version had to be the right one. Didn't it?

Asai was shaking his head, but his smile was still warm and approving. "An unfortunate side effect, perhaps, but no, not punishment. I doubt the Ancestors foresaw the toll their laws would take on their Voices.

"No, I think rather the Ancestors were well intentioned but ultimately shortsighted. Even the full-Blood is not powerful enough to see so far ahead into the future. One would need the Blood of..." Asai paused, narrowing his eyes at the table. "The dilution and subsequent reduction of power in the Jin as a whole is likely what has caused the Voices of the Ancestors to diverge from the paths of wisdom and into madness." He peered at Jacin, dark eyes intense. "All of it made possible by the interference and machinations of the *Temshiel*. That is why, my boy, we must do as we can to save your people from their bondage, and thus restore the Voices to sanity. With every bound soul the Adan stamp out or enslave, the Ancestors' cries intensify. We must stop it before the full-Blood lines are permanently eradicated."

Jacin thought of Joori, of his mother, and held back a shudder.

"It is why you must dedicate yourself to your training." Asai's voice was gentler now. "I know sometimes I can be... harsh."

"No, Beishin." Jacin shook his head. "My control—"

"*Is* improving, Jacin-rei, never lose heart." The sincerity, the approval in Asai's gaze made Jacin's heart flip. "You have come a long way, my boy. You've a long way to go, yet, but there is time. You will be what you need to be when the time is right."

My boy. It always made stupid, embarrassing tears rise to the backs of Jacin's eyes.

"I will be what you need me to be, Beishin."

Jacin knew very well it involved killing. He didn't know whom, but... did it matter? He'd be doing it for Asai, for Joori, for his mother, for his people. Any who would enslave and use an entire people, any who threatened the ones Jacin loved... surely they deserved whatever they got.

"I know you will, Jacin-rei." Asai stood, rubbing his hands together. "And now, I must prepare for my guest. You will remember about the charm, yes?"

Jacin touched the little amulet. "Of course, Beishin."

"Of course." Asai gave Jacin another pat on the shoulder as he passed him on the way to the door. "It would not do for word to spread that Lord Asai is thwarting law and tradition by treating an Untouchable with love and respect."

That one brought the idiotic tears back, and this time, Jacin's throat clogged. Love and respect. *Love* and respect.

"And Jacin-rei?" Asai paused in the doorway, peering back at Jacin over his shoulder.

"Yes, Beishin?"

"Should you… overhear something…" Asai tilted a knowing little smile that heated Jacin's cheeks. "Always remember that what one says is not always what one believes, nor is it that for which he will fight, in the end. Sometimes we must say what another wants to hear, in order to gain or keep an ally."

⛩

"I understand what you're saying, Asai. But you must see—arranging a judgeship is… delicate, to say the least."

Asai's eyebrows rose. "Why, Sonji, are you saying there is something you cannot do?"

Jacin almost snorted when the fat lord flushed and scowled.

"'Cannot' is one thing. 'Will not' is quite another."

"Ah." Asai took a sip of his tea. "Tell me, Sonji—does Jin magic frighten you?"

Sonji's teabowl hit his saucer with enough force to slop the tea over its rim. "I *beg* your pardon!"

Asai held up a hand, placating. "I mean no insult. It's only that I should like things to be clear between us. If you won't because you fear the magic, well, then…" He shrugged, unconcerned. "However, if you won't because you don't believe in the Adan's policies…"

Sedition hung in the air, so thick Jacin could almost feel it himself from the shadows crouching on the narrow gallery above the two men in Asai's formal parlor.

"An accusation of treason from Lord Asai," Sonji said slowly, "could surely ruin a man."

"Oh, worse, I'm quite certain." Asai smiled cordially and waved it away, dismissive. "I do not accuse, dear Sonji. I merely inquire." He set his bowl on its saucer, leaned forward. "Taru is a like-minded man. If he were set into a judgeship, he would be… beneficial to other like-minded men. It is no secret that the Courts funnel the doomed to those who are willing to pay for their magic. The people of Ada would not approve. And yet it continues, because the judges are men who appreciate their comforts a little too much. However." Asai eyed Sonji sharply. "If the Courts were peopled by the right judges, men who would, perhaps… ensure such valuable Blood was not spilled and wasted…" He picked up his tea, and sat back. "Taru would ensure that the Blood would, shall we say, travel the proper channels."

"And you have a particular proper channel in mind, I assume?"

Asai merely looked at Sonji steadily. The affirmation was unspoken but clear.

That… couldn't be right. It sounded like Asai was arguing *for* using Jin Blood to… No, he was just being careful in his wording, phrasing it so his words couldn't be used against him. Protecting himself. And Jacin certainly wanted Asai to protect himself. Jacin thought of what could happen, should Sonji leave here and go to the Courts, level a charge against Asai.

Disaster. On too many levels to count.

The men were silent for quite a while, before Sonji finally sighed and shook his head. "It is not an easy thing, what you propose."

Asai smiled, wide and pleased. "Which is why it is a task for a man who can do the impossible."

It made sense, now that Jacin thought about it, latched onto the political thread, and followed it through the noise. Perhaps these men they were talking about—these judges who sold doomed full-Bloods to those who stole their magic—were the very ones Jacin would one day be called upon to execute. Cut their throats or stick a knife through their ribs, then remove their hearts from their chests to be sure they could never be reborn. The thought failed to horrify.

Always remember that what one says is not always what one believes, Asai had told Jacin. And Asai had already made it abundantly clear what he really believed. He'd risked his life, he'd risked everything when he took Jacin from that camp. He continued to risk it all to save the Jin. Save Joori. Save their mother.

The talk moved on to more mundane, social matters while Jacin pondered and half-listened. It segued into mutual invitations and well-wishing to Sonji's family while Asai led Sonji cordially to the door and saw him out.

Jacin kept his shadows, crouched up on the gallery, watching Asai walk slowly back into the parlor, pick up his tea again and take a sip, grimace; it must have gone cold. Relaxed, careless, Asai set the bowl back in its saucer and sank into the cushions of the couch with a sigh.

"Have you any questions, Jacin-rei?" He stared straight ahead, out the window and over the lush grounds.

Jacin stood slowly, whispering the spell to drop the shadows. "No, Beishin."

Because he really didn't. Because this was Beishin.

And Jacin believed.

7

"I *know* there was a botched raid six weeks ago." Malick leaned over the cup warmer and the cards they weren't really playing, letting the temperature of his gaze drop a few obvious degrees. "I want to know what *exactly* happened and why no one will talk about it."

Denchai cut a glance to all points, taking in the crowd and the noise and the smoke, hopefully concluding that they wouldn't be overheard. "It was just—" His voice broke and he cleared his throat. Young, poor, and a little too easily intimidated for a doujoun, which made him rather useful to Malick, generally. Until now, anyway. "It was just another raid. That's all anyone knew. It's only... well, it didn't quite... work out." Denchai's fingers nervously twiddled with the silver buttons of his surcoat.

"Didn't work out how?"

"Well, the raids don't often end in dead hunters, for one." Denchai reached for one of the cups and tossed the liquor back. He shook his head. "I wasn't on duty, Mal, and no one who was will talk about it. Timura was *there*, and it's like he doesn't even remember it."

Malick cut a surreptitious glance to Shig over at the Luck table as he refilled Denchai's cup. Shig didn't even look up at him, only angled a small, casual nod and threw her stones. Malick sighed. Brilliant.

So, whatever else happened the night Fen's mother was taken, it appeared that—one way or another—there were no witnesses, and so no one who could give Malick a clear trail to follow. And this was the first Malick was hearing apparent evidence that the Doujou had the ability to mess with people's minds so blatantly. The only magic they'd used up 'til now had been that contained in the hunters' amulets. The implications of Denchai's news were not good. And considering that Malick had got fuck-all else so far...

A waste of another night. Malick had already spent the last several here on the public floor of the Girou, chatting with the regulars, listening, digging, but this wasn't a subject that arose in casual conversation.

Even those with senses dulled from drink or poppy were careful to keep away from even talking about magic, and walked quickly away when it came up. Perhaps individual chats with Umeia's lads and ladies were in order. It couldn't hurt. And it wasn't as though anything else was working.

"Well, fuck it all, then." Malick sighed, and folded his cards down on the table. He slid what was left of his stake over to Denchai. "But if you hear anything..."

"Right." Denchai said it with obvious relief. A nervous smile ticced at the corner of his mouth as he eagerly snatched up the koins. "Anything at all, Mal, you know you can count on me."

Yeah, all the way to the bottom of my purse.

Malick merely put on an easy grin and stood, gaze slanting over toward the bar where he'd last seen Madi. If Malick was going to start covertly questioning the help, he might as well enjoy it.

ᛏ

"And exactly how does catting about downstairs count as looking for my mother?"

Fen's tone was, if not exactly deadly, at least fairly dangerous. Everything else about him, though, was blank with stiff-necked control.

Malick was only half-aware of it. He was too busy watching through a still-bleary haze as Fen prepared his breakfast. Malick had twigged to Fen's strange meal routines by lunch of the second full day of Fen's residence, and since then, they'd become Malick's favorite daily entertainment.

"It *is* looking of a sort." Good old Samin. A decent sort for a cold-blooded killer. "You'd be surprised what people will tell a whore sometimes."

Malick had missed breakfast and lunch the first day, but he'd joined the others in their new shared common room thereafter without fail. They sat, as Umeia had teased, like a family, all gathered at the table, sharing the large dishes of various courses Samin and the girls took turns fetching from the kitchens.

It was... odd, in the beginning, the new arrangement, and Malick didn't know why at first, but he got it pretty quickly. Besides what he was finding to be very interesting conversation over the shared meals, there was the surprising realization that he was getting to know Samin and Shig and Yori better in a week of casual togetherness than he had in the years previous. Who knew Shig ever even looked at men, let alone had a crush on one of the bouncers? And who knew Samin would come over all protective auntie when he heard it?

Mostly, though, there was also the added fascination of watching Fen.

"Exactly which 'whore' are we talking about?" Fen muttered, snide.

Yori barked a laugh. Even Shig chuckled.

Malick just kept staring, absently chewing on… well, he had no idea what he was eating, actually. Almost every bit of his attention was on what Fen was doing. Because Malick's favorite part would be coming aaaaaaany minute now.

Tea, with every meal—one bowl, strong and scalding hot, with nothing added to weaken its natural flavor; always set to the upper left of Fen's rice bowl. One small mound of rice, the portion of which was so precise Malick thought he could probably count the grains each time, and each time, he'd come up with the same number; the rice was always centered exactly in the middle of the bowl before Fen broke the egg yolk over it with the tips of his henjiisticks. At breakfast and lunch, there was a small cup of broth set to the right of the rice bowl and a slice of bread to the left—for breakfast, exactly two equal-sized dollops of clover honey were added to the bread, spread out in a precise, thin layer; for lunch, it was a single spoonful of monyo-butter and a half helping of cabbage. Supper was the same as lunch, except there was a serving of whatever meat or fish was sent up, minus the cabbage but plus a half mugful of watered beer, and one of the sweet bean-paste squares Malick had covertly asked Ragi to add to their evening meals once he'd learned of the new routine. Again, as it had apparently been at Asai's, no one but Fen ate the nasty little things.

Breakfast, though… breakfast was what Malick thought he lived for these first several days, and was sorry as hell that he'd missed the first one. Because Fen had his one vegetable a day with lunch, his one serving of meat a day with supper, but at breakfast, he had his serving of fruit. An oblate, to be precise. And watching him eat it had to be one of the more arousing, riveting things Malick had seen in his life.

The skin peeling away at the tips of nimble fingers, sticky with juice. The pieces opening into succulent, ruby sections, segmented individually and set like a burst of wet, rosy petals on the plate. Pink tongue sliding from between full lips, white teeth sinking into fleshy red fruit, juice in a tiny spray caught by roseate lips and licked from fingers with meticulous deliberation.

The first time Malick had watched it, he'd had to make a run for his room halfway through, and that only because he knew all the whores would still be asleep. Umeia would kill him if one of them complained he'd woken them because he'd just watched Fen make love to an oblate and needed relief *right now*.

Fen's lips would be sour-sweet, Malick decided as he watched Fen take his first bite. A little cool from the chill of juice. He'd taste tangy, and his tongue would have a fizzy zing that would trickle into Malick's mouth as he—

"…tonight."

Malick vaguely heard Fen's clipped tone, but he was more interested in the tiny pink droplet of juice hovering just at the edge of Fen's bottom lip as he spoke.

"…join me…"

It took another second or two, but the sense of the words finally wriggled through the remnants of poppy and liquor and lust and lack of sleep that hovered around Malick's head like a sticky cloud.

Tonight. Join me.

Malick's bloodshot eyes popped wide and he sat up straight. "Sorry, what?"

Fen's lip curled, but not before his slick, pink tongue poked out to slide over his lip and catch the stray droplet of juice.

"I said I'm going to Pon's. Tonight. Join me or not, but I'm going, and you won't stop me."

Malick merely blinked several times, ignored Yori's muffled snorts, and gave Fen a nod.

"Pon's. Tonight. Right."

Because the others would likely notice if Malick ripped the damned oblate out of Fen's hands and fucked him right there on the floor. It would probably piss Fen off a little too.

⚊

"Get your bloody hands *off* of me!"

"As soon as you calm the hell down and stop fighting me!"

Fen stopped, but Malick could still feel the muscles under his hands, tensed and wound tight to spring.

"I can't…" Fen paused and sucked in a shaky breath. "Stop. Fucking. *Touching me.*"

He'd tried to break away from Malick the second the light in Pon's bedroom was put out. Tried to bolt to the house and ruin every moment of the last three hours he and Malick had just spent surveying the place, learning its routines, counting its staff. Tried to drive right in and kill Pon in his bed so he could search the house for the source of the magic Malick could feel slithering out in a weak pulse.

Malick had Fen now in an almost full-body hold, trying to make sure none of those damned knives came at him while still keeping Fen from doing what Malick had to admit he'd want to do himself, if their positions were reversed. Then again, if their positions were reversed, Malick didn't think he'd be fighting so hard to get out of it.

Still, Malick had been on the receiving end of Fen's offense before—if Fen *really* wanted to get loose, he could've done it already. Which meant Fen didn't really mind the hold. And Malick didn't think it was all about the quiet anymore.

"We can't go get him now. Understand? We *can't*." They could, actually. It would be pretty easy. But then Malick would have to use magic, and he didn't want to give that away if he didn't have to. "We go home tonight, we plan tomorrow, and *then* we can go in."

"And what if she's there?"

"Then she'll still be there tomorrow or the night after." Malick tightened his grip when Fen gave a little jerk in his arms, but Fen still didn't fight with everything. "She's not going anywhere, Fen."

Clearly the wrong thing to say, because *then* Fen fought with everything.

It was abruptly like trying to hold an eel—*twist, jerk, slip, jolt*, before Fen's elbow slammed into Malick's ribs as Fen snapped sideways and out of Malick's hold. Malick had to bend over and press at his ribs.

"Fucking *ow*, Fen!"

"Fuck you." Raspy and a little bit shaky. "Just…*fuck you*." Fen backed a pace, seething, before he turned and stalked away. Luckily in the opposite direction of Pon's house and out of the paths of the guards' circuits.

Malick supposed he should be grateful Fen spent most of his time controlling every minute reaction, or Malick might have ended up with a knife in the ribs, as opposed to an elbow. With a scowl, Malick followed Fen's retreat back the way they'd come.

"Don't fucking touch me," Fen snapped when Malick caught up to him. He rounded on Malick only briefly, but it was with a glare so malevolent Malick stopped where he was and pulled back the hand that had been mindlessly reaching for Fen's shoulder. "If she's—" Fen clenched his teeth, visibly pulling his control down around him in a tight fist. "It'll be on *your* head. Understand? *Your fault*. And I. Will fucking. *Kill* you."

He didn't wait for Malick to reply; he merely spun and stalked away again. Which was kind of good, because Malick didn't really have a reply, anyway. He merely followed after Fen again, thinking, keeping the stiff back in his sight as they made their way back home.

Blame. Well, that was at least a change from being alternately sneered at or ignored. Fen couldn't take his anger out on Asai, where it belonged, so he'd take it out on Malick because Malick was handy.

Or maybe Fen just didn't like that Malick could get reactions out of him.

Because Fen wanted Malick. Other people might mistake Fen's attitude for loathing, but Malick was very good at reading a body—even one that couldn't be "touched" with magic—and he knew bloody well what Fen's was telling him. So why was Fen fighting it so hard, damn it?

Don't fucking touch me.

Malick couldn't help miming the words and making a face at Fen's back like a five-year-old.

Damn it, Fen would have let Malick have him that day in Malick's rooms, all Malick would have had to do was swoop in and seize him in his weak moment. And it either pissed Fen off that he wanted Malick, or that Malick hadn't taken the opportunity. Or maybe that he'd had a weak moment at all.

Malick only wished he knew which.

╥

He was almost getting used to waking up with Madi scrunched against him. Almost getting used to the bit of disappointment at realizing where he was and who he was with—and who he *wasn't* with—and the slow throb of too much liquor the night before still wending through his veins. Almost getting used to wondering a little blearily whose name he'd been muttering into skin that was smooth and damp with sweat but didn't smell of almonds.

Shit. He should probably put a stop to this before it got out of hand. This made it… well, at least three nights this week with Madi. That Malick could remember. Madi was a sweet lad, and Malick didn't want things to get… unpleasant. He gently extracted himself from the loose grip, got dressed, and left his koin on the press.

He'd slept through breakfast. Which only added to the low level of irritation that had been steadily building in Malick for days. He shut the door silently and headed upstairs, stopping at Umeia's door only long enough to be told that no, there'd been no new notes waiting in the jar, before the door shut in his face.

Yeah, well, fuck you too.

A week, and still no answer from the Mage. And it was pissing Malick off. Almost enough that he considered simply not fulfilling tonight's commission, but… only almost. He couldn't take this one away from Fen. If, however, Malick still hadn't got an answer from the Mage when the next job came—or if he got an answer he didn't like—he would reconsider his loyalties.

It was too quiet when Malick climbed the attic stairs. He hadn't been paying attention to the sounds of the Girou around him, nor had he noticed the set of the suns, but damn it, he'd apparently missed lunch too.

Fine, then. He'd just go up to watch the sparring, kill some time, because he was pissy and at loose ends and a little antsy about the job tonight, and… well, what else did he have to do with himself? Despite what Fen obviously thought, Malick really was trying. Because Malick would give just about anything to find Fen's mother someplace other than where he was growing more certain every day she actually was.

All obvious avenues had been temporarily exhausted, though.

Samin had put the word out to his two doujoun contacts, but wouldn't hear back from either of them unless they heard something pertinent. Umeia had put a whisper into Judge Canti's ear, but it would likely take days before he could give her anything useful. A visit needed to be paid to Malick's informant in the east camp. Malick had promised Fen it was next on the list, after this job was done tonight.

A damned lot of care needed to be taken in hunting up information on Asai's doings. Tread very lightly, be bloody sure of sources before asking them the wrong questions, that was the key. And it was all a lot more difficult than Fen seemed to think it was. Damn it, Malick *deserved* to dip down into drink and debauchery every chance he got. He was working bloody hard at all this.

"Bloody hell," Samin was saying when Malick reached the roof door. "Give a man a chance, why don't you. Here, when you block with the cross like that, bring your other arm up and you can get a good punch in right under the jaw. See? Do it hard enough and you'll break some teeth, at least—send a man's jawbone up into his brain at best."

Malick hung back and watched, noting with keen interest how Fen listened attentively to Samin's instructions in hand-to-hand then did exactly what Samin told him to do in exactly the way Samin had told him to do it. No mistakes, no deviations, and Fen always got it right the first time. He hit every mark, and always remembered to keep his guard up. *Step-turn-jab-hook-cross-counter.*

Still doing things by rote—perfectly by rote, but still rote. They were going to have to work on the principle behind the words *lateral thinking*, but Malick would see how Fen did on the job tonight before making any suggestions.

They switched to the knives while Yori and Shig went back and forth between lazily wrestling and stopping to watch Samin and Fen. This time, Fen was the teacher, and it was really something to watch.

They worked in a strange alchemy of nonverbal expression on Fen's part and a near-constant stream of banter on Samin's. He joked good-naturedly with Fen, providing both the straight lines and the punch lines, with the laughter supplied by Shig and Yori, if they weren't busy putting each other into headlocks. Fen never answered, never laughed, but Samin seemed to interpret the silence in any way he felt appropriate, just like he did with the apparently mute instructions in knife work. Whether Samin really could deduce what Fen wanted from him by a shift of eyes alone or not, neither of them ended up seriously hacked, so Malick supposed it was working for them. And Samin could use a better offense than just his fists. He'd not needed it thus far, but one never knew, and Malick preferred all his people be as well prepared as possible. And it would be nice to know that no one was ever going to get Fen down in the way Malick had done.

All in all, Malick approved.

He waited for an opening. When Fen and Samin disentangled from a particularly intense deadlock, backing away from each other with knives lowered and bowed heads, signaling the finish or at least a break, Malick stepped up.

"Nice work." He smiled, all easy affability, and peered specifically at Fen. "Care for a go?"

Because the idea of having an excuse to be so close again was making Malick's mouth water. The oblates were bloody *killing* him.

Fen wanted. He just didn't *want* to want. And he had no problem punishing Malick for it.

Stubborn prick.

So Malick figured that sparring was a good excuse. Get in close, give Fen another taste of the silence, get him wanting—get him admitting to the wanting.

But Fen merely stared at Malick for a bit too long, slipped his knives into the sheaths at his belt, and shook his head. And then he walked off, Shig following happily after him.

No "thank you, anyway," no "perhaps another time"—Fen merely made his way across the roof, opened the door for Shig, and then let himself through it without looking back.

Fucking stubborn prick.

"It isn't you." Samin was smirking. He jerked his chin at the door. "It's only that we have lunch, he meditates for half an hour, we spar, then he has a bath. I didn't realize it was going to be a daily thing. Caught me out the second day when I found him haunting my door with his knives strapped on. Didn't say anything, either, just walked off down the hall and waited for me by the stairs."

"Routines," Yori put in. She smiled when Malick turned to her, stretched her legs out in front of her where she lounged up on the wide ledge, hands propped behind her, deftly missing the spatters of old bird shit, dried and baked to flat, gray powder on the clay by the suns. "I didn't get it, either. But Shig got pissy with me the other day when I laughed about it. Said if I had no control over anything in my own head, I'd probably want it over everything else too." She shrugged, closed her eyes, and tilted her face up into the sunlight, her midlength gold hair, loosed from its habitual tail and slightly mussed, catching the light in a bright corona. "Doesn't really make it less funny, though."

Malick toed a pebble. "Shig's quite taken with him."

Yori snorted. "Shig's dying to braid his hair, and he keeps not letting her. But yeah, she really likes him. I guess I do, too, though he's more work than I'd put up with if you weren't making me. You really have to watch his eyes to know what he's thinking. Surprisingly, he's not generally thinking of murdering us, even if his face says so."

Bloody—

Malick had to clench his teeth. Did *everyone* get along with Fen better than Malick did? Like Fen was a sun, pulling them inexorably into his orbit without even trying. Probably without even wanting to.

No, not like a sun—like a black fucking hole, sucking Malick into a hopeless trajectory, eating up reason like a void ate light.

"Sounds about right." Samin dug an oily cloth out of his tunic and started wiping down his knife. "He's still here—he's got a use for us."

Malick studied Samin carefully. "Still don't trust him?"

"Depends on what you want me to trust him for." Samin eyed the knife's tip before giving the blade another swipe. "He takes the job seriously. We go out tonight with a new man we had to almost knock unconscious and threaten to assassinate if he didn't come along, and strangely, I trust him to watch my back while we're on the job. He needs structure, routine. He probably needs it like we need food. Right now, we're giving it to him."

"Didn't know you were such a people watcher."

"Don't usually need to be." Samin didn't look up, only watched what his hands were doing. "There are three kinds of people to someone like Fen—those he thinks of as 'mine,' those who don't matter, and those who need to die. We moved from 'those who need to die' when you promised to help find his mother. Right now, we're all hovering just outside of 'mine,' and making ourselves part of his structure will move us into it by the time our job is done tonight." Samin flicked at the tip of his knife with a fingernail, slanting Malick a look. "You wanted him, you've got him. But break his structure, and you're likely to break *him*. I'd have a care, if I were you."

There was a wealth of meaning in both the statement and the look. "A warning, seyh?"

"If you'd care to take it as such, seyh." Samin slipped the knife into his belt, and made a business of stuffing the cloth back into his tunic. "I like him. More than I thought I would. We get on. Even when he's not saying a damn thing, he's more honest than just about anyone I've ever known. His silences don't 'say' anything, but he doesn't fill them up with shit, either."

It made odd sense that Samin and Fen would get along, now that Malick really thought about it. Both of them were brutally blunt, neither of them seemed to know or give a shit when that bluntness went unappreciated, or even when it wounded. And Malick rather thought Samin understood that "three kinds of people" thing so well because it was a view he held himself.

"I trust him." Samin looked back at the door again. "But if he breaks, I'd be the first to take him out. Because if the foundation goes, there's not a whole lot he's got to keep the rest from coming down too. And that man can take someone's head off with one swipe of a blade better than any executioner with an ax in his hand. I don't want to see the poor sap who starts the first crack." He turned back to Malick with a level look. "He's temporary, Mal. More than anyone I've ever met before. That man is measured in moments, not years. You won't hold him, and if you try…"

A definite warning.

Malick thought about swatting Samin down, putting him in his place, but he didn't. However it came out, it was done out of loyalty, worry for Malick himself, and it was quite a lot more astute, for all its wrongness, than Malick ever would have given Samin credit for.

Weirdly accurate, when Malick thought about it—for Samin. Not for Fen.

Samin saw what he saw because he felt a surface kinship with Fen, so he assumed everything on the inside was the same too. But a superficial similarity was all it was. *Samin* liked his routines, *Samin* liked his structure, *Samin* needed to know what to expect. Samin saw structures and walls and crumbling foundations and only insanity waiting behind it, because that's all Samin *could* see. He'd had his own foundation shimmy beneath him in the Doujou, disintegrate shortly after he'd left it, and his sanity ground down beneath his shattering walls until Umeia'd got hold of him.

Malick didn't see walls and structures and stanchions when he looked at Fen. Malick saw a dense layer of ice, and so much more biding beneath it—he just didn't know what yet. Passion, for certain. So much of it beneath all the frost that Malick wondered if there would be any survivors when it finally broke the surface. Malick hoped he was there to find out.

Shig had it righter than Samin did, but control wasn't all it was about, either.

Perfection—that was what Fen was after. All you really had to do was watch him for a day to see it. You merely had to look past the snarls.

Malick met Samin's direct gaze, then tipped a nod. "I expect we'll all have to be careful, then."

⋒

It should've gone beautifully. They'd planned it perfectly. There shouldn't have been a single snag or hitch.

Too bad no one told Pon.

Yori looked down over the small crest that ran along the eastern side of the property. The best vantage, Malick had told them, and only patrolled in a regular circuit, a sentry passing routinely once every half hour or so. It had looked so easy on the drawing, sounded easy when Malick explained the plan. Two sentries around the perimeter, and once all the day staff went home, only a steward and two maids were in residence overnight, besides Pon himself.

Fen and Malick had watched for hours only a few days ago, timed it all, and come back with the plan. No inconvenient wife to try not to accidentally kill, no children who might get in the way. Malick and Shig would go in, question then take out Pon, Fen would locate and take care of the full-Blood, and Yori and Samin would tend to any unlucky sentries who might stumble into an ill-timed circuit. Get in, kill those needing killing, get out, go home.

Yori should have known it sounded too easy.

Samin peered over Malick's shoulder. "Son of a bitch looks like he's packing for an extended holiday. We'll have to call it."

"Someone's warned him." The leather of Fen's gloves creaked as he fisted his hands.

Malick nodded. "I expect that's probably why our orders were for tonight. If we don't get him now…"

"Then we live to tell about it." Samin jerked his chin toward the house. "There are too many, Mal."

Personally, Yori agreed with Samin. There was a ridiculous number of guards and minders swarming the small estate, helping to pack and load carts. A man who looked very close to the description Fen had given them of Pon was directing. It looked like he'd commandeered Sonji's own mercenaries for himself. That was the Sonji heraldry on their hauberks.

But Malick was the boss and he was looking rather ambivalent. "Shig?"

Shig wandered up beside Malick and surveyed the scene. "They're all charmed." She squinted. "Good charms too."

Meaning made from full-Blood, over which Shig had very little influence, half-Blood that she was.

Strange. Yori could understand it with Pon himself, but why hand out protections to all the guards too?

"I could maybe get in through a few of the weaker ones." Shig chewed her lip. "Maybe. That would take care of…" She shut her eyes. "I can do five." Pause. Blink. "Maybe."

Samin grunted. "Definitely warned."

"Shig." Malick's voice had gone tight. "You can or you can't."

Shig scowled first, then looked guiltily at Malick. "Probably not."

"Shit." Malick sighed then ruffled Shig's hair. "It's not your fault, love, no worries. You just keep alert to anyone approaching, yeah? Let's keep this as quiet as we can."

He blew out a breath, irritated. "All right, that's… looks like twenty, at least." His hand flexed over his sword's grip. "What the *fuck*. What does one bloody jumped-up prefect need with all *this*?"

Twenty. Or more. Who knew if there were more in the house they couldn't see?

Yori considered it. She could get at least three from up here before they started to notice, considering their current distraction. Another three or five when they started to charge, and that was assuming her aim was true each time. But with the time for renocking, they'd be on her before she could get many more, even taking into account that they'd be huffing up the rise after her. Those boys looked fit.

That would still leave at least twelve—four or more each for Malick, Samin, and Fen.

Any way Yori looked at it, there were too many of them. Even if they managed to get Pon as ordered, and took out every one of these men in the process, they were still too likely to limp away from it at least one less than they'd come with. She peered around her, unwilling to imagine the group without one of the faces now present. They were her family. Even Fen.

Speaking of…

"Hey." Yori jostled an elbow into Malick's ribs. "Where's Fen?"

Samin frowned. "Fen?"

"Yeah—tall fellow, braid, scary fondness for knives?"

Malick whipped around, eyes quickly studying each of them in turn, as though he thought perhaps Fen might be wearing a Samin-mask and if he looked hard enough…

"Good bloody question." Malick turned again to scan the surroundings, gaze roving over the green, the garden, the roof—

"Fucking *shit*." He jerked forward, as though he meant to make a run for the house, but Samin grabbed his arm and yanked him back. "What the *hell* does he think he's *doing*?"

Shig grinned, her bright head bobbing in the moonlight. Yori followed her gaze, almost laughed when she spied the skulking figure on the roof of the porch, but… it wasn't really funny. Before Yori could even form an opinion on what Fen might be up to, he was swirling down from the rain gutter and right into the center of the clustered guards. Without a single sound, knives flashing, Fen went to work.

Malick just stood there for a second, shaking his head. "Can't help it." He blew out a resigned huff. "I bloody love it when he does that." He shrugged off Samin's grip and jerked his chin at Yori. "We're on."

It was messy. It was chaotic. It was bloodier than Yori had seen in a long time.

It was fucking *exhilarating*.

Fen had got four down before Yori let fly her first arrow—she'd forgotten about his little throwing knives. Everyone else was so busy wondering what was going on, heads turning to look at the sudden commotion in their midst, that they didn't even see Malick coming. He took out three before Yori stopped counting. Samin had moved around to flank them, planting himself between the house and the overgrown gulley at the bottom of the ridge where Yori and Shig still stood.

Yori's bow sang and her arrows flew. She loved when it all narrowed down around her like that—just her and her targets, nothing else in the world but willing her arrows home. It was like her own kind of magic.

A spray of blood caught the corner of Yori's eye. She shifted her glance in time to catch the crumpling form of one of the guards trying to flank Samin, the side of the man's skull blown out.

"I thought you couldn't get any of them." Yori sighted down the line of her arrow as someone made a run at Fen's back.

Shig shrugged. "It looked like too much fun not to try."

Yori couldn't help the grin.

She herself ended up getting Pon. After the initial confusion settled into actual battle, a good number of the men moved in to try to manhandle Pon back inside, forming a circle around him and hustling him behind a cart. When Fen carved his way through three of them, they made a run for the house. Yori picked off the two guards first, then Pon himself—one, two, three.

Easy.

"Fen's going to be pissed." Shig's tone held the tiniest touch of reprimand, but amusement too. "Now we can't question Pon."

…Oh. Right. Yori had kind of forgotten about that part. If Malick didn't kill her, Fen probably would.

"There he goes." Shig sighed. "He'll be looking for the full-Blood."

Yori looked over her shoulder in time to see Fen disappear at a run into the house. Malick and Samin were finishing up the dregs, so all Malick could do was call after Fen then curse—loud and eye-poppingly filthy, even for Malick—when he was ignored.

"He won't find her." Shig sounded… sad, maybe. "She's gone. She was a present."

It was only a moment later when Fen stormed out the house, face set hard and fists still balled tight. He walked right past Malick—who was still cursing—and started sorting through the dead, collecting his knives and searching the corpses for the charms.

"What the *fuck* did you think you were *doing*?" Malick snagged Fen's arm and spun him to his feet.

Fen merely snarled back, wordless, and shook Malick off, then went back to sorting.

They were both blood-spattered, the whole left side of Fen's face dripping with it. Samin came out the better of the three of them, now that Yori could see him.

"You could've got us all *killed*." Malick was clearly livid, and not backing down. "You stupid son of a bitch, just what did you—?"

"I didn't make you engage." Jaw tight, eyes flat, Fen straightened and began to stalk up the hill toward Yori and Shig.

Malick only watched in disbelief for a few seconds before he gathered himself and went after him. Yori prudently stepped back and out of their path and tugged Shig along with her.

"You didn't *make*—?" Malick's eyes had gone dark and dangerous, even in the uncertain light of the half faces of Raven and Dragon and the crescent koin of Wolf. "You didn't *make* us engage? Are you bloody *kidding* me? In case it's escaped you, *I'm* the one in charge here!"

Fen stopped abruptly, stalked back to Malick, knife still drawn and clenched in his hand, but not raised or threatening.

"You were taking too long." He said it in a way that someone else might say, *Die, you slimy fuck!*

Malick looked like he couldn't decide between laughing and punching Fen in the mouth. "I was *taking too long?*"

"He was leaving. Someone warned him off. If we didn't get him tonight, we never would've got him at all. As it is, he's got rid of his full-Blood."

"She was a present."

Fen turned sharply to Shig. "*She?*"

Shig nodded. "She was a present."

Fen merely paced swiftly over to Shig and shoved the bloody charms into her hands. Without a word or so much as another snarl, he pushed past Malick.

Malick grabbed him again. "Where d'you think you're going?"

Fen shook him off. "Sonji-onna." He stalked away. "*She* was a fucking *present.*"

"A... present." Malick stared after Fen, jaw clenched, then turned to Samin. "Anyone hurt?"

Samin sighed, resigned. "I'll get the girls home."

"See Umeia as soon as you get in," Malick said, and took off after Fen.

Samin only gave their backs a sour look, then flapped a hand at Yori and Shig. "Well, let's get on, then." He paused, squinted at Shig through the dark. "What's got you so gloomy, lovie? We won, didn't we?"

Shig merely scowled with an unhappy shrug. "I wanted to go with Fen."

"Oh, for fuck's sake," Yori muttered, rolled her eyes and went to retrieve her arrows.

⛩

The knob of the crooked door turned almost soundlessly. Joori started, then quickly scraped a match against the rough floor, and set it to the candle's wick. He sat back and peered levelly at the door.

Jacin was blinking, eyes adjusting to the sudden light, holding a bulky sack to his chest like a shield. He stared at Joori, sitting calmly against the wall, fully dressed, waiting patiently for his brother.

"You look like shit." Joori kept his voice down; he didn't want to wake the younger ones yet. "Have you slept at all?"

Jacin only kept staring. Joori thought perhaps Jacin was debating just turning around and leaving again without a word, and the fact that it seemed like a very real possibility almost broke Joori's heart.

"I didn't think you'd be awake," Jacin finally said, subdued.

Joori merely gave him a twist of a smile. "Yeah, I figured."

Jacin frowned, looked down. "How did you—?"

"I didn't." Joori shrugged. "But our supplies were getting low, and there's been nothing 'magically' appearing in three mornings. If not tonight, it would've been tomorrow." He narrowed his eyes. "Is that blood on your face?" And then he peered more closely. "For pity's sake, Jacin, you're *covered* in it."

He'd been out again. Hunting.

Wordless, Joori dug through the pile of shirts Jacin had brought him, and threw over a black tunic that was a little too big in the shoulders for Joori. Jacin had filled out quite a lot in the time they'd been apart.

"Did you get them?"

Jacin dropped the sack by his filthy boots and started to change his shirt. "You shouldn't have waited for me. You shouldn't—"

"Shouldn't what? Shouldn't want to see my brother? Shouldn't feel shunned when my brother doesn't want to see me? Shouldn't—" Joori's small tirade died in midquestion. His eyes went wide. "For fuck's sake, Jacin, what've you *done* to yourself?"

Jacin only slipped the clean tunic over his head then torso, covering old scars and new gashes all up and down his upper body, some of them deep and still oozing. A disturbing band of silver nearly ringed his upper arm, one scar on top of the other.

Joori started to rise. "Some of those are fresh. You need to be band—"

"It isn't that I don't want to see you." Jacin's voice was still quiet, almost diffident, but it still stopped Joori and made him sink back down. "You know that, Joori." Jacin pulled the sleeves down over the knives strapped to wrists and forearms then tucked the shirt's tails beneath the belts crisscrossing his hips.

"Do I?" There were tears in Joori's eyes—damn it, he'd wanted to be calm and adult about this, but the distance, the absences, what Jacin was risking during them, all the knives and those fucking *scars*. It all rose up, choking, and Joori locked his jaw tight against it. "What am I to think, Jacin? You come and go like the ghost they name you, only you leave the offerings instead of taking them. You wait 'til we're all asleep, sneak in here in the dead of night and don't even wake me—*me*, Jacin—don't leave so much as a note or even a fucking *footprint*, just food and clothes and blankets, like having those things is better than having *you*. And in between, I don't even know if you're *alive*! Look at yourself—it looks like you've been to war!"

Joori's voice had grown steadily louder as he'd gone on, first stirring then waking Morin and Caidi, who sat up on their mats and blinked blearily between them. Morin stared at Jacin with contempt and a curled lip, but Caidi's pretty face opened in delighted surprise as she leapt up from her blankets, instantly awake.

"I knew you'd come back! *Joori* was worried, but *I* wasn't." She hopped over Morin, darting at Jacin with ingenuous glee. "Morin, Jacin-rei's here!" She glomped onto Jacin and wound her arms around his waist.

"*Jacin*," Joori snapped.

Caidi jerked back like she'd been burned. Her hazel eyes were wide, her face gone abruptly from pleasure to dejection. Damn it, why'd she have to look so like their mother?

A hot twist went through Joori's chest, and he melted—any man would.

"I'm sorry, Caidi, I didn't mean to... you didn't do..." Joori slumped against the wall. "I'm sorry."

Jacin, hadn't so much as lifted a hand toward Caidi when she'd dived at him, hadn't even looked at anything but the floor, that sack once again held between him and everyone else like a shield. Like he needed one.

Joori's throat was tight. "I'm sorry, Jacin. It's only... I've missed you. And I do worry."

The silence stretched, long and uncomfortable.

Morin broke it. "What'd you bring?"

Jacin stirred from his frozen stance, hugged the sack reflexively before jerking it away from his chest. Eyes still on the floor, he swept a soft touch to Caidi's hair then stepped slowly over to the long board fastened to the wall. A dwindling pile of foodstuffs was sorted in one corner. Jacin began unloading his sack.

Morin was watching it all with hostile eyes. "You didn't get that rubbish from any market." He caught Joori's eye and jerked his chin. "Look at it—he's been stealing from the shrines again. He's going to get caught." He swiveled the glare at Jacin's back. "Why don't you just—?"

"It isn't *stealing*." Joori could barely force it through his teeth. "It's what they're *for*, you bloody troll. And I've not seen *you* refuse it. Your belly's full, isn't it, you little prick."

Jacin kept his back turned, kept piling the things he'd brought onto the board, smacking a packet of dried plums that were obviously not from any shrine down with enough force to threaten the flimsy support of the board.

"I was delayed tonight." Amazingly, Jacin's voice was still quiet and even. "The markets were all shut up by the time—" His mouth twisted. "I don't know when I'll be able to come back."

"You shouldn't be coming back at all."

Bloody Morin. Whether he loved or hated Jacin, he was relatively safe, fed, dressed in much better than rags, and had clean bedding on which to sleep—and Jacin had provided every scrap of it. Apparently, the concept of "gratitude" was completely alien to Morin.

"Are those plums?" Caidi's voice was small and hopeful.

Jacin's entire stance softened as he peered at her over his shoulder, and a faint smile Joori thought might make him cry finally curled softly at Jacin's mouth. Save him, for a while there, Joori'd thought perhaps Jacin had forgotten how.

Without a word, Jacin took up the small packet and tossed it gently to land in Caidi's lap.

She beamed at him. "Thank you, *Jacin*." With a smug look at Morin, she pried the packet open.

Joori stood, gave Caidi an approving grin and glared evilly at the troll, then paced the few steps over to Jacin. He stopped abruptly when Jacin's shoulders stiffened.

"Jacin." Joori hadn't intended for it to come out so cautious, but he couldn't seem to help it. "I don't mean to... to sound greedy, but... I know you—"

"Things are not... not in my control at the moment." Jacin's back was still rigid, his posture wound tight, and everything about him vibrated tension in the close little hut. "I don't have..." He clenched his teeth. "I lost the shadow charm. It's harder getting supplies without it."

"You *lost* it?" As if Morin got to have an opinion. "How could you bloody *lose*—?"

"Shut *up*, Morin." Joori glared until Morin knew he meant it.

"Yeah, shut up, *Moooooorin*," Caidi echoed, smacking her lips around her sticky treat and pulling faces at Morin.

"I'll come as often as I can." Jacin said it to the food still in his hands, rather than to Joori. "I swear to you, you won't starve, I won't just leave you here. Only..." Finally, he turned and looked Joori in the eye. "A little more time. I'm trying to arrange a safer place for you, but I don't... I just can't tell yet if the people are to be trusted. If nothing else, there's a caravan that leaves for Heldesan midmonth. I've almost enough koin to buy your way onto it, but I can't... the drover won't take partial payment, and I need one more—" He looked away. "Give me... perhaps a few days. Maybe a little more. One way or another, I'll have two hundred tomorrow and then another two hundred next week. It'll be enough. I *won't* fail you."

"Jacin..." It almost made Joori weep. "When have you ever failed at anything?"

Jacin didn't answer, only shut his eyes tight and clamped his jaw. When he looked up again, his face was almost completely blank.

"I've another name."

"Another..." Joori's gut took slow sliding turn. "You think... maybe...?"

Jacin shrugged. "I always think maybe. I thought tonight, but."

The silence fell again. Caidi had burrowed back into her blankets, sitting beside Morin the troll, both of them watching their brothers calmly discuss assassinating the one responsible for the destruction of their already difficult lives. The troll was still sneering, obviously wanting to snark his way into the conversation but not quite daring. Caidi was watching Jacin with shining eyes, a strange awe Joori wouldn't have credited before she'd watched Jacin emerge from the ruin of their home, flames at his back and blood on his knives, and a shadow charm that got them past the few doujoun Jacin had left alive, and out of the camp.

With a determined set to his jaw, bracing himself, Joori laid a firm hand to Jacin's arm. He expected the flinch but was still dismayed when he got it.

"Jacin... you keep talking like you plan to bundle us into wagons and wave us goodbye." Joori tightened his grip. "You *said* you'd think about it. You said you'd—"

"I can't have this conversation right now." Jacin pushed off Joori's hand, stepped back, and crouched down to give Caidi a quick hug and a kiss to the top of her head, but peeled her off again before she was ready to let go. "We'll talk again." As though that ended the conversation, Jacin turned and walked to the door.

"When?" Joori followed, but Jacin was already out and swishing his way through scrub and weed and vine. "*When* will we talk, Jacin? When you're watching the back of me?"

"Keep your voice down!" Jacin hissed, but he didn't stop, just kept walking away, leaving Joori behind like it didn't matter.

Joori blinked after him, watched until Jacin disappeared into the trees. Heedless, Joori shouted, "I'm the one, Jacin! She said so! No laws, remember?" He listened, but heard nothing but Jacin's footsteps slowly getting less and less audible with each swift step. Slumping, Joori stared out into the yard, breathing hard, trying not to weep. "You're supposed to be the one too." He dropped his chin to his chest and leaned into the ancient, splintered wood of the doorjamb.

"Let him go." Morin's petulant tone was just too much. "You can't keep expecting him to—"

"*Don't.*" Joori turned slowly, leveled a glare at Morin, keeping the rumble in his core under control by nothing more than will and the insidious knowledge that if he allowed so much as a tremor beneath his feet, it would likely take hold of everything seething in his chest and open up the ground from here to Subie. And then they'd *really* be fucked. "One more time, Morin. *One more fucking word*, and we'll just see who's the bloody ghost in the family. *Won't* we?"

Somehow, when Morin paled and looked away, Joori wasn't nearly as satisfied as he should have been.

Sleep wouldn't come for Samin, and for no good reason. He wasn't particularly worried about anything. All was well as far as he knew. Fen and Malick had been late, but they'd made it home, Samin had heard them come in—Fen first, then Malick about half an hour later—so it wasn't that.

It wasn't the job tonight. That had actually been sort of fun. They'd gone, they'd done the job, they'd made a bit of a mess, but they'd all walked away without injury as far as Samin knew, though he didn't know if Malick or Fen had had any trouble at Sonji-onna's; if they had, Samin figured he would've heard Umeia shrilling by now. And the fact that Fen was up on the roof as usual rather implied they were both fine. So, it couldn't be that.

It was a little early for Samin to be abed, maybe, but Fen had been wearing him out lately, and it was beginning to catch up. Samin was bone-weary. And still, no matter how heavy his eyelids got, sleep eluded him. He could blame it on the noise from downstairs, he supposed, but he'd got used to that years ago, so it wasn't a good excuse. And it was perhaps a little warm for the time of year, but a cool breeze was sliding pleasantly into the room from his open window, so that wasn't it, either.

The light, rhythmic thudding from above, that was it. Had to be. Another thing that had quickly become a routine when Fen arrived, and it hadn't bothered Samin before, but this time...

Not Fen's fault—Samin reminded himself sternly of that. If Samin hadn't been listening for it, he never would have heard it. Fen was obviously a night person. He couldn't go traipsing about the city, not without Shig or Malick, and somehow Samin didn't think the idea of dragging Shig around back alleys in the middle of the night would even occur to Fen. And he certainly wouldn't ask Malick. So he'd taken to sparring shadows on the roof. And tonight, for whatever reason, it was bothering Samin. Actually, this morning, now that Samin looked at the set of the moons out the window.

Grumbling, he flung the sheets back, bullied his way into the trousers he'd left in a heap on the floor, and stomped out of the room, heading for the stairs. To do what, he had no idea. He couldn't exactly send Fen to bed. But it was either this or go find himself some company downstairs, and if it was this late—early—all the good ones would be otherwise occupied. Malick had probably already dug in with one of the girls,

Samin thought sourly. Or one of the boys, more likely—Malick had been tending toward pretty dark-haired lads these days more often than not. Which made Samin smirk, and not terribly kindly.

Except Malick apparently wasn't getting busy with one of the lads—he was at the top of the roof stairs, slouching against the open door, utterly still and silent. Samin didn't know whether to snort or scowl. Fuck, but Malick was gone on Fen already, and he didn't even know it. The lust was bad enough—if Samin had to watch Malick watch Fen eat an oblate *one more time*—but the fascination was getting entirely out of control. And all the snapping and snarling in the world from Fen wasn't going to dampen it. In fact, it seemed to do exactly the opposite. Samin had never thought the words "Malick" and "idiot" at the same time so often in his life as he had over the past week. And the really sad part about it was that it wasn't exactly one-sided. The little Ghost wanted too—he just didn't want to *let* himself want.

Everything was proceeding exactly as Samin had been afraid it would. Except somehow, he'd actually come to like Fen, which just pissed Samin off more. And if Samin ended up having to kill Fen, he'd have both Malick and Shig pissed off at him.

With a sigh, Samin plodded up the steps. Malick heard him immediately, turned when Samin hit the third step, and silently placed a finger to his lips. Samin rolled his eyes and kept coming.

Spin, lunge, feint, attack. Just as Samin had known.

He scrubbed at his hair. "Did you take care of things with Sonji-onna?"

Malick didn't take his eyes off Fen. "Not nearly as many guards. Must've given them all to Pon. And Fen got a name out of her. He was... something to watch. Fucking *ruthless.*" He smiled, soft and admiring. "After he thought I'd gone, he went back and raided her larder. Can you imagine?"

Samin thought about that for a minute but decided it was just too... bizarre for comment. "Will the Mage be... upset?"

"We took care of the full-Blood. If he's upset, he's not someone I want to work for." Malick bobbed a nod toward Fen. "D'you know he makes pyres for them, sends them to the gods?"

"Uh... no." Neither did Samin necessarily care, but he did wonder why it impressed Malick enough to make the comment. "So, it wasn't his mother, then?"

Malick only shook his head.

Too damn bad. Samin thought maybe these all-night sparring sessions might drop off a little, if they could find the lad's mother for him and put her soul to rest.

"He went for another walk tonight, after," Malick said, out of the blue, as though having a conversation with someone else entirely. "I followed him again."

Samin frowned. "Another?" He hadn't known Fen had been for any "walks." He hadn't thought Malick would allow it.

"Same place he went that first night." Malick leaned more heavily into the door. "I almost let him see me, almost let him know I knew, but..."

Samin waited, but when Malick didn't go on, he asked, "Knew what?"

"That thing you were talking about before—routines. D'you know he even has them for that?" Malick whiffled a small grim laugh, vague and bemused. "Over the gate, stand up there and watch the moons for a while, jump down, stare at the bodies—even the ones still weeping for rescue, or just twitching away the last of themselves—then shudder, go on his way. And then he stares again on his way back through. Morbid, our little Ghost. He doesn't even need his shadows, really. He's so bloody quiet, they never even know he's there. He climbs the gate twenty paces away from them, and they never even look. Like he really is a ghost.

"I think he'll tell us soon enough." Malick paused, narrowing his eyes when Fen stopped and tilted his head to the side. "I was coming at it all wrong before. I almost made it worse. Too edgy. It's bubbling up in him, and I don't think he can keep it back for long. Too much pressure. Everything about tonight made it worse. I've always had shit timing." He sighed a little sadly. "It must kill him to see them. He weeps every time. Just stops where he's standing for... maybe ten seconds, that's it, and then he just..." Malick turned to Samin, thoughtful. "Ten seconds can't be enough for anyone. Can't get rid of it in ten seconds, can you?" He turned back to watch Fen. "Failure—that's what it is, y'know. Fear of failure."

It made Samin's teeth clench. The roundabout twists made him feel like he was talking to Shig. "Malick, what the *fuck* are you on about?"

Malick eyed Samin through the moonlit dark, smiled at him in a way that almost made Samin want to deck him—all soft and faraway—before he turned back and set his distant gaze once again on Fen.

"His name's Jacin-rei, but he doesn't like it. That was a mistake, too, calling him that. Those people he considers his, you said—they call him Jacin."

How the fuck d'you know? Samin wanted to snap, *And who the fuck cares, anyway?* but instead, he ventured, "I didn't know he had a name," because he really hadn't, hadn't even thought about it. Fen had told Samin to call him Fen, and that was as far as Samin had ever thought to consider.

"That..." It was like Malick hadn't heard, staring as Fen went down on one knee and dropped one of his knives with a clatter. "That doesn't look right."

"It never looks right." Samin couldn't help the irritable grimace. "Damn disconcerting, it is. Yori was worried it would happen during a job. What's he doing, anyway?"

Malick flashed Samin a short glare over his shoulder, then turned back to watch as Fen's empty hand came up, took hold of his braid, and yanked. Hard.

"Listening, I think, but..." Malick leaned forward, head cocked just like Fen's. "D'you hear it?"

Samin frowned, leaned in too. He wouldn't have noticed it, unless Malick had pointed it out, but now that he had... yes. Whispering. Fen was whispering to himself in a steady stream, low hisses through his teeth, then heavy bursts of breath, like he was having a hard time getting a good one.

"That isn't right." Malick wasn't even trying to be quiet anymore, speaking with authority, like he knew. Maybe he did—no one watched Fen with as much rapt attention as Malick did. He abandoned Samin at the door and headed toward Fen.

"He's still got a knife." Samin trotted along after Malick, wishing he'd thought to bring a weapon. He'd meant what he'd told Malick before: Fen was dangerous, and would only be more so if his mind finally went. Fen might've dropped one knife, but he still had another, and even if he didn't, Samin thought Fen could probably kill a man with his teeth if he thought he had to. And who knew what a man in the grip of... whatever this was might think he had to do? "Malick, watch—"

"I *know*, Samin." Malick approached Fen's hunched figure cautiously enough, but still in a hurry. "If all you're going to do is nag, then go back downstairs. I'll take care of this."

Yeah? Well, fuck you, too, then, *Take care of what, exactly?* were the only coherent things that came to Samin's mind, so he shut his mouth, watching, covering Malick's back because Malick was being too stupid right now to know he needed it.

"...back to Zero," Fen was whispering, "start again," and something else about Raven and Wolf Samin couldn't make out. Clutching at his hair like he wanted to yank it right out of his head, eyes shut tight and teeth clenched, a bright trickle of blood leaking from the corner of his mouth, glistening black in the moonlight. "Shifts, shifts, rumbling and quaking, the ground trembles and shifts to Null—" He bit down on it then gasped, like he was in pain.

The knife arced up, glittered in the light of the moons—

Malick lurched forward. "Fucking *shit!*"

—then swept down in a bow of silver.

It took a second for what Samin was seeing to travel from his eyes to his brain. Another for his brain to talk him into believing it.

Fen hadn't just gutted Malick; he'd slashed a stripe to his own thigh. A neat, precise line of cut fabric and seeping blood. And there Fen knelt, wheezing in great gulps like a man drowning, and raising the knife again.

Malick caught Fen's hand—"Shh, little Ghost"—braced himself like he was expecting a fight, but Fen went immediately still at Malick's touch, breath held. Malick set both hands over Fen's fist around the knife. "How about you don't slash yourself to bits, and we can—"

"Are you the Null?" Fen snatched hold of Malick's shirt with his free hand and dragged him in. "Are you the *Null*?" A snarl this time, louder, but no less fraught.

Samin stood back, watching, waiting himself for an answer, because he had no idea what Fen was talking about. Since the moment Samin had run into Malick on the stairs, it was like everyone had gone and switched languages on him and he was the only one left who wasn't speaking in tongues. What the *fuck* was a "null" and... and why was Malick bloody *nodding*?

"Yeah. Some call me so."

Fen's mouth worked, but for a long, uncomfortable moment, nothing came out of it. He just kept staring at Malick, the closest to open emotion on his face as Samin had ever seen, and yet Samin still couldn't tell what it was. Anger was easy, but this was... different. Despair? Disbelief? Confusion? All of it?

Then, finally: "I think..." Fen clenched his teeth, peered down at the long stripe carved into his thigh, steadily leaking blood into the surrounding fabric of his trousers and pattering quietly onto the pocked clay of the roof. "I think it's supposed to be you." Misery laced with blatant distrust. "You've hidden people before."

There was a slight curve at the corner of Malick's mouth, as though this was all somehow an expectation fulfilled. "I have."

"How much?"

Malick's eyebrows rose. "How much?"

Fen growled, let go of Malick's shirt, but didn't try to get his other hand free. "Three of them. I've got koin. I can get more. How *much*?"

Malick sat back, eyeing Fen levelly, but Samin had known Malick a long time, could see the calculating grin beneath the bland expression, the victory.

"Let's talk about exactly what you want first. Then we'll talk price." Malick turned to Samin. "Go get Umeia. Tell her to come quick, Fen's hurt himself."

Fen looked away. "I'm fine."

"'Fine' doesn't bleed, does it?" Malick shifted his glance back up to Samin. "And scare us up a bottle while you're down there. We'll be in my rooms." He gave Fen a small smile. "Make it two. I'm thinking it's going to be a long night."

ᛏᛉᛏ

Change-month, Year 1316, Cycle of the Wolf

Dearest Joori—

Beishin tells me you are well and that you managed blah blah drivel blather blah.

Asai lowered the letter with a sigh, already both bored and annoyed. Bad enough Jacin-rei was growing harder to read and his very nature prevented Asai from seeing him clearly. Or at all. But for someone like Asai to be reduced to reading an adolescent boy's *mail* for an ounce of insight was flat embarrassing.

Blah blah, miss you, blah blah, how is Mother, blah blah, failed... keep failing, so sorry, jabber, more jabber...

By all the gods, Asai was actually thankful the boy *didn't* say all this out loud. There'd never be any peace!

...so beautiful... made me feel... I wanted... liked it—

Asai sat up straight. The parchment gave an odd little creak between fingers he hadn't meant to clench so tight.

Dani. The boy was telling his *brother* about a craven little tryst that—

No. Not the point. Asai did not read these letters for an excuse to punish the boy. And he had to admit he'd handled the situation rather badly. He should have allowed Jacin-rei to keep the trainer. Young boys did have their needs, after all. And Dani had been pliable. Asai wasn't going to find another so skilled who'd be willing to remain confined to the estate for the length of his engagement, nor one who could disappear so easily afterward.

A shame, really. And annoying that Asai hadn't foreseen it, but it was so hard to see anything clearly where Jacin-rei was involved. Then again, Dani had served his purpose, had trained Jacin-rei in all the basics of what he needed, and even exceeded Asai's expectations in the time he'd been with them. Asai would take it from here, and Jacin-rei would be ready.

Blah blah, Beishin says, blah blah, promised to arrange a visit with you, but I failed to blah blah, so sorry... perhaps someday... can see you when I do better... control and perfection... more blah blah, a bit of groveling...

Good. Back to more acceptable topics. Asai read the rest of the letter more carefully, finger tapping at his lip, trying to discern deeper meanings within the words, when he'd never had to do such a thing before. The boy didn't *have* depth. At least Asai hadn't previously found it necessary to consider the possibility. But with the next bit, he rather had no choice.

I keep the hope that these letters find you, as Beishin has promised they do.

(Do they, Beishin? Do you read them? Do you send them? Or do you merely peer inside my messy head through them? What confessions are you looking for? And would you really want to hear them?)

Asai sat back, mouth tight. The cheeky little—

He shook it off, caught between a scowl and a satisfied smile. Perhaps things had taken an unexpected, and rather salacious turn, but the boy *was* coming along exactly as Asai had foreseen in most ways. In other ways… he couldn't decide. Asai hadn't planned for nor expected to be the object of adolescent lust or—dare he think or believe it?—honest young love. Though since he'd become aware of it, he thought his own lack of vision rather absurd. Even without Sight, he should have seen it coming. He had, after all, rescued a young, suggestible boy on the verge of madness, pulled him back from both it and the choking life of a Jin camp, and dropped him into the middle of luxury and purpose.

And the boy *was* tempting.

No. Out of the question. For the moment, at least. Asai had grown fond of the boy, cared more than he'd thought he would, which might well make things difficult later, but that was later and he'd deal with it then. He'd made greater sacrifices, after all. But actually allowing what Jacin-rei wanted right now could be disastrous. Asai had made that mistake before, and it still haunted him. Nothing was more unpredictable than young love.

Damn it all. It wasn't bad enough Asai had the Ancestors to contend with, but he was forced to deal with raging hormones, as well. He'd forgotten how unsettled young boys could be.

The balancing act was exhausting.

…but everything Beishin has given me, I would give it all back for another day with you.

That was… disturbing. No—it was unacceptable.

The strength of the bond between the brothers had bothered Asai from the beginning. Some attachment was necessary, of course—fond memories and a tragic view of their separation would have been more than enough—but Jacin-rei's near-obsessive reliance on the memory of his brother… It had the feel of a situation that might slip out of Asai's control, if he didn't handle it exactly right. And control of the brother would be essential, eventually.

Perhaps Asai should fulfill his next promise, instead of finding excuses not to. Perhaps allowing the boys an afternoon together might dull the sharp edge of Jacin-rei's fixation. Asai could arrange it easily. Simply request the boy specifically for a work detail. He could even quietly buy him and bring him here to live.

Asai considered the idea. Surely the father could be persuaded again. A weak man, and weak men were easy to… convince.

No. Impossible. It would put too many possibilities into play, and things were already chancy as a result of the involvement of an Untouchable. Anyway, how would the brother's eventual fate be explained or excused, if Asai brought him here to live? It was entirely too impractical. And the eventual reunion Asai had foreseen had to happen as he'd seen it, or it might as well not happen at all. Everything had to be exactly right, or as right as Asai could make it, and the strength of Jacin-rei's love for his brother, and his brother's love for him, made them both less predictable than Asai would like.

Then again, no future was truly set, only as set as Asai could make it. Everything was changeable, whether Asai liked it or not, and all he could do was try to trim away possibilities. Thus far, things were still on course. As long as he kept Jacin-rei's fundamental framework in mind, and used it accordingly, things should work out as Asai had seen. Feed the despair with subtle reminders of what Jacin-rei was and what he would have been by now had it not been for his beishin. Nurture the guilt with an almost free run of luxury, while the family he loved still dwelt in destitute misery. Maintain the loneliness with the deprivation of the company he most wanted.

Harden him. Mold him. Perfect him.

Give him a purpose and make him believe it was his own.

Dangle his fear of failure in front of his nose, and make him believe the only way around it was through Asai himself.

Maintain the adolescent love but keep it unrequited, and yet not without hope. Keep the Ghost biddable.

Give him just the right balance between strength and tragedy. The perfect allure to the right eyes.

It should work.

Mouth set, Asai stepped softly over to the hearth, and tossed the letter onto the fire. Stood there until every scrap and corner was a curl of fragile black.

Do you read them? Do you send them?

Asai poked at the ash.

Yes, little Ghost, I read them. And no, little Ghost, I do not send them.

And do you know what you will do about that, Jacin-rei? Absolutely nothing. Because perhaps you doubt, but you still believe. And that's all I need.

Still. It wouldn't do for the boy to find the remnants. Platitudes, assurances and uncertainty would keep him manageable for now.

Asai found the boy in the kitchen, seated at the table with a fine-haired brush clutched in his hand. Vonshi was leaning over Jacin-rei's shoulder, watching careful efforts bear fruit on paper.

Asai had a peek too, and raised his eyebrows. Vonshi shot Asai a look out the corner of his eye, at which Asai merely rolled his eyes and made for the wine rack. Vonshi ignored him.

A little irritating, but Jacin-rei liked Vonshi, enjoyed their "lessons" together, and they did help Jacin-rei's concentration. And Asai had given his permission. Still, Asai had a perfectly good steward and here he was, getting his own wine. He was too good to the help sometimes.

"You're losing it, lad." Vonshi set his bony hand on Jacin-rei's shoulder. "Focus on the graze of ink on the paper. Concentrate on the hairs of the brush, how they bend as you sweep it along the curve. Bring that and only that to the front of your mind."

Jacin-rei paused, hunching over the table, and took a long, deep breath. "It's getting too loud." His voice was admirably controlled but there was a slight quaver beneath it.

Asai would have to work on that with him. Jacin-rei still gave too much away with his voice and his eyes.

"That's because you're putting it in the wrong part of your mind," Vonshi said, all kindness and reassurance.

"It crowds out all else sometimes. They... demand."

Vonshi patted Jacin-rei's shoulder. "I'm afraid that is the point, lad. But there is no reason you can't listen while you concentrate on something else."

"But—"

"I'll hear no buts, lad." Vonshi's craggy voice had gone stern. "I can polish Beishin's silver while cooking his supper, baking tea squares, and singing. Surely you can manage to listen whilst you draw a simple circle."

"A *perfect* circle," Jacin-rei muttered irritably. Getting near the edge; he always got snarly when his control was teetering.

"Beishin demands perfection, and perfection demands concentration."

Jacin-rei went quiet again and resumed his task.

Asai poured his wine then stepped lightly over to the table and had another look over Jacin-rei's shoulder. Asai had never considered this tactic, but... it was clever. Drawing a perfect circle? Without tracing it from a bowl or dinner plate? Impossible. There was no such thing as a perfect circle.

The side of his mouth curled up and he took a sip of his wine as he peered at Vonshi.

Ingenious, really. Asai wished he'd thought of it. Set the boy to an impossible task that required all his concentration and control, convince him it was possible, and when he failed, set him to it again. And again. And again. He'd never complete a perfect circle, but he'd achieve Asai's goals nicely.

Flattening his small smile to a frown, Asai sighed, said, "Hardly perfect, is it, Jacin-rei?"

The effect was predictable: Jacin-rei jumped, as though Asai had just touched him with a hot branding rod, brush scrawling a smeary trail across the paper, where dapples of at least two-score approximations of very near to perfect circles stood in dark relief. Jacin-rei lurched from the table so fast his chair went over with a hard clatter.

"Beishin." His voice was tight, as though he was trying to control his breathing. "I didn't hear you come in."

"Mm." Asai set his lips thin in disapproval as Jacin-rei mumbled anxious apologies and righted the chair. Asai looked pointedly at the smeared paper and sighed. "Perhaps if your emotions did not... interfere..." He let it hang there. No sense in taxing himself searching for the harsher implication. Jacin-rei would invent that all by himself.

Already, Jacin-rei had paled, his jaw was tightening, and the brush would soon be nothing more than blots of ink and splinters in his clenched fist. He dipped his head, stammered, "Yes, seyh, I… I'm sorry, I—"

"May I have a word with you, Beishin?" Vonshi put in softly, his hand going once again to Jacin-rei's shoulder, a calm, respectful smile on his wizened face. "In private, seyh, if I may."

Asai regarded the bony hand with narrowed eyes. The way its presence seemed to calm the quivering. An odd little cramp tweaked in his chest, and for some unfathomable reason, Dani rose to mind. Asai frowned and shook it away.

He nodded. "Carry on, Jacin-rei."

He led Vonshi to his sitting room.

Vonshi took the time to pull the double doors shut behind him before he got to it. "Forgive me, seyh." His hands were tucked behind his back, chin up. "I do not mean to overstep, but I cannot complete the boy's lessons if you interfere." He paused, mouth pursed. "May I be blunt, seyh?"

Asai's eyebrows went up. It was all he could do not to snort. "Is it possible for you to be any other way, Vonshi?"

Vonshi's thin lips lifted in a small, conciliatory smile. "And you are gracious and generous to allow me, Beishin." The smile dropped. "The boy has begun cutting himself, seyh. With knives. You've seen the bandages?"

"On his arm."

"Since Dani… left, seyh. I fear—"

"You will leave it, Vonshi."

Asai had rather been expecting this, but sometimes Vonshi bordered on insolence. Asai believed in allowing his people their own opinions, but not when they tried to interfere with his.

Vonshi tilted his head. "Seyh?"

"You will leave it. He must be allowed to find his own ways to cope. We will not always be at his side to help him through his more difficult moments."

"But, seyh, the concentration exercises—"

"Should help him to learn to utilize an alternative. In time. *Then*, perhaps, he will no longer need other coping methods." Asai paused, lifted an eyebrow. "If you teach him well, yes?"

Vonshi's stance had gone rigid, and his gaze pointed straight ahead. "Yes, Beishin."

Asai nodded, satisfied. "Your heart is a credit to you, Vonshi. And Jacin-rei was indeed blessed when the gods led me to you." He sighed. "There will come a day when he will not need such drastic measures. But that day is not yet. Until then…" It wasn't as though Asai *liked* to see the boy hurt. "If we take this away from him, we take away his mind. He *must* be allowed to cope on his own. You know as well as I how important he is to your people. If we allow him to slip inside the voices—or worse, allow him to allow himself—our chance will be lost. So very much depends on him."

"Yes, Beishin."

Too quick, and Vonshi still wasn't looking at Asai. But Asai had made his point, even if he hadn't quite convinced Vonshi to agree with it. And Vonshi—for all his impertinence—obeyed all of Asai's orders with admirably strict attention, even if he too obviously didn't agree with them. It would have to do.

"Go." Asai waved Vonshi away. "Continue your lessons. Spoil the boy with sweets when he draws you a circle, and…" He paused and gave Vonshi his warmest smile. "Treat yourself to a glass of wine." He held up his own, swirling it so the light flared ruby facets out from the base. "Very dry, as you like it."

Vonshi bent his neck low, and placed a fist over his breastbone. "Thank you, Beishin," he said then turned and made his silent way from the room.

Asai sighed—probably for the fiftieth time this evening—and rubbed at his brow. He swirled his wine and peered down into its rich depths.

"Jacin-rei." He shook his head. "One day, you will thank me." A small, weary smile tilted at his mouth, and he lifted his glass, toasted his little Catalyst. "They will all thank me, but yours… yours will *mean* something."

And then, perhaps, if they both lived, if the boy didn't hate him when it was all through, perhaps then there might be time for requiting.

Asai tipped the glass back and drank deeply.

8

Storm-month, Year 1322, Cycle of the Wolf

"I thought Samin said no one got hurt tonight."

Umeia eyed the gaping slice in Fen's trouser leg then the still-blooded knife on the tea table. What she could see of Fen's thigh was already so scarred up, she didn't know if stitches would even take, and the depth of the wound was going to make them necessary.

She tilted a stern look over at Malick, standing behind Fen's chair, hand set lightly to Fen's shoulder.

"And how did you say this happened, again?"

Malick made a business of looking at the wound, then angled to peer at Fen's face. He lifted his eyebrows, expectant. When Fen didn't look up, didn't speak, barely breathed, Malick straightened, shrugged.

"I didn't."

Umeia clenched her teeth, tore at the bloody fabric to expose the wound, not necessarily caring that she was likely inflicting more pain. And anyway, it wasn't like Fen was about to moan or whimper or even react. He'd been sitting still as stone since she'd walked in, a half glass of uzin sloshing in his hand.

She shook her head, disgusted. "You'll have to take them off." It snapped out of her, patience having been left behind altogether in her warm, comfortable bed, out of which she'd been dragged for the third time this week. And all three times, one way or another, had been the result of this man's presence in her house. She prodded at Fen's knee. "C'mon, then, I haven't all night, get them—"

"No." Flat.

Umeia narrowed her eyes first at the top of Fen's bowed head, then up at Malick's badly concealed snort and smirk. Calmly, she slapped a thick cloth over the wound, withdrew her now bloody hands, careful to keep them away from her robe, and sat back on her perch on the tea table in front of Fen.

"I can't treat and bandage it properly unless you take off the trousers."

"Then don't."

This time, Umeia's jaw clenched so tight she accidentally scraped her molars together. She fisted her hands, grimacing at the sticky feel between her fingers.

"Listen, Trouble, I don't think you—"

"Umeia." Malick's tone was chiding, too calm.

"He's leaking all over the chair." Umeia paused, because, really, a few bloodstains would hardly make that chair worse. "And it'll never come out of the floorboards." She stopped altogether, because this was Malick's room, where disarray, old food, and discolored blotches were merely part of the ambiance. Instead, she shifted to an argument she knew Malick might hear: "It needs to be cleaned and sutured. Otherwise, it's likely to get infected, and he could lose the leg. Ada law says I'm not even supposed to do that much for an Untouchable—accept my generosity now, because it won't be on offer very long."

Fen didn't seem to care much, just sat slumped in the chair with Malick's hand on his shoulder, staring down into his uzin.

Malick, on the other hand, shot Umeia a narrow look. "Wolf's law says different, doesn't it?" Nonetheless, he nodded. "He's got a few along his ribs need looking at too. It'd be best if—"

"How would you know that?" Fen angled a suspicious squint up at Malick through his fringe.

Ugh, he had blood clotted in his hair, too, now that Umeia looked.

Malick ignored him. "Fen's asked our price for harboring refugees, Umeia. Three of them."

His gaze burned into hers, though what he was trying to relay, Umeia had no idea, and he was keeping his veil too damned tight for her to get a hint. Considering the way she'd flubbed it when Fen had approached her earlier in the week, Umeia thought perhaps Malick was trying to tell her to shut the fuck up and let him handle it.

"I told him," Malick went on, "that we'd need to know exactly who, and why, before we could give him an answer."

All fine and reasonable, except Umeia still had no idea what Malick was expecting from her. If he'd just lighten his veil for a second… He didn't.

So Umeia merely did what she would have done otherwise: she turned to Fen, reached out and took his chin, ignoring the reflexive jerk back and the low growl, and maintained the pressure until Fen looked her in the eye.

"Who?"

Fen's jaw was already tight. Now it quivered slightly, and a distinct flicker of anxiety and distrust moved through his gaze. He angled his head until Umeia let go of his chin, then he lifted it.

"Fugitives from the east camp."

Umeia shook her head. "*Who?*"

It took a heavy moment of teeth-gnashing silence, Fen clearly reluctant and furious about it, before he answered, barely audible: "My... my brothers and sister."

It seemed like it sucked everything out of him, the one simple sentence that wasn't simple at all. All the breath went out of him, and seemingly all the strength. The only thing holding him upright and in the chair was Malick's relentless grip on his shoulder.

Umeia sat back, eyeing Fen critically. He really did look terrible. Blood loss couldn't be helping. She didn't know how long ago he'd got hurt, but he'd been bleeding pretty steadily since Umeia showed up. Dried splotches of blood were scattered irregularly through his hair, brown smudges and smears of it on his face and neck where he'd missed a few places when he'd apparently wiped the bulk of it off. His hands looked filthy, but Umeia rather suspected that was the effect of dried blood embedded in the crevices of his knuckles and the whorls of his fingertips.

It must've been a hell of a night.

Umeia softened. She knew what Fen was risking, knew he had to be doing it out of desperation, knew he didn't quite trust them yet, and here he was, risking that trust for people—children, from what Malick had said—apparently quite precious to him. A Jin Untouchable with Jin runaway siblings, and really—who *could* they trust?

Was this why the Mage had bid them take him?

Umeia shot a quick, decisive look up at Malick—a warning, because she was going to do this, whether it was what he wanted or not—then leaned in. She almost laid a hand to Fen's knee, but set it atop the lump of linen soaking up the blood from his thigh instead.

"I don't give oaths lightly." Umeia didn't even have to try to put sincerity into it, because she meant what she was about to say. "I rarely give them at all because I am bound by the oaths I grant." Umeia dipped her head, waited until Fen met her gaze. "*Bound*, Fen—do you understand? I cannot go back on an oath, or I risk the suns."

"Umeia." There was light warning in Malick's tone. Very light. Umeia had guessed right—this was exactly what Malick wanted. But he was still making it clear it was Umeia's choice. "You've not yet even heard—"

"Shut up, Kamen." Umeia kept her gaze locked to Fen's. "I don't need to hear it all. I've already made up my mind. Did you doubt it?"

It was, after all, what she did, how she honored Wolf in their self-imposed exile, and moreover, it was what she *was*. It was why Malick brought each of them here eventually—Samin first, then Yori and Shig, and now Fen—to sit before Umeia and hear words they didn't fully understand and meant very different things to them than they did to her. It was why Malick had pulled Umeia from her bed now.

Malick was direction and action; Umeia was protection.

Fen only stared, exhausted eyes resigned to... Umeia couldn't tell. Rejection, maybe, because he really didn't look like he expected to get what he needed here.

It should have pissed Umeia off—what did Fen think she *was*, after all?—but it wouldn't come. Frankly, he had every right to his disbelief. Because, in truth, Umeia wasn't about to give Fen anything at all.

"I don't tell you this to impress you." Umeia held Fen's gaze steadily. "I tell you this so you'll know you've not chosen wrongly. As long as you consent to entrusting your brothers and sister to my care, my oath is yours." She placed her fist over her heart and dipped her head, an echo of the formal bow Fen had given her when he'd tested his trust against Umeia's heart and Umeia had failed. "By my heart, by my body, by my breath and spirit, I pledge my oath to—" She paused. "What are their names?"

Fen was still staring at her. "Joori." Soft; cautious. "And Morin and Caidi."

"I pledge my oath of shelter and protection to Fen Joori, Fen Morin, Fen Caidi, 'til the day they dwell no longer beneath my sight. Should my life be required in bond for their mortal safety, I pledge it willingly, by forfeit—"

"—by forfeit of my..." Fen's eyes had gone wide, the hand around his glass so lax Malick gently retrieved it before Fen could drop it. "By forfeit of my soul—"

"—by forfeit of my soul should I fail." Umeia peered a little nervously up at Malick, but he looked calm and assured, like he'd expected exactly this. Still, the way Fen recited the latter part of the ancient oath along with Umeia gave her pause.

"The oath of the *Temshiel*." Fen's gaze drew inward. "Why would you... what...?"

Jaw tightening, he shook off Malick's hand for the first time since Umeia had come in. Immediately, Fen's back went straight and his head tilted to the side, eyes shut tight, and brow scrunched down in concentration. Listening.

Umeia slid Malick a quick glance, but Malick just kept looking at Fen, calm and cool.

A small growl made Umeia drag her gaze back to Fen in time to see a vicious sneer curl at his mouth, hands fisting and coming together to press brutally into the wound on his thigh as he shook his head.

"Nothing, they say *nothing*." He shot up from the chair, bloody lump of linen splatting to the floor. He nearly teetered over Umeia as he backed away from both of them, wild-eyed, careful to angle out of Malick's reach. "Who *are* you?! How d'you... how *can* you...?" He looked at Umeia, all lost and hovering over some mental brink, then back at Malick, shocky gaze tightening down to anger then winding back up to alarm. "Please." A whisper this time. "*Please.* What do you want, why have you… why *me*, what…?" Fen shook his head, hand going once again to his thigh, fingers actually dipping *inside* the wound, pressing so hard it made Umeia wince. "What are you?"

Malick hadn't moved from his place behind Fen's chair, not once—only kept watching with something so deep in his eyes Umeia knew he'd deny it if she ever told him it was there. An hour ago, it would have made her wish for Fen's name on a scrap of paper in the crock at the end of the bar downstairs. Now, it only made her somewhat sad for her little brother who would hear no oath from Umeia, but never seemed to understand that not speaking it aloud didn't mean she hadn't given it.

"We're the ones who are going to help you," Malick said gently, "starting with getting you sewn up and bathed. Tomorrow, we help you by getting your brothers and sister for you, and bringing them here safely." He leaned down, retrieved the bottle of uzin from the table, and joggled it so it sloshed sweetly against the glass. "Right now, I'm just the man who's going to get you pleasantly drunk, so the sewing part won't hurt so much."

᛭

He'd poured four shots down Fen's throat before Umeia had got to the stitching, and then another two while she was doing it. Fen accepted each one without argument, without reaction, without expression or so much as a harsh breath as the uzin went down. Malick had no idea if Fen generally drank, besides his watered beer at supper, or if he did, what his limits might be, so Malick stopped at six. It didn't seem to matter— there wasn't so much as a twitch or creasing of Fen's brow as Umeia's hooked needle dug in and out of his skin. Either he was too used to pain for it to matter, or the liquor was doing its job. Or he was too deep inside himself for any of it to register.

He seemed all right going down the stairs, though, hobbling along with his torn trouser leg flapping down over his knee and bouncing against the top of his boot. He'd refused to let Umeia get him out of the trousers, no matter how reasonably or snappishly she'd insisted. Malick figured it was because Fen wouldn't have been able to do it without help, and he didn't want to show himself so vulnerable. Malick understood this for two reasons: one, because he was male, and grasped fully the idiotic things testosterone could do to the logical part of a brain; and two, because he'd learned more about Fen tonight than he had all week.

Malick kept a good eye as they descended, but Fen had yet to seriously stumble. Slight wobbles now and then, which Fen handled by pointedly gripping the banister instead of Malick's offered arm, but he didn't go headfirst, so Malick let it pass. No banister on the stairway down to the baths, though. Fen paused at the top of them, seemed to measure his chances of getting down them unaided, then looked down at his boots, at the stone stairs, at his boots, at the stairs…

With a grunt, he abruptly sat down on the top riser, right leg held out stiffly, bobbed a little nod to himself, then yanked his left leg up by the knee and dragged off his boot. Then his stocking, toes unconsciously giving a brief wriggle of freedom that, for whatever reason, made Malick smile. It figured Fen would have pretty feet too. Without even looking, Fen merely tossed both boot and stocking over his shoulder and bent to do the same to the right.

Malick stopped him much the same way he'd stopped the knife from doing further damage: he crouched down on the top step and laid his hand firmly over Fen's. Tightened his grip when Fen tensed and tried to wrench away.

"Put a strain on it, and you'll tear the sutures." Malick said it calmly. "And then Umeia will have to do it again, and I don't think she'll be happy with us if we try to get her out of bed again."

Fen's head was bowed, but his whole body was rigid, his breath coming fast and shallow. Malick waited until the hand beneath his loosened, uncurling slowly from its fist, and Fen's shoulders went just the slightest bit slack. Without a word, Fen jerked a tiny nod and slowly pulled his hand from Malick's. The message was all too clear: *Don't touch unless you absolutely have to.*

So Malick tried to touch as little as possible, gripping the back of Fen's knee only briefly so he didn't yank him down the steps on his ass as he pulled the boot off by the heel. The wool of the stocking stretched as Malick dragged it free and tossed it and the boot to lay with the others. And then he let go, stood on the step below Fen, and waited.

Fen peered at him steadily out the corner of his eye through the messy clumps of chestnut clotted over his brow. Not quite suspicious, but not trusting, either.

Ah, well. Uzin could only do so much.

It didn't matter. Malick had found patience tonight, hadn't even had to dig for it, but found it just lying there at the top of his chest, waiting. Stirred to life when he'd watched Fen with his brother, watched the nonreactions and complete lack of expression when they'd spoken. Then watched everything Fen had been holding back fly across his face, bash around inside his eyes, when he'd left his family behind again.

Malick hadn't quite understood it before, and he didn't altogether now, but he understood it a lot better than he had. He'd seen it all in the brother's eyes, seen Fen beating back its twin in his own. Not only did Fen love, but he was loved in return, and more deeply than he could apparently bear. Malick had known there was passion down there beneath all that ice. He'd seen it in the way Fen had driven into those guards at Pon's with such grim abandon. He just hadn't understood entirely.

Hopelessness. Guilt. Loneliness. All of it seething inside Fen, bubbling up like a boiling-over pot, and Fen was practically throwing himself over the lid to keep it all in.

Insight too long in coming had hit Malick tonight with a slow, spreading ache.

Malick had been going about it all wrong before, adding to the pressure because he'd thought it would be fun, had been intrigued and challenged. Now, he'd seen at least the murky outlines of what lay beneath the ice, and found himself wanting to see it all, wanting Fen to show it to him—wanting to be the sort of person Fen could trust enough to let him see.

He paced slowly down the stone steps, braced and ready to be a buttress if necessary for Fen—limping and wobbling behind him— should he slip. He didn't. Fen made it to the baths, blinking a bit myopically at the closed door, until Malick dug the key out of his pocket and let him through.

Empty, all business tonight—this morning—having been concluded and the evidence cleaned away for a fresh start tomorrow. They were alone, as they'd been that first night—full circle. Strange, how things had changed in so short a time.

"You can leave now." Fen's quiet voice rang against the silence as his bare feet padded toward the shower-boxes, the stone of the walls snapping up the aggressive tone and bouncing it between them. "I don't need your help."

He hadn't let Umeia have a look at his other wounds; now Malick had himself a good one as Fen clumsily shed his shirt behind him on the floor. Malick marked the lengths and depths of the cuts and slices down Fen's ribs and across his torso, judged them bad but not serious, and so let it pass. Already dried and beginning to scab over—a good cleaning could be nothing but beneficial.

"No?" Malick turned up two of the low lamps and strode slowly after Fen, close enough to catch if Fen fell, but not close enough to unnerve. "How d'you think you're going to get those trousers off, then?"

Fen paused with his hand on the reed screen, muscles tensing, head down. Malick could almost see the angry scowl darkening Fen's face as he realized his quandary.

A week ago, this small fissure in the ice would have had Malick driving in for the kill. It was intensely arousing, that suspense in posture, strangely erotic—and forlornly dangerous. The fact that Fen was leaving his boots and clothes behind him in a messy trail told Malick that Fen was… off, not himself, control still slipping steadily, and the uzin had to be adding to it all.

Not the time to be taking advantage.

Down, boy. Sit. Good dog.

"You never…" With an irritable huff, Fen slouched into the wall, face pressed to his arm, shoulders vibrating with strange, silent little chuckles. "You never told me how much, but I think... You don't want my koin, do you?" Muffled and slightly slurred. "I suppose it hardly matters now." He turned unsteadily, and leaned back against the wall, peering at Malick through his fringe with a small smile-that-wasn't. Moving probably less elegantly than Malick had ever seen him, Fen pulled the braid over his shoulder, fingers clumsy as he loosened the bit of leather that held the tail of the queue in place. He wagged it at Malick like a mother would wag her finger at a child, almost brushed it along the tip of Malick's nose, but missed. "Not supposed to see it undone." It was low and... fuck, *please* don't let that be seduction. "But you've been wanting to." The strange little smile turned sly, and Fen's voice went deep and hoarse. "Haven't you?"

More than anything. Wanting to see *Fen* undone, but now...

Fen's long fingers untangled the leather, slipped into the seams of the plait and began unthreading them. Strands of chestnut, crimped by the braid, caught the lamplight in gleaming folds of gold with flashes of deep-set russet.

Malick couldn't take his eyes away. "Fen." He forced himself to take a breath. "There is no payment for my help."

Well, there might be. Could be. Probably was.

But.

Malick dragged his gaze away from the hair and the fingers entwined in it and locked it onto Fen's. "You need to get cleaned up."

Fen paused, eyes narrowing, then the not-smile came back, and he nodded, fingers once again unwinding yards and yards of braid into a glossy stream of wavy silk. "Yes. Cleaned up." His eyes misted up, and for a second, an awful mix of grief and shame flashed over his face. "Lots of blood tonight." He shook his head, set his face back into the lines of seduction, and turned his mouth back up into that not-smile again. "You don't care, though, do you?" His hand came up, fingers reaching, tracing lightly over the shape of Malick's lips. "It doesn't matter what you are. You're just as foul as I am."

"Is that what you think you are?" Malick had to fight the very real temptation to slide out his tongue, catch the tip of Fen's finger with it. "You think what you do makes you... unclean?"

"I think..." Fen trailed off, took his hand away, and went back to loosening the braid, eyes cast down, dark lashes splashed long and full over high cheekbones. "I think what I did tonight makes it not matter what I think."

He'd been ruthless, a dervish of death, and Malick had watched it all with lust and admiration. They'd slashed their way through men who likely had nothing to do with what their lady and her lover had been up to, and done it with no more thought than that which went into the strategy of it all, such as it was. Sonji-onna's guards had worn Blood-amulets; that was all Fen saw, all he cared about. He'd got a name and more out of Sonji-onna, and hadn't flinched once at what he'd had to do to get it. And what he'd had to do had been... messy.

Malick had only watched, hadn't even cared that the name that finally came from Sonji-onna was the one he'd been dreading. He probably would have slit Yakuli's throat right there, and the gods and their orders be damned, if Fen had asked him to. Nothing and no one had mattered but Fen, with his tragic eyes and his blood-streaked face, twisted into a strange mix of fury and hate and shame and relief.

"You want to know what I am." Malick slipped his fingers over Fen's jawline, noting abstractly that there was no flinch or gasp at the touch anymore—Fen had got used to these moments of silence, or he'd simply stopped reacting to them. "I'm the man who is telling you... there is no foul, there is no clean. There is no good or bad. There's only better and worse. Sometimes we're better, sometimes we're worse. Tonight, I think we were a bit of both, but... Fen—you're exquisite. You're Wolf's own treasure, he stole you right out from under Raven, and he watches you with a smile on his face. I know. Look at me, Fen." Malick waited until Fen did, a slow lift of thick lashes, a slight shimmer to gilt-gray eyes. "D'you believe me?"

Fen only stared, steady and thoughtful, then: "Do you honestly think," he answered, low and soft, "I give even the slightest fuck?"

Oh, bloody *hell*, and why did that land in Malick's groin like a ball of fire?

Yeah, I do. I think you give more of a fuck than is good for anyone.

Malick had leaned in, without even realizing it, fingers sliding into softest silk, lips almost brushing Fen's, and fuck, Fen was *letting* him, tilting his chin up, looking Malick in the eye with... desire, yes, it *was* there, but not the right kind. Acknowledgement, resignation to some kind of compensation he'd invented from words and not their meaning. Words Malick himself had spoken, but he'd never meant them like this.

Malick drew back, watched Fen's brow twist in thwarted confusion, and jerked away.

With a will he didn't know he had, Malick coerced his legs to move and take him across to the cupboard. He kept his eyes on his own hands as he collected two buckets and a bathsheet, thought better and snagged another, along with soap and a clump of sponge. Turned back to find Fen's eyes on him, no smile this time, loose waves draped over his shoulder and swathing down the whole right side of his body, all the way down to the tops of his feet. Everything in Malick seized up and started babbling as Fen slowly undid his belt.

"Going to help me with these?" All smoke and sex.

Right, so. Fen was trying to kill him.

It was Malick's own bloody fault. He deserved every agonizing twitch in his trousers, every sharp ache of want. He'd been prowling around Fen's edges like a tom in a roomful of mollies since he'd laid eyes on him, and now that an actual invitation was being handed to him, Malick couldn't take it. Wouldn't. Not like this, not... not when it would make him something he'd been convinced he was but abruptly and too sharply realized he didn't want to be.

Malick snatched his gaze away from Fen's, and firmed his shoulders. With a groan he hoped was only internal, he threw the bathsheets over his shoulder and stepped over to the pool, dipped the buckets in and carried them over, then squeezed past Fen to set them on the floor of the shower-box. Mind deliberately blank, Malick roughly opened Fen's trousers the rest of the way, stopped himself before he yanked them down and ruined all Umeia's work, and slid them carefully from Fen's hips, dragging the linens along with them, and. And. *And.*

Bloody fucking *fuckfuckfuck*, Fen was half-hard, Fen was... Fen was—

No. Not like this.

Jaw set, Malick dropped down to one knee, eyes steadfastly on his own hands and nothing else. He tapped lightly at the back of Fen's left calf until Fen lifted his foot, then his right, and slipped the trousers from him completely. Bared, hair unbound, aroused, waiting, expectant.

Malick didn't know what he wanted to touch more.

He thought he might've blacked out for a few seconds, because the next thing he knew, he was standing, arm locked at the elbow and propped to the wall—support, because bloody *damn* did he need it— while his other hand pushed Fen into the shower-box and slid the screen shut. And all Malick could do was stand there, breathing as quietly as he could. Eyes shut tight. Listening to the *splish* of water. Trying not to imagine it runneling down all those too-tempting dips and angles.

Teeth actually grinding now, Malick dangled the soap and sponge over the top of the screen until wet fingers took them. With the very last of his self-control, he draped the bathsheets over the screen and dragged himself over to the door, then leaned his back to the wall and rubbed roughly at his face.

"Try not to get the stitches wet," he managed to shove out, then he let his head fall back and stared at the uneven curve of the stone ceiling. Cursed silently. Clenched his hands into fists and pounded them to the wall behind him. Again. Listened to the sporadic splash and trickle of water and really, *really* tried not to let the mental pictures take hold. Tried—though he knew he'd fail—to talk himself out of the thumping arousal knocking all through him, making every sense he owned more acute, honed. The mineral scent of the water, the flicker and flare of the lamplight, the bloody *sounds* coming from behind that screen, and knowing—*knowing*—that if he threw it back, stepped in, Fen would let him.

The abrupt slide of the screen against the stone floor almost made Malick yip and startle like an old woman. He kept still, shut his eyes.

Fen's soft voice came at him, all uncertainty and diffidence: "I need more water."

Malick blinked, blew out a thin breath.

Fen leaned demurely around the screen, body sheltered behind it, arm extended and bucket swinging by its rope from his hand.

"Would you mind?"

A jerky bit of a nod was all Malick managed, but he did get his legs to move again, eyes carefully focused only on the bucket as he approached. Except when he took hold of it, gave it a tug, Fen didn't let go.

There was no leverage problem this time, no awkward angle. The punch came straight from the shoulder, slammed into Malick's jaw, and knocked him down flat.

"...the *fuck?*"

Huh. Seemed if you got hit hard enough, you really did see stars.

Malick's ears were ringing, and *painpainpain* radiated from the point of impact and out through his head, right down his spine. He blinked up to see Fen standing over him—gah, still naked, and wet now too—all that hair hanging heavy and sticking to him everywhere, the ragged fringe dripping down into his eyes. Improbably, Malick's gaze caught on the chunky, ugly tracks of the sutures, strange fascination, as he watched the scarred skin shift over thick-hewn thigh muscles.

"I've just been thinking." Fen was amazingly calm and cool as he stared down at Malick. "You've been mocking me since the moment I met you. I don't like it."

Malick cradled his jaw with a careful hand, blinked some more. "*Mocking.*" He shook his head. Augh, bad idea.

"Not as much fun when it's offered freely?"

Malick sat up, indignant. "It wathn't *off*—" Damn it, had he lost a tooth? He stuck a finger in his mouth, gingerly poked around... No, all still accounted for, but it seemed he'd bitten his tongue rather smartly. Damn Fen and his... his... whatever the fuck this was. "It wasn't offered *freely*. It was offered in *payment*. There's a difference, and I'd prefer to keep on this side of it."

Fen frowned, eyes narrowed. "This side."

Frustrated, Malick flailed. "Yeah, *this* side... the better side, the, the... the not-disgusting side." And then he remembered how that might sound to Fen's ears, so he clarified: "The side that doesn't make me feel like I'm demanding sex in payment for doing someone I like a good turn. The side that doesn't make me feel like some sick deviant for getting what I want. You know—*that* side."

Fen only stared at him, calculating, before he shook his head. He shrugged.

"It wasn't in payment. It would've been, if you'd demanded it. But it wasn't."

Malick's mouth flapped, brow twisting. "No?" Could a person die of confusion?

"No." Apparently, that was all the answer Fen was going to give, because he merely turned—all that hair covering the good bits, naturally—and limped back into the shower-box, pulling the screen shut behind him. "I still need more water."

Malick... stared. Rubbed at his jaw some more. Scrubbed a hand through his hair.

What he needed was to make it a point to meet and begin associating with not-crazy people. The novelty alone should keep him entertained for... all right, probably minutes. But still.

Growling, Malick hauled himself up from the floor and found the bucket that Fen had apparently dropped while Malick had been admiring the stars grinding up from his jaw and bursting behind his eyes. He dipped it into the pool, pausing briefly when all the blood rushed to his head and settled, hot and pounding, at the base of his teeth. Fucking Fen. Malick hoped he'd at least bruised his knuckles good.

"It was the other things," Fen said as Malick set the bucket just outside the shower-box.

Malick straightened, squinting at the screen. "All right, it's in the right language and all the words make sense."

The screen rattled aside again. Malick couldn't help the bit of a flinch backward, but Fen merely cut him a wary look as he leaned around it and pulled the bucket through before sliding it closed.

"The other things you said. I was trying to pretend you meant them. And it's been a while, so... I wanted to."

Quiet. Subdued. Said to the floor, Malick could tell just by the way the stone nearly absorbed the words before they reached his ears.

He was afraid to guess what he'd said that might've meant enough to Fen that he'd wanted to—

Gah, he'd *wanted* to, and Malick had...

Fuck. Fucking fuck fuckitty *fuck*.

"Fen—"

"I understand."

Yeah? Well, maybe he could explain it Malick, then, because shit, he'd had the best intentions he could recall having in a very long time, and Fen had *wanted* to, and... *and.*

"Understand what, Fen?"

One of the bathsheets slipped from over the top of the screen. Half a moment later, Fen slid the screen aside, water dripping over his shoulders, down his chest, and into the fold of the sheet knotted around his hips. He reached for the other, pulling all that hair over his shoulder, and began working excess water from the base of his skull and down. His face was blank, his movements all unconscious reflex, and his gaze divided its time between the hair and the floor.

"I haven't any clothes."

Damn it, Malick hadn't even thought of that. And didn't much care now. "No one's up," he said, troubled by the statement he *did* care about. "Fen—understand what?"

Fen sighed, shut his eyes. "You think I'm too distracted. You think I don't see anything." He opened his eyes, but he still wouldn't look at Malick. "You didn't want it—you wanted me to want it. You win." He opened his mouth, like he meant to go on, but then just shut it and went back to squeezing water from his hair. "I think I might need help with the stairs."

Malick couldn't do a single thing but stare as Fen turned and slowly limped toward the door. What was that—four sentences? Five? And inside them, an entire lifetime of rejection, and calm acceptance of it, like he didn't expect anything else. Bloody hell, if that was what Fen thought was going on, it was amazing Malick had got away with only a sore jaw.

"Was that how it was with Asai?"

Fen stopped dead, every muscle in his back and shoulders tightening. His head turned slightly to the side, dipped down, but still, he wouldn't look at Malick.

"I'll take the stairs myself."

And Malick couldn't stand it, couldn't stand anything about it. That Fen loved that son of a bitch enough that Malick could still hurt him with only a name. That Fen thought Malick would do what Fen thought he'd been doing. That Malick's own behavior since he'd met Fen had probably made it all too believable.

He stood there like an idiot, gaping, until Fen was three shuffling steps away from the door, then Malick stalked over, shoved it back the two inches Fen had got it open, spun Fen's back into it, and pressed in. Fen's fists were clenched just as stiffly as his jaw, but they didn't come at Malick this time, just locked in tight to his sides, body rigid, the damp warmth of the bathsheet seeping all down the front of Malick and heating him through. Words were not Malick's friends tonight, and Fen was never good at them, so Malick avoided them, just leaned in and kissed him.

Not as hard as Malick's flaring temper would've otherwise made it, but deep and sweeping, aggressive and immediately intense. Fen kissed like he fought—all-in and no backing down, driving in and taking Malick over absolutely. There was a directness to it, the strange candor of wanting in the harsh breaths through his nose, the soft, demanding moans rumbling at the back of his throat, and the way his hands came up and sank into Malick's hair, closed into fists, held him still.

This is what I want, it said. *Give it to me.*

Simple; much more clear and unguarded than anything else about Fen.

His hair—the scent of almonds came from Fen's hair, winding right through the blander smell of the pine soap he'd used to wash it. Malick could smell it so clearly as he took a handful of it in his fist, let his fingers curl through the chill-wet of it, like he'd been wanting to do since the first time he'd seen Fen out on the floor of the Girou.

Panting, aroused almost beyond rational thought, Malick pulled back, trailed his lips along Fen's jawline, slipped a little nip to his earlobe.

"D'you still love him?"

He hadn't known he was going to ask it, almost appalled that it had come out his mouth, and *now*, but it was suddenly imperative that Malick know. Even more imperative than the aching arousal at his groin, Fen's answer to it jutting against Malick's hip.

"Does he love you? Does he even pretend to?"

Fen pulled in a tight breath, and Malick... smiled. There it was—there was the way in. The right one, the one that would stick.

Malick slipped a kiss to Fen's temple. "Would you like me to pretend for you? I'm fucking brilliant at it."

And the best part about it—the exploitation would be mutual and by conscious consent.

Fen tensed at the question, still distracted enough by Malick's mouth at his throat and ear that he didn't shove him away. "Please."

Please don't ask me that? Please keep doing what you're doing? Please just shut up and fuck me stupid and let me pretend this is whatever I need it to be to keep my fucked-up head from exploding into a million tiny pieces?

"Please what, Fen?" Malick soothed it just a little with a quick snap of his hips, crushing his erection into Fen's until Fen gasped and pushed back. "D'you want to close your eyes and pretend I'm him?" Ran his hands over Fen's arms, his shoulders, swept one hand in until it rested lightly around Fen's throat. Traced the other down the dips and swells of chest and torso. "Take from me what your beishin wouldn't give you and scream his name when you come?"

"Fuck you."

Malick grinned as he sank in to run his tongue over the cords of Fen's throat. As though he couldn't help it, Fen tilted his head to the side obligingly. Fen's body was so much more eloquent than he was, asking, so Malick answered, settled his hand around the side of Fen's neck, thumb brushing the small jutting bumps of the trachea. Fen's fingers dug in to the thick muscles just below Malick's shoulder blades, ruthless pressure, then jabbed almost right through the skin when Malick's hand settled over Fen's erection through the bathsheet.

"Tell me, Fen." Malick pressed in tight, letting Fen rock into his hand a few times before Malick squeezed, stones and throat both, tight enough to still all movement. "Say it so I'll know. Who are you going to see tonight while I'm fucking you?"

He didn't think he really wanted an answer, but he had to have one, had to know. And even if Fen said it, said the name that could rouse such pain in his heart that it completely stilled his body—a body he controlled so completely otherwise—Malick thought he *still* might not be able to walk away, *still* might not be able to stop himself from giving Fen exactly what he wanted.

Fen's eyes were squeezed shut, his head resting back against the smooth cedar of the door. Panting. Trembling with need. Hips swaying little stutter-stops, both fighting Malick's grip and rocking into it. His hands had bunched in Malick's shirt, knuckles digging into his backbone.

Fuck, he was beautiful. Color high and swathing his cheeks; muscles tense and quivering, scars and gashes and cuts standing out in soft relief against supple lines and curves; dark hair contrasting like a splash of ink down his entire body; face pulled into wanton lines of unthinking expression, silently shouting his need and hunger. One thing Fen couldn't hide, one thing he couldn't blank from his face and pretend to be unaffected— the effect was vibrating in Malick's hands, in the fluttering pulse at Fen's throat, the undeniable heat and solidity at his groin.

Couldn't keep it all from leaking from his eyes, either, Malick decided, dazed, as Fen slid them open slowly, looked right at Malick, swallowed so the muscles in his throat shifted against Malick's thumb, and pushed his hips in hard to Malick's hand. Eyes still locked to Malick's, Fen tipped his head back, bared his throat—submission; deliberate and cognizant.

"I *am* the ghost," Fen said, hoarse and low, "I don't see them," then he leaned in and brushed his lips over Malick's—

—took him by the shoulders and spun him, shoved his back into the door before Malick even realized he'd lost the leverage advantage.

Turnabout.

Oh, yeah. That'll teach me.

Malick grinned, arousal redoubling so fast it almost made his knees give. Somehow that half inch Fen had on Malick was looking like a lot more right now, and it gave Malick a wanton little thrill.

Smug, Fen swept his hands down over the breadth of Malick's chest, stirring warm little shudders, then tipped in, nipped at his throat.

"Dumbass. Help me upstairs."

They argued over whose room. Well, Malick argued. After he'd cleared the last step of the three flights up—four, if one counted the steps from the bath—Fen just shoved Malick off, said he needed to braid his hair, and ignored Malick's argument that his bed was bigger and his room not right next to Samin's. And anyway, Malick had pointed out—well, all right, whined—he wanted Fen to leave all that hair down, wanted to see what it looked like spread out beneath him, wanted Fen above him and to see what it was like to have it all fall around them, what it looked like when they moved.

He didn't say all of that, of course, but Fen probably knew. Definitely didn't care.

Braided, because it was the law, and because it would knot and tangle if he didn't, and anyway, "D'you want to do this or not?"

Oh, fuck, yes, but Malick kept a little bit of self-respect and merely rolled his eyes, followed Fen into his room, and shut the door.

Almond oil—that was where the scent of Fen came from. Almond oil combed through his hair to make it easier to untangle, easier to weave into the long, smooth plait. Malick watched the process for a little while, lounging back, propped on one elbow on Fen's bed. Fen was perched on the other side, hair over his shoulder and streaming down to the floor over the edge of the mattress as he combed it through. Malick watched it until he couldn't help touching, running his fingers all through it. Smooth and satiny, everything he'd imagined. Malick had to lean in and dip his mouth to Fen's shoulder, hand catching on Fen's through the thick drape of damp hair and pushing it away, taking the comb from his fingers and guiding him to his back on the sheets. Fen let him, arched up into him and pulled him in, demanding.

It shouldn't have been so good. Malick had built it up in his mind so heavily the reality shouldn't have even come close. But oh, save him, the reality of Fen bending to Malick's hand, curling his body up and in to meet Malick's, the reality of Fen's impatience as he pushed away Malick's shirt and yanked at his belt until Malick half-snorted and had to draw away for ten seconds. Ten seconds during which Fen growled in annoyance and whipped the bottle of almond oil at his Malick's head, snapped, "*Come* on, then," and yanked Malick back down before he'd even got his trousers kicked completely from his feet.

Almost no patience at all for foreplay, Fen.

"You said you'd pretend." Quiet. Cautious. "Pretend you… you meant—"

"No pretending about this, love."

Fen arched like a wanton cat when Malick entered him. Impatience appeased, the jagged edges of want smoothed down by the press of bodies, the slick of sweat-hot skin, the slow rock and push-drag-push of sensual rhythm. The light of the moons shattered silver-red through the window, a delicate filigree strewn over angled planes, fracturing over lean muscle, shadowing each dip and pulling every shift of breath into individual relief.

Malick had expected to spend all his time on the hair, running his fingers through it, winding it around limbs, fanning it out on the sheets, just to see what it looked like. He was apparently not half as obsessed as he'd thought he was. Just another part of Fen, another one of his fascinating edges, and deserving of attention, certainly, but not at the expense of ignoring the rest of him—the feel of him, the scent of him, the sound of his raspy breaths and whispered demands through his teeth.

Bloody damn, though, that hair did get everywhere, winding around limbs like clinging ivy.

"Exquisite, Fen." Malick dragged his mouth over brow and temple and sharp cheekbone. Firmed his grip on the blade of Fen's hip and rocked, quick and blunt, until it spiked a cry loose from Fen's throat.

Fen's gray eyes were open, glazed and shameless, expression lax in abandon. He reached, touched, arched, met every move with equal force and more craving. It drove into the heat down deep in the core of Malick, churned it hotter, sent it in a coiling squall through his limbs, through his chest, through his mind.

"I meant it, every fucking word."

Fen's brow creased then immediately smoothed out again when Malick took him in hand, momentary bemusement forgotten as Malick shifted the angle. Kisses, because Malick couldn't seem to stop, all long and deep then shallow and importunate, going from languid to frantic and back to languid again. Drawing it out, making it last, because now that Malick had it, he never wanted it to end. His every breath was put into making it good, giving pleasure, thigh muscles burning with the strain of keeping his strokes long and slow and deep and forceful. He shifted again and gave a little *pushpushpush* that had Fen cursing and grinding helplessly up into it.

Malick's heart stopped—actually *stopped*, he was sure of it—when Fen's head dropped back, throat a smooth, arced stretch of vulnerable skin beneath Malick's mouth as Fen shoved out a sharp curse and writhed a shudder, face blank with desire, open and unguarded—fucking *beautiful*—as he came. Powerless to pleasure, shaking and sweating and climaxing in Malick's arms. Shattering.

Malick followed, he had no choice. Just the sight, the feel of Fen's body seizing around him, pushed him down into a spiral of grinding pleasure, took him under, mind and body and soul swathed entirely in blank-white bliss.

Fen fell asleep directly after, returned a kiss sluggishly with eyes closed, and then just didn't open them again. Passed out, maybe, Malick supposed. It had been a long, difficult day and night, and there'd been the uzin too. He shoved Fen into a more comfortable position, reminded about the stitches only when he saw them as he arranged Fen's legs, guilt assuaged by the fact that none of them had torn.

Malick padded to his own room for the bandages Umeia had left, and wrapped a good several coils around Fen's thigh before climbing in beside him and pulling the sheet and quilt up over them both. Dragged and prodded until he had Fen curled into his chest, warm skin all along the side of his body.

He half-considered combing out and braiding Fen's hair for him—it did look a little tangled, and would likely be more so in the morning—but instead settled for running his fingers through as much of it as he could reach and gently unknotting whatever snags he ran into. Anyway, he hadn't the first clue how to braid hair. Maybe Fen would teach him.

"Tomorrow." Malick set a light kiss to the crown of Fen's head, breathing in almonds as his fingers gently unraveled a particularly stubborn snarl. "Tonight," he amended after a glance out the window as he took hold of Fen's hand and dragged his arm to rest across Malick's torso. "We'll go and fetch them for you tonight. And then we'll find her and put her soul to rest. And perhaps unlock yours while we're at it."

He didn't care anymore what he was going to have to do to get Fen's mother back for him, didn't care about the laws he was going to have to break, or the risk he took in doing it. Fen was Wolf's, and it was Malick's job to save him if he could.

Because Malick might be a bit of a romantic, but he wasn't stupid— one night of permitting a semi-thaw wasn't going to solve all Fen's problems, wasn't going to appease all his demons.

For a man who was known to the world around him as a Ghost, he had more haunting him than any man should have to bear. There was blinding passion beneath all that icy exterior, Malick had known it from the beginning—save him, he'd seen it tonight, felt it, wanted to drown in it—but it belonged to Jacin. Not Jacin-rei. Not Fen.

Jacin-rei used it to hate and threaten a man he'd loved, perhaps still loved, used it to break himself free from whatever had held him to Asai, used it to carve slices into himself to keep his sanity.

Fen used it to kill, to seek out those who would take from him and bleed them, stare blank-faced at them while they screamed.

Jacin didn't use it; Jacin invested it, allowed it to possess him through his love for his family, through the twist and curl of his body against Malick's. Jacin had had too much taken from him, and one night with the Almighty Cock wasn't going to give it all back. Perhaps nothing could. But Malick figured giving Fen his brothers and sister back would be a good place to start. And saving Fen's mother's soul would be the next logical stepping stone. After that...

They'd have to see. It might just turn out that Fen was the answer to long-withheld justice, and if Malick had to use Fen to get it… well, maybe Fen wouldn't actually mind it too much. He might have to be used to be saved, and Malick was beginning to think he knew now where to start.

Fen was a paladin searching for a lord to lead him. Asai had lost his hold on him and now that hold was, quite literally, at Malick's fingertips. All he had to do was tighten his grip.

He'd start with real wooing. He hadn't done that in… he didn't think he'd ever actually wooed anyone, not sincerely, anyway, and not for ages. Gifts—you were supposed to give gifts, right? He'd have to ask Umeia. Gifts and compliments and… no, not flowers. Fen would probably beat him over the head with them. Or make him eat them. Or shove them up—

Right. Ow. No flowers.

Small kindnesses. That sounded less soppy. Affection, if Fen would take it. And Malick actually wanted to give it. He might not be able to stop himself. Because, along with all the other revelations Malick had uncovered tonight, he understood now that he didn't merely want Fen— he wanted Fen and Jacin-rei and Jacin. And Jacin was the core—the heart—of the trinity.

Malick had seen unintended glimpses of Jacin. Now, he wanted Fen to introduce him to him.

ᛟ

Festival-month, Year 1319, Cycle of the Wolf

Asai was waiting on the straight-backed chair in Jacin's room when Jacin shimmied back in through the window. It was ugly and painful, the small burst of fear and shame that wrenched through Jacin's gut, but the heat of still-fresh anger kept him balanced. Kept his stare cool and calm as he stood straight, tucked his hands to the small of his back, and lifted his chin.

Asai was silent, watching him, dark eyes furious, but a thin, scornful smile curled at his mouth.

Any other time, it would have made heat bloom on Jacin's cheeks, risen helpless, stuttered apologies from him. Not tonight. Tonight, he held onto the anger. Tonight, he kept his mouth shut and his chin up. Defiant.

"You have added flying to your skills, Ghost?"

The name was a dart, meant to hurt, because he *knew*, Jacin had let him see. Mistakes. One after another since he'd come here.

Jacin shrugged, indifferent. "Merely landing, Beishin."

It had been a chancy thing, and he hadn't been sure he could do it. It was two stories from the porch roof beneath his window down to the ground, after all. But with a bit of lift, and some calculated twisting before he hit the ground, Jacin had managed it with minimal damage to ankles and shins. The real worry had been climbing back up, but he hadn't thought of that until he'd got back and the lack of handholds registered. Drainpipes were such wonderfully useful things.

Asai was still staring, expectant. Waiting for Jacin to break down, no doubt. Waiting for the blubbering apologies. He could keep waiting. Jacin could stand here all night, and he doubted Asai had the patience to watch him do it.

It only took another few minutes: Asai's mouth set in a thin line, and he stood, paced slowly over to Jacin, dark eyes piercing as always, but Jacin *would not* allow the gaze to fuzz his mind as it so often did. Not this time. He kept his own gaze locked to the angry one staring back at him and stood straight and unflinching as Asai advanced. Trying to tower, when he really didn't anymore. Jacin had marked his own height slowly creeping past Asai's only this past summer. He wondered if Asai had noticed yet. If he had, he gave no indication that it mattered.

"Where did you go, Jacin-rei?"

Jacin let his mouth turn up at the corner. "Why, Beishin, I didn't know you cared."

A hard slap to his cheek made his head rock to the side. His ears rang. Jacin made the smirk twist wider, straightened, and met Asai's gaze again.

Asai shook out his hand. "I *care* that if you get yourself caught, I face death in the Courts for having harbored you. I *care* that the amulet you stole for whatever illicit jaunt you took tonight damns me without question if you're found with it. I *care* that insolence and stupidity can ruin all we've worked for with one careless step by a Ghost who can't—"

"And what about *my* damnation, Beishin?" Quiet. Calm. "Oh, that's right—I'm only a Ghost and already damned. What's one more to the tally?"

"Where do you get such ideas, Jacin-rei? What have I ever—?"

"Interesting, the things a Ghost can learn when even his master thinks he's deaf and blind and *stupid*." Jacin stepped in right up close. "I *heard* you, Beishin. Were you trying to impress her? Did it work? Did she let you spirit her upstairs in the middle of your gathering and fuck her on your bed? Or maybe she couldn't wait, and let you have at her in the kitchen. She looked like she was gagging for it."

Understanding unfurled over Asai's face, and again, it might have made Jacin bow his head and look away in shame before, but Asai *didn't* understand, not at all.

Years, Jacin had spent in this house, learning and trying to please an unpleasant man, striving for perfection, killing himself reaching for control, training for a purpose he wasn't allowed to know, trusting and believing. *Years*, he'd spent pretending he didn't exist to anyone but Asai and Vonshi, hiding behind shadows, *being* a damned ghost, because he'd been told it was necessary, believed it. Even the guards weren't allowed to know Jacin existed.

And then... *tonight*. One charming smile from that... that *tart*, one subtle promise in the form of innuendo, and stark betrayal had come wearing Beishin's pleasant smile.

"Ah." Asai smiled. "Jacin-rei, I have told you before. Sometimes one must say things that—"

"No." It was all Jacin could do to keep his voice even. "'Pitiable, wretched animals,' isn't that what you said? 'Damned by arrogant demigods, poor things, they should all be put out of their misery.'" He leaned in, darkly satisfied when Asai took an involuntary step back. "'As doomed as the people who have made them outcasts.'" Low now and taking on a feral edge. "'The Jin wasted all they had so foolishly—they cannot be trusted with magic. Perhaps wiping them out altogether would be best all around.'" Jacin's hands were fisted behind his back now, and he was glad, because he didn't think he wanted to know if they were actually trembling.

Asai's smile turned condescending. "You have heard me say such things before. You know I must keep some semblance of cooperation to outside eyes, Jacin-rei, you know how—"

"Not about *this*." Jacin took another step in; Asai retreated again. "Not about..."

Not about me.

Jacin couldn't make himself say it. He'd shown Asai the things inside him before, let him see, and this was what Asai had chosen to do with it.

"You knew I was there. You said those things because you *knew* I was there."

"In the middle of a Festival gathering where the man who saved you would have been arrested, tortured, and killed, if you'd been found out." Asai's expression hardened. "Your emotions make you weak and foolish, little Ghost. A lesson was necessary."

"And your eyes needed to be glued to her cleavage while you taught it?"

Jacin clamped his jaw shut. Shit.

"And jealousy," said Asai, smooth and arrogant, "is the basest of emotions."

Jacin had to clench his hands behind his back to keep from clouting Asai's superior smile right off his face.

"What about anger? What about betrayal?" Jacin stepped in again, but Asai didn't back away this time. "What *do* you believe of the Jin, Beishin? What do you believe at all? You lecture me on the gods and their laws, and yet you thwart them by hiding a 'pitiable wretched animal,' teach him to fight, to kill. You tell me the withering of Jin magic is what keeps the Ancestors shrieking in my head, yet you entertain judges and prefects and lords in your home, men who steal that very magic, and yet here I sit—*your weapon*—idle and watching you leer at the wife of a man who would happily bleed my brother dry. You *seduce* her by maligning me *and* my people, and yet you still want me to believe that whatever plan you have for me will save the people you speak of as foolish dupes who would be best got off the world."

"Your belief is not entirely necessary," Asai said softly. "But it would be… beneficial."

This time, he couldn't help it: Jacin whipped his hands out from behind his back and *shoved* Asai into the wall.

Surprise flushed Asai's face, made his eyes go wide. "You would *dare*—"

"I would dare so much more than this, Beishin. I would dare to demand to know what it is you want with me, what you've seen, why you've risked so much, invested so much to make me believe, if my belief is *unnecessary*." Jacin leaned in until he was directly in Asai's face. The thought of sliding out one of his knives, waving it threateningly, came fleetingly to mind, but only fleetingly. Even with all the fury and hurt writhing inside him, Jacin couldn't bring himself to actually threaten the life of his beishin. It did not mean, however, that he had to let Asai know it. He blanked his face into hostile lines, let his gaze go dangerous. "What is my purpose, Beishin?"

Asai watched Jacin closely, trying to see inside, perhaps, or trying to *see* at all. "Your purpose is to be that which I have foreseen for you. My purpose is to save your people—yours is to trust. If you cannot…" Asai paused, raised an eyebrow. "If you cannot, then your purpose is lost and you will fail. Fail your brother, fail your mother, and the Jin as a whole." He tilted his head. "How difficult would it be, do you think, my angry little Ghost, to keep your mind your own, should you fail so spectacularly? Can you accept the responsibility for the horrible fates of those you love when you yourself allow that failure?"

"Stop it. You will not manipulate me so easily, not anymore. You won't use me to—"

"To save those you love? To save me?"

It made Jacin suck in a sharp breath, too telling, but he couldn't help it.

Asai sighed. "Ah, my boy, my own, I would not have burdened you with it, but… I understand your anger and your doubt. I had merely hoped…" He paused, looked away. "I had hoped that you might trust me enough, dare I think… love me enough, to keep your faith, your belief." His gaze drifted back to Jacin's, sorrow in its dark depths, but it was the disappointment that cut, even as Asai stroked Jacin's cheek where he'd slapped it before. "To touch the Untouchable. Love the unlovable. None would dare love the Ghost, but I am… weak." Asai shut his eyes. "You think I scorn what you would give."

Damn it, there were tears crowding Jacin's eyes, blurring his vision. He had no answer, or at least not one he could give without choking. And what did it matter?—Asai *knew*.

"Never." Asai slid his fingers up, pushing messy tangles from out of Jacin's eyes. "You cannot know how difficult..." His hand fisted, and he jerked it away. "I would not have what you would give from gratitude, Jacin."

Jacin. *Jacin.* Had Asai ever called him that before?

It... stunned. Every emotion that had been boiling in Jacin's chest all night abruptly turned on him, razed him, then abandoned him. The betrayal was a burnt-out husk, barely even a memory. The anger—Jacin's friend, his safety—was just... gone. Without either to hold, Jacin was adrift, lost in the mangled maze of his noisy mind, couldn't even remember what had driven him from Asai's house hours ago, fury so tight in his throat his breath had almost whistled through it.

"Not..." Jacin shook his head, dazed, took hold of Asai's hand and pressed it to his cheek. "It was never... no, Beishin."

It was thoughtless, the impulse, driven by years of denial and then a single crystalline moment of having what he'd been denied edging at his fingertips. The voices were blank-white anarchy, Jacin's mind a clapper in a struck bell; Jacin ignored them, leaned in, slow and careful. Asai watched him all the way, let him, and when Jacin's mouth hovered only a breath from Asai's, Asai tipped in.

It was...

Words wouldn't do. It just *was*. So long wanting it, so long wishing for it. Desire spiraled through Jacin, took him, slid between the ribs of every bit of reason and bitter knowledge, and skewered them like cancerous growths.

Asai's mouth was softer than Jacin had thought it would be, damp and full and responsive. Not at all the stern thing that reminded Jacin constantly of his imperfections. Not the laughing thing that curled in mild, disenchanted disdain when Jacin failed a task to which he'd been set. Giving, willing, a sharpness of fervency around its edges.

Sensation was a live thing, curling over Jacin's skin, stirring it to sentience, waking an urgency he'd kept throttled down deep because he'd had no choice. Except now Asai's warm hands were cupping Jacin's face, Asai's fingers were skimming into the wispy hairs at Jacin's temples, Asai's thumbs were stroking over Jacin's cheekbones.

Receiving Jacin's clumsy enthusiasm, and guiding it into breathless passion. Taking awkward jerks and tugs, and sliding them languid.

Real. All of it, *real*. All this time, all that want and longing, and now...

Had Asai wanted too? Had he refused Jacin because he'd thought offered love mere indebted gratitude?

Jacin almost laughed, giddy and dizzy with lust. A seer, and Asai couldn't see *this*?

He pressed in, the lines of his body fitting easily against Asai's, the deep-down awesome *joy* of finally having what he wanted overriding any doubt or anger that had brought him to it. Asai was hard against Jacin's hip, panting against his mouth. Boldly, Jacin rocked into him, almost came in his trousers when Asai gasped in response.

"Jacin." Asai pulled away, but allowed Jacin to draw him back again with a trail of kisses down his throat, then another, deeper and more insistent, to his mouth.

Fuck, Asai smelled of… jasmine, like he always did, and clean linen and a little bit of wine. But over it all, *her* perfume had oozed into his clothes, and bled all over him. Jacin wanted to wipe it out, obliterate it, smear himself all over Asai and lay his own scent over him, make him—

"*Jacin.*" A push this time, firm and purposeful. Asai's hands gripped Jacin's shoulders, holding him away.

Oh, but Asai was beautiful like this, flushed skin and gaze a little vague and burning, lips red and damp and wantonly plumped. Even as Jacin stared at them, Asai pulled them into a thin line.

"My boy… we cannot. *I* cannot." Asai firmed his hold before Jacin could push back in. "Everything we have worked for, everything I have seen—I cannot risk it all, not even for you."

Jacin could have cried. In fact, he just might. His chest had gone tight again, and there was an aching burn behind his brow.

"There *is* no risk. I'll do whatever you want, everything you want, you don't have to—"

"Then this is payment?"

Jacin hadn't seen the neat lines of the trap, not until he'd barreled right into them. "That isn't… *no*, Asai, you don't understand. It's nothing to do with—"

"My boy." Asai slipped his hand to Jacin's cheek again, stroked it. "My Ghost, my gentle mercenary. If we do this, we place all at risk. We will both fail in the things we want, but this failure will be mine. I would not be your brother's doom." He laid a gentle kiss to Jacin's brow. "Would you?"

Unfair. Un-fucking-*fair*.

"*No*, but—"

"If you love me, you *must* trust me." Asai's voice was soft. He pressed his body forward, too quick, before he pulled back again, but the surprise and the overwhelming need that flared at Asai's touch still made Jacin gasp. "You see now that you are not alone in your… wish. It has been no easy thing to bury my desire all these years, but bury it I must, and you must."

Asai's fingers were tight on Jacin's shoulders, digging into tendon and muscle, but the near-pain of it brought no clarity, only more hurt.

"Jacin, I cannot tell you what you wish to know. The future is a chancy thing, and sometimes, the mere speaking of it can change it in ways I cannot allow. If I were to tell you right now that I foresaw you skulking down to the kitchen tonight to filch a biscuit, would you still do it? Or would you refuse merely to assert your control over your own actions? Or would I have indeed planted the idea by voicing the prediction, and thus have altered the future myself by my carelessness?"

There was sense in there somewhere, Jacin knew there was, but he couldn't quite follow it, not now. Everything in his head was white and loud, and he didn't want to know any of this anyway.

But he couldn't not try. "If you told me what I must do, I would do it. My future is what you make of it."

"So, I should either risk the future and our goals, along with your mother and your brother, or I should command you to love me—to make love to me—because you would do it, if I said you must."

"No! That isn't what I meant, you're twisting—"

"Jacin-rei." Stern now, the voice of Beishin, hard and unyielding, where Asai's had been sad and tender only a second ago. "Would you be the doom of your brother? Would you fail your mother?"

Jacin shook his head, the tears burning hotter now, crowding his eyes. "*No, I—*"

"And do you trust me, Jacin-rei? Do you *believe?*"

Jacin didn't want to answer, because he knew exactly where this was going, knew exactly what answer he had to give, and the demand that would follow it. Except, as with everything else, he had no choice.

"…Yes."

Because he was Beishin. And Jacin believed. Most of the time. Sometimes. Fuck, he just didn't *know* anymore.

"Then trust me in this, Jacin-rei: we cannot do this. It is not for us. At least… not now."

Jacin was going to cry. He was going to start leaking all these humiliating tears that were cramming against the backs of his eyes, and then it wouldn't matter, because Asai wouldn't want a simpering weakling anyway.

Control.

Control.

But, damn it, he'd *had* it, right in his hands. Asai wanted him, perhaps had wanted him as long as Jacin had wanted back, and none of this was bloody *fair.*

"Tell me where you went tonight, Jacin-rei. I must know if there is even a small chance someone saw you."

"No one saw me." Jacin whispered it to the floor, unable to bring his gaze up to Asai's, not wanting to fall into the dark depths of it again, because Jacin could drown in there, and Asai wouldn't save him. "I went to the camp. I went to see them."

"Did you." Asai sighed. "And…?"

"And." Jacin walked slowly over to his bed, sank down and propped his elbows to his knees, head hanging. "And I didn't let them see me."

He'd stood outside the house that was once his home, and watched the people who were once his family carry on without him. Like he really was a ghost, hovering at their edges. His father, with his hard views soured further; his mother, gentle and half-mad, but still so kind and at peace with it; Morin tormenting little Caidi, but with more good-natured teasing inside it than Jacin had ever seen; and Joori…

Not a half of anyone, not anymore. Grown strong and assertive, the head of the household in truth, if not in name. The mirror image of Jacin himself, but somehow more substantial, more real, more… *there*. Lounging in their sleeping room, too early for bed, but apparently the end of a long day, because Joori had looked tired, but content. He'd had a book on his lap—old and yellowed, its pages almost disintegrating in his careful, callused hands—reading quietly as the others gathered in the kitchen. No empty mat beside him, waiting, nor one curled up against the wall, out of the way. Not a twin anymore, his own man, whole and complete, his Self intact, and certainly not missing another half.

"I couldn't…" It hardly made a sound. "I didn't… didn't want them to… to…"

To see.

Or worse—*not see.*

Asai sighed. "It is best you don't venture there again, Jacin-rei. This too, you must trust."

Jacin nodded automatically, but he couldn't help the frown, the slight tilt of his head. "Does he truly never write to me, Beishin?"

Does he know I write him?

How often do you betray me, Beishin?

…Have you ever not?

Asai was silent for long enough to make it heavy, before he stepped over to the window, peered out. "Do you believe, Jacin-rei, that I would not give them to you, if he did?"

Yes, Jacin almost said, but it was an answer he didn't think he owed Asai. Just another confession that would amount to nothing more than a fresh weapon for Asai to use against him. And anyway, Jacin had already humiliated himself enough tonight.

Instead, he said, "I don't think I'll be going back."

It had hurt far more than he'd thought it would. Hurt even more because he hadn't once been tempted to reveal himself, even when his mother had sensed him, spoken to the Ghost hiding inside his shadows in her dooryard.

Asai merely nodded, and turned for the door. "Then I shall not need to ask for the amulet back." He laid a hand to the doorknob and paused. "Jacin-rei—"

"I will be what you want, Beishin." It was true, and Jacin meant it, but he said it mostly because he really didn't want to hear whatever sympathetic platitudes Asai might offer in an attempt to placate the lovesick Ghost. "I will be ready."

Asai merely nodded then let himself through the door without looking back.

Jacin sat there for a long time, staring at the floor, thinking of very little, just letting the sadness take him, dwelling inside it one last time, because it was the last time he intended to let it through. Asai was right, in this, at least: it was weakness. All of it. The profound, soul-killing *futility* of it all. It made Jacin a pawn, a biddable puppet, willing to sell his soul to the first person who answered to the simpering little fool who crouched at the bottom of his heart. Selling himself into slavery for a kind touch, selling his own fate for an obsessive love that would never be anyway.

Jacin was done with it. Done with sentiment, done with bloody Asai and his deep-dark eyes, done with pining like an idiot, because it fucking *hurt*, and almost having it hurt even more, and he was just… just *done*.

Save his brother, save his mother, all by saving the Jin, if he could. He would use Asai as Asai was using him, and in the end, Jacin would walk away with his sanity and the safety of his family. Not a bad trade for his heart.

And as for Asai? Well.

"I'm not perfect, Beishin." Jacin licked his lips, sucked in a bracing breath. "But neither are you."

9

Storm-month, Year 1322, Cycle of the Wolf

Samin couldn't help it—he stared when Fen sat down at the table in the common room, just as he'd done every morning at breakfast for the past week. And just like every other morning for the past week, Fen was fully dressed, his hair was braided neat and straight, and his face was… completely blank. No soft, private smile, no soppy love-struck gaze, no quiet sighs as he dished out his rice. Fen greeted Samin and the girls with his usual silent nod and poured his tea, only giving the slightest of second glances to the new green streaks in Shig's hair to go with the red and blue.

He didn't seem like he was absurdly smitten, nor had he apparently needed to be peeled off Malick, and in fact seemed fully able to function without him. And Samin *knew* they'd been at it last night. The walls weren't thin but they weren't soundproof, either, and Fen's room *was* right next to his.

Maybe Samin had been wrong. Because if ever there was a man ready to shatter, it was Fen as he'd been last night on the roof, and Samin had been sure that what Fen and Malick got up to after would push Fen further along. Instead, he was just as prickly and borderline hostile as he'd ever been—his own version of normal. Samin had to wonder, though, if Fen had yet seen those very distinctive marks on his neck just beneath his ear, and if he had, whether Malick wasn't up yet because Fen had killed him for them.

Samin cleared his throat. "How's the leg?"

"Fine." Fen dribbled some honey onto his bread then reached for his tea and said, "Thank you," like he'd almost forgotten to add it.

Shig was abruptly more awake than she'd been five minutes ago. "What's wrong with your leg?"

Fen shot a quick glance across the table, opened his mouth like he might actually answer, but then merely shook his head and took a sip of tea.

Samin answered for him—"A nasty slice to his thigh last night"—still watching Fen, but all Fen did was tighten his mouth.

Samin wondered what would happen if he told the girls exactly how nasty the slice was and exactly how nasty the circumstances under which Fen had got it had been, but he wasn't going to. It seemed a private thing, something to which Samin himself shouldn't have been witness, and since it was sheer accident of circumstance that he had been, he kept that bit to himself.

"Umeia sewed him up," was all he said.

Let the girls assume what they wanted. There'd been plenty of opportunity last night for nasty slices, after all.

"Sewed him up?" Yori blinked between Fen and Samin. "How many stitches?"

Fen's hand tightened around his teabowl. "I wasn't counting."

"Well, how bad is it?" Yori's tone was somewhere between anger and concern. She turned to Samin. "Will it take him out if we get a job?" And then back to Fen. "You didn't look like you were limping."

Samin snatched up a couple of dumplings before Shig got them all. "I expect we'll figure that out if and when we get a job."

"It won't." Fen's tone was cool and hard.

Yori huffed. "Did it happen at Sonji-onna's?"

Again, Samin turned to watch Fen, curious how he'd answer. If he'd answer. There were still things about Fen that were unpredictable, and downright incomprehensible—take last night, for a good example—but Samin liked to think he'd got rather adept at interpreting him.

As Samin had rather thought, Fen simply chose not to answer, just kept sipping his tea, eyes on the table, completely uncaring that the expectant silence that fell around him grew more prickly with each passing second. He hadn't touched his breakfast yet, and it didn't look like he was going to, which was telling in itself: breaking routine, on edge still, and trying not to be. Not the backlash Samin had expected after Malick finally got his way, but... Fen clearly wasn't all right, either.

"What happened at Sonji-onna's?" Shig's soft voice was slightly accusing, miffed.

It broke some of the tension that had built itself into the silence, loosened something in Samin's chest that had wound up with it. Samin tucked his snort back into his throat and sank his teeth into his grilled fish.

"She gave us a name," Fen replied.

Yori and Shig were obviously waiting for him to go on, but Fen didn't seem to notice, sipping his tea and staring at the table.

Yori rolled her eyes. "*And...?*"

Fen raised his eyebrows at Yori over the rim of his bowl. "And I'm going to kill him." The *obviously* went unsaid but rang clear, and his brow furrowed like he couldn't understand why she'd even asked the question.

Shig's fist pounding into the tabletop made them all jump. "You don't get to do this one by yourself too!" She looked at Samin, bottom lip gone wibbly. "It's not fair."

Samin almost choked on his fish. He swallowed, took a good gulp of tea, before he turned to Fen.

"Shig was a little… unhappy that—"

"Pissed." Shig gave Fen a betrayed look. "I was pissed."

"Oh, for the love of—" Yori growled and made a great show of noisily slapping a helping of seasoned kelp into her bowl. "Shig, honestly, if I have to hear this *one more*—"

"It isn't *my* fault you always listen when I talk. All you have to do is *not listen*. I hardly ever listen to *you*."

"Yeah, like when I tell you to *stop bloody moaning* about last night before my head explodes."

Samin had to bite the inside of his cheek this time but he managed to give Shig a nod in acknowledgement. He was quite proud of himself for not laughing outright at Fen's expression of utter bewilderment.

"Shig was pissed that you and Malick went off without her last night."

Shig turned to Fen. "The thing at Pon's was a fluke. I usually do a lot more than that, but they were all charmed, which *never* happens, and they were full-Blood charms, so I couldn't—"

"You don't need to justify yourself," Yori chided. "Fen knows all that. *Don't* you, Fen?"

She pointed a meaningful look at Fen, who was still staring between the two sisters with his bowl of tea poised at his mouth, almost frozen. Honestly, Samin was going to burst something important if he couldn't let the chuckles loose pretty soon.

"I wasn't *justifying* myself. I was just explaining to Fen that last night—"

"That last night was unusual, and you'll be sure to impress him next time?" Yori's voice and expression had both turned sweet, which would normally be unnerving, but right now was just fucking hilarious. "Honestly, Shig, get in line behind Malick, why don't you. I won't be able to stand watching the *both* of you preening like slutty cats."

Shig mimicked her sister's sugary smile, all teeth and dimples and wide, blinking eyes. "You mean like you do with Umeia?"

"*I* don't want to *sleep* with Umeia."

"I don't want to sleep with Fen, either!" Shig turned to Fen. "I would, you're very cute, but you're very noisy, too, and Malick sort of called dibs, so it's only fair." She paused, eyebrows lifting. "Unless you really want to? You don't want to, right?"

Fen's mouth had dropped open, gaze blank and a little dazed as he peered back at Shig. His lack of an answer didn't seem to have anything to do with surliness this time—it looked like he was just plain scunnered.

It was pretty fucking funny, in a painful sort of way. The socially clumsy not quite propositioning the socially useless.

"Ha!" Yori still wore that scary smile, but now her eyes had gone a bit narrow. "Even Fen's not *that* clueless. You keep looking at him like you want to sprinkle him with honey and tuck in. Like we can't tell *exactly* what you—"

"And *you*, sister dear, have got sex-on-the-brain so bad you think everyone else's mind is right down in the gutter with yours. Why don't you just go down and buy one of the boys tonight and give us all a rest? Umeia will be happy to find you one who doesn't mind getting topped by a woman."

Yori's face turned pink and her eyes took on a malicious glitter. She kept the syrupy smile as she opened her mouth to retort—something vicious and cutting, no doubt; the sisters could really go at it sometimes. Samin was denied the spectacle, because it all seemed too much for Fen— he jerked up from his chair and set his tea carefully on the table.

"I beg your pardon." He bowed his head at Shig. "It was not my intention to…" He frowned, searching. "…to exclude you."

"Exclude who from what?" Malick came sauntering into the common room with a bright grin and far too much satisfaction behind his eyes. His gaze lit immediately on Fen, and his grin grew wider as he leaned his shoulder into the wall, all lazy good humor. "G' morning everyone."

"Mal, you're up!" Yori's face went bright, likely wondering exactly how much of that last exchange Malick had heard, and hoping for none of it.

"Yeah, and not in a fun way." Malick's tone had dipped slightly accusing as he stared at Fen, probably put out he hadn't got a morning cuddle or another go. He slipped a mollifying wink at Yori as he ambled up beside Fen and threw an arm over his shoulders. "Sleep well?" Clearly possessive. Clearly an announcement—*mine*.

It only took a half a second for Fen to shrug Malick off. Samin had no idea why he was so pleased to see the familiar little snarl, but he was. It had no effect on Malick, and if it did, it wasn't the one Samin was sure Fen intended: Malick merely grinned wider, swung his arm back up, and held on tighter this time.

Fen growled and jammed his elbow into Malick's ribs hard enough to make him puff a sharp little gasp and let go. "What are we, boyfriends now?"

"Ooh!" Shig clapped her hands with a happy grin. "Are you?"

Samin's eyebrows shot up, and those snorts he'd been trying to hold back before redoubled to nearly choke him.

"*No!*" Fen barked then muttered something irritable about "fucking *dibs!*" under his breath.

"Ooh, ow." Shig gave Malick a sympathetic look. "Where'd you get that bruise?"

Malick dabbed gingerly at his jaw. "Fen clocked me." He was absurdly cheerful about it as he mussed at the already mussed fringe hanging over Fen's eyes.

Fen knocked Malick's hand away. "Leave off, or I'll match it on the other side for you."

Oh, yeah, Samin didn't say with the proper amount of sarcasm, *that'll teach him.*

Malick only rolled his eyes and gestured to Fen's chair. "Sit back down, would you, please? We should fill them all in on the job tonight."

Fen glared, mouth tightening and ticcing, but he stopped the snarling, seemed to think about the request for a moment, then did as Malick had asked. Sullenly. Wound up tighter than he'd been before. Obviously not reacting the way Samin had been sure he would after Malick finally had him, but this... was no less troublesome. Mostly because Samin didn't know what to make of it. Malick was the one who was acting all handsy and chipper, and Fen was the one who seemed like he'd got what he wanted and was done now, thank you.

It was really quite funny, when Samin thought about it, and with two different people, he might've got enough entertainment out of the ludicrous situation to last him for months. Except there was a new tension about Fen that Samin didn't like at all, a strange knowing light in Malick's eyes, and a curious patience that Samin had never seen before.

"Another job? Tonight?" Yori frowned at Malick as he took his seat between her and Shig. "We've never had two in a week."

"Then this will be new." Malick helped himself to fish and bread and casually planted an oblate beside Fen's bowl. "You didn't tell them, Fen?" He said it with an innocuous lift of his eyebrows as he snapped up the last dumpling.

It took a moment, but Fen eventually, slowly, took the oblate and began working at its rind.

Malick didn't even look smug. "It should be fairly easy. It's a personal commission. Your bonuses will be coming from the House till, not the Mage. We're going to get Fen's brothers and sister and bring them back here." As though it hadn't been a bolt from the blue, Malick turned to Yori. "Is there anything that could pass for furniture in that room next to yours? We'll need someplace to put them."

Samin likely looked as shocked as the girls did, and he'd been there last night, he'd heard Fen's question about the refugees. Still, he somehow hadn't even considered this.

"Is this another snatch from one of the camps?"

Not that Samin objected, but they were risky, and Malick and Shig both had to use a lot of magic to pull the last one off. And with the hunters always watching, using magic, no matter how skilled one was, it was always dangerous.

Somehow, though it made every bit of sense when he thought about it, Samin was still surprised when Fen was the one to answer.

"No." Fen kept his eyes on his fingers as he slowly peeled his oblate. "They're... elsewhere. And they don't need to be 'snatched', only..." He trailed off, frowning at the sticky, ruby fruit in his hands.

"Rescued," Malick put in, tone weirdly gentle, and eyes...

Oh, save the bloody idiot, he was completely gone. Samin only just kept from groaning in near-despair. How had he got it all so completely backward? This was so much worse than how he'd thought it was going to go. How, after all, did Malick ever expect someone like Fen to deal with something as chancy and incomprehensible as another's heart?

That was it—Samin was done. He just wasn't smart enough for this, and guessing was making his brain all hurty. They were both grown men, after all, though granted, they were both off in too many ways for anything between them to be even close to healthy or safe. But Samin was done with it. If Fen ended up crazy—craz*ier*—and Malick ended up gutted, well, then. Samin would just have to keep himself and the girls out of collateral-damage range.

Maybe it was time for him to cultivate a handy drinking problem.

"Rescued." Fen laid the oblate on the table next to his untouched breakfast. "Yes. Thank you." He sucked in a long breath and twitched his shoulders straight. "If you've a map, I can show you where. It won't take long. Though we might need..." He shot a quick glance at Malick and then let his gaze settle on Shig. "I thought... if you..." It was like he was having a hard time coming up with the words. With a frustrated sigh and a clench of his teeth, Fen shook his head and tried again. "I'd like to buy a small dray. My..." His eyes flicked to every one of them, gauging. "My sister... she's only little. The walk might be difficult for her." He looked at Shig again. "Will you help?"

Shig actually *beamed*. "Of course!" She shot a smug look at Malick. "After breakfast, yeah?"

"Yeah." Fen's voice was nearly a hoarse whisper as he flushed and went back to mangling his oblate. "Thank you."

Making amends for having "excluded" Shig last night?

Damn it, all of it, it was just too... too *touching*. Why did almost everything wrung from this man's mouth have to poke at Samin's soft spots? And now there was a little sister. Apparently, a *little* little sister.

Oh, just fuck it. Fuck it all. Samin was already neck-deep in sop; he might as well go under with the rest of them.

He cleared his throat. "No worries, if you can't find one. We'll take your sister pig-a-back if we have to."

"*No!*" Shig's scowl was a mix of offense and petulance. "I want to go buy a dray with Fen."

Malick snorted, nearly choking on a chunk of fish as he shook his head. "Yer killin' me, Shig."

"Yeah?" That made Shig brighten up a little. "Can I have your room, then?"

Asai watched the storm gather from the porch overlooking the pond, fingers idly combing the thick fur between the ken-ken's ears. Until now Storm-month had hardly lived up to its name in obvious terms, but metaphorically...

The news of Pon had not been unexpected, but was still disturbing. The news of Pon's lady-whore was... well. Asai had mixed feelings about that one. He'd foreseen Pon in time to give warning, but the idiot had delayed to *pack*, of all things, so he rather deserved his fate. Sonji-onna he hadn't foreseen at all. Between the blank spot of Jacin-rei and Pon's impulsive, unthinking nature—what the hell had he thought he was *doing*, hiding the full-Blood there, of all places?—last night had been little more than a blur of faces and possibilities in Asai's sight.

No significant loss in the greater scheme, Sonji-onna, but Pon's lack might complicate things in the Courts. Asai would have to find another go-between to Yakuli. It was... disappointing. Asai had spent a lot of years cultivating Pon. All his time and work wasted now, and all for Sonji's slut.

Asai's fault. He saw that now. He should have set Jacin-rei loose sooner, should have pointed all the wrath so carefully cultivated at those variables whose idiocy was now carving shapes in Fate's construct that could very well ripple to the core, if Asai didn't step in. Now he could only see the aftermath of the boy's course, and though most of those Jacin-rei had executed thus far had been those to whom Asai would have eventually directed him anyway, some had still been unexpected. And the veil obscuring every individual fated to intersect with the Ghost was... damned annoying.

Faint flashes of lightning flickered in the distant clouds, the faces of the suns still burning through the gathering gloom and dulling the brewing storm's threatening brilliance. The ken-ken piped a little whine in its throat, leaned harder into Asai's leg. Asai merely sighed and turned his absent scratching into long, soothing strokes.

"Only a storm." He crooned it, calming. "Nothing so tumultuous as what might be coming in its wake."

A bleak little sigh whiffled from his throat. Too many possibilities. Too many opportunities for everything to go wrong. Too many futures were suddenly running parallel to the right one, but only one course would set it firm. And now the timing had been thrown into disarray.

He'd needed Jacin-rei to flush out the *Temshiel*, and it appeared Jacin-rei had done so. Except Asai had counted on having control over the boy when it happened, guiding him to the right conclusions, channeling his rage onto the paths for the proper outcome.

No magic—not even *Temshiel* magic—could touch an Untouchable, but Jacin-rei was still susceptible to influence. Asai had built him that way. Except he'd built him to be susceptible to *Asai's* influence, damn it. And Asai absolutely *could not*, no matter how he railed and bashed himself against it, penetrate the veil that had been cast over the Untouchable and those who intersected his future. He'd expected it eventually, but not *yet*, damn it—later, when the future was set irrevocably, when Asai could merely sit back and watch all his work come to glorious reality. Now, the only thing keeping Asai from tearing through the city to find his disobedient Ghost was the blank spot where the brother should be.

Another mistake. Asai had wavered on the brother from year to year, month to month, sometimes even day to day, and he was only just now able to see how it should have gone. He should have had the midwife twist the boy's neck fresh from his mother's womb, like she'd done the year before. That future had been so clear, so easily seen: fated to save the brother he loved, the one he refused to call "Ghost," and in the process, tear the fabric of the Balance into unforeseeable scraps—Asai couldn't have that. And yet, that very love, and its answer in Jacin-rei's core, was the only thing that could have provoked Jacin-rei onto the course Asai had set for him, the only thing that could have rooted the rage so deep, turned the need for vengeance into blind obedience. A grievous sacrifice, to be sure—Asai truly didn't like to see Jacin-rei hurt—but a necessary one.

Except now that the brother had gone from a set piece to a variable, the proper fate of the Jin had been neatly bisected into two murky possibilities. One of which Asai had thought he'd tidily stamped out in a muddy Jin camp more than twenty years ago when he'd bargained for a Ghost.

Damn the boy for his inconvenient rescue, damn him for his stubborn secrecy, and damn him, *damn him,* for taking vengeance into his own hands, slaughtering men whose fortunes had not yet been realized to Fate's satisfaction. And damn him to the suns and back for finding the *Temshiel* before his course was irrevocable.

Thunder rumbled inside the bruises on the horizon, as if in answer to the anger growling in Asai's own chest. The dog whimpered another complaint, and made several close orbits around Asai's legs before settling again at his side, leaning its head to his knee. Vicious man-eater, indeed. Asai snorted. Then sighed.

It wasn't irretrievable, not yet. The right fate was still in futures-possible, and still brighter, clearer than the others. Asai hadn't supposed Jacin-rei's distrust of him could possibly work to his advantage, but it seemed it might still be a useful tool. He'd allowed the boy, after all, to bear witness to Asai's stacking of the Courts, and with Jacin-rei's trail of kills leading him directly to the heart of the nest, perhaps believing Asai had put them all there for different reasons would still lead to the same conclusion.

If the earthbound died before standing witness to his Untouchable brother's fall. *If* the brother's resulting and fate-shattering paroxysm of grief and anger was stopped before it could take hold. *If* Jacin-rei led the *Temshiel* to Asai and did what must be done to prevent the wrong future. *If* it all happened in the proper order.

Asai *hated* the word "if." And if he could just get Fate to realign into its proper shapes, he'd never have to employ it again. Because he'd *know*.

Annoyed, he watched the darkening veil of the clouds put out the suns, watched the swell of lightning burble inside them, watched it all churn together into a threatening soup of mindless intensity. Storm-month had come, in all ways possible. All he could do was ride it out, rely on all the work he'd done to get here, and guide it along as he could.

Find the brother—that was the first task. The younger two were inconsequential, but the twin was vital. Find him and perhaps even take him, allow Jacin-rei to know Asai had taken him, and then… use him as leverage?

Asai paused, focused on the stratum of building thunderheads, let his gaze roam inward on the thread of this new possibility…

Smiled. Yes. It could work.

In the meantime, the beishin would have to allow the apprentice's hatred, cultivate it, poke and prod it, and hopefully avoid becoming a victim of his own weapon. The one unpredictable rub in the otherwise precise pattern of this future-possible. Eventual confrontation would be unavoidable, and too many risks fanned out from that one crux— Asai's own lack of a future prominent among them. Asai might have taught his Ghost a little too well. Still, he was not unskilled himself. And if he could avoid actually killing the brother while still preventing him from fulfilling his most obvious fate, turn him hostage to Jacin-rei's failure to protect him, if he could show Jacin-rei the necessity of all the machinations…

Well, then.

Every lord needed his paladin, did he not? And paladins so often made the best lovers and companions. It was, after all, what Jacin-rei had been wanting for years.

The brother could have an "accident" afterward. Asai would not appreciate being compelled to share. And helping another through their grief forged such fascinating bonds with mortals. Asai should know. His Catalyst would never question him again. And gods on their moons, wouldn't *that* be a nice change.

"Tea, Beishin?" Vonshi was smiling benignly from the frame of the sitting room doors.

One bit of foresight that had played out exactly as Asai had seen— Vonshi had been extraordinarily useful over the years, always seeming to know what Asai wanted and when. Vonshi had been mentor to the Ghost almost as much as Asai had been, and his help in maintaining the boy's sanity so he could be used appropriately had been invaluable. The gods had indeed led Asai to Vonshi's door that night after Wolf's long sleep had ended.

"Thank you, Vonshi. Tea would sit very well just now." Asai gave the dog one last scritch between its ears before following Vonshi into the sitting room.

Find the brother and Jacin-rei would follow. Asai had built him to have no choice. If Asai had done his work properly, where Jacin-rei went, the *Temshiel* would have no choice but to come along. And if Fate was at all kind, the Ghost would already hold the *Temshiel* tethered, and all else would simply fall into place. Asai could lay everything on either outcome, with no possibility of failure.

Either way, he decided as he watched Vonshi pour his tea, Asai couldn't lose.

It had begun to storm by the time Fen managed to force down a little rice and half an oblate—and he *had* forced it, Malick could tell. Nerves, most likely, and who could blame him? After all the weeks hiding his family, nearly buckling beneath all the stress Malick had seen for himself, and now they were just going to walk in, pick them up, and bring them back. It must all seem too easy, and Fen obviously didn't trust "easy." He also didn't seem to entirely trust them yet, either, but that would be put to rest tonight.

There was an initial fuss over finding Fen a suitable cover from the rain—Shig and Yori insisting, and Fen silently refusing; most likely because he didn't have anything, and didn't want the fact to interfere with his intended errand—until Malick inserted himself into the mild fray and settled it. One of Malick's own lighter, oiled dusters; Fen accepted it with a look that clearly said he was doing it to get them all to shut up.

Fen was alone in the hallway, waiting for Shig, when Malick found him. Malick didn't touch this time, only leaned against the wall next to Fen and waited with him.

"Last night..." The part where Fen spoke without prompting was surprising; the part where he seemed to have decided to not finish the thought was not.

Malick made himself not snort. *Last night was mind-blowing*, he wanted to say. *Staggering. Wondrous.* And any other adjective that meant *really fucking good*.

He settled for, "Last night was brilliant. You were brilliant."

Because Fen needed to be pushed and poked at sometimes, or he'd just keep working on thickening up that ice again.

A light blush crept over Fen's cheeks, and he looked away. "It changes nothing."

Sure. You keep telling yourself that.

Malick stuck his hands in his pockets. "Whatever you say, Fen."

"I wanted it, and I figured you'd be good at it. That's all."

"Uh-huh." Malick tilted his head. "And was I?"

Because you were yowling like a cat for a little bit there, so I sort of assumed...

"You are *not* my responsibility."

...Um.

Malick frowned. Because that one had been just plain weird. "All right?"

"I won't—" Edging on surly now, Fen set his teeth tight. "It isn't a beginning."

"It doesn't have to be an anything, Fen. It can be whatever you want it to be."

Tell yourself anything that makes you feel better, just as long as you keep wanting it.

"I know what you are." Fen's voice was... almost small, as close to tentative as Malick had ever heard it. He paused, peered at Malick sideways. Expectant.

There wasn't much Malick could answer to that. Fen was an intelligent man, and Malick had done a worse job of hiding what he was from Fen in the past several days than he'd done of hiding it from the others for years. And Fen had too obviously known the words of an ancient oath he had no business knowing before Umeia had even spoken it.

Malick should be worried. Asai had set Fen up specifically to draw out a *Temshiel* of Wolf, and Malick still didn't know why. And yet.

He shrugged. "All right."

It seemed to confuse Fen. "Why are you—?"

"Mal!" Shig bounced down the hall toward them. "C'mon, then, give over. It's my turn."

Malick leaned in toward Fen, but not too close. "Come see me after we get your brothers and sister settled in tonight, all right? We'll talk."

Fen only jerked a nod, pulling Malick's coat more firmly around his shoulders as he followed after Shig. He wasn't limping, Malick noted. Or, rather, he refused to limp when Malick knew that thigh had to be throbbing and painful; wounds like that were always worse the second day, damaged muscles tightening and stiffening up in self-defense. He'd have to get Umeia upstairs later and have her take a look to make sure it wasn't swelling or reddening. Fen wouldn't like it, but his acquiescence to Umeia's commands was slightly less snarly than his mulish balking against Malick's.

Malick set it away, along with all of the other soft, squishy things that had been curling in his chest all morning. Concentration. There was still a job tonight to prepare for, and Malick had errands of his own today.

He collected Samin on his way downstairs. Malick had no doubt the name of his destination would pique Samin's interest.

"The Rutting Stallion? Seriously?" Samin's expression was a cross between dubious and amused. "Why not just call it The Thrusting Hips and have done?"

Malick grinned and dragged the hood of his waxed cloak up over his head as they stepped out into the rain. "I expect the former has a more vivid imagery to it and thus makes a man more willing to bring his purse along for the ride."

"And you haven't got enough of that at home lately?"

"Your smart-assedness knows no bounds, does it, Samin?"

Samin was unrepentant. "It's why you love me." They walked in comfortable silence for a few blocks, then: "You think Madi will mind?"

"Madi?" Malick's eyebrows snapped up. "Mind what?"

Samin only gave him a *what d'you think?* look.

Malick shook his head, bemused. "Madi might miss the extra koin, Samin. That's all."

"Uh-huh." Samin rolled his eyes. "So, what's for us at The Rutting Stallion?"

The question was inevitable, and at least this one was expected, but Malick wasn't prepared to answer it with words. He'd rather wait and let it explain itself.

"Oh, you know, a drink for luck, a virgin sacrifice. Sorry, you're the only one who qualifies."

This time Samin's look was more along the lines of *I have sharp knives.*

No fun at all. "Business," Malick said.

"The Sonji-onna business or tonight's business?"

Malick looked away. It was rather seeming now that they were one and the same. "Bigger business."

"Want to tell me the name?" A real question, not a sarcastic prompt.

And there was no way to sugarcoat the answer. "Yakuli."

Samin stopped in his tracks. "Mal, that's..." He trailed off, stunned and perhaps a little fearful, which was unusual for Samin. All the better that Malick had brought him along on this trip. They would all have to know what they were getting into eventually. "A bloody *councilor*, Mal."

"I know." Malick started walking again.

As far as Samin was right now concerned, it was as simple as closing in on the inner circles of the Judiciary itself. While Yakuli wasn't a judge, he was tight enough with those who were, and powerful enough he might as well be. Taking him out could have repercussions that could turn Malick and his little band from the hunters to the hunted. Fen had already taken out a judge—there was no way these men would miss connecting the dots, and it was only a matter of time before they started striking back with everything they had.

Samin took another few moments, but he followed Malick in due course. He was quieter than was his usual wont. It could have been the weather, but Malick rather suspected not. He didn't ask. Anyway, there would be a lot more on Samin's mind when they were through at the Stallion, so they might as well get it all over with at once then.

A pleasant enough walk, normally, but with the rain growing heavier, and the storm churning steadily, the trek to the seedier reaches of the Iron District seemed longer than it should have been. The closeness of the air snagged at the stench of the ironworks and neighboring tanneries, mixed with the fishy-salt reek of the bay, and mutated to a pungent miasma of decay and acidic sulfur. The cobbles ran with a layer of swift-moving water and bits of garbage it had picked up along the way, prisms of oily dross floating on puddles like filthy little rainbows. This quarter would have a fresh, clean look to it, however temporary, when the storm was through with it, but right now, the flavor of it all was just plain depressing.

They were cold and soaked nearly through by the time they reached the Stallion. The blazing fire in the central hearth and the aromatic smells coming from the little grills scattered around the room like small constellations whorled around them in a warm, thick welcome. Malick and Samin stomped through the doors and shed their cloaks with matching relief.

Trade was light right now, more clients coming in for the food—which was surprisingly good here—and a warm, dry spot, and perhaps a bit of flirtation and tame entertainment, rather than the other services for which the Stallion was better known. More sedate and bordering on respectable at this time of day, at least for this part of the city, but at night, the Stallion had Umeia's House beat in the darker side of the trade. Anything a body wanted could be found here, if you knew whom to ask and phrased your questions carefully. And if you were willing to pay for it. Not a place Malick frequented unless he needed information not easily got elsewhere—some things even a hedonist didn't want to know, or have to look at—but the service he needed right now couldn't be found anywhere else.

"I need to see Xari." Malick slid three koins across the rutted, sticky surface of the bar toward the great big ogre tending it. "Tell her..." He paused, peered at Samin over his shoulder, thoughtful. Last chance to spare the rest of them from what Malick thought was coming down. Somehow, he thought Samin would be fairly pissed if he knew Malick was even considering it. "Tell her the Eremite begs audience."

A long, solid look from the man's black eyes, but he didn't ask any questions, merely snatched up the koins and pocketed them. Without so much as a nod or a "Wait here," he made his way out from behind the bar and through a frayed, faded curtain in the western corner.

Malick turned around, propped his elbows on the bar, and leaned back, surveying the scene. Done up more in the old Jin style, the room was dark-lit, low tables set around the central hearth, patrons reclining on plump cushions on the floor, and watching the various cooks grill their lunches through aromatic smoke. Some had obvious doxies for company, but most seemed to have come for the food. Several of the doujoun were scattered about, perhaps having just finished a shift, or on their way to one. An entire table of middle-aged women giggled and flirted loudly with their assigned cook, having apparently come in out of the rain for the dual purpose of treating their eyes as well as their stomachs—the cook was young and handsome. And apparently quite willing to flatter and play along for his tips as he grilled shrimp and onions while the women got pleasantly, mildly squiffy in the early-afternoon anonymity of a whore-house's common room. As though what went on here after dark existed in another world entirely and had nothing to do with their own.

A perfect place for *banpair*, Malick reflected, though he knew Xari hated the epithet. He wondered why more of them didn't think of places like this. There was, after all, plenty of run-off angst and avarice to suck in and keep both need and appetite sated with no call whatsoever to go and hunt it down. Or cause it yourself. It must be like having a feast served up every night.

Samin was quietly taking it all in, any curiosity he might have about their purpose here, or Malick's cryptic request, apparently willing to wait for eventual explanation when Malick wanted to give it. That was why Malick liked Samin—opinionated as hell, and fairly vocal about it when he thought he ought to be, but willing, for the most part, to wait out a situation and see if Malick actually knew what he was doing before shouldering his way in because he suspected Malick didn't. And even though Samin sometimes came to a very wrong conclusion when he disagreed with Malick, it was always out of loyalty and his own distinct brand of cantankerous love. Samin was the sort you could count on to put you out of your misery if you were too far gone to do it yourself. The only problem was, he couldn't always tell, and he might cut your throat out of mercy just when you were sucking in your first curative breath.

The great big ogre-bartender-probable-bouncer emerged from behind the curtain, jerked his head at Malick, then disappeared through a door to what Malick suspected was the stairway to the private rooms, but he'd never ventured that far into the bowels of this place, so he couldn't be sure. Either way, Malick didn't worry—he was safe here, and though he'd come armed, he had no concerns that he'd have to use anything more lethal when he left than a woeful lightening of his purse. Malick nodded to Samin to come along then made his way across the dim-lit room, pushed the curtain aside for Samin, and then followed him through.

It took a moment for Malick's eyes to adjust. No light here but the ethereal glow of the small amber globe in the center of the table and the tiny sparks of three sticks of incense set to smoking fragrantly on the mantel of the cold fireplace beside it. Pine and sage—honoring Wolf today. Malick's mouth curled up at the corners on a wry smile. Of course she'd known he was coming. She always did.

Xari sat like a bony little spider at her table, painted reed screens at her back, the dim glimmer of her stone loaning soft radiance to her pinched, weathered face. Her long, gray hair was tucked back neatly in a bun at the nape of her neck, and folds of fringed silk were draped over her thin shoulders. She appeared swathed in black, what with the dark set of the room, but Malick knew those silks were as brilliant as Shig's hair in the light. Xari liked color almost as much as she liked the dark; the room itself was swathed in it, enough to pain the eyes, when it was lit properly.

Dipping her head on a creaky little bow, Xari slithered something at them that might have been a smile, but with Xari, you could never quite tell—it could just as easily have been a grimace.

"So, the Eremite's pilgrimage has brought him thus once again." She puffed a wheezy chuckle and waved at the chairs set to either side of her. "You have brought a novice to my table, Wolf's-own?" There was a mild chiding tone to her crow's caw of a voice.

Malick felt more than saw Samin stiffen beside him, and had to flatten a smile. Samin probably didn't think himself a novice at anything, but in some things, he was even more naïve than… actually, Malick didn't know anyone who was entirely naïve, now that he thought about it. The heart of Ada was a difficult place to maintain innocence.

"And who better to initiate a novice?" Malick gave Xari a smile meant to both charm and flatter.

It apparently did neither. Xari merely rolled her eyes and gestured again to the chairs, more impatiently this time.

Malick smothered a grin. He gave Samin a bit of a poke in the ribs, bowed his head respectfully, and then took a seat to Xari's right. Samin didn't seem to like it much, but he took the place to Xari's left. Not without a sharp look at Malick that promised lots of questions and the expectation of answers when they were through here. Which was fine with Malick.

"So, tell me, my fledgling, self-styled renegade." Xari waved her bony hand in front of Samin's nose, a deck of cards fanning out from her previously empty palm. "What bit of advice can I give you to ignore this time?"

"I've not come for advice." Malick dismissed the chastisement because it was unwarranted and Xari knew it. "I've come for information."

Xari snorted, and began dealing her cards. "And what sort of information would an old woman such as I have that one of Wolf's-own could not get for himself?"

Samin kept admirably still and watchful, though Malick could tell he was writhing with curiosity about just what the hell was going on. Malick put him out of his mind for now. One didn't match wits with Xari with only half of them at his disposal.

"An answer as to what one of your kind would want with a Catalyst."

He watched Xari purse her lips in annoyance, her crooked hands pausing only minutely in the dealing of her cards, but the almost unnoticeable reaction was more telling than she'd obviously like: her glamour slipped for half a breath. Malick didn't see her without it often, but he knew well the smooth olive skin, the silky black hair.

"I know about Asai, Xari."

"You've known about him since the moment you came here." Xari slapped two cards facedown with force enough to rock her little stone on its perch in the center of the table. "'Twas no secret I kept from you, since you were already busy keeping it from me."

"We both know that's smudging the truth. I couldn't keep that from you any more than he could. He's your kind, after all. He's your own."

"My kind, *my kind*." Xari shook her head, cards going down faster and harder now. "He's no kind of mine, and he is no longer *my own*. Exiled he is, even more so than you, for you've always the choice of going back. Asai knew what he was choosing when he rocked the Balance so. I've nothing to do with him, nor do any of *my kind*."

"But you know what he's up to, don't you?" Malick leaned in and set a hand over Xari's, halting the flurry of cards. "He's interfered with Wolf's Catalyst. That's against your laws."

"Aye, so off he flies from Raven and takes allegiance to Wolf, because it isn't against yours, is it?—*Wolf's-own*."

She swatted off Malick's grip and went back to dealing her cards, more calmly this time. "Catalyst." Her wrinkled mouth pursed tight. "The pin in the crux of the fulcrum that would shake the world." She flipped a card over. "The Fool." Her eyes lifted slowly, turned up to Malick's. "The divine breath of inspiration. All sums dividing into Zero, forever seeking substance, an inborn ache for the coherence of One. Pure potential. Neither good nor evil, but always the capability for either or both. Always with one foot hovering over the abyss. This is your Catalyst. This is Asai's Fool."

Annoyingly smug, Xari tilted her head. "Will he be enough to drag you from your gentle rebellion, *Temshiel*?" She paused, mouth turning up in a sly little smile when Samin huffed a sharp curse under his breath that Malick ignored. "You spurn your magic, hide your light, turn your face from Wolf, and all for a lover who was not, a brother who was not, a silly-headed fool who gave his heart and scruples to pretty words and open lust. You skirt the edges of your nature, risk your own soul—all because you were denied the fortune of sullying your blade with maijin blood."

Malick sat back in his chair, eyeing Xari narrowly. "I couldn't prove he'd taken Skel's Blood. The gods were silent as always, and no maijin would bear witness against him." He lifted an eyebrow. "Not even you."

"And no *Temshiel* may take life without just cause that it keeps the Balance. And yet you flirt with your own laws by taking life by order of...?" Xari waited for a moment, but when Malick only gave her a stony stare, she smirked. "'Tis fortunate your Mage chooses your victims well."

Malick ignored the jab. "I've asked you before who the Mage is."

"And I've chosen not to answer." Xari stared, no expression on her cragged face, dark eyes glittering in the goblin-light glowing softly from her stone.

"And what do you choose now?"

Xari didn't look away from Malick as she flipped over another card, laid it crosswise atop the Fool. "The Sorcerer." She hadn't even looked down. "Only he can take Zero and make One of him. Channel to the power of the gods and all the spirits. The will to take potential and realize it." She paused, giving Malick a reproachful scowl. "This should be *your* card, mutinous *Temshiel*. And yet you hold stubbornly to the Eremite, force your own into her Paladin's role, though she doom her own soul, and all for you. You've searched for your knowledge—it can only become wisdom when you've earned it through sacrifice. When will you step from your exile of flesh and vice, and stop dimming your light beneath mortal cloaks?"

Malick sighed. He'd heard it all before. "Are you going to tell me who the Mage is or not?"

Xari growled at him. "Seek that answer in your own House."

She turned to Samin with a glare. "Yes, I spoke truly, Templar of Swords, with your dual-edged justice, and now you know what your Eremite is, what you truly fight for, all unknowing. He is *Temshiel*, reborn to the flesh times uncounted, power unnameable, and yet dimmed and hidden while he sulks like a five-year-old." She turned back to Malick, dark eyes blazing. "*Your* kind have permitted Asai this liberty, *your* kind have threatened the Balance. And now your Catalyst hangs over the precipice—a tool, a ready weapon. Which hand will take him up? Will it be yours that sets him toward the suns?"

Silence, thick and choking, while Malick took this in. More than she'd ever given him before, and now he almost wished she hadn't.

He kept his face blank. "Not if I can avoid it."

"And how will you do that?" Xari snorted, thin and derisive, and thumped the rest of the deck down to the table. "Drag your veil tight around you as you've done? Try to pull him under with you? Watch him spiral down into the chasm and blame your Mage for not warning you?" She shook her head, held up the Sorcerer card again. "Take it up while you still can, for Asai seeks it for himself, and he cares not whose Blood must spill to have it so. If you would save your Catalyst and the Balance that hangs around his neck like a noose, do that which you have scorned for too long now."

Her hand shook, the bright-painted card blurring in Malick's vision as she waved it in front of his nose. Insistent.

He took it, turned it over in his hand then, deliberately impudent, flicked it back down onto the table. It landed face-up and dead center of the configuration she'd made of the rest of the deck. Malick wasn't sure what to make of that, but Xari was looking annoyingly satisfied, so it probably wasn't good.

She cut a sideways glance to Samin. "Breathe easy, Templar of Swords. There is hope yet for the Balance, and Wolf may yet smile again."

Her expression faded into solemn dignity when she turned back to Malick. "Swear the Catalyst no oaths, Kamen Wolf's-child, though it pierce your heart to withhold them. He will not thank you for them in the end."

"I'll take care of my own, Xari." Malick's patience was going threadbare and his temper was flaring. "Just tell me what Asai is up to."

"And what redemption do you offer me in recompense?"

Well, that had to come eventually. Xari had been punished for her silence when Asai was judged, saving him from the suns while Skel burned. Now she dwelled in exile from her god's sight for it, reduced to *banpair* while she sought her redemption, while Asai was left free to seek allegiance as he willed.

It wasn't fucking fair, and it *still* burned like acid in Malick's gut.

Malick thought about what Xari was too obviously implying, but the promise she was looking for belonged to Fen, if he wanted it.

"I offer you the chance to make your own redemption. *But.*" Malick held up his hand, warning, when Xari's sere face cracked into a smile. "It's an opportunity, Xari. Not a promise. Not a guarantee. The Catalyst is already three steps ahead of you, and you're going to have to be damned fast to beat him to his vengeance. Now. *Tell me.*" He sat back again. Waited her out.

Xari stared at him for a long while, measuring, before her hand settled over the stone, its fey light pulsing slowly through her fingers.

"The Jin have always been a people easily led." Her voice was soft. "Like a parent who coddles a child, the Ancestors gave to them their magic and traditions, when they should have allowed them to gain such for themselves through erudition and respect for the gods. Too easily mastered, are spoilt children. And when their Voices were lost, so was the will of the Jin."

She tsked, shook her head, then peered up at Malick, intent. "Asai broke no laws when he took *Temshiel* Blood, for your foolish Skel gave it all too willing. Thus, Asai walks free to seek Heart's Blood, to claim the power for himself.

"And if their Adan masters were to let go the leash of the Jin, who better to guide them and all their magic than the demigod who saved them from their self-inflicted doom?"

"The Blood…" The card Malick had tossed to the table pulsed at the edge of his vision as though it were giving off its own light, burning. "Holy… *fuck*." His heart had tripped over itself, everything in his chest plummeting down to the bottom of his stomach. He stared at Xari, unselfconsciously wide-eyed, shocked right down to marrow. This was beyond even his wildest suspicions. "He means to take the power of a *Temshiel* and set himself up as the Jin's master."

Asai really did mean to "save" the Jin, only he meant to do it in such a way as to yoke them to his own will instead.

Xari only shrugged, though it looked uneasy. Her hand came away from the stone, gaze dipping down to where Malick had tossed the card she'd pushed on him.

"He would think to rival even Wolf, only no moon to wait out the centuries until his Cycle for Asai."

Malick shook his head. "The gods would—"

"The gods would do *nothing*," Xari spat. "The gods would watch, as always they have done, and wait for Asai to cross their line, blaspheme, call himself one of their own. *Then* perhaps they would act; *then* perhaps they would set the *Temshiel* on him." She paused, mouth turned down and expression gone sour. "He will dance the line, perhaps, but he will not cross it. He will not spill the Blood himself. Arrogant though he be, I have birthed no fool."

"More's the pity." Malick glanced up at Samin, saw his mental gears slipping and grinding all over his granite face, and sighed. "What is the Catalyst to him?" Malick asked Xari, though he was pretty sure he already knew the answer.

Xari gave him another of those scathing snorts. "A better question would be: What is the Catalyst to *you*?" Her mouth turned up, sly. "Who better to obtain Heart's Blood from the *Temshiel* than the one who holds that heart already in his hand?"

Samin sucked in a light, hissing breath, but otherwise kept quiet.

"Fate's Fool has been made Fate's tool." Xari pulled another card from the mess on the table. "The Contradiction, the Paradox." She tapped the edge of the card to the stone. "The last child of Raven who can save or doom the first child of Wolf. Thus hangs the Balance around the Catalyst's neck."

"His brother." Malick narrowed his eyes. "The twin."

Xari shrugged, weary now. "Set the Catalyst free as he watches him die, perhaps, give him the essence of One at last, make him whole—

mind and spirit. Or take mind and spirit from the Ghost forever by sacrificing himself for Wolf's Catalyst and the brother he loves." She sighed. "Hearts are such chancy things. What gods could set the Fool and the Paradox as brothers and think themselves kind and just?"

"The same ones who judged Asai blameless generations ago. And you wonder why I retreated from their purview."

"I never wondered."

"You named me recreant."

A twitch of dry lips. "Even so."

Malick rolled his eyes. With a look at Samin, he reached down, untied the purse from his belt, and dropped it to the table. He didn't bother to count it. Whatever was in there, it wasn't enough. He stood, Samin taking his cue and heaving his bulk from the too-small chair.

"Thank you, Xari." Malick bowed his head, fist lightly thumping his breastbone. "Be careful. If he's getting close to his goals, he'll be sending his eye out farther and deeper. As you said: you've birthed no fool."

"The veil of Kamen Malick has shielded me well these last years. I fear not."

"Then *you* are the fool. Cultivate your fear and watch your back. Never forget my veil dies with me."

"*Feh!*" Harsh and derisive. "If a maijin of Raven can undo a *Temshiel* of Wolf, I am done with this world anyway." Xari waved him off, impatient. "Go. You've wearied me. Dare not darken my door again before my vile progeny has been brought to heel. And..." For the first time, she paused, hesitant. "Remember me to Wolf, Kamen Malick, for Dragon turned her face from me when your Skel went to the suns."

"Another injustice, *misin*." Malick set a gentle hand to Xari's cheek, smiling when her glamour wavered and his palm slid over skin smooth as satin. "If Wolf will heed my appeal, your name will be the first he hears. The sins of the scion are not the sins of the dam."

"No, but perhaps the fault is." Xari batted his hand away. "Go. I have other trade, and you have other matters to attend."

Malick did, but he had one more question. "The Catalyst's mother. She's spiritbound and Disappeared. I think Asai turned her over." He paused when Xari's eyes closed and her fists clenched. His tone was purposefully gentler when he went on: "Can you tell me where she is?"

Xari sagged, a sigh that came right up from her soul whistling out from her thin chest. Her hand crept over the Fool, resting there, while the other slipped over the stone. She was still and silent as Malick and Samin stood there and waited. With a bit of a shudder, she slipped her spidery fingers beneath the Fool's card, flipped another over. A bright-painted grin leered up from its face, a man with both hands on the crisscrossed slats of wood from which strings dangled and snapped.

Xari shook her head and opened her eyes. "The Puppet Master." She peered up at Malick, resentful. "But then perhaps this does not surprise you as it should."

Malick could have said some choice things to her, but this was not an argument he wanted to have in front of Samin. "Where?"

Xari shut her eyes again, only for a moment this time, her hand on the stone. When she looked up at Malick again, it was with a glare.

"Horses. All I see are horses."

Not precise, but not as vague as it could have been. Not many men owned horses. And Malick knew all too well that Yakuli was one of the few.

There was no way out of it now.

Malick dipped Xari another respectful bow, then jerked a nod at Samin. "Thank you, *misin*. I'll…" He paused. What could he say? *I half hope you get to kill your son and earn your way back to your god, but I'm going to help Fen beat you to it?*

Xari seemed to understand his dilemma. "We all do what we must." She waved him away. "Go. I have nothing more for you."

There was nothing for Malick to do but what she'd asked.

He didn't speak as they made their way through the common room, Samin's mien thoughtful but calm and composed as they collected their still soggy cloaks and strode through the doors.

Still, Malick was fairly surprised when Samin stopped just outside the doors of the Stallion and, instead of the hundreds of other questions he must have had, asked, "Would you be doing this if you didn't love him?"

Malick blinked against the rain, pulled his hood up to stall and get his bearings, and then shook his head at Samin. "Bloody hell, Samin, I don't *love* him. I've only—"

"*Bullshit.* I see it, that crone sees it, everybody bloody sees it. That's your problem, Mal—you love everybody, but you only love them a little bit until they start to bore you, and then you walk away. And I have to hand it to you—most of them walk away still adoring you and with no hard feelings. But Fen…" Samin blew out a frustrated breath, and scrubbed a hand through his short brown hair, droplets of rain flying out from beneath his fingers. "Mal, the man isn't right in the head. You use him like that woman says you should and you could break this one. And no matter what you tell yourself after, it'll eat you alive. If he doesn't gouge your heart from your chest in whatever madness you trigger, you'll *wish* for the suns."

Malick stared, shoved out a heavy breath, and then started walking. "You can't believe everything she says, Samin. She's maijin. It's their job to fuck things up. It's what they do. Xari's better than most, but only because she's trying to buy her way back into Dragon's good graces."

Of course, she'd take Wolf. She'd take anything that would get the yoke of Asai off her shoulders, and take away the stigma of *banpair*. And she'd say anything she thought might help her get it.

Love. *Ha.* What kind of idiot would Malick be if he fell in love with a cold little prick with a chip the size of Subie on his shoulder, an unnatural fondness for all things sharp and pointy, and a hard-on for bloody Asai?

"You keep telling yourself that, Mal, but I know better, and so would you, if you weren't being so monumentally blind. And I'll tell you something else." Samin took hold of Malick's arm, held on until Malick stopped and turned to look at him. "Even if he loves you back, he isn't capable of knowing it, because yes, there actually *is* someone in the world more heart-stupid than you. If it comes down to a choice between you and someone he *does* know he loves, he's not picking you. Asai needs a heart, and you've made yours awfully damned handy to the one who's supposed to get it for him."

"Fen's not as oblivious as you think he is."

Samin blinked like he was trying to recover from a knock to the head. "Have you *met* him?"

…This was *really* not what Malick had thought they'd be discussing on their way home.

"All I need from you, Samin, is to know if you're in or out." He shook his head when Samin flinched. "I'm giving you a chance to walk away. That's all. No repercussions, no hard feelings. If you want out, this is your chance, and you might do well to take it. This is looking like it's going to get ugly."

"Ya think?"

Samin's jaw twitched and ticced. Angry. Thinking. Standing in the street, rain pouring down his face, unmindful. It took less time than Malick thought it would, less time than he thought perhaps it should, before Samin growled then gave Malick a sharp glare.

"Fuck you, if you think so little of me."

Malick should have smiled, but he found he couldn't do it. "I think the world of you, Samin. It's why I gave you the choice."

"Yeah, well, fuck you anyway." Samin started walking again. Malick only stared after him for a second or two before following, watching Samin's back as he strode down the dirty street. Samin's broad shoulders were straight and locked tight, not even hunched in against the rain. Everything about him screamed tension and worry, but he covered it with blunt impatience, the same way Fen covered his with rage.

"Fen needs mail," Samin said as Malick caught up to him. "Something light and flexible. I know a man. You're buying."

Malick blinked. "I gave Xari all my money."

"Then you'll owe me."

Malick pulled the hood of his cloak in tighter. Yes, he supposed he'd owe Samin. One way or another. He just hoped Samin wouldn't actually take it out of Malick's hide.

"What's your name, then?" Samin asked it somewhat grudgingly.

"Kamen is the name Wolf gave me. Malick was from my mother. I… chose not to discard it."

Malick didn't say why. And he didn't say how the two truths had come in useful now and then. It didn't make anything less true. Anyway, Samin already knew Malick was a manipulative bastard.

As though he'd heard, Samin flicked Malick a sideways glare. Malick really couldn't help the grin.

☖

Xari slumped back into her chair, and ran the tip of a finger over the smooth, round surface of the stone, its power thrumming through her hand and all up her arm. Soothing.

She rubbed tiredly at her eyes and dropped her glamour. "He is right to be angry." She looked over her shoulder. "I cannot blame him for his withdrawal. Nor can his god, else he would already be damned."

The Mage stepped from behind the screens, glamour falling from him like so much smoke, handsome face emerging from beneath its mask of wrinkles, iron-gray hair going nearly black as he paced slowly over and took a seat beside Xari. His hand went to her cheek, as Kamen's had done a moment ago.

"Wolf believes in allowing his children their meditations. And Kamen is ever careful to step within the bounds of the law, though he thinks himself quite corrupt and daring." The Mage shook his head. "His pilgrimage toward wisdom has come to its logical end. He will choose as he must."

"He means to find you, *Temshiel*. He has handed his heart to the Catalyst. It is for him Kamen Malick will end his rebellion."

The Mage merely shrugged with a dim little smile. "He will choose as he must."

Xari rolled her eyes, but didn't disagree. "Asai…" She paused, lips pursed, simply unable to say the words: *my son*. "Asai threatens the Balance. Again. If he breaks it—"

"He will burn, Xari. I cannot help him. I won't. You knew that."

She swallowed, eyes stinging, but she nodded. She'd known. And she knew Asai had to be stopped. It didn't help. She'd disowned him over a century ago, but somehow, her heart wouldn't allow her to sever its tie to him altogether. Even though she knew Asai wouldn't think twice about cutting Xari's heart out and imprisoning her soul. He'd already tried it the once, after all.

"His sins are not yours, Xari." A heavy sigh wafted from the Mage's chest and stirred the cards scattered over the tabletop. "Our children are ever both joy and bane, are they not?"

Xari had to agree. And at least she still had a child over whom to fret. For now.

"You have done all you can to set his path aright, and make amends for his arrogance. There is naught to do now but wait and watch."

"No." Xari stared down into her stone, watching fates and futures whirl and snarl together inside it. She sighed, weary and sad. "There is still more to do."

The Mage merely shrugged, opened a hand. "If that is your wish, Xari."

It wasn't. But she'd do it anyway.

"The sins of the scion," she muttered unhappily and set to restacking her cards.

⛩

Tides-month, Year 1321, Cycle of the Wolf

Vonshi pursed his lips to keep them from trembling, or perhaps curling up into a smile—he wasn't quite sure. Anticipation. Fear. Tugging at him all day, distracting him.

He sucked in a long, steadying breath as he stood at the end of the second-floor hallway, peering out over the rolling estate from the great window that overlooked the eastern sward and the surrounding trees. Watching the guards' steps pick up pace and their postures tighten, wary. He couldn't hear the hoofbeats himself, but he could almost feel them. The dogs were reluctantly obeying their masters' hushing commands, but they were all alert, vibrating, staring anxiously through the fence and straining at their leashes.

It wouldn't do for the boy to miss it all, not when it seemed like the world was standing on the razor-edge of the beginning of the end.

Vonshi craned his neck so he could see Wolf's leering face, tipped a nod then pried open the window—only a little, only enough he could just make out the guards' low conversation in the yard below, could be sure nothing would be missed. Then he turned, focused on the boy's door until it slipped its latch, creaked softly open. Subtle and yet not a thing easily ignored. This all had to appear happenstance. He'd worked too long for this.

He could hear the horses now, the steady *thump-kadathump-thump* of hoofs to ground, the occasional thick grunt of protest as a beast was driven a little too hard over unknown terrain in the dark. He stared at the boy's door, mouth going tight and fists clenching unconsciously.

Hurry.

It only took a moment that seemed far too long, but the stir of shadows beneath the door foretold the boy's curiosity. Vonshi could see only a slash of the boy's profile through the narrow gap—frowning, guarded—as he took hold of the latch, joggled it a few times experimentally, then opened the door wider. Had a look at its mechanism in the doorframe then flashed a glance out into the hallway. Wary.

Locked in his room tonight, the window nailed shut, because Beishin was unhappy—jealous. Vonshi smirked. Too many forays out on his own for the boy, too many nights spent discovering the underbelly of the city, where some could be paid to ignore the braid and lie with a Ghost, sate the penury Asai stoked but refused to mitigate. Too many nights haunting the camp and the family he wasn't allowed to see, and he'd promised Asai he wouldn't, but Vonshi knew the boy did, and he knew Asai knew it too.

"He's been lying to me, Vonshi," Asai had growled. "*Me!*"

As though it wasn't a betrayal he'd earned. As though he had every right to ensnare a Catalyst, manipulate his course—*lock him in his room*—when he wasn't even supposed to lay hands on the boy. It made sense, Vonshi grudgingly admitted. The Wheels would turn this night, one way or the other, and Asai would of course take every precaution to ensure the Catalyst could not interfere.

The boy peered carefully up and down the hallway, suspicious but hopeful, eyebrows raised and a small smile quirking at the corner of his mouth when he realized his fortune.

Vonshi smiled too.

He'd come to quite like the boy, done everything he could to negate Asai's influence—oh so very carefully, of course—and had watched him grow from the quivering mess he'd been when he'd arrived to a young man with a sharp mind and a good heart. And a rebellious streak that was more than Vonshi could have ever hoped for when he'd felt the tug of a soul pulled from Raven and over to Wolf.

A whisper from the gods, a command, Vonshi had known it all those years ago. It had been a chancy thing, planting the revelation into a seer's own sight, leading him to that empty little cottage on that rainy night just after Wolf's first dawning in over a century. Maintaining the veil for all these years had been difficult, but easier when Asai simply stopped looking. Secure in his own machinations. And why not? Fate was Asai's game, people his pawns, and the boy his personal tool.

Vonshi could have told him tools had a way of developing sharp edges, turning on the hand that wielded them. Of course, he hadn't.

They'd reached the gates now, a hail from the guards halting the thud of hoofbeats. The jingle of bits and halters mixed with a demand for the master wafted up through the open window. A shrill bark was quickly throttled by a sharp jerk on a leash.

Vonshi at first thought the boy hadn't heard it, so thrilled with his sudden and surreptitious freedom, mind probably already whirling toward what he might do with it. But the boy paused when he heard the din out in the yard, turned toward the window. Took a hesitant step.

Come on, lad. His permission or lack of it hasn't stopped you from spying for years.

Vonshi had almost despaired for the first several months after the boy had arrived. He'd seen no rebellion at all, no indication whatsoever that the boy would ever be anything besides Asai's besotted instrument, and that was only if he could hold onto sanity long enough. Dani had been the turning point, Vonshi thought. Or rather, Asai's reaction to Dani. No interference from Vonshi or even Wolf himself had been necessary—Asai had knotted that noose all by himself. And he *still* didn't see it. It would be amusing, if the stakes weren't so high.

"…dare to come to my home!" Asai was scolding from the front porch. Vonshi couldn't see him, the porch's roof blocked his sight, but three hooded men with no heraldry on their battle gear stood on the walk, heads canted at an angle toward Asai's voice. "*Fools*! If you're seen—"

"Then the Court will be advised in no uncertain terms that Lord Asai has been most helpful to its interests."

The deep voice caught the boy's attention. He narrowed his eyes at the window, paced swiftly up beside Vonshi, and peered down.

"We were not told there was an earthbound, as well as the spirit-bound," the voice went on. "We've come for amulets."

The boy sucked in a sharp breath, hands gripping the windowsill so tight he might rip the wood from its joints. A heartbreaking mix of fear and disbelief washed over his sharp-boned face, driven stark and deathly pale in the moonlight through the window.

"You were given them." Asai's tone was angry. "They are not toys to be doled out to—"

"We were not given enough. One spiritbound, we were told. Additional men are needed for the earthbound." The dark figure stepped in, and the voice dipped down, but was still audible. "Perhaps it was a purposeful deficiency in information on Lord Asai's part. Perhaps Lord Asai—friend to the Courts, frequent host to judge and councilor alike— had meant for hidden magic to slip its traces. The northern camp has only just been quelled and subdued. Another riot so soon after the last might well—"

"*Enough!*" Asai lowered his voice, but still Vonshi was able to make out "The earthbound is not to be taken alive," so he was sure the boy heard it too.

The door slammed downstairs. The movement of Asai's heavy footsteps was easy to trace as he apparently swept to his sitting room to retrieve from behind a bed of loose mortar the hateful amulets Vonshi knew resided in the hollows beneath the stone of the fireplace. It had been all Vonshi could do over the years to let them lie where they were.

The door slammed again as Asai stepped back out onto the porch. "Take them and go. And do not dare to breach my borders again."

The man said not a word, only dipped his head on an ironic bow. He gestured sharply to the two standing at his sides, and wheeled around to head back to the gate and his horses.

Vonshi watched the boy watching it all, watched the horror and betrayal swath pain all over his face, watched the harsh in-and-out of budding hyperventilation, before the boy collected himself, pushed it all down into rage. Vonshi watched it blossom, watched it set the fine features into cut stone, watched it lay a dangerous glitter to eyes gone hard and sharp.

With a feral snarl, the boy shoved away from the window, pelted down the hallway and into his room, reemerged only a moment later with knives strapped to his hips and thighs, and the shadow charm gripped in his fist. Face set and eyes hard little coals, he raced down the steps.

Vonshi swept over to the gallery, watching as the boy very nearly plowed Asai under in his single-minded haste toward the door, the frantic attempt to catch men on horseback both pitiful and admirable.

"Jacin-rei." Asai staggered, and reached out to snag hold. "*Jacin-rei*, where are you—?"

"*Fuck* you, Beishin." The boy shook off Asai's ineffectual grip and shouldered past him. "I heard. I heard *everything*!"

Asai followed after, throwing himself in front of the door before the boy could open it. "Jacin-rei, I *forbid* you to leave this house. What you heard… it wasn't what—"

"I know *exactly* what it was." Low and through teeth bared and clenched tight. "Get out of my way—*Beishin*."

He didn't wait for Asai to move; he merely snapped up his arm and leveled Asai with a right hook to the side of his head. Asai hadn't even hit the floor yet before the boy threw open the door and bolted through it.

Vonshi took a long, deep breath, leaned into the banister that framed the gallery, and closed his eyes. He'd been right—the beginning of the end. And the gods help and keep the boy this night. It was difficult not to imagine the scene that might greet him. Vonshi hoped the boy got there in time. He might. Hard to beat men on horseback, but the boy wouldn't have the inconvenience of the necessity of riding over roads, and he was certainly inspired to speed. He did love his family so.

Asai slowly pulled himself up from his sprawl in front of the door, sat for a moment with his hand to his head. Likely reeling. Dazed.

Vonshi had to smile.

"Vonshi!" Asai dipped his head and pinched at the bridge of his nose. "Vonshi, I need you!"

He wasn't through yet, there was still much to do, so he couldn't answer that summons as he wanted to. Vonshi composed himself, set his face into its usual grim lines, and dropped his veil. He leaned over the banister.

"Yes, Beishin?"

Asai snapped his glance up, relief and gratitude. "Our Ghost has taken flight, Vonshi." He shook his head with a sigh. "The Wheels of Fate have begun to turn." Grimacing, he pulled himself slowly off the floor until he was on his feet. He peered up again at Vonshi, rubbing gingerly at the side of his head. "I could do with some ice."

Years of watching and careful, cautious preparation. Arranging the players, lending subtle influence when he was able without being detected. Coaching the boy delicately, helping him as he could, guiding him into a close approximation of what Asai wanted of him, but with a will of his own that Asai could not break. Finding Kamen and snaring him with the lure of duty while he indulged his anger at perfidious gods.

Playing dutiful, devoted servant to the maijin who'd murdered his son.

A smile, a slow dip of the head on a respectful bow, all obedience and careful manners.

"Yes, Beishin," said the Mage.

10

Storm-month, Year 1322, Cycle of the Wolf

The reek of the bay hung heavy, briny and brackish and curling into his nostrils in a murky blur of near-tangible misery. Even the gulls were lethargic in their forlorn, warbling circuits of the rooftops.

Jacin tucked down farther into the borrowed coat, concentrated on not limping, and not moving his head too much while he was at it. Fucking uzin. Off his routine, out of sorts, cold and wet and hurting. The only good thing about today was that every minute of it was another step toward getting his brothers and sister to safety.

The dray had been easy. A small wainwright's outside the Gates, a handful of koin, and mental nudges from Shig. It had been more interesting than unnerving to watch her work, and Jacin had found himself almost envying her, wondering why she didn't use something like that to her own advantage more often. Why hadn't she just walked onto some lord's estate and convinced him he wanted to give it to her? Or even declared herself Empress of Ada? Then again, she didn't really seem the type—Shig used her magic for more... practical things.

Like convincing a wainwright that he really did want to sell her the little dray he'd made for someone who'd already paid in advance and would be picking it up tomorrow, and that he wanted to sell it to her for half of what it was probably worth. Sturdy enough to pull Caidi and whatever gear they wanted to tote along, but light enough that Jacin wouldn't have to ask anyone to help him pull it. Shig had made it look so easy. The hard part had been finding a place to stash the thing where it wouldn't be spotted and stolen, but wouldn't be too hard to get to later.

The rain was doing some good, Jacin supposed. There weren't many passersby for Shig to "tweak."

He wondered if his mother had been able to do the things Shig could do. Wildly different in appearance, and somehow shrewder, too, but in some things, Shig reminded Jacin of his mother in ways that were sometimes excruciating.

"It must hurt awfully."

Jacin was more startled by the hand on his arm than by the question. He kept from flinching back by the simple expedient of stilling his entire body, *making* himself not lash out. Touch seemed to be the way of it with these people, but not with Shig—she hung all over everyone else, but actively avoided touching Jacin—so he paused to examine the anomaly before reacting to it.

They were several lengths from the gates, just past a tiny, solitary stall from which an old woman sold squid breaded and fried in a deep, cast-iron kettle; the smell of it was making Jacin's stomach want to curl in on itself. The woman didn't even look at them, nor did any of the stray travelers who made their way in and out of Ikata's main gate, bundled in cloaks or heavier gear against the weather.

Jacin blinked rain out of his eyes, tried to take his focus from the smells and turn it to the thumping heat radiating from his right thigh. If he ignored his stomach, perhaps he wouldn't vomit all over the squid vendor. Or Shig. And if he ignored the hand on him, he might be able to come up with an answer to whatever she'd just said.

He carded back, tried to remember what it was she'd been talking about—she'd been chattering at him almost all morning, and him tracking what she was talking about didn't seem to be a requirement to her "conversation." He carved a channel through all the inner noise, and came up with what appeared to be some sort of worry for his own person.

"Why d—?" He stopped just short of *Why do you care?* He might not understand why people felt the need to express concern for strangers, but he did understand it was rude to snipe at them for it. Unless they were being intrusive, which was rude in itself, and for which he felt perfectly justified in biting back.

Shig didn't seem intrusive. Shig seemed... like something Jacin couldn't think about right now.

"You're quiet today." Shig tipped a sympathetic smile through the rain, her motley braids darker with the wet, and her jade eyes somehow brighter and greener in the murk of the day. "You're not all buzzy. I guess it shuts them up for you, yeah? The pain?"

No, not really. It shoved them back, coiled something louder than their voices, gave him something else on which to focus his attention. Nothing shut them up except a touch he loathed himself for craving, for allowing, for *inviting.*

You would doom your soul for something so ordinary?

It would seem so, Vonshi. If there's anything left of it.

And somehow, damnation wasn't feeling as unbearable as Jacin had always imagined. Maybe because there was nothing ordinary about any of this.

If you're determined to risk yourself, boy, be sure of the cost beforehand. And be sure it's a price you can pay.

Except Malick had told him there *was* no price.

Jacin shut his eyes, throttled the hope that crept behind his breast-bone like a ghoul from a crypt.

Even if Malick believed it himself, Jacin knew better. It was the nature of… people—beings? creatures?—like Malick. They weren't normal, they didn't value life the way mortals did. *Temshiel* didn't do anything for anyone without a reason, and the penalties were usually paid by the mortals left staggering in their wakes.

And still, here Jacin was. And there he'd been last night, not only saying *yes* but *please* to seduction and silence, and damn if he hadn't thoroughly enjoyed himself.

It was the attention with which Malick pinned him, he supposed. The obsessive focus. Jacin had never had anything like it leveled at him, and apparently, his body couldn't care less from which direction it came. All those years, wishing for it, *burning* for it, from a man he'd at least thought he'd loved, and now he had it. And he was a little too close to terrified to realize it was feeding some deep, empty place inside him he hadn't wanted to acknowledge. Even Shig's touch terrified him, because he *liked* it—the simplicity of it, the… normalness. Jacin didn't do "terri-fied" very well, and the only way he knew of dealing with emotions he didn't understand was to strike back with the one emotion he under-stood completely. Except the anger had only seemed to pique Malick's interest further, and Malick wouldn't let up, he'd never *let up*, and the rage inside Jacin had turned in his hand like an ill-balanced blade.

Bloody hell, Jacin must've been a real son of a bitch in a previous life to have deserved this one. He hoped he'd at least enjoyed himself.

He didn't answer Shig—he'd forgotten the question again and didn't feel like digging for it—just dragged his arm back, and pulled the borrowed duster up closer around his neck, trying to ignore the smell of pine soap, smoke and sage, and light, musky sex. Of temptation. Fucking hell, was Malick *made* of lust? The reek of it permeated even his clothes.

Teeth set, Jacin shook it off and started walking again. Refused to limp.

The pain was a hot, throbbing spike skewering his entire leg, and he was pretty sure he'd blown a couple of stitches somehow. It at least dulled the pulse of the heavy, squishy lump of bruised fruit that was his head, the low-level churning of his gut. Too much of that liquor last night. Too much of a lot of things last night. Giving in had felt like dying for a little while, and then it had felt like living, and the sharp edge of bliss had been agonizing. Dreamlike now, with the distance of a few hours, except for the scent he couldn't get away from, because he kept wrap-ping it more firmly around himself.

But the pain was *his*, it was real, a reminder that he was still here, still in control, still had command over his own body and the abuse he inflicted upon it, his own reactions to it. Except he'd cut himself much deeper than he'd meant. And he couldn't allow it to interfere with tonight. *Couldn't.*

The one thing the Ancestors had said of which he could make sense, the one almost-clear command since they'd roosted in his head like noisy grackles—he couldn't fail, not at this. If this Malick, this *Temshiel*, was the key to getting Jacin's family to safety, perhaps even out of Ada entirely—

"So, how was Mal?" Shig bumped an elbow into Jacin's ribs with a leering waggle of eyebrows.

Jacin blinked, shot her sideways frown. "...Sorry?"

Shig shoved back a clump of striated braid and pushed her arm through the crook of Jacin's. "I hear things around the Girou all the time." She gave his arm a squeeze and leaned her wet head to Jacin's wet shoulder. "A bloody good lay, Mal. At least that's what I've heard. And the ones who have him always want him again, so I figured—"

"I don't."

Shig smirked. "Uh-huh. Sure, Fen." Her smile was sly as she slid it up to him. "C'mon, you can say, I won't tell."

Tell who? Jacin wondered, irritated, but the answer was probably everyone.

No, no, and *fuck* no.

These people... *talked.* All the time. Malick especially. Bloody magpies, all of them, even Samin sometimes. Jacin couldn't understand it. Couldn't understand how they could just... *say* things, hemorrhage words, entire life stories, like it didn't matter. All of them. Didn't they know words were power? They all seemed like intelligent people—didn't they know that voicing the things inside you, letting another know, was handing that power over, betraying yourself? And if you betrayed yourself to the wrong person...

Maybe that was it. Maybe none of them had ever shown another everything they had inside them and had it all turned back on them, used against them. That, he could understand. He'd been naïve once too.

"Was it quiet for you?" Shig's question was sincere and hopeful, all amusement gone. Her head was still on Jacin's shoulder, her arm wound through his as they strolled back in through the city's gates.

Traffic was lighter than usual with the weather, and those who made their way in and out, flowing around them like they were stones in a river, didn't even seem to see them. Not even the doujoun, who checked papers and inflicted mini-interrogations on seemingly random travelers. It was like the shadow magic that made Jacin shudder to think about, now that he knew what it was made of—*sure, Jacin, tell yourself you didn't know on some level all along*—but he missed it all the same.

This—walking down a city street, a pretty woman willingly holding his arm, no one stopping to stare or pretend they weren't—it was… disconcertingly comforting, though Jacin supposed the disconcertion was merely an excuse. He was, he'd only recently discovered, rather a whore for touch.

"Yes," Jacin answered, because silence didn't work on Shig, she wouldn't *shut up*, she was bloody *worse* than Malick, and maybe an answer would make her stop. And anyway, what could it hurt?—they all knew. He shifted a look up at the pikes and crows' cages as they passed beneath them, and allowed his arm to tighten around Shig's. "It was quiet."

It was. Had been. Like living inside a hurricane made of fire, and then it all drops away, leaving nothing but a cool, calm breeze to soothe the conflagration of your own mind. Jacin had nearly wept—would've done, had Malick not kept feeding him pleasure to distract him.

Jacin had never been done to before. It had been difficult enough to find the rare whore willing to thwart tradition so blatantly as to let an Untouchable touch them, but impossible to find one willing to touch. A simple kiss was sacrilege. A touch with intent was unthinkable.

Malick had kissed. Malick had *touched*.

And Jacin had no idea what to do with any of the aftermath. It was as though he'd spent his life teetering on a wire and then suddenly found himself standing on solid ground. Except his body kept trying to catch a balance that was abruptly crushing it, ripping away the cockeyed moorings he'd worked so hard to build, replacing what false balance he'd managed to achieve with the weight of reality and planting anchors in his feet.

He knew now what Malick was. He knew *Temshiel* were not to be trusted, any more than maijin. Thing was, Malick was a fucking *master* at pretending. And now Jacin couldn't stop wishing even a second of it had been real. He'd traded control for a few moments of pretense, of belief, and now it was all fucking with his head.

Such a hazardous, alluring thing, ceding control. Letting someone's voice be his Voice, telling him where to go, what to do, who to kill, how to die, and when. And then taking back that control, just to be sure he could. Except now he had no idea if he wanted it. If he should even have it.

He couldn't do this on his own—couldn't protect them, couldn't provide for them. Every day was a new failure.

All his life, he'd been told where to go, what to do, until… until he'd stopped believing. And the one thing he'd done on his own, he'd failed at it. Failed so spectacularly he'd been caught, put into a position of either joining a group of dubious purpose or risking them taking him out altogether. And now he'd *slept* with one of them. Was strolling down the street with another like some cow-eyed suitor.

His mother hanging somewhere in the in-between of not-death, her soul doomed to wander, feeding on seeds left in scattered circles, if he didn't find her. His brothers and sister living like hunted animals, somehow still skirting beneath the probes of Asai and anyone else who might be looking. Jacin couldn't just keep leaving them there merely because he didn't know what else to do. It was shocking they hadn't been found already. Even now, the desperation shrieked at him to go there, *now*, make sure it hadn't happened. The constant terror that he'd show up one night and find the mangled corpses of everyone he had left, or worse, blank spaces and the empty necessity of a new hunt, new vengeance.

His heart gave a hard jolt behind his ribs and his breath stuttered sharp. Everything, all of this, it had been so easy last night when he was just *feeling*, except now he was *thinking* again, and it wasn't easy anymore, not at all.

"You know, unhappy Ghost," Shig said softly, "tonight is… it's what he does. You know what he is."

Not a question, but still, it startled a "Yes" out of Jacin. He shouldn't have been surprised; if any of them knew, it would be Shig.

Shig quaked a little shiver and snugged around Jacin's arm more firmly. "But did you know he's Wolf's?" When Jacin didn't answer, Shig nodded against his shoulder. "The strongest of them all, and now he's in his own Cycle. Almost every kind of magic in him, and the skill to take it from others too." She tilted a knowing smile up at Jacin. "And Umeia's gone and sworn for your family, hasn't she?"

Something hard and hot swelled in Jacin's throat. He couldn't have answered if he wanted to.

"It'll be all right." Shig drew in closer to Jacin's side, her curves fitting against him in a way that made him wonder if she was deliberately trying to distract him. "You don't have to do everything by yourself, and not everyone will steal what you don't give them, use it against you, and pretend they're doing it for you."

It twanged things inside Jacin he couldn't—*wouldn't*—name. He stopped short, breath coming harsh and sharp, the dull pounding in his head winding tighter and sending sick, heavy thumps of pain down to his leg with each pulse of blood to damaged muscle and tissue. *Fuck*, she reminded him so much of his mother it hurt, tore something wide inside him and filled it up with saw-toothed acid. He'd wanted to be nice to her, make up for whatever insult he'd caused last night, but fuck, he couldn't be expected to *take* this when he'd been avoiding her from the first to prevent it.

He shouldn't have tried, shouldn't have asked her along. He wasn't good at "nice" and it just provoked people when he made the attempt; they saw it as invitation, and that was simply intolerable.

Scattered, too confused, Jacin jolted away and sidestepped a few clumsy paces. He almost let his hand wander to his thigh, poked and prodded, but he needed to be able to walk tonight.

As if she knew, Shig took up Jacin's hand. Her grip was wet with the rain, but harder than he'd imagined, her small hands ruthless.

"He uses." Her eyes were bright and clear in a face set firm with eldritch knowledge. "They all do. It's their nature. And he'll try to use you, but he won't be able to."

Jacin tried to pull his hand away again—failed.

"I'm telling you what I know, unhappy Ghost, because I know *him*— I watch, I *see*. Giving his life for another means nothing to him, because he can always have more. But for you, he'll give up his soul. Do you really want that?"

Spiritbound or no, she was spewing absurdity like Asai spouted prophecy. Except Jacin used to think Asai's made sense, and this just *didn't*.

"He doesn't even know me."

Shig chuffed a small snort. "So you say." The rain had spiked her blonde lashes, turned them to a darker ring around sharp jade eyes; one blink, two, then she crushed in close and laid a soft, warm kiss to Jacin's wet cheek. "And neither does anyone else, right?" Breathed hot into Jacin's ear, and even through the heat and proximity, it wasn't the slightest bit seductive. "So, how come you're so easily used?"

It hit something prideful inside Jacin, spangled out hot and tight. This time, when he wrenched away from Shig, he managed to loosen her grip, step back. Shig only smiled, nodding, like they'd just agreed to something, which pissed Jacin off, because he hadn't agreed to *any* of what had just happened. And anyway—what the *fuck* had just happened?

"You're going to make such a mess of things." Shig set a light pat to Jacin's cheek. "No wonder Umeia calls you Trouble."

Mute, Jacin whipped around and headed back up the street. They were winding along backstreets and alleys now, and he knew how to remain unseen, even without his shadows. He didn't need the resident cheeky spiritbound hanging on him anymore.

Make a mess—as if everything wasn't already a mess, and he'd had precious little to do with any of it. Used, indeed. All he wanted from these people right now was for them to help him get his brothers and sister then find his mother, and he might have to tolerate them in exchange, but he didn't have to *listen*.

"Fen!"

He stopped as he turned the corner that would eventually take him to the path toward the dingy alley behind the Girou. His teeth were set tight and his breath was coming more harshly than it should be doing, but he turned to look at Shig. He had to. There was just something about her that wouldn't let him ignore her.

She was leaning with her shoulder against the outer wall of the bath-house two buildings down, her smile soft and kind, blinking those shrewd green eyes at him against the rain. She'd lit one of those cherry things she smoked, a substantial plume gusting from her smirk, hanging heavy in the sodden air and obscuring her face until the rain scattered it.

"Life sucks." She cupped the smoke in her hand. "But no one says you can't have a little fun when it's offered. You're not the only one who's had a shitty time of it." Smirking, she shrugged. "We'll go and get them for you, like we promised. And then we'll find her for you. You drive yourself with the pain, but it's all right to snatch the things that take it away too. They'd want you to, don't you think?"

Blah, blah, fucking blah. Platitudes and pseudo-insight and utter *shit* from the mouth of a bizarre, incomprehensible walking augury. And Jacin had neither the wit nor the want to decipher it.

Shig pushed away from the building, ambling over to Jacin with that same knowing smirk until she stood a mere pace away. She looked older with her bedraggled braids and sharp eyes. Her small hand came up to stroke Jacin's cheek, but this time Jacin didn't stop the flinch back, or the glare that shoved his eyebrows down and tightened his jaw. Shig's smirk turned to a grin, and she was herself again—just a pretty young woman with a faraway look and odd hair.

"Back to Zero, love." Almost bloody twinkling at him. "He's already started again. No worries." Shig held out the smoke, inviting. "Bet you never thought you'd be someone else's redemption, did you?"

Jacin stared at the smoke, too close to seething, before he accepted it, took a long drag. Debating with himself over just how much he might reveal through either silence or the question that was pounding behind his brow. Redemption?

"What the fuck does that mean?" he finally asked, aggravated and edgy, and not in the mood for games.

Shig stepped beneath the curled eaves of the teahouse where Jacin had stopped, leaned her back to the wall, and lit herself another smoke.

"You know what he is."

A being who was supposed to act as sentinel for his god's laws on mortal lands. And who was, at least at the moment, passing his time playing slut and assassin.

"So?"

"*So.*" Shig rolled her eyes, took a drag, and blew a neat little smoke ring in Jacin's face with that same cheeky grin. "You're so adorable when you're pissy. No wonder Mal's besotted." Her grin only widened at Jacin's angry growl. Sly, she beckoned him close, and when he complied, irritably, she leaned in until her mouth was altogether too intimate with his ear again. "You've a *Temshiel* punch-drunk over you, bloody idiot. How much clearer d'you need your portents to be?"

Jacin clenched his teeth, took a long draw of the smoke to keep himself from biting her head off, and blew out a long, fat plume before crushing the thing under his boot. Control—*ha*. The only thing he was controlling right now was the wish to lash out and kill something.

"Clearer than whatever the fuck you just said."

"He'll try to use you, but he won't be able to. But I've a feeling you'll be able to use him." Shig raised her eyebrows. "Think you can live with that?"

If it got him what he needed? "Yes."

Shig threw her head back and laughed, deep and full. "Poor Fen." The laughter tapered to chuckles, then a rueful sigh. "Have it your way, then. Pretend you *don't* hear your own voice inside the din. Pretend it's not telling you things you don't want to know. Pretend that your deepest, most secret wish *isn't* that someone would love you like you know Malick can, if you let him."

He was going to hit her. He wasn't going to be able to stop himself. And then they wouldn't help him.

A long, deep breath, all his control—it wasn't going to do it. With the very last of his restraint, Jacin wheeled away from Shig and strode across the street. Fast.

A high giggle was all the warning he got before Shig thumped her palms between his shoulder blades, grabbed his arm, and flung him against the building.

"Ooh, you do hate it when you have to *hear*, don't you?" She grinned, all dimples and bright green eyes, like it was all some grand joke and she wasn't spouting things that were driving into Jacin's chest with the force of blows. "You hate it when someone offers help because you can't trust that they'll actually give it. Shit, Fen, no wonder you're so easy to use."

Jacin's hands were already balled into fists to prevent them from reaching for a knife. His body was so tense he thought he might snap in half if he moved too quickly.

"Stay the fuck *away* from me."

Shig flicked her smoke out into the gutter, and gave him another grin, all sweetness and good humor. "No worries. We're all Wolf's, y'know—even Samin, except he doesn't know he switched gods when he switched sides. We'll help. All of us. Can't get rid of us now." Her smile turned wicked. "I don't think the one you hunt has any idea what a pack of wolves can do when one of its own is threatened."

All the anger, all the roiling confusion inside Jacin—it stilled, just like that.

"The one I hunt?" His stomach was curling again, all his blood rushing down from his thumping head to churn, viscous, in his gut. "Do you know who it is?"

His voice was far too small, far too tentative. Like he didn't really want to know, except he *did*. Then again, if he really did want to know, why hadn't he ever thought to ask Shig? He'd watched her enough to know she might at least have some idea.

Shig slid her arm through Jacin's again and tugged until he started walking. "I don't." She laid her head to his shoulder again. "But you at least know where to start."

Bile rose. Because he did. He always had. And he'd walked away from at least two opportunities to gut the man he'd known from the beginning was responsible because he couldn't bear to believe it.

Failed. Again. Allowed his emotions to make him weak. *Allowed* it.

Jacin shut his eyes, let Shig lead him, pushed away the pain in his leg and his head and his heart. Tried to keep from stumbling as the noise rose, blurry static filling his head, drowning out everything, and he let it, didn't even try to listen, just let his mind buzz and drift into the white. He'd rein it all back when they got to the Girou.

And then he'd let himself throw up.

🕍

The first thing Malick did when they got back, after relieving Samin of his share of the load of bundles, was to arrow up the stairs, dig through his rooms for his various stashes of koin, and pay Samin back. Samin would never have even mentioned it, if Malick didn't reimburse him, but it was important that these things came from Malick.

The mail had taken a little longer than Samin had predicted. They'd arrived at the tiny wood-framed armorer's to find only an apprentice on duty, and Samin had insisted on waiting for the man himself. It had turned out for the best—Malick couldn't find a single fault with the light vest—but it had put Malick behind in what he wanted to accomplish today.

They arrived back during the in-between lull that came after lunch and before supper. Shig and Yori greeted them from their comfortable puppy pile on one of the couches in the common room, though when Malick asked Shig if she'd helped Fen get what he needed, she only giggled. Malick took it as an affirmative.

Fen's door was shut, and with the rain and the stitches, Malick assumed he wasn't sparring on the roof. Maybe resting up for tonight. Or brooding. And since Fen brooded like it was his job…

Malick left him to it and dumped the bundles on the couch in his sitting room. He had something he needed to do before presenting his loot to Fen anyway. He wrote the note quickly then headed downstairs.

The main floor of the Girou was nearly deserted, all the kitchen help busy preparing for the evening, and all the other help busy bathing and primping. He had a few hours yet.

Malick made his way into the kitchen, skirting the grills heating beneath the narrow window vents. Coolly casual, he paused once or twice along the way to greet the cooks and lackeys, but his gaze roved all the while, watching. Carefully. Because his target was very, very good.

Warm, fragrant steam filled his nostrils, and clanging pots made a happy din. He loved the kitchens. Busy as a hive, and seemingly chaotic, but there were patterns to the traffic, logic to the flow. Those who didn't do their jobs well and efficiently didn't last long back here. More than one promising talent had fled weeping through the back-alley doors.

Malick bent to accept a motherly kiss on the brow from Sendi as she hacked a rack of ribs into chops. Wire-muscled and just on the edge of attractive, she was still entirely do-able in her middle-age, and could sing the roof down besides when the mood took her. Malick took a moment to let her chatter on about her grandchildren, nodding and smiling like he had the first clue when baby teeth were supposed to show up, before he moved along.

He kept the slip of paper carelessly in his hand as he grinned and flirted his way through the kitchen, stopping by the baking counter to accept a sample of the pork buns from Keki. Malick had almost suspected Keki of being his target once upon a time, but that was before he'd started really paying attention. Keki had his own secrets, but not the ones important right now. Soft-spoken, almost mousy, if one didn't know him, but he was the only one who actually scared Ragi as far as Malick knew. Well, besides Umeia.

Speaking of Ragi...

Malick found him at the bank of stoves against the back wall, berating the boys supervising the soups. Already, Malick could feel the heavy thump of antagonistic energy vibrating from the sinewy frame. No wonder Ragi gave Shig headaches. Malick actually had to touch Keki to feel it, but not Ragi. Malick had suspected right from the beginning how Ragi had managed to stay hidden from both the hunters and his own kind, but it had never actually mattered before. And he'd never really wanted to know until now.

Malick waited politely and with a rueful smile slanted at the boys, until Ragi's diatribe was through.

"Bad night?"

Ragi's scowl smoothed when he turned to Malick, scrubbing a hand through ragged waves of brown strung through with copper. Tall and rangy, almost as tall as Malick. He might have been handsome, but ill-temper cragged his face and hardened its lines.

"Bad help." Ragi dipped his head respectfully. "What can I do for you, seyh?"

"Confections." Malick smiled at Ragi's raised eyebrow, and waved his hand around, the note flapping in the breeze he stirred. Ragi didn't seem to notice. "For supper tonight. I want something special. I'll leave the selection up to you, but make it good. I'm wooing."

Both eyebrows went up this time. "Wooing."

"And I'll want the portions doubled starting with breakfast tomorrow."

There were a thousand questions flitting over Ragi's dour face. He voiced none of them.

Malick knew what the staff speculated about him—an ex-lover of Umeia's turned hanger-on; an orphaned relative she'd taken in, the first of her ducklings; a ne'er-do-well who'd found something incriminating in Umeia's murky past and was using it to blackmail her, his silence in exchange for her generosity of room and board. Those who needed protecting, needed to hide their magic, knew Malick could do that for them, and that was *all* they knew. What they guessed was up to them. Malick didn't care what any of them thought, so long as they acknowledged his authority—dubious though they might think it—and did what he asked of them on the rare occasions he wanted something from them.

With Ragi, it hardly mattered. Ragi had to have known damned well what Malick was from the beginning. Malick was pretty sure it was why Ragi was here.

Ragi merely bowed his head. "Yes, seyh. Is that all?"

"No. One more thing." Malick leaned in, lacing his tone through with a tiny bit of menace. "I think we've a spy. I've felt… eyes on me, if you know what I mean."

Ragi's blank face ostensibly told Malick that no, Ragi didn't.

"If you notice anyone paying untoward attention to my doings, or what goes on upstairs, I want you to tell me. Immediately. Understood?"

A narrow-eyed stare this time, but that was all. Ragi dipped his head again. "Yes, seyh."

No cracks, no twitches. He was very good, but Malick had already known that. Except Ragi didn't seem to be wondering why Malick would seek out the kitchen supervisor, of all people, for help in ferreting out a spy.

Malick gave Ragi a bright grin—the one that usually blinded, turned gentle prey wide-eyed—and tipped a friendly nod. "Good. Thank you." He waved the note in salute then sauntered out of the kitchen.

He took his time ambling behind the bar, pausing to pour himself a cup of rice wine, swallowing a nip of it quicker than he should do—it was the good stuff, the stuff Umeia wouldn't let him have unless he paid for it—then topped it off and made his way down to the end. Not even bothering to look around for possible watchers, he noisily shifted the heavy lid off the crock, dropped the note in, and set the warding spell known only by Malick, Umeia, and whomever the Mage had running messages. He took his time leaving, too, a careless saunter as he angled across the floor and to the doors that led to the stairs. Allowed his tread to fall heavily on each step as he took the first flight.

When he got to the top of the stairs, he spun his veil.

Amiable banter drifted from one room to the next and across the hall. Beautiful men and women darted back and forth to exchange lacy undergarments or silks or lewd "toys" in anticipation of specific guests. Madi, half-dressed in silky drawers and wide-open velvet lace-up shirt, flittered out of his room and down the hall a few doors to murmur something to its occupant then laughed at whatever response he got and danced away again.

Malick smiled. He'd have to stop in soon and see Madi again, just to say hello and see how he was doing. Madi was sweet and extraordinary at what he did, and Malick was glad Fen's arrival had prompted him to get to know the boy a little.

When he judged enough time had passed, Malick headed back down. The spot just on the other side of the bath stairway had the clearest view, so he leaned his back to the wall and waited.

It took almost no time at all. Ragi must have calculated—just as Malick had—that if he didn't act now, he'd have to wait until the end of the night, and things would be too geared up in the kitchen very shortly for Ragi to slip away. As soon as his gnarled hand lifted the lid from the crock, Malick dropped his veil. Ragi's usual stern composure abandoned him completely when Malick abruptly appeared in front of him.

"I'm giving you the next couple of hours off." Malick let his smirk slide into something more dangerous. "Take me to him. Now."

⛩

For a surreal moment, when Ragi fetched up in front of the sedately modest holding in the Judicial District, Malick thought he'd made a colossal blunder.

"The Mage is *here?*"

"Where better?" Ragi creased something like a smile, mocking. "He'll be out anon. You won't need your veil." He dipped his head. "Seyh," he murmured then turned around and went back the way they'd come, disappearing down the street into the murk of rain and low-sitting fog.

Malick frowned after him, uneasy. Then frowned up at the stately façade of Asai's city residence. He couldn't have been this wrong. The Mage *couldn't* be—

"Ah." Malick wanted to punch something. "This just gets better and better." Because the lean figure strolling out from spiral-shaped hedges lining the perimeter of the small manor's yard wasn't exactly a relief. "*Shit.*"

"It's looking that way." A small, humorless smile curled Husao's mouth. "It has been a long time, Kamen."

Not long enough, Malick thought, fairly certain the sentiment showed on his face, because Husao's smile turned sardonic.

"So." Malick sighed, annoyed now and warier than ever. "You're this 'Vonshi' who helped Fen rive reason from insanity."

Husao dipped his head low. "I know the boy as Jacin-rei. And he knows me as this." For a moment, the glamour of a bony old man stood in front of Malick, iron-gray hair and face cragged and stern. And then it was once again Husao, jet hair framing a face that held just enough hints of his son Malick almost had to look away. "I did what I could for the boy."

"Why? What's this about? And what are you doing here?"

Skel had been Bear's, and Husao belonged to Dragon—these were matters for Wolf, and Husao had no right.

Husao shrugged. "The same as you. Watching. Waiting." The smile once again morphed, this time sliding sly. "A great lord such as Asai has need of a trustworthy steward."

"I'll bet." Malick rolled his eyes. "So you've known about Fen all along."

"Of course. One wonders why you didn't."

All right, now Malick *really* wanted to punch something.

Husao sighed. "Peace, Kamen. I have no intention of chiding you for seeking your own balance. It is the way of it with Wolf's-own—a small catch in the wisdom of drawing to his purview those whose hearts will survive the centuries, those who still remember being mortal."

"I've not come to—"

"I know why you're here."

"Our deal was that you wouldn't interfere. Our deal—"

"Our *deal* was that I would pay you very well for dispensing with men who needed dispensing, and in return for your services, I would not seek you out or interfere in any way with your life." Husao put out a hand. "I have done neither. *You* sought *me* out."

The truth of it only pissed Malick off more. "What d'you call sending Fen to the Girou?"

"Fate, if you will." Husao waved it away. "I did not send him, Kamen— I merely alerted you that he would come, and bid you take a skilled assassin into your fold." He lifted his eyebrows. "Has he not proven... useful?"

I don't need a pimp, Fen had sneered at Malick once. It appeared he'd had two all along. And one just as manipulative as the other.

"Oh, *fuck* you. You knew *exactly*—"

"The maijin who doomed my son has been subtly trying to attract the attention of the *Temshiel* by using my son's Blood to enslave the Jin— Wolf's people, *your* people." The rage and pain Malick had seen all those years ago, and found so hard to look at, was now plain on Husao's face, in the fine tremors shivering over his lean frame. "Have you any idea how hard it's been to watch? To *help*?"

Somewhat. Not entirely. Malick had thought his own wish for revenge and blood had been keen until he'd seen Fen's. It wasn't the same for Malick. It wasn't even the same for Husao. Dragon chose her own for their strict senses of justice, their remove, their indifference to mortals in the greater scheme of the Balance. When Dragon's Cycle came 'round, Malick wouldn't be surprised to see the Jin wiped out entirely, just for being dupes to the folly of the Ancestors, for even threatening the Balance, let alone rocking it as Asai and Skel had done. Husao's rage came not from the loss of Skel, but from the loss of his own, from pride, from anger at having been blind to the machinations, from having failed his god. Someone like Skel—Bear's because of his fierceness, his recklessness—was altogether too ripe for the schemes of Asai.

Neither Malick's grief at Skel's loss, nor Husao's, held a candle to Fen's over the loss of his mother, the threat of the loss of the rest of his family. It was... a cleaner thing, Malick mused, regardless of the bloody way Fen went about it. More to Wolf's liking, which... Shit.

Husao took a step closer. "*Years* I have listened to the last of my son wail from within drops of his Blood in the hands of the one who murdered him. And all so Fen Jacin-rei—"

"*Your* choice, Dragon's-own. You would use the Catalyst just as surely as Asai intends to."

"No. I would help him to become a true creature of Wolf, and I have done. You'll wring no apologies or regrets from me for it. I was within the law. The rest..."

The rest is up to you. Malick saw it in the infuriating smirk, heard it in the heavy not-silence of the steady patter of rain.

Husao sighed, abruptly weary. "Skel was your friend, Kamen. You vowed vengeance to me the last time I saw you. You raged against the gods for their refusal to step in, their denial of your wish to take justice to yourself. You still want it. I can see it clear on your brow, like a brand. So tell me, Wolf's-own—now that it's within your reach, will you rebuff the tool that's been set in your hand?" He stepped in close, set his hand to Malick's arm, gripped tight, but his voice remained low and soft. "Asai is looking for the brother now, Kamen. And it will only be a matter of days—perhaps hours—before he finds the mother. Two hearts to hold against the Catalyst, and all in exchange for Heart's Blood from Wolf's *Temshiel*. Which do you think the Catalyst will choose?"

That was the second time today Malick had heard the same threat. "You son of a bitch. You've got Xari bridled too. *You're* why Asai can't see the brother anymore." He'd known there was a veil, that *Temshiel* were somehow involved, but knowing it was Husao was something else altogether. "You'd let him have him, too, wouldn't you? You'd let him have them all, just to make sure Fen goes after him."

"And you would not?" Husao shrugged. "I would have been well pleased had the boy slit Asai's throat on his way out the door and been done with it the night he watched Asai betray his family, but..." He shook his head, disdainful. "He was besotted before I laid eyes on him for the first time. Mortal hearts can be so very… inconvenient." He narrowed his eyes at Malick. "I like the boy. I would prefer it if he survived and got what he wanted. And make no mistake—he wants Asai's heart in his fist just as much as Asai wants yours. Or…" Husao lifted an eyebrow. "I've no doubt Asai would settle for another *Temshiel* of Wolf." He tilted his head. "How is your sister?"

Malick hadn't really known he was going to do it until he was shaking out his hand in the aftermath, knuckles aching. "Touch Umeia and I kill you."

Husao rubbed at his mouth, smiling at the blood that stained the back of his hand, quickly washed away by the rain. "Rage away at Fate and the gods, Kamen Wolf's-own. Hate me for seizing the opportunity to serve the Balance and avenge my son at the same time. Blame me for taking up Asai's tools and using them against him." His smile disappeared, and his face went hard. "Do what you must, but *take up your duty* to your god. Honor the memory of your friend by guiding his replacement dupe.

"Your rebellion is at an end, Kamen, and you've no one to blame but yourself for how it came about. The Balance hangs around the Catalyst's neck. Do you want the noose in Asai's hands or yours?"

It didn't matter that Husao was right. It didn't matter that what he was demanding was exactly what Fen wanted anyway, what Malick wanted, had been wanting. The manipulation and inevitability of it still flared rage and loathing in Malick's chest, still seethed through his veins.

"You've left me shit choices in the matter, haven't you? You're no better than Asai." And because he was pissed off, because he wanted to *hurt*, Malick leaned in and lowered his voice. "Xari was right, Husao—Skel was a fool. He let Asai fuck him into stupidity, and handed him the seed that's only now trying to bear fruit. I loved him like a brother, but if I had been the one sitting in judgment…" He paused, flexing his hand, feeling the burn in his knuckles, and watched Husao's face set itself in stone as he stood in the rain and listened.

"Asai deserves the suns for taking Skel's Blood," Malick said, low and harsh, then he spoke the words he'd known all along, but until now, could never bear to allow into coherent thought: "But Skel deserved to burn along with him. *He's* the one who broke the laws, *he's* the one who couldn't stand it that the Jin had used their magic against those who didn't have it, *he's* the one who taught Asai how to make the amulets."

He'd got right down into Husao's face, teeth clenched so tight his jaw was aching. He drew back and shook his head.

"*I'm* to blame. Right. *Fuck you*, I'm to blame. *I* wasn't the one who stood back and watched it all happen and didn't even know it until it was over."

Husao had gone pale in the fading gray of late afternoon, his mien unflinching, cold, apparently untouched, but the curled fists and the visible trembling gave him away. He sucked in a long breath.

"You know your duty, Kamen. My part is almost done. You'd do well to rescue the brother before the night is through." He slid his hand over his brow, shut his eyes, then smiled, peered at Malick, mocking. "He is unveiled now and vulnerable."

Malick took a step toward him. "You son of a—"

"Beishin has guests just now." Husao stepped back and gathered his glamour around him. "But he will be sending out his eye, perhaps even reading the cards in only a matter of hours. You'd best get along. Vengeance awaits."

It took a moment for Malick to send out his own veil toward the little grover's hut, and by the time it was secure, Husao was already heading back toward the side of Asai's house.

"I'll get you your vengeance," Malick called after him. "But it won't be for Skel."

"As long as you do," Husao said, "it hardly matters," but he didn't look back.

ㅠ

The sill was wide enough to almost fit him sideways. Jacin propped his thigh on it, leaned his head against the thick, cool glass, and watched the rain. The view wasn't really a view—merely an up-close look at the dingy brick of the laundry next door—but it could've been much worse: it could've been a smelter's with its stench of burnt oil and liquid ore, instead of lye soap and clean steam.

Today, though, everything smelled of fish and rot and decay. He tried not to take it as an omen.

His stomach had calmed down, once he'd purged it. Still, a cup of tea would probably settle it better, but it wasn't time for supper yet, and he'd deliberately missed lunch. He would wait. The chill of the glass against his brow was soothing his head well enough for now, though it was doing more unpleasant things to the rest of him. He hadn't yet been able to rid himself of the clammy-damp, even after a change of clothes and an extra shirt. It was the fucking braid—it took forever to dry, and the heavy wet of it wound right through the rest of him.

He dozed, fitfully, foot planted to the floor and his throbbing leg locked at the knee to support him, because he didn't dare bend it. Not altogether comfortable, but he'd learned to catch at least shallow snatches of sleep standing or kneeling—whichever was Beishin's pleasure that day—and meditating on whatever it was Asai had been trying to teach him that Jacin hadn't performed to perfection.

I don't do this out of cruelty, Jacin-rei, but you must understand how imperative this is. Now you will stand there and think about it, go through it in your mind, until your body can perform it to my satisfaction.

Except there was no such thing. Ever. Jacin knew that now. Knew a lot of things he'd known all along but couldn't admit.

The noise had muffled down to a sludgy wail beneath the aching of his head and his leg and the almost forgotten burn of smaller hurts along his ribs and torso. But the residue of the uzin and its morning-after repercussions was getting in the way of actual thought.

Fuck it. Focus on tonight, and let the rest wait until tomorrow. He had a name, a direction to follow toward the man who had taken his mother, and he had almost-proof that it was Asai who had, for whatever his own twisted reasons, engineered it. Get Joori and Morin and Caidi tonight, then find Yakuli and Asai, and take care of them both.

He'd take his time with Asai. Make it hurt. Make him see. Make him *sorry*. Make—

"What'd you do, perch up there and die?"

Jacin snapped his eyes open, hand instinctively reaching for the sheath at his hip, before Malick's clamped down on it, stilled it. Stilled *him*.

"Sorry, didn't mean to startle you. You looked all..." Malick waved a hand up and down. "Sorta stiff and gray."

He'd sauntered in like he had the right, munching on what looked like roasted almonds out of a little cup made of waxed paper. He offered one to Jacin, shrugging affably when Jacin merely tightened his mouth and scowled. There was no grin or smirk stretching Malick's too-handsome face, not this time, but his eyes danced, and Jacin could tell there wanted to be.

"I knocked, but..." Malick trailed off, gesturing vaguely toward the closed door of Jacin's room. His head tilted to the side. "You all right?"

Tea. His eyes were the color of strong tea, tinged light but hung with murk, like tarnished bronze. A slight crook at the bridge of an otherwise perfect nose lent reality, mortality, to his too-striking good looks. His hair was filigreed umber, wavy, and flared to a light curl just touching his shoulders. Worn loose, for vanity, even when he went out to hunt, because binding it into a tail would have been too practical for someone like Malick. It looked just as soft as Jacin knew it was; his fingers remembered the feel of it as he'd gripped, held on, rocking into—

Shit.

No, Jacin wasn't all right. He was ridiculously entranced and pissed off about it.

He snatched his hand away. Shuddered at the loss of contact, of that stillness. A heavy chill wobbled all through him and somehow flared sick heat at the same time.

"What d'you want?"

Malick put his hands up, palms out. "I wanted to warn you that Umeia will be up shortly to check your stitches. And I've brought you something. Several somethings, in fact. Also, I've news."

Jacin didn't really hear any of it but the first part. It curled a hard knot of anxiety in his gut. The tight burn and thudding pain told him what was likely under the bandage wound around his leg, and if any of them saw it...

Damn it, tonight *could not* be put off, he couldn't allow it. He'd go out of his mind if they tried to stop him—last night would be nothing by comparison, and last night had been... bad. And then it had been good. And then he'd nearly lost his mind anyway.

Fuck.

"I want to go now."

Malick looked as surprised by the statement as Jacin was himself. His eyebrows shot up and he stopped chomping on those stupid almonds.

"Now?"

Now that Jacin thought about it—"Why not?"

"Wait, go where?"

It was all Jacin could do to keep his teeth from grinding. What a stupid question. Malick was full of stupid questions. *Go where? Who sent you? Do you still love him?* Did he do it on purpose?

"I want to go get them. Now."

"Now." Malick still wasn't grinning or smirking, but he was halfway to frowning. "What's the matter?" He narrowed his eyes. "Did Shig say something?"

The question—so blunt, so... intuitive—threw Jacin. He didn't have a single answer, so he gave none. Just stared. Angry. Because why should he have to explain?

Because you need his help, and they need his protection, even if you can't trust his reasons.

And still, nothing would come. There was too much, all clogged somewhere in his chest, pushing behind his eyes, and if he opened his mouth, he might not be able to stem the flow once it started.

"All right." Malick sighed, the frown that had been working at his brow now set there in clear confusion and concern. "We don't have to wait until the middle of the night, I suppose. It would be easier, but..." He trailed off, eyes too cogent, too aware. "Tell me why."

It was fair. It was prudent. And Jacin still couldn't do it.

Staring didn't work on Malick. Glares amused him. And he'd only do something for another if there was something in it for him.

Except.

You've a Temshiel punch-drunk over you, bloody idiot.

It... could work.

These people used touch as some sort of silent communication;

Malick in particular used it as a kind of control. And to a degree that almost shamed him, Jacin allowed it. Malick had been watching Jacin since he'd got here, but Jacin had been watching him back. He knew what made Malick tick. What moved him.

Jacin did "coy" just as well as he did "nice," and "seductive" was quite frankly beyond him. Best he went with "slutty and needy." "Slutty," at least, he knew Malick understood, and he rather seemed the sort who liked to think himself the hero in whatever drama he fancied himself playing at, so "needy" should work too.

Jacin allowed the burning behind his eyes to seep outward, allowed the fear and uncertain misery to rise, tried not to let it swallow him even as he let it show. He stepped forward.

The kiss was desperate. Clutching. Pleading. All of it authentic, even in its calculation.

Malick pulled back, wary. "Am I going to get a punch in the jaw for this?"

Jacin had no idea what the hell he was talking about, so he ignored it. Dragged Malick in and kissed him again.

Salt on his lips and the taste of almonds on his tongue, rich and robust. Eyes closed and body pressed in tight. Deep and driving; heavy breaths and grasping fingers.

Silence gave coherence to vague anxieties and spiked them sharper. Stillness made sense of slow arousal, gave Jacin a place to direct scattered passion, focus it all down to this one thing. Yielding, surrender through overture, giving to get, and he really didn't mind the giving part. It would terrify him later, when the touch withdrew, when all he was once again rose inside him, crowded out the perfect, pristine sense of it all that was so clear and sharp right now he could cut himself on it, slice raw to bone. Right now, he sank into it, let it rise right over his head, and didn't even try to keep himself from drowning in it.

Fuck, but the man could kiss.

Jacin's fingers wound into thick, tawny waves, clung, and his body molded to hard planes and pleasing lines. He shoved his hips in, presenting his arousal as proof of intent, satisfied when he felt an answer burning a solid line into the top of his thigh. Firm hands took hold of Jacin's wrists. His fingers were pried away from Malick's hair, then his shoulders when they tried to latch on there; Jacin allowed it, allowed his hands to be guided outward then downward, curling his torso a little more, then arching when Malick pushed Jacin's hands behind his back, pressed them to the small of it. Kept them there. Broke the kiss, panting. Reluctant but dogged.

Malick pressed his brow to Jacin's, just stood there and breathed for a moment. His smile was soft when he opened his tea-colored eyes to skewer Jacin with a look too knowing.

"I see how it is." Malick dipped in to run his mouth slowly over Jacin's cheekbone, gave Jacin's wrists a sharp squeeze to remind him of the position into which he'd allowed himself to be maneuvered—the position into which he'd stepped willingly. "You've almost got what you want, and the nearness of it is terrifying you. So you want to fuck it all away for a while. And if giving me a tumble gets you what you want..." Right in Jacin's ear, hot and soft and dulcet, like it wasn't nailing pieces of him to the wall and hammering him to a quivering pulp.

There was no point in trying to fight his way loose—Jacin had given away his leverage. Offered it. He was stronger than this, and yet he kept getting himself into these positions. It wasn't fair. And anyway, if he started fighting now, he didn't know if he'd be able to stop, and who knew where that could end? What was the price for murdering a *Temshiel* in a fit of insane impatience? Not that he'd be able to. No wonder Malick had laughed at Jacin's knives that night in the alley. Jacin was more likely to end up with one through his own heart than he was to kill this man— accidentally-on-purpose or otherwise—and there was too much at stake. Jacin couldn't allow it all to end with a knife to his ribs in the midst of a "lovers' quarrel," his blood wasn't his to spill, and he no longer had any illusions that he could kill Malick, not knowing what he was.

Malick set a light nip to Jacin's earlobe. "Is this what you learned at Asai's knee?"

Jacin stilled, shut his eyes tight. The accusation spitted him, held him there, quivering. Because maybe it wasn't so far off. Maybe manipulation was the sum of his choices, and yes, he knew from whom he'd learned it. After all, it had worked so well on him, hadn't it?

His hands twitched reflexively, testing the hold on his wrists; it merely tightened again, near to painful now.

With a soft chuckle that was closer to dark and sad than humorous, Malick pulled Jacin in tight against his chest, dipped his mouth down to the sensitive skin just below Jacin's ear.

"Tell me what he was to you, Fen. Tell me what he *is*."

Jacin... *couldn't*. How was he supposed to find the words? How was he supposed to voice them, give them power, give Malick power by hearing them? Jacin was already next to powerless. He couldn't allow what little control he had to slip away from him in his own treacherous voice.

Malick's mouth was still ghosting over Jacin's throat, sliding heat beneath his already burning skin. Stoking reluctant arousal and twisting it in his gut. Tangling doubt with need, hesitation with the agony of craving.

"Please." Jacin swallowed, a shiver rolling up from the base of his spine as Malick's teeth sank lightly into his throat. "Please, I want..." What did he want? Why had he even started this? "I want to go—"

"I know." Malick firmed the strange embrace. "And we will. I promise. I've already promised. But that isn't how it's going to be between us, Fen. You're not going to be fucking me to get what you want unless what you want is the fucking. There are some games I won't play."

"I... I didn't..."

Didn't what? Didn't mean to? Yes he did. Didn't think it would matter? Why should it? They'd both get something out of it. Didn't think Malick would twig? He might play charmingly dim and cavalier, but the man was scary-sharp when he wanted to be, and he was obviously much better at manipulation than Jacin was.

...Didn't even consider the tacit contract might be rejected?

He shouldn't have allowed all that emotion to rise. Meant to aid exploitation before, and now it was only serving to choke him. Familiar lust and too damned much feeling laced with the even more familiar promise of bitter disappointment.

Boneless, hopeless, weak and fuzzy, Jacin's head fell forward to rest on Malick's shoulder. His eyes seared in their sockets.

"I don't want Umeia to look at my leg." Thick and strangled as Jacin wilted into Malick's hold, bone-weary all of a sudden, and sick, head thumping and stomach roiling, and heavy thuds driving up from his leg to his chest.

Malick gusted a light snort and turned his grip on Jacin's wrists from restraint to something oddly comforting.

"One day, I'll learn to follow your twisty turns in conversation."

Jacin doubted it. And he didn't care. When was the last time someone had actually held him like this? When was the last time he'd been rejected and consoled at the same time? Why wasn't Malick pushing him away?

"It's got infected, hasn't it?" Malick asked quietly. "You're burning up."

Probably the most reasonable explanation. Jacin hadn't had the nerve to actually look. He'd made the cut countless times, but the repercussions had never been like this.

"It was deeper than I'd meant. And I hadn't cleaned the knife."

Fucking idiot. He always cleaned his knives, first thing, *always*. Except last night, everything had been... too much. Too loud. He hadn't been able to think, to even track his own actions. Even now, he still couldn't remember how he'd got from the city gates to the roof of the Girou, or from the roof down to Malick's rooms. Bits and snatches were all that came to him, and most of it too humiliating to be worth remembering.

"Well, you were a little out of it," Malick answered, calm and compassionate rather than sickened and scornful.

The hold turned to a true embrace: hands releasing Jacin's wrists and sliding comforting swipes of fingertips where they'd pinched muscle into bone; arms reeling him in more firmly, winding around him, making it hard for Jacin to breathe through the tangled mess in his chest that was clogging his throat. Jacin's arms dangled limp at his sides—he didn't know what to do with them.

He didn't know what to do at all.

So he simply endured it, waited it out, until Malick gave him a gentle squeeze then pulled back, led him over to the bed and made him sit. Watched closely the whole while until Jacin remembered too late that he'd forgotten not to limp.

"All right." There was a touch more command in Malick's voice than there'd been before. "I can see how it is. And before you get yourself into a twist, your brothers and sister *will* be here tonight." He laid a hand to the side of Jacin's face then shook his head with a heavy breath. "You're… bloody hell, you're hot as a forge fire. *Shit.*" Malick scrubbed a hand over his face. "I don't suppose you could be talked into staying here tonight and letting me do this for you?" He merely nodded at Jacin's glare, like he'd expected it, then rolled his eyes. "Right. Stay here."

He left Jacin sitting there on the bed, staring blankly at the door as all at once the noise rose, blurring out reality. He'd come to accept it, that initial wave of sticky incoherence in the first several moments after Malick's touch went away. It was harder to ride it out today. Harder to do anything today but sit and stare, or close his burning eyes and try to drift, try to listen, but the Ancestors didn't have anything to say, nothing Jacin could understand, and anyway, he hurt too much. It was just as well Malick had refused him. Jacin didn't think he would've been able to carry through in the end, and that would have been embarrassing, as well as detrimental to… whatever it was he'd been trying to do at the time.

"Shifts to Null." He wheezed a small snort and curled himself down, propped his elbows to his knees and laid his head in his hands. "Son of a *bitch.*" Pulled back and blinked muzzily at his fingers, wet with clammy sweat.

No wonder his clumsy manipulations hadn't worked—he probably looked like shit. Who would want to see that writhing beneath them? Anyway, he'd already given in, Malick had already got what he wanted, he'd won, so what would be the point? Malick had wanted to touch the Untouchable, and Jacin had given it to him. Why come back to clean up the sloppy afters? Hand the crazy Ghost promises instead, he'd believe them, he always did. Look at what he'd done for Asai—what he'd been willing to do—for nothing more than promises.

He wished Malick had left him over by the window. He missed the chill of the glass against his face. Missed the touch that had shifted his focus from tangled voices to incomprehensible emotions because he wasn't capable right now of fretting over things he didn't understand. There was comfort in just giving in to the chaos.

Malick announced his return with a cursory knock before he barged back in, a small bowl in his hand and a bulky sack slung over his shoulder. He kicked the door shut behind him, and set the bowl to the little cupboard beside the bed.

"I've put Umeia off for now. Drink that. Hangover remedy—works wonders. I know." Jacin just bet he did. "I threw in some boneset. None of it's a cure, and we really should have Umeia see to that leg now, but she'll just try to keep you here tonight, and I think whatever you'll get up to while trying to follow after the rest of us will end up more dangerous than just letting you come along."

Come along. Honestly. Was there no end to the presumptions?

"They're *my* family."

"Yeah, yeah." Malick swung the sack around to bounce on the bed and started rooting through it. "Drink the damn potion. I'm trying to woo you here, and you're not making it easy."

…What?

"These don't really count." Malick tossed a pair of curved steel and boiled leather vambraces into Jacin's lap. "Those are more just because you're clearly too careless with yourself to know you need them, so." Malick shrugged and dug deeper. "Ah, here it is." With a grin, he pulled out a long wooden box and set it on the mattress. "You can open it after you've drunk the brew."

Jacin was still stuck on "woo."

He stared at the vambraces. Then the box. He shot a frown up at Malick, but Malick only raised his eyebrows and glanced pointedly at the bedside cupboard. Jacin followed his gaze, picked up the bowl, and took a cautious whiff, surprised when his mouth watered at the thick, spicy scent of the steam. He hadn't realized he was so thirsty. Interest piqued despite himself, he took several healthy gulps, scalding his mouth and throat.

"Watch it, it's strong." Malick took the bowl and set it back on the cupboard. "I'll get you another before we leave if you need it, but only the one for now. All right, open the box."

Still wary but absurdly curious, Jacin did. Stared.

"I know very well," Malick said, "that by rights I should've had you with me. It's better to try before you buy, make sure your hand fits the grip, but I tried them, and I don't think I've ever felt such perfect balance. And I thought they were quite beautiful."

They were. Twin long knives, the steel tempered nearly blue and scored down the flat with acid-etched leafy vines curling into and over the fuller, winding down from just below the point all the way to the choil. The compound bevel, from tip to return, was sharpened to near silver-white. The handles were straight-grained ironwood, cut from the same block, if Jacin's assessment was correct; the uniformity was that close. The scales securing the tang were virgin ivory. No etchings or frivolities marred the handles, only a subtle series of leather strips set into evenly spaced grooves in a satin-smooth finish so as not to detract, even minutely, from the individual grip.

Beautiful. A far cry from the utilitarian long knives Jacin used. Those hadn't exactly been gifts from Asai—more like accessories to make his tool more useful—but they were efficient and they served Jacin's purposes. These were actual pieces of functional art.

Malick gave Jacin a nudge. "Well, give them a try."

"Give..." Jacin peered up, frowned. "Why?" He'd never let another handle his knives—well, at least the good ones—and he saw no reason to insult these weapons by smudging them up with his sweaty fingers. They looked very expensive. In fact, there was no reason to insult them by selling them to their new apparent owner, but Jacin supposed the craftsman couldn't be blamed for making some koin when he could. It was almost a crime that Malick had bought them. Certainly it had been for vanity's sake—Malick didn't use long knives, and these belonged in the hands of someone who knew what to do with them.

"Remember we talked about wooing?" Malick dragged out a matched set of belted snakeskin sheaths, supple-looking as they coiled around his hand, as though the spirit of the snake they'd come from still possessed them. He waved at the knives. "They're for you, bonehead."

Jacin gave the knives a bit of a glower. "I'm not paying for these." Beauty and form were all well and good, but Jacin's koin was limited, and he needed it all to get his family out of Ada.

"Of course you're not paying for them." Malick rolled his eyes. "Wouldn't be much of a present if I made you pay for it, would it?"

...The fuck?

"A skillful assassin must have tools to match his skill." Malick dropped a small, authoritative nod. "It's in the rule book."

Jacin blinked. Rule book?

"It's a joke, Fen." Smirking now. "There isn't really a rule book."

...All right. But still. None of this was making sense.

"Present." Jacin couldn't stop frowning.

Malick's grin made a comeback, along with a waggle of eyebrows. "And there's more." He dug back into the sack, tugging out bundles of what looked like waxed wool. "I doubt your brothers and sister have raingear, and I know you don't. Think this'll fit your sister?" He held up a small hooded cloak, rich dark blue, with decorative carved-bone buttons and ribbons at the throat. "These, I admit, were Samin's idea, though *I* paid for them. And this."

A vest of lace-thin silvery mail chimed elegantly as Malick pulled it from the sack and held it up. It was cool and light through Jacin's trousers when Malick laid it over his lap. Nothing pretty or fancy about it, but close-meshed and flexible as linen.

Jacin stared. Utterly mystified. He leaned back, hands curled to his chest, unwilling to actually touch any of it.

Malick nudged him again. "Feeling wooed yet?"

Jacin just kept staring. The headache had receded—whatever that brew was had set right to doing its promised work—but he could feel the heat of fever flushing his cheeks, and a renewed solid pulse thumped through him, flaring heavily up his thigh.

"I don't understand."

Malick's grin was… strange. Soft. "I know you don't. That's what makes it fun. It's not important." He jerked his chin at the box with the knives. "Try them."

Presents.

Wooed.

Confounded, Jacin ran a fingertip over the butt of one of the knives, then slipped his hand around it. The wood was like warm silk against his palm. He tested the grip as he lifted it from its bed of dark velvet, and gave it an experimental twirl.

"Full tang." The blade caught the light as Jacin spun it, then flipped it to lay crosswise over his palm. "Perfectly balanced."

"I said it was, didn't I?" Malick's tone was perhaps a little miffed. "I may not do a lot of knife work, but I at least know how to look for quality."

Well… that seemed true enough. Jacin laid the knife back in the box. "I'll pay for the cloaks." Because he hadn't thought of them, and they would be necessary. "The rest—"

"The rest you'll be needing." Malick's smile was gone, gaze abruptly sober. "I told you I've news, as well."

The sudden turn to gravity made Jacin's eyes narrow. "Does it have to do with tonight?"

"It has to do with the things most precious to you, so yeah, I guess you could say it does, in a roundabout way." Malick paused, like he was thinking about what he wanted to say and exactly how he wanted to say it, then tipped a sharp nod, looked Jacin in the eye. "You know Asai's been lying to you."

It wasn't a question, and the baldness of it made Jacin look away, duck his head, eyes hot and throat tight. Mostly because it didn't need to be a question.

"I… He—"

"If I wanted someone completely under my control…" Malick trailed off, eyes bright with… something—sympathy, maybe—before the light abruptly went out, turned cool, and he tried again. "If I wanted someone completely under my control, do you know what I'd do?" He didn't wait for an answer. "I'd find out what mattered to him, what he loved, and control that. I'd take it and hold it hostage, and make him believe I was

the only thing standing between that thing he loved and complete anni-
hilation."

It had the sound of a threat, but not the feel. Still, Jacin's stomach
curled in then dropped altogether. Malick was capable of it, all of it;
there was a coldness in him sometimes that Jacin didn't doubt. And
Jacin had practically begged a *Temshiel* to "rescue" his family.

"And if I was *very* clever, I'd do it all in a way that made me the hero."
Malick's gaze never left Jacin. "I might even persuade my target that I
was everything he ever wanted, pretend I loved him, and do everything
I could to make sure he loved me. I'd become his savior. Show him I
could be the savior of everything he loved."

Just exactly how much did Malick know about Jacin's years with
Asai? And how had he found out? Was he rubbing Jacin's nose in his
own stupidity? Or was he arrogantly laying out his own plans and
showing Jacin how powerless he was to stop any of it?

"Is that...?" Jacin had to pause, suck in a long breath. "Is that what
you're doing now?"

Malick only stared at him, anger edging his gaze, then he clenched
his fists, unclenched them. He didn't answer the question.

"I've known Asai for... a long time, Fen. You might say we've a bit of
a history. And not a pleasant one." He paused while Jacin took this in,
then said, surprisingly gently, "You had no idea he's maijin, did you?"

Everything... *tilted*. Just a little, but enough to throw off whatever
balance Jacin had been maintaining between confusion, noise, and pain.
He shook his head, hand shifting along his thigh, pressing just enough.

"He..."

He couldn't be was what hovered on Jacin's tongue, but... why
couldn't he be? The full-Blood ran through Jacin's veins, but none of its
magic—how would he be able to tell? Abruptly, this *Temshiel's* invasive
presence in his life, and his absurd interest in Jacin himself, made a little
bit more sense.

Jason's head went light. "And you're here to balance him out."

Because it was what they did. It was their nature. Maijin influenced
mortals to make a mess of things, and *Temshiel* followed after, mopping
up, wiping out any—even the duped mortals—who weren't smart
enough to get out of their way. All except for the maijin. Exquisitely
unfair, Jacin had always thought—they could and did kill everyone but
each other, waged war on each other through those they manipulated.

"No. I was here to..." Malick raked a hand through his hair. "Some
would say 'hide'—some *have* said as much—but I prefer to call it a strategic retreat. Which is what it was. Except... well, then, you came along,
and... here you are."

"...Here I am." Fear sat high in Jacin's chest, stuttered his breath.
"What d'you—?"

No, that would do no good—these people didn't explain themselves to mortals. And Jacin had... Had he broken any laws? Adan laws, certainly, but it wasn't the same as breaking the laws of the gods. What *were* the laws of the gods? Everyone had their own versions. And Jacin hadn't done anything worse than what this *Temshiel* had done—did that count for anything? Shig had said Malick belonged to Wolf; did Wolf give a damn about the Adan and their laws? The Jin were his favored people, or so they liked to claim—not that it seemed to have done them any good—but Wolf's laws seemed to have more to do with...

Temshiel, children of the gods, and the Ancestors were the children of the *Temshiel*. Except the Ancestors had angered Wolf when they'd bound their magic to their people, changed their natures, altered the Balance, and when Wolf's Cycle had ended, the Jin had been abandoned by their guides and their god. Only the Ancestors had been left to lead the people, direct their magic. And when the Ancestors' long lives stretched too thin, they cast themselves into Subie, chose their Untouchables who spoke with their Voices, and lived on through them.

Oh... *shit.*

How many times had Jacin heard the speculation that the Adan's quick success in subduing the Jin was overdue punishment for the Ancestors' folly and the Jin's continued compliance with it? The Jin had won the Binding War, but it had cost them their guiding Voices, driven the Ancestors mad, and the Untouchables in their wake. Left the Jin open to that final and decisive invasion only decades ago, placed the bootheels of the Adan firmly on their necks. And now their magic was being stamped out where possible, covertly stolen when it could be managed. Surely it must be the final retribution of an angry god? The *Temshiel* had been set against the Jin before—why not again?

"Please don't hurt them." Likely no good, either, but Jacin had to try. Beg. Whatever it took, even if he had to kill... everyone.

Had he told Malick that Joori had magic? No, Jacin had kept that to himself, but was it possible to hide something like that from *Temshiel?* Malick had to know—why else all the interest? No wonder he was so keen to go and get them, bring them here, and Jacin was going to lead him right to them.

"Do you love him?"

The question, so seemingly random, threw Jacin. He stared, trying to make his mind move from the fear and dread of a second ago to the shame and confusion the question provoked.

"Love?"

"Asai, Fen. Do you love Asai?"

Did he love Asai? Jacin wanted to snarl, snap, *No! What the fuck do you think I am?* but indignation came from pride and honor, and Jacin didn't think he had any of those. He wanted to say he hated Asai—for what he'd done, for whatever it was he was planning to do—but the thick tangle in Jacin's chest felt too much like the one that had choked him since he'd seen dark eyes and a kind, handsome face lit by the moonlight in his father's dooryard. Love and hate were too closely entwined as a rule, and Jacin had no idea how to tell one from the other.

"Did you sleep with him?"

"He wouldn't have me." It came all too quickly, spilling out of Jacin's mouth before he could dam it up. Humiliated, damage done, the anger spiked again, and Jacin lifted his head, glared at Malick. "I would've done. I wanted to." Defiant. Strangled with years of frustration and hurt and rage, and he was more than willing to take it out on Malick, since he was handy, and *Temshiel* besides, and also full of fucking questions when he had yet to address Jacin's.

"Don't hurt them." Jacin said it through his teeth this time, but it wobbled and fell from threat to plea by the end. And he was already in it, so he might as well add, "*Please,*" though he had no illusions that anything he said would change a damned thing.

"I'm not going to hurt them."

Jacin heard it only dimly through the driving buzz, but he did hear it.

"I'm going to do whatever I need to do to make sure no one gets hurt at all. Fen, look at me."

Shit, Jacin's eyes had clamped shut. He pried them open, dragged in a painful, heavy breath. Looked up.

"I'm not going to hurt them," Malick repeated. "I told you, I'm going to help."

"Why?" Strung through with dread and despair and horrible foreboding.

Malick shrugged, careless, as though everything Jacin had left wasn't dangling from the fingers of immortal beings like the strings of helpless puppets.

"Well, for one, because Umeia's already sworn oath to you, and she'd kill me if she ended up going to the suns because of me."

"Umeia…" Right. Jacin had forgotten about Umeia for a minute there. "Your… mate?"

"No. What? *No!*" Malick reared back with a shudder. "*Fuck,* no. Sister."

Huh. Jacin hadn't known *Temshiel* had siblings.

He cleared his throat. "She swore to my brothers and sister. She didn't swear to me."

Malick's gaze snapped over to Jacin, sharp and narrowed. "Hm," he said, like he hadn't realized it until Jacin had pointed it out. He stared, thoughtful, brow drawn and expression gone dark, before he shook it off. "Nonetheless, she's sworn to your family, and unless I'm willing to

risk her—which I'm not—I'll be making sure nothing happens to them."
He paused, swept the mess on the bed to the side, and sat down so his
gaze was level with Jacin's. "Fen, believe me on this—you *will* have your
family here, safe and sound, tonight."

"And then what?"

"What d'you…?" Malick shook his head. "I told you there's no price
for tonight."

"But you never said anything about *after* tonight." Jacin set his jaw.
"And *then* what?"

"Why does there have to be an 'and then'?"

Why? *Why?*

Because you're Temshiel *and I don't trust you*, but Jacin didn't dare say it.

There was a price, there had to be because there always was, and Jacin
needed to know it, know it *now*, so it wouldn't creep up behind him some
day and bite him on the ass. He didn't know how to say it, not in a way that
didn't sound vicious and ungrateful, and he needed to at least *sound* grateful, because this *Temshiel* now held everything Jacin had left in his hand.

"They're my *family*." It came out thin and raw, but there was nothing
Jacin could do about that.

Malick huffed. "And everything has to be a fucking trade, dunnit?" It
was strangely soft, and… disappointed? Not sad, surely. "Fine, then, if that's
what you need. I get your family for you, and then you return the favor."

There it was. Jacin almost buckled. It was… bizarre relief.

"How?"

"You kill Asai."

"I was going to do that any—"

"And you do it so he stays dead."

"What does that—?"

"You take out his heart, Fen. You pull it from his chest and you bind
his spirit to the earth."

Jacin paused, sucked in a slow breath. Tried to picture it, and
stopped himself when he found he wasn't quite as disturbed as he ought
to be, considering what Asai had been to him. Considering that Asai
himself had taught Jacin how to do that very thing, except Jacin was
pretty sure Asai hadn't meant for "his Ghost" to use it on him. So, who
had Asai meant for Jacin to use it on? Jacin's gaze settled on Malick's,
hung there as vague suspicion wound its way to almost certainty.

…Oh.

The irony was both fitting and horrifying.

"There is no price for bringing them here." Malick's tone was low and
even, like he was afraid Jacin would bolt. "But that's not all you want.
And it's not really enough, in the end, is it?" He leaned in, right up close,
gaze intense. "You want a trade, Fen, there it is. Asai for them, and I'll
give you what you want. I'll get them *out*."

Jacin narrowed his eyes. It couldn't be that easy.

"I can't kill him," Malick said, soft and serious. "I'm bound by different laws than you are. But he *needs* killing, Fen. Besides what he's done to your family—and I know now it was him who betrayed them—there's so much more you don't know."

"Yes." Jacin almost didn't recognize his own voice, faraway and flat.

His hand reached, all on its own, to stroke a fingertip down the edge of one of the knives. Agreement, maybe, or just final verbal acknowledgement of the truth—it didn't matter. He'd been planning on doing it anyway. Just not… that way.

The potion Malick had given him had dulled all the aches and calmed Jacin's stomach, taken his mind back to almost as "normal" as he got. He wished he hadn't drunk it. Near-agonizing pain and overwhelming noise seemed almost like welcome distraction now.

Malick leaned down, caught Jacin's gaze, held it. "I don't know how long he's been planning this, though I've my suspicions. But his machinations began in earnest when Wolf pulled you away from Raven."

Jacin looked down at his fingers, hovering along the knife's beveled edge. A wheezy little laugh rolled loose from his throat.

"He came to my father the night I was born." Still soft, almost insubstantial. "Traded me on my Change for…" Jacin paused. He'd almost mentioned Joori. "…for my mother's safety."

"And your brother's."

Fuck. Jacin's fingers slid down the blade of the knife, wrapped lightly about the handle.

Malick tsked. "It's impolite to kill a man with a knife he gave you for a present."

Jacin snapped his gaze up, searching, but for maybe the first time since he'd laid eyes on Malick, there was no mockery or amusement in the clear gaze.

"I don't know what you're talking about. My brother—"

"Oh, please." Malick rolled his eyes. "You really thought I didn't know? Or wouldn't find out, once he got here?"

Maybe. No. But he'd been willing to give it a try for as long as it took to get his family back, and figure the rest out later. Not great as strategies went, but thinking ahead—planning and scheming—were not exactly Jacin's areas of aptitude. And reading people… Hell, he'd spent his entire adolescence in love with a maijin who was all the while planning to hand over his mother and brother, and probably have Morin and Caidi killed. What the fuck did Jacin know?

"Anyway." Malick pointed his gaze downward. "I, um… I followed you that first night." He peered up, guilty. "I've known from the start, Fen."

How…? No, it didn't matter. Almost every kind of magic, Shig had said. It must have been laughably easy. And there Jacin had been—so careful, so pathetic—thinking he was doing at least that part right.

"Son of a *bitch*."

"Yeah, so I'm told." Malick shrugged. "Sorry."

Jacin didn't think he was, not really.

"Did you know that little hut sits well inside Asai's holdings?" Malick lifted an eyebrow. "He's got his own ways of watching what goes on in the lands he's claimed. It's good luck for you the Mage was watching out for you and yours."

Jacin hadn't known. He hadn't had even the faintest clue. Fuck, what had he been *thinking*? They could have all been dead that first awful night. The horror of the possibility drained the blood from Jacin's head, sent it driving down into his gut, twisting it.

There it is, Joori—even you'd have to see this failure for what it is.

Malick set a hand, warm, to Jacin's arm; shockingly, Jacin didn't even flinch, and the fact that he didn't made his face burn. Improbably, the silence was merely secondary. Comfort, and he didn't even care from whom it came. A whore for touch, even now. Practically begging his father for it, like a cat winding around its owner's legs, then lapping up the sparing little he'd got from Asai, and latching on to Vonshi's bony grip that always seemed to slide a sliver of sanity through the mangled mess of Jacin's mind. And now...

He couldn't shake it off. Wouldn't. And he couldn't fool himself anymore that it was only the silence inside it he craved. This was older, this need, ingrained and dangerous, and much stronger than he was.

"You said Asai never told you why he was training you." The compassion in Malick's soft voice slid through Jacin like a knife to the chest. "You were to use your training on me. Or whatever *Temshiel* came to stop him—it's his bad luck it happened to be me." He paused, too obviously stifling a growl, then shook his head. "He doesn't love you, Fen. He never did."

"So what?" It came out humiliatingly thick. "Neither do you."

"Ah, but I can pretend. I'm fucking brilliant at it." Malick's tone was abruptly low, a subtle note of sex clinging to its edge as he leaned in close to murmur in Jacin's ear. "Wouldn't you like to believe it? Just for a little while?"

Yeah. He would. He'd probably hand over his soul to Malick right now, just to believe *someone* did. That someone *could*. That he was worthy of it. That he wasn't *nothing*.

And fucking hell, but he was pretty sure Malick knew it.

Jacin shut his eyes so they wouldn't start leaking again. "What do you want from me?"

"Oh, baby..." Malick chuckled, but somehow, it didn't feel derisive or insulting. "You don't know the half of it. So much more than this, but this'll have to do for now." He dipped in close again and set a soft, damp kiss to Jacin's temple. "Just like I can't kill him, he can't kill me. But he wants my Blood, and you're meant to get it for him.

"So, you have a decision to make here, Fen."

Malick pulled back, gaze intense but otherwise unreadable. He kept his hand where it was, and Jacin continued to let him.

"You're with me or against me. You're his dog or you're mine. There is no in-between. There is no price but what you choose. If you choose him, we go tonight, get your family if you still want us to, then you go on your way—no harm, no foul.

"But if you choose me, I won't just go and get them, I'll keep them safe. I'll get them out." Malick paused, leaned in close. "Think about it, Fen, because there's no going back. And by that I mean: if you cross me, I'll kill you. The Adan's laws do not apply to me. So."

Malick took his hand back, waited for a moment, like he knew Jacin needed him to, then stood and stepped slowly over to the window before turning back. He leveled his gaze with Jacin's.

"*Now* d'you feel wooed?"

- BOOK TWO -
WEREGILD

1

Storm-month, Year 1322, Cycle of the Wolf

He hadn't been expecting to see Jacin again so soon. And yet here Jacin stood, rain-soaked and hollow-eyed, in the doorway of the little hut, blinking around like he'd forgotten why he'd come.

Joori's mouth quirked up in an uncertain half smile—right until he saw the two men behind Jacin.

His first instinct—*hunters? bandits? was Jacin some kind of hostage?*—was to yank Jacin through the door and slam it shut. Too bad his body's first reaction was to freeze like a rodent beneath the shadow of a hawk's wings.

"*Jacin!*"

Joori was still gaping and didn't catch Caidi before she made a run at Jacin, so she was rather open prey for the man who stepped forward to intercept her. Jacin didn't move. Joori couldn't. Just watched the man swing Caidi up onto his hip with a grin Joori didn't quite believe—more wolfish than friendly—then cut a narrow glance at Morin and a mocking one at Joori.

"Kamen Malick." The man tipped a nod at Morin. "You can call me Malick." He spared a quick smile for Caidi, tweaked her nose, before turning his cool glance back on Joori. "Friends of your brother's. We're here to take you somewhere safe."

The other man, the big one, pursed his mouth in clear disapproval. "You plan on telling everyone you meet your real name?"

You-can-call-me-Malick grinned. "It's Fen's family."

Handsome. Friendly-seeming enough. The other man was big and blocky, a little bit scary, maybe, but not threatening, despite the broadsword hung at his hip. The one who called himself Kamen Malick was armed as well, but no weapons were drawn, which had to be a good sign.

…Right?

With Jacin just standing there, somewhat glassy-eyed, You-can-call-me-Malick smiling, all amiable amusement, and the big one waiting in the doorway like an attentive steward, it all seemed absurdly unthreatening for a sudden appearance in the dark of night with a storm rolling steadily. And the statement—*safe*; could it be possible?—really should have set elation through Joori, not raise his hackles the way it did.

It was the hand on Jacin's shoulder. The casual way You-can-call-me-Malick tipped in and spoke something quietly into Jacin's ear as he set Caidi down and gently pushed her away. The impossible-to-mistake marks just below Jacin's ear.

For years, Joori had his suspicions about what Asai had wanted with his brother—hell, he'd been pretty sure he knew exactly what Asai was about the night he stepped arrogantly into their dooryard—and Jacin's reticence and unwillingness to talk in detail about any of it had drawn conclusions of every abuse and exploitation Joori could fathom. And he'd be damned if he'd see it done again—not in *his* name, never again.

He pushed past the cocky stranger with the too-easy grin. Brazen, You-can-call-me-Malick angled in front of Jacin, like he was trying to keep Joori away—keep *Joori* away from his brother; how *dare* he. More brazen, in fact outright hostile, Joori bared his teeth, shoved through, and took hold of Jacin's elbow.

"Jacin, what's going on? Who are these people?" Joori looked closer. "Are you *drunk*? Or...?" His eyes narrowed, and he wheeled on the grinning stranger. "What've you got him on?"

You-can-call-me-Malick's eyebrows drew down. "What've I *got* him—?"

"I can barely see the color of his eyes for the pupils, and he looks like he's about to fall over!"

"Joori, not now." It was snappish and short. Jacin pulled his arm from Joori's grip. "They're who they say they are. This is Malick. And that's Samin."

He waved at the man still standing like a block of stone just outside the door. Good thing too, because the hut was only so big, and Caidi was taking up half the floor with the pile of clothes through which she was sorting with Morin's help. Caidi was chattering excitedly, while Morin kept half a cagey eye on everyone in the room.

"Yori and Shig are keeping watch outside." Jacin crouched down beside Morin to help shove balled-up clothes into a sack. "We're taking you to a safe place in the city. Get your things. Take what you can carry; the cart's only big enough for Caidi and a few provisions."

"A safe...?" Had he really said "a safe place"? In *Ikata*? Was there such a thing?

Joori looked around. At Caidi and Morin obediently stuffing their packs. At the man Jacin had called Samin standing out in the rain on the other side of the door, watching everything going on inside while simultaneously scanning the yard. At the other man—this Malick—smiling that self-satisfied smile, eyes too focused on Jacin. At Jacin, making his stiff way over to the board and staring down at the piles of food like he couldn't decide what to do about them—

"Leave it," Malick said quietly. "You won't need to worry about it anymore."

—at the way Jacin just nodded vaguely, compliant.

Joori stepped up behind Jacin, shot Malick a glare. Malick merely widened his smirk and shook his head. *Amused.*

Teeth tight, Joori leaned in and lowered his voice. "Jacin. Are you sure this is real?"

"As real as I can manage."

"What's wrong with you? You look awful."

Jacin was pale, going sallow, with twin spots of hectic color on each cheekbone. Half moons like bruises blotted the thin skin beneath his eyes, and his jaw was clenched so hard Joori would swear he heard teeth squeak.

"Nothing that won't keep." Jacin tried to smile, but the ghastly thing that crooked his mouth only knocked up the worry blooming in Joori's gut. "We don't have much time. I didn't know… I had no idea…" Jacin paused, rubbed at his temple. "Asai… *Fuck*, Joori, I'm so sorry. I never thought—"

"I think that's got it all." Malick shouldered past Joori and set a hand to Jacin's arm. Tawny eyes settled far too keenly on Joori. Possessive. Smirking. Silent laughter bubbling just beneath it. As if Malick knew exactly what Joori was thinking, and thought it terribly funny. "We should go, Fen."

"I… yes." Jacin gave Joori's shoulder a quick brush as he squeezed around him.

Biddable. Like what this Malick person said *mattered.*

Joori took hold of Jacin's elbow and stopped him. "Jacin." He kept his narrow gaze locked onto Malick's smug one. "Are you *sure* this is real?"

Jacin frowned. "I said it was." Then why did he look so damned miserable? "It'll be all right. I… this wasn't… I'm sorry."

"For what?" Joori flared a look at Malick, who somehow had Jacin's braid in his hand like it was a bloody leash. Joori tugged until Jacin took a step away. "Why are you sorry, Jacin?" He dropped his voice as low as it could go and still make sound. "What are you paying for this?"

Rising dread turned to unfocused alarm when Jacin whiffed a tired laugh. "No price."

He met Malick's even gaze for a long, heavy moment, face unreadable, then straightened and pulled away. Joori was ridiculously relieved when Jacin irritably yanked his braid from Malick's fingers, and even more so when Malick let go.

"We have to leave now." Jacin turned to face Joori squarely, eyes flicking over Joori's shoulder at the smirking man who watched a little too closely, then back again to Joori. "Please, Joori."

Joori looked at Jacin hard then turned his glance once again on Malick, let it narrow at the steady look he got back. "I don't trust him." He kept his voice deliberately loud enough that Malick could hear.

Malick shrugged, indifferent. "*He* never asked you to." It seemed as though he made it a point to drop a quick touch to Jacin's shoulder as he sauntered out the door, collecting Samin as he went.

Joori turned back to Jacin, anger receding and worry crowding back in at the weariness and wan cast to Jacin's face. "Jacin—"

"Brother." Jacin closed his eyes, sucked in a deep breath. "Please."

Joori could only stare, mouth tight and unease roiling up his backbone. Because really—what choice did he have?

⁂

For all the rush and worry, Yori decided, this "job" was turning out to be the most boring one she'd ever been on. Irritably, she rolled her neck, mouth pinching tight as rain trickled down between her shoulder blades. She wondered why she was even here. She clearly wasn't needed— neither were Samin or Shig, or even Fen, when it came right down to it. Maybe Shig, now that Yori thought about it. Malick always kept Shig close while he was using his magic, laying hands on her more than Yori thought entirely necessary. But Shig didn't mind and Malick was Malick, so Yori didn't say anything. Still, it seemed Malick could have done this job all by himself.

…Well. She supposed Fen's presence was necessary, or Malick might have had some trouble getting the three refugees to come along as compliantly as they'd done, but other than that.

She wasn't *too* put out. She'd only seen Malick do his trick with the gates once before—most of their jobs fell inside the city's walls, and he used his magic so rarely Yori sometimes forgot he had it at all—and she rather enjoyed the high the aftereffects gave her. Nothing she cared to understand, but Malick once half-explained it as fazing their corporeal realities while altering the perceptions of any who might cross their paths. Yori had just sort of nodded a "Yeah, yeah, whatever" at him, and enjoyed the bit of euphoria.

It didn't work with Fen, which surprised Yori, but wouldn't have done, had she stopped and thought about it. Magic didn't work on an Untouchable. Too bad for him. It was a heady thing while it was happening, Malick's magic, a little like coming down from poppy. But even that bit of a thrill— and the knowledge there'd be another like it when they returned—wasn't enough to offset the squishiness in Yori's boots now, the too-steady rain seeping through her oiled cloak, and the annoyance that was Fen's little brother. And Yori had thought *Fen* was hard to get along with.

"Why couldn't they have got a cart big enough for all of us?" It seemed as though the only way Morin knew how to speak was through snark.

Fen mumbled something back at him Yori didn't catch, and though the tone sounded almost mellow—or at least as mellow as Fen got—Morin's mouth shut up tight and didn't open again.

Yori rolled her eyes.

The strangest reunion she'd ever seen, though admittedly, she couldn't recall ever having seen one before. She'd sort of expected hugs and shouts of relief; what she'd got were intense looks from Fen's twin, clear distrust and hostility, particularly toward Malick. The little one, Caidi, seemed to be rather a limpet where Fen was concerned, to which Fen submitted with some softening of his usual stony expression. Morin was a bit of a puzzle.

Not hatred in his eyes when he looked at Fen, but... Yori couldn't tell, really. Morin was too obviously afraid of both his elder brothers, but that wasn't it. His distrust of Shig was harsh, and clear from the second he laid eyes on her—the hair was apparently too much for him—and turned to outright anxiety when Shig spoke. Though, Yori mused, the fact that Shig's first words had been "Damn, but you're an angry little rabbit, aren't you? Stop thinking so loud, you're giving me a headache" probably hadn't helped. Not the best way to introduce herself to a boy who'd been taught that magic, or even one's proximity to it, meant painful death. Pretty amusing, though, at least to Yori, but then, lots of inappropriate things amused her.

Samin's granite face and hard eyes terrified the boy, though that might've been because Samin made the mistake of trying to smile at him. Not a pretty thing, Samin's smile, at least not 'til you got to know him. For whatever reason moved little girls, it stirred a giggling fit in Caidi, and she'd allowed Samin to lift her and plop her on top of the things they'd packed into the dray. She even obediently complied when Samin gruffly directed her to fan out her cloak to cover what it would. Yori thought perhaps she better understood the girl's good humor when she saw Caidi surreptitiously poke her tongue out at Morin as Samin settled her in for the ride.

Morin stuck to a loosely defined middle ground between his two elder brothers. Fen kept his head down, jaw set, silent but for occasional monosyllabic answers to Caidi's chatter behind him in the cart that he refused to allow anyone else to help him pull, all the while pretending not to limp.

The twin, Joori, engaged Malick in a conversation Yori hadn't been able to hear above the rain and the squishy grind of the dray's wheels on the road. But she'd heard Asai's name spoken sharply twice—first by Joori then later by Malick—before Malick had stopped abruptly. He'd jerked his head at Yori to take point then pulled the brother to the side to growl something at him, low and intense and strangely cross. Malick's eyes stayed on Fen the whole while, though Fen hadn't seemed to notice anything but his own feet and the death grip he had on the dray's handles. Samin had offered four times now to pull it for him, and four times had been ignored.

"You're Yori, right?"

Yori shifted a glance sideways. "And you're Joori." She couldn't help the silly grin. "Sorta rhymes."

The chuckle out of the dark sounded more tense than sincere. "So, how long have you known my brother?"

With an irritable swat at some fringe that wouldn't stay put beneath her hood, Yori blinked rain out of her eyes, squinting at the blob of murk walking beside her that was Fen's twin brother.

"About..." She paused.

Besides whatever had passed between him and Malick, Yori had watched this one trying to wring conversation out of Fen since they'd maneuvered the little cart out of the scraggy yard of the hut where they'd been staying. He'd been just as unsuccessful as Yori had ever been. She would've thought Fen would be more communicative with his family, at least, considering what he'd apparently gone through to protect them. All things considered, perhaps it wasn't her place to be blabbing things Fen didn't choose to disclose.

She kept her answer to "A little while." At the resultant sigh that was nearly a growl, Yori changed the subject: "Has anyone told you we've a hot-spring bath where we're going? Bet it'll be nice for you to sink into *that*, won't it? I know I can't wait."

Joori changed it right back: "You've come very well armed." His voice was just as deep as Fen's, but with a different nuance Yori couldn't quite ken. "I take it you don't have the same magic as that other one with the hair."

Yori snickered; she'd have to remember to repeat that to Shig later. "That's Shig. My sister."

"I figured. You look a lot alike."

"Except for the hair, yeah?"

"And you're prettier."

Yori only just kept from rolling her eyes. Honestly—men were so transparent.

"So, you tried wringing answers out of Fen, then arguing them out of Malick, and now you're down to flattery." Yori shook her head. "You're not even very good at it."

"Huh." Yori could just make out Joori's shrug in the dark, then a frown momentarily illuminated by a fleeting streak of lightning. "Strange, because I meant it. I won't say I'm above sweet talk. And I do want answers. But it's still the truth."

Yori gave him a slit-eyed stare as a quiet rumble of thunder rolled. Joori looked right back, eyes a mere dull gleam through the gloom.

She had to admit he was attractive. Identical to Fen in respect to facial features, but there was something about Fen—his hardness, maybe; the way Yori had to decipher him all the time and couldn't just *be*. It had… not repelled her, really, but at least put her off from the start. Unlike *some* infatuated dimwits, Yori had never had a single carnal thought about their newest duckling. This one, though.

Yori huffed and shook it off. "Fen works with us."

"And you rescue the families of everyone who works with you?"

"Everyone who works with us *is* family."

Joori went quiet, taking that in. "He's been looking for our mother."

"Uh-huh."

"And you—?"

"Yes."

Joori brooded over that for a while. Yori let him, only lifting an eyebrow when Joori spun every now and then to walk backward for a pace or two, likely eyeing his brother, before turning back.

"He looks like shit." It was low and just for Yori. "What's going on with him?"

It was the accent—that was what was different. Joori had the same voice as Fen, but Fen didn't have the twangy Jin accent.

Yori looked back over her shoulder, squinting, but all she could make out was Fen's hunched figure, stubbornly pulling the dray and trying to keep up with the pace she and Joori were setting. Malick was walking beside him now, and Morin hovered a little closer than he'd done before. Fen had stopped even the quiet, one-word answers he'd been giving his sister, a chore that Malick had seemingly taken to himself, though Caidi didn't seem to mind. In fact, she seemed charmed. Samin had moved up to walk behind the cart, leaving Shig to watch their backs, which he wouldn't ordinarily have done unless Malick had told him to.

It appeared Joori wasn't the only one waiting for Fen to drop, though Yori was putting her koin on Fen. He was too mulish to let his body stop if he wanted it to keep going. In Yori's observation, when Fen hit a wall, he just rammed until it fell down.

Joori sighed, all put up and impatient. "At least tell me why he's limping."

"Oh, that." That was easy enough. "He got a cut on his leg last night. Umeia had to sew him up. Probably just needs a painkiller. And to stop insisting on pulling that dray by himself." Bloody bonehead.

"I saw him last night." Joori turned again, cloak billowing around his knees as he pivoted to walk backward. Yori could see more of his face now, though he was still little more than a dim smudge against the foggy black. "I didn't notice anything wrong with his leg. Although." A shrug. "He was covered in blood."

"Yeah?" Yori shrugged too, but didn't volunteer anything.

Like how Fen's descent from the top of the gate had been more like a fall, and that he'd landed awkwardly then snarled off any concerned attempts to help. And how Yori was almost certain she'd heard a strangled wheeze of a scream when he was trying to drag the dray from the culvert where he and Shig had stashed it, and then nearly bitten Malick's hand off when he bulled his way in to help. Obstinate idiot.

Yori would have to make sure Umeia knew about it when they got back. Umeia would take care of it, whatever it was. Fen had probably gone and got the thing infected, and Yori would bet some stitches gave when he'd wrestled with that cart. What the hell were they supposed to do with all these people if Fen up and died on them? And anyway, what would...?

Wait.

"You saw him last night?" Yori frowned. "How? When?"

"Is he sleeping with that man? That Malick?"

Yori blinked, eyebrows snapping upward. Apparently, flapping from subject to subject was a family trait. She almost barked a laugh, but the question had been posed so... almost angrily, and the tone of it, the suspicion inside it, roused something oddly protective in Yori. Fen's brother or not, this Joori wasn't theirs, at least not yet, and what Malick and Fen got up to wasn't even Yori's business, let alone Joori's.

"I'm not quite certain that's your concern." Yori made her tone deliberately cool. "Or mine. P'raps you'd best ask Fen."

Joori took his scrutiny off his brother, turned it to Yori for several strides, then huffed. The "Yeah, thanks" he shot over his shoulder as he walked off toward Fen was rudely scornful.

Damn. Yori wished she could warn Fen, and apologize in advance for apparently setting his brother on him, but. Well. Maybe it would stop him dragging that stupid cart for a minute, at least. Joori was right about that—Fen looked like shit.

Deliberately, Yori looked away, sent a glance ahead and to all points, scanning the shadows, but if anything was going to come at them, she wasn't going to see it before it saw them, not tonight. No moons, low-hanging fog, and trees bloody everywhere. She'd have to rely on Shig and Malick twigging in time. Anyway, they were halfway home, and nothing had happened so far, and she had more magic at the gates to look forward to.

Biting back a sigh, Yori ignored the steady rise of Joori's voice, tried to ignore her numbing toes with rather less success, and tucked her hands up under her cloak to warm her fingers. If there was trouble, she'd need them flexible. Although, she mused—trying not to snort as Joori's voice went higher, and the sound of the dray's wheels on the road ceased abruptly—perhaps any trouble that might come wouldn't be from anything lurking out there in the dark.

Then again—

"Yori, look sharp!"

Malick flew past her, sword drawn, and a hot welter of power like Yori'd never felt in her life nearly swatted her aside. Had that come from *Malick?*

All instinct now, Yori swung her bow around and nocked an arrow, planting her feet in an offensive stance, even as she squinted ahead in the direction Malick was stalking. Trees and more trees, shadows and more shadows, and she'd been looking right at them only a second ago, but now...

Well, bloody damn.

Now the shadows were *moving.* And not in any way people moved—at least not people with bones beneath their skin. Vague man-shapes then hunched... somethings. It was fascinating and revolting at the same time, and Yori hadn't even got a good look yet. She wished for a flash of lightning, just so she could see what the hell they were dealing with.

She spared a quick glance around, taking in the configurations, so she'd know if things got messy. Fen had shoved his siblings behind him; Morin and Caidi both huddled in the cart, Joori between them and Fen. Samin stood by the dray, sword drawn, watching Malick. Shig was turned to face the rear, bright head atilt in the way it did when she let her own magic loose, seeking.

Satisfied, Yori turned back, eyes flicking back and forth between the smoky curls of... whatever they were farther up the road and Malick as he strode up to them, planted himself mere paces away, and drew up straight. Threatening. Frightening. Powerful.

"Three of you?" Malick swung his sword in a lazy figure eight. "That's all?"

Rolling hisses gathered from the writhing murk as it wound into three distinct shapes then fanned out again.

"No." Shig sounded annoyed. "There's more."

Yori glanced back, just long enough to see more smoky shapes pooling to either side of the dray like twisting skeins of the stormy sky. It was as though she almost recognized the contours they were thrashing them-selves into, but couldn't quite settle them in her head yet.

"Fucking Husao." Malick shoved it out between his teeth. "Manipula-tive prick." He shifted into attack stance. "Whatever you see, remember it's all glamour. They're only maijin. They bleed and die like everything else."

Terrific, Yori thought sourly, *good to know,* then sucked in a long breath and sighted down.

It had to be Husao, Malick decided, or Vonshi, or whatever Husao was calling himself at the moment.

They were still on Asai's lands, which made these Asai's creatures, but Malick had been covering all his people since they stepped foot out the Girou, and Husao and Umeia were the only ones who knew they were coming. Even if Husao hadn't told Asai directly, that split second when he'd dropped his protections over Fen's brothers and sister might have been enough for Asai to have twigged.

Arrogant fucking manipulative prick.

The shapes were taking on substance, hunched beasts vaguely wolfen, snarling through slobbering, jag-toothed maws. Going for effect, hoping for shock and fear and a quick surrender.

Clearly, they had no idea who they were dealing with.

Strip away all their glamours? No, Malick didn't want to give himself away if he didn't have to, and it wouldn't necessarily stop them, anyway—they weren't after Malick, after all.

Veiling everyone could work, but then Fen would be exposed. None but Wolf's-own could touch Wolf's Untouchable, but if even a single one of them *was* Wolf's...

And Asai was smart—he'd have thought of that.

Which was really starting to piss Malick off.

"Well, bloody *fine*, then, if that's how we're playing it." Malick huffed. "Fen? Don't get excited, all right?"

The veil dropping over Joori, Morin, and Caidi clearly surprised Fen anyway, because he shouted when they disappeared in front of him, but that was all.

"Shig, I need you up here." Malick was going to be throwing around a lot of magic in the next minute or two, and he could use all the help he could get.

Fortunately, Shig didn't employ her usual *I'll get there when I get there* gait, but was at Malick's side inside three breaths. Malick reached out with his free hand and latched onto Shig's arm, let her magic curl in through his palm, and found Joori.

Take them out of the cart, and bring them over here behind me. Malick felt the alarm, the confusion, the anger, and cut through it: *Be a little bitch about it later. Do as I tell you now, and your family will live. Stay there and glare, and your brother will throw himself in front of every one of these things to protect you.*

"*Temshiel.*" The creature's voice was like scraped stone, guttural and garbled through a throat and mouth not meant for speech.

Another one made a quick dive for the dray, prancing back with a leering grin as Fen's knives just missed its nose. Teasing. Taunting.

The one in front of Malick snapped its long teeth. "Kamen."

Well, fuck it all. Whoever this was, they knew him. Which meant Asai would know before the night was through.

"Uh-huh." Malick flipped his sword. "And you're apparently exactly as smart as you look, and don't choose your allies very well. But don't worry—you won't be regretting it for long."

Something like a graveled growl went up. The loose orbit of shadowy not-wolves snorted through soggy muzzles. Improbable bodies moved inward, tightened the circle, long jaws pulling back in feral grins.

Surrounded.

The one in front of Malick morphed again. Wet fur turned to gleaming scales, multihued beneath a metallic matte, as teeth became barbed fangs, paws became rough talons.

"Ooh." Malick blew out a soft whistle. "D'you breathe fire too?"

"Give us the earthbound," it hissed.

Well, at least this was exactly what Malick thought it was.

He creased a grin. "Naw, don't fancy it. Anyway, it's more trouble than you want, getting past his brother." He jerked a nod over his shoulder. "See, thing is, Fen there is Wolf's Untouchable. Only Wolf's-own can touch him. And if any of you *are* Wolf's... well." Malick shrugged. "Let's just say this is an old coat and I won't mind the blood. So maybe just take your scary teeth and pack it in, yeah? 'Cause if you don't, there are very few maijin I know who'd like to see me enjoy myself, and I promise"—he braced back on one leg—"I'm gonna have *a lot* of fun in just a minute."

He reached a touch to Shig again. *Joori, I swear, if you don't move your bloody ass—*

Joori was already moving, but the prod quickened his pace.

The dragon-thing flexed its claws. "Kill us and burn, Kamen."

"Oh, I know." Malick winked. "But I'm *really good* at hitting the bits that hurt." He shoved a sharp whistle through his teeth, called, "Fen!" and swung his sword.

Fen lunged at the closest man-sized pseudowolf, knives whirling. Malick waded into the thick of the three before him.

Safe—*almost* safe—inside Malick's veil, Joori swept his little sister onto his hip, and shoved Morin ahead of him, angling between Fen and Samin and through the small pocket of calm in the middle of the abrupt melee. Just in time too; every one of the creatures that wasn't already engaged with either Malick or Fen went surging in for the dray.

"Keep down!" Malick called to Joori. He flipped his sword in the middle of an upswing and hacked at the rigid scales covering the dragon-thing's long neck. No blood spurted—yet—and he had to twitch sideways to avoid the swat of a claw at his face. Annoying.

He glanced back to place Joori and the children. Yori's bow was twanging, and she wouldn't be able to see them if they got in her way.

"Fen, I've got them," Malick called, then, "Yori, shoot high—go for the eyes," just in case, as Fen's siblings made a huddled knot close to the ground behind Malick.

Shig liberated a knife from one of Malick's sheaths, but seemed to be concentrating mostly on pulling apart the glamours, distracting the maijin as they tried to maintain them. Samin swung his broadsword in wide, efficient arcs, and followed them up with blows from his massive fist when he could manage it. Fen was doing what Fen did—nothing more than a whirling flash of metal in the dark.

Malick parried a set of long, black talons with a sweeping drive, then lunged in right up close with a brutal swipe at a scaly thigh, boosting the blow with a shock of magic this time. The satisfying sensation of flesh and meat parting beneath his blade wound up through steel and into his palm.

Grinning, Malick waggled his eyebrows. "I've always wanted to be a dragon slayer."

He flipped the sword up into his palm and drove it down, just so. It sank in just below where a clavicle would have been. Malick was careful to keep the plunge shallow—painful but not deadly. Even as he pulled back, thrashing claws lashed across his midsection, slicing easily through cloak and shirt, but only striking dull sparks from the mail underneath.

"Careful." Malick shot a wink at the dragon-thing. "That could've been fatal. If I wasn't bloody *awesome*."

This was why maijin shouldn't play with glamours. They got too caught up in what they were projecting to remember who they weren't supposed to kill.

And that they weren't *actually* as invincible as the things they pretended to be.

Malick swung with a quick twirl and flip of his sword, then lunged in with a hard swoop of magic backing the blade. It sank through the scales just as easily as it did through flesh.

A feral, hissing shriek turned to an angry scream. Malick took advantage of the creature's distraction and stripped its glamour away.

"Aw, *shit*." Malick stared into eyes gone from cat-slitted yellow to just plain hazel. "Leu, what the hell were you *thinking*?"

One of Wolf's, as he'd suspected, but he hadn't suspected her. Leu was smarter than this. At least Malick had thought so.

Shouts and hisses and low, rolling screeches were going on all around him, and all he could do was stare. Blood dribbled down Leu's chin as she stared back, hanging in Malick's grip, shiny haftless spikes dropping from her hands and falling to the mud. Malick slid the sword loose from where he'd lodged it in her between her ribs. She stumbled back, gasping, trying to draw in breath and choking on blood. He must've hit a lung. It would hurt like hell for a while and make it hard to breathe, but she'd live.

Which was… good. He supposed. Though, if he were allowed to kill her, he was pissed off enough right now to do it.

Enough. He was going to end up tripping himself into the suns, or one of his people was going to end up hurt.

Malick dragged his gaze away from Leu and narrowed it over at Fen. Fighting side by side with Samin, but none of these maijin were going after Samin. Instead, they were focusing their attacks on Fen, lunging in to swipe and snap, but.

It wasn't right. Yori had dropped back, bow nocked and cocked, but the creatures were positioning themselves so she couldn't shoot without the risk of hitting Fen. They wound in front of Samin so he couldn't get through them to aid. And yet, they weren't driving in for the finish—harassing Fen, swiping to wound but not to kill, mauling him. They could have had him twice just since Malick had been watching, and they'd foregone both opportunities.

They weren't all Wolf's—couldn't be. They didn't quite dare kill Wolf's Catalyst, but it seemed they were willing to risk damaging him.

Malick set his jaw, turned back to Leu, catching her as she tried to make her slow way into the trees and go to shadow. He yanked her around and leveled a swift rabbit punch to the bleeding wound he'd given her. She wheezed a thin curse and she went to her knees.

"Call them off, Leu." Through his teeth, and to make sure she knew he meant it, Malick drew his fist back again. "Don't fuck with me—I'm not in the mood."

"Kamen, I only—"

"I know why you're here, and you've already lost the earthbound."

He took her by her collar, snapped another blow between her eyes, all knuckles. Leu gasped and tried to writhe away. Malick only reeled her in closer, drew back his fist again, and jerked his chin back toward Fen.

"Maybe I can't kill you, but I can hold you down while he does. *Call* them *off*."

She believed him. Still gasping for breath, Leu slumped, head bowed, and shut her eyes. Only a few seconds later, the creatures surrounding Fen widened their circle, fur morphing back to flesh as they withdrew, until Fen, the cart, and Samin were surrounded by eight men and women of varying sizes and ages. All of them held double handfuls of spiked weapons, some obviously limping or clutching at various limbs in suppressed pain. One of them had a white-fletched arrow jutting from her bicep.

"Yori, Shig, stand down."

Yori had just snapped her bow up to take aim at now-clear targets. She didn't gripe out loud, but Malick could tell she was doing it silently.

Samin was already holding Fen back, keeping him from going after the retreating attackers. Fen looked supremely pissed off about it.

Malick left Samin to it. He could only concentrate on one idiotic drama at a time.

He dragged Leu to her feet. "The fact Asai has claimed Wolf does not mean Wolf has accepted Asai to the Cycle. You might do well to give that some thought the next time he sends you out after me and mine." He shoved her away, indifferent to her gasp of pain and the way she had to stumble to keep her feet. "Go back and tell Asai his message has been received. And bring him back one from me." Malick dropped his veil from around Joori, Morin, and Caidi, and took a step toward Leu, satisfied when she took one back. "Tell him Kamen sends him greetings from Skel. Tell him if he wants the earthbound, or the Catalyst, he'll need to come through me. They're mine."

"Still an arrogant prick, I see." Leu spat blood and wiped her mouth with the back of her hand. "We weren't to kill them, there's no need—"

"No, I imagine you weren't. You were only meant to take the earthbound, if you could, retreat if you couldn't. Wanna know why?"

Leu shook her head. "I didn't know it was you, Kamen." She kept her hands out and open at her sides. "I didn't even know..." She paused, caught her breath. "I heard you'd gone to spirit."

"You heard wrong."

"I didn't know. I wouldn't challenge Wolf's *Temshiel*."

"But you'd challenge *Temshiel* in general?"

"*No.*" Leu clenched her teeth, spat another mouthful of blood. "I didn't know until you veiled the earthbound." Her gaze turned sullen, almost accusing. "I thought you were just another mortal. You were concealing."

"And apparently with good reason." Malick took a step in, looming. "What the hell are you doing here, Leu?"

Leu couldn't seem to hold Malick's gaze. "We were to take the earthbound and allow the Catalyst to follow. Asai needed one of Wolf's... needed me to..." Her glance shot quickly over Malick's shoulder before turning to the ground. "He needed me to control the Catalyst."

"Yeah, well, from what I saw, the rest of them didn't have a problem helping you out with that." Malick was afraid to even look to see how torn up Fen was.

"They'll be punished. They weren't meant to attack him. They belong to Owl." Leu caught Malick's glower. She put her hands out, warding. "We were sent to watch for the Catalyst, and take the earthbound while he watched. Asai said the Catalyst would fight us and then follow—I was to let him. That's all I know. I don't want to know anything else. I don't want anything to do with this. Nothing Asai offered could be worth—" Leu wheezed in a thin breath, foamy pink spit leaking from the corner of her mouth. "Just let me walk away while I still can."

Malick shoved her back. "Yeah, walk away, Leu. And if you've got a brain in your head, you'll keep bloody walking. You don't want to find yourself on the wrong side of me in this."

Leu backed away, gaze wary, hazel eyes never leaving Malick as she drifted backward toward the trees. "No," she said, "I don't," and then she was gone, a lazy whirl of shadows covering her as she vanished into mist and rain.

Silence fell, the transitory brilliance of distant lightning marking the still figures of Malick's little band like bright-lit sentinels. The rain was steady but light now, its constant patter a soft contradiction to the sporadic blat of thunder rolling overhead. It was… nice, after what had just happened, a small pocket of peace in the aftermath of chaos, until—

"Who the fuck was *that?*"

Malick turned to Fen, still held tight against Samin's chest. A wide burst of sheet lightning dazzled a hectic glitter to Fen's eyes.

"That…" Malick sighed as he wiped the rain from his face then raked his hand through his hair. "*That* was apparently Asai's first sally."

And he'd gone right for the jugular, first thing.

"I thought he wanted *you.*"

"Yeah, well—"

"You said he wanted *you.* You said they'd be *safe.* You said Umeia was protecting them."

"I did, they are, and she is." Malick found himself abruptly pleased Samin hadn't released his hold on Fen yet. The rage and suspicion were almost tangible things. "Look, what d'you want from me? I'm not a bloody seer."

"Why not?"

"Why…?" Malick sheathed his sword, flummoxed. What the hell kind of question was that? "Because—" He ground his teeth.

He knew what Fen was thinking—the distrust and hostility were all over him. Right now, Malick should probably be trying to soothe and placate.

He wasn't in the mood. All his careful caution to keep who he was, and exactly where he was, from Asai had just been blown to shit. And now he'd put Umeia in the middle of it, too, along with Samin, Shig, Yori, and everyone he knew named Fen. Not to mention everyone at the Girou, because now that Asai knew who Malick was, he'd know how to look for him. It was only a matter of time.

The next time Malick saw Husao, he was going to fucking kill him. Slowly and with a smile.

"Joori," Fen said, "get Caidi back in the cart. We're going. Samin, let me the fuck go. *Now.*"

Samin didn't. "Mal?"

Malick frowned, bemused by the clear warning in Samin's tone. *Now what?*

"Where you gonna go, Fen?" Shig's voice was quiet beneath the drum of the rain, honeyed in that singsong way she had when she was going all spiritbound on them.

Terrific. Just what Malick needed.

"Away from here." Fen jerked in Samin's hold. "Away from *you*."

"Back to the little hut in the wilderness?"

"Samin, let me *go*!"

Again, Samin didn't. "Not 'til Mal says so."

Shig snorted. "If he lets you go, you'll fall over."

"Then I'll fall over." Fen bared his teeth. "Fuck off, Shig."

A slippery little giggle warbled up Shig's throat. "Think you're gonna go after Asai now?" She *tsked*. "Angry ghosts with raging infections don't make for good assassins."

"Infection?" Joori took a step toward Fen, but Shig snagged hold of him and kept him back.

Morin, weeping little sister's hand in his, turned a narrow look up at Malick, head atilt. "Infection?"

"Looks like." Malick laid a staying hand on Morin's shoulder. "Leg. Long story."

"Think you could do it this time?" Shig leaned in with a wicked little grin. "Or will you just bare your throat and beg him for what you can't have?"

"You don't know what the fuck you're talking about." Fen had gone still, but his eyes took on a malevolent glitter. "Your voices make just as much sense as mine do."

"You don't want to know, but you'll go anyway, won't you?" Shig's voice dipped low, uncharacteristically vicious. "You hate him as you hate yourself, so much hate you could raze the world, because no one else can hurt you like he can."

"Shig, don't fuck with me, I'm warning you."

"The pain's the only thing you understand, so you'll go to him to make sense of it all. You'll walk right into your own murder just to spite the man who would make himself your master."

"Samin, if you don't let me go, I'll—"

"That's a pretty suicide, innit? Can't hate what you love and can't love what you hate."

"Why won't you just *shut* the fuck *up*?"

"Can't scream, so you'll let your knives do it for you, or let Asai make all your pain go away."

"Suicide." Joori stared at Shig, brow drawn down in a frown that turned him to the mirror image of his brother. He turned wary eyes on Fen. "Jacin—"

"Your blood's not yours to spill, isn't that how it goes, angry Ghost?" Shig hugged Joori's arm tighter as he tried to push away from her. "Can't keep the Blood of the ones you love in their veins, and can't sweat enough of your own to save them."

Fen actually snapped his teeth, startling Joori into stillness. "Shut up, Shig." Clear warning.

"Mal?" Samin asked quietly.

Malick cut him a glance, shook his head. Shig didn't do something like this unless it was important.

Shig ignored it all. "Can't spill your own blood, so you'll corner the man who won't love you into sticking a knife in you instead of sticking his cock—"

"Shut up, *shut the fuck up!*" So feral it was almost unrecognizable. Fen lunged.

Samin held tight. With a heave and a grunt, he got Fen's wrists locked in both his big hands, arms crisscrossed over Fen's chest.

It didn't stop Fen from trying to break loose. "You don't know a *fucking* thing about me, just shut—"

"Can't take care of them the way you think you should, so you'll leave them all to the *Temshiel* who's handed you his promise, and if he burns for it—"

"Leave him alone!" Caidi broke loose from Morin's grip and skirted in to stand in front of Fen, all childish impudence and Fenlike audacity. "He's *not* a ghost, Joori said so. I thought you were a nice lady, but you're not, you're *mean*, and, and… and your hair looks funny."

Malick shut his eyes, pinched at the bridge of his nose, burying a tense and highly inappropriate snort inside a light cough.

Shig had no such qualms: she threw her head back and laughed. "Such a fucked-up family." She turned a grin on Yori. "And you thought we had it bad." She leaned down toward Caidi, amiable, almost conspiratory. "No one should ever, ever leave him alone, pretty little forfeit. Alone is the one thing that'll truly break him."

Forfeit.

That… didn't sound good. Come to think of it, none of this sounded good, and Shig was on a very rare roll. Despite the edge over which he could see Fen lurching, Malick had no choice but to let Shig keep going.

Yori took a cautious step in. "Shig, I think maybe—"

"Get away from her, Caidi." Fen jerked in Samin's grip. Caidi didn't move, but Fen didn't even seem to notice. Wild eyes all but *blazed* at Shig. "Stay away from her. Stay away from *all* of them, and stay away from *me!*"

"Aw, poor Fen." Somehow, Shig made her sigh mocking. "Standing here in the rain and watching yourself fail them all." She took a step forward, shaking loose from Joori and shoving him backward. "Except no one sees living as a failure but you, Ghost. You think I don't know why you stare so at the gates?" She shook her head. "Dying is the failure, Fen."

"Someone..." Fen's voice was mangled, rough, like it had to get through physical obstacles to claw its way up his throat. "Get her the fuck *away from me!*"

"Mal." Samin's voice was low with caution. "I swear by the suns and every moon in the sky, I can hear the fucking cracks."

Malick could almost see them.

"Sorry, can't." Shig gave Fen a fake grin full of teeth. "You're all part of the pack now. And our alpha bitch won't stand for a forfeit of the weak and small."

Malick's eyebrows rose, despite the steady erosion of the entire situation. "Alpha bitch"—he'd have to tell Umeia that one.

"What are you gonna do about your mother, Fen?" Shig went on, relentless.

"My mother is none of your damned—"

"You limp off to your self-destruction now, she'll spend eternity bound to the earth—"

"Fucking bitch, I swear—"

"—vying with the crows for seeds to sate her hungry soul, until her spirit's madder than your Voices."

"Stop it." Thin and wound tight. *"Don't."*

Shig leaned in, right in Fen's face. "Shall we just pack up your brother now, and send him off to join her? At least she'll have company."

And Fen... *snapped.* Malick actually saw the break in reason.

Fen's eyes went blank, face pulling into a savage snarl so full of despair and deranged fury it actually *hurt* to look at him. A wordless roar broke loose from his chest and rolled up his throat, and he lunged with the strength of a wild beast. He managed to get an arm loose from Samin and went for Shig's throat, fingers hooked into lethal claws.

Malick had to shake himself out of momentary shock.

"Shig, that's enough."

Too late, naturally—his timing was always shit—he swept over to Samin to help hold Fen back.

Fen writhed like an oiled mink, kicking and punching and gouging. Incoherent curses grated out his mouth, until Samin actually threw his arms around Fen's torso and lifted him off his feet. Fen didn't stop, in fact intensified his struggles. He swung his head back, trying to connect with Samin's and only managing to beat at Samin's shoulder with it.

Joori wasn't helping—just as Malick got a good hold on Fen's flailing right arm, Joori latched on to Malick's, snarling, "Get off him, let him go!" until Yori joined the fray and pulled Joori away. Caidi was screaming back there somewhere, high-pitched and discordant. It made Malick's teeth hurt, so he clenched them as he grimly held on, buffeted by a mad strength he wouldn't have credited, until Fen actually threw Malick off. Malick stumbled sideways, spun, braced to surge back in.

"No." Shig held Malick back. "Just…" She jerked her chin at Fen.

"Shifts to Null." Slippery vowels; slurred consonants. Fen's voice was thin and breathless as he struggled, eyes shut tight and teeth clenched. "Wolf calls the Prime to his own he sees the Eye and calls the… the Prime the *Prime* fuck… leers through a… Raven's *Raven's* duplicity the gods speak no more silent silent dead and quiet, aw *fuck*, shutupshutup-shutup—"

"Jacin!" Joori tried to writhe out of Yori's grip. "Jacin, it'll be all right, just—" He managed to drag Yori in a step closer. "Let me go, I can help him!"

Malick didn't want Joori to help him. As hard as it was to watch, he knew now why Shig had pushed so. Because he understood what Fen was saying. Where it was coming from. What it *meant*.

This was worlds different from what Malick had heard last night on the roof.

"Dying magic Catalyst slides to Zero the Null veils the Eye a cloak of night sound the vaults of Raven cast acid to the sky they don't see like Owl won't hear mockery it's all gone sour worm-ridden carcass of faith and hope the gods won't save them they've all gone… spitted… spitted… *Joori!*" Gasping now, strength running thin, and *still*, Fen kept bloody *fighting*. "Our boy clinging to corpses wandering both edges… crux… crux of…" A harsh burst of air, and, "Aw, fuck, Beishin, *please!*"

It did something in Malick—a hard twist of honest concern and compassion wound too tightly with fascination and darkling jealousy. That name—*that name*.

Joori loosed a fraught cry. "Damn it, let me *go!*"

Yori and Shig were both hanging on to Joori now. Caidi was fluttering around the edges of the commotion, weeping, unsure to which brother she should go. Morin was just standing where Malick had left him, watching it all, his face unreadable.

Joori's desperate glance fell on Malick, pinned him. "Stop it! He's falling apart, can't you see it?"

Yes, Malick could see it.

"Stop it or I will, Mal," Samin growled, all caustic accusation. "Enough."

And yes, it was enough.

Except, before Malick could decide what to do about it, how to bring Fen out of it, Morin stalked past him, gave Joori a look that was half apology and half disgust on his way by, and stopped in front of Fen. Stood there for a moment and watched Fen struggle, listened to him mutter and scream. Waited for an opening then leveled a solid kick to Fen's thigh, right where the chunky line of stitches wound over thick muscle beneath the cover of his trousers. Morin couldn't have aimed it better if he'd inflicted the wound himself.

"For the love of—" Samin gaped at Morin then Malick. "Mal…"

Nothing squeezed out of Fen's chest but a thin, wheezy scream. His eyes went wide and shock-blank in clear agony, then his back arched and his eyes rolled back. He went limp, head lolling back on Samin's shoulder.

They stared, all of them, the silence a live thing, until Joori stepped slowly over to Fen.

"What…?"

He shot Samin a murderous look before laying a hand to the side of Fen's face then sliding it down to his chest. A long breath of relief sighed out when he apparently felt Fen's heart beating. Joori's arms went deliberately to hang at his sides, fists clenched, the muscles in his jaw ticcing and jumping, then he whirled on Shig, a too-familiar snarl curling at his mouth, but it didn't have the same fire behind it Fen's did. When he got no reaction from Shig, he turned on Malick.

"*Temshiel? You're* bloody *Temshiel?* And *this* is the best you can fucking do?"

"It's not my fault!" Malick protested, reflexive, because, really—whose fault was it? He'd known what Shig was doing, and he'd let her do it, because there were things he needed to hear, and he apparently needed to hear them from right inside the madness of the Ancestors. And he wasn't sorry.

Except.

How had Shig seen this, and Malick had missed it entirely? *Now* he recognized Fen's recurring derring-do for the repeated attempts at passive suicide they were. Malick might've taken too long to twig otherwise, and then it would've been too late. He'd bloody *admired* it. Stood there and watched Fen try to drive himself into apparently welcome death with a twirl of knives, and thought it was pretty.

Shig wandered up to stand beside Joori. "Don't hate, jealous lad. He had to say it so Malick could hear." She turned to Malick, reproachful. "And I had to show it so Malick would see."

Malick's mouth tightened. "Yeah, yeah. I get it, all right? Leave off."

"I tried to tell him you could help him make sense of it, but he doesn't listen."

"Yeah, I've noticed."

"Give him to me," Joori said, staring down Samin, who still held Fen, though he'd adjusted him somewhat so the rain wasn't pelting his face. Fen was now draped rather awkwardly over Samin's shoulder.

Samin sighed, shot a look over to Malick, then shook his head at Joori. "I'll put him in the cart." He didn't wait for Joori to protest, just turned and did as he'd said.

Malick frowned. Something about the way Fen dangled over Samin's arm, the bonelessness of his neck as his head rolled with Samin's stride, the way the tail of the braid dragged in the mud… It bothered Malick more than it should've done.

He looked away, uneasy, only to have his gaze clash with the puppy-dog eyes of Caidi. She was staring at Malick, eyes a bit swollen, and he could only talk himself out of the uncomfortable thought that she was still crying and he was expected to do something about it because, what with the rain, he couldn't really tell, right?

"Is Jacin going to die?" Her voice was high and wobbly.

Oh, hell.

"No." Malick put as much force into the word as he could without turning it sharp and frightening her more. "No, he's not going to die."

Caidi seemed to unknot, just a little. She took a cautious step closer, big, worried eyes stubbornly holding Malick's.

"Were those really maijin?"

Malick swiped at his face. "Yeah."

"And…" Her lip quivered. "And they were going to take Joori away?"

Malick sighed, only just kept himself from growling and snapping at her. What did she bloody *want* from him, after all?

"I don't intend to let that happen." Malick left it there, because it was simple, reassuring, and the truth.

Caidi thought about that for a moment, then took another step.

It was all Malick could do not to step back in absurd retreat. From a *little girl*. Those wide, earnest eyes were sucking the swagger right out of him.

"And you're really—"

"Come along, Caidi." Joori's hand landed on Caidi's shoulder, his angry gaze locking onto Malick. "I'm sure Kamen-seyh has Important Things to take care of." The sarcasm all but dripped. Eyes still on Malick, Joori tugged Caidi away, like he suspected Malick might eat her just to be a prick. "C'mon, I'll give you a pig-a-back." He turned Caidi around and pushed her over toward the cart, where Samin was adjusting Fen's cloak to cover as much of him against the rain as possible.

That left Morin. He was staring at Malick like his sister had been doing, only his eyes were measuring… interested. When Malick had watched the brothers that night in the hut, Morin sneering and snarking and generally making everything more difficult than it had to be, Malick had thought he didn't much like the little shit. After tonight, he thought perhaps he'd jumped to conclusions.

Fen covered every emotion he had with anger; this one covered them with pragmatism, and managed to keep a clear head because of it. Born to fear, knowing he'd lose one brother, the constant threat of losing another and his mother.

Morin might be the sanest one in the whole bloody family.

"She was going to ask if you're really *Temshiel*." Morin offered it up like he was only doing his sister a favor and didn't really want to know himself.

Malick lifted his eyebrows. "And you're not?"

Morin shrugged, threw his cloak's hood off and scraped his fringe out of his eyes before pulling the hood back down. "It's only that I didn't see you do any magic."

"Ah. Well." Malick gave him a small, conspiratory smile. "Just because you didn't see a thing…" He sighed when Morin just stared at him. "You should go see if your brother needs help."

Morin rolled his eyes. "Which one?"

Yeah, good point.

Malick cocked his head. "How did you know?"

Morin's brow twisted, quizzical.

Malick waved at his thigh. "I didn't tell you exactly where to kick him." He paused once he'd said it—he hadn't told Morin to kick Fen at all, but… well, it had turned the trick better and faster than anything Malick had been able to come up with in the moment.

"Lucky guess." Morin's mouth screwed down into a grimace as he looked over toward the dray. He turned back to Malick. "He used to wait 'til we were all asleep before he'd go out to the wash barrel. I wanted to know why, so I…" He shifted uncomfortably. "I pretended to sleep. He's got… lots of scars. And those things chewed him up pretty good. Someone better have a look at that leg." Morin huffed out a dubious sigh. "Joori's going to kill me when he calms down."

Malick couldn't help the smile.

"We're ready, Mal." Yori sidled up and bumped shoulders with him. "Samin's going to lug the cart, and Joori's going to carry Caidi. How we're going to get Fen back in through the gates is for you to figure out. Can't exactly climb it this time, can he?"

"Oh, fucking *hell*." Malick slumped sideways into Yori and put his head on her shoulder. "If you love me, you'll just kill me now. Before Umeia gets me."

"Yeah, *if*." Yori shoved him off with a grin. "All this bother about maijin and *Temshiel*, and all I get is rain down my back, sore feet, and two lost arrows." She gave Malick a poke in the ribs. "*I* want to see the magic next time too. C'mon, Morin, you're with me." She didn't roll her eyes as she prodded at Morin until he went along, but Malick could tell it was a near thing. "And here I thought tonight was going to be boring."

Ha. So had Malick. Wouldn't that have been lovely?

Shig was the last one left, waiting for Malick several paces away, too placid for all the trouble she'd caused. It would take a while for the headache to hit her, but Malick had no doubt it was coming. And he couldn't be altogether sympathetic about it. Yes, making sense of what the Ancestors were apparently screaming in Fen's head was going to be necessary; Malick could tell just by the little he'd heard tonight. But the way Shig had proven her point had been… rather brutal. And clumsy, when it came to it. They weren't going to get reason by provoking madness.

This was exactly why Malick disliked dealing with spirits in general—one careless push in the wrong direction and they came over all raving and dramatic and useless. And the person channeling them bore the brunt.

He only scowled as Shig strolled up to him, looking for all the world like she'd just woken from a particularly pleasant nap. When she failed to wither beneath his glare, Malick just shook his head, and started after the dray.

"Not a word, Shig," he growled, annoyed when she only snorted and followed along. "Not one bloody word."

🜍

"Not a word, Malick," Umeia growled as she slipped Fen's arm over her shoulders. "Not one bloody word."

"Umeia, you—"

"I don't want to hear it. Samin and Yori already told me the important bits, and anything you have to say will be colored all too brightly with *The World According to Kamen Malick* paint. Just stuff it before you make me kill you."

Fen snorted. "Kill 'm anyway. Fucker."

He tried to pull his arm from around Malick's shoulders, but only managed to stagger against Umeia. Too bendy and wobbly and, unfortunately, his usual hostile self as they lugged him up the steps. Wet and shivering too, though Umeia could feel the fever burning through the chill.

Her mouth went tight. "I see you two are getting on as pleasantly as usual." She turned a scowl on Fen. "And you're no better. You knew that leg was infected and you went anyway. Stupid. It was *stupid*, Fen."

"Yeah, yeah."

Umeia turned her wrath on Malick. "I'd ask what you were thinking, but I suspect you weren't thinking at all. At least not with the big brain. If you even have one."

"It wasn't my fault! It was his decision. He was going to go, one way or another. What did you want me to do—drug him and tie him to the bed?"

"*Yes!*"

They cleared the top step to the third floor, and started down the hall to the attic stairs. It was creeping up on the small hours, the doors to the rooms all shut and their occupants occupied. With any luck, no one would poke their head out. Umeia didn't want to have to drag Shig down here to adjust inconvenient memories, not after she'd just got everyone dried off and settled in upstairs.

"I don't think you understand how serious this is, Malick. Magic doesn't work on him, which means I can't fix this. All I can do is what a surgeon would do. He could lose the leg or die."

"*His* choice."

"Pfft." As though to emphasize his erudite observation, Fen stumbled again.

Umeia shot Malick a glare over Fen's head. "And it no doubt suited your purposes. No, shut up, I don't want to hear it. Just get him upstairs before that brother of his has an apoplectic fit."

Speaking of whom—

Joori stood up from the bottom step of the attic stairs as they approached.

Umeai was ready to kill someone. "I thought I told you not to come downstairs."

Joori didn't even glance her way. His eyes glittered in the low lamplight from the sconces, narrowed at Malick, mostly, distrustful, but softening when they landed on Fen.

"You all right?"

Fen stared at the toes of his boots instead of his brother. "Fine."

"He's always *fine*." Malick rolled his eyes. "We won't count the trail of blood behind us." He moved to push past Joori and up the stairs.

Joori merely angled into a firmer obstacle. "I'll take him." His eyes were narrow little slits now, jaw clenched in very clear malice as he shoved his arm between Malick and Fen.

Malick slanted his stance to block. "I've got him."

The resulting shoving match was restrained, but it still jostled Fen into Umeia. Fen let out a yip then a hiss. Umeia tipped sideways, nearly rolled her ankle as she tried to keep upright.

Malick and Joori were still too busy puffing their chests at each other to notice. It was like Fen was a bloody wishbone, and they were going to snap him in two to see who got the bigger piece.

Umeia was *this close* to knocking all their heads together. "How about *I* take him while you two whip 'em out and start measuring?"

Fen tried to pull away again. "Let go. I can do it myself."

Umeia almost did, just to spite them all.

She jerked her chin at Joori. "*You*—go tell Yori I need my bag then take the sheets off his bed so we don't foul them." She turned to Malick. "*You*—get a better hold and take more of his weight before he takes us all down." And then to Fen. "*You*—shut up and start hobbling. You're heavier than you look, and if I go tumbling and break a leg, I'll beat you with my crutch."

They all shut their mouths and complied, which was good, because Fen really was heavier than he looked; Umeia's shoulder was going numb and her balance was chancy, with him pointedly hanging mostly on her rather than Malick. Fen might look lean and rangy, but he was apparently all dense, compact muscle under the angles and sharp lines.

Yori trotted down as they reached the third step. She spared a sympathetic shrug for Umeia then a smirk at Malick as she bounded past them without a word.

"Tell Samin to hurry it up while you're down there," Umeia said over her shoulder. She'd sent Samin down to bring up tea and something to eat for the new arrivals as soon as he'd dried off and changed, and he was certainly taking his bloody time about it.

They were halfway up the steps when Umeia remembered to ask, "How did you get him through the gates?"

She'd fretted after Yori and Samin had shown up with only the children. Malick had got them all in then sent them ahead while he went back for Fen and Shig, Samin had told Umeia. All well and good, but Umeia had been starting to wonder if Malick and Shig and Fen were going to have to spend the night outside the city, and what Umeia was supposed to do with Fen's frantic brother if they did.

"I was going to go with old-fashioned bribery." Malick kept a careful eye on his feet. "Even got them to open up one of the accessory doors, but then they saw the braid." He shrugged. "It was either have Shig take care of them, or let them arrest me for interfering with an Untouchable. Or killing them all, but."

No wonder Shig had merely stomped past Umeia and gone right to bed. Her head must be near to exploding. Umeia would stop in after she finished with Fen.

Joori was waiting at the door to Fen's room, vibrating, when they finally crested the top of the stairs. He didn't advance to try to take his brother back again, but Umeia could tell it was all Joori could do to keep still and wait.

The younger ones—Caidi and Morin—were standing in the hallway between their new room and the one Yori shared with Shig. They were wrapped in blankets, goggling as Malick and Umeia got Fen up the stairs.

Fen didn't look up, just hung his head, fringe nearly covering his face. Hiding. He stayed silent as Umeia and Malick maneuvered him down the hall and through the door to his room.

"All right, let's see what we've got here." Umeia gratefully lowered Fen to sit on the bed, shaking out her arm as she stepped back.

Fen wasn't even seated properly yet before he was shrugging off Malick's grip like he couldn't stand the touch for another second. Except, as soon as Malick let go, Fen's whole body curled in on a sharp gasp, eyes abruptly sprung wide and anxious. Frantic, he reached out, grabbed for

Malick, catching only a loose shirttail at first, groping desperately, until Malick reached back and took Fen's hand. The reaction was immediate: instant calm and instant frustrated shame for needing it.

Umeia watched it all with… too many emotions that pissed her off. She sighed.

"Help him with the shirt and trousers, M—" She caught Joori's look, and shook her head. "Never mind." She tapped at Fen's nearest elbow. "C'mon, lad, let's get 'em off. No sass this time, yeah?"

Umeia was surprised but satisfied when Fen only sighed and reached up to unlace his tunic, though she noted—and noted Joori noting—that Malick's hand went to rest on Fen's knee, and Fen didn't try to kill him for it, tightening his mouth only when the tunic gave him trouble. The tie was leather and soaked through, and squeaked when he tried to unknot it. Mouth set, Fen reached down to the sheath on his hip—stopped. He lifted a glare up at Malick.

"Who took my knives?"

"Samin's got them."

Fen chewed his lip. "Did… was I…?"

"Yeah, you were." Malick slicked his fingers through Fen's fringe, pushed it back. "'S all right, no worries. We're all used to you being a massive git."

The bizarre part wasn't Malick's too-tender smile—it was the part where Fen tried to smile *back*.

Umeia blinked. Right, then. Fine. A lovely, tender moment—or at least as tender as these two got, she supposed—but none of it was getting the job done.

She shook it off and went for Fen's boot. "Cut it for him, Mal, and let's get this done. Joori, help me with his boots and get the— *Shit!*" Umeia snapped a look up at Malick. "What chewed through his boot like that? And…" Oh, for pity's sake. She'd been supporting Fen on the left, and it had been dark when they'd finally staggered through the alley doors. Umeia hadn't got a good look at him until now. There was a small puddle of blood pooling on the floor around the sole of his boot, and now that she looked, there really was a trail of it. "What got at you, lad?"

"Wolves." Joori shot another glare at Malick.

Malick ignored it.

The wolf-things Yori had told Umeia about, no doubt, and about which that little Caidi was likely to have nightmares for weeks. These were no blade wounds, and the way the boot and trouser leg were torn to hell—

"Asai bought himself a coven." Malick's tone was muted fury. "Came at us all wolfen. Cocky bastards. Leu and a mishmash from Owl and Snake. Tried to pull on a dragon glamour when she recognized me, like she thought it would make some kind of difference."

"*Leu?*" Umeia would have thought Leu smart enough to stay out of something like this altogether. "She wouldn't do *this*, surely."

"She didn't, but her thugs did. Said they'd be punished for touching him." A roll of his eyes relayed exactly how appeased Malick was with that.

Umeia looked down at Fen's leg, ran her fingertips gently over shredded fabric, and poked very lightly at the bloody, mangled flesh exposed through the tears. She stopped immediately when Fen hissed and flinched. It must really be excruciating if *Fen* was reacting like that to such a light touch, and with the infection she knew was already twisting beneath the torn stitches she could see...

"*Damn* it." She nodded at Joori. "Boots."

"No." Fen shot Umeia a quick glance then leveled his gaze with Joori's. "Go. Take care of Caidi and Morin. Malick will help me."

If Umeia hadn't already been getting a pretty good idea of what the budding dynamic was between these three, the clench of Joori's jaw and the flare of his glower at Malick would have told her in no uncertain terms.

Joori shook his head. "I'm not leaving you alone with him." He made a snatch for Fen's boot.

Fen snapped his leg out. Not *quite* a kick but a definite push. It nearly knocked Joori to the floor. It must've jarred Fen too, because he went a frightening shade of gray and swayed to the side.

"I don't..." Fen sucked in short, shaky breaths, and most telling, allowed Malick to hold him up. "I don't want you here, Joori. Get out." Hard and cold, like he was trying to take the concern in his brother's eyes and turn it into contempt.

To his credit—and Umeia's astonishment—Malick stayed silent, watching. His hand was firm on Fen's shoulder now.

Joori's gaze narrowed on it. He shot Fen a steady look.

No trained assassin like his brother, but Joori was still quick. He surged in, angling between Malick and Fen, and tried to shove Malick away. A solid right hook hit Malick's temple and sent him backward on the bed with Joori on top of him.

Fen went over to the side, rasping out a harsh yip when the raw meat of his leg hit the corner of the mattress. He would have fallen off the bed altogether if Umeia hadn't lunged in to catch hold of him and drag him away from the sudden brawl.

"No, no, no." Fen shook his head, crushed his palms into his temples. "Stopstopstop, I can't... I *can't*, not..." His eyes were squeezed tight and his muscles were rigid beneath Umeia's hand.

Malick got the better of Joori quickly, flipping him to his back on the mattress, knee pressing into his stomach and one arm pinned. He grabbed for the other one.

"What the *fuck* is wrong with you?" He snapped his head to the side to avoid a clumsy swipe of Joori's curled fist.

"He's paid *enough!*" Joori kept swinging. "He's not some kind of—"

"Oh, for *fuck's* sake!" Samin thundered from the door. "Are you *bloody* kidding me?"

Yori stood beside him, shaking her head in consternation, steaming basin and Umeia's satchel in hand. Caidi and Morin stared, wide-eyed, behind them.

Fen's gaze shot up, plummeting right down into desolate when he saw his brother and sister. "Get them out of here." Thin. *Panicked.* "Get them out, get them out, *get them out!*"

Umeia caught Yori's shocked gaze. "Take the children down for a bath. Right now."

Immediately, Yori did exactly as she was told, settling the bag and the basin on the clothespress beside the door then hustling the children away.

The pause in action was just long enough for Malick to get hold of Joori's flailing arm and slam it down to the mattress, pinning him.

"No! *Get off!*" Joori's legs were still free; he kicked wild, body twisting, trying to buck Malick off him. "He's not your whore!"

Fen took hold of Umeia's sleeve with shaking, clawlike fingers. "Not now, not *now*, I can't... the noise, I..." He fisted his fringe, *pulled.* "Shifts... shifts to... ours—" He clenched his teeth, eyes shut tight. "Stop. *Stop.* I can't *hear*, I can't—"

Yes. Right. The noise—too much of it, and too much pain. Fen was losing whatever control he usually managed right in front of her.

Umeia spun a helpless look around the room then settled it on Malick. "You're going to have to do something."

Samin had deposited the tray he was carrying on the clothespress by Umeia's bag. His glance snapped up and locked with Malick's. A quick look sparked between them

Square jaw set, Samin stalked across the room. He braced to the side of the bed, gave Malick a short nod, and when Malick broke quickly to the side, Samin swooped in, took hold of Joori—still cursing and spitting—and hauled him to his feet.

"You son of a *bitch!*" Joori flailed out, trying to catch hold of Malick's shirt, then kicked at Samin's shins—"No, stop, let me go!"—as Samin dragged him just outside the door in the hallway.

Malick seemed to hear only Fen's raspy little "*Pleasepleaseplease.*" He left Samin to deal with Joori, rushing over to wedge a shoulder under Fen's arm. Murmuring things Umeia couldn't hear beneath all the other noise, Malick took Fen's weight from Umeia just as Fen went boneless, gasping, allowing Malick to draw him in and push his face into the hollow between Malick's chin and chest.

Umeia used the opportunity to hustle over and retrieve the tea and her bag. Quickly, she threw a sleeping powder in—xsinzaua, because it worked damned fast, and getting Fen to pass out seemed like a very good idea right now. In fact, she wouldn't mind if every damned one of them lost consciousness. She added some painkiller, not even bothering with spices to soothe the bitter taste, and carried it over.

"*Fuck.*" Fen's wheezy rasp was muffled by Malick's still-wet tunic. "I can't… can't *listen* now, I can't… they can't ask it of me, not… it's not *fair*."

"Shh, now. I've got you." Malick shot a sharp scowl toward where Samin was still holding onto Joori in the doorway, and began carefully leading Fen back over to the bed. "It's unquestionably not fair, and you don't have to, not now. I'll keep it quiet for you, all right?"

"Quiet." Fen choked on a groan. "I don't want him here. *Please.*" With a shudder, he buried his face in Malick's shoulder as they sank to the mattress, burrowed close in a way that was almost touching, but mostly unnerving. It was so un-*Fen*-like.

"Here, drink this." Umeia held the bowl to Fen's lips until he turned his head, eyes still shut, and let her pour the tea down his throat.

"What's in that?" Joori asked, all suspicion and anxious bravado.

Samin rolled his eyes over Joori's head. Joori had stopped fighting, but Samin still kept a solid hold on him.

Shaking her head, Umeia looked Joori up and down—heavens, but he did look like his brother, especially with that glare burning holes in Malick—then pinched at the bridge of her nose.

She only had secondhand knowledge of what had gone on tonight, but she'd heard enough, and now she'd seen enough. With a heavy sigh, she left Fen to Malick and stepped over to Joori. She set her face into lines as nonjudgmental as she could manage toward someone who'd just spat poison at her brother and all but accused her of drugging Fen for purposes all too clear. Then again, if she'd suspected someone was doing to Malick what this one obviously thought Malick was doing to Fen…

"He doesn't want you to see him like this." Umeia kept her tone even, her voice quiet. "It isn't that he doesn't love you—it's that he does."

Jaw clenched tight, Joori jerked his chin at Malick. "But he doesn't mind *him* seeing him like—?"

"Malick can make it quiet for him. Understand? *Quiet.* After whatever went on tonight, I think he'll take anything that comes along with the quiet. Wouldn't you?" Umeia took a step in closer. "He's clinging to the edge by his fingernails, lad."

And the gods help them all if Fen lost his grip, because Umeia was sure it wouldn't be pretty—it wasn't pretty now. Good job they'd thought to take his weapons away.

"He—" Joori's eyes filled; he blinked it away. Gaze pleading, he jerked in Samin's hold, but when Samin didn't let go, Joori stopped. He shoved out a shaky breath, leaned in toward Umeia. "Please—what does he make him *pay* for it?"

Umeai could have smacked him. She could have hugged him.

She rolled her eyes. "Just because he lives in a whorehouse, doesn't mean he *is* one. Or that anyone expects him to be. Save your worry for someone who needs worrying about."

"Have you *met* my brother?"

Umeia didn't answer, only gave Samin a nod. "Let him go. He'll behave." She leveled a narrow glare at Joori. "*Won't* you, lad?"

With a look that wasn't entirely unpleasant but mostly was, Joori shrugged out of Samin's grip, stared at Umeia, like he was thinking about saying something, then just shook his head and pushed past her into the room. He didn't so much as acknowledge Malick's existence as he approached the bed. Crouching by Fen's knee, Joori grimaced at the mess that was Fen's right leg.

"Jacin." When Fen only shook his head, Joori reached up, hands coming up to either side of Fen's face, turning his head and holding him still. He leaned in until they were brow to brow. "Jacin. Look at me."

Tentative, Fen laid a shaking hand to Joori's arm. "Sorry. I'm *sorry*." Pushed out on a strangled whisper.

"No." Joori pushed Fen's hair out of his eyes. "Look at me."

It took a moment, but Fen eventually did, tears spilling out the corners of his eyes the second he opened them.

Joori pulled in a wobbly breath. "I won't look, if you don't want me to see." His tone was soft, artless. "But you're my hero, Jacin. You always have been. Don't you know that?"

It was sweet. It was touching. And still, it made Umeia's teeth clench. Couldn't the lad see he was only making it worse? Couldn't he see Fen was already under too much pressure to rescue... well, everyone he loved? And now Joori wanted to go and wrap "hero" around his neck?

"You're the other half of me." It looked like Joori was trying to smile. "You're my heart. I could *never, ever* see whatever it is you see when you look at yourself." Now his eyes were leaking too. "Don't make me lose you so soon after I got you back."

"Joori. Brother." Fen opened his eyes. His voice was slurred, only barely above a whisper. "You can't get back what you never had. Jacin will always be lost. I'm all that's left."

Joori jerked back, stood. Stared. Mouth tight, he swiped at his face with the crook of his elbow.

"The one who will be there, Jacin. Fight me all you like. I'm not letting go." His face crumpled, and he put his hands out, asking. "She told me not to."

Fen only stared, expression devastated, as though Joori had just broken his heart. It was gone quickly, flattening smooth and blanking out.

"Yeah," Fen said, "I know," then just turned away, eyes shut, and wilted into Malick.

Joori blinked eyes wet and swollen, and set his jaw. He directed a level look at Malick, hands fisting then flexing as Malick merely looked back. With a deep, shaky breath, Joori dragged his gaze away, nodded to Umeia, and left.

Silence lurched into the room, uncomfortable, until Umeia shook it off. She sent Samin a speaking look. Without a word, Samin left, too, casting one last glance at the bed as he pulled the door shut.

Malick gave Fen a careful jostle. "He's out."

The xsinzaua had finally kicked in. Thank all the gods.

Umeia sighed. "Right, then. If we're done with the melodrama, let's see what we're dealing with. I'll get the boots, you get the shirt." She shook her head in dismay as Malick laid Fen out on the bed and she looked him over, taking in all the tears in wet fabric and the no doubt gory wounds waiting for her to uncover. "We'd better just cut off the trousers. Honestly, Malick, what were you thinking?"

Malick's mouth tightened as he sliced through the ties on the tunic that had started the whole mess. "I was thinking he'd been manipulated enough."

"Lovely." Umeia braced to tug the unmangled boot off. "And trying to manipulate him into coming 'round to your way of thinking never once occurred to you, I'm sure, what with your motivations being all pure and innocent."

"His father *sold* him, Umeia." Malick pushed it out through his teeth, caustic, hands pausing on Fen's chest and curling into fists. "Sold him to fucking Asai when he was still a child. Now, if you want to tell me *Asai's* motivations are pure and innocent, and Wolf would approve, I'll be happy to—"

"And you're going to tell me indulging his every whim—even the ones that might kill him—has nothing to do with trying to gain his trust for yourself? You're going to tell me you didn't sneak him out tonight behind my back because you knew he was in bad shape and I wouldn't allow it if I knew? You're going to tell me you don't plan to use and manipulate him and his brother, *and* those children, if you have to, just as much as As—"

"*Do not* put me in the same sentence with Asai. I've got shit choices here, Umeia, but at least I don't dress up what I do with lies of salvation and promises I don't intend to keep. I haven't asked of Fen anything he didn't intend to do anyway, and I won't promise him anything I'm not damned sure I can give him. I can't help that he's the best chance I've got of getting Asai. *I* didn't do this to him, and I'm bloody well not about to watch while he goes to the suns for *that* son of a bitch. Fucking *manipulation.* You want to talk about manipu—"

"Fine, you're made of good intentions and upright scruples." Umeia rolled her eyes at Malick's glare. Bloody hell, he was in deep, telling himself he wasn't all the way down. "Let's assume he'll take care of Asai for you. You have to know it won't solve all his… problems. And I won't allow you to use those children. I've sworn. I'll fight you, if you make me."

She would too.

Drawing Asai out before he was ready, holding out as bait the very leverage they all knew he needed, was exactly the sort of thing Malick would do. What he probably should do. What Umeia should let him do.

But Malick had brought Fen to Umeia for a reason. Maybe Malick hadn't known what that reason was—probably still didn't know—but Umeia did. Better than she had when she'd blithely sworn oath, all too confident she'd known exactly what she was doing.

She wasn't just precautionary protection for Fen's siblings. She was the empress, hunching on her square of the chensuboard, shielding her pawns as both Malick and Asai maneuvered the rest of the board around them. Shielding *Malick*, keeping him from straying too far from Wolf while he wended through what was to come. And making sure he could live with what he'd have to do, what he'd have to become, before it was over.

Wolf smiled on Umeia's little brother—oh yes, surely, the aloof prick—because Malick bloody *suffered* for what he was, and suffered harder when he tried to be something else.

No wonder he and Skel had understood each other so well.

Umeia sighed. "Sometimes I wish you really were the ass you pretend to be, little brother."

Malick clenched his teeth and started moving again. "We can't stay here for long." He kept his eyes on his hands as he maneuvered Fen out of his tunic, pausing to shake his head and growl at the bloody, twisted flesh of his forearm—that was going to need sutures too, damn it. "It's only a matter of time before Asai finds me. And when he finds me, he finds you and everyone else. They were after his brother tonight. I've absolutely no doubt Asai plans to use him to blackmail Fen into doing what he wants, and he won't stop, even if he has to tear down the Girou around us. Or, more likely, pay someone else to do it for him. Fucking prick, he never has stooped to doing his own wet work."

Malick paused, shoulders hunching, the muscles of his back heaving with two long, deep breaths, but he still didn't look up. "I'm sorry."

Umeia dropped Fen's boot to the floor and went for the other. "Save 'sorry' for when I ask for it. Cut that trouser leg right up the center. We'll talk about the rest in the morning."

Because she'd be damned if she'd let Asai, of all people, drive her out of the home they'd made, or harm the people who made up their family.

It had been too long since they'd had one. And she wasn't about to argue with her obstinate brother over it now.

Anyway, with what she saw when she finally got a look at Fen's leg, they likely wouldn't be going anywhere for a while.

Umeia stepped back, hands on her hips. "Go get my bag off the clothespress."

She had work to do here, a duckling to tend.

Asai could just fuck off for now.

2

It had been the briefest, tiniest of glimpses, but it was... almost enough. A flash of potential, all in a smeary whirl—more like glimpses of images, really, and far too much cryptic symbology—but enough to see that the Wheels were still turning. Fate was lumbering forward.

Strangely, it all seemed to flower outward from the little one, not from the twin, as Asai had rather expected, but youth did burn brightest in his general experience. Jacin-rei's little sister was burning like the last gasp of a dying star.

Asai frowned. He had a bit of a soft spot for mortal youth. They were such fascinating little portents, even the ones without magic, their funda-mental *belief* in all things splaying them open like porous possibility. And he'd truly hate to see Jacin-rei lose more than he had to. Still, the boy might well make it necessary to take a ruthless step or two.

The value of laying the responsibility at Jacin-rei's feet could be debated later, after Fate had set the Cycle, when Asai was better able to gauge the feasibility of keeping his Ghost. Guilt was always an efficient tool when it came to Jacin-rei, but there was such a thing as too much of a good thing. Asai was going to have to be very careful when Jacin-rei found his way back to his beishin.

Still, Asai'd had his glimpse. He knew now. Knew the who, the what and the where—*on his own lands*, for pity's sake!—but he couldn't help the frisson of unease that curled up his backbone. He needed *Temshiel*, certainly, but he hadn't counted on Kamen. And why should he? By all accounts, Kamen had retreated to spirit after... well.

Asai fisted his hands. *Bloody* Kamen! Of all the *Temshiel* out there, Jacin-rei had to stumble into *Kamen*.

It could complicate matters beyond repair if Asai wasn't extraordi-narily careful, and there wasn't time to start again. There was less than a decade left in the Cycle, and he saw no possibilities in any of the other pitiable Untouchables—whether born or as yet unborn—fated to be crushed in the Wheels before the Cycle was through. Not a true Catalyst among them. It was, and had always been, Jacin-rei who held the Balance.

Damn, damn, *damn* the boy for slipping his traces before Asai had set his course.

"Seyh?" Vonshi knocked softly on the jamb of the open door and entered the study with his head bowed in apology. "She will not leave, seyh. She insists she must see you."

Asai sighed. He'd rather thought she wouldn't take *Lord Asai is abed, come back tomorrow* for an answer, but he'd hoped. He knew what he needed to know, and he saw no real reason to listen to her tell it to him. He'd caught the "where" from the little one, but the "who" came directly from Leu not an hour after she'd gone to collect her thugs. Asai had known she failed before she'd even crossed onto his lands.

He gave Vonshi a weary nod, and rubbed at the headache winding at his temples. "Show her in, then."

Brief as his glimpse through the little one had been, it was enough to show him what he had to work with now, before the veil had clamped down tight over her and hers again, even more impenetrable than it had been for all the months preceding. And no wonder—he was dealing with Kamen, Wolf's-own, already the strongest of the *Temshiel*, handed unprecedented power by his god when Wolf made him, and now in his own Cycle, apparently emerged from his retreat and taking up his place again.

Tantalizing, to imagine all that power at Asai's own fingertips. The possibility was nearly torment for its lack of present reality, but that unease wouldn't leave him.

Kamen didn't take losing well, and he'd lost spectacularly. And now he knew Asai was here, perhaps had known all along, and it was too much to hope he didn't know what Asai was after. If he was still angry over Skel—and of course he would be; Kamen had petitioned to have Asai sent to the *suns*, for pity's sake—he might well do his best to interfere, would not hear the sense in the liberation of the Jin. And if Kamen learned Skel's Blood had been instrumental in obtaining the Blood of others—*Skel's* Blood...

Asai couldn't help the shudder.

Still.

He knew what appealed to Kamen. Knew what set Kamen's too-naked, mortalbound heart to thumping. Knew Kamen's rage, when all was said and done, was less on Skel's behalf than it was unreasonable emotional reaction to an affront to his senses of loyalty and justice. Knew why Kamen had loved Skel, what had attracted him. And Asai himself had built the Catalyst. Perhaps he'd foreseen more than even he'd suspected.

"This way, please, *misin*."

Vonshi's soft, creaky voice preceded Leu by mere seconds as she stormed past him and into Asai's study. Wet and bedraggled, a little bit bloody, and apparently altogether too angry for manners as she shoved the door shut in Vonshi's face and advanced toward Asai. Hazel eyes were sliding yellow and cat-slitted then back to hazel again as Leu tried and failed to keep her temper in check.

Asai flattened his mouth. "You did not acquire the earthbound." He said it bluntly, hoping to stem her anger with an oblique accusation of failure.

Leu didn't seem inclined to cooperate. "How much of tonight did you *see*? Did you know about the *Temshiel*?"

It was a difficult question to answer truthfully. In its broadest sense, yes, of course he had. It was the whole point, after all. But Leu might kill him for that, and she could, quite easily. She was in her own Cycle, too, and Asai was still a mere aspirant, suffering the lesser powers of Raven while abiding Wolf, and always with the threat of *banpair* over his head if he ended up rejected by both. He couldn't allow it. He would accomplish great things, he'd foreseen it, and Wolf would welcome him. It would be Asai's *right*.

He chose to answer the question in the narrower spectrum of specific truth: "No, I did not."

Because he truly hadn't known Kamen himself would stoop to the rescue of a mere mortal—a waste of *Temshiel* power and resources, surely—and it only made that same unease tighten Asai's chest while at the same time stirring hope. It was all happening, what he'd foreseen, but it was too early, out of sequence, and the future had yet to set itself into unbendable shapes. The *Temshiel* was supposed to follow the Catalyst, damn it, not the earthbound, and *not yet*.

Had Kamen done it for the earthbound or for the Catalyst? And *why*? The earthbound could be no possible use to *Temshiel*, but perhaps, if Kamen had done it for Jacin-rei…

The answers were imperative, and Asai had no illusions that Leu would have them. He wished she'd just crawl back to the rock under which he'd found her, and leave him to his contemplation. Except she was the only one of Wolf's maijin who would suffer him in his exile. He'd wrung compliance from her through her mewling cries of completion, but women had an annoying tendency to gain clearer heads when they were vertical. Sometimes he missed Skel with burning regret.

Asai clenched his teeth and bowed his head respectfully. "I am sorry, Leu. I saw only—"

"No, you know what? I don't want to know what you *saw*. I don't want to know what you plan. I don't want to know *you*. I'm done, Asai."

Keeping Leu in the corner of his eye, Asai angled behind the desk and sat down. Putting a bit of a barrier between them, however thin, but it wouldn't do to let her know it.

"You would abandon your god's favored people so swiftly, Leu?"

Her eyes went slit-yellow again. "I would abandon *you* and whatever you've done to draw Kamen's interest. Bloody *Kamen*, Asai." She stepped over to the front of the desk, propped her hands on it, and leaned in. "He sends you 'greetings' from Skel."

Asai rolled his eyes, though his stomach dropped. "And isn't it just like Kamen to hold on to that old grudge to justify his opposition?"

"His opposition to *what*?" Leu held up her hand and pushed her back straight. "No. I don't want to know. I'm finished, Asai. Find yourself another of Wolf's to plead your case. If you can."

"You know I cannot."

And the more he thought about it, the angrier it made him. He was in the position he was in now *because* of Kamen. Forced to supplication. Forced to seek acceptance with Wolf, when it should have been *offered* centuries ago. Forced to kowtow to an inferior maijin to help him achieve what should have been given him.

"I would bring glory to Wolf, Leu, you know I would, but I must have the earthbound to do it. Your failure tonight has set back Fate—"

"Bloody *hell*, you're an arrogant piece of work." Leu shook her head, eyes gone back to mere hazel again. "I'll admit I thought perhaps you'd been banished unfairly. I'll admit I thought your skills and your hopes for the Jin would please Wolf. But you can't think to pursue whatever it is you're pursuing now. Kamen's taken both the earthbound and the Catalyst to himself. He all but challenged you to try to take them from him. You can't continue on this course, Asai. I've no desire to see another war between maijin and *Temshiel*, and I won't stand by and watch you start one. As Wolf's, I can't allow it."

And there it was again—rubbing Asai's nose in his status, or lack thereof. And this one was no better than a mercenary. Nothing—she was *nothing*, and she *dared*. Didn't she know what Asai would be when Wolf accepted him? What difference could it possibly make to her how he did it? And what could possibly make her think she had the right? The bloody gall of the woman.

Asai took a long, deep breath to quell his rising anger, stood, and paced slowly to stand beside Leu.

Perhaps it was only Fate that had put Kamen in Asai's path as a too-wrathful barrier. Kamen was the most powerful of the *Temshiel*, yes, but Asai was—*had been* the most powerful of the maijin. And he would be again. And once he had Heart's Blood—Heart's Blood of not just *Temshiel*, but a *Null*...

A fair exchange for leading Wolf's favored tribes out of bondage, was it not? Asai was more than certain Wolf would see it that way, even if Wolf's-own refused to. Heart's Blood might wobble the Balance some, but what Asai did with it would set it back where it belonged, set it in stone for ages to come. Wasn't that worth the loss of one *Temshiel* and a few insignificant mortals?

Asai allowed a rueful smile to curl at his mouth. "You're right, of course." He took Leu's hand, pleased when she allowed it. "The war years were hellish, and their reflection through the mortal realm only hastened the Jin's subjugation."

It had done more than that—it had made it inevitable. *Temshiel* and maijin choosing sides, defining mortal boundaries to complement their own, and using their dupes as proxies in their own war. Pitting Jin against Adan, removing all too easily the centuries-old brotherhood between the two peoples. Except no one had foreseen the Jin unleashing their magic, knowing their mortal war for a thinly disguised divine one. Razing their own lands to rid themselves of the troublemaking trespassers of the gods, and sacrificing countless Adan in the process. And all with the justification that it would reinstate their own balance while the minions of the gods battled over the world's. Charged with using their magic only to serve the Balance, forbidden from ever using it against those who had none, they'd thought the Adan would understand, would approve when all was said and done—they were brothers, in the end, were they not? They'd allowed the Adan to bind with them through their Blood, after all. They'd almost become different tribes of the same people. The end of a war that wasn't their own would surely justify the means.

Except it was merely a horrible beginning. They'd been warned by their Untouchables, and the Voices of the Ancestors had, for the first time ever, been ignored. Because no one—not even Wolf's *Temshiel*— had understood until then that the Ancestors had not merely bound their magic to their people, but had bound themselves to their people through the lands. And when the Jin had turned their magic on their own lands to evict the sentinels of the gods—rent earth from bedrock, broke forests from their beds and burned whole cities—it was more damage than the Ancestors could take. It wrung their sanity from them and took their guidance from their people, sent their Untouchables shrieking, made them living Ghosts, and opened a chasm between the Adan and the Jin that could not be repaired or forgotten.

The two peoples would not come together again, they would be forevermore out of balance, one enslaving the other. And now Wolf was in his Cycle, the prospect of freeing his people from their bondage never more possible—and Asai was in a position to hand it to his new god. And he *needed* the twin to do it. Because if Asai held the earthbound—Jacin-rei's *heart*—in his hands, not even Kamen would be a match for the Ghost.

Considering all of that, everything that was at stake, everything Asai had done to bring about this particular future…

Did Leu really think Asai would pause to await her *permission*? "Asai?"

Asai blinked. Leu was looking at him with a mix between irritation and concern, her hand still trustingly between his, her guard almost nonexistent.

With a smile and a self-deprecating chuckle, Asai patted Leu's hand. "My apologies, I seem to have wandered." He let the smile falter. "I had such hopes for the Jin, you see."

Leu huffed. "Asai, I think—"

She never saw it coming, the fool. One quick jerk of Asai's arm, and two fingers set swiftly to her temple. Hazel eyes flew open, already blooming with petechiae, and then Leu merely crumpled at Asai's feet.

Asai stepped back, prodding Leu's ribs with the toe of his slipper until her body rolled to the side. A temporary measure—she'd be back and there'd be others—but it would take time, and perhaps it would be enough. She'd never plead Asai's case to Wolf now, but she probably wouldn't have done anyway, and if Fate conformed to the paths Asai set, he'd hardly need her to. By that time, there'd be little choice but for all to see her folly and the necessity of her removal.

"Nothing personal," he told the corpse. "You made a lovely obstacle, but an obstacle nonetheless."

At least there was no danger now that she might ally with Kamen and—

Kamen. Damn. Asai had almost managed to put Kamen out of his mind for a few moments. Almost, but not entirely, which was… good. Kamen was a danger to everything Asai hoped to accomplish, and Asai still had no idea if Kamen's presence was part of the future-possible he'd foreseen, that had led him here, or if he was to be the destruction of it.

Asai had wanted *Temshiel*, but not this *Temshiel*, damn it. Why couldn't Jacin-rei ever do anything bloody *right*?

Back to the cards, Asai supposed. Back to his meditations. Back to the bones and the stones, and every divination tool he had, and the frustration of too-vague allusions and not enough distinct auguries. Another long night. And he didn't intend to spend it with Leu's empty shell.

"Vonshi!" Asai's shoulders slumped wearily as he slouched back around the desk, and threw himself into the chair. "Vonshi, I need you!"

ᛟ

Not at all the same tableau as the one he remembered so fondly, and yet it had only been yesterday. When had he got so soppy? For pity's sake, it wasn't even long enough yet to be considered nostalgia.

Samin set the tray in the middle of the table, watching Caidi's eyes light up at the sugary lumps of fried dough and the mound of fresh fruit. Samin quirked a smile and dropped a wink when Caidi's shining eyes met his.

"Rice and fish first," Joori chided as both Morin and Caidi made grabs for the treats before he'd even finished pouring them their tea.

Morin glowered, mutinous, but Joori death-glared him into compliance. Sullen, Morin reached for the paddle, dropping a mound of rice into Caidi's bowl before he got his own.

Samin exchanged a smirk with Yori over the teapot.

"Let them have them." Yori reached over to ruffle Morin's blond mop with a challenging smile at Joori. "When's the last time you had anything fresh-cooked, eh?" The smile she gave Joori was one of those worrisome sweet ones as she dropped two dough balls onto each of the children's plates, along with an oblate each. She widened the smile to a grin, and propped her chin in her hand. Batted her eyes.

Shig didn't even try to hide her snort. Joori's gaze snapped over to her, hardened. Yori cleared her throat, and when Joori looked back at her, she batted her eyes again.

He huffed, but there was a small smile ticcing at the corner of his mouth. He nodded at Caidi and Morin.

"Whatever Yori-onna says."

The children dove for the sweets, all wide eyes and happy grins.

Yori snorted. "Yori-*onna*."

It was so strange to see a smile on that face that was Fen's, but wasn't. It was strange to see that face across the table in Fen's accustomed place but without Fen's accustomed precisely portioned breakfast, without his chronic ready tension, and without the braid. It was even stranger to hear strings of words and actual conversation come from that mouth in a cadence and accent that was twangy and somewhat lilting, rather than the smooth, dulcet rhythm Samin had got used to. And the expressions, the glares—they were almost funny.

When Fen glared at you, you instinctively checked to make sure you were armed, and when he spoke, you listened for the snarl and made sure you had a clear shot to the exits, just in case. When Joori came at you, it was more like being scolded by an unhappy duck, all squawks and flapping about, and empty attempts at offense he couldn't carry through.

The lad was strong, Samin would give him that, no life of idle luxury, certainly, but restraining him after having spent most of last night restraining his brother had shown Samin a marked difference. Joori might be able to defend himself, if armed, but if someone skilled came at him with intent, it would be the end. And offense was out of the question.

Samin would have to speak to Malick about teaching Joori some things.

"You saw my brother this morning?"

Joori's voice had changed from the light teasing note of only a moment ago into something cool and hard. Samin looked up from his rice to see Joori's still-angry gaze leveled at Shig.

Shig was sitting sideways in her chair, half-sprawled over the back of it. She was staring at the ceiling like she was reading invisible sonnets scribbled over the beams and plaster.

"Mal wanted me to see if I could read him when his head's not so busy."

Morin stopped munching on his sugared dough ball. Slowly, he set it back on his plate, expression going from happy indulgence to almost sick.

Joori's mouth screwed down into an angry line. "And could you?"

Shig sighed, gaze drifting slowly down to meet Joori's squarely—unapologetic, which Samin could tell pissed Joori off more than he already was. Shig wasn't about to apologize for last night, and Joori wouldn't accept it if she did. The lines had been drawn between these two, and Samin couldn't say he really blamed Joori. Last night had been hard enough for Samin to watch. He couldn't imagine what it must have been like for Fen's own brother.

"Magic doesn't really work on him." Shig shrugged. "I can usually hear his voices, because the Ancestors don't so much speak to him as blare the crazy at him." If Shig saw Joori's wince, she didn't acknowledge it. "I can only get little bits and pieces of what they're saying sometimes, but most of the time I just hear a noisy white buzz."

Joori shut his eyes for an uncomfortable moment, jaw clamped tight, then shook himself and gave Shig a glare. "You didn't answer my question."

Shig's mouth curled up at one corner, sly. "Imagine that."

"Shig." Yori turned to Joori. "She's not always this annoying. You just have to get used to her."

A disgusted snort was all Joori offered by way of reply.

"Can you read me?" Caidi's eyes were wide with fascination and a little bit of fear as she methodically obliterated her breakfast while staring at Shig.

"If I wanted to. But Mal doesn't like it when I poke about our own."

Joori narrowed his eyes. "But it's all right to 'poke about' with Jacin?"

Samin stepped in before it could degenerate. "He's not exactly in any shape to tell us anything, is he?" He held up a hand when Joori opened his mouth on what was likely meant to be a scathing retort. "I know what last night looked like to you, and I know what all this might look like to you now. But we like Fen, he's our own, and we all want to do right by him. He keeps things very close, your brother." Samin met Joori's hostile gaze with a clear one of his own. "Last night wouldn't've had to happen, if he'd just told us before."

"Told you *what*? That he's been used and hurt, and *keeps on* getting used and hurt, and now he wants to d-die?"

Joori's voice cracked on that last. Samin could tell it was taking everything in Joori not to let his eyes fill and spill over.

"He was hanging on for you." Shig leveled an intense gaze on Joori. "If he thought you wouldn't starve out there in the wilderness, he'd've walked into a knife on our last job."

Joori flinched like she'd slapped him. Caidi seemed to have lost interest in her breakfast for the first time since she'd sat down at the table. Morin gnawed on a pickle, gaze flicking back and forth between Shig and Joori, watching.

"But... but my..." Joori swallowed. "My mother."

Shig's gaze went back up to the ceiling. "We'd already promised him that."

Joori stared, expectant, before he lost his patience. "What the hell does *that* mean?"

"He doesn't want to have to look." Samin set down his tea. The face of his own pretty, long-dead reason for vengeance rose to his mind's eye before he thought to push it away. "*You* wouldn't want to have to look. And you sure as shit wouldn't want to have to take a knife to your own mother."

Shig opened her eyes at Joori's throttled gasp, peering at Samin sideways. She smiled, soft and sad, then closed her eyes again.

Samin looked Joori in the eye. "His only reasons to keep fighting were your safety and putting your mother to rest. You're safe now, and we promised the first night he came to us that we'd find your mother. Apparently, he trusts us to do it, even if he's not around to make sure we do." He paused, just to ponder that small revelation, and to make sure Joori was listening so he wouldn't have to say it again. "He doesn't have any reasons anymore. And like you said—he keeps getting hurt. How long d'you think *you* could take living your brother's life?"

It made Samin sad to say it out loud. It made him a little bit angry to watch the hurt rise in Joori's eyes, the betrayal. It had taken Samin perhaps a day to see the desperation in Fen, five minutes to see the constant struggle for sanity, and the occasional loss of it, the despair afterward. Fen's own brother couldn't possibly have missed it, not unless he'd been trying not to see it.

Fen's candle was flaring toward the end of the wick. Either the insanity would finally win, or death would take him, one way or another. And Samin could tell just by looking that Joori would never accept it.

There were two kinds of compassion, in Samin's experience—the kind that wept over a wounded animal and watched helplessly as it thrashed in its final agony, and the kind that put it out of its misery, quick and clean. Fen was the latter, something Samin shared and understood, but this brother of his was definitely the former.

Last night had been just as bad as Samin had been expecting since that first night in the alley, except it had been pointed in a direction that had surprised him—Fen had really meant to kill Shig, and anyone who got between them. He might have even killed one of his brothers or his sister in his madness, because for several terrible moments there, Fen hadn't been *seeing* any of them. And if Fen ever got past the point where his sanity was salvageable… well. At least Samin knew he could deal with it. He was quite certain Joori couldn't.

"I want to see my brother." Joori's voice was quiet but forceful, as though expecting a challenge.

Yori and Shig both looked at Samin, expectant, like it was his to give or deny permission. His mouth set tight when, eventually, every gaze at the table drifted toward him and hung there, waiting.

Samin sighed. "Umeia's in there now."

"I *need* to see my brother."

"Yeah, well—"

"I'll take him in after breakfast." Yori lifted her eyebrow at Samin, waiting for him to object; when he didn't, she turned to Joori. "Umeia says he's been kind of out of it. He's… he's not well." She set her hand lightly over Joori's. "Get it? It won't be fun. It won't make you feel any better. It'll likely make you feel worse."

Fen, too, if he was even aware enough by now to track the people around him.

Joori looked down. "It's not me I'm worried about."

Samin didn't think he quite agreed, but Joori at least believed it. Samin gave Yori a shrug and a nod.

"If Umeia says it's all right."

"Can I go too?" Caidi asked, soft and hopeful.

Samin could see the protective, likely harsh denial rise in Joori, so he cut it off.

"Then who will help me pick out pretty linens?"

He slid his expression into exaggerated disappointment as Caidi turned to him, looked him over, skeptical. "What do *you* want with pretty linens?" Stern directive in her incongruously high little voice.

Samin folded his hands on the table, leaned over them, and dropped his voice to a confidential murmur. "There's a pretty little girl I've just met, and pretty little girls need pretty bedcovers. I think it's a rule."

Caidi stared, almost smiling, but still unsure. "I've never had a real bed before. Mother and Father had a bed, but we only ever had mats. And my mat burnt up. Everything burnt up."

There were no tears, and her face didn't crumple, but the strange practicality of the statements twisted in Samin's chest. They weren't even real beds—just wood-framed cots with straw mattresses all crammed in one communal room—but this little girl acted like it was all something new and wonderful.

Joori was staring at Caidi, pained. Morin was focusing on his unfinished breakfast, mangling a sugary dough ball between nervous fingers.

"Well, then." Samin tilted Caidi a smile. "You'll be needing new linens for your new bed. I know a place in the district, not too far. And if you're very good, Shig knows a doll maker who uses real silk ribbons."

Joori startled. "You want to take her out into the city?"

Caidi's eyes sprang wide, like the implications hadn't hit her until Joori had said it. "I've never been in the *city* before."

She'd never been anywhere before—nowhere but a run-down Jin camp and a run-down little hut by the coast. And strangely, Samin wanted to be there and watch those expressive eyes when she saw what she'd been missing.

"It's safe," Yori put in. "Shig will make sure no one notices."

Her hand was still resting lightly atop Joori's, Samin noted with a mix of chagrin and amusement, and Joori was letting her keep it there. Shig had been taunting Yori only recently about... such things, but Samin wasn't sure he approved of the direction Yori's attentions were currently pointing. Not that it was any of his business. And maybe getting laid would get the stick out of Joori's ass.

Samin cleared his throat. "Umeia's working on getting you all papers."

Caidi stared at Shig, brow crinkled down in a stern pout that was just too adorable on her pretty face. She leaned in toward Samin, waiting until he ducked down so she could whisper in his ear.

"Does she have to come with us?"

Samin throttled the smirk and choked back the snort. It wasn't really funny. Caidi was obviously still smarting over last night, but the protectiveness and ire in her sweet little voice was just so disconsonant he couldn't help but be amused.

"Well, if she doesn't," Samin whispered back, "how will we ever find the doll maker's?"

Samin watched Caidi's gaze go suspiciously to Shig again, hang there as Shig lifted an eyebrow. Caidi looked at Joori. She widened her eyes, asking, and when Yori squeezed Joori's hand, he sagged, and gave Caidi a defeated smile. He nodded, though he shifted a warning glare at Samin directly after.

Samin wasn't the least bit offended. "It'll be safe. I promise."

Caidi sat up straight. "Can Morin come too?" She was almost vibrating with glee.

Samin grinned at the way Morin's expression went hopeful, even though he was very clearly trying to look disinterested.

"Well, he'll have to, won't he?" Samin tweaked Caidi's nose and made her giggle. "Who else will we get to carry back all the sweets?"

They'd near demolished all the confections leftover from last night's supper. Samin hadn't been quite sure if it was real hunger, a bid to distract themselves from what was going on behind their brother's closed door, or just the new experience of being spoiled. Considering the blissful sighs and groans they'd oozed when Yori and Samin took them down to the baths, Samin was betting on the latter.

"Sweets?" Caidi's eyebrows shot up, and her clear hazel gaze sparkled. "Can we bring back some for Jacin and Joori?"

Bloody damn, she was cute as a bug. Samin had to really work at it to not go all melty inside. He throttled the *Whatever you want* that tried to blurt itself and molded it into "If you're very good and listen to Shig and me while we're out and about." But he could tell by Shig's smirk that she had at least some idea of what Samin hadn't said.

Shig stood, and held out her hand to Caidi. "C'mon, we'll see if your cloaks are dry, and then I'll help you fix your hair."

Both Morin's and Caidi's gazes went to Shig's hair, faces pinching in worry, before drifting back down to Joori, as though for help. Joori had his hand over his mouth, but Samin caught the slant of amusement he directed at Yori, and then the roll of Yori's eyes.

"No dye," Yori told her sister firmly. "And no braids."

Shig flipped her off with a grin.

⏶

Its wings were dusky white, just this side of gray, flaring translucent as it rammed against the glass of the lamp. Fitful sparks glimmered through as they *thwip-thwip-thwipped*, beating their urgent rhythm—*thwip-thwip-thwip-thwip-thwip*—then a defeated plunge to the bedside cupboard.

Fly as you fall. His voice was strange inside his head. Echoing. Empty. *Even falling feels like flying.*

He wanted to fly.

A wobble of wisp-thin antennae, a flutter and surge; mindless, it flipped back into pathetic flight. Powdery wings, delicately veined, made an elegant *ching* sound against the glass that separated a frantic, useless life from a single instant of burning, excruciating brilliance.

Jacin? Are you awake? A shift that set his head whirling and his stomach tumbling, and pain—*pain*—striating out through every nerve ending. *Jacin, can you hear me?*

Something—no, someone—squeezed his hand. He wanted to do something, but he couldn't decide if he should squeeze back or shove the grip off him. He didn't do either.

He shut his eyes. Drifted.

Has he woken at all? Said anything?

He's... very sick, lad. The wounds are healing already, but the infection... It's got into his blood.

So much blood, and none of it his own, and fuck, he *ached*.

Boiling skies of verdigris, bruised with violet. Cherry blossom petals coasted on a gust of warmth, spiraled above him in a whirl like a miniature blizzard. They pattered down to settle over his face, his eyelids, his hair. Entombed in a sweet-soft shroud, and inside the silky miasma, it was silent. He thought he should be glad, but he only felt naked and terrified and alone.

He was freezing, but the petals stuck to the sweat slicking his skin. They itched. He wanted to shake them off, scratch everywhere, but if he moved, the shadows flickered at the corners of his eyes, and he didn't want to see what was inside them. There was hopelessness in there, way down in the murky depths, and something inside them whispered at him—*nothing, you're nothing*. He didn't want to listen. Maybe if he didn't look, he wouldn't have to hear.

The cherry trees rustled—*thwip-thwip-thwip*—and shadows fluttered over his closed lids. The sound made him sad, so fucking tragic, but he didn't know why. Something about wings and flames, and falling, falling, falling, tumbling down to start all over again, and even falling felt like flying for a little while until you burnt up your wings in your headlong plunge into the fire.

Burning. Cleansing. Resting, finally *resting*.

Except there was something he hadn't finished. He wasn't done.

Hurts.

Everything hurt, even his heart. Maybe if he took a knife, carved it out…

No. They'd taken his knives away. Defenseless.

He's in pain, Umeia.

I know.

He tried to open his eyes. The petals weighed them down, so heavy. He stopped trying.

I can't do much more, Mal.

Something cold and wet touched his brow. He shivered. Choked as something strong and bitter was poured down his throat.

Just keep it quiet for him. He shouldn't have to fight the fever and the damned Ancestors at the same time.

The Ancestors. Wasn't he supposed to be listening? Shake off the petals, and maybe the noise would block out the pain, or—

The silence was so seductive. He kept still.

Quiet. Beautiful. Just the sporadic *thwip-thwip-thwip* and the closing of a door.

But the shadows hid the noise. He could see them out the corners of his eyes, even with them shut and covered by petals.

Tired. So fucking tired.

I know, Fen. You're very sick.

Sick? Well, yes, he'd been that for a while, but.

No—tired.

Fucking exhausted. Wasn't he finished yet?

Your brother wants to see you. D'you think you can keep your eyes open for a bit?

No. He shook his head, a strange muffled fear in his gut. *The shadows will see me.*

He curled in, shied from the gloom at the edge of everything, and coiled into a tight knot inside his own mind. All alone. Desperation and relief all at once, because it was a *quiet* place, but it wasn't a *safe* place. Sharp and dangerous. Feelings he didn't understand lashed out like whips, cut him. Each blow crackled in his mind with a voice of its own, echoing in the silence and slipping away before he could put a name to it.

I got a new doll, Jacin, see? Her hair's like mine.

His eyes slid open. He never could refuse her anything.

The scream that wanted to come only shoved out his throat in a thin whimper.

Blood in her gold hair, streaming down into hazel eyes, so blank-empty.

He hadn't saved her.

She kept *smiling* at him, a cold, dead thing.

I'm Wolf's creature too, Jacin. We're all made for sacrifice. Didn't you know?

Tatty gray wings beat at the shadows behind her, frantic and useless. His mother's eyes stared vacantly from Caidi's heart-shaped little face. Shig, smirked—*Come along, pretty forfeit*—and Jacin shut his eyes tight.

You're not the only one who's had a shitty time of it, angry Ghost.

Jacin clenched his teeth. *Why can't you ever shut up?*

You still fear death. Blue eyes flashed with lust and disdain, thick dying sunlight catching at caramel-colored hair and setting it aflame. Pine soap, smoke and sage, and light, musky sex.

Jacin shook his head, pushed his body into Dani's. Begging. Shameless. *I don't. I can't.*

Liar.

No, I—

Failure.

Fuck you.

Dani only laughed, so Jacin let go. Fell down into the darkness and pretended he was flying.

C'mon, Fen, open your eyes. Talk to me.

He frowned. How was he supposed to open his eyes when the petals weighted them shut? And anyway, talk about what?

He didn't want to. He didn't have time.

…Wasn't he supposed to be doing something?

I have to listen. They'll only say it once, and when you touch me I can't listen.

A soft rustle, a rough hand at his cheek, and then that pine-sex-sage smell was all over him, overwhelming the fragile scent of the cherry blossoms.

D'you want me to let go?

...No.

Too weak. Too many emotions he couldn't not feel, even when he buried them deep and snarled them into silence, strangled them until he couldn't breathe. And still he couldn't make himself pull away from that touch.

Not... not perfect.

Tears burned behind his eyes.

Fuck, Fen. Soft and sad, then gentle, callused fingers threading the sweaty tangles off his brow. *You're not supposed to be. It's what makes you beautiful.*

Beautiful. Time lost, and yes, he was beautiful in the silence and the not-hours of blank, empty nothing.

Warmth settled at his back. An arm curled over his ribs. The steady rise and fall of another's breath heated his nape.

Held. Cradled. Like he was someone's lover.

It felt so fucking *good* he could've cried.

Was this what it felt like to die? Had he gone to the suns?

'S not so bad.

It felt a little bit like flying, so he didn't mind the fall.

A shift behind him, then beneath him, and his body rolled, limp and lifeless. He waited for someone to light the pyre.

You're not dead. Angry. Impatient. *You're just stubborn and broody, and you're pissing me off.* Stillness. Silence. Then, softer: *Fen. Please.*

He opened his eyes, watched the moth thump against the glass—*thwip-thwip-thwip*—its wings like ragged lace around the edges now. The lamp was wicked lower, persuading the shadows from out of their corners, but the frantic bashing went on and on and on. He shut his eyes again.

So fucking tragic. Such a waste.

It didn't stop. It never ended. Smoke rings, the arcs feeding into themselves, eating themselves, spiraling into infinity, because there was no such thing as a perfect circle.

You're losing it, lad. Focus on the graze of ink on the paper.

Careful brushstrokes, but he couldn't stop his hand from shaking. It didn't matter. He was losing himself in the ink drops, letting them suck him down into the pitch.

Hardly perfect, is it, Jacin-rei?

He tried not to weep, but the tears were searing his eyes, and they *hurt*.

Nothing, you're nothing.

Yes. I know.

He'd never thought otherwise.

Fen, damn it, open your fucking eyes. Stop being so bloody dramatic.

Rough, that voice, like fine liquor, and it brought the quiet with it, kept the shadows cowering in their corners, so he let himself hear it.

Can't, he wanted to say, but the petals crept down his throat, wedged in his chest, sprouted and took root. It hurt, but he couldn't cough and dislodge them. He wondered if a sapling would shoot from his mouth if he tried to talk, so he didn't, and the silence—inside and out—made him wonder again if he was dead.

Is that what you want?

Malick had him shoved up against the door of the baths, and his hands were running over Jacin's bare shoulders, hot and callus-rough, thumbs settling first in the dual grooves of his collarbones then sliding up to rest—no, *dig in*—at the pulse points at his throat. Jacin let his head fall back, arched his neck, defenseless, because there was no true surrender without risk.

You want this, Fen, is that it? The smile was flat, all teeth and contempt, and the gliding strokes of Malick's thumbs increased in pressure, cutting off air.

Jacin was mortified to realize it was making him hard.

Malick dipped in, dragged his mouth up the line of Jacin's jaw. *Did you think I wouldn't give it to you if you asked me to?* He squeezed.

Jacin shut his eyes, the shadows of moth's wings rippling through his lids—*thwip-thwip-thwip* in time to the flurry of his heart—so he opened them. Watched the petals settle in Malick's hair like snow, watched them reflect, white and empty, in the smoky tea of his eyes. The pressure knocked up, not just cutting off air this time but stealing it. Jacin's pulse thudded through the silence in his head.

No. He pushed it out through the bracken in his throat. *No, I—*

You like it when you're outnumbered, don't you? You need *the risk. You love all the pristine possibility.*

Jacin's eyes slid shut, and he couldn't stop them. He didn't understand, and he couldn't think—all the blood was blocked from his brain and pooling in his groin. *Possibility of what?* But when he opened his mouth to ask, petals and moths came fluttering out, and something warm and garlicky went in, and he didn't have the energy to choke, so he swallowed it.

Sorry, I know it's disgusting, but Umeia will kill me if I don't make you drink it all.

I don't do this out of cruelty, Jacin-rei.

No, Beishin had saved him, saved his family, and was going to save the Jin, so Jacin let him pour the brew down his throat and made himself not throw it back up. Except Beishin was maijin, and didn't love Jacin at all.

Jacin opened his eyes, stared into the deep-dark of Asai's, furious and humiliated when his vision blurred and hot tears ran like water down his cheeks.

Hate you. Fucking hate *you. I loved you. I would've done* anything *for you. How could you do this to me?*

And *still*, he was reaching out, leaning in, desperate for everything that wasn't his. Love that didn't hurt. Silence he didn't have to ask for.

Please, please, *just… just say you love me, just once, lie, promise me, I'll believe it, I can't do this anymore, I can't—*

Untouchable! His father shoved him away.

Asai only smiled that shark's smile that made Jacin want to scream and weep and fuck him right into the ground.

Jacin-rei, cover yourself.

Jacin looked down, almost sobbed. Naked. Exposed. Showing him everything. Giving it all away so Beishin could use it to flay him, again and again and again. Smash his face into his failures. Make him look at them up close.

Jacin… When have you ever failed at anything?

No. Not you. Go away. Please!

He couldn't look up. Couldn't stand to see the forgiveness for his sin of survival. Couldn't bear the love.

It wasn't a pretty thing for Jacin, love. Not something warm and comforting in which to hunker when a storm set to brewing. It was loss. It was bitter hope. Another soul strapped to his back, another danger of grief, another motive to wear like armor when his knives sang.

Ah, my own. A soft touch to his cheek, cool against his hot skin. *Don't cry, love.*

Mother. Jacin kissed her palm.

Mustn't fail them. Promise me.

The steady faint tattoo of petals on his bare skin and *thwip-thwip-thwip* in the back of his head, and *I promise* fell out his mouth. He could have dropped to his knees and howled, it hurt that bad, so *heavy*. But the shadows were curling again, restless, and he didn't want them to see him, so he stayed still and silent.

No laws. She kissed his brow, and Malick squeezed his hand, but Jacin didn't squeeze back.

I'm sorry. Useless, but it was all he could manage, hoarse and hollow. *Sorry, I'm so sorry.*

Malick only shook his head, peering at Jacin's mother, contemplative. *She wouldn't want you to be.* He turned back to Jacin. *Open your eyes, Fen. C'mon, wake up.*

Are you dead? Jacin asked his mother.

She smiled, and he could see it in his mind, but he couldn't open his eyes, he *couldn't*.

No. I can't die 'til you save my soul.

He thought about that for a long time. With a reckless snatch at hope, he asked, *Am I?*

There was a touch at his brow, and he worried that someone was trying to paint the prayers on his skin. He didn't want them. He didn't want to go to the gods. Fuck the gods. He batted the hand away.

Wolf will have you, Fate's Fool. His father stood before the blazing suns, burning. *You must set the Balance before you rest.*

Fool. Of course.

He opened his eyes, looked at Malick, but Malick looked sad, so he shut them again.

Mother smiled at him, soft. *My twice-born, my boy of too many lives.* Save him, her hands felt so good on his face. *It was you that first time, too, though that wasn't* your *first time, oh no. Lives uncounted, my lonely little Ghost. I knew when you came to me again. They thought I wouldn't know my own, but I did. Snapped your neck the first time because I couldn't bear for the Ancestors to have you.*

He took her hands. *You should've done it this time too.*

Mother sighed, stroked his cheek, wiped his tears like she'd done when he was small and his father wasn't looking. *You were determined. You* would *be born, and Wolf* would *have you.*

Is that what you want, Fen? Malick asked him, except there was no stranglehold this time, only a hand gripping his own. *You think dying will fix it all for you?*

No.

He opened his eyes, watched the petals fall and coat the little cupboard where the moth lay, brittle and ragged-winged, dead. No more *thwip-thwip-thwip,* just a soft fall of cherry blossoms threading itself into a shroud.

No, not fix it—just... make it stop hurting so much.

Everything hurt. Everything.

I know. A heavy sigh, and more cool-wet at his brow. *But dying won't fix it. Living is your sacrifice, Fen. I'm sorry.*

Jacin snorted, squinted through tears at the husk of the moth. *We're all made for sacrifice.*

He shut his eyes, let himself fall—

Yes. Soft and faraway. *But I can help you endure this one.*

—and for a little while, it felt like flying.

⌘

Malick stretched, bones not quite realigning and muscles too tight, wound through with knots. He wasn't used to spending so much time in one place, and certainly not used to spending so much time on a metaphorical tether. He made sure his socked foot stayed in contact with Fen's shin through the blanket and stretched again.

Joori shot him a blatant sneer from where he sat next to Fen on the bed. "D'you have to put your feet all over him?"

Malick rolled his eyes. "You had a hissy when I curled up with him, and my hands are starting to cramp. So, yes—since this is the most comfortable I've been in two bloody days, and I'm a little tired of giving a shit about your delicate sensibilities—I absolutely do."

"You didn't *curl up* with him—you were all over him. You think I don't know what—"

"Yeah, I'm pretty sure you know fuck-all about your brother. And I *know* you know fuck-all about me. So maybe you could just keep your bloody unhelpful opinions to yourself."

"You're *Temshiel.*" Joori said it like it was the vilest curse he could muster. "What more do I need to know? You use and hurt and kill, and you aren't capable of caring who—"

"Yeah, I want to watch while you say that to Umeia. I'll make snacks and charge admission. Should be fun, since she's not slept much the past couple of days, what with trying to *keep your brother alive* and all, and she gets a little… cranky when she's tired."

Joori snapped to his feet, abrupt enough to jostle the bed, but Fen didn't stir. For a moment Malick had hope he'd finally pissed Joori off enough to storm out, but no such luck. Joori only paced the room, a rapid back-and-forth, hands fisted and back rigid. He fetched up by the press, set his hands to it and hunched over. He hung his head.

"What d'you want with him?"

It was quiet, and with as little rancor as Malick had heard from him yet.

It did nothing to assuage the annoyance. Malick leaned his head to the back of the chair and shut his eyes.

"You're a rude, nosy little shit, Joori, and I don't like the way you ask that question."

Joori huffed. Malick could hear him turn, could feel eyes on him as Joori settled back against the press.

"I tried to kill him once."

That got Malick to open his eyes.

Joori's head was bowed, arms folded across his chest. "On the day of his Change. Except I couldn't do it. And later, when *he* came for him, he watched me cut Jacin to calm him down…" He trailed off, shook his head, looked up and past Malick toward the window. "It was the only way—at least the only way *I* could figure out, the only thing that… that made it a little quieter for him. And *he* just watched me do it. And d'you know what he said?"

He looked at Malick, mouth curled up in a bitter smile. "He said, 'How very… interesting.' *Interesting.*" He clenched his jaw. "And then he used what I did, what *I* showed him, to…" He didn't finish. It looked like he couldn't.

Bloody hell, this family's fucked-up-ness was so monumental Malick could earn himself a blissful eternity on Wolf's moon just by pulling *one* of their asses out of the fire.

"Your brother used it to stay sane." Malick kept his tone even—neither forgiving nor accusing, because it wasn't his place to tender either.

"Sane." Joori snorted, scornful. "He's my brother. He's my other Self. I love him more than I love myself. And I couldn't do what needed to be done to save him. Not… not then."

That… sounded like a threat.

"And you could now?"

Joori stared, for quite a while, gaze cold on Malick, assessing. When Malick only stared back, Joori chewed his lip, looked away.

"When Asai came for him, I let him go." Soft and faraway. "Jacin said 'let me' and I did, because I didn't know what else to do and I was terrified, even though I knew, I *knew* he couldn't… he wasn't… he wasn't capable of making a decision then, not like that, not so soon after…" His voice had started to shake, and he shut his eyes, took a long, deep breath. "The other night with Shig—the first time it hit him, it was worse than that. He wasn't in his own eyes. I tried to kill him, tried to end it for him, and I *couldn't*. And a few hours later, I was watching him make a life decision, *knowing* he couldn't, because I didn't know what else to do. I could kill Asai and run and hope, but I would've had to kill my father too—maybe Morin—and I…"

His gaze went to Fen, hung there. "Our father wouldn't love him. Refused to love him. He treated Jacin like a Ghost from the moment he was born. Our mother was mad for as long as I can remember, and only got worse as the years passed. She loved him, but…" Joori shrugged, gaze lifting to meet Malick's, unflinching. "Sometimes I wonder if I love him the way I do to make up for everybody else. And it still wasn't enough."

Bloody hell. It certainly explained a lot.

Malick shifted in the chair, propped an elbow to the arm of it, and set his chin in his hand. He kept the other resting over his knife. Just in case.

"And that bothers you? That you're apparently not all things to your brother?"

Joori shook his head. "No, you misunderstand. I love him, he knows I love him, and that didn't used to hurt him, but now…" Frustration shook his voice. "This isn't jealousy, all right? This is… this is…*fuck*." He thumped a fist to his chest. "*I'm* firstborn. If there's something that needs doing, *I* should be the one doing it. I *owe* him, d'you get that? And I failed him. *Everyone* fucking *fails* him. They always have. *We* always have. *Always*." More agitated with each word, Joori shoved away from the press, nearly stumbling as he stepped over to kneel on the floor beside the bed. Gaze locked to Malick's, Joori snatched up Fen's hand, squeezed. "He's been treated like he was nothing from the time we were born. He believes it, he always has. But whatever that man did to him, it made him believe it more. And now you."

It wasn't a question, and it wasn't exactly a statement. Neither of which mattered, because whatever Joori had meant by it, he'd almost certainly meant it to be just as offensive as it sounded.

Malick didn't know how to react, so he didn't, just said, "And now me."

Joori glared, mouth set tight. "Is this a fucking *joke* to you?"

"Yeah, actually." Malick's patience was nearly used up after the last two days he'd had, and having to deal with *this* one for far too many hours of them. "Yeah, it's a fucking joke to me to watch you strutting around here, thinking you know everything about him, when you actually know shit and can't admit it."

"Oh, and I expect *you* know every—"

"It's a fucking joke that you've apparently been regretting not putting him out of his misery when you had the chance—"

"That's a fucking *lie*, I never—"

"—and now you're trying to use the fact that you're pretty sure you can do it now as some kind of threat to make me say whatever the fuck it is you want me to say to put your guilty conscience at ease. It's a great big *monstrous* fucking joke that you seem to think you've got all his answers, and if we hadn't interfered with our inconvenient rescue, your brother and sister wouldn't right now be dead, and you wouldn't be a snotty, belligerent little bargaining chip for Asai to use against him—and *stop* squeezing his hand so tight! You think he's not in enough pain, you want to break his fingers too?"

Joori snatched his hand away, startled, and belatedly pissed that Malick had startled him. "If it hadn't been for your *inconvenient rescue,* my brother wouldn't have to be drugged into unconsciousness, and he wouldn't need you fucking *touching* him all the time! Or was that why you sicced Shig on him? To push him over the edge so you could 'rescue' him too? He was handling it, he didn't need—"

"Yeah, yeah, big bad *Temshiel.* Destroyer of lives, seducer of innocents, and kicker of puppies." Malick rolled his eyes. "Honestly, what *have* they been teaching you?"

"*Seducer.*" Joori's lip curled. "So you *are* fucking him."

"Not right this second, but yeah, kinda thought that was obvious."

Joori flinched. "Yeah. It was." Oddly, he didn't seem angry and hateful; he seemed... winded. "I just... I didn't think..." He slid his hand over Fen's again. "Why can't you just leave him alone?"

"Because he doesn't want me to."

"And you give everybody what they want, 'cause you're just generous by nature."

Malick's tolerance was already stretched thin. That remark, and the flat look that came along with it, snapped the fraying edges of it.

"Listen, you little prick. You want to pretend you've got your drawers in a twist out of concern for your brother, you keep living the fantasy, but don't expect me to—"

"Don't you even *care*? Can't you see what it's doing to him? You're *using* him—just like Asai did."

"And you're a jealous little bitch who's so intent on not sharing his toys you won't even see that maybe *you're* not what's best for him right now."

"I'm not *jealous*, you arrogant *ass*, I—"

"Oh, for fuck's sake, you're not that deep. You think I can't see what—?"

"I think you see very little but what you *want* to see. Even Umeia-onna said it: he'll take anything that comes with the quiet. And *you're* what comes with the quiet. I'm not that deep?—well, *you're* not that *special.*

"Yori keeps telling me what a great man you are, how you saved her and taught her how to shoot, how you saved Shig, how smart you are, and, 'Don't worry, Joori, Mal will take care of Fen.' But then I ask her what you plan to do about Asai, and *she doesn't know.* She doesn't *care* if she doesn't know. She just assumes you're too smart to do the wrong thing. And that's fine, I get it, you've always come through for her. But see, I *know* about *Temshiel*, I *know* about maijin, and I *know* you wouldn't've staged your *inconvenient rescue* without some kind of payment from Jacin, and I'm telling you—*he can't pay it.*"

Malick sat back, eyes narrowed. And here he'd thought this imaginary "payment" Joori was all worked up about was of a sexual nature, and if it was, Fen was obviously already "paying" it. So… what the fuck was *this*, now?

"Care to expand on that?"

"You can't know—" Joori pressed his mouth tight, raked a hand through his hair, clearly trying to calm himself. "Our father made it his life's work to not love his second son. And *still*, that night the hunters raided and Jacin came for us… he fucking *wept*, Malick. He picked our father's dead body up from the ground and put him in the fire, said the *rites*, and he *wept* over the man who wouldn't love him. *And he didn't even know it.* He didn't know he was weeping, all the way to that bloody little hut on the coast. He didn't know how much he was hurting. How much the death of the man from whom he'd only ever wanted love and couldn't have it was killing him. He *still* doesn't know.

"If my father had been alive that night when Jacin came, if he'd come at Jacin with a knife, Jacin would have let him. *Suicide*, Shig said—and since I have to assume you keep her around for a reason, I know you believe it. And now you want to send him to kill Asai."

Malick… stared. Peered down at Fen with a frown he didn't try to hide.

All right, so maybe the annoying twin wasn't so annoying merely out of jealousy. And maybe he had a point. Several points.

There had to be a reason Asai had refused Fen all those years, and Malick knew it hadn't been out of honor. Asai wasn't exactly the self-denial sort, and he rarely did anything without checking his cards and stones and visions first. Asai had done what he'd done to Fen deliberately, and perhaps the whole unrequited aspect, torturing Fen with it all through the hormonal ambushes of adolescence... well, perhaps Joori did see that bit a little more clearly than Malick had been doing. And maybe Shig's taunts about Fen walking into knives had a lot more bite than Malick would like to admit.

And yet there were still things about Fen—about people in general, but his brother in particular—that Joori would never understand. He hadn't walked through the same fires, hadn't seen enough beyond the seclusion of a Jin camp to know some of the things Malick could see without even having to look.

"D'you know what the hardest substance in the world is?"

Joori frowned at the seemingly blind turn in conversation. He blinked.

Malick relaxed back into his chair. "It's a diamond. Harder than steel, harder than iron—it can cut through stone, if you know how to do it. D'you know how diamonds are formed?"

The look Joori was giving Malick was narrow and suspicious, but he shook his head.

"Deep down in the bowels of the world—extreme pressure, unbearable weight. Anything else would crack or buckle. And when all of that comes together to form a diamond..." Malick paused. "Ever seen one?"

"No." Joori huffed it, impatient now.

A smile twitched at Malick's mouth. "Umeia's got mine. She stole it two nights ago, but shh." He set a finger to his lips, winked. "She doesn't know I know, so let's keep that between us for now."

Only for now. Malick was going to be needing it as soon as Fen could stay awake for longer than five minutes, so Malick was going to have to confront Umeia very soon. And wasn't *that* going to be an interesting conversation. Malick knew why she took it—what he didn't know was how she'd got past his wards to nick something that could literally end him if it came into the wrong hands.

"What...?" Everything about Joori was saying *What the fuck is wrong with you?* "I have no idea what—"

"Anyway, I'll have to show you. They're fucking beautiful. There's nothing else like them. You hold it up to the light, look way down deep inside all its facets, and you're... overwhelmed. Something so strong and so beautiful at the same time, and if you look at it just right, it's even more beautiful. But the most interesting part about it is that the only thing that can cut a diamond is another diamond." Malick gave Joori a level look. "Asai is no diamond."

Joori's scowl was gone now, his expression thoughtful rather than hostile. "And what about you?"

"What? Am I a diamond?" Malick snorted. "Part of what makes diamonds so precious is their rarity. And those who manage to get hold of one tend to take proper care."

Malick watched Joori closely to see which part of that last statement he was going to latch onto. But all he did was push out a heavy sigh and turn a tired look on his brother.

"Why can't you just teach me how to do it?"

Malick blinked. "Do...?"

"Teach me how to kill Asai." The "you idiot" was implicit in Joori's tone.

"Right, and why don't I just take that lamp there and set myself on fire, and spare your brother the trouble of killing me?"

"Why should he take all the risks? Why should you, even, or Yori or Shig or Samin? It's me he wants to use, and it's Jacin he wants to... whatever the fuck he still wants from him. Why should—?"

"He wants Fen to kill me." Malick paused, watched Joori's eyes narrow, surprise and the faint dawning of calculation blooming behind them. Malick had to grin. It was probably the most he'd seen Joori resemble his brother yet. "Don't get any ideas. I'd hate to have to kill you in self-defense. Fen would be... unhappy."

Joori rolled his eyes. "Why does he want Jacin to kill you?"

So many reasons, Malick thought, but said, "Blood magic," and left it there.

"So, why hasn't Jacin killed you, then?"

The question was so frank and ingenuous, Malick almost laughed. He choked it back and merely shrugged.

"Well, I'd like to think it's because he'd miss me." He crooked a sly smile. "But it's more likely that he's recently had cause to doubt Asai's motives. And he's no longer Asai's dog."

"He's yours, then, is he?"

"Yeah, sure. If that's the only way your narrow mind can understand it."

Joori looked down at his hand, curled tight around Fen's. "So, what happens next?" He looked at Malick. "I mean, you've got the others out at that Yakuli's now. If they find my mother there..." He trailed off, the honest question all too plain in his gray eyes.

"They were sent to spy and nothing else." Malick sighed, trying not to worry about the others out there without him, doing what he couldn't do. "Unless they find Yakuli alone. Which they won't."

Of that, at least, Malick was sure.

The buzz in the city had been ramping up for days. Almost every lord or official was calling in his prefecture army and beefing up his private guard. They were on alert, especially those who "owned" stolen magic. No way would Samin and the girls have a crack at getting to Yakuli that easily.

Malick looked away, mouth tight. "If they find your mother, they'll come back here and report it to me, at which point I'll decide what to do about it."

Joori looked startled. "But, surely you mean to—"

"Yes, surely I do—*if* Fen isn't well enough by the time we find her to do it himself. I won't take that away from him."

"And what about me?"

"What about you?"

Joori rolled his eyes. "Asai's obviously expecting me to be a helpless hostage. Why can't I just—?"

"*No.*" For the first time, Malick jolted enough he almost lurched from the chair and took away the contact with Fen. He controlled it. "Listen to me, Joori—he's done all this for you and your brother and sister. You won't—"

"But my mother—"

"He already knows she's gone, he has no illusions, and he'd sacrifice what's left of her to save you. Don't piss all over that—don't fuck up everything he's put himself through, everything Asai put him through— by thinking you can step in and play the hero."

"But if you show me how—"

"For fuck's sake, what part of *'no'* do you not understand?"

It was probably a touch dramatic, but Malick did it anyway—he leaned in, unleashed a touch of power and let it curl around him, watched Joori feel it and not quite understand, but his eyes widened and his expression tilted into worry. Dramatic, yes, but it always seemed to do the job more effectively than forceful words did, or actual physical force. Malick had wished more than once that it worked on Fen.

"You can't just *learn* everything you'd need in the next two days." Malick tried to make it firm and reasonable. "You can't close your eyes and wish yourself a warrior. Not against maijin, and certainly not against *this* maijin. What you *can* do is get yourself caught or killed." He pointed at Fen. "Either of which will break him. Now, if you love him as much as you say you do, the *only* thing you can do here, Joori, is to make sure neither of those things happen. Are we clear?"

Joori stared at him, wariness that turned to resentment from one breath to the next. His hand was clamped to Fen's like some kind of security blanket. With a subtle grimace, he looked away.

"Why are you doing this?"

"It's my job. It's what I do. He belongs to Wolf, and Wolf—"

"No." Joori shook his head. "You actually give a shit. You care about him. I didn't think you could."

Malick looked away, unaccountably uncomfortable. It was too close to Samin's accusations the other day. *Would you be doing this if...?* He shoved it away before he could complete the thought. Fucking Samin.

"Yeah, well... you don't know everything."

That... hadn't come out as cutting as Malick would've liked. Mostly because he was absurdly irritated, and irritated *because* he was irritated, so it was all rather doing his head in.

"I heard you and Umeia-onna shouting about hiding this morning."

Malick didn't react. He'd been done with Fen Joori for two long days. Now he was *more* than done.

Anyway, everyone had probably heard the quarrel this morning. Malick had rather lost his temper when Umeia refused to leave, and Umeia had lost her temper right back. It hadn't been until Fen started to twitch, groaning weakly as they'd stared each other down over the bed, that Malick realized he'd let go of Fen to stand and face off with Umeia. It hadn't ended the argument, at least as far as Malick was concerned, merely postponed it.

"It sounded like she won." Joori's tone was suspiciously calm and casual. "So I'm assuming we're staying here, and Asai will know we're here shortly."

Malick merely scowled.

Joori seemed to take it as confirmation. "Right. So, I'm also assuming you want Asai to know I'm here and you want him to try to come after me."

"What I *want* is for him to curl up and die, but he's damned uncooperative."

Joori levered up from his crouch beside the bed, and angled his hip to the mattress.

Oh, good—it looked like he was staying.

"Yeah, well." Joori shrugged. "So, I'm to be bait, then."

It was so straightforward, so pragmatic. From willing hostage to willing bait. Idiot.

"I think," Malick said slowly, carefully, "Umeia and your brother both would kill me if I proposed such a thing."

Joori's eyebrow rose. "You think Umeia-onna doesn't know? Seems *you* don't know everything, either." He seemed quite satisfied with himself, the little prick. "That Leu woman knew you. Even I can see where that leads. And even if Asai wasn't a seer, he's still a powerful lord. He'll find us. Umeia-onna has to know that."

Malick nearly snarled. The little prick was right—Umeia knew. Which meant she had plans of her own she wasn't telling him.

Malick *hated* it when little pricks were right.

…And just exactly where was *Umeia, anyway?*

"So," Joori went on, "we're under Umeia-onna's protection, which means Asai can't kill us, but it seems—"

"*No*, you bloody clod, that's *not* what it means. What the fuck are they teaching you anymore, anyway?"

Bloody hell, every day of Malick's existence put together couldn't be as exhausting as two days with fucking Fen Joori. Malick wished he *could* let Joori just toddle off with his arrogant attitude and deadly misinformation, and get himself conveniently killed so Malick wouldn't have to deal with him ever again. But Malick hadn't been exaggerating before—it really would break Fen.

He scrubbed at his hair. "Being under Umeia's protection means it would be extraordinarily difficult for Asai to kill you, for anyone to kill you, but it could be done. And it would be nothing at all for him to do to you what's been done to your mother. The only guarantee that comes with the protection is that no one can sniff you out using magic, and anyone who wants you would have to go through Umeia's magic to get to you, which very few could. It's not done for *Temshiel* or maijin to go after those marked as another's, but there are no laws against it. And if Umeia's killed…" Malick made the shrug and the wave of his hand look unconcerned, he hoped, but he still didn't like the way the words felt on his tongue.

"All right, that makes things a little less… safe, but…" Joori shrugged. "It doesn't really change anything. I want Asai dead. It's the only way Jacin will be safe from you both. If you won't let me do it, let me stop hiding. Let him find me."

"Uh… huh." It would probably not be helpful, Malick decided, to fall out of his chair laughing just now. "And then what?"

Joori looked at him like he'd lost his mind. "And then Jacin will kill him, of course."

"Of course." Malick opened a hand. "But you said he wouldn't be able to."

"And you said he would. Or was all that 'diamond' twaddle just bull-shit?"

There was a trick in there somewhere, some kind of ambush waiting inside it all. This one was a bit slippery, sometimes deliberately unreadable, where Fen was just mostly hard to read by nature.

"No." Malick folded his hands across his stomach, watching closely. "It wasn't bullshit."

It wasn't. Malick had meant it. Every word.

"Good." Joori looked a little too pleased for someone who seemed to believe he'd just talked himself into being bait for a maijin. "I think we're agreed that Jacin doesn't need to know about this?"

"You know…" A small smile curled at the corner of Malick's mouth.

Perhaps he'd just found the ambush. "If I agreed to this and your brother found out, he'd kill me."

And it wasn't just a euphemism.

Joori met Malick's gaze head-on. "You say that like I give a shit."

"Ah."

Well, that was easy. Half-formed and rather half-assed, but Malick had to hand it to Joori—it *was* actually a plan. Just not nearly as clever as Joori seemed to think it was.

Maybe Joori honestly didn't think he was jealous. Maybe he really did think every one of his motivations was out of a pure, perfect love for his brother. But what all this "bravery" in volunteering as bait came down to was that he would—at least he thought he would—hold the key to getting Fen away from the big, bad *Temshiel*, once all was said and done. Possibly even before—who knew? He might just spill it all to Fen as soon as Fen opened his eyes, and coerce him to gather the family and skulk away before they drew Asai's eye. They could do it now—Fen had money, and Umeia had handed Joori all the papers just this morning.

Fen might kill Malick, or he might not, but he certainly wouldn't have another thing to do with him, not even if Malick was the only one in the world who could save his mother's soul. And though Malick wouldn't let that stop him if it turned out to be the best or only solution, he didn't like Joori thinking he'd manipulated him into it. The little prick was already too smug by half. Malick was torn between punching him in his smirking mouth and patting him on the head and giving him a biscuit.

Good dog. Clever boy.

Trying to outmanipulate a manipulator. This should be fun.

3

It annoyed Umeia that she had to jump through such hoops, but she dressed carefully nonetheless. No plunging neckline today, no swinging skirts or clacking heels. Traditional layered robes, held closed by a thick sash, and flat-soled leather shoes that squeaked when she walked and made her feel too short. She winced as she slipped the wig on—she looked dull and washed-out as a brunette, and she hated the feel of it swinging down her back—but steadfastly tucked brassy curls beneath it and carefully pinned it in place.

No glamour today, not where she was going. She couldn't take the chance that a hunter would smell her magic coming. And she'd had no choice but to shut herself off from Malick, which meant shutting herself off from his veil; with all the magic she spent keeping those to whom she'd sworn oath protected, her own veil just wasn't as strong.

"*Him* again?" Lex was propped on an elbow on the pillows, sheets in a tangle around his hips, pouting.

Umeia rolled her eyes. Honestly, men were so… competitive. Or something. Sleep with them a time or several hundred, and they thought you should never, ever want another. As if anyone was *that* good.

"Who is he?" Lex's gaze was a bit fiery and all too becoming, for all his annoying attitude. He did look rather decadent and tempting, lying there in the rumpled sheets, broad chest bare and black hair distinctly disheveled.

Too bad Umeia couldn't be late today.

She turned to the glass above her vanity table, checking the set of the wig and the kohl around her eyes. "Someone who owes me some favors."

Lex's expression turned sour. "Oh, I'll just *bet* he—"

"Lex." Umeia turned, snatched up her bag—small and plain, ridiculously sedate; she was supposed to be a lady, after all—and stepped over to the bed. She slipped her fingers into Lex's tangled hair and gently combed through a few snarls. "You're the Girou's right hand. You're not my mate." She patted his cheek and made for the door. "See that Haru and Fee are up in an hour—they're working lunch today, and I want

Haru bright-eyed and smiling or he's going to the kitchens. I've wasted enough time on him."

She huffed an aggravated sigh when she got out into the hallway, turning just in time to avoid walking directly into Malick's chest. Bloody hell. She'd assumed he was still plastered to Fen where she'd left him.

"What are you doing down here?" She slid the door shut behind her. "Why aren't you with Fen?" Maybe redirection would spare her from an argument she didn't feel like having.

Or not.

Malick only lifted an eyebrow at the wig, but rolled his eyes when his gaze landed on the shoes.

"Off on business, I see." He smirked—that cold one that turned him cruel. "What more've you got to discuss with the good judge?"

Damn it. "Who says we're going to 'discuss' anything? I run a brothel, brother dear. Men have needs." Umeia made a business of smoothing the long hair of the wig over her shoulder. "Have to keep up appearances, yeah?"

Malick's expression didn't outwardly change, but somehow it seemed his gaze got a little cooler and his smirk turned to a jackal's leer.

Umeia rarely had cause to be afraid of Malick. He could make her nervous when he wanted to, but hardly ever afraid. But the cold calculation in his eyes had a little too much potential right now. It almost never did Umeia's nerves good to remember exactly what her little brother could do.

"I want to know what you're up to, Umeia." Malick's voice was low, his tone laced with threat. "You've got your own little game going on. What's it to do with Judge Canti?"

Despite her discomfort, Umeia's eyes narrowed. He had the *nerve* to accuse *her* of playing games.

"It's no game." Umeia tried to make her tone just as cool. "I won't let you play with the lives of those children. I'm doing what I need to do to protect them."

"From me?"

"Yes." There was no sense in trying to dissemble. Malick wouldn't have asked if he hadn't already known. "From any who might be a threat to them, which includes you. I swore oath, in case you forgot. At *your* request."

"And somehow, you neglected to include Fen in that oath."

She'd been wondering when he'd notice that. Fine. He wanted to draw lines in the sand?

Umeia shrugged. "I'm not the one with the death wish."

"And that means…?"

Idiot. He knew exactly what it meant.

"It means I won't swear an oath of protection to one who takes his own knives to himself so casually. I won't risk my soul for one whose time has been counted in hours instead of years since the moment he was born." Umeia lifted her chin. "You want to pretend he's not doomed, little brother, you go ahead and keep those blinders on. But I won't let you risk those to whom I *have* sworn oath, *and* me, for someone who won't live out the month."

And it pissed her off—*hurt* her more deeply than she wanted to admit—that Malick would want her to. Fine, he had a big, sloppy heart, and it was currently tangled around Fen, even if he wouldn't admit it. But damn it, Malick was the one who'd drawn Umeia into all this. She'd accepted Wolf's charge *because* of Malick, so she could watch out for him. Didn't that count for anything? Could he really risk her so blithely?

"He's *not* doomed." Malick's tone was scornful, and so was his glare. "He's meant to set the Balance, Umeia. Can't you see the convergence coming?"

"Oh, I see it. And you'll be the first with a knife through the heart when your pet Untouchable sees it." Umeia stepped in, teeth set. "What d'you think he'll do when he understands that setting the Balance means the destruction of his people? What would he think if he knew on which side you fought in the Binding War?" Her hands clenched into helpless fists. "Get the Blood of the *Temshiel* and save the Jin, that's what Asai ground into him, and once he understands that Kamen Wolf's-own tried to take away the magic of his own people—"

"I'm not debating this with you again."

"There *is* no debate! They were never meant to have it, Malick. The Ancestors thumbed their noses at the Balance when they bound them-selves to the Jin, and the Jin nearly destroyed it altogether when they used their magic as a weapon. They only still exist because Wolf wishes it. And d'you think your pretty *Jin* Untouchable is going to give a *damn* that the *Temshiel* who helped put his people down did it with a protest and a petulant scowl?"

Malick was silent for a moment, the rage down to a smolder. The pause gave Umeia hope. Right up until Malick shook his head with that too-familiar obstinate set to his jaw.

"Fen is Wolf's too. He'll see the sense in—"

"Fen can't see sense in the change of the seasons right now! Fen sees his family and their safety, and *that's all*. If he sees you as a threat to them, Malick…"

Umeia slumped against the door. "I'm getting them out. For *your* own good. *That's* my business with Judge Canti, since you're so keen to know. I'm doing it before you have the chance to use them as bait. And what's more, I'm getting papers for Fen too.

"There's a caravan that leaves for Heldesan at the turn of the week. Funny thing—the drover says he'll take an Untouchable for a little more koin, and isn't it ironic, because one's been haunting his wagons off and on for several weeks, trying to talk him into taking half payment for getting three others out when he goes."

There was no surprise on Malick's face. Umeia should've known.

She curled her lip. "Judge Canti needed a little more time to get Fen's papers through. Asai's spies are watching, and he had to be careful. I'm going to pick them up now, and you're making me late." She pushed away from the door and tried to bully past Malick.

He gripped her elbow, squeezed. "You're not taking Fen." Calm and blunt, but his fingers dug into the tendon and sinew in the joint of Umeia's arm. "Take the other three, I don't give a shit, but Fen stays."

This was why Umeia hadn't wanted Malick to know what she was up to.

"They don't shun Untouchables in Heldesan, Malick, they don't treat them like animals. He'll be—"

"He'll be right here, with me, taking care of Asai."

"You'd *really* risk the one who rules your heart to avenge someone you used to love?"

"Ridding the world of Asai for good serves the Balance."

Umeia almost laughed, but she was afraid she'd end up either braying like a madwoman or weeping hysterically.

"And whether you want to admit it or not," she said instead, "what Asai proposes to do will set it for centuries to come."

"A *maijin* ruling over both the Jin and the Adan will set the Balance?" Malick snorted. "I think you've been sampling the poppy again."

Umeia wished she had been. "Think about it, Malick. When the Ancestors gave their magic to their children, it rocked the Balance. When Skel gave Asai his Blood, it rocked it back again. The only thing that'll set it for good is if the magic is taken away altogether. But if Wolf won't allow the Jin to be stamped out, what other solution is there but to control it?" She paused, pulled her arm out of Malick's looser grip, and took his hand. "Killing Asai only puts things back the way they were. Do you *really* think that's all Wolf wants of you now?" She stepped in, peered at him closely, watching, and dipped her voice low. "And do you really think Fen will thank you for making him watch while you do what you *know* has to be done?"

Malick only stared, blank-faced, and with ice floes for eyes. Emotionless. *Frightening*. Umeia couldn't move, it pinned her that tight, until Malick snapped his hand away, clamped down on her wrist, and dragged her in close. Teeth clenched, gaze all at once wrathful, he leaned down, right in her face.

"Are you going to tell me that you want to *allow* Asai to do what he plans?"

Umeia was suddenly finding it hard to swallow. "Not with your Blood, no." She kept her expression calm, but her heart was battering behind her breastbone. "But we're not the only *Temshiel* in Ada. We're not the only ones who sense a convergence. You can't tell me you haven't felt them."

Malick was looking at her like he had no idea who she was. Perhaps he didn't, if he thought Umeia would give him up like that, or just blindly go along with his plans for vengeance while he risked his own soul for a mortal—an *Untouchable*, of all people.

"You'd set someone else in my place," he said slowly, "hand Asai what he needs to completely enslave an entire people—*Wolf's* people—all to keep from having to leave the whorehouse you call home?"

It sounded so selfish when he said it like that. And it hurt.

"I would do what I must to keep the Balance and protect my own. You'd see that, if you weren't being so blind. I wouldn't deliberately put another in your place, but I won't mourn if someone other than you is drawn into Asai's sight.

"We find ourselves in Ada, in Wolf's own Cycle, and if you were using your head, you'd see there's a reason for it. The Catalyst has done his part—pointed the way to setting the Balance—Fen is now unnecessary, a risk we don't need. You should've killed him that first night, but since you didn't, I'll see that he and his family are safe, because I don't think you can. If I'd known the whole of it when you brought him to me, I wouldn't have sworn anyone oath at all." Umeia shook her head, sad and achingly disappointed. "Bloody hell, little brother, you can't even be haunted by your own demons, you had to go and take on someone else's. You've done this entirely to yourself. I'm only fixing it."

She made to move away again, but this time, Malick took hold of her and slammed her back into the door, teeth bared. "Umeia?" came from the other side of it, Lex's voice with a good dose of worry, but he didn't try to open it. Umeia just kept staring into Malick's furious gaze, called, "It's all right, love, don't come out," and tried not to wince at the strength and viciousness of Malick's grip on her arms.

"Take the others," Malick snarled, "I don't give a fuck. But you keep your traitorous claws off Fen."

Umeia's eyes widened. She'd known Malick wouldn't like any of this, but... *traitorous*?

"Malick, if you'd only—"

"Stay away from him, understand? No more nursing, no more potions, because I no longer trust you not to poison him."

Shocked, and she really shouldn't have been. It was only that it had been far too long since Umeia'd been reminded how cold and cruel Malick could be.

"I wouldn't bloody *poison*—"

Malick slammed her into the door again. "My heart is what made me Wolf's, remember?—*you* keep telling me that. You've just broken it,

Umeia. Well done, you." Seething with rage, for all the words were sorrowful. "You've gone against your own kind, your own Blood, and I should kill you for it."

Right now, Umeia thought maybe he would.

"I won't. Not now, anyway. But you'll take Fen's family with you, and you'll go. You're done here. Perhaps I'll see you in another few lives."

Umeia's stomach dropped, and her head went light. "This is *my* home. You can't—"

"Watch me. I can't trust you now. I've no use for you."

"Just because I see the merit in Asai's—"

"There *is* no merit in Asai's plots. Not if they come from betraying one of our own. Not if the means go against Wolf's own laws."

"The end would *justify* the means!"

Surely Malick couldn't be *this* blind. He *had* to see—he was smarter than this.

But Malick only shook his head, some of the anger leaching into weary grief as he peered at her like he couldn't believe any of it was really happening.

"You know..." Malick huffed a disbelieving laugh. "That was exactly the Jin's argument for using their magic against the Adan in the first place. And if I knew Skel, it was his too."

Umeia flinched. "The Balance—"

"The Balance will be served, and you'll have no part in it. A *Temshiel* who'd allow... *enable* the murder of another—"

"I *wouldn't*! You're deliberately misunderstanding, Malick!"

"When Skel went to the suns, you mourned just as deeply as I did. You swore that one day Asai would—"

"And he *will*! Nothing's changed, damn it, why won't you see this? You act as though I've just ruined some grand scheme you've been plotting for decades, when in truth all you've been doing is lying back and pretending to watch. You've done only as much of Wolf's work as you had to, and that was only by happy coincidence."

Umeia sucked in a breath and tried to calm the slamming of her heart. She laid a shaky hand to Malick's arm.

"Now is your chance to set your hand to the Balance, Malick. Let Asai do all the work, let him take all the risk, use whoever blunders through his sights if they're not smart enough to get out of his way. If he gets his Heart's Blood, he'll have set the Balance, but if he doesn't, he'll end the Cycle with no god. He'll be *banpair*, little brother, godless and vulnerable. He'll try to cast his lot with Snake next, of course, but in the in-between— when Wolf wanes and before Snake waxes—he won't be maijin anymore."

She left the *And then you can kill him without risking your soul* just sitting there, all too obvious. But Malick's hard gaze hadn't softened, his grip on Umeia's arms hadn't relaxed.

"You miss the point, sister dear. A *Temshiel* who would hinge the Balance on the fulcrum of the murder of another, and place it in the hands of fucking *Asai*—"

"Is that what you're *really* worried about, little brother?" Umeia kept her voice deliberately soft. "Or is it more that you no longer have any real reason to control the Untouchable? I'm about to take him out of your hands, and you can't stand it."

"You," Malick said, low and deadly soft, "break my fucking heart. You're no better than Asai." He shook his head, let go of Umeia like he couldn't stand to touch her for another second, and took a step back. "You're done here, Umeia. You've got two days. Best get your affairs in order. Oh." He snapped his fingers. "It was a nice try with the ring, but I'll be wanting it back before you go." His eyes narrowed down to slits. "Did you think I wouldn't notice? That I couldn't tell whose magic is all over the broken wards?"

Umeia had been reeling back and forth between terrified and frustrated. Now it all went numb.

"You can't give something like that to someone like Fen, Malick, you can't—"

"It's Kamen to you. The others will be warned against you. I won't have the murder of one of our own on *my* soul."

Umeia couldn't believe Malick—*her brother*—was actually saying this. Couldn't believe he meant it.

"You'd see me shunned? You'd cast me out for an Untouchable who—"

"Don't even pretend it's got a damned thing to do with Fen."

And he really believed it too; that was what rose Umeia's own anger and blotted out a little of the grief.

"You're going to break him." Umeia said it through her teeth, shock slowly turning to wrath. "You're going to fail Wolf, and you're going to break his Catalyst. You're going to end up dead by the hand of the one you *won't* cast out, and the Balance will be served with *your* Blood anyway."

This time, Malick *smiled*—a flat and deadly thing that curled dread in Umeia's gut, and crawled up her backbone.

"He won't break." The cavalier tone was worse than the coldness and fury of before. "He'll submit. He's dying to. He doesn't know any other way. He's almost there already, and I'll have everything I need from the Ancestors themselves. I might even manage to sic him on Yakuli while I'm at it. Did you really think I didn't have a plan?"

Malick took a step closer, looming. Umeia was dismayed to find herself pressing back into the door again, caught in those dead eyes, that bitter smile.

"The Balance will be served, Asai will be dead, and Fen will keep his mind, and all of this without touching your precious charges and risking your soul." Malick shook his head, breathed a small laugh. "Now don't you wish you'd asked me before you betrayed me?"

Umeia shut her eyes, clenching her teeth to keep from weeping. Perhaps she'd underestimated him. Perhaps she'd been too worried about his heart and forgotten too easily that Wolf had chosen him for reasons that had been made all too clear in the past terrible minutes.

"Malick, please—"

"Ah-ah."

Still with that smile. Umeia wanted to… she didn't know what she wanted to do—smack it off his face, throw herself at him and beg him to forgive her, warn him again that Asai had managed to bend someone as smart as Skel to his thinking, so what chance did Fen have against him? And what chance did Malick have against Fen when he refused to see what a danger Fen was to him?

"Kamen." It stuck in her throat. "Please. I only wanted—"

"I know what you wanted. And I know why. It's the only reason you're not already dead."

Umeia flinched. Because she knew he meant it. Bloody hell, how could she have forgotten what a cold-hearted bastard he could be?

"Then you know I would never—"

"Two days," Malick told her. "Don't test my generosity."

"Umeia-onna? Is that you?"

The voice, so soft and tentative, made Umeia jump. Her gaze snapped toward it, landed on Madi, standing in the hallway in a silken robe, sleep-tousled and frowning, his eyes drifting back and forth between Umeia and Malick.

"Madi." Umeia ran shaking fingers through the wig. "Yes, it's me. What d'you need, lad?"

Madi looked between them, diffident. Umeia wasn't surprised. The tension was likely so thick, he could probably feel it.

"Aki-seyh says he was too drunk last night to remember anything, and now he wants another round for free. He won't leave."

An hour ago, it would have been a problem of the highest priority.

"Go get Bone," Umeia told him wearily.

Let Bone handle it in any way he wanted to. Maybe seeing someone else beat to shit would make Umeia feel less alone.

"Right." Madi's gaze drifted to Malick, a soft, hesitant smile tilting at his mouth. "Hello, Malick. I've been looking for you."

Didn't they all? Damn Malick, why couldn't he see?

"I've been busy." The way Malick said it… Easy and charming and cavalier, like he hadn't just completely destroyed Umeia a minute ago, and that fucking *smile* that made her want to fall down on the floor and sob. "How've you been?" Genuinely interested—Malick bloody *gave* a shit about how *Madi* was, when Umeia was standing here shattering.

"All right." Madi leaned hip-shot on one leg, unconsciously seductive. "Missing you a little."

Too late, Umeia wanted to tell him. *Start picking up the little bits of your heart now, because he's got what he's been wanting for too long, and he's not even going to notice he's broken you along the way to getting it.*

Malick grinned, stepping away from Umeia and toward Madi. "Only a little?" He laid a hand to Madi's shoulder then turned the grin on Umeia over his shoulder, a shark's grin, cold and hard, not a trace of the warmth directed at Madi only a second ago. "Two days, Umeia." He turned back to Madi, gently prodding him down the hallway. "C'mon, let's go see if we can't charm Aki-seyh out of your room without bloodshed."

Umeia watched them go, numb. Disbelieving. Because this *couldn't* be happening. Two days, but Malick would come to his senses before then, surely. *Not* betrayal, because Umeia *couldn't* betray him, she loved him, she'd followed him into immortality, and immortality was fucking *hard*, but she'd done it, and continued to do it for *him*. Malick would remember all that. Umeia just had to give him a little while to cool down and think about it calmly.

She wouldn't even make him apologize.

"Umeia?" Cautious and low, from the other side of the door. Umeia only just had the wits to pull herself away from it before Lex pulled it open behind her and sent her tumbling. He peered at her closely, frowning, concerned. "All right, love?"

Umeia only stared, shook her head.

No, she wasn't all right. She'd just joined the ranks of all the shattered hearts Malick left behind him. All the more cutting because Umeia had always thought she'd be exempt in the end.

"Come back to bed, love."

Lex laid a hand on her arm and gave it a light tug. No demands for an explanation, no accusations, no hard stare that made her want to curl up in a ball. Just a soft gaze and real distress—for *her*—and the offer of whatever she wanted to take from him. Lex had always been so easy to be with.

Umeia was going to miss him.

"Yes," Umeia said, half-dazed, abruptly bone-tired and going weak in the knees. "Yes," she repeated, and let Lex tug her through the door, kept repeating it as he gently rid her body of its disguise and then rid her mind of everything else.

⧌

Yori was loitering in the hall outside Fen's door, absently chatting with Caidi and pretending she wasn't waiting for Joori to emerge, when Malick plodded up the stairs. His head was bowed, eyes bloodshot and hung with bruised half moons, and his gaze was turned inward, troubled, like Yori had never seen him. It gave her a nasty little turn. Malick didn't *get* troubled.

Maybe it was the business with Yakuli. They'd had a good look last night, Yori and Samin and Shig. Malick's orders had been to stay out of sight of all of the guards and keepers, which had been just fine with Yori—there'd been far too many for comfort. But they'd come back with all the information Malick had wanted. They hadn't got a look inside the manor but for what they could see through windows from a distance, but Shig had confirmed Fen's mother's presence, so Yori knew something would be happening soon.

It wasn't the only information they'd gathered, though. The knowledge that Yakuli had horses was what Malick said led him to the councilor, but saying Yakuli had horses was like saying there was sand on the beach. Hundreds of them, running in loose herds in their fenced pastures that took up most of the swath of land on which the manor was sat. Secluded, ideal for a secret horse farm, farther outside Ikata than even Asai's lands, and too close to the camps for any "respectable" lord to want to venture there. Funny thing, though—Yori hadn't really thought about why anyone would want to keep horses a secret until she'd got a look at Samin's face.

"Warhorses." He'd cursed vilely, scanning the perimeter, calculating, his wide body vibrating like it was all he could do to merely look and not act. "This isn't a farm. It's a training camp."

And Samin would know.

He'd walked into Fen's room without announcement or a request for permission as soon as they'd got back, and unceremoniously ousted Joori. It was all right with Yori. It meant Joori had to cool his heels with her in the common room, and they'd had a nice… chat.

…*Fine*, so they'd rutted like minks. Right there in the common room. Anyone could have walked in. It made Yori's cheeks heat every time she thought about it. It really wasn't like her. And she'd only known him for a couple of days. But. Well.

Whatever Malick clearly thought, in Yori's opinion Joori was bloody *adorable*, and sweet to her, and with just enough of a hard edge beneath it all to make Yori quiver. And anyway, anyone who loved as hard as Joori did had to be worth a bit of indiscretion.

Yori blinked it away. "Everything all right, Mal?"

It wasn't. Obviously. Malick looked… subdued, or… no, *angry*, or… No, that wasn't it either.

"Everything all right, Mal?"

It gave Yori a start, coming from behind her like that, because she wasn't used to little girls following her around like lost puppies, so she'd been trying to ignore it. But there Caidi was, propped against the wall, mimicking Yori's pose with her arms crossed over her chest.

Malick's gaze jerked from Yori down to Caidi, pensive now, and just… unlike him. *Broody*. That was it. Except.

Malick didn't *brood*. He didn't have the patience for it. Or enough self-doubt.

Between one blink and the next, it was gone, quick as a feather aflame. Malick creased a grin, tawny eyes bright and dancing, and winked at Caidi.

"Everything's fine, love, no worries." He gave Caidi's pigtail a tug, and made her giggle. "Listen, I've been thinking…" He turned back to Yori, once again all easy charm. "Umeia's going on a trip day after tomorrow, and… I'm thinking you might want to go with her."

Another time, it would thrill Yori. Now, she had to stop herself from slumping, though she couldn't keep her gaze from flicking toward the door of Fen's room.

Malick caught her at it and gave her another grin. "No worries. I wouldn't interfere with young love. I'm not taking you away from him. You'll understand when it's time."

Yori looked away, annoyed her cheeks were heating again. "But what about Yakuli?"

"Yeah, what about Yakuli?" Caidi chimed.

Damn, Yori'd forgotten she was there again. What was it the laundress next door always said? *Little pitchers, big ears.*

"Let me worry about Yakuli for now." Malick gave Caidi's nose a tweak this time, to which she proved just as susceptible: she giggled again. Malick's gaze came back up to Yori, more intent this time. "You'll go with Umeia, yeah?"

"Yeah. Of course." As though Yori would ever say no—to Malick *or* Umeia. She gave Malick a smirk, because somehow it looked like he needed… something. "But you'd better make it worth my while."

"Yeah, yeah." Malick turned for Fen's room. "Your reward will be out shortly. Preferably on his ear." He dropped Caidi another wink as he shut Fen's door behind him.

"Why is Malick-seyh sad?" Caidi's voice was low in what she probably thought was a whisper.

Yori frowned first at Caidi then at the door. "Sad?"

Caidi didn't get a chance to answer; Joori was abruptly in the hallway, glaring at Fen's door as it shut firmly behind him. He pulled up short when he saw Yori, dark scowl going wobbly, like he was trying not to aim it at her, before he pointedly turned it to a smile.

"Um… h'llo." Joori sent a tight look back at the door. "Your *boss* said you wanted me." Spoken with heavy sarcasm and a healthy dose of rancor, but Yori could tell neither was for her.

"Uh-huh." Yori let the side of her mouth curl up. "Are you complaining?"

Joori turned back to her, frowning, querulous, before his eyes widened and his cheeks pinked.

Gah, he was adorable. And he wouldn't stand for someone bleeding another for their magic. And he was polite to Shig—well, acidly polite, but still polite. And he was *really* good in bed. Well, it had actually been on the couch, but still—*really* good.

"Oh!" Joori said—*finally*. Adorable, sure, but a little on the slow side, apparently. "No, of course not, I..." He kept opening his mouth but not actually saying anything, all discomposure and awkward charm, before he huffed and shoved his hands in his pockets. "You look pretty today."

Yori rolled her eyes—like she'd washed and twisted up her hair just for *him*. She hadn't. Obviously.

"Samin-seyh was right." Caidi made a little gagging sound, then swept a dainty pivot to flounce toward the common room. "Too bloody precious."

Joori yipped, scunnered, before he gathered himself enough to sputter, "Caidi, *language!*"

Her high, and distinctly *evil*, little laugh carried down the hallway even after she made the turn out of sight.

Joori stared after her, shaking his head. "Somebody needs to put a bell on her," he muttered then turned to Yori. "You wanted me?"

Oh, yeah. But first: "How's your brother?"

Joori shrugged with a tired sigh. "Better, I think. Quieter. Malick says he's healing a lot faster than he thought was possible, and the wounds have just about closed over, so..." He still looked worried, but he pulled in a breath, bracing, and straightened his shoulders. "He'll make it."

"Of course he will. He's too stubborn not to."

Joori didn't look quite convinced, and Yori knew he'd brood and stew unless he was... distracted. Not that she had any selfish motives.

"I, um..." Yori waved toward the door of the room she shared with her sister. "Shig's down in the baths. She usually takes all morning."

Hint, hint.

Joori's eyebrow lifted, gaze going down the hall where Caidi had disappeared into the common room. "My sister..."

It was halfhearted enough to make Yori grin. "Your sister's got Samin wrapped around her tiny little finger, and Morin's not too far behind. Samin's down in the common room, showing Morin how to properly wrap a sword hilt in wire in between bites of sugar dumplings."

"I... hm." Joori frowned, gaze drifting down the hallway again. "I'm not quite certain I like that."

Yori pushed away from the wall, and took a step toward her room. "Would it make you feel any better if I told you it'll keep them all busy for at least another twenty minutes?"

Joori stared at Fen's door for half a second, then up the hall to the common room for another. Gnawing on his bottom lip, his gaze finally landed on Yori as she sauntered away, and after a brief, obvious struggle, settled on her ass. He straightened his shoulders and followed.

Apparently, it made him feel *much* better.

⚏

It was nearly nightfall when Fen's fever finally broke. Malick could tell because the sluggish thrashing finally stopped, and the room fell silent. No more disconnected ramblings that made too much sense. No more pain-filled groans and tears that came from inside the agony of near-madness.

The mutterings about cherry blossoms had been… disturbing. Malick knew the symbolism the Jin placed on the petals. Though Fen was rather morbid by nature, so there was that.

Malick didn't suppose it mattered much. Fen was healing fast. Faster than he should. Either Umeia's magic was leaking through somehow, or Fen really was *that* stubborn. Anyway, the worst seemed to be over.

Exhausted, Malick abandoned the chair to crawl in beside Fen, and slept like he hadn't in days.

He was woken not by whimpering or too much heat baking off sweated skin, or even a hard shove off the bed and an indignant *How dare you, get the fuck off me*. He was woken by a soft, dry kiss to his mouth, a shaky fingertip sliding along his jaw. He dragged his eyes open, blinked slowly into somber gilt-gray. The fitful light of the low-wicked lamp dropped ashed-gold shadow over Fen's angular face, limned the contours of his bare shoulder and chest. Fen's straight nose was only inches from Malick's, head sunk low on the pillow they shared.

Malick didn't think he'd ever seen Fen's gaze so open, so calm. He wanted to see more clearly. Gently, he fingered strands of matted chestnut out of Fen's eyes.

There were things that needed saying. Nothing would come. Malick stopped trying. Only held Fen's solemn gaze, let careful fingertips explore the stubble on his jaw, slide up and settle lightly on his lips. Chaste. Intimate. Meaningful, somehow, but Malick couldn't quite ken the import yet.

The second kiss, when it came, was light and sweet and warm, and… private. Profound, maybe.

People's mouths didn't have their own special taste, not like sentimental saps would wax. People tended to taste like what they'd last consumed. Fen tasted medicinal, like the cherry liquor laced with poppy and myrrh and cloves that Malick had last coaxed him to drink through semiconsciousness.

And yet.

The kiss did things inside Malick's chest, took hold and turned everything on its head. Nothing sexual about it, no heavy, panting breaths or rise in libido. Only soft intimacy, warmth, a strange comfort, when he hadn't suspected he needed comforting.

He didn't protest when Fen pulled back, only opened his eyes. Waited.

"My mother wasn't here. Was she?"

It should have sounded a little bit insane, or at least strangely random, but Malick had been privy to quite a lot of things he perhaps shouldn't have been. He knew what Fen was talking about. He'd known what Fen was talking about since the first spate of vitriol and madness had come spiking from his tongue as he'd thrown himself at Shig.

Malick lightly kissed Fen's palm. "No. I'm sorry."

Fen bit his lip, looked down. His fingers twitched in Malick's hand, but he didn't pull away.

"How, um." Malick kept his voice to a whisper in fear of breaking the spell. "How are you feeling?"

A small shrug was all Fen deigned to answer.

"D'you want something to drink?"

He should. To replace what he'd sweated away the past few days, and to flush the rest of the infection out of his system.

But Fen shook his head.

"Fen. C'mon." Malick squeezed Fen's fingers, made his tone stern. "Don't turn me into a nagging nursemaid. Yori'll never let me live it down."

Malick hadn't really expected a reaction, so he was altogether wrongfooted when Fen... *smiled*. A tiny, reclusive thing. Not the bit of a flicker he'd given Samin that first day; not the sly thing he'd trotted out in some half-assed attempt at seduction down in the baths. A real smile, a Fen-smile: a warm curve of the mouth, and a small lightening of gray eyes. And all for Malick.

It should have pleased him, turned him smug. Instead, it made him uncomfortable.

Fen wasn't himself. And Malick needed him to be.

The poppy in that last elixir, Malick realized with a jolt that shouldn't have stung but did. He should have twigged first thing, once he'd had a look at Fen's eyes. None of this was real, and it likely wouldn't stick, once the effects wore off. The absurdly alluring vulnerability was like some kind of drug, going straight to Malick's head and blurring thought and sense, but it had to go. And Malick was going to have to *make* it go.

The low light spiked Fen's lashes into shadows like the spines of a clover's petals on his cheek. He looked so young, all soft and drowsy like this, defenseless without his shield of anger and the constant suggestion of violence just beneath his surface. His brow twitched; he licked his lips, opened his mouth, closed it, then:

"They're here?"

Considering all the phantoms with whom Fen had been conversing just recently, Malick shouldn't've understood the question.

"They're here. Safe. They're all asleep now, but they've been wanting to see you."

Fen lifted his gaze slowly, somber now, the strange little smile gone altogether. "No."

Malick should let it go. He should let Fen hold onto whatever safety to which he thought he was clinging. He should let Fen keep whatever illusions he'd invented in his delirium, and break them gently when Fen himself was less breakable.

He should do a lot of things he had no intention of doing.

Surrender without fracture—there was no other way this could work.

"You have to." Malick squeezed Fen's fingers. "They need to see you. They're leaving day after tomorrow."

And Malick would never get Joori in the bloody wagon if Fen wasn't the one sending Joori away.

Fen's eyes snapped open. "Leaving?"

"I told you I'd get them out."

"...Where?"

"Umeia's taking them to Heldesan. They'll be safe."

Fen shut his eyes, relief flowing out of him in a long, even breath. "Safe."

"Yes. Safe." Malick joggled Fen's hand. "But they need to see you first. They need to know you're all right."

Fen snorted, scornful. "Am I?" His mouth pressed tight. "No. I don't... just... no."

"After all this? Everything they've been through?" Malick bent his tone accusing. "They're your family. All you've got. You're all *they've* got." He paused, dropped his voice to a dulcet whisper. "Have you no feelings, Fen?"

Stirring embers and hoping to fan them into flames.

"Too damned many." Fen opened his eyes, all of a sudden overbright and piercing. "I wasn't always like this, y'know. I was a boy once. I wanted things." He shut his eyes again. Went silent. Like that said everything.

It was strange to imagine Fen as a child. Playing. Laughing. Hugging his mother, maybe, or even... no, not his father. Malick could imagine Joori doing all those things, somehow, but not Fen.

"You need to talk to Joori, at least," Malick told him, almost an order, really, but he shied from it at the last second.

Actually, Malick should talk to Fen first, put his own spin on everything before Joori got his nose wedged in, but... He wasn't going to. Some games Malick wouldn't play, and he'd be damned if he was going to allow that jealous twat to manipulate him.

"I don't want to." There was a tremor going through Fen's hand that hadn't been there before. "Stop. Just let me sleep, and... *stop*."

Ashamed, likely. Unable to face those who'd seen him at his worst. Fen was probably right now doubling and trebling what had happened in his head, and coming up with someone who didn't deserve what his brothers and sister wanted to give him. But Fen needed poking and prodding sometimes. He needed something to fight for. To live for.

Malick only hesitated for a second before he leaned in, laid a soft kiss to Fen's brow. "They love you."

Fen didn't open his eyes, didn't flinch or shake his head or clench his teeth. And still, Malick felt like he'd just kicked him when he was down. Too easy to see, now that he knew what he was looking at. Damn Shig, anyway.

"It hurts." Malick kept his voice soft, but his tone demanding. "Doesn't it?"

"You knew it would."

Malick had, but he was a little surprised to hear Fen admit it.

"It's too heavy." Fen pushed it out on a thin breath laced with pain and shame and more guilt than could belong to any one person.

Admittance—*I can't do this*—and one Malick never thought he'd hear, never thought Fen was capable of knowing, acknowledging, *permitting*. And once again, it made everything in his chest tighten and twist.

He wasn't talking to Fen now; he was talking to Jacin. Malick had wanted exactly this, only days ago.

Except Jacin was a man far too young who'd lost far too much, was in danger of losing even more, losing it all, too many fates yoked to his back. He wasn't equipped. It was breaking him.

No. It had already broken him. Malick had watched him shatter. Now Fen was groping about, trying to find all the pieces to put himself back together again. And failing.

Thing was, Malick knew what he was doing here. It was only that the doing was a little harder than he'd thought it would be.

"You don't have to do this alone." Malick slid his hand up to cup Fen's jaw. "This is bigger than you, Fen. You don't have to carry it all yourself."

A tear slipped from the corner of Fen's eye, meandered down the side of his nose. Malick swept it away with his thumb, and then the one that came after it.

"She was wrong," Fen said. "It isn't suicide."

Malick only hummed a noncommittal "Hmm." Because there was a lot Fen didn't know about himself, and Malick knew what a death wish looked like.

"It *isn't*." Fen's voice was steadier than it had been. He looked up, met Malick's gaze squarely. "She thinks she can read me, but she can't. She thinks she understands, but she doesn't."

"All right." Because Fen believed what he was saying, even if Malick didn't. "Then why don't you explain it to me?"

Fen looked away again, brow creasing in mild frustration. "I'll hold up my end." Not exactly an answer to Malick's question, but... maybe Fen thought it was. "I'll kill Asai. As soon as I can walk. I swore it and

I will. You can't let Umeia withdraw her oath if I die doing it. You *can't*."

Ah. That.

"And what comes after, Fen?"

By the way Fen's frown deepened and he lifted his gaze to Malick's, questioning, Malick thought it was quite likely Fen had never thought beyond "Save my family, kill Asai." Which was more of an answer than Malick thought he really wanted, but it wasn't anything he hadn't already had shoved in his face two nights ago, and then again this morning.

"When your mother's put to rest, when your brothers and sister are safe, when Asai is dead—what happens then?"

Fen dropped his gaze. "I don't know."

"No?" Malick's eyebrows rose. "You wanted to save the Jin once. Have you changed your mind?"

"It was shit fed to me that I swallowed because I was in l—" Fen clenched his teeth, shook it off. "The Jin can't be saved. And if they could, I'm not the one to do it. I'm no one's savior. I'm Untouchable. Mad. A Ghost."

"And yet I'm touching you." Malick thumbed away another tear. "You're the Voice of the Ancestors."

A spark of Fen pushed itself through Jacin's more temperate gaze. "Like I said—mad."

Malick had been waiting for it, gently guiding the conversation to this particular end point, laden with potential. True surrender; complete submission. He needed it, and he needed Fen to give it to him, and it had nothing to do with Malick's own ego this time. It was the only way he was going to be able to save Fen from himself. And strangely, that was right now more important than Umeia's doubts and perfidy, Asai's plots, Yakuli's significance, or even the Balance itself. Malick told himself it was because he needed Fen whole, unbroken, he needed that diamond inside Fen and he needed it deadly sharp.

"You're not mad, Fen. The Ancestors are. And I can help you." Malick pushed up onto his elbow, and rolled Fen to his back. Contrarily gentle, Malick laid his hand flat to Fen's scarred chest and pressed his palm in until he felt the rhythmic thump of Fen's heart. "I can help you make sense of it, Fen, but you have to let me hear it."

It was like Malick had just punched him in the gut. Fen shoved out a harsh breath, shut his eyes. His heart lurched beneath Malick's palm.

"So quiet." Fen pressed his mouth tight. "I *want*… I don't… *can't*—"

He went still. Everything did. Not even a breath spilled to warn Malick before Fen's arm snapped up and his hand latched onto Malick's nape, dragged him down. The move was too sudden, too importunate. Malick didn't have a chance to even try for leverage; his knee came up to brace himself and knocked into Fen's mangled leg.

Fen didn't even seem to notice, just pushed a harsh "*Please*" into

Malick's mouth, hoarse and grating. The kiss was rough, desperate, all *push* but no *give*, not even trying for affection or pleasure.

Malick went with it, allowed his mouth to open, accommodated without reserve or complaint when Fen's tongue pushed in. Harsh, Fen gripped a fistful of Malick's hair and tugged. Harsher still, Fen curled and coiled his spine until his hip pressed into Malick's groin. And when that didn't make Malick fuck him through the mattress, Fen tried latching onto Malick through his trousers. Except, instead of the rush of lust Fen no doubt intended, a rush of… something else hit Malick: anger mixed with a strange sort of hurt he couldn't fathom, and that twist in his chest clenched into a tight fist.

Damn it, he ought to give Fen what he was asking for, just to teach him a bloody lesson.

Except.

Umeia had lost count at forty-five when she'd stitched up the mangled mess that was Fen's leg. Leu's idiots had taken an actual chunk out of his calf muscle, and miraculous healing or no, it *had* to still be hurting him. There'd been another twenty or so stitches to his arm. And he'd spent nearly two days in fever-induced delirium. He'd been awake less than half an hour, and already, he was trying to get around Malick by throwing sex at him like he'd throw a dog a bone. Fen had some pretty fucked up ideas about what sex was for, and Malick had no intention of proving him right.

Malick pulled back—and how had *he* got to be the one who was apparently bent on some convoluted idea of honor here?—kept pulling back even as Fen's grip tightened, strengthened. It was less a half-assed seduction now, and more of a fight. Fen's other hand came up, latched onto Malick's shirt, and bunched it into a grip Malick wouldn't have thought Fen capable of, not after how sick he'd been, how weak.

Fen clenched his teeth, shunted out "*Please*" between them, furious and forlorn, all at the same time.

Malick was not a man who said no very often. He wasn't liking it now.

"*Fen.*" Almost a shout. "I'm not going to take it from you. I won't take away the quiet."

He wasn't sure Fen even heard him. The struggle didn't stop, the grip didn't loosen. Until Fen's gaze caromed away, looking for escape, perhaps, then settled quite suddenly on the cupboard beside the bed. Hung there. Everything about him went still, except his face; it twisted into the shapes of alarm first, then shuddered into outraged misery.

Malick frowned and followed Fen's stare, but all he saw was the lamp and a dead moth lying beneath it.

"Oh," Fen said, stricken, and he… sagged. He turned his head and looked up at Malick. The animosity and distrust all but punched Malick in the face.

"I won't take it from you." Malick kept it soft, steady. "Not until you're ready. And when you're ready, I'll give you a way to keep it if you want to, a way for you to choose. But you *will* have to listen. You *will* have to let me hear what you hear."

"Everything's a fucking trade, isn't it?" Rage was sliding into Fen's eyes, but the despondency still had too firm a foothold to let it bloom. "*Temshiel, maijin*, Balance, like I'm supposed to give a fuck. You'll save them if I kill Asai. You'll give me the quiet if I—" Fen's jaw clenched, chin trembling, and he was too obviously trying desperately to hold back the tears that were already trickling down his temples. "I would've anyway. I was all right, I didn't know what I was even *missing* anymore, I'd forgotten what quiet was *like*, and then you... you... *damn you!*" His fingers at Malick's nape dug in painfully, and his face twisted in resentment and betrayal. "*I would have done it anyway!* You didn't have to... have to *do* this to me, I would've—"

"Fen, this isn't—"

"—killed him already if you just left me the fuck *alone*, and I don't want to listen anymore." Fen's grip on Malick loosened, but he didn't let go. "I can't." Flat, steady, but fear rumbled beneath it. "You ruined it. If I have to hear it I'll be as mad as they are."

"Not if you let me help you." Malick's tone was as gentle and persuasive as he could make it, because if he tried to force this, Fen probably really would lose his mind altogether, and for good this time. Malick shouldn't care, not if Fen still did what Malick needed him to do, but—"I won't let it happen. It won't send you mad. Not if you let me show you." Malick set a hand to Fen's cheek, heartened when Fen merely closed his eyes and didn't jerk away. "You trusted me this far. Just a little more."

"I've never trusted you." Detached—no true insult, just a flat statement of fact.

It should have pissed Malick off, but it didn't. Because there was a lot Fen didn't know about himself. And Jacin trusted everyone, no matter how they repeatedly gutted him for it.

"D'you even have feelings? D'you have *any idea* what you've—?" Fen's tone was dull, despondent, but not broken. *Not* broken. "You're not even pretending. You *said* you'd pretend. That was the deal."

The defeated rebuke in it was like a fine-honed blade slipping through Malick's ribs. He couldn't speak.

"Did you do it on purpose?" Bitterness was seeping into Fen's soft voice, twisting it harder. "Did you give it to me just so you could take it away? Make me beg so you could refuse?"

Like it had done when Joori had spat an accusation too similar, it curled anger in Malick's gut, only this time it was laced through with that same odd hurt he'd felt a moment ago, sharper now. Resonant. And he had no idea why.

Not broken. The anger inside Fen's indictment proved it. That was the important thing. Malick repeated that to himself—twice. He should be feeling quite satisfied. He felt rather vile.

"Whose dog are you, Fen?" Malick made his tone gentler than the harsh question should merit.

Fen looked away, gaze sliding to the moth's husk again, hollow. Slowly, he let go of both Malick's neck and his shirt, arms flopping boneless to the mattress.

"Yours, it seems." Emotionless. Gaze still glued to the dead moth on the cupboard. Then, quiet, "Fuck you."

Painful to look at, this surrender. But necessary.

Mine, Malick thought, bleak with anger that had no real direction and self-rebuke that most certainly did. But still—*Mine*.

Somehow, it didn't have the sweet ring to it he'd been imagining

⊤⊤

Everything hurt. It seemed like the ghost of every wound Jacin had ever had was rising up to haunt him. He couldn't recall it ever affecting him this way before. He couldn't recall ever *feeling* it like this before. Maybe it was because he didn't have the screeching to distract him. Maybe it was because his hurts were scattered, too many, when always before there'd been a single, neat pinpoint of near-sanity.

Maybe there was just too much room in his head now, and his mind was trying to fill up the corners left empty by the quiet.

Jacin shunted a growl to the back of his throat, and tried not to enjoy the swath of heat at his back, the steady breaths rhythmically swaying him in a cadence that should probably induce sleep, but he'd been doing that for almost two days, and there were things he had to do. He'd got lightheaded when Malick helped him down the hall to the too-small washroom they all shared, and that was just not on. So he'd eaten the noodles and cabbage with broth Malick told him to eat, drank the tea and cherry elixir Malick told him to drink, obedient and compliant. All the while keeping a hold, making sure a hold was kept on him, beyond humiliation now, personal space a thing of the past, and Jacin... was somehow all right with it.

Like the trained dog Malick wouldn't shut up about.

Shouldn't that... take a swipe at Jacin's pride, or something?

...Did he have any?

Clearly, he was incapable of functioning on his own. Quite frankly, Jacin couldn't understand why Malick thought he might be useful. He'd already failed to kill Asai twice, and damn Shig to the suns for exposing those failures so cruelly.

Still. Jacin's family was here and safe. At least one promise Malick had kept. And if Jacin didn't hold up his end...

An involuntary shudder wracked through him. He rode it out, waited for all the flares and throbs of his body to settle back down to their steady sharp hum.

Not *his* pain, that was what this was, why it refused to check itself like it had always done before. It wasn't his, it had been inflicted by someone else, and he'd had no control over it. Somehow, that distinction took it from pain to *pain*.

There was something profound in there somewhere, probably. Jacin had no idea what.

Brittle. He felt brittle. Cold, frosted over and breakable.

He opened his eyes, squinting against the low-wicked lamplight, gaze going immediately to the dead moth on the cupboard. He couldn't stop staring at it, like it was supposed to mean something to him, but if it was, he'd forgotten. He wished he could turn over, but the trip to the toilet had nearly undone him, and he'd been trying his best not to move too much since he'd been dumped back to the mattress with a groan. Anyway, if he turned over, he wouldn't be able to pretend the body at his back was some nameless, faceless someone who wanted nothing more from him than his presence. He'd be forced to acknowledge he was actually sleeping with Malick, and *liking* it, and pretty much willing to do anything to keep Malick and what he offered right where he was.

Damn it. If there was anything at all good about a scattered mind and constantly trying to concentrate through too much noise, it was that it only allowed Jacin to focus on one thing at a time. Now that there was no noise, his own thoughts shrieked just as loudly as the Ancestors ever had. And made just as much sense.

He'd forgotten how to think like a normal person. Every thought brought corresponding emotion with it. He hated it. Poked warily at its edges, tried to find focal points inside it, but his mind wouldn't stop going where he didn't want it to go. It was too much.

He blew a soft breath at the moth, watched its ragged wings stir, flutter, then still.

"You're luckier than you know."

Realized what he'd said and rolled his eyes. No wonder Shig accused him of attempted suicide.

"It isn't suicide."

It wasn't. Jacin wasn't done yet. And if he died before he'd kept up his end of Malick's bargain, who knew what would happen to his family? *Temshiel* weren't exactly known for their concern for mortals. Passage out of Ada was already arranged, thank every god—but if Jacin didn't do what he'd promised, he had no illusions the bargain would hold. He couldn't die yet. Shig was right about at least that, though Jacin was loath to admit it: dying would be a failure right now.

Living is your sacrifice.

He remembered that from… somewhere. Probably because it felt so true. It made him tired all over again.

Your emotions make you weak and foolish, little Ghost.

"Yes," he whispered to the moth, "I know."

He'd tried and failed countless times to kill them. And yet.

When have you ever failed at anything?

Jacin clenched his teeth, hands fisting.

Every time you say something like that is another failure, he thought bleakly. *Fuck, Joori, how have you managed to stay so innocent?*

And when had innocence become something to both resent and envy?

The rain lashed against the window. It stirred a memory-scent of cherry blossoms from somewhere. Jacin imagined them swirling on the wind, making abstract patterns of pink-tinged white, settling over everything like a warm, silent blanket. It comforted him, though he had a vague idea it shouldn't, but he'd apparently just recently become a person who took any comfort offered to him, regardless of price, so he ignored the uneasy confusion.

A creak of floorboards in the hallway made him squint through the gloom, watching as the door slid ajar, and a sliver of light spilled in around the small figure that peered in. He'd been expecting Umeia. He'd've been fractionally happier to see her than he was to see Caidi.

"Jacin?" Caidi's small, high voice was pitched to a low whisper in the dark. "Are you awake?"

Jacin shut his eyes and pretended he wasn't. He couldn't see her, couldn't face her, couldn't face any of them. Didn't they know what he was? Why did they keep coming back to be shown again?

"Jacin?" Closer now, and a little bit wobbly. There were throttled tears inside it. "I had a bad dream."

Predictably, Jacin's heart gave a little twist, because that was the way it always was with Caidi. He remembered her as a chubby little toddler, all golden curls and sunny smiles, and clinging arms around his calves. Giggles, and bright hazel eyes that Jacin now couldn't help imagining dull and dead. His mind instinctively shied away from it, curled inward, because perhaps if he stopped loving, he'd stop hurting.

Except he couldn't. Caidi had hardly changed at all—still bright as the suns and constant smiles, and an adoration in her eyes that made Jacin want to howl. He *had* to love her; she gave him no choice.

"Jacin? Please?"

Jacin braced himself, and opened his eyes. No blood in her hair, no empty eyes that still somehow mocked and accused at the same time. Just a little girl who'd had a bad dream, a doll clutched to her chest, and her heart in her eyes.

Jacin licked dry lips. "Are you all right?"

Tears spilled down Caidi's full cheeks, and *still*, she smiled—all wobbly and full of trying. She took a hesitant step closer.

"I had a bad dream."

"Shh, you're all right." Jacin didn't ask what it was about. He didn't think he wanted to know. "Why don't you climb in with Joori?"

Caidi picked at the yellow curls on her doll's head. "He's sleeping on the couch down the hall."

"The couch?" Jacin frowned, but it didn't seem worth trying to decipher. "What about Morin?"

A scowl pursed Caidi's bow lips and crinkled her brow into much older shapes. It was sweetly incongruous on her little face.

"He doesn't let me sleep with him, and anyway, he kicks." Caidi peered at Jacin with wide eyes—blink… blink… blink—with just the right amount of tears collecting at the corners, and dropped her trilling imp's voice down to a pathetic murmur: "*Pleeeeeease?*"

Jacin almost laughed. Because Caidi knew exactly what she was doing. She proved it when she grinned as he sighed and lifted the covers, all hints of tears and trembling lips instantly evaporating as she carefully climbed in. The exaggerated care with which she made sure not to bump any of the too-numerous bandages swathed over leg, arm, and torso touched Jacin all unwilling, and his throat burned.

Malick stirred, slid an unconscious squeeze around Jacin's ribs, ghosted a soft indecipherable mutter into his nape, and the warmth at his back and the warmth at his front did things inside Jacin that felt too much like some kind of rapture, bright and pristine and shocking for its novelty. Unaccountably, Jacin's eyes filled.

He cleared his throat. "Have enough room?"

In answer, Caidi burrowed into his chest, the chill porcelain of the doll between them, and pushed her head beneath his chin, like a cat butting at its owner for a thorough stroking. Jacin couldn't help but oblige. His hand lifted all by itself, laid a caress to her hair, fingers idly toying with the wave and curl of individual strands, the twinge it stirred under the bandage on his arm only a faint nuisance.

"Are you better now?" Caidi's whisper was light and warm against Jacin's throat. "Joori thought you were going to die, I could tell, and anyway, he *always* worries about *everything*, but Umeia-onna said you weren't, and Malick-seyh was sad this morning, so I worried a little bit, too, but then he said at suppertime that you were getting better really quickly, and he wouldn't let you die, and he's got magic, after all, so I felt better." All of it said in one breath in a low murmur as Caidi's hand crept about until it found Jacin's and latched on.

Jacin's head was spinning, but he found the wit to whisper, "Yes, I'm better now," even though it felt like a lie, so he amended it with "I'm not going to die," and left it there.

"Good. I'd miss you. And anyway, who would take care of us then?"

It was like a knife in the chest. "Joori would take care of you." Said less with soothing assurance for Caidi than desperate shame for himself. Take care of them? Was that what she thought Jacin had been doing?

"Joori can't kill the monsters like you can." Caidi's small fingers squeezed around two of Jacin's. "I wish you could be in my dream. You could've killed the monsters for me, and then I wouldn't've cried."

She had to shut up. Jacin had to get her to *shut up*.

"It was just a dream." Jacin only just kept the tremor from his voice, though he'd tensed again and reminded his body it was torn up and hurting. He tried to concentrate on the pain, instead of the things coming out his little sister's mouth.

"Mother always said there's no such thing as 'just dreams'," Caidi informed him sagely. "She dreamed once that Tai-onna died, and she really did, and Mother said she knew because she'd talked to her ghost in a dream, but Father told her she couldn't say things like that out loud. She dreamed about me once, too, but she said she couldn't tell me what it was because it would be like sealing my fate and it wasn't her place to seal anyone's but her own. D'you want to know what she dreamed about you?"

"Caidi…" Jacin couldn't keep the tremble from his voice this time. "I don't think—"

"She dreamed you were walking in cherry blossom petals." Caidi's tone was warm, almost excited. "She said they were deep as snow, and you were limping, but you were smiling too. She said there was a big wolf walking with you, and it growled at her until you told it not to, and then you hugged her and told her it didn't hurt anymore."

Bloody hell, his mother must have deteriorated steadily over the years if she'd taken to telling her tiny daughter her dreams.

"Caidi, go to *sleep*." If Jacin's throat wasn't so tight, it would have come out as a bark. This was somehow worse than Shig's rambling accusations.

"But it made her *happy*, Jacin. And maybe she dreamed about those bad maijin hurting you, because you were limping, and I bet you'd limp now if you tried to walk, but you told Mother it didn't hurt anymore, so it must be going to be all—"

"Sleep, Wolf's daughter," Malick murmured. His hand had come up to rest at Caidi's brow, and Jacin hadn't even noticed, but he didn't chide himself for his lack of attention or his agitation, nor did he snarl at Malick for the liberty. Caidi's chatter abruptly stopped, and her small body sagged into the mattress, rolling into Jacin's chest, limp in deep sleep.

Jacin should be angry. He should be outraged. He should be plotting Malick's death for even touching Caidi.

He was relieved. And ashamed because he was relieved, and it all rose again to choke him.

"I…" He couldn't get any words out. He couldn't shove Malick away from him and protect his little sister. He couldn't drag his hand from Caidi's. He couldn't do anything at all but lie there and shake.

"Shh." Malick set his hand to Jacin's cheek, stroking lightly, then to the crown of his head and on down his arm, over and over again, skimming over the bandage with gentle fingertips. "You don't have to say things, if you don't know how." He slipped a tender, sleepy kiss just beneath Jacin's ear. "I know it hurts. You don't know how to be anything but damaged, so you run away from the pure things people offer you until they corner you with love and there's no place to run anymore. But it's really the running bit that does the hurting."

Jacin heard it, but couldn't make any real sense of it. He had a vague idea it should piss him off—*right, because you know me so well*—and he could feel a comforting rage pooling in his gut, but he couldn't take hold of it.

"You can't stand to be content," Malick went on, gently relentless, "because you don't understand it, and things you don't understand frighten the hell out of you."

Bloody hell, was *every*one a fucking oracle?

Jacin's teeth clenched. "I don't—"

"I know you don't." Malick stretched against Jacin's back and nestled in closer. "That's all right. I'll show you."

"Show me *what?*" Jacin snapped, too loud, but it didn't make Caidi even twitch, and Malick didn't answer, the steady rise and fall of his chest against Jacin's back speaking sleep, as though the past two minutes hadn't even happened.

Maybe they hadn't. Maybe Jacin was dead after all, and this was what it was like to have been sent to the suns—not the blissful oblivion of nothing at all, but enforced life that you couldn't make sense of, but went on and on and on. Maybe Shig had driven him completely insane and this was all the twisted conjuring of his own sick, guilty mind. Maybe he was still unconscious and delirious, lying on the road in Asai's lands in the rain, the torn corpses of everyone he loved scattered around him.

Maybe he was wounded and sick and exhausted, and living with silence for the first time in years. Maybe this was what sanity was like, and he'd just forgotten.

"If this is what sanity's like," he muttered, cutting a grim glance at the corpse of the moth, "I think I retract my wish for it."

Malick tightened his arm around Jacin's ribs. "Too late now."

"Oh, for—" A growl rolled up Jacin's throat, and he let it come. "Just shut up and go to sleep."

Thankfully, Malick did.

4

The rain, Samin decided as he stared moodily out his small window, was only making things worse. And if there was one thing he'd learned over the years, it was that things could always get worse.

The revelation that he'd been working for a *Temshiel* all these years had been somewhat staggering, certainly, but it rather put some things Samin hadn't really thought about before into perspective. That icy look Malick could get sometimes, like all his emotions had just dried up and he could kill you without giving it a second thought, regardless of the years and experiences between you. How they'd walked away from every job over the years without serious damage, even those they shouldn't've walked away from at all. How Samin had only rarely seen Malick use magic, but when he had, it had been a different sort every time, like Malick had every kind there was, and Samin had never been able to pin down exactly what Malick was—spiritbound, earthbound, elemental-bound… Apparently, Malick could do it all. It made sense, now, once you added in the word *Temshiel*.

Unexpected, certainly, but then Samin had been more or less making an effort not to see it, so it hadn't been shocking.

Lord Asai a maijin? *That* had been shocking, but again, it had put Fen's apparent past with him somewhat into perspective. Samin couldn't exactly blame the lad for getting as deeply entangled as it seemed he'd done, not when the man entangling him was centuries old and made to manipulate. It made Samin glad Malick hadn't allowed him to kill Fen that first night in the alley. He liked to think his kills were morally justi-fied, that he served the gods in some way by doing what he did. Killing Fen for what had been made of him, what he'd been duped into being, would've been an injustice. Samin didn't need more black marks on his soul. Anyway, he truly liked Fen, which had made the business of the other night actually hurt, and Samin hadn't thought that possible.

Now, the business of the other night—getting attacked by a pack of not-wolf maijin, and then watching Shig drive Fen into some kind of mental break—that was pushing things. Samin had worried that first night they'd taken Fen in the alley that Fen had the potential to be a real danger to Malick. Now he thought perhaps Malick was the bigger danger to Fen, and that if Fen one of these days put a knife through Malick's heart, it would be because Malick deserved it.

Samin's jaw clenched.

And yet, none of the recent events and revelations had shaken Samin's resolve to see it all through. What he'd seen at Yakuli's had, if not shaken it, at least wobbled it. Warhorses, gates and guard towers, barracks, and… more barracks. Something more was there, something big, Samin knew it, but he couldn't set it in its proper shape in his mind. And Shig's reaction… *that* had shaken him. She knew a hell of a lot more than she was saying, and everyone else was too preoccupied to notice. Malick was more obsessed with Fen than usual, Yori was so sickeningly smitten with Joori that Samin had taken to avoiding them both, and Umeia…

Fuck.

Samin quit the room, and stalked down the hall to the common room. It was Shig and Yori's turn to bring up breakfast, and he saw when he got there that they'd already done so, everyone already seated and digging in.

Caidi called a cheery "G'morning, Samin-seyh!" and he couldn't help but smile back at her. He nodded at the more subdued greetings from the others, his gaze turning to Shig, not at all surprised when he noted she was looking at him expectantly and hadn't bothered to fill her plate yet. And Samin hadn't even known he was going to do this until ten minutes ago.

Shig lifted an eyebrow. "Ready when you are."

Samin merely grimaced, and poured a cup of tea to take with him. "Anyone take them breakfast yet?" He kept his eyes on his hands as he added honey, but he'd have to be blind to miss the abrupt tension in the set of Joori's shoulders.

"I was hoping—"

"You will." Samin stirred his tea. "Shig and I have some business to discuss first, but you have my word that you won't be kept from your brother today." Samin didn't give a shit what Malick's reasons were for keeping Joori at bay. It wasn't right, and Samin'd had enough.

Joori subsided.

Yori, however, had turned suspicious. "What business?"

"Business we can't discuss here." Samin shunted a pointed look around the table, again a little thrown by Caidi's sudden but very sincere smile when he caught her eye. Save him, she was so bloody cute, and always happy to see him. If Malick was half as smitten with Fen as Samin was with Caidi, they were probably all in some very deep shit.

Yori half stood. "Should I—?"

"No." Samin turned the remnants of the smile Caidi had prompted to Yori, and then darted a quick look at Joori. Winked. "You keep everyone else company, yeah? We'll fill you in later."

Yori sat back down with a slight blush. All the better. With things out of kilter between Malick and Umeia… well, Samin didn't know. Yori had been circumspect enough not to tell Joori yet that they'd found his mother—there would've been a hell of a scene already if she had—but there was always a chance Yori would take up for Umeia in whatever this falling-out had been. Samin didn't like to think loyalties might be split, but Yori had always been Umeia's devotee, and her new involvement with Fen's brother might end up being a problem. Best Samin leave this one to Malick.

Anyway, Yori didn't seem to mind the slight. She didn't even seem to realize there'd been one. If Samin was not very much mistaken, she and Joori were actually holding hands under the table. Samin rolled his eyes. Apparently, regular sex made one's brain go all slushy. Then again, that was hardly a revelation—look at Malick.

Samin gave Shig a rough nudge. "Let's go."

Shig merely tilted a faraway smile, tossed an oblate absently from hand to hand, and gestured to the tray at the end of the table. Two covered dishes, two teabowls and a teapot, with all the necessary trappings. Samin tried not to see it as further evidence that Shig was at least one step ahead of him in everything. He only bit his tongue, and took up the tray, sparing a nod all around as Shig sauntered past him and down the hall.

"Bye, Samin-seyh!" Caidi chirped.

Samin merely grunted and followed Shig to Fen's door. She didn't pause for the courtesy of a knock, but slid the door open and turned to Samin, tossed the oblate lightly in the air and caught it with a small shrug. The eerie little smile she'd been sporting tweaked just slightly 'til it took on a hint of… malice. That was definitely malice.

"Hey!" Malick's voice was still a little sleep-scratchy. "Don't you people bloody *knock*?"

Shig was blocking the way into the room. Samin only lifted an eyebrow. Waited. He really wasn't in the mood for her games, and they *were* games. The other night on the road had been too carefully calculated for her to not have known what she was doing. "Heeding the spirits" Samin's great ass, and even if she had been, a person just didn't *do* the sort of thing she'd done to Fen. It was things like that—the *abuse* of what some called a "gift"—that made Samin hate the idea of magic.

"Don't look at *me*." Shig tossed and caught the oblate again, outwardly insouciant but her green eyes were glinting borderline cruel. "This one's all on you." She leaned up, lowered her voice so she was almost whispering in Samin's ear. "Who d'you think'll be left to deal with the afters? Shall we take bets?"

Funny. Things that, perhaps a week ago, Samin had thought a little unnerving but mostly cute and "just Shig" were suddenly grating on his nerves like sandpaper on sunburn.

He set his jaw. "Out of the way."

Shig merely shrugged, pushed the door wider, and stepped aside.

Samin's expression was probably fairly thunderous as he stalked into the room. He didn't care.

He was surprised that Malick was the one in the bed, and that he was in it alone. Fen sat slumped in the chair beside it, thick-bandaged leg set stiffly in front of him, extended far enough that his toes remained in contact with Malick's hip. Malick blinked blearily, propped against the pillows. He was fully dressed but for his boots. Fen was clad only in linen drawers and an open tunic that exposed the swathes of bandages around his torso, but hid the one Samin knew had to be around his right arm. Samin had watched one of those things latch onto Fen's arm and shake its head like a terrier with a rat; Fen had merely snatched his arm out of the clamped jaws without much apparent concern that he was leaving chunks of meat behind. It had to be almost as messy as his leg.

Samin cleared his throat. "You're looking better." It was... mostly true. Fen still looked like death, but still better than Samin had been expecting him to. "More color to you."

Fen didn't answer, didn't even spare Samin a glance. His gaze was nailed to Shig, all narrow and murderously hostile, but with a glint of fear beneath the glare. Samin understood and was immediately sorry for it, but he'd had no choice—Malick wouldn't leave the room, and this couldn't wait anymore.

Samin set the tray on the edge of the bed, lifted the cover on one of the plates, and shoved it at Malick. The other made him pause—a neat mound of rice in the center, a bowl of broth to one side and a slice of bread with honey on the other. There was a soft chirp of a whistle from Shig, and when Samin looked over, she tossed him the oblate she'd been playing with. Samin didn't know who'd filled the tray for Fen, but now he suspected it was Shig, and the incongruity of the thoughtfulness of the gesture threw him.

For five seconds. Because whatever. One small kindness didn't change anything.

Samin poured some tea and carried it and Fen's breakfast over to him. The tea Samin set on the little bedside cupboard, within easy reach, but the rest he set right in Fen's lap, said, Eat," and purposely blocked Fen's line of sight to Shig.

Samin was still trying to out-glare Fen into compliance when Malick spoke up behind him.

"Shig, I need you to go down to Umeia's room and get me something."

Samin scowled. "We're here for a reason, Mal. I think—"

"Yeah, I gathered. And you'll have your say, but I need this first." Malick jerked his chin at Shig. "Umeia's got a ring in the little black-lacquered chest she's got on her vanity. A thick gold band with a diamond set in a bed of onyx. You'll know it when you see it."

"And what shall I say if Umeia—?"

"She won't. Anyway, it's mine. Do it now."

Shig looked unhappy but not surprised as she quietly let herself out.

Samin turned to Fen. "I promised Joori he could come see you after we're done."

He'd expected an objection from Malick, but there wasn't one, just a sideways glance at Fen then a lift of eyebrows at Samin. Nothing at all from Fen but absent picking at the rind of the oblate. His head was bowed, stringy fringe hanging over his eyes.

After a moment, Malick sighed, hand absently moving to settle over Fen's foot. Fen didn't kick it off. Malick's gaze was even when he turned it on Samin.

"They should all come see him when we're done. They're leaving tomorrow."

Samin's mouth tightened. "And they don't know it yet."

"No."

"Damn it, Mal." Samin nearly groaned, several things clicking into place. "Umeia's taking them." That explained her apparent upcoming trip, at least.

"Yes." Malick's tone was flat this time, borderline hostile.

"Are you going to tell me what happened?" More to the point: did Samin really want to know?

Malick scraped a hand roughly through his hair. With a weary sigh, he set his untouched breakfast to the side and leaned forward to pour himself a bowl of tea from the tray at the foot of the bed.

"A long time ago..." Malick trailed off. Mouth pursed, he sat back, took a quick sip of tea, hand going once again to settle over Fen's foot. "A *very* long time ago, Asai managed to get hold of *Temshiel* Blood. The circumstances matter, but I'm not in the mood to go into them now. The long and short of it is that he's been using that Blood to make amulets for the Adan hunters. The *Temshiel* who..." Malick scrubbed a hand over his face. "The *Temshiel* who *donated* the Blood was a Null. Like me." He shot a glance at Fen, and when Fen just sat there, head down, Malick turned back to Samin. "With the right spells, the amulets can take away the magic of another. It's how the hunters can snatch their victims without getting set on fire or buried in a sudden earthquake."

Samin frowned. He'd always wondered how the Jin who fell to the hunters had done so without much resistance. Like most things, he hadn't wondered too deeply, and a flush burned at his face as he realized he'd more or less written it off to innate weakness in the Jin. He flashed a discomfited glance at Fen, but Fen seemed perfectly content to just slouch in the ugly chair and make crosshatch scores in the rind of the oblate with his thumbnail.

Malick huffed a cynical snort. "Asai is apparently not satisfied with the power in his hands. He wants more. He intends to get himself Heart's Blood from a *Temshiel*." He shot another glance at Fen then back to Samin, his gaze steady. "Fen was supposed to get it for him."

Heart's Blood. Not something one could bleed from another's veins, not if it was what it sounded like.

Samin's eyes narrowed. "How—?"

"From a *Temshiel's* still-beating heart."

It rather confirmed the grisly picture that had been forming unwilling in Samin's mind. That crone had almost said as much just the other day, but Samin had hoped maybe it was some kind of maudlin euphemism. Now that he knew it wasn't...

Samin shot a speculative look at Fen.

Malick seemed to know what Samin was thinking. "He wasn't told who he was supposed to kill." His tone was patient, almost gentle. "He was told only that playing the part Asai instructed him to play would save the Jin."

All right. Now the rest of that strange conversation between Malick and the crone made a whole lot more sense. Take the power of the *Temshiel* and Asai would set himself up as a demigod—that was the conclusion drawn then, and it seemed the most reasonable, Samin supposed. But now the situation at Yakuli's made even less sense.

"Asai must've seen that it wouldn't work." Even as he said it, Samin was trying to wend through the maze of the circumstances presented. "If Yakuli is his man, Asai must've foreseen something that would make him start building that army he's got. It's not a new thing. What Yakuli's got going on out there has been going on for a long time."

There it was again, fizzing at the base of Samin's spine. There was something too wrong about it all, but he just couldn't lay hands on it.

"You're assuming Yakuli is Asai's man." Fen lifted his head for the first time since Samin had come in. "What if it's the other way around? What if Asai's sight has been blocked, and he doesn't know anything about it?"

Samin frowned at Malick. "Is that possible?"

Malick shrugged. "If Yakuli's got enough spiritbounds covering his footprints in Fate." He clearly didn't believe it, though.

Fen's gaze snapped over to Malick. "The man who... who came to Asai for amulets." His fingers tightened around the oblate until pink juice ran between the fissures in the skin he'd made with his fingernail. "He was on horseback. And he spoke as though Asai was his servant."

"Or like he *thought* Asai was his servant. If Yakuli thinks Asai works for him, believe me, Asai's got a reason for it. Asai serves no one, not even the gods, unless he absolutely has to."

Fen took this in silently, and with no outward reaction. His hollow gaze shifted slowly to Samin.

"What did you see at Yakuli's?"

Was my mother there? It was what the question really meant.

Samin peered at Malick, waiting for direction. Malick gave him a slight nod that only made Samin's throat go a little dry. Damn it, why did people keep giving Samin meaningful looks, like he had any say in *any* of this?

"Shig said she's there." Samin made it as gentle as he could. "I'm not sure how she knows, but she was damned sure."

Malick waved at the door. "She's hovering outside in the hall. I suppose we should let her tell us."

His gaze cut over to Samin's, unreadable, before shifting back to the door just as Shig slid it open and stepped through. Samin wasn't sure he'd ever actually seen Shig look uncomfortable before, but by the hard look Malick was pointing at her, and the way her gaze looked all too knowing, if a little chagrined, Samin suspected she'd just been caught "listening."

Shig's guilty shrug all but confirmed it. "I know what her spirit tastes like." Her gaze went to Fen, though Fen missed the genuine sympathy in it, because he wouldn't look up. "It's in your own Blood. She tastes like you."

Samin couldn't help the way his mouth twisted. "You've tasted Fen's *blood*?" The revulsion was no doubt in his voice, and he couldn't suppress the shudder.

Shig ignored him, watching Fen with soft sympathy, so at odds with the way she'd been behaving just lately. "Shall I tell you what she—?"

"*No!*" Fen's jaw was clenched, but even that couldn't stop it quivering. "Yes." He shook his head. "I... I don't know."

Lips pursed and brow twisted in compassion, Shig stepped slowly to the bed, though she didn't round it to stand near Fen. Instead, she sidled over to Malick, held out her hand, and when he lifted his own, palm-up, she dropped a thick, glittering ring into it.

"Umeia didn't say anything."

Malick closed his hand around the ring. "I didn't expect her to."

Samin again wanted to ask what was going on between Malick and Umeia, but it seemed like it wasn't the right time. Instead, he tried to be patient as he waited for whatever Shig's newest drama was to play out.

Shig crouched down, leaned an elbow on the side of the mattress, and leveled her gaze with Fen, though Fen refused to look up.

"I won't say unless you ask it." Shig's voice was soft, uncharacteristically compassionate. "It's yours to choose."

Fen's gaze finally jerked up, bitter and angry. "Since when has what I wanted meant a damn to you?"

"Since always."

Shig leaned in, right over Malick's knees, like Malick wasn't even there anymore. Samin had the uncomfortable notion that he and Malick had just gone completely invisible.

"You don't want to know, but you have to, yeah?" Shig shook her head. "Poor Fen."

Almost condescending, but... not. Still, it made Samin uneasy, like he should be coming to Fen's defense for something he didn't even really understand yet. Malick caught his eye, intent, and gave a minute shake of his head.

Fen said nothing, just stared at Shig, stone-faced.

Shig seemed to think she understood what it meant, because she gave Fen that sad smile she'd been flashing around recently. "Maybe later, yeah? After Mal's done what he should've done days ago."

"You—" Malick jerked his knee, and knocked Shig off him. "You can be a real bitch sometimes, you know?"

Shig blinked, all wide-eyed innocence. "And you can be a lazy, stubborn bastard when there's something in it for you." She turned to Fen. "You can't ever trust him all the way. He could've given it to you when you made your promise, but he had his reasons for waiting."

Malick glared. "Yeah. I did. So why don't you just shut the fuck up, if you're not going to say anything helpful?"

Fen looked like he wasn't quite tracking everything they were saying, or what it might mean, but he didn't open his mouth to ask.

Samin wasn't quite getting it either, but—"Give him what?" Because there was a time for restraint, and now was not it.

Shig mimed shutting her mouth with lock and key, and sat back on her heels on the floor.

Malick's fists were both clenched as tight as his jaw, but when he turned back to Fen, he made a visible effort at relaxing. He held the ring up so the diamond gleamed in the lamplight, its bed of onyx giving it the relief it needed to practically dazzle the eye.

"See that?" Malick was looking only at Fen. "The flaw in the center—look deep." He reached out, snatched up Fen's hand, turned it over, and dropped the ring into his palm.

Fen gave Malick a wary scowl as he took the ring, but he did as Malick told him to. He squinted as he held it up in front of the lamp.

"It isn't a flaw."

"No. It isn't. It's my Blood. I don't give it lightly. This is how Skel damned himself. One talisman, one person I must choose very carefully." Malick set his teeth, as though bracing. He tilted his head until Fen met his eye. "Wear it, if you like, or keep it in a pocket, but keep it *safe*. You don't know what I risk handing this over." He sat back, clearly unhappy with what he was doing, but doing it anyway. "It's not as strong as touch, but it'll keep things quieter than what you can do yourself with the pain. It's yours for as long as our bargain stands, and if you keep your end, it's yours for as long as you want it." He slanted a harsh glower at Shig. "Happy now?"

Shig lifted an eyebrow. "Well, I'm not done yet, am I?"

"Gods on their moons." Samin threw his hands up. "Can *someone* speak plainly for once? What the fuck is she not done with? What the fuck is going on with you and Umeia? What the fuck are we going to do about Yakuli and Fen's mother, and what the *fuck* are we going to do about Asai?"

Malick shot another sour glance at Shig. "She's not done because I want her here when Fen lets me hear the Ancestors." Fen stiffened, but Malick didn't pause. "Umeia decided that Asai may have a point in what he's been plotting. I disagreed. Therefore, she's no longer welcome here." He opened a hand when Samin let a gasp slip loose. "She's taking Morin and Caidi and Joori to Heldesan in the morning, and she's not coming back." He shifted his gaze to Fen again, softer this time. "It's Fen's to decide about his mother, and I have to think a bit more about Yakuli. As far as Asai..." Malick shrugged. "Fen's agreed to take care of him for me."

Samin eyed Fen dubiously. Not that he had any doubt Fen was skilled enough, but... he didn't look like he was entirely capable just now. There were more bandages showing than there was skin, after all, and the other night... Well, it was still fresh and somehow terribly raw.

Fen wasn't even listening, really—he'd been scrutinizing the ring since Malick dropped it in his palm, and now he was slowly inching his foot away from Malick, the ring held in white-tipped fingers and face screwed up in skeptical hope. A long, bracing breath preceded the complete removal of contact. Fen's eyes shut tight as he went still, breath held.

Samin wasn't the only one staring; Malick and Shig had both turned to watch, their expressions remarkably similar—hopeful but nearly as cautious as Fen's.

It was almost as though a great, silent sigh went through the room when Fen went loose, closed his fist tight over the ring and sank back into the chair. Relief. *Profound* relief.

It lumped something thick and mushy in Samin's throat, so he cleared it.

A crisis of sanity avoided for a change, rather than plowed into or exacerbated apurpose. Samin couldn't help but approve. But it seemed he now had more questions than when he'd walked in. The thing with Umeia was disturbing, but at the moment, not tactically significant. The thing with Yakuli, though...

"Shig?" Samin was rather hoping she just knew, like it seemed she'd known all morning, what he was going to say or do before he did. But when she merely blinked at him—almost sly and challenging—Samin sucked in a calming breath and turned to Malick instead. "She knows more about Yakuli than what she's telling."

"Yeah." Shig shrugged, calm and casual. "But you saw more than you want to say out loud. I don't know any more than what you've already figured. You just don't want to be the one who makes it true."

Samin was caught between embarrassment and anger. Because it wasn't anything that was at the top of his mind, even though he'd been pawing at it since last night, but as soon as it came out Shig's mouth, he knew, *knew* what had been bothering him about those barracks. And damn it, he really didn't like it that someone else could know better what was in his head than he did.

"*Fine*." He turned a frustrated glare on Malick. "There was a set of barracks on the southern end of the estate. Enough to house two hundred men, at least. They were normal enough—the little I saw through the windows was standard military. Bunks and trunks and the usual. But there was another row of barracks to the west." Samin paused, swallowed. Shig was right: he didn't want to have to say this, and especially not with Fen in the room.

Malick tilted his head. "You already told me this."

Samin had. And had wondered at the time why Malick questioned him so intensely about what Samin thought very small, unimportant matters in the scheme of all the bigger observations. But Samin hadn't made the connection to the barracks before. Possibly deliberately hadn't made the connection because he hadn't wanted to know. And he'd just assumed Malick would question Shig, or Shig would volunteer what she knew, and what needed to happen would happen. Except Malick hadn't questioned Shig. And Shig hadn't volunteered. Like they were each waiting for the other to say something both of them already knew.

Samin shook it off. "I didn't mention they had no windows. It didn't seem important last night. I didn't really think much of it, except to estimate a count, but... well, and I couldn't get a look in. Yori was going to give sneaking past the guard a go, but Shig wouldn't let her."

"Too many charms." Shig looked away. "They would've caught her." She turned her gaze to Malick, sharp and fully "here" now. "There was too much magic flying around for me to be able to protect her."

Malick's gaze took on that detached look he got when he stopped pretending he wasn't too smart for anyone's good. "How *much* magic? And what kind?"

"Funny you never felt it, huh?" There was no taunting in Shig's soft tone this time, and none of her games, and the real meaning of it—just outside the reach of Samin's too-practical grasp—made ghost fingers crawl up Samin's backbone. "How d'you suppose anyone could hide all that magic from *Temshiel*?"

Fen had been removed enough from what was going on around him as to almost not be there at all. Now his eyes opened, narrowed on Malick, and his slouched posture went stiff and alert.

Malick didn't answer Shig's question. He met Fen's gaze somberly, all too knowing, and turned his glance slowly back to Samin, pinned him.

"Samin?"

Samin's throat had gone tight. It was the look on Malick's face; it was what Samin was going to have to say next; it was the fact that Malick's expression seemed to imply that perhaps he already knew.

"I think they were prisoner barracks." Samin's palms had gone sweaty, his heart skipping beats all over the place. "I think perhaps we know now what's happened to all the Jin who've been Disappeared."

How could anyone keep something this big from Temshiel? Shig had speculated. Samin was fairly certain they couldn't. Not Wolf's *Temshiel*, and not in his own Cycle. Which left the disconcerting, quite frightening conclusion: Wolf's *Temshiel* had known. And apparently done nothing.

⛩

Joori skulked down the hallway, aware this was a bad idea, but he didn't have much choice. He'd already exposed himself, though the boy from whom he'd asked directions had seemed pleasant enough and unlikely to go running off for the Doujou or anything. By the way he'd talked, he'd assumed Joori to be a "new boy" and amiably pointed to the door Joori wanted then went on his way, clad only in a long, silky robe, completely unselfconscious.

Joori didn't think he could ever get used to a place like this.

He stood at the door, contemplating the veracity of what he planned to do. So far as "plan" went, anyway. More like posture and bluff and demand, and pretend he knew more than he actually did.

But the alternative was to do what bloody *Malick* was so dead-set against Joori doing, and that really would be a betrayal to Jacin in a way. Still, Joori would rather save Jacin by betrayal than allow him to sacrifice himself for reasons that weren't even real. Which was likely why bloody *Malick* was so eager to be rid of everyone who wasn't Jacin. And Joori would be damned if he'd just bow his head and say *Yes, seyh* like a good little Jin. Because he'd never see Jacin again if he did.

Jacin wasn't going to go. Jacin had never had any intention of going. Jacin had always meant to put Joori and Caidi and Morin on that caravan and wave them goodbye. And these people were going to be all too happy to help him do it. Even Yori, and strangely, that one hurt.

Joori wasn't a fool—they'd had sex, not sworn their undying devotion. Yori killed people for a living, and what was more, she liked it. He'd never slept with anyone before who could probably snap his neck in the throes of orgasm with a flick of her wrist. And strangely, he found it bizarrely arousing in a way he probably never wanted to scrutinize.

He could love Yori very easily, and he knew she liked him—*she* sought *him* out most of the time, and it wasn't for any kind of distraction so he wouldn't realize what they were all up to. She liked him, wanted to be with him.

Which made the duplicity hurt.

He expected it from Jacin. Jacin would lie, cheat, steal and sell his soul to keep them safe. But while Joori didn't know exactly what Asai had done to Jacin in the years he'd had him, it was clear that Jacin's mind and heart had been twisted around the bastard somehow. A man who had very little unencumbered access to his own mind had little other choice. And if Asai ruled Jacin's heart, Asai ruled Jacin.

It pierced Joori to think it, to know it, but Shig, the flighty bitch, had been right: Jacin would go to Asai, and he'd go armed and willing, but he'd be going to Asai to die.

Joori's options were limited. They were all basically helpless to these people, caught as they were in the heart of Ada and with only fake papers that proclaimed them Umeia's "property" to protect them. And Joori had no illusions that he could get through to Jacin. There was no one in the world more single-minded than Jacin once he'd narrowed his focus to a specific goal. Jacin's goal right now was to get them all out of Ada then go to Asai and accept his end, and he wouldn't hear Joori's arguments or pleas. Joori had to accept it as simply the way Jacin showed his love, but he didn't have to accept it as the only option.

He squared his shoulders and raised his arm to knock on Umeia's door. It slid open before he'd had a chance to even curl his hand into a fist.

"Done hovering, then, are you?" Umeia's expression was wry.

Joori chewed his lip and tucked his hands at the small of his back. He gave Umeia a quick bow of his head. "I—"

"Yes, yes, I know." Umeia crooked a cockeyed smirk. "In. Before someone else sees you."

Joori didn't even think twice, just obeyed, stepping past Umeia and into her rooms. He was tempted to goggle a little—quite a lot more plush than anywhere he'd seen before—but didn't like the idea of exposing himself as the green provincial he knew he was. They already thought him dim, apparently. Joori saw no reason to bolster their opinions.

"Where does Malick think you are?" Umeia asked bluntly.

"I don't think he cares." Joori shrugged. "He's been holed up in my brother's room and throwing me out every chance he gets. I've not been let in since Jacin woke."

"And Yori?"

That made Joori flush. "No one has seen fit to tell me what's been decided for my life. I saw no need to burden any of the others with the little control over it I may still have."

Umeia gestured to the ornate chair in front of her vanity. Joori sat down while Umeia perched on the edge of her unmade bed.

"So, you're a clever lad, then, are you?" Umeia's tone was lightly mocking, but Joori detected no real rancor. She was testing him, somehow.

He wished he knew for what. "In some things." He lifted his chin. "You've had a falling-out with Malick."

"That's not being clever. That's merely stating the obvious."

"All right, then." Joori made himself sit back, made his muscles unknot. "It's obvious that whatever you rowed about, my brother is at the center of it. And since I know you don't want to leave, and you're doing it anyway, the disagreement must have something to do with that."

Umeia stared at him, narrow-eyed and calculating. Joori made himself stay still beneath her scrutiny, made himself look back.

Finally, Umeia looked away. "You people know so very little of our kind." She huffed, half a laugh, and half… something else. "Not your fault. You can't be expected to know. Not when the agents of the gods themselves keep it from you."

Joori frowned. "What does—?"

"You came down here for answers. So, hush while I give them to you."

Surprised by the softness of the tone, Joori merely shut his mouth.

"You can't trust him." Umeia had folded her hands in her lap before. Now her fingers picked and pried at each other. "Don't misunderstand me. He wants your brother to live. He wants you to live because your brother wants it. He won't lie to get his way. He won't promise you or anyone else anything he doesn't intend fully to give. But Malick can make a person…" Umeia paused, thoughtful, then pursed her full mouth into an unhappy line. "A man like your brother—someone who needs love like he needs breath; someone who's been denied it his whole life— a man like that will see his deepest, most secret wants in the smallest of promises. A tender touch is all it takes, and Malick… well." She snorted grimly. "Malick's had lots of practice at loving. Our little Untouchable has had next to none at *being* loved." Umeia met Joori's gaze squarely. "Malick has promised your brother he'll get you out of Ada safely in exchange for killing Asai."

"I know." Joori kept the anger and hurt of it to himself.

"And he will. He's ordered me to get you out, and I've little choice. I've already sworn oath to protect you, and forgive me for being so blunt, but you're simply not worth burning for. So I'll do it—I'll get you out of Ada. Whether you want it or not, I'll load you into a caravan bound for Heldesan, ride with you to the border to make sure you make it across safely, and will defend you with my life if I must, if you're pursued. And then, once we're in Heldesan, I'll leave you, my oath fulfilled." Umeia lifted an eyebrow. "I'm oathbound only for as long as you're in my care. Understand?"

Oh, Joori understood all right. They'd be dumped in a foreign land, refugees, unschooled in the hows of defense, making a living, or even speaking the language. And completely unprotected by the shielding veil of a *Temshiel*. If Asai decided he still wanted to use them against Jacin, all he'd have to do was come and get them. They might as well have targets painted on their backs.

"Then what's the *point?*"

"The point, Fen Joori, is that Malick's promise will have been kept, a beacon of trust for your brother, who already trusts too much." Umeia leaned forward. "And now the one Untouchable in decades who's managed to stay sane has no Voices to hear. Malick has given your brother the quiet he needs to keep his mind—stanchions on which to lay more trust—but he's taken away the Voices that were meant to guide him."

"They've never *guided* him. They've only ever—"

"And how d'you think he ended up here, with the very *Temshiel* who's got more reasons than anyone else in the world to want Asai dead? How d'you think he decided to put you into our hands? And however dangerous it may be for you to *be* in our hands, it's still safer for you than being in Asai's." Umeia shook her head, strangely sympathetic. "Whether they said so in words or not, the Ancestors *have* guided him. For whatever reason, they wanted him here, they wanted *you* here. And now that you are, their Voices have been silenced."

Joori thought about it for a moment, just to make sure he wasn't hearing it wrong. "Are you saying you *want* him to be driven mad by them?"

"I'm saying your brother's fate has been interrupted. So has yours. He's supposed to listen, Joori. It's what he's for."

"You're talking about him like he's not even a *person*. Like he's nothing but a tool for everyone else to use. You sound just like—"

"They've found your mother, lad."

It stopped Joori cold. And she'd known it would. For that, he could have throttled her.

"Where?"

Umeia's eyes were keener than they'd been before. "Exactly where Malick has known all along they would."

"Wh… what?" Joori couldn't gain enough breath to even suck in a good lungful.

"I have to give him credit." Umeia waved a hand, cavalier, like she wasn't crushing Joori's heart in her fist with every word. "He did everything right. He sent out his probes first, did his investigating, gathered his information." She paused, her half smile almost condescending but not quite. "Let your brother see him do it all."

The implication was all too clear: "He set him up."

"See? You *are* a clever lad." Umeia stood, paced over to Joori slowly. She took hold of Joori's chin gently, forcing eye contact. "Your kind were never meant to have magic. No mortal is, but some have earned the right. The Jin didn't have to. The *Temshiel* abandoned the Ancestors when they gave their magic to you, and then the *Temshiel* assisted the Adan in trying to tame it. *That's* what your Binding War was really about."

Joori's throat clogged on a negation he couldn't quite voice, unable to do anything but keep his gaze locked with Umeia's. He couldn't even jerk back from her touch.

For all her soft tones and sympathetic eyes, Umeia was relentless. "Malick fought on the side of the Adan. So did I. All *Temshiel* did, because that was what our gods commanded. But the rest of us walked away when a balance was struck, because that's the way of it with us. The Adan and the Jin have perhaps come to an unhappy standstill, but Malick has never stopped fighting the war, even when he was refusing to fight at all.

"What Asai wants to do would turn the Jin's slavery to regency. Do you understand what that means?" Umeia was fervent now, almost like she'd forgotten she was even talking to Joori, merely ranting to excise whatever anger had too obviously been boiling in her chest. "The Jin and the Adan would switch places. Your people would no longer be hunted, slaughtered, bled." She took a long breath, as if to calm herself. "They would not direct themselves, granted, but they never have, really. They've always had their Ancestors for that."

She pulled back and tilted her head to the side. A knowing smile curled at her mouth, and she waved at the door just as a soft knock gently rattled the wood. Umeia placed a finger over her lips, gave Joori a wink.

"Enter!"

Joori almost jolted when the door slid open to reveal Shig on the other side of it, but Umeia's hand clamped on his shoulder, keeping him still. Shig peered at him with no surprise, only a bit of melancholy in her green gaze. Still, it had the feel of admonishment to Joori, and it was all he could do to meet it squarely.

Shig turned to Umeia. "I expect you know what I've come for."

It was colder than Joori had been expecting. For all that he'd only "known" Shig for a short while, he'd rather judged everything she did or said as abstractly passionate: listening to her spirits and following their guidance because she believed in their truths. Even when she'd been taunting Jacin into a mental breakdown, Joori had still been able to tell that she'd *felt* something, that she wasn't doing it just for fun.

This cold remove seemed… strange on her.

Umeia didn't seem to notice or care. She merely reached behind Joori to a small black chest on the vanity, whispered a quiet spell he couldn't hear until the lid popped open, and then she extracted a chunky, flashing ring. Without a word, she tossed it to Shig.

Shig caught it, still with that hard gaze, nearly glittering now. She closed the ring tight in her fist

"So, it all comes to this, then. Gentle, secondhand betrayal, 'for his own good.'"

Umeia only sighed, her expression almost as hard now as Shig's.

Shig turned to Joori. "Perfidy is perfidy, Fen Joori. All sides in a war can be justified. It only depends on which side you're standing when the justifications start spilling from angry hearts." She turned back to Umeia, eyes narrowed. "And exactly where the betrayals began." She held Umeia's gaze for a long time—so long Joori began to wonder if they were having some kind of mental conversation and had forgotten him entirely—before Shig turned her jade eyes back on Joori, harder and sharper than he'd ever seen them. "Love gives even the weakest among us the power of cruelty. And nothing rends a heart so cruelly as the misjudgment of it by one who's supposed to know it."

Joori didn't know exactly why he bristled, but he did. "What's that supposed to mean?"

Shig gave him a look brimming with frustration, before she shook it away. "Their souls are ever dipped in blood. It's *their* way—not ours. A bargain with a *Temshiel*, a bargain with a maijin. It's all the same. It all depends on the *Temshiel*. Or the maijin. Either one will betray you for their own ends, even if they love you. But betrayal of the Blood…" Her gaze slid over to Umeia again, accusing this time, though with a strange glimmer of mourning at odds with the ruthlessness. "Hasn't he endured enough?"

Joori had no idea who she was talking about. Had no idea what this even *was*.

Shig sighed and stepped over to Umeia. "Yori loves you hard, but in the end, our Blood wills out. She isn't yours. She's mine. I'm sorry." A long look passed between them, another silent conversation, then Shig leaned in, kissed Umeia's cheek. Umeia shut her eyes, her chin quivering as Shig laid her head to Umeia's shoulder. "Goodbye, my Wolf-mother. You've weakened the pack, but I still love you."

Umeia was silent, but the grief coming off her was almost as strong as the burst of power Malick had thrown at Joori a few nights ago. Joori wondered if this was part of Umeia's power—making others feel what she felt—and whether she even realized she was doing it, because his heart was actually hurting, and he didn't even *like* these people.

Umeia hugged Shig tight for a long, long time, until Shig pulled slowly away. With one last quick look back that Joori couldn't read, Shig quit the room, shutting the door softly behind her.

"Blood wills out, spiteful little earthbound," Shig said through it, and then it was silent.

Umeia stood rigid for a few uncomfortable moments, gathering herself, then pushed out, "*Well*, then." It was brisk, almost blithe.

Only then did Joori realize that Umeia hadn't said a single word while Shig had been in the room. He had no idea what to make of that, but Umeia clearly wasn't as together as she wanted Joori to think she was. She wavered as she made her way back over to the bed and inelegantly dropped to the edge of the mattress.

"I've just handed over your brother's salvation and his noose, all in one." She said it so softly Joori thought perhaps he'd heard wrong.

Except he knew he hadn't. "What does that mean?"

"She's right." Umeia's shrug seemed incongruously helpless. "Betrayal is a common thing for our kind. Love is rare. But, oh, I do love my brother."

"Brother?"

Umeia smiled, soft and sad. "Malick. He's my brother."

...Right. Yori had told him that, had apparently only recently discovered it herself, and been strangely awed by this new additional facet to the people who made up her "family."

"I love my brother." Umeia laughed, a fragile, hopeless thing. "Just as you love yours. And just like you, I'm apparently willing to betray him to save him, even though I never would've believed it last week." Her hands curled into fists. "And he hates me for it, but at least he'll be *alive*, he'll have his soul."

She stood abruptly, paced in front of Joori. Her smile turned... scary, for all the grief packed inside it.

"The Ancestors have led the Catalyst here, they've led you here, and all of this heard by their Voice through their shouts of insanity. So, tell me, clever Jin lad: what d'you think the Ancestors would say to their Voice now? How would they guide him next, if only he would hear? If someone wasn't right this second handing him the key to never having to listen to them again?" Umeia stopped in front of Joori, grabbed hold of his chin, and jerked his head up, her eyes hectic, nearly blazing. "Would they ask for pseudosalvation for their children, or another century of misery?"

Joori opened his mouth, but Umeia gave his chin a sharp shake.

"Think very carefully, Fen Joori, because you may be called upon to make the same decision for yourself."

She was terrifying in her heartrending anger. And just like it had been back in that hut when Malick had shown up, Joori couldn't move. He had no idea if he was truly frozen, or if Umeia was using some sort of magic to keep him that way, but he couldn't make himself move or look away.

"Salvation," he heard himself answer, low and breathy, and completely unlike his own voice, and perhaps it wasn't, but it was the truth nonetheless. Anyone would choose salvation.

"Salvation." Tears filled Umeia's eyes before she blinked them away, turning her firm grip on Joori's chin to a soft caress to his cheek. "Yes." She took her hand away and turned her back on him. "Malick hasn't seen clearly since your brother walked into my House. And the rest of them are all his, even Yori, though it's going to break her heart to choose." She shook her head, then bowed it. "Why d'you suppose it is that you and I are the only ones who can see?"

Something went cold in Joori, spangled out into shivers he only just managed to suppress. This one scared him even more than Malick did, and having his own thoughts and feelings compared to hers... it unnerved him. And the things Shig had said...

It had been a mistake to come here. It had been a mistake to think he knew what the fuck he was doing. That he could outguess these people. That he had even the smallest chance against them.

He swallowed, his throat only squeezing out a dry clicking sound. "I'm not sure I know what you mean." And he had a feeling it was going to be important that he understand whatever this was very clearly.

Umeia turned around, all the sadness abruptly dashed. Her entire being went hard and cold as she leveled an even stare on Joori.

"Malick loves him, but he can't save him. And the only way either of them can save themselves is to let go. There's nothing we can do, lad." She shrugged, like none of it really mattered, like she could stop caring, just like that. "You came to me for answers, and there are none. None of us truly owns our own heart. The only things we truly own are our choices. Go now, please. I want to be alone."

"But..." Joori stood, fear giving way to renewed anger. "But *what* choices? I don't know what you're talking about! How am I supposed to choose something when I don't know—?"

"I never said anything about *your* choices." Umeia stepped over to the door and shoved it open. "Best get along. They'll be done soon, and you don't want Malick knowing where you've been."

"But—"

"*Go*, Joori. I've had all I can take of this mortal business. Leave me to my own."

Joori had no choice. She wasn't to be argued with, not now, and if he tried, he had no idea what might happen. He didn't know these people, and he only knew enough about what they were capable of to be afraid.

He left, finding himself once again out in the hallway, in the same spot where he'd started, staring at the door again.

Love and betrayal; cruelty and salvation. What the *hell* had just happened? And why did he feel even more unsettled and confused than he had before he'd come? And why did he find himself feeling oddly sorry for Umeia? It was as though she—

"So. Who are you really, then?"

Joori spun at the voice behind him, heart in his throat. And found that same young man who'd cheerfully pointed him to Umeia's door standing just down the hall.

Doe eyes, lightly kohled and slightly smeary, blinking at Joori with a sadness that hadn't been there before. The boy's pale skin was dewy, the ends of his silky black hair wetting dark splotches on the neck and shoulders of his robe.

"You're not a new boy. Are you." Not hostile, but not really a question, either.

Joori's mouth flapped. "I…" He didn't know what to say. He wasn't even supposed to be down here, wasn't supposed to let anyone see him, so how was he supposed to explain himself?

"I didn't realize until I was halfway through my bath, but…" The boy paused, eyes narrowing. "Umeia would've introduced you around. I would've met you already. So that means you're not a new boy." Soft eyes gone slightly sharper looked Joori over, appraising. "And you don't look like a customer."

Shit. What the hell was he supposed to do now?

"You're Malick's lover." The boy's tone bent softly accusing, but mostly disappointed. Dark hair fell over his brow as he blinked his pretty eyes at Joori. "You're the one he was talking about."

It was all Joori could do not to turn his head and spit on the floor. Not only for being assumed Malick's *lover*, but for the fact that apparently Malick had been talking to some stranger about Jacin. Like he had some kind of *right*.

Amazingly, Joori managed to keep at least most of his wits. "I, um. Sorry, I'm not sure I should—"

"No, you probably shouldn't." The boy sighed and gave Joori a small smile.

Not so much a boy, now that Joori was paying attention—he was probably a little older than Joori himself—but his manner and his wide eyes made him seem young. He likely got more trade that way, Joori thought with a little bit of discomfort. With a languidness that was probably ordinarily seductive, but now just seemed to be his natural state of being, the young man leaned his shoulder against the wall and shrugged.

"I knew I couldn't keep him. Everyone knows they don't get to keep Malick. But they all try."

And how had Joori known that Malick was a promiscuous asshole? It figured. What was it about Jacin that attracted the most reprehensible sorts?

The young man was looking Joori up and down, as though trying to figure out what Malick's new "lover" had that he didn't. Clad only in that silky robe, dark hair tousled and damp, and his stance a study in seduction. Joori had never looked twice at another man, but he'd make an exception for this one. He was already making an exception for this one.

An unconscious toss of the head, though it did no good—the boy's thick hair flopped back over his brow and into his eye again almost instantly.

"He said you're what he's been looking for, for a very long time." It was said with a bit of skepticism, but mostly curiosity.

Joori *did not* loose the derisive snort that was knocking at the back of his throat. Of all the predictable kiss-off lines.

"He didn't say you were Jin."

That made Joori start. If this young man was jealous and thinking to take some sort of vengeance, go running for the Doujou—

"Don't worry yourself." The boy smirked; it was almost friendly. "I'm half Jin myself, and have just as many reasons for wanting to stay out from under the Adan's eye." A sudden grin flashed his small white teeth. "I wouldn't've even mentioned it, only I thought it was interesting."

"Interesting how?" Joori asked, strangely not frightened, or even uneasy anymore in the presence of this young man who thought Joori was Malick's lover.

"Interesting because he must really love you to risk so much for you."

Joori looked away. Umeia had said nearly the same thing. Except she'd also said Malick couldn't save Jacin. She'd said a lot of things, and so had Shig, and Joori hadn't yet had time to figure out how much of it he believed.

The boy's smirk came back, turned a little sly. "You're very beautiful, y'know. I imagine that's what caught his eye. You'd have quite a flock of admirers if you *were* a new boy."

It was so strange, standing here and listening to this young man speak to him like he was Jacin. Giving him Jacin's compliments, flashing him Jacin's smiles. It made Joori wonder what Jacin would do if he were the one standing here, listening to this apparent former lover of Malick's tell him he was beautiful and he'd make a good whore. It depended on which Jacin, Joori supposed—the Jacin he'd grown up with would likely have blushed and cast his eyes to the floor, mumbled polite thanks and edged away as quickly as possible. This new Jacin, the one it almost made Joori sick to admit he didn't really know anymore, this new Jacin would probably glare the boy into silence then stalk past him without looking back. Maybe even flash a knife at him to keep him from ever attempting conversation again.

Joori couldn't see himself doing any of those things.

"I'm sorry if you've been... hurt."

The boy lofted an elegant wave. "It's what we're made for, isn't it?"

"Who?"

"The Jin. A race made for pain. I'm only half, but that's the half the pain comes from." The boy's expression grew concerned, apparently at whatever had blossomed on Joori's face. "Don't look so glum." He tilted another of those soft smiles. "This is a good place. Pain-free, I promise. And anyway, Malick's one of the good ones. If someone like Malick loves you, you're not likely to ever feel pain again. It would've been nice if... Ah, well." The boy's smile had gone wistful for a few seconds before he shook it off. "I'm Madi, by the way."

"F—" Joori caught himself. He couldn't just go about blurting his name, even if this young man did seem kind and harmless. And anyway, the boy—Madi—thought he was talking to Jacin.

Madi laughed, a gentle thing. "Right. Probably wise, though it doesn't really matter—he's called me by your name more than once. You'll understand why I made it a point to forget it. I'll forget it for... other reasons, now. I'll just call you Beautiful, then." Madi winked, and pushed away from the wall. "I need some tea. And you need to get yourself back upstairs before someone sees you. The others will be dragging themselves out of bed for their baths soon, too, and some of the customers stay overnight. We take care of our own here, but you can't stop talk once it starts." He flowed through a shallow, graceful bow. "It was nice to meet you, Beautiful. Make sure Malick takes care of you, yeah?"

He gave Joori a lazy wave, turned, and sauntered away. Joori only stared after him for a moment, frowning.

This morning had just been too fucked up for coherent thought. He was going to have to clear his head and think about it anyway.

Slowly, he made his way back to the attic stairs, climbed halfway up, then sat on a step to consider. He could hear Caidi chattering at someone, a light, pleasant drone; he let it wash over him and took a long breath.

And discovered it really didn't require a whole lot of thought, after all. It was easy, really. All he'd needed was a moment to catch his breath to reach the same conclusion he'd reached when he'd watched Shig push his brother into a complete break in reason.

Watched Malick allow it.

Malick loves him...

Joori was willing to concede that, as much as it surprised him. Annoyed him. Jacin was ridiculously lovable, and if it had been anyone else doing the loving, Joori would have rejoiced. He might be selfish, but he wasn't a total bastard. And Malick's... obsession with Jacin did look suspiciously like something more than concern for the deal they'd made. So, it wasn't hard to believe Malick might love Jacin—*Temshiel* or no.

It was just hard to believe someone like Malick knew how to do it properly.

If someone like Malick loves you, you're not likely to ever feel pain again.
Uh-huh. That seemed to have been working out *real* well so far.

Joori shook his head, his mouth thinning down into a sour line. If Malick really did love Jacin, Joori would hate to see what he did to someone he didn't much like.

But Umeia wasn't much of an alternative. The way she talked, it sounded like she *approved* of Asai and what he'd done, what he meant to do. Joori would bet just about anything that the real reason behind the row between Malick and Umeia had been that strange confession. Which was a reluctant point in Malick's favor, Joori supposed.

From slavery to regency, Umeia had said. Joori had laid eyes on Asai once in his life, but even he knew that someone like Asai wouldn't offer something like that without demanding a terrible price in return. Joori had a sick, sinking certainty he knew who was supposed to pay it. And Malick, no matter if he really did love Jacin or not, was sending him right into the teeth of the bargain to get chewed up and mangled.

This entire morning had been a complete waste of time, all confusion, because Joori had known before he'd ventured down to see Umeia what needed to be done. What *he* needed to do.

Temshiel and maijin prowling around his brother like he was a coveted bone; assassins living in the attic of a whorehouse; death plots and stolen magic and *Exactly where Malick has known all along...*

Didn't that say it all, really? What was there to think about?
Blood wills out...
Too bloody right it did.

He needed to get his family out of here. He needed to get *Jacin* out of here.

Now.

5

Xari hadn't read her cards last night. She'd been weary. She'd had more trade than usual—too many young men abruptly called up to serve their lord or prefect for reasons vague but urgent, protection against the growing shadow-threat of assassination, and wanting to know if there was danger ahead, would they live out their conscription—so she'd been tired. Tired but well paid.

She hadn't read her cards.

The conflict and sorrow hit her first, and she sipped at it, allowing the strength of it to fill her before she recognized the taste and looked up.

She sighed. "I did not expect you, Wolf's Daughter." Weary all over again, and her day had only just started.

Umeia shifted a shrug and took the chair across from Xari, demure. "Then that's one for me." Her manner was respectful but… hard. Angry, perhaps?

A practical woman, this Paladin of Souls, not chosen by Wolf but conscripted by Blood, and she wore her duties well. The Gift of healing, for it pleased her to right wrongs, and she was not afraid to unbind her heart to sway those gone to despair. Asai had scoffed once, predicted that Umeia's heart would one day bleed a little too much, likely for her brother, and there would be no more lifeblood to spare for herself. Xari judged Umeia too sensible and so had ignored him. Arrogant enough to make predictions without the tools necessary, her errant son, and Xari put him out of her mind.

She had not come veiled today, this proud child of Wolf, but wore the trappings of the Adan: formal robe, wide sash, sensible shoes, and a silky black wig to cloak the brasher style she favored. A respectable woman. No one would guess her preferred nighttime doings. No one would think to look twice at the plain woman, perhaps the mate of a midlevel noble, strolling the city on business that was her own and of no interest to them.

"The color does not suit you." Xari lifted her gaze pointedly to the wig. It made Umeia look tired and wan.

Umeia ignored it, reached into her small bag and withdrew a handful of koin, counting ten onto the table. "I should like to see my cards, please."

Xari hesitated. Not like her brother, this one—Kamen "allowed" Xari to read his cards, he never asked for it, he didn't approve, and he rarely ever listened when she did it anyway. Xari had read once for this daughter of Wolf, just before Umeia had Kamen buy the Girou for her, and then never again. Xari's cards hadn't seen far for Umeia—they never did for *Temshiel*—but what they'd shown had been good.

"Perhaps you'd prefer to tell me what it is you seek, child." Xari's hands had already taken up the deck, the gnarled fingers of her glamour coaxing them into their proper places. "A reading can set a chancy future too firmly, if one does not understand the message entire."

"The cards, Xari." Flat. Then, more insistent, "There are already too many chancy things. I'd like *something*, at least, I can see clearly."

Xari bit her tongue on the admonishments that wanted to come. The cards were not for building a future. Not even for predicting one, truly. She should refuse. Trading in possibilities was a heavy responsibility, one Xari accepted with all due gravity, one that was too easily abused—just look at her son. But her curiosity had been stirred, and the chill just beneath the demeanor of this very warm woman worried Xari.

Kamen could be a bastard, but he loved his sister. And Umeia would not have come here for something as simple as a row between siblings. Surely whatever this was had nothing to do with…?

Speculation was just as irresponsible as reading one's cards without the proper instruction in their meanings first, and useless, in the end. Xari straightened the deck then fanned it out.

Obediently, Umeia reached tentative fingers, chose a card, and slipped it from between its fellows. She held it to her breast for a moment, eyes shut, as though afraid to see, before she slowly turned it over to lie between them on the table.

It was all Xari could do not to gasp.

"Your card has changed." A slow trickle of fear wound down Xari's backbone. "Paladin of Souls you are no more." She denied the shudder that wanted to ripple through her and lifted her gaze slowly to Umeia's. "What have you done, child?"

Umeia didn't answer, merely tapped the card on the table. "What does it mean?"

"Choices." Xari swallowed, laying a bony hand over the Obelisk. "To fall or to fly. Let go or risk being shaken off." She shook her head. "You must tell me why you've come, child. I cannot read properly unless I know—"

"The card, Xari." It was a touch harsh, just enough to remind Xari across from whom she sat. Kamen might overshadow his sister in power, but that didn't mean Umeia hadn't been bestowed with plenty of her own.

Xari drew herself up, met Umeia's eyes squarely. "Change." She kept her tone even and bland. "Disastrous change." She tapped the card. "The Obelisk of falsehoods, its foundation built on sand and gravel. Lies you have told yourself. Lies that set it too heavy on its perilous foundation. If you do not push it over yourself with elucidation, it will fall beneath its own weight." Her fingertips drifted to the orange flames licking at the peak of the Obelisk. "Fire purifies. Its ash is virtue."

"So, I've been lying to myself." Umeia's eyes filled.

"That is one interpretation." Xari resisted the urge to reach over and take up Umeia's hand. "I cannot know unless you tell me why—"

"Do you still love your son, Xari?"

Xari sat back, eyeing Umeia carefully. "Blood is Blood. There are many things that can take the love in one's heart and change it, but very few that can wipe it out altogether. Even if we might wish it."

"And you do what you do now—you plot with my brother—because you hope to save your blood, even though you know it will hurt him. Make him hate you. Perhaps kill him."

"He already hates me. Were it not for your brother, my arrogant get would've already sought me out and sent me to spirit. And only one sort of death means anything to our kind. Hurt...?" Xari shrugged. "We have not the same goals, you and I. I am godless; you have never been. I would dig out the heart of Asai myself, if Dragon would but ask it and give me back my place. My own redemption is why I help your brother."

"And what about Wolf? What if one of Wolf's-own were willing to speak for you, swear for you? Would you take Wolf for your god if he'd have you?"

"No *Temshiel* or maijin would refuse Wolf, should he call." Xari paused, thoughtful. "And what would Wolf's-own ask for in return for this boon?"

She didn't mention that Kamen had already made her the same promise, and a petition from him would likely go further. Dragon might take Xari back before the Cycle shifted, if she had a hand in stunting Asai's plots, but a call from *Wolf*...

Xari would never have to fear her son again. Even if he escaped the suns a second time.

Umeia leaned forward, her eyes bright with new zeal. "Warn my brother off. Lie to him, if you have to. He's no longer necessary to this grand plot you have between you, both of you tools of vengeance for Husao and nothing more. Leave the Catalyst to me."

Xari kept the shock from her face. "And what would you do with the Catalyst, Wolf's Daughter?"

Umeia's eyes hardened. Her mouth remained stubbornly shut.

A strange grief rose to Xari's heart. "Kamen Wolf's-own has claimed the Catalyst as his own. They are bound as tightly as souls can be without the pledge of oath. You yourself have sworn to those the Catalyst holds most dear." Xari leaned in, met Umeia's cool gaze squarely. "What use for a Catalyst has Wolf's Daughter, Paladin of Souls that was?"

For a long moment, Xari thought Umeia would remain silent. But then her gaze shifted away, flickering down to the card on the table before lifting again to Xari.

"Blood is Blood. And I stand now on an Obelisk of lies. I would taste the ashes of virtue."

"The Obelisk is Death and Temperance both," Xari warned. "Even falling can feel like flying until you're broken on the ground. You cannot know which it is that awaits you unless you tell me what answer it is you seek. Always more than one meaning in the cards—it is not the cards themselves that guide but the one who reads them."

Umeia only stared, implacable, just as stubborn as her brother.

Xari's mouth tightened, and she shook her head. She set to irritably dealing out the rest of the configuration.

"If you will not tell me, I shall read the rest myself. Impudent children who think they can interpret for themselves what it takes centuries to—"

Umeia pushed Xari's hand away, snatched up a clump of cards, and swept them to the floor. Xari wouldn't have been as appalled if Umeia had just plunged a blade through her heart.

"Wretched girl! What—?"

"Some things I would keep for myself." Umeia stood calmly and stared down at Xari, her face unreadable. "You've been as helpful as I expected you to be, Xari." She bowed her head, bizarrely deferential, considering her blatant disrespect for Xari's craft and tools. "Goodbye," she said, then turned and pushed through the curtains that hung in the doorway, their dangle and sway holding Xari's stunned eye longer than they should have done.

Xari shook herself, rubbed at her brow. She hated to be taken by surprise. She should have read her cards last night. She should have been more prepared. These precarious days called for vigilance, and she'd been caught lacking.

Sighing, Xari heaved herself up from the table and hobbled over to the cards scattered over the floor. Damn it, it was going to take an annoying amount of time she apparently didn't have to purify them so they'd read properly again.

She needed to speak to Husao. And she needed to send for Kamen.

"This…" Xari bent to one knee on the floor and reverently began to collect her cards, unsure whether to be dismayed or relieved that the

Obelisk sat face up atop the otherwise haphazard mess. "This absolutely will not do."

ͲΨͲ

"*Yes*," Malick growled, wanting to be anywhere but where he was at the moment—sitting on Fen's bed with three sets of eyes staring at him in different degrees of accusation. "Yes, I thought we'd likely find your mother through Yakuli, but I hoped we wouldn't, because I—no, *no*, don't give me that look." Malick held up a hand, trying to stave off the wrath too apparent on Fen's face. "I wanted to find her, Fen. I just didn't want to find her *there*."

"What the fuck is that supposed to mean?"

Amazing what a little fury could do for Fen—he was healing faster than Malick had thought, faster than he should be doing, but a minute ago Fen had been gray and exhausted. Now color flooded his face, and anger livened up his eyes.

Malick raked a hand through his hair. He'd known this was coming, and he supposed he was lucky Fen hadn't already killed him. Damn it, how had he let himself get so mired in how he'd hoped this would go, as opposed to planning for contingencies when it inevitably went the way he knew it would?

Oh, right—optimism and libido.

Malick put out his hands, calming. "I'm subject to different laws than you are. We don't have the same… values, morality, whatever you want to call it."

"So, that means you can turn a blind eye while all those people—?"

"*No*. It means I *should*. It means I'm supposed to. Except I can't. I've never been able to, I've never… *fuck*."

With a vicious glare at Shig, Malick shuffled across the mattress until he was right in front of Fen. Fen made it a point to move his leg to the side to avoid Malick's touch. Samin had conspicuously taken up a place right behind Fen's chair, a not so subtle way of informing Malick that, on this subject at least, Samin was firmly on Fen's side.

Malick sighed, trying to order his thoughts, irritated they were so messy. He should've had a speech prepared, a ready defense. Except he'd never been able to find one in him, not for this, and *Yeah, it pissed me off, so I flipped off the gods and went to sulk for a few decades* didn't sound good even in his own head. He expected it would get an even less enthusiastic reception out loud, considering his current audience.

"We serve the Balance." Malick kept his gaze on Fen, as open and honest as he could make it. "Sometimes the defense of innocents is a tool to do that. Sometimes looking the other way is. There *is* no moral choice for us. We do as the gods tell us, and if the gods are silent, we use our judgment, our knowledge of our gods and what they wish, and hope we don't fuck it up and burn for it."

Fen was still glaring. But he had Malick's ring clutched tight in his fist.

Malick pointed at it. "You know, that won't work anymore if you kill me."

A lie, of course. The fact that it *didn't* lose its magic upon the death of its contributor was rather the appeal of *Temshiel* Blood in the first place.

Samin was frowning, skeptical. "So you're saying the gods want Yakuli to keep doing what he's doing?"

"No, not exactly." Malick shot a look at Shig, but he'd already known she'd be no help. At least she wasn't glowering at him like everyone else was. "The gods don't care about right or fair or just. The gods want Balance." No, that wasn't going to work. He was going to have to start at the beginning.

"There were *Temshiel* who made the mistake of loving mortals. And from that love came the Ancestors. The gods were angry, they wanted to wipe out the Ancestors and the *Temshiel* who made them, because they were a potential threat to the Balance. Mortals aren't supposed to have magic just *given* to them. But Wolf called the Ancestors to his Cycle. In a sense, they all became Wolf's children."

Fen tilted his head. "And their children became the Jin."

Malick was a little surprised—Fen was actually *participating* in a conversation, with *him*, and without having to be forced to it—but not terribly encouraged. Fen was still glaring.

"Yeah." Malick nodded. "The Jin have always been Wolf's favored children. But then the Ancestors pushed too hard. They bound their magic to their people. Even Wolf wouldn't come to their defense that time. They hadn't just threatened the Balance; they'd rocked it. The *Temshiel* were ordered to abandon the Jin or burn. Most of those who'd either sired or birthed the Ancestors burned. But still, Wolf wouldn't allow the Jin to be destroyed, and none of the other gods had the strength to defy him. So they simply waited until Wolf was no longer in his Cycle."

"The Binding War."

Malick stared. "...Yeah."

What would he think if he knew on which side you fought in the Binding War? Umeia had asked, and for all it had clogged anger and betrayal in Malick's chest at the time, it had still stoked the low simmer of unease to a smoldering coal. Because, yeah, what *would* Fen think? Except it appeared he already knew.

"How did you know that?"

Fen only stared, face unreadable, then he shrugged. "I had a good teacher."

"Not Asai, surely."

"No."

Right. Husao. Maybe his pain-in-the-ass interference had actually proven helpful this time, because Fen had known for days that Malick was *Temshiel*, and he'd obviously already known what the *Temshiel* had been to the Jin, and he hadn't actually tried to kill Malick.

"Maybe *he* knows," Samin put in irritably, "but some of us would like to know what the fuck you're talking about."

"Yeah, yeah." Malick scrubbed at his face. "No one knew the Ancestors had also bound their magic to their lands. And when the Jin used their magic against the Adan, it was the last straw. Some believe Raven's Incendiary influenced them, but it doesn't really matter, in the end—they did it and they had to be punished. So Raven set the *Temshiel* on them. Even those of us who aren't Raven's had to obey. And since maijin and *Temshiel* are equal parts of the—"

"The maijin fought for the Jin." Fen tried to stand, back away, but only ended up with his back pressed more firmly into the cushions of the chair. "Asai—"

"*No*, Fen." Malick reached out, clamped down on Fen's wrist. Fen stilled, but Malick could feel the vibrations in the taut muscles beneath his fingers. "He'll tell you he fought for the Jin and he serves Wolf, but it's only true enough that it can't be entirely negated. He wants to get the Jin out from beneath Adan rule, it's true, but only so that *he* can rule them."

Fen snarled, tried to jerk his arm away.

Malick jerked it right back. "Those charms, Fen—don't forget where they came from. Don't forget what Asai's done with them. Skel made them, but Asai used them. *He's* why all those people have been Disappeared. The Adan never would've known it could be done, were it not for Asai.

"He got hold of *Temshiel* Blood, and he saw what could be done with it, but he saw too late—he'd already betrayed the one who gave him the amulets and taught him the spells. Skel went to the suns for it, but if he hadn't, Asai would've seen him murdered for Heart's Blood."

"I don't understand," Samin put in. "Why wasn't Asai sent to the suns too?"

Malick held back a growl, mouth pinched up in a sour grimace. He pointed at the ring.

"One. We can make one. It's against the law to make more, but it's not against the law to take it when it's given. It's not against the law to use it however one sees fit. It's why we have to be careful when we hand them over. *We're* responsible for when they're misused, not the one misusing them. It may be difficult to believe it, but Skel had the best intentions, except..." Malick sat back, abruptly saddened and a little winded. "He made dozens. Maybe hundreds. The *only* intelligent thing he did was to keep the stronger spells to himself."

Because as bad as it was now, it could have been so much worse.

"What's any of this to me?" Fen asked through his teeth. "What are you trying to convince me of here? You've already said whose side you're on—shall I help you destroy the Jin altogether? Would that please your *gods?*"

"It probably would," Malick snapped back. "But it wouldn't please *me*. Why d'you think I walked away? Why d'you think I'm *here?* I waited—for the first decade of Wolf's Cycle, I *waited*, I watched, but there was nothing. *Nothing.* No guidance, no direction, no call. I couldn't watch it done anymore. I couldn't stand to not *do* something. Except I have limits—I can't kill the men who are behind it all."

"Mal…" Samin shook his head. "I've *seen* you kill men who've—"

"I can take out the small fish, the ones who don't affect the Balance, the ones who serve it by their deaths, who aren't protected by Fate. But I can't take out the ones who serve the Balance by living, no matter how repugnant they are. And Yakuli—*somehow*—serves the Balance. His existence serves Fate."

Malick looked away, the rage that never really left him all at once boiling behind his sternum. His lip curled, scornful.

"I've slaughtered those who've stolen magic because I *wanted* to, because I *enjoyed* it, because the idea of allowing them to keep doing it makes me bloody sick to my stomach, and I couldn't stand *not* doing something about it anymore. If I could prove beyond a doubt that Asai is the one pulling Yakuli's strings…" Malick's hands fisted. "If it was my choice, I'd walk into that compound Yakuli's got going, tear it down around his ears, and cut Asai's throat while I was at it, but I *can't*. The whole place has invisible 'Hands Off' signs all over it."

"Why would it—?"

"I don't *know*. I'm a fucking minion. The gods don't bother to give me the bigger picture, and I don't always get to have morals, all right? I don't know why I can't touch him, I just know that I can't."

"So, why couldn't *we?*" Samin's tone was no longer accusing, but genuinely curious, too obviously already calculating strategies and points of attack in his mind.

Malick threw his hands out. "Because there's magic all over the place. Shig already said as much." He turned his gaze squarely to Samin. "I couldn't risk you when I knew I wouldn't be able to help you. I couldn't risk Umeia, who'd sworn you all oath."

I didn't want to send you all out on a moral quest, only to watch you all cut to pieces.

Malick didn't say it, but Samin was a practical man, a man who understood "acceptable risk" and recognized it when he was looking at "*un*acceptable risk." He didn't acknowledge Malick's tacit apology with words, but his nod spoke the acknowledgment for him.

Well, that was one of them.

"So, Heart's Blood really would free the Jin." Fen's hostile gaze was still pinned to Malick, just as suspicious as he'd ever been. And yet he still held that ring protectively in his fist. "Asai wasn't lying."

Was that hope, deep down in that gray gaze? Fuck, Malick hoped not.

Shig shifted forward. "It depends on your definition of *free*."

Malick braced himself. He could never tell these days if he was going to be sorry or vindicated when Shig finally shut up.

Shig crawled up onto the bed beside Malick, sat on her knees, and looked Fen in the eye. "Ever been imprisoned in your own body, angry Ghost? Ever had your magic forced from you at someone else's will? Ever had your body move to someone else's tune, like you were a puppet, but one with a *mind*—one who *knew* what was being done to them and couldn't stop it?"

She paused, staring at Fen, the silence filling with heavy tension, until Fen finally shook his head and looked away.

Shig's smile was poignant. "It hurts. Whatever state your mother's mind is in right now, her soul is in agony."

Fen's teeth clenched, and he shut his eyes tight.

Shig leaned in, took hold of Fen's chin, and turned his head. She waited until he opened his eyes.

"Would you be the one to justify the means to Asai's end?"

It was so like the argument Malick had made to Umeia. He squinted at Shig with a jaundiced eye. She didn't appear to be playing by his rules anymore—she'd obviously been "listening." It'd been so long since he'd had to worry about it, he hadn't even thought to keep her from doing it. And he had to wonder whose rules she *was* playing by... if any.

"You've not even heard the plan yet." Shig said it to Fen but nodded over at Malick. "He's got one. He always does." She leaned in until her mouth was right next to Fen's ear. "Punch-drunk, angry Ghost. The risk of a soul. You sure you can live with it?"

Malick heard it, but he had no idea what it meant.

Fen apparently did, though. He snapped back, stared at Shig for a long time with narrowed eyes, then turned his piercing gaze over to Malick. Scrutinized him. Malick was finding it hard to sit still beneath the hard glare before Fen finally turned back to Shig.

Fen only said, "Yes," then knocked Shig's hand away, and spiked a harsh look at Malick. "What d'you intend to do?"

"Exactly what I promised to do." Malick blew out a heavy breath. "Exactly what I'm forbidden to do." Fuck, fuck, *fuck*. He flopped back against the headboard and rubbed at his brow, trying to pretend he wasn't risking everything with a promise he'd already made once. "I'm going to help you get your mother."

And in order to do that, he was going to have to lead his people into the heart of Yakuli's compound. And he couldn't pretend he didn't hope

Yakuli was there, would force Malick to kill him in "self-defense." And he couldn't fool himself that it would be defense enough for the gods. In all likelihood, Malick was going to end up killing a man he was forbidden to kill, and he'd end up burning for it.

Maybe it really was love. Why else would he have just more or less sworn to give up his soul for someone who could barely stand to look at him?

"What did she say, Shig?" Fen's voice was hoarse, his eyes shut tight again, head down, the ring clenched in his fist.

Shig bowed her head. "She said..." She bit her lip, but neither she nor Fen looked up. "She said, 'No laws, my twice-born. All things come to Zero.'"

Fen sat very still for a moment before he took a long, deep breath, and blew it out slowly. With a small shudder, he lifted his head, met Malick's gaze calmly, dry-eyed. He held up Malick's ring between long fingers.

"What exactly are you hoping to hear?"

Malick thought about how he should answer, *if* he should answer. Decided he'd come this far.

"I won't know until I hear it."

Fen didn't lunge for Malick's throat, and he didn't actually snarl this time. He rubbed at his eyes, then propped his elbow on the arm of the chair. He folded his fingers around the ring again and rested his chin on his fist.

"Fine. Do it."

⛩

He felt distinctly uncomfortable with Samin watching, and he had no idea what the hell Malick thought Shig could "help" with, but Jacin submitted to it all without growling. It was necessary, or at least Malick seemed to think so, part of the deal, and if it meant he'd never have to listen again, Jacin could endure it.

Letting go of the ring was... bad. The first waves of noise nearly took him under. His mind already felt brittle, almost fragile, and the screeching, after not having to hear it for days, was like a punch to the brain. Only the frantically held-to knowledge that he could reach out and silence it with a touch allowed him to keep hold of himself.

And save him, he missed the touch.

What was *wrong* with him? He'd been so long without the quiet he'd nearly forgotten what it was like to have it, and now that he'd had it again, he was having a hard time doing without it. Had he always been this hollow, grasping thing? A slave to touch, all right, he'd known that, but... like *this*? Ruination by his own reaching hand, and he couldn't make himself stop *wanting* it.

Shame crept at his edges, and he waited for it to hook him in, but nothing could touch him but a swirling confusion that was worse and more senseless than the usual insanity. Blathering in his head, bouncing against the inside of his skull, pulsing through his own confused angst and trebling it. Cherry blossom petals whirled inside it, blinding him and ramping the noise to levels that felt like they'd split Jacin's skull.

Too fucking loud, too fucking insane, and the *touch me please* that was ringing inside it was only making everything worse.

"All right, you're doing really well, Fen." Malick's voice came through amazingly clearly, and it was strange, because Jacin didn't think he was only hearing it with his ears. "Try to narrow it down to the words alone. I've got hold of the Ancestors' magic. I'm going to boost it, all right? Can you feel it?"

Jacin frowned, because he *could* feel it, and he really didn't like it. Too strong, too resonant, too... everything. Malick's hand was clamped to Shig's instead of Jacin's, and Jacin wondered vaguely why that was, but he only had so much concentration, so he dismissed it. Dismissed his own pathetic worries and fears and wants, and tried to blank out everything but the shrieking.

"Try to picture it in your head. Like a... like a wave."

A wave. Yes. A wave of...*colors*. Jacin could taste them. Slithering over his tongue, down his throat, choking him. Red smacked of fire. Blue of words he couldn't understand, blurring together. Bitterness was petal-pink, and suffocating. Anger chittered at the edges with the grit of black, clogging his nose with its cloying silty rot.

"Ride it out, Fen. Set yourself astride it and ride it out."

Buzzing, almost vibrating his teeth, and Jacin couldn't reach for the pain this time to dull it. Madness crowded in, he could almost feel it like a stalking brute, trying to shove him from out his own mind. It took everything in him to keep his hands clamped to the arms of the chair, keep them from clawing for pain or silence.

"There it is. You're doing really well, Fen. Feel it?"

He felt... something. Jacin latched onto Malick's voice like a piece of driftwood in turbulent seas. Cherry blossom petals swarmed in, obscuring, filling Jacin's mouth with sweet-bitter so thick he couldn't breathe. The tidal wave in his mind shifted—not a wave anymore, but a cool wind, comforting somehow. The petals skirled away in its wake, lifted from his lungs; Jacin sucked in clean air that smelled of pine and sage. Not dragging Jacin under and drowning him. It was softly sweeping away debris. Not reducing the volume, but... clarifying what was left.

Wordswordswords, always too many and too close together, and he could taste-touch-smell them this time, nearly overwhelming, but only nearly. Still clogging, still cloying, and treacherous if he got caught in it, but not taking him under. How was he holding on? What was he holding on *to*?

"Out loud, Fen. Anything you hear that's actual words, I want you to say them out loud."

"They don't make sense." Jacin shoved it out from between gritted teeth, hands cramped into fists, and *holdonholdonholdon, don't let it all the way in, don't let go.* The focus of his life for years had been keeping the insanity *in,* only spilling it when he couldn't help himself, and each time he'd let it out, he'd edged further from sanity, and it had been harder to claw his way back. "It's all just… frenzied."

"It doesn't matter what it sounds like. We all know it's not you, Fen. We all know the madness doesn't come from you, all right?"

That cool wind again, like… like *Malick.* Like it had been that night when Jacin had given up, given himself over to both Malick and silence, and a breeze had blown through his mind and settled it for a little while. Settled *him.* Calmed him like he hadn't been since… he couldn't remember.

Focus.

He was fulfilling a bargain he'd made with a *Temshiel,* and he was necessary to what Malick wanted. Malick wouldn't *let* Jacin get lost inside the insanity. Malick wasn't done with him yet. It was a cold thing, but a comfort nonetheless. Jacin's mental wind of noise and color was diligently sloughing away, without him even paying it any attention at all, and *wordswordswords* crowded behind it.

Not yours to spill rolled through Jacin's head, and he let it out in an unwilling whisper. And then the floodgates screeched open, and he couldn't stop it: "Sound the vaults of Raven, Wolf calls the Prime to his own."

It slid through his mind and out his mouth, slippery and too fast. His hands made a reach—for Malick, for the ring; Jacin didn't know—and he willfully restrained them.

"Wolf will *not* be thwarted, he sees the Eye and calls the Prime to his own, leers through a veil of burning skies to Raven's duplicity, and sends his call, start again, start again, the Prime has started again, back to Zero and rise to One, take up the call, Wolf's-own, the Blood of the Catalyst showers the Eye, plucks it, plucks it—"

"It's getting away from you." Malick's voice, calm and soothing. "You're letting the noise crowd in again, Fen. Relax. You won't get caught in it. You can have the quiet anytime you want."

Jacin latched onto it with a mental fist

"Malick." Shig's voice was high-pitched, excited. "It's like hearing the voices of the gods!"

"No shit," Malick snapped impatiently. "Now, shut up for a minute, can't you."

Jacin had squeezed his eyes shut somewhere along the way, but he could almost feel Malick turning back to him, could almost see his countenance softening.

"You're there, Fen, you've got it. Don't worry about what any of these words mean. Don't worry about how any of it sounds or where it's coming from."

Right. Don't worry about any of it, let Malick keep doing whatever it was he was doing—and what exactly *was* he doing, anyway? Taking Shig's power somehow and using it to turn Jacin into some kind of channel, or maybe just boosting it with his own. Jacin wasn't sure he cared. He just wanted it over. He let himself ride on the wave of nonreality, on the wind that Malick stirred inside him, and let the rest ride along with it.

"The earth shifts to Prime, the key, the Paradox, the Paradox, the key, mustn't take the key from the hand of the Prime, the gods have all gone silent and Wolf calls us home, your Blood, our Blood, our boy, clinging to corpses, only say it once, *listenlistenlisten*—"

"Fen, you're letting it get too much again, just—"

"*Eremite!*" It rocked out of Jacin's chest, loud and resonant, like it hadn't even come from him. Colors swamped through him again, bleeding out his mouth, he could taste them all, all at once, until the wave washed him under completely, bleached out to white and engulfed him. "Wolf waits for you to take up your Sorcerer's mantle. The Obelisk falls even now. Will you hear your god?"

Without his permission, Jacin's eyes popped open to see Malick's expression gone intense, his gaze instantly locked to Jacin's, light brown eyes all but burning. Jacin couldn't pull his own eyes away, couldn't control his own body. Panic, sharp and bright; he was drowning in white as utter silence broke through, heavy inside his head, pregnant and waiting. He leaned in, helpless to stop it, words forming on his tongue, booming out his mouth.

"Will you *hear*?"

"*Yes*," Malick breathed, too keyed-up for volume, but he took the time to tip a reassuring nod. "It's all right, Fen, just let it come."

Jacin couldn't have stopped it if he'd wanted to. It was stoppered up back there somewhere, *push-push-pushing* like something wanting to be born, and it wasn't about to be denied. It *shoved*.

"Justice is balance" came rolling from his mouth, deeper and clearer than anything that had ever twisted sense from the noise before. Everything else faded to a chaotic quiet at the back of his mind—even Jacin. "All fates rest on the Heart of the Null, yet the hand of Fate herself safeguards those who would mock Balance. Flout Fate to your own damnation. Fail the Fool and fail the Cycle. Wolf suffers not the duplicity of weaker gods. He calls the Prime to his duty. He calls his children home."

And then it all left him, like someone had just drained Jacin's mind, all color gone, all sense gone with it, all strength. The waves turned to a tempest and blanked into howls.

Shig was literally bouncing on the bed, beatific.

Malick was staring, dumbstruck, like he was the one with a precarious mind, thoughts rocketing around behind his eyes too fast for sense.

"Fen?" Malick leaned in, brow furrowing as his eyes cleared and he looked at Jacin with blooming worry. "Fen, are you—?"

"I need…" The clarity was gone, all at once—*pop!*—leaving Jacin muddled and lightheaded, the shrieking risen again and pulling him under. His hand flailed out, desperate and directionless. "I need…"

Malick's hand snapped up, took firm hold of Jacin's. The silence covered Jacin like a warm, petal-soft blanket, and he smelled pine.

"What the hell just happened?" Samin's voice, too fuzzy—from behind Jacin, from all around, from far, far away, from the other side of the world.

"Dizzy," Jacin heard himself mutter.

Malick snorted. "Yeah, I have that effect on people sometimes."

"That was Wolf's voice!" Shig was semi-euphoric, her voice bounding around the sudden quiet in Jacin's head, echoing 'til it made no sense at all. "Malick's been given—"

"Whoa, hey, *Fen!*" was all Jacin heard, then everything went black.

ᛝ

He came to with his head hanging heavily between his knees, a cold, wet cloth pressed to the back of his neck, and a gentle hand settled over his shoulder blade. It took him a moment, but Jacin eventually understood all the noise was gone again. He was alone in his head. The only sounds he heard were the soft drone of the rain and the voices of people with corporeal bodies attached to them.

"Shig, you've got to calm. The fuck. *Down.*" Malick. From right beside Jacin.

There was no surprise; even without the silence, Jacin would've recognized the touch. Wanted to keep it. Wanted to take a nice, heavy mallet to his pounding head for allowing the notion to slip into conscious thought.

Bloody hell, he was craving a cuddle. He wanted a fucking *cuddle*. He wanted to wake up all over again with a warm body snugged against his back and the pleasant weight of an arm draped over his ribs.

It was humiliating. Had he no dignity left at *all*?

"No, *you've* got to get more excited." Even without seeing her, Jacin could tell Shig was grinning and giddy. "Fuck's sake, Mal, you've just heard the voice of your *god*, you can't tell me—"

"Yeah, and he's ordered me to put everyone I know on the line. He's told me to break the laws. And did you happen to notice how there was no assurance I wouldn't end up sent to the suns for it? Ever heard 'damned if you do, damned if you don't'?"

"But... surely..." Samin's voice, strained and hesitant.

"Surely *nothing*. It changes *nothing*. Except now I have the very slim comfort that at least my god has as much morality as I do. I was beginning to wonder."

They all went quiet. Jacin could almost imagine them all frowning, broody.

Samin breached the silence with a skeptical tone. "I thought magic wasn't supposed to work on Fen."

"It didn't really work on *Fen*." Malick sounded thoughtful. "It worked on the Ancestors."

"What's the difference?"

"Plenty." Curt and clipped. A gentle squeeze to Jacin's shoulder. "You going to make it?"

Jacin gathered himself, and tried to straighten up. He growled when Malick had to help him, but it was mostly at himself.

"Bloody damn." Samin winced. "You look like shit."

Jacin was sure he did. He certainly felt like it.

"You want us to go?" Malick asked. Someone had slipped the ring onto Jacin's finger, he noticed, but Malick's hand still stayed where it was. "We could take this to my—"

"No. I need to..." Jacin paused, then turned to Malick. "Was that really Wolf?"

"Yeah, it was."

"Has that ever happened before?"

"What, a god speaking through a Catalyst?" Malick shook his head. "No. The gods used to speak through the Incendiary, but there are no Incendiary anymore—they were of the old magic, back when the world was still called Daichi, and most of them didn't survive long into the new world. Only one lasted... no, that doesn't matter right now. The point is sometimes the gods will speak through *Temshiel* if they have to. Catalysts have always been the Voices of the Ancestors, and the gods have never approved of them."

Incendiary echoed in Jacin's mind. The scent of cherry blossom petals came with it. He sniffed and shook it away.

Shig was still far too bouncy. "Except for Wolf."

Her openly pleased awe almost made Jacin smile until he remembered he was still pissed at her for the other night. Which reminded him that he was pissed at Malick for withholding the Yakuli thing. He shrugged Malick's hand off his shoulder.

Malick let him without protest. "Except for Wolf. But even Wolf has never spoken through any but the Incendiary and the *Temshiel*." He tipped a wink and a small grin at Jacin. "Guess that makes you special."

Oh good. Because *that* couldn't set Jacin skidding more quickly on his road to ruin.

He shook that away too. "How d'you know it really was Wolf?"

The voice had been different than what normally shrieked through Jacin's head. All of it had been different. But the Ancestors were long-dead lunatics with magic. Impersonating a god didn't seem to be something too far outside the realm of believability.

"It was," Malick said, firm, if a little reluctant.

Jacin supposed he had to take Malick's word for it. He didn't like taking Malick's word for anything. Malick was too good at telling only partial truths and making it look like it was your own fault for not seeing what he hadn't told you.

Except.

There was a too-evident sense of morality in there, a strangely consistent opinion on right and wrong, and a willingness to skirt the laws that bound him to keep his own conscience. Such as it apparently was.

Jacin hadn't understood Malick at all, at first. He still didn't mostly. It should be unsettling. What Malick had said last night had hit something, something that hurt, because Jacin had known it for truth right away—things Jacin didn't understand scared the shit out of him. Because, for the most part, he didn't have the resources normal people had to figure them out.

Funny thing, though—he didn't necessarily need those resources with Malick.

Not the hard, cold, manipulative bastard he was trying to be; Jacin could see that now. Hard, cold, manipulative bastards didn't cuddle and stroke, and soothe, even when they weren't aware the one being cuddled, stroked, and soothed was awake to notice. No matter how much Malick supposedly needed Jacin for his plots and plans, there was something else in there, something soft and smushy armored only by craft and calluses.

Temshiel with a mortal heart—it was almost worth a bit of pity.

Jacin chewed his lip. "What does all this mean?"

"It means…" Malick scrubbed at his hair, everything about him all at once exhausted and unhappy. "Apparently Wolf and Raven are having a little pissing contest, and we get to be good little toadies and put ourselves on the line so they don't have to." He shook his head. "I think I know what Umeia was talking about now." It was baleful, quiet, seemingly to himself. He lifted his head, giving them all a steady look, one after the other. "There's no one way to keep the Balance. If Asai gets his way, it *would* set it firm in its fulcrum for… centuries, maybe forever. But his way isn't the *right* way, damn it, I wish Umeia would…" Malick sighed and knuckled his eyes. "Although, the 'right' way depends on which perspective you're looking at it from, I guess."

"And you've been commanded to look at it from your own." Shig was still a little high, and smiling more than was probably appropriate, considering the subject matter.

"Commanded, but not guaranteed protection." Malick curled his lip. "But yeah. In the end, I'm Wolf's and Wolf wants it. About fucking time too."

It gave Jacin an odd feeling he didn't quite know how to parse. Compassion, maybe. Jacin could kill Asai and stand before the gods with a firm defense. Malick couldn't. He'd offered to risk his soul, before his god told him he should; Jacin believed Malick meant it. Even if he'd been intending to do it in a way that minimized the risk as much as possible. But who wouldn't, really? And if Malick truly was punch-drunk, like Shig said, and taking all that risk for Jacin... well. Compassion or no, it was a mark on the soul Jacin would accept.

"'Fail the Fool and Fail the Cycle.'" Jacin peered up at Malick. "What does that mean? Fail how? Who is the Fool?"

Malick looked at Jacin straight. "I don't know."

No hitch or twitch, no telltale. Still, Jacin narrowed his eyes. It felt like a lie. And Malick was a difficult person to read when he wanted to be.

Had Jacin just been thinking he could almost trust a *Temshiel*?

"So." Samin scrubbed at his short brown hair. "We're going after Yakuli, then."

A light knock on the door made them all turn in time to see a folded piece of paper slip beneath it. Shig got up to retrieve it, read it with a frown, then handed it over to Malick as she climbed back up beside him on the bed.

"It's from Ragi."

Malick frowned at it, too, but merely slipped it into the pocket of his shirt. "It'll have to wait. Can't do six things at once."

He looked at each of them in turn. "We're going after Yakuli. We go back tonight. I want to see the place for myself. And once we see, we come back here, and you'll think long and hard about whether or not you really want to do this." He turned to Samin. "I gave you the choice before. I'm going to give it to you again. Once more. I want no decisions until tomorrow, but once you've made them, there's no going back. Understand?"

Samin pursed his mouth, but he nodded. Shig had finally lost all the bounce from before.

Jacin noticed Malick didn't look at him while making the offer. Jacin was in it until the end, one way or another. Which was exactly where he wanted to be, so he didn't take offense.

"Which way d'you think Yori will jump?" Malick asked Shig reluctantly. "She's always been Umeia's. I only—"

"No she hasn't." Shig was clearly offended. "She's mine. She always has been. Just as much as I'm hers. And we all know which way *I'll* jump."

It seemed to be enough for Malick.

Jacin didn't necessarily care what Yori might do. "So, when do we go? I mean… it's only…" He set his jaw. It was too late for sentiment. "My family leaves in the morning. I… I should… see them for a little while."

"You should." Malick shrugged. "And you can see them all night, because you're not coming."

Jacin jolted. "You can't keep me from—"

"Yeah, I can, actually." It was hard, and colder than Jacin had seen Malick for a while now. He made a visible effort to soften it. "Fen, be reasonable. You can't even walk."

"I can walk! I'm fine."

"Yeah, *fine*." Malick rolled his eyes. "You're always *fine*. And what happens if we get halfway there and you're not *fine* anymore?"

"I've got the dray." Jacin frowned. "Haven't I?" He couldn't remember. In fact, he had no idea if they'd brought it back to the Girou or if they'd abandoned it outside the gates.

"A dray would blare our arrival to anyone within a mile, and I can't veil you." Malick sighed. "Fen, think about it. You know it's how it has to be. We couldn't attack tonight, even if you did manage to limp there. There's no way in hell we can get to your mother until we know exactly what we're up against. I need to see it for myself, because there are things even Shig can't see."

It all made sense. And Jacin hated him for it.

"And what the fuck am I supposed to do? This is my *mother*! You promised. We made a *deal*. You *swore* you'd—"

"And I'll *keep* it, damn it." Malick was trying very hard not to be offended, Jacin could tell, and didn't entirely care. "I'm sorry I won't be able to keep it before the others leave, but that's not *your* failure, it's mine. You can face them without hiding this time, all right?"

Jacin flinched. Damn it all, how did Malick keep… *understanding* like that, when Jacin hadn't even been aware of exactly what he'd been thinking?

"You can be really cold sometimes, Mal." Shig nearly chirped it, like she was admiring, rather than chiding.

"Yeah, well, sometimes he needs a kick in the ass. And since he's already beat to shit…" Malick gave Jacin a bit of a glare before turning to Shig. "Did you get all of what he was saying before written down?"

Jacin winced when Shig nodded and retrieved a marked-up slate from the mattress behind her. No one had told him they'd be writing it down, which probably meant they'd be reading it, and he was going to have to *hear* how crazy he'd sounded. It was different when it was happening—he didn't have enough of his mind to know how bad it sounded out loud when he lost hold of it like that, because he was usually too busy trying to keep it in. And now his mind was relatively his own, wreathed in a quiet to which he was getting far too accustomed and far too quickly, and they were going to make him hear it anyway.

At least this time, no one seemed to notice Jacin's internal flailing.

Malick held out his hand to Shig. "All right, let's have a look and see if we can decode it." He shifted a quick look up at Samin. "You should probably find someplace comfortable. This'll likely take a while." And then to Jacin. He held up the slate, waved it between them. "None of it's you. So, stop it."

Jacin glared and sank back into the cushions of the chair.

Damn it, how did he always *know?*

Yori was getting a little sick of playing babysitter. She was getting *really* sick of cooling her heels while the others discussed... whatever they were discussing. And she was getting *bloody* sick and damned tired of playing messenger.

"Another one?" She couldn't help her churlish tone.

It didn't matter, anyway, because Ragi not only ignored it but topped it. "It can't wait." He stood just below the top step on the attic stairs, not quite daring to broach the attic itself. All the staff and all the help had been threatened with immediate expulsion from the Girou and possible death—depending on Malick's mood—should they trespass, and Ragi was keeping to the letter of the warning, grudgingly, if not entirely the spirit. "I need to see him *now.*"

Well, at least it was a little excitement to break up what was otherwise a ridiculously monotonous morning. Not that Yori minded being "stuck" with Joori—even though he'd been annoyingly antsy and short-tempered— but she did sort of mind being "stuck" with Morin and Caidi, because their presence rather ruled out doing anything good to pass the time. They'd played cards—Suns and Moons because it was the only game Caidi could win once in a while—until they couldn't stand to look at them anymore, and then watched the rain until it stopped. In the lull, Morin and Joori had filled the silence by snarking at each other until Yori was ready to bash their heads together, and then did it some more until she actually threatened it. They'd been reduced to nursery songs before Ragi came along, so Yori had to concede that his annoying presence was at least distracting.

Yori rolled her eyes. "What d'you need *Mal* for, anyway? He's got nothing to do with the bloody kitchens. Go bother Lex or Umeia."

"I don't need Lex or Umeia."

"Is the kitchen actually on fire?"

Ragi's mouth set tight, and his eyes narrowed. "I need Malick. *Now.*"

Yori's mouth tightened too. Ragi was *so* not the boss of her. "Well, you'll just have to write him another note, because he's not to be disturbed."

Ragi was not a huge man—tall, surely, and sinewy, no wider than Malick, really—but he seemed to expand right in front of Yori as his expression shut down into blank determination. He braved the last step, took Yori by the arms, lifted her off her feet, and set her to the side. Yori was so stunned she almost didn't gather her wits before he'd started down the hall. Did the man not understand he was imperiously stomping his way right into the middle of a den of assassins?

Then again, no, Yori supposed he didn't.

"Hey!" She set her pace to a fast trot as she tried to catch up with Ragi's longer stride. "*Hey*! You can't—"

"*Malick!*"

A bellow, deep and clear, and echoing down the hallway at a tooth-jarring volume. Yori only just got her hand latched onto Ragi's sleeve before he snatched his arm away and opened the first door he came to.

"*Malick!*"

Bloody hell, if Ragi was going to try going door to door, and if Yori didn't stop him, he was going to end up seeing Joori and the children, and Yori couldn't allow that. Damn it all, Joori probably had his ear plastered to the other side of the door, and would end up with a concussion if Ragi threw that one open like he'd just done Malick's. Not for the first time, Yori rued the fact that her weapon of choice wasn't something she could handily tote around in a sheath at her belt or tuck neatly into a boot.

"*Malick!*"

"Ragi, you can't *do* this! You're not even supposed to be up here! Mal's going to kill you if you don't—"

"*Malick!*"

Yori was just darting around Ragi, trying to get between him and the next door, which happened to be hers and Shig's, when Fen's door opened across the hall, and Malick slammed through it, knife in hand and murder on his face.

"What the *fuck* is—?" He stopped dead when he saw who it was, brow twisting. "Ragi. What are—?"

"No time." Ragi looked relieved but no less determined. "We have to go."

"*We* nothing. I'm busy. Tell Hus—" Malick darted a look at Yori and pursed his mouth. "Tell your boss it'll have to wait."

"It can't. Didn't you get my note?" Ragi shot Yori an accusing look.

Yori bristled, but she didn't have time to retort.

"I got it." Malick's eyes took on that cool look they got sometimes when he was trying to decide which would be the easiest way to kill a person. "He's *your* boss, not mine. I told you, I'm busy." He tucked the knife back into its sheath, then opened Fen's door behind him and turned to go back inside. "I'll come when I—"

"Xari says the cards have changed."

Oddly, Ragi's tone sounded to Yori like it had an edge of desperation beneath it.

Maybe it did, because it stopped Malick, made him snap his glance back to Ragi over his shoulder. "Which cards?"

"All of them."

Malick stared at him like he could look right through him to bone, then turned an intense look on Yori. "Where's Umeia?"

It was all Yori could do not to take a flinching step backward. "I don't know."

Yori hadn't seen Umeia since before Malick told her they'd be taking Joori and the others to Heldesan tomorrow. She'd tried—had herself a look around the Girou last night, sent three messages through Lex, and if Umeia had been in her rooms either of the times Yori'd knocked, she hadn't chosen to answer.

Malick was still looking at her, his expression perhaps not quite as gritty as it had been a moment ago, a little softer but by no means soft. It hardened again when he turned to Ragi.

"Go. I'll follow shortly."

Ragi shook his head, jaw set tight. "He said—"

"It's the best answer you're going to get. Give me a fucking minute, will you? Tell him I'll be there within the hour."

Ragi stared, obviously having some internal debate with himself, before he growled with a grudging nod. "Go to Xari's." He turned a dour look on Yori then back to Malick. "And go veiled." His usual scowl set firmly back in place, Ragi turned and left, his steps heavy as he made his way down the stairs.

Malick glared after him. Clenching his teeth on a throttled growl, he muttered, "*Shit,*" under his breath, then turned to Yori. He glanced down at her feet. "Go get some shoes on. You're coming with me."

Yori barely had time to gape before Shig was poking her head out Fen's door. She lifted her eyebrows at Yori for a second, but only gave her a small smile before tugging at Malick's sleeve.

"Mal?"

Malick was staring down the stairwell again, distracted. His fists were curling and uncurling at his sides, and he still hadn't unclenched his jaw.

"She has to be told sometime, Shig. Everyone's got decisions to make and sides to choose." He shook his head then turned around to look at Shig. "D'you know what's going on with Umeia?"

Oddly, Shig couldn't seem to hold Malick's eye. She shot another glance at Yori then pointed her gaze to the floor.

"I've said my goodbyes."

"You want to tell me what that means?"

"What d'you think it means?"

Malick seemed to know, because he looked like he wanted to deck

Shig, or maybe just whoever happened to be nearest. He turned back to Yori.

"Shoes. And get Little Lord Pain-in-the-ass. Get them all, and bring them here."

Yori already had the door to her room open when she heard Malick mutter, presumably to Shig, "Fen's going to fucking kill me," but Yori didn't stop or look back. If Malick's mood was anything to go by, speed was highly recommended. She'd seen Malick really pissed once or twice, but it was usually because some target hadn't died as quickly and easily as assumed, or he'd lost more at cards downstairs than he thought right and proper. He'd *never* been angry with Yori. She didn't want to find out what it felt like.

She threw open her wardrobe and shoved her feet into stockings and boots, and herself into Shig's waxed duster. Her bow and quiver stood in the back corner; she paused as she reached for them—only briefly—then followed her instinct and shouldered them.

Malick's order to collect Joori and the others turned out to be wasted breath. Joori was already hanging on Fen's doorjamb when Yori emerged back into the hallway. Caidi and Morin were still hovering at the door to their own room, eyes a little anxious, so Yori gave them an easy smile and a little push down the hall.

"What's going on?" Morin demanded.

"Nothing bad." Yori planted him and Caidi behind Joori outside Fen's door, laying a brief squeeze to Joori's shoulder as she pushed past him. She had no idea what was going on, in truth, and the tableau she walked in on seemed to belie her assurance.

She was fairly surprised to see Fen standing, with only a hand braced to the back of the chair for support. Yori would've thought it would take at least a week or so to get him upright, considering.

Fen was glaring at Malick. Nothing new, so not worrisome.

Malick wasn't answering it with his usual smirk or leer, though; he was glaring right back.

"I'm not doing this again. If we can still do it tonight, we will, but I'm not—"

"That's not what I was talking about, and you know it." Fen's voice was venomous. He shot a quick look over at the doorway, mouth crimping at Joori's unabashed smirk—Yori had to roll her eyes—then he leaned in and lowered his voice. "I don't care about any bloody paradox, *or* any key. We agreed." He took hold of Malick's sleeve. "You *promised*."

"I know. I was there. And I'll deal with this when I get back."

"From *where*? What are you plotting now, and what—?"

"*I can't fucking do this now, Fen!*" Loud and strung far too tight.

It stopped everyone.

Malick looked at no one but Fen, who met his gaze with as much fire in it as Yori had ever seen. Gently but firmly, Malick took hold of Fen's arms and pushed him back into the chair. Fen had no choice but to buckle his good leg and make the descent as pain-free as possible, growling all the way down.

"This is important." Malick leaned over Fen, tone solemn, gaze intense. "I wouldn't be going, else, damn it. You think I *want* to go? *Now?*" With an annoyed grunt, he straightened, and turned to take in everyone else crammed into the room. "Whatever else Umeia's doing, she's still veiling all of you. But watch. No one is to be left alone."

Odd. It sounded like Malick was warning them against trouble here at the Girou, which was… ridiculous. Obviously. And odder still, it sounded like he was warning them against Umeia.

Malick turned back to Fen, hands out. "I'm not taking it back, all right? I swear. Just… give me 'til I get back, and we'll figure it out. Please."

Fen's scowl was fierce as he waved angrily at his leg. "I haven't much choice, have I?"

"The only thing that's gone halfway right today," Malick muttered irritably then turned to Yori. "Let's go."

Yori jumped, startled, and shot her glance to Shig with a lift of her eyebrows, asking. Shig only gave her an unhappy smile and a shrug, but she nodded in reassurance. Yori breathed a tiny bit easier. Her normally calm and pleasant life seemed to be erupting into doubt and chaos with every passing moment, but Shig *knew* things, and that nod told Yori that it would work out in the end.

She let Malick take her arm and all but shove her through the door, but stopped when she came face-to-face with Joori. Yori peered up at Malick, quirking an eyebrow.

Malick rolled his eyes, let go of her arm, and stalked away. "I'm going to get my coat. You've got thirty seconds."

Yori didn't wait for him to stomp across the hall and disappear into his room before she reached out for Joori's hand and clamped onto it.

"What's going on?" Joori was clearly anxious.

Yori couldn't blame him. "I don't know. But it appears I'm about to find out."

And about bloody time too. She hadn't realized how much had been going on just beneath her sight until now, and it wasn't like she could blame anyone else for it. She'd been smitten and enjoying herself, and letting everyone else pick up the slack. If she'd demanded answers the moment she realized she didn't have them, they would've stopped and given them to her, but she hadn't. For the first time in her life, she'd had a real lover—not someone who used her body because they could, and not someone she'd paid to be nice to her for an evening and pretend she mattered. Joori liked her, wanted to be with her, and it seemed like it had made Yori's brain go a little wobbly.

No more.

She straightened when Malick slammed back out of his room, blew past her toward the stairs, and gave her a brusque wave over his shoulder without looking back. He grunted something that sounded like "Come on" and kept going.

Yori gave Joori a reassuring smile, squeezed his hand tight before letting it go. "I'll see you when I get back." She took off after Malick. "Don't fight with Shig while I'm gone!"

"Be careful!"

Yori paused on the stairs, then turned around to give Joori a grin. She'd heard it hundreds of times from Shig, from Malick, from Samin, from Umeia, but from Joori… it just sounded different. Made affection bloom in her belly and warm her through.

She thumped her fist to her breastbone, said "Yes, seyh!" then headed off, taking the steps two at a time to catch up with Malick.

She had no idea where they were going, nor what they were going to be doing once they got there. But she was with Malick, and Malick would make sure everything turned out all right. He always had.

Yori leapt the last three steps down to the third-floor hallway, pushing past a few of Umeia's lads and ladies loitering outside their doors. She gave Umeia's door a brief glance as she passed it then quickened her pace and trotted after Malick.

"All right," Malick said as Yori caught up to him, and they started down the stairs to the second floor. "Let's get you up to speed on what's been going on."

※

"You're going to do yourself more damage." Joori watched unhappily as Jacin hobbled from the chair to the clothespress. "Hasn't anyone thought to get you a crutch or something?" His glare was accusing when he strafed it around the room.

Shig merely gave Joori a blithe little smile and no comment whatsoever. Samin turned and frowned at him, surprised and not happy about it, like he hadn't thought of a crutch and was annoyed with himself that he hadn't.

Jacin merely shrugged as he hitched up against the clothespress. "They don't want me up yet." He was breathing heavier than he apparently wanted to show, face set into stony lines, and a light scrim of sweat on his brow. "And I don't need a crutch."

Samin snorted a querulous little grunt, but said nothing.

A strange man, Samin. Big and blocky, yet still strangely approachable. Predator or protector, depending on which side of his line you stood. Edgy and on watch now, but he'd quietly and casually been helping a resentful and embarrassed Jacin into a pair of trousers when

Joori had herded Morin and Caidi through the door, sliding the fabric up over the heavy bandages with a matter-of-fact gentleness that somehow didn't seem out of place. And the way he doted on Caidi was just... cute.

Speaking of—

"I'm so *boooooored*," Caidi moaned. She'd been sitting in the middle of the rumpled bed next to Morin, but now she threw herself facedown into the mound of sheets and blankets with a disgruntled sigh. "And I'm *huuuuuungry*."

Joori seized on it. "Yeah, isn't it past lunchtime?"

He shifted significant, expectant looks between Shig and Samin, pleased when, unbidden, Caidi lifted her head and gave the room in general hopeful puppy eyes. Even Morin unintentionally cooperated, sliding his bored glance from its contemplation of the gray day through the window and letting it flick around, eyebrows raised. Joori buried a smirk when Samin's gruff face turned resigned.

They'd all been corralled in Jacin's room since Malick stalked off with Yori. They hadn't been left alone for even a second; they couldn't even travel down the hallway to the washroom unaccompanied.

Samin and Shig were both armed. Samin paced the room, agitated. Shig merely leaned with her back to the far wall, arms crossed over her chest. Her gaze was distant, but weirdly intent, as though watching things no one else could see.

Joori wasn't sure if they were being protected or imprisoned, but since the presence of Samin and Shig prevented him from talking openly to Jacin, like he desperately needed to, it all amounted to the same thing. Time was running out all too quickly, and Joori was stuck just *sitting* here in limbo, waiting it out. It was making him insane.

"I expect they need to be fed." Samin peered at Shig with a lift of eyebrows, as though looking for agreement.

Shig only stared, blinking slowly. Apparently, she had no intention of being the one to feed them.

Samin's mouth clamped into a sour line. "Can you at least tell me nothing's going to happen if I go down for some trays?"

"Maybe—if I were a seer."

"Damn it, Shig, this is not the time for your games!" Samin turned scary when he was pissed. "Are we all right or not?"

Shig sighed, her expression and her stance both drooping. "I'm not a seer, Samin." It was almost gentle. "I can't tell you what's going to happen."

So why did Joori get the feeling she knew anyway? And why was he the only one who seemed to notice that she hadn't actually answered the question?

"...Fine." Samin sounded resigned, but his gaze was still flinty. "I'll go and collect a tray or two. *You.*" He jabbed a finger at Shig. "Pay attention. Do whatever it is you do, and *watch.* Understand?"

Joori was dying to ask exactly what they were supposed to be watching *for,* but didn't necessarily care. One thing was just as bad as another, he supposed, and danger was danger. All the more reason to get them all the fuck *out* of here, and the removal of Samin as a blockade was something to be encouraged.

"I get it, Samin." Shig's green eyes were sharper than Joori thought he'd ever seen them, no amusement in her expression now, no dreamy abstraction. "Go get some lunch."

Jacin hadn't seemed to be paying much attention, instead slowly making his way over to the door, where his belts and straps and sheaths hung from hooks on the back. He threw the longer ones to dangle loose over his shoulders; the others he bunched into one hand and used his other hand to hold himself up as he carefully made his way back to the clothespress.

Joori scowled. "I would've got those for you if you'd asked."

Jacin might not have even heard him, for all the reaction he offered. Joori watched him flop the belts and sheaths over the knives laid out on top of the press before he began to methodically strap them on. Jaw clamped, Joori looked away and sent a steady look at Samin, who was peering at Jacin with something soft-ish and faintly approving.

Joori shook his head. "Is there anything we're supposed to do while you're gone?"

"Stay here." Samin sucked a tooth, clearly unhappy. "And do what Shig tells you."

Joori merely lifted an eyebrow, his skepticism over being "protected" and possibly ordered around by someone who rarely even spared the attention to follow a conversation purposely plain.

Samin ignored it, shot one more dark look at Shig, flipped it over to Jacin, then quit the room with a gruff "I'll be back anon."

Silence fell; the occasional slap-and-slide of leather and steel as Jacin armed himself was loud inside it. Joori watched him for a while, watched the sweat build up on Jacin's too-pale face, the fine tremor in his fingers, the way his jaw tightened once in a while on a thwarted wince as he tied the butt of a sheath to his thigh with a leather thong to keep it in place.

Joori looked away, shaking his head. What did Jacin think he was going to be able to do if they were attacked? He couldn't even walk without limping.

It would do no good to say as much. Jacin wouldn't listen, and that would just piss Joori off more.

Instead, Joori asked, "What's that ring?" It had been bothering him since he'd spotted it—partly because of what Umeia had said when she'd handed it over to Shig, but mostly because Jacin had obviously accepted it.

"Yeah." Morin tilted his head, openly curious. "Is it real? Looks like it'd feed a whole family for five years. Malick give it to you?"

Predictably, Jacin didn't answer, though Joori couldn't tell if it was because he didn't want to or if he simply hadn't heard the question. He'd seemed rather removed from them all since they'd been herded in, even Caidi, and Joori had seen Jacin sink inside himself and his Voices before.

"Hey!" Morin raised his voice. "Jacin-rei, I asked—"

"*Jacin*." It snapped out of Joori, reflex, probably a little sharper than it should've been, but he was on edge and not in the mood for Morin's shit right now. "Why d'you have to do that? Father's not even here anymore, and nobody else in the world but you calls him Jacin-rei. D'you hate him that much?"

Jacin didn't react, steadily strapping on belts and sheaths then sliding knives into them.

Morin watched him for a moment before turning to Joori. "I called him that when I was little because Father demanded it and it pissed you off. I call him that now because it's what he is." He didn't blush or look away when Joori gaped at him, only shrugged. "I don't hate him." He went back to watching Jacin, who was still behaving as though he was in the room by himself. "But you've done him no favors by pretending he isn't what he is."

"What the hell is *that* supposed to mean?"

"It doesn't matter, because you'll never see it. You've always refused to look." Morin met Joori's gaze squarely. "You're a good brother, Joori. But you're crap at accepting people for what they are."

"Have you lost your small mind? I'm the *only one* who—"

"You taught him how to stay sane," Shig put in quietly. "But you also taught him to hope for the impossible. He was always going to be what he is. Pretending he wasn't and convincing him to believe it seems… kinda cruel."

Joori's mouth flapped, dozens of hot retorts and plenty of vicious profanity accumulating at the back of his throat.

Jacin beat him to it. "Shut up, Shig." It was quiet and low but laden with threat. "You've no right to an opinion when it comes to my family." Jacin turned slowly, his eyes burning out of their bruised hollows from beneath stringy, uneven fringe.

Shig looked back calmly, but she seemed… odd now. Strained.

"Umeia's coming."

Shit. Did that mean Umeia was going to try to take them away now? Were they still expected to go with her? They *still* hadn't been told who they were being "protected" from, and Joori had no idea if they were going to be handed over to Umeia and expected to follow after her meekly, or if all this sudden tension was a result of whatever had happened between Malick and Umeia.

Joori shot his glance between Shig and Jacin. "What does that mean?"

"It means we're leaving now." Jacin opened the clothespress and took out a hefty little purse that clinked with promise as he stuffed it down his shirt. "It means we're not waiting for Umeia, we're not depending on Malick, and we're not asking permission. We'll meet the caravan tonight, but we're leaving here now. Get your shoes on."

"Stunned" was probably a good word for the silence that settled. Probably a good word for the wave of relief and elation that swamped through Joori too. He thought he might be grinning.

"Yeah?"

"Yeah." Jacin limped back over to the door and snagged the long duster that hung on a hook, slipping it on to cover the crisscross of belts and straps that entwined him.

"You sure you want to do that, Fen?" Shig asked softly. "She's not alone."

"All the more reason." Jacin's mouth tightened, and if possible, his eyes blazed harder. "Malick wants to keep them here. I can't allow that. It's *my* duty—not theirs."

Wait, what duty? And what did Jacin mean by *Malick wants to keep them here*? Had Malick broken his promise to get them out safely?

"True." Shig's mouth turned down. "But the Ancestors told him to."

"*Fuck* the Ancestors!" Jacin snapped. "We're getting out of here. Now." He gave Shig a look of clear challenge. "You going to try to stop us?"

What would happen if it came down to a fight? Joori had seen Jacin at work before, but he wasn't in very good shape right now, and Shig could do things with her *mind*. Joori skimmed quick glances at Caidi and Morin, both of them staring wide-eyed, thankfully quiet and waiting to see how it all shook out, keeping an eye on Jacin for cues.

"No." Shig closed her eyes, hand coming up to rub distractedly at her forehead. "I wouldn't be able to if I wanted to." She dropped her hand and leveled an intent gaze on Jacin. Joori was surprised and dismayed to see a small trickle of blood leaking from her left nostril. "Don't forget what you are, Fen Jacin-rei. Don't forget what any of them are." And then her eyes rolled back, and she slid down the wall into a heap on the floor.

Caidi gave a little *meep!* but stayed where she was, her huge hazel eyes going from Shig to Joori to Jacin then back again.

Jacin watched Shig's descent with abrupt alarm, breathed, "*Shit*," then jerked his chin at Joori and shoved the door open. "Move. *Now*. Go get their shoes and—"

"No need to panic, lad." Umeia's shapely figure was framed in the open doorway. She held a crutch in her hand—the irony of it thoroughly stunting any sense Joori might have made of it, and any gratitude he might have had for it otherwise. Her eyes slid to the knives Jacin had unsheathed and clenched tight in his fists, then up to his face. "You look... better."

Everything about Jacin was blaring furious threat. "What did you do to Shig?"

"Worried about her, are you? You don't even like her." Umeia's gaze went to the huddled heap on the floor across the room. "Nothing too serious. Unfortunately, I caught Samin on the steps, but he's only got a bump on the head. Well, that and your lunch all over his trousers. Van and Bone are trying to move him now, but he's rather large, so." She shrugged. "They'll both be fine. I only needed them out for a while."

"Why?"

"You already know why. Malick wants to keep them here, doesn't he? You don't want it, and I can't allow it. I'm getting you all out." Umeia shot a look at Joori. "Do as your brother told you. Get ready to leave. There's not much time."

Joori looked at Jacin, waiting, because he wasn't about to trust any of these people, no matter that what he was hearing now seemed to be exactly what he'd been wanting since... ever. Jacin just looked back at him, then gave his head a little jerk toward the door—permission; command—so Joori chivvied Morin and Caidi off the bed and out of the room.

He paused in the doorway and then turned to Jacin. "We go together. Right?"

Because he knew bloody well that Jacin had had no intention of leaving with them before all of... whatever all this was.

Jacin didn't look at him. "Not now, Joori."

And since Caidi was already halfway down the hallway and Morin was staring at Joori with something between blame and gloom, Joori decided to leave it until he saw what happened next. What choice did he have?

With one last look at Shig crumpled on the floor, Joori followed Caidi down the hall to the room they'd been loaned. Caidi already had her shoes and cloak on, busy now collecting what few things they'd removed from the packs and sacks and shoving them wherever she found room.

"Is Umeia-onna taking us somewhere good?" She picked up the porcelain doll Samin had bought her, her heart-shaped little face twisted in concern. "Is Samin-seyh hurt? It sounded like he's hurt. Should we ask her? Is he coming too? We're not gonna leave Shig-onna on the floor, are we? Won't Malick-seyh be mad if we leave while he's—?"

"Caidi." Joori dragged on a pair of Jacin's boots and caught up his cloak and Morin's. "Let's just go now, and we'll talk about it on the way, all right?" Because any second now she was going to ask about Yori, and Joori was doing everything he could not to wonder if he'd ever see her again.

"On the way where?" Morin buckled a pack shut. "Does Jacin-rei trust her?"

"I doubt it." Joori threw Morin's cloak at him and swung the sack Caidi had loaded over his shoulder. "But *Jacin* won't let anything bad happen."

Morin pulled the cloak on, then took one of the smaller packs and settled it over Caidi's shoulders. He took the bigger one for himself.

"You really think he can stop a determined *Temshiel*?"

Joori wasn't sure of anything right now. "Let's go."

He pushed Morin out the door and waited for Caidi to trot past him before taking a quick look around the little room that wasn't home but almost could have been. He shut the door behind him, deliberately not thinking.

Jacin and Umeia were waiting for them in the hall, engaged in a low-voiced conversation that didn't look terribly friendly.

"…know all that." Fire might as well have been shooting from Jacin's mouth, the way he was spitting the words. "Did you think I'm a fucking idiot? I know what Malick is, I know what Asai is, and I know what I have to do."

Umeia looked unhappy. "And I can't change your mind?"

"Why would you try?"

"Because you don't have to *do* this, lad."

"Yeah, I do. She's my *mother*."

Joori herded Caidi and Morin in front of him. "Do what, exactly?"

Jacin clamped his mouth shut and looked away, sending an angry gaze down the steps. Umeia merely stared at Jacin. She looked genuinely sad about something, but with all the confusion under which he'd been flailing since Malick and Yori had bolted out of here, Joori had no idea what to make of any of it.

"Your choice, Fen." Umeia tipped a nod at Joori. "Help him with the steps."

Jacin wouldn't let him. And he knocked the crutch out of Umeia's hand with a sneer, glaring as it clattered to the floor. Umeia only looked at it with a lift of her eyebrow, shrugged, and waved at the steps. Jacin descended more slowly than he would've done a few days ago, but he was steadier than Joori thought he'd be. Either he'd been overdoing the limp before to fool Shig and Samin, or he was underdoing it now to fool Umeia. Joori didn't know which, or why Jacin would do either, but it showed that Jacin was thinking, planning, and it gave Joori hope.

Joori had expected to be stared at as they went. The "lads and ladies" were all up and about now, socializing with each other or berobed and headed for the baths. But no one seemed to even notice them. It wasn't like that night when Malick had got them through the gates—there was no swell of magic, no vertigo or lingering high. It was just a complete lack of notice on the parts of everyone around them. Umeia's magic, Joori had to assume, though he hadn't known she could do something like this. Then again, she was *Temshiel*, and what did he really know about their limits?—if they even had any.

The back stairs past the kitchens still had evidence of the spilled trays Samin must have been carrying—rice and noodles everywhere on the landing—but there was no sign of Samin himself. Joori was surprised to find himself hoping Samin would be all right. Besides Yori, Joori thought he probably liked Samin the most out of any of these people. Straightforward and… what? Honorable, maybe. Or at least as honorable as an assassin could be, Joori supposed.

Umeia laid a hand on the handle of the door at the bottom of the stairs, the one that led in from the back alley. She turned to look at Jacin as she swung the door open.

"I'm sorry, lad. But you won't listen, and I can't take any more chances."

Too cryptic to make sense of, but it still made fear rise in Joori's chest, sharp and cold, because Jacin… froze.

Froze.

Everything blurred. Too fast to track. When Joori could mark what was happening again, Umeia had already got behind Jacin, and shoved him facefirst into the wall beside the open door. Another blur, then she had Jacin's arms twisted behind his back, held at the wrists and hiked up at too-sharp angles between his shoulder blades. Pinned. Jacin fought it, wild, but Umeia didn't budge, and Joori's brain hummed *she's Temshiel, too strong, shit!*

Joori tried to surge forward, knock her away… couldn't move. Just like that night when the hunters had come for his mother. Paralyzed, forced to do nothing but watch, Morin and Caidi sentient dolls to either side of him.

"You fucking *bitch*!" Jacin's roar was fathoms deep with pain and betrayal and deep-dark rage as his gaze found and held something Joori couldn't yet see out in the alley. "You can't do this, you swore *oath*, you can't—"

"I swore oath to your family, Fen. And I'll keep it. I didn't swear to you." Umeia held on as Jacin struggled and snarled, but he was weak and hurt, and Umeia had *Temshiel* strength. She angled flush behind Jacin, pressed him harder into the wall then closed her eyes and laid her cheek to his. "I'm sorry, lad. You chose your brother and I chose mine. I'll keep my promise. They'll be all right."

"No, they *won't!*" Jacin bucked his whole body, managing to jostle Umeia but not enough to get loose. "Fucking *bitch*, don't you know what—?"

"I expect I know a great deal more about all this than you do." Umeia adjusted her grip and flattened Jacin brutally into the wall, shaking her head as he grunted. "Believe me or don't, but I'll keep them safe. Heart and body; breath and spirit."

She turned her glance out the door. "He'll need to be bound or he'll—"

Jacin tried again to jerk in her grip, tried to get loose from her impossible hold.

Umeia set her teeth and held on. "Probably sedated too."

The day was gray and damp, almost oppressive with the heavy warmth and the stench of the alley seeping in through the door. There was no real sunlight for shadows, but Joori could swear he saw one darkening the doorway, and the scent of jasmine leached in, cloying.

Jacin kept glaring and snarling and fighting as light footsteps approached. One cheek was still mashed into the wall, but his wild eyes never left whatever—whomever—they were watching.

"No. *No.*" Little more than a brittle wheeze, and Jacin all at once sagged, breath coming in harsh little hitches, face so filled with pain Joori could almost feel it twisting in his own chest.

Defeated, powerless, Jacin shut his eyes, teeth clenched tight.

"Beishin… *please.*"

6

It hurt. There was a time when that plea would have meant entirely different things, and there would not have been that heavy thrum of betrayal beneath it. There was a time when Jacin-rei would have begged his beishin for other things, and there was a time when Asai had been so sure in his refusal. He wasn't sure anymore. And seeing Jacin-rei's eyes devoid now of their dedication, their blatant love, seeing it all replaced with bleak despair and distrust…

It hurt.

Asai never would've thought it.

He hadn't wanted it to be this way. He hadn't wanted to have to resort to such measures to regain his hold on his Ghost, and he certainly hadn't wanted to be forced to accept the wolfling's "deal" to get Jacin-rei back. But Jacin-rei had proven more unpredictable than even Asai had guessed, and there'd been little choice.

It was heart-stopping disaster Asai was flirting with now. Kamen would be blood-mad when he found out what his sister had done, and he *would* come. There would be nowhere for Asai to hide.

So he wouldn't.

There was, after all, still one card left to play. When Kamen came after Asai, the Ghost would not allow his beishin to fall to the *Temshiel*. Asai had built Jacin-rei to have no such choice. And the boy was a very skilled killer. Asai would get what he wanted out of this, in the end; it would merely be in a very different way than he'd foreseen.

Asai stepped forward.

"I've permitted this pointless rebellion too long, my wayward Ghost."

Paralyzed as he was, the earthbound—the key to Jacin-rei's absolute obedience and cooperation—managed to slide a shocked gaze to Asai. It was all Asai could do not to snatch him up too. So close and yet now as untouchable as his brother. Asai refused to allow his disappointment to show.

He held out his hand to… he couldn't remember the man's name—one of Snake's thugs who happened to be for sale when he'd sent out an eye for biddable minions… Itai, that was it. He held out his hand to Itai and accepted the length of rope he'd hoped wouldn't be necessary. He wound it around his hand with a level look at Jacin-rei.

"It's time to come home."

And none too soon, from what Asai could see. Jacin-rei looked ill-used and hollow-eyed. He wasn't physically well, the offense of which curled much deeper in Asai than he'd supposed it would or should.

"Only me?" Jacin-rei's hoarse voice held heartbreaking hope and far too much damnable suspicion.

Damn Kamen for the way he'd twisted the boy from the devoted Ghost he'd been to this sad, chary, defeated shadow. Asai hadn't *wanted* to use Jacin-rei's family against him; he'd only wanted to motivate his Ghost in the right direction. Well, he hadn't wanted Jacin-rei to *know* he was using his family against him. Moot, anyway, since Asai couldn't have them.

He took a step closer, raised an eyebrow at the wolfling when her mouth and grip both tightened, then dismissed her. She could distrust and hate Asai all she liked. It would have no effect whatsoever on his place with Wolf when this was through.

Frowning, Asai swept gentle fingertips over Jacin-rei's sweat-clammy cheekbone, pushed stringy hair out of his eyes. Jacin-rei neither tried to flinch nor lean into the touch.

"Your hair, Jacin-rei." Asai *tsked*. "These people haven't been taking care of you properly."

Certainly he was no longer the clean, impeccable youth Asai had seen every day for almost a decade. And there would be words later about those marks on Jacin-rei's neck. Bloody Kamen.

"You need your beishin to see to you, lad. You always have done. None other can love the unlovable, not like your beishin. Whatever these people have told you, little Ghost, whatever you might want you to believe, only I can give you what you truly want. What you *need*, Jacin-rei. You do not exist but in my eyes."

No babbling pleas. No worried tears. No reaction at all. Only a blank-bitter glare and harsh breaths through clenched teeth.

It wouldn't do.

Asai leaned in close, and went for the gut.

"You have not yet attained perfection, little Ghost. How it must pain you, knowing they all look to you, and knowing you can never make the measure."

Failure. A not-so-gentle reminder. Cheap, perhaps, and a shortcut, certainly, but Asai needed his Ghost back. Needed him walking the path set for him. Needed the promise of the Fate only this Catalyst could bring.

Except Jacin-rei's gaze hardened, and his teeth tightened impossibly.

"Only. *Me*."

Asai pulled back, keeping the snarl from his face with a great deal of effort. He'd known this was going to take work; he reminded himself it was all going to be worth the effort. And that Jacin-rei would thank him when it was over.

A kiss, perhaps, might sway him. Still him. At the very least confuse him. Clearly, it had worked for Kamen; it ought to work even better for Asai.

Not here. The promise of it, though…?

Asai smiled. "You are, and have ever been, the only one I need, Jacin-rei. For you, I touch the Untouchable."

Sincere, because it was true, the way things should've been, had Asai not miscalculated that fateful night so badly, had Yakuli and his disastrous arrival at Asai's door not slipped right through Asai's sight and taken him so unaware. Yakuli—so arrogant and disdainful of "Lord Asai"—would pay for it in pain and true terror when Asai finally revealed to him what he was up against. And if Asai played everything exactly right, Jacin-rei would believe Asai was doing it all for him.

"Fen." The wolfling's tone was calm yet commanding—so much like her brother Asai's mouth tightened in distaste. "You for them. That was the deal. He'll take you with him and he'll leave them here with me. I promised you I'd see to them, I swore oath. You know I can't break it."

Jacin-rei stared at Asai, narrow-eyed, searching, and… damn. Calculating. What *had* these people done to Asai's Ghost? Jacin-rei did not calculate; Jacin-rei did what he was told. All the work Asai had done over the years to ensure obedience was the only way to ensure his control and influence over the Catalyst's effect on Fate. Now, Jacin-rei was taking in what was happening around him, thinking about it, planning.

It really wouldn't do.

"Let them go." Jacin-rei slid his gaze sideways to where his siblings were all but staked to the floor, still and silent as they should be. "Take off the spell, and I'll come with you."

As though he had a choice. Still, it would probably be best if he thought he did.

Asai spread his hands out, palms-up. "You can see it isn't I who—"

"I *know* it's you." An actual *snarl*, complete with hate-filled gaze and bared teeth. "Umeia might be a reprehensible traitor, but even she wouldn't stoop to Blood-magic."

The wolfling pinched her mouth up tight but said nothing.

Asai lifted an eyebrow. "You walk a very fine line here, Jacin-rei. You would do well to remember who—"

"And *you* would do well, *Beishin*, to understand that I know what you are. And I know what you've done."

The vitriol gave Asai pause. He'd been expecting anger, had seen as much the night Jacin-rei came to kill him and couldn't, years of confused affections doing their job and stilling his hand. Now, it appeared they were even more confused, stirred with rage. Whatever else Kamen's influence had done, it had rocked Jacin-rei down to a core of which Asai hadn't been aware.

Damn Kamen, and damn Asai's own sight for not showing him that the *Temshiel* he needed would end up being the very one who could turn the boy against him. It hadn't altered what Asai could still see of Fate, but it was making it damned difficult to keep his head in the midst of all the upheaval.

Asai carefully kept his smile. "After we're safely away, Jacin-rei." Kind and indulgent, to counteract the sting of denial. "Your brother will not—"

"My brother will do as I tell him. Let them go, or you'll have to try to get that rope on me before I get to a knife and gut you." Jacin-rei tilted a disturbing little smile—sickly and full of loathing. "I'm very fast, Beishin." Low, almost seductive. "I did, after all, have an excellent teacher."

Impertinent little reprobate. Clearly, this was going to be more work than Asai had thought. *Damn* Vonshi for disappearing right when he would've been the most useful. More than two decades, Asai had groomed the ungrateful baseborn for this, and now that it was here and Asai needed him...

"He *is* extraordinarily fast." The wolfling's smirk and snarky tone were enough to coil a hot coal of anger in Asai's chest. "And I have no intention of allowing my charges to risk themselves. Give him this. He'll keep his word."

As if Asai needed this poor excuse for a *Temshiel* to tell him what his Ghost would and wouldn't do. Asai only just kept the sneer from his face.

"Anyway, he won't have much fight to spare in a moment." The wolfling shifted her hold, wrenched Jacin-rei's arms higher up his back with one hand, nearly snapping his hands up to his nape, and with the other, she twisted a ring from his finger.

Asai hadn't noticed it before, but he knew right away what it was. Jacin-rei's reaction when it was taken from him merely confirmed it. Jacin-rei squeezed his eyes shut, jaw clenching so hard Asai thought it likely he was fissuring hairline cracks in his teeth.

No wonder Jacin-rei had seemed so clearheaded. What had Kamen been thinking, entrusting such a thing to a Catalyst?

Had it been bribe or gift?

Asai had a feeling it mattered.

The effect of its loss had done more than any force or coaxing Asai might have tried. Jacin-rei was a quivering mess.

Sharp eyes pinned to Asai, the wolfling took the ring and ran it lightly against Jacin-rei's cheek; Jacin-rei hissed, stilled, eyes shot wide and fixed once again on Asai, off-balance, but clearer now. A deliberate demonstration, and Asai had no trouble at all recognizing the wolfling's threat: give the Ghost what he asked for, or she would give him back the talisman that gave him sanity and walk away from their deal. Asai would never get his Ghost out of this dirty back alley without a horrible battle. Tirin and Itai had already demonstrated that they couldn't control themselves when it came to a fight, and the boy was already damaged enough—Asai needed Jacin-rei, and he needed him able. And the wolfling knew it.

"Why do you even care?" Asai asked the wolfling, irritated that his tone bent petulant. He couldn't help it. She hated him just as much as her brother did, and Asai had been able to detect no soft feelings for Jacin-rei whatsoever when she'd come to him with this trade.

The wolfling apparently heard Asai's confusion and annoyance all too clearly. Her smirk broadened, and she shrugged.

"Because he *is* fast. And you won't be the only target his knives will seek when I let him loose." Her eyes narrowed, her smirk gone. "I'm not doing any of this for you, Asai, and I have no ill will toward him or his. Give the lad one thing he wants, one bit of reassurance that he's giving himself away for a reason." She took the ring away again, shaking her head when Jacin-rei once again reacted as though someone were placing a hot iron to him. "He's not well, and he hasn't got much fight left, but he can do you and himself more damage than you want. *Give him this.*"

Damn. She sounded like Vonshi, and yes, she was right, though it made Asai grimace to even think it. And what wouldn't he give to have that ring? If he'd known the spells to make it years ago, Jacin-rei would be nothing more than an extension of Asai's own will by now, but Skel had been… reticent. In that, at least. Back then, Asai hadn't yet foreseen the use of an Untouchable, and so hadn't pressed it. Yet another reason to regret his own premature… well, Kamen would surely call it a betrayal, but it was merely a parting of ways. Still, that ring would have been a damnably useful tool to make Asai's own tool even more effective.

Asai eyed the earthbound, frozen with an almost pitiable look of panic on his face. Strong, certainly, but his strength thus far had been invested in throttling and denying his magic. He wouldn't know how to use it now if he held it physically in his hands. Asai didn't think there'd be much danger in letting him free. His role in possible futures had been voided. One thing, at least, that had played out as Asai had foreseen. And the other two… Feh. Mortals and nothing more. They wouldn't've even been worth his notice at all, had it not been for their importance to his Catalyst. Still, all this would have been so much easier if Yakuli had just done as he'd been instructed. Asai would make him pay, of course, but that wasn't helping him *now*.

He sighed at the mess Kamen had made of his Ghost. So much work undone, and now Asai would have to spend time redoing it. And this bold move would certainly shorten what time was left to him. Kamen would waste none of it in coming after what he deigned his.

Disgusted, Asai retrieved the amulet from where it hung around his neck, held it in his palm, and whispered the spell. As soon as the earthbound staggered forward, the wolfling shoved Jacin-rei at Asai and moved to restrain his brothers and sister. The strength of a *Temshiel*, obviously, but they had the audacity of youth and the ignorance of mortals. All three surged in at once, shouting and flailing. The littlest managed to writhe and twist her way through bodies and limbs to almost-freedom; she eschewed it in favor of throwing herself at Jacin-rei, even as Asai caught him.

Mouth set tight, and grip tighter, Asai motioned for Tirin and Itai to hold and start disarming his Ghost. They each took an arm, though Jacin-rei wasn't fighting them, merely allowing Asai to set him upright on his feet as the little girl clung to him, limpetlike.

"Jacin!" She wrapped her arms around his waist, weeping. "Jacin, don't go, don't let that man take you away, *please!*"

"Let me *go!*" The earthbound was caught up tight in the wolfling's chokehold. "You can't do this, you can't let him have him, you can't—"

"Joori, stop."

Jacin-rei tried to drag his arms away, apparently intending to reach down toward his little sister, who was still entwined around his waist, but Asai's men didn't let him loose, and he didn't struggle very hard. Just stood there as Tirin and Itai began taking his knives from their sheaths. A little more roughly than necessary, they pushed the little girl back now and then to reach a belt or a strap, but each time, she used the daring and limber-limbed slipperiness of youth to shove right back in. Jacin-rei only sagged, and let his sister wind around him as Asai's men went about disarming him. Beaten. If he weren't being held as he was, he'd be lying facefirst on the dirty stone of the alley.

"Caidi." Thin and thready. Poor little Ghost. "Caidi, go to Joori. Please. Before they—"

"They won't do anything to your sister." The wolfling's tone was imperious, threatening. She watched Asai and his men with keen attention. "They can't."

All too true, unfortunately.

"And we're supposed to trust *your* word?" The earthbound shoved at the wolfling, unable to break loose. "You bloody traitorous—"

"Stop, Joori." The younger brother's tone was far older than his apparent age, and the anger in his eyes calm and focused, where the earthbound's was panicked and wild. The boy was just as caught as his brothers were, but he didn't struggle. He only stood in the wolfling's grip, and split an all too familiar glare between his captor and Asai. "You don't really think Malick-seyh is going to stand for any of this, do you?"

"Malick-seyh." Asai slid a sardonic look to the wolfling. "Is Kamen *still* using his mortal name?"

Such foolishness. Why not just have *WEAKNESS* tattooed on his forehead?

"He's going to kill you both. Jacin-rei sort of brings that out in people." The little brother smirked—all brass—and set his eyes directly on Asai. "He won't have to kill you, I guess. My brother will do that, first chance he gets."

"Oh?" Asai lifted an eyebrow. He really had to smile at the brash impertinence. "Which one?" The one in the wolfling's chokehold, or the one held between Asai's own men, arms spread wide and pinned like a man crucified?

"Take your pick, I guess." The boy smiled back, as though they shared a private joke between them. "Depends on which one gets the drop on you." He shrugged. "Maybe even me."

"Morin." Jacin-rei shoved it out from between teeth clenched tight. "Shut up. *Please*."

A look passed between them, something Asai would have to remember and analyze later, but it made the arrogant little misanthrope nod and shut his mouth, so Asai let it pass for now. Probably something noble and self-sacrificing on Jacin-rei's part, and selfish acceptance on the brat's. That, at least, was predictable. Ah, Jacin-rei—always and ever looking out for those he loved, never seeing them for the weaknesses they were, which was a little disappointing, but worked in Asai's favor this time.

Jacin-rei's gaze lifted to his twin, commanding and pleading all at once. "Don't do anything stupid. Don't let them do anything stupid. Caidi, go to Joori."

The little girl's big eyes welled over, cheeks pale and stained with tears. "But—"

"*Jacin*," the earthbound whined. "You can't just—"

"C'mon, Caidi." The brat's gaze was still on Asai, mouth still curled in that overconfident smirk.

Asai marked it all for another time. Marked it very carefully, and with great relish. Someone needed to be taught a lesson about having the arrogance to challenge a maijin.

"Don't make it worse for him." The brat all but dismissed Asai—*dismissed*—turning his gaze to the earthbound. "He needs us to stay alive. He'll take care of himself, and what he can't take care of, Malick-seyh will. Let him be what he is, Joori. You just be what *you* are." A speaking look Asai couldn't interpret passed between them before the boy's gaze slid back to the wolfling. "You can't think you'll be forgiven for this."

The wolfling grimaced, released her hold on the boy, and used both arms now to restrain the twin. "Hush and go get your sister, lad."

And why was Asai even wasting his time on this absurd little drama? He had what he needed for now, and he could turn Jacin-rei back onto the proper path without this nattering troupe of incompetents. Asai had given his Ghost what he'd asked for; it was time to collect on his end of the bargain.

"Enough." Asai gave his men an impatient wave toward the mouth of the alley. "Get him to the carriage, and make sure the curtains are drawn." He tossed the length of rope to Tirin. "Secure his hands, and don't let his state of apparent dysphoria take you in. He *is* fast, and he *will* kill you, if you give him half a chance."

"*No!*" The earthbound redoubled his efforts in breaking loose from the wolfling, but she grimly held on as he flailed. "I won't let you take him, not this time. Jacin! *Jacin!*"

The little one screamed as Tirin shoved her away from Jacin-rei; she fell to the ground in a tumbling little heap.

It was a mistake—Asai could tell before she even hit the stones.

The look of vague, helpless rage that had settled over Jacin-rei abruptly lifted and cleared, and his gray eyes burned. He turned, swift as lightning, and head-butted Itai, stunning him. Almost an indistinct streak of movement, Jacin-rei lunged out of Itai's grip, and right into Tirin, grappling at Tirin's belts where Jacin-rei's own weapons had been thrust. Worrying, certainly, but not dire. Tirin still had the strength of a maijin to rely on, and Jacin-rei was more a frenzied madman right now than the efficient assassin Asai had made him.

Still… the lad was something to watch. He *was* fast. Nearly a blur to the eye. Asai couldn't help the bit of admiration and loving pride. He'd seen Jacin-rei spar—with that… unfortunate young degenerate, and then with the shadows—but he'd never seen his Ghost actually fight before. Asai could only imagine what it would look like if he hadn't had the boy's knives taken from him, but this… this was something to see, all economical, unthinking grace and lethal instinct.

The twin was still struggling with the wolfling, the little one still sitting on the stones, shrieking, the younger brother trying to duck around the perimeter of the fray to reach her. Itai was hovering at the fringes, trying to clear his head, watching it all and waiting for a signal from Tirin to join in or take over. And all Asai could see was the Untouchable. Dodging and striking. An airborne kick to Tirin's gut that left him gasping. Jacin-rei spun back, braid flying; he landed already poised in an offensive stance, and used the momentum to spring back in again.

There was no holding back in that narrow gray stare, no mercy. There was caged malevolence. Intense concentration on his own body and that of his opponent's. Cool, deadly intent. Artful violence.

Jacin-rei was at an obvious disadvantage—Tirin and Itai were among the idiots who'd torn him up the other night, and Jacin-rei was clearly favoring his right leg as he fought. That, and he was currently locked in combat with a maijin. And still, he attacked and parried Tirin as though he was the one with supernatural talent. And Jacin-rei was *unarmed*. Tirin's blade never touched him.

Oh yes, this one would do the job on Kamen quite well, when his head was finally put back to where Asai needed it. *If* Jacin-rei put the appropriate effort into relearning his place and purpose. And with the added advantage of being someone Kamen *wanted* up close...

It might work out after all.

With efficiency and skill Asai just had to admire, Jacin-rei blocked punches and deflected sword strikes, waiting for his moment, before he finally whirled across the dirty cobbles in a flying, twisting leap. He hit Tirin low, driving in with his shoulder and knocking the sword to clatter across the alley.

They rolled. Tirin landed on top. With one hand, he tried to restrain; the other wrapped around Jacin-rei's throat. Asai almost put a stop to it there, but perhaps, if he allowed it until Jacin-rei lost consciousness...

The little girl screamed again. Scrambling away from the fray, she retreated back toward the wolfling, propelling right past the younger brother and throwing herself at the twin. He managed to get an arm loose and reach for her. Asai only just caught a glint of dull metal out the corner of his eye, only just registered what he was seeing pass from sister to brother. He turned back to shout to Itai and Tirin, but Jacin-rei had managed to get one of his knives back and was currently carving a wide, precise gash through Tirin's chest. And Itai was merely standing there, *watching* it in obvious disbelief

Magic swelled, thick and oppressive, raw and unfocused. Enough crude power filled the alley to set Asai's skin buzzing and make his mouth go dry. The wolfling shouted something, the ground rumbled beneath Asai's feet, and before he even had the time to acknowledge what it meant, everything went to hell.

┯╤

Malick was extraordinarily unhappy, and he didn't much care who he brought down with him. He'd been terse and snappish with Yori as they'd made their swift way to the Stallion, his longer stride and urgent pace somewhat trying for Yori to keep up with. He'd ignored her huffing and the light scrim of sweat on her red face, and kept rattling off what had happened, what was happening now, what he thought might happen next, and how he was all kinds of pissed off that so little of it was under his control.

"So, Joori's not going anywhere, then?"

Yori's hopeful question had only pissed Malick off more, though he shouldn't blame her for being pleased. She'd never formed an attachment to anyone in all the years he'd known her. He should be delighted for her. But it was so far beyond what was actually important Malick almost smacked her.

"The Ancestors seem to think he's significant to what's going on."

Malick had said it as evenly as he could, because it was just one more thing on which Fen would lay distrust, and it wasn't bloody *fair*, damn it. Malick had *meant* to get them out, he'd *wanted* to get them out—who wanted the annoying, jealous twin around mucking up the works, anyway?—but he'd forced the issue with the Ancestors for a reason. Now he had to suck it up and deal with what he'd got. Joori was some kind of key, according to the Ancestors, and there were bigger issues at stake here than Fen's fury at Malick for breaking a promise.

They sat now in Xari's dark little parlor, listening to Husao blather about changing fates and what Wolf *really* meant. Because, of course, Husao, one of Dragon's, *would* know better than Malick how to interpret Wolf's directives; Malick didn't even try not to roll his eyes.

Yori listened attentively to Xari and Husao debate, while Malick ground his teeth down to almost nothing. The day just kept getting better and better.

"But he clearly said he was calling Kamen to his *duty*," Husao argued. "'All fates rest on the Heart of the Null'. Surely that means—"

"The hand of Fate herself safeguards those who would mock Balance," Xari put in wearily. "What Asai is safeguards Asai. Fate safeguards Yakuli. It does not mean what you want it to mean, and no amount of debating and choosing those things you want to hear will make it so. The Balance comes before your vengeance, Husao." She turned to Malick. "Your god has commanded you to risk your soul to do his work, to see to Asai, to see to Yakuli. And, I would hazard, any other who has dared to use Wolf's children so badly. But you have not been given leave to destroy out of hand. You risk the suns only if you disobey your laws while obeying Wolf. That is your conundrum. Only you are Wolf's-own. Only you can judge best what your god wishes of you."

"Yeah." Malick set his jaw. "All I have to do now is kill Yakuli without actually going near him, and then let Asai walk away because Fate says I get to kill everyone but the people who badly need killing."

"You do not need to let Asai walk away." Xari pursed her lips. "You agreed—"

"*No*. I didn't." Malick kept his tone firm, his stare hard. "I told you there'd be opportunity, but neither Fen nor I will wait for you to take it. It's up to you to be quick enough."

Xari might well want redemption in the eyes of her god, but Malick wasn't about to let Asai slip away while she dithered about taking it. If Malick had made any promise at all about Asai's intended fate, it had been to Fen.

Xari's eyes flashed. "So you would—"

"I would do what I must. And none of it's exactly thrilling me, Xari, so bottle your bloody unhelpful reprimands. I don't need *more* shit right now. See, because, aside from everything else, I *also* get to keep Fen's brother here—where Asai *knows* he is—and defend him against Asai, *also* without killing him, even though it's already pissed Fen off so badly he may never trust me again." Malick slouched in his chair, crossed his arms over his chest, and glared like a petulant child. "Oh yeah, and—*and*—not only can I not fail Wolf or I burn, but I also can't fail Fen or I burn, even though keeping Fen's family here and *not* sending them safely away is already a pretty big failure. I might as well just say *fuck it*, and kill everyone, because I'm fucked any way I turn. So what *you* want out of this, Dragon's-own That Was, is pretty much *last* on my bloody list."

Xari *tsked*. "Always you think in terms of who to kill and how to do so. Do you never consider other paths?"

"Like *what*? Tattle on Yakuli to the Doujou? *Right*. There are two judges I know of who don't have a full-Blood of their own or aren't waiting for one—*two*. Probably half the lords and prefects have been bought, and those who haven't are being steadily plotted against by those who have. The only people in Ada who *aren't* abusing magic, or are unaware that it's being abused at all, are the people themselves."

A grim, muffled snort from Yori's direction caught his attention, and he turned to her, barked, "*What?*"

Yori flushed, and sank in her seat, green eyes flicking around the table, overfaced. She hadn't said a word since introductions were made but for a soft "No, thank you, *misin*" when Xari had offered her tea, merely sitting quietly and trying not to stare at Ragi, who'd been equally as silent. Now, she gave Malick a wide-eyed look full of nerves that made him feel even worse. Made of stern stuff, Yori, a little biddable, perhaps, but not easily intimidated.

"Nothing." Yori cleared her throat, glanced at Xari then Husao, then settled her gaze on Malick. "I mean." She shifted a self-conscious shrug. "You just said it: the people don't know. And the Adan fear magic, above all else." She paused and waited for a beat, but when no one shushed her, she went on, "They're not going to like finding out they've been ruled by it all this time."

"True." Husao sat back, his face, for the first time since they'd got here, thoughtful rather than imperious. He studied Yori, so intense Yori was clearly trying not to squirm, then he peered at Malick, head atilt. "I imagine that's what Yakuli's for."

Xari scoffed. "Even my arrogant get would not think to so blatantly usurp the Adan. Free the Jin and enable their rise back from enslavement, yes, but true rule? Such open involvement by a maijin—for *that* the gods would never stand. No." She shook her head, eyes narrowed.

"No, he is more subtle than simple revolution. Yakuli is a distraction and a tool, else Asai would have hidden the magic better. Yakuli might think he's to lead a coup, but Asai has no use for the Adan, for they have no power." She shot Malick a meaningful look. "His cards still strive beyond his reach. He would grasp for the Sorcerer's mantle still."

Husao answered something, but Malick was no longer listening.

Subtle.

Asai was subtle, yes. Too subtle for armies and revolts, unless there was something else beneath it that served his purposes. He might want a revolt, but if he stayed true to his patterns—and he hadn't done anything yet to make Malick think he wouldn't—Yakuli was a tool to be used and betrayed. Not meant to succeed, but to be conveniently disposed of by other hands besides Asai's. No blame to Lord Asai. No crimes of which to accuse him. Asai meant to come out of this as a savior, clean of all blame and able to stand before the gods and claim his place with Wolf.

Banished by Raven, but… had he been? Really? Could he have been sent to finish what had long been suspected Raven had started?

Wolf suffers not the duplicity of weaker gods.

Right.

And was it possible that Asai was actually weaving between the two gods? Covering his steps in his intricate dance to appear as though he were adhering to the wishes of both, and all the while plotting for his own ascent to a status that rivaled them all?

The Adan would find the will to stand against magic. They'd done it before, when they'd marched on the Jin. They didn't hate the Jin—the tribes had blended too much; there were too many among them who had Jin blood in them for that—they feared them. They feared the magic that ran through Jin veins. The people of Ada didn't want the extermination of the Jin, or they wouldn't've bothered with camps. They wanted the extermination of magic. And if they knew that the elite who governed them—those who condemned and punished magic; those who made them fear even the smallest hint of it in themselves or their children—if the Adan people knew those men had all the while been torturing full-Bloods and using their magic themselves…

"Revolution" would be putting it mildly.

The government of Ada would be lynched wholesale. The people would be leaderless, directionless, ripe for subjugation. A repeat of the pattern that had been the doom of the Jin when they'd lost their Ancestors.

A liberating raid on the camps would be the first step, Malick decided. That was what Yakuli was for, though Yakuli likely had no idea he'd be saving the Jin, rather than destroying them. In fact, he likely had no idea he was to be a mere captain to Asai and not a leader in his own right.

Malick had no doubt Yakuli had very different objectives, probably implanted by Asai himself, or at least seized and encouraged. Because Xari was right—Asai didn't want rule, Asai wanted power. And what better way to get it than to have it handed to him willingly by those who'd been persecuted for it for a century and a half?

Free the Jin from their imprisonment, subtly guide them toward vengeance, because Asai was a subtle man. And while the Adan were distracted by the upheaval of their government, their beliefs, their lives, the Jin would walk back into their city and take back what had been theirs. Asai wouldn't march at the front of the mob, but behind it somewhere, lending little pushes where necessary, using his talisman of Heart's Blood to "guide" them all, keeping his influence oh so subtle, because Asai was an oh so subtle man.

"Bloody damn." Malick looked up and caught Yori's eye, ignoring the droning of Husao as he continued to speculate with Xari.

It wasn't a bad plan, really. Malick even grudgingly approved of some of it. If it hadn't been Asai, who perverted everything in which he had a hand, and if it hadn't been for the fact that it happened to require Blood—*any* Blood; the Heart's Blood had become more and more academic as Malick thought the plan through—he might just sit back and watch it all happen. He was no longer just incensed by the fact that Asai had "purchased" Fen, made him a killer, manipulated him and used him, and all to crack open Malick's chest and siphon off his Blood. He was incensed that Asai thought he had the right to wield the power of gods. He was incensed that Asai had enabled Yakuli to build himself a full-Blood "farm" for the purpose. And he was *profoundly offended* that Asai could very well walk away from this with ostensibly clean hands and everything he wanted.

"You've got it, Yori." Malick sat forward. "I think you—"

Pain first, driving right between his eyes, hitting him like a spike, then an overwhelming awareness of *wrongwrongwrong*.

"Shig," Malick gasped, because it felt like her, and then it was gone, all at once, winked out, like a shout cut off. He snapped his glance back to Yori, saw that she'd felt it too; her face had gone pale, and her eyes had sprung wide and worried.

"Not dead." It felt wrong, but not *that* wrong. Still, Malick jerked Yori out of her seat. "Let's go." Because wrong was wrong, and speed felt very necessary. He didn't need to drag Yori after him, she was already on her feet and headed to the curtain that hung at the doorway, but he latched on anyway, told Husao, "We've got trouble," and yanked Yori out.

Yori, more than any of them, appreciated the experience of being one place one second and another the next. Malick had always brushed off her inquiries about the hows of it with vague explanations of altering perceptions and sleight-of-hand, because it was a lot easier than trying to really explain it. Anyway, it fit with her reality of Malick as a lazy reprobate who happened to be good at killing the people she wanted dead—a lazy reprobate who had a little magic she couldn't quite classify. It worked for both of them, but it wasn't that simple.

Even as Malick stalked through the Stallion, dragging Yori behind him, Husao and Xari following after with a mix of annoyance and worry between them, Malick was already dismantling their physicality, breaking it down and dissipating it through the winds. Sternly, he called the captive ghosts of the earth, drawing in the life force of the air, blurring the reality all around them, and warning the spirits against laying claim to Yori's soul while he heaved her through their bounds. Still, they reached for her as Malick hauled her through. He could feel their euphoria at once again touching a living soul, a beacon of corporeal strength and the physical existence they either couldn't or wouldn't leave behind. Hungry ghosts, bound to the earth for so many reasons Malick had stopped caring, craving the flesh they could see but not have so fervently it scattered their reason like the seeds that fed them but never satisfied.

Their whispers and pleas crowded in, but Malick didn't hear them as well as he did when Shig was with him. Yori might love it when he did this, but Shig hated it, and Malick couldn't blame her. For Shig it was like living for a second's-worth of eternity inside Fen's head, except Fen's spirits shrieked, where these only sighed and muttered longingly. It wasn't nearly as intrusive for Malick or Yori as it was for those two, and not for the first time, Malick was thankful he didn't have to hear it all the time.

He bulled through them all, ignored their shadowy grasping. Tightening his hold on Yori, Malick launched them through the periphery of reality and took them home.

He guided them to the roof of the Girou. He might be in a hurry and more alarmed than he could remember having been in a very long time, but he wouldn't help anything by blundering into an ambush.

He let go of Yori's hand and pushed her to lean against the door of the stair. "All right?"

Yori's knees seemed a bit wobbly, and she was somewhat shaky, but the dreamy little grin she usually got when they did this was notably absent. She made a visible effort to clear the exhilaration from her mind and channel it into the job at hand.

"Yeah." She nodded sharply, took a long, cleansing breath, and straightened. "Ready."

Good girl. More clearheaded and dedicated to her job than even Samin. Malick wanted to give her a quick hug, but she was working so hard at gaining back her concentration, and he didn't want to break it. He could already hear an alarming clamor from the back alley, and he felt Yori tense as she heard it too.

Malick patted Yori's shoulder, said, "I'm going down," and made his careful way to the edge of the roof that overlooked the street, noting a black carriage—horse-drawn, of all things—that was collecting a bit of attention from a few curious children and their mothers. It was past midday, and those who'd broken for lunch and crowded the streets for a few hours had already returned to their occupations, but the presence of an actual horse and the rich-looking carriage to which it was harnessed was attracting everyone that happened by. Good. Malick had no doubt to whom it belonged and why it was here, and he might need every distraction he could get.

Mouth tightening, Malick stepped carefully to the edge that overlooked the alley, saw Asai as expected, saw Fen, head bowed, defeated, held between two thugs—maijin, Malick could tell, and if he wasn't mistaken, two of those who'd been with Leu the other night. Saw Caidi clinging to Fen while the two maijin alternately tried to pry her off and work around her. Malick couldn't see Morin or Joori, but he heard Joori—"I won't let you take him, not this time. Jacin! *Jacin!*"—wondered vaguely where the fuck Umeia was, because whatever happened, she wouldn't have left her charges so open to ambush like this. But she'd been veiling against Malick since that day outside her door, and he couldn't tell.

He saw Caidi go flying, saw the flash of metal as her cloak flapped and tangled around her. Saw, even from four stories up, the look of knowing dismay on Asai's face and the abrupt focus in Fen's eyes.

Watched as Fen came alive and began to do what Fen did.

Damn, but those sparring sessions with Samin in hand-to-hand had done more than Malick could've hoped. He'd have to give Samin a raise. Even as the maijin got Fen down and ostensibly pinned, Malick didn't worry.

"Give me a count of ten, then go check on Shig and bring her up here if you can. Make yourself a little sniper's nest." He shot Yori a grin. "Double pay if you get Asai between the eyes. *Triple.*"

Yori grinned back as Malick turned and began to gather the air around him again, recalling the spirits. A swell of magic that wasn't his made him pause, half pleased and half uneasy. It was too crude, too direction-less—dangerous for its untried simplicity—and filled with rage and fear that could only be Joori.

Malick frowned, surprised, then almost fell off the roof altogether when the pain hit him again. Visceral this time, bone-deep and agonizing. It striated through his chest in sharp waves, scattering his concentration and his hold on the spirits. The shock of it nearly doubled him over.

"Umeia."

No more than a weak breath, because it didn't just feel like her—it *was* her. And so much wronger than it had been with Shig's truncated warning.

"What the… *fuck.*"

Umeia's veil dropped. Protections went shattering. And with them, Malick felt the shocking agony of losing a part of himself, an almost physical wrench to his spirit.

Not like when Skel had gone to the suns, Malick told himself. Umeia's soul wasn't crying out, but Malick felt it as it was forced from her body, felt it with a gut-twisting grief as she moved from physical to spirit.

"*Mal!*" Yori shouted, impatient, like she'd already done it a few times, and he didn't blame her—the roof was shimmying beneath their feet, and he could hear the uneven grumble of the earth shifting beneath the building.

He took in a long breath and gave his head a sharp shake. No time.

"Forget about getting Shig." Malick's throat was too tight, his vision too blurry. "Just give me enough time to set up a gallery for you and start shooting. Get into position now. *Move!*"

☗

Joori honestly didn't know if he'd really meant to do it. He supposed he must have done. He was furious enough—the betrayals, the lies, the bloody "protection" Umeia dangled in front of Jacin's nose to turn him compliant. And Joori supposed he couldn't truthfully say he didn't know he had it in him. His wrath was leaking out through his pores, combining with the spirit of the earth throttled inside him, letting it stretch its atrophied limbs and shake them loose, and he really didn't care who might get in the way once he really let them go. So he couldn't say his intentions had been to ask nicely.

But even as hope had coiled bright in his chest when Caidi pushed the smooth handle of the knife into his hand, Joori hadn't really been sure he'd be able to do anything with it but wave it around until someone saw through the bravado and took it away. Funny, though, how his fist had curled around the knife, how he'd braced. And still, there hadn't been any real thought—just action.

The blade slid through Umeia's ribs much easier than Joori would have expected. She spasmed at first, her grip tightening painfully before it loosened. Still without thought, Joori threw her off him altogether, pulled the knife back as he turned, and sank it into her chest.

The shock on her face made Joori want to start babbling stunned apologies. The blood that pumped from around the blade and soaked his hand with sticky, wet heat made him want to vomit. He wrenched the knife loose, backed away, watched, dazed, as Umeia's hands fluttered for a half second, as a trickle of blood leaked from the corner of her mouth… as her gaze latched onto his. Confused accusation flared then snuffed like a star sparking out, and Umeia fell gracelessly to the floor at the bottom of the kitchen stairs.

"Oh." Joori staggered back, knife still clutched tight as he stumbled out the door and into the alley. "Oh... *no*."

It wasn't possible. He was only mortal—he *couldn't* have just killed a *Temshiel*, and certainly not taken one so utterly by surprise and so easily. But there she was, dead on the floor, and here he was, blood all over him.

The ground was seizing up beneath him, he could feel it all the way down through the rock, could almost feel its veins where the molten blood of the earth ran in honeycombed passages fathoms below. A fissure opened up, right between Joori's feet clad in Jacin's borrowed boots, and Joori merely watched as steam billowed out and bathed his face, searing. The rest of the world clamored around him—Jacin fighting with the thugs Asai had brought, Asai shouting something to... someone, Morin doing... something. Joori registered none of it, only the nauseating tackiness of the blood all over his hands and how it both slicked and stuck his hand to the grip of the knife, like it was fusing with his skin. He wondered if this was how Jacin felt when he killed—just an extension of his weapon, the machine behind the tool that allowed it to do its blood-hungry work.

"Umeia," someone said, breathless and full of dismay.

Joori looked up into the eyes of a mousy little man dressed in loose linen and a stained white apron. *Kitchen help*, Joori's mind supplied uselessly, and he flinched back as the man took hold of his arm, barked, "*Stop it!*" and backhanded Joori so hard his ears rang. He reeled, the wiry man's grip keeping him on his feet, and it was only very vaguely that Joori noted the ground had stopped shaking.

He turned back to the man, said, "What...?" but the man wasn't even looking at him, just holding onto his arm, his quick glance scanning up and down the alley and landing on...

"Oh, fuck." Joori all but whimpered it.

Malick stalked the alley, face like thunder, eyes flat pools of obsidian. The air crackled around him, singing with wrath. His pace was swift and sure, his dark gaze lethal and strafing everywhere at once.

A young woman paced steadily behind him, her face murderous but calm. A tall man with dark hair walked beside her.

A small crowd was gathering at the mouth of the alley. Two people came to stand behind the man who held onto Joori. The new man was clearly from the kitchens, too. The woman must be one of the doxies, apparently come from the middle of a bath because her hair was streaming wet and her robe was stuck to damp skin.

Joori barely noticed, only watched, terrified and awestruck, as Malick advanced down the alley like a slow-moving storm. Violence sat like a promise on his shoulders, at his brow. Cruelty roared from eyes like twin crucibles. His presence filled the alley, engulfing, as he prowled it. The brick walls of the Girou all but rattled in his wake, thunder booming overhead, and tension gathering to him like a curling fist.

He looked right at Joori. There was no pretending Malick didn't see the bloody knife in Joori's hand. There was no pretending Malick didn't know exactly what it meant and what Joori had done. The knowledge was all over his face. But Malick didn't come after Joori.

His hand came up, slashed through the air. The air wavered like warped glass, billowing out in a dense wave.

The scorching *whoosh* of unfurling power pushed Joori back, made him stumble.

Asai went flying back into brick and mortar. Malick slashed again, and the two men Asai brought with him went to join him—one just as bloody and dead as Umeia, but Malick didn't seem like he cared.

Malick bared his teeth. "You would *dare*." It was a snarl, savage, and aimed at Asai. "You've got some balls using *his* Blood where I can get my hands on you."

"You never did approve of even odds." Asai rose to his feet along with the harsh crackle of swelling magic, raising the hairs on Joori's nape and setting actual weight to his skin. Asai swung his hand out, fisted it, then *shoved*.

Malick jerked, took a lurching step back, as though he'd been struck by an invisible mallet. He smiled, awful and all teeth. His hands turned out, sparks like tiny bolts of lightning between spread fingers.

"I'm gonna *enjoy* ending you."

"Kill me and risk the suns, Kamen. And you're just not the sacrificing sort."

Asai swept both hands out this time, pushed. Magic thumped out, an invisible surge, and hit Joori square in the chest, taking his breath. And it wasn't even aimed at him.

A slight stagger was the only reaction Malick showed as he moved slowly toward Asai, taking his time, all seething rage and murderous intent. His bootheels clocked on the cobbles—*scuff-drag; scuff-drag*—resonant as a struck bell, and inevitable as a predator stalking crippled prey.

And all at once, Joori could almost understand what Jacin might see in Malick. He was blinding in his righteousness, adamantine in his wrathful grief, beautiful in his extremity of pure and perfect rage.

He stopped in the center, put his hands together in front of his chest, then slowly opened his arms. Joori watched, dumbstruck, as Caidi and Morin were gently pushed from between Malick and Asai then nudged to relative safety a few feet away from Joori.

Jacin didn't move—hadn't *been* moved—magic moving around him like waves around a surge break. He stood right where he was, knife in his hand.

"Fen." Malick kept his eyes on Asai. "Get out of the way."

Jacin was breathing too heavily, sweating too much, and his arm was bleeding right through the bandages and into the light brown of his duster's sleeve. And still, he stood calmly between maijin and *Temshiel*, and twirled the knife absently along his fingers.

"No."

Asai smirked. Malick's jaw clenched, his hatred and malice almost physical things, swirling with the magic weighting the air.

Samin and Shig came spilling out into the alley directly behind Joori, but he almost didn't notice them. Not until arrows started hailing down from the rooftop. One hit the man Jacin had fought with, the one bleeding from a gory chest wound on the stone of the alley; if he wasn't dead already, the arrow through the eye had certainly finished the job.

Asai and his one remaining man shot their glances upward. Asai looked unconcerned, but the other man flinched to the side when another arrow sailed down to hit the wall right behind where his head had just been.

Samin made his way over to Caidi and pushed her behind him. Shig trotted down the alleyway toward Morin.

"He is mine, Kamen." Asai's tone was going for snide but shaking a little around the edges.

Fear? It sounded like fear. Scared of Malick, maybe. Joori could understand that.

"Is he?" Malick bit back.

Before Joori could figure out if that was as ominous as it sounded, a fist closed around him, took his air, took his sense and all ability to move. It wasn't until the reality of the sensation hit him that Joori realized he'd effectively killed their protection when he'd killed Umeia.

It was worse than the spell from the charm—at least with that Joori had been able to breathe. Not with whatever this magic was. Tiny spasms shook him, and reedy noises were forced from his throat. He was almost immediately lightheaded, but he heard Malick curse, saw Jacin start toward him.

Malick curled his fist and drew his arm back.

"*Now*, Fen."

Fire whizzed across the alley, spattered all around Asai. It didn't touch him, as though there was an invisible wall around him, but whatever had held Joori let him go.

Abruptly, Joori could breathe again. He sagged, the small man who'd struck him earlier gasping along with him, but still holding on, holding Joori up as he gagged and wrenched air back into lungs that felt altogether too small.

Malick took a step toward Asai. Jacin was right behind him. Both of Malick's hands were seemingly on fire now. The ground shifted again, but it wasn't Joori this time, though he could swear he felt a thread of... *something* running out of him, twining and twisting and curling into something bigger, stronger.

Piercing whistles sounded the air from a few blocks away, and a reedy horn took up the call, sending it farther into the city. The alarm for the Doujou had been raised. Magic had been unleashed in the heart of Ada, and the hunters would be out and homing in within minutes.

A hail of arrows pelted down from the roof, one right after the other. All of them pinged off an invisible barrier and fell to the ground at Asai's feet.

Joori could hear Yori cursing.

Asai laughed, full and rich. "The hunters come, Jacin-rei. They've already caught the scent of your earthbound brother. Who will protect the ones you love, now that their paladin is gone?"

Another ball of fire came hurling from Malick's hand and toward Asai. Malick took another step, Jacin flanking him, as flames splashed around Asai but didn't touch him.

"Keki!" Malick pointed a glowing hand down to the mouth of the alley. "Get them down there to Sia."

Immediately, the man holding Joori's arm—Keki, apparently—started tugging him down to where Malick had pointed. Joori resisted until he met Jacin's gaze, read every plea and command inside it; Joori submitted, let himself be pulled away, even as his brother advanced on a maijin.

"Mika!" The young woman who was still in her robe snapped to almost-attention at Malick's shout. "Get every 'bound out of here before the Doujou shows up. *Now*."

Joori's head was spinning. He hadn't had any idea there were others here with magic. What was this place? Some kind of haven for them?

"It will do you and them little good." Asai's smile was arrogant, cool.

It stopped Joori, made him dig in his heels, even as Keki kept tugging at him.

Asai swept out a hand, though no magic came with it this time. "The alarm has been raised and the hunters called out. Will you veil them all, Kamen? Or will you leave it to your...? Oh!" He paused, the look of regret and sympathy on his face so overdone it was insulting even to Joori. "That's right. Your sister's *dead*, by the hand of one of her own charges." He swung a sharp look to Jacin. "How many of your own people fell at the hands of *Temshiel*? What vengeance do you suppose this *Temshiel* will take upon your kin for the murder of his own, little Ghost?"

Jacin's gaze slid from Asai to Malick and back again. His face was blank.

Malick loosed a chuckle that couldn't have been less sincere. "Oh, for fuck's sake."

"Do what you were saved for, Jacin-rei." Asai's voice was strangely soft, crooning, a lover asking for favor. "He will kill me. You failed your mother because you would not listen to your beishin. *This* is what I have foreseen. *This* is the time for Wolf's Catalyst to do as his beishin has taught him. You *must* trust me, Jacin-rei. Stand with the *Temshiel* and you will fail them all. You will fail *me*. Would you see me fall to treacherous *Temshiel*?"

Joori was dismayed down to his core to see that Jacin was *listening*.

"You are a sigh's breadth from perfection, Ghost. So little have I seen for the Untouchable, but this... I saved you for *this*, Jacin-rei. I *made* you for this. Do it now and save your family, save your *people*."

Malick only stood there, looking at Jacin. His smile was grim, knowing, as he held his arms out from his body. Open. *Inviting*.

"If this is what it takes, Fen."

Joori couldn't tell if it was sincere or mocking. He wondered if Jacin could.

"You're not his dog." Malick had eyes only for Jacin. "You're not anyone's yet. But give him what he wants, and he'll own you and yours utterly. Do what you promised, and no one owns you. Either way..." Malick spread his arms wider, teeth clenched, anger creeping in. "Make a fucking decision, Fen."

"*Temshiel* lied about loving the Jin right up until they turned on them." Asai took a step away from the wall, hands out. Another arrow flew at him, but he merely snapped out a hand and flicked it aside. "You've no choice. You *must* come with me. You must do that for which you were made, before the vengeance of the *Temshiel* takes all you love from you. I have *seen* it, little Ghost." Asai's dark gaze cambered over to Joori for just a second, a tiny smirk curling up one corner of his mouth. "Your brother killed his *sister*, Jacin-rei."

Jacin shut his eyes, hand curling more tightly around the knife, shaking.

It hit Joori then, the full weight of what he'd done when he'd killed Umeia. In that one, impulsive, bloody act, he'd put every single tool Asai needed to use against "his Ghost" right into his hands. Joori had done this.

"By my heart." Malick took another step toward Asai. "By my body. By my breath and spirit. I pledge my oath to Fen Joori—"

"*No!*" Asai flung his arm up.

Shadows curled around Caidi, thrashing like live things, coiling over her skin, down her throat as she opened her mouth to scream.

"What...?" Samin frantically brushed at Caidi's skin as though he might loosen the shadows that were choking her just by the force of his will and brute strength.

Joori lurched toward his sister, but Keki still had hold of him. As though abruptly reminded, Keki started pulling at Joori again, his strength nearly shocking for someone a full head smaller. Keki only paused for a second to latch onto Morin and start dragging him too.

"Leave it to Malick-*seyh*."

Jacin had surged toward Caidi. Malick was holding him back.

"Then *do* something!" Jacin spat, the second half of an argument Joori hadn't heard but the direction of which was all too apparent.

"I'm doing it!"

Malick pushed Jacin aside. A nest of shadows swarmed from his palm, whorled out toward Caidi. They twisted, converged, dark mist spiking out then digging in. *Pulling.* Caidi had faded to a dim little smudge inside the formless black mass, but now Joori could make out facial features, the gold of her hair.

Joori almost got hold of hope, almost began to think this wouldn't end as badly as he thought it might, when Caidi was jolted then lifted up. She shot into the air, right out of Samin's grip, little feet kicking. There were no screams as she sailed up and up, right past Yori, who still hung over the edge of the roof with her bow. Yori flung it over her shoulder as she watched Caidi ascend, made a grab for her, but Caidi was wrenched away in midair, still dark with shadows, and writhing.

"*Fuck!*" Malick grimaced like he was in pain, flinching as though from an invisible blow, but his hand reached up, curled into a fist. Caidi was wrenched again, this time toward Yori, who reached so far past the roof's edge Joori thought she might fall. "Keki!" Malick shouted.

Keki had started to vibrate, power leaking from him, raising the hairs on Joori's arms even as Keki let him go and stepped away. Joori could feel the change in the air right away—the thickening of it, the shift of eddying currents. And again, that weird boost he couldn't feel with anything he could name, but he *knew* it was coming from Malick.

Caidi's abrupt up-and-down evened out as Keki steadily weaved his hand back and forth in front of his chest. The dark cloud that was all Joori could see of his little sister mimicked Keki's movement. Joori could see Asai's own hand moving frantically, but whatever he was commanding wasn't responding. Keki and Malick had taken over this bit of magic completely.

People were hanging out the windows of the Girou now, some screaming, some just staring slack-jawed. All of them alternated their disbelieving gazes between the ground and the air. A crowd was surging in from the mouth of the alley, some of them butting up against an invisible barrier, but most of them only gaped at the dark shape lurching over the rooftops.

Keki abruptly stopped vibrating. That same malignant magic that had paralyzed Joori before took hold again.

Joori had forgotten about Asai's lackey. Right until he appeared from a swirl of shadows to tackle Malick from behind, driving his head into the stones with an audible *thud.*

The horror in Jacin's panicked "*No!*" was terrible. Jacin lunged for the man on Malick, wrestling the sword from his hand with the savagery of a wild animal. Turned it on him, nearly sliced his head clean off. Jacin screamed again, "Malick—*help her!*" as he sent a desperate glance at the sky.

Asai moved in behind Jacin, eyes alive with clear intent as he reached for him. Malick stirred sluggishly on the ground just as Asai latched onto Jacin's braid, wrenched him close enough to whisper something into his ear. Whatever he said made Jacin arch, snarl, "*No!*" and turn on Asai, knife flashing in his hand, even as Asai swept his arm down in a wide, dramatic arc.

The shadows dissipated from around Caidi all at once, her little body thrashing out against nothing as she plummeted. Yori lurched after her again, reached out and made a desperate grab for her, but she stumbled, arm tangled in her bow, and her balance teetered into nothing.

The magic held Joori still. Wouldn't let him look away.

Caidi didn't make a sound, but Yori yelped in surprise and panic as she fell, plunging down the four stories to the stone of the alley. She hit in a crunch of bone just after Caidi.

Strange, Joori thought—dazed and sickened, and oh so horrified—he would've thought it would go the other way 'round, with Caidi crying out and Yori going silently, the good soldier to the last, and maybe it was because Caidi had already been dead, choked to death on fucking shadows, *Caidi, please, I'm sorry*, or at least unconscious, *please let her have been unconscious*, because perhaps hitting the ground would obliterate all pain, but the falling, the *knowing*, the last few seconds of that bright little life spent in terror, and maybe she'd dreamt she was flying, yes, she'd been flying, never expecting a tangle of blonde hair and broken bodies, and *ah fuck, so much blood*, and Joori couldn't even close his eyes.

Morin's wild screams and denials blended in Joori's ears with Samin's bellow of rage and grief as they both rushed over to the shattered bodies. Blind hope flared on both their faces, like anything that might be left of either Caidi or Yori could be saved. Joori vaguely wondered why he didn't hear Shig scream, why she wasn't going to her ruined sister, but then he remembered she'd be just as rooted as he was.

My fault, my fault, oh fuck, Caidi, I'm so sorry.

Eight men from the Doujou were forcing their way through the crowd that had gathered at the mouth of the alley, three with the claret sashes of hunters striding ahead of them. Malick was just getting to his feet, the look of a man who'd lost all control entirely, and didn't know whether to rage or cry. The maijin who'd attacked him was lying in his own twisted heap at Malick's feet, but Malick looked like he wasn't even sure if he'd done it or not. And if he had, it wasn't enough.

Joori could only watch the men coming down the alley, watch one of the three hunters pointing out Shig then two others from the Girou Joori didn't know. And then, finally, Joori.

It was almost a relief. Let them take him. Let them do whatever it was they did with his sort, and then maybe little sisters wouldn't fall from the sky, and budding romances wouldn't be wiped out in a spray of blood over stone. Let him stop being the noose around Jacin's neck, and the stone around Morin's. No more leverage for Asai, no more threat to Jacin, no more Yori rocking beneath him with her bright green gaze and constant half smile.

Fuck, Joori wished he could shut his eyes.

"Fen," Malick kept his voice quiet, his tone smooth. Fen had been sitting on the ground by the time Malick disentangled himself from Snake's maijin, the bastard who'd blindsided Malick and caused him to lose his grip on Caidi. Fen had nailed Itai with his own sword, even as he'd turned on Asai, but now Malick had no idea if he should be expecting an attack from Fen for failing him so spectacularly, or the loss of sanity altogether.

Fen was too calm, too quiet, sitting there in the alley with Asai's bloody corpse beside him. And as much as Malick's heart broke for him, as much as it broke for himself, as much as he was right now mourning both Yori, whom he'd loved like a little sister, and Caidi, whom he'd been growing to, he still regretted that he'd missed it when Fen finally took Asai down.

Umeia, he wouldn't mourn—death didn't mean to him what it meant to mortals, and while Malick was pissed as hell that Joori would dare to do what he'd done, he was still just as happy to have Umeia out of his way. Because however this had all spiraled out of control, Malick knew it started with Umeia.

Grim, he toed at Asai's corpse.

The Blood of the Catalyst showers the Eye. Plucks it.

Perhaps not exactly what Malick had thought it meant, but Fen had a way of taking the predictable and twisting it around until even the color of the sky seemed impossible to foresee. Even without "Untouchable" in the mix, Malick thought Asai could never've seen Fen coming. Malick wondered if even Wolf could predict Fen completely.

He could see how it happened, how Fen had got Asai, just by the tale the corpse told: one of those little throwing knives jutted out from Asai's left eye. Whether Asai's men—*Snake's-own*—had missed it when they'd disarmed Fen or Fen had somehow managed to get it back, along with one of his long knives, didn't matter. Fen had blinded Asai first then taken him down. A knife to the heart, and a slit to the throat for good measure. Apparently, Fen wanted to make bloody sure Asai was dead.

Just after his little sister had crashed to the stones? Or during? Just how removed from himself *was* Fen right now?

The Doujou were slowly containing the crowd, and the hunters had moved in, carefully inspecting one 'bound after another. Husao and Xari were still watching from down the alley, waiting for a cue from Malick. He was surprised they were still here. They'd both more or less got what they'd wanted—it lay beside Fen in a bloody heap. As did Yori. As did Caidi. And they'd just stood there and watched it all happen.

Anger burned in Malick's chest, but he put it aside.

Later.

"Fen, can you hear me?"

Blood trickled down Malick's scalp, into his eye, and he flicked it away impatiently. He had to get some kind of control over this, had to get the Doujou and the hunters out of here, and without taking any of his people with them, and he had to get started on it now, before… shit. One of them was peering a little too closely at Joori, a look of satisfaction on his face. Perhaps Joori had just been figured for the earthbound who'd escaped the raid all those weeks ago.

"Fen." Malick crouched down, very carefully out of easy reach of the knife in Fen's hand, but it wouldn't make a difference, really—if Fen wanted Malick dead, he'd find a way. *"Fen,* can you *hear* me?"

"'M… falling." Flat. No emotion of any kind. Like there'd been so much it had burst its dam and left only empty desolation behind. "Even falling feels like… like flying." Fen's teeth clenched tight, jaw quivering. "Falling… falling, for a little while… feels… just a little while, just—" His brow twisted. "D'you think she flew?"

He might as well have punched Malick in the throat.

"Hey." Malick reached out but slowly drew back without touching. "Fen, why don't you let me—"

"You… you have to…*say it*. Say you… say you…"

Malick jolted, unsure whether Fen was talking to him or Asai's corpse. But undeniably sure what Fen was saying.

"You promised. A trade, a… it's all a…" Fen kept staring down at Asai's still face. "Everything's a *trade*. I give you what you want, you promise to pretend." His gaze lifted, skimmed right over Malick and farther up the alley to where his sister lay and his younger brother mourned. "I kill Asai, you keep them *safe*."

"Fen. I *tried.*"

Even as Malick said it, he knew it wasn't enough. Intentions aside, he hadn't got the oath out in time. Hadn't been quick enough when Snake's maijin blindsided him. His timing was always shit. And he couldn't expect any of it to matter to Fen. His little sister was dead, and telling Fen her soul was intact, they'd meet again in another lifetime, wasn't going to make the hurt Fen was clearly refusing to feel any less.

"You said you'd pretend." Desolation leaked through Fen's dull tone. "I don't want to fall anymore. *Say it.* You *promised.* Say it so I can… so I…"

Malick shut his eyes. He'd remembered in his head what it was like for mortals to love, to lose, but his heart had rejected the memories, rejected the pain that came with them. He'd remembered just enough to see the value of love as leverage, so he'd risked more than he should've done, things that weren't his to risk. And *I'm sorry, I didn't mean to* wasn't going to be enough.

Wolf chose those who wouldn't lose their mortality in immortality, who never forgot the pain of being crushed by Fate, who sought balance to the Balance and always remembered the millions of smaller pictures inside the bigger one. Malick was Wolf's-own, but he hadn't been Wolf's-*own* since Skel, since… since almost the beginning.

If he'd known then… if he could get back there and start again…

"You made this trade. *You* did." Fen was staring at Asai's face again, as though studying the set of each curve, each splotch of blood. "A broken life for a few words. You don't have to mean it. You can lie." He lifted his head, but his eyes slipped shut before Malick could get a look at what was in them. "I can't fall yet. I can't. I'm not done. Say it so I can pretend for *one fucking minute* this isn't for nothing."

"Fuck, Fen, this is no *trade*! I think maybe I…" Malick trailed off, unable actually say it—*I think I do love you*—no matter how true, so, he settled for "I think I do, but it's been too long. I'm not sure I remember how to do it right. You can pretend having that from me is worth something, but you don't have to pretend it's there."

Fen only nodded slowly. "Fly as I fall."

Hollow eyes in a filthy face. Tone measured, calm, and expression flat. And yet tears leaked riverine, cleaning smeary stripes down grimy cheeks through blood and dirt.

…he fucking wept, Malick… And he didn't even know it.

"There's only ever falling. I want to pretend she flew. I want to pretend *I*…" Fen's eyes opened slowly, focused down on Asai as his fingers—tacky with blood—traced a sticky line over Asai's cheekbone, gentle and so reverent it almost made Malick want to look away.

"He can just come back, can't he?" The tender stroking never stopped.

Malick took a long, deep breath. "Yeah. Not right away, but yeah, he can come back."

Fen nodded, slow, distant. "But not if I take his heart, right?"

It didn't necessarily matter that it was exactly what Asai had wanted Fen to do to Malick. It still stirred a shudder, the very idea repulsive. Malick was, after all, as vulnerable to it as Asai. Take the heart of *Temshiel* or maijin, bury it instead of burning it, and bind them to the earth, along with all the other hungry ghosts. A cruel fate, however one looked at it.

Still. If anyone deserved it…

Malick sighed. "That was the deal."

And Fen had been trained for it.

"Untouchable," someone muttered from a few feet away. "Lord Asai" and "murdered." Too close, too curious. They had to get whatever Fen needed to do here done, so he could keep his tenuous hold on this odd, quiet sanity. And so Malick could begin the business of mopping up this staggering disaster.

Still calm, Fen leaned down and ran his fingertips lightly over Asai's bloody lips. Kissed them.

"I loved you once, you treacherous fuck. It never had to be like this."

He pulled in one shaky breath, two, bracing, then snapped his back straight and plunged his long knife into Asai's chest with a nauseating force that broke through the breastbone on the first strike.

Malick honestly hadn't thought Fen would have the physical strength left for it. Clearly, Fen somehow found enough.

The sick crunch of bone breaking and ribs parting was nothing compared to the sounds of Yori and Caidi plunging to their deaths. Those sounds would haunt Malick for a long time to come. This was merely… anticlimactic. Justice by proxy wasn't nearly as gratifying as Malick had hoped it would be.

"I wanted this to hurt." A new spray of blood speckled Fen's face and mouth as he dug into Asai's chest. He licked it away from his bottom lip. "I wanted to make you watch it."

"Bloody… *hell*."

It came from behind Malick, soft and breathy. Fen didn't even seem to notice it, but Malick turned and saw one of the men with the hunters' colors staring down in apparent horror at Fen's gruesome task. Which was a bit of a laugh, really. Considering all the butchery for which this man was likely responsible, a little blood and soft tissue couldn't be *that* bad.

"Is that…?" The man wrenched his incredulous gaze away, fixed it on Malick. "What in the name of—"

"I'll have you release your captives now."

Fen's flat voice surprised Malick just as much as it seemed to surprise the hunter.

Hard and cool, Fen slid flinty gray eyes upward and shook the worst of the blood from one hand, looking for all the world like he didn't have a man's heart sitting in the palm of the other. He set his gaze on the hunter, jerked his head so at least the top half of the braid slithered over his shoulder; the bottom half seemed to be tangled beneath him.

"I'll have you release your captives. Now." Fen repeated it calmly, a steady thread of menace beneath it. He tilted his head, eyes narrow slits. "Or have you been purchased, as well?"

The man's eyes widened at the braid. Widened further at the seemingly coherent orders coming from the mouth of an Untouchable who sat in the middle of rather startling carnage with Lord Asai's heart in his hand.

"You are—"

"Obviously." Fen angled his chin toward the doujoun trying to restore order. "And I expect those men back there know the law. Are you interfering, seyh?"

The man looked at Malick like he really thought Malick was going to step in and save him from the bizarre situation. Malick was just pleased that someone other than him was on the receiving end of that glare. He didn't think he'd ever seen Fen so cold, so… distant.

He'd never really worried about Fen before, not even when he perhaps should've done. For all his problems, Fen could take care of himself extraordinarily well. Malick was worried now. The man's sister was splattered across the alley, his brother paralyzed by these men who wanted to take him away to the Courts, and he'd just killed the man he'd loved through years of adolescent fixation and dug his heart from his chest. And he didn't seem to have the ring, was wading through all this with the Ancestors shrieking steadily in his head. So why was he looking saner than Malick had ever seen him?

"Fen." Malick leaned down close so only Fen could hear. "What exactly are you doing?"

For the first time since all this started, Fen met Malick's eyes. Malick straightened, took a reflexive step back.

He'd been wrong—Fen's gaze wasn't flat and it wasn't cold.

You're going to break him, Umeia had warned. Malick didn't think so. Malick thought perhaps breaking wasn't the danger here. Not with what was looking back at him. Because in Fen's eyes was the deepest pit of smoldering grief and rage Malick had ever seen. And Fen was burning inside it. A star blazing too brightly until it tripped into supernova before collapsing in on itself. And the problem with implosion was that it sucked everyone else down into the deep, dense void with it.

"I'm a Catalyst." Gritty. Like chewing on broken glass. "I'm tired of shit happening *to* me." Fen held up a bloody hand and waited until Malick reached down and helped him to his feet. Teeth set grimly, Fen pulled the braid so it dangled plainly over his shoulder, leaning on Malick and favoring his leg as he dropped Asai's heart to the stones and crushed it under his boot. Several times. "I'm interfering," he said, then jerked away from Malick and limped off.

Malick only turned his head, watched him go.

You don't have to mean it. You can lie.

Malick didn't think any of the things churning in his chest had a single thing to do with lying.

He turned to the still-gaping hunter, shrugged with an *I'm just following orders* look, then smirked evilly down at Asai's corpse. Gave it a swift kick.

"Bet you didn't see *that* one coming."

7

Failure. Peerless and profound.

He had, in a sick, convoluted way, finally achieved perfection as reality fractured around him, riven to blood-edged fragments, and he—

fell

was strangling on jasmine, all-over jasmine, bound within Beishin's whisper

you did this, little ghost

amidst latent ruin, only a whisper, ringing, out-shouting the Ancestors in a voice that curled everything inside him to a hard, cluttered little knot

your lessons always came to you too hard and too late

then a scream, but not his, because he was choking on cherry blossom petals and the end of everything as he whirled and *struck*

i loved you, i loved *you*

and if he could just move fast enough, be good enough, live for a second in that impossible state of perfection, he could call it all back, and

help her

the hard *thud* of impact wouldn't somehow twine with Beishin's voice in accusation

you did this, little ghost

no blood in gold hair, no blank hazel eyes staring, staring

i'm wolf's creature too, jacin. we're all made for sacrifice. didn't you know?

blank-eyed on a reality wholly shattered and so utterly

splintered to ruination

wrong, it was all so *wrong*, too loud, too true, too real, and hot blood on his hands didn't make it go back to the way it should be, because that broken little body wasn't meant for reality

wrongwrongwrong

and he couldn't

feel

call it all back, couldn't batten down the voices with pain, because the agony inside shoved everything down a sharded void

down and down and down
until there was nothing left but the shrieking and the deep-clawed rawness in his chest, in his mind
my fault, my fault
and he could hear but he couldn't *listen*, he'd refused to listen, *failed*, and it had to go
falling
away, *all* of it, it had to go
listen
away, and he
thwip-thwip-thwip
cast himself over the precipice and spread tattered wings
fell
waited for the ground to rise up and mangle him or the fire to burn him
listenlistenlisten, our boy, only say it once
because he hadn't been listening, he'd missed it, so he
flew
—shattered the first amulet easily. Lapis ripped from its chain around the neck of a hunter who just stood there and let him take it—*let him*—just watched as Jacin dropped it to the bloody stone—*her blood, standing in a lake of her blood, wrong, so wrong, and why wouldn't it drown him?*—and crushed it under the heel of his boot. And then he merely held out his hand, just held it out, didn't say a word, and two others were dropped into his palm. Cut amethyst, both of them, and they wouldn't shatter, and he hadn't even realized he'd been stomping for so long until Malick laid a hand to his arm, and he flinched away like he'd been burnt, because *that* he felt. Silence, fleeting and dead-cold, and the *painshock-grief* all rose up at once inside it, and he couldn't… *couldn't.*

He yanked away, watched the sympathy in Malick's tea-colored eyes, the helplessness, and hissed, because fuck him, too, fuck them all with their sad eyes that only watched her fall as they'd watched the Jin fall for decades. He snarled, let his good leg give beneath him and sank to the bloody cobbles, sat next to his sister's ruined little body and dropped the amulets into the blooming puddle of her blood. Took his long knife by the hilt and crushed them.

A shrilling shriek slammed into him, and it took him a second to understand it came from outside his head and not inside. Shig was a vague shape in his periphery as she wended her unsteady way down the alley toward Yori, grief in everything about her. Joori's voice came to him, as though from miles away, hollow and calling his name, then Morin's, and good, alive, both of them—at least for now—but Jacin couldn't hear it now, that was it, all he could take, had to go away, didn't want any of it, blocked it from his consciousness. He concentrated instead on the shrieking inside, because it was louder now than it had ever been before, cacophonous, but it was also more garbled because all the voices were his, no sanity left inside them, and so safer than what was happening outside his head.

"The Girou is mine," he said, shards of bloody amethyst cutting into the tips of his fingers, then he looked up, narrowed his eyes at the Adan man who thought it was all right to hunt Jin and take their Blood. "The Girou and everyone in it. We have dead to mourn. Leave us now."

He didn't know what happened after that. He had vague recollections of Malick speaking to the men of the Doujou, making up explanations on the fly and leveling threats—*He's already said the Girou is his. You would interfere with the Untouchable? Leave him to tend to his dead*—

His dead.

A thready gasp whiffled from Jacin's chest. He skimmed shaking fingers through sticky gold.

"Need to... need to wash her hair."

Would he be able to without her skull falling away in pieces?

He hadn't had the courage to actually look at her yet, only quick glimpses out the corner of his eye. Gold hair trailing in a puddle of scarlet. A little hand curled into a loose fist palm-up on the stones. He didn't know if he could wash her body, paint the prayers on her brow, say the rites, wrap the linens, light the pyre. He didn't even know if he could look at her all at once, see the damage, without losing his grip.

He couldn't see Yori, because he'd have to look past Caidi, and he couldn't, just *couldn't*. Couldn't make himself face these splinters of skewed reality, because if he looked, if he accepted, it would *be* reality.

Refused to look at Beishin, because his dead eye—the one without a knife jutting from it—kept going tea-colored, and Jacin didn't want to know why.

Say it, just say it, because... because...

He didn't know.

A trade, and for what? Someone who couldn't truly die? Someone who'd fight dirty, lie, cheat, and steal his way out of it, and never leave Jacin with this hollow nothing burning him up from inside?

Reality broken into tiny little pieces, like a shattered mirror, and he could see himself deep-deep down in each one, and he was screaming inside them. Bashing himself into oblivion as broken as this reality where little girls fell silently from the sky, and sharded reflections caught the not-sun and blinded him.

Samin's tears leaked from a face that looked like it couldn't support them—water from stone. Mute, he lifted Caidi's small, broken body, hugged her gently to his chest as he stood. His eyes were hard and cold when he turned them on the hunters and the doujoun all around him, big body vibrating for want of blood and vengeance, heart too obviously wrapped around the small bundle in his arms.

That, Jacin remembered. The look in Samin's eyes, the sounds of grief coming from Shig, her warbling voice whispering, whispering—*you're all right, Yori-love, Umeia will see to you, she'll take you to Wolf*—and Joori, pleading, *I'm sorry, I'm sorry.*

Hands on Jacin's shoulders, his arms, stroking his cheek, but he kept snarling and knocking them off, because he'd taken the silence before, and they'd punished him for it. Except the hands wouldn't *let up*, wouldn't *stop*, just kept pushing gentle comfort like petals down his throat 'til he thought he'd choke. *C'mon, Fen, you can't see to your sister like this*, and he wanted to ask, *Like what?* but he couldn't push it past the petals.

Husao, I need you to see to these people—we can't let them remember all this, and especially not the Doujou.

It made sense somewhere, but Jacin didn't even reach for it. It didn't matter, he didn't care. Just went along and let the hands lead him... somewhere. Heard the steady *thwip-thwip-thwip* of a moth's battered wings, smelled jasmine twined with sage and pine, reached instead for the scent of cherry blossoms, and let them shroud him.

Faces going by, staring at him, and he stared back, wondering at the tears and the looks of pain and sympathy on the faces of strangers. Or maybe they weren't strangers, maybe he knew them and had forgotten. Maybe none of this was really happening, just another fever dream, more broken reality, and Caidi would wander in any second now to wake him from it and climb in next to him—*Pleeeeeease, Jacin*—and curl a warm swath against his chest with Malick at his back. Safe, safe, reality whole and unbroken, no dead sisters, no stolen mothers, no voices in his head throttling reason with madness, no dark, lying eyes or knives red with his beishin's blood, and—

"*Stop!*"

Hunched in, curling into the pain he couldn't feel that shattered all through him—inside and out—and those hands on him again, still, and he let them guide him, take him, show him.

Never loved me, never loved me, so blind, he'd been so blind, and, *Shit, Fen, no wonder you're so easy to use.* He shut his eyes and tried not to pretend the hands on him were long-fingered and demanding, and not callused and almost tender.

Didn't kill him soon enough, failed, refused the chance—twice—because I didn't want to see, didn't want to know.

Hands, more hands, the same hands, they wouldn't go away, wouldn't leave him be. Peeling away layers and layers of blood, *sayitsayitsayit*, layers and layers of cloth, layers and layers of self, *please just* say *it*, like a snake sloughing skin, except nothing new grew back to take its place. Just raw, all over raw, and he wanted to roll in broken glass, grind it, because he could feel pain, but he couldn't *feel pain*, and surely it wasn't real punishment unless he could *feel* it, writhe inside it, scream in its extremity. Only numb and cold and nothing and more nothing. Voices riding over him, except they all sounded like his, *screaming*, and hands *pushpulldragging* him away from blissful ruination.

Damn it, Fen, don't let go now, not after all this.

A knife. He needed a knife, because he knew what he was when he had a knife in his hand. Muscle and bone and sinew melding with steel and turning him into something *other*. Something that moved with *almost*-perfection, that didn't need any voice to drive it, any touch to silence it. And always, *always* the sweet potential of oblivion in the turn of the blade, rounding on him like a faithful dog turning on its master, except *he* was the dog, no one's master, not even his own. No reprieve, not even in that, no knife in his hand, someone had taken them all away, *not your blood to spill*, replaced his weapons with a ring shoved onto his finger that gave him silence he shouldn't have but couldn't refuse. Soft voices and soothing touches, blunting the sharp edges of his mind so he couldn't even turn that on himself, rip and tear and gnash and scream.

No, I'll take care of this, you see to the others. Get Ragi to help you with Joori and Morin, but stay close to Shig.

It echoed strangely, too resonant, like his skull had just opened up and everything was falling into his brain, *everything. Nothing, you're nothing*, and *thwip-thwip-thwip*, tattered gray wings beating against the silence, so why could he still *hear*?

Jasmine, fucking everywhere jasmine, sage and pine leaking through it, drowning him, and petals, blinding him, sticking to his skin.

Water drizzled, burning and prickling, rinsing away petals and searing little pinpricks at the lacework of stitches. It shocked him, throttled the numb agony in his head and chest and heart downward until he knew he was hunched on the bench of one of the shower-boxes. Air heavy with the thick scent of minerals. Hot water trickling down his spine, puddling at his bare feet in an ungodly cloud of pink as blood came loose from skin and hair. Hands on his scalp, the scent of pine soap in his nose, and Malick's voice a steady patter:

"…can't give up, all right? Not now, Fen, you're better than this."

A splash, and the soothing sluice of water runnelling over his head and down his shoulders. Jacin shut his eyes.

"Fucking gods and their fucking cryptic fucking orders." A soft growl this time, and the hands in his hair turned rougher. "I won't stand for it, Fen, y'hear? I don't give a shit anymore what Wolf wants, this all stops now."

…for you, he'll risk his soul. A mischievous grin beneath too-sharp jade eyes. *Think you can live with that?*

"I don't… know."

He didn't know anything anymore, except he hurt, and he couldn't feel it, a great ball of agony locked inside his chest like a drop of Blood that wasn't a flaw in the facets of a diamond, and he wanted it but he feared it, because when it shattered—

"Fen?" The hands had stopped tangling at Jacin's hair. Tea-smoky eyes peered sharply through the wavering lamplight and the last *pit-pit-pat* of falling petals. "Fen?"

Jacin blinked.

He was… naked. Letting Malick tend him. Clean him. Wash his hair.

Shame should've come with the realization, or anger or… something. There was nothing there. Only the heat of the water searing him to bone, but still setting shivers all through him, and a throng of emotions he couldn't name. He poked and nudged their periphery, wary of setting them loose in a slurry of insanity, but they bunched in tight, curled in on themselves, and it was so new he couldn't stop himself from worrying at it. Silence howled in his head, and he couldn't figure out why it *hurt* so much more than the noise, and yet it was numb, like a dead limb.

It was too much. It was nothing at all.

You think I don't know why you stare so at the gates? And maybe she did understand his horrified fascination, and maybe it mattered, he thought maybe it did, because it was reality now, his obsession with the near-dead. Watching them waiting to become ghosts, soul-hungry, watching the world around them pretend they weren't there, except he'd never *really* understood the emptiness of true hunger before. Strange and absurd, because he'd been a ghost for years—he really should've got it before now.

"Stop it, Fen. You're *not* a ghost, damn it."

Except Malick didn't understand, couldn't know. *Living is your sacrifice*, yes, right, but *survival* was a ghost's unforgivable sin, unending penury its penance.

"No more. I can't."

"Fen, you—"

"I *can't!*"

All of it wrong. Everything out of true.

Punishment without pain was meaningless; grief without heartache was… nothing at all. He owed Caidi more than that.

But *this*—whatever this agony-apathy was writhing through his every thought, his every sense, his every breath… it had to *go away*.

"I need…" He didn't know what he needed—he just. "I *need*."

He latched onto Beishin's shirt and dragged himself up.

The kiss tasted metal-bitter, like blood, and even as Malick tried to wrench back and away, Jacin held on, pushed in. His patchwork leg bumped stone as he shoved them both into the wall, and it hurt, but he still couldn't *feel* it, so he drove himself into Beishin harder. Clamped his fingers to the hinges of Malick's jaw and *squeezed* until Beishin opened for him, gave in, let Jacin shove his tongue in his mouth, let him rock them together. Let him keep doing it until he dragged reaction from them both, until his breath ran out and he had to pull back.

"*Fen*." A growl, and dark eyes narrowed with worry. "This isn't what you—"

"*Fuck* you!" Jacin *snarled* it. "Always telling me what I need, what I am, what I'm *made* for, teaching me how to *fail* and nothing more, but you never really gave a shit, you only ever—"

"For fuck's sake—*Fen!*"

"—wanted someone to love you, *worship* you, but you wouldn't give any of it *back*, you never—"

"*Fen!*" A sharp shake this time, enough to rattle his teeth, then: "Who are you seeing, Fen?"

Dark-dark-dark had gone to old bronze again, so Jacin shut his eyes tight. "I…" Confused. Straddling an unfamiliar edge, and he didn't know if he should let himself fall.

"Open your eyes, Fen." Malick's hands—*Malick's* hands—slid up, fingers tangling in Jacin's hair. "*Look* at me, damn it."

Wary, abruptly *terrified*, Jacin… did. Squinted past the blur and distortion. Whispered, "Please," and wished he knew what he was asking for.

"Who d'you see, Fen?" Calm on the surface, but a little shaky beneath it. "Say my name."

Jacin swallowed, teeth clenched tight, because his chin wanted to quiver. Looked into light-brown eyes gone dark with concern and pain and compassion. Licked his lips and said,

"Malick." Thin and reedy. "Your name is Malick."

No more blurring, no more mourning one who shouldn't be mourned, no more wishing for things he shouldn't want, shouldn't *need*, but—

"Malick." *This close* to falling. "I need to… I can't—" *hold on, I can't, I can't, I can't*, and all Jacin could do was sag in Malick's grip and whisper, "*Please*."

Because it was Malick. *Malick*, not… not *him*. And Malick had made it all go away before.

Dark eyes slid to tarnished bronze to dark to light, staring him down, measuring, and Jacin could only hang there and drown in silence. In nothing. In the deadness inside him that kept crowding him toward a precarious edge, goading him to fly when he knew he'd only fall.

Then, finally: "If this is what you need, then," Malick said, and he let Jacin kiss him again, deep and heavy, while Jacin pushed in, in, in, trying to obliterate himself inside skin and bone and sinew, and it was such a fucking *relief* he could've cried.

Your emotions make you weak, little Ghost.

"No." Malick breathed it against Jacin's mouth, fanned it out over his tongue, his teeth, down his throat. "Not a ghost, Fen, understand me?"

As if Jacin had said it out loud.

...Had he?

"You're alive, and I know you don't want to be, but you're *here*."

Talk-talk-talking, he never just *shut* the fuck *up*, but his hands were moving, sliding over Jacin's back and pulling him in.

"You can't be alive and a ghost at the same time. One or the other. Right now you're *here*, with *me*, and you're going to *stay* here—got it?"

Who are you going to see tonight while I'm fucking you?

Sick nausea curled in Jacin's gut, and he fisted his hands in hair that wasn't quite right between his fingers. "Why d'you *care* what I—?"

"Because *you* wanted a trade."

Everything... *tilted*. Only for a second, then Jacin was shoved back, and forced to look into eyes that kept sliding from dark-dark-dark to light, smoky tea.

"Except I don't need to pretend, Fen. Do you?"

Make a fucking decision, Fen.

So Jacin did. He angled away, backed up until he hit the other wall. Turned, propped himself up with his elbows, and bowed his head.

Submitted.

Waited.

"Fen," Malick said—*Malick, it's Malick*—hesitant, and Jacin could tell he was going to balk, and he *couldn't*, because Jacin could still smell jasmine, and Malick's eyes wouldn't stop going dark and deep.

Malick had made it all go away before. *Malick* had made it go *away*. Everything. And Jacin *needed*.

He didn't look back, didn't move—merely dipped his head 'til his brow touched wet stone, said, "Trade me this," and didn't even care what he was bargaining for. Desperate and pathetic, and he didn't care about that, either. Added, "*Please*," again, because it was jammed up in his throat and he had to push it out.

Beishin picked her up and Malick dropped her. Joori killed her protection and Jacin killed Beishin too late. A perfect circle; perfect failure. And all of Jacin's trying came to nothing more than a ring of smoke, a split-second illusion of perfection that broke apart the moment he tried to touch it. So many ways reality could have remained whole, and yet it hadn't, had shattered into a world where Caidi was dead and Jacin was alive and lost and drowning inside silence and not-pain, and—

"Fucking son of a bitch, just *give me this!*"

It bounced against damp stone, echoed in the blank spaces inside Jacin's head.

Malick pushed a rough breath through it. "Whatever you need, Fen." All at once tinged with husky seduction.

Just like that, Malick was a solid line of rangy muscle through damp linen at Jacin's back. Warmth bled through the chill on Jacin's skin. Cold stone on his cheek was uncanny contrast when Malick shoved him face-first into the wall, held him there with a harsh grip on his nape.

"You need it and you need it from *me*, Fen." Malick's voice was almost a growl, a rumble from the chest that somehow came out sonorous and sultry. "You want to make it a trade, then here are my terms." The grip on Jacin's neck tightened; Malick pushed him harder into the wall. "You'll see me and only me. You won't shut your eyes and pretend I'm him. You'll call *my* name. You'll stay *here*, with *me*."

"I... yes, I—" Jacin tried to nod, but all he could do was twitch in Malick's grip. "You're Malick."

"What else, Fen?"

Jacin had to think about it, had to card back over the demand, tried to say the words—*I'm here*—and... *couldn't*. Even unspoken the words reeked of too much risk.

"*More*, Fen." Malick's voice was dulcet and low this time, right next to Jacin's ear. The grip on Jacin's neck softened. "You have to say it."

Jasmine rose, choking, and it wasn't right, it was supposed to be cherry blossoms. Pine crept in, sage on its heels, and swirled in a smeary mix that slid through Jacin's mind, cooling the crucible of *too much*, soothing the wreckage of *not enough*.

A knot slipped in Jacin's chest; he clawed a great whoop of air in past it.

"Fen, you have to—"

"*Bloody*—" Jacin pushed back against Malick, demanding. "I'm *here*."

...Except the words unfurled this time, coiling shapes inside Jacin that took on sharp edges as he spoke them, gave them power.

"You're *here*, with *me*."

Jacin shut burning eyes, clenched his teeth. Because now that he'd made the bargain, *here* seemed like the most dangerous place he could be.

Too late. Malick pushed into him, hard and fast, made it *hurt*, as if he knew Jacin needed it to. Rough, reckless, he flattened Jacin to the wall, pinned him there, his grip on the back of Jacin's neck never letting up, anchoring him to this pinpoint of space between blank cold nothing before him and the living conflagration that was Malick at his back.

A spark flickered in Jacin somewhere, a spent coal cracking open and sputtering out embers, and he *felt* it. A vague emptiness filling up, a relinquishing of control, of his own body as it was pushed and shoved and rocked, and raspy words spider-walked through senses like dead things abruptly stirred at life.

"Here. You're here, Fen. Not a ghost, understand? You're—"

"Shut up, just *shut up*, just make it *go away*."

"Oh, Fen." Malick pushed rough, panting breaths into the crook of Jacin's shoulder. "I don't think you have any idea what you've done here."

"Stop, shut up, just let me—"

Feel.

Forget.

Fly.

Jacin shut his eyes, all at once overwhelmed, burning. Free fall snagged him, dragged him, and Malick pulled him back and grounded him. Jacin had no choice but to bend his neck to a rhythm both blind and graceless, raking and breaking him. Sensation spiraled—a brushfire kindling up his backbone, the sting and scrip-scrape of his cheek against the stone, a shove and grunt from Malick that lit something incomprehensible in Jacin's core, bloomed out and up and *up*.

It was beautiful. It was terrifying. It was too much, not enough. It was everything he'd asked for, and nothing he'd expected. He couldn't move, could only lurch with Malick's body, submit to his rough cadence, and let Malick keep *pushpushpushing*.

Except it was pushing everything *in*. It wasn't taking it *away*.

This wasn't what Jacin had bargained for.

He couldn't say it. The sluggish burn at the bottom of his skin was scaring the shit out of him, and yet he couldn't tell Malick to stop, he'd made a mistake. He couldn't do anything but *feel* it, and shut his eyes against everything that wanted to swarm in with it.

Long, driving strokes, hard and rough, and it was sending Jacin somewhere too deep inside himself where sanity lived and reality threatened, and he had no choice but to let it enwind him, bind him. Hot, searing webs wrapped around him, coiled up from his thighs and into his chest. No control, closer and closer to that edge, and a solid brutal bite to his shoulder sent sparks beneath his skin that doused him in sensation, unlocked a groan from his throat that shattered out his mouth in ragged desperation.

"Say it." Malick sped his strokes, twisted his hips, growled when Jacin couldn't hold onto a sob. Wrapped Jacin's unbound hair in his fist and yanked. "*Tell me.*"

"Here," splintered from Jacin's throat, and it *burned* this time, seared down to his gullet, because it wasn't taking away reality—it was making it *more real*. "Malick." Too soft, too hoarse, too broken, and he couldn't keep it back: "Help."

"*Fuck.*"

Malick's rhythm picked up, driving what breath was left in Jacin's lungs out into harsh little pants that heated the stone against his cheek.

"Fucking… *shit*, Fen, love you."

The shaky tone of confession slid a hot knife through all the knots tangled in Jacin's chest. That cool, calm wind inside him that said *Malick* to him, like even the physicality of Malick himself couldn't do, skimmed through every sense Jacin owned, took him.

Orgasm clamped him in a hard fist, wrung him and flung him. The dazed detachment that tethered him to sense jinked and snapped, tore him loose and sent him spiraling. It whited him out, shook every raw thing inside him in a long, sharp, jacksaw wave of searing *hereness*. Shoved his face in it until he couldn't breathe.

Silence—absolute and profound. Stillness so complete he could feel the sweat drying on his skin.

Inescapable *knowledge*.

Gold hair stained crimson. A tiny, dimpled fist curled loose in a lake of blood.

Failure.

Thwip-thwip-thwip.

He came to still in the shower-box, still slumped against the wall, Malick still a swath of heat at his back, panting now, shaking from his own release, but everything inside Jacin had altered and shifted around in a jumbled welter of... *everything*. All the things that had been hovering at his edges before now bunched tight in his chest, knotting and wedging behind his breastbone, spreading out like a fist uncurling. *Feeling*. Agonizing life. Terrifying reality.

It caved inward, striped his soul like welts from a whip. He couldn't push it away this time, couldn't unfeel it. It shot him up, sucked him down, and he had no choice but to let himself be battered in the rush.

Unraveling.

Shattering.

Undone. Unmade.

Pressure—inside and winding out.

It was too much. He couldn't keep it in.

Jacin's head fell back to Malick's shoulder, breath curling out in a long, winding whimper that grew too fast into a moan then a sob. Pressing him down, crushing him with grief and rage and *too much, too much, too much.*

Long, strap-muscled arms wound around his chest, tightened—"It's all right, Fen, you're not alone, let it come"—and it all clustered together, built and built and built inside him, *hurt* him, *burned* him, scraped him raw and too open. That great, unfeelable ball of agony locked in his chest gathered into itself, burst, splintered up his throat, and shoved out his mouth in a deep-dark, soul-scouring scream.

It drove right down into Malick's soul. He'd never heard anything like it. And there was nothing he could do but wait it out.

And wonder how he'd ever, *ever* looked at the surface of everything that was Fen and decided he wanted to watch as it all snapped its traces.

Since he'd laid eyes on Fen, he'd seen the storm coming. Had watched it build and build. Had known when he'd watched Fen crush Asai's heart that a break was coming.

He just hadn't suspected its violence.

Dimly, Malick noted Samin bursting through the heavy door of the bath, sword drawn and face set in the same grim lines they'd taken on since their comfortable little world had slipped and skewed. Drawn by Fen's screams, no doubt; on alert and assuming attack. Malick merely leaned a little backward out of the shower-box, and gave Samin a small shake of his head. Samin's shoulders slumped, and his eyes shut tight for a moment, before he tipped a jerky little nod and backed out the door again.

Malick curled in more tightly around Fen. Rocked and stroked and murmured through the keening that was less piercing than it had been, but Malick thought it was likely due to exhaustion, rather than a mellowing of the sharp emotion that had borne it.

Until Fen choked. Spat blood.

And just... kept screaming.

He was going to rupture his throat. Maybe had already.

It had to stop.

"You're alive, Fen. Alive, not a ghost, and I know it doesn't take away the pain of losing your sister, but your brothers are still here, and they need you."

Responsibility. Principles. Guilt, maybe, because Malick was pretty sure Fen thought his own survival was unforgivable when it had come at the price of Caidi. Malick didn't like appealing to any of it, but it was the only thing that might drag Fen out from so deep inside himself.

And it did—it forced calm where even the most tender, soothing words had been failing. Fen's shivering kept up, his lurching breaths didn't subside, but Malick almost felt the shift in attention, the lift of a thin layer of haze.

"I thought..." Fen's voice was harsh, hardly even there. He wrenched in a choppy breath that ended in a strangled sob. "I thought I was... I *tried* to... save... but I—"

"You *did* save them, Fen."

Malick had to pause for a moment to consider what he needed to say here, now that Fen was actually listening, because one couldn't speak to Fen like one would speak to any other. There was too much muddled inside him, too much ground in from a father who pretended he didn't have a son, and a "mentor" who fed on the self-hate and confusion it had wrought. And that wasn't even counting everything that came along with trying to keep his sanity through the desperate shrieking of the Ancestors.

I won't swear an oath of protection to one who takes his own knives to himself so casually, Umeia had said. Except there was nothing casual about Fen. Certainly not his pain, or his self-inflicted sanity. Fen thought his failings and weaknesses through very carefully.

"You were set up, Fen. Asai meant for them all to die months ago, and you saved them then. You stole more time for your little sister, tricked a few more months for her out of a maijin, and Fen—she *lived* for those few months. She pushed new life into everyone around her."

"And now she's dead." Too weak and thready, but Fen was following Malick's words, he was *here*, and that was better than it had been a few minutes ago.

"She is. And I know it doesn't help now, but Wolf will take care of her, and you *will* meet her again. She's not really gone—she's just not here right now."

Fen didn't answer, only pulled a defeated silence around himself. Disturbing, perhaps, but not actually distressing, like before.

They were speaking two different languages. Though Malick had endured today's losses with what felt too much like a mortal heart, he also had the knowledge of an immortal. He'd *seen* souls come back, had seen loved ones find each other again. Malick's pain wasn't nearly so deep. And Fen knew it.

He couldn't expect Fen to take any real comfort from it. Limited time and the nonremembrance of lives past were gifts, in their ways, but... not for something like this. Malick had jarred Fen back into *here and now*, except here and now, Fen had just killed the man he'd been in love with for years and torn his heart from his chest. Here and now, his little sister had just died horrifically in front of him. Even Shig—who regularly spoke to the spirits, who *knew* she'd see her sister again—was grieving and curled further into herself than Malick had seen her since she and Yori had first come to the Girou.

Shig. Damn. He needed to see to Shig too. Fen's sanity wasn't the only worry right now, though Malick had made it his priority, and for reasons he knew but wouldn't even try to define. There just wasn't time.

Husao had taken care of the Doujou, but he couldn't take care of the entire city, and the alarm had gone up. There would be an investigation, probably underway already, and sooner or later, the vague nonexplanations and apparent blank spaces in memory—not to mention the sudden loss of three amulets—were going to result in at the very least an enquiry centered on the Girou. Husao could buy more time, but not forever. Those Adan who gave the orders were all too familiar with what magic looked like, and they knew even better what the seemingly invisible traces of hidden magic looked like. They'd figure it out. Soon.

Before Malick could come up with a gentle way to prod Fen into even a tenuous acceptance, Fen was pulling that iron control around himself again, settling his breathing, shoving everything back down to wherever it lived when he tried to deny its existence. Everything about him stiffened, like he'd only just now realized where he was and the position he was in—that he was allowing it.

He moved, trying to pull away and get to his feet, so Malick angled back and up then dragged Fen up with him. Gave him a brief once-over—

some popped stitches on both arm and leg, but most of the wounds had already knit new skin anyway, so a few bandages would do. Fen had never entirely shaken the fever, but Malick had been in the closest contact possible for the past however long it had been, and he didn't think it was anything to worry about right now. Fen seemed to heal himself, whether he wanted to or not, by sheer force of subconscious will.

He was shivering now, skin mottled with gooseflesh. The hob hadn't been tended for too long, the uproar outside having drawn any who'd been bathing to the alley, and there'd been other things to worry about when Malick brought Fen here. The jasmine oil he'd snapped up with the vague idea of washing Fen's hair then combing it out for him, giving the braid a go—and which he'd ended up using for an altogether different purpose—had toppled from the bench and now mixed with the bloody water at their feet. The bathsheets Malick had retrieved from the cupboard had fallen over the drain; they looked like viscous clots on the floor now. Malick grimaced, didn't even bother to inspect his boots and trousers after having been kneeling in the mess, just made sure Fen was propped against the wall before he left him there to get fresh bathsheets.

Fen was staring off into somewhere that wasn't *here* when Malick returned. But he allowed Malick to wrap one bathsheet around his shoulders and mop at the miles of hair with the other.

"It doesn't end with Asai." It was low, Fen's voice barely there, but it still rang loud.

Malick's eyebrows rose, but he kept his gaze on his hands. "No. It doesn't." He dropped the bathsheet to the already ruined heap on the floor then gently steered Fen out of the shower-box.

Fen limped along silently, then halted when they reached the door. "What will you do?" His gray eyes, for the first time since the alley, peered straight at Malick, and there was no question at all that Fen was *seeing* him.

Like he'd done several times today, Malick paused, thought carefully about what he wanted to say. What he *should* say. What Fen needed to hear.

"What d'you want me to do?"

Because Malick really wanted to know. And he really wanted to give Fen whatever he wanted, if it was in his power to give.

Fen didn't blink, didn't hesitate. "I want you to do what you promised. I want you to keep Morin and Joori safe and help me… take care of my mother."

No concerns about the Balance. No thought to any orders given from gods, or vague permissions with no promises attached to them. Fen wanted what he'd always wanted, his focus jarred and taken from him forcibly for a time, perhaps, but unchanged: *Save my family, kill Asai.* He'd accomplished the second part, but the more important part had got mangled and skewed in terrible ways today. It wasn't surprising that Fen would merely shift that narrow focus and keep trying until he was dead or broken completely. Because Fen didn't seem to know how to quit. And after everything that had happened, after watching Fen drag himself from the abyss and force himself to sanity when the call of oblivious madness must have been so sweet and seductive, Malick had no real choice.

All he could do was sigh, nod slowly, then lead Fen through the door of the baths and toward the stairs.

"Then that's what I'll do."

⎕

So many people needed to die, Samin would have to spend his next sixteen lives hunting them all down. Thing was, most of the ones responsible for the current wrongness of the universe were already dead. And he hadn't got to kill any of them.

He stood silent in this new impotence, merely watching as Joori methodically and gently peeled the blood-sticky clothes off his little sister's body. Joori's tears flowed steadily while he tried not to wince every time his fingers glanced over a knot of bone or a gaping wound. Shig was doing the same for Yori, though Shig had stopped her weeping, gone silent. Umeia lay sheet-draped and untended on one of the steam tables where only an hour ago the kitchen boys had been preparing rice and setting up for supper.

There'd been nowhere else to bring the bodies. Upstairs hadn't seemed right, and the floor of the Girou was too open. And there was no telling if they were going to have the time for a proper pyre. The practical part of Samin had remembered the cold-storage room, so he'd brought them all to the kitchens, evicted any who were still lingering.

Some had begun the mourning of their surrogate "mother" and patroness. Some had tried to flee after the blatant display of magic. The man Malick called Husao corralled them back, and that crone-who-wasn't-a-crone from the Stallion was now keeping them relatively quiet, either up in their own rooms or congregated out on the floor. Most had stayed, gathered out on the floor where they made their living, getting slowly drunk and discussing the open secret of the Girou, which was a lot more open than Samin had known.

Protected all this time beneath Malick's veil, but Umeia had been the face of it all. Umeia had been the one everyone thought really in charge—even Samin. Even now, he couldn't tell how many were hiding magic of some kind, how many were just as shocked as he was by the number of those who'd somehow known to seek open refuge here, and how many had no magic themselves but had willingly accompliced those who did. Accompliced the woman who'd taken them in and sheltered them, and only now were they beginning to get the faintest clue that it had really been Malick all along. Malick's magic hiding them, Malick's money giving them new names, buying them papers, getting some out of Ada altogether, if that was what they'd wanted, and if they'd earned the help.

And now the woman they'd all thought of as some kind of House Mother lay dead on a steam table in her own kitchen. Samin didn't think it was entirely inappropriate of him that he was glad it was Umeia and not Malick.

It seemed wrong, though, that no one was tending to Umeia like they were for Caidi and Yori, but Lex was still trying to pull himself together, and anyway, it wasn't really his place. Lex wasn't Umeia's mate, merely her favored companion, but certainly not the only one. It was Malick's place, but Malick was... busy.

Samin's mouth turned down, and he bowed his head.

The incense was heavy in the air; it burned his nose, stung his eyes. Shig had lit too much of it, but Samin hadn't wanted to tell her to quit at the traditional three.

Morin was staring around with his red, puffy eyes. Unaccountably, Samin wanted to hug him.

He liked the whole family. Maybe even loved them a little bit. He hadn't thought he even *liked* children, but Caidi had got to him in ways—

Samin blinked. Damned incense.

That little girl had been taken right out of Samin's hands. Out of his *hands*. The feel of her quivering as he'd tried to brush away the shadows. The look in her eyes through the murk. The fear. The confusion. The sick sinking of his gut when he'd grabbed for her foot as she lifted up past him and... *missed*. Just missed.

Another failure among... so many. An entire day of them. Weeks, maybe, months, *years* leading up to this—who really knew?

A thousand horrible, painful deaths for Asai, with Samin himself twisting the blade—it still wouldn't be enough.

"I need more water, Morin." Joori's voice was mildly startling, for all it was quiet. He didn't look up, head bowed over Caidi, shoulders tight and trembling as the cloth he used to bathe his little sister's body grew redder.

Morin sucked in a shaky breath as he retrieved the basin to clean and refill it. He hadn't gone three steps before he stopped, wary-eyed and tense, swollen hazel eyes riveted to a spot behind where Samin stood.

Samin didn't need to turn, but he did anyway.

Malick took in the scene with a look that was pained, sad. Fen was leaning into him heavily, a bathsheet wrapped around him like a blanket. He carefully looked at nothing.

Joori stared at Malick with eyes both terrified and defiant, clearly confused when Malick did nothing but meet Joori's eye then move on to Morin.

Malick looked tired. Exhausted, really. Grief-stricken and just plain *done*.

He scrubbed at his face, then set his jaw. "By my heart, by my body, by my breath and spirit, I pledge my oath to Kel Saminil, Kojoi Shig, Fen Joori, and Fen Morin. Should my life be required in return for their safety, I pledge it willingly, by forfeit of my soul should I fail."

The silence was complete, though the delivery had lacked any sort of dramatics. Even Samin was stunned. Malick just wasn't the sort. Or hadn't been.

"Mal." Samin had to clear his throat. "We haven't even—"

"It doesn't matter. Whether you stay or you go, you've earned it and more."

"What about my brother?"

Surprisingly, it came from Morin, not Joori. Morin was a little too pale, like he expected to be struck down for his impertinence, but his chin was up and his gaze was steady, if a little too obviously terrified.

"Your brother won't accept it." Malick's mouth turned down in obvious disapproval. "Anyway, I'm not sure it would work. Magic just kind of… slides off him."

"Oh." Morin rolled his eyes. *"Brilliant."*

He was a snarky little shit who gave his brothers grief at almost every opportunity, but he loved them in his way. Samin had seen it that first night, counterintuitive though it seemed, when Morin had kicked Fen to put him down.

Malick merely shifted his gaze to Joori. "Take your brother upstairs and help him dress."

"But." Joori frowned, blinking, then he looked down at the red-soaked cloth in his hand, at his little sister. "I was—"

"I know. Morin can take over." With a slight flicker of his gaze toward Caidi, Malick shook his head and gave Fen's shoulder a squeeze. "She's not going anywhere."

Joori winced, but he didn't snap back. Only ran a gentle hand over Caidi's brow, whispered something to her that Samin didn't try to hear, then turned to rinse his hands.

"Still think you can live with it, angry Ghost?"

Shig hadn't said a word since they'd begun their mournful tasks. To hear her speak so calmly now—without the spirit-driven singsong it seemed they'd all expected when she finally decided to speak again—was strange and disconcerting.

Samin didn't know what the question meant, but Fen seemed to. He didn't answer it, though, merely gave Shig a flat stare, too wrung out and stricken to muster much else. He looked, in fact, now that Samin was letting himself *really* look, like a man who was gazing directly into the empty perdition of the suns, and just barely hanging onto whatever precarious hold he'd been able to snatch.

Malick was right—the lad needed his brother. Samin was just surprised it had been Malick's idea.

Shig's jade eyes were too sharp for someone who was so deeply in mourning, but not hostile, though the question had almost sounded so. She looked… interested. Curious. She merely shrugged when Fen didn't answer, looked away, and went back to her task.

They were all silent as Joori took Fen's weight from Malick and began leading him from the kitchen.

"Watch it on the stairs," Malick said. "And take him to my room. There are rolls of bandages and a jar of salve in the cupboard under the washstand."

Joori didn't answer, but he turned back to look over his shoulder as he went, searched Malick's face, even more confused than he'd been before.

Malick waited until Joori and Fen were well gone before he turned back. With a soft look, he gestured Shig over. She came quietly, with a subtle show of relief, but the tears that had dried up a while ago were once again misting her eyes as she stepped willingly beneath Malick's arm and laid her head on his shoulder.

"Better, love?"

Shig merely nodded and began to sob almost silently into Malick's shirt.

Malick looked at Samin. "Fen still intends to go after his mother." His glance cut briefly to Morin then down to Shig before it settled again on Samin. "If either of you has any objections, now's the time to voice them. Any debt either of you ever thought you might owe me has been…" His eyes went to Yori's body then back again to Shig. He shut them briefly and looked away. "It's been *paid*."

Giving them yet another opportunity to back out, now that the warning of things getting ugly had been made terrible truth. As if any of them could have witnessed what went on today and merely bowed their heads and stepped back. Malick had to know better, but Samin supposed he respected that Malick took care to make the offer. Still, Samin didn't justify the opportunity for cowardice; he merely waited until Malick's gaze lifted again and settled on him.

"Plan?"

The ghost of a familiar cocky smirk flickered at Malick's mouth. "Sorry, have we met?"

Excellent. Mayhem.

Samin shot a quick look at Shig, returned her watery smile, then turned back to Malick.

"When?"

How could it be possible that Joori was still standing here? That the blood on his hands had washed off?—just *washed off*. That life, *his* life, just kept going, when the lives of his sister and his too-new lover were just… over? Gone and done, and here he was, still breathing, still functioning, when it was supposed to have been him, it should have been *him*, and he knew they all knew it. That they all wished it had been.

That was all right. He wished it too.

"Brother."

Jacin's voice was hoarse, because he'd been screaming, they'd all heard it, all the way from down in the baths.

Joori couldn't answer. If he opened his mouth, *he* might start screaming.

"Joori." Jacin took hold of Joori's hand around the comb. Stilled it. Pushed it away. He turned.

Joori couldn't meet Jacin's eyes. Couldn't do anything but stare down at the comb in his hand, a long rope of Jacin's hair still twisted between his fingers. He was supposed to be braiding it, like he'd used to do when he'd known Jacin like he'd known himself. When life still had dubious hope, but *hope*. When Joori could almost always find the right words to say, the right reassurances—*I won't let it happen, Jacin, you're not a Ghost, you'll never be a Ghost*.

Except now Morin's words—*you've done him no favors by pretending he isn't what he is*—kept coming back to him. Joori had a vague notion he should understand them. That they meant something he wasn't seeing. Something that could've made today not happen if he'd only understood, only seen, because it was all down to him, all his fault, every bit of it, and they all knew it.

Morin's knowledge poured out from hazel eyes so like Caidi's, so like their mother's; shone in those strange, soft looks he kept shooting Joori. Except Morin kept not saying it, kept not rubbing Joori's nose in it. It was so unlike Morin. Joori couldn't wrap his mind around it.

Be what you are, Morin had told him, and Joori had, or at least he'd tried. It hadn't mattered, hadn't made a single bit of difference. Now Joori wondered if it meant something else altogether. Perhaps it had been an admonishment, a sarcastic prediction of coming failure, because Morin *knew*, Joori knew he knew, even if no one would say it.

Shig's knowledge was too quiet, too composed for someone who'd never seemed interested in or able to care about the corporeal life that went on outside her multicolored head. "Too many are bleeding just as red as you today, angry earthbound." Her hands had been just as drenched in murky scarlet as Joori's were as she lovingly bathed her sister's face, dropped soft kisses to Yori's closed eyelids. Joori wished he could do the same, but he hadn't had the nerve to presume Shig would allow him near. "It wasn't yours to die today, and it was never yours to save them." She'd lifted her head then, looked right at Joori, her jade eyes red-rimmed and far too bright. "You're just not that special."

It had cut, and it shouldn't've. Shig was no one to him, just one more obstacle to saving his brother. Except now Joori had to wonder if he'd thought her an obstacle because she—just as much as everyone here, the world in general—was a threat to Jacin, or merely a threat to Joori's place beside him. Because Malick had told him, had accused him, had *warned* him, and now they were dead, gone, dropped from the sky to—

"Brother, *please*."

Jacin's voice was shaky, right on the edge of... something. The bottom of whatever abyss from which he'd been screaming, maybe, and it hadn't been Joori who'd pulled him out.

"Joori, I can't... Please, I need you."

It drove through Joori like a spike, buckled his knees. All at once breathless, he crumpled, laid his head in Jacin's lap. He wept, a long clump of silky-damp hair gripped too tight in his fist.

"I'm sorry. Jacin, I'm so *sorry*."

"Don't. I can't—"

It took more than Joori knew he had to get hold of himself, to breathe again, to lift his head and look into eyes that were so like his own, and yet so much deeper, with so much more inside them. Dry now, no tears, but swollen and bloodshot, and hollow with grief. Grief that Joori was forcing on Jacin, making him watch and feel, lose himself inside again. And Malick wasn't here this time to pull Jacin back out. Only Joori.

Jacin swept his thumbs over Joori's cheeks. His fingers were gentle in Joori's hair. Comfort. Understanding.

It was wrong, somehow. It should be the other way around. It should be Joori offering solace. It should be Joori padding the edges of the madness that perpetually hovered around Jacin.

Maybe Joori didn't know everything he'd thought he did. Maybe Malick was right and Joori didn't know Jacin at all anymore. But he knew who Jacin had been. He knew that everything inside Joori himself—every whisper of blame, every accusation of failure—was trebled and quadrupled in Jacin's precarious mind.

"Jacin." Joori took hold of Jacin's hands. "Whatever you're thinking, you're wrong." Joori swallowed. "It wasn't supposed to be you. It wasn't your fault. You couldn't have stopped any of it."

Somehow, it was the wrong thing to say. Jacin hadn't been shaking a few seconds ago, Joori was sure of it.

He was doing this wrong. He had no idea *how* to do this, how to reach the boy Jacin had been back when they'd truly been two halves of the same Self. Back before the world had taken away their shared life, imperfect as it had been, and given them only this unending penury to take its place.

"Jacin… tell me what you need. Tell me what to do."

Jacin's hollow gaze lit with a fire so abrupt and fierce it almost singed Joori's skin. Jacin turned his callused hands in Joori's, gripped so tight Joori almost yipped.

"*Don't die.*" Nearly violent in its strange sibilance.

Joori almost jerked away. Because he wasn't looking at Jacin anymore.

This was Fen. This was Jacin-rei. This was the Ghost, feeding on rage and grief like others fed on seeds, bound to a reality Joori had tried so hard to pretend away.

"I need you to *live*, Joori. I need Morin to *live*."

Jacin's hands were so strong, long fingers that looked so much like Joori's, but Jacin had always been more dexterous. Jacin had always been able to set his hand to a task and pull from it exactly what he wanted. Joori hadn't ever been able to even whittle without clumsy mistakes and mangled fingers. The only thing Joori had ever been able to make his hands do with any alacrity was weave that fucking braid, and he thought the irony of that might just kill him if he let himself think about it too hard.

Jacin snatched his hands away, cupped Joori's face between them, so gentle, so earnest.

"Brother. *Please.*"

No laws, their mother had told them. But she'd never said anything about a request from the one person Joori couldn't refuse. And like anything Jacin asked of him, Joori had no choice but to give it to him.

⚊

Xari scrutinized the motley assembly grieving for their mistress on the floor of a whorehouse, wondering, as mortals were wont, what came next. The man they called Lex had emerged from his grief for his apparent lover and begun the mundane business of picking up pieces, showing others by calm example how to do the same. Mortals were so alike in the ways they dealt with what they knew but never quite believed was only temporary death. Xari absorbed the pain and sorrow like another would absorb a good meal.

Kamen would not allow Lex to tend to Umeia's body. Xari could feel how that rankled, how it hurt; she pulled that into herself as well, ignoring Husao's curled lip when he realized what she was doing. She didn't look away. It was what she was. *Banpair*; the accusation lay broody in Husao's stare. Xari merely shrugged. Husao took his strength from his god; Xari had no such luxury. Not yet. And it was kinder to bleed off—feed off—misery than take from gentler emotions. At least in Xari's opinion.

There were *banpair* who sucked away any emotion they could gather, obsessed by it, who harmed or maimed or even seduced only to incite such passion, and then slurped it like addicts. Xari took what she needed, and only when she needed. A true *banpair*, after all, could not hope to be claimed by any god. And a godless maijin needed the strength and power to do the deeds required for that divine acceptance.

Xari did not intend to remain godless, and she trusted no promises. She would earn her place again—with Dragon, if she would take her; with Wolf, if she wouldn't—and standing by and watching her son destroyed was simply not enough.

The Obelisk had taken Xari's intended penance out of her hands. Her own fear had stalled her feet when she'd had a brief flicker of a chance to redeem herself through her son's death, but she'd foreseen her own in the doing, and had hesitated. And the Catalyst had not waited for Xari to catch up. Kamen had warned her, and still, Xari hadn't been quick enough.

There were no choices left to her now, only one moment left to seize. She would have to find her redemption through the salvation of one who had no intention of being saved.

"It is not done." Xari gave Husao an assessing look across the table. "There is more to do."

Husao sighed. "Kamen will—"

"Kamen sees naught but his Catalyst. Kamen lets it blind him, and too many will fall with him." Xari looked away. "You have your vengeance, Husao, and you have your god. You've none left to please, no redemption for which to beg. The Untouchable is Kamen's redemption. Asai was to be *mine*. Kamen will understand."

Husao's smile was frustratingly shrewd.

"No, Xari. He will not."

8

What comes after?

Someone had asked him that. He could hear the echo of Malick's voice inside it, so maybe it had been him. Jacin hadn't really thought about it before, hadn't an answer then, but he knew now what had been at the back of his mind, tucked away inside some twisted bit of hope that still inexplicably lived.

Kill Asai. Fix his mother. Bring his father back to life and make him love him. Stop the screeching in his head. Stop the madness. Stop the hurt.

The list went on. Foolish and deluded, but it had been there. It was there still, even knowing none of it was possible.

There was nothing to do but start picking up the pieces of his shattered reality, fit the ragged edges into shapes that didn't make him scream. Keep Malick's ring on his finger because it was already too late, Jacin had missed… something. Beishin was dead, Caidi was dead, Yori was dead, and the Ancestors might have told him how to save them, but he hadn't been listening.

…Or maybe they wouldn't have told him at all. Maybe they merely would've kept shrieking their agony at him. Because what difference did it make to them?

It didn't matter. He hadn't been listening. Couldn't bring himself to listen now. He needed the silence, needed to think, wake up the bits of his mind that'd gone to sleep inside the Ancestors' nightmares, and use them to save what he had left.

He kept the ring on his finger. Clung to the bits of himself that still felt like sanity.

"What now, Jacin?" Joori's voice was soft as he slowly plaited Jacin's braid.

It felt nice. It felt like home somehow, so Jacin let Joori do it. Even when Joori'd had to start over twice for the shaking, it still felt nice.

Jacin shut his eyes. "Now, we go on." Because it was all he knew.

Joori was silent for a while, braiding more carefully than he really needed to, stretching the process into curling silence. Jacin didn't mind, so he didn't say anything.

"Malick…" Joori's voice quavered. "I mean Kamen… *damn* it." Joori unwove a few inches of the braid then started again. "Did he ever tell you how he… how he was made, or…?" Joori's touch turned rougher. "I mean. Jacin. What d'you even know about him?"

Jacin's mouth turned up at one corner, bitter irony. He leaned his head back against the top of the chair's cushion.

"He was made—turned; whatever they call it—by Wolf in the last Cycle before the Binding Wars. He's apparently young for *Temshiel*, and he thinks he's more jaded than he is, and he had the brass to strike a bargain with Wolf to bring Umeia along with him."

It was actually sort of amusing to imagine—Malick, still mortal, offered immortality and power by a god, and still having the audacity to level conditions. Because it probably never occurred to him that he shouldn't. Vanity, apparently, did wonders for a person's expectations.

"He fought on the side of the Adan."

Jacin shrugged. "He's *Temshiel*."

It wasn't something he could hold against Malick like perhaps Joori did, because Jacin understood it. War was an ugly thing, impersonal, waged by the minions of jealous gods who seized on the too-personal fears of mortals to sway them to one side or the other. Malick was no different from that Adan doujoun who'd wanted to help Jacin the night he left the camp, and couldn't, bound by the laws and the reprimands of his superior. If you were someone's dog, you did what they told you.

"He's scary," Joori said.

"Hm." Jacin opened his eyes to look up at the ceiling, the gray light of the waning day casting goblin shadows through the rain on the window. "He's always felt like a cool, calm wind to me." Pine and sage, clean, where Beishin had always smelled of jasmine, cloying; Jacin shunted the memory-scent away like he shunted Beishin's voice away, whispering in the back of Jacin's head—*You did this, little Ghost.* "He says…" Jacin swallowed, his throat raw and burning, like trying to talk through hot ash. "He says he loves me."

Just like Beishin had done. When he'd thought it would get his Ghost to do what he'd wanted.

Joori drew in a shaky breath. "And…?"

"And." Jacin shut his eyes again, Beishin's shark's smile curling behind them. "People lie. But sometimes the lies they tell are telling in themselves."

"But you trust him anyway."

"I suppose."

"With your life?"

"It's not that simple. Our… purposes are the same. For now. I trust that."

I had hoped that you might trust me enough, dare I think... love me enough, to keep your faith, your belief.

Jacin's mouth tightened.

Shut up, Beishin.

"Mm," Joori hummed. "Not much reassurance, I think, when you don't give a shit if you live or die."

It wasn't deliberate. That wasn't Joori's way, not with Jacin. It cut anyway.

Anger swelled, all at once. Jacin jerked the half-woven braid from Joori's hands.

"I can finish."

Because he really didn't need this. Not now.

"Jacin, I... I'm sorry." Cautious, Joori gently took the braid back. "I don't mean to... I only..."

Jacin chanced a look upward, saw tears thicken Joori's gaze, so looked away.

"She's already gone, Jacin. We've sacrificed Caidi to avenging her, and she's still gone. I don't want... I *can't* lose any more. Neither can you, and you know it."

It wound in Jacin's chest, tightened. How was it that Joori could hurt him like this, when Jacin knew he only ever tried not to?

Jacin centered his focus on the ring on his finger. "I've heard the voices of mad spirits for what feels like thousands of years. Desperate agony, terrible knowledge, and the excruciating inability to do anything with it, to even understand the knowing, just having it inside you, gnawing at you, and you can never quite catch it, force it into sensible shapes. It's maddening. It's unbearable."

Joori had stopped braiding again, likely horrified, but there could be no mercy in this.

Jacin turned his hand, watched the gem on the ring catch the gray light. Watched the drop of Malick's Blood inside it darken, shapeshift inside the facets.

"I won't leave her soul to that." Jacin made it hard, ruthless, because it was true, and because love was a weapon, and Joori wielded it with too-sharp precision. Jacin didn't want it anymore; it made him weak, it distracted him, it made his heart a soft, dangerous thing, and the howling loss inside him for Caidi only drove that home in ways that could crush him if he let them. He couldn't let them. "I won't allow another to leave her to it, not if I can stop it happening. If you can leave the woman who bore you to such a fate, you're no brother of mine."

And yet you could doom the man who taught you, who cared for you, who lov—

Shut up, shut up, you didn't, you don't.

Everything about Joori went rigid.

Jacin almost went on, almost drove the knife in deeper. If he couldn't cut the love out of his own chest, maybe he could cut it from Joori's. Kill the weakness inside himself by proxy.

Would you be the doom of your brother? Would you fail your mother?

Shutupshutupshutup—

But Joori only snorted, something bitter and disbelieving. "And you'd sacrifice us for it?"

Your emotions make you weak and foolish, little Ghost. A lesson was necessary.

I'm trying very hard to learn it, Beishin.

"If I had to."

"Malick said you wouldn't."

"Malick was wrong."

"Yeah?" Joori shifted back behind the chair again, resumed weaving Jacin's hair into its hated braid. "You're a liar, Jacin. And the lies you tell are telling in themselves. Five minutes ago, you were *begging* me to live, and now you're trying to cut me out, cut Morin out, cut your own *heart* out like you cut out—"

"Believe what you—"

"Oh, don't worry." There was a smile in Joori's voice, cold and calculating. "You'll get what you want out of me. I'll live because you've asked it of me. I'll make sure Morin lives because you've asked it of me. And I know what it would do to you if you had to watch us die too. I'll live and I'll make sure Morin lives because I owe it to Caidi. I owe it to you, because I'm firstborn. All of this should've been my—"

"Joori, none of this—"

"—burden. I owe it to Yori too. I even owe it to Umeia."

"You don't owe—"

"We'll live, even though it's profoundly unfair that I don't get to make the same demand of you." Joori set both hands to Jacin's shoulders, laid a kiss to the crown of his head. "And you can go and save Mother knowing there'll be no more bodies for you to prepare, no more pyres to light."

Save him, Joori could be even more ruthless, could out-cruel Jacin without even batting an eye.

Proved it when he lowered his voice, whispered into Jacin's hair, "He wasn't supposed to love you. Was he, Jacin-rei?"

The name—*rei*—from Joori's mouth shocked Jacin, stilled him.

"*Temshiel* don't know how, do they, and you thought you were safe. He was supposed to use you and leave you, and instead he handed you his heart, offered you his soul, and now you have to figure out what to do with it. Because love isn't a safe thing for you, is it… *Ghost?*"

It was soft, right next to Jacin's ear, warm breath and sonorous accusation. It was only vaguely that Jacin felt the hot splash of tears hit his neck and realized Joori was weeping inside the words that came through a smile Jacin couldn't see.

"Love only means you'll have to watch someone else die. You were down to two and now you're back up to three, and you can't take it, I know you can't take it, and it's all right." Joori's arms wrapped about Jacin's shoulders from behind, locked his back into the cushions of the chair, and only now did Jacin realize he'd stopped breathing. His heart was battering beneath Joori's palm where it rested over Jacin's breastbone. "You can stop loving us for a while if you need to, Jacin. I won't fight you anymore."

Abruptly, Joori let go, came around to the front of the chair. He leaned in, set his hands to both sides of Jacin's head, eyes both soft and intense.

"Be the Ghost." Fierce and from between clenched teeth. "Give Fen Jacin-rei all the pain and power, because he's the only one who can bring my brother back to me. Because if we have to be alive, then so do you."

ᛏ

Vengeance was... *almost* satisfying. Husao had got it without risk, had skirted the shifting lines of true interference, and could stand before his god with no need for defense. But for the matter of the amulets bearing his son's Blood, he could walk away, and make no enemies.

Xari could lay no blame on Husao for her failure. She'd hesitated, and the Catalyst had beaten her to her redemption.

And Kamen... No one wanted to make an enemy of Kamen. Even those *Temshiel* who'd been drawn by the swell of power in the city, the aura of conflict, were hovering the edges, staying close but not venturing into Kamen's sight. Husao could feel them, biding and watching, and wondered if any of them would be foolish enough or think themselves strong enough to take a stand against Kamen when his intentions became clear. Because it wasn't difficult to see that Wolf's aim was very different from that of the other gods, and where Wolf pointed, Kamen led. Even when he didn't think he did. Wolf too obviously intended to save his children, and as far as Husao could tell, none of the other gods had yet ventured to gainsay him openly—or at least, none of them had deigned to guide their *Temshiel* to do so.

To be expected, he supposed. It was Wolf's Cycle, his power at its apex, and Kamen was the bloody hand at the end of Wolf's long arm. And none, thus far, not even Kamen, had broken the laws of the gods. Raven and Dragon risked, at the very least, bending them, if they moved against Wolf now. It would be interesting to see if Kamen could manage to achieve his god's goals without crossing the oft-blurry lines of the others', but if anyone could maneuver around the ambiguities, it would be Kamen. Reason enough for Xari to throw her lot in with Wolf's-own, in Husao's considered opinion, but Xari did not trust easily, and had witnessed too often the machinations and duplicity of the gods and their servants to count on Kamen's promise of entreaty to Wolf.

The gods offered no guarantees.

The harsh judgment of Husao's own son had proven it. Intention meant nothing; only action mattered. Skel had intended to set the Balance back on its fulcrum, empower the Adan to remove the Jin entirely, take magic from mortals who never should have had it. What he'd actually done had sent him to the suns. Even had he achieved what he'd wanted, singlehandedly set the Balance, it would not have mattered. Not when he'd broken the laws to do it.

The laws were not theirs to break. Fate did not suffer tests to her intentions. Even the gods didn't dare.

Xari would not be judged by her hopes and attempts. Only by what she accomplished before the end of the Cycle. So far, that had been little. She had not taken the brief instant of opportunity. Her chances of being forgiven and reclaimed by Dragon were better than her chances of being accepted by Wolf, and pleasing Dragon by ridding the world of the Jin abomination would secure her endorsement.

Husao had no such dilemma. Dragon had not directed her *Temshiel* to take a side, and so he didn't. He'd got mostly what he'd wanted. He backed neither Jin nor Adan. And though Xari and Husao shared a god, they'd only very briefly shared goals. They were not allies, not unless Dragon told them to be, and Husao had one last promise to keep, one last task to arrange, if he could, about which he'd told Xari nothing. He kept it that way now. If honoring the Mage's promise got him that last thing he needed, he would keep it.

He led Xari up the flights of stairs to the attic floor, following the throb of the earth at the bottom of his spine. The Paradox had allowed his power to unfurl, had allowed Kamen to take it and treble it, use it. Husao didn't know how the earthbound had managed to keep it suffocated all this time, but he didn't think it would willingly go back down to wherever the boy had shoved it before. He was pulsing out power like a beacon, ripe for the hunters, were it not for Kamen's veil. Ripe for ground-shaking disaster, as well, if provoked. The boy had no real control.

There were reasons most mortals should not have magic. Ironically, the Adan had put themselves in even more danger by taking away the ability of those who had it to learn to use it. The amulets had always been a shaky stopgap—proven as such through the riots that still sprang from the camps now and then—because Asai had at least been wise enough or manipulative enough not to hand those who used them their full power. If the Jin were a different people, they would've already risen up and crushed the Adan, amulets or no.

They found the Paradox and the Catalyst in a modest set of rooms at the top of the stairs. Jacin-rei was sitting, stiff-backed and blank-eyed, in an ugly overstuffed chair, clean and put together. Husao still winced at the change in the boy who'd fled Asai's only a little over two months ago.

The earthbound stiffened in challenge as Husao and Xari entered. Jacin-rei merely stared.

Both sets of gray eyes were wary, taking in beautiful Xari without her glamour, Husao, a stranger to them both without his. They watched with hostile curiosity.

Jacin-rei's left hand went behind his back; the other went openly to the hilt of one of the several knives at his belt. Lazy tension wound around him.

"Yes?" Hoarse but very calm.

Husao politely directed Xari to the couch opposite the brothers. They all stared over the divide of the tea table.

"Hello, Jacin-rei." Husao smiled and nodded at Xari. "I am Husao. This is Xari. We are…" He paused, his smile going a bit crooked. "We are old acquaintances of Kamen's. We have—"

"Acquaintances." Jacin-rei lifted his eyebrows. "Not… friends? Allies?" He tilted his head. "Enemies?"

Xari snorted. "Enemies of Kamen's would not live past the doorstop." She slid a warm smile between the brothers, all easy charm. "And our kind do not have friends. Allies?" She shrugged. "When it suits us."

Husao had forgotten how lovely and appealing Xari could be when she didn't wear her crone's face.

The earthbound's mouth tightened. "You're *Temshiel*."

"I am maijin." Xari lifted her chin. "Husao is *Temshiel*."

Jacin-rei merely blinked at them, unimpressed. "What d'you want?"

Blunt and to the point. Husao had always liked the boy.

An almost imperceptible stir of magic trickled into the dark depths of Husao's perception. He shot a look at Xari, but she didn't look back, so he couldn't tell if she'd felt it too. Likely not. It was so light and subtle a touch Husao wouldn't have felt it himself, had he not been stretching his senses to keep sentinel for the probes of hunters. And he recognized the talent and technique. Kamen was keeping a close eye on those under his veil. Quite possibly unfortunate for Xari; she was still included in that number.

Husao sat back. He was merely here to observe and wait for opportunity to present itself. Xari's business interested Husao only as much as it intersected with what remained of his. Even Kamen couldn't find fault with that.

"Not all is darkness this day." Xari leaned in, raven hair falling loose over her shoulder, the beaded tassels of her bright violet shawl chiming softly as she moved—not *quite* seductive, not yet, but not ruling out the possibility, either, should she need to fall back on it. "The Catalyst has today served the justice of the gods." Her voice was smooth and honeyed. Nothing at all like the creaky-hinge sound when she wore her glamour. "The treachery of Asai has stood as mocking example for too long. Wolf is well pleased."

Jacin-rei just kept staring. He didn't say a word, but Husao knew the boy, had made it his business to know the boy, and *I don't care* managed to ooze out from the blank-bored expression like a physical taste of bitter metal.

"We have come…" Xari paused when Husao subtly cleared his throat. Her mouth tightened only slightly, but she merely went on, "*I* have come to offer retreat and safety to you and yours."

Her smile was warm, almost sweet, directed at the earthbound, who seemed to be the better choice for charm. Trying to charm Jacin-rei right now would be like trying to seduce a stone. The way to Jacin-rei was—had always been, would always be—through those he loved.

The lack of reaction seemed to confuse Xari. "I can do what has already been promised to you. I can get you out. You seek now vengeance, and for that you cannot be blamed." Her expression went sympathetic, kind. "Your grief is profound and just. What happened today was…" Xari shook her head, almost reached out but seemed to think better. "I can see that your sorrow is oceans deep. Today should not have happened, and were it not for Kamen's desire for vengeance, it would not have done. He has used you, lad. You know this."

All through the little speech, Jacin-rei neither flinched nor looked away. He hadn't reacted at all. Now, he merely blinked, then shot a flat look up at the earthbound, who only shrugged.

Jacin-rei turned back to Xari. "And?"

Xari frowned. "And he has used those you love to a horrible end. Not his intent, to be fair, but reality nonetheless. You have already been betrayed by Kamen's own blood. Do not allow your grief to swottle you into allowing him to further that betrayal." She searched Jacin-rei's face, clearly bemused. "He would use you still. He would set you against Yakuli, risk you and yours, and all so he needs not risk his soul."

"He's sworn us oath." The earthbound slid an uncertain glance at Jacin-rei, but when Jacin-rei didn't chide him, he turned back to Xari. "Have you got something better than a *Temshiel's* oath?"

Xari had abruptly lost her smile. Husao understood why—Kamen had never sworn oath to another soul. Ever.

Xari shook off her shock. "And what good has such an oath done you, lad? You have—"

"That was my doing." It looked like it gutted the earthbound to say it, but he still squared his shoulders, lifted his chin. "I killed Umeia. I took away the protection of her oath." He clenched his jaw, looked away. "I won't defend Malick—your Kamen. I don't much like him. But he's—"

"He has set aside the wishes of the gods for the obsession of his lust. He has—" Xari cut herself off, mouth pinched up tight, and she looked at Jacin-rei with such rueful sympathy that Husao almost believed her himself. "Forgive my audacity, lad, but Kamen's passion for you has set aside his reason. He would tie the world in knots if he thought they might bind you to him. He would not mean to harm your own, but he is both well intentioned and ruthless. It makes him dangerous."

Jacin-rei continued to look unimpressed. "And what is the advice of a maijin on the matter?"

Xari didn't hesitate. "Get you gone from here. Leave the Adan and the Jin to their own misery. Leave Kamen to his machinations. Any servant of the gods who must use mortals to achieve his ends cannot own the power necessary to hand you what you would wish. Asai has taught you that cruel lesson. I have no goal but to aid the Catalyst. My power is at your disposal."

Husao only just managed to choke back a snort. Propping the power of a godless maijin against that of Wolf's *Temshiel* in his own Cycle—indeed. Had no one informed Xari that this Catalyst would know better? That Husao himself had taught him better? No, he supposed not. At least Husao had never seen the need to inform Xari of anything but what he wanted her to know, and it appeared Kamen had been just as circumspect.

The earthbound's eyes went a bit wistful at the promise. After the tragedies of the day, he was likely ripe for any promise at all that would keep him from losing the rest of those he obviously loved, including his Catalyst twin, upon whose shoulder his hand gripped tight.

Jacin-rei's eyes, however, sparked with something dark, dangerous. "And this from a maijin."

Husao could tell that Xari was treading very perilous ground, and by the way she stiffened, he could tell she did too. Still, she had a great deal to lose, and Husao had seen her wend through much worse and come out bruised and a little battered, but victorious.

"A maijin," Jacin-rei went on, "who scoffs at the 'plots' of a *Temshiel*, as though the very word isn't breath and bone to her, as though she herself has never—"

"A maijin who can offer you what none other will." Xari's tone went deep and imperious. "Who *has* offered you what none other can." She fisted her hand, set it to her breastbone, and thumped once. "The mother of Asai offers you and yours safety and protection for the rest of your days."

That got a reaction—from both brothers. The earthbound heaved out a sharp gasp and clutched even tighter at Jacin-rei's shoulder. Jacin-rei went rigid, all color draining so quickly from his face it was like watching someone turn to wax.

Xari's mouth quirked up in a not-smile, careful to keep her mien sincere. She tilted her chin to indicate Husao next to her.

"The father of Skel, he who was betrayed by Asai, offers you his thanks."

Very carefully speaking only the truth, nothing Husao would move himself to negate, but in such a way that implied Husao was willing to offer much more.

He didn't gainsay it. He merely dipped his head in acknowledgement, because it was true, he *was* grateful, and it wasn't up to him how Xari's words were to be interpreted by hopeful minds.

"*What* do you *want?*" Jacin-rei's tone was sharper this time, full of threat.

"But I've already told you." Xari let her smile bloom again, though she kept the triumph from it. "I want to take you away from here. I want to reward you by doing what's been promised to you over and over, and yet has never actually been granted."

Jacin-rei was silent for a while, thinking, then he jerked his chin up, brusque. "I've other matters I must see to. I won't leave yet. And I no longer trust any other to take my kin from my sight."

All too reasonable, as far as Husao was concerned. Jacin-rei had never had to be taught a lesson twice.

Xari shook her head. "Do not allow your wish for vengeance to put your own into the very danger from which you wish to save them. I know who you seek, and I know what you will be up against, should you do what I see burning in your eyes." She stood, then slipped down to her knees at Jacin-rei's feet. This time, she did reach out, laying a slender hand over the one curled into a tight fist over the hilt of a knife at Jacin-rei's belt. "Yakuli will come to his just end. I have seen it."

It was a lie—Husao knew she'd seen no such thing. His own sight was much deeper and far-reaching than Xari's, and he'd seen a very different possible future for Yakuli, now that Asai's machinations had come to an abrupt end and left Yakuli's ambition unchecked. With the army Asai had helped build, and the host of mindless full-Bloods both stolen and grown, Yakuli's potential for power was almost limitless. Only one future-possible remained beyond Husao's sight, and he was quite confident that the reason for his blindness was sitting right in front of him.

Jacin-rei couldn't possibly know all this, but it didn't seem to matter. The anger that had been swelling in his gaze now flared bright into rage. And still, he kept himself motionless, that control Husao had watched him build like a suit of armor over the years, plate by torturous plate, now wrapped around him in unbending rule of Self.

"You've *seen* it."

Xari clearly knew there was something lethal crouching inside it, but she didn't seem to know what. She kept still, only narrowing her eyes when Jacin-rei's head tipped to the side, questioning, and he subtly shifted his elbow, nudging, until the earthbound angled behind the chair.

"What else have you seen?" Jacin-rei's raspy voice curled sinister. "Did you *see* what happened today?" His fearsome gaze snapped to Husao. "Did it serve your gods? Is that why you stood there and watched them fall?"

"I have not the power to pluck a child from the sky and bend the air around her." Xari said it with just the right amount of contrition and accusation, leaving Jacin-rei free to draw the conclusion that Kamen had the power and yet had failed.

Jacin-rei didn't seem to be cooperating. "What power *do* you have? You make promises of protection, and yet admit you haven't the power." With a curl of his lip, he knocked Xari's hand away, leaning forward in his chair until his nose was only inches away from hers. "*You* sent for Malick this morning. *You* drew him away. *You* made it possible for Asai to come here and do what he did."

Drawing all the wrong conclusions, but harboring all the right suspicions. Xari most certainly had not colluded with Asai, but she very well might collude with Yakuli—one or the other didn't really matter to Jacin-rei, and Husao saw no need to correct him.

"The cards had changed." Xari was all soft caution now. "I sent for Kamen to warn him of the duplicity of his own."

"And by doing so allowed that duplicity to come to pass. The future is a chancy thing, and sometimes, the mere speaking of it can change it in ways that can't be foreseen. One who deals in it should know that."

Husao recognized the words, could almost hear Asai's voice inside them. He suppressed a sneer.

Jacin-rei only kept glaring at Xari. "Who is your god?"

Xari blinked, hesitated for only a second before she lied, "Dragon."

Husao understood her reluctance to admit she had no god and thus no power to carry through on what she was offering, but he thought it a mistake nonetheless. The jump in direction might seem like it came from scattered reasoning, but there was purpose beneath it, and it was never wise to bluff when one didn't have at least an informed guess as to what one's opponent held in his hand.

Jacin-rei's gray gaze settled on Husao, still near-wild with building wrath, but leashed and held back tight. "And you?"

"Dragon." There was no need for hesitation or prevarication on Husao's part.

"So, you cannot touch Wolf's Catalyst." Jacin-rei's hoarse voice was low, but still managed to ooze menace and derision. "And yet you need Wolf's Catalyst gone from Ada. Away from Yakuli." He sat back, his hand coming out from behind his back, a chunky ring Husao recognized right away flashing in the watery light through the window. "Care to tell me why?"

Husao had watched enough. And that ring told him things for which he needed no cards or stones or portents. Xari had just roundly lost, had lost before she'd even mounted the attic stair, and Husao had no wish to sit here and watch her try to recover the unrecoverable. Jacin-rei's suspicions, though wrong, were not going to be assuaged, certainly not by Xari.

With a sigh that was sincerely sympathetic, Husao patted Xari's arm.

"Perhaps that question would be best answered by Kamen."

He turned to look over his shoulder. Husao merely lifted an eyebrow when Kamen wavered into sight, but Xari went rigid and shot up from her crouch at Jacin-rei's feet.

So she truly hadn't felt the stir before. Husao couldn't help but feel a little sorry for her.

"Oh, I don't know." Kamen sauntered around the back of the couch and hitched up beside Xari. He slid his arm around her shoulders. "Fen seems to be doing fine on his own." Anger rumbled beneath the blithe tone, and when he turned his eyes on Husao, only the knowledge that Kamen was much angrier with Xari than he could be with Husao kept Husao from tightening his shields. "But perhaps we should have *proper* introductions first, yeah?" Kamen flashed a grin that most would probably perceive as charming, but Husao had seen that ruthless spite before. "Why, Husao. No reunion? No glad embraces for the one you nearly helped raise? Everyone's all dressed up for the occasion, not a glamour in sight. Surely you've nothing to hide from the Catalyst?"

Damn. This was entirely unnecessary. And a brief flash of the very near future told Husao it was also quite dangerous. But then, that would be Kamen's point.

"Kamen." Husao kept his tone even. "There is no reason to hurt the boy."

"No, there isn't. Nor was there any reason for him to have to watch his sister die while you just stood there and watched him carry out your vengeance for you. You could have helped, Husao. You didn't."

"I saw to the rabble, and that was a gift. Surely you didn't expect more from me. You knew my role in this, Kamen. And you know Dragon's—"

"Don't hide behind your god, Husao, it's beneath you. Dragon issued no decree against saving the lives of a little girl and a young woman who managed in their short years to earn more grace than you've done in centuries."

"You seem, Kamen, to have refound your tender sympathies for mortals. One wonders if it can do anything but harm to those mortals. Even when you try to save them, they seem to just… slip through your fingers."

Unfair and rather cheap, but Husao had to at least try a tentative defense. Kamen's wrath had been stirred, his Catalyst toyed with. There would be no quarter, not even for those who were just here to watch.

Kamen bared his teeth—a wolf's leer, fitting to his namesake god—and turned to Jacin-rei.

"Fen, I'd like you to meet the *Temshiel* who's been posing as my patron, the Mage, though I think you'll be more familiar with the name by which his glamour is known." He swept his hand out toward Husao. "Fen, this is Vonshi."

It seemed to take far too long for it to sink in. Jacin-rei went blank, hand tightening then relaxing, tightening then relaxing, while his expression slid from stunned-empty to confused to pure and profound rage. Both hands snapped to the knives at his belts, and he was on his feet and coming for Husao in the time it took for the earthbound to gasp, "I know that name," in bewildered surprise.

Jacin-rei kicked the tea table out of the way, and leveled his blades at Husao's throat.

"You *knew*."

Husao didn't move. Damn it, he *liked* the boy. He'd made him those revolting sweet bean-paste cakes for the gods' sakes, for *years*. Shouldn't that count for something?

"I knew."

"Did you know where she was?"

Husao cut a look at Kamen, lifted his eyebrow.

"Don't look at *him*." Jacin-rei's knives pressed harder. "*Did you know* Yakuli took my mother?"

There was no reason why the hatred roiling at him should bother Husao so much—Catalyst or no, the boy was still only mortal—but it did.

Husao very gently pushed the blade closest to his throat away. Jacin-rei merely whirled it smoothly and resettled it against the blue veins at Husao's wrist, effectively pinning his hand to the arm of the couch, then flicked the other knife beneath Husao's chin. Precise and faster than even Husao could follow. He could feel the fine-honed tips of both blades and yet neither of them even pricked his skin.

"Better tell him the truth." Kamen's smirk was blatant, cold. "I doubt even you can foresee his next move."

Too right. Husao grimaced. The boy was not only Untouchable, but he moved almost entirely on instinct, without thought, which made him almost impossible to foresee. Like Asai, Husao had only ever been able to predict Jacin-rei by concentrating on those around him, and though Husao's sight was fathoms deeper than Asai's, he'd still never been able to see Fen Jacin-rei himself with any real accuracy.

He had, however, just witnessed a too-quick vision of quite a lot of blood, so he'd best to tread very carefully. Under other circumstances, death now would be inconvenient, at worst, but Jacin-rei knew how to make it so Husao couldn't come back. And Husao wasn't altogether sure Kamen wouldn't just stand there and watch.

Husao sighed, annoyed. "I saw."

Jacin-rei's gaze turned murderous. The earthbound hissed a string of foul invective.

Husao kept all his attention on the knives. "You must understand, Jacin-rei: one mortal life carries no weight within the Balance. You would not have moved against Asai without cause, and you were the only one who could remove him with neither damnation from the gods nor the forewarning of his own sight. It only made it more… poetic that he taught you how to bring about his own end." Husao shrugged, careful not to shift those parts of himself still pinned at knifepoint. "You have lost very little, in truth. As Xari says, you could very well leave Ada now with your brothers and your sanity, and still be leagues ahead of any other Untouchable in the last century or so."

"You…" Disbelieving. Stricken.

Husao frowned. The boy needed a better grip on his emotions. His eyes had gone glassy, and his skin was going to ash.

"Fen?" Kamen shot a furious glare at Husao. "Fen, are you—?"

"My father, dead. My mother… taken. My brother almost taken, my… my sister…" Jacin-rei swallowed, mouth quivering. "And you knew. All your teachings, all your kindnesses."

"Fucking hell." The earthbound huffed, windless. "And I thought Malick was bad."

"Oh, I am. Just in a different way." Kamen tightened his arm around Xari. "Right, love?"

Husao ignored them. "They were meant truly, lad. I wanted you—"

"You wanted me to do your wet work for you." Jacin-rei's voice was still hoarse, but the shakiness of only a second ago was morphing into something harder, colder. "And a mad Untouchable would've been worthless."

It would likely be a mistake to smile and pat the boy approvingly for his deductions, so Husao remained still and silent.

"That night." Jacin-rei's gaze went a little foggy, and both knives relaxed their pinions very slightly. "The door opened. It was locked, I *know* it was locked, but it opened. I heard…" He shook his head, betrayal and deep, dark wrath in eyes gone turbulent. "You knew even before he did."

Husao breathed a little easier. He recognized this look. Jacin-rei was nothing if not ever-anxious for stern direction when his mind began to wander into places he didn't really want to see.

"Look at it with your head, boy, and not with your heart. Your emotions make you addled, they always have done." Husao was gratified when Jacin-rei's eyes snapped into focus, a little less so when they narrowed, sharpened. "Of course I knew. It was I who veiled your brothers and your sister as they huddled in Asai's wilderness. Had I not,

Asai would've had them before that first night was through. I protected them to the very limits of my laws—for *you*."

"Because you needed me sane. Because you needed the threat. Because my emotions make me addled and weak, and you needed me just sane enough to obey when you pointed the Catalyst at his beishin."

"Of course not." Husao huffed an impatient sigh, almost shook his head, but couldn't move for the blade. "I needed you strong. I needed you ready. I needed you to draw Kamen to you, to give you the proof that would incite you and the strength that would enable you."

"He told me you'd come." Kamen, maliciously helpful.

And how did all of this get to be a veritable trial for Husao, when it was Xari who'd been attempting to take Kamen's Untouchable away? It wasn't fair.

"And told you to kill me if I didn't." Jacin-rei paused, head atilt. "And my family?"

Husao didn't answer. Without Jacin-rei to dangle them over as impetus, his family had no value. Husao *might* have alerted Kamen to their existence, left it to him, but then... he might just as easily have forgotten about them altogether, left them to starve or survive as Fate decided. Looking into Jacin-rei's eyes, Husao didn't need to be told that admitting as much would be... unhealthy. And yet, he somehow couldn't make himself speak a lie.

He needn't have done either—Jacin-rei knew. Husao could see it in the wrathful cant to his expression, the pain beneath it.

"I... see." Soft, almost distant, before Jacin-rei jolted. His eyes squeezed shut, and his hands tightened around his knives. "Shut up, *shut up!*"

For a moment, Husao thought the half-crazed command had been directed at him, and only the awareness of the knives overrode the indignant annoyance at the impudence.

But then Kamen stilled, said, "Fen?" in such a way it made Husao take a sharper look at Jacin-rei.

Jacin-rei's eyes slid open. Anger. Confusion. Betrayal. And very little clarity.

"You told him to kill me."

Husao should perhaps tread a little more carefully. "I did not want you dead, lad. Understand." Husao took a moment to think about what he should say, because he'd seen that vagueness in Jacin-rei's eyes before, but he'd never seen it mixed with such hatred. "If you didn't join them, yes, you would have been got out of the way. Your Samin would've done the deed; even that first night, Kamen was too besotted and would've balked. I couldn't have you going back to Asai, Jacin-rei. Nor could I have you running about loose. And I knew that you would... appeal to Kamen."

Kamen snorted. "Perfect, Husao. That'll calm him down."

The earthbound muttered back there somewhere, low, indecipherable, but Husao was almost certain he made out the word *pimp* hissed out on a sneer. He scowled.

"So, you used me to gain his complicity." Jacin-rei's head tilted to the side, a listening posture Husao had seen too many times, but now... it just didn't seem right. The boy had Kamen's ring, after all. "Why?"

"They are using *my son's Blood!*" It all but burst from Husao. He sucked in a quick breath and made his heart slow its rhythm, made his breathing even out. "Control—that was all Skel ever wanted. To level the ground, arm both sides equally. *Balance.* He never would've used the amulets and spells the way Asai has done—he would have killed Asai himself and damn the suns, if he'd known. But he was in love, just as you—"

"Shut up, shut up, shut up, *enough!*"

Jacin-rei's voice was low and rust-raspy, and again, Husao wasn't even sure it was directed at him. It stopped him anyway.

Not Xari, though. "You see now, lad. The machinations are too large and far-reaching. They began before you were even born. Husao saw you before Asai did—he attached himself to Asai the night Asai bargained with your father. *He* showed Asai the vision, pushed it into his mind as though it were Asai's own."

Husao's mouth pinched in tight. *Thank you, Xari.*

Rather brave of her, though, considering Kamen's arm was still locked around her, and his jaw was set in cold anger. Then again, Kamen couldn't kill her, and though he could be maliciously creative in the ways of hurting a person, one could recover from hurt.

It was... annoying. Husao had only come to observe, after all. He'd had no intention of making things more difficult for Xari, but it seemed she had no compunction about making things more difficult for him. And the damnable flashes of splattered blood would *not* stop lurking just at the edges of Husao's sight.

"I needed you, Jacin-rei." It was easy for Husao to make it earnest, because he meant it. "I needed Kamen. Neither of us could kill Asai ourselves, and he was more powerful than any maijin, even his own mother. He was virtually invulnerable, except to the one person he couldn't foresee. Planning was his mistake. I could see his ripples in Fate and work them against him, but he couldn't see yours. It's why your presence was imperative. No one knows what you'll do—not even you. It makes the future harder to predict. You're already a blank spot in Fate. Your effect on it is colored ever in gray. But put you with Kamen, the one who craved vengeance almost as deeply as I, the one who would gladly help you find yours..."

He trailed off, let Jacin-rei fill in the rest, because Jacin-rei wanted to see it, wanted it all to have a purpose he could understand and take for his own. A directionless paladin looking for a lord to lead him, and Husao had given him Kamen. Had virtually handed them Asai. What more could they want from him?

"What d'you want to do, Fen?" Kamen clearly didn't care what answer he got. And he clearly intended to do whatever Jacin-rei wanted him to.

Husao nearly rolled his eyes. He respected Kamen, truly was grateful for the role he'd played in Husao's own vengeance, but sometimes he couldn't help but feel that all that power was wasted on one who was still too close to mortal.

Jacin-rei was still glaring at Husao, cold and maybe slightly less deranged than before, but with no less hatred. It still twisted foolish regret in Husao's chest. He truly did like the boy, after all.

"I don't know." Jacin-rei assessed the positions of his knives, minutely adjusted the angle of the one at Husao's throat. "D'you want him dead?"

Kamen shot Husao a look that was both snide and appraising.

Husao's lip curled. How very… sweet. Offering cold-blooded murder like a gift to a lover. Husao wondered if this was their idea of romance.

"Don't care, really." Kamen shrugged. "It's your quarrel."

Jacin-rei jerked his chin. "What about her?"

"Xari?" Kamen's arm tightened around Xari's shoulders. He grinned. "Aw, she only wants what's best for *you*, dontcha know." The sarcasm was sharp enough to cut. "It's up to you. She'll walk out of here and head right to Yakuli, so think about it."

Kamen shook his head and peered down at Xari, clear regret in his chiding look.

"Wolf would've taken you, y'know. Even without your son's blood on your hands. You should've thought this through. You watched Umeia make her mistakes, then came right behind her and made them yourself." Kamen's mouth went thin, cruel. "You're veiled until you leave the Girou, and that's only to protect everyone else. After you leave here, you're on your own. If Fen doesn't kill you now, I mean."

Jaw set, clear distrust, Jacin-rei lowered his knives. "I was promised by the Mage that the man I wanted would twitch at the end of my blade."

It was all Husao could do not to show his relief. His cautious exhilaration. The blood spatters slowly faded from the edges of his vision, but that was now almost inconsequential. *This* was what he'd been watching for.

Husao nodded. "You were."

"I was also told the Mage keeps his promises."

"He does." Husao shot a look at Xari. "Kamen is right—she will leave here and go to Yakuli, warn him."

Xari's mouth tightened, but she said nothing. And what had she expected? She'd hardly shown Husao any loyalty.

"It won't matter." Jacin-rei sheathed his knives and began a slow limp toward the door, pausing only long enough to snap up a clump of fabric on the couch beside Husao that resolved itself into a rumpled duster. Jacin-rei dragged it on as he walked away. "I've already made other plans. I don't really expect you to keep your word, but it would be nice."

"Wait, what?" Kamen let go of Xari and followed after Jacin-rei. "What plans? Hey, *Fen*." He disappeared down the small foyer that led to the hallway. He was only out of sight for a second before he returned. "Either of you touches the earthbound, I'll do to you what Fen did to Asai, and damn the suns." He pointed at Xari. "You—run away. I see you again, you die." He turned to Husao, hooked a thumb at the earthbound. "Keep him here and don't let her touch him."

As though he had the *right* to make demands. Husao didn't have time to even form a protest before Kamen was gone again.

Husao was left with the earthbound and Xari. Both Husao and the earthbound merely watched as Xari backed away from them with a cagey look then lifted her chin and faded to shadow. The earthbound shifted a flat look at Husao, kept it there. Husao gazed back levelly, expecting to be compelled to sit through an indignant defense, perhaps, or acidic vitriol for all the manipulations just laid bare.

The earthbound only shook his head, curled his lip.

"Fucking *Temshiel*."

⛩

"Fen, damn it, hold up!"

How, Malick wondered, could Fen still move so fast, when he was making an obvious effort not to limp? Malick only caught up relatively quickly because the inevitability of the stairs slowed Fen down.

"*What* other plans, Fen?"

Fen ignored him, merely concentrated on his first step down. He'd clearly got his control back, which... all right, good. Great. Brilliant. But Malick had been getting some pretty up-close experience with Fen's "plans" just lately, and they all seemed to be something along the lines of "I'm going to walk into knives and see what happens."

"*Fen*." Malick hitched up on the second step and grabbed Fen's arm to make sure he did too. "Talk to me. What's going on?"

Fen tugged at his arm, but when Malick didn't let go, he seemed to consider his own chancy balance, weigh a tumble down the steps against all the other injuries, and come up with "Malick = the lesser of two evils." He turned to Malick, no longer hazy-eyed and tottering on the edge, but clear and calm, gray eyes like twin lakes on a winter's night, flecked with the phantoms of amber stars.

"If I can't get them out, I'm not going to sit here and wait for someone to take them. You keep saying you want to help me, but you want to keep Joori here because insane ghosts told you he's a key. You can't help me get Yakuli because some god who's not even yours says you can't. Fine. I understand. I don't even fault you for it. Your laws aren't the same as mine, but it works both ways."

"Both ways how?"

"I don't have the same power as you." Fen tipped his chin up. "But I also don't have the same restrictions. And I've a city full of people who still believe in Untouchables enough to keep shrines and obey the laws concerning them. My kind were the Ancestors' Voices once." He pulled his arm out of Malick's grip.

Malick let him, only watching as Fen took hold of the railing and began making his way down the stairs again. That last sentence might have been cryptic, if Fen had said it to someone else. Malick was very much afraid he understood exactly what it meant.

"Fen." He took the three steps down Fen had managed then took another and angled himself into a blockade. "Fen. Tell me you don't plan to announce yourself to the Courts and try to have Yakuli arrested. Because I gotta tell you—that's a really terrible plan."

"I don't plan to announce myself to the Courts and try to have Yakuli arrested."

"And is that the truth?"

Because one had to be very clear, when it came to Fen.

Fen shrugged. "Sure."

"Hm." Malick eyed Fen suspiciously, leaned his shoulder into the wall. "So, what *are* you planning?"

Fen stared at him for a long time, measuring, maybe, but Malick couldn't tell. It was intense, anyway—more intense than he'd thought Fen capable.

"You're really not like them, y'know." Fen pitched a vague wave over his shoulder. "Husao and Xari. Even Umeia. You're not like them. You plot too much, and you manipulate when most of the time all you have to do is ask, but. You could've been a lot worse, I guess."

Malick had no idea if he should be pleased or insulted. And he wasn't about to be distracted.

"Fen—"

"I saw you grieve for those you love, which means you can. It surprised me. And I see the disgust every time Yakuli comes up. I think you really do want to stop him."

"Well, of *course* I do, I wouldn't—"

"Shig says you'd give up your soul for me."

Malick blinked, his eyebrows shooting up into his hairline. "...Sorry?"

Would he?

He shook his head, scowled. No, of course not.

Wait, would he?

"I don't want that." Fen looked away. "I don't want your oath. I don't want anything but what you've already sworn to Joori and Morin. Let the woman do what she will. Don't let anything happen to my brothers. Leave Yakuli to me."

All right, that *really* didn't sound good.

"What are you planning, Fen?"

"I'm planning to be a Catalyst." Too calm, too cool. "I'm going to be Untouchable. I'm going to see who dares to touch me."

"What the fuck is that supposed to mean?"

Fen only shook his head, prodded Malick backward until there was no choice but to move out of the way or flip ass over elbow down the steps.

"Honestly." Fen hobbled down one step then two, "I would've thought *Temshiel* would recognize a simple plot when he saw one."

"Maybe I'm dim." Malick kept pace beside Fen, ready to catch if necessary. "Humor me."

Fen stopped, turned slowly, gaze all at once burning, a little bit scary. His mouth turned up in a smile Malick had never seen before—sly and cold and just one shade shy of creepy. He leaned in, right up close.

"He's still here."

Malick frowned. "Who?"

"He's not bound to the earth. He's bound to me." It should've been impossible for so much fear and desperation to come through in a voice that could barely climb above a whisper. "One more hungry ghost haunting me." Fen held up his hand, flashed Malick's ring. "Got rid of the Ancestors, and now I've got him." His mouth twisted. "Fucking figures."

Malick stomach dropped. He leaned back, a little sad that the intermittent clarity and confidence seemed to be coming from a diseased root. And more profoundly disappointed than he might've suspected that Fen's sanity was once again—no, still—in serious question.

"Uh-huh." Malick kept it calm, but with a slight tinge of panic he sent, *Shig! I need you upstairs—right now,* and even managed to smile as he did it. At least he thought he did. Everything had gone kind of numb. "And is he the one made this plan for you, whatever it is?"

Fen snorted. "He only ever planned for me to fail." His eyes filled. "I've had… enough of that."

There wasn't enough time and there weren't enough words to make Fen believe he wasn't what his father and Asai had taught him he was. There was no time at all, really.

"Fen. What *plan*?"

Fen leaned down 'til they were almost nose to nose, teeth set tight, and lip curled back on a snarl.

"The same plan I've *always* had! The same plan I had when you mugged me in the alley and told me I could kill for you or die. The same plan I had when you promised to help me, except you keep. Not. *Doing it.*"

"I'm doing it! I'm doing it now, today, ask Samin. I've a plan of my own, and if you'll just give me—"

"I've had enough of *your* plans. The point of a plan is that it should eventually become action. Yours never do. I'm not waiting for you anymore—I'm going to find my mother."

"By yourself?"

"Who else? You can't do it. You go after Yakuli and you risk your soul. I have no gods, and I doubt there's anything worth saving of my soul."

"I know you'd like to think that, but you—"

"Burn your dead, *Kamen.* Joori's agreed to see to Caidi."

"Has he, then."

Malick shot his glance up the stairs. Joori was hovering, watching. He said nothing, but he tipped a subtle nod and made small shooing motions with his hand. Malick's eyebrow went up, and his mouth turned down. Apparently, there were things Malick had missed and needed to know, and if he couldn't get them out of Fen, he'd get them out of Joori.

He turned back to Fen. "And you'll be doing what?"

Slowly, Fen twisted a hard, sharp grin. It made his eyes go flinty and… empty. Like a dead man's eyes.

"Am I your dog, Kamen?" Throaty and low, with a cruel jag toward twisted seduction.

It gave Malick a shudder.

It was a weird relief when a tiny whiff of cherry smoke curled into his nose, and Shig's light touch tendriled at the back of his mind. Malick pushed into it.

Have a look at Fen. Is Asai still here?

He didn't spend nearly as much time with the spirits as Shig did. He wanted no mistakes.

There was only a short pause before Shig answered, *No. They can't find him. They never could. Caidi was looking for him, but I sent her to Joori and Morin then guided her to Umeia. They'll all go peacefully when the fire frees them.*

All right. So.

…So?

Malick rubbed at his brow, tried to remember where he'd left off with Fen—*Am I your dog, Kamen?*—and decided there was no reason in the world to answer it less than truthfully.

"You're no one's dog, Fen. You never have been, not really."

And the way things had worked out, it was rather seeming the other way around.

Fen leaned down, very slowly, and brushed his lips over Malick's, hovering just at the edge of a kiss.

"Then stop asking me stupid questions, and get the fuck *out of my way.*"

Right. So. Clearly, Fen thought the way around Malick was through his trousers. And clearly, he wasn't going to give Malick anything useful.

Malick stepped aside. "Woof."

Fen smirked, but it was flat; when he caught sight of Shig at the bottom of the stairs, it curled wider, almost wicked.

Shig was leaning against the wall, smoking, hair pulled back into a neat, subdued tail at the back of her neck. A crutch was propped beside her.

"I've decided I can live with it." Fen's eerie little smile turned bitter when he pointed it at Shig. "But it seems I won't have to. I'm no one's redemption."

He didn't look at either of them again, just made a point of trotting a little too carelessly down the steps, refusing to limp. He paused when Shig stuck the crutch out, blocking his path.

"Sure, Fen." She took a long drag and blew a thin stream of smoke into Fen's face. "But then, you still think you have to do everything by yourself, even though you know damned well you can't." She shrugged, pulled the crutch back, and shoved it into Fen's chest. "Here. This'll help you get to your suicide faster. You can hold Caidi's hand when we put you both on the pyre."

Everything about Fen turned rigid. Slowly, he pulled a breath in through his nose, as though trying to calm himself. It didn't work. Teeth clenched, he snatched the crutch, and whipped it in a whistling arc to angle over his shoulder the way Samin readied his sword just before he decapitated someone.

Malick tensed to jump between them.

Shig didn't even blink. In fact, she smiled. She held her smoke out to Fen.

Fen didn't move. "Don't touch Joori." His voice was low and thick, the threat even more clear than the crutch raised over his shoulder like a ready bludgeon. "It wasn't his fault."

"You Fens punish yourselves so thoroughly, anything I might do would be redundant." Shig turned a slow look up the stairs, past Malick, before she let it drift back down to Fen. She shrugged and waved the cherry smoke under Fen's nose. "Kinda takes the fun out of it."

Fen's glare was close to murderous. He didn't attack, though. Jaw tight and ticcing, he flipped the crutch down, and shoved it back at Shig. His glare was just as vicious when he snagged the smoke, stuck it in the side of his mouth, and walked away.

Malick and Shig merely watched him go. Strangely, so did Joori.

"He thinks it's Asai." Shig shook her head with a sad sigh. "But it's really just him."

Malick slanted a curious look at her. "You can 'hear' him?"

"No." Shig snorted dully and lit herself another smoke. She propped the crutch against the wall. "I just know how he thinks." She tipped a wink through a puff of smoke. "I watch. I see."

"If there's no one around to tell him he's a failure," Joori put in behind Malick, "he'll invent someone."

Malick turned to him. "All right, what's his too-likely very stupid and almost certainly suicidal plan?"

Joori scowled. "Jacin doesn't *plan*. Jacin *does*. The Ancestors said I'm a key, so he's going to destroy the lock." He darted a glance over his shoulder as Husao drifted up behind him. Joori's sneer spoke worlds as he pointed it at Husao then Malick. "It's a bit simple for a grand plot, so I guess I'm not surprised you had to have it explained to you."

Malick rolled his eyes. "And you agreed to it?" Joori was the last person Malick suspected would let Fen walk out of here by himself and with his dubious "plan."

"You won't let him go alone, even if you *have* been forbidden." Joori shrugged. "I don't really care if you risk your soul, as long as he walks away from whatever's to come. And this one"—he jerked his head over his shoulder at Husao— "he can't stand that his son's Blood is being used." His mouth pulled down, and he turned to face Husao squarely. "That's why you promised Jacin what you did. You never actually cared about my brother. You helped him because he meant something to your schemes, not because he meant something to you. And the worst part? You've no idea, nor do you care, what that's done to him. *On top* of everything else."

Husao had the good grace to look away, but his expression showed none of the remorse Joori was probably looking for. Joori's mouth tightened, and he turned back to Malick. He placed his fist over his heart and dipped his head low.

"Kamen-seyh, I c—" He had to stop and clear the wobble from his voice. "Kamen-seyh, there's nothing I can say to—"

"There isn't." Malick didn't want to hear it. Partly because there really was nothing Joori could say that could mean anything, and partly because the entire family truly had suffered more than their share, and he saw no point in adding to it. "It was a mistake, Joori, but you should never've been put into the position of making it. We all share the burden of what happened today, but it was Umeia and Asai who allowed it to happen. I might've done exactly what you did when the dust settled. I don't mourn Umeia."

"But." Tears were crowding Joori's eyes as he turned a quick glance at Shig then winced and looked down. "Yori. And Cai… Caidi. They—"

"Will go to Wolf and be reborn. You'll see them again, and that's the best I can offer you. You made a mistake. So did I."

Malick had always had shit timing, and it just kept getting worse. And his mistake was the biggest, when it came down to it. Umeia might not've had Malick's power, but she'd always been more *Temshiel* than Malick, no matter how he'd tried to outdo her in hardness and indifference. He'd trusted her with his mortal's heart, and he should've known better. He'd been shown better only days ago, and today still happened.

Joori shook his head, but couldn't seem to lift his gaze from the floor. "And Shig?"

"Shig's forgiveness is up to Shig, and I don't have time to concern myself with it now." Malick cut a rueful look at Shig. "At least we know she's not going to kill you."

Shig managed to pull up a smirk, though it was weary and quite sad.

Malick turned to Husao. "Is he right? Did you make your promise to Fen for the amulets?"

Husao's mouth twisted down. "I'm not quite certain an explanation of my reasons is either necessary or yours for the asking."

"Then try *demanding*. Let's don't forget, Husao—*you* I can kill."

"He loves Fen in his way." Shig's tone was distant and dull. "He just doesn't recognize the sentiment." She sat on the bottom of the stairs, staring at the lit end of her smoke, absently bobbing it up and down to force tiny smoke rings from the end. "You *Temshiel* with your hard hearts. You work so hard to forget what love is that you have no idea what to do with it when you have it. P'raps if you could remember what it was, you wouldn't have to manipulate so much to get what you want." She took a drag and blew the smoke out slowly. "And p'raps mortals wouldn't hate and distrust you so much."

She shot Malick a hard look sidelong. "You're back at Zero, Kamen. You've started again. Don't fuck it up this time, yeah?"

Husao stiffened. "Impudent tripe. You dare to interpret the mind of—"

"Oh, *shut* the fuck *up!*" Malick jabbed a finger at Husao. "That right there—that's what I've always hated about this business. That's what made me want to walk away from every one of you and never have to deal with you again. Immortality doesn't make us better; it makes us afraid to lose it. Power doesn't make us superior; it makes us lazy. We're supposed to be the teachers of mortals, guide them to keep the laws of the gods, and yet when those laws were broken by our own kind, I asked for justice and found I stood alone." He set his teeth. "Even Skel's father wouldn't demand a reckoning from his god, because he was too afraid he might be turned away.

"Yori lived less than two decades, and still, I'd put her honor against yours any day. Now, make up your fucking mind—are you prepared to take a stand or not?"

Husao looked away, jaw tight. "I intend to do what I can to the limits of the laws." His chin lifted, and he looked back at Malick. "That is all I will promise. *However*"—he held up his hand when Malick's lip curled up in a sneer—"your Catalyst already changes the future. I can see the ripples in Fate winding out from the void of his presence even now. And the laws glance off him just as fluidly as magic does. The Paradox is perhaps the key, but the Catalyst is a battering ram."

Malick narrowed his eyes, but it wasn't at what Husao had said. There was a light tug at his veil. It almost felt as though—

He angled a sharp look at Joori. "Where's Morin?"

Joori blinked, his brow beetling. Shig barked out a surprised laugh.

Which rather answered Malick's question. Damn it *all*.

He nearly slapped his forehead. "How was Fen planning on getting out to Yakuli's?"

"Steal Asai's coach." Joori was frowning, clearly aware something was happening, but unsure what. "Limp if he had to."

"Well, fuck it all, then."

Malick shut his eyes, thought about it. He could stop Morin easily, but… maybe it was better this way. At least if Malick knew where everyone was and he kept them close, he could keep an eye on them all. And Fen was less likely to do something deadly stupid if his brother was with him.

"He's not limping." Malick opened his eyes and sighed. "And I imagine he'll get more than one surprise when he gets to Yakuli's." He looked at Joori's confused frown and rolled his eyes. "You Fens just can't seem to take simple instruction, can you? A fucking family trait, innit?"

"What? I don't know what you're—"

"Shig." Malick didn't have the patience for Joori right now. "Go find Samin and tell him we're moving the plan up a few hours. I'll want you both ready in five minutes."

Shig said nothing, just kept chuckling to herself, something dark and without real humor. But she went to do as Malick had bidden.

Malick turned back to Joori. "Your brothers are both being idiotically brave. I don't imagine I could stop you from doing likewise unless I chained you up and left you here with an armed guard."

"I assumed you'd take me along, whatever happened." Joori stared, suspicious. "Your 'key,' after all."

"Yeah, well, I was thinking of picking the locks myself."

Funny thing—it was completely sincere. Malick had planned to take Fen along to Yakuli's because he knew Fen wouldn't allow him a choice, but Joori's presence had been conspicuously absent from the scenario of anarchy and mayhem Malick had sketched out for Samin earlier. Somewhere in the back of Malick's mind, at the bottom of his heart, the suns had stopped being such a horrifying threat, and been replaced with the peril of causing Fen one more second of pain.

Malick huffed, annoyed. "Your brothers have altered the plan a little, but they haven't ruined it, yet."

"…Wait." Joori leaned in, fury all over him. "Your *plan* was to let Jacin go and do whatever—?"

"Why would I stop him, Joori? This is his *right*. It's *your* right, it's Morin's. I swore to help him, and I intend to."

Malick waved at the door to his rooms. "There are weapons in the chest beside the bed. Arm yourself as you prefer. We haven't time for lessons on how to use them all, so only take what you think you can swing and do some damage."

Joori only stared, surprised and bitter and outraged, before he shook his head with a clench of teeth then stomped off.

Husao turned a narrow look on Malick. "Just exactly what *do* you plan?"

"Oh, all sorts of mayhem, just you watch." Malick put on a grin, all teeth. "Yakuli's not the only one with his own private army."

9

He chose a small axe first, because he knew how to swing one—all out and from the shoulder, aim for the joints, and make the cut clean. He chose a long, curved knife, because the one he'd had at home for slaughtering had the same arc, and he'd appreciated the way the curve lent a certain neatness and precision. He chose several others simply for their look, the way they fit his grip, and though one looked suspiciously like a boning knife, it was sharp and the small serration at the tip would likely…

Joori sucked in a breath. Made himself stop thinking.

He'd never thought himself particularly bloodthirsty. He'd learned quite a lot about himself today. He didn't think he liked any of it.

"It isn't how many you take."

Shig's soft voice came from behind where Joori crouched on Malick's floor, beside Malick's bed, arming himself with Malick's weapons. He didn't turn, only paused for a slow breath, curled the short sword he was holding in his palm, testing its weight.

"No?"

"It's how you use what you have. Here."

Joori turned in time to see a flash of silver netting coming at him. He reached instinctively to catch it. The mail runnelled over his hand like musical water, catching the light of the lamp on Malick's bedside table.

"It's Fen's." Shig shrugged. "Guess he forgot it."

Joori's mouth tightened. Sure he had.

"What am I supposed to do with it?"

"Huh." Shig's eyebrow went up, mocking. "If you really need me to tell you, no amount of weapons is going to help you." She lofted a *hurry up* wave. "Wear it. You made your brother a promise. I assume you want to at least try to keep it."

"How did you—?"

Joori looked away. He knew exactly how she'd known. She probably even knew exactly what he was thinking now. And what did it matter? There was nothing in his head for which he didn't wish he could find words, and she'd been right before: he didn't bleed any redder than she did.

He cleared his throat. "Thank you."

It was only fair that Shig didn't acknowledge it.

Frowning, Joori turned the mail in his hands then laid it carefully on Malick's bed and stripped his jacket. He dared a glance over his shoulder as he pulled on the mail, trying not to remember what had happened the last time Jacin had worn it. At least there was no blood on it.

"I brought this for you." Shig's voice was very soft this time—no scorn, no disdain Joori could detect.

Joori turned around slowly.

A broken arrow lay across Shig's outstretched hand, its fletching snow-white, straight and intact. There was no question where it had come from. Joori had watched Shig carefully maneuver the quiver from Yori's body as he'd just as carefully maneuvered the cloak from Caidi's.

Not absolution, this gesture. Joori supposed that was a relief. He didn't think he could stand such an offer. Anyway, it wasn't really Shig's to give.

Only when Shig shrugged did Joori notice she had Yori's bow slung over her back.

"It was Umeia's garden." Shig took a shaky breath. "On the roof. Yori... there were pots knocked over, and..." She looked down at the arrow in her hand. "Malick always teased Umeia about it. Her garden. Said it was a good thing she never had children because she'd forget them every autumn, and they'd blow away in the wintertime. Yori... *tripped*." She licked her lips, then pressed her mouth tight. "She *never* trips, she's always so... so *graceful*, but the pots, they must've... she was trying to—"

"Stop."

Joori paced slowly over to Shig, gently took the arrow from her hand. Shig just let it go, but her hand curled into a tight fist as it fell back to her side. Joori wanted more than anything to reach out, lay a hand to her shoulder, but he didn't have that right. He didn't know what to say. Everything he said anymore turned out terribly wrong. And Shig might actually kill him if he said he was sorry, even though she, more than anyone else, would know how much he meant it.

"I could've loved her." It came out before Joori even realized he was going to speak at all, but he couldn't regret having said it, even if Shig didn't want to hear it from him. "I think I did. Love her, I mean. If I could turn it back, trade, I'd do it in a second. For both of them. For all of them. But all I can do is try to be someone she would've loved back."

It wasn't enough. Nothing would ever be enough.

Joori skimmed his fingers over the jagged ends where the arrow had broken in the middle, tracing the feathery splines of the fletching, careful not to spoil their pristine set.

"It's not meant as a weapon." Shig set the tip of her finger to the arrow's fractured shaft, pressing until the splinters broke the skin. Her gaze lifted slowly, locked onto Joori's. "It's meant as remembrance. It's meant as… a talisman." Somber, she lifted her hand to her mouth and licked the blood from her finger, then turned toward the door. "C'mon. Everyone's ready. Malick doesn't like to be kept waiting."

"Yeah, I'll bet." Joori turned back to the bed to retrieve his jacket. He laid the arrow on the coverlet more carefully than he needed to while he dressed again. Checking himself over, feeling like a bit of a pretender with all the weapons strapped over him—like he was trying to be Jacin, and maybe in a way he was—he slid the arrow into his belt along with the knives; the axe hung solidly against his hip, but somehow, the arrow that weighed next to nothing felt heavier.

"He wants to save your brother."

Joori shut his eyes, bowed his head. "He wanted to save Caidi too." He turned back to Shig.

He hadn't meant it as recrimination, or blame, because it wasn't Malick's fault. But it was still the truth. Even if Malick loved Jacin more than himself, more than anyone or anything, it still wasn't a guarantee. Every one of them could lose everything today. And for all his apparent magic, Malick couldn't just wave his hands and make it so they wouldn't.

"I'm not trying to reassure you." Shig's tone was less cautious, more stern. "I'm trying to tell you how it is, how it's going to be. He doesn't only want to save Fen's life—he wants to save his mind. He wants to save *Jacin*." She opened her hand, as if in apology. "To save Jacin, he needs to save you, he needs to save Morin, he needs to save your mother's soul. D'you understand what I'm saying?"

Joori wished he could say "yes" because it seemed so important to her.

"I'm sorry, but I don't."

Shig didn't seem like it upset her. Her mouth curved up, almost a smile but not quite.

"He won't be looking out for himself. He's immortal, but he's not invulnerable. And he risks far more than any of us. Your brother thinks he could take it if Malick gave up his soul for him. What d'you think about that?"

It almost made Joori groan. Jacin could barely take having damned Asai's soul, and Asai had done more damage to Jacin's sanity than the Ancestors. Malick had told Jacin he loved him, was launching an assault where he wasn't supposed to go for him.

Even if Jacin walked away from Yakuli's with Joori on one side and Morin on the other, their mother between them, sacrificing Malick's soul would haunt him. Just like the ghost he'd conjured of Asai was doing now.

Now Joori understood what Shig was trying to tell him.

"You want *me* to watch Malick's back?"

"Whatever else you are or are not, you're a key, set in Malick's hand. Keep close. Fen can look after himself."

"No. He really can't."

"When he's got a knife in his hand?" Shig snorted, a real snort with real amusement inside it. "Yeah, he really can." She patted Joori's cheek. "Let's go. They're waiting."

┯

Untouchable. Nothing.

Perhaps, Father. Then again, you couldn't save anyone, either. So, what does that make you?

He lost time as he drove. He didn't know if the horse simply followed the road or if he'd actually steered it while his mind buzzed and fuzzed in a gray limbo that wasn't real thought but not really *not*-thought, either. He ignored the malicious whisperings of his own personal ghosts, but found himself strangely relaxed when Caidi rode beside him, silent and smiling, small fingers making designs in the raindrops puddling on the puckered leather of the box's seat. He thought maybe he wept, because the water on his face felt hot, but he was smiling, too, so he didn't think about it too much.

"We're here, Jacin-rei." It sounded strange, that name in her small, high voice, but her hazel eyes were kind, full of love, for *him*, so that made it all right. He'd already lost her; loving her back couldn't hurt more than it already did.

Jacin turned his glance outward, noting the walls that rose up through the surrounding pines, the towers set to either side of the tall, sturdy gates. Torches were set at strategic intervals—enough to give the guards light by which to see, but not enough for a potential enemy to get a line on them in the dark. Jacin could hear the faint *siss* of the rain hitting the flames, see the vague shadows of the men walking sentry, carefully avoiding the flickering pools of light the torches threw outward. One of the men had paused, stock-still and alert. Jacin could almost feel the hard gaze squinting through the dark, watching him.

More shadows twisted all around, too insubstantial to be mortal, and too animate to be actual shadows. Maijin, perhaps? More of Asai's cronies come to stop Asai's Ghost? Or just more of Yakuli's stolen magic, forewarned by Asai's mother?

It didn't matter—none of them moved toward Jacin, none of them seemed to be advancing, trying to block his way, so he ignored them. They were watching, surely, but not yet challenging.

"We'll see." Jacin gave Caidi a flick of a smile. "We'll see if they'll touch an Untouchable."

The rain had turned into cherry blossom petals, fluttering down to cover his lap, coat his skin. A thick layer weighted Caidi's gold curls like a veil, and she stuck her hand out to catch some, like one would catch snowflakes.

"What do they mean?" Her eyes weren't wide-open and ingenuous, but knowing and expectant.

Jacin peeled off his glove and put out his hand. The slight flash of Malick's ring in the dark distracted him for a second before he turned his hand palm-up. The petals pattered into it like hundreds of silent, sweet-smelling auguries. A warrior dead in battle, each one of them, and he was holding their spirits in his hand. Perhaps Joori would one day hold Jacin's spirit just so, make a wish on an errant petal, and blow it into the wind. Release his haunted soul from its hopeless sentry of earthly planes.

Was Jacin a warrior? He'd like to think so.

"Tell me." Caidi settled warm against Jacin's arm. "Say it."

The corner of Jacin's mouth ticced up. "Death."

"Nooooo." Caidi giggled, high-pitched and so engaging it was like a punch to the heart. "Transience."

"A big word for such a little thing." Jacin blinked away the petals that had stuck to his lashes. "D'you even know what it means?"

Caidi's smile changed, slid into something too old for her heart-shaped little face. "The Ghost won't survive the night." She laid her small hand over the petals in Jacin's palm. "Perhaps we'll go to Wolf together with Mother. Perhaps we'll say goodbye over the flames of the pyre until the next time we meet. It all depends on who rises from Fen Jacin-rei's ashes." Caidi squeezed Jacin's hand, laid a kiss to his cheek. "What do you fight for, lordless paladin? How many souls would you damn to have your vengeance?"

"All of them." Jacin turned his face so he could bury his nose in gold curls and their mantle of cherry blossom petals. "For you, for her—damn them all."

"Sure, Fen." It was Shig's voice, but Caidi who rubbed her warm nose into the crook of Jacin's neck. "Back to Zero, love," Caidi whispered in their mother's voice, soft puffs of breath warming Jacin's cheek. "A paladin can be his own lord, y'know."

There was no *pop* or *hiss*. Caidi was just all at once gone.

Jacin's cheek was cold. His hand was empty. Not even a single cherry blossom clung to his fingers. He could smell them, though. Sweet and fresh against the rain.

He ran his thumb over the tips of his fingers, Caidi's touch still tingling through the petals that weren't there.

"The Ghost won't survive the night."

He thought of Joori, his love and his anger, his refusal to admit the long-ago ruin of his twin. He thought of Morin, his quiet contempt that wasn't really contemptuous, a remnant of their father that Morin had somehow managed to rise above in ways Jacin couldn't even fathom, had managed to love around it where their father had been afraid to try.

He thought of Malick, who was indeed well-intentioned and ruthless, and more than dangerous, in ways Jacin never would've thought to consider before. Who handed a Ghost silence in exchange for justice. Who bargained away his own soul in trade for someone else's vengeance.

Jacin shook wet hair out of his eyes, then sucked in a long breath. With a shift of his shoulders, he tightened his jaw and levered himself to his feet.

A dim flash of gold sparked in the dark out the corner of his eye. "Are you the lord to lead me, then?" Jacin turned, a smile ready for Caidi. "Your paladin will—"

A gasp of dismay cut it off. Jacin's knees gave, all at once, and he fell back, windless, onto the cushioned seat of the carriage.

"Um." Morin—*Morin!*—peered up cautiously from beneath damp-lank fringe, the toe of his shoe making idle patterns in the mud. "H'llo, Jacin-rei." He looked away with a self-conscious shrug. "Who are you talking to?"

"Who's there?" came from the gate, harsh and challenging. "Approach and be seen."

Jacin turned to peer in the direction of the voice, noted the wide shape of a man striding swiftly toward them, noted the shadows pooling lazily between Jacin himself and the gate... and then he turned back to stare blankly at his brother. Ridiculous with a broadsword almost as long as he was sheathed at his hip, one of Jacin's own knives clutched in his hand, and a hard set to his hazel eyes that made Jacin's stomach bottom out and go cold. Too small in the dark, too vulnerable, too... mortal.

"Who's *there?*" the guard barked again, more hostile this time, and he just kept coming toward them.

Shoulders squared, jaw set, Morin dragged the long sword from its sheath in a clumsy stop-and-start 'til he finally cleared it from the stiff leather.

Jacin squinted at the guard closing in on them, then peered back at Morin.

"Well, *shit.*"

⛩

"Oh, brilliant! Just in time."

"For what?" Joori crowded in close to Malick, trying to focus through the dark.

Malick took hold of Joori and pointed. "Watch this."

It was quicksilver whirls and silver on black when Fen spun down from the box of the carriage. A dark blur through gray mist when he waded in. A smear of torchfire on a spinning blade when he went for the kill.

One down. Two.

Malick grinned.

"I've seen it before." Joori was nearly vibrating with nerves. "Aren't you going to go and help him?"

"You want I should distract him?"

Malick's little "army" stood on the small rise above the drainage culvert across the road from Yakuli's gates, veiled securely and watching. Maijin and *Temshiel* both had gathered, a picket between Fen and Yakuli. Good for show, maybe, but useless, in the end. None of them could touch Fen, and the guards who could were clearly no match for him, even injured as he was.

"Fen on a mission." Malick shook his head, awed, as he watched Fen shove Morin behind him then take down two men with the same swipe of a long knife. "A bloody force all his own."

Never more sane than when he was focused. And Fen was never more focused than when he had a knife in his hand. He *needed* this. Left to himself, Fen's mind turned inward, and gnashed itself to pieces. Silence gave him a center, but he sabotaged it by inventing ghosts to fill the void of quietude. Battle gave him no choice *but* to focus.

Joori gave Malick a look full of venom. "I thought the point of all this was so he wouldn't *be* on his own!"

"For the love of—" Malick rolled his eyes. "Can you just belt up for a *minute* and let me enjoy this?"

"Enjoy it? *Enjoy* it? *This?*" Joori flailed. "He could *die!* And you're just going to stand there and *watch!*"

"He's not going to *die.* He's going to get his blood pumping and his muscles primed, and put on a pretty show while he's at it."

"You're a sick son of a bitch."

"And incredibly sexy. You forgot incredibly sexy."

"No, I really didn't."

Two more guards detached from the contingent at the gate and moved toward the ruckus. Morin kept hedging away from the carriage, waving a giant sword that had to be Samin's. Fen kept trying to shove him back and make him stay. It seemed stubbornness ran in the family.

With a growl Malick could hear clear across the green, Fen leapt back up into the carriage, climbed atop it, then flipped down the other side. A spin then a twist, and he nailed one of the advancing men with a hard blow of a knife hilt to the temple.

Malick pushed a soft whistle between his teeth. "*Gah*, look at him go."

Samin sidled up. "You might want to pay attention to the reinforcements coming around from the west side."

"Pfft. There's only ten of them. That's just a warmup for Fen. Let him have his fun."

"Well, but, he's got Morin to worry about."

"He's doing just— Damn it." Malick elbowed Samin in the ribs. "You broke my concentration and ruined the fantasy I had going in my head. And it was a *very nice* fantasy. Now I've got to start all over again."

"Like you ever *stop!*" Joori looked like he wanted to punch Malick in the face but didn't quite dare. "Those are my brothers over there, and Morin has no idea what he's doing! If you're not going to—"

"Morin is in less danger than Fen is. I've got him under my protection, remember? And if you think these men are any danger to Fen, you haven't been paying attention, so just shut your bloody..."

Malick trailed off as Fen took hold of the horse's mane, and used it to lever himself into some flippy move Malick'd never seen him do before. Midspin, Fen kicked out and took the legs out from under a guard; they both went down, but Fen didn't stop moving—he rolled, twisting back up to his feet and underhanding a throwing knife with a casual little flick. The guard stayed down, gurgling his last wet breaths through the knife in his throat. Fen backed up, slid like he was all bend and no bones beneath the carriage's hitch and out the other side, then slapped at the horse's rump, sending it and the carriage careening into—no, *over* another guard.

"Did you see that? Did you *see* that?" Malick laughed, absolutely rapt. He threw his hands up. "Yeah, I give up. It's definitely love."

"No, really?" Samin rolled his eyes. "What about all those shadows?"

They were all around the perimeter now. Still dark smudges in the dark night, twisting and coiling, but shying from curling into shapes, taking on substance.

It annoyed Malick. Made him lose his smile.

"I guess they're here to keep me out. But they can't touch Fen, and they can't stop Shig from tapping into my magic. After Fen gets past these stooges, I'll take care of the shadows, and you just slide on through. Shig and I will take care of the rest. Just like we planned."

Shig leaned around Malick's shoulder. "Did you plan that?" She pointed to the gate.

It was creaking open too slowly to allow the ten men trying to come through it past all at once. They streamed out, only one of them stopping to engage Fen. The rest of them headed right for Morin.

There it was. One way or another, Yakuli was watching what was going on at his gates, and had either figured out Fen's weakness or Xari had told him long before Fen even got here. Samin made to surge forward, but Malick held him back. He couldn't veil Morin without Fen freaking out, so Malick turned to Shig.

"That's you, love."

The pull immediately wound through him. Malick gave to it, pushed into it.

Shig hadn't done this before. It had always been Malick taking her power and boosting it, using it like it was his own. Now it was reversed, and there hadn't been much time to coach Shig through the skill. Her aim was good, but there was no finesse, her assault clumsy and heavy-handed. Three men went down in a spray of blood and brains. The others fell in varying forms of distress, gushers of blood spurting from every visible orifice.

"Hmm." A grimace flattened Malick's mouth. "Not pretty, Shig."

"I can't decide between the head and the heart. The head's faster, but the heart's easier." Shig sniffed, shrugged. "Anyway, it's not supposed to be pretty."

Well. That was true.

"All right, Samin." Malick let go of Samin's arm as Fen grabbed hold of Morin and dragged him through the now unmanned gate of Yakuli's estate. "Stick with them. No one can find any of you using magic, and by the time you get done with your end, Yakuli will have a lot less of it than he does now." Samin nodded and made to trot after Fen and Morin, but Malick grabbed his arm. "Watch his back, Samin." He opened his mouth to say more, but there was nothing else there, except, "Please."

Samin merely clamped his hand briefly over Malick's, then hustled after Fen and Morin, hop-scotching with surprising grace over the scattered bodies of Yakuli's guards and disappearing through the open gates.

Malick turned to Shig. "All right, love." He planted a firm kiss to her brow. "You know what to do."

Shig tipped a smile that was grim and eager, all at the same time. With a long look at Joori, she turned slowly and headed back out into the trees.

Malick surveyed the shadows. Finally, they were calling substance to themselves, forms solidifying. Some faces Malick knew; some he'd never seen before. An even dozen, three of them maijin, and not a single damned one of them Wolf's-own.

What the hell? Was he the only one here? He'd've thought at least Imara would've shown up. She *owed* him.

Then again… no. He knew what he was in for if this went wrong. It was probably better this way.

"So, then." Malick drew his sword and nodded for Joori to draw a weapon of his own. "Haven't you just been *dying* to kick some *Temshiel* ass?"

☗

There was no ass kicking. Not that Joori had really expected there to be, at least not from him. They were *Temshiel*, after all, and he was just… nobody, really. Still, Joori had rather been expecting… well, something other than this.

The rain had stopped, at least, the clouds rolling back to reveal Wolf's silver face through heavy banks of bruised gray. Joori wondered if that was a good or a bad thing, and decided it didn't matter, because no one would probably tell him anyway. The air was salty and warm, and it seemed like every single night insect in the world had congregated around them and started to sing, grating at his nerves almost as badly as Malick was.

"This is the part where they try to intimidate me through numbers."

Joori had no idea if he should laugh or growl. The last of his family had just disappeared into, from what Samin had said, something that was closer to a military complex than a lord's estate, crawling with magic, and Malick was out here cracking wise. And Joori was having a hard time not barking a nervous little giggle in response.

Malick was insane, clearly. Joori just hadn't realized until now it was catching.

"Peace, Kamen." The woman who stepped forward from the loose picket of immortals was really too beautiful to be real.

Malick huffed and threw his hands out. "Why do people always start conversations with me like that?"

"I wonder." The woman smiled, though it looked like she was trying not to. "How are you, Kamen?"

"Why, what've you heard?"

The woman smirked, absently adjusting the two belts that crisscrossed her hips, the ornate hilts of short swords jutting from their sheaths. Dark as the night and twice as lovely, hair like slick jet and eyes that were bright, alive, and full of a sharp humor Joori thought a bit insulting, considering the circumstances.

"Lots of things." Her bearing was alert but her tone was mild. "First, that you'd gone off to spirit to sulk for a while."

"Naw, didn't fancy it." Malick's stance went from aggressive to flirty. "Spirit's no fun. You know me, Sora—I prefer more… physical stimulation."

Joori rolled his eyes. Honestly.

"And then that you'd gone mercenary." Sora's tone slid just this side of sultry. "Just what *kind* of 'physical stimulation' are we talking about, Kamen? Getting it up without a weapon in your hand becoming a problem?"

"Ah, love. When used properly, it *is* a weapon."

"Oh, for pity's *sake*." Joori wanted to smack their heads together. "You can't just *hand* him straight lines like that. Can we just get to the bit where we decide if we're on the same side or not?"

Sora turned her cool gaze on him, looked him up and down, then lifted an eyebrow at Malick. "New toy?"

Joori stiffened. "That would be my brother. Who happens to be—in case all the all-knowing, all-powerful *degenerates* present have forgotten—walking into a nest of minions and their pet Jin slaves, among which happens to be *my mother*. So if you *don't* mind, I'd prefer it if we could either get on with killing each other or get on with helping!"

Sora turned a bland look on Malick. "Excitable little earthbound, isn't he?"

"Eh." Malick waved it away. "Mortals."

Joori growled, his hand fisting tightly around the knife in his grip. Before he could snap out a retort, one of the men broke loose from the rest of the picket and came forward.

"Excitable or no, the lad has a point." The man turned a brilliant smile on Malick, and held out his hand. "It's good to see you, Kamen."

Malick eschewed the hand and instead sheathed his sword. He embraced the man with a rumbling chuckle.

"It's been a long time, Tatsu."

Bloody hell, were all immortals fucking gorgeous? Did the gods pick them for prettiness? This one's hair was a little longer than Malick's, dark gold shot through with copper and pulled into a loose tail at his nape. His pale skin was gilded by the torchlight, and silvered by Wolf, highlighting the sharp cheekbones and perfect nose. The muted glow of Raven and Dragon pulled sparks of claret and tawny amber from the loose bits of fluff that framed his face.

No wonder every *Temshiel* Joori had met so far seemed sex-obsessed. They could probably get it any damned time they wanted it.

"Now, Kamen." Tatsu thumped Malick firmly between the shoulder blades before he drew back. "Tell me."

"You might prefer I didn't." Malick jerked his chin toward two men hovering just at the edge of a circle of torchlight. "And not with those two here. They attacked Wolf's Untouchable on Asai's orders last week. Get rid of them, and I'll tell you what you want to know."

Joori narrowed his eyes at the men, a little startled. He hadn't recognized them—he really only remembered that Leu woman—but he supposed Malick would know. Strange. Joori'd been picturing them in his remembrance as ugly and perhaps even malformed to match their reprehensible actions of that night, but it appeared maijin were just as beautiful as their *Temshiel* counterparts. His teeth tightened, and he couldn't help glaring.

Tatsu merely shook his head. "They are Owl's. They were not trying to kill your Untouchable. They were trying to put him out of the way. They were trying to help."

"By nearly ripping off his leg?"

The abrupt malice in Malick's voice shouldn't have surprised Joori, but it did. Malick could go from cavalier seducer to vicious sorcerer in the turn of a breath, and it appeared nothing could do it so predictably as a threat to Jacin. Joori should've been heartened by it. But Jacin and

Morin had gone through those gates at least five minutes ago—anything could happen in five minutes.

"By making it impossible for him to participate in Asai's plots." Sora's mouth twisted wry. "Obviously, it didn't quite work out that way."

"Obviously." Malick's eyes narrowed. "And what d'you know about Asai's plots?"

"Nothing." One of the maijin took a bold step closer, though he kept his distance. "But one only needs to know of Asai's existence to know he had at least one bubbling. Owl commanded, so we followed."

"Owl *commanded*?" Malick shot a quick glance around, calculating, taking in all the faces, before turning back to the maijin. "Asai sent Leu to spirit for it."

"No." The man shook his head. "Asai sent Leu to spirit because she was Wolf's, and her usefulness to his plots had ended. She did not move against you that night, Kamen. And so he knew she *would* not."

Once again, Malick's gaze swept them all, thoughtful, before his grin bloomed again, turned wicked. "I see Owl, Snake, and Bear. Raven is not represented here this evening."

Tatsu shrugged. "The gods do not choose sides against one another."

"Uh-huh, right, of course not."

"Raven has avoided the appearance of duplicity." Tatsu grimaced and shook his head. "Asai, after all, acted alone, and for the—"

"Yeah, yeah, for the glory of Wolf." Malick rolled his eyes. "And Wolf hasn't commanded his *Temshiel* to act on his behalf. *Now* I see why none other of Wolf's-own have come."

"Our task tonight is to see that none of Raven's interfere. Nor any of Wolf's." Tatsu stopped, frowning, as though unhappy with what he'd been apparently commanded by his god to say. "None but you, Kamen."

"Hung out to dry. Yeah, I know, I was told. So, why all this?" Malick waved to indicate the others hanging back and watching silently.

"The gods do not choose sides against one another." Sora gave Malick a *yes, yes, I know* look. "But they often change their minds. And after the… disturbance today…" She paused, shot Joori a glance, but it was quick and nearly disdainful. "The Untouchable could no longer be dismissed as ambiguous anomaly."

"It is Wolf's Cycle," Tatsu said. "A time of change. It is not ours to know what the gods foresee, and Bear certainly has not confided her divine sight to me. It would seem to me, though, that the gods bide and watch. The Ancestors have lost their Voice, and the Jin have been set as a wedge in the Balance." His eyes cut to Joori then back to Malick. "You alone hold the key, placed in your hands by Wolf himself."

"Yeah, and if I fuck it up…" Malick tilted his head. "So, what if I *do* fuck it up? Are you saying the gods will move against Wolf?"

Grinning, Sora patted Malick's cheek. "Ever the inflated ego,

Wolf's-own." It was chiding, though she winked and her smile seemed real enough. "No god would rest on one possibility—even one with such possibilities as Kamen."

"Aw, you say the sweetest things."

"The spiritbound wields your power." Tatsu raised his eyebrows like it was a question; when Malick nodded, Tatsu held up a hand. "I don't want to know your intentions. None can testify to what they don't know. Yakuli was claimed by Fate, Kamen, and so is protected by the gods. He is as untouchable to you as your Catalyst is to me." He set a hand firmly to Malick's shoulder. "Let those you would lead do what you've trained them to do. You know what happens if you fuck it up. So, *don't* fuck it up."

"Damn, Tatsu." Malick knuckled at the corner of his eye. "You make me teary when you go all poetic and squishy like that."

It was bloody surreal. Joori only just kept himself from making the rounds and punching each and every one of them in their pretty faces.

"If you all don't mind," he said through clenched teeth, "some of us lowly mortals have families in danger. D'you think we could possibly—"

"Right." Malick gave Joori's shoulder a condescending pat that Joori managed to take without growling. "One more thing." Malick turned a serious gaze on Tatsu and Sora. "Where does Dragon stand in this?"

Sora rolled her eyes. "Dragon stands as ever, where it is most beneficial to stand. Her *Temshiel* abets the Untouchable, and her maijin abets the would-be usurper, and neither of them do so by her command." She shook her head. "Dragon will have someone on whom to place all blame when you're through, Kamen, regardless of whether or not you're still standing amidst the rubble."

It sounded awfully damned cold to Joori.

Malick merely nodded. "Good enough." He turned his full attention on Joori, nodding at the gates. "Tatsu's been keeping the guards away while we've talked, but once we're through the gates, we're on our own."

"Yeah, I figured that out." Joori shot a disdainful glance at Sora and Tatsu, and then all the others for good measure. "Standing back and watching the lowly mortals fight it out, yeah? I've never seen so many machinations and manipulations in all my life. Why can't you people just *do* once in a while?"

Tatsu merely opened a hand. "Then what would be the use for lowly mortals?"

"Are you *fucking* ki—"

Malick jerked Joori away by the arm and shoved him toward the gates. "Play nice, children."

Joori wanted to clock Malick's smirk right off his face, but at least they were *moving* again, *finally*, so he let Malick prod him along.

"Oh, and Tatsu." Malick turned and walked backwards. "I think you still owe me a drink from that time in Thesia. You remember—you said she had twelve tattoos; she had fourteen."

Tatsu grinned. "I'll buy you a whole bottle."

Joori pushed out an irritated sigh and set his teeth.

Fucking *Temshiel*.

Samin knew exactly where Fen would be heading. Both he and Malick had predicted it so firmly there wasn't even any leeway to lay odds. Neither Fen nor Morin—*especially* Morin—should be charging into something like that without someone there to steady them, so Samin hastened his pace. He needed to get his own part of the plan done before bullying his way into Fen's.

Timing was going to be everything tonight.

Yakuli's men were already on alert, the commotion at the gates having stirred them, and more of them wandered the paths and perimeter of this hideaway fortress than made Samin comfortable. Most of the attention, however, seemed to be centered on the walls and towers and secondary gates, so Samin had so far been able to get about his business.

He stopped as briefly as was possible to unhook the various hasps on the corrals and pens then quietly shoo the horses out of them. One or two would usually do the trick. When the others saw their fellows wandering by with horsey-smirks on their faces, they typically ambled out too.

He'd taken the western side when they'd been divvying up who was going to be doing what tonight. Because that was where the prisoner barracks were, and he knew Fen knew it too.

As though his thought had called it, Samin caught a flash of blooming moonlight refracted by Morin's gold head up the slope. Farther ahead than Samin had hoped, though. He'd have to double-time it.

Malick had wanted to wait until full night to begin the assault, but Fen had rather screwed that strategy all to hell, so the camp wasn't near fully asleep with only a skeleton watch. Too many were venturing out, now the rain had stopped, and with Wolf deciding at the most inopportune time to have himself a wide-eyed look through parting clouds, Samin was far too exposed for his liking. Wolf splashed silver over the earth, while the scimitar-splinters of Raven and Dragon lent bloody shadows. Samin had never thought the effect particularly eerie, but now it curled something uneasy in his gut.

Quiet and as low to the ground as he could get and still stay on his feet, he made his way to another pen, unlatched it, then dug his knife into the wood and popped the hasp off. His eyes all the while scanned up ahead, trying to spot another glimpse of Morin's bright head bobbing along in the moonlight, but it appeared that Fen was being even more careful than Samin.

Subie gave a rumbling little burp in the distance. Samin's mouth tightened as he worked at the iron latch, queering it so it couldn't shut once he was done. Wouldn't now just be a *spectacular* time for an eruption or an inopportune quake? Fucking Ancestors. If it hadn't been for them...

Finished, Samin pocketed the hardware. He'd throw the hinges and bolts later when there was no chance he'd be seen doing it. He didn't want any of Yakuli's men finding them and fixing the gates too quickly. Cautiously, Samin turned and scanned again, using the thick post of the pen against which he crouched as flimsy cov—

All right, not *enough* cover, apparently, because the slender chill suddenly striping against his jugular was very definitely a blade. A wickedly sharp one. From behind.

"What the fuck are you doing here?"

Samin let his breath go, watery with relief. He'd know that snarl anywhere.

"Bloody hell, you scared the shit out of me."

Fen withdrew the knife so Samin could turn around to look at him where he crouched on the other side of the fence. He blended into the shadows much better than Samin ever would, the bloody streaks and spatters on his face working almost like gruesome camouflage. He was glaring, but that was normal, so Samin ignored it.

"What the fuck are *you* doing here? By *yourself*, for pity's sake. No, not by yourself, you've got your little brother—" Samin shot a quick look around, then frowned at Fen. "Where's Morin?"

A darker pool of shadows to Fen's flank swirled in a way that was unmistakable to Samin, but then he'd seen it rather often just lately. As they settled and dissipated, Morin crouched, grinning, beside his brother, a chunky flash of a ring Samin was dismayed to recognize set loosely on his index finger.

Samin narrowed his eyes at Fen. "Aren't you supposed to be wearing that?"

"It was given to me. As far as I know, there were no restrictions on its use."

Now was really not the time to argue semantics with Fen. And especially now that Samin knew it might not get through all the noise.

Morin's grin brightened. "Isn't it brilliant?"

"Mm, brilliant." Samin gave Fen a dubious frown.

"Don't look at me like that. Morin needs it more than I do. Now what the hell are you doing here? And what's with the horses?"

"I'm here because *you* moved up the plan for tonight, and left the rest of us little choice."

Fen glared. "I wasn't about to wait for another—"

"We've already been sitting here too long, and haven't time to debate it. We're here now, so we might as well get on." Samin waved at the gate of the pen. "I'm letting the horses loose, so when the alarm goes up, and it will, it'll at least cut down one advantage, and hopefully distract while we're at it. After I'm done, I'm to signal Shig so she can get them to bolt. It'll be one bit of ammunition moved from Yakuli's pocket and into the blue. Then I'm to head to the prisoner barracks and..." He trailed off, kept his gaze even on Fen, unflinching.

Fen stared at him. "Malick's here?"

"You know he is, or at least you should." Samin was a little tired of watching the two of them wend through their trust issues. Now was not the time. "He bloody *told* you he had—"

"He bloody *told* me a lot of things. Where's Joori?"

Samin opened his mouth, cut a glance down to the great big knife gripped in the gloved hand resting on Fen's knee... He shut his mouth.

Fen drove his knife into the ground. "Son of a *bitch!*"

Seething, he shot a tight-lipped glare at Morin, who had the good sense to shrink back and keep quiet. With a long, heavy breath, Fen shut his eyes, pinched at the bridge of his nose. Morin shot an asking glance at Samin, but Samin could only shrug and tilt him what he hoped was a reassuring smile.

"Fine." Fen retrieved his knife and waved it at the buggered latch on the post. "Show me how to do that. We'll move a lot faster if Morin and I help you." He gave Samin one of his more lethal looks. "And then you can help us."

ᛘ

They did move a lot faster. By the time they'd got through all the pens and stables and corrals, the guards had discovered the problem with two of them, and a low buzz was humming. Suspicion flared almost visibly in the straightened backs and the way their eyes flickered everywhere at once.

Samin waited for an opening, then pulled Fen and Morin toward the nearest building—a small tack shed, apparently—made sure they were all on the shadowed side with their bodies pressed flat, and gave Shig the signal. Morin had to cover his mouth and stifle a laugh when all the horses suddenly grunted or squealed or blew then took off at a dead run in the direction of the main gates. Shouts went up and whistles shrilled. In the confusion that ensued, Fen said the spell that would cover Morin once again in shadows, and they all took off for the first set of barracks.

Fen couldn't run. It was only now that Samin thought to wonder how he'd been walking. Adrenaline, likely, but whatever it was, it was wearing off, and Fen's limp was so pronounced it was almost a hobble. Hobble, hell—it was a full-fledged loping shamble. Samin discreetly adjusted his gait to Fen's slower pace, and hoped like hell that bit of shadow to Fen's left was Morin.

A heavy *pop!* sounded from the south end of the complex. Samin turned with an anticipatory grin, and took hold of Fen's elbow to turn him too. The northwestern side of the estate, where they stood, was set in the dip of a midsized rise then angled back up to where Yakuli's manor overlooked the whole of the tree- and wall-ringed camp. Samin's grin broadened when he imagined the man himself peering down to watch the distant flames curl up over the rise as red-orange bloomed against the sky. Shouts went up, and were immediately drowned out by another *pop!* that Samin thought probably sounded much more dramatic when one was right up close to it.

"That'll be Malick taking out the soldiers' barracks." Samin breathed in deep, not yet able to catch a whiff of the smoke he knew would be black and thick once the flames took hold of the wet wood. It didn't matter—he knew it was there. "Ah, mayhem."

Fen rolled his eyes and took off again. Samin watched the brilliance of the fires coat the sky then followed.

Fen was panting by the time they hitched up at the first of four long, squat buildings that Samin was all too sure housed what was left of the Disappeared. Windowless and wood-framed, the buildings were all walled and roofed with woven reeds, wet and sharp-smelling with the rain. There were no guards here, which was what had piqued Samin's suspicions the other night when they'd come to spy. Though now that those suspicions were all but foregone knowledge, he understood why. There'd be no need to spend men and resources guarding those he knew would be inside. He'd seen it in another life, when he'd worn the livery of an arrogant lord who lusted after a pretty young Jin girl, not for her looks or what was between her legs, but for what ran through her veins.

Samin turned to face Fen squarely, though he knew before he even opened his mouth he'd be wasting his breath. Still, decency demanded, so Samin obeyed:

"Fen…" He paused, set his teeth. "You don't have to do this." He nodded down at Morin as the shadows once again swirled and revealed him, leaning against Fen—Samin wasn't sure if it was comfort for Morin or support for Fen. "He shouldn't see this. This isn't—"

"I'm not a child." Indeed, Morin's voice was low and calm. Not the reedy denial of a thwarted not-yet-grownup, but a reasonable statement of fact. "You said this was my right."

"You're not a child, and it is your right." Samin looked at Fen again. "I've seen this before. So have you. You know what's in there. One at a time is hard enough to look at, but this is…" He trailed off with a helpless shrug.

Fen didn't answer, only turned to Morin and took one of his knives from a sheath strapped to his thigh. It was long with a mean curve, and glinted with what seemed like its own malicious wink in the moonlight. He curled Morin's hand around the hilt.

"From here"—Fen laid his finger to one side of Morin's throat, just below his ear, then swept it across to the other—"to here." An invisible smile-shaped outline. "Firm and steady. Keep to the side and back so the blood spray doesn't hit you. If there's no spray, you're not doing it right."

Stone-cold and emotionless. It made Samin shudder.

Morin paled. His hand came up to lay over where Fen's gloved finger had just traced, as though trying to erase the touch, or protecting himself from the reality of it.

"They won't feel it." Samin shot an annoyed glance at Fen, but kept his tone calm and quiet for Morin. "They've all gone beyond feeling their bodies. What we're doing tonight is a mercy."

"Yeah." It came out shaky and thin as Morin cut Fen a look Samin couldn't read.

Fen, apparently done with it all, merely gave them each a flat, flinty stare then pushed past Samin and opened the flimsy door to the long hut. Morin took a long, deep breath, loosed a full-body shudder, then firmed his jaw and followed his brother. With a grimace, Samin shot one more glance down toward the flames at the other end of the camp, sent *We're going in* to Shig, and took up the rear.

10

"**B**loody… *hell*."

The abrupt inferno was, apparently, Malick's signal to start burning the place down around them. Except he hadn't bothered to tell Joori as much. He'd merely shoved Joori out of the way of a herd of terrified horses and toward the barracks. And then started lobbing fire.

The barracks exploded into a great splatter of flame. The blast was nearly deafening, the flare nearly blinding, a great *whoosh* out and up. The heat and intensity sucked all the breath from Joori's lungs, baking his skin. The roar of the flames drowned out the thunder of hoofs.

Malick grinned as shouts and screams went up from the conflagration. Pleased with himself.

Joori only stared, jaw hanging. He'd thought Malick scary before—he'd had no idea.

"There are men in there." Joori's voice was thin and thready.

"Yeah, no shit." Malick yanked Joori toward the next building. Another nut-sized ball of fire twitched at the ends of his fingers as they dodged out of the path of more fleeing horses. "Kinda the point."

"But." Joori watched the macabre scene over his shoulder as he stumbled after Malick. Vaguely man-shaped globs of flame lurched out of the building, their ghastly garbled screams lancing into Joori's head and grinding right down his backbone. He had no love for these men, certainly, but… what a horrible way to die. "Isn't there another—?"

"Heads up."

Malick shoved Joori so hard he landed on his ass. Joori thought at first it was merely an overcautious way for Malick to spare him from the side effects of another conflagration as the little ball of flame left his hand and headed for the second barracks. But then he noted the shapes of men, not on fire but silhouetted by it, and headed straight for them.

"Ah, *here* we go." Malick gave Joori an exhilarated grin over his shoulder. "Draw a weapon, and stay back." He flipped his sword in his hand, then barreled in.

What looked like at least two score men were rushing toward the first fire. Some broke off and headed toward the second blaze when it went up. None seemed to notice Malick and Joori yet but for the few who'd caught Malick's attention. Most of the men Joori could see looked like they were attempting to either help the screaming masses of melting flesh and bone that used to be their comrades or gathering in some semblance of order to fight the fire.

A distraction, Malick had told Joori. To give Samin time to find Jacin and Morin. And to give them all time to do what they'd come here for.

And, well. This was certainly distracting.

Joori climbed slowly to his feet, pulled the little axe from his belt, and stared. He'd already watched Malick quietly garrote three men as he and Joori had crept their way down here. Had watched him engage in the briefest of sword battles and thoroughly rout the guard with whom he'd engaged so quickly and easily Joori had to wonder why Malick would even bother hiding at all. If he just marched in here like he'd marched down the alley before, surely they'd all just lay down their weapons and run.

Maybe it was his ruthlessness. Malick *enjoyed* the fighting. He used every cheap trick, went for every soft spot and weakness, aimed for the quickest kill.

Malick, in short, fought dirty. Nothing was beneath him. For pity's sake, he was sneaking up on men asleep in their beds and *setting them on fire*.

…Which, now that Joori thought about it, was more merciful than what these men did to the Jin they managed to get hold of. At least they got a pyre of sorts, they'd be reborn—as pigs or hens for a Jin's table, if there was even a tiny bit of justice, but still.

There were six men now, the reddish glint of their weapons swirling around them, smearing into Joori's vision as they all centered on Malick. Joori didn't have to see their faces to know their intent was to kill and not capture. They ran right past Joori without even seeing him. Joori wondered for a moment if Malick had veiled him and he'd missed it, but it didn't feel like it had that night on the road, and Malick had aimed pretty well for the shadows as he'd thrown Joori down. So Joori sank a little deeper into the murk and watched.

Malick's smile was wicked and hard. His sword glittered and his knife arced. He dodged and drove and sliced like he was dancing. And loving it.

Thing was, Malick wasn't Jacin. Jacin had taken down twice this number in half the time at Yakuli's gates. These men were getting in far too close for Joori's nerves. Their blades hadn't yet connected but they were at least grazing, and Malick…

Malick wasn't using his magic.

Defending almost as much as attacking. Dropping back two steps for every one gained. The sole center of attention for six armed men who were out for blood.

And five more were coming.

The problem, as Joori saw it—well, one of the problems, the immediate problem—was that Jacin was going to be *pissed* if Joori just stood here and watched Malick die.

"Joori!" Malick whirled away from his closest opponent, drove his knife into the chest of the one coming up behind him, and spun right back into the center again. "Two more! Get them and then run for the gates! *Go!*"

It took a second for the command to make sense to Joori, because there were actually four more, and another five would be close enough to engage in seconds. And then he realized what Malick was saying.

Take care of the other two barracks. And then run away.

Run away to *what*? What good would living do now, if Malick was right this second in the middle of failing? And if Malick failed, what happened to Jacin and Morin?

You have a brain, Joori. Try using it instead of being baggage for a change.

Taking out the barracks now would do no good. They were all either empty or in the process of emptying. Everyone was alerted. Those not scrambling to deal with the fire were scrambling to regroup and figure out where the attack was coming from. And only if the entirety of the men here were complete morons would it escape their notice that the attack was coming from where it obviously appeared the attack was coming—right where Joori and Malick were standing.

So. No.

Whatever Malick's grand plan had been, that part of it was as complete as it was going to get. There was only one thing Joori could do right now to have any effect on how tonight played out. And it wasn't running away.

Jaw set, Joori tossed the axe a few times, familiarizing himself with the grip. Yori's arrow was wedged in his belt; he slid his fingers over the shaft. He was a key, he reminded himself as he watched the men approach. Not something important, probably, but something that unlocked something important. Maybe this was what he was *supposed* to be doing.

He stepped from the darkness and met the men coming to join the battle head-on.

Surprise got him his first kill, coming out of the shadows as he did. The axe hit the joint between neck and shoulder with a squelching *thunk*, and the man took another two steps before he realized he was dead and went down. Unfortunately, he took the axe with him, and Joori lost the advantage when he forgot he had other weapons to draw and spent a few too-precious seconds trying to work the axe's edge loose from bone.

The second one was pure luck. Panicking, trying to get his axe loose, Joori finally remembered he was still heavily armed. He tried to pull a knife, ended up with the broken arrow. He waved it clumsily to the side as he crouched for leverage and yanked at the axe. The second man died when Joori tripped backward as the axe came loose. Their feet tangled and the man ended up with Yori's arrow through his throat.

Nice one, Yori!

Bloody damn, Joori was going to love her *forever*.

"Joori, you *idiot!*" The clash of metal on metal was a strangely sweet harmony to Malick's shout. "Bloody *run!*"

Joori didn't. Wouldn't. Buzzed, high on panic and adrenaline, he laughed. It came out chillingly feral. The scent of blood, hot and metallic, was all over him, all around him. The scent of battle and his own rank sweat swamped him, blending with the reek of smoke and sizzling fat, hazing his mind, his sight.

Violence had a taste, saccharine and sickening, and Joori drank it in.

Instinct took him, and he let it. Rolled because it told him to. Felt a peculiar little grin stretch his mouth as he watched the wide blade of a sword sweep the space where his head had just been. He came up swinging the axe, spun like he'd seen Jacin do. He didn't hit anything this time, but he didn't trip, and the four men surrounding him all flinched back. Instinct again moved him, took him back several paces 'til he was no longer surrounded.

But instinct couldn't suddenly turn him into a master warrior. And it couldn't make him disappear so he was no longer the center of attention to three men who were.

Restless, Subie gave another annoyed rumble in the distance, enough of a tremor that Joori felt it through his feet. Something in him seized it, took the strength of it in through his skin and twined it with the spirit that crouched in his core. Instinct again, all over him, a tingle over his skin, almost a warm whisper in his ear. Overwhelming and worryingly seductive.

He set it loose, everything.

Something in him that *wasn't him* was abruptly pulsing out a strange sense of gratitude. As though the unfurling spirit at his core wasn't really a part of him. Not *his*, but something *other* that lived inside him.

The sheer might and fury of it almost sent him to his knees. Stubborn, he kept his feet. Took the adrenaline washing his nerves and twined that too. It wound out, and Joori let it, could almost see it as it spiraled from his body and back down into the earth, shook it.

This time, when a split in the ground opened at his feet, Joori didn't panic—he aimed.

It was… ingenious, if extremely risky. Husao had never seen nor heard of another instance in all time when a Null handed over his power to a mortal. There were no laws against it because it simply wasn't done, would likely never have occurred to anyone but Kamen.

Temshiel of Kamen's sort were rare. Even Skel hadn't been ready for the Null power Bear had given him as a sort of answer to Wolf's making of Kamen. And none had ever been made without having first served for centuries before as *Temshiel*. Many had thought Wolf soft or even reckless when he made Kamen.

Husao had reserved judgment and merely waited. He, better than most, knew the vagaries of sight, and he wasn't foolish enough to think his own on a par with a god's. Wolf had a purpose for Kamen, and Husao wanted to watch as he served it.

He nodded at Tatsu as he walked calmly through the Puppet Master's gates, waited for a challenge, but neither *Temshiel* nor maijin objected, merely stood to either side of the gates and watched Husao pass. Sora gave him the smallest of smiles, but Husao didn't know if it was merely courtesy, or if her sight had shown her something his hadn't. It was certainly possible. His sight was deep and wide-reaching, hers more short range and immediate; he wouldn't be surprised if she were able to see and interpret the night's events better than he could. He thought about stopping and consulting with her, but she might say something that would change his mind, and he didn't want that.

Husao kept walking, following the call of his son's Blood that had settled a sick weight in the center of his chest over a century ago, calling to his own Blood wordlessly with the low-level howl of a mindless revenant. The one mercy of the suns was that death was immediate, oblivion complete. Husao wondered if Asai had known that making and continuing to use those amulets would only perpetuate the torture of the last of Skel's sentience. Skel's death had been neither immediate nor complete. Asai hadn't paid nearly enough.

Perhaps this night, Husao could finally put the last of his son to rest, even as Jacin-rei did the same for his mother.

Calmly, Husao stepped out of the path of a clutch of white-eyed horses, galloping past him toward the gates. He smiled as one of the buildings on the southern end of the camp went up in flames.

Kamen's plan was simple in its audacity, sublime in its cunning. Draw all eyes to himself with chaos and mayhem. Allow the spiritbound to use his magic, interlace it with the power of all those around her and slip it into the wash of magic all over this place. Mask it, diffuse it, so none would feel it when the Puppet Master's Disappeared were put to rest, one by one, because unlike *Temshiel* magic, mortal magic died when the body did.

Sleight-of-hand at its craftiest, and in more ways than the one.

Kamen would get for his Catalyst everything he wanted, would destroy the Puppet Master and his "farm" like he'd been wanting to do since Husao had put him on the scent, and would break no laws in the doing. No Blood was exchanged, neither given nor taken, only Kamen's power, and that merely borrowed.

It was brilliant.

Husao's sight had refused to show him the possibility until Jacin-rei had walked out Kamen's door, so his own plan was much simpler: follow the call of his son's Blood, find the amulets and destroy them while Kamen and his people took all the risks. Husao would break no laws, and though it might put him out of favor with Dragon for quite a long time, he could not be punished.

The earth shuddered beneath Husao's feet, just as another several dozen horses bolted past him, frothing and obviously panicked, and for a moment Husao thought the rumble had come from their hoofs. It was the tingle of magic moving with the tremors that told him he'd misinterpreted. This swell of power was over and above that of the *Temshiel* and maijin and half-Blood mortals that still bided at the gates. It even washed out the pulse that came from the Puppet Master's estate like a sick, thumping heartbeat.

The futures-possible slipped through Husao's sight like so much smoke, roiling and changing from one breath to the next. Jacin-rei was here, after all, his shifting directions determining one possibility then distorting it as his course altered and his focus adapted. Not thinking things through, because Jacin-rei didn't think things through unless he was forced. Jacin-rei *did*, surrendered his mind to the din and moved on instinct alone.

Husao instead fixed on the others. Watched the earthbound die in endless horrible ways. Saw him live as a result of miniscule changes in actions around him. Saw the same with the younger brother. Kamen's own people. The Puppet Master's men. The Puppet Master himself.

There were just too many. Prediction was impossible.

All but one.

Husao followed the call to the place from where it wailed the loudest. Not, as he'd speculated, to the manor that sat atop the place, but to a long, squat reed and thatch building on the northwestern end. One of several, but the pulse pounded from one in particular.

Eager, Husao let it pull him.

ᛗ

Samin had expected it to be dark, and it wasn't. He'd expected to have to take care of perhaps a few guards or at least caretakers, and he hadn't. He'd expected to be overcome by the sight, and in that he wasn't disappointed.

It hit him as soon as he neared the threshold—the stench of lye and soap, nearly overpowered by the scent of blood. Not the smell of decay and waste he'd been expecting, but not any better, really. He'd seen this before, so he shouldn't allow it to affect him the way it was doing, but the sheer *scale*…

Not even beds, but slatted frames, one atop the other like bunks, stretched out along both walls in straight rows. Pale, nude bodies lay on each of them, all with clean swaths of linen wrapped around both wrists, eyes thankfully closed in most cases, but some stared sightless up into nothing.

They looked clean, which surprised Samin. They weren't emaciated and wasting away, which surprised him more. He could still see the sunken face of that little Jin girl all those years ago, the brittle set of starvation and dehydration in her wasted body; could feel the dry bristle of her hair between his fingers, the thin bones in her neck as they snapped against his palms.

Morin pushed out a shaky breath. "They've no hair."

Samin had been so caught up in his own revulsion, he'd nearly forgotten he wasn't alone here. Nearly forgotten what he was supposed to be doing.

Gently, he angled Morin behind him.

Fen took it all in without apparent emotion, scanning the aisles of bunks and bodies with eyes gone blank. Searching for one that looked familiar, perhaps, or maybe just deciding on the most efficient method of doing the job they'd come to do. Samin couldn't tell. Either was just as likely when it came to Fen.

So it was extraordinarily inopportune, and wasn't it just their luck, that the bloody Ancestors would pick *now* to start wailing at Fen. Samin recognized the listening posture, the stillness, and came *this close* to swatting Fen out of it. If he did it hard enough, maybe the Ancestors themselves would come bouncing out Fen's ears. Or at least shut the fuck up and die like they were supposed to. There were enough unpleasant sensations crawling up Samin's backbone just now, thank you. But he waited it out, grateful that at least he didn't have to know what those lunatics in Fen's head were screeching about now.

It took a moment for Fen's eyes to clear. When they did, he merely turned a detached gaze on Samin.

"I'll start down the other end."

A little stunned when he shouldn't be, Samin just watched him go. He'd seen Fen put away everything but the killer before. But this—

"Why don't they have hair?"

Samin dragged his gaze to Morin.

Wide, hazel eyes glittered in the low lamplight, tears dammed but only just. *I'm not a child*, and no, he wasn't, really, but he *was*. And one of these mindless lumps of mortality used to be his mother. They were all someone's mother or sister or father or son, so how was Samin supposed to explain to this boy why, among all the other, more atrocious atrocities and degradations, they'd had their hair taken from them too?

Samin couldn't quite look Morin in the eye. "To make it easier to keep them clean, I guess."

It was a relief when Morin just accepted it silently and didn't ask more.

Because the cold, observant part of Samin supposed the shaved heads made practical sense—no lice or fleas to worry about, none of the diseases they carried. But the part that thundered profound offense in his chest wondered if it was just another way to make these people seem more like nameless animals.

There were no wounds on their heads, like the one that had scabbed over on that little girl by the time Mizin had arrogantly led Samin down into his cellar and shown her off with a loathsome show of pride. *Pride.* As though she were some sort of pelt he'd made into a coat to boast of his prowess. So Samin really had to wonder how these people had been turned mindless without the evidence of the spike to the brain he'd seen on all the others.

And how was it they weren't emaciated and steadily dying? They were being fed somehow, or there wouldn't be so many of them, and what there were would be skin and bones, lasting maybe a month, if the "caretakers" were careful, two if they were lucky. There were at least a hundred in this barracks alone, and another five buildings besides.

Some kept their pet full-Bloods alive and compliant through drugs, but that altered the Blood in ways Malick understood and Samin didn't. But he believed Malick when he said it made the amulets weaker and the spells not as reliable. The men who'd bought Shig and Yori had kept Shig alive and bleeding for them only because they hadn't the funds or connections to pay one of those skilled enough to jam a spike into her brain without killing her. They'd kept Shig compliant through drugs, and Yori compliant through Shig.

These people didn't look drugged. They looked... asleep. Pale, perhaps, but healthy enough. The only evidence of harm was those bandages on their wrists, and even those looked clean.

Confused, deeply uneasy, Samin sent his thoughts out to Shig, even more uneasy when nothing came back to him. If she was—

"Morin! *Run!*"

Fen's urgent tone snapped everything in Samin back into focus. Without thought, he shoved Morin behind him, whirled, then raised his sword.

Shadows came to life to either side of Fen. Fen stood rigid, knives ready, backing up a few paces so he could watch them as they solidified between him and the set of bunks over which he'd been working.

Samin made out the bright glistening tracks of blood on the throats of two of the prone bodies, his ears picking up the wheezy gasps of emptying lungs and the steady *drip-drip-drip* of blood hitting the rush-covered floor. But his eyes watched the shadows recede, watched that Xari woman emerge from them with a man Samin guessed was Yakuli, because that was just how Fen's luck seemed to run.

"There is no need for panic." The man—*Yakuli*—flashed a sad smile at Fen then a cordial nod down to Samin.

Samin's gut gave a twist.

"Nor is there a need for violence." Yakuli waved gracefully at Fen's knives, and the blood dripping from them, then the gaping wounds on the throats of the two soon-to-be-corpses. "I intend no harm to you or yours. In fact, I think you and I can come to a satisfactory arrangement between us, young Fen-seyh."

Xari stepped forward and bowed her head to Fen, by all appearances deferential and respectful.

Samin reminded himself she was maijin. They all knew how to lie and make it look good.

"Things are not as you see them, lad." There was a thick thread of condescension in Xari's tone, like she was speaking to a small, stupid child. Her smile was beautiful, but there was nothing real about it.

Samin wondered if Fen could see it, too. Wondered if Fen could see anything clearly, or even think. Malick's ring was, after all, wedged on Morin's finger and not Fen's.

"I tried to explain it to you, but Kamen will not..." Xari shook her head, mouth turning down. "Kamen sees only you, and would give you what you ask for, even if it is not his to give. You asked for his head." She shot a sidelong look at Yakuli. "Kamen would give it to you, even knowing it would mean his soul. I warned him that death and violence were not the only ways—"

"I didn't, actually." Fen's voice was hoarse and low, still with that flat quality to it, but Samin could hear the anger building beneath it. "I didn't ask for Yakuli's head." Fen nodded at Yakuli. "*Your* head. I didn't ask for it. I asked M—Kamen to help me find my mother." The knife in his hand turned and twirled, spinning along his fingers, blade-hilt-blade-hilt, casual, unconcerned. "If there's a better way, perhaps you'd like to tell me now, before I, um..." A thin, scary-looking grin bloomed. "The Ancestors are very loud tonight."

"Bloody hell." Samin kept his voice at a very low murmur. "You'd better be bluffing."

"Yes, yes, of course." Yakuli gave Fen an agreeable nod. "We can come to an accord like reasonable men. Asai often spoke of his Untouch-able. Told me proudly more than once that you were unlike any other in decades. That you were sharp and strong enough to do what he needed of you, though…" He paused, smile falling down into sympathy. "Xari has told me how you turned on your master. I am very sorry it became necessary, lad. I know he loved you in his way."

Fen… flinched.

"Oh, shit." Samin took a quick step forward. "Fen."

"Don't." Morin clamped on to Samin's coat and held him back. "He knows what he's doing, and they'll kill you if you interfere."

The hard look Xari shot Samin confirmed it, but… damn it, was he supposed to just stand here while they ripped away whatever flimsy stanchions Fen was standing on? How much could Fen take before he broke completely?

"I see it grieves you. And I am sorry for the losses you have suffered." Yakuli took a step in toward Fen—not too close, and he didn't reach out for him. "It can stop now, Fen-seyh. You and yours can walk away from here now, with my blessing. As Xari has already promised, you can leave Ada, and leave behind forever the shadow of threat that hangs over your earthbound brother."

As if the mention had called it, the ground beneath their feet rumbled enough to nearly unbalance Samin. The lamps swayed on their rope fixtures on the ceiling, flinging shadows everywhere. The frames of the bunks creaked and shivered. Samin hoped like hell none of those bodies got dumped from them. That would be just a little *too* much creepiness.

Fen only stood still and waited for the ground to stop shaking. Staring. Calm. Outwardly, at least. Samin wasn't close enough to see Fen's eyes, but he imagined they'd gone stormy and confused.

When the ground stopped moving, Fen merely tilted his head.

"My mother."

"Ah!" Yakuli smiled, warm and gracious. "Yes, where is my head? Of course, of course. My apologies, but your mother is not here in this room. I moved her somewhere safe. You understand, lad. One cannot strike a proper bargain if one hands everything over too quickly." He reached into his high-necked tunic and pulled out an amulet.

Even from where he stood, Samin could hear Fen's growl.

Yakuli merely reached out to the body lying nearest him, and whispered a spell.

Samin didn't have the wits to watch Fen's reaction. He was too caught up in his own. He took an involuntary step backward when the "body" sat up, blinked against the lamps, turned its head from side to side, and settled its gaze on Yakuli. A gasp left Samin when its mouth turned up in an obsequious smile, and it dipped its head.

"Good evening, Beishin. How may I serve you?"

"You see, Fen-seyh." Yakuli waved toward the… thing. "Circumstances are not as you seem to think them. There is hope yet for your mother."

Fen only stared, narrow-eyed, then flicked a wary glance at Yakuli, and a downright distrustful one at Xari. He didn't seem to like what he found there. But he stayed there, not going for throats but keeping his knives at his sides and listening.

Samin wasn't sure what it meant. Surely Fen wasn't falling for this bullshit?

The… thing's eyes were as empty as Fen's had ever been. The voice was hoarse from disuse. The movements were too mechanical, the facial expression a weird imitation of Yakuli's.

Hadn't someone called this man a "Puppet Master"?

Morin tightened his hold on Samin's sleeve. "Watch." Just that, just that one word, but it was soft and firm, like Morin knew exactly what was coming next.

Samin made himself look back at Fen, lungs filling with air again when he saw the disgust and rage well up in Fen's face, and his hands grip tight around his knives. Fen didn't believe these people were still inside themselves any more than Samin did.

It was clever, Samin had to give Yakuli that, and if Fen were a man who didn't expect to get fucked over by everyone at every opportunity, he might have fallen for it. Fen hadn't, though. Proved it when he shot a speaking glance at Samin. Samin might not know exactly what that look was saying, but he knew Fen well enough to understand it at least alluded to *MAYHEM* in big, bold, capital characters.

Yakuli must have seen it, too, because the bodies on the frames all began to stir at once. The motions were loose-limbed and jerky, as though invisible strings were clumsily pulling them from their prone positions and to their feet.

Samin could only stare for a moment, more revolted than he'd ever been in his life. This man wasn't only Disappearing these people and using their Blood to arm his men with the amulets he made from it—he was turning them into an army of revenants he could control *using their own magic.*

All of them came for Samin and Morin. Clearly meant as hindrance, rather than attack, because they did nothing but make themselves into a wall and keep crowding, but Samin didn't wait to start swinging his sword. He'd told Morin that death for what was left of these people would be a mercy, and he'd meant it. And they dropped at a blade through the heart just like anything else.

They were slow, but they were effective. No matter how many Samin cut down, the sheer number of them kept him and Morin penned on the opposite side from where Fen was. And who knew what might be happening down there now, because the wall of puppets was blocking the view. They'd backed Samin and Morin almost to the door; Samin was running out of room to swing his sword, and there were just *so many* of them.

Morin, quick thinker that he was, snagged on a better strategy. With a wild little "Hyah!" he swung around Samin and launched himself at the nearest bunk, flew up it like a monkey climbing a ladder, and cut the rope that held the nearest lamp to the ceiling. Oil splashed out over the damp reeds on the floor. Fire followed immediately, catching the pools and drops of oil and climbing to the thin wood of the bunks.

Yakuli's puppets just kept coming, stepping into the flames like they didn't feel them, body hair catching fire and burning down to skin.

Samin nearly jumped out of his own skin when a firm hand landed on his shoulder. And then he almost gutted Husao, just for making him nearly jump out of his skin.

"Get the boy." Husao jerked his chin toward Morin. "There are more souls to save than these."

Samin saw the sense in it and tried to see the stomach-curling roast going on in front of him in terms of saved souls, rather than senseless horror. Except he couldn't quite get past the horror.

Shig! he sent as he snagged Morin down and pushed him along, swinging his sword at anything in reach. *I think we're going off plan here!*

⛩

The look in Joori's eye must have been a little wild, maybe even crazed, because the three men, trained as warriors, armed well and thoroughly competent, stared at him, frozen—*afraid*. And then they began to back away.

Joori laughed, a deranged little titter that sounded nothing like him. He sidestepped the loose, cracked earth at his feet, moving deliberately toward the men, instead of away, like he should be doing. He had no idea what he intended to do—make a great big hole and drop them into it, maybe, or bury them alive—but he was vibrating with strength, with power. Every bit of him shuddered with something deep and driven.

He *liked* it. Had no wish to crush it down again, to stuff it back inside himself where it had lain somnolent for so long he'd almost forgotten it was there.

Except Malick laid a hand to Joori's arm, and it all went away. Just went away. Gone. Everything around Joori went dull, muffled, as though someone had just thrown a thick blanket over him.

Malick only stared the men down, gave them one of his scary grins. He opened his hand and rolled a little fireball along his fingers.

"You should run."

They didn't even turn to check with each other—they spun around and ran.

Joori watched them go, a strange sense of loss burning through the weird, heavy fog. It felt too much like thwarted lust, and if it turned out that was what it was, he didn't want to know it. Anger curled through him, and he didn't know if it was at them, at himself, or at the spirit of the earth that lived inside him and turned him into something he didn't want to look at. It could have been any of it, all of it, and he had no idea what to do with it. So he pointed it at Malick.

He wrenched his arm from Malick's grip.

"*Now* you decide to use your magic? Where the fuck was it when you were over there fighting for your life, huh? What am I supposed to do if—?"

"You're supposed do what I bloody *told* you to and *get out!*" Malick snuffed the fireball, bared his teeth. "My magic is being used for other things at the moment, and what isn't is being spent on protecting everyone else, which includes *you* and *your brother.* So I'd prefer it if you didn't take stupid chances like wading into a clutch of professional soldiers and *not running* when I tell you to!"

Damn, Malick could be terrifying when he wanted to be. With the wavering light of the fires crawling all over him, throwing his face into alternate flame and shadow, and his eyes catching the conflagration, flaring it out like it was inside him...

Joori deflated. "Oh." He let Malick shove him away from the great crevice Joori had wrought when he'd been pretending to be someone strong.

"Yeah, *oh.*"

Rolling his eyes like Joori was the most tiresome trial he'd ever had to endure, Malick dragged them into a run, away from the barracks and up the incline. Joori didn't doubt the pace Malick set was deliberately punishing, an increasingly faster clip, weaving and out of intermittent copses of pine and larch. They kept to the shadows as much as possible, moving more stealthily than they'd been doing down at the barracks.

Finally, Malick halted them when they reached a stand of pines about fifty paces from the closest building, just outside the ring of fence enclosing an empty paddock. Joori didn't even protest when Malick turned him roughly so they were facing each other. Panting, they both bent over, clutching their knees.

"Look." Malick was too obviously forcing calm into his tone, pausing another few seconds to catch his breath. "I know you don't like me much, and I know you don't trust me." He straightened, pushing at Joori's shoulder until Joori stood straight to face him. "I don't care if you like me, and I don't need your trust. What I *do* care about is Fen walking away from here tonight with everything he needs to keep his mind. That means you and your brother alive and walking, your mother put to rest, and Yakuli with a gaping hole in whatever part of his body will bring death the quickest. If you want to help him get all that, you'll do *what* I tell you, *when* I tell you. And you *won't* take another chance like that."

Joori... stared. He almost didn't know what to make of this new person he was seeing who not only professed to love Jacin but was in the process of *proving* it, until he realized—

To save Jacin, he needs to save you, he needs to save Morin, he needs to save your mother's soul.

This was *Malick*—not Kamen, not Wolf's *Temshiel*, and not the smirky smartass who'd cavalierly flirted and bickered with immortals at Yakuli's gates.

This was the man who still lived inside the immortal. The man who'd set his sights on the pretty Untouchable, and ended up with his heart and soul wound too tightly around Fen Jacin-rei.

Damn Shig and her annoying insights, anyway.

"It was…" Joori hesitated, pretending he needed to catch his breath, but it was more to stall, because he hadn't really meant to speak at all and now he was caught. He licked his lips. "You looked like you needed help. I'm supposed to be your key, and you told me to run. What's the point? And if you haven't enough magic to go around, it seems like—"

"I've exactly enough magic to do exactly what I need to do. And speaking of which." Malick peered closely at Joori in the dark, glaring. Then shocked him by abruptly giving Joori a firm clap on the shoulder. "Good going back there. Be careful how you use it—you're about as elegant with it as Shig is with mine—but *damn*, you've a lot of it, and you could too easily take yourself out next time. Just because it comes from you doesn't mean you're invulnerable to it."

Joori was… annoyingly touched and absurdly pleased.

"Why can't you direct it?" A little rush wound through Joori's chest as the idea bloomed and took shape. "I mean, take it like you did before, make it stronger, and we could just crumble the whole place, open it right up, and everyone—"

"And everyone here would go down with it. Which would be fine, if it were only Yakuli and his men, except it's not." Malick paused, grim but strangely sympathetic. "Your mother's not the only one in need of saving, Joori."

Oh. Right. As Malick had said before—kinda the point.

"Anyway." Malick scanned the area around them. "I can't actually kill Yakuli."

And *that*…

Joori scowled. He'd known it, but he supposed he hadn't quite believed it. It seemed so… arbitrary. So unnecessarily complex. Malick could walk in and direct chaos and destruction, but he couldn't actually kill the one man who desperately needed killing. He could give his magic to Shig to do whatever the hell it was she was doing with it, but he couldn't let her use it to kill Yakuli.

"That's…" Joori shook his head, teeth tight. "That's really stupid."

"Yeah." Malick turned back to Joori. "All right, the good news is, whatever Xari's up to, she didn't warn Yakuli we were coming. Or at least it looks that way. The bad news is—"

Malick straightened. His eyes went vague for a second, narrowed, then widened, and he shot his glance up the hill.

Joori turned to follow it, scanned the rise but saw nothing. He was just about to turn back to Malick, ask him what was wrong, when a brief flicker in his periphery caught his eye, disappeared for a second, then flared up like a fist unfurling. It took a moment for Joori to make out the shape of another barracks through the flames, another moment for him to realize that what he'd been unconsciously waiting for wasn't happening—there were no men stumbling from the building, aflame and screaming.

Malick stared, drew his sword. "That," he said slowly, "wasn't supposed to happen yet."

ᛏ

He was selfishly sorry he'd given Malick's ring to Morin. The Ancestors were loud, insistent, the chaos a crescendo that would have deafened him, had he been hearing it with his ears. It was making it too difficult to think, to track, to do anything at all but what his body told him to do. The residual pain of mostly healing injuries couldn't cut through it like it had always done before.

not be thwarted Wolf acid to the skies Raven duplicity our boy only one only one

A big man, Yakuli. Younger than Jacin had thought, and not nearly as revolting-looking as he'd imagined. Men like this should be ugly, twisted out of shape and plagued with growths, so people could tell just by looking that they should turn and run the other way. This man was almost handsome. Bronze-blond hair, and eyes the color of winter pine. Wide and fit, a full head taller than Jacin. A voice that could either command or seduce, depending upon how he wielded it.

That was what had been seared into Jacin's memory. That voice. He'd listened from a hallway window as it demanded more ammunition against his family. And Asai's response had delivered the first real blow in the violent deconstruction of Jacin's life. And so to hear Yakuli nearly *cooing* at him, trying to pretend to be a friendly, reasonable man...

It burned through the noise where thought and pain could not.

"My patience wears thin, Fen-seyh." Yakuli swept a hand out toward the soulless bodies, standing still now as fire crept over them, one after another. "I've shown you in good faith that I can restore your mother to you, and in return your accomplices murder my children."

Caidi leaned up on tiptoe to murmur in Jacin's ear. "Ever had your body move to someone else's tune, like you were a puppet?"

Xari narrowed her eyes, peering around as though she'd heard something but wasn't sure what it was or where it had come from.

The Ancestors were singing, *singing*, loud and nearly painful in their harmonic perfection.

clinging to corpses Wolf leers through a veil of burning skies to Raven's duplicity.

Look at them, Asai whispered. *Alive. Your mother is still alive. You can still save her. You can save them all.*

Except Asai was a liar. He always had been.

I know he loved you in his way, Yakuli had said, all sincerity and somber compassion, but Yakuli was a liar, too, and Jacin knew better, had finally learned better. Beishin had never loved him, Jacin would never be perfect, and so he would always fail. It still hurt, but at least now he knew what to expect.

The hut was going up like a candle. The creatures that used to be people stood there and burned. It made Jacin's stomach flop about, but he didn't move, didn't react. Yakuli was trying to distract him, and Jacin was already too distracted as it was.

He set his jaw. "Where is she?"

"She is waiting for you." Yakuli smiled, that kind, condescending thing. "Let me take you to her."

The Ancestors *shrieked*, agonized and wordless, the volume nearly crowding out everything else, but Jacin couldn't let it. He kept his hands from flying uselessly to his head to try to block them out.

"Tell me where she is."

"Do you know what Asai wanted?" Yakuli's tone was calm, curious, as though the place wasn't on fire and almost-corpses weren't roasting only feet away. "How much did he tell his Ghost, I wonder…?" Yakuli leaned casually against the bunk behind him, eyeing Jacin thoughtfully. "Asai was an ambitious man. He wanted to provoke chaos then rein it in, make himself the hero of the Jin as he was the hero to the Catalyst."

Xari hadn't moved, hadn't spoken. At the mention of Asai, her mouth turned down, and she looked away.

Smoke curled into Jacin's nostrils, the sick-sweet stench of roasting meat. He forced himself to breathe shallowly.

"I don't want chaos. I want order." Yakuli tilted his head. "Do you know why my careful plans, half of my painstaking *work* is now lying in smoking heaps around my estate?"

burning skies clinging to corpses our boy listen

Yakuli held out a hand. "It is because I cannot see *you*, Wolf's Catalyst. The Voice of the Ancestors. The Abomination that should have never been at all."

once only once our boy we've chosen only say it once

"Look around you." Yakuli waved over his shoulder to the fire that steadily ate away the other half of the long hut, creeping closer, then to the blank wall behind Jacin, presumably to indicate the encampment in general. "Asai is now dead because he could not see you clearly enough to know the knife was coming for him. Such treachery he must have felt in his last moment, betrayed so profoundly by the one he loved so well." He grinned. "Your accomplices even now waste precious magic with each of my children they cut down."

will not be thwarted cast acid to the sky

Yakuli's teeth tightened, and the friendly façade vanished. Those of his "children" that had still been on their feet abruptly dropped like dead things.

"And all because the Abomination wants his mother back."

Caidi grinned at Jacin. Jacin grinned back.

It seemed to throw Yakuli. It seemed to downright startle Xari.

balk batter baffle them all crushed and craven Wolf will not be thwarted he sees the Eye and calls the Prime to his own leers through a veil of burning skies to Raven's duplicity the gods speak no more silent silent dead and quiet

"Tell me where she is," Jacin said evenly, "and I'll go." And he wasn't even sure if he was lying or not. He couldn't think clearly enough.

Yakuli pulled out of his slouch against the bunk. "She is merely one more spiritbound to me. Her worth does not approach what you have cost me tonight. But do you know what *your* worth could be?"

"He wants to make you one of his 'children.'" Caidi's lip curled in disgust. "He wants to see if the magic that took their spirits from them would work on you."

Jacin's gut roiled.

Yakuli took a step closer. "A blank spot, Untouchable even to Fate, defying sight by your mere presence." He turned a calculating glance on Xari. "Surely the spells—"

"You cannot touch the Untouchable." Xari's expression was unreadable. "The gods—"

"The gods approve. If they did not, they would have moved the *Temshiel*, and we would not be here talking about it."

"He doesn't know about Malick." Caidi laid her small hand to Jacin's arm. "If he did, he wouldn't be piddling about here, he'd be trying to add him to his 'fold.'" She smirked. "Xari didn't warn him."

Good. As long as Malick stayed alive, so would Joori and Morin.

"Where is my mother?"

One last time. Jacin twirled his knives to make that clear.

Yakuli laughed this time—*laughed*—and shook his head. "Do you really think I *know?* Did you suppose she had some special import for me? That she was somehow more than all my other children, merely because she is special to *you?*"

Yes, Jacin supposed he had.

"She is one Jin among hundreds. She is clean. She is cared for. She will live longer than perhaps even you will, and her magic is being used as it ought, not hidden away in a prison camp and wasted on one who has neither the wit nor will to use it. You should be thanking me. I have done more for the Jin and their magic than the Ancestors and the gods combined since before the Binding War." Yakuli dipped his head on an ironic bow. "And I thank you for bringing the possible value of the Untouchable to my attention. I don't believe I would have thought of it, had the little lost Ghost not been so... persistent in his want for his mother."

Mocking. Taking because he could. Withholding because it amused him. Threatening to take even more.

And Xari was just *standing* there.

It wasn't right. It wasn't fucking *fair*.

Jacin couldn't decide which one to go for first, but he had two hands, after all, so he went for both of them at once. He lunged in, blades twirling horizontal, aiming for quick double-decapitation—let them try to use their magic to fix *that*—but they were both too fast. Shadows swirled around them, and they were suddenly behind him.

Jacin spun, brought his knives up in defense. Xari didn't move on him, just stood there and watched, but Yakuli drove in with a hard fist to the side of Jacin's head that set him staggering. Fucking shadows.

Furious, Jacin raised his knives again, and again, Yakuli was gone in a swirl of shadows. This time, Jacin spun around and aimed for the empty space behind him, but Yakuli apparently didn't use the same tricks twice—he rematerialized right back where he'd started and nailed Jacin again, this time in the temple.

Go with the impact, don't resist it, don't try to absorb it, you'll take less damage that way—Samin's voice, steadily instructive, somewhere in the back of Jacin's head. He followed the advice without thought, yet still, it was all Jacin could do to keep his feet. He reached for the frame of a bunk, clung.

"Told you, I did." Xari took Yakuli by the collar like a recalcitrant child and shook him. "Mortals with your foolish attempts to finesse and beguile with all the cunning of a gullible newborn. *Told* you, did I not? You cannot touch the Untouchable." She turned her glare on Jacin. "He bargains with what he does not have. He cannot give you your mother back, this you know. But he can take more than you can give and keep your mind." She shoved Yakuli away. "A trade. A *true* bargain. Take your brothers and go. Take Kamen with you. Do it and I will place your mother on the pyre myself." She put out her hands. "You don't know what I've seen, child. You don't know what Kamen will forf—"

"*Lie.*"

Jacin gave his head a bit of a shake to try to clear it, but his vision was doubling. Smoke curled into his nose, down his throat, and he tried to keep himself from choking on it, tried to keep himself from panicking when the other end of the hut suddenly went up in a great *whoosh* of flames and the walls collapsed outward.

"All you know is self-interest and betrayal." He pushed away from the bunk and stood straight. "Come a little closer, and I'll show you what happens to those who betray me."

Raven's duplicity Wolf will not be thwarted

Xari's eyes narrowed. Jacin had no idea if it was a giveaway on her part or instinct on his.

He whirled, slashed at darkness, almost giddy with satisfaction when Yakuli barked a curse, voice edged brittle with pain. He solidified a few feet away from Jacin, his arm bleeding and rage twisting his face. Jacin snorted, head still a little light, knees still a little weak, but the look on Yakuli's face—surprise, indignant anger—Jacin had to laugh. He couldn't help it.

the one the only one listen always listen our boy we've chosen

Enraged, Yakuli swirled into shadow, came up at Jacin's flank and leveled a solid blow to his kidney then twisted away again.

Gasping now, the snorts more like animal grunts, Jacin tried to turn, came up short when Yakuli was there again. This time, he got an elbow to the jaw. Sweet copper exploded in his mouth, and his head throbbed with *noisepainvoicesrage*.

Jacin swung wild, knife flashing out. He aimed for the throat, only got a good gouge down the side of Yakuli's face. The yelp of pain was satisfying, but Jacin had stupidly left himself open for a ruthless thump to the ribs in payment, and it took his breath.

He checked his backward momentum with a quick jag and pivot, and turned it to a surge forward instead. Teeth set, he lashed out, felt one blade sink home somewhere, but he couldn't tell where. More shadows, too fast to track, then his head was yanked back by the braid, so hard and quick he felt the heat of strained joints and tendons burning up behind his jaw. He had perhaps a second and a half to register the smoke gathering in great, thick clouds at the ceiling. He jammed an elbow back, hoping to hit ribs, before Yakuli's fist again eclipsed his vision.

Jacin managed somehow to keep his feet when everything went black for a second, managed not to sway when the pain finally hit him and made him wonder if Yakuli hadn't actually taken off the top of his head.

And all the while, he managed to keep slashing, keep swinging, keep whirling until he made himself dizzy. His knives missed more than they hit, but they *were* hitting, and he had to be doing *some* damage. Not nearly as much as Yakuli was doing to him, but at least Jacin wasn't bleeding yet, and he knew Yakuli was. He couldn't get a long enough look to confirm it, but the blood on the edges of Jacin's knives told him so.

Once again, his braid was gripped, yanked, only this time, Yakuli used it as a tether and swung Jacin headfirst into a wooden bunk. Jacin's chest and face took the brunt as the bunk shattered beneath him and he went to the floor amidst a pile of kindling. It took him a few seconds longer than was healthy for him to get to his feet again.

Too strong, too fast. Jacin had taken out a maijin, had held his own with a *Temshiel* who made it a pastime to fight dirty, and this man who couldn't even use magic against him was beating the shit out of him. It was ironically fucking hilarious.

the one the only one listen always listen our boy we've chosen

Chosen.

Chosen.

It was too fucking funny.

He laughed when Yakuli's sweeping kick took his legs out from under him. Laughed some more when Yakuli's hands on the back of his coat—Malick's coat… where the fuck was Malick?—lifted him back up and pulled the coat down so his arms were clumsily pinned to his sides. Jacin had lost a knife somewhere, and he couldn't even get his vision under enough control to look around for it, but he gripped the other more tightly, slashed out blind. Reeling, he wheezed out a truncated snort when another blow landed on his temple and his vision blacked again.

When it came back, he was on his knees on the floor, the coat half-on and half-off. He dragged himself up, coughing through the chuckles as smoke filled his lungs and took all the breath he'd managed to get back.

the one the only one listen always listen our boy we've chosen

"Stop it!" Yakuli was agitated now. "Stop fighting. I need you alive, boy, but I don't need you undamaged."

Jacin couldn't. Couldn't stop fighting, couldn't stop laughing because he couldn't stop fighting, even though he knew he'd already failed.

He'd finally lost it. He was standing here—well, wobbling—in the middle of Yakuli's compound, on a mission to put his mother's soul to rest, the walls on fire and spreading to the part of the roof that hadn't collapsed yet, right over his head, and his sanity was finally dripping from him like so much wax from a high-wicked candle.

chosen our boy only say it once

Because they'd *chosen*. All these years, all the madness splitting his head, his self, and *this* was what the Ancestors had chosen. He wasn't even really surprised—after all, they were even more insane than he was.

Jacin was still laughing when Yakuli drew the shadows in once more and came barreling at him. The force hit Jacin in the chest, pounding all the air out of his lungs. Like he was a giddy twig in a hurricane, Jacin flew through the burning reed walls and slammed to his back in the grass. Small flames crept all around him, burning through Malick's coat and down to skin before Jacin could gather the wits to thump them out.

Yakuli drew two long swords from the scabbards at his sides and went to shadow again.

Caidi stood limned in flame, watching with a sympathetic smile.

I made you for this, Beishin told him.

"Yeah." Jacin laughed harder. "I *know!*"

Malick couldn't chance going to spirit to get him and Joori up the hill. There was too much going on, too much magic flying around, and it was hard enough to make the spirits cooperate when they weren't so distracted. So they ran, and when the guards were too thick of an obstacle, they ran veiled.

He knew when Shig disobeyed his orders and abandoned her position outside Yakuli's gates. Malick felt the shift in focus, felt Shig's intentions. Even had he not approved, he wouldn't have argued with her. She wouldn't have listened. And anyway, the whole point of what she'd been doing had been rendered moot by that fire at the prisoners' barracks, so leaving her out there idle would be a waste.

The whole fucking thing had been a waste. Plan—*ha!* It would've been bloody *beautiful,* if everything had stayed on track, but it had all depended on timing, and Malick's timing had always been shit. No, not just shit—a great big steaming pile of it. Only this time, it had been Fen's fault.

Your friends at the gates are following me, Shig told him.

Malick just rolled his eyes. *Ignore them. As long as they don't get in the way, I don't give a flying fuck what they do.* He thought about it as he ran, then sent *Get everyone with you up to the prisoner barracks. Use whatever you have to use to get Yakuli's men out of your way, but double-time it. Everything's going to shit way too fast.*

Sure, Mal was all he got back.

"Are those…?" Joori slowed, huffing and blowing as he squinted up to the top of the rise. "Malick, what the hell *is* that?"

Malick followed his gaze, knowing, but even knowing didn't stop his stomach from turning over when he actually *saw.*

"What d'you think? It's your brother trying to take on the world all by himself again."

Joori jerked back, eyes huge and wild. "Is that… is he…?"

Malick didn't know what Joori couldn't finish, and he didn't have time to wonder. His attention was nailed to the two figures silhouetted by flames atop the rise. And then completely arrested by something else altogether.

"Fucking *shit!*"

Malick grabbed hold of Joori's arm again and shoved him back into a run, up toward the fifty or more armed men making their way steadily toward the spot where the two figures whirled and clashed. More flames flared on the other side of them—another barracks going up—

and Malick's heart tripped up into his throat when he saw the lean figure of Fen stumble backward, almost falling into the fire before he caught his balance again.

Subie growled again, louder this time, and the ground shook, harder than before, harder even than when it had been Joori. Malick spared a glance up toward the mountain, small puffs of smoke belching from its peak and silhouetted by Wolf. It might have been portentous, or even picturesque, under different circumstances, but Malick didn't have the time.

"Oh, no. *Jacin!*" Joori doubled his pace, running through guards who were too busy trying to figure out what was going on to snatch for him or try to stop him. Joori barreled through and knocked them aside like he didn't even see them.

Malick reached out, snapped his veil down around Joori, stopping him, and then down around himself so he could get close enough to assess the situation before he barreled in too.

Coming up behind you, Mal, Shig told him, and went silent again.

Malick watched Yakuli point downward. *And you've got at least fifty coming at you,* he sent back. *And they're all charmed.*

Yakuli's men would be concentrating on Shig and her band, instead of outnumbering Fen. A little more dangerous for Shig than Malick would like, but she'd always enjoyed a down-and-dirty.

Husao rushed down the slope past Malick and toward Shig. Malick only stared, eyebrows high. Finally moved to help, maybe? Still merely watching it all for his own weird entertainment? Malick didn't really care, so long as Husao stayed out of the way.

Husao's on his way down, he told Shig, then shut it all away. Shig had Malick's magic, and her own little army at her back—she could take care of herself.

But Fen...

Two figures, framed by flames, spun and swept and swirled. One went down, staggered back up, and twisted into a clumsy whirl. Malick couldn't mistake the long tail of the braid streaming out behind Fen as Yakuli caught him in midleap with what looked like a hard kick to the gut. Fen flew back and went down again. There was no efficient grace or straightforward elegance to Fen's movements this time. There was merely a blow then an ungainly plunge to the ground. A bone-saving roll like an afterthought or maybe instinct, then Fen dragged himself up to his knees.

Son of a bitch had no idea how to quit.

He was at least on his feet again by the time Malick reached Joori and dropped his veil. Joori was livid, but Malick had expected him to be. Malick merely ignored the snarling and cursing and kept a firm grip as Samin trotted up to Malick's side, dragging Morin and his too-big broadsword along behind him. Morin's sword was bloodied; there were dark, wet streaks on his face. His eyes had that wild, half-shocked, half-exhilarated look to them that was too distinctive of a first kill. Malick might spend time later lamenting that the boy had been forced to it, but the world was tough all over, and Malick had other things to worry about right now. He looked Samin and Morin over, judged them both unhurt, and saved the rest for later. With the unspoken order to hold him back, Malick shoved Joori, still cursing, at Samin, sucked in a long breath, and took stock.

Shig and her party had been engaged about fifty yards down the hill, and though Malick could feel that Yakuli's men all had amulets, none of them were those the hunters carried, the ones made from Skel's Blood. One lucky break in this night severely lacking them. Still, it made Malick wonder uneasily why, and if Yakuli had a nasty surprise tucked up his sleeve and waiting.

Maybe Yakuli really hadn't known they were coming. Which made no sense at all, because Xari had warned him.

…Hadn't she?

Malick's magic through Shig was nulling out the magic of the amulets Yakuli's men wore. The only weapons of any use to them were those made of steel. Shig's party returned the fight in kind, kept it to physical weapons and hand-to-hand. It was riskier, but Malick approved. Throwing magic around was how the Jin had got into this whole mess to begin with. Regardless of their foolishness and the suffering they'd caused their own children, the Ancestors had never meant their magic to be used that way.

Satisfied that Shig had her end under control, Malick turned back to Fen, glad he was at least on his feet, but dismayed down to the ground that he looked so… not-Fen.

Laughing. His grin was downright deranged as he chuckled and muttered things Malick couldn't hear and probably didn't want to. He looked like every Jin Untouchable Malick had seen in the last century or so—blank-eyed and tattered, mumbling to himself, and just… *not well*. He was limping worse than he'd been before, and he didn't even seem to notice. Blood dripped from a split in his lip, down his face from an apparent head wound, and wide swaths of what Malick was pretty sure weren't shadows bloomed all along the left side of his face and his right temple. How the hell had—?

And then Yakuli went to shadow halfway through a charge, and Malick knew.

Bloody hell, and Fen had thought Malick fought dirty.

Joori was still snarling at Samin. He latched on to Malick's sleeve, tug-tug-tugging then *wrenching*.

Malick just shook him off, called, "Fen!" and started running.

The whistle of air on steel was what moved Jacin to roll to the side and to his feet, surprised he could hear it through the singing and the screeching, and the low, humming roar of the flames. Or maybe he felt it, Yakuli's sword coming for him. Didn't matter.

Yakuli didn't even bother with his shadows for a while, just came at Jacin, both swords swinging. Jacin was surprised, because they looked like good weapons—heavy, quality steel—but Yakuli twirled them with no apparent effort, aiming to damage, maim, or at least cripple with every swipe.

Jacin flew and spun and slashed, taking hits when necessary, and inflicting them every chance he got. And he couldn't stop laughing.

Catalyst and Incendiary light the lamps of the sky and burn the heavens whet your blades with the rites of vengeance our boy chosen the key rites of vengeance

Too many disadvantages. Jacin had to get up close to use his weapons, and Yakuli didn't. He blooded Jacin at least a little more every time he attacked. And with access to the shadows any time he wanted them, it was only going to be a matter of time. The throwing knives were useless against someone who could disappear every time Jacin reached for one.

Meant to fail, and maybe so. Jacin didn't expect to get out of this alive. But he did expect to do a hell of a lot of damage before he went down. Maybe give Malick enough time to find Jacin's mother and get everyone else out, because Malick had promised. And now, in what were likely his last moments, Jacin chose to believe it.

He clung to it, laughing as he went flying backward and landed hard on his ass. A pounding kick to his ribs splintered little snaps and cracks through his chest. Pain, white-hot and staggering, exploded through him. Ribs were the fucking *worst*.

Jacin's sniggers skewed breathless as he went down on his back in the grass. The red-gold-orange of more fire than he remembered smeared through the trails of the stars spangling at the edges of his vision.

Subie snarled out another complaint. The ground shook, making Jacin's teeth rattle. And even as he watched Yakuli coming for him, watched the flames curl and snap all around him, heard Joori's voice coming to him from far away, shouting, *"Jacin!"* in a voice edged with stress and panic, Jacin couldn't stop laughing.

"The ground trembles and shifts to Null." He snorted then let it all bubble up his throat, spill out his mouth: "The gods have all gone silent and Wolf calls us home your Blood our Blood our boy clinging to corpses only say it once—"

Yakuli moved in. "Stand *down*, boy!"

"—*listenlistenlisten* Wolf suffers not the duplicity of weaker gods he calls the Prime to his duty, the key, the *key*—"

Jacin was still laughing as he pushed himself along the grass on his back, but it felt more like sobbing in disguise. His chest was burning, and his mouth was moving with no more control over what came out of it than Yakuli's creatures had over theirs. *Fuck*, his head hurt.

"—Wolf speaks we've chosen our boy say it once—"

"*Stop it!*"

Jacin couldn't. Could only shuffle back when Yakuli advanced on him. Not bothering with his shadows anymore, because what was the point? Jacin was lying on his back in the grass, crazed laughter and incoherent Voices frothing from his mouth like a rabid animal—what kind of threat could he possibly be?

Out of breath, ribs on fire, everything else just *hurting*, Jacin throttled the snorting down some when Yakuli drew the swords at his sides up and to the ready. Let it burble back up when Yakuli took a step in. Saw Malick out the corner of his eye, careening in toward Yakuli, sword swinging in a glittering arc to his side. Watched some man he'd never seen before step in and hold Malick back, and then a woman with skin as black as the night hustle in to help him.

Good. Jacin had already been responsible for the damnation of one soul; he didn't want Malick's on his conscience too. He didn't think he could take it, not after tonight, not after actually seeing what it meant to have one's spirit taken away. And who would be left to help these people if Jacin was dead and Malick was damned? Who would see to Jacin's mother? Who would take care of Joori and Morin?

"You've always known you couldn't live with it." Caidi crouched down, ran her warm palm over Jacin's bloody temple. She leaned in, laid a kiss to his cheek, soft and sweet, then pulled back, her hazel eyes glinting gold and dangerous in the wavering firelight. "The Ghost breathes his last and the Catalyst moves back to Zero." She grinned, a Caidi-grin, all bright eyes and dimples. "Time to start again, love."

"Yeah. All right."

Jacin matched the grin, windless chuckles jostling his ribs, thumping at his head. He had no idea what the fuck she was talking about, but he was breathing his last, Caidi said so, and it made him giddy. He rolled slowly, got an arm and a knee beneath him. Yakuli's boot crashed into his gut and shoved all the air out of him.

Jacin collapsed like a baby deer on ice, tried, *tried* to get back up, but only managed to flop to his back. He couldn't breathe for the smoke and the laughter, and his arms were too shaky to hold him up.

Wolf was bright in the sky, too bright, hazing Jacin's vision. He watched Yakuli lift his sword, saw the reflection of Wolf on the flat of the blade as it glinted and gleamed. Jacin winced as Wolf's mirrored light speared into his eyes.

"Leers through a veil of burning skies." Jacin huffed; a fine mist of blood sprayed through it. He squinted through the flames at Wolf's face. "I think... I think I'm... done now."

Caidi tilted her head. "Are you?"

He was failing. Meant to fail. *Made* for it.

The Ghost would not survive the night. Caidi had told him so, and Caidi was the only one Jacin could believe.

Wolf grinned down, watching him fail, Raven and Dragon ghost-red splinters behind him. Jacin could almost hear Wolf laughing through the Ancestors' lunatic shrieking, louder and louder, taking him over. He couldn't think, so he stopped trying, gave himself to the voices and the madness, and narrowed himself down to instinct alone.

"Fen!" someone shouted. He thought it was Malick.

"Jacin-rei," Caidi corrected, gold hair washed crimson in the firelight. "*Ghost.*"

Jacin grinned, then shoved himself back when Yakuli's blades came at him. Kicked out and managed to send Yakuli sailing back. Because he was Jacin-rei, he was the Ghost, and the Ghost would not survive the night, but he wasn't going down alone, and it was just too fucking funny.

"You must be what you are." Caidi's smile was approving, hazel eyes on fire. "Be the Ghost, Jacin-rei."

"*Yes,*" Jacin answered, because everyone lied, but Caidi never did.

Galvanized, Jacin laughed, loud and full, as he rolled to the side. Yakuli's crossed swords came down, a glittering X aiming to take his head from his shoulders. Jacin rolled again, twisted, and leapt to his feet.

"Catalyst and Incendiary"—Jacin dodged away from a swipe—"light the lamps of the sky and burn the heavens whet your blades with the rites of vengeance."

Diving to the side, no thought, Jacin's hand drew a small knife all on its own from the straps on his forearm, flicked it at Yakuli. Some hard little coal in his mind that burned through the madness purred in satisfaction as it sank into a meaty thigh.

"Wolf will *not* be thwarted the Ghost unlocks the door to our grave the Prime turns the key to rebirth Wolf opens his arms and brings us home."

"Get him, Jacin-rei." Caidi's grin was feral. "No one can kill the monster like you can."

⚏

Joori "saw" it half a second before it actually happened. Caught somewhere in someone else's dream, time slowing down around him, moving with syrupy lethargy as battles clashed and fires flared, and Wolf stared down from the sky and watched it all. It was like seeing one reality overlay another, witnessing the tiniest snatch of *What Will Be* while *What Is* played out all around him.

He watched himself watching as Malick charged in toward Jacin, obviously intent on helping, and was stopped and held by Tatsu and Sora.

Watched as Jacin flew in at Yakuli, knives aglitter in the wash of fire and moon, and landed a solid slash across Yakuli's chest before being driven back again.

Watched as Yakuli looked down at where his tunic had been sliced and then smiled as the glimmer of mail flashed out. He drove in at Jacin, returned the favor. Except Joori was wearing Jacin's mail. Yakuli's hit drew a splash of blood that turned Joori's stomach and made Jacin stagger.

Watched Jacin go to his knees, and Yakuli raise his sword.

Watched himself tear loose from Samin and rush in toward Jacin, just as Malick used a short burst of magic to knock Sora and Tatsu off him then raced in toward Jacin too.

Watched himself get to Jacin first, try to drag him away and to safety, only to get Yakuli's blade through the throat. Joori actually felt the pain of it as he watched Malick charge in—radiant in his dread; terrifying in his rage—and cut Yakuli down.

Felt the elation, too short-lived, before he heard Jacin's screams of grief then the laughter as Joori watched himself fall into his brother's arms. The sky rumbled and roiled, and Wolf grew, grew, until he filled it, filled Joori's vision. Malick looked up, sad and resigned, but not sorry, *not sorry*. He smiled down at Jacin with a shrug like it didn't matter as fire flared bright as the suns and Wolf swallowed him up.

Watched the battles rage and the not-dead burn. Watched Samin try to protect Morin and save Shig at the same time. Watched as he staggered away when they fell beneath a swarm of hauberks and Yakuli's coat of arms.

Heard the laughter, the screams, coming from Jacin, and knew, *knew* they'd never stop. All that was Jacin was gone, and what was left was laughing itself to death on the trampled grass of Yakuli's compound beside Joori's dead body.

Samin wept as he cut Jacin's throat, stopped the laughter and gave him the only sort of brutal mercy a man like Samin knew. Tatsu and Sora withdrew, mourning one of their own, and Husao looked down into Joori's dead gaze, his eyes hard and his expression angry.

"Let him be what he is. You must be what *you* are."

Not a dream—a vision. A vision from a *Temshiel* seer.

"The future is such a chancy thing." Husao lifted an eyebrow, like he thought Joori might be too stupid to understand what he was saying. "Chancy and all too changeable, if we know what to do with it."

Think very carefully, Fen Joori, because you may be called upon to make the same decision for yourself.

Horrible, sickening irony that Umeia's advice would come to Joori now.

And then he was back in Samin's grip, watching blood splash as Yakuli's sword connected with Jacin's chest. Joori lifted a hand to his own breastbone, felt the mail beneath his palm as Jacin went to his knees.

Watching it all happen again, reliving it—Malick charging toward Jacin, Tatsu and Sora stopping him then being shoved away as Jacin fell and Malick shouted and Joori shoved at Samin's hand on his arm.

He'd tried so hard, right from the beginning. To protect Jacin, to love him by keeping him. And everything he'd done had turned out wrong. He'd stepped in where he shouldn't, and Caidi and Yori were dead because of it. *He must be what he must be* their mother had told him, and then Morin, years later, had echoed almost the exact same words, and Joori hadn't understood them, denied them. He wasn't sure he understood them now, but he'd just been shown a future where Malick had given up his soul for Jacin, and Jacin had given up himself to the madness as he watched.

And all because Joori had stepped in again where he shouldn't.

Don't die. It was the only thing Jacin had asked of him—possibly ever. *I need you to live.*

This time, when he shoved loose from Samin, Joori still ran to Jacin, but he didn't step in, didn't try to drag him away like he'd watched himself do before. He only stood there, kept watching as Malick raised his sword on Yakuli, his eyes on fire, that scent of ozone snapping around him like it had done in the alley, and raising the hairs on the back of Joori's neck. Joori wanted to shout out, warn Malick, tell him what he'd seen. Any warning he might have given turned to ash in his throat when Jacin rolled up to his feet and angled his body in front of Yakuli—

"*Don't!*"

—just as Malick's blade completed its plunge.

Time froze again, but Joori didn't think it was only him this time.

He stared at the sword in Malick's hand, sunken halfway through Jacin's gut. Malick was just *looking* at it, shock-blank as his eyes slowly rose to Jacin's, his expression horrified and betrayed.

"I dec—" Jacin wasn't laughing anymore. His voice was thick, like he was pushing the words out from under water. His awful smile was gone now, his eyes clear and lucid. "I d-decided I c… couldn't live with it."

Malick caught Jacin carefully as he went down to his knees, staring out around him, vague and distant, until his gaze landed on Joori. Unbelievably, horribly, Jacin smiled, that soft, warm one Joori thought he'd never see on his brother's face again, untroubled and sweet and… peaceful.

Joori's paralysis finally broke. He lurched in toward Jacin, helped Malick lower him gently to his back.

Malick was nearly babbling—"You *bastard*, you can't… Fen, I'm sorry, don't do this"—over and over again as he carefully pulled the sword from the wound then covered it with his hand to staunch the bleeding.

Joori shoved Malick away, because he couldn't make himself not do it, and replaced Malick's hand with his own, holding his brother's guts in and feeling his brother's blood spilling out all over his hand. Morin was yelling back there somewhere, hurling curses, presumably at Yakuli, but Yakuli was running away—*running away!*—and Samin was still holding onto Morin, so maybe some of them were for Samin too.

"Wolf will *not* be thwarted"—blood leaked from the corner of Jacin's mouth—"the Ghost unlocks the door to our grave the Prime turns the key to rebirth Wolf opens his arms and brings us home the Prime turns the key the key only say it once—"

"Jacin, stop." Joori couldn't stand another word, not now. "Stop, just... *stop.*"

Except it seemed like Jacin couldn't. "Catalyst and Incendiary light the lamps of the sky cast acid—"

"Incendiary." Malick jerked back, shocked. "*Incendiary.*" He turned, looked at Joori, almost-horror. "*Shit.*" Breathless and stunned. He turned back to Jacin, shook him. "Fen. *Fen!* You can't do this. *Incendiary,* Fen, you don't know what—"

"Told you, did I not?" Xari was there, just looking, eyes riveted to Joori, like she was waiting for him to do something, and when he didn't, she turned her stare on Malick. Her full mouth turned down, her beautiful face twisted into regret. "He would not have thanked you for your oath. 'Tis better that you did not give it."

"I couldn't." It was shocking how helpless Malick sounded, how frantic. "He wouldn't let me, and then it didn't stick anyway." He lifted his head, looking everywhere. "*Tatsu!*"

"So, you tried. Of course you did." Xari shot another look at Joori but quickly looked away again. "I have shown Wolf's key the path, in the end. My lot is cast."

With a half bow of her head, she held out her hands, and amulets dropped from them, one after another, like they were coming from nowhere at all. They piled up impossibly high—dozens and dozens of them—and then she paused, dangling one that perhaps had more significance than the others, because it seemed like she shuddered just from touching it. She tossed it over Malick's head, and Husao was suddenly there to catch it. Husao stared at it and drew in a shaky breath, strangely reverent.

Xari pushed out a long, tired sigh. "My part is done."

Malick didn't look, didn't thank her, didn't try to kill her, didn't even answer. Just turned back to stare down at Jacin.

Jacin smirked back up. "Always a..." He sucked in a breath, arched like it hurt him. "...a fucking... trade."

And Joori abruptly *knew.* Whatever it was he'd seen, it had been Xari's doing—she'd shown Joori a possible future and manipulated him into changing it, used his own hard-learned lessons against him, and turned it all into *this.* Maneuvered him into killing his brother.

All she'd wanted, from the very beginning, was to save Malick, and apparently, the "trade" had been Jacin, just like it had been with Umeia. And Husao had known, had helped her do it.

How could Joori have trusted, even for a second, anything that came from the man who'd pretended to be his brother's confidant and caretaker, when all along he'd been setting Jacin up to be Asai's killer?

Fury welled in Joori's chest, all jumbled together with grief and regret. He choked down a sob that seized his throat, strangled him as he pulled his hand away from Jacin's wound, listened to Malick calling for Tatsu, like there was something he could do.

Subie shoved out another heavy rumble, and like it had done before, even as he watched Xari dissolve into shadow, the rage inside Joori reached for it, twined with the spirit that was bound to his own and curled, purring, through his core. Everything rammed up and out with the scream of rage that hurtled from Joori's chest. The Blood in Joori's veins joined with the fiery blood in the veins of the earth that ran beneath him, pulsing toward the heart that was Subie. The air shimmered, the ground broke and steepled then warped, dirt flying, rocks and pebbles pelting.

Joori didn't see any of it—*you could too easily take yourself out next time*—and Joori didn't care.

What did it matter? Jacin's blood was everywhere, leaking out and away, eyes going cloudy. But his smile was still there as he whispered the Ancestors' nonsense to Malick and reached for Joori with his blood-soaked hand.

Men scattered, and screamed. The earth trembled beneath them all and swallowed indiscriminately.

Joori felt Malick's eyes on him and met the stare, challenging. But Malick was looking at Joori like he was shocked and grieved and thrilled all at once, like he was exalted in the throes of some sublime epiphany.

And still, Joori didn't care.

Grief, fury, betrayal—all of it roiled through Joori and wended into the ground around him. Curled in when his fist did, and thumped when he pounded at the ground as he watched Malick lean down, tenderly lay a kiss to Jacin's brow.

Malick's mouth formed the word "Key" as he squeezed Jacin's hand then… smiled.

How could he fucking *smile*, when Joori was sitting here watching his brother die and the world convulse and collapse around him, echoing the shattering of his heart? But Jacin was smiling, too, as Malick, weeping, reached out a hand covered in Jacin's blood, and clamped on to Joori's.

The shaking didn't stop like it had done the last time Malick had touched him—it grew, trebled and quadrupled. And when Malick gently lowered Jacin to his back in the grass, freed his arm then lifted it, snapped it straight with his palm out, everything in Joori followed the shove.

Samin had a good hold on Morin when the first tremor shuddered beneath his boots—he'd had to, because Morin was too intent on getting between his brother and Yakuli. But when everything rippled and erupted beneath him, Samin lost his grip along with his balance, and Morin slithered loose. He didn't get far; he couldn't. The ground was shaking, caving in around the barracks like it was aimed, uprooting trees. Samin was just thankful he'd dragged Morin out as far from the fight as he'd done. They'd been too open to attack for his liking at the time, but now he was glad there was nothing big enough to collapse on top of them and crush them. That was, if the ground itself didn't do the job.

Rocking and shaking, almost in time to Joori's shouts and screams of despair that echoed so disturbingly those of Fen only hours before down in the baths. Except these screams seemed to have a destructive power all their own. The jink and snap of the earth kept their undulating rhythm, until it all shifted, took on a new tone, and altered from an all-encompassing shudder to something deeper, something driven, something with purpose.

Teeth gritted, Samin crawled over the rocking, broken earth to Morin and gripped the back of his collar. Held on tight. The barracks went down, flattened to sticks and smoldering. Bodies were everywhere. And Fen was down on the ground right in the center of it. Malick was with him—where else would he be?—leaning over Fen, one hand clutching Joori's in a tableau of shared grief and comfort, and the other raised... aimed.

Samin only just had time to understand that the quakes were coming from Joori, that Malick was taking them, directing them, before thunder rolled, lightning streaked, and Subie erupted with a great, spurting *roar*.

Fire vomited from its peak, spewed from its vents. Great chunks of rock broke loose from all sides, hurled up and out, and careened back down its flanks. Lava flowed, beautiful in its lethal indifference to everything in its path.

Samin idly wondered if the rivers of scorching slag would reach the city, and decided it could only be an improvement.

Gouts of liquid fire gushed from the mountain. Wolf's grinning face watched it all, long arms of flame crawling up the sky, as though reaching for the moons themselves. Clouds of thick smoke and pulverized debris flashed and glittered as ropes of lightning stretched to flitter over the falling peak.

The sound was deafening, all-consuming, as Subie pummeled itself. The ground continued to rock and sway, and Samin continued to keep his grip on Morin. Joori's face went from grief-stricken to awed to viciously exultant as one hand gripped Malick's, and the other gripped Fen's.

Malick's face stayed the same, focused, but stone-hard and blank as he aimed everything in himself and Joori at the mountain like it had, all by itself, ruined everything that was good in his life. Samin peered down at Fen's still shape, looking smaller than it should, and wondered if it had.

Samin's ears were ringing, his whole body numb but for the deep-set thumping that rattled his ribs and his teeth and jarred all up and down his backbone. And still, Subie kept snarling and crumbling and shaking, spewing out ash and smoke and fire, blotting out the moons as it collapsed on itself. Gone in only a few timeless minutes, from a mountain that hunched over Ada and what used to be Jejin like a stern sentinel, to a bad-tempered smoking crater the size of the bay itself.

And then it all stopped, just like that, all at once. All that was left were the aftershocks, tiny tremors that slithered through the ground then shook themselves out.

Samin couldn't hear a thing, just a dull ringing behind his teeth, but he pulled himself up to his feet then dragged Morin up after him. He surveyed the chaos.

Everyone had gone flat to the ground. Samin couldn't distinguish the live bodies from the dead ones, so he didn't try. Just searched for Shig's distinctive multicolored head, relieved when he saw her getting to her feet farther down the hill, shaking her head as if to clear it, and then turning her glance his way. Samin tried to ask her if she was all right, but he didn't get an answer, so he waved. Shig waved back as she started up the hill.

Samin let Morin do what he'd been wanting to do since he'd started that fire in the barracks—drag Samin toward Fen and Joori.

They picked their way over broken earth and crevices wide enough that Samin had to toss Morin over them first then jump after. Men in Yakuli's livery stirred, peering up cautiously from their flattened positions on the ground like gophers poking their heads from their holes. They seemed willing to ignore Samin and Morin as they stepped their way over and around them, so Samin returned the favor.

None of Yakuli's creatures stirred, though. Samin wasn't quite sure what to make of that. He hoped it meant Yakuli was dead, but he'd learned over the years that good luck was for other people, so he didn't count on it.

Husao was standing over Malick, two others Samin didn't know just behind him. They didn't look like they belonged to Yakuli, and the woman was bloody gorgeous with her dark skin and dark eyes, so Samin was willing to hold off on killing them until he found out if he should.

Anyway, he was bone-fucking-weary, and the numb, shaky vibrations still working under his skin told him he was going to be sore as hell tomorrow. Cautiously, he scanned around for Xari, but he saw neither her nor Yakuli, and counted it as a good thing.

"Is he dead?" Morin's voice was overloud to be heard over the probable ringing in his ears, but his tone was dull, detached. Like a boy who'd known all along he was meant to lose something, and was determined to accept it like a man when he finally did.

Poor lad; just when he'd allowed his surly veneer to retreat behind the true one.

Another aftershock fluttered beneath their feet, and more fountains of fire belched up from Subie's ruin.

Shig fetched up beside Samin, looking unhurt but strangely confused, her expression flat and unreadable. Samin wondered if Morin knew he was clinging to Samin's arm hard enough to leave marks, but nothing in the world would move him to ask it out loud.

"He is not dead," Husao answered, when neither Joori nor Malick turned to do it.

"The Ghost will not..." Fen's voice was no more than a shaky whisper, his eyes half-shut and dull. He gusted a snort that loosed a tiny spray of blood from his mouth, then smiled, all bleary and wistful. "Caidi said..."

Samin didn't find out what Caidi said, because Fen closed his eyes and passed out.

"Tatsu." Malick's tone might as well have been a predator's growl. "Don't fucking argue with me. I want—"

"I will not." The man Malick called Tatsu stood unbending, gaze hard. "I *cannot* touch the Untouchable."

Malick held out his bloody hand, eyes blazing, the muscles in his jaw ticing and twitching. "Then give me—"

"*No.*" Tatsu took a step back, out of Malick's immediate reach. "You know what you ask, Kamen, and you know what it would mean to a *Temshiel* not of Wolf. Threaten all you like, but I will not—"

"You will. You can." Shig's voice was soft, and her faint flutter of a laugh sad, maybe a little lost. She leaned in closer to Samin, like she was afraid she might fall down. "They're gone." She looked at Malick, shaking her colorful head like even she didn't understand what she was saying. "It's all... it's gone quiet."

Malick stared, piercing at first, then his gaze twisted with sympathy Samin didn't understood.

"It worked, then." Malick huffed a dazed laugh. "It *worked.*"

He was an abrupt burst of movement, all frantic energy, as he snatched up one of Fen's knives from the ground—one of the ones he'd bought the day he and Samin had gone to the Stallion—then made sure

Joori was watching. The silence was complete as Malick took Fen's braid in his hand, slid his fingers along it, deliberate and tender, then gripped it in his fist and sliced it off just above Fen's shoulder. A collective gasp went up from all around, but Malick ignored it, gave Joori a grim smile, then turned back to Tatsu.

"The Ancestors have gone home. He's not Untouchable anymore." Malick's eyes hardened, his mouth went tight, and he jerked his head down toward Fen. "Now *fix* him!"

11

"You have to wake up now." Caidi's whisper was all warm, sweet breath in Jacin's ear.

But he was falling and it felt like flying. It was silent and it felt like rapture. Not a sound, not even *thwip-thwip-thwip.*

Jacin didn't want to wake up.

So he didn't.

⋀

The sirens cranked, the wail reaching even as far outside the city as Lord Yakuli's estate. It took several hours for the Kiwa Shuua to hit, the lethal waves that crawled as high as the sky and rolled over the coast with deadly force. And if it wreaked even more havoc on a city already in near-chaos, at least it went a little way toward putting out some of the fires that had sprung up from falling ash.

The little grover's hut on the coast was pounded into driftwood and swept away as though it had never been.

The waves extended their destructive reach through Ada's Iron District, stretched their tendrils all through the Industrial Quarter, and inched in toward the Judicial District, edging up the bottom steps of the Statehouse itself before they finally receded, taking ships anchored in the harbor out to sea with them. It would be weeks before a final count could be tallied in the wake of Subie's decisive fit of supreme wrath. Days of night before the ash and smoke cleared enough to allow the suns to burn through.

Retribution from the gods—the assumption ran rampant. Mortals tended toward divine explanations when there wasn't another. In this case, they weren't entirely wrong, though the distinction would remain indistinct to most for a while yet.

Judges Canti and Girosui were not most. They'd arrived at Yakuli's gates with a sizable company of the Doujou in time for the first tremors, and witnessed the anarchy and resultant destruction. They followed in the aftermath with grave faces as the *Temshiel* Husao guided them through the surviving barracks and explained to them what they'd already suspected but could never prove. Neither of the men was able to keep his composure entirely. Girosui's cheeks were pale and wet when he emerged from the last barracks and called an order for the search for and arrest of Yakuli and his men, though all but those who'd been killed or injured too gravely to escape had already scattered.

"I have promised the Untouchable that Yakuli would twitch at the end of his blade," the *Temshiel* told the judges, and though neither man could vouchsafe the promise, they both left pondering the possible advantages of an Untouchable testifying before the Courts, exposing the corruption of their fellows in public testimony. Justice's blade, so to speak. If the Untouchable survived, and if he remained as sane as the *Temshiel* claimed him…

The judges left Yakuli's estate already in deep discussion, planning their approach and debating details, with no doubt between them that what they did next would change worlds. The *Temshiel* Sora and the maijin Xari accompanied them. It would not do for the last two uncorrupted Court officials to fall to the treachery of the corrupt, just as the wheels of true justice began to turn. The fruition of the years-long conspiracy of Canti and Girosui to break the back of the Court was within their reach, and they were determined to see Ada once more a state in which they could take pride. With no magic to fear, the Adan could no longer justify the imprisonment of the Jin, and once the Court was exposed for the den of snakes Canti and Girosui had known it to be for too many years, perhaps they could begin the process of restoring honor and morality to Ada.

The end, they decided as they mobilized the Doujou and began the search for Yakuli, should begin in the Courts, from which the dishonor had taken seed and its rotted, twisted roots had spread.

The end should begin with the Untouchable.

⻢

"It's time to open your eyes now, Jacin."

Caidi's voice was soft, cajoling. Almost wheedling.

It made him smile.

The scent of cherry blossoms was thick, comforting. Jacin felt them pattering on his skin, settling feather-light on his closed eyelids.

"C'mon, Jacin, *pleeeeeeeease?*"

If she'd been anyone else, it would've been annoying, the whiny tone grating. But she was Caidi, so it was neither.

Jacin flickered open his eyes, blinked and blinked as the layer of cherry blossom petals scattered and flittered off his lashes. He was blanketed in them, thick as a fresh fall of snow, warm and soft. He breathed in, sucking their light scent down deep into his lungs.

Caidi held out her hand, caught a palmful, then blew them gently away. Her smile was as sweet and dear as the scent of the petals when she turned to Jacin.

"Transience."

It was so *easy* for Jacin to smile back. "Death."

"Oh, Jacin." Hazel eyes sparked mischief. "You're so morbid."

Long, gold curls whorled around Caidi's open, smiling face as she leaned over Jacin, almost nose to nose. She dropped a light kiss to his brow, and a swarm of moths flurried from the sea of petals, rising up through the branches of the cherry trees. Jacin watched them, squinting against the soft sunlight quivering through leaf and blossom, until he lost them in the patches of sky he could see through the thick puffs of the treetops.

He hadn't heard a single, frantic beat of wings.

"It's so quiet here."

The fluted peal of Caidi's laughter was like bells. She sat back, hair and cloak dusted with petals.

"It has nothing to do with *here*. Wolf called the Ancestors home, and Joori and Malick set them free. You don't have to listen to them anymore." Caidi stroked Jacin's cheek, her small fingers just as soft as the petals against his skin. "You did well, Jacin. Wolf is pleased. You've earned his favor. Even salvation will be in your grasp, if you choose to reach for it." She pulled her hand way, smile tilting down to rue. "But not yet. You can't stay here."

"No?" There was no alarm; only curiosity. "Where, then?"

Caidi pursed her bow lips. "You have to go back."

Now there was alarm.

Jacin sat up, petals scattering everywhere. "But you said—"

"The Ghost will not survive the night." Caidi shrugged guiltily, even blushed a little. "The Ghost is gone. Jacin-rei is gone. There is only Fen Jacin now."

It wasn't silent anymore. Jacin's head was pounding with the thumping drumbeat of his own heart.

"I don't want it."

Caidi's eyes glistened. Her smile trembled. She launched herself at Jacin, wrapping her small arms around his neck.

Jacin shut his eyes tight, breathed her in.

"You can't stay." Caidi snugged in closer. "You have to open your eyes now."

Jacin held Caidi in a grip that was likely strangling the breath out of her, but he couldn't help it.

"I can't—"

"*Yes.*" Caidi's tone was gentle but firm. "You can. When have you ever failed at anything?" Brutal for its sweetness. She turned her face into Jacin's neck. "No laws, Jacin. The one whose face hovers over yours when you wake from your death-sleep—that will be the one."

"I don't want—"

"We're all made for sacrifice."

With a sigh and a soft sniffle, Caidi laid a warm kiss to Jacin's cheek, then pulled back. Jacin resisted, clung, but she wrested away just enough that she could lay her brow to his.

"Since when have any of us had a choice?" Caidi gripped Jacin's shoulder, shook, and her voice deepened, a harsh note of command. "You have to wake up now."

"*No.*"

Weak protest, but it did no good. Already, the light was thickening, going smoky, and it was getting harder and harder to catch the sweetness of the cherry blossoms.

Caidi pulled away entirely, tears on her full cheeks, and she leaned in, kissed away Jacin's. When she drew back from him again, Jacin could see the shapes of the trees through her.

His throat clenched. His chest hurt.

"I'm tired." He couldn't even find shame that his tone was edged in desperation. "I can't... I want..." It lost itself before he finished, because when had it ever mattered what he wanted? He tightened his jaw to make it stop quivering. "Where is Mother?"

Mother had always loved him, even though she wasn't supposed to. Had touched her Untouchable son. Dried his tears. Because he was Wolf's but he was her own, and she'd held to him even through her husband's condemnation, her own madness. Mother would let him stay. He'd weep and let her wipe away his shame, and she'd let him stay.

"Mother isn't here." Caidi's voice was growing fainter as she faded. "She awaits the fire."

It made the tears come harder, the anger rise.

"So do you!"

"But I have to go now too. You only needed me for a little while. You don't need me anymore."

"Yes I do!" Jacin tried to snatch at her, but it was like trying to catch water. "Caidi, don't, *please*—"

"The Ghost is gone. Back to Zero. You have to start again, Jacin."

He didn't want to start again. He wanted an *end.*

"I'm so tired, Caidi. I'm *so tired.*" Weeping. Sniveling like a child. He didn't know what to say, how to make her stay, how to make her let *him* stay, except, "*Please.* Don't go."

But Caidi only smiled at him, that bright Caidi-grin, as she faded to almost nothing, shook him again and snapped, "Damn it, Fen, *wake* the fuck *up!*"

Jacin's eyes flew open, squinting against sunlight that wasn't there, lashes thick and clumped with tears. Pain stitched itself to the corners of his awareness, but it wasn't sharp and focused like a knifepoint; it was dull and dissipated, a low ache that throbbed beneath his skin, wound into muscle and sinew, just enough to let him know it was there. The ceiling was familiar, but not quite, rough beams and whorls of plaster he almost recognized, but wouldn't, because he didn't want to. He breathed in, trying to catch the scent of cherry blossoms, but all he smelled was sage and pine.

His vision was smudgy. Reluctant, he blinked at the blur, focused on smoky-brown hair and a handsome face hovering just above him, tea-colored eyes watching, narrowed in worry.

"About fucking time." Malick gave Jacin a grin that held not even the slightest hint of snark or a gleam of disingenuous pretense. Relieved. *Glad.*

That will be the one, Caidi whispered.

No. It was supposed to be Joori, maybe Morin, or… anyone else.

Instead it was Malick. It was *always* Malick—dragging Jacin back, making him stay, telling him he was things he knew he wasn't, almost making him believe them, when he *knew* it would only rip him up later.

"Oh." Jacin shut his eyes and tried not to start bawling again. "It's you."

☖

The days passed in clear spots between long periods of fugue. There was no great ball of emotion in the middle of his chest threatening to shatter. There was silence, deafening, and there were his brothers, hovering close, almost clinging, and there was a pyre that was almost too big for the shrine's altar, but it was somehow fitting that they all burned together.

It was Morin who'd found their mother, and it was Morin who'd ended her torture. Jacin thought the torture had only just begun for Morin.

He took their word for it that the tight-wound mass of linen held his mother's body, and that Joori had painted the prayers on her brow and Caidi's before they'd been lovingly and securely wrapped for the fire. He didn't demand they be unwrapped so he could see them one last time, so he could see for himself that the prayers were flawless with no errors to prevent their acceptance and eventual rebirth. He didn't want to have to see his mother the way Morin and Joori had seen her, didn't want to see her naked scalp, the ragged smile-that-wasn't-a-smile torn into her smooth throat.

He only watched the blaze catch and climb, tried not to gag on the thick haze of incense. Looked for Caidi's face through the flames but didn't see it. Listened for her voice telling him goodbye, that he'd see her again, but he didn't hear it. He wondered if it would be unseemly for him to stretch his hands out over the fire to warm them—he was cold, all the time, *freezing*—but he didn't know, so he didn't chance it.

It took him a week to notice that all his knives were missing. He didn't care enough to wonder where they were.

A very near thing, the gut wound, Joori had told him. Another *Temshiel* had tried to heal him, but it hadn't worked until Malick shoved his magic into the mix and *made* it work. Apparently, Jacin was still mostly immune to magic. Except for Malick's.

He wondered if he hated Malick for that.

Scabbed over and just raw enough that Jacin could poke and pick at it now and then if he wanted to feel something. Except Malick always seemed to show up, fussing and cursing and redressing just when Jacin got a good flow going. Like he could smell the blood or something. Jacin stopped picking at it.

The Girou went on. Malick told Jacin that Umeia would have wanted it to, like Jacin might care, told him he'd signed it over to Lex, and since Jacin had no idea who Lex was, he didn't answer. He never answered, but that didn't stop Malick from talking. Because Malick never let up.

Shig slept with Samin now, because she couldn't sleep alone, and Morin and Joori couldn't stay in the room where Caidi's first real bed sat with its pretty linens, so they shared Jacin's. Malick didn't exactly tell Jacin to share his bed with him, but it was where Jacin had woken up that first day, and it was where he always ended up shuffling back to when he was forced from its seclusion. Sometimes Malick would make him move to the couch in his little sitting room, but most of the time, he just let Jacin stare at the wall from his little cave of blankets and bedding, and ignore time.

Sometimes Jacin heard Beishin, heckling him, telling him it hadn't been the Ancestors who'd made him insane. Sometimes he saw his father, looking at him with disdain and disgust.

But then there would be Joori, holding on, weeping into Jacin's shoulder, maybe, or just sitting quietly beside him, nudging when Jacin forgot halfway through a bowl of rice that he was supposed to be eating. Or Morin, snarking about idleness as Jacin lay on Malick's great big bed, burrowed in and barricaded, though it didn't keep them out. Sometimes Morin read aloud from books Samin found for him, pretending he was just doing it because he felt like it and not because he was trying to get something from Jacin that Jacin suspected he couldn't give. He never remembered the stories.

"You would've been proud of him," Samin had told Jacin, his gruff voice a weird anchor in the silence that had felt somewhat comfortable between them before it was broken, and now in hindsight seemed tenuous, like it had never felt with Samin. "He almost couldn't see for the tears, but I told him he wouldn't be a man if he hadn't wept, and that seemed to make him feel better." A long, timeless pause before Samin went on, "His hand was steady. He gave her a clean end. Just like you showed him."

Jacin thought Samin made a better father for Morin than their own had done. He thought perhaps he should tell Samin this, but he lost time, and when he found it again, it had gone dark and Samin was gone.

Shig, it seemed, was always curled up in Malick's big, ugly chair whenever Malick would drag Jacin from the warm cocoon of the wide, goose-down mattress and fine, heavy linens and dump him on the couch for a while. Jacin didn't try to decide if it annoyed him. Anyway, he was forever cold anymore, and the fire was out in the sitting room.

He still had a limp, some of his wounds bone-deep, the mangled muscle of his calf beyond full healing, but the short, enforced walks didn't pain him as much as he'd pretend if Malick tried to make him leave the room for a trip any farther than the baths. Somehow, though he always started out on the couch alone, with Shig in the chair across from him, Jacin usually managed to drift from his haze after a while to notice that she'd moved to the couch to curl up against him like a cat on a hearthstone

"Malick wants to take us to Tambalon after Yakuli's trial." Shig puffed a light, humorless snort, and shrugged. "I wonder if I get seasick?"

The streaks of green and blue and red weren't as vibrant a contrast to Shig's blonde hair as they'd been, like all her losses had dulled her on the outside as well as on the inside. She missed her sister. She probably missed Umeia. She missed her spirits.

Jacin almost understood it. It was hard to get used to all the empty space, all the silence, when you were so accustomed to shoving your thoughts through the noise. Like trying to batter through a stone wall, and then the wall crumbles, and you go careening off the cliff on the other side of it. And you can't even pretend you're flying.

"How d'you go on?" Shig asked him, her voice weirdly solid without its edge of singsong. "What do you hide behind, now that the braid can't hide you anymore?"

Jacin had thought maybe he'd like her more without all her spirits telling her how to sucker-punch him. He didn't. With the exception of a reflexive touch to the ragged ends of his now shoulder-length hair, he didn't bother to answer her.

"You have to start again now too." Shig wrapped herself around Jacin's arm like ivy. "You wanted an end, and instead you got a beginning. Poor Fen."

He almost wanted to shove her away, tell her to fuck off, but he couldn't make himself muster the will. And still, he didn't bother to answer her.

He didn't bother to answer anyone. Not even his father. Not even Beishin. He would have answered Caidi, maybe, but she never came.

Instead, always, right beside him—holding him up, pushing him forward, telling him he wasn't nothing, poking him, prodding him, annoying him enough he was sometimes moved to growl a warning—it was Malick, tarnished bronze eyes watching, waiting for something. Except Jacin didn't know what it was, and he couldn't make himself care. But he let Malick do it, let Malick take him to bed at night and curl around him, hold him, warm him, and Jacin slept and felt improbably safe and distantly... something.

The statehouse loomed up, a penumbra of shadow slinking down the marble steps and onto the slate path that led from the street. Jacin toed the line of sunshine that edged the shadow, peered up, and squinted, looking for the blue hulking haze of distant Subie that wasn't there anymore. Smoke still tendriled from its sunken caldera, a thin, gray line linking heaven to earth, and he fancied he could see the ghost of Wolf hovering above it, grinning, so he cut his gaze downward.

It still smelled of seaweed and rotten fish. The floods had reached right to these very steps; he could still see the mudline on the riser of the second. He imagined there was probably a great deal of detritus lingering as a result of the destruction of the Kiwa Shuua, and he also imagined they must have passed at least some of it on the way here. He hadn't looked.

"Just ignore them." Malick's arm was heavy across Jacin's shoulders as he frowned at the gathered onlookers, mouth set grim. "There'll be a crowd in the courtroom, too, but they'll at least have to be quiet in there."

Jacin hadn't noticed the din. He was good at ignoring noise. He noticed the stares, though, because they were different than the brief glances, the shocks of recognition, then the quick aversion of gazes. These gazes drilled into him, *looked* at him—curiosity, hostility, sympathy, expectation. No one got too close, though, as if an invisible bubble kept them back. Jacin vaguely wondered if Malick was doing it, but it didn't really matter.

Joori frowned at Malick. "What do I do about the carriage?"

Jacin peered back over his shoulder, saw Asai's expensive coach hitched to Asai's expensive horse, Morin with a hand on its rein, staring about, wide-eyed. Samin—as he always seemed to be these days—was standing just beside Morin, eyes sharp on the crowd, watching for threat.

Jacin really should thank him some time.

The weight of Malick's arm shifted on Jacin's shoulders. Thin stripes of chill bloomed where his warmth had rested just a second ago. Jacin shivered.

"Just hand it over to him." Malick jerked his chin at a thin boy—a page, perhaps—clomping down the steps of the Statehouse, preceding a stout man with a somber smile.

The man's bald head caught a stray glint of sun-through-shadow as he descended and stepped up in front of them. The toes of the man's flat, leather shoes, like the toes of Jacin's scuffed boots, edged along the band of light and shadow on the walk.

"Fen, this is Judge Canti." Malick paused while the man dipped his head respectfully, seemingly not offended when Jacin only stared. "He'll be leading the questioning."

"Your Husao has told me much about you, Fen-seyh." The judge met Jacin's flat stare with apparent interest, his pale blue eyes bright with intelligence and a hint of craft. "I trust you're prepared for what is to take place today?"

The upward slant of the tone made it into a question. Canti's eyes shifted from Jacin to Malick, directing the query at him.

Malick's hand tightened on Jacin's shoulder. "Fen will—"

"Jacin will do what he can." Joori slid a dark, warning look at Malick, but he didn't snarl or growl, like he might've done before. He looked at Jacin, his mouth dragging slightly upward in a grim smile. "He's had a… a bad time." He was either talking to Malick or Canti, but he was still looking at Jacin. "We never promised anything." He stared, as though waiting for something; when Jacin didn't give it to him, couldn't, Joori turned to the judge. "We don't know what to expect today. But Jacin… well, he's Jacin. He comes through. It's what he does."

Jacin didn't know if he was inspired or horrified.

He knew what today was about in a vague, esoteric sort of way. Knew what they were expecting of him, what was at stake. He just didn't know if he could do it.

"It is fitting," Judge Canti said with a somber smile, "that great change should come through Wolf's Catalyst."

Jacin wanted to vomit.

He'd been a catalyst. Nothing more. The stumbling, fumbling center around which great things had occurred. He hadn't saved the Jin. He hadn't saved his mother. He hadn't saved anyone.

It had been bad enough knowing Asai had always meant for him to fail. What was Jacin supposed to do with the knowledge that his god had intended the same?

Meant to fail. Made for it.

Perfection at last.

They'd quarreled about today, Joori and Malick. Malick had contended that Jacin needed to be pushed; Joori had countered that Jacin couldn't take being pushed any more.

Jacin had merely watched and listened, and wondered if Joori realized they were bickering right in front of him, over him, around him, like Joori used to argue with their father about their mother. It was Jacin's own fault, he supposed. If he could manage to argue for himself, they wouldn't have to do it for him. Except that would require Jacin to make a decision first. The last time he'd done that, his whole world had ended.

He let everything sink into the background—whatever Judge Canti was saying to Malick and Joori, and whatever they were saying back, the steady murmur of the crowd as they watched—and let Malick hold onto his arm as he hobbled up the steps in Canti's wake. He didn't even curl his lip, just let Malick give him a little push as they stepped into the courtroom, and Canti gestured for Jacin to follow him. Canti ushered him to a small, raised platform edged with a polished walnut railing, and Jacin let his mind drift inward, let all the expectant gazes recede to irrelevance.

Found Yakuli's hate-filled glare, and let himself smile, just a little.

He shut his eyes. Let himself remember.

Dark eyes and the scent of jasmine. A deep, smooth voice in the dark of night demanding magic from a maijin. The squelching *crunch* of a small body caroming into the cobbles. Soft, hazel eyes, and a slender hand *touching* him when touching was forbidden.

And when Canti raised his voice, asked the Untouchable to speak… Jacin let his mouth open.

Let himself tell them everything.

᛭

The breeze was cool and crisp for all it was briny. It ruffled at his fringe, obscuring his vision then blowing back and clearing it again.

He hadn't got used to the hair yet. His head still felt too light. He couldn't keep it out of his face, so he'd let Joori pull it back into a stumpy tail at the back of his neck this morning. Joori had grinned like Jacin had just asked him if he wouldn't mind taking a bag of gold off his hands.

The voyage to Tambalon would take three weeks, if the weather was good, and the captain had assured Malick it would be. A thick, swart man, pierced and tattooed and unexpectedly jolly, the captain had seemed to take great pleasure in accepting their papers when they'd boarded. It was the first time ever, he'd said, he'd taken a Jin onto his ship without the risk of the gallows, and if there was anything they needed in the coming weeks, they'd only to ask him.

Jacin didn't need anything. Jacin had spent the first week exactly as he planned to spend the rest of them—planted in a spindly deck chair, watching the waves, smelling the sea, feeling the wind on his skin, and the vague sting of salt.

The crew was small, and went about their business with comforting ease, their chatter gruff and their looks at Jacin cursory and pleasant enough. A mix of Heldes and Thecians, their mingled accents were strangely reassuring in their distant snark and banter, a soothing background hum beneath the sound of the sea and the frustrating buzz of incomprehensible thoughts. No one stared, and no one sneered. They did what needed to be done and left Jacin to his solitude, such as it was.

Malick was forever hovering, poking, prodding, trying to get conversation that Jacin wasn't equipped to give. Morin and Joori were almost as bad. Samin more or less respected Jacin's wish for silence, but Shig didn't. Sometimes Jacin thought she annoyed him more than Malick did.

It wasn't until just two days ago, when he'd found himself alone on the deck and realized it was for the first time—and that only for perhaps five minutes or so before Joori swung up on deck, a bit wild-eyed then too obviously relieved when he spotted Jacin—that it dawned on him why he was so rarely free of company. He'd almost snorted. Almost. The call of the depths might have been enticing, if he could bring himself to bother caring. For the first time, he connected it with the missing knives. He couldn't decide if he was offended or amused.

The water was pleasantly calm today, the breeze light, so the crew had finished whatever it was they did before Jacin had even got up here this morning. He'd only seen one or two a few times since, adjusting and checking sails and doing incomprehensible things with ropes. Jacin ignored them, and they never seemed to mind.

Shig sat in one of the chairs, two down from Jacin's. She looked tired and drawn, so Jacin pretended not to see her. He wasn't the only one who'd had a shitty time of it, and he probably had it a little better than she did right now. He didn't miss his voices, and he had another on whom to lean, even if he told himself most of the time he'd rather not. Not that it mattered—Malick didn't let up. And he apparently owned more patience than Jacin would have suspected.

Odd. Unfathomable, really. Jacin was extraneous now. He'd done what he'd promised, fulfilled his end, and so had Malick. They were square.

So why was Malick still here?

"Are you that determined to be a ghost?" Shig had asked, just last night, as she'd sat in that same spot and held a smoke out, eyeing Jacin narrowly as he took it and sucked in a long drag.

It had been windy last night, more than usual, and he hadn't been able to see the stream of smoke as he'd blown it back out. But he'd tasted the sharp cherry tang on his tongue, felt the low burn in his lungs.

"You don't have to drive yourself with the pain anymore." Shig's voice was soft, just loud enough to hear above the wind and waves. She flicked the butt of her own smoke over the rail. "And it's still all right to snatch the things that take this new pain away. They'd want you to, don't you think?" She leaned back in her chair, turned her head, and looked at Jacin straight, eyes sharp and lucid. "Alone is the only thing that'll truly break you, Fen. I know love's not a safe thing for you, but he loves you.

He risked his soul for you because he loves you, and you couldn't let him do it, because…" She paused, lifted her eyebrows. "Why d'you think that is?"

She'd asked it like she didn't think she already knew the answer. And Jacin didn't think she'd like it if he gave her the real one.

He hadn't wanted to be responsible for the damnation of one more soul. That was all it had been. He'd thought the gods might let him rest if his last act was one of repentance and sacrifice.

And then Malick had snatched it away from him.

Shig snorted, like Jacin had said it all aloud. "You're the only one who's ever seen living as a failure, Fen. Maybe you didn't do all the saving, but none would have been saved without you." She frowned. "You saved their souls, Catalyst, including his. What more did you want?"

Jacin had merely stared, for quite a long time. Shig had stared back with a small, weary smile. She wouldn't look away, so Jacin did. He'd got up, taken one last drag from the smoke, then pitched it over the side and headed below deck.

"You're just a living ghost, Fen," Shig called after him. "Did he risk it all for nothing?"

Jacin found the energy to flip her off over his shoulder.

Malick hadn't been in the tiny cabin. Hadn't been there to chatter at Jacin and drown out Shig's voice with snarky teasing, or news of Ada and the release of the Jin, or just his presence. Somehow, the emptiness of the cabin stung.

The bunks were hard and small enough that Jacin wondered if mats wouldn't have been better. But he hadn't complained that first night after they'd boarded and Malick squeezed into Jacin's with him, crammed him up against the curve of the hull. He'd got used to Malick's shape against him as he slept, had got used to the particular level of heat he generated. Always with Jacin's silent permission, his acceptance.

Malick never touched him, except to hold him, talk to him softly until he drifted into sleep, and that queer feeling of safety kept hovering at Jacin's edges. It bothered him, because he'd never really thought safety was a thing he craved.

It didn't seem fair that he had it. Others who'd actually deserved it were gone. All the people he'd loved and couldn't save, and he'd ended up surviving because—

He shut his eyes.

He wasn't supposed to love you, was he, Jacin-rei?

No.

No one was.

It was supposed to have been him. All the sly digs, all the knowing remarks, all the shrewd questions—*What about after, Fen? What comes next, Jacin?*—and Jacin never had an answer, because he didn't think he'd need one. He'd thought it would all be over. He'd never have to deal with hurt or shock or pain or questionable sanity ever again. And he didn't know what to do with himself, now that even that had been denied him.

Perhaps Shig was right: perhaps Jacin really was a living ghost. Because whatever this was he was doing, it couldn't possibly be living. Then again, how would he really know? He'd never had an actual life before.

He was supposed to use you and leave you, and instead he handed you his heart, offered you his soul, and now you have to figure out what to do with it.

What *was* he supposed to do with it? What did he know about *any* of this? He was trapped in reality, snared in a life he didn't know how to live, and it was fucking *cold*. A shiver rippled through him, as if he'd called it, and he admitted the wish for a wide stripe of heat at his back, warm whispers at the crown of his head.

Because love isn't a safe thing for you, is it... Ghost?

"Not a Ghost." He whispered it. Tried it out. And waited.

Nothing. Still. Nothing but the chill and... that was it.

He'd spent a lot of time lately feeling numb and cold, or just nothing at all. There were days at a stretch that passed him by and he didn't even notice. He liked Malick's warmth. It had taken a while for it to leak through the cold, the numb nothing, but it was one of the few things Jacin knew now, and he liked it. It placated... something. Something down deep.

He was biding in some odd limbo, a place where he could see life, touch it, but he couldn't feel it. Malick made him feel. *Made* him.

Forced him to acknowledge that he was sick of the cold. Sick of himself.

A living ghost.

Malick's relentless presence was a persistent, bizarre comfort, and Jacin had allowed it to prod him into staying *here* when he really didn't want to. Last night, Shig's voice haunting him, the taste of cherry smoke burning his tongue, he'd allowed it to prod him into turning to Malick when he'd finally entered the cabin quietly, climbed in, and wrapped himself around Jacin. Allowed it to guide his hands. Watched Malick's expressions change as Jacin allowed his fingers to roam and explore. Allowed himself to *feel* every detail beneath his fingertips—time the pulse, map the dips between muscles, trace bone and sinew, stalk the thump of blood through vein—until Malick met his eyes, asking.

Jacin answered. Slowly and with all his attention.

No bargains this time, nothing to trade but mutual want.

Malick had made it all go away for him before. Maybe he could make it come back.

Sayitsayitsayit—

"D'you love him?" Joori had asked Jacin only a few days ago, leaning against the railing as Jacin sat, otherwise alone on the deck, staring out to where the bruised line of the horizon smudged from sea to sky. No anger that Jacin could detect. No derision. Only curiosity, with perhaps a touch of worry.

Jacin had snorted, pushed his hair out of his eyes. He hadn't answered, but he figured Joori knew what he meant, even if he wasn't sure himself.

He thought he might be getting used to Malick, but that might have just been because he was *there*, wouldn't let up, and Malick had at least believed it when he'd told Jacin he loved him, or he'd seemed to. And if it was all still part of the trade, well. Jacin imagined he'd find out what his end of this new bargain was eventually.

"Don't lie to me," Jacin had told Malick last night, afterward, when they were both still flushed and sweaty, skin sticking to skin, and the smell of sex down deep in their pores. "Don't manipulate me. Don't manipulate them."

A warning of sorts, and Malick seemed to get it, even if the threat was minimal. He was *Temshiel*, after all; what could Jacin *really* do to him besides walk away? But Malick hadn't smiled or smirked, or even rolled his eyes. He'd only nodded, his expression this close to grave, and sincere, as far as Jacin could tell.

"I won't."

"You really want this?" Jacin had to ask it, had to know.

You really want me? Why? What's to want?

There was no hesitation from Malick, no apparent equivocation. Only a simple, and apparently sincere "Yes. I do."

Touch the Untouchable. Love the unlovable.

In that moment, peering into tarnished bronze, looking for prevarication and finding only somber confession, Jacin thought maybe he could love Malick, if Jacin were a different person.

"Well." Jacin's answer had come slow, confused, not quite believing. "All right, I guess."

For as long as it lasted, at least. Until Malick one day looked into Jacin's eyes and realized there was nothing there.

Malick had merely snorted and buried his face in Jacin's hair.

It might be possible for Jacin to be an actual person one day, to love someone. Someday. Maybe. When love stopped feeling like such a terrifying risk. Right now, "love" was, quite simply, beyond him. At least until he figured out what real life was supposed to be. And what he was supposed to do with it.

He didn't have Beishin to tell him anymore. No more braid or traditions to label him, no more vengeance to define him, no more fear to cage him, no more knives to show him the hard reflection of a face he didn't know mirrored back at him in their polished blades. He was going to have to define himself, because for all that Malick wouldn't let up, wouldn't let Jacin retreat, he still never forced anything on Jacin but the present. He wouldn't tell Jacin what to be, even if Jacin asked him to.

Jacin might be able to love that. Eventually. Maybe.

Maybe that was what "starting again" meant.

"Bloody Fens." Malick came stomping up from the direction of the bow, and fetched up at Jacin's shoulder.

A second later, Joori flopped into the chair at Jacin's right, and Morin into the one at his left. Jacin hadn't heard them coming, but Morin and Joori at least were looking awfully smug and pleased with themselves.

"Throw the whole lot of you overboard, that's what I'm going to do." Malick pointed an accusing finger at Morin. "*Then* we'll see how bloody clever you are. Try those smartass remarks when you're choking down sea water. *Ha!*"

Morin unfurled over the chair like a particularly satisfied cat, gangly limbs longer than Jacin had noticed before. Morin's gold hair flopped into his face as the salt-wind licked at it. He slid a sly grin at Joori.

"Try it." He shot a wicked flick of his glance at Malick over Jacin's shoulder. "Samin will have your guts." He pointed his grin at Jacin then oozed back into the chair, all relaxed confidence and easy snark. "Samin likes me."

"Are you threatening my lads, Mal?"

Even without the comment, Jacin wouldn't have needed to turn to know Samin was trailing the others; his heavy tread was unmistakable, even on the deck of the small ship.

Casually, Malick leaned against Jacin's chair, his hands on the back of it, fingers just touching Jacin's shoulders through his light coat.

I'm Untouchable. Mad. A Ghost.

And yet I'm touching you.

A spark of brilliance caught the corner of Jacin's eye as the sun reflected off the ring on Malick's finger—the one he'd given up trying to get Jacin to take back—and then an oblate appeared over Jacin's shoulder. Jacin took it and didn't even roll his eyes.

"*Your lads.*" Malick flipped Samin off with one hand, but the other one stayed on Jacin's shoulder. "*Your lads* have taken to torturing me for sport just lately. Do something before I kill them." Jacin felt the shift in weight as Malick turned toward Shig. "How are you, love?"

Shig gave Malick a small smile. "It's nice here."

Samin was smirking when he sidled around the chairs and hitched up against the rail, leaning over to have a look at the foamy curl of the ship's wake. He'd spent most of the first two days below deck, retching his guts out, and the few times he'd ventured up, he'd had a sickly greenish cast to his skin. He looked much better now.

"C'mon, lovie." He gestured over to Shig.

Shig only hesitated for a second before she rose from her chair and shuffled over to Samin. She even gave him a small grin with a touch of cheek in it as Samin lifted her by the hips and planted her on the railing, legs dangling over the side of the hull. Samin was careful to keep a good hold as Shig leaned over and spread her arms like she was flying.

Jacin turned to Morin. "What did you do to Malick?" His voice was still just as raspy as the last time he'd used it. It probably always would be now, just like his leg would never be right again.

The look of wide-eyed surprise Morin shot him was… odd. Morin covered it quickly with an open smile that made him look so much like their mother Jacin's heart took a bit of a lumping lurch behind his breastbone.

"I didn't *do* anything." Morin's smile turned devious. "I only said I was surprised he wasn't as pretty as all those other *Temshiel*." He widened his eyes, all innocence. "It was sort of a compliment!"

"*How*," Malick growled, "was that a bloody *compliment?*"

Morin grinned wider. "Jacin never liked his men pretty." As if he would really know, but Jacin didn't contradict him. "He likes 'em wide and stocky." Morin looked Malick up and down, then shot an appraising glance at Samin; Samin caught it, rolled his eyes at Jacin, but he didn't ruin Morin's fun, either. "You'd better watch yourself." Morin dripped his voice and looked over his shoulder at Malick. "I dunno. You look more butch than those other *Temshiel*, but I think Samin might be more—"

"*Bloody*—" Malick gave Morin a light cuff behind the ear. "Stop, or you'll give Joori a nosebleed."

"*Help!*" Morin shot up from his chair, knocking it with a clatter to the deck as he leapt over toward Samin and wedged in under Shig's outflung arm. "Save me from the big, bad *Temshiel!*"

"See?" Joori put out his hands, eyebrows high. "Kicker of puppies."

The rabbit-punch Joori laid on Malick's arm was apparently in retaliation for the cuff Malick gave him to match Morin's.

Jacin… stared.

They were all smiling. *Laughing.* Like they were normal people, living normal lives.

How long had that been going on?

Jacin shook his head, letting his glance rove over all of them, one after another, looking closely, as though they were completely new people. Perhaps they were. Perhaps they'd all started again.

So… where did that leave Jacin?

You can't stand to be content, because you don't understand it…

Pensive, Jacin turned his chin up, peered at Malick. Malick grinned back down at him and waggled his eyebrows.

That will be the one.

His mother's voice, soothing like it had always been.

"So, what'll it be?" Malick gave Jacin's shoulder a light squeeze. "Going to defend me or leave me at their mercy?"

So, you have a decision to make here, Fen.

It was so much easier not to make them. He was horrible at it, anyway.

...if you choose me, there's no going back.

Someone who couldn't die. Someone who'd fight dirty, lie, cheat, and steal his way out of it. Never leave Jacin with a hollow nothing burning him up from inside.

He'd get sick of Jacin eventually. It was inevitable, once Malick really got to know him. Once he looked deep enough to see the empty, hollow nothing Jacin really was. But *here* and *now*...

Alone is the only thing that can truly break you.

And there it was—that simple. Almost the *only* thing Jacin knew right now was that he didn't want to be alone anymore.

Jacin stared up, refused to let the confusion that was hovering at the back of his brain bloom, pushed back everything but *here* and *now*, just so he could get a good look at it.

His brothers were *here*, a new life spread out before them—*now* they had a chance to actually live it.

Malick was *here*, offering—*now* Jacin could accept what Malick was giving, and just *not think* about what might come after.

Here and *now*, there was a mild soreness lingering from last night; it was pleasant, and it had nothing whatever to do with pain. *Here* and *now*, Jacin's mind was calm, his thoughts his own. *Here* and *now*, he wasn't cold, a weird, creeping thaw going on inside him somewhere, and he coveted the warmth.

He turned his face back up to Malick and shrugged. "You're plenty pretty." He didn't smirk, only aimed his gaze back out to the water, daring Malick to try to cuff *him*.

Malick didn't. Instead, he paused for a moment, silent, then let loose a breathy little chuckle.

"Well, I'll be damned. Fen, did you just make a joke *and* say something kinda nice to me? At the *same time*?"

Jacin squinted over at Shig, caught her knowing little grin, the sly look of conspiracy, and refrained from growling at her.

"I guess I did."

He slanted a look over at Joori, raised his eyebrows to see Joori smiling at him so hard his eyes were starting to water. Jacin was a bit bemused but didn't comment. Instead, he drove his fingertips into the rough rind of the oblate before he craned his neck to look at Malick again, flicked a chunk of peel at him, and nailed him right between the eyes with it.

"Now, leave my brothers alone or I'll gut you."

Malick's hands went to Jacin's shoulders, clamped on and kneaded—strong and sure but gentle. Joori was smiling, almost smug as he slouched down in his chair beside Jacin. Morin's grin was wide and untroubled as he climbed up beside Shig, Samin gripping them both securely, while Morin leaned over the railing, arms outstretched, whooping a pleased cry as he pretended to fly.

Yori was missing, the hole she would've filled with her dry, careless wit noticeable. Caidi was missing, the lack of her laughter like a mournful cry in Jacin's chest.

Silly Ghost. Caidi's voice was more memory than phantasm. *You don't need to be so morbid* all *the time.*

And, well. Yes.

Jacin sank down in his seat and decided he could always brood later. Decided he was still a little crazy, maybe, but whatever he was *here* and *now,* he didn't feel Untouchable anymore.

Maybe this was the way it was supposed to feel when you started again.

Back to Zero. Maybe he was capable of it.

Anyway, it was a place to start.

TURN THE PAGE

FOR A SNEAK PEEK AT THE NEXT AND FINAL
INSTALLMENT IN CAROLE CUMMINGS'

WOLF'S-OWN
SERIES

Raven Inconjunct

Men and women in a wild array of apparent wealth, from moneyed to beggared, and yet all mixed together in conversation with no apparent awareness or concern about station. A young woman clad in the rich robes of the Heldes, cheekbones highlighted by the sepia strokes of elaborate tattoos; she lounged on cushions at a squat table, delicately smoking from a water pipe while speaking quietly and earnestly to an elderly man who looked like he was keeping his raggedy coat on by a few stitches and a wish. A girl who couldn't be older than Morin wagged a grubby finger at a young woman dressed in a fine satin longcoat and who appeared to be listening like her life might depend on what the girl said next. Jacin pegged the woman as Temshiel or maijin, because she was beautiful, without flaw, and mortals just didn't look like that.

The buzz of conversation was quiet, but more noticeable for the fact that Jacin could hear it at all. No musicians strummed or sang in a corner, no drunks bawled epithets, no doxies strolled the perimeter proffering favors.

It only took a second or two for the poppy smoke to curl into Jacin's nostrils, overlain by the yeasty smell of cheap beer and the more palpable sting of strong liquor. He wondered if everyone here was already stoned. Would that be a good thing, or a bad thing?

No one paid Jacin any mind as he wandered into the dim-lit room, just cut the occasional curious glance his way and then went back to what they'd been doing. He almost wished someone would challenge him, because there was no one tending the shabby bar, there were no maids or lads waiting tables, no clear direction for Jacin to point himself. Jacin was almost beginning to wonder if he hadn't perhaps stumbled into someone's private party when a great, whiskered man detached himself from a pile of low cushions and lumbered toward him with something a little too close to intent in his dark eyes. His hair and beard were as white as snow, both sprouting straight and lank in unkempt tufts. He was bigger than he'd looked while lounging on his cushions, a full head taller than Jacin and at least twice as wide. And nearly every bit of visible skin besides his face was covered in tattoos.

Jacin kept his hands from reaching for a weapon. He didn't want to start anything with this giant unless he absolutely had to.

"There is no magic here." The man spoke angrily, as though Jacin had offered some sort of offense.

Jacin gave him a wary stare. "All right."

"Take it off."

Jacin flexed his fingers, body tensing when he sensed another presence at his back, hovering. Yeah, well, he'd figured it was a trap of some sort.

"Take what off?"

There was the faintest of stirrings at Jacin's nape; he sidestepped quickly, only catching a minute flash of substance out the corner of his eye before it was gone and he was backing into a very wide, very solid-feeling chest. Where he knew no one had been a half a second ago. Bloody hell. He stilled completely when a great hand roughly gripped his shoulder from behind.

"What kind of magic have you got here, seyh? And how did you get it past the wards?"

The chatter had stopped. Every patron of the dingy little tavern who'd politely disregarded Jacin before now stared at him with varying degrees of interest.

Jacin only snapped a glare at the white-haired man in front of him. "I paid your little friend for the damned stick. If he told you otherwise—"

He already had a knife in his hand by the time the man in front of him had completed his lunge forward and snatched away the stick. Jacin let him, countering with a warning swipe of the knife that just grazed the man's beard, but the man behind him prevented Jacin from lopping a hunk of it off like he'd wanted to. Jacin stilled again, the man behind him now gripping his right shoulder and his left wrist while the man in front of him inspected the walking stick like he thought it might explode in his hands. He stroked at his beard with a narrow glare at Jacin and a curl to his lip.

All right. Jacin could still get out of this. The grip on his wrist was pretty firm, but the one on his shoulder was only just firm enough. And his right hand was still free. The man was probably used to being able to subdue anyone he wanted to with size and strength alone. Except Samin was very nearly as big as these two, and had put Jacin into this kind of hold numerous times. And had taught him very well how to break it. Plus, neither of these men had yet tried to disarm him. Jacin wasn't trapped quite yet.

"I can sense nothing from this." The man in front of Jacin was looking the walking stick over with a frown cut deep between his spiky white eyebrows. "Is it possible to disguise magic as nothing at all?"

Available from
FOREST PATH BOOKS

Carole Cummings

lives with her husband and family in
Pennsylvania, USA, where she spends
her time trying to find time to write.
Recipient of various amateur and
professional writing awards, several
of her short stories have been trans-
lated into Spanish, German, Chinese
and Polish.

Author of the Aisling and Wolf's-own series, Carole is currently in
the process of developing several other works, including more
short stories than anyone will ever want to read, and novels that
turn into series when she's not looking. Carole is an avid reader of
just about anything that's written well and has good characters.
She is a lifelong writer of the 'movies' that run constantly in her
head. Surprisingly, she does manage sleep in there somewhere,
and though she is rumored to live on coffee and Pixy Stix™, no one
has as yet suggested she might be more comfortable in a padded
room.

...Well. Not to her face.

www.carolecummings.com

To the villain.
Because everyone has a backstory.

PART ONE

TRAVIS

I worked so hard to get the three of us here tonight and now I wondered if it was all a huge fucking mistake. Too late now. I fiddled with the crystal champagne flute. It was nearly empty, and I finished it off before the server came over with refills. If I was going to make it through this evening, I needed something much stronger than champagne. A few stiff drinks might do the trick, but I needed to keep a clear head.

The forty guests crowding the overfilled room were all dressed to the nines in designer suits and overpriced gowns. They gushed backhanded compliments to one another like the superficial assholes they were bred to be. I was out of place here, but I guess that's the price I paid when my two best friends were classy AF. They were expected to have elegant parties with their fancy family and friends and I stuck out like a sore thumb at the head table with the lucky couple.

It seemed everyone wanted to give a speech tonight, celebrating the happy pair, though currently, neither the bride nor groom-to-be looked especially joyful. I saw through their fake smiles and wondered if anyone else noticed or even cared that the happy couple actually looked miserable. Most guests seemed too self-absorbed, caught up in how they sounded during their failed attempts at being witty or sentimental in their tributes to Addison and Oliver. I had not been to many wedding rehearsals, so I didn't know if this was the way they always went.

My gaze slid over the unhappy lovebirds and Oliver held my eye. He wasn't glaring at me, but his typical carefree smile was noticeably absent. I shifted my sights from my best friend's sad blue eyes to Addison's. The two of them shouldn't be so depressed the evening before their wedding, but the day had been a whirlwind of high-stakes drama. That shit was draining, and I think the three of us were all a little shellshocked and tired. I knew none of us were enjoying these damn speeches.

Addison wore a fake smile, her lips painted a soft pink to match the pink ribbon on her short white dress. Her blonde hair was pulled out of her face, tucked back into a loose updo. Her hand rested on the table next to Oliver's and I knew she was waiting for him to twine his fingers through hers. I wondered how close she was to tears . . . or vomiting. Oliver appeared too lost in thought to reach out, and I had to suppress the urge to go comfort her myself.

I hadn't even had a chance to properly speak to Oliver. I didn't know when he'd had time in the last twelve hours to get a haircut, but his dark hair had been cut short and styled, and his face was clean-shaven. He wore a chip on his shoulder that I had personally seen to and a suit that Addison probably chose.

I was nervous to be here tonight. I didn't know how

Oliver would act towards me. I was the worst best man, but I would be here for as long as they would allow me. They meant too much to me, and I'd spent way too much money on my custom made navy suit. I was a big guy. Not fat. Just big-boned and muscular with linebacker shoulders. It was hard for me to blend in with most crowds. I knew I would never fit in here, not that I actually wanted to, but I would put in the effort for my two best friends.

I had tamed my unruly short brown hair that always grew too fast, and I'd trimmed my facial hair so it was less grizzly and more GQ. I was tan from the Arizona sun, but this week in New York seemed to drain the color from my face.

Addison had stopped me on my way into the church before rehearsal. I hadn't slept in almost thirty-six hours and she pulled me aside and put some shit on my face. She said it was to cover the bags under my eyes. I was too tired to object and even I had to admit she did a good job covering the dark circles. My brown eyes were only slightly bloodshot which no one had commented on. Not even the judge, though he usually avoided me these days.

Addison's old college roommate and current maid of honor finally finished her long-winded speech, and I decided it was my turn. I was going to shut this speech business down.

I stood, and Addison gave me a hesitant smile, while Oliver looked slightly murderous.

I hoped my anxious sleep-deprived mind could conjure up the right words. I cleared my throat and began. "I don't think there are two people in this world who were meant to be together more than Addison and Oliver. I've witnessed their love over the last eleven years and . . ." *it was torture* ". . . it only solidified how perfect these two are for each other."

There was an aww from the crowd like they actually fucking cared. Assholes.

"Oli has always been the kindest man I've ever known. He's the type of guy who will thank a police officer for writing him a ticket. Not that he'd ever give them a reason to pull him over. I've watched him give the shoes off his feet to a total stranger to help them through a hard winter."

I chanced another glance at him and he looked less angry and more heartbroken. Fuck. "I have no idea why you chose me to be your best friend. I mean, I'm the guy who tries to talk my way out of a ticket and usually end up with a bigger fine." Muted laughter filled the room. "Most of you know Oliver and I have been best friends since preschool. We met on the playground and as usual, I was the bad influence."

It was recess and all the kids were playing, but I didn't want to play with these kids. I wanted my old friends back. I sat on a bench and watched everyone run and skip around me. The trees were bare from winter, but it was warm enough that I peeled off my coat. It was too tight because mom said I was growing like a weed. I didn't know how weeds grew, but I figured if the coat was too small, I must be too big for preschool. But mom still made me go.

I looked around at all the kids playing. I recognized the skinny kid from my class getting pushed by an older boy.

I heard the younger kid say, "Please give it back."

The older boy laughed and shoved my classmate to the ground. I jumped off the bench, too mad to feel scared of the bully.

When I got close, I said, "Give him his toy."

The bully turned his mean freckled face toward me. "Finders keepers."

I pointed at the boy on the ground. "It's his."

"It's mine now," said the bully.

My dad taught me how to be brave. He said that only babies got scared and I wasn't a baby, so I stepped forward. "I said, give it back!"

"Are you gonna tattle?" he teased.

"I'm not afraid of you," I said, so he would know I wasn't a baby, but he laughed, so I clenched my teeth and kicked his ankle.

He dropped to the ground to rub at it. "Oww! You butthead!" he shouted, throwing the toy.

I walked over to where it lay on the ground and picked it up, surprised to find a barbie. The bully was already running away, and I yelled, "Go tattle, scaredy-cat!"

I turned back to my classmate on the ground and held my hand out to help him up. His eyes were wide as he hesitated to take my hand. Eventually, he grabbed it, and I pulled him to his feet. I held out the doll. "Here's your barbie."

He huffed, "It's not a barbie! It's a G.I. Joe."

"Looks like a barbie to me."

The kid shook his head. "Look, he's got his army uniform on, and he even has weapons."

"My dad was in the army," I said, leaning in to see what kind of weapons.

He looked suspicious. "How come I've never seen you before?"

"It's my first day. I liked my old school, but mom said I have to come here now."

He looked at me for a minute. "What's your name?"

"Travis."

There was a pause, and he asked, "Aren't you gonna ask my name?"

I shrugged. "What's your name?"

"I'm Oliver." He pulled a hand full of plastic weapons out of his

jacket pocket and held them out. "See, look."

I moved closer. "That's cool."

"Wanna play with me?" Oliver asked.

I shrugged. "Sure."

Oliver replied, "And tomorrow, I'll bring another G.I. Joe, so we can both have one."

I smiled at my new friend. "Cool."

The following day, my mom kissed my forehead as she dropped me off outside my preschool classroom.

"Mom, don't kiss me," I said, pulling away from her.

"Travis!" I heard from behind and turned to see Oliver running toward me.

"Hi, Oli!"

He stopped in front of me, his face twisted. "What'd you call me?"

"Oli. It's like Oliver but shorter."

He smiled, seeming to approve, and held out a G.I. Joe. "This one's for you. Look, he has brown eyes and hair like you do."

I grabbed it, and he was already asking, "Wanna come to my birthday party. I'm gonna be five. Are you five?"

"I've been five for like a hundred years," I said. "Is there gonna be cake at your birthday?"

"Yeah, and there's gonna be ice cream and presents."

"I'll ask my mom."

I SNAPPED back to the present.

Continuing my speech. "Oliver deserves the best kind of person. So when he started dating Addison, I was skeptical. Then I got to know her and found out that she's not only amazing. She's a great fit for Oli.

"So let's raise our glasses to the happy couple." I held up my glass. "I can't wait to see the two of you become husband and wife. Cheers."

Addison delicately dabbed at her tears, and I knew they'd had enough of the speeches. I'm pretty sure they were over this whole evening, so I announced, "That will be all the speeches for tonight. We've gotta save something for tomorrow," I joked, turning up the smile meter. "I mean aside from these two becoming husband and wife."

I took a seat, continuing to smile, though I was dead tired and filled with regret. I excused myself shortly after and left the banquette room to get a stiff drink from the restaurant bar. I didn't want people from the party to see how much alcohol it took to get me through this evening. I stepped outside for some fresh air before going back to the party. I was still on best man duty.

When the evening was finally over, Oli stopped me before I could leave.

"Thanks for the speech and playing the part," he told me. "Then again, I guess you're used to playing the role of best friend."

I looked around. There was no one nearby, so I stepped forward. "Oli, I'm glad she told you. It's been killing me, but I didn't want to hurt you. I never meant for anything to happen."

He shook his head, glaring at me. "Why did it happen?"

I sighed. "My feelings for Addison have always been complicated."

Complicated was putting it simply.

It all began eleven and a half years ago...

TRAVIS

I saw her first.

Someone had messed up my schedule, putting me in precalculus instead of weightlifting. I didn't know how the teachers got it so wrong, but I barely passed Algebra two and had no desire to work hard my last year of high school. I had no one to impress, and it's not like I had plans to go to college. I was preparing to coast through my senior year, but then I met the new girl, and my life's trajectory shifted.

She should've been wearing a warning sign. Something like *this chick will fuck up your life and destroy you forever*, but there was no warning. In fact, when I saw her, I had the urge to yell, "Dibs!" It wasn't a dibs kind of situation, but perhaps if I had called it, things wouldn't have gotten so messy.

I swung the clunky hall pass around on its lanyard as I walked into the school's office. There was a teenage girl standing with her back to me and it gave me time to look her over. She was tall for a girl, and I wasn't a butt guy, but dammit, her ass was enough to convert me. Her shorts showed off long silky legs, and I instantly pictured them wrapped around me. Shit. I had to focus on something else.

Straight blonde hair fell to the middle of her back, and her fair skin was tanned from the summer. She turned around to see who walked in, and that was it. Her light blue eyes found me, and I wanted to stumble back like cupid had shot me with a fucking arrow. I wasn't sappy, so the idea that I thought of a fucking flying baby threw me. That should have been my cue to run.

The secretary pulled my attention to her, asking, "What did you do this time, Travis?"

It wasn't good when the office staff knew a student's name because either they were a troublemaker or a suck-up. Obviously, I wasn't a suck-up, but I didn't want the new girl to think I was a troublemaker either, so I tried for charming.

"Now, Patty, you're looking stunning as always. I like the new do."

She blushed a bit but called me out. "Don't try to butter me up. What'd you do?"

"I just need a slight schedule rearrangement." I handed her my schedule, and she looked it over.

"You're in precalculus?" she said with a surprised laugh, making me look dumb in front of my dream girl.

Pride made me do something I would later regret, but I pulled the paper out of her hands and said, "Precalc isn't the issue." I looked over my schedule, trying to come up with something else that could be wrong. "It's lunch," I said, "I can't eat that early. I'll be starving before football practice." That made me sound like a well-rounded individual. I'd come back later to switch out of advanced math.

"I'm sorry, but we can't switch lunches around. You'll just have to bring a snack for after school."

I sighed. "Maybe you could bring one for me," I said to the secretary.

"I'm afraid not, Mr. Rose. But you could escort Miss Arthur to her first class." She motioned toward the new girl, which gave me an excuse to look at her. She had a faint redness to her cheeks as if she were embarrassed. Patty said to the girl, "Really, it's you I need to make sure this one," she pointed at me, "gets back to where he's supposed to be."

I pretended to be offended, but I had a reputation for skipping class. "Hey," I objected, "You know I don't skip during football season."

Patty shook her head, saying, "Addison, this is Travis Rose. Travis, this nice young lady, is Addison Arthur. Do not corrupt her."

I had every intention of doing just that. "It's an absolute delight to meet you, Addison Arthur. Don't listen to a thing Patty says about me. She's just sad there can never be a future between us."

Patty made a noise of annoyance.

"Hush, Patty. We mustn't. You're married." Before she got angry at me for taking it too far, I grabbed Addison's hand and whisked her out of the office.

I let go of her hand out in the hall, and she was giggling.

I made her laugh before he did.

And I loved her laugh before he did.

"So where'd you come from?" I asked, wondering how this angel of a woman had just fallen into my lap.

Her smile was shy. "I've always lived in the area, but I went to private school before transferring here."

"Private school? Did they kick you out for being too hot? You seem like a fire hazard to me."

She arched an eyebrow, clearly unimpressed, so I continued, "Or maybe you got in trouble. What was it? Did you skip school? Or maybe you were caught skinny dipping?"

She rolled her eyes. "None of the above. I don't skinny dip, and I would never skip class. I wasn't forced to come here. I chose to transfer."

"Why?"

There was an intensity in her bright blue eyes as she said, "To help my father's career."

I smiled at her. "Nope, that wasn't it. It was definitely the skinny dipping."

She fought a grin as she shook her head. I don't think she knew what to make of me, and I didn't want to push my luck, so I steered the conversation into safer territory.

"What's your first class?"

"AP English Lit." She wasn't just beautiful. She was smart.

"That's right across from Precalculus, which is my first class," I said in case she wasn't listening earlier.

"I have that next."

I peeked over at the schedule she held in front of her. "Holy shit, your schedule is packed. Those are all college prep classes."

"I know. I'm taking several college courses too. At this rate, I'll finish my undergrad a year early. I mean, if I want to have my own medical practice by the time I'm thirty, then I need to pack in as much as I can now."

"You want to be a doctor."

"No, I'm going to be a doctor."

I smirked, liking her confidence. "So, since you're so smart, if I would happen to need any help with precalculus, you'd be able to tutor me if you had the time."

She blushed and with a bashful smile, said, "I'd make time for you."

She flirted with me first, and if I hadn't been so afraid of coming on too strong, I would have asked her to marry me at that moment. Instead, I walked her to her class and went to my own, thinking I had plenty of time. I didn't realize when I dropped her off at her class that she would sit down next to Oliver.

He wasn't blind, or stupid, so he asked her on a date. She said yes. It was just a date. I still teased her, and she continued to flirt with me right up until she learned Oli and I were best friends.

Addison and I gravitated toward each other, until I bailed, giving her the cold shoulder so there would be no confusion. Two weeks later, Addison and Oliver were a couple.

I may have loved her first, but Oliver asked her out first, kissed her first, and fucked her first.

What I felt for her wasn't an insta-love infatuation that faded after getting to know her. The more I learned about her, the harder I fell. And the more our friendship grew, the more my heart broke.

She made good on her promise and tutored me through a vigorous year of precalculus where she found out I wasn't smart at all, but she seemed to like me anyway. She saw something in me that no one else seemed to notice. She believed so strongly that I was meant for more, and even I started buying into the idea. When I was with her, I felt I was qualified for more than just a laugh and a touchdown on the football field. She made me feel like I could make something of myself.

She usually tutored me in the school library, but in the spring we had to meet outside of school because the library was closed off for academic clubs. Oliver had baseball practice, or we would've gone to his house. Addison offered to meet me at my place, but I didn't want her to see where I lived. I knew she came from money, and not everyone was as comfortable coming to my trailer as Oliver was. It didn't seem to phase him, and I never felt like he looked down on me for my upbringing, but not everyone felt that way. It already seemed against the odds to have a friend like Addison, and I loved her encouragement and her blind belief in me. I didn't want to give her more reasons to stop working with me.

"Why don't I come to you?" I offered as we stepped outside. The early April air was warmer than usual for Upstate New York, and the days were stretching longer.

She made a doubtful face. "I live at the edge of the district. It's a drive."

"You're doing me a favor. Driving to your house is the least of my worries."

With a shrug of her shoulders, she said, "Fine. Works for me. I live in a gated community, but if you follow me, I can put the code in for both of us."

"You live in a gated community?"

"Yeah, my father's a judge and likes the extra security."

My eyes narrowed. "So why'd he pull you out of private school and dump you here?"

She rolled her eyes. "He didn't dump me here. I offered. It would look better for his reelection to have me in public school. It made him more relatable. I knew the AP classes here would be less of a challenge, which would give me more time to focus on my college courses. Plus, I would finally be free from the all-girls' school." She gave a cheeky smile.

"Oh, I see. So it was all about the boys."

She scoffed. "Well, you don't hear me complaining." She started walking toward her car, saying, "Follow me."

I got in my car and tailed her. When we reached the gated community, I watched her punch in the code for both of us. I followed her down a winding road through well-landscaped mansions. There was no other way to describe them, except when we pulled into Addison's driveway, the word castle came to mind. Her house was a towering stone structure, looking like a modernized victorian castle. I parked behind Addison in the driveway even though I was sure she had a spot somewhere in their gigantic garage. She got out of her car and met me by the double front doors.

As I walked toward the house, I said, "Damn, Addie. Didn't know you lived in a castle."

She laughed. "My dad would certainly like to think so, but to be a castle, it would need a moat, or curtain wall, or at the very least a portcullis. It's also missing battlements and arrow slits. The only defense is a home security system. So it'd make for a very poor castle."

I didn't know what half of the shit that came out of her mouth meant, but it made me smile. "You're a huge fucking nerd. You know that?"

"Why do you think you're here? You need this nerd!" She flipped her hair over her shoulder as she turned to unlock the front door.

Her words were true in more ways than she would ever know. Even now, I itched to touch her. I reached out and tugged playfully at her hair. She glanced back at me, and I said, "Lead the way, princess."

She pushed the door open, and I followed her in. I wasn't surprised to see such an amazing interior. It was part medieval museum and part domestic. It did not, however, look lived-in. The spacious stone foyer echoed with hollowness. It was a place to show off—a place where children were seen but never heard. I quickly formed a vision in my head of Addison's father, and I instantly disliked him.

Their house felt like a museum of expensive artifacts rather than a home. "Is your dad a collector?"

"A collector of envy perhaps, but I don't think any of these things actually bring him joy. He covets them because their value makes him feel important. He gets the most joy out of making his friends and colleagues jealous." She spun to me, eyes wide. "Don't ever repeat that." She covered her mouth, looking shocked by her own admission. "I can't believe I just said that to you."

"My lips are sealed." I made a motion of locking my lips.

She bit hers, and it drew my attention to her mouth. Damn. I looked away, avoiding eye contact and close proximity.

She led me to her home library, where an entire wall was nothing but built-in bookshelves holding hundreds of books while the other side of the room overlooked the lush land-scape of the front yard. A long table ran down the center of the room while matching chaise lounges sat in front of the oversized windows.

I snorted. "Glad we came here instead of my house."

Addison's brows dipped. "Your house would've been fine."

"Princess, I live in a trailer."

"There is nothing wrong with that."

I arched an eyebrow, opening my mouth to speak when a woman walked in.

"Addison?" A tall brunette woman stood in the doorway.

Addison spun toward her. "Oh, hi. I didn't think you were home. Mom, this is Travis, Oliver's best friend." She gestured to me with a glance. "Travis, this is my mother."

Her mom stepped into the library and held her hand out to me. "It's very nice to meet you, Travis."

I shook her hand. "Nice to meet you too. You have a beautiful home."

"You're too kind." She looked around the space. "There are parts that are beautiful, I suppose, but it does feel a bit too stately and masculine for my own tastes sometimes." She shrugged and then addressed Addison. "What are your plans this evening?"

"I'm helping Travis with calculus."

She nodded, and her eyes fell on me. "Travis, will you be joining us for dinner?"

"No, ma'am."

"Alright, I'll leave you to study. Dinner is at six."

Once she left, I said, "Your mom seems nice."

Addie gave a half-smile. "She is." She seemed to hesitate before adding, "My biological mother died when I was five. Jeanine has been Mom ever since."

I grimaced. "I didn't know. Sorry you lost your mom. I'm sure you miss her."

She shrugged. "I can barely remember her now." She paused. "That's terrible. I feel guilty for not remembering more, but I never got to know who she was or what she loved. To me, she was just my mommy, and as far as I was concerned, she was put on this earth just for me." She shook her head. "Why am I telling you this? Sorry." She walked to the table and set her bag on it. "Let's get to work."

I sat down beside her. "It's okay to want to talk about her. Your mom."

She gave me a sharp look that would shutout a lesser man, but I was determined. "Do you feel like you can't talk about her in front of your stepmom?"

"We don't use that word."

I snorted. "That's a yes. They made you feel guilty for missing your mom, so you stopped talking about her, and now you feel like you've forgotten her."

She looked up at me. "What is it about you that I always tell you too much? Way more than I mean to."

"It's okay. Your secrets are safe with me. Anyway, who would I tell? Oli?" I laughed. "Like he doesn't already know all of your deepest, darkest secrets."

She froze, her lips pressed into a determined line.

My eyes narrowed on her. "What?

"Let's get to work." She opened her book and looked down, her hair falling over her shoulder onto the page.

I moved the hair out of her face, feeling a zing between us. This proximity made my pulse beat double time.

"Addie, it's okay to be sad."

She sniffled, pushing back from the table. "Excuse me for a moment."

I shoved away from the table and stepped in front of her. "No. What's wrong? Why are you sad?"

Her bottom lip trembled as she looked up at me. I wanted to kiss her and make the pain I saw in her eyes disappear, but she wasn't mine to kiss. She was Oliver's girlfriend, and this wasn't about what I wanted. She was going through something, and instead of letting her stuff it down inside like she was trying to do, I was forcing her to bring it into the light.

With annoyance, Addison blurted, "Today is the anniversary of her death."

I stepped back and grabbed my bag from the table. Throwing the strap over my shoulder, I said, "Let's go."

"What? Where? What about calculus?"

"Calculus can wait. You need a milkshake, or hot fudge

sundae or some kind of comfort food, and you have two hours before what is sure to be a healthy dinner."

"You're taking me for a milkshake?"

"Yeah, you got a problem with that, princess?"

"No, but—"

"Come on." I grabbed her hand and pulled her with me out of the library.

She called out, "Mom, I'll be back before six. We have an errand to run."

"Okay, sweetie."

Addison climbed into my car even though hers would've been a smoother ride. She didn't comment about my POS other than to tell me it smelled surprisingly pleasant. It smelled like my cologne which meant she thought I smelled pleasant. I grinned as I pulled out of the driveway. I drove past all the mansions and out of the gated community with a dumbass smile on my face.

"Why are you smiling like that?" she asked.

Of course she would notice. "Just thinking about what flavor I'm gonna get."

"You're pretty excited about these milkshakes."

"Aren't you?"

"They're a lot of calories."

I narrowed my gaze on her. "Do you always count your calories?"

She tilted her head. "I'd say I'm pretty calorie conscious."

"You should relax a bit."

"We can't all eat six thousand calorie diets like you."

"That's only during football season."

"That's disgusting. I don't know how you can eat that much."

"And how many calories do you consume, princess?"

She looked out the passenger window. "Enough that I can have a milkshake." She sounded melancholy.

"You thinking about your mom?"

"That's where she's buried," Addison noted as we passed a cemetery. "I haven't ever been able to bring myself to go."

"Ever?"

She shook her head.

I slowed the car and pulled a U-turn at the next light.

"Travis, no! I can't. I don't even remember where her grave is."

I lifted a shoulder as I drove toward the cemetery's entrance. "Then we'll find it."

"Travis," she complained again as I pulled in the open gate.

When I noticed how ghostly white she looked, I pulled over and put the car in park. Turning to face her, I rested a hand on her anxiously wringing fingers. "Addison."

She looked up with storm clouds in her blue eyes.

I whispered, "Do you want to visit your mom's grave?"

She stared at me for a long time before sucking in a breath and nodding her head.

"Together?" I offered.

She nodded faster.

"You have any idea which direction? This is a popular place. Lots of people're dyin' to get in."

She snorted, saying, "That's so inappropriate."

"Made you smile, though."

She pointed to a structure a little ways off. "I remember that building. I think it's over that hill somewhere."

I nodded and drove the narrow path over the hill and down to a small parking area. There were hundreds of graves, but she seemed to be zeroed in on a specific section. When we got out, I let her lead the way.

We walked down several rows, and I wondered if she realized her movements started slowing the further we went. Her breath seemed shaky as she stared at a polished headstone a few graves away. She blew out a breath. "I should've brought flowers or something."

"You're enough." I encouraged, "Just visiting is a great first step."

"Thanks for bringing me here, Travis."

I nodded and followed her down a few more graves before she stopped. A fresh bouquet of lilies lay on the grave, and I checked the name and dates to verify it was her mother.

In Loving Memory
Vivian Alana Arthur
March 7, 1963
April 16, 1995

She wrapped her arms around herself. "Life feels so permanent, but we're all going to end up here in the end, aren't we?"

"Not me. I'm gonna be cremated and scattered in the wind so you guys can continue to choke on my sick sense of humor."

A small laugh escaped her lips, and I wrapped my arm around her shoulders.

She leaned her head into me. "My dad's been here. I never knew he thought of her, let alone visited her grave."

I looked at the lilies and wondered their significance. "He should've asked you to come with him."

"My dad isn't big on emotions. We, Arthurs, have a reputation to uphold, and emotions are nasty little things that get in the way of common sense." She pulled away from me. "You, Travis Rose, bring out the worst in me."

I gave a sarcastic laugh. "You mean the human part. Not the beep boop I am a robot, my name is Addison Arthur, and I feel no emotion." I gave her a doubtful look. "That's not the best part of you."

She fought a smile as she glared at me. Then with a sigh, she turned back to the grave. "Lilies were Mom's favorite. My father used to bring them home all the time for her. It was so sweet. He doesn't do that for Jeanine, but she's the kind of woman who would buy her own flowers." She stepped closer to the grave.

I moved back. "I'll give you some privacy to talk to her."

She looked at me. "She's not really here, Travis. She can't hear me here any better than anywhere."

I nodded. "I know, but you should talk anyway."

She stared at the grave. "But what do I say?"

"Talk to her as if she were standing right in front of you."

"Pretty sure I'd scream and run from my zombified mother."

I smirked. Nothing like dark humor to make a depressing situation light. "I think you'll be fine. But I'll go get a bat from the car just in case." I walked back toward the car, pulling out my phone. It was nearly five. Oliver would be finishing baseball practice soon. I shot him a text, telling him to meet us at the ice cream shop.

Once I got to the car, I turned back toward Addie to see if she was talking, but her back was to me. At least she had let me bring her here, and now she was hopefully talking to the mother she hadn't spoken to in thirteen years. I felt like that was a big step for her.

She didn't stay at the graveside for long. She jogged back

to the car, and I pushed away from where I was leaning and stepped forward just as she slammed into me, giving me a full-body hug. With her head buried in my shoulder, she said, "Thank you, Travis."

I loved the feel of her body against mine, which was exactly why I needed her to let go. I thanked my lucky stars that my dick had cooperated so far, but I didn't know how long I could hold out. "Come on. It's milkshake time."

When she pulled away, she smiled, her eyes brighter than before. "Mmm, I want strawberry!" She raced around to the passenger side.

When I got in the car, she was already fastening her seatbelt. As we drove, she reached over and laid her hand on mine. "You're a good friend, Travis. At least I hope you see me as a friend, and you're not just putting up with me because I'm Oli's girlfriend."

I didn't mean to laugh, but one escaped. "Shit, Addie. Do I seem like the kind of guy who would play nice with a girl just because she's dating my best friend? The answer is no, and I sure as shit wouldn't take her for milkshakes."

"Or to her mother's grave?"

"Especially not to her mother's grave."

"So is this your way of telling me we're friends?"

I glanced at her. "Do you think I'd let just anyone tutor this brilliant mind?"

"Well, I kind of got the impression that I annoyed you."

I'd done that on purpose—given her the cold shoulder, so she didn't feel torn between Oliver and me. I practically gift-wrapped her for him because I knew she'd end up with the better man, and that would never be me. I shrugged and said, "I didn't want you feeling like you had an in with Oli."

She jerked away. "You think I was using you to get closer to Oliver?"

"Wouldn't be the first time."

"Seriously?" she asked.

I lifted a shoulder and said, "Oli is a catch."

"So are you," she argued.

I snorted. "Princess, I live in a trailer park, barely pass my classes, and drive this POS. I don't have a whole lot going for me. Oli on the other hand—"

"That is not true." Addison's voice was stone. "You are one of the best people I've ever met."

"Then I have you fooled."

Her head shook. "No. I think you have everyone else fooled." She was getting heated. "You're smart. You've just never applied yourself because you were scared you'd fail."

"I don't get scared," I corrected.

"We all have moments of fear. And your fear stems from the fact that no one has ever believed in you the way you deserve. You work full-time hours on top of your school load, and I know you could've bought a nicer car, but you used it to help your mom pay the bills."

"How the fuck do you know that?"

"Oli accidentally let it slip. But that's not something to be embarrassed about or ashamed of. Travis, you—"

"Do you guys just sit around and talk about me?"

"Yeah, Travis, we have meetings about you a few times a week. God, of course we don't sit around and talk about you, but you do come up in conversation because you're important to Oliver. You're important to me too. Is that such a bad thing?"

I didn't answer. I didn't know how to. I didn't know what I thought anymore.

"Travis, your biggest flaw is that you don't believe in yourself because you can't recognize what a rare breed you are."

"Rare breed? Ha. Like I'm some kind of hypoallergenic Shih Tzu mix. Damn, Addie, that was poetic."

She glared at me. "Being a sarcastic prick is a lame coping mechanism."

"And being a self-important bitch falls into what category?"

"Screw you!"

I raised a brow. "I think Oli would be upset at both of us if I took you up on that."

"You're incorrigible."

What the hell was I doing? Why was I letting her get to me? I swallowed my pride and didn't give her the retort on the tip of my tongue. I quickly changed the subject. "Oli is meeting us at the ice cream shop. He's out of practice."

She jerked to me with panic-filled eyes. "Did you tell him where we were?"

"No, but what's the big deal?"

"Oliver doesn't know Jeanine isn't my biological mother."

I glanced at her, waiting for an explanation.

Addison shifted in her seat. "It didn't come up right away, and now it's been so long that I feel like I've been keeping this big secret, but I don't know how to bring it up casually."

"Then don't do it casually. Tell him straight. Tell him what you told me just now."

She sighed.

I laughed. "You can't seriously be afraid to talk to Oli?"

"Shut up."

We pulled into the ice cream shop's parking lot and

ordered our milkshakes. We drank them outside on a bench where we soaked in the warm spring air.

Oliver surprised Addie by coming up behind her and wrapping her in a hug. I liked to see my friends happy, and that made the pain of seeing them together worth it. But after today, it hurt extra. I sucked down the last of my milkshake, giving myself brain freeze.

I stood. "Oli, can you take Addison home?"

"Of course."

"Good. I'll see you guys later." The thing about being a dick was people never second guess my rudeness. They just thought it was part of my jackassery, which worked for me. Especially when it covered the feelings I was hiding for a certain blonde who was so far off-limits. But she had opened up to me and told me things she hadn't even told Oliver. That was a mind-fuck for sure. But, then again, that's what friends did. They confided in each other, and she had put me in the friend zone, which is right where I belonged.

Before I could climb in my car, I heard footsteps and turned to find Addison rushing toward me. She leaned up on her toes and kissed my cheek.

"Thanks for today, Travis." She gave a meaningful smile and added. "You're a great friend, and I promise to help you with calculus tomorrow."

I smiled. "You'd better. There's a test coming up, and if I fail, I'm blaming you."

She laughed, reminding me how much I loved her laugh. And I loved this new weightlessness that seemed to come from facing her past. I'd helped her today. We were good together, but damn did we have a knack for arguing.

Addison is the reason I passed my senior year with better grades than I'd ever managed before. She helped me apply for scholarships and grants and because of her, I headed to college in North Carolina the next year. It wasn't the college she and Oliver got into, but I was only an hour away which worked out for the best because I was close, but not close enough to hear him and Addie going at it every night.

People gave them nicknames like Addiver or Olison, mashing their names together like they belonged together while I was the perpetual third wheel. We spent a lot of time together, and even when Oliver wasn't around, I still gravitated toward Addie without realizing what I was doing.

I went from girl to girl, trying to fuck Addison out of my system. Except none of the girls were her, and it left me feeling like shit because I knew what love was. I knew how good it could be. I wanted what she and Oliver had, but I wanted it with her, and I knew that wasn't an option.

2

TRAVIS

THE FIRST SEMESTER of my sophomore year of college, my feelings for Addison grew stronger and being around her became even more painful. I regretted picking a college in North Carolina to be closer to them.

I distanced myself, but Oliver came to me, thinking something was wrong. Of course, he brought Addison along with him because he knew we had become good friends. He felt that together, they would cheer me up.

They dragged me out to a party that night, and we all had too much to drink. It was college. We went back to my one-bedroom campus apartment, and Oliver passed out in my bed while Addison and I sat on the couch watching crap TV in the living room. I was still a little drunk, so I didn't catch myself falling into dangerous territory.

She caught me staring at her and gave me a look that said, *dude?* But I couldn't stop looking at her. I blamed it on the booze, but with her so close and the two of us alone, it physically hurt not to touch her. My blood burned with the need to make physical contact, and my heart yearned for her, knowing no one else would ever fill the perfect Addison shaped hole she'd begun carving into my chest since the day I met her.

I jumped off the couch and went into the kitchen, distancing myself from her, but she followed me. "Travis, what's going on with you?" Her hand landed on my arm.

It was just a touch, but I reacted like she'd begged me to kiss her. I grabbed her face and put my whole heart into a kiss I knew would get rejected, but I needed her to reject me. I fully expected her to jerk away and slap me.

I thought my love for her was completely one-sided until she kissed me back. Her fingers curled into the front of my jacket, and she pulled me closer. Once our kiss ended, we stood together, breathing each other's air. I was so shocked that I didn't know what to do next. She was supposed to make this easier on me, but she had just made it so much more difficult.

As if just realizing what had happened, she unfroze and pushed away from me, walking to the other side of the kitchen before coming back. Her eyes were on the floor, searching for the answers. She lifted her head, looking bewildered. "You kissed me."

"You kissed me back?" It wasn't a question, but I said it like it was because I couldn't wrap my mind around it.

"You're Oliver's best friend," she accused, making me feel even more like a shit bag.

"I know."

She leaned against the counter, asking, "Why did you kiss me?"

"I had to. And you were supposed to push me away and slap me."

Her frantic eyes searched mine. "I did push you away."

She wanted to deny her part in our kiss, or that it had ever happened at all, and that was fine with me. I didn't know what to do after that anyway.

But she didn't leave it alone. "We're just drunk. That's all. We're not thinking straight because we drank too much."

I sighed, knowing we weren't that drunk. "Must be."

She looked at me. "What do you mean you had to?"

I bit my lip to keep myself from saying anything. She reached out for me, but I pulled away, saying, "You can't touch me, Addie."

She moved closer. "Why can't I touch you? I've been touching you for years without anything like that happening."

She wanted me to spell it out for her.

I couldn't.

Kissing her was one thing, but telling her that I loved her —that she was and would always be the love of my life and that watching her with my best friend tore me apart—was out of the question. I thought they were happy, but she had kissed me back.

"Are you and Oliver happy?" I asked.

She took a step back and avoided my eyes. "We're very happy," she said in a soft voice.

"Then why did you kiss me back?"

She shook her head, wanting to deny it but knowing she couldn't. "Because I . . . I got confused."

I stepped forward with a racing heart and uneven breaths. "Addie," I whispered, "are you confused now?"

She looked up at me, her eyes sad, and her cheeks pink. I ran my knuckles over the warm skin, and her eyelids fluttered closed, but her words felt like a slap. "Are you just horny tonight, and I'm the only one around with boobs?"

Her baby blue eyes opened and narrowed. "I mean, I've been with Oliver for three years, and in that time, I've seen you go through woman after woman, Travis. I think you're confused too."

"I'm not confused. It's just that the one I've wanted hasn't been available."

She sucked in a breath, saying, "I've heard you use some pretty smooth lines before. You'll say anything to get girls to fall for you. But I never expected you to use that shit on me."

I stepped forward, breathing too heavily as I said, "It's not a line and if this was premeditated, it sure as shit wouldn't be happening while Oliver is in the other room. I meant what I said, and I've stopped myself from telling you so many times."

That's when she told me the truth, and I knew my life was truly fucked.

"I liked you first, Travis." Tears glistened in her eyes. "You flirted but never did anything about it. I didn't think you were interested. I tried to get your attention but got Oliver's instead. I'm happy with Oliver. Happier than I knew I could be, but I guess the feelings I've had for you never really went away. I just thought you didn't see me that way. Why didn't you tell me?" A lone tear trickled down her cheek, and I knew I'd royally fucked up.

"I don't deserve you, Addie. Oliver is the better choice, and we both know it, but it doesn't keep me from wanting you for myself."

Her eyes searched mine as if they were searching my soul. Lips parting, it appeared she had more to say, but she hesitated. She took a big breath like she was ramping up for a speech, but even as her lips danced with uncertainty, her voice remained silent. Then her mouth stilled and she covered her face with both hands for a brief moment.

"Addie." I stepped forward.

She held out a hand to fend me off, dropping her other hand to her side, while she clenched her jaw. This time when she looked at me, there was a healthy dose of anger mixed with her sadness. Without another word, she left the room, spinning away so quickly, I caught a whiff of her long hair as it fluttered out behind her.

I wanted to follow her, but I held tight to what little self control I had left. Instead of making everything worse, I poured myself a strong drink, and hoped I could forget the whole thing had ever happened.

But I couldn't forget. I knew I would never forget what her lips felt like against mine. I would always remember how she made my heart sing and how my soul had come alive like never before.

If that night had never happened, then maybe we would've eventually been fine. We could have gone on denying there was anything between us, but after that night, our cards were on the table. She knew my most sacred secret, and I knew hers.

We also knew we couldn't act on it because Oliver was too important to both of us. But knowing that I could kiss her and she wouldn't tell me to go to Hell was a dangerous temptation.

Nothing else happened that night, but the foundation had been laid.

3

ADDISON

WITH ARRESTING BLUE EYES, a chiseled jaw, and a tall, muscular body, Oliver's looks were the first thing that should have drawn me to him, but they weren't. I heard him speak before I ever saw his face. I was sitting at the front of the classroom while he was in the back. Being the new girl, I already felt like I was on display, so I had taken the first available seat and ignored the rest of the students. When the class began, they discussed the summer reading. Because of changing schools just a week before school started, I hadn't read it, but it appeared the main character was universally disliked. And then Oliver spoke. He stuck up for the unlikeable character, diving deeper into their motivation. He saw things differently than everyone else, and I enjoyed his optimism.

He had said, "There are always things we can't see, and without understanding a person's history, it's easy to judge them harshly."

His words resonated so profoundly that I spun in my chair because I had to see who said them. Only then did I realize he wasn't just smart and compassionate. He was gorgeous with his dark hair, tan skin, and those blue eyes that stared right back at me.

Now, I gazed at his side profile while he drove us home to New York for Thanksgiving break. Travis left a few days earlier, so he could fix his mother's leaky roof. I missed my friend and felt disappointed at his continued avoidance. But part of me was relieved Travis hadn't sought me out. I knew I should've had it all worked out, but I still could not wrap my head around what had happened between us. It didn't seem real, and spending eight hours in a car together would have been uncomfortable, especially because we couldn't discuss what happened in front of Oliver.

Travis's actions had always confused me. That first day, he had walked me to class, and I swooned over his easy smile and wit. His honey-brown eyes melted me, and I couldn't wait to get to know him better. He was a giant of a man, and I felt safe next to him. Like nothing could touch me. At five foot ten inches, I wasn't used to feeling petite and girly, but Travis made me feel both.

He flirted with everyone, so of course, he flirted with me over the years. I thought it was harmless. He was too loyal to make a move on me. And then he'd gone and kissed me, confessing deeper feelings, and all the emotions I had held back flooded me every time I was near him.

Guilt ate at me, and I almost told Oliver about the kiss dozens of times. But telling him would destroy everything, and it's not like it would happen again.

We pulled up to my parent's house just after six in the evening. Oliver carried my bags inside, and Jeanine greeted us.

"So glad you two made it safely." She gave us soft hugs and kissed Oliver's cheek. "Dinner is almost ready. Your father is in his study finishing up some business. Go get settled in, and we'll meet in the dining-room at six-thirty."

Oliver lifted my bags. "Can't wait. The food smells delicious."

Jeanine seemed pleased with his compliment, tossing him a smile before retreating into the kitchen.

We unloaded my bags in my room. When I was sixteen, Jeanine redecorated my room with soft pinks and creams. The fabrics were plush, the chandelier was dripping with pearls and crystals, and a sheer canopy floated over my bed. I think she was trying to compensate for the cold, masculine feel that overwhelmed the rest of the house.

I enjoyed the soft pillows and blankets, but I had always been too busy to care what my room looked like. All I really cared about was that it was clean and organized so that it wouldn't distract from my studies. This left it feeling impersonal, more like an elegant hotel room, rather than a teenager's bedroom. The trunk at the foot of the bed is where I stored the things that mattered to me.

I opened it now and pulled out my violin case. I was never a master, but I missed playing and wanted to take it with me when we drove back to school. Oliver wrapped his arm around my middle. "I haven't heard you play in a long time."

Setting the case down, I spun in his arms. His blue eyes focused on my lips a moment before he was kissing me. He was a great kisser, and we could've easily gotten carried away. Still, I knew my father wouldn't appreciate us showing up to dinner looking disheveled, so after a few moments, I pushed back and caught my breath, regaining my composure.

Oliver pushed my hair back behind my ears, his palm soft on my jaw as he whispered, "To be continued?"

I smiled at him. He didn't just make me feel desired. I felt cherished. My hands wrapped around his neck, and I pulled his lips to mine once more for a simple kiss. "To be continued," I promised.

Soon dinner was ready. Oliver, Jeanine, and I waited at the table for my father to join us. He finally walked in after several moments, and Oliver stood to take his hand. "Judge Arthur, thank you for having me for dinner."

My father wasn't a very large man, but the way he held himself made everyone feel small in his presence. He commanded respect in and out of the courtroom, and I never wanted to challenge him. Once, he had scolded me for wearing two-inch heels because it brought me eye-level with his six-foot frame. He told me it wasn't feminine to be so tall.

Oliver towered over him, but he never seemed to mind, probably because Oli didn't have a threatening bone in his body. I witnessed the approval in my father's gaze as he accepted Oliver's hand. He had always approved of Oliver.

"So glad the two of you made it home safely." He spoke with fondness, and after they shook hands, my father's gaze landed on me. There was a table between us, and I knew he wouldn't make his way over to hug me. He wasn't an overly affectionate man, but he looked genuinely pleased to see me. It was the best I could expect from him.

Dinner conversation flowed, going over all the subjects most families avoided. Oliver could hold his own against

Judge Arthur. He seemed to know just what to say to defuse the conversations when they got tense. Meanwhile, I danced around disagreements with frivolous details and distractions. It was a technique Jeanine had taught me. Our tense family meals all felt very orchestrated and normal to me, but I knew this wasn't how other families interacted.

I briefly wondered how Travis would fair with tonight's dinner conversations, but I already knew exactly how that would go. I surprised myself with a laugh, and all eyes turned to me in question.

"Sorry, I just remembered something that happened during one of my exams the other day."

"Care to share?" My father asked.

My eyes found Oliver, and he looked curious.

My mind went blank. I couldn't come up with a single thing.

Oliver rescued me with a laugh. "Was it about the kid who drooled all over his desk?"

I nodded, forcing a smile. "Yeah, during the exam, and yet, he somehow still passed the class."

"That sounds irresponsible," my father added. "I would fail them on principle."

I nodded, my eyes still locked with Oliver's. I swallowed, so grateful for him in that moment and all the moments. He fit so perfectly into my life, so why had I kissed his friend?

AFTER DINNER, I walked Oliver to the front door.

"So what really made you laugh?" he whispered conspiratorially.

I smiled up at him. "I remembered the family dinner Travis attended."

His eyes widened. "Never again. Mixing your father and Travis is like mixing bleach with ammonia."

I smiled but inwardly groaned. It was my fault Travis hated my father. Travis antagonized him for fun, welcoming Judge Arthur's disdain.

"You get along with my father so well," I complimented.

He shrugged. "He might be a little tough sometimes, but he's a good man. I respect him."

I grinned up at him, and he leaned forward to brush his lips over mine. "I love you, and I'll see you tomorrow."

I nodded, watching him leave.

He was so good. Way too good for me.

I wanted to tell him what happened between Travis and me. He might forgive me. He probably would. It was just a kiss, and we had been drinking.

I sighed, watching until his taillights disappeared out of view. I bit my lip.

"You better hold on to him, Addison."

I spun toward the voice, startled by my father's sudden appearance in the foyer. I hadn't heard him approach. I swallowed. "That's my intention."

"You don't seem especially resolute." His brow dipped, and he pressed his lips into a firm line, appraising me.

"I am." My words felt weak.

"Trust me. It is better to receive love than to give it. Giving love leaves you vulnerable, but being loved gives you power. Always remember that. Oliver adores you. You've made me proud in picking such a refined and malleable partner. Your life will be easy with him. You're a smart woman."

His praise was so rare, and the child inside of me ate up

his words of approval. I was starving for them. He didn't used to be so stingy with his affection, but after Mom died, I was lucky to get anything out of him.

He stepped forward, and his palm landed on my bicep. My heart leaped at the contact. He squeezed. Not painfully, but firm enough that I could pretend it was a hug. I needed the reassurance. I needed to know I was making the right decision, and hearing my father's approval solidified my decision. I would do anything to keep Oliver. He was my future, and one day I would be good enough to deserve him.

My father smiled at me, subtle and warm, before dropping his hand and moving away.

I replayed his words in my head. I let them wrap around my heart. He didn't say I love you, but he showed a rare vulnerability, which showed he cared.

Before he walked out of the room, he turned, his brows furrowing. "Don't disappoint me, Addison." His voice held a certain edge that sent a chill through me.

"I won't, sir."

His face softened once more, and he smiled before turning back around and leaving the room.

I tried to remember his words from a moment ago, wanting to bask in his praise a while longer, but I felt like the air had been knocked out of me. I pressed a hand to my sternum, remembering to breathe. It was so hard to fill my lungs when all I could remember was his glimpse of disappointment. If I lost Oliver, I would lose my father's respect, and I didn't know how to live without either one.

I didn't wait to catch my breath. I pulled out my phone and sent a text. Almost immediately, I got a text back. I stepped into the library, where my stepmother sat, reading a book.

"I'm going to meet up with the girls while I'm in town. May I use your car?"

Her smile was warm and motherly as she nodded. "Of course. Have fun."

"Thank you."

Fifteen minutes later, I was pulling into the park. It was late, so the dark lot was empty. I parked in my usual spot and got out of the car, searching. Trees lined the back of the playground, and on the other side was the trailer park where Travis grew up. He appeared out of the shadows as soon as I climbed out of my stepmother's car.

His brows drew together in concern. "What's wrong?"

"I'm okay," I reassured as I met up with him.

He didn't look relieved. I couldn't blame him. He reached out, but I stepped back. This felt different from all the times before. Maybe because before I could pretend Travis was like a brother. He was a confidant that I went to in times of trouble, but now—now he was more, and my feelings toward him were no longer virtuous or familial. I felt guilty for even being here, like I was cheating on Oliver just by talking to him. And I hated it.

"You look like you're gonna cry," he said, folding his muscled arms over his broad chest.

"I'm not hurt. I just— We can't do this anymore."

His lips parted, and his eyes narrowed. "Do what? Talk?"

"I can't come to you like this anymore. My future is with Oliver, and now I feel guilty for even coming here, but I needed to tell you in person."

His eyes shifted, and he let out a breath. "Don't make this into something it's not." He dropped his arms to his sides. "We're friends, Addie. Just friends, and we won't cross that line again."

I stared at him as my vision clouded. For the last three years, I'd been telling myself that Travis was unattainable. Sure he knew some of my deepest secrets, and as long as we remained friends, I could keep him. But the moment we became more—the moment I gave him my heart, he would soon get bored and toss me aside. I'd seen it too many times. There was an expiration date on his relationships, and I'd once had a gallon of milk that outlasted three of his girlfriends. He was not the kind of guy that settled down. It's why I pursued his handsome and compassionate best friend.

Oliver and I didn't have that deep connection that Travis and I shared, but Oliver was reliable and consistent. He had a heart of gold and treated me like a princess where Travis had continuously pushed me away. Oliver was not only the safer choice, he was really the only choice.

Travis was just the sex on a stick bad boy who would only break my heart. But I was too smart to let him. I had big goals and was on course with my life's plan. I couldn't let my feelings for Travis derail everything I'd worked so hard to accomplish. Especially not when I had Oliver, who was so . . . perfect. Even my dad knew it.

I had always been stronger than my emotions, so I knew I could beat this. We could beat this.

It was just a crush.

A stupid, horrible, debilitating crush.

"I just don't think we should spend any more time together."

He stared at me, his hands tucked into his pockets. "You're not here to tell me you're ending our friendship. You're here because your dad made you doubt yourself, and you don't know how to handle everything you're feeling. You can't go to Oliver because he worships the judge, and you don't have anyone else who understands you like I do."

I blinked. Was he right? He always thought he was smarter than me. "There's no room in my life for a romantic relationship with you, Travis."

He scoffed. "Don't flatter yourself, princess. I know how to keep my hands to myself. It was one kiss."

We both knew that wasn't true, but maybe he was just as unprepared to face the truth as I was.

I gulped in a breath. "Not only would this destroy you and Oli's friendship, but also my father would disown me, and I would lose Oliver. I can't do that. I might care about you both, but I already chose him."

"Add, I get it!" His voice was rough, but his honey brown eyes stayed soft. I knew I was hurting him, but I needed him to hear me.

"I just want to be clear."

He nodded, keeping his distance. "I read you. Loud and clear."

"Good." I nodded as dread filled my body. The heaviness of it weighed me down, making my limbs move slower. I didn't know what I'd do without these talks with him. I always felt lighter after unloading my burdens, but now I clung tight to the bulky encumbrance and spun away from him. I moved in slow motion toward the car. It wasn't deliberate. It was just that I felt like I was climbing a sand dune, my feet slipping out from under me as I trudged ahead.

The kiss wouldn't happen again. I wouldn't become that person. The bitch, the cheater, the weak-minded woman who put her emotions before everything else.

I hadn't heard Travis move, but he unexpectedly twirled me toward him, tucking my face into the crook of his shoulder as he wrapped his arms around me. The night was chilly, but his body warmed me. The tears and tension I'd barely been containing escaped on a sob. I clung to him, my fingers fisting in his jacket as I cried—the heaviness melting away as we stood together.

His cheek rested on my head while one of his hands ran through my hair in a soothing motion. "Let it go. Everything's gonna be fine. I'm not going anywhere."

I tried to pull away. "But—"

His grip tightened. "Shh. We're friends, Add. Just friends. That's all we'll ever be."

Great relief washed over me.

I believed him. We were adults. We knew how to control ourselves.

4

—————

TRAVIS

OVER WINTER BREAK, we gathered at Oliver's dad's house for Christmas Eve's eve. His parents had gotten divorced when Oli and I were in middle school. It was an amicable separation that went against everything I had ever heard about divorce. His parents remained friends even after they both remarried.

We always celebrated Christmas with his dad on Christmas Eve's Eve. It was a tradition that started after Oliver's parents split up. He was with his mom for Christmas, so he had his own night with his dad, and since I was practically family, I was there every year for as long as I can remember.

And just like the last two years, Addison came home with Oliver. The three of us traveled together. It had only been two months since the kiss, and a month since we talked, and I still believed I had self-control. At twenty years old, I should have been able to control myself. At least that's what I told myself. We acted as if it had never happened, going right back to being nothing more than friends.

Oli and I unpacked the car while Addison ran inside to use the bathroom.

"I swear that woman's bladder is the size of a pea," Oli complained.

"Not ideal for road trips," I seconded as we trudged up the steps to the front door.

Oli and I said hello to Buck as we entered the house. The tall burly man with olive skin was basically my second father. Oliver looked a lot like him minus fifty or so pounds, and Oliver had his mom's blue eyes while Buck's were brown. Buck was a handsome guy and a good man. There were many times I'd wished he was my own dad. I gave him a big hug, cutting in front of Oliver. "We all know you missed me the most," I teased.

Buck laughed, and I stepped back, looking around, noting his wife's absence. "Where's Janet?"

"She had a work party tonight. She won't be home until late."

Oliver stepped in to hug his dad. "Spouses weren't invited to her work thing?"

"Not this year, but you won't hear me complain. There are some good games on tonight."

Addison came down the hall from the bathroom and Buck said, "Now, there's my girl."

Addison's smile was so easy. They wrapped each other in a tight hug.

Buck said, "My boy still treating you like a princess?"

She let out a light laugh. "He's practically my knight in shining armor."

"Good, that's what I like to hear. You tell me if that changes."

Oliver lifted his and Addison's bags. "I'm gonna go throw these in my room."

He left and I was about to follow when Buck said, "Are you staying here tonight?"

"No, my mom is working late at the diner, but she has tomorrow off, so I'm going to meet her later tonight."

His voice dropped. "Are you gonna see your dad while you're in town?"

I lifted a shoulder and let it fall. "I don't know. We'll see."

He eyed the duffle bag on my shoulder. "If you're not staying, then what's with the bag?"

I adjusted the strap on my shoulder while Addison helpfully offered, "He needs to shower."

"Are you laughing?" I tried to stay serious, but her smile was contagious. "You are! You're laughing at me when it was your fault."

She broke out into a fit of giggles. "I'm sorry, I'm trying not to laugh. I don't mean it."

Buck scratched his head. "What am I missing?"

"Miss Priss over there, spilled her drink all over me."

"It was an accident," she voiced.

"You have no defense. Who doesn't put their damn cup in the cupholder?"

"The cup holder was full, and I was distracted, passing out the food."

"And it took you forever because you couldn't stop looking at those damn flashcards," I said to her, before turning to Buck. "So Oliver was driving and Addison had shotgun. Meanwhile, I'm half asleep in the back seat. We go through a drive-thru, and Addison orders a large soda to help keep her awake so she can study."

Addison added, "The MCAT is coming up. Do you know how big of a deal that is?"

I scoffed. "You wanna be a doctor, yet the simplicity of putting your cup in a cupholder is lost on you." I turned back to Buck. "Her flashcards took up the cupholder so she set her large drink on the center console."

She cut in, "I was passing out the food. I didn't know Oliver was going to pull out onto the road just then," she added.

The smile on Buck's face grew, knowing what was coming next.

"Yeah," I said, confirming his suspicions. "Her entire drink flips into my lap. The lid popped off, soaking me in freezing sticky liquid an hour into our eight-hour drive. I'm dry now, but I'm still sticky as fuck and feel disgusting."

Addison held her hands against her lips like she was praying or begging for forgiveness. "I'm so sorry, Travis."

I puffed. "Sure you are," I said, messing with her. It was fun to mess with miss perfection. She got so flustered.

Buck laughed. "Cut her some slack, at least it wasn't hot coffee."

I grimaced because the majority spilled right in my lap. My dick shriveled just thinking about it. I guess I'd rather get a sticky ice bath than second-degree burns.

Addison threw her hands out. "See, there is a bright side."

I shook my head, adjusting the bag's strap again. "I'm gonna go shower. Don't have too much fun without me, and make sure to give Addison a sippy cup."

I headed through the living room and down the hall that led to the bedrooms. The bathroom was at the back of the house, and just as I was about to walk in, Oliver jumped out from a doorway, yelling.

I jumped back, throwing my bag at the fucker.

He laughed, while I bent at the waist, clutching my chest, catching my breath.

"That was awesome!" he gloated.

"Fuck you, man," I said, regaining my ability to stand straight. "I fucking hate you."

He smirked. "At least we know what you'll do if you ever get mugged," he said, picking up my bag. He held the bag in front of him and in a high voice, said, "Please, just take my things. Please don't hurt me."

"I can't wait to get you back. Wipe that smug smile right off your face."

He handed me the bag and headed in the other direction, laughing the whole way while I stepped into the bathroom, locked the door, and checked for booby traps. I plotted my revenge while I showered.

AFTER MY SHOWER, I heard Oliver in the kitchen and snuck behind the wall separating the rooms. When I heard footsteps coming toward me, I readied myself, and just before he came around the corner, I jumped out and shouted.

Addison jumped. "Oh my god!" she squealed, throwing the mug of hot chocolate she just made down the front of me.

The drink was hot but not scalding. Still, I was soaked…again.

"What the fuck, Travis?"

I pinched the front of my soaked T-shirt and held it away from my skin, laughing. "Geez, you should seriously consider sippy cups from now on."

"I wasn't expecting to be ambushed."

"I thought you were Oliver."

She rolled her eyes. "Oli and Buck left. They had some last-minute Christmas shopping to do."

"So, it's just us?" I swallowed, making it weird. Shit.

Addison pointed to the floor. "You're helping me clean this up!"

"Of course."

After we mopped up the floor, I went to Oliver's room to change my shirt. She followed, needing new socks since hers got wet. I didn't hesitate to take my shirt off in front of her. She'd seen me shirtless before. It wasn't a big deal. I'd also been working out, and part of me wanted her to see me. I wanted to tempt her like she tempted me.

Addison was not impulsive. She made very long and thought-out plans for her life. She knew she wanted to be a doctor and had a ten-year plan to reach all of her goals. I'd seen her list. It was insane.

So I knew she'd been thinking about me when her hands grabbed the clean shirt out of my hands and chucked it across the room. Her hands roamed my torso, her fingertips sending a shockwave of desire through me. She was tall for a girl, but I still had several inches on her. She tipped her head up, eyeing my mouth. "Travis . . ."

"Addie," I said, wrapping my hands around her waist, my fingers digging into the small of her back. I wanted to pull her forward but knew I should hold her back. This was a mistake. Her tongue wet her lips, and I inhaled sharply, my resistance slipping. She inched forward painfully slow. Her soft lips pressed into mine.

I hesitated, but only for a second because I was a weak bastard. Her tongue slipped into my mouth, and my restraint failed. A moan escaped me as her tongue swept along mine. My grip on her tightened, and I pulled her against me, pressing my straining cock against her pelvis. I walked her backward until she was pushed against a wall. I slid my thigh between her legs and rocked against her as we inhaled each other's pleasure noises.

"Travis," she whimpered, and all I could think of was putting my dick inside of her.

She pulled back, panting, "I know we agreed this would never happen, but maybe this thing between us is just physical. Maybe you just need to get me out of your system, and then we can go back to the way things used to be. Nothing more tempting than what you can't have."

She had a point, and she always had the right answers, so in that moment, while thinking with my dick and Addison's fucked up logic, it all made sense. She closed the bedroom door and locked it before shedding all of her clothes.

Before I could think of a reason not to, I was slipping out of my jeans and boxers. She attacked, kissing and groping, braver than I expected. She grabbed my cock and stroked. I tried to reach between her thighs, but she said, "No time. Do you have a condom?"

I had to bend down to get the condom from my wallet, and then we were in business. There was no time for foreplay, or perhaps the last three years had been our own version of foreplay.

Part of me remembered where I was, and I knew I couldn't fuck her on Oli's bed, so I sat her on the dresser, and she separated her thighs. I stepped between them and pulled her to the very edge before sinking into her warm wet center. Long silky legs wrapped around my hips, and I tried to show her my best moves, but our position made it challenging.

I couldn't believe it was happening. Her nails scraped my back, and she bit my shoulder in an attempt to quiet herself. I did my best to draw it out, making it last because I knew once it was over, it would never happen again.

As I was buried deep inside her, I pulled back to take her in. Her eyes fluttered shut as her head fell back, her full pink lips parted with a deep intake of breath. She lifted her head. Her heavy-lidded eyes opened to show azure irises that sparkled with desire as her gaze locked on mine. At that moment, I knew there was no fucking her out of my system. If anything, she was ruining every other woman for me, forever.

It wasn't just lust that drew us together. It wasn't just her pretty face and gorgeous body that made me crave her. We knew so many intimate details about one another. I knew her mind, her heart, and now I was learning her body. I wanted to worship her. I wanted to watch her shatter with pleasure. My hands ran through her long blonde strands and skimmed down her body, everywhere I could reach.

When it came to Addison, I found every complex layer devastatingly beautiful. She was single-handedly destroying me. I needed to remember every single detail about her because I could feel her slipping away even as I moved inside of her.

The garage door was noisy, so we knew the moment it opened. Someone was home.

Her eyes widened in panic, but we didn't stop. I pounded into her harder, needing her to feel me later, needing her to remember that I gave her that ache between her legs. I bit her shoulder as I shuttered to a stop. As soon as I was still, she pushed me back.

I hadn't bit her hard enough to leave a mark, but she inspected her shoulder to make sure, and then she slipped off the dresser and threw on her clothes, saying, "I'll tell him I dumped my hot cocoa on you and you're changing." She turned to me once she was dressed, running her hands through her hair, she asked, "Do I look okay?"

I was in a state of shock. "Beautiful," I managed to say.

She nodded, and then she was gone, shutting the door behind her. I was still naked, the condom hanging from my limp dick as I tried to figure out what the fuck just happened. I saw myself in the mirror and was sickened at the sight. I felt used—destroyed and I barely got to enjoy the destruction before it was over and I was left behind without a second glance. She ran out like our moment meant nothing, like one time with me couldn't be over fast enough.

I guess Oliver was better in bed than I was. She didn't even give me a chance. I covered my face, disgusted with myself. I just had sex with my friend's girlfriend in his childhood bedroom while he was out buying her a gift. And what the fuck was I supposed to do with the condom?

I got cleaned up, tied the condom off, wrapped it in tissues, and threw it in the garbage. I looked down at the little garbage can and imagined Oliver's used condoms thrown on top of mine. He would probably assume it was his own if he came across it. I hated the idea of them having sex. I wanted to be possessive of her but had absolutely no right. I still couldn't stomach thinking about our condoms touching, so I took the garbage bag out of the small can, tied it up, and threw it in the bag with my clothes.

I pulled on my boxers, jeans, and a clean t-shirt. Zipping

my bag, I lugged it onto my shoulder. Running my fingers through my hair one last time, I glared at myself in the mirror before leaving. On my way out, I turned on the ceiling fan to get rid of any lingering sex smells.

I pulled myself together as I went out to join the others, worried I'd taken too much time and that they would be wondering what was taking me so long. But when I reached the living room, Buck was alone on the couch watching the football game.

"Where's Oliver?"

He didn't look up at me as he answered, "You know how bad he is at surprises. He needed to give Addison her gift right away."

"Oh," I said, "What'd he get her?"

"A TV. It's a nice one. He said hers broke a few weeks ago. You should go out and look."

I hesitated to go, but I felt antsy and weird and needed to do something because the longer I sat with Buck, the more I felt like he could hear every thought in my head, despite him being lost in the football game.

I went through the kitchen to the garage. I started to step out when I heard panting. Addison moaned, and I caught a glimpse of Oliver's bare ass as he fucked his girlfriend against his dad's car.

Addison was facing me, and our eyes caught for a second before she looked away, and I turned around and went back inside. Scrubbing my hands over my face, I paced the kitchen before pulling out my phone.

I walked back into the living room with the phone to my ear, saying, "Stay where you are. I'll be right there." I hung up my nonexistent call, and Buck was already looking at me. "Everything alright?"

I was going to Hell for this. "No, my dad's drunk again. I guess he's trying to drive home from the bar. I'm gonna go get him."

"Piece of shit," Buck grumbled. He always let me know what he thought of my alcohol dependent father.

After grabbing my bag and coat, I told Buck, "Tell Oli I'll bring the car back tomorrow."

He nodded, and I ran out the door, fleeing into the cold winter night.

5

ADDISON

I didn't know that it was possible to hate myself so much. All the feelings I had convinced myself I could overcome had turned around and destroyed me. I had drowned myself in my own emotions.

My drink dumped on Travis in the car because I was so flustered by his close proximity, especially with those sexy, sleepy eyes. I was too busy squirming in my seat to care where my drink was until it spilled in Travis's crotch.

I didn't know how I was going to get through the week with him around. I didn't know how to undo these feelings that grew inside like a wild inferno. I was burning with lust —with need and being with Oliver only took the edge off.

So when I saw Travis not so innocently flaunting his bare chest in front of me, I knew what he wanted, and I was dying to give in to the need. I was praying I could get him out of my system or that he could get me out of his. If we couldn't ignore our attraction, then maybe we could get over it together. But seeing him gloriously naked only increased my need for him, and the feel of him between my legs was heavenly. But what chilled me to the bone was the passionate look in his eyes as he was buried inside me. It was no fling for him. He wouldn't betray his friend unless he felt I was worth it. It flooded me with so much shame that I couldn't enjoy what was happening. I let him have his way with me while thoughts of Oliver assaulted me, making me feel like the shitty person I'd become.

Afterward, the look of pain on Travis's handsome face when I pulled away so quickly nearly broke my heart. I'd hurt him. I wanted to apologize, but that seemed like it would only make things worse. I was selfish and stupid and was too consumed with my desires that I didn't think of the consequences. And there were so many consequences.

When I found Oliver in the living room, I was sure he'd be able to see my guilt, but he was too excited to give me my present. He took my traitorous hand and led me out to the garage to show off the TV he bought for me. I didn't care about his gift. I cared about him, and I wanted the mistake I'd just made to go away. I wished there was an undo button. I prayed for an undo button, but those didn't exist in real life.

He leaned in to kiss me, and I felt relief. He still loved me. He didn't know I was a terrible person. I thought about telling him what I had done, but he would hate me. It was too late to take it back. I had already fucked up. If I told Oliver the truth, it would hurt him. Travis and I were already hurting, but Oliver didn't deserve this.

Oliver was the best thing that had ever happened to me, and I couldn't hit undo, but I could reset. I could focus on him. Our kiss deepened, and I knew how to make it better. At least temporarily.

I unbuttoned his pants and took down his zipper, reaching for him.

"Babe?" he had questioned.

But I was too focused on how I was going to make it better. I needed him inside me. I needed him to claim me, and it would be as if Travis had never been there.

I stripped out of my pants and sat on the side of the car with my legs spread. Oliver looked like he'd just won the jackpot. He reached for a condom, but I pulled him in. I was on the pill, and right now, I needed him raw.

He didn't argue. He slid between my thighs, and I wanted to cry. This wasn't right. This felt so very wrong, but I couldn't pull away now. Then I would be a tease on top of an unfaithful whore. I faked a moan and grabbed onto Oliver's shoulders. The door to the kitchen opened, and Travis stood there for a second. I couldn't look him in the eye. I knew what it must have looked like to him, and I couldn't stomach his disappointment. The next time I looked up, Travis was gone.

My attempt at making the situation better had only made things so much worse. I clung to Oliver until he finished, but when he pulled back, I knew I couldn't contain my tears.

"Hey, what's wrong?" he asked, his blue eyes filled with concern as he wiped my cheeks.

I fought the urge to pull away. "I'm just emotional, I guess."

"Did I do something wrong?"

I wanted to shout, *Yes, you chose me!* But instead, I shook my head. "No, Oli. You're perfect."

I slid off the car onto my feet, feeling Oliver's release slide down my inner thigh. What if I had just gotten pregnant? I wouldn't be certain who the father was. That thought sent me into a downward spiral of self-loathing, and I knew I'd never look at myself the same.

How had everything happened so quickly? And how did I make it better?

Oliver helped me with my pants, saying, "You've been studying too much, Addie. All that stress has to be getting to you."

I nodded. Because what could I say?

As we went into the house, I said, "I think I'm going to shower and go to bed early tonight. You're probably right about the stress."

A little while later, I stripped naked in front of the bathroom mirror. I'd let two men fuck me today. Two best friends. Within minutes of each other. And worse. I might be in love with both of them.

My father had seen my weakness over Thanksgiving and warned me against following my emotions. He would be so disappointed in me if he knew how badly I messed up.

I cranked the hot water and steam slowly fogged up the mirror, hiding my reflection. I stepped into the scalding heat of the shower, right under the spray. The water stung against my skin, turning it bright red. It burned, but I didn't turn it down. I deserved the pain. It was my punishment.

6

***

TRAVIS

MY LIE WASN'T that far from the truth. I did go check on my dad. He was a sore excuse for a father growing up, but the older I got, the more I felt sorry for him. Charles Rose had been dealt a rough hand in life and never recovered after his time in the army.

He used to be a handsome man, tall and fit, but that had long disappeared. His muscles had deteriorated, leaving his easily bruised skin saggy beyond his years. He was too skinny aside from the beer belly that hung over his pants, looking like he was five months pregnant. His hair had thinned, and his sunken face had an unnatural yellow tint.

He didn't appear surprised when I showed up at his door. He didn't ask why I was there or make a big deal about me visiting. In fact, he didn't ask me anything. He just handed me a beer and invited me into his crappy apartment that reeked of cigarettes and stale beer.

I tried for ten years to get him to stop drinking, but I'd come to accept it. It was the only way he knew how to cope, and even though he was showing signs of liver failure, I took the beer he offered and clinked it to his. I sat on his musty sagging couch, drinking with him in silence while we watched his small fuzzy TV. It was the same football game on across town at Buck's house on his big screen television with cozy couches and clean air.

I owed a lot to Oliver's family. When I was young, and my dad couldn't be trusted with his own life, let alone a child's life, I followed Oliver around. My mom was always working, so I would go home with Oli after school. I spent the summers with him, vacationed with him. His family took me in and never complained about me being around. I got used to being part of their family, forgetting *this* is actually where I belonged, on this worn-down sofa in this run-down apartment with the broken man that was my father.

How different would my life have turned out if it weren't for Oliver? I owed him a hell of a lot, and he never asked for anything in return. He never expected anything from me, and how did I repay him for everything he'd done for me? I fucked his girlfriend like the piece of shit I really was. And since he always saw the good in everyone, he didn't know that I was a threat. That I could fuck up his life.

I wanted to be better, but my blood was tainted, and I would never be good enough for the life I wanted. I could pretend that I belonged in Oliver's world, but I would never be good enough for Addison, and we all knew it.

It reminded me of the first time I went to Oliver's house. The first couple summers after we met, our moms took us to parks to play together, but the summer after first grade I visited Oliver's house for the first time, and it became very clear how different our worlds were.

~

STIFLING summer heat wafted through the open windows. My mom had set up all the fans around the trailer, but they did nothing but recycle the same hot air. I peeled myself off the sofa, my sweat leaving a damp imprint behind. My mom wasn't gonna like that. I had stripped out of my shirt and wore only my swim trunks. Mom said when she got off work, she would take me swimming.

She also told me to stay in the house and not to answer the door. I didn't know why. I wasn't a baby. I was seven years old, and I looked like I was eight. I stepped outside, knowing we lived too close to all of our neighbors to go completely unnoticed, but if I behaved then hopefully no one would tell my mom that I had been outside.

There was no breeze between the trailers so it was just as hot outdoors as it was inside. I got the hose out, twisting the knob with both hands because it always stuck. Once I succeeded, I pointed the nozzle straight up in the air, letting the water fall over me like rain. The blissfully cold water felt good in the heat. It cooled my skin and I lowered the nozzle to take a drink.

A shiny dark green minivan with tinted windows crunched along the narrow gravel drive. It was nice—too nice for this neighborhood. It was either stolen or they were lost. Either way, I knew to mind my own business.

I looked away, spraying my feet. That's when the van pulled into our driveway. The sun reflected off the dark windows so I couldn't see who was inside. I gripped the hose tighter and looked for something I could use as a weapon. I was eyeing my neighbor's garden gnome when the van door slid open. I looked up in time to see Oliver jump out. "Travis!"

I dropped the hose, about to greet him when I remembered how loud Mom yelled last time I left the hose on. By the time I turned it off, Oli stood a couple feet away. His skin got really tan in the summer, much darker than mine ever got, and his dark brown hair looked almost as light as mine did.

People had mistaken us for brothers, but we didn't look alike. His eyes were bright blue while mine were brown. I stood several inches above him even though we were the same age. Oli was grinning, like always. I couldn't smile as much as he did. Too much smiling made my cheeks hurt.

But seeing him now, I was smiling. "What're you doin' here?'

"I missed you. Do you want to come to my house and play?"

"I can't. I have to wait until my mom comes home."

"Where is she?"

"At work."

"Do you want to come over tomorrow? Mom said we can pick you up," he said, pointing at the van.

I looked at the fancy van and then back to Oli. "I'll ask my mom."

THE FOLLOWING DAY, Mom agreed to drop me off at Oliver's on her way to work. It wasn't rainy but the hot air felt wet as it blew through the open car windows on the drive over to Oli's. The houses in his neighborhood looked huge, with multiple floors and big porches. The yards were big and green. The grass at the trailer park was mostly brown, except Miss Kiddy's yard, but that's because she covered it in that grass carpet stuff.

Mom pulled the car onto the side of the road, gawking at the house as her fingers plucked the cigarette out of her mouth. "Travis, hun, I don't know if I wrote down the right address? I swear this is the address Kim told me, but . . . " she stared out the window at the house. "You said, they came to the trailer yesterday?"

"Yeah."

Her brows scrunched together and her lips twisted. She tapped her fingers on the steering wheel.

Oliver bound out of the house, looking tiny on the massive porch.

Mom sighed, stubbing out her cigarette in the ashtray. She unbuckled her seatbelt and I undid mine, grabbing my backpack.

She was in her mustard yellow waitress dress as she walked me to the front door. Before we went up the porch steps, she turned to me, saying, "Travis, I can't afford to pay for stuff you break so please don't break nothing."

That made me nervous, but if I didn't agree, she wouldn't let me stay. "Okay."

Oliver walked us inside. Despite the hot day it was cold inside the house and it didn't feel so wet. I decided I'd stay just for the cold air. And Oliver probably had cool toys.

Mom bit her lip while she looked me over. She looked unsure. Then she pulled me aside. "Travis, are you sure you want to stay the night here?

"Yeah."

"Are you sure?"

"I promise I won't break nothing."

Oliver's mom came to talk to my mom, and Oli pulled me away so he could show me his toy room.

"You have a room just for your toys?"

"Yeah, don't you?"

I shook my head and followed him through the biggest house I'd ever stepped foot in.

It felt weird to sleep at someone else's house but I loved Oli's cold house with his room of toys. His family was really nice and they had the best snacks. I was excited for my first sleepover and Oliver had a bunk bed, so I wouldn't have to sleep on the floor like I thought.

As we got ready for bed that evening, Oliver claimed the top bunk. That was fine by me. I could protect us both better from the bottom bunk. Once he climbed to the top, I got up and closed the door, flipping the lock.

"What are you doing?" Oli asked.

I crawled into bed. "Locking the door so nobody can get to us."

"Who would get us?" he asked, leaning over the railing to look down at me. "I always sleep with the door open."

"But what if your dad has a bad dream?"

Oliver's face scrunched. "Dad's don't have bad dreams. They're grownups."

"My dad has bad dreams," I said, rubbing at the scar at my throat.

Oliver looked confused. "My sister used to sleepwalk."

I nodded. "My dad does that too. My mom called it flashbacks. He talks and fights sometimes too."

Oli hung over further, sounding impressed. "All while he's sleeping? That's so cool!"

I grimaced. "No, it's not."

Oliver climbed down the ladder. "Well, no one sleepwalks here so we can keep it open." He opened the door and I stared through it, frightened, but I couldn't tell my friend that I was scared. My dad said boys weren't supposed to be afraid.

I stayed quiet as Oli climbed back to the top bunk. Once he was settled, I pulled my overnight bag closer to the bed and slipped the black bar under the blankets next to me. It was heavy and kinda sharp at the curved end. I'd snuck it out of the tool chest this morning before leaving my house. I held it tight as I watched the door.

Oliver was telling me about a TV show I'd never heard of before. At home we only had six channels, but Oli had hundreds of channels and some of them played nothing but cartoons. I wondered why we didn't get those channels.

Oli talked nonstop about this show and ended up falling asleep right in the middle of a sentence. I was shocked by how quickly he fell asleep. Maybe because he felt he was safe, but I knew I needed to lock us in to make sure.

I got up, carrying the heavy black rod with me. I closed the door and slid the lock in place.

THE NEXT MORNING while we were eating breakfast, Oli got in trouble for locking his door. When I tried to admit that it was my fault, Oli talked right over me, taking the blame.

I prepared for yelling, but his mom stayed calm, saying, "I know you're growing up, but what if there had been an accident, we wouldn't have been able to get to you."

Oli hung his head. "Sorry, mom. It won't happen again."

After breakfast, I asked Oli, "Why'd you take the blame?"

Oli shrugged. "We're buddies, right? That's what buddies do."

"I won't lock the door next time," I promised.

Oli smiled really big. "Next time, there will be boobytraps. We can set them to catch any bad guys or sleepwalkers."

At that thought, I smiled so big, my cheeks hurt, but it was worth it.

WE CAME from different worlds but Oli invited me into his life and I swallowed up everything he and his family gave me. I always knew I didn't belong but they never made me feel inferior. But sitting here next to my father was a brutal reminder of where I really belonged.

I avoided Addison and Oli for the remainder of winter break, and on the drive back to school, I pretended to sleep the whole way. I was too hungover to drive and too heartsick to make conversation. So as usual, I contributed nothing, and no one blinked an eye or expected more from me.

TRAVIS

THE STICKY JULY heat of upstate New York stuck to my skin as I entered the sliding glass doors of the emergency department. The cool sterile air was a balm to my frazzled nerves. My mom had been in hysterics when she'd called from the back of the ambulance.

I went to the desk, and they showed me back to my dad's room. I found my mom biting her nails as she paced the hall outside his closed door.

"Travis," she called through her tears when she spotted me.

I moved to her, wrapping her in a hug. "Mom, why aren't you in there?"

"They found out we're not married anymore and shoved me out of there like I'm nothing," she admitted.

Even though they'd been divorced for sixteen years, she still loved my father. She just couldn't handle him. It's excruciating to watch someone you love slowly destroy themselves.

She was already a petite woman, barely above five feet, and as I held her, I realized how skinny she was getting. She was a chain smoker and often forgot to eat during her shifts at work.

"Mom, you need to eat more."

"How can I eat when he's just lyin' there dying?"

This was his third time in the hospital this month for his ever-worsening cirrhosis of the liver. We knew his liver was failing, and things were only going to get worse from here. A transplant was out of the question as he refused to quit drinking. Arguing wouldn't get me anywhere, so I kissed the top of her head before pulling away.

She didn't let me go far, grabbing my hands as she looked up at me. "You know, your dad used to be so handsome." Her hand reached up to cradle my cheek. "You look so much like him," she said with adoration, but it was a reminder I didn't want. I never wanted to be anything like my father.

"What are we gonna do without him?" she said as if she'd forgotten the man had been nothing but a detriment to both of our lives.

Oliver and Addison showed up just then, saving me from the conversation. Oliver said a quick *hello* to me, slapping a hand on my shoulder and squeezing before wrapping his arm around my mom, consoling her in a way only Oliver could.

"Oli, I'm so glad you came." She touched his cheek the same way she'd just touched mine, but perhaps with more affection than I'd seen. "What did we ever do to deserve you?"

Oliver smiled, saying, "Let's go grab a coffee."

She nodded, and the two of them walked away, leaving Addie and me alone in the hall. I stared after them even after they had gone. Addison and I hadn't seen each other since Christmas break. It took some meticulous planning, but I managed to get time with just Oliver. I was under the impression that she hadn't wanted to see me any more than I wanted to see her. Yet, here she was, and I didn't know why.

Addison's hand touched my arm as she asked, "How are you?"

I turned and made eye contact with her for the first time since I caught her and Oliver having sex. Her eyebrows pinched with concern as she bit her lip, the depth of her blue eyes shining with so many unspoken emotions.

All the anger and hurt I'd been holding onto disappeared at the sight of her. Stepping forward, I wrapped her in a hug, touched that she'd come. She wasn't there as Oli's girl-friend. She was there as my friend, and I needed her. I was moved that our friendship meant enough that she'd come. Holding her gave me hope that we hadn't fucked everything up.

When she pulled away, she had tears in her eyes. "I'm so sorry, Travis," she whispered, "I missed you. It was such a dumb idea. It didn't make anything better. I felt so guilty, and I just, I needed to forget that it ever happened. I thought that if Oli and I—"

Shaking my head, I took her hand in mine. "Stop," I begged. "I don't want to think about that night."

"Okay," she whispered, squeezing my hand. "So, you never did answer. How are you?"

"Better with you guys here. Oliver has a way with my mom. I can only do so much. Before I got here, I guess she was wailing and carrying on."

"Have you talked to your dad about his drinking?" she asked.

"He's forty-eight years old, Addie. If he hasn't stopped yet, I don't think he's going to."

"Maybe this was a wake-up call," she suggested.

I let out a breath, knowing this was the beginning of the end for him. I said, "Did you know he has night terrors and flashbacks?"

She shook her head.

I looked toward his hospital room. "He screams in his sleep and sometimes wakes up thinking he's under attack. When I was four, before my parents were divorced, he dragged me out of bed in the middle of the night, put a knife to my throat, and held me in front of him to keep my mother from coming closer. He thought he was at war, and we were the enemy. He seemed to wake up or snap out of it before he really hurt me, but afterward, he cradled me and sobbed. I had a few scratches on my neck. That was it as far as physical harm, but it fucked me up, Add.

"My mom moved us out after that, and for the next five years, I was terrified of my dad. I wouldn't sleep in the dark. My mom had to take the lock off my door because I kept locking myself in at night. I still have trouble sleeping because of what happened when I was four years old. I didn't go to war. I didn't kill anyone. I didn't watch my best friend die.

"My dad doesn't want to get better, Addie. He wants to numb the pain until he dies. He's suffered enough. Would I rather he stopped drinking and get the help he needs? Of course, but I can't force him to do those things, and he's had plenty of opportunities. I don't want him to die, but sometimes people don't need medical treatment. They need acceptance."

"That feels hopeless. There has to be something—"

I moved my gaze to her. "It's inevitable, Addie. He's the only one who can save himself, and he's not going to. Even the doctors have given up on him. Everyone here knows he's a dead man walking. I know you want to heal everyone, but some people don't get better."

"That's sad."

I nodded, looking back toward my father's hospital room.

"So, what are they going to do?"

Drawing out my next inhale, I confessed, "I'm moving here."

Addison's chin jerked toward me. I didn't have the heart to look at her. I knew there would be accusation and disappointment written on her face. She'd worked so hard to get me into college—determined for me to make something of myself.

I continued to look straight ahead at my dad's door. "My mom can't do this on her own. She's still in love with the man, and he's destroying himself. She's a basket-case whenever they're together. I'm transferring back here. I might not be able to take classes for a while, but I'll get a job and get a place with my dad. They said once a person is at this stage, it usually goes pretty quickly, but it could be another year. No one really knows."

She squeezed my hand, and with her other, she turned my chin toward her, forcing me to look at her. "They don't deserve you, T. You're amazing." She kissed my cheek before stepping back. "But you have to promise me that you'll go back to school. You've come so far since precalc. You're smart. I won't let you waste that brain of yours."

"I'll do my best," I said, glancing back to the door.

"Have you been in there yet?"

I shook my head. "No, but I should before my mom gets back."

She took my hand. "I'll go with you."

I nodded, and together we stepped forward.

8

ADDISON

THERE WAS a little nip in the October air. I didn't expect it to be this cold in North Carolina, but the evening breeze caused a chill to spread over my exposed legs. Part of the reason I moved south for college was to bask in more temperate climates. It was warmer than New York, but the seasons still changed. I knew it was time to break out my jackets, but I held off for one more night.

Luckily it was a quick walk into the new, upscale restaurant I'd been dying to visit. Oliver had told me to get dolled up, so even though it was chilly, I still wore a cute red dress that didn't fit the weather. Its boatneck ended in short sleeves, while the waistline cinched before flaring out in a full skirt that ended a few inches above my knee. It gave the illusion of curves, accentuating what little I had. My long blonde strands were pulled up into a chignon, keeping it simple but elegant.

I had a black wrap and a clutch that matched the dress. Oliver wore a suit. He always looked handsome, but I loved him in a suit. I wasn't sure how he got the reservation at this restaurant, but if the past had taught me anything, it was that Oliver knew how to wow me on my birthday. The gorgeous dining room was filled with well-dressed patrons, murmuring over the soft music and delicious smells. Looking around, I saw the portions looked like tiny pieces of art.

Oliver pulled out my chair. He helped remove my wrap and waited for me to sit before pushing me toward the table. The man knew his manners. He took his seat across from me and ordered a bottle of wine for the table. I knew this wasn't the typical place most would choose to spend their twenty-first birthday. This was the kind of place one would expect a proposal, and for a minute, I got nervous, but Oliver knew the plan. I wouldn't get married until I finished med school. Twenty-one was far too young to think about marriage.

I knew I acted older than my age, but I had big goals and wanted to be taken seriously.

Oliver leaned across the table, holding my hands in his. "Happy birthday, Addison. You look absolutely stunning. You know I love you, and I'm not proposing so you can wipe that worried look off your face. This restaurant was your idea."

I laughed. He knew me too well. "Sorry," I said, chagrined, "Thank you for bringing me here. It's beautiful, and you look handsome as always. Everything is perfect, thanks to you."

"You haven't even opened my gift yet," he said, pulling a long Tiffany's jewelry box from his pocket.

I smiled at his impatience. "You couldn't even wait until we order our meals. You're so impatient."

He slid the box across the table. "At least I made it to the restaurant."

"This is true."

"Open it," he insisted.

I took the blue box in my hand and opened it. A delicate chain held a diamond encrusted infinity pendant.

"It's not a proposal, but that doesn't mean I don't plan on being with you forever. Think of it as a promise."

I looked up from the beautiful and meaningful gift to stare into Oliver's indigo eyes. "It's perfect."

I lifted it out of the box and clasped it around my bare neck. The delicate pendant hit just below my neckline, the sparkle standing out against the red background.

"Gorgeous," he chimed.

I fingered the pendant as I said, "Thank you, Oli."

Our waiter came with our wine, and we both took a moment to look over our menus. After ordering, Oliver asked, "Did you volunteer yesterday?"

I held in my eye-roll. He loved that I volunteered with the homeless. He thought it spoke volumes about my character that I wanted to give back. I only started volunteering to pad my resume, and I continued because it was something Oliver loved about me, and sometimes he'd go with me. I never told him how much I hated it. Volunteering made me feel guilty for being privileged. It was depressing, but the way Oliver looked at me made me feel like a better person. "Yes. I spent the afternoon at the homeless shelter helping with the coat drive."

I almost stopped there, but then confessed, "The staff kept talking about one of the family's that came through. A single mom named Sandra and her two little girls. Gracie is her ten-year-old, and Marley is seven. They left an abusive situation a few years before, and within a month of leaving, the oldest daughter, Gracie, was diagnosed with cancer. She fought it and finally got the all-clear earlier this year, but between the medical bills and missing work, Sandra lost her job and they got evicted. Social services is thinking about placing the girls with their abusive father because there is no record of the abuse."

One of the reasons I hated volunteering so much was because of situations like this one. Situations that felt hopeless. "I wanted to take them all home with me," I said before realizing the words were out of my mouth. It felt like a weakness to care so much for near strangers.

Oliver leaned forward, offering. "So, what can we do to help them?"

I shrugged. I wasn't supposed to make things personal. "There are programs that can help, and I got them pointed in the right direction, but I also gave them the entire stash of gift cards I kept in my car." I always kept a stack of random gift cards, usually to fast-food restaurants, but sometimes grocery stores and gas stations. I gave them out instead of cash, making it easier for people to feed themselves instead of their addictions.

"That had to be like five hundred bucks worth of gift cards."

I nodded. He didn't seem angry, just surprised. Then I went on, exposing my weakness. "I paid for them to stay in a motel. It was only one-hundred dollars for two nights, and I'll sleep better knowing they're safe." It was selfish—my way of evening the scales so I didn't feel so guilty for having so much.

"Volunteering is becoming expensive for you," he said with a grin.

I straightened in my seat. "She's not an addict, and the others at the shelter had nothing but good things to say about them, and you should've seen those little girls' faces light up."

Oliver's smile grew. "You don't have to defend your decisions. I love it when your big heart shows. Let me know if I can do anything to help."

I stared at him, thinking for the millionth time that I didn't deserve him.

"I feel better knowing they'll get the things they need. I'm stopping to check on them tomorrow. If the assistance programs haven't found a place for them yet, then I'm going to pay for as many nights as they need until they get on their feet."

"That's amazing, Addie."

"Maybe you can come with me tomorrow so you can meet them."

"I'd love to."

Our meals came, and it was a perfectly romantic evening with tiny portions of delicious food. And I left feeling a little tipsy from the wine.

We went to my apartment after dinner, and as I took my shoes off right inside my door, I saw the package I had gotten earlier in the day. I found it outside when Oliver came to pick me up, but I didn't have time to open it then. Now, I was curious.

Oliver picked up the box and carried it to the kitchen table where the giant bouquet of purple roses sat. Oliver had them delivered this morning. He always brought me purple roses. It was a tradition that started in high school when on Valentine's Day, they were out of all the other colors. Oliver said it was meant to be because purple roses symbolized mystical, enchanting love at first sight.

After that, purple became my favorite color.

Oliver set the package next to the flowers, saying, "Travis

said he was sending something, but he wouldn't tell me what. It's kinda heavy."

"Well, now I'm even more intrigued," I said, stepping into the kitchen.

"Open it."

I grabbed a knife to slide through the tape. I unfolded the box flaps, finding a card on top. I opened it, and the damn thing started singing at me.

"Leave it to Travis to make it obnoxious," Oliver said.

In his handwriting he wrote, *Sorry I couldn't be there to experience your twenty-first birthday. Welcome to the club!*

I set the card aside and continued unpacking, sifting through the confetti and tissue paper. Next, I unwrapped a sippy cup followed by a two-liter of the same soda I'd dumped all over Travis the year before. Oliver burst into laughter while I smiled at the gift.

Inside the sippy cup, there was a note that read: *These lids are guaranteed spill-proof. Great for road trips.* Winky face.

Oliver read the note over my shoulder and continued to laugh.

I rolled my eyes, touched by the ridiculous gift, but it also reminded me of what happened later that same day, after I spilled my hot cocoa on Travis and then helped him out of his clothes. I bit my lip, remembering the sight of him wonderfully naked with his broad muscled shoulders and washboard abs. But it was the look in his eyes while he was buried inside me that still haunted me. Just thinking of it flooded me with shame and arousal.

Travis was so wrong for me. We worked as friends, and obviously, there was a mutual attraction. I loved him, but we would kill each other if we ever tried to date. We weren't a viable option, and the thought shouldn't have been running through my head, especially while Oliver stood right next to me looking so delicious in his suit. His dark hair was trimmed short and styled, and his easy smile belonged to a toothpaste model. I loved everything about Oliver, but still, Travis never entirely left my mind. He enticed me, and I couldn't understand why.

Oliver ran a hand over my shoulder and down my arm. "Holly said she'd be out of the apartment tonight, which leaves us all alone." He kissed my neck. "What ever will the two of us do?" he teased as he nipped at my ear.

"Mmm," I moaned, tilting my head to the side.

He grabbed my hand and led me to the bedroom.

9

ADDISON

THE ARTHUR'S New Year's Eve Party was a refined event. All the well-to-dos came, and I always looked for an excuse to get Oliver and myself out of going, but we couldn't skip every year, so here we were standing in the formal dining room, making our appearance. I held my champagne flute in one hand, while my other hand was in the crook of Oliver's arm.

Oliver looked sexy in his black tux with silk amethyst accents to match my gown. I regretted wearing the two-inch heels because with them, I was just shy of six feet tall. Oliver still had a few inches on me, which I loved, but I'd always wanted to be petite and feminine. I was thin, but my curves were few and I felt like a behemoth standing next to these tiny women with their hourglass figures.

I suspected these obligatory parties were a power trip for my father. No one called him by his first name. I was beginning to think people didn't actually know his name. To everyone here, he was Judge Arthur. Only my stepmother, Jeanine, called him Jonathon.

Jeanine was an anomaly. She was stately yet petite, appearing kind and gentle, but had a backbone strong enough to withstand Judge Arthur. He'd married Jeanine a year after my mother's death. I was only six, and my father introduced her to me as my mother. I remember being confused, but I never argued. I had learned at a very young age that my father hated being questioned.

In those first few years of Jeanine being my new mother, I told people that I had two mommies, but one died. People often referred to my mommies as partners or lesbians and consoled Jeanine for my mother's passing. I thought that was odd because Jeanine hadn't even known my first mommy. Things got even more confusing when Jeanine mentioned my dad, and at the time, I didn't understand the miscommunication until Jeanine sat me down and gently explained it to me.

My father rarely came to any of my school events, and the one and only parent-teacher conference he had attended was when everyone still thought Jeanine was my single lesbian mother. He didn't appreciate the miscommunication, and when a teacher referred to Jeanine as my stepmother, the vein in his forehead had bulged, ready to pop. Stepmother was a bad word as far as my father was concerned. He said there were negative connotations that went along with the phrase stepmother. I nodded like I understood, and when we got home, I looked up the words connotation and lesbian.

Jeanine had always been kind to me. She was encouraging in a motherly way, but despite the title my father had given her, she was not my mother. My father always had the final say and Jeanine never argued with his decisions, though she would tell me later that he expected too much of me. I aimed to prove her wrong. His expectations were high, but I strived to exceed the projections set for me. I hated disappointing him because I thrived on his praise, even if it was rare.

I was graduating with my undergraduate a year early. Although my father wasn't one to gush over my accomplishments with me, I overheard him bragging about me to his friends and colleagues. It warmed my heart.

A man stopped in front of Oliver and me, and since both of my hands were occupied, the man placed his hand on my upper arm.

"Addison Arthur, you're growing into a lovely young woman."

I had a moment of panic before I recalled his name. "Senator Jamison, it's so nice to see you this evening."

He looked me up and down as his hand slid down my arm, his thumb grazing against the side of my breast. I knew it wasn't an accident. "My, you have grown up, haven't you? I've missed seeing you the last several years."

Oliver cut in, "Addison has been busy working on getting into medical school. She starts this fall."

He turned his attention to Oliver as if just noticing him.

"Oliver Riser," Oli offered, reaching out for a handshake, which made the senator remove his hand from my elbow.

"Oh, you must be Addison's boyfriend." He took his hand for a quick shake. "Judge Arthur speaks highly of you."

I smiled at Oli with hearts in my eyes, or at least that's how it felt. "High school sweethearts til the end of time," I said.

"What a romantic notion," said the senator. "You'll make a brilliant doctor one day, Addison. Now, I must go rescue my wife from Charles. He's one hell of a prosecutor, and once he's had a few drinks, he becomes even more argumentative."

"Sounds like he chose the right profession," Oliver said.

"That he did," Jamison agreed before moving away.

To Oliver, I whispered, "I hate these things."

"You mean, you don't like when married senators with grabby hands and hungry eyes feed you compliments like he's sugaring you up before he eats you?"

"Exactly."

Oliver moved in close, his lips at my ear. "How would you feel if I sugared you up?"

My eyes fell shut as I leaned in closer. "Yes, please."

"Let's go upstairs," he whispered.

I nodded, and his hand fell to the small of my back, propelling me forward as we began our journey to sneak away. We were walking toward the stairs when my father stepped in front of us. Jeanine had attached herself to his arm like a good politician's wife.

My father said, "Oliver, I'm glad you finally persuaded my daughter to attend. She's been woefully distant since starting college." His voice was pleasant and teasing, but I knew he was disappointed I didn't visit more. It felt like a double standard because he was the one to break plans with me too many times to count. I knew he was important, and his job demanded a lot of his time, but he couldn't expect me to wait around on him forever. But he had, and I'd spend my entire school breaks bending to his schedule. I decided it was not always worth the effort to come home most of the time.

Oliver smiled. "She's been studying incessantly. I can barely get her out of the library most nights. You've raised a very determined woman." He eyed my father, "Looks like she inherited your drive, Judge."

This made Judge Arthur beam with pride. "She's always been hard-headed. She'll need that drive to make it through medical school, but I have faith she will graduate the top of her class. She's an Arthur after all," he said, clapping Oliver on the shoulder while directing a pointed look my way.

My smile wobbled but held as my heart rate climbed even after his attention drifted back to Oliver, asking him questions about his classes. Questions without expectation.

My smile must have waned because a delicate hand wrapped around mine, and my eyes jerked to Jeanine, who gave me a small smile while giving my hand a reassuring squeeze. Her reassurance made me feel weak. I gave her a more convincing smile, and her hand fell away.

I tuned back into the conversation, focusing on Oliver so my smile wouldn't feel so forced. Oliver was too good for this world. Everyone in this house was playing some kind of game, trying desperately to elevate their social standing, but Oliver wasn't. He was genuine, polite, smart, and handsome enough that people enjoyed talking to him. And he seemed to enjoy everything, even making small talk in a room full of pretentious assholes. My grip on his arm tightened.

"— your doctorate in Economics?" my father asked.

Oliver glanced at me. "That's the goal, but it depends on where Addison ends up. It's killing me to spend next year apart."

While I made plans to pursue my dream of becoming a doctor, Oliver made plans that would align with mine. I hated to move away from him for my first year of medical school, but I knew Oliver would be there the following year. I would never be good enough for him. I knew that, and it stung, but he was rare—a unicorn, and for some reason, he chose me.

I'd be stupid to let him go.

A big hand landed on my father's shoulder. "Hey Johnny, this is some party you've got going tonight."

My father's eyes hardened, his jaw grinding before throwing a contemptuous smile over his shoulder at Travis.

Travis had his short brown hair parted on the side and slicked down. His face was clean-shaven, advertising his square jaw. He was wearing a black tux, and I wondered how he had afforded a tux. Then I wondered if anyone had ever filled out a tuxedo better than Travis. I mean, except for Oliver, of course.

With a fake smile and a cruel glint, my father asked, "How's that father of yours, son?"

I cringed, but Travis just shrugged. "He claims he wants to die, but he just won't quit living. He's a stubborn bastard like that."

I bit my lip to hold in my smile as my father's face turned red, and he growled, "Alcoholism is often passed down through generations. Do you have a drinking problem?"

"Nope, I can drink just fine. Thanks for your concern." He patted my father's shoulder again before turning his attention to my mother. Reaching out to take her hand, Travis struck her with the full force of his irresistible charm. "Jeanine, you're looking lovely as ever this evening." His lips brushed her knuckles before releasing her hand.

She blushed because even she was not immune to Travis. "Thank you, Travis. You're looking quite handsome."

Then his eyes landed on mine, and a shiver ran through me. Oliver felt my shiver. "Are you cold?"

I was about to deny it but then thought better of it. "A little. I have a wrap upstairs."

"Jonathon, the Wilson's just arrived." Jeanine gestured toward the entryway. "Let's go say hello."

My father nodded, then shot one more glare towards Travis. His eyes slid back to me, giving me a disappointed look before he and Jeanine excused themselves and glided away. I swallowed and watched his back as he moved toward the new guests. I wanted to know what his look meant.

As soon as they were gone, Oliver elbowed Travis. "Dude, you've gotta stop aggravating him. I thought the vein in his forehead might burst."

Travis broke out his shit-eating-grin. "It's good to give his heart a little work out every now and then."

"Where'd you get the tux?" Oliver added.

Travis folded his arms over his chest. "Knocked someone out on the way in and stole it."

I gawked at him, waiting for him to tell me he was joking. Apparently, Oliver was making a similar face, because Travis scoffed. "Wow! Your faith in me is staggering. Either you guys are that gullible, or you think as highly of me as the dear ol' judge."

OLI PASSED out in the bed of my childhood bedroom. It was a little after midnight, and the party was still going on down-stairs. I sat on the floor in my dress and took another swig of champagne straight from the bottle.

There was a soft knock at the door, and then it opened. Travis poked his head in, and when he saw we were decent, the rest of him followed.

I said, "I wondered what happened to you."

He shrugged. "I love to bullshit a bullshitter, and your house is filled with them."

I laughed.

He took his tux jacket off and slid down the wall, sitting next to me, a beer bottle in hand. His shoulder leaned into mine, nudging me. "Are you still upset because you can't figure out what your father's look meant."

I swung my gaze to him. "So, you saw it?"

He snorted. "Of course, I did. I see everything that fucker does."

"Travis. That's my father you're talking about."

"Princess, I don't give a rat's ass who he is. He's a condescending asshole, and one glance from him ruined your night."

"It didn't ruin my night."

"He always ruins your night."

I shook my head. "Things have been better, Travis. It's been a long time since he lost his temper."

I could feel him looking at me, but I didn't want to see the accusation in his eyes.

He scoffed. "You're wallowing?"

"I am not." I gestured to the bed. "Oliver fell asleep."

Travis glanced toward Oliver. "Oli always falls asleep. Does that mean you have to babysit him?"

I turned to glare at him. "Must you always be so rude to me? I don't need to hear that I'm pathetic and wallowing."

He laughed. "Never called you pathetic."

I shrugged. "Might as well have."

Travis moved to sit on the floor in front of me with his legs crossed. He reached his hand out to tilt my chin up. "I hear there's an after-party next door for the younger crowd. Go with me."

I tried not to smile. "Do you even want to hang out with those people?" Travis had been around this group a few times before. And after the last time, he had said he would rather take a cheese grater to his balls than hang out with them again. They weren't my favorite people either, but they were the people I'd been thrown together with my whole life. They were at all the same events, so at least they were familiar. "I believe you've told me you'd rather have your pubes pulled out one by one than to spend one more second with those pretentious assholes."

With fake enthusiasm, he said, "That was before. I've matured a lot since then."

"You said that at Thanksgiving."

He frowned at me. "Do you wanna go or not?"

I bit my lip to keep from smiling as I nodded.

He stood, offering me his free hand. I took it and he hoisted me to my feet. I grabbed my coat, and Travis slipped back into his jacket for the trek next door. There was a path between the houses, but each property was expansive, so the walk through the bitter cold was miserable. I gasped as air found its way up my skirt.

Travis wrapped his arm around my shoulder, and mine slipped behind his back as I asked, "So, not to be depressing, but how is your dad?"

"He has some okay days, but mostly they suck. And he still has those fucking nightmares."

"Sounds like you need fun more than I do."

"Don't try to turn this around on me, princess. I'm handling things just fine."

"Have you thought about going to a grief counselor?"

"Fuck no. Don't worry about me. I got people."

"Who? Who do you have? Oli said you haven't talked to him about it."

"I fuckin' hate it when you guys talk about me."

"We care about you."

He shook his head. "I don't want you guys worrying

about me. I found some people who've been through this kind of thing before. They're helping me."

"Well, I'm glad you have people," I said, letting it drop.

As soon as we arrived next door, there was a barrage of greetings. It appeared everyone was drunk, high, or both. A bartender was serving drinks, so Travis and I made our way toward the bar. I ordered a cocktail while Travis got another beer.

I glanced at him. "Not drinking the hard stuff tonight?"

"Nah. I gotta keep an eye on you."

I rolled my eyes. "Yeah, right."

"I also don't wanna be hungover tomorrow while I'm taking care of my dad."

"Is someone with him tonight?"

His voice was flat. "My mom insisted on staying."

"Is she gonna be okay?"

He sighed. "I think it's a bad idea, but they're adults." He shrugged. "I can't babysit them."

"You always kind of have, though, haven't you? Parenting your parents."

His eyes shifted to me. "Unsuccessfully, maybe. Hopefully, I'll be better at it if I ever have kids."

"Awww. That'll be the day! Travis as a daddy. I can't wait for you to get all soft and protective."

He harrumphed, and I added, "You know that's not true what my dad said, right. The alcoholism thing. I know you're not an alcoholic."

"Fuck him. My dad didn't start drinking heavily until he got back from war. His issues go deeper. Alcohol is just the weapon he's chosen to kill himself."

I frowned. "Sounds like a miserable way to go."

Travis held up his drink, tapping it to mine. "Cheers to

that." I laughed, at his dark humor, taking the last sip from my glass.

He turned to the bartender. "Hey, she'll have another, please."

Travis reached into his coat pocket, pulling cash out to slip across the bar.

"It's an open bar," I said.

He nodded. "I know, but it's New Years, and this guy's stuck with a bunch of spoiled rich kids."

"Technically, we're adults, T."

Travis gestured between the two of us. "We are, but the rest of them?" He eyed the space with skepticism, noting the group of guys carrying a mattress into the foyer. "I doubt some of them have ever worked a day in their lives. They happily live off mommy and daddy."

"You could lump me in with the rest of them because my dad pays all of my bills."

"Addie, I've never met anyone who works as hard as you do. And you should take that fucker's money for as long as you can. Drain him dry for all I care."

"He's not evil, T."

He stared at me, a smirk slowly curling his lips.

I lifted a brow. "What?"

He continued to stare without saying anything.

"What, he's not."

Without breaking eye contact, or his stupid grin, he took a sip of his beer.

"Shut up," I protested.

He laughed at that, saying, "I didn't say anything."

"You said it with that smug look."

I was distracted by his smile which is why I didn't see Tinsley and Ingram approach. "Hey, Addison! Who's your friend?"

We swiveled toward them. "Hello, ladies! This is my good friend, Travis. Travis, this is Ingram," I said, gesturing to the skeleton of a woman in the ten-thousand-dollar sequined mini dress that barely covered her ass, let alone her suspiciously perky double D breasts. "And Tinsley." Her dress was just as expensive, but it was long and wispy, flowing in a trail behind her naturally curvy body.

Travis took them both in, his eyes skimming right over Ingram to linger on Tinsley's voluptuous figure.

Ingram moved closer to Travis, running her hand over his shoulder, asking, "Are you in medical school, too?"

Travis let out a bark of laughter. "No."

"So, what do you do?"

With a smug grin, he eyed Ingram. "I dropped out of school to take care of my impoverished father while he dies."

I stifled a laugh.

"Eww!" Ingram stepped away with a look of horror. "You shouldn't tell people that."

"You asked," he said simply.

She rolled her eyes, looking at me. "I knew you volunteered with the homeless, but they don't belong at events like this." To him, she warned, "There are security cameras here."

I leaned forward, the alcohol loosening my tongue. "The security cameras won't catch him. He stole that tux off of a corpse during the guy's funeral without anyone noticing."

Ingram's eyes bugged out, and she huffed in disgust before demanding, "Come on, Tinsley."

Tinsley smiled at me. "I'll catch up later."

"Whatever!" Ingram said with an eye roll.

Once she was out of earshot, Tinsley said, "That was amazing! I've been trying to get rid of her all evening." To

Travis, she clarified, "She thinks we're friends because our parents work together."

"Bummer."

Tinsley's eyes roamed his body while his did the same to her. I suddenly felt like a third wheel.

Part of me wanted to crawl into Travis's lap to claim him. I didn't want him to ditch me for a woman who would give him the things I couldn't. But out of everyone here, Tinsley was one of the few I liked enough to introduce to Travis. So instead of keeping him for myself, I became his wingman. Or wingwoman.

"Travis is Oliver's best friend. He took leave from school to care for his terminally ill father. He's one of the best people I know," I said.

Travis's lips twisted in a smirk as he lifted an eyebrow at me. "Talking me up, princess?"

I ignored him, saying, "Tinsley is in veterinary school. She's always had a soft spot for animals. Her mother works in the courthouse with my dad."

Tinsley cut in, "I wouldn't say they work together. Pretty sure, my mom has had her fair share of arguments with Judge Arthur."

I added, "Her mom is a defense attorney."

Travis nodded. "You mean there's someone who stands up to Johnny, the Judge, Arthur?"

Tinsley's tinkling laugher made Travis smile, and I flinched. I couldn't justify the feelings that overwhelmed me. "Excuse me. I need to find the ladies' room."

Travis gave me a strange look, but I turned away. When I left my seat, Tinsley slipped into it, and I didn't dare look back. I couldn't begin to digest these emotions that were tugging at my heart.

I loved Travis, but I was with Oliver. I'd seen Travis with other women, and it didn't bother me. So why was this different? Maybe I knew those other women weren't a threat, but Tinsley was the whole package, and I should be excited about the prospect, but dread pooled in my stomach. That wasn't fair.

I slipped into the bathroom, locking the door. My pale skin was flushed when I looked in the mirror, and I couldn't help comparing myself to Tinsley, with her creamy dark skin and curves for days. She was a sweet seductress. She was everything I wasn't. She was soft and warm, where I was reserved and driven. It was second nature to hide my emotions, where Tinsley wore them on her sleeve. I always envied that about her.

I was being ridiculous. They would be great together. They would be a couple Oliver and I could go on a double date with, and I think Travis would really like her. She wouldn't be bothered by his status or upbringing. This could be perfect.

Once I got my emotions in order, I opened the door and stepped out.

"You okay?"

My hand flew to my heart as I startled, gasping, "Travis, you scared me."

He was leaning against the wall by the bathroom door, a smirk on his face.

I looked around. "Where's Tinsley?"

His brows climbed his forehead. "You that desperate to get rid of me tonight?"

I shook my head. "No, of course not. I thought you would hit it off."

There was commotion from the front entrance, and

Travis took my hand, pulling me toward the action. A crowd had gathered around the two-story foyer as a guy I didn't recognize stood at the ledge of the upstairs balcony. He had a hold of the spiral raindrop chandelier and looked like he was about to jump. Half the crowd was yelling for him to do it while the other half pleaded with him to stop.

My heart thumped in my chest. It was a bad idea. The guy could get seriously hurt, and the mattresses they laid across the floor wouldn't do anything if the entire chandelier fell on top of him.

As if Travis didn't care what happened to the guy or the chandelier, he turned to me. "She wasn't my type."

I was distracted by him, pulled from the disaster in the foyer. I faced Travis. "Was she too gorgeous and curvy, or was it her sweet intelligence?" I looked back out at the dumbass standing on the ledge. "This guy is an idiot. Almost as big of an idiot as you are. I saw the way you looked at Tinsley, like she was a snow cone on the Fourth of July, and you were dying for a lick."

His bark of laughter took me by surprise. "Where'd that come from?"

I glanced at him and shrugged. "Some guy said that to me once."

He marveled, "That's possibly the best worst line. Incredible."

I glanced at him. "But seriously, Tinsley is an amazing woman."

"Sounds like you wanna date her." He made a noise of approval, saying, "Now that sounds hot."

I slapped his shoulder. "Don't be a degenerate."

He leaned into my ear to be heard over the crowd. "I'm

here with you tonight. I'm not gonna ditch you for some woman, no matter how amazing and hot you think she is."

I laughed, and the crowd seemed to shout all at once. I turned in time to see the guy jump. I gasped as he swung over the foyer, the chandelier holding his weight.

Travis's hand lifted to my neck, and I pivoted toward him. His palm rested on my jaw while his thumb ran across my cheek. The way his eyes focused on me had me holding my breath. His touch was soft and reassuring. His lips pulled at the corners as he leaned in. "I can't help who I'm attracted to, princess," he breathed.

My lips parted in anticipation, and I desperately needed a reminder of what his lips felt like against mine.

A loud crash, followed by screams, pulled our attention back to the idiot in the foyer. He had fallen, landing half on one of the mattresses while the chandelier was in pieces scattered across the space. Drywall dust rained down from the ceiling.

I rolled my eyes. At least the guy was moving. Travis was no longer touching me, and when I turned to him, he said, "Since you're so insistent, I'll let you know, I got Tinsley's number, but right now, we should probably call the squad." He pulled out his phone and dialed. "That dumbass just broke his leg, and people are taking pictures instead of calling for help."

10

ADDISON

Four months later, Travis knocked on my door. I was back at school in North Carolina, and Travis still lived in New York, so when I opened the door and found him standing there, I was confused.

He didn't look up at me. He stood there staring at the floor, his body unmoving except for his breath. The stubble on his jaw had grown into a short beard and his clothes were rumpled. He ran a hand through his tousled hair.

"Travis?"

His chin lifted, and his bloodshot eyes flicked up to mine. The pain I found in their depths reached out and made a fist around my heart. I stepped forward, wrapping my arms around him, holding on tight. Eventually, his arms circled me, and he leaned into my shoulder, saying, "He died."

No one expected him to live this long, but Travis had taken good care of him, taking the year off school. I hugged him tighter.

When he pulled away, he was fighting tears. "I'm not ready to tell my mom, so after they took his body, I just got in my car and drove. Oliver isn't home. I didn't know where else to go."

"You've been up all night?"

He nodded.

I pulled him inside. My roommate was studying on the couch in the living room, so I guided Travis down the hall to my room to give him some privacy to grieve.

I closed my bedroom door behind us. Travis sat in my desk chair while I sat on my bed. There was a distance between us, and it felt wrong to comfort him from across the room, but I think he did that on purpose. I sat cross-legged on the bed, putting my hands in my lap. I felt uncomfortable. Like when I shut the door, I trapped all the inappropriate feelings in here with us.

I stood up to grab my phone from the desk, so I could tell Oliver that Travis was here. As I walked back to my bed, he asked. "Are you texting Oli?"

I nodded and then realized he wasn't looking at me, so I said, "Yes."

"Good."

There was silence for a moment as I typed out a text.

Suddenly Travis stood. "I gotta go."

"Already?" I said, hesitating to send the text. I set my phone down, taking a step toward him. "You just got here. Travis, you need to rest. When was the last time you slept?"

He shrugged.

"Why don't you just take a nap."

He shook his head, his jaw clenching as he reached for the doorknob. "It smells like you in here."

That statement sent a spike of pain through me. I thought we'd worked through our attraction to one another, but perhaps he was more susceptible to the temptation in his emotional state.

He raked a hand through his hair and under his breath, he muttered, "He's a lucky sonofabitch."

I hated this. I wanted to comfort my hurting friend, but I didn't know how to do that without causing him more pain.

"Travis," I said, stepping forward. "Stay."

He turned to me, hand still on the knob. "I can't."

I put my hand on his cheek, saying, "Let me be your friend, T. Take a nap. You can have the room. I'll study at the kitchen table and try to get a hold of Oliver. Please, Travis. Stay."

I let my hand slide from his jaw and stepped back. I moved back to the bed, folding down the covers in invitation. When I finished, I stood there and watched as he stood by the door, staring at the blankets I just folded back.

I continued, "You need to sleep, and I'll be just outside if you need anything."

His eyes flicked to mine and he slowly moved forward. He sunk down on the side of the bed, and I stepped back, but he grabbed my hand, pulling me forward until I stood between his spread thighs. His arms pulled me in, wrapping around my hips, holding me in place while his forehead rested against my abdomen. "Thank you, Addie."

I combed my fingers through his messy hair. I felt strong and in control when I promised to be nothing more than his friend, but standing in his arms was dangerous as my body recognized him, remembering the depth of my desires. I had kept them hidden below layers of denial, but now they floated to the surface.

His face tucked just below my breasts—each warm breath whispering a silent seductive promise through the thin material of my shirt. My self-control was quickly crumbling like it always did around Travis. He sighed in contentment, and I closed my eyes as desire sparked through me, sending my nerve endings into a blazing storm of sensation.

Experiencing Travis raw and unguarded was like holding heroin in front of an addict. I tried to dislodge my body from his hold, but that just prompted his hands to land at my hips while he lifted his honey brown eyes to gaze up at me. His fingers swept against the bare skin at my sides as my shirt fell over his hands.

I whimpered, and my eyes flitted closed, unable to contain my reaction to his touch. I bit my lip to hold back the rest of the noises on the tip of my tongue.

I squeezed my eyes closed while I worked to catch my breath and regain my control. I was not an impulsive person, yet Travis destroyed even my best-laid plans. He was looking for comfort, and I'd talked him into staying, forgetting that he devastated my equilibrium, especially when he seemed so vulnerable.

I chanced a look at him and saw his eyes darken as he watched my heaving chest. His fingers at my sides slid to the small of my back and guided me closer. I gasped even as I stepped forward.

He leaned in, his lips caressing the exposed skin of my abdomen, while his hands slid up my back.

"Travis, you have to stop." I meant it as a demand, but my voice was breathy and barely audible.

His lips broke contact, and he nodded against my abdomen. Then to my body's utter dismay, he listened to my words and pulled away completely, his hands leaving my skin as he sat up straight.

I stepped back, just outside of his reach. It's all the further

I could go, held in place by an invisible rubber band that seemed to tether us to one another.

Suddenly, he stood, putting him right back in my personal space. He was a bigger build than Oliver, his muscles more pronounced. Oliver never made me feel big, but Travis made me feel downright dainty. His size and bulk overwhelmed me as he stepped forward. I knew I should have pulled away. He had given me a chance to escape, and I should have taken it. But it was Travis. All the logic in the world couldn't help me.

His lips fell on mine, and I hesitated. I didn't kiss him back, but I didn't push him away either. His hands cradled my jaw, before sliding to the back of my neck and threading into my hair. I couldn't resist anymore. My lips moved with his, my mouth welcoming his tongue with reckless abandon. My hands twined around him as he devoured me. Hand in my hair, he tugged my head back, and his lips traveled my jaw and down my neck.

With Oliver, I could think, but with Travis this close, his strong arms crushing me against his body, I knew I would give him anything he wanted. I would let him own me and likely beg for more.

He pivoted our bodies, moving us, but I didn't care where just as long as he didn't stop. I felt the bed behind my knees and gasped as the pulsing sensation between my thighs increased, demanding attention. He lowered me onto the bed, my back pressing into the mattress before he pulled away, breaking our connection.

He took a step back, his hands dragging down his face. He laced his palms together on top of his head and spun toward the door.

"Travis," I begged, halfway to orgasm and in desperate

need of release. He paced a few steps back and forth while I caught my breath and sat up.

"I need you," I panted, my voice beckoning him. He dropped his arms, and his intense gaze locked on my half-lidded eyes. His eyes flashed with something that looked like carnal hunger, and he came forward, holding nothing back. His hands were on me, and he tugged my shirt over my head in a fluid movement that should have felt rough but felt just right. Then he slipped his fingers beneath my bralette and slipped that off too. He laid me back and tugged at my yoga pants and underwear, sliding them both down my legs. He stripped me naked so quickly. I tried not to think about how much practice he'd had in this area. I'd only ever been with him and Oliver.

He was still fully dressed, kneeling partly on the bed. His hand cupped my cheek, ran down my neck to my collar bone, and then lower, between my breasts, down to my navel until it stopped between my legs.

"You're so beautiful," he said as he separated my thighs, exposing all of me. It would have felt awkward if I wasn't overcome with need and he wasn't looking at me with such fascination. He lowered his body, and I squeezed my eyes as I felt his breath against my thigh. Then his tongue ran up my crease, and my hands slid into his messy cropped hair.

He moaned, and I felt his breath against my most sensitive area as he said, "You taste so sweet, Addison. So damn sweet."

Then he went right back to it, his teeth nipping, his tongue lapping. He teased me for a long time, long enough for me to beg for more as my hips writhed against him, searching for the more I needed. He added a finger and then two, finding that perfect angle, knowing exactly what to do to make me lose my mind. I grabbed my pillow, covering my face to muffle my scream as an intense orgasm rocked my body. My god, it was so powerful.

After a moment, Travis pulled the pillow away. He wore a confident smirk as he knelt over me, holding most of his weight above me. Then I felt the pressure against my opening and peeked down. His jeans were undone, a condom already wrapped securely around his girth.

He leaned forward, his mouth at my ear, he warned, "I'm going to fuck you so hard you'll be feeling me for days."

My eyes flared as his words registered, and he sunk into me in one swift motion.

"Fuck, Addie," he sighed, stilling deep inside me, giving me time to adjust before he began moving. Thoughts of Oliver flitted through my head, but I forced them away, because this was already happening, and I'd be damned if I didn't make the best of it.

He pulled away, and we stared at one another for a moment before my hands went to his shirt, and I said, "Take it off."

He did as I instructed, his cock still firmly inside of me. "Pants too," I said, and then I lost him. He pulled out and I whimpered at the loss. He smirked as he stood to slide out of his jeans.

He stood before me, a naked man. He was gorgeous. He leaned back in, and I let my hand run down the ridges of his six-pack and bit my lip. Then he was pushing between my legs again, spreading me and stretching me. He went slow, painfully slow, and I was squirming. His pace quickened, hard and fast. It was rough, rougher than I was used to, and I loved it. I came again, but he still wasn't done.

I was exhausted and needed time to recover, but then his

soft strokes had me raising my hips to meet his. "How are you not done?" I asked.

"Fuck, Addie. I'm not about to fail you like I did last time."

He was kissing me, and I didn't hesitate to kiss him back. They were long, languid kisses.

"I'm never going to forget this, and I'm not going to let myself regret this, Addie. Don't regret me."

"I won't."

"Promise me you won't forget this," he said.

"I promise I won't forget."

"Say my name," he demanded, pumping hard and fast into me.

"Travis, I'll never forget the way you feel inside of me, and I'll never forget the way I feel about you."

His strokes became more powerful before abruptly shuddering to a stop. He closed his eyes, and his head rested against my shoulder. "I fucking love you, Addie. You're a dream come to life," he whispered into my ear. He kissed my shoulder and inhaled before pulling away. He removed the condom and was starting to get dressed. His pants and boxers were in place, but I grabbed his shirt before he could put it on. He looked at me, sitting at the head of my bed, holding his shirt against my chest. I wanted to cry, but that was so irrational.

He looked concerned, and his voice was filled with it too as he asked, "What, Addie?"

I wanted to yell at him for getting dressed so quickly. I wasn't ready for him to leave. He made me promise to remember him, but he made no promises. I knew it wasn't safe for us to be in here naked together, so it made sense for him to get dressed, but I didn't want him to. I wanted him to hold me, but that's not what this was.

I held his shirt out to him, and as he put it on, I said, "I'll leave him, Travis."

He froze, looking at me. "What?"

"I'll leave Oliver."

He shook his head, looking panicked. "No. No, Addie."

"What? Isn't that what you want?"

"No, it's, I mean yes, but no. I—fuck."

I was grabbing my clothes. I didn't want him to look at me. I didn't want him to see what he was doing to me. I fucking knew it! He wasn't the kind of guy that settles down. It's why I pursued Oliver instead of him. Travis was just the bad boy player who would break my heart, but I was too smart to let him. I got into med school a year early and was starting in just a few months. I was on track with my life goals, and these feelings for Travis weren't part of the plan. I can't believe I even offered to give up Oliver. For what? For Travis, who dropped out of college to help his alcoholic father. He had no idea what he was doing with his life.

He was a mess. He just fucked his best friend's girlfriend because he confused our friendship for love. I was an idiot for falling victim to his charm.

I was fully dressed, and Travis hadn't stopped watching me. When I gave him my attention, he said, "You and Oliver were meant for each other, Addie. My life is a mess. I didn't mean to drag you down with me. I'm so sorry, Addie. This won't happen again."

I was not going to let myself cry over him. Either he wanted me, or he didn't, but he couldn't profess his love for me and then tell me to stay with his friend.

My phone saved me from having to respond. It was on

the floor, having fallen off the bed when I had my major lapse in judgment. I picked it up, seeing a text from Oliver.

Oliver: Thinking of you. Have you heard from Travis?

Oliver was sweet as fucking pie, and I was a whore who slept with his best friend. Below his text was the message I had typed out about Travis being here, but I never hit send. I deleted my earlier words and spoke my new message aloud as I typed.

Me: Travis just left.

I hit send as Travis walked to my bedroom door. I didn't stop him. I needed him gone.

Then I remembered why he was here in the first place, and I cursed myself. I ran out after him, running past Holly in the living room. She had her earbuds in and didn't even notice me. I made it outside just in time to see Oliver giving Travis a hug in the parking lot.

11

TRAVIS

ADDISON and I spoke about our fuckup at my father's funeral in April. We concluded that it had only happened because I was grieving and she was stressed about maintaining her perfect GPA as college graduation grew nearer. We vowed never to talk about our mistake again, agreeing to pretend it had never happened. But Addison avoided me all summer. It wasn't until August that I saw her again and only because I got roped into helping her move.

Oliver had another year in North Carolina to finish his degree, but Addison was preparing for medical school, which meant moving into her own New York Apartment. It made us neighbors—sort of. There was still a half-hour drive between her apartment and mine, but that was nothing, considering it was an eight-hour drive to see Oliver. I wondered how the lovebirds would fair with the long distance.

"What are you gonna do without Addie?" I asked Oliver, who held the other end of the couch.

"It's only a year," he said while we set the heavy piece of furniture down and pushed it back against the wall.

"A year without sex." My brows shot up. "Or are you gonna find a side piece? Get a taste of something different. See what you've been missing."

Oliver didn't look amused. "I'm not going to cheat on her."

I flopped down onto the couch. "Shouldn't you guys both get a hall pass? I know you're committed, but everyone has needs, and you've never been with anyone else. Doesn't that bother you?"

"No," Oliver said, resting on the arm of the couch. "Why would I want anyone else when I have Addie?"

"Aren't you a little curious? Come on. Girls hit on you all the time. You're saying you've never been tempted?"

"Not enough to hurt Addison or risk losing her, and I'd lose my mind thinking she was hooking up with other dudes. We're committed, T."

I was so close to saying something I shouldn't. But I had to admit, if I had Addie, other women couldn't tempt me away either. Oliver was smart enough to know what he had, and I knew he would never stray. It just made me feel worse.

Addison walked in, carrying a box labeled kitchen. She walked past us, saying, "Are you guys taking a break? There is still furniture out there."

I groaned, "Didn't daddy offer to pay for movers."

She disappeared into the kitchen, yelling back, "He did, but I told him I already had movers. Plus, I didn't want them to break my stuff or misplace anything."

"Control freak," I coughed.

Addison popped back into the living room. "Are you that

out of shape that moving a few boxes already has you whining?"

"Shut it, princess. I could be out doing something fun, instead of being used for free labor."

"It definitely feels like I'm paying for it," Addison shouted as she disappeared back into the kitchen.

Oliver laughed as he walked toward the front door. "Come on, man. There are only a few more big pieces. It won't be that bad."

I stood, following him out. "Easy for you to say. You're getting paid with sex."

Oliver climbed into the moving truck, a grin spreading across his face. "What can I say? She makes it well worth my time."

I plugged my ears. "Don't want to hear what kinky shit you guys are into." But I couldn't get the image of her naked —and begging for more—out of my head.

We picked up a tall dresser, Oliver tipping it so I could lift it from the bottom. I had to get us onto a different topic. "So you have to leave this afternoon. That's too quick."

"My classes start tomorrow, and this was the first day her apartment was available. The timing sucks, but at least we've had the last few days together."

We carried the dresser into the apartment and took it to the bedroom. After setting it down, Oliver said, "Promise you'll keep an eye on her. Sometimes she gets too focused on school and forgets to take breaks. It's not good for her."

"I'll be my usual annoying self and make sure to drag her out sometimes."

"I know you guys give each other a hard time, but I'm lucky that you get along as well as you do. I hate that if something would happen to her, I'm so far away. It makes me feel better that you're so close."

Cue my self-loathing. Fuck me.

OLIVER VOLUNTEERED to pick up lunch for all of us and as soon as he left, Addison started snapping at me as I helped her unpack her apartment. I tried to avoid her by unpacking her bathroom. I was crouched down, in the middle of putting towels on a shelf when she stepped into the room, snapping, "Those don't go there."

I was in the middle of reaching for more towels, but stopped and looked up at her in the doorway. I sighed. "You still pissed at me, or something?"

She rolled her eyes. "I don't want to have to undo everything you're doing wrong."

"Okay, princess, then where do these damn towels go?"

She leaned against the door frame. "Why are you even here today?"

I sat back on the floor. "Because I was dying to be verbally assaulted while moving heavy shit around all day. Why else?"

"I'm serious. Why are you here?"

"Because Oliver asked me to help. I would've found an excuse to get out of it if I knew you were still so pissed. I thought we worked things out at my dad's funeral. You were stressed about finals and I was grieving. We had amazing sex and that's all it was. It won't happen again."

She folded her arms over her chest. "Yeah and you made me promise not to regret fucking you, but I do. It's the biggest mistake I've ever made."

I wanted to wince, but I nodded. "That's fair."

"Do you regret it?"

I looked her in the eye, seeing the challenge in their depth. "Do you want me to regret it?"

She pressed her lips together, glaring down at me.

I got to my feet and stepped toward her. I brushed a stray strand of hair out of her face. "I regret hurting you. I regret what it did to us. I regret betraying my friend. But I can't bring myself to regret being inside of you."

Her eyelids fell closed and she took a breath before they snapped back open to glare at me. "I want you gone as soon as we're finished eating."

I grinned. "You say the sweetest things to me."

"I mean it, Travis. Find an excuse to leave and go."

"You want some alone time with Oli? Break in the new apartment." I twisted the knife in my own heart, hoping that by beating her to it, I could take away some of her power to hurt me. I fought dirty, but then so did she.

She arched a brow. "Why would you like to stay and watch?"

I stepped closer to her. "I'm not really one to sit back and watch." I leaned in, my lips brushing her ear. "I prefer experiencing the action firsthand."

She pulled away from me, her eyes wide.

I chuckled as I brushed past her. Walking away, I said, "Don't worry, princess. I'll be gone before you know it."

But I didn't get to escape after we ate because Oliver needed me to follow him as he returned the moving truck. I drove him back to Addison's and was planning to take off but Oliver roped me into fixing her laptop. I didn't have my degree yet, but when it came to computers, I knew a great deal more than either of them. The laptop had a nasty virus and it wasn't difficult for me to fix, but it was time consuming.

I could hear Addison and Oli talking in the other room. They were discussing Oli's sister, Shelby, and her new husband, Brad. The couple were planning a trip down to North Carolina to visit Oli, and they offered to take Addison with them. I already knew there was no way that was happening. Brad was a total douche, and I didn't like the glances he sent Addie's way.

"Oli, I'm going to be studying all the time. I probably won't be able to get away to come see you."

"If you rode down with them, you could study in the car," Oli suggested.

Addison confessed, "Brad gives me the creeps."

Oli snickered. "You're overreacting. He's an okay guy."

I winced. My friend was an idiot. Addison had every right to feel uncomfortable around Brad, but of course Oli didn't see it.

After a long silence, I heard Oliver say, "What?"

I waited for Addison to hand Oli his ass, but instead, she said, "I'm not comfortable traveling with them. If you want to see me so badly, you can come visit me."

I blinked. What the fuck? Oli invalidated her feelings and she didn't retaliate or even stick up for herself. If I had said that to her, Addison would give me a piece of her mind, so why didn't she argue with Oliver? Was this what real mature relationships looked like or was their connection completely lacking passion?

I tried to recall a time when I heard them argue. Had they ever raised their voices? They yelled at me all the time, but they never actually bickered. That seemed like a sign things were going well, but Addison was a passionate person. She needed someone to argue with her.

WHEN I FINISHED with the computer, I joined Addie and Oli in the living room. They were sitting cuddled on the couch, and I was hoping to say a quick goodbye and be on my way, but I was intrigued by their conversation.

Before realizing I was there, Addison said, "Promise me you'll check on Gracie."

The way she said it with so much concern in her voice made me pause in the doorway. Who the hell was Gracie?

Oliver nodded, giving Addison another kiss. "I will."

Walking in, I asked, "Who are you talking about?"

Oliver's hand reached up to fiddle with Addison's hair as if he couldn't help but touch her. "Gracie. A little girl Addison met through volunteering just found out that her cancer is back. She's starting treatments this week." To Addison, he said, "I'll check on her, and I'll make sure Sandra doesn't lose her job or their home this time."

Addison cupped his face. "What would I do without you?"

"Let's hope we never have to find out." He kissed the tip of her nose. "I'll see you in a few months over Thanksgiving break. It's not that long."

She frowned. "I hate being away from you."

"It's only temporary. Then we'll have the rest of our lives."

She smiled.

I made gagging noises, and Addison turned to glare while Oliver smiled, saying, "I really do need to get on the road. Don't forget, Travis is close by if you need anything, and I can't get here."

She nodded without making eye contact. Together they climbed off the couch. I gave Oliver a hug and then Addison was walking him to his car. She gave him one last kiss through the open car window, and then she stepped back and let him pull away. She stared after him, a mournful expression on her face as she watched his car disappear.

I stepped out the door, about to walk out to her when she began walking back toward the apartment. They had their issues, but they loved one another.

I felt uneasy about Addie living so close, worried we'd fuck it up worse than we already had.

When she approached, she just glanced at me as she walked past into her apartment. I came in behind her, shutting the door.

"Like Oli said, I'm only twenty-five minutes away if you need anything. I have a spare room if you'd ever need it, and I promise not to hit on you or touch you." I hesitated. "I know I haven't been the best at showing it, but I'm rooting for you and Oli. I hope you know that, and I'll do better."

"Thanks, T." There was a quiet pause before she confessed, "I do love him."

"I know you do."

I left soon after, and Addison never called on me for anything. We may have lived close but our lives were going in opposite directions. The only time I saw her was when Oliver came back for a few weeks around Christmas, but even then our visit was brief. Our friendship was drifting apart. It felt necessary, but I didn't like it.

TRAVIS

IT WAS a rainy April day the next time I saw Addison. Her first year of med school had kept her busy, and I hadn't had much time to reach out between starting classes and continuing my full-time job at the gym. Oli was still in North Carolina, but would be moving back soon.

I was running late to a second date with a sultry psych major I really liked. She had interesting things to say and had worked her way up in the world. She hadn't put out right away, and I didn't expect to get any tonight, yet I was still fucking excited.

Spotting the rain outside, I grabbed my jacket off the hook and stepped out the door. I was about to run for my car but stopped short. Addison sat on the concrete stoop, her grey t-shirt streaked black by the rain.

Her shoulders seemed to fight a shiver, and she folded her legs up to her chest. Her arms clasped around her drenched leggings while her light hair clung to her pale face.

She stared out into the small parking lot as the downpour attempted to swallow her up.

"Addison, what are you doing?"

She startled, looking up at me for a second before tilting her face away from the rain. I knelt down, throwing my jacket around her and pulling the hood over her head. I pushed the hair out of her face, uncovering the purple mark on her cheek. My fingers brushed over the bruise, and she winced.

"Fuck, Addie."

Her skin was ice cold, and everything about this situation made me want to beat the shit out of the fucker who did this to her . . . again. He did it again. My blood boiled, but I suppressed the anger for her sake.

"Addie, come inside."

She nodded and I helped her stand before leading her into my apartment. I took her to my room and got clothes out for her. It was all going to be too big, but it would do the job while her clothes were drying. I stepped out, giving her privacy to change.

I leaned against the wall outside my room and breathed through my anger. It had been years since the last incident, and I didn't think there would be another one. If I had, I wouldn't have stayed quiet.

ADDISON *and I moved the rest of our tutoring sessions to the library at her house. It was quieter there than the high school library, and it became our routine once or twice a week through the end of our senior year. She would help me with Precalculus for an hour and then Oliver would come over or meet up with us when he was finished at baseball practice.*

With our final exams creeping closer, our tutoring sessions ran longer. The house was often empty as Addison's parents worked long hours. Oli started having baseball games so sometimes we would go cheer him on after studying.

We had been meeting at her house for a month before I actually saw her father. Oliver had an away game and Addison's stepmom brought us snacks as we studied through dinner. The library windows overlooked the driveway so we knew the moment her father came home. Addison stiffened as he called out, "Jeanine, is dinner ready?"

I heard talking but couldn't make out her response. Then the man was beckoning Addison. The fear I saw in her eyes made me instantly hate him.

Breathless, she told me, "I'll be right back."

She rushed out of the room, and I heard her down the hall. "Yes, father?"

"Your mother told me you got a B in biochemistry. Now, I'm wondering, are you stupid, or are you trying to embarrass this family? Arthurs don't get B's, Addison. We don't do mediocre. Arthurs get A's. Otherwise, you'll never be more than a pretty face, and beauty fades. Is that what you want? To just get by on your looks. Do we need to send you somewhere to prepare you how to be a trophy wife?"

Addison's mom chimed in, "Jonathon, she's tutoring. She has a student waiting on her in the library."

It was her polite way of saying, "Shut up, there are witnesses."

I scooted my chair loud enough to be heard as a way of saying, "Fuck you, I heard you, you piece of shit."

"Is that why your grades have fallen behind?" Her father asked, "Are you tutoring too much? Some kids are just unteachable."

"No, sir, I was sick last week and missed a quiz. I've already made it up. I have an A in every class. Tutoring looks good on

college transcripts," she sounded so pleasant. I was sweating, ready to beat the motherfucker's ass.

He harrumphed. "I don't want to take any chances. Wrap this session up early tonight, and come see me when you've finished."

Then Addison said something bold. "Without my help, he will fail. He has his final exam tomorrow, and I promised the teacher I would help him. Arthurs don't go back on their word."

Fuck, I loved her. Everything she said was a lie except for the without her help I would fail, but the teacher couldn't wait for me to fail. He was angry I was even in his class and even more blown away when I started passing.

"See me when you're finished."

"Yes, sir."

Who the fuck calls their dad, sir?

"She has to practice violin tonight," her mother chimed in, and I wondered if it was true or if she was trying to help her daughter.

"Fine, then see to it. I'll talk to you tomorrow."

She came back into the library and I was standing, gripping the back of my chair. She wore a smile like everything was fine, ignoring my angry look. She nodded to my seat. I took it, and before I could ask who the fuck her father thought he was, she pointed to a math problem on the page and said, "You see, the problem you made here is—"

She kept talking, but my eyes shifted as the dickwad she called sir walked by, checking me out and assessing the situation. I turned back to the book and pretended to listen to Addison explain the problem. I already knew I got the question right. I checked, so she was just doing this for show. Really, we were finished for the night, but she didn't want me to leave, and I wasn't going anywhere. After the man walked away and a door shut down the hall, Addison's whole body sagged. She let out a long breath. Her eyes glistened, and she swallowed, then swallowed again.

Softly, I asked, "Does that happen a lot?"

She glanced up, a tear marring her perfect face. With a shrug, she said, "Sometimes. It really wasn't that bad. I don't know why I'm so emotional." She wiped her cheeks, reigning in her remaining tears as she avoided direct eye contact. "I don't like disappointing him, but sometimes I screw up. He only gets angry because he wants what's best for me."

She couldn't be serious! I barely contained my anger. I had murder on my mind while she sat there feeling like she wasn't good enough for that piece of shit.

She glanced up at me, saying, "What?"

"Does he hit you?"

Her eyes shifted, and her body stiffened. "Of course not. He . . . he just—It's my fault. I need to do better."

"That's a bunch of bullshit."

She looked up at me, terrified, "You can't tell anyone. Please. You can't say anything. He doesn't hurt me. He just expects perfection, and sometimes I can't be perfect."

I grabbed her face, saying, "You are perfect. Don't let that bastard tell you any different."

"That bastard is my father."

I scoffed. "Yeah, I got that by the way you call him father. So fucking proper. I've never called my dad father, and I sure as shit never called him sir, but then again, I don't think we live in the same world. Does Oliver know about this?"

There was that fear again. "No," she said, "Please don't tell him. There is really nothing he can do about it anyway. And I don't want him to look at me the way you're looking at me right now."

"And how am I looking at you?"

She shook her head. "He's a judge, Travis. That's why he's so hard on me."

The more she spoke, the more worked up she was getting, so I grabbed her hands. And she swiveled toward me. "I swear I won't tell a soul, just as long as you promise that you will call me if it ever gets out of hand or when you need someone to build you up after he tears you down."

At my words, tears streamed down her cheeks, and I continued, "The truth is, you're a rockstar. You're acing all your classes, including the college courses. You tutor dumb kids like me in your spare time. You volunteer on the weekends, and apparently, you play the violin."

She made a face, shifting her eyes to the side. "My mom may have exaggerated. She knows how hard he is on me. I do play the violin, but I've only mastered a few songs. I don't practice for hours like she implied. I turn on violin music while I study."

"You, Addison Arthur, are a very persuasive liar."

"It's the Arthur way," she said with a fake smile.

That was only the beginning. I kept my promise not to tell anyone, and she kept her end of the deal, calling me after her dad tore her down. Once, she showed up at my house in the middle of the night with a red handprint emblazoned across her cheek. I hugged her while she cried, and I told her how awesome she was while I plotted how to end him.

NEVER BEFORE HAVE I found her sitting in the rain waiting for a pick-me-up before.

When she emerged from my bedroom, her head was down, her wet hair dripping onto the clothes I had given her. They were way too big, but they'd work for now.

I pulled her into a hug, and she sobbed. I ran my hand through her hair. "What did he do to you, Addie?"

She shook her head, refusing to talk about it, like she

usually did, only this time I needed more. She deserved to be heard.

"Addie, you need to tell me what happened."

She only cried harder, and I continued to hold her as I ground my molars down to nothing in an attempt to repress my rage.

"There is no excuse for him to put his hands on you. He's a fucking bastard. Report him, Addie." I was pleading. "Report him."

She pushed away from me. "I shouldn't have come here."

"I've kept my promise, but if you don't report him, at least tell Oli. He needs to know what's going on."

She backed up another step, her eyes wide. "I can't tell Oliver. He won't understand."

"Won't understand what? That your father beats you. Yeah, that's because it's unfucking believable, but your face will convince him. I mean, how are you gonna hide that bruise?"

Tears shown in her eyes, and her voice was timid. "Tattoo concealer."

I gawked at her, speechless. She had already thought it through. Hell, I bet she already had the tattoo concealer for this purpose. "You have an answer for everything, don't you?"

She pressed her lips together, her eyes shimmering.

Emitting a long sigh, I said, "Oliver needs to know."

Her face paled, and she distanced herself further as her voice grew. "He won't ever look at me the same, Trav. I don't want him to see me as a victim. It's not like that. I got back-handed. I'm not a beaten woman. His ring hit me just right to make it look worse than it is."

Rage shivered through me. "Unfucking believable."

"What?" she snapped.

I threw my arms out toward her, no longer able to control the anger I'd been holding back. "You're defending him!" I closed my eyes and ran my hands over my face, pulling my shit together.

When I finally opened my eyes, her tears had dried up, and her nostrils flared. She swallowed before saying, "You're supposed to build me up, not judge me, and try to fix everything. It can't be fixed, Travis. You should understand that. My birthmother's death changed him. He is a good man, and I shouldn't have to defend him to you."

"A good man doesn't hit his daughter! A good man doesn't break people down for sport!"

Her eyes narrowed on me from across the room. "How would you know what a good man would do? You're sleeping your way through the city. Tell me, how many women have you hurt, Travis?" Her face was turning red, and her voice shook. "Don't act like you're in any place to judge."

I counted my breaths, exhaling the insults she slung my way. I knew how to take a good jab. It just hurt more coming from her. Here I was missing a date with an awesome girl only to be verbally assaulted by the only woman I'd ever fallen for.

It was sad. *I* was sad, pathetic, pining away for the one person off-limits.

I pulled my phone from my pocket and hit Oliver's number, holding it out to her.

She eyed the phone. "What are you doing?"

"Calling a good man, so he can help you decide what to do."

She grabbed the phone and hung up, slipping the phone

into the pocket of the too-big sweats she was wearing. "I can't tell him."

"Why?"

"He's never been verbally or physically abused by a parent. He looks up to my father. This will ruin everything."

"The only thing it will ruin is the illusion that you've built. Why are you trying to maintain a lie? Do you think he won't understand, or do you think you aren't good enough for Oli?"

"I know I'm not good enough!" she shouted. "He's never been touched by tragedy. My mom died when I was five and was replaced within months by someone prettier and younger, and my dad made me call her mother the moment they got married. I've been torn down my whole life by a man who expects perfection. I'm not perfect. But Oliver thinks I am. He's the best thing to ever happen to me. He's the whole package. He's perfect, and I'm. . . I'm a mess. I'm sleeping with his best friend because I don't know how to stop. I know how messed up this is. I shouldn't even be here, but my friends can't know, and even if I told them, they would never understand. You've lived it, T. You know what it's like to defend a dad that by all rights you should hate. I don't want that to be my life, so no one can know."

Silence stretched after her admission, and I didn't know where to begin unraveling that clusterfuck.

She decided for me as she confessed, "You understand me better than anyone, T."

"Me? The man sleeping with half the city, the heart-breaker. And you think the reason I understand is because we both grew up with fucked up parents?"

She shrugged.

"So let me get this right. You come to me with all the

things you're ashamed about. Meanwhile, Oliver only gets the shiny airbrushed parts. How sustainable is that? I mean, how long do you think you can keep that up?"

She swallowed, her voice shaky, "For as long as it takes."

"He already fucking loves you." I was shaking. She was making me crazy. "Goddamnit, Addison." I bit my lip and shook my head. "You're such a bitch."

She cringed. "I know, but I want to be the person Oliver believes I am. I want to be that shiny, perfect woman that everyone thinks I am. I want to be better. It's the life I've always dreamed of, which is why Oliver can't know—" she gestured to her face, "any of this."

"You're really not giving him enough credit."

"It's not even about him. It's about what I want."

"And you expect me to stay quiet and continue taking all the shit you throw at me, expecting me to build you back up without reacting, but I'm a person, Addie. I react because I care about you. I can't just turn that off, and I'm not okay with you being so self-destructive."

"Friends share their problems. I know Oliver is your best friend, but . . . but you're mine."

I tilted my head to the side, confused as I folded my arms over my chest. "How do you figure? You don't talk to me for months at a time and then come to me when something like this happens and you're falling apart."

"Oh, I forgot friends don't come to each other in times of crisis." She hit her forehead, sarcasm thick as she said, "How crazy of me!"

"Addison, you don't even like me. You just think you do because I'm the only person who knows you. You could have real friends if you would just stop pretending and let people see the real you."

She rolled her eyes. "Forget it." She turned and walked back into my bedroom. "I don't know what I expected."

"What are you doing?" I said, following her.

"I'm changing back into my clothes, and I'm leaving."

"Why?"

She tried to close the door between us, but I held it open.

"Close the door!" she demanded.

"No. Not until you tell me why."

She pressed her lips together and stared me down, waiting expectantly.

When I did nothing, she said, "Fine." With a shrug, she lifted the shirt over her head and chucked it at me before grabbing her wet t-shirt from the floor. Before she could put it on, I shifted forward and ripped the soaked shirt out of her hands.

"Wha—" she gasped as I spun her around to look at her back.

The bruises spread along her lower back. She tried to pull away when she realized what she had exposed. "Let go!"

I stepped back. "You're not fucking leaving."

"We aren't Neanderthals. You can't keep me here against my will." One of her arms covered her breast while the other attempted to grab her shirt, but I pulled it away.

"Addie, you can't seriously think this is fine. You have bruises all over you."

"Travis, give me my shirt!"

I handed her the dry shirt of mine she just took off. She ripped it out of my hand and covered her chest with it. "It's not as bad as it seems."

"Just stop it, Addie! Stop lying!"

She slapped me with her free hand.

I grabbed her wrist, but she started kicking my shins, so I let go, which gave her time to slip into the shirt as she ran out into the hall. I caught up to her and pinned her to the living room wall. "Addie, stop running and listen to me for a second."

"Let go."

I pressed my whole body into hers as she tried to kick. She continued to struggle for a few moments before finally giving up and sagging against the wall, breathing, "I hate you."

"Yeah, I know, but I don't really give a shit. Addie, you're too smart for this. What would you say to your patient if she came in with bruises like yours?"

"That's different."

"How?"

"You're not my doctor."

I stepped back, giving her a little room. "Nope, just the best friend you hate. But I'm happy to drive you to your doctor. Let's see what they think."

Her eyes glistened as she looked up at me. "I hate you so much."

"No, you don't."

"Yes." She tried to shove me back. "I do!"

"No, you're just scared of me because I know who you are. That scares the shit out of you."

She shoved me again. "Fuck you!"

I held her arms above her head. "You're miserable, so scared to tarnish your pristine reputation, that you'll let your father break you down over and over again."

"Let go of me." She struggled against me.

"Not until you admit it."

She lifted her chin. "You're an asshole."

I leaned in, whispering against her cheek. "At least everyone knows what I am. I'm not hiding from anyone."

I let go of her arms and stepped back, but stayed close.

Her palms hit my chest, and she pushed against me a few times before her hands fisted in my shirt and pulled me in. Her breath was heavy as she tilted her chin, lifting up on her toes. Her lips pressed against mine in a sloppy kiss. Her tongue was in my mouth, and I was pushing her back. We broke our connection, and I tried to pull away, but her hands clung to my shirt. Her cheeks flushed and her breath was erratic against my neck.

I grabbed her shoulders and held her back. "You can't do that."

She nodded, letting go. Her eyes followed her hands as they lingered against my chest and started roaming.

My dick jumped in response. So ready. It didn't matter how awful she treated me. It was always ready for her.

Her blue eyes pierced through me as her chest rose and fell. I grabbed her hands and pulled them away, but our fingers intertwined and my mouth found hers. She ripped her hands out of mine, breaking our kiss and shoving me away.

I moved back, needing the distance to tamp down my desires. I walked to the middle of the living room before turning to face her. I was in great shape, yet she winded me. Addison broke all rules and logic. She'd moved to the kitchen, burying her hands in her hair.

We were grown adults who could use our brains. At least that's what I thought until she looked toward me, and the passion I saw drew me to her like a magnet. We rushed together, helpless against the pull.

Our kiss was angry, passionate, aggressive, needy. Her

arms clung around my neck while I grabbed her ass, pulling her in. She rubbed her body against mine while I ground my erection into her center. She let out a noise deep in her throat while her teeth raked my bottom lip. Her nails skated up to my scalp. I kept one hand on her ass while the other slid under her shirt, gliding up her smooth skin to the soft lift of her breasts. My thumb rubbed over her puckered nipple, and I breathed in her responding moan. My erection grew harder, stretching the limit of my pants as we worked ourselves into a frenzy.

Her mouth pulled away, breathing a desperate, "I need you," as she reached for my fly.

"Fuck, baby." She ran her palm up the length of my shaft while her other hand fumbled with the button of my jeans.

My phone rang and Addison gasped, stumbling back, falling against the wall. I pulled the other way, putting distance between myself and the mistake I was about to make. From the mistake we had already made.

Addison pulled my phone out of her pocket, checking the screen. "It's not Oliver," she breathed with a sigh of relief as she slid down the wall, holding the phone out to me.

The ringing ceased, and I ignored the phone, staring at my shoes. I rubbed a hand over the back of my neck. "Fuck, Addison, we can't do this again."

I looked at her crumpled on the floor, her tears falling. She was beautiful, even in her fallen glory, even with her cracks on full display. It pissed me off that my head automatically went straight towards attraction. I knew the real Addison, and I loved her even though she saw no real value in herself. Her insecurities were woven into the fabric of her making—down to her marrow. She couldn't love herself, so she tried to make others love her. And they did. Everyone loved Addison. But it was all surface. No one really knew her. She didn't let them know her because to be genuine meant showing her flaws.

I picked up the phone she left on the floor between us. Nope, it wasn't Oliver. It was the date I had stood up. The one I was excited about. The one who probably was too good to give me a second chance, and that was okay because I didn't deserve her.

I slipped the phone in my pocket with no intention of calling her back. I was a dick, better she learns now than be disappointed down the road.

I walked toward the door. "Stay as long as you need," I said, "I'm gonna get some fresh air." I twisted the knob, and the cool damp breeze washed over me, clearing my head.

She sniffled, and I paused in the doorway. I turned back to her, saying, "You have to tell Oliver. About us. About your dad. This isn't right. He has to know. If you don't tell him, I will."

Her frightened eyes shot to me, and before I backed down, I closed the door between us, walking out into the biting rain.

As soon as I climbed into my car, I pulled out my phone, hovering over Oli's number. If I called him right now, I could lay it all out. Come clean. Tell him about our slip ups and about her bastard of a father. My thumb hovered over the send button, hesitating. My eyes fell closed and I backed out of my contacts. Damn it. I couldn't do it over the phone.

I set my phone down, but picked it right back up, knowing if I didn't tell him now, I'd probably talk myself out of it. He deserved to know. He deserved better than Addie and me. He also deserved to hear it from Addison, but I didn't know if she'd do it. I'd give her until morning.

Before I could put the phone down, it began ringing in my hand, Oliver's face lighting up the screen.

Had Addie called him already?

I inhaled deeply before letting it out and answering the phone. "Hey, Oli."

"Hey . . ."

My heart jackhammered as I realized how badly I'd fucked up. He was more than my friend, he was like a brother to me, and I didn't know what to do if he never wanted to speak to me again. And why the long pause?

"Oli?"

"Yeah, man. I'm afraid I have some bad news."

I stopped breathing. "Oh-kay."

"My gran passed away this afternoon."

That wiped out all the thoughts I had circulating in my mind. "Are you serious?" I cringed. It's not like he would make this shit up. He loved his gran. "I'm sorry, man. That really sucks."

Oliver had a special connection with his gran. She mothered him more than his mother. Gran always stuck her nose in Oliver's life and meddled like it was a professional sport. He didn't seem to mind too much, and she had always treated me like part of the family. She was impossible not to love, and I knew how much this would hurt Oli.

"I've got a flight home tonight," he said.

I asked, "Was she sick?"

"No. She, eh, she had a stroke."

"I'm sorry. Are you gonna stay with Addie?"

"Nah, I don't want to distract her from school. I know she has a big test tomorrow that she's been stressing about, so I was going to get home tonight and get settled at my parents. I'll let her know tomorrow after her exam."

"I'm here for you. Just let me know what you need."

"Yeah, I will. I'll text you later."

After we hung up, I rested my forehead against the steering wheel. Well, fuck.

I climbed out of my car and ran back into my apartment. Addison was just reaching for the doorknob when I walked in.

"Change of plans, princess. Oliver just called me. Gran died. He doesn't want to upset you before the big test you have tomorrow, but he's catching a flight here tonight."

She paled, her hand reaching up to cover the bruise on her face, and I knew she was going to continue hiding everything from him.

It would be up to me, and I didn't know if I could do it.

13

ADDISON

THE DAY after my misstep with Travis, Oliver surprised me with Chinese carryout. He showed up at my apartment unannounced but, thanks to Travis, I'd been prepared, using tattoo coverup and makeup to camouflage the bruising.

Oliver told me about Gran and I feigned shock, but my grief was real. I loved Gran. As we ate and drank wine, we reminisced about her. He didn't seem like he was in the mood for sex, but as a precaution, I faked cramps. I couldn't have him seeing the other bruises, or he'd jump to conclusions the same way Travis had.

Oliver respected my father, and I didn't want to break that respect over an argument. I knew it wasn't right that my father hit me, but it didn't make him a monster, and I didn't want him to lose his career over it.

He wanted me to be my best and obviously I wasn't making the best decisions which was made evident by my decision to go to Travis the day before.

My father hadn't beaten me mercilessly like Travis made it sound. He had backhanded me and the ring he wore landed just so as to make it look worse. I had backed away from him, my back hitting one of the custom book-cases in his office. He held me against it, making sure I heard his words. He hadn't known the ornamental detail of the bookcase was digging into my lower back. I hadn't even realized how much it hurt until afterward. I could've explained the bruises to Travis, but he wouldn't have believed me anyway. He'd made up his mind about Judge Arthur, and it was my fault for going to him after my father was harsh with me. Travis only saw the worst and would never know about the things my father had done to help us all.

THE FOLLOWING DAY, all the people closest to Gran converged at Oli's mom and stepdad's house. It was mostly family—a few aunts and cousins, Oli's dad, Buck, and his wife, Janet, were there, and of course, Travis came too.

Oli's sister, Shelby, showed up with her husband, Brad. I didn't care for the man. I felt like his eyes lingered too long and his hands roamed whenever he hugged me. I may have been unfaithful to Oli, but not the way Brad was to Shelby. He hit on anything in a skirt. Shelby deserved better. I saw divorce in their future, and I hoped it was sooner rather than later for everyone's sake.

Family was scattered through the large house, leaving only a handful of people in the kitchen. I was sitting next to Oliver at the breakfast nook and thinking of ways to talk to Shelby while simultaneously avoiding Brad.

Oliver snapped me out of my thoughts, asking, "Have you talked to Sandra recently?"

I shook my head. "Not for a few weeks. School has been really busy. Why?"

He sighed. "Gracie isn't responding to the treatments."

I gasped. "What?" Guilt ate at me, but I forced my voice to calm. "I've been so busy. The treatments worked before. I assumed they were working since Sandra hadn't called."

"She reached out to me," he said. "She knows how busy you are with school."

I stared at my empty plate on the granite counter as the food started to turn sour in my gut. "I should've checked on her." The little girl's face danced through my mind. Gracie had been so happy the last time I saw her. She'd come such a long way from the small sickly girl I'd first met. I didn't want her to go through it all again. "So what are they going to do?"

Oliver's solemn smile wasn't encouraging. "They might try surgery again."

And the punches just kept coming. I felt sick. "But that's so risky."

Oliver pressed his lips into a grim line and nodded. "They know the risks, but—"

I didn't want to hear the *but,* so I interrupted. "I'm coming down to see her. I'll fly down with you and catch a flight back."

Oliver nodded. "I'm sorry to bring it up. I didn't know how to tell you."

I sighed, needing to move on to a different subject. But as Oliver spoke, I tuned him out, staring at my glass plate and wondering how everyone would react if I threw it at the wall. I wondered if the visceral action would relieve any of the tension and nausea that was growing inside me. As if realizing I needed a moment to process everything, Oliver said, "I need to talk to my mom for a minute. I'll be back."

I nodded and he left. I stared at the granite counter beneath the plate, following the pattern until it became blurry, reminding me of those magic eye puzzles I did as a kid. Were those still around? Had Gracie ever done one? My breath caught.

"You really care about this girl?" Travis said, sitting down next to me.

I glanced his way. "Yeah, I do."

"Why?"

I shot him a murderous glare, wanting to chuck the plate at him instead.

He held up his hands in surrender. "I mean, no kid should have to suffer through cancer, but I didn't know you were close to the family."

I continued to glare at him, which prompted him to explain, "You tend to keep people at a distance. What is it about this family in particular?"

"This girl and her family have already been through too much. Sandra's a single mom who hasn't had it easy, yet she's fought for her girls every step of the way. She's doing everything to make her daughters' lives better and life just keeps throwing them curve balls. It makes me angry. They deserve better. These girls are so sweet and you know I don't love kids."

He raised a brow. "But you love these kids."

"Yes."

"Is there any extended family that can help them?"

"No and Sandra said the girls' father was abusive. He never raised a hand to the girls, but he beat Sandra unconscious one night. The next morning, she packed up the girls and left him. Only a month later, Gracie started getting sick."

Travis drank in my story, sipping up every last detail and

looked to be deep in thought as he worked it through his mind. He leaned forward. "I'm glad they mean so much to you."

"And yet, I'm failing them." I stood, needing to get away. I gathered the dirty plates on the table and took them to the kitchen sink. I busied myself with the dishes, getting halfway through when the anger and disappointment became too much. I needed to scream, or throw something, but I couldn't do either. Not here. Not where there were witnesses.

Skin is the largest organ in the body and I knew how much it could take before causing permanent damage. I turned the hot water to full blast, washing the remaining plates in searing water. Then the plates were finished and I held my hands under the scalding water, angry with myself. It hurt, but I deserved to feel the pain.

"What the fuck are you doing?" Travis pulled me back from the sink.

I stepped away from him, eyes wide. I hadn't realized he was watching me.

"Jesus, Addison!" He wrapped my hands in a towel and held them between us, demanding eye contact. "Why would you do that?"

I didn't speak. I had never been caught before, and wasn't sure what to say. My reasoning would fall on deaf ears. He wouldn't believe a lie, but he also wouldn't accept the truth. He would tell me I didn't deserve the self-inflicted pain, but he was wrong. I deserved it. He was too easy on me—too forgiving.

My anger poured out of me in harsh words. "I don't have to explain myself to you."

Travis looked disappointed, but instead of lashing out, he

pulled me in, holding me against him. He kissed the side of my head, whispering, "It's not your fault."

I tried to push away, but he wouldn't let me go without a fight, and I wasn't going to cause a scene while surrounded by Oli's family.

"You don't know what you're talking about," I said in a huff.

"Sandra withholding how sick Gracie is, is no one's fault. She was trying to protect you from the devastation she's living. She doesn't want the burden to fall on your shoulders because there isn't anything you can do."

"And how do you know there's nothing I can do?" I said into his shoulder. "I could do some research, find a better surgeon. I could—"

"Finish school, become a doctor, and save people's lives." He pulled back, holding onto my shoulders to keep me close. "It sounds like Oliver is helping while you're doing what you're meant to do."

I felt the tears in my eyes as I stared at him. His gaze shifted over my shoulder and his posture changed.

"Well, well, what's going on here?" Brad said, stepping into the kitchen.

Travis pulled me into his side, not so subtly putting himself between me and Brad.

"Looks like I interrupted a private moment. Does Oli know about you two or is this a threesome kind of arrangement?"

Travis's muscles stiffened. "Get your head out of the fucking gutter. She's grieving, just like the rest of the family."

Brad snickered, "But neither of you are family, are you?"

"We're more family than you'll ever be," Travis said. "It's a disgrace that you're here at all. Gran never liked you."

"I don't give a fuck about Gran." Brad stepped closer. "I wanna know how many times you've fucked behind Oli's back?"

If he was anyone else, I probably would've felt guilty at his accusation, but it was Brad. My lips curled in revulsion. "You're disgusting."

He eyed me. "When you're ready for a real man, let me know." He walked out the back door and I stepped away from Travis.

Travis stared at the back door. "What does Shelby see in that piece of shit?"

I blew out a breath. "Buck can't stand him. He hired a private investigator so he'd have proof to show Shelby."

"Damn. Does Oli know?"

"No, he's in denial too. You know he always sees the best in people."

Travis scoffed. "Oh, the blinding optimism."

Oliver walked into the kitchen and Travis excused himself to go give his condolences to Oliver's mom.

14

———

TRAVIS

OLI'S MOM was never super affectionate or overly motherly, but Gran more than made up for what his mom lacked. Oliver had always been close to Gran. She was warm and loving, and that warmth spilled over into my life, most significantly when we were twelve.

WE'D HAD a sleepover at Gran's, and when she dropped us off at school the next morning, she planted a kiss on Oliver's cheek right outside the school. She wasn't ashamed to show love, and Oliver didn't seem embarrassed to receive it. But I wasn't used to the affection and was very aware of all the eyes on us.

We walked into the school and were immediately confronted by three boys. Kevin was their ringleader. I went on guard the moment I saw them, but Oliver seemed unaware until they spoke.

Kevin shouldered Oli, saying, "Does she kiss your boo-boos, too?'

Oliver was unprepared for the insult, but I was ready. "Why?

You want her number?"

Kevin ignored me, zeroing in on Oli, who wasn't built for this kind of thing. He was too nice for his own good, but I wasn't.

Kevin glared at Oli. "I don't need her number. I'm not a baby."

"Loving my grandma doesn't make me a baby," Oliver said.

Kevin laughed, mocking in a high voice, "I'm not a baby for loving my grandma."

I stepped closer to Kevin. I was bigger than him, and I used it to my advantage, making him take a step back.

He turned his gaze on me. "And what are you, his bodyguard or his boyfriend?"

"Why? You jealous?" I said, stepping forward.

Oliver grabbed my arm. "It's not worth it."

"Yeah, be a good little boy and listen to your boyfriend," Kevin snickered.

That stopped Oliver in his tracks, and he said, "I can't tell if you're just immature and think it's funny to make gay jokes, but being homophobic doesn't make you cool. It makes you ignorant."

I held in a laugh. Oliver was being genuine, but to them, it sounded like a taunt.

"Come on, Oli, he's just trying to overcompensate so his friends don't find out he has a crush on you," I said.

"Fuck you. I'm no fag!" Kevin shouted.

"It's okay if you are," Oliver said with a sincerity that only pissed Kevin off more, but I didn't expect the kid to get violent.

I was wrong. Kevin's hands balled into fists, and before I could react, he socked Oliver in the eye. He drew back to throw another punch, but I sprung forward, cracking my fist into his face over and over. He landed a couple of punches as I followed him down to the tile floor before Oli was pulling me off the asshole.

The other two boys looked scared as I stood. Kevin stayed on the floor with his arms covering his face in case I came back. My adrenaline was pumping, and I wasn't done fighting. I stepped toward the other two. "You got more to say?"

"T, drop it," Oli said.

I stalked toward them. "I'm not done."

They were smart enough to back up, one of them saying, "What the hell? We were just messing. You didn't need to beat the shit out of him."

I laughed and spit blood out of my mouth from a punch Kevin had landed. "He threw the first punch. I was just defending my friend."

A teacher approached. "What's happening over here?" Quickly taking in the scene, he skewered me with a glare that would've made most kids squirm. I wasn't most kids.

I stepped forward to show him he didn't scare me. "Kevin sucker-punched Oliver. I was teaching him a lesson."

My mom got called to the school. She slapped the back of my head as soon as she saw me. "What's wrong with you? You wanna get kicked out of school? You sure don't ever see Oli getting in trouble like this. You've got too much of your father in you." She was resigned to the fact that I was at fault for everything that happened.

That's when Oliver's Gran showed up. The small woman whirled into the room, smelling of powder and roses. The smell clogged my nose as she swept me into a hug. It was the kind of reassuring hug that made me forget all my troubles. I felt protected in her arms, like nothing could get to me for as long as she was there.

"Boy, you're clinging to me like a life raft." She pulled back, but held onto my shoulders. "I heard what you did to protect Oliver after those boys were being nasty little shits."

I smirked at Gran's cursing. "Stop giving me that look. I'm seventy-four. I'm old enough to swear whenever I feel like it."

My mom had never actually met Gran before, and she was giving us a dirty look.

"Gran, this is my mom," I said, afraid my mom was about to do something to embarrass us both.

Gran turned to her, giving her the same kind of hug she just gave me. "Bless you for creating such an amazing boy." She pulled back. "You must be so proud. Can you believe they want to get him in trouble when he was only defending Oli after that kid sucker punched him?"

My mom blinked, looking from me to the older woman. She finally settled on me. "Is that what happened?"

I nodded.

"They said you were pummeling the kid."

Gran spoke. "Defending his friend, like the loyal guy he is. Oli's lucky to have you."

Her words settled in my chest, filling me with a pride I'd never felt before. Never had I considered that I contributed anything positive to Oli's life. I was so used to hearing people tell me how lucky I was that Oli and his family accepted me.

The principal's door opened and the kid I'd whaled on, stepped out with a split lip and bruises already forming across his face. Kevin's parents narrowed in on me, marching over in a huff, but Gran slid in front of me like a momma grizzly even though I towered over her. Her size didn't seem to matter because she still shut them down.

"Before you go blaming this on anyone else, you best take a good look at your son," she said to Kevin's parents. "You're raising a homophobic bully, and Travis," she pointed at me, "stood up to your son after he assaulted my grandson. You better redirect that anger!"

It was so rare that anyone stood up for me, and I knew if I wasn't careful, I could get used to that warm sensation that filled my chest.

~

I LOVED that little firecracker of a woman, and as I looked down at her casket, my heart exploded with pain. I owed Gran so much. That day so many years ago, she changed my life. I'm positive if it weren't for her fighting for me, I would've been expelled, separating me from Oliver. I never would've met Addison. I never would've gone to college. I would not be the man I am today without Gran.

Oli came to stand next to me, saying, "Seems like it wasn't that long ago since we were having sleepovers at her house."

I nodded. "It's hard to believe she's gone. How did she pack all that attitude into such a little body?"

There was a moment of silence between us before Oliver said, "I'm really gonna miss her."

"Me too."

"I'm sad I lived so far from her these last few years."

I felt the same way. I wish I had told her how much I loved and appreciated her. We stood by her casket in a long stretch of silence while people mingled, making small talk around us.

When we stepped away, we were both clearing our throats where our tears stuck.

When I regained my composure, I said, "So when do you go back to school?"

"In a couple days, but I wanted to talk to you about next year."

I turned to him. "Yeah?"

"In the spring, when I graduate, I was looking to move back to New York, but Addison's apartment is cramped and it's so far from where I'll be getting my masters. I was thinking since you lived so close to the university and you have that spare room, maybe I can stay with you for a year. It'll cut your rent in half and it could be like old times."

I already got a break on my rent by helping with building maintenance. It was the only way I could afford the two bedroom apartment without a roommate. I enjoyed living alone, but I knew living with Oli wouldn't be difficult. I used to spend summers with him. Of course, it meant Addison would visit more frequently, but only when Oli was around so it was unlikely to be a problem.

"Of course you can stay with me," I said. "It'll be fun. Like old times but with less supervision."

He laughed, but his smile disappeared when he caught sight of Addison.

I asked, "Is she okay?"

Oli shook his head. "She's pretty upset about Gracie. I hope I didn't do the wrong thing by telling her. She insists on coming back with me so she can be there during Gracie's surgery. It's an all-day thing and she's going to be a wreck if it doesn't go well."

I shrugged, offering, "At least she can keep Sandra company. They can go crazy together. Misery loves company and all that." I tried to lighten the situation, but seeing it wasn't working, I said, "Addie is strong. She'll be okay. It's good she knows. She would've been pissed if she found out about the surgery after the fact."

With a brisk laugh, he said, "You're right about that."

"Life isn't for the faint of heart."

Oli sighed. "I just wish I could protect her from all the bad and unfair things out there."

"You can't and shouldn't shield her from the truth. All you can do is support her through the harsh realities."

15

TRAVIS

OLIVER MOVED in with me over the summer. Having him there while he got his masters seemed like a great idea, but it meant that Addison visited a lot. She was in her second year of medical school, and sometimes she came over only to study the entire time, but it was nice having her around. I was even getting used to her and Oliver's canoodling, and most of the time, I managed to ignore the pull she had on me. She haunted my dreams less and less, but it still sucked to hear them going at it through the apartment walls.

Gracie underwent a risky surgery shortly after Oliver moved in, and he and Addison went down to wait with Sandra during the operation. Gracie pulled through, feeling stronger than ever, and the doctors estimated she would be cancer-free after a few more treatments. I got to celebrate with Addison and Oliver when they got back to New York.

The more I was around Addison, the more I remembered why we made such good friends. She was smarter than she let on and more opinionated than she wanted anyone to know. She was witty with a dark humor she kept hidden. I thoroughly enjoyed picking on her with her type A personality that she tried desperately to keep under wraps. It was a trait she deemed less than perfect, and she airbrushed her imperfections, determined to conceal the characteristics she saw as flaws. She was doing everyone a gross injustice, but she was too stubborn to recognize the limits she placed upon herself by hiding behind her perfect image.

Refusing to let her pull that shit with me, I excelled at drawing out the real Addison. I knew exactly how to get under her skin and drive her just crazy enough to get her to break her precious facade. There were times I wondered if Oliver ever questioned her little inconsistencies. Oliver wasn't an idiot. He had to notice the slight changes in her behavior, but ultimately, I decided he didn't want to see them. He was stupid in love, insanely happy, and he'd always had an optimism that made him gloss right over those small things that should've made him ask deeper questions.

I could've popped their happy little bubble, but that felt unusually cruel. Despite all of Addison's pretenses, I knew how much she loved Oliver.

In October, Addison turned twenty-three, and we went out to celebrate like old times. The tension between us never entirely went away, but we were getting better at knowing our limits without stepping over the line. We were doing well until Halloween rolled around.

My dedication to seeing my friends happy together had me trying to liken Addison to something of a sister. It was my way of trying to lessen my attraction to her, but the moment she stepped out in her skimpy Little Red Riding Hood costume, I knew that was a joke. My feelings toward her were far from familial, and the image of her in the scraps of red fabric and lace would forever be burned into my memory, filed away under the ever-growing Addison Arthur spank bank.

There wasn't a single bit of her that didn't tempt me, from her red *fuck-me* heels, which elongated her already long legs to her loose *just-been-fucked* blonde curls. A corset I was dying to unlace bound the sexy crimson dress, and the micro mini skirt flared out in lace ruffles that barely covered her ass. I instantly had visions of bending her over the counter where she stood and taking her from behind. But the nail in my coffin was the diamond pattern thigh-high tights. They ended halfway up her thighs, leaving a good portion of smooth bare skin. That stretch of sensitive skin begged to be touched, preferably while her legs were wrapped over my shoulders, and I was tasting the sweet honey between her spread thighs.

She bit her lip as if she knew exactly what was going through my mind, which she probably did as I couldn't fucking tear my eyes away from her, and I was growing rock hard in my pants. I shifted, trying to hide my reaction to her. And it couldn't have come a second too soon as Oliver stepped out in his Big Bad Wolf costume. His much less elaborate costume was a thin hoodie with a faux fur hood with wolf's ears and matching furry fingerless gloves. It wasn't anything special, but it indicated to everyone that he and Addison were together.

"Are you a cop or a stripper," Oliver asked, regarding my sleeveless police costume.

"Both," I said, twirling the plastic black baton. "The cuffs are real."

"You just wanted to show off your biceps," Addison accused.

I gave a cocky shrug. "Gotta show off my best assets, and

I can't go with my dick out, so I had to settle for second best. But the pants tear away like stripper pants." I waggled my brows. "Easy access."

"Just try to keep your pants on until you leave the party," Oliver noted.

"I can't promise anything. I might have to do a striptease just to take attention off Addison in that fucking scrap of a costume."

Oliver took his time looking over Addison. "I'm not sure how long we'll be at the party, anyway."

I laughed. "You're already coming in your pants, aren't you?"

THE NEIGHBOR'S Halloween party was in full swing, and Addison and Oliver left shortly after we had arrived. I wasn't in the mood to be there anymore, but I couldn't go home. I didn't think I'd survive the noises coming from Oliver's room, and I definitely didn't want to go home alone.

I wasn't feeling the slutty costume parade with one woman after another coming onto me. I didn't really see any of them. Addison had been burnt into my retinas, ruining me, and not for the first time.

Out of all the girls that had been hitting on me, I decided I liked the blonde in the slutty nurse costume best. She was tipsy but sober enough that I didn't feel like I was taking advantage of her. I may have slept with my fair share of women, but they were always happy, willing participants.

This one's name was Tiffany, and she was in school to be a dental hygienist or something like that. I only knew because she told me she had an unusually large mouth compared to the average woman. To prove her claims, she fit her whole fist inside her mouth. And me, being a classy asshole, asked what else she could fit in there. She batted her lashes and said she would be happy to show me.

On the short walk back to my apartment, Tiffany claimed she was a pro at deep throating because she had very little gag reflex. I almost choked as I opened my apartment door.

I glimpsed Addison stepping into the hall bathroom. The door closed with a click, and the shower turned on as I led Tiffany to my bedroom. As soon as my bedroom door closed, she pulled me in front of the floor-length mirror.

There was no kissing or any prelude to her ripping off my pants and boxers. Tiffany went straight for my erection, smiling at me as she got down on her knees and unceremoniously began working to prove she gave amazing blowjobs. She took me in root to tip, sucking deep. She was right. Even taking me all the way in, she didn't gag, and it was a huge turn-on. Her eyes peered up at me as her head bobbed. My hand wound in her blonde-Addison like-hair, and I deeply regretted choosing a blonde.

I shouldn't have been thinking about Addison, but I couldn't keep myself from picturing her in that skimpy little costume. There were so many things I wished I could do to her and with her. Tiffany was cute, but I didn't feel for her what I felt for Addison. There was no deeper connection with Tiffany. We were just using each other for the night.

I thought that's what I wanted, but now a night of meaningless sex just felt . . . meaningless. Joyless. Even if I managed to push the thoughts of Addison out of my head, I couldn't extricate her from my heart. My feelings for Addison were ruining me.

16

———

ADDISON

THAT SKANKY WOMAN walked into the apartment with Travis, and even though I didn't actually know a thing about her, I knew she wasn't right for him. I stayed in the bathroom long after my shower, trying to understand my irrational anger. I tried to convince myself that I was just looking out for Travis. He deserved more than a one-night stand. He warranted someone who knew him for more than just the physical pleasure he promised.

But my anger wasn't just because of a selfless need to watch out for my friend. I was jealous and angry that she got a piece of him when I couldn't. I turned away from the mirror, unable to look myself in the eye while I pictured myself wrapped up in his arms. His soft eyes filled with adoration as he moved inside me, making love to me. I pushed away from the vanity and walked to the bathroom door, gripping the handle. I needed to crawl back in bed with Oliver. I needed to stare at him while he slept so I could remember all the reasons I was with Oliver instead of Travis.

I twisted the handle but paused as a thought occurred to me. The woman he brought home was blonde. Was Travis pretending she was me? I had seen the look he gave me earlier when I came out in my costume. He wanted me. He was tempted to take me right there, and what did it say about me that part of me wanted him to?

I dropped my forehead against the door. My heart was so mixed up, and I knew I'd become a disgusting person.

This had gotten so out of hand, but I couldn't stop thinking about him. Me, Addison Arthur, Miss Determination, Miss Perfection. I had big plans and did anything to achieve them. I never let anything distract me—except Travis.

Guilt ate at me, and I had to get out of this bathroom. I threw the door open and stepped out into the hall. The bathroom was right across from Travis's closed door, and I could hear the noises from his room growing louder. The woman was moaning and screaming his name. Though obnoxious, her noises weren't what bothered me. It was Travis's gruff voice that tore at my heart.

I had no right to him or these feelings. Travis could make his own decisions and mistakes. He could sleep with whomever he wanted.

Instead of going back to bed with Oliver, I went to the kitchen. I couldn't lie in Oliver's loving arms while my mind was still on Travis. I made a cup of tea and sat at the kitchen table, stirring my drink to keep my hands busy.

Their sex noises were quieter in the kitchen, but it didn't make it hurt any less. I loved Oliver. I did. So why was I so upset?

I could feel my heart splitting—pulled in opposite directions. I pretended for so long that I started believing the lies I told myself when, in truth, I had fallen in love with both men a long time ago, and my love for them remained. They both owned a piece of me, and while I sat drinking tea, that love was ripping me in two.

17

TRAVIS

CHAMOMILE TEA. It's the first thing I noticed as I stepped out into the hall. Since Addison, the tea snob, practically lived here now, I had grown accustomed to the distinct smells of tea. I could name them by scent, and right now, I smelled Chamomile, which meant Addison was having trouble sleeping. I could have figured that out without the tea being that it was the middle of the night.

I closed my bedroom door behind me and followed my nose.

Addison sat cross-legged at the kitchen table, staring down into her mug. She wore nothing but flimsy cotton shorts and a tank top with no bra. Her nipples were hard. I cleared my throat. "Addie."

She startled, her chin coming up as a palm flew to her chest. Her eyes met mine and held. Oliver had to be sleeping. Addison probably thoroughly wore him out before she got in the shower.

I felt my brows knit together. "You couldn't sleep either?"

She shook her head and picked up her mug to take a sip.

I felt awkward standing there in nothing but my boxers. I probably should've put more clothes on, but I snuck out after Tiffany had fallen asleep, and I didn't expect anyone to be up. Also, this was still my apartment. I should be able to wear or not wear whatever I wanted.

Addison seemed to be in an unusually quiet, sullen mood as I crossed the kitchen and opened the fridge. I had finished off the orange juice that morning, but a new one sat in its place. I pulled it out of the refrigerator, turning to Addison. "Did you buy this?"

She nodded. "I picked some up when I was out today."

I looked at the juice and back to her. "Thank you. Do you want some?"

Addison shook her head like I knew she would because neither she nor Oli liked orange juice, which meant she bought it just for me. I tried not to read anything into her thoughtfulness and poured a glass, feeling Addison's eyes on me.

I twisted the lid back on and leaned a hip against the counter, facing Addison as I took a drink.

We stared at each other, and eventually, her eyebrows pinched together, and she said, "I hope you never develop diabetes."

I laughed. "Where'd that come from?"

"The orange juice," she said like that explained it.

I tried to hide my smile. "Does orange juice fuck with your blood sugar or something?"

She nodded. "It can cause it to spike."

I grinned at her. She was such a nerd.

She remained unsmiling as her head tilted up to appraise me. "Do you usually walk around in your boxers after we go to sleep?"

I looked down at myself with a shrug. "I didn't think anyone would be up, and I didn't want to wake Tiffany."

"Tiffany." She repeated the name with disdain. "She's um . . . loud."

I let out a sigh. "Yeah, sorry about that."

"Why aren't you in there asleep next to her?"

I shrugged. "She's in the middle of the bed, and I'm not really in the mood to cuddle. What about you? Why aren't you asleep next to Oli?"

She stared at me. "I couldn't sleep through your sexcapade."

I wanted to tell her I regretted bringing Tiffany home, but that seemed like a pretty shitty thing to say about a woman who just got me off twice, so I winced and said, "Sorry."

She looked down at her tea and tucked a wayward strand of hair behind her ear. "Oli and I are never that loud, are we? I mean, no one is *that* loud, but do you hear us?"

I replayed all the times I'd heard them. With a sigh, I admitted, "Yeah, Addie. I hear you."

I caught her mortified look before she studied her lap, her hands picking invisible fuzz from her shorts.

"It's okay, Add. I knew what I was getting myself into when I told Oliver he could live here."

She looked up, and there was an intensity in her eyes. "I don't know how you do it. I was instantly angry when I heard you two. I had the irrational urge to burst in and stop it from happening. She's not good enough for you, T."

My blood thickened to concrete, making me feel heavy as everything came to a screeching halt: my breathing, my heart, my brain. And then, just as quickly as it stopped, everything started moving again, kicked into hyper speed.

My heart galloped. My ears rang. I felt dizzy as my mind started working over her words. I set my glass on the counter and stared at her. "Why?"

She looked heartbroken at my question, her eyes welling with tears. I didn't move to comfort her. I couldn't. She would have to figure it out on her own.

Her head shook, and she grabbed her now empty mug, holding it as if it would warm her up, but the warmth was gone. It was just an act to busy herself so she wouldn't have to face me.

I stalked forward. "Why, Addie?"

Her eyes were stormy oceans when she made eye contact, and her voice was hesitant. "I don't know, I just heard you and—"

I shook my head as my shock turned to anger. "I'm not asking why you wanted to barge in. I know exactly why you wanted it to stop. I'm asking why the hell you would tell me something like that when you're with my best friend?"

Her eyes widened before closing tightly. Her face fell into her hands.

I stood on the opposite side of the table, leaning forward onto my palms. "You wanna know how I deal with it?"

She peeked up at me, and I continued, "I don't come to you and tell you how difficult it is for me to hear you and Oliver's very active sex life. I just endure it because I want my friends to be happy."

She swallowed, looking up at me. "Why wouldn't you say something? Tonight has been torture. If this is what you've been feeling this whole time, why wouldn't you want me to know so I could make it easier?"

I tilted my head. "How, Addie? How am I supposed to have that conversation with you or Oli? It's better that I keep it to myself. Whether I can hear your sex noises or not, it doesn't matter. You're always on my mind—constantly occupying space in my head. And you're not helping any of us by buying me orange juice."

"What's wrong with the orange juice?"

I glared at her. "It was thoughtful."

She sat with her mouth gaped, a dumb expression on her face like she thought I was crazy. Maybe I was.

She took a calming breath and said, "I noticed you were out of juice, and I was at the store, so I picked it up. Stop acting like I wrote you a love letter."

I was still hovering over her, standing with my fingers splayed out on the table. I stood straight. "It's not just the orange juice. It's all the nice little things you do for me. You drive me crazy!"

She stood, the chair scooting back with the movement. It was her turn to lean forward on the table to whisper-yell at me. "I drive you crazy? You're yelling at me for being selfish in one breath and too nice in the next. I don't know what you want from me."

I folded my arms over my chest. "You'll never understand how hard it is to be on my end of this relationship, Addie."

"It's not all roses on my end either." She pushed back from the table and mimicked my stance. "Do you really think your suffering is greater than my own?"

"Yes." I looked at her, bewildered. "A thousand times, yes. How do you not understand that? You have Oliver. You may get jealous hearing me with someone else, but I get to witness the woman I love living her happily ever after with my best friend." Saying it out loud made me cringe. It made it more real, and I choked on the guilt in my own admission. It only made me angrier, and I added, "You don't know shit about my pain."

She shook her head as if disappointed. Her arms dropped to her sides, and I could practically taste the sadness in each word as she breathed, "Is that what you think?"

She turned away and paused, whispering, "You don't know me at all." She took a shaky breath and started to walk past me, going toward the bedrooms. I reached out, my hand encircling her wrist.

It was the wrong move.

She spun so quickly; I didn't see her palm coming in time to dodge it. My cheek stung with the slap, and I jerked away, dropping her wrist. She followed me, moving into my space, assaulting me with her accusations. "Were you pretending she was me? That's why you chose the blonde, isn't it?"

I took another step back, trying to escape her words, as shame flooded me.

All the meticulous work I'd done to piece our friendship back together was falling apart just like a house made of straw. I don't know why the three little pigs came to mind, but it seemed appropriate. Addison and I were both wolves in disguise, and poor Oliver never stood a chance. He thought his foundation was stone and mortar. He had no idea the slightest breeze could destroy everything. My brain must have shorted. Why was I thinking about children's fables?

"I know your pain, Travis. Trust me, I know. My heart is constantly being pulled between the two of you. Do you think I want to be the cause of your pain? Tell me, how do you feel when you hurt the people you love most?"

Angry and defeated, I closed my eyes, but when I felt her move closer, they reopened to peer down at her, witnessing her sullen expression. Her soft palm slid against the sting in my cheek, holding me like I was something precious while she continued destroying me.

Her breath tickled my face as she spoke. "I don't know how to handle these feelings. You're the only one who understands. I don't want to keep hurting you. I'll do better —be better, but you have to tell me when I do something wrong."

It wasn't just me she was destroying. She was wrecking herself and Oli, too. It was just a matter of time until we all imploded.

I reached out, gingerly sliding my hand behind her neck to pull her into a hug. She came willingly, and I buried my face in her hair so I wouldn't kiss her.

We clung to each other for several moments before she pulled away. Her eyes shimmered with unspoken emotions as she lifted onto her toes and placed a soft kiss against my lips. And then she left, going back to Oliver's bedroom. I heard the door close and felt my heart crumble.

TRAVIS

NOVEMBER, December, and January were fucking uncomfortable. I skipped Christmas at Bucks and avoided the apartment as much as possible. I was tired of trying, tired of screwing up, and tired of hating myself and the woman I loved. There was no more room for screw-ups. I was determined to get through the rest of the school year, and then Oliver would be out of my apartment. That was the plan until I woke up one day and found Addison in my room.

After a restless night's sleep, I was staring at the ceiling. That's when I heard a noise and tilted my head. I almost jumped out of my fucking skin when I saw a person right next to my bed sitting stock straight in a chair, watching me. "Holy shit, Addison!" Jolting up in bed, I demanded, "What the fuck are you doing?"

Her eyes took in my naked chest before her attention returned to my face. Her jean-clad legs uncrossed as she leaned forward. "We need to talk." With the movement, her oversized sweater slid to hang off one of her shoulders, revealing the smooth skin beneath.

I drew my eyes away from her exposed skin to look her in the eye. "I have nothing to say to you."

She sighed, leaning back. "You can't just decide to end our friendship without giving me an explanation. And Oliver keeps asking what's up with you. You've been a dick to both of us, T."

"Would you like me to tell Oliver what's crawled up my ass? It would ruin both of you."

Her eyes flared. "Is that what you want? You're upset, so you're going to ruin all of our relationships?"

I narrowed my eyes. "You're being selfish, princess. Daddy must not be beating the bad manners out of you anymore."

She gaped at me, her face going slack. "I forget how mean you can be."

"Me? How mean *I* am? You are the one who seems determined to ruin our friendship," I accused.

I wasn't proud of what I'd said. I slid my legs off the bed to face her, making sure my blanket covered my junk. "You wanna be real? Let's talk. Did you get jealous hearing me with someone else?"

She stared at me, her eyes glistening, but I wasn't backing down. She'd started this. "You think I don't get jealous. There are times I hate you and Oliver for the noises coming from his room. And what? Did you think if I couldn't be with you, I would remain abstinent?"

"Travis, what is it that you want from me?"

I ran a hand over my face. "I want you to be faithful to Oliver."

"I want that too," she said immediately.

I put my head in my hands. "I'm so fucking tired of this battle, Addie. If he's what you want, then you two should live together. Cut me out of the equation. Take away the temptation. That's the rational choice."

Her head shook. "I don't want that."

"You can't have us both." I wanted to stand or pace, but I was naked under my sheets, and the last thing we needed was for me to have my dick out during this conversation. I rubbed at my scalp, putting it all out in the open. "It hurts to be around you, and I can barely stand being around Oli. We're the bad guys, Add. The guilt is eating at me, and my feelings for you are so fucked up. I'm so angry all the time. I can't afford to love you anymore."

She closed her eyes. "The thought of losing you makes me sick," she whispered.

"But holding on is hurting all of us."

She nodded, looking down at her lap. "You're right. I'll go pack up my things, and I'll stop coming by so much."

"It's only a few months until Oli finishes his masters."

She nodded, keeping her eyes down. Standing from the chair, she walked to the door. But before leaving, she said, "I love you, Travis. I'm sorry everything got so messed up. I'm sorry that I've hurt you and let you down so many times. You deserve so much better." Finally, she looked at me. "I don't know why it's taken me so long to say that out loud. I'll always love you, and I don't think it will ever be the way I'm supposed to love you. Thank you for being my friend, even when I really didn't deserve your friendship."

She took a slow breath, fighting tears as she stared at me from across the room.

I didn't know what I could say to all of that. I wanted to get up and comfort her, but again, the whole being naked thing was working against me. I could toga it, but with our track record, that was a bad idea.

"I love you too, Addie."

She bit her lip and, without another word, slipped out the door. I heard her moving around in Oli's room for a while before her footsteps moved to the living room, and then the apartment door squeaked open and closed with a thud. Something felt so wrong about this.

I had the whole day off, which was rare as a student who worked full-time. It was supposed to be my day to relax, but all morning I had a bad feeling that I couldn't shake. Oliver would be home in the afternoon, but it felt so quiet in the apartment. Too quiet. The ticking clock sounded loud in the silence.

I was supposed to go to the gym because I'd accidentally left my phone charger there. Now my phone was dying, but I was not in the mood for the gym today. I had no motivation to work on homework. I wanted to take a nap or sleep all day, which I intended to do after I went into Oliver's room to borrow his charger. But while I was there, I saw the note on his bed. The necklace Addison always wore was lying beside the note, and the unsettling feelings I'd had grew into bone-chilling dread.

Fuck their privacy. I reached for the note, unfolding the little card. Of course Addison would have stationary. I read the short message and stuck the card in my pocket before snatching the necklace off the bed and leaving his room without the charger. My phone would charge in the car on my way to Addison's.

The drive wasn't long, but it felt like a lifetime as all the scenarios ran through my mind. When I got there, I pounded at her apartment door. When she didn't open it, I used my key. The key she'd given me for emergencies.

I barged in, calling, "Addison!"

There was no response, and she was clearly not in the living room, so I checked the kitchen and bathroom before reaching the bedroom. The door was closed, but she had to have heard me. "Addie, I'm coming in," I warned, cracking the door.

She was in bed with a box of tissues. She had changed into pajamas and had a pile of used tissues next to her. Streaks of mascara marred her blotchy cheeks.

Tissue in hand, she sat up. "What are you doing here, Travis? Didn't you just beg me to leave?"

I softened my tone. "What the fuck do you think you're doing breaking up with Oliver?"

"What?" she asked innocently.

"Don't play stupid." I pulled the card out of my pocket and held it in the air. "I went into Oli's room to borrow his charger and found your breakup note on his bed. What the fuck is wrong with you?"

Her brows knit together as she stared at me. "I'm in love with you, Travis. It's not fair to him."

I sucked in her confession, letting it wind around my traumatized heart before rejecting it. "But you're in love with him, right?"

"Of course. How could I not be? But like you said, we're the bad guys, and Oliver deserves more."

"So you left him a note? Don't you think he deserves more than that?"

"Of course he does. Do you know how many times I've tried to break up with him? Do you think it feels good to be me? I hate myself for what I've done to him. I don't want to hurt him. I'm not strong enough to break up with him in person, so I wrote a fucking note because it's the only way I'll go through with it. I'll lose both of you, but you'll have each other. There is no scenario in which this works for the three of us, and I'm the one that came between you. He's your family, and I won't be responsible for taking that away from you."

Blinking slowly, I processed her words. She was plunging her pretty little life off a cliff in order to save mine and Oliver's relationship.

I came forward. "Stupid, sweet, Addison. Oliver is in love with you. You're in love with him. I can still be his friend. No one has to lose him. You don't have to break his fucking heart. Our relationship is the only one that has to change." I stared at her, hoping she would understand. "Our friendship has to end. From now on, I'll treat you like you are nothing more than Oliver's girlfriend. We'll see each other, but only when Oli's there."

"I already made my decision," she said, turning her back to me and laying back down.

"Your decision was stupid and rash and made out of guilt instead of love," I said to her back. "I told you I'm rooting for you and Oli. I meant it."

"But everything is a mess, and I don't know how to do it anymore," she mumbled into her pillow. "I can't do it anymore."

I walked around the queen-sized bed and laid next to her. She tried to turn away, but I forced her into a hug.

"What are you doing?" she said, panic lacing through her words.

I tucked her face into my shoulder. "Addie, I know how much courage this had to have taken. You're going to do right by him. Please don't destroy his happiness, or he'll end up jaded like the rest of us."

She nodded into my shoulder, clinging to me. We stayed

that way for a long time, knowing once we pulled apart, we didn't know when we'd see each other again.

Finally, I kissed her forehead and pulled back. I took her necklace out of my pocket and handed it to her. As I dropped the delicate chain into her open palm, I said, "This is the right move." I don't know who I was trying to convince more, her or myself.

I left before I changed my mind, and within the next month, Oliver had moved in with Addison, deciding to make the commute for the last few months of school. And Addie and I went a whole year without seeing or speaking to each other at all.

19

ADDISON

I CHEERED as Travis walked across the stage. His mom stood next to me, cheering just as loudly. It was summer, and I hadn't seen Travis in over a year. According to our agreement, I shouldn't be here, but I couldn't miss this. I had to watch Travis accomplish something he had once thought was impossible.

He was the first person in his family to graduate from college, and his mom had tears of pride falling from her thin face. We came from different worlds, but despite all of our differences, his mom took to me when we'd met six years ago, and I was never sure why. She had confided in me and I knew life hadn't been kind to her, but seeing the pride on her face as she watched her only son graduate, brought it all home for me. He was her life. She wasn't a perfect mother by any means, but given that she was raised by parents who barely tolerated her existence, I was impressed by her affection and dedication to her son.

When Travis approached our little group, I knew he'd expected Oliver and his mom, but his brows shot up when he spotted me, his smile growing. "Addie! I didn't expect you to come."

I'd been nervous about coming, unsure how he'd react to me breaking our no contact rule, but I was too proud of him to sit this out. I was thrilled and relieved at his smile.

"You think I'd miss this." I threw my arms around his neck, surprising him. He recovered quickly, his arms folding in around me. I kissed his cheek, and he stiffened a little. I knew I was pushing it. I pulled away, smiling. "You did it!"

He stared at me like I was the only person in the world, and my chest grew tight. "Thanks to you." His look filled me with so much warmth that it burned, and I couldn't wait for him to open his gift.

"I only encouraged you. You did the rest." I backed up another step, running into Oli, who wrapped his arms around me. Travis took in Oli's hold, and his eyes shifted to Theresa, who was in tears.

"My college graduate," she said, sounding so proud of her son.

After giving his mom a long hug, he hugged Oli.

"Proud of you, man," I heard Oli say.

Travis stepped back. "Where are we eating. I'm starving."

Oli and I had picked up Theresa on our way, but she rode with Travis to the steakhouse. It wasn't a long drive, but it gave me plenty of time to second guess going to dinner. My nerves rattled as I thought of the gift we had gotten Travis. I knew he would love it, but now that I'd seen him in person and remembered his touch, the present felt too personal.

I couldn't watch him open it. I couldn't handle the look on his face. I knew how he would react, and I wasn't so sure my heart could withstand the meaningful look he would give me. The worry I felt was eating away at the lining of my stomach—sure to cause an ulcer. I felt queasy.

"I'm not feeling well," I said suddenly.

Oliver looked over at me from behind the wheel. "What's wrong?"

"I feel nauseated. Will you drop me off at home?"

We were about to pass our exit, but Oliver changed lanes just in time. "Are you sure? Maybe you're just hungry?"

I shook my head. "No, I think I need to throw up."

We got off the exit, and he turned the car toward our apartment. "I'm sorry. Do you want me to stay with you?"

I put a hand over my mouth. "No. You have to give Travis his gift."

"I can't give it to him without you."

I closed my eyes, inhaling. "Yes, you have to give it to him." I cradled my head in my hands. I was having a panic attack, but he didn't know that. To him, I just looked ill.

"Hold on. We're almost there," he said, placing a hand on my back to rub little circles. It was sweet. Oliver was sweet.

I definitely couldn't go to dinner. I couldn't do anything that would jeopardize my relationship with Oliver or make me question past decisions. Oli was the one I chose. He was the one Travis and I both chose. And being near Travis made me question too many things. We'd done the right thing by putting distance between ourselves, and I knew he would understand why I wasn't at dinner.

We made it home, and Oliver stayed with me until I shooed him out the door. As soon as he left, I ran a bubble bath, congratulating myself on doing something right even though it felt so wrong.

Distance was good. Distance was necessary. I closed my eyes and went back six years.

~

"PEOPLE like me don't go to college, Addie. That's just the way it is," Travis said with a shrug as we walked down the hall toward the school library.

"There are scholarships and grants you can apply for," I said amidst the locker doors slamming and the clamoring of excited teens who were escaping the confines of school for the day.

Travis snickered. "Yes, because everyone is looking to help the white male of the lower-middle-class with poor grades and no extracurriculars except football. I worked my ass off at that, and it didn't result in a football scholarship. I'm not qualified for anything else."

I rolled my eyes. "You really fit yourself into a tiny little box, didn't you?"

"I'm just being realistic," he said.

I stopped him, turning him toward me. "The only people who succeed are the ones who fight for it. You're never going to improve yourself by giving up."

He snorted and continued walking. "One, that's bullshit, and who said I wanted to improve myself?"

"You did when you asked me to tutor you," I said, following him.

His head dropped back with a groan. "You were the new girl. I was just hitting on you. I didn't know you were actually going to only tutor me."

"And, yet, here we are four months into the school year, and you're still asking me to tutor you with no strings attached."

We stopped in front of the library, standing across from one another in a stare-down.

He reached for the door. "You're a pain in my ass. If you weren't dating my friend, I wouldn't even be here."

"Oh, so you're doing this all for Oliver?" I said doubtfully as he held the door open for me.

He shrugged.

As we walked to our regular study table, I thought of a different way to approach this. When we sat down, I said. "I'm not saying college is right for everyone, but if you want to work with computers, you're going to need it."

He set his bag on the table. "God, it was a mistake to tell you that. I swear you have vaults of information on people. You just keep things tucked away until you can use them for your benefit."

I laughed as I pulled out my books. "We had that conversation last week."

He quieted his voice as he sat next to me. "Listen. I already have a mom to lecture me, and even she understands I'm not really cut out for that kind of life."

"What does your football coach think?" I asked, pulling a folder out of my bag.

"Coach Miller doesn't give a shit about me off the football field."

I pulled the letter out of the folder. Handing it to him, I said, "That's not what he had to say."

He looked like I offered him a snake. "What the fuck is this?"

"I asked if he would write a character reference letter for you. I didn't even have to tell him why I needed it. He was happy to write it. He said he'd write as many as you need."

His mouth gaped, and his eyes were wide with disbelief.

"He doesn't want you to give up on yourself," I clarified.

His jaw hardened, and he made a face like he'd tasted something sour. His voice was low and menacing. "Who the hell do you think you are?"

"I'm—" he cut me off.

"That was a rhetorical question. Miss Queen Bee, who never had a problem in her pretty little life, thinks she can fix poor ol'

Travis. Well, fuck you, Addison." He gathered up his things and walked out of the library.

I sat there, holding my breath. The people at the table next to me were staring. I glanced over, and they gave me looks of sympathy before going back to their work.

Oliver was so easy going, genuine, and kind, but his best friend was the antithesis of kindness. Travis Rose had long spiked thorns, and I had just experienced how deeply they stuck. His words hurt, and my eyes started to cloud up, but I shook off the irrational emotion. His lashing out had nothing to do with me.

I worked on homework since I was already there, but my mind kept going back to his words. "Miss Queen Bee, who never had a problem in her pretty little life . . ." Is that really what he thought of me?

After half an hour of stewing, I gathered my things and left. The halls were empty, and the parking lot was sparse, making my car easy to spot. My feet slowed when I saw the figure leaning against my car.

I debated going back inside, but I knew I wasn't in any danger. Oliver's friend might have a mean streak, but he wasn't someone who would wait around in the parking lot to assault me.

His arms were crossed, eyes on the ground as he leaned back against my driver's side door. It was only thirty-degrees outside, and I wondered how long he'd been waiting there. I gripped the straps of my backpack to keep me from fidgeting and moved forward.

He must have sensed my presence because he looked up as I approached. Stepping away from my car, he said, "I might have overreacted."

I didn't say anything, just kept a cautious eye on him.

"Okay, I definitely overreacted," he admitted.

I released my straps and crossed my arms. "You know, we all have problems, Travis. No one's life is perfect."

"I know. I'm sorry. I just . . ." He sighed. "I read Coach's letter."

I stared at him, waiting for more, but his eyes went back to the pavement. Finally, he said, "I'm not used to people believing in me. It's better to have low expectations. Less disappointment that way."

"Minimum effort. Minimum rewards," I said, and he looked at me.

"I do want more," he admitted. "I just know it's gonna be an uphill battle the whole way, and—"

"You're scared?" I raised an eyebrow in challenge.

He gave me a dirty look. "Not scared. Practical. I don't have anyone to back me financially."

"Is that what worries you the most?"

"Yeah, college is expensive. I mean, if a shit-ton of money just dropped into my lap, that'd be great, but I don't see that happening."

I shrugged. "You never know."

He gave me a side-eye and I continued, "I'll help you figure out the financial part."

"I'm a dick. Why would you do that?"

"Because I want to see you succeed. And because one day after you've graduated college and have an amazing job, I want to watch you come back here to this school and dump a shit-ton of money in some unsuspecting kids lap to make things a little easier for them."

"Yeah right."

I grinned. "I'm serious."

He laughed. "I know you are. Your faith in me makes no sense."

"But that would be pretty cool, right?"

He nodded. "Yeah, it would."

∾

MY PHONE CHIMED with another text from Oliver. He had met up with Travis and Theresa at the steakhouse and kept checking in on me. This message had a video attached. It was Travis opening his gift.

He pulled the papers out of the envelope, looking confused as he held up pictures of the teenage boys. "You got me a boyband?"

I could hear Oliver laugh, saying, "Look at the rest of it."

My heart dropped, and I worried he thought it was stupid. Did he even remember our conversation? It had been over six years. It was quite likely he didn't remember at all. In fact, I felt stupid for recalling it so clearly, but I thought back to it a lot. Maybe it all meant more to me than it did to him.

Travis inspected the papers beneath the pictures and looked back up to the camera, his lips parted and voice sounding a little breathless. "What is this?"

I heard the smile in Oli's words, "It's the Rose Scholarship."

Travis's eyebrows pinched together, creating a groove as his head tilted to the side. "This was Addison's idea, wasn't it?"

Oliver didn't answer verbally, and I could only assume he nodded as Travis said, "That woman's mind is a steel trap. I can't believe you guys did this."

Oli said, "The pictures are the boys that Coach Miller recommended. You can choose one or split it between the three or pick someone entirely different. Basically, you can give the money to whoever you want."

"A graduation gift with homework. Just what I wanted." Travis laughed. "I'm kidding. This is incredible! I would complain that ten-thousand dollars is way too much fucking money, but it's not going to me."

"Addison started the fund when we were still in high school. This was her pet project."

Travis's eyes zeroed in on the camera, his look so intense, "Of course it was."

Theresa chimed in, "She always believed in you."

I held my breath as Travis said thank you to Oliver and mouthed it again as he looked directly into the camera.

2 0

ADDISON

Oliver and I fit in occasional trips down to see Sandra and her girls. Gracie's cancer had come back with a vengeance, and I learned everything I could about her type of cancer. I spent my whole third year in med school soaking up as much as possible, but everything I suggested to Gracie's doctors, they had already tried or said wasn't an option. I realized the doctors were likely annoyed by me, thinking I was a know-it-all med student, but really, I wish I had known it all. I was frustrated by all the things I didn't know—desperate to learn of some new cure to save her.

In the break before starting my fourth year of med school, Oliver and I packed up to visit Gracie and her family before my life got too hectic.

Our layover flight was delayed, making us several hours later than we had expected. By the time we arrived at Sandra's apartment, it was creeping toward eleven o'clock. We told her we could come in the morning, but she insisted we come straight from the airport. Sandra opened the door, and we exchanged hugs before she said, "The girls insisted on staying awake because they're so excited to see the two of you."

"I'm so sorry we're so late."

She shrugged. "It's fine. Things rarely go how we plan them. We roll with the punches here."

"Hi, Miss Addie!" Marley ran at me full speed, throwing her arms around me. She was small for twelve, but the impact still had me taking a step back as my arms went around her.

"Hey, Marley."

Sandra admonished, "Give the woman some room to breathe."

"I'm just so happy to see you." Then she saw Oliver and leapt on him next.

Sandra said, "Okay, Marley, it's time for bed."

"But they just got here," she whined.

I smiled and said, "I'm gonna go say hi to Gracie."

Marley pouted, "See, Miss Addie will keep Gracie company, and we can catch up with Oli."

Sandra and I exchanged a look. Both Gracie and Marley had a crush on Oliver. I walked down the hall and let Oli fend for himself.

I cracked Gracie's bedroom door. Dim lamplight glowed from the nightstand while Gracie rested with her back elevated at a thirty-five-degree angle in a hospital bed that was way too big for her. Gracie's eyes flicked open at my little tap on the door. "Hey, Princess Gracie."

"I'm not a little kid anymore. I'm fifteen."

"That doesn't make you any less of a princess."

She smiled, closing her eyes, and seemingly struggled to reopen them, which gave away just how tired she was.

With her eyes closed, she said, "They tell you I'm dying?"

I swallowed, pressing my lips together. I nodded.

She peeked at me. "Cat got your tongue?"

I sniffed. "How are you feeling?"

She looked up at me and sighed. "It's not that bad. They give me medicine that makes me a little loopy so I don't feel the pain. But it does make the room spin sometimes. Come here." She patted the bed.

Lying next to her in the hospital bed, we both stared up at the ceiling in silence.

She patted around until she found my hand on the mattress between us. She linked it with hers and asked, "Will you do something for me?"

"Anything."

She took a breath and said, "Tell me what it's like to be in love."

I hadn't expected that. I didn't want to give her a hallmark answer. I wanted to be honest. She deserved that much. "It's. . . like you found the other half of your heart. Someone who will crawl into the pits with you just to comfort you." I paused, thinking of not only Oliver, but of Travis too. "They'll make you laugh at things that wouldn't be funny to anyone else. You have a thousand inside jokes. They know what you're thinking based on your expression. And you can't get enough of them. You cherish every detail. You learn all their weird little flaws and find them cute or at least learn to live with them." I laughed softly. "Your whole world could fall apart, but when you're in their arms, you feel safe. You hurt when they hurt, and you're happy when they're happy. You celebrate their accomplishments as if they're your own, and you'll do anything to see them smile."

Her next question was already on the tip of her lips. "What about sex? What does that feel like?"

I thought about whether or not it was ethical to answer. She was only fifteen, but I'd promised her, and I knew aside from a miracle, Gracie wouldn't get to experience it for herself.

"I don't know what it's like for other people. I can only tell you from my own experience, and for me, sex goes hand in hand with love. Sex is the closest you can get to another person, and I couldn't imagine having sex with someone I didn't love. It's so intimate. You expose your body, but also your heart and soul. And your partner is at their most vulnerable too. It's beautiful and powerful and feels amazing. I don't know if it would be the same if you didn't love them. I would imagine it would still feel good, but there would be an awkwardness that isn't there when you fully trust someone."

"I bet Oliver is good at sex," she said with a wicked grin.

I smiled. "No complaints here."

She giggled. "If I had time to fall in love, I'd want it to be with someone like him."

That statement hurt. I closed my eyes. *How much had I taken for granted?* She was only a teenager, and she was thankful for every single day she had left.

After another long pause, she asked, "Do you think my mom will be okay?"

She was the one dying, and she was worried about her family. "Your mom is a strong woman. She'll keep going for Marley's sake, but you're her baby too. She's going to miss you like crazy."

Gracie's voice shook. "Promise me you'll keep an eye on them."

I turned toward her. "Of course, I will. We might not be related by blood, but we get to decide who we call family, and I consider all three of you my kin. And I have something to tell you."

She turned her head towards me, her eyes heavy with exhaustion. "What?"

"You know how I said I wasn't sure what kind of doctor I wanted to be. Well, I've decided." I swallowed, trying to hold back my tears. "I'm going to help kids like you. I'm going to try my hardest to kick cancer's ass."

Gracie's eyes opened wide, looking terrified. "Why would you want to do that?"

"Because I want to save lives so other kids can grow up and experience the good things in life. If there is a chance for me to help even one kid, it will be worth it. I just wish I could save you." Tears fell in rivulets down my cheeks.

"Miss Addie, you're already crying. You can't do this. I don't want you to be sad forever. Do something that makes you happy."

I wiped my tears. "Just because something makes me cry doesn't mean it doesn't make me happy. Being here with you makes me both happy and sad. It won't be easy, but that'll make it all the more rewarding."

She let out a sigh. "You're a good person, Doctor Addison Arthur. I wish you could've been my doctor." Her eyes closed and her breathing slowed. I watched her sleep for a few moments before rolling out of bed. I tried to pull my hand from hers, but she squeezed, holding on.

I looked down at her, and her eyes were open. "In the future, you probably shouldn't talk to your patients about sex."

I laughed. "Good thing you're not my patient. You're family." I leaned forward and kissed her forehead. "I love you, Princess Gracie."

"I love you too, Doctor Addie."

Before I was through the door, she said, "Addie," I spun to face her. "You're going to save a lot of lives, but I'll look after the kids you can't save."

My trembling hand covered my mouth, holding back the sob that wanted to break free. It took a moment for me to pull myself together enough to respond. "Of course you will, Gracie. You've always been an angel awaiting your wings. Thank you."

Oliver and I had set up a fund for people to donate money to Sandra so she could stay home with her daughter for her final weeks. So far, we had raised over forty-two thousand dollars, which would help with some of the crushing medical bills.

Gracie slept through most of our weekend visit. I spoke to her one more time before our final goodbye, and the flight back to New York was a quiet one. I was grateful Oli and I were seated next to one another, as I couldn't keep from crying. I kept checking my phone, worried I would miss a text or call. It's an awful feeling, waiting for that call. None of us knew when Gracie would breathe her last breath, and my heart raced with every text and call until the actual call came.

21

TRAVIS

After graduation, I moved a couple of hours away for a job. Addison was a fourth-year med student and she was busy with clinical rotations. Oliver received his masters in economics and then went the other direction into commercial real estate. He said it made sense temporarily while Addison finished school and then residency. It was a chore to coordinate schedules, but Oliver insisted on us getting together. He said it had to be before Addison went back to school. So it was the end of summer by the time I drove back to Upstate New York to meet up with them.

We met at a restaurant and by the time I arrived, they were on the patio with a table and drinks.

Oli spotted me as I approached the table. With a big smile, he stood and gave me a hug, thumping me on the back. "Good to see you, man."

"You too," I said as we separated.

I turned to Addison who wore a short loose-fitting summer dress and my first thought was *easy access*. Damn, I was rusty. I hadn't been around her in quite a while and it showed. I'd forgotten how my whole body reacted so irrationally to her. It didn't help that she was showing so much skin. There was no cleavage, just toned arms and long sexy legs.

As I hugged her, I definitely wasn't thinking about how soft her skin was, or how sexy she smelled, or how good she felt in my arms. I absolutely did not sprout a hard on at the sight of her like a fucking twelve-year-old boy going through puberty. No, I did none of those things because that would be insane and I'd learned a long time ago how to control my dick.

I pulled away quickly before she felt my reaction to her. I took the empty seat and jumped into conversation. "How's the new condo?"

Oli shrugged. "It's nice for now. Addison is never home, but there is a pool and I've improved my swim time considerably."

I smirked. "I bet I could still beat you."

"That's awfully cocky of you," Oliver retorted.

"You're forgetting I used to teach aquatic therapy to middle-age women. It's a hell of an exercise, so I've kept it up."

Addison sat forward with a laugh, "Did you just admit to doing water aerobics without getting paid for it?"

I nodded. "It's a good work out and I'm not that dude at the gym posting selfies of my workouts."

"Yeah because you're doing water aerobics," she snickered.

"It works a lot of muscle groups. A lot of athletes do *aquatic therapy.*"

The waitress stopped by to get my drink order, interrupting us.

~

AFTER WE ATE DINNER, we ordered another round of drinks. I was on my second long island iced tea. Oliver was on his second bourbon, and Addison was on her third cocktail which was more than she ever drank.

"So how's dating life for our wild single friend?" Oliver asked.

I laughed, looking into my drink. "You know I don't kiss and tell."

"Since when?" Oliver asked. "What happened to your rating system." He turned to Addison. "He rates how good each woman is in bed."

I kicked Oliver under the table while Addison's gaze flicked to me. She was not impressed.

Oliver kept talking, "Extra points for blow jobs."

Her lip curled. "Congrats," Addison said, "you just won the douchebag seal of approval."

"I haven't done that for years," I backpedaled. "I realized the error of my ways." I glared at Oliver, "What the fuck, man?"

"What? It's just Addie. She already knows you're a douchebag."

"Maybe I was a douchebag. Not anymore."

Oliver leaned forward, resting his elbows on the table. "Come on, you've gotta have some good dating stories."

I glanced at Addison, seeing how she felt about this. She seemed to tune us out as her body swayed to the live music. She must have had a good buzz which was so unusual, but I loved when straitlaced Addison forgot to hold back.

The girl loved to dance, but she didn't let herself often. I pulled my focus off of Addison and back to Oli. I needed to get my head back on straight and I did have some good fail dates.

"Okay," I hedged. "There was this one date that was pretty fuckin' terrible."

Oliver shouted, "I knew it!"

Addison looked startled by Oliver's outburst, but soon the music caught her again and her head started bobbing.

It was fucking adorable. "Damn, Addie, you lightweight."

Addison shrugged. "I don't get out much these days." She did a shimmy in her seat.

Oliver smirked, watching her dance. "That's my girl."

She shook her head, as if trying to clear it. "No, I want to hear T's story." She stilled her body and leaned forward, elbows on the table and her face in her hands, staring at me. "Go on."

"You're adorable when you're drunk."

"Don't try to distract us with your charm. Get to talking mister."

I laughed. "Okay, so I met a girl on this dating app, and we had several conversations before we met in person. She seemed normal, cute, funny, but dear God, she showed up looking like she ate the woman from her profile picture. I mean she had at least 120 pounds on the woman from her picture. That wasn't a deal breaker, but it was surprising. The first thing she said to me was, 'I don't date white guys.' Clearly, I'm white, so obviously our date was off to a great start."

Addison asked, "Didn't she see your pictures from the dating app?"

"Yeah, which is why it was so confusing. Then she jumped right into talking politics. She has some very, eh, controversial views. She wasn't shy to tell me we're all going to Hell for all our evil ways. Then immediately, without prompting, jumped into talking about her favorite kind of porn, which is stepfather porn, by the way, in case you were wondering. Which I was not wondering, but she told me anyway."

Addison stifled her laughter, and I continued, "When we were finished eating, she asked if she could stay at my house. When I told her no—"

"You said no!" Oliver howled. "Why? She sounds like a great marriage material."

I laughed, continuing, "So when I said no, she offered me blow in the bathroom. I mean, I don't think I'm being especially picky, but I would like someone who at least looks like their picture and isn't a fascist drug addict."

Addison rested her chin on her folded hands. With a serious face, she asked, "So when's the wedding?"

While Oliver and I laughed, Addison flagged down our waitress. "He needs another drink," she said, pointing to me.

Our waitress smiled. "I can make that happen."

As she walked away, Addison, said, "What about her? She's cute."

"I don't need you guys to play matchmaker. Sometimes, I just want to go out with my friends."

"That's not a no," Oliver noted.

"I'll ask her out just as soon as Addison gets up to dance," I said.

She looked around. "I can't do that. Or maybe I can. Let's go to a club!"

"How drunk are you?" I asked.

"More drunk than you. You need to catch up." She jumped up, announcing, "I'm going to the little girl's power room."

"Where?" I asked, but she was already walking away.

"I think she meant powder room," Oli clarified.

I looked at Oliver. "I haven't seen Addison get drunk in . . . a long time."

"Remember Gracie?"

"Of course. The girl with cancer."

"She lost her battle yesterday. She was fifteen." He gave a sad smile. "Addie made me promise not to talk about it tonight. I don't think she knows how to cope. I haven't seen her cry since she got the call. She loved that girl. We were down there two weeks ago to say goodbye."

"That sucks and it explains why she's all over the place tonight."

Oliver nodded. "Maybe she's in denial. We leave in two days to fly down for the funeral."

The bill came and we had already paid by the time Addison finally came back to the table laughing. We were about to go check on her.

She didn't sit down but instead said, "I almost went into the men's room. Well, I might've walked in a little bit, saw urinals, and walked right back out, running into a man. Oops, I think we should probably leave now."

We stood from the table and Oliver bit his cheek, trying to keep from laughing. "Did you find the ladies room?"

"Yes and the ladies in there were very supportive of my decision to go clubbing."

Oliver looked concerned. "I don't know if that's a good idea."

She spun on him, giving a pouty frown. "Pleeease!"

Oliver glanced over at me, his brows raised. "What do you think?"

I shrugged. "It could be fun. If for no other reason than to watch drunk Addie."

She ran ahead to the car and I asked Oli, "Are you okay to drive?"

He nodded and we climbed into the car. Addison sat shotgun and immediately cranked the music all the way to the club.

On our way in, I leaned into Oliver. "You know we're gonna be playing body guard all night."

He nodded, looking nervous. "Whatever makes her happy."

WITH ARMS RAISED above her head, her body moved to the music. It'd been so long since I had seen Addison look so carefree.

I sat at the table with our drinks while Oliver went out to the dance floor with Addison. After a few songs, Addison came running up to the table, dragging Oli behind her.

She stopped only a hair from my face and shouted, "Travis!"

I pushed her back a little, holding her at arms length. "Yeah, Addie?"

"I'ma help kids fight cancer, cause fuck cancer!"

"Fuck cancer!" Oliver repeated, lilting to the side as he came forward to stand next to her.

"I'ma be a pediatric 'cologist, a'cause fuck cancer!"

I smiled at her. "You guys doin' okay?"

She held her drink up, saying, "This one's for Gracie. She never even gotta taste alcohol. She never gotta love a boy. She'll never getta have sex or pick a college. She won't have a job or kids. And here we are feelin' sorry for ourselves. Gracie didn't even feel sorry for herself when she knew she was dying. What does that say 'bout us?" Her mood had quickly turned solemn.

I held my drink up. "To Gracie."

She smiled, and she and Oliver tapped their glasses to mine, saying, "To Gracie!"

We all chugged our drinks and I wondered briefly how we were going to get home. None of us had stayed sober enough.

"I'm gonna get us a ride," I said, pulling out my phone.

Before long, we piled into the back of the car which was a tight squeeze, but I managed to close the door. Addison sat between me and Oli. About a minute into the ride Oliver passed out against the window, but Addison wasn't so much tired as she was sad. I watched as she sat in absolute silence with tears dripping from her chin. She didn't even attempt to stop them. I wrapped my arm around her and pulled her against me.

"Let it out," I whispered, rubbing a hand over her back.

She sniffled, turning her body into my chest as one of her hands fisted in the front of my shirt. Her silent tears turned ugly as her body shook with violent sobs. She struggled to breathe through her grief. It was the kind of heart wrenching cry that had her whimpering and gasping, while her tears, snot, and mascara dripped onto my shirt. It broke my heart.

"It's not fair," she sobbed.

"I know."

"Why her?" she whispered.

I shook my head. "I don't know," I said into her hair.

Once she managed to quiet herself a little, she complained, "It hurts, Travis."

I held her tighter, grinding my teeth to hold in my own damn tears—tears she seemed determined to wrench out of me. "I know it does, Add. But you're going to be okay. And you're going to make the world a better place."

She rested the side of her face against my chest, admitting, "I'm scared. I know they won't all make it. Kids die. I'm not stupid. I know I won't be able to save them all."

I blew out a breath. "But you will save some. You'll walk straight into Hell and you'll save the ones you can. Not many people could do that, Addie. You're incredible and you're going to make a difference."

I pulled her blonde strands out of her face as I peered down at her.

"Thank you," she whispered. "After all these years, and you're still building me up."

I kissed the top of her head. "Of course I am. That's what we do."

Her voice was soft. "I don't feel like I do that for you."

"I wouldn't have gotten into college if it weren't for all your encouragement. You believed in me when no one else did."

She held on tighter, whispering, "You might have to carry both Oli and me out of this car."

I scoffed. "Is that so?"

She nodded before going still. Her grip on me loosened a bit and her breath became even.

I caught the driver eyeing us in the rearview mirror and wondered if I should feel guilty about holding her, but we hadn't done anything wrong. I was comforting a friend and that's all it was. Everything happening on the inside couldn't be held against me, right?

22

TRAVIS

OVER THE NEXT two years I communicated with Addison and Oliver mostly through an ongoing group text. Between social media and our messages, I kept track of my friends, but we rarely saw each other. Addison was in her second year of residency and Oli and I both had busy work schedules. But we always showed up for the big events. Always. Which was why I had agreed to go to the charity event Addison helped coordinate.

It was a black-tie event that required spending several hundred dollars just for tickets to get in the door and then there were the silent auction items. All proceeds went toward cancer research.

Oliver made me promise to behave in front of the judge who would surely be there. I made no promises. I had tried to tell Oliver he was a shit human, but without breaking Addison's confidence, I couldn't tell him all of my reasons for hating the man. As my best friend, I feel like he should've taken my word for it. I was rarely wrong about people. He knew this, yet he seemed to have an unwavering respect for the man that I couldn't understand.

What I hadn't realized was I would be seated at a table with Addison, Oliver, Judge Arthur, Jeanine, and Oliver's mom and her husband. It wasn't until I arrived that I found out that tidbit of information.

Oliver's mom and stepdad, Kim and Harry were up bidding on auction items and Jeanine was off talking to a group at another table. Then it was just Oliver, the judge, and myself left at our table. Oliver was seated next to the judge and they seemed to be having a deep discussion about politics which was something I had no interest in discussing with Mr. Arthur.

I decided it was time to make my way to the bar. After I got my drink, I stayed next to the bar, leaning against it as I took in the room. Addison had been running around all evening and she finally sat down at the table next to Oli. He acknowledged her, giving her a kiss on her cheek before going back to his conversation with the judge. It didn't take long for Addison to look as if she'd rather be elsewhere. Earlier in the evening she had given a heartfelt speech about the despair of losing children to cancer and I knew she was not in the frame of mind to want to talk ugly politics. Addison's political opinions didn't line up with her father's beliefs, but she would never contradict him.

A song came on and she immediately looked at Oliver. She was about to grab his arm, but stopped herself as she realized he was still deep in conversation. She knew better than to interrupt. Her excitement fizzled for a second before she looked out to the dance floor and her smile came back slowly as she watched everyone dancing.

I watched as her body began moving to the beat. I was

hoping she would get up on her own. She didn't need Oliver to dance. Come on, Oliver. He had to know this song reminded her of Gracie.

It's like he didn't even see her tonight. It pissed me off. It wasn't often that Oli let me down, but I was disappointed in him tonight. I knew how much of herself she poured into this evening and now he couldn't even see her.

Fuck it. If Oliver wasn't going to do anything, I was going to step in because I couldn't let my friend sit this out. I downed the rest of my drink and set my glass on the bar before going to Addison.

I approached the table dancing between Oli and Addie, bumping the table, purposely being extra obnoxious because that was sure to break Oliver's attention and piss off her bastard father at the same time.

Once I had everyone's attention, I said, "Addie, it's Gracie's song!"

Oliver smiled like he always did and I wanted to shake that damn smile off his face and tell him to take care of Addie. Mr. Arthur glared at me like always while Addie beamed at me. "You remembered."

I gritted my teeth and tried to look happy and not constipated or pissed. "You wanna dance? Come on guys."

Addison would have sprung from her chair if her father hadn't been there, instead she went back to looking nervous.

"Sorry," Oliver said, "We're in the middle of something. Maybe later."

He meant him and Mr. Arthur. I wasn't just disappointed he didn't encourage Addison to dance, but I was officially pissed at him. He was too caught up in whatever they were discussing to notice anything around him. I wasn't going to let her sit this song out. I offered her my hand. "Addie, you comin'?"

She smiled up at me, my insistence giving her the permission she needed. I looked back at the table as we went to the dance floor, watching as Oli turned back to the judge. He was a fucking moron.

He didn't even want to watch Addie dance. A spoiled fucking asshole. He'd grown complacent. He missed the sheer joy on her face as she danced and lip synced every word.

It wasn't long before I forgot all about Oliver. Getting gifts was great, but watching the joy on someone's face as they opened the perfect gift was a thousand times better. And that's what I felt like I was doing. Watching someone who rarely let herself be happy, totally let go. It was a beautiful thing.

When we came off the dance floor laughing, we swung by the bar to get water and then we wandered out on the edge of the ballroom.

As we stood in the entryway, I said, "Addie, I'm so impressed. Tonight was a great turn out."

She beamed. "You haven't even seen what the silent auction brought in. I couldn't be more excited with how things have gone tonight. I mean, there were a few hiccups but I would say it's been a success."

I couldn't have been more surprised by her response which must have shown because she asked, "What?"

I shook my head. "Nothing. I'm just not used to you being proud of yourself. It's a good look on you."

In a small voice, she admitted, "I am proud of this." She looked a little bashful.

Addison's father approached and without greeting or

preamble, he ripped his daughter to shreds. He kept his voice low, not wanting to be overheard. "You think anyone will respect you as a doctor when you're dancing like a childish whore."

Gone was her bashful smile. She swallowed, her beautiful face frozen as her eyes glazed over. She kept her composure, and with a gracious smile, she said, Excuse me." She walked away, disappearing into the women's bathroom.

Fuck. I hated that she cared what he thought. I tried my best to keep my fists at my sides as I glared at her father, but he wasn't concerned with the likes of me as he walked away like I didn't exist.

My fists tightened and I held myself still, attempting to breathe through my fury. But as he entered the men's room, I knew what I had to do. I burst in behind him, grabbed his pristine white collar and shoved him against the glossy stone wall, getting right in his face.

"How dare you call your own daughter a childish whore, you miserable piece of human garbage! I've never seen someone so determined to break their child's confidence. The next time I hear you insult your daughter, I promise you, I will break your fucking face."

Once he realized I wasn't going to hurt him just then, he started saying, "How dare—"

I lifted the chubby man off the floor and he shut up. "I wasn't asking for your feedback. I'm just letting you know where we stand."

I dropped him and left the room, but swung back when I heard him mumble, "Trailer trash."

His look of fear made me smirk. "That's right. Proud trailer trash. It could've been worse." I ran my eyes over him in disgust. "I might've ended up like you."

After that, I left and waited outside the ladies' room. After a few minutes, Addison emerged, looking as beautiful as ever, but her composure was fragile like the cracked shell of a baby bird and I wanted to peel her out of that damn armor she hid behind. But she had to do that on her own.

I stepped up to one of the decorative pillars along the wall. I held onto it as I dipped down doing my most provocative stripper dance, "Wanna come dance with this slut?"

Her smile was weak, but she stepped forward. "This childish whore would love to dance with such a seductive slut."

I bit my lip, loving the fact that I could make her smile no matter how faint. I held my hand out and she took it. I led her straight out to the dance floor and let go of her hand. Her touch still set me on fire, no matter how many times I told myself that I was just her friend. The less we touched, the better. Somewhere between Mr. Arthur's words and now, things had changed, and I had a hard time controlling the pull she had on me. I distanced myself from her as her hips moved with the beat. This wasn't just attraction, this was that soul sucking desire that tortured me. I thought by twenty-seven I had finally gained control over my feelings, but it seemed I couldn't control who I fell in love with any more than I could control the weather.

I looked around, trying to figure out where the fuck Oliver was. Why wasn't he here with her? Didn't he realize he shouldn't leave his beautiful woman out here on her own. I'd already tracked four guys who were waiting for me to leave her so they could move in.

I sucked it up, focused on one of my two best friends and we danced together, pulling out all of our best moves while I simultaneously looked for Oliver. He was nowhere in sight. What the fuck.

The fucking DJ put on a slow song, and I wondered if my panic was as evident as hers. Addison and I stared at each other, the distance between us amplified by the couples who were already pairing up. I held out my hand and she stepped forward, both of us knowing this was a very bad idea.

Then out of nowhere, Oliver swooped in, kissing Addison's cheek and wrapping his arms around her from behind. I was shocked that her look of relief tore me open. And through the heartache, I stood there and smiled at my friends, even though I still wanted to sock Oli in the eye for having his head shoved so far up his ass tonight.

I thought I could do this. It had to get easier. It wouldn't always suck, right? I just had to keep control of my dick and all these fantasies that crept in when we got too close. The trouble was, it wasn't just my dick driving my fantasies anymore. No, my heart was so tangled up in it that I imagined normal shit, like waking up with her in my bed and spending a lazy weekend together in our pajamas. I wanted to feed her chocolate cheesecake with strawberry drizzle, not to get in her panties, but because it was her favorite and I desperately wanted to be the person to make her smile.

Did Oliver know she didn't like roses? Did he even see her? Not the version of her she showed the world but the real her? She confessed he hadn't in the past, but had that changed? Was it possible that I could actually be a better fit for Addie? Of the two of us, he was unquestionably the better man, but was he the better man for her? I'd always thought I had known the answer, but I wasn't so sure anymore.

Someone tapped on my shoulder and I spun to face a

gorgeous woman in a silk black gown. It was skintight and the neckline was generous, giving me a great preview of her full breasts. Dark eye liner, with fuck me eyes and blood red lipstick gave a come-hither look. Her dark hair was pulled into a sleek ponytail. Everything about her gave me the impression that I'd be going home with her that night and she hadn't even spoken to me yet.

"Want to dance?"

I reluctantly pushed Addison out of my thoughts as I stepped forward, saying, "I'd love to."

Her smile was pretty. "I'm Chelsie."

"Travis," I said, offering my hand. She took it, guiding it low on her hip before wrapping her arms around my shoulders. She was petite, but her heels had to be close to five inches. Her breasts pressed into my chest as our bodies moved together. I couldn't help but wonder how different Addison's body would feel against me. I looked toward her and Oliver. A jolt of desire ran through me when our eyes met. Fuck.

23

ADDISON

IT WASN'T fair how just a look from Travis could set my whole body on fire. I could feel my cheeks flush and tried to hide my reaction by resting my cheek on Oliver's shoulder. Thank God Oliver showed up when he had. I didn't think I could touch Travis without kissing him. I heard him threaten my father in the men's room, and then he pretended it never happened, going to any length to make me smile.

I loved him, and I didn't like the picture-perfect model he was dancing with. She looked easy, and Travis didn't need an easy girl. He needed someone he could love. He deserved the world. I wished I could be the one to give that to him, but if I did, he would lose his family. Travis still had his mom, who continued to ignore the signs of a serious lung disease. If something happened to her, Oliver would be the only family that remained. As much as we love each other, it would destroy Travis to lose Oliver.

So I had to sever this possessiveness I felt over him. I was going to be a doctor. I was smart. I knew these feelings I had for Travis were just a physical response, and I wouldn't let it ruin both of our lives.

I loved Oliver. And if he knew about my history with Travis, it would destroy him.

However, if Travis confessed his undying love for me and asked me to leave Oliver, then I wasn't sure what I would do. But even if he did feel that strongly for me, I knew Travis would never do that to Oliver.

TRAVIS JOINED Oli and me at the bar. I sipped at my drink, asking, "Where's the woman you were dancing with?"

"She had to leave early, but I got her number. We're gonna get together in the next few days."

"Of course you are," I said with a smirk.

"Nice, man," Oliver congratulated, then swooped in to kiss my cheek. "I'm going to go check the items I bid on."

I ran my hand over his chest, giving him a warm smile. "Thanks, babe."

Once it was just Travis and me, things felt awkward. He slipped his hands in his pockets, saying, "So, it seems like people are having a good time."

"Yeah," I nodded. "But don't small talk with me. You hate small talk."

He shrugged. "I was just making an observation."

I downed the rest of my drink. "You were trying to make this feel less awkward."

"That too."

"The Cupid Shuffle" came on, and Travis smiled, his brows lifting. I grabbed his arm, tugging him to follow me back out to dance.

By the time we were sweaty, laughing, and relaxed, a slow song came on. We looked at one another for a moment before I decided it would be better not to tempt ourselves. I started walking off the dance floor, but his hand caught my wrist. I looked over my shoulder.

"It's one dance. We can do this. We've gotta be able to do this." He sounded desperate, and I figured if our friendship couldn't handle one slow dance, then what were we doing?

I ignored the electricity that zapped between us like a live wire. I couldn't lose him, so I nodded, resolved to prove we could do this.

Oliver was all lean muscle, where Travis's muscles were bulky. I always felt petite in his arms. Maybe it wasn't as difficult for him as it was for me. Perhaps he didn't feel everything I felt.

His hands remained at an appropriate height and didn't roam or explore, but his touch alone made me crave more. I tightened my grip around his neck, needing to pull closer, desperate to feel his body against mine. I would cling to the feel of him for as long as I could. But as I pressed into him, he hissed, and I drew in a quick breath, realizing there was nothing one-sided about this. His erection was long and hard, and I had to restrain myself from grinding against the length of him.

His grip on me tensed, and his movements stiffened as if withstanding the temptation was taking all his focus. He tilted his face into my hair and his lips found my temple, but he didn't kiss me.

I tighten my arms around his shoulders, barely holding in the urge to run my fingertips up into his hair. I knew he loved the feel of my nails raking his scalp in a moment of passion. I knew he'd come unhinged if I nipped at him, anywhere—his shoulders, his neck, his pecks. He would groan in ecstasy when my teeth tugged at his bottom lip. I whimpered at the thought, and he rewarded me with a rough growl.

I closed my eyes to hide the fact that they rolled back in my head. My hips squirmed, my lady parts were desperate to find relief. The heat between my legs could have set fire to my thong if it hadn't been soaking wet from that damn growl.

We were crossing a line, but we didn't talk about it. If we acknowledged it fully, we knew we would need to stop. And I don't think either of us wanted to put an end to it.

Had I ever felt this out of control with Oliver? Was it just that Travis was forbidden, or was there something more here? I already knew the answers. It wasn't that Travis was forbidden. I was still in love with him. The distance we'd put between us the last few years didn't dampen any of my feelings for him.

I could tell he was trying to keep things platonic, but did he feel the fire between us? Was it only lust on his end? Lust wouldn't have him standing up to my father. Travis loved me. So did Oliver. And I loved both of them. It was evident to me that I thought about Travis more than I should, and at times when I should've been focusing on Oliver. I guess I thought of Oli when I was with Travis, but only because the guilt ate at me.

Oliver was the safer choice. He would do anything for me, and I called all the shots. Travis was a wild card. He made me crazy. And he practically handed me to Oliver on a silver platter when I tried to break up with him.

"Why didn't you let me break up with Oliver?" I whispered.

"He's the better man."

I shook my head in disagreement. "You underestimate yourself."

His fingers curled into my back.

My voice was barely a whisper. "You're mad at him tonight. Don't think that I don't see it. I see you, Travis. The same way you see me. We're trapped. Both of us."

He released his grip and pushed back to look at me. His brown eyes were razor-sharp. He grabbed my hand and pulled me off the dance floor, out of the ballroom, and down the hall.

"Where are we going?" I asked.

"Somewhere to talk in private."

He led us up a staircase, and we passed a couple of doors before he wiggled the handle of one, and it opened into a dark room with only the glow of the exit sign. Travis moved away and flipped a switch that lit two out of the ten recessed ceiling lights. It filled the space with a soft glow, and I took in the room. It appeared to be a small event room they converted into a storage area. There were various centerpieces, piles of fake floral arrangements, and a cluster of potted trees. There were rows of stacked chairs, and he grabbed a chair and propped it in front of the door, essentially locking us in. He led me toward a baby grand piano in the back corner. Leaning against the piano, his elbows rested on top while his face fell into his hands.

I continued to look around the space. Finding a corner stuffed full of artificial Christmas trees. I asked, "How did you know this was here?"

He spun to face me. "I worked here as a caterer in college. It was just a side job, but apparently, they never fixed the lock on that door." He took a step toward me. "What did you mean when you said we're both trapped?"

I sighed and stepped forward. "When I'm around you, it's like my whole body is going to spontaneously combust, and I think you feel it just as strongly as I do." My hand cupped the bulge in his pants, and he hissed. I let go, stepping back. "It's what we do to each other."

His eyes closed tightly.

As I looked him over, my desire grew, and I breathed, "It's not safe for us to be in here alone."

His eyes shot open, and he ran a hand over his face before moving forward. He reached out to me, taking my hands in his. It looked like he wanted to say something, but maybe he couldn't find the words.

He untwined one of his hands from mine and reached up to cup my cheek in his palm. "You're right. I am mad at him tonight. If he wouldn't have spent half the night ignoring you, then we wouldn't be here, alone right now. I wouldn't be so tempted."

I put my hand over his, holding it to my jaw as I leaned into it. "These events are usually dull and a little stressful. I'm either running around or bored out of my mind. I've had more fun with you tonight than I thought was possible. Thank you for making my night."

He blew out a breath, his forehead falling against mine. "Don't say nice things to me right now, Addie."

Our bodies drifted closer. "You want me to be mean?"

"Yes, please." His breath brushed against my face.

"You want me to call you trash like my father did?"

With a little intake of breath, he moved back, his brows drawn in concern.

I stepped away and smiled. "Or as you say, 'proud trailer

trash.'" I shook my head. "Why would you stick up for me like that?"

"With everything he's done to you, he's lucky I haven't killed him, or at least roughed him up a little."

I swallowed. "No one stands up to Judge Arthur. It's reckless. He could make your life hell."

"And I could make his life hell."

I tilted my head, with a grin tugging at my lips. "You're so cocky."

"You're the doctor and you're calling me cocky."

I inhaled deeply. "I know how to handle myself."

"No offense, princess. But no, you don't."

I snorted. "You can't just preface an insult with no offense and expect me not to take offense."

With a smirk, he said, "No offense, but yes, I can."

I smiled.

His voice turned wistful. "God, I love to make you smile."

My smile melted as I searched his face, looking for a sign that he was experiencing the same desire that was burning through my veins. "Travis," I whispered as I stepped forward, lifting my chin. "It terrifies me."

He reached out, running his fingers from my shoulders down to my wrists. "What terrifies you?"

"This pull you have on me. The things I feel when I'm with you."

His eyes found mine. "Four years," he said.

"What?"

"It's been four years since our last fuckup. Four years since I felt you—tasted you."

My palms met his chest when he moved forward.

"Push me away, Addie." His heavy-lidded honey-brown eyes begged me to reject him. "Push me away. Please."

My hands ran up his chest, feeling the muscles beneath his suit's expensive material. "I can't."

His arms wound around my waist, pulling me in. One of his hands ran up my spine as he breathed, "Addison, we can't do this."

My eyes fell closed at the feel of his breath against my skin. "Can't we?" I whispered.

His face nuzzled in next to mine. The stubble of his short beard felt rough against my cheek. My eyes opened, and I tilted my face toward him. His lips brushed mine so softly that I couldn't be sure they actually touched. We were both breathing as if winded by the strain of holding back.

The tension between us stretched so thin—like a rubber band pulled too tight. The snap was almost audible as we reached our limit, pulling free of the bonds that held us apart. Too late to turn back, his lips fell heavily against mine. My mouth opened for him, welcoming his demanding tongue, but as soon as I got a taste, I moaned into his mouth, needing more. His teeth raked my lip, tugging.

My hands gripped onto his broad shoulders, pressing my chest against his as our mouths found a desperate rhythm. We were mouths, teeth, lips, and tongues. The energy between us was urgent and unrelenting. The more I kissed him, the less it felt like a mistake. The longer we kissed, the quieter my conscience grew, drowned out by our passion. Any reasons I might have for stopping what we started seemed flawed.

My body moved against him without conscious thought, undulating against the erection he hid inside his trousers. Travis suddenly pulled away, and I made a noise of complaint, his absence assaulting my mind and body as I opened my eyes and reached for him, but he was too far away.

I forced my eyes to focus, and I watched as he unbuttoned his tux jacket and slid it off his shoulders. He smirked at my obvious desperation, saying, "It's too hot."

He laid his jacket across the baby grand piano, and I moved toward him. I stopped just in front of him, my hands reaching up to land on both sides of his jaw. "You're beautiful."

"That's my line," he said, leaning forward to kiss me, but I held him back.

"Wait," I whispered. My eyes drank in every part of him as my hands ran across his jaw, down his neck, and over his broad shoulders. "You make me dizzy, and I don't want to rush this. I want to savor every minute with you."

His straight lips curled in an uneven smile. I ran my fingers over his smooth mouth before lifting for another kiss. I wanted to memorize the feel of his lips against mine, so soft, yet so powerfully firm—life-altering.

Our pace was unhurried. We savored every touch as our kiss progressed into more. Needing to feel his body without barriers, I went to work on his shirt, unfastening one button at a time. It was slow torture.

I undressed him, pulling his shirt off his shoulders and forcing his undershirt over his head until his chest was bare. I knelt down so I could run my tongue up his abs to his pecks. It's something I'd fantasized about since the first time I saw him shirtless.

When our faces lined up again, I breathed, "I've always wanted to do that."

He smiled and then he was kissing me again. I guided his

hand to the zipper hidden in the side seam of my dress. He pulled it down with patience I found agonizingly slow. I wore only a black thong under the strapless dress, and as my dress fell to the floor, his body guided mine back until my bare ass was leaning against the closed keyboard of the baby grand piano.

My hands went to his fly, and as I unfastened him, he pulled something out of his pocket and set it next to me on the closed keyboard.

"Open that."

I grabbed the little metal compact-looking case and popped the latch. The top sprung open, and a stack of condoms lay inside. I fought a smile as I took one out. "You have a little case for your condoms?"

"Safety first," he mumbled.

My smartass retort died on my lips as his pants and boxers slid down his muscular thighs. His legs were tree trunks, thick and strong, and I was dying to sink my teeth into them. But his thighs weren't the only thing thick and hard. My free hand went to his erection without pause. I stroked him with one hand while the other hand held the condom. I used my teeth to open it, and Travis's deep growl made me feel powerful.

His hands went to my hips, and he pulled me off the keyboard to slide my thong down my legs. One of his hands slid between my thighs. His fingers grazed down my center, and he cursed under his breath. "Fuck, you're wet."

It was hard to concentrate as his finger sunk into me, pumping in and out as my legs shook beneath me. I tightened my grip on his cock, while the hand with the condom held tight to his shoulder for balance.

My head fell against his chest as I let out unintelligible

noises, unable to control myself. His free hand lifted my chin and he kissed me, absorbing my noises—my breaths.

An orgasm flooded me, and my legs refused to hold me up any longer, but he held on to me, lowering me back to the piano. He took the open condom, sheathing himself before pulling my legs around him and tucking himself between my thighs.

I inhaled a sharp breath as his cock slid between my folds. I gasped into his mouth as he sunk to the hilt. He kissed my lips, my cheek, my jaw. He sucked at my neck, distracting me, but then our lips met again, and we inhaled each other's moans as our hips moved together.

We weren't just having sex. We were making sweet love, rocking together like we had nowhere to be but in each other's arms. Our connection went beyond the physical act of making love. Our hearts and souls coalesced as the love we had held back from one another flowed freely.

How could this be wrong when it felt so right?

We found a slow rhythm as we continued to kiss, our hands roaming each other. I was a fool. I loved him too much to let him make love to me. Next thing I knew I'd be confessing my love. My heart and brain were at war, tangled in the dizzying loop we had been running in for the past nine years. It was painful to be apart yet more painful to be together. We were in ruins, only pretending to be whole.

"Travis," I moaned. He paused, but I shifted my hips forward, and he resumed his pace. "Please don't stop. Don't ever stop."

I wanted to run away with him, but neither of us could justify hurting Oli that way. If I broke up with Oliver, I would lose them both. Oliver was the glue that bound us. He was the reason we couldn't be together and the reason we couldn't stay apart. If I left Oliver, his best friend would always be off-limits. I would be the ex, and I would lose them both.

Sneaking around was the only relationship that could work with Travis. And as awful as it made me feel, I couldn't give him up.

I needed Travis, and Oliver didn't have to know. We were good at keeping secrets.

His tongue was in my mouth, his arms around my body, his dick deep inside me. Slow. It was deliberately slow, allowing me to feel every ridge, and the feel of him was magnificent. I knew tonight, when I was falling asleep, I'd be closing my eyes and remembering Travis.

My breath caught as a terrifying thought filled my head. Years from now, after I had married Oliver, would I still be thinking of Travis?

TRAVIS

WHEN WE FINISHED MAKING LOVE, our arms locked tightly around one another. Her legs curled around my hips. We were as close as two people could get, but I wanted more. I wanted to do this for the rest of my life.

As if reading my thoughts, Addie confessed, "I'm in love with you, Travis. Madly, deeply in love with you. It hurts to be with you knowing we can't be more, but it hurts worse to be away from you. I don't know how to do this. I'm not strong enough to let you go." Her tears gathered, gleaming, and then they fell. Her breaths came so quickly that she was gasping. I didn't know what to do, so I held her tighter.

I tried to think of a way to make this work, but I had no better answers than she did. I held her in silence until her breaths evened out, and she whispered, "I think he bought a ring. I'm pretty sure he was getting my father's blessing tonight. He's going to propose to me, Travis."

Dread pooled in my stomach, and I almost begged her to refuse him. But I knew she would say yes. And I should want her to say yes. I should want my friends to be happy, but I had to leave the equation for them to be truly happy.

I held her tighter, so tight, she probably couldn't breathe. "I'm sorry, Addie. I'm so sorry. This should be great news, but I've ruined it."

I pulled out of her and pulled back. She slid off the piano onto her feet and collected her clothes. "There's a bathroom through here." I showed her the bathroom where we both cleaned up and redressed.

"Will you take me home? If Oliver sees me . . ." She didn't finish her sentence. She didn't have to. Her lips were swollen, hair a mess. Her puffy eyes and mascara smeared face spoke for her.

"I'll take you," I said.

We got cleaned up, and I zipped her into her dress, kissing her shoulder, knowing this was the last time. She was going to marry Oliver and have his babies.

She texted Oli, claiming she had a terrible headache and couldn't find him, so I was taking her home. I was disappointed when he didn't even question how sketchy it sounded. He only promised her he would be home soon.

We were quiet the whole way home, but when we pulled up to their house, I said, "I'll always be here for you, Addie. Call me or text me whenever. I just can't be near you for a while."

"Let's not say goodbye, okay?"

When I didn't answer, she looked over at me with tears clouding her eyes. It killed me not to pull her toward me—not to comfort her. I nodded. It was all I could do.

She reached across the space, and her thumb ran across my bottom lip. She pulled away before her tears fell, and she got out of my truck without looking back. I watched her unlock her door and go inside, waiting for her to turn, wanting one last look. But she didn't turn around. She didn't fucking turn around. And I shouldn't have wanted her to.

As soon as her door closed behind her, I pulled away from the curb and drove out of her life.

I DIDN'T SLEEP that night, and worse, the next day, Oli came over to show me the ring he planned to propose with. He had indeed been getting Judge Arthur's approval. And through the silent auction, he made sure to win a Caribbean trip where he planned to propose to Addison. I thought he was being an asshole by ignoring her all evening when, in reality, he was working on an elaborate proposal for the woman of his dreams.

Fuck.

I didn't know if it was possible to hate myself more.

I knew I needed a way to escape both of them before I repeated the same mistakes.

I had been headhunted a month prior. The position would've been an advancement to my current job, but I turned it down when I learned it was in Arizona. Now, I was desperate to get away and praying the position was still open.

I sent an email as soon as Oli left. The next day I received an email back, asking how soon I could start. The position meant more money and more responsibility. I was hoping it was enough to keep my mind off Addison.

Before the end of the week, I was packed up and moving across the country.

25

ADDISON

I FELT HOLLOW for the next month after Travis left. I knew this wouldn't be like the last times. When Travis moved across the country, I knew it was to get away from me, and I knew I'd lost him for good. We'd gone long periods between seeing each other, but this felt final. And worse, I felt like he had taken a part of me with him.

I couldn't find the energy to fake happiness, so Oliver knew something was bothering me. However, the correlation between Travis leaving and my deep depression didn't seem to occur to him, probably because he didn't see it as a loss. Our group texts stopped, but Oli still talked to his friend. He could always visit him. I knew those things were forbidden for me.

After a few weeks, my residency became demanding, which distracted me. In addition, I picked up extra hours because I was trying to forget my own sorrow and guilt.

A month later, Oli surprised me with a trip to the Caribbean. And just like that, I was engaged. Oli and I face-timed with Travis. He looked and sounded happy for us, and his easy acceptance hurt. Everything hurt. He said he couldn't make it back for our engagement party because of his new job. I suspected maybe he was doing the same thing I was doing—working to keep his mind off the things he couldn't control.

Everything felt wrong. But I had to let him go and hope he found his own happiness.

I knew I loved Oliver, but my love for him got wrapped up in guilt and regret. I wanted to call off the engagement, and if there were a way to do it without hurting Oliver, I would have. I just needed to step back from my life to take a breather, but instead, life continued forward at full speed. I ignored the growing issues as I built invisible walls between myself and everyone around me.

My relationships felt empty. All I had to give were surface smiles and courtesy appearances. I wore a smile while I withered away inside. My career advanced, propelling me through the monotony of days, weeks, and months. I saved children's lives. I made sure families left the hospital intact. My work fulfilled me when nothing else could.

PART TWO

2 6

TRAVIS

Six months after my move to Phoenix, I finally adjusted to my new job.

I stifled a yawn, struggling to keep my eyes open. I should have grabbed a coffee. I glanced at the clock and only five minutes had passed. How was I going to make it through this? Hadn't we had enough meetings about implementing the new system? My boss droned on while I focused on getting through the next half-hour.

I wondered if the other dozen people here were just as bored. They certainly seemed like they were paying attention. My eyes grew too heavy to keep open, and my buddy, Paul, kicked me under the table. Shit.

"It looks like Deena made it," my boss announced, and I looked up just in time to see a petite woman walk into the conference room. She wore a black power suit with spiked heels and black-rimmed glasses.

"Sorry I'm late," she said.

"No problem," my boss said, "Everyone, this is Deena, the consultant who will help us through the transition."

Her sleek brown hair hung just above her shoulders. She had sharp eyes that took in the room, assessing the group. Her eyes passed over me without a second glance, but my eyes were glued to her. She reminded me of a young nerdy Lucy Liu in those adorable glasses. "It's nice to meet everyone. We'll have plenty of one-on-one time, but for now, let's get into the nitty-gritty."

I wasn't nearly as tired anymore. Instead, I focused on her movements, her words, her dark eyes, and nude lips that smiled wide. She was friendly and professional, and I was hoping under all those layers of professionalism was a sex kitten just waiting to rip off her glasses and pounce.

There was no wedding ring, and even though I didn't date people I worked with, I could justify it because she was only a consultant. She'd only be here for a time, and I very much looked forward to working closely with her. I would make the most of it.

After our meeting, she made rounds, working individually with everyone on our team. I kept my eye on her as she went from desk to desk, and finally, it was my turn.

"Mr. Rose, you are the lead BI developer, correct?" I stared at the nameplate on my desk that read, Travis Rose, Lead Business Intelligence Developer.

"Yes, ma'am." I smirked. "At least that's what my nameplate says."

"Please, call me Deena," she corrected without looking at me as she typed on her iPad.

"Yes, ma'am."

She glanced over the iPad at me, unsmiling. Her eyebrow quirked, and her look made me feel small, foolish. Her eyes flicked back to the screen in her hands.

We went over the details of the project plan, and she

asked if there was anything I needed. Dozens of dirty thoughts sprang through my head, but I answered with a grin. "I can't think of anything, but I'll let you know if that changes."

She tilted her head, looking unimpressed. She set her iPad down next to my keyboard and sighed. "Just so we're clear, Mr. Rose, I do not have romantic relationships with my coworkers. I will report any advances to HR. This is a business relationship. Are we clear?"

Grinning ear to ear, I said, "Crystal. And I'd like to extend the same gracious warning to you. And since we're on the subject." I let my smile drop as I used my pen to push her iPad a few inches away from my keyboard. "I'm a firm believer in personal space."

She watched the movement, her face blank. I smiled inwardly. I enjoyed confusing her and couldn't wait to watch her squirm for the next few months. I knew how to be sweet while keeping my distance, and in my experience, the results would drive her mad. She'd be begging for my attention by the end of this project.

THERE WASN'T much progress during the first month, but I knew I was on Deena's radar. At the end of the month, our team went out for happy hour after the implementation went live. It was a success with only minimal snags, but we had a few more months of transitioning ahead. I avoided her during happy hour, even after I felt her eyes on me.

The second month was a clusterfuck of problems. My plan fell apart as I was too exhausted to focus on anything but fixing the issues with the software. Most days, I worked well into the evenings, and Deena was there helping me. I was too tired and frustrated to be cute, and most of the problems were things I felt she should have caught before the transition went live, but here I was, cleaning up her mess.

"For the last time! This wasn't my fault," she snapped at me.

"How did you not see this coming?" I growled.

Her voice grew louder. "I've never had this snag before. It's your company's fault. Not mine."

I buried my hands in my hair and went back to looking at the screen. It was ten o'clock at night. My eyes burned and I'd lost my tie hours ago. She had shed her suit jacket, and within the last hour, she'd taken off her shoes. She removed her glasses and rubbed at the bridge of her nose. Her short hair was pulled back into a messy ponytail, with dark strands falling loose.

It was cute, and if I wasn't so angry at her, I might be tempted by her.

"Are you hungry?" she asked suddenly.

"I just want to get this done," I huffed.

She stood up. "Well, I'm leaving. We're not getting anywhere, and we're both grouchy. I'm starving. Let's get dinner. This disaster will be here tomorrow."

I put my face in my hands. "I'd rather just finish and go home and sleep."

"No. We've been working on it too long. We need a break! Come on, or I'll turn the lights off on you."

Reluctantly, I pushed back from my desk. "Fine, but you're paying."

"The company will be paying for our meal and drinks. God, there will be drinks," she groaned as she grabbed her bag and slipped back into her shoes.

I stood up and made sure I had my keys, wallet, and both my personal and work cellphones. "I'm not driving your ass home."

"Pfft. I bet I could drink you under the table, but we're not driving. There is a bar just down the street. They have the best wings."

That, I couldn't resist seeing. Wings were messy and Deena seemed so clean and professional. I couldn't wait to see her spill sauce on her crisp white shirt.

It was a five-minute walk, but it was a cool night for Phoenix. The fresh air felt good. The bar was a little hole in the wall. This seemed like a place where I would be comfortable, but it was rough around the edges, and Deena stuck out here.

We sat on stools at the bar, and after we ordered our drinks and wings, Deena asked, "Have you always lived in Phoenix?"

"No. I've only been here six months."

"Oh, where were you before?"

"I'm from Upstate New York. I started my degree in North Carolina but had to transfer back home when my dad got sick."

"Oh, I'm sorry. Is he okay? What's wrong with him?" she asked.

"A lot was wrong with him, but liver failure is what killed him."

"I'm sorry to hear that," she said as our drinks arrived.

I shrugged away her concern. "It was years ago."

She struck me as a sweet cocktail kind of woman, and something about her drinking a beer was sexy in a girl next door sort of way. I cleared my throat. "So, where are you from? Tell me about yourself."

She set down her beer and studied it, saying, "I grew up in a small town in Indiana. I got my degree and then got a job close to where I grew up." She peered up at me with a smirk. "Believe it or not, my background is in writing code, but I got bored staring at a computer all day. And bored with living in a small town. I wanted a job that allowed me to travel, meet new people, and experience life. My sister moved out here a year ago and talked it up so much that I thought I'd give it a try. So here I am."

"Nice. It's good to know that you're usually good at your jobs."

She winced. "Ouch. Normally, I have very few issues transitioning old platforms to the new platform. I don't know what the issue is this time."

"I know it's not you," I admitted. "I'm just new to this position, and it's making me look bad."

"It's making both of us look bad," she corrected.

"So, I'm curious." I leaned forward. "What do you do for fun? I'm gonna be honest. I never pictured you drinking beer at a dive bar."

She smiled. "I got the impression you didn't care what I did in my free time."

I shrugged. "Well, the last time I was friendly, you threatened to report me to HR."

"I did do that." She laughed. "I may have gotten the wrong first impression of you."

"Nah, you got it right. But then you started making my life a living hell with this damn project, and I was too tired and pissed to make you fall for me."

She was mid-sip and almost choked. She coughed a few times, setting her drink on the bar. "I'm sorry. Did you say you were going to make me fall for you?"

I smiled. "If you made the first move, you couldn't really report me, could you?"

The arrival of our chicken wings interrupted her glare, and the subject was dropped.

By the time we finished eating and paid, I'd learned a lot about her, and I liked what I heard. I liked her and not just because she had sex kitten written all over her. I like that she was nerdy and adventurous. She enjoyed visiting museums but also went bungee jumping for her last birthday. She was complex and down to earth. The kind of woman a man would take home to meet his mother.

She was in the middle of telling me about her trip to Vegas when she stopped short.

"Wait! That's it!" She picked up the pen she used to sign the bill and looked around like she needed something to write on. I slid her an unused napkin, and she started scribbling furiously.

I let her work and continued to sip my beer. After a few moments, she slammed the pen down and jumped up. "Got it! Let's go."

She didn't wait for me. She just took off, and I chugged the rest of my drink before catching up to her on the sidewalk.

"You have an epiphany?"

She waved a hand at me. "Don't talk. I'm still thinking."

We walked back to the office in silence, aside from her random mumbling. I hoped all this acting crazy led to an actual answer.

She went in without flipping on the lights, so I turned them on while she was booting up her computer. It was nearing midnight, and if I hadn't been curious, I would've been tempted to leave her there and call it a night.

She was squinting at the computer as she wrote code, working in silence as the seconds turned into minutes and the minutes turned into an hour. I'd dragged a lounge chair over by her computer, and when it was clear I didn't understand what she was doing, I fell asleep.

I woke to Deena shouting. "Yes!" My eyes flew open in time to watch Deena stand and do a fist pump.

I asked, "Did you fix it?"

She spun to me. "I think so!"

"Let me look." She backed up and I moved in. It looked like she had fixed it, but I would not get excited until I was sure. I spent the next half hour trying to look for a flaw. Realizing she'd done it, I turned to tell her, but she was fast asleep in the lounge chair. I watched her for a moment. She was beautiful, and I hadn't been giving her enough credit on this project. She'd been left a mess, and she had spent hours upon hours fixing it. She was a brilliant woman. Who knew that would be such a turn on?

I guess Addison was brilliant too. So it appeared I had a type. Smart, beautiful, and way out of my league.

I reached out, resting my hand on her shoulder, whispering, "Deena."

"Mmm Travis," she moaned, a noise that went directly to my cock. I narrowed my eyes on her. Was she dreaming about me?

"Deena," I said louder, pulling my hand away.

She woke with a start. "Huh!"

"You did it," I gave her a proud smile. "You fixed it."

Her eyes fell closed. "Finally!"

"Let's go the fuck home!"

"What time is it?" she asked, looking for her phone.

"Two AM."

She groaned, and I helped pull her out of the seat. We straightened up and collected our things before leaving.

As we walked out to the parking lot, I saw that our cars were just a few spaces away from each other. I thought about sneaking a kiss, but I wanted her to make the first move.

I went to my car, and she went to hers. We hesitated before separating.

"Thanks, Travis. We make an excellent team."

I smirked. "We do, don't we?"

"I'll see you tomorrow," she said before climbing into her driver's seat.

"Sweet dreams," I said, giving her a wink before sliding into my car.

Her eyes narrowed, and I gave her a knowing grin, closing my car door. She shut hers and we both drove away.

THE FOLLOWING WEEK, Deena came to my desk. "Travis, may I have a word with you?"

Her tone was authoritative, and I was worried she had actually called HR, but I'd been careful about crossing lines. I knew I hadn't gone too far. I followed her to a small conference room, and once the door closed behind us, she pushed me back against it. I was getting mixed signals. Then she grabbed my tie and pulled me down while she stood on her toes. Her lips pressed into mine, and as soon as I kissed her back, she pulled away.

"Travis, I would like to date you. And while we're dating, I don't want you seeing anyone else. As far as work is concerned, we either pretend we aren't dating or disclose our relationship to HR and sign a paper. Honestly, I'm fine either way. Those are my terms. Are you interested?"

I grinned at her. "You want to date me?"

"I already established that. Do you want me or not?"

"Sweetheart, I've wanted you from the moment I saw you walk into that conference room."

"Good. What about HR?"

"I'd rather not get them involved. It's none of their damn business anyway."

"I was hoping you'd say that because I don't have anything on under this skirt, and I was really hoping we could make good use of this room."

All of the blood drained out of my face and went straight to my dick. "Are you serious right now?"

She took her glasses off and set them on the table. "That door doesn't have a lock, and it'll have to be quick, but yes, I'm very serious." She held up a condom between two of her fingers. "Plus, it'll take the pressure off our first date and the will we or won't we."

I looked around the room, figuring out the logistics. "Are you a screamer?"

Her lips curved into a sly grin. "I know how to be quiet."

"Have you done this before? At work?"

She bit her lip and shook her head. "No, I've never wanted to until now."

I pulled her in, my lips fell on hers, and she opened for me, her tongue slipping into my mouth. My hand ran up the outside of her thigh, pulling her skirt up to her hips. My fingers slipped between her thighs. I groaned when I found no barrier. I pulled away from her lips to whisper, "You were having a sex dream about me that night we stayed so late, weren't you?"

"Yes, one of many," she confessed.

I rubbed against her wetness while she unlatched my belt. As she unfastened my pants, she said, "That feels really good, but we don't have time for all of that."

Her hands found me, and she was rolling the condom on before I could process how quickly this was going.

She stared up at me. "Okay, how are we doing this, big guy?"

I picked her up, and she made a little "Whoa" sound as she clung to my shoulders, her legs automatically going around me. She positioned herself, and then I lowered her tight little pussy onto my cock. Her breath was heavy as I pumped into her, guiding her hips. I worked out when I was stressed, so I'd been hitting the gym a lot which now seemed totally worth it.

Deena held on for dear life while staying as quiet as she could. She bit my shoulder as an orgasm ripped out of her. It was fucking sexy.

When we finished, we put ourselves back together, and she said, "I think you'll do just fine."

"Excuse me?"

With her hand on the doorknob, she looked back at me. "You exceeded expectations."

"Are you reviewing my performance?"

"Yes," she answered, totally blasé. "Are you free for dinner tonight?"

"Yes."

"Perfect! Looking forward to a repeat performance." She smirked and then walked out the door.

She blew me away. Her confidence and directness left me speechless. I should probably feel a little used, but instead, I felt like a smitten puppy ready to follow her anywhere.

After work, we had a real date. After dinner, she came to my place, and we had one hell of a repeat performance. By the time we finished several rounds of vertical tango, it was late, and we were exhausted, so Deena stayed the night. It wasn't even discussed. I didn't want her to go, and she didn't seem to want to leave, so she stayed. After that, we had many more sleepovers. Three months later, she moved in with me.

For the first time in my life, I realized how easy it was to love a woman. It felt almost effortless when the woman in question wasn't your best friend's girl. It was a relief not to have to continually fight my desires. And there was no guilt associated with my attraction to Deena. I didn't feel like I was in competition with anyone or as if I had to compare myself to Oliver and all the ways I didn't measure up. It was freeing.

Deena and I worked well together. She was an amazing woman, and for the first time in ten years, I wasn't hung up on Addison.

27

ADDISON

I WAS in my third year of residency, and I was so close to having everything I had always wanted . . . the career, the man, the house we just purchased with a pool in the back-yard. Everything was going according to plan, and my father admitted how proud he was of me. Everything was perfect—except for all the things that weren't.

City lights flashed by as I drove home from the hospital. There, in the privacy of my car, I let the tears fall. I wanted to help kids like Gracie so they didn't lose their battle with cancer, but today, I failed. I had to tell the parents of a three-year-old that there was nothing else to do but stop treatments. I was compassionate yet professional as I relayed our failure in treating their child. The cancer had spread and continuing treatments would only kill their child faster. No parent should have to experience what those parents went through.

It shocked me when they thanked me for everything I had done. I wanted to remind them that I had been unsuccessful, but they seemed relieved to take their baby home and spend the rest of their time together outside of the hospital.

I wasn't ready to go home, so I drove around for a while, thinking. Oliver was sometimes suffocating. He cared about me and went out of his way to make my day better, but sometimes I wished he cared less. Things had changed between us since our engagement. Or maybe it was just me who had changed.

When I arrived home, Oli was in his office working on his computer. "Hey," I said from the doorway.

He spun around. "Addie." He looked at the clock, confirming the time. "That was a long day."

I nodded. "It was," I confirmed.

"You okay?" He approached, his arms wrapping around me.

I leaned into him, letting him take my burdens for a moment. I kissed him, needing him to give me something else to think about, but he pulled back, apparently not understanding my intentions.

"I made dinner. Leftovers are in the fridge. Why don't I warm them up while you shower?"

I nodded, feeling rejected.

I showered, spending a little extra time shaving, and then just standing in the spray, letting the water wash away my failures. Once I was out of the shower, I slipped into my robe and met Oliver in the kitchen. He set my plate on the table, but I ignored it and walked straight to him. My hair was still wet, my body damp, and I was hungry, but not for the food Oli set out. He was standing at the kitchen island. I untied my robe and left the front open as I walked toward him. I slid it off my shoulders, and Oli watched with eager eyes. I let the robe fall to the floor, and my hands met Oli's chest. I lifted his t-shirt and helped him pull it over his head.

I ran my hands over his chest and shoulders while his ran over my skin, his mouth finding mine. We kissed for a while. But I needed more. Oliver seemed determined to make love to me, taking it slow, treating me like I was precious, but I wanted rough, mind-numbing sex. I tugged at his sweatpants, reaching inside his boxers. He was trying to slow it down, so I said, "Oli, I don't want slow and sweet right now. I need you to bend me over this counter and fuck me as hard as you can."

His eyes flared, looking shocked at my words, but he complied, letting me have it my way. He usually did. A second later and he was naked and bending me over the kitchen island. My breasts rested on the cool granite counter while he fit himself between my thighs. He gave it to me hard and rough, just as I wanted. He did everything perfectly, but something was missing. Something was wrong with me. I gave him the show he deserved, but I felt hollow. The relief I felt when it was over only increased that feeling of emptiness.

Afterward, I pulled my robe back on and pretended I was starving. I ate the vegan dinner he had prepared. I'd converted him, determined to stay healthy. We would be thirty soon, and I didn't want to show my age. My mother was only thirty-two when she passed from an aneurysm. I was always conscious of my health. It was an obsession carried over from childhood and became worse as I got older.

Oli sat with me while I ate, and I asked him about his day, almost immediately tuning him out. Sometimes his positivity drove me insane. I wanted to yell at him to stop being so optimistic, and those thoughts made me feel guilty. For a long time, I thought his positivity would rub off on me, but it didn't. If anything, it made me more cynical.

We were watching the news one night after a mass shooting. There were no fatalities, but ten people were injured. Oliver had said, "It's a miracle no one died."

I just stared at the screen and thought about those ten injured people. Was it a miracle? Did they feel lucky to be alive? What about the guy with the severe brain injury who would live out his days as a vegetable? Did his family think it was a miracle he didn't die? Maybe I had just seen too much bad to feel so positive.

Oli stood up, and I tuned back into what he was saying, "I found that wine you like. Want a glass?"

"The Pink Moscato?"

"Yeah, I stocked up."

"That was thoughtful. Thank you. I'd love a glass."

He uncorked the bottle, and I had a glass of wine while he had bourbon. When we finished, I took the dishes to the sink and began washing them by hand since Oli had just emptied the dishwasher.

The water was hot, and at first, I pulled my hands away and went to adjust the temperature. Then I remembered I deserved to suffer the sting of scalding water. I'd failed a child today, and now I was failing Oliver. Travis was so sure I'd do right by him, but he was wrong.

The water burned, but I held my hands in place. I wouldn't leave them in long enough to cause permanent damage, but I deserved the punishment. I was failing too much.

Most hot water heaters were set between one-hundred-twenty to one-hundred-forty degrees Fahrenheit, which can cause burns in just a few minutes. I'd once seen a baby in the Emergency Department with horrific burns from being placed in scalding water. I don't understand how anyone could do that to any child, especially their own.

"Addison!"

The water abruptly turned off and Oliver pulled me away from the sink. I hadn't heard him come up behind me, but he was right there. Turning me toward him, his hands gently cupped mine, inspecting my blazing red skin.

He gawked at me. "What the hell, Addie?"

I blinked. "I was so lost in thought. I didn't even feel the heat."

"What the hell were you thinking about?"

I gave him a truth. "I sent a family home with hospice today."

All the shock and anger I saw on his face melted into soft concern. "Oh, Addie." He pulled me into his chest, but I couldn't cry. I was cried out and all that was left was anger and disappointment, but he didn't need to know that.

"Add, I'm worried about you. The things you see and experience every day." He hesitated. "I don't know how you do it."

"I failed that family," I confessed. "Cancer won."

He pulled back, holding my shoulders, and staring at me hard. "You did not fail them, Addison Marie Arthur! You fought with them. You willingly went into the trenches to fight for another child. I know you did all you could, but cancer cheats. It sneaks in and steals, but it doesn't win, just like a robber doesn't win. Cancer loots, taking what doesn't belong to it. It might rob that family of their child, but you did everything you could to give them more time together. You're a guardian angel for all your patients, Addie."

God, this man. I swallowed as tears fell. "I love you, Oli."

He leaned in, kissing the tip of my nose. "You're one of the best people I know, Addie. I hate that you're so hard on yourself. I love you."

I sighed and tugged at his t-shirt to bring him closer. I pressed my lips against his, saying, "Let's go to bed."

28

TRAVIS

A YEAR after moving to Phoenix, I got a call from Addison. I was sitting on the couch with Deena when my phone vibrated and Addie's picture popped up on my screen. It had been three months since Deena moved in with me, and she knew of Addison. We hadn't spoken at length about her, just that she was Oliver's girlfriend and had become my friend too.

But a call out of the blue was unusual, and at first, I thought about ignoring it. I was happy. I didn't need Addison creeping back into my life and opening old wounds. I had closed the door on that chapter in my life.

I shut her out of my heart and put her out of mind. The further I removed myself from her, the more my affection for her turned to bitter dislike. I forgot what it was about her that drew me in, especially when faced with the facts. It seemed pretty black and white, and I didn't know how I'd let myself fall into her trap.

I wasn't going to answer. I didn't need Addison messing

things up. But then I worried something terrible had happened to Oli.

Deena seemed to sense my tension. "You okay?"

I let out a breath. "Yeah. I think so. Addison doesn't usually call me."

I didn't want to answer, but I couldn't let it go to voicemail, especially if something was wrong. "Hello?"

"Hi, Travis. Sorry to call you so unexpectedly," she said before a pause. Her voice was hesitant as she continued, "Have you spoken to your mother recently?"

"I spoke to her last week. Why?"

She inhaled deeply. "Travis, you should come home."

I didn't like the sound of that. "Why? What's going on?"

On a sigh, she answered, "I went to the diner for lunch today. Your mom wasn't working. When I asked about her, they said she hadn't been at work for the last month. You know I worry about her, so I stopped by to make sure she was okay. Her oxygen was set to ten liters, and her lips were cyanotic."

"English, Addie."

"Her lips were blue, and it's dangerous for her to be on that much oxygen with her condition because—" She stopped herself before going into medical jargon. "Just . . . because. I tried to explain it to your mom, but she appeared confused and lethargic. I mean, her body clearly isn't absorbing enough oxygen. I tried to talk her into letting me take her to the hospital, but she refused and got angry. I left but not before witnessing her pull out a cigarette and smoke it while her nasal cannula was on."

My head fell into my hand. "Shit."

Addie rushed to add, "I stopped her and took all the lighters, matches, and cigarettes I could find. She is really unhappy with me, but I told her she was going to blow herself up."

I sighed and glanced at Deena, who looked concerned. To Addie, I asked, "Why did you go to the diner? That's not close to you, and I doubt they serve anything you could eat."

"I could've ordered a salad, and I hadn't seen her in a while. You know I've been trying to get her to take care of herself for years."

That was true, and my mom loved Addison, though she didn't love her health lectures. "Thanks for going to the house and checking on her. I'll call her and have the neighbor check on her to make sure she hasn't found another way to blow herself up. I'll fly back as soon as I can."

ONCE I GOT off the phone, I explained what was going on to Deena, and then I called my mom. After discovering Mom couldn't remember Addison's visit, I knew things were worse than even Addison had told me.

Deena offered to fly home with me, but I insisted it wasn't necessary. I wanted her to meet my mom, but not like this.

I arrived in New York the next morning, relieved to see my mom's trailer was still standing. As I neared the trailer door, I caught a whiff of Mom's favorite menthols. When I stepped inside, the stench of cigarette smoke assaulted me. It had coated the once cream walls, turning them a jaundiced yellow, the same color my father had been before he died. The stained beige carpets were worn thin with the occasional burn marks here and there. My mom used to clean obsessively, but apparently she'd let things go the last few years.

How had I not realized it had gotten so bad? She always made me think she was doing just fine, but I hadn't been to her house for a visit in a long time. She had always come to me.

As soon as I entered, I realized how dire the situation was and packed Mom up and took her straight to the place she hated most. She may loathe the hospital, but she looked desperate enough to go just about anywhere if it would make her feel better. She kept calling me by my father's name. She asked me, "Charles, are we going to the hospital? Am I in labor?"

I glanced at her, and she looked so hopeful, so I nodded. Whatever got her to cooperate.

She got a room in the emergency department, and soon they were admitting her. The doctors found multiple masses in her lungs as well as fluid. She had pneumonia along with a slew of other illnesses. Her labs didn't look good, and they suspected she hadn't been eating, which she confirmed, saying it was too hard to swallow.

After a couple of days, we finally had some semi-concrete answers. The doctor came into my mother's hospital room and gave me a forced smile. "Please have a seat."

"Shit." They never ask you to sit when they had good news. I sat in the chair next to my mother's bed. She was only half awake, not that she understood what was happening anyway.

Mom reached for my hand. "Charles, is Travis still in the nursery?"

The doctor cleared his throat before he began, "She has what we call squamous cell lung tumors. I'm sure her preexisting conditions masked many of the symptoms she may have noticed as they manifest similar traits, like coughing and shortness of breath. The location of the tumors explain why she has so much trouble breathing and swallowing. It also explains the blood in her sputum.

"The tumors have spread. We detected spots in her adrenal glands, liver, and brain, which explains her memory impairment. Expect her confusion to worsen. You will need to attain medical power of attorney so you can legally begin making decisions for her."

I swallowed, glad he told me to sit down. My palms began sweating as I clamped them together. "What about treatments?" I asked as I looked at my mother, now sound asleep in bed. Even in her sleep, she looked uncomfortable.

I heard sympathy in the doctor's voice. "She's pretty sick. I can't tell you what to do, but if she were my mother, and the cancer has spread as we think, I would seek palliative care. Some localized treatments may help shrink the tumors to make her more comfortable in the time she has left. I know this isn't the news you wanted, but I would make her comfort your top priority."

She was only fifty-two years young. Twenty-eight years didn't seem like enough time with her. I wasn't ready for any of this.

The doctor cleared his throat. "I'll give you some time to digest this information."

"Thanks, doc."

He left the room, and my composure cracked. I leaned over my mother, grabbing her hands. I wasn't ready to let her go.

~

As soon as I pulled myself together, I called Addison and explained what the doctor had said. "Addie, tell me how bad this is? Is it as bad as I think?"

There was a pause. "It's not good, Travis."

I pulled my face out of my palm, asking, "So, what would you do if it was you?"

"I would do whatever would make her the most comfortable. Cancer at this stage, combined with her heart and lung issues, I agree with your doctor. I think you should look into palliative care. That doesn't mean hospice. That just means something to help her feel comfortable while you get more definitive answers."

"She's going to die, isn't she?"

"I don't know for sure, but from everything you just told me, I think it'd be a good idea to get her affairs in order."

"How long? How long do we have?" I fought my emotions.

"I don't have that answer." I hated the sadness in her voice.

"If you had to guess?"

"You know I hate when people do that to me," she said. "I really don't know."

"Ballpark?"

She sighed. "Without all the facts, I'd say less than six months, but with intervention, it could be a few years. I'll know more when I see her records."

I took a moment to digest that information.

"Travis, do you want me to come down there now?"

"No." I appreciated her opinion as a doctor, but I wasn't ready to see her. "I appreciate your help. I . . . I'm really glad you checked on her that day."

"Me too."

When I hung up, I called Deena. When she answered, I couldn't say anything right away.

"Travis, are you okay?"

"I need you," I whispered. "Will you come to New York?"

"I already have a bag packed," she said, which instantly lifted some weight from my chest. She had started a new consulting project, and since we no longer worked together, I didn't know if she could get away.

She asked, "Did you get some answers today?"

I ran a hand over my head. "Yes. It's much worse than I anticipated."

"Oh, Travis. I'm so sorry. I'm on my computer now. It looks like the next flight leaves in a few hours. I can be there late this evening. Or I can come tomorrow if it's better."

"No, tonight." I pulled my thoughts together and said, "Please come tonight."

THIS WASN'T how I wanted Mom and Deena to meet, but I was grateful to have both of them with me.

"Mom," I said, stepping into her hospital room hoping she'd recognize me today.

Her eyes zeroed in on me. "Travis, baby, why am I here? Nothing's wrong with me, but they won't let me leave."

I stepped forward. "They want to keep you here to keep an eye on your oxygen levels."

"Those bastards won't let me smoke," she huffed.

"That's because it's dangerous to smoke in your condition."

Her voice rose, "Ain't nothing wrong with me."

Time to change the subject. "Mom, I have someone with me. Someone I want you to meet."

"It better be the fuckin' doctor dischargin' me."

"No, mom." I held my arm out to the open door, beckoning Deena. "Mom, this is Deena. Remember me telling you about her?"

Mom glared at Deena for a split second before asking, "What about Addison?"

What the fuck? She knew nothing about Addie and me being anything more than friends. "What about Addison?"

"She's a doctor. Can't she discharge me?"

I closed my eyes and took a breath. "Mom, Addison doesn't work at this hospital. She works with kids."

Mom glanced at Deena and said, "Who's she?"

I put my arm around Deena. "This is my girlfriend."

"Your girlfriend?" She gave Deena a once over and asked, "Do you have a cigarette?"

I winced, embarrassed. This was not the way I'd imagined things going when I finally brought a girl to meet my mom. "Mom—"

Deena nudged me, answering, "Not on me, but let me see if I can find one for you."

My mom smiled. "She's a good woman." She choked on the last word and coughed so hard, her face turned red. She hacked up blood-tinged mucus. I cringed, rethinking bringing Deena here.

Deena stepped forward and hit the call button.

"What are you doing?" I asked.

She pointed at the dry erase board on the wall where the nurses wrote their names and other pertinent information. "It looks like she's almost due for medication, and hopefully, they have something to help calm her cravings and the coughing."

I nodded, thankful she was here with me. For the second time in as many days, I felt the weight ease from my chest. Had I told her how much she meant to me? "I love you," I said, unable to hold it in. "You're incredible."

She quickly covered her surprise with a cheeky smile. "About time you realize how amazing I am."

I looked back at my mom, who was left breathless from her coughing fit. "Mom, I'm going to marry this woman someday."

"What the hell did you call me? I ain't nobody's momma."

And she was back to not remembering who I was. I didn't think it would change that quickly, but between her medications, low oxygen levels, and the tumors, her brain function swung back and forth, and I never knew which way the pendulum was going to swing.

"Fuck cancer," I mumbled.

Deena rubbed her hand over my back. The nurse entered the room, and my mother screamed a line of profanity so harsh that even I was blushing. The nurse seemed completely unfazed, and Deena coughed to cover her laughter. I apologized, which only made my mother croak out some more mean words before violent coughing interrupted her tirade.

The nurse went to her bedside to help her while Deena leaned toward me to whisper, "I guess I know where you learned to curse like a sailor."

I gave a huff. "I'm lucky you never met my dad. He'd have you running back to Phoenix in a heartbeat."

DEENA and I reserved a hotel room and rented a car for the week. It was nice to have her support while I spent days at the hospital making decisions on my mom's treatment plan.

Deena helped me clean Mom's trailer in preparation for her coming home. I replaced most of the furniture, and the curtains—everything that had absorbed too many years of smoke to salvage, and I'd hired people to paint and replace the carpet.

There was still a lot of cleaning and sorting to do, so while I sorted, Deena cleaned.

It was late afternoon when I found a box of old photos. "Deena!" I called, interrupting her deep clean of the kitchen.

She came in with rubber gloves on. "What?"

"Look." I held out a picture, and she slipped off her gloves before taking it.

She laughed. "You were always a big kid, weren't you?"

There was a knock at the front door, and then I heard Oli's voice. "The cavalry has arrived."

I jumped up, and wrapped an arm around Deena, leading her out to the living room.

"Look who could finally make the time." I was messing with him. I had told him and Addison not to come. They had busy lives, and I had Deena with me. But they'd insisted on coming today.

Addison walked in, saying, "We didn't come to see you. We came to meet this wonderful woman you've tricked into falling for you. I'm assuming she has Stockholm syndrome and requires council."

Deena laughed. "Oh, I like her."

I did too, which had always been a problem. When Addie was around, I seemed to revert back to a hormonal eighteen-year-old, but this time was different. Things had changed.

The pull Deena had on me lessened what had been there with Addison. This was good.

I hugged Oliver, and Addison stepped forward, giving me a quick side hug while Oliver offered a hand to Deena. "It's really nice to finally meet you, Deena. I'm Oliver. I've heard a little bit about you, which says a lot as Travis is not usually a talker."

Deena laughed. "A little. I'm flattered. He's mentioned you and Addie a time or two."

I clapped my hands together. "Alright, enough chitchat. There's a lot of work to be done."

"This place already looks so different than it did a few days ago," Addison said, walking toward the pile in the kitchen. "Smells a lot better too. Where can we help?"

"Deena's cleaning the kitchen while I go through the stuff in my closet. I went through a good chunk of the stuff already. Mom's room is ready for the hospital bed they're delivering tomorrow."

"I'll help Deena clean," Addison offered brightly.

"I guess that means I'm helping you sort," Oli noted, walking back to my bedroom.

I was nervous leaving Deena and Addison alone together, but Deena gave me a reassuring smile and pulled me in for a kiss which made me breathe easier.

ADDISON

BEFORE THE GUYS disappeared into Travis's old room, Deena pulled Travis in for a kiss. It was weird to see Travis returning her affection with such ease. It was obvious they were comfortable with one another, and she seemed really good for him. But something in me rebelled at the reality of him being with someone else. In my mind, no one was good enough for him. For his sake, I tried my best to be someone Deena could call a friend.

She slipped on rubber gloves and handed me a pair, whispering, "These cabinets are disgusting."

"Thanks."

We made small talk for several minutes as we cleaned, and eventually, she noted, "You were the one who told him something was wrong with his mom. I know he's grateful you checked in on her."

"I love Theresa. She might be a little rough, but she's special—a fighter. To come from what she did and still be able to love Travis the way she has, says all you need to know about her."

That piqued her interest. "What did she come from?"

I wondered how much she knew about Travis. He held most things close to his chest, but Deena wasn't a fling. She was here with him in the trenches, cleaning these disgusting cabinets. She deserved to know about Travis. "I don't know everything, but I know her parents were abusive, and she was always an inconvenience. She dropped out of school at fifteen and ran away to the city to start a life of her own. She fell in love with a man who became a violent drunk, and she packed up Travis and left even though she never stopped loving the man. That takes strength. I always hoped she would find someone to love her—someone she could settle down and retire with, but it doesn't look like that's in the cards."

She seemed at a loss for words as she stared at me, her eyes calculating. I didn't expect the words that came out of Deena's mouth next. "I think I'm a little jealous of you. He's a hard man to crack, but you truly know him, don't you?"

I suspected she didn't want to like me, just like I didn't want to like her, but we bonded over our mutual love. "Travis has been one of my best friends for a long time, and during that time, I've watched him break open wide after his father died, and Oli and I were there to help put him back together." I swallowed. "But you're going to be the one holding him together as he watches his mom die. And his mom means a whole lot more to him than his dad ever did."

"I never hear him talk about his dad. I mean, he mentions him, but never actually talks about him."

"And he won't because it's painful. Don't take it personally. As much as his dad let him down, Travis never blamed him. Trust me. I can tell you mean everything to him. Oli and I both offered to come to the hospital, and he told us not to come. He doesn't need us like he used to because he has you." I sighed. "Travis has never had a long-term relationship, and for him to bring you here and show you what he came from puts him in a very vulnerable position. It speaks volumes about what he thinks of you. He not only loves you, but he trusts you. Please don't break that trust."

She bit her lip, looking uneasy. "That's a lot of information."

"Sorry if I'm overwhelming you. I've grown protective over him."

"It's okay. I feel like you're giving me the sibling talk. Half-welcoming and half-threatening." She laughed. "So you and Oliver are getting married next summer?"

"Yes. In June."

"And you've been together since high school? Why wait so long?"

"I wanted to finish med school and be a little more established."

"Well, that's exciting."

The guys came out of the bedroom, and Travis was carrying a box of old toys. He set it on the kitchen counter and said, "Do you think these are in good enough shape to give to goodwill, or should I throw them away?"

I peered into the box, spotting a G.I. Joe that I had never seen before but heard about all too often. I picked it up, shocked that he wasn't keeping it. "How can you get rid of this?" I looked at Travis and then at Oli, wondering why neither of them cared.

Travis shrugged. "What am I gonna do with it?"

I knew guys weren't sentimental, but this surprised me. "You could give it to your kid someday."

"I'm not going to keep it for that. I'll buy them a new toy," Travis said.

I held it closer, protecting it. I was going to take it if neither of them wanted it.

Oli held out a picture to Deena of him and Travis when they were young.

"Awe, look how cute you two were. And look how cool you're pretending to be." Deena laughed, asking, "How old were you in this picture?"

Oliver said, "It was at my fifth birthday party at Chuck E Cheese. I think that's probably the first picture of us together."

Deena shook her head. "Do you remember when you decided you were going to be BFFs?"

They exchanged a look, and Travis shrugged, "Sometime in preschool. I can't remember that far back."

I leaned against the counter and held up the G.I. Joe. "Do either of you remember the significance behind this guy?"

Travis shook his head. "No, I guess not."

Curious eyes turned to me, and I laughed, wondering how it was possible. I looked at Travis. "I can't believe your mom never told you. She told me the story at least five times."

"Are you gonna share with the rest of us?" Travis asked.

I nodded. "Your mom said it was your first day at the new preschool, and you saw a bully trying to steal Oliver's G.I. Joe on the playground. Of course you got it back for him." I held up the toy. "You thought it was a barbie, and Oli had to explain the difference between the Barbies and G.I. Joes. The next day, Oli gave you your own G.I. Joe so you guys could play together."

I looked at Oliver and Travis. "And you never stopped

playing together." I stared at them. "I can't believe neither of you knew this." I pointed at Travis. "Your mom was relieved because you had a history of behavior issues and got kicked out of your previous preschool. Oli, your mom was happy because you were painfully shy until Travis came along." I looked at Deena. "Travis gave Oli confidence, bringing him out of his shell while Oliver tamed Travis's wild side. You two were better together, and your mom said even the teachers saw it."

"Really?" Travis asked.

I shrugged. "That's what she told me."

Oli and Travis looked at one another.

Oliver said, "Thanks for sticking up for me even when you thought I played with Barbies."

Deena said, "There is nothing wrong with a little boy playing with Barbies."

Travis snickered, "My dad would've disagreed."

"Everything I hear about your dad leads me to believe he was a terrible father."

I laughed. "That's an understatement."

Travis glared at me.

I rolled my eyes. "I know you loved him, but you were always kinder to him than he was to you."

Travis's glare lingered on me, and I knew he wanted to say something about my own father, but he wouldn't. Not in front of everyone.

I held up the G.I. Joe. "Please tell me you're going to keep it now. It's the first thing Oli ever gave you. It solidified your friendship."

Travis nodded, taking the doll from my hand. "So what other stories has my mom told you?"

Most of the stories Theresa told me were embarrassing

or private things that only Travis should share. It took me a minute to come up with something I knew he would be okay with me sharing. "When Travis was about ten, he wanted a dog so badly that he tried to prove how responsible he could be by taking care of an egg. He broke the first egg before he even got it out of the fridge and wasted an entire carton of eggs in one day. He never asked for a dog again after that."

Deena's brows knitted together. "That's not fair. Dogs are much more durable than eggs."

Travis shrugged. "It's fine. A dog was a bad idea, anyway."

TRAVIS

I THOUGHT I'd have more time with her. Christmas was only a few days away, but I knew she wouldn't make it. Everything had happened so quickly. I still felt like I had whiplash. I'd been staying with my mom for the past two months, ever since she left the hospital. The palliative treatment helped her comfort level, but it was too hard on her body to continue.

Deena had been making trips to New York whenever she could squeeze them in, and having her with me was a breath of fresh air. Addison and Oliver also visited often. Sometimes Oli would come by himself, but Addison never visited unless she knew we wouldn't be alone. It was an unspoken rule.

Mom had barely been awake in the past three weeks. Even with supplemental oxygen, her levels stayed in the low eighties, and as of last week, the nurses said I could start giving morphine more regularly for discomfort. It seemed to help her breathe easier and lessen her moaning. I gave it as often as it appeared she needed it.

Tonight, her skin was splotchy, and she looked different —worse. I called the nurse to come check on her, and after she did a quick scan of my mother's body, she decided she would stay for a while. It confirmed what I already knew. This was the end.

My hand curled around my mother's fingers, and I waited for a responding squeeze, but her hand remained limp, her fingers icy against my warm palm. I scooted a wooden chair across the room to sit next to her bed. I listened for her labored wheezes and watched her chest rise and fall in uneven intervals. It was a sign of life, proof that she was still with me, but I knew it wouldn't be long now. I had heard the nurses talk about the death rattle. I never experienced it with my father. Or maybe I had missed it, but there was no missing my mother's rattled breaths. The nurse was in the other room, and I thought about calling for her, but she'd just given my mother pain medication, and there was nothing more she could do.

This was my time to say goodbye. Her face was pale, almost ghostly white, and her steroid swollen cheeks looked sunken. Her mouth was open wide, her lips colorless and chapped. This was what death looked like, and as the tears collected in my eyes, I reminded myself that not everyone got to say goodbye to their loved ones. Leaning forward, I gathered both of her hands in mine.

"Mom," I cleared my throat, "It's Travis. I just want you to know, I'm gonna be okay, so if you're holding on for me, you can let go."

There was no response. I lean in, kissing her icy hands. "You can let go, Mom."

～

I DIALED the only remaining family member.

"Hey, bro," Oliver answered, "How's Mom?"

"She just passed."

There was silence for a beat, and then Oliver said, "I'm sorry, man. Where are you?"

"I'm with her now. The funeral home is coming for her body."

"I'm on my way."

"Oliver," I complained, ready to argue.

"Travis, fuck you, man. Don't you dare insult me by telling me not to come. We're family. It's what we do."

Addison and Oliver arrived a few minutes before the funeral home, so they had a moment to say their own good-byes to the woman who gave me life.

I'd held off their hugs, wanting to be left alone. I sat on the couch, holding in all the emotions until I was alone, but Addison squashed that plan. She stood in front of me and held out her hands.

"Not now, Addison."

She ignored me, wrapping her hands around mine. She knelt in front of me, lifting my arms so she could wrap her arms around my torso. She leaned into me, her cheek pressing against my chest. It annoyed me. I didn't want people here to witness my grief. I glanced toward the door frame where Oliver stood. He wiped a hand over his eyes, and Addison's hot breath brushed against my arm as her body trembled against me. I closed my eyes, pressing my face into her hair. My arms tightened, holding onto her as I realized they weren't here just to be spectators. They were here to grieve with me for a woman important to all of us.

I had just lost the woman who made sure I survived my

childhood. Flawed though she was, she had loved me the best she knew how, and it was more than enough.

"I'm so sorry, T," Addison breathed once her tears slowed.

This wasn't like my dad's death. So much had changed since then. We were no longer kids fucking around. We were grown adults, and Addison would always be one of my best friends. I'd been trying to blame all of our mistakes on her, but that had been selfish and dumb. She was important to me. I needed her and not the way I had in the past. She and Oli were the only constant I had left in my life.

She pulled away from me and pivoted, sitting on the couch next to me.

"You're not alone, man," Oli said, drawing my attention to the doorway. "You got us." He looked down at his phone as it started ringing. "It's my dad. I'm gonna step outside to take this."

Once he stepped out, Addie asked, "Is Deena on her way?"

"Her flight was delayed. She's stuck at the airport waiting for her connecting flight. She said she'd text me once she knew more."

"The airports are always a little busier around the holidays," she offered.

"Fuck. The holidays." I was supposed to meet Deena's family over Christmas. I leaned my head back against the couch and ran a hand over my face. My facial hair had gotten scruffy. I tried to comb it down.

Addison threaded her fingers through my free hand, saying, "One thing at a time. You just lost your mom. Don't worry about Christmas right now."

We were quiet for a moment before she sighed, saying, "It doesn't seem fair, does it? You lost both parents. Meanwhile, Oli still has all of his parents and stepparents."

I already knew life wasn't fair. "I broke the eggs on purpose," I admitted.

She turned her head toward me. "What?"

"When I was ten and wanted a dog. The first couple were an accident, but after seeing how upset my mom was about the mess and wasted food, I realized we would never get a dog no matter how badly I wanted it. We couldn't afford it, just like we couldn't afford most of the other things I wanted. I stopped asking for things after that. She didn't believe that I could keep an egg intact, and after a while, I stopped trying because I knew even if I did, people like me didn't get the things they dreamed about. It's why I gave up on the dog. It's why I gave up on a lot of things, including college. I didn't think I was smart enough or rich enough, so what was the point of trying? Those kinds of things happened to other people, like Oli.

"My mom didn't want to see me get crushed the way she'd been crushed. She never encouraged me to go after the things I wanted. She gave up on my dreams before I did and by the time I got to high school, even the teachers stopped believing in me."

I turned my face toward Addison. "Then you showed up, and after a few conversations with you, college felt doable. I might've backed out, but you went and ran your mouth to my mom."

"You made yourself at home next to her in the stands at one of our football games. You introduced yourself and then gave her all these grand plans that you had for me. My mom wouldn't shut up about it. She said you were bossy and direct as you promised not to give up on me. You made her realize that it was good to encourage me to reach for the most in life, that we all have the opportunity to improve our lives."

Addison smiled.

I continued, "She told me to marry you. I told her you were Oli's girlfriend, and she never said another thing about it, but she loved you. She wanted you to be her doctor at the end. I had no idea how close the two of you were." I rubbed my forehead. "Thanks for checking in on her."

"I loved her too," Addison said. "And I'm glad she got a chance to meet Deena. She seems like a fantastic woman. I'm happy for you, Travis. I'm happy you have her, and of course, Oli and I will always be your family."

DEENA ARRIVED LATE THAT EVENING. Addison and Oliver hadn't left my side, and it was nice to have them around. But when Deena came, I felt the heaviness of the day lift a little. I knew she must have been exhausted from spending her entire day traveling, but she rallied for me.

If I hadn't already known I wanted to marry her, I knew it then. I had purchased an engagement ring, but knew now wasn't the time to propose, no matter how strongly I felt.

Addison and Oli left shortly after Deena arrived. We exchanged a round of hugs. Addison hugged Deena first and I heard her say, "Take care of him."

Deena nodded, and then Addison wrapped her arms around me, holding on longer than usual, and when she pulled away, she had tears in her eyes. "Love you, T." She gave a sad grin, and then she was spinning toward Oliver who was waiting for her.

"Love you guys. Thanks for coming today."

Once they left, Deena and I sat in the living room and

talked about the plan for the next few days. Then our conversation drifted.

Deena said, "I'm so glad they were here with you today."

I nodded. "Me too."

"You and Addison seem close," Deena observed.

"We used to be."

"You aren't anymore?'

"She's one of my oldest friends, but life gets busy, and we got busy with our own lives, so we don't stay in touch as well as we used to."

"But you make time for Oliver."

"Oliver is family."

Her eyes narrowed. "Was Addison ever more than your friend?"

Deena watched us interact twice, and she caught on to our connection while Oliver was still blissfully ignorant. Perhaps Deena wasn't as trusting as Oli. Not many people were. Or maybe she was just feeling jealous. At this moment there was no way I could tell her the truth, so I looked her in the eye and lied.

"Addie and I have never been more than friends. We come from very different backgrounds, and we tend to drive each other crazy, but we're there if we need each other."

"That sounds like family."

"Yeah, she's kinda like a sister," I said, remembering the time I tried to liken her to a sister. I had failed miserably.

3 1

TRAVIS

DEENA CAME FROM THE KITCHEN, bringing me my phone. "Addison is calling you. She's called three times."

I hadn't seen Addison since Mom's funeral six months ago, and the last time she called me out of the blue was to tell me bad news about my mom. What now? What was so urgent she'd call three times in a row?

I took the phone from Deena, worried something terrible had happened.

Reading my concern, Deena offered, "Maybe it's about groomsman duties. Their wedding is only a week away."

I nodded, answering the phone. "Addie?"

There was a long pause, and I repeated her name. "Addie?" When there was no answer, I pulled the phone away to make sure we hadn't gotten disconnected. The call time kept ticking away, and I heard a sniffle when I brought the phone back to my ear.

Her words were broken, and I almost couldn't make them out. "I told Oliver."

"Told him what?" I asked with no idea what she was talking about.

"About us."

"Us?"

It was then her words registered on a deeper level. "Fuuuck."

"Yeah!"

Deena was watching me with curious concern. I held my finger out to her, gesturing I'd be a moment, and then I closed myself in the bedroom. I paced a moment before going a step further and locking myself inside the master bathroom—as if I could hide from this.

Addison didn't get hysterical. She was quiet and reserved, but at that moment, she was crying so hard she was gasping.

I covered my face as I slid down the bathroom wall. "Breathe, Addie."

She sounded like she was trying to catch her breath.

So was I.

"Breathe with me." I took deep breaths, blowing them out slowly until she mimicked me and calmed her hysteria.

"Everything is going to be okay, Addie."

"No it won't. I'm so sorry, Travis. I never meant to mess up you and Oli's relationship."

"I did that all on my own, Addie. How did . . . why . . . how did he find out?"

"I told him. I couldn't let him marry me without knowing. It wasn't right, and it's not just about me anymore."

I scrubbed at my face. "Oliver loves you. He'll get over this. Where is he now?"

"He drove off hours ago. He turned off his phone, and I don't know what to do. I'm so worried and I . . . I didn't get to tell him everything."

I shook my head. "Shit, Addie, he doesn't need to know everything. You want to give him a play by play?"

"I'm pregnant," she sobbed.

It's like a bomb had gone off, and it left me with this horrible ringing in my ears as I sat there trying to wrap my head around it. At first, in my panic, I wondered if it was mine, and then I remembered it'd been years since we'd been together.

"I didn't get to tell him. He just left in the middle of dinner."

I ducked my head back into my palm. "You told him over dinner?"

"Yeah. I thought his favorite food might soften the blow, but . . ."

"Fuck, Addie. How far along are you?"

"Not far."

A thought occurred, and I tried to swallow it down, but I had to ask because Addison was too careful. She planned every second of her future without exception. "Were you trying to get pregnant?"

She choked, like the question was asinine. "No! We had a plan, and it certainly wasn't to get knocked up right before the wedding. I was stress eating, so I stopped taking the pill in an attempt to lose a little weight, and I guess Oliver wasn't very careful with the condoms. They don't always work, you know."

I didn't want to think about them not working. "So you're saying I could have several kids out there running around."

"No, I'm just saying I wasn't trying to get pregnant, but it happened."

"So because you're pregnant, you decided to tell him about us? Why? The baby is his, right?"

"Jesus, T! Is that really what you think of me?"

I raked a hand through my hair. "Sorry." My brain had stalled out. "It's a lot to process." Then I remembered she said Oliver left hours ago. I wondered if he had hopped a plane to Phoenix to come kick my ass. I deserved it.

"T, I don't know what to do," she sobbed. "What do I do?"

"He'll come back. You guys have been together for eleven years. He's not just gonna leave you."

"Except that's exactly what he did." She gasped, "What if something happened to him?"

"Breathe, Addie."

Breathless, she whimpered, "I can't. I can't fucking breathe. I fucked up, T. We both fucked up."

Yet I couldn't bring myself to regret her. No matter how I tried to smother my feelings for her, I couldn't. Even now, it hurt just hearing her pain. And I couldn't even think what this meant for him. I'd deal with that later. Right now, I needed to fix this. Oliver didn't have a vindictive bone in his body, so I knew he wasn't coming for me. It would've been easier if he had, but that's just not how he processed things. He probably went somewhere to hide out so he could sort out his head.

"T, what if he doesn't want to marry me anymore?"

"Addie, that's crazy. He loves you so much."

"But what if it's not enough?"

"God, Addie, it's enough. He'd be crazy not to come back to you."

After a moment of silence, I asked, "Does anyone else know about any of this?"

"No. Only you. It's not something I want people to know."

There was another pause, and she admitted, "I have so many things to do this week to prepare for the wedding. I don't know how to proceed. I never expected him to run off."

"Did he say anything before he left?"

"He said he needed time."

"He's probably just processing. He'll come back. I can be there by morning, and if he hasn't come back, I'll track him down myself and drag his ass back."

"He hasn't done anything wrong, T."

"He ran out on his pregnant fiancée the week of your wedding."

"He doesn't know I'm pregnant. We didn't get to that part." She gasped, "Oh my god! What if he doesn't believe me that it's his? I swear to you, Travis, there has been no one else, ever. Just the two of you, and it's been years. I'm not a whore," she choked, and the phone muffled before I heard retching.

"Addie!" I called, pacing the bathroom, unsure when I even stood up. I listened helplessly as she continued to get sick. So worked up, it was making her sick. After several moments, I heard a flush and water running.

Her unsteady voice came through the phone, "Travis?"

"What the fuck, Addison? You have to calm down, so you don't keep getting sick."

"I vomit at least three times a day. It's how I first suspected I was pregnant. I've ruined the best thing in my life, and I feel sick all the time. This baby seems determined to make me as miserable as possible."

"There are options, Addie," I said carefully, "If you're not ready for this."

With a half-laugh, half sob, she said, "I would say the same thing to someone going through my situation, and I know this will not make sense, but I would do anything for this little embryo in my womb. Motherhood was something that was expected of me, but it wasn't something I was ever desperate for. I've always been more focused on my career. Then I saw this little fluttering heartbeat on the ultrasound, and maybe it's just the hormones, but I was so overcome with emotions."

"Isn't there someone there that you can talk to? One of your bridesmaids, maybe?"

"I don't want to have that conversation with Oliver's sister, and I don't have that kind of relationship with my bridesmaids. Most of them are colleagues."

"You need better friends."

"I don't have time for friends."

I sighed. "That makes me sad."

"You're doing a poor job of cheering me up."

"I've never been good at this whole comforting thing. You know that."

AFTER I GOT off the phone with Addison, I started making new flight arrangements. It was Sunday night and Deena and I were supposed to fly out on Wednesday. I canceled our flights and purchased a ticket for the next day instead. I told Deena what was happening. At least partly. As far as she knew, Addison had confessed to cheating, but she didn't think it was with me.

Deena stood in the doorway, watching me pack. "Why is it up to you? It's between the two of them."

I turned to her. "If your sister was about to throw away the love of her life, wouldn't you try to talk sense into her?"

She crossed her arms. "But Oliver has the right to leave her. She cheated."

I dropped my clothes on the bed. "You're right," I said, walking to her. "Addison made a mistake, and the wedding might not happen, but I don't think Oliver will ever forgive himself if he walks away from her." I reached out to her, my palms cupping her cheeks as I planted a gentle kiss against her lips.

When I pulled back, her stare was a little softer, and she seemed to relent. "Okay, just don't get sucked into picking sides. I know you care about both of them, but if you have to choose a side, choose Oli. He's the one who has been wronged."

I nodded, hating myself. I gave her a kiss. "I'll let you know when things are sorted so you can come join me."

"If work wasn't so busy, I'd be coming with you now."

IT WAS LATE when I arrived in Upstate New York. I rented a car and drove to Oli and Addison's house. Before I could knock, the door flung open, and Addison launched herself at me. I caught her and held on as she clung to me.

We stood that way for a long time before she pulled me inside. She closed the door behind us, saying, "I'm so glad you're here."

I gave her a sad smile. "How are you holding up?"

"I've been better."

Addison sat down on the leather sectional in the living room. She didn't look like herself. She was in loungewear with greasy hair pulled back in a messy bun. I sat at the other end of the couch.

She noticed the extra space. "Why are you all the way over there like I have cooties?"

"If Oliver walked through that door right now, I don't want him getting the wrong idea. I want to be here for you, but I'm going to do it from over here. I know Deena and I were going to stay in your guest room but given the change in events, I thought it was better to get a hotel room."

She put her head in her hands, mumbling, "What if he comes back and demands that we can't be friends?"

"Then you do what he says."

She pulled her face out of her palms. "You'd be okay with that?"

"Of course not, but I'd understand it. And isn't that what we've been doing anyway, avoiding each other."

"Yeah, but you're in love with Deena. You don't have those feelings for me anymore."

"I do love Deena, and I'm committed, but you should know better than anyone that loving one person doesn't mean your love for everyone else ceases to exist."

"You still have feelings for me?"

I gawked at her. Was she serious? "Addison, what are you doing? I have Deena, and you have Oli."

"Do I?" She made a show of looking around the room. "Where?"

"He'll come back."

She shook her head. "I don't know if that's true. It's been over twenty-four hours. What if something happened to him?" She sighed. "It's so unlike him to disappear without letting anyone know what's going on."

"You're not alone, Addie. No matter what happens. You're not alone."

She stared at me. "Thank you for coming. Your hair is getting shaggy, and your beard is very lumberjack."

"Yeah, I was going to get it cut before I came, but now, I suppose I should find someone here."

"I'll schedule an appointment for you with my stylist." She said on a sigh which turned into a yawn.

"It's late." I stood from the couch and moved toward her. "I just wanted to stop and see you before getting settled in at my hotel. I'll be back in the morning."

I helped her to her feet, saying, "I can pick up breakfast on my way." I hesitated. "If I can find something that qualifies as vegan." I made a face, and she laughed.

"How about you bring me green tea, and I'll make breakfast."

"I don't want to eat that vegan shit."

"That vegan shit is going be the reason I outlive you."

I snorted. "I don't mind dying early if it means I get to eat whatever I want."

She shook her head. "Whatever you say. Now get out so I can go pretend to sleep."

ADDISON

MY TEXTS to Oliver went unanswered, and my calls kept going straight to voicemail. I already filled up his voicemail box last night. He very rarely posted on social media, but I checked there too. There was nothing. Travis and I even went to some of the places he loved most but didn't find any trace of him.

Oliver was in the wind.

I stared at my phone screen, willing Oli to call. "Travis, what am I going to do?" It was a question I'd already asked him several times today, and each time he'd lied and told me everything would be fine. It was the reassurance that I needed even if I didn't believe it.

A few moments went by, and I looked up at Travis, who hadn't responded. His big frame filled the oversized chair across from the sectional. He slouched in the seat, his arms stretched out on the armrests. His posture was relaxed, and his expression was blank, giving me no indication of what he was thinking.

Finally, he leaned forward. "I'm not a cheerleader. I don't

have Oli's overzealous optimism. I still think he'll come back, but I don't know what's going to happen. Do you know what you'll do if he doesn't come back?"

The panic started rising in my chest, but he was right. I needed to plan for the worst and hope for the best.

"I'll cancel the wedding. I don't even know how to go about doing that. I guess through email and calls. I could delegate and have Oliver's immediate family tell his extended family." Dread pooled in my stomach. "I'd have to tell my father." I felt sick.

"I can take care of him," Travis offered. "That kind of stress isn't good for the baby, and if that fucker lays his hands on you while you're pregnant, I'll fucking kill him."

I sighed. "My father has lightened up in the last year."

Travis ignored that, prompting, "After notifying the guests, what would you do?"

"I'd cancel vendors and—" My phone started ringing. I looked down at the blocked number. "Do you think—"

He sat forward in the chair. "Answer it!"

I fumbled with it but got it to my ear. "Hello."

"Addison." Oliver's voice sent a chill down my spine. His voice was so cold. He'd never spoken to me this way. It hurt, and my tears fell.

"Oli, Oh my god!" I cried, "I was so worried about you. Where are you?"

There was a pause, and his voice sounded detached as he said, "Addison, why does my dad think we're still getting married this weekend?"

Pain speared through me, and I gasped, my eyes flying to Travis, who had moved closer. "Oli, you don't mean that."

"Are you gonna throw up?" Travis asked as the color drained out of my face, nausea making a quick arrival.

An anger I'd never heard before came from Oliver. "You've gotta be fucking kidding me, Addison. He's there with you right now?"

"Umm . . ." I hesitated, "Yeah, but only because we were both so worried about you."

"Worried about me?" he scoffed, "Fuck, Addison. Cancel the goddamn wedding. I can't marry you."

"Oli," I cried, knowing I would never make it to the bathroom in time, but I threw the phone at Travis and flew off the couch, running into the kitchen.

"Oli, it's not what you think," I heard Travis say while I was throwing up in the garbage can. Then he cursed. "What a fucking idiot! When he comes back, I'm gonna kick his ass!"

I held my hair in one hand while bracing the other against the wall. I wasn't sure if I was done retching, but the smell of the garbage made my nausea worse, so I took a risk and moved to the kitchen sink. I leaned against the counter and rinsed my mouth out. Travis's hand gently rubbed back and forth over my back.

"So, is that it?" I whispered into the sink.

His hand stilled. "That's up to you. You can stop trying and cancel the wedding, or you can track him down and make sure he knows all the facts before making that decision."

I stared at the drain. "I don't want him to marry me out of obligation or because he feels coerced."

"He wouldn't be marrying you just because of the baby. You guys have a history. He's feeling hurt and betrayed right now, but I know he loves you."

I rested my elbows against the counter, feeling breathless as I held my face in my hands and cried. "I love him, Travis. I should've announced the pregnancy before confessing the infidelity. I just never thought he'd leave and not come back."

His hand moved, resuming its comforting motion over my back. "It's late, and it's been a long day. Why don't you try to get some sleep?"

I knew I wouldn't be able to sleep, but I straightened, standing to my full height. I sucked in my tears, feeling guilty for putting this on him. I didn't want to be alone, but this wasn't his mess. I bit my lip to hide the trembling and nodded, unable to trust my voice.

I walked toward the door, hoping he'd follow. I was barely holding it together, and I needed him to leave right away, or he would have a front-row seat to my devastation.

He followed me to the door, and I opened it for him. Avoiding his eyes, I stared at my hand on the knob. "I'll see you tomorrow?" I heard the desperation in my request but prayed he hadn't.

His fingers landed on my jaw and gently tilted my face toward him. His speckled brown eyes had flecks of gold in them, highlighting their depth and beauty. And right now, they were appraising me. I pressed my lips together, giving him a shaky smile.

His laugh was soft, and he shook his head. "Your acting skills are rusty, Addie. But you've never been good at hiding from me."

He pulled me against his chest, forcing me to let go of the door. He shut it with his foot and led me back toward the sectional. Pulling me down to sit next to him, his arm slid around my shoulders. "Addison, cry, scream, do whatever you need to do. Your emotions are justified. It's okay if you're not okay." He pulled the hair out of my face, and I relaxed into his side.

I confessed, "I just found out I'm going to be a mother, and I'm already messing up my kid's life."

He ran his fingers through my hair. "You're going to be an amazing mom. You're already putting the baby first. You risked your relationship with Oli by confessing the truth. You did that because of the baby. I have no doubt you'll be an incredible mom, no matter what your relationship status is with Oli."

"I don't know how to be a mother." I rested my head against his chest, using him as a pillow while I pulled my legs up onto the couch.

He continued gliding his fingers through my hair in a calming rhythmic motion. "From what I hear, even the best-prepared parents don't know what they're doing until they're doing it. And you'll do a much better job than our parents did."

I exhaled wistfully, wanting that to be true. My ear pressed over his steady heartbeat. Its pace seemed to stabilize my emotions, and I felt stronger with him next to me. His presence was soothing, and his fingers in my hair were lulling me to sleep.

If he were anyone else, I would have gotten rid of him hours ago, but this was Travis. His presence reassured me. As my eyelids became heavy, I breathed, "Will you stay here tonight? I feel better knowing I'm not alone."

"Yeah, I'll stay," he agreed. "I'll sleep in the guest room."

I went to say *thank you*, but as my mouth opened, I resolved that thank you wasn't enough. "I love you, Travis. I don't mean that romantically. I just need to tell you how valuable you are to me."

"I love you too, Addie. I mean that platonically, of course," he snickered, likely trying to lighten the mood.

But I was just getting started. "We've been friends for a long time, and you've seen me at my worst, over and over again, yet you still accept me. You still love me." I shook my head. "Not the way you love Deena. Romantic love is deep and possessive, prettied up with lust and sex. Familial love leaves little choice. It's in our nature to love our family even if they're awful. But the love between friends is the kind where you see all the flaws and the ugly, and you still choose to love that person—not because you're having sex with them or because you're bound by blood, but because you've claimed them as part of your tribe, even though nothing actually binds you."

His hand paused in my hair. "But we have had sex. Doesn't that muddy the waters?"

"I don't think so because we have no plans to have sex with one another in the future." I glanced up at him. "You didn't come here because you were hoping to get lucky. You aren't here now, just waiting to have sex. You're here because, for some reason, you love me. Not romantically, just deep mutual love."

"I've never thought about it like that before." It was quiet for a moment before he added, "You have that same friendship bond with Oliver. I mean, you have the sex part too, but—"

"If I had that kind of bond with Oliver, then where is he? I slept with someone else, and he felt betrayed because sexually, emotionally, I was supposed to belong to him. He didn't wait around to see how I was feeling or hear me out. It's what is to be expected from romantic love, but a friendship bond doesn't have those same restraints. I could fuck up huge, and you would still be there for me. It's different. One love is unconditional, while the other has conditions."

"We hurt Oliver. I don't think it matters what kind of love it is. Oli and I don't have a romantic relationship, but he's not talking to me either. I think there are conditions."

"But that's only because you messed with his romantic life. If you slept with anyone else, he wouldn't've cared. But romantic love is more possessive and easier to mess up."

"You make it sound like romantic love is inferior."

"No. It's just different. And there's something else that's bothered me for a long time." I sat up, pulling my legs under me on the couch while I faced him. "This is probably one of those things we're not supposed to talk about, but I can't let it go. He's not the better man. You've said that to me so many times, but it's not true, and it's important that you realize that. You are different men with different strengths and temperaments, but you've proven over and over that you're an incredible man. You showed your father compassion he could never return. You were a constant for your mom, even when she was unstable. You repeatedly put Oliver's needs first over your own. You were born into very different lives, and Oliver never had to deal with the things you have. I'm not putting Oli down. He's a wonderful man, but so are you."

He took in my words. "Thanks, Addie. Being with Deena has helped me see some of those things."

I'd never seen him so self-confident. I swallowed. "Good. I'm glad she can make you see your worth." I sighed, wishing I could've been the one to help him realize it, but I was grateful Deena had. "What have you told her?"

"Nothing about the two of us. I told her Oliver left because you confessed to cheating." He rubbed a hand down his face. "I should've told her the whole truth, but I didn't know how she would react. I just feel like there was a window of time when I should've told her, but it didn't seem important. It was a mistake in the past, but now I'm afraid she's going to think I'm keeping other things from her."

"We really fucked up, T. I'm sorry."

"Me too." He pursed his lips, looking like he had more to say, but he blew out a breath and looked away. "It's too late to change things."

I nodded, my thoughts going back to Oli. "How am I going to find Oliver?"

He shrugged, slumping further into the couch. "We'll figure something out tomorrow."

I pulled the blanket off the back of the couch and covered my legs as I stretched them out onto the ottoman. I leaned against him, confessing, "I'm not ready to go to bed."

"Let's watch something to help you clear your head." He grabbed the remote from the side table and flipped on the TV.

I fell asleep against him, only waking when he nudged me. "Bedtime," he whispered, helping me up to my feet. He went to his room, and I went to mine. And after a long while staring at the ceiling, I finally fell asleep.

WEDNESDAY, I compiled a list of everyone I needed to contact should the wedding be canceled. I barely slept the night before, and today had been another day filled with dread and regret. It was exhausting, and nothing I ate sat right with me.

All my attempts at sleuthing had been unsuccessful. Oli had spent no money from our joint account, but I looked into his credit cards and noticed recent purchases. One of those purchases was at a hotel. I went to Oliver's email and searched for a hotel confirmation. This was my last-ditch effort to find him, and it looked like I hit the jackpot.

Travis stood over my shoulder while I clicked on the email from a hotel. I knew Oli didn't want to be found, but I had to tell him about the pregnancy. If he was canceling our wedding, he needed all the facts.

"Who or what is in Michigan?" I asked.

"I guess we'll find out." He dialed the hotel's phone number and had the clerk connect him to Oliver's room. He handed me his phone, and I listened to it ring and ring, but no one answered.

I hung up. "I mean, it is kind of late."

I tried not to think of the reasons Oli wouldn't be in his hotel room at nine in the evening.

Travis said, "We can try again in a little bit, or we can try again in the morning."

I handed him his phone. "I'll try it tomorrow. I'm tired." And terrified he would reject me.

"I'm gonna head back to the hotel if you're okay," Travis said.

I nodded. "I'll be fine. Thank you."

He pulled me against him, and I felt a flash of desire as he wrapped his arms around me, pulling me against his solid chest. My palms ran over his back, reminding me of his strength. His muscular build always affected me, but these last few days, I thought I had finally outgrown these carnal desires. But here they were, flaring to life at the most inconvenient moment. It took me off guard, but I shoved it aside. My hormones were on the fritz, but the impulse, however involuntary, only reassured me that he should leave.

I stepped away. "Travis, you don't have to come back tomorrow. Either I get a hold of him, or I don't, but there's no need for me to drag you down with me any more than I already have."

He frowned. "Unless Oli comes back sometime in the night, I'll be back tomorrow morning."

"But—"

"Addie, go to bed. I'll see you tomorrow." He walked to the door and spun before leaving. "Goodnight."

I watched the door long after he left. What the hell was wrong with me? I was desperately trying to get my fiancé back. Travis was here with the same goal, yet my attraction to him still had me clenching my thighs together. This had to be the baby hormones.

MORNING SICKNESS WAS A FUCKING LIE. It wasn't just in the morning. And Thursday was the worst day so far. I called the hotel a few times, never getting an answer. Travis had his hair appointment mid-afternoon, and I took a nap, too sick to care if I had to call off the wedding. I would cancel it right then and there if it meant my "morning" sickness would go away.

By evening, I was moping. I was lying prone, my body sprawled out on the couch, when Travis said, "Let's go."

He had been pacing for the better part of an hour, and he finally stopped. I lifted my head to look at him. "Huh?"

"Let's drive to Michigan tonight."

I laid my head back down. "That's a long drive, T."

"That's why we need to leave tonight."

"I'll probably throw up in the car."

"We'll bring those disposable puke bags you took from the hospital, and we can always pull over."

I glanced up at him again. "That sounds miserable."

"You're already miserable."

"I meant for you," I clarified.

"I used to wipe my father's ass. You think you're gonna traumatize me with a little puke?"

I shrugged.

"Grab a bag, Add."

"Fine," I groaned, rolling off the couch in such an unlady-like way. My father was probably cringing wherever he was, just sensing the massive lapse in etiquette.

To mine and Travis's relief, I only got sick twice in the car before finally falling asleep. To his credit, he didn't seem to flinch, just rolled down the windows to give us both some fresh air before pulling over at the next stop so I could clean up and dump the disposable puke bags.

When I woke, it was still dark, and the SUV was slowing. The clock on the dash said it was five in the morning. Travis must have noticed I was awake because he said, "We're almost there. I just need to fill up the tank. How are you feeling?"

I rubbed my head as my body stretched. "I'm okay."

He pulled into the gas station, and the overhead lights momentarily blinded me while he asked, "Are you going in?"

I nodded. "Yeah, I need to stretch and use the ladies' room."

While he pumped gas, I went inside. When I came out of the bathroom, Travis was in the candy aisle. I met him there.

He glanced at me. "Maybe the baby disagrees with your vegan diet. Don't you want some candy or maybe some beef jerky? Is it even a road trip if you don't get five pounds of snacks?"

I scrunched up my nose. "No thank you. You can have

your diabetes in a bag and meat bark. I'll grab a banana or something."

He smirked at me. "Suit yourself."

I walked away as he grabbed junk food. We met at the register, where he bought an entire grocery sack full of garbage foods.

He threw my banana and water in with his stuff, and then we were headed back to the truck. Once we were inside, he started pulling things out of his bag.

"I thought you said we were close. Why did you get so much stuff?"

He smirked. "We still have a trip back."

I sighed. "I swear pregnancy brain is a thing."

He gave me a pity laugh. "You make pregnancy seem so fun."

"You better treat Deena like a goddess when she's pregnant with your children."

He laughed. "Don't get ahead of yourself. That's not gonna happen anytime soon."

"I bet she'll be one of those crazy women who enjoys being pregnant. She'll glow the entire time and only gain weight in her belly." I made a gagging noise. "Gross."

His smile grew. "You're probably right. That woman is crazy. She would be the kind of woman to kick pregnancy's ass."

I smiled as I watched him. "Your hair looks really nice, by the way. I just realized I never said that."

He'd had an appointment with my stylist earlier in the day. Or was it yesterday at this point? His grizzly beard and wild hair had been tamed and trimmed short.

"Thanks for getting me an appointment," he said as he pulled out of the gas station. When we pulled back onto the highway, he added, "It's only about twenty minutes away. But we can park when we get there and maybe get some sleep."

"I'm sorry. You haven't slept at all."

"It's fine. I'll take a catnap once we get there."

"Well, depending on how all this plays out, I might be the one driving you home. That way you can sleep," I said.

He shook his head. "No, that won't happen."

"I don't know how I'm supposed to win him back, looking like I've been hit by a bus. It's not my best look."

"Addison, you're beautiful. He's a fucking moron if he doesn't come to his senses."

A thought suddenly occurred to me. "How am I going to find his room? They won't just give that to me."

Travis laughed. "Leave it to me, princess. I'll get the number. Shit. I could probably get the room key, too."

"You're awfully cocky about that."

"I worked at a hotel for a while. I know a few tricks, and I can be quite charming, and nightshift is usually easier to deal with."

Once we arrived, Travis hopped out of the SUV, saying, "Wait here."

About five minutes later, he returned with an arrogant grin and climbed into the backseat.

"What are you doing?" I asked from the front.

"These seats lay back. I'm gonna close my eyes for an hour or so before you go to room three-fourteen and talk to Oli."

I smiled. "How'd you get it?"

"I just gave them the Travis charm."

"No, really, how'd you get it?"

With a sigh, he admitted, "The computer was unattended, and I messed around with it until I found Oli's room."

I snorted. "That sounds more like it."

He reclined the seat back, saying, "You're welcome."

He deserved so much more than a thank you. "Thank you feels incredibly inadequate. I wouldn't even be here without you. I don't deserve you."

He stared up at the ceiling. "You're wrong. I'm incredibly selfish. I love you guys and want you both to be happy. And I don't know how to live with myself knowing I was the reason you guys didn't get your fairytale ending."

IT WAS A COOL MORNING, and the sun was still creeping over the horizon as I entered the hotel lobby. Something was wrong with the sensor on the sliding doors. They kept gliding open, though no one else was around to activate them. The lobby looked brand new, and it looked as if the hotel staff was setting up the continental breakfast.

As soon as I hit the button for the elevator, it opened for me. I climbed on, remembering to breathe the entire ride up to the third floor. I stepped off and followed the signs to room three-fourteen.

I stared at the door for a long time before finding the courage to knock. I knew it was early, but it was a long drive back to New York and tonight was the rehearsal dinner. I needed to know whether or not I needed to cancel.

I knocked again, but realized he may not want to answer, so I called, "Oli, are you in there? I really need to talk to you."

It was quiet. "Oliver, please," I begged, sounding beyond desperate.

The door opened a crack, and Oliver stood there bare-chested. It was painful looking at him because he was gorgeous in nothing but boxers and because I knew he was just as beautiful on the inside. And I'd hurt him so badly that he left me. I tried not to let his sympathetic gaze break my pride. I knew I looked awful. My hair was a mess, my eyes were puffy, and my face was blotchy.

"Addie, what are you doing here?" he asked.

"Your phone is dead or off, but I have to talk to you, so I followed your credit card charges," I said.

"That's not what I asked. Why are you here, Addison?"

I placed a palm softly on the door. "Can I come in?"

He sighed, shaking his head. "How about I meet you in the lobby in a few minutes, and we can talk?"

"Okay," I agreed, embarrassed at the tear that slid down my cheek. I wiped it away quickly. But he'd seen it.

I WENT DOWN to the lobby, and Travis walked up to me. "That was quick."

"He told me he'd meet me down here."

"He wouldn't let you in his room?" He seemed taken aback, and I knew his mind went to the same place mine did.

I shook my head, trying not to think of all the reasons he wouldn't want me in his room. Was he afraid if I came in, I'd refuse to leave? Did he have someone in there with him? Or several someones? I had no idea, and I didn't want the answers anyway. I just needed him to listen to me for five minutes, and it didn't matter where.

"I'll make myself scarce," he said, his hand lingering on my shoulder. "You can do this, Addie. And no matter what, you've got me in your corner." He squeezed my shoulder before walking away.

I went to grab a cup of tea where they were serving breakfast—then thought to grab two. I took a seat at the edge of the lobby and watched the people checking in and out. The lobby door was still gliding open and closed as it pleased.

There was a line for the waffle makers, and I watched three children with their parents at a table in the far corner. The youngest was crying, her mother consoling her, while the two older boys were having a low-key food fight. The dad seemed oblivious as he scrolled through his phone. The mom, realizing the boys were tossing food at each other, glared at her husband, and words were spoken. The dad lowered his phone and looked at the mess on the table. His eyes darted between the boys, and instead of screaming, he started laughing. The mom rolled her eyes, and I looked away.

Is that what motherhood would look like for me? A syrup covered table and crying children. Or would I be at a table for two? A single mother? I tried not to let fear get the best of me, sipping my drink just for something to do.

That's how Oliver found me. "Addie," he said, sitting down across from me.

I pushed the second cup across the table toward him. "Green tea."

He looked at it and then back at me. "Addie, why are you here?"

I moved my cup aside and sat with my hands clasped on the table. "Oliver, I'm pregnant. The baby is yours. I'm not a whore. I made a mistake with Travis years ago, but there is nothing between us but friendship now. After you left, I called him and told him what happened and that I was pregnant. He came to town to help me find you so I could tell you about the baby." I continued, needing to get it all out in the open. "I compiled a list of everyone I need to notify that the wedding is off. I will contact them all today if that's what you want, but I thought you needed all the facts before you made your decision."

His hands wrapped around my clasped fingers, and I sucked in a breath.

His eyes glistened with unshed tears and a look of adoration I thought I'd never see from him again. I swallowed my tears and gripped his hands tightly. Maybe it wasn't too late. "Oliver, I'm so sorry. I love you, and whether you want this baby or not, I'm keeping it. If you don't want to be a part of our baby's life, I'll never ask anything more of you." The words hurt, and tears poured from my eyes. "Oli, say something. Please."

Oliver pulled his hands out of mine as he slid out of his seat. For a second, I thought I might lose him, but then he came around the table. I pivoted in my chair, and he kneeled in front of me, coming to eye level. His words were feather soft and filled with awe. "We're going to have a baby." He leaned forward, giving me a quick peck on the side of my lips before his arms were around me.

I choked on a sob, pulling him closer and holding on for dear life. After a moment, I let him pull away. His smile melted as something over my shoulder seemed to catch his eye. "Shit." He jumped up. "Excuse me for a minute." He was already moving away, and I turned in time to watch a dark-haired woman walking out of the hotel, dragging her wheeled suitcase behind her. Oliver was dodging people as he ran out of the lobby.

Who was she?

33

TRAVIS

I STOOD with my back against my rented SUV. I was too anxious to wait in the car, and besides, I needed to stretch my legs. I'd just texted Deena, keeping her posted on what was happening and telling her for the fifth time this week to stay home.

I knew how busy she was at work and it didn't make sense for her to come now. Even if the wedding happened, I was nervous Oliver would tell Deena that I was the one who slept with Addie. I planned on telling her, but not over the phone and I didn't want Oli beating me to the punch.

I knew Deena would understand when I laid it out for her. It's not like I had ever cheated on her. I could've been more open, but it wasn't just my secret, it was also Addison's.

"Willa, wait!"

Oliver's voice grabbed my attention, and I turned, watching a beautiful curvy woman with dark hair rushing away from him. She looked as if she was about to chuck her luggage at him in order to escape, but she stopped at a car, popping the trunk.

Oliver caught up to her as she loaded her luggage, "Willa," he said, his voice pleading.

"Addison will see us together," she warned.

My eyes narrowed. What the fuck was happening?

"I don't care," Oli said in a rush.

She slammed her trunk and glared at him.

"I don't," he repeated.

"Honest, ugly truth," she said. "Did Addison call off the wedding?"

His shoulders slumped. "No."

"Are you going to marry her?" she asked.

Hell yeah, he was, or I was going to drag his ass down the aisle myself. His answer was too quiet for me to hear, but I watched the emotions swarm her.

She asked, "Did you tell her about us, *Oli*? I get that you are confused, but how dare you let me think you were done with her. You made me the other woman, Oliver!"

My brows shot up. What the fuck?

I was only getting parts of the conversation, and I didn't care if I was being nosey. I glanced toward the hotel and saw Addison watching from the lobby doors. I doubt she could hear anything, but she could see them together.

The woman's voice drew my attention back to her and Oli. "Glad I could help you clear that up."

"Willa," he tried.

She shouted up at him. "I told you I didn't want to be your goddamn rebound, Oliver! You had women offer to be that for you, but I wasn't offering. You made me fall for you. Or at least the *you* I thought you were."

She moved to get in the car.

"Willa, would you just listen?"

She spun on him, crossing her arms over her chest in

preparation for what he was going to say. I wanted to hear this too.

"She . . ." He suddenly seemed unsure of what to say next.

Her words were too quiet for me to make out, but his response was immediate. "It's, well . . . fuck!"

"Honest, ugly truth," she said. "I wish I had never met you."

He stumbled back while she climbed into the car and slammed her door. She backed out of her space and drove away.

I looked to the hotel in time to catch Addison disappear back through the lobby doors. I didn't know what to think anymore. The Oliver I knew would never cheat on Addison, but maybe he really thought things were over between them. Oh, how the tables have turned.

Oli stood, bent at the waist with his hands on his hips like he was winded. He continued to stare after the woman long after she was gone. His look was riddled with guilt and misery. It was a feeling I knew all too well.

After a long moment, Oli seemed to pull himself together and turned back toward the hotel. He was walking back when his eyes fell on me. His eyes widened in surprise, and I watched a dozen emotions flit across his face before he settled on defeat. We didn't speak. We didn't need to. Our drama had spilled over onto that poor woman who apparently had fallen for Oliver, but we all knew Oli and Addison belonged together. And Oli would do the right thing. There was only one right move at this point. He and Addison would get married, and all of this would be a blip in an otherwise happy relationship.

After a moment, Addison texted, asking me to meet her in the lobby. I rushed inside, worried Oli had canceled the wedding. I found her sitting on a bench just inside the door. She was bent over, her face in her palms.

I sat next to her, wrapping my arm over her shoulders. "Addie?"

She wiped her tears as she sat up to face me. "T, am I doing the wrong thing?"

"Of course not."

She wouldn't meet my eyes. "Who was that woman?"

A casualty was my first thought, but I said, "I tell you who she isn't. She isn't you. She isn't carrying Oli's baby. She hasn't spent eleven years at his side. She's not important, Addie."

"Do you think they had sex? Do you think she was in his room when I knocked? Is that why he wouldn't let me in."

Yes, I did think that, but I wouldn't admit it. "Is he coming back with you?"

She nodded.

"Then what does it matter? He chose you, just like he always has and always will."

"What if it was wrong to come here?"

"Addison, do you want to marry him?"

She pushed her hair out of her face. "Of course I do."

"Then, stop it. We slept together, and you chose Oli. He slept with someone, and he still chooses you." It sounded fucked up when I said it, but she nodded, understanding my point.

I added, "Don't be too hard on him. He was hurting, and if he can forgive you, then you better be able to forgive him."

She nodded again.

I stood. "I'm gonna go before he comes down and sees us together."

34

ADDISON

OLIVER CHECKED OUT, and we walked to his truck in silence. We climbed inside, and he looked over at me wistfully.

"Why are you looking at me like that?" I asked.

He shook his head and shrugged before putting the truck in gear and pulling out onto the road.

"Did you sleep with her?" I asked because I couldn't help it.

He stared ahead as he nodded. "Yeah."

He was so sad, and it was my fault. "Oliver, I know I hurt you, and we have some things to work through. I'm sorry."

The silence lingered between us, bringing with it a dark cloud of shame and doubt that filled the cab of the truck. I was suffocating on my own contrition by the time Oli broke the stifling quiet. "I hurt her."

"Who?"

"The woman you saw me with."

"The one you slept with?"

He nodded, and I had no idea what to say to that. How do you comfort your fiancé after they sleep with someone else?

"I'm sure she'll be okay. You couldn't have known each other that well. You've only been gone for five days."

He took a deep breath and blew it out in a long sigh. The silence that followed wasn't as uncomfortable as before, and I was grateful for the change. My gratitude was short-lived. Before we got on the freeway, he pulled into a drive thru.

I shot him a look of horror. "Oli, what are you doing?"

"I want a cheeseburger."

He sounded blasé and dread pooled in my stomach. Did they even serve burgers this early? I didn't know because we'd given up fast-food when I went vegan. I knew he wasn't vegan, but he was usually more sensitive when we were together. Was this how things would be from now on? Was he doing this on purpose? I felt like I couldn't complain, but the smell alone was bound to make me sick. "But you . . . you don't eat meat or fast food."

His tone was defiant. "No, Addison, you don't eat those things. I do." He ordered his food and pulled around.

I sat in shock. He was angry and wasn't taking my morning sickness into consideration. Of course, he wasn't. He didn't know about the morning sickness, and instead of telling him about it, I said, "But Oli, they're so bad for you."

He glared at me. "So is sleeping with Travis. Do you even know how many times he's been treated for STDs?"

"Oli!"

"You think I'm kidding? I was legitimately concerned he'd catch something that antibiotics couldn't fix. You're the doctor. You know what I'm talking about. Hell, you probably wrote him a prescription or two."

I sucked in a breath, holding back a sob. I looked away, staring out the window, unable to face him. Who was this man? He wasn't the man I had spent the last eleven years with. I'd never seen him be so cruel, and here he was tearing Travis and me to pieces, and I couldn't say a damn thing to defend either of us because we were the ones who broke him.

I covered my mouth, trying to hide my uneven breath as tears fell in rivulets down my face. Oliver collected his food, and the smell assaulted me. I ground my teeth and cracked the window.

He sighed as he pulled the truck back out onto the road. "I'm sorry, Addie."

I pulled a tissue from my purse, attempting to look like a lady as I mopped up my face. "You have nothing to be sorry for, Oli. I know I hurt you."

"Why did it have to be Travis?"

I shrugged. That was too complicated and our relationship wasn't stable enough for me to be honest, so I tried to blow it off. "Because he was always around. Do we have to talk about this?"

"I think we should."

I needed to get his mind off Travis. "Why does it matter? I messed up, but I want to spend the rest of my life with you. You have always been there for me. We're going to have a baby together. I don't want to trudge up the past. I never meant to hurt you, and part of me wishes I had never told you because then you wouldn't be hurting like this."

"You wish you would have just lied to me for the rest of our lives?" He sounded incredulous.

I barely kept myself from screaming, *yes!* "Oliver, I want to stand in front of all of our loved ones tomorrow and publicly tell them how much you mean to me. I would do anything for you. If I could take it back, I would, but it's in the past, and it will never happen again. Do you believe me?"

He nodded. "Yes."

"Do you still love me?"

With a sigh, he confessed, "Yes."

I pretended to sleep for most of the trip to keep from vomiting and because I was afraid anything I said would make him change his mind.

When we got closer to New York, I made a last-minute hair appointment for Oliver with my stylist. His hair was long enough to put in a bun, and he had promised to cut it short for the wedding. It also looked as if he hadn't shaved for the five days he'd been gone. He looked so different from the Oliver I was used to, but the hair appointment would fix that.

Rehearsal dinner started at seven, and we were short on time to get ready. I was already fielding calls from brides-maids and family. When we arrived in New York, we drove straight to the salon. While Oli got his hair cut, I caught a ride home so I could start getting ready.

While I styled my hair, my cellphone rang. It was Sandra, Gracie and Marley's mom. Marley, now fifteen, was in my wedding party, and since they were out-of-towners, I figured she was calling for directions.

"Hey, Sandra."

"Addison, I'm so sorry. Our flight has been delayed. We won't make it to rehearsal."

I was usually so organized that something like this would feel like a disaster to me, but everything was already a disaster, so this was nothing. I sighed. "I'm sorry to hear you won't make it, but don't worry about missing it. What time do you think you'll arrive?"

"They're saying close to midnight."

"Just be safe, and we can fill Marley in tomorrow."

"Thanks. Sorry about that."

"It's no big deal. I'm sorry you're stuck at the airport."

"As long as we make it there by tomorrow, we're fine."

They were still under the impression Oli and I were a perfect couple, and I felt bad about deceiving them. But people preferred the fairytale to the actual story, so I'd let them keep believing.

I heard Oliver arrive home as I disconnected the call. I was wearing a robe and applying makeup when he walked into the master bath. I paused to take him in, and without the facial stubble and long hair, he looked a lot more like the handsome man I fell in love with, but he felt like a stranger. "Your hair looks really nice. I hung your suit on the closet door."

He didn't respond, and after a moment, I turned back to the mirror to continue applying my makeup. He remained in the door frame, watching me. I did my best to ignore his stare. I didn't know what he was doing, but it was making me nervous. I never expected this level of tension.

After several moments, he stepped into the room. "I'm gonna shower in the hall bathroom." He reached into the shower to grab his body wash and shampoo.

I turned to him. "You can shower in here."

"It's okay. You're getting ready."

As he walked away, I reminded him. "We need to leave in fifteen minutes."

He spun back to me. "If anyone has that big of a problem with us being five minutes late to our rehearsal, I'll be glad to uninvite them."

He sounded as though he were itching for a fight, which made me pause. I had feared how deeply our betrayal would cut Oli, but witnessing the most diplomatic man I had ever known lose his temper over something so small knocked the wind out of me.

WE WERE ONLY two minutes late to the church, and no one said a thing. Oliver separated from me as soon as we arrived, and I caught Travis on his way in. He looked like shit. He had slept for one hour out of the last thirty-six hours. The dark circles under his eyes looked like bruises on his otherwise striking face.

"You look like you were in a fight," I said, dragging him along with me. "Come on. Let me put some concealer under your eyes."

"I don't think we're the same shade," he said with humor.

I pulled him into a private hallway and took out my concealer. "Anything would be better than those bags under your eyes."

After applying, he looked less tired, though I could do nothing for his bloodshot eyes. I looked over him in his suit. "You look really nice," I said as my fingers ran down the collar of his jacket.

"Thanks. I had to have it tailored to fit right."

I grinned, already figuring that part out. No part of him was little, but his waist was small compared to his herculean shoulders. "It was worth it. I'm sorry Deena's not here to see you in it."

"Probably for the best because then she'd know I let you put makeup on me."

I laughed. "God forbid."

Even as I laughed, I wondered what he had told Deena to get her to stay in Phoenix.

～

REHEARSAL DINNER WAS in full swing. The private event room overflowed with crystal champagne flutes and the forty guests who wielded them. The wedding was black tie, but the rehearsal was not. It didn't stop people from dressing like they were going to a fancy gala. It appeared everyone was trying to one-up everyone else with their glitzy gowns and sleek tuxes. I felt underdressed and plump at my own party. I couldn't wait to take my hair down from this damn updo that was giving me a headache. And why did I have to pick a mostly white dress for rehearsal? I feared it made my waist more obvious. I hadn't actually gained any weight, what with all the vomiting, but I felt like a swamp monster when I should have felt like a glowing beauty.

I was exhausted. And, more than anything, I wanted to be at home in my pajamas with a bowl of popcorn. I was practically drooling over the idea of sweatpants, but at the rate this evening was going, I would never get there. Why was everyone determined to give a speech? Maybe I should've felt touched by their kind words, but I couldn't help feeling like no one here knew me.

I had non-alcoholic champagne in my first glass, but when they refilled the crystal flute, they poured the real stuff. I hadn't anticipated refills because I hadn't expected people going off book and being so insistent on saying a few words. A *few words,* my ass. These were chapter book speeches, and apparently, everyone felt it was their right to be heard since we made them wait so long to tie the knot. They were excited to see the forever couple get married. Meanwhile, I couldn't even catch Oli's eye. I left my hand close to his on the table, hoping he would take it, but as far as I could tell, he was too busy glaring at Travis.

People didn't seem to notice the discord between Oli and me. We smiled and laughed and kissed at the right moments, and no one saw through it except Travis, but he was pretending too—playing his own role of best man. His eyes skipped over mine, and I felt an invisible knife twist in my gut. Or maybe that was just the pregnancy indigestion. Travis was the one I wanted to go to for comfort, but with Oliver here, I felt like I had to hide our friendship. I sighed inwardly and tried to pull myself out of my thoughts as I heard the crowd aww over something sappy my old roommate was saying about me.

I gave her a meaningful smile even though I kind of hated her. Neither of us really knew or cared to know much about the other. Our friendship started as a mutually beneficial surface relationship, and at some point, she accidentally became my oldest friend. So even though she was a bitch I barely knew, she became my maid of honor by default. She was happy to do it for the attention and the connections.

How the hell had my life gotten to this point? I had a lot of friends, but I never actually connected with anyone other than Oli and Travis. I'd always been envious of their easy friendship, and now I had severed that friendship down the middle. No wonder I didn't have any real friends.

Everyone lifted their glasses as the toast came to an end, and I took the tiniest of sips. Travis was the next to toast us. I was surprised but then remembered it would look strange if the best man didn't say something. I gave him a hesitant smile, sorry I put him in this situation. I glanced at Oli, and he looked worried.

Travis spoke, his voice steady and filled with warmth. "I

don't think there are two people in this world who were meant to be together more than Addison and Oliver. I've witnessed their love over the last eleven years, and it only solidifies how perfect these two are for each other."

There was a collective aww, and Oliver actually took my hand.

Travis continued, "Oli has always been the kindest man I've ever known. He's the type of guy who will thank a police officer for writing him a ticket. Not that he'd ever give them a reason to pull him over. I've watched him give the shoes off his feet to a total stranger to help them through a hard winter."

His eyes zeroed in on Oli. "I have no idea why you chose me to be your best friend. I mean, I'm the guy who tries to talk my way out of a ticket and usually ends up with a bigger fine." Laughter filled the room. "Most of you know Oliver and I have been best friends since preschool. We met on the playground, and as usual, I was a bad influence." Another laugh.

"Oliver deserves the best kind of person. So when he started dating Addison, I was skeptical. Then I got to know her and found out that she's not only amazing. She's a great fit for Oli."

"So let's raise our glasses to the happy couple." He held up his glass and everyone followed suit. "I can't wait to see the two of you become husband and wife. Cheers."

I pulled a tissue from my purse and dabbed at my tears, realizing Travis hadn't sat down. He announced, "That will be all the speeches for tonight. We've gotta save something for tomorrow." His smile grew, looking so carefree. "I mean aside from these two becoming husband and wife."

I watched his smile even after he sat down, and I

wondered how long he could keep it up. He excused himself and left the event room, probably to give his cheeks some time to relax.

An hour later and the party had finally ended. I was already in the car, waiting on Oli when I saw him and Travis talking just outside the restaurant. I desperately wanted to eavesdrop, but I was too far away. Their conversation was brief, and soon Oli got in the car.

"What was that about?"

He glanced at me. "Just thanking him for playing the role one last time."

"Oli, you've been friends for too long for this to ruin your friendship."

His eyes narrowed. "But have we? Our friendship ended the first time you two slept together, and I don't even know when that was. After college, during college, high school? He would've gone on pretending to be my friend forever if you hadn't confessed."

I sighed, wanting to skip ahead in time, to skip over this emotionally exhausting part. Since I couldn't do that, I stayed quiet, and when I did finally get to change into my sweatpants, it was to go straight to bed.

35

ADDISON

BARELY AWAKE, I hurdled out of bed and ran to the bathroom. I dry heaved for several moments before something finally made its way up. Once I was finished, I rested my forehead on the cold toilet seat.

This was not how I ever envisioned myself the morning of my wedding, but here I was with my face in the toilet, worrying that my fiancé didn't love me enough to go through with the wedding. It was so far from the Cinderella fairytale I'd envisioned that I laughed. It was that or cry, but I didn't want a swollen face today.

I sat back and rested my head against the glass shower door. Oliver was standing in the doorway to the bathroom. He had slept in the guest room last night, and I wasn't sure how he had heard me, but there he was, looking concerned.

He stepped forward. "Are you okay?"

I assumed he was talking about the vomiting. "It's usually the worst in the mornings."

He leaned back against the counter. "How long have you been having morning sickness?"

"Two weeks."

He gawked at me. "Why haven't I noticed you getting sick?"

I gave him a sad smile. I could lie, give half-truths, or blow it off. Or there was another option that I was ashamed hadn't been my first and only. I could be honest, as I'd promised him. When had lying become so much easier than telling the truth? "You heard me the first time, and we thought it was food poisoning, but I quickly realized it felt different, and I started having other symptoms. Once I knew what it was, I set my alarm for earlier in the morning. You can sleep through about anything. But I'd go to the guest bathroom just to be safe, and I usually felt better by the time you woke up."

His eyes were wide, looking at me like I was crazy. "Why?"

"Why what?" I asked.

"Why lie? Why wouldn't you want me to know? Why wasn't I by your side at the ultrasound? Why were you sneaking around like you were doing something wrong?"

I hid things, so I didn't have to answer the whys. I took a breath and with a sigh, confessed, "I was embarrassed."

His eyes narrowed. "Embarrassed about what?"

"I got pregnant. I don't regret it, but it was an unplanned pregnancy. It was irresponsible. I stopped my birth control so I could look better on my wedding day. That's a pretty vain reason to end up pregnant."

His fingers pressed against his forehead as he digested the information. He stayed that way for a long time before lifting his head. "Addison, your logic is ten shades of fucked. You did all of that because you didn't want me to think you were vain?"

If there was ever a moment to have morning sickness, it seemed like then was the time. I would take vomiting over his accusation and disappointment anytime. Travis told me I wouldn't be able to keep up with my sparkly facade, but I never dreamed I'd be the one to purposefully sabotage it.

When it was clear I had no response, he asked, "How much have you kept hidden from me?"

And here we went. "I don't know. They were mostly little things."

He ran a hand through his short hair. "Why? I mean, did I do something to make you believe you were better off hiding things from me?"

"You're perfect, Oli. I've always known I wasn't good enough for you, so I tried to be."

He shook his head, letting out a huff of frustration. "Jesus Addie. Where the hell is all this insecurity coming from?"

I was doing a poor job of convincing him to marry me. "It's not insecurity. I have high standards for myself."

"High standards? Or unrealistic expectations? Have you been setting yourself up for failure all these years?"

"I . . . don't know. I shoot for the stars and hope to make it to outer space. I don't think it's wrong to have big goals."

His brows knit together as he pinched the bridge of his nose. "Travis saw through your bullshit, didn't he?"

When I didn't answer, he nodded, noting, "That's hard to swallow." He folded his arms. "My supposed best friend knew you've been lying to me, and he didn't tell me."

"I didn't lie. I just didn't want you to see all my ugly parts."

"The ugly parts make you human." He sounded bewildered. "You must think so little of me. I'm sorry if I ever led you to believe you weren't good enough for me, Addie. If you just would've talked to me, I could've cleared it up, but you never did, Addie! It really blows my mind that you couldn't trust me. You feel like a stranger right now, but I know you. Being a little vain on your wedding day is fine. Shit, I think it's expected. That's surface shit. I know your heart."

Did he?

I sighed. "Please don't give up on me. I'm doing my best to be open and honest. I love you, Oliver. Don't give up on us." I put my hand on my belly.

His eyes followed the movement and then shot to mine. "You say I'm perfect in one breath, and in the next, you act as if I'd run out on you and our baby." He blinked. "No matter what happens, I'm not going to leave you to raise our baby alone."

"I feel like you're going to back out of the wedding on me," I said in a rush before I chickened out.

"I'm here, Addison. We have a lot to work through, but I wouldn't be here if I didn't love you."

Yes, you would, I thought. He was the type of man who would go through with it because it was the right thing to do. I would've voiced my fear, but I was too scared he would realize I was right, and he would leave. I already spent the week without him, and it terrified me to think of spending my whole life without him.

"Do you think you can stomach some breakfast?" he asked.

I nodded, and he helped me up from the floor.

AFTER A SEMI-UNCOMFORTABLE PRIVATE breakfast with Oliver, the rest of the morning was a mess of appointments and people. I met my four bridesmaids at the salon where we began primping, starting with manis and pedis. We drank mimosa—well, they drank mimosa's—Marley and I drank orange juice. I called ahead of time to inform the salon manager of my situation, and she assured me they would be discreet about my drinks. After our nails, we had our hair styled. Then we headed to the church, where a talented makeup artist made us look like living photoshop filters.

Jeanine helped me into my lace fitted bridal gown while my bridesmaids slipped into their wispy lavender chiffon dresses. They all had slightly different tops that I'd meticulously coordinated to flatter everyone's body shapes. Oliver's niece was the flower girl and also the only child invited to the wedding.

All my planning had paid off. The decorations, flowers, dresses, and tuxes were perfect, but none of it mattered if the groom got cold feet. At least it would be a tastefully beautiful disaster, instead of a tacky one.

The day was filled with so many fake smiles and hurried trips to the bathroom. I didn't know if it was nerves or the baby, but the nausea had me excusing myself constantly. I tried to vomit as quietly as possible, and I had a travel-sized mouthwash stuffed into the hidden pocket in my gown. My mouthwash was almost gone before the pictures even began.

Travis knocked as he entered the room where the bridesmaids and I were getting ready. "Incoming ladies," he warned, but we were all dressed. "I need to steal the bride for a moment." He spoke with enough authority that no one second-guessed it. I followed him into the hall where he assured me everything was fine. He led me into a private room just a little way down the hall. He locked us in, and when he spun to face me, he said, "Breathe."

I hadn't realized I was holding my breath. I dropped the fake smile, and my shoulders sagged.

He stared, taking me in. "I thought you might need a break. How're you holding up?"

"Not amazing," I said with a shrug. "I just keep imagining him bailing on me at the altar."

He pulled me into a hug, being extra careful with my hair and dress. "He loves you. He wouldn't do that to you." He kissed the top of my head and released me.

"Thanks, Travis."

"How's the nausea?"

"It's under control now."

"Good. I need to get back to my best man duties, but I had to come check on you." He stepped toward the door.

I wanted to steal him from his best man duties and make him the equivalent of my maid of honor. What would that be? Bridesman or maybe a friend of honor. It didn't matter. He wasn't mine to claim. I realized he was staring at me with a brow raised, hesitating to leave. I gave him a fake smile, and he unlocked the door.

Before walking out, he said, "I didn't know you could get more beautiful, but even with your fake smile and almost tears, you look stunning."

The door swung closed behind him, and I blinked back my tears. This was going to be a very long day.

TRAVIS

I WENT BACK to the groomsman's quarters. It had been a weird morning. I tried to give Oliver space while also staying close by in case I was needed. I had already run some last-minute errands for Oli, and now that things had slowed down, I went over to join the other groomsmen who were playing pool. They were okay guys, but I could get along with most people when I wanted to.

"Travis," Oli called when I got back from talking to Addison.

"Yeah."

"How is she?" He sounded genuinely concerned.

"Huh?"

"You did just go see Addison, didn't you?"

This looked bad. "Yeah," I hedged.

He didn't seem angry, so I continued, "I just wanted to make sure she was okay, you know, with the nausea and all the stress."

He folded his arms over his chest. "Uh-huh, and?"

"She said the nausea is under control. But she's scared shitless you're going to leave her at the altar."

Oli emitted a long sigh. "I'm in it now. Did you always know how insecure she was?"

The question felt random. "Uh . . . yeah."

"Why didn't you tell me?"

I shrugged, feeling restricted in my tux jacket. "She's good at hiding things, but her insecurities seemed obvious to me. Honestly, they should've been obvious to you too. I thought you might be ignoring them on purpose, or maybe subconsciously. I didn't feel it was my place to intervene when you two seemed so happy."

Oliver gave me a pointed stare. "You didn't want to intervene?"

"More than I already had. And I tried to tell you. I was constantly pulling the truth out of her in front of you."

Oli looked thoughtful, staring out the window that overlooked the church's garden. "I just don't understand why she's so insecure. She's always been an overachiever, but I didn't realize it stemmed from feeling like she's not good enough. Why would she feel that way?"

Her fucking father. The words were on the tip of my tongue, and I knew it would be better if Oli knew. "Her father is an asshole with a God complex who goes out of his way to make his daughter feel like she's not good enough."

He turned his face back to me, accusing, "Is that why you hate him so much? Because you blame him for her being insecure? Travis, you have no idea what you're talking about. You don't give the man enough credit. He adores his daughter. He might be tough on Addison, but he would do anything for her."

I drew in a deep breath. "He's an asshole, Oliver. He talks

her up to make himself look good. But does he ever praise her when it's just the two of you? He always has an agenda."

Oliver shook his head. "You don't like him because he's always been able to see through your shit. He warned me that you'd bring me down. I should've listened."

I wanted to punch my friend in the fucking face. Even if I told him straight out that the judge beat his daughter, I doubted Oliver would believe me. Addison was right. He had her father on a pedestal. He looked up to him. And I'd never been more disappointed in Oliver.

"Oli, I don't know why you have such a hard-on for the judge but—"

The photographer interrupted. "Oliver, we're ready to take the groomsman photos and some family shots before the ceremony."

I'd never been more pissed at Oli, so of course, it was time for fake smiles and about six million photos. Oliver seemed just as angry with me, and if it weren't for pictures, I would've started a fight. Maybe it would help both of us feel better.

The closer to the ceremony it got, the more Oliver looked like a flight risk. I would tackle him if I had to. I would make sure there was a wedding today. This was the way things were supposed to be. Everyone knew it.

Oliver's parents and their spouses stopped in to say hello to Oliver before the ceremony began. Everyone looked calm and happy, without a hint of fear that the bride and groom wouldn't make it to Mr. and Mrs.

Jeanine, Addison's stepmom, even cried happy tears as she patted Oliver's cheek before the ceremony.

At one-thirty on the dot, I patted Oliver's back to get his attention. It was time for us to walk to the front of the church. Oliver looked a little queasy, and once we were in place at the head of the room, I leaned toward Oli, asking, "You okay?"

"I don't know if I can do this," he whispered back.

Fuck, I knew he was a flight risk. I subdued my panic and whispered, "Oliver, I know you. If you leave her at the altar, you won't be able to live with yourself."

Oliver took a steadying breath, and I knew my words had sunk in deep, hitting home.

The bridesmaids came down the aisle in light purple dresses, carrying roses that matched. I couldn't focus on the bridesmaids. I was too focused on my kinda best friend, who looked a little more relaxed.

The flower girl scattered petals up the aisle, and then the music changed. Addison appeared in the doorway, and I lost focus for a moment. I'd never been eager to get married, but watching Addison walk towards me, changed my perspective. I would be ecstatic to be in Oliver's shoes, and yet here I was leaning in to whisper in Oliver's ear, "You can do this, Oli. You love her."

37

ADDISON

I WALKED down the aisle on my father's arm, focusing on Oliver as I moved forward, relieved he hadn't run off. Travis leaned in, whispering something to him while I fought the urge to throw up. My father released me to Oliver, and then we were touching. He took my unsteady hands in his, and my heartbeat slowed. I let out a breath. We were almost there.

Oliver turned, looking out over the crowd, and I followed his gaze, wondering what he was looking for. His eyes turned back to me, but he wasn't looking at me. There was a war going on inside him, and his breathing shuddered as the pastor started speaking.

Then it was my turn to steady his hands as tears came to his eyes. My panic returned tenfold. My pulse galloped while I clenched my jaw, holding my composure as fear devoured me. To the crowd, we looked like a couple so overwhelmed with love that we couldn't contain our emotions.

Our guests were here to witness the happiest day of our lives, but they were all unknowingly watching our relationship fall apart. I begged Oliver with my eyes, pleading for him to see this through. I would give him anything he wanted just to stick it out.

What would I do if he ran out? What would I say? How would I ever face any of these people ever again?

Part of him loved me, and I hoped it was enough. I knew I hurt him, but him leaving now would destroy me. My father would be so ashamed.

We seemed to come up with a nonverbal truce, and to my relief, we recited our vows, knowing we would break them. I knew it was over even as we kissed for the first time as husband and wife. We walked up the aisle holding hands as the room cheered. He tried to steer us toward an empty room, but the wedding coordinator kept us busy talking to guests and thanking people for coming. We had more pictures, and people surrounded us for the next hour. We even rode to the reception in a limo with the bridal party.

Our first dance was the first time we were alone enough to talk, but we had hundreds of eyes on us. Oliver held me tight and said, "Addison—"

"I know, Oli," I whispered. "Just don't do this here. Please," I begged, tears clogging my throat.

We were deceiving everyone but each other. I held it together as I danced with my father. I smiled like the perfect daughter, relishing his approval while I could, knowing it would all be gone as soon as he knew the truth.

Travis approached on the dance floor, asking, "Is this okay? Are we allowed to dance?"

I grabbed hold of him and began crying as we swayed. The truth was, we could do whatever we wanted because Oliver wasn't really my husband. At least not for long. He would never really be my husband.

My shoulders shook as I sobbed, and Travis's shoulders blocked me from the crowd. He didn't ask what was wrong. He just held me closer until I pulled myself together.

Oli and I rushed through our duties like cutting the cake and the stupid garter and bouquet toss. Then we bailed. We only said goodbye to a few people but skipped the big send-off we had planned.

I could only withstand so much torture for one day, and I'd met my limit. I wanted sweatpants and a case of extra-soft tissues.

We were silent on the drive back to our house. I just kept wondering how we would split everything up and what was the etiquette for our bridal gifts? Once we were inside, I changed out of my gown. I wore a new pair of cotton pajama pants and pulled on a tank top. I pulled my hair out of its updo but kept my smudge-proof makeup in place. It felt like my last layer of armor. I wasn't ready to let it go.

Without discussing it, I knew to meet him in the living room. He sat at one end of the sectional, leaning forward with his elbows resting on his knees and his gaze on the floor. He hadn't changed out of his tux, and I wondered if it was his own version of armor. I was glad I hadn't washed off my makeup. I sat at the other end of the sectional but felt ridiculous and moved closer.

We sat in silence for a moment before he said, "Addison, I want to be at the next ultrasound. I want to be involved. I will always be part of your life, but I can't stay married to you. We might be able to work through our problems, but neither of us would be happy. I know part of you loves me but I don't think you're in love with me, and I'm not sure if you ever were."

"I was. I might still be. I don't know. I'm scared and filled with regret. I don't want to lose you. I swear I never meant to hurt you. This week without you has been the worst week of my life, and I don't know if it's because it's the first time you've ever hated me or because I don't know how to live without you or because of the pregnancy hormones."

"I never hated you. Well, maybe a little, but mostly I hated me. I should've seen all the things Travis saw. I should've noticed you keeping things from me. I should've picked up on a lot of things I didn't."

"Please don't hate me," I cried.

"Addie, I still love you. I'll always care about you, but I can't be your husband."

"Why?"

"Other than you not being in love with me, I'll resent you. I'm afraid I'll become bitter, and we'll grow to hate each other. I don't want it to get ugly. I don't want to hate you, especially with a child involved. I want to end on good terms, and I think you want that too."

I nodded furiously, too choked up to speak. The realization that I was no longer in love with him had come so gradually that I hadn't allowed myself to recognize it. Living in denial felt better than losing him completely.

The pregnancy had been an eye opener. I knew the life we had built could crumble so easily if my secrets were exposed. I was so terrified that our baby would get caught up in the wreckage that I derailed the train myself, confessing the infidelity. I was relieved Oliver still wanted to be in our child's life, and hopefully we could figure out the messy parts before the baby came.

"We'll figure this out," he said, sliding over to me. His hand caressed my cheek, and he tilted my face toward him. He was blurry through my tears but still looked like he had himself together. "We don't have to have it all figured out. I'm not running out on you. I'll stay in the guest room until we know our next step, but I don't expect us to figure it out tonight. It's been a long exhausting day, and Travis told me you've been throwing up half the day."

I nodded again, and he slid off the couch. He knelt on the floor right in front of me and pulled me into a tight hug. I clung to him, needing the physical reassurance that I wasn't alone.

It struck me as odd. I'd never been afraid to do things on my own, but motherhood terrified me, and I'd come to rely on Oli without ever realizing how much.

After several moments, he pulled away. He searched my face, and when he seemed sure I was okay, he said, "I'm going to go move a few of my things into the guest room."

I nodded, making myself speak, "Okay."

He seemed reluctant to leave me, walking away slowly in case I called him back. I didn't. This was going to hurt, but we were mature adults who loved each other. If anyone could make this work, it was us.

I hoped.

38

TRAVIS

THE SUMMER EVENING FELT NICE, and the sun was just beginning to lower in the sky. I rolled the windows down on my drive over to Addison and Oli's place. It had been a long fucking week. I couldn't wait to get home to Deena. I missed her, and part of me wished she was here, while the other part of me really didn't want her to witness this fucked-up part of my life.

I rolled up the windows and called her. I just wanted to hear her voice. "Travis."

"Hey, babe."

"How was the wedding? According to social media, they are officially married."

"Yeah, but something's up. Addison was in tears earlier, and they left the reception early."

"Maybe they needed makeup sex."

I flipped my turn signal and said, "I don't think that's it. It's been over an hour since they left, and neither of them are answering their phone."

"Because makeup sex," she repeated.

"No, that's not it. Something's been off since they said their vows. I was going to ask Addison while we danced, but then she started sobbing. I'm headed over there now to see what's going on."

She groaned. "Travis, I know you love them, but you can't fix all their problems. They're married now. They're going to have to figure these things out by themselves."

I exited off the highway, saying, "I know. I just wanted to check on them one last time before I leave."

"Are you still coming back in the morning?"

"Yeah, I'm taking the redeye." I paused before admitting, "I miss you."

"Oh, yeah?" she chimed playfully, "I could've been there, you know."

"This week has been a big fucking disaster. I'm glad you weren't drawn into the mess."

My phone beeped with another call. "Oh shit, Addie's calling me."

She sighed. "I love you, Travis."

"I love you. I'll see you soon, babe."

She disconnected, and I clicked over to Addison. "Hey, Addie. What the hell is going on?"

Her voice was calm as she relayed, "Oliver and I broke up. It's permanent this time, and we're not mad at him."

"We?"

"Yeah. I don't want you to be mad at him. He only said I do today because he couldn't hurt me, but we both knew it was over."

I turned into their neighborhood. "I don't understand. You two love each other."

"Yeah, we do, but not as husband and wife." She sniffed like she was holding back tears.

It made me angry. I pulled up in front of their house, wondering how the fuck I was supposed to respond to that. How could he do this to her? We spent the whole week tracking him down, dragging his ass back, only for him to renege at the wedding reception. I wanted to murder him, but there were no cars in the driveway. Maybe they were both in the garage. "Where are you guys?"

"At home. He's staying in the guest room until we can figure things out."

"What about the honeymoon—the wedding gifts? How are you going to explain this to people?"

"We don't have everything figured out. We're trying to find out if we can change the reservation or move it, but honestly, that's not a priority. If we can't change it, then I'm going to try to talk Oliver into going alone."

"You sound too calm."

"I'm exhausted."

I could hear the weariness in her voice. "I'm outside. I think you should let me in."

"You're here?" she cried in surprise.

"Yeah."

The front door opened, beckoning me as the sun sunk below the skyline. I exited my SUV and walked to the open door. Addison stood there, her hair pooled in soft waves around her shoulders, while her makeup remained mostly intact. But instead of her white gown, she wore cotton pajama pants and a white tank with nothing beneath. I forced myself not to focus on the thin shirt and stepped into the house.

Even drained, she still looked good. I noticed her engagement ring and brand-new wedding band were no longer on her finger. It felt so surreal. How many times had I secretly hoped for this to happen? Just as many times as I back-tracked, remembering how much I wanted them to be happy.

I changed my life around so they could be happy. If I would've known he would walk away in the end, I would've fought for her. I would've fought with everything I had, but now, it was too late. I was in love with someone else. I was in a committed relationship for the first time in my life. Even so, Addison was pregnant with his baby. How would that work?

Anger, red-hot, pulsed through my veins. I was going to beat the shit out of him—the asshole. I walked through the living room down the hall until I found him in the guest bedroom. He didn't see me coming. He had his back turned, removing his tux jacket. He turned just in time to give me a perfect shot at his left eye. The hit connected, and Oliver stumbled back.

"What the fuck!" he shouted.

"Are you out of your goddamn mind, Oliver?"

The corner of his eye was bleeding as he stared in bewilderment. I watched his confusion fade away, and his eyes turned hard. He straightened and stalked toward me, throwing his own punches.

I wanted to beat the shit out of him, but I didn't want him dead, so I pulled my punches. Oli wasn't a fighter, not like I was, but we used to scrap back in the day for fun. I taught him how to fight, and he put that knowledge to use.

Addison had followed behind me into the room, screaming at us to stop, but we didn't, not until we were both too worn out to continue. The pain felt good. The tension in my body had built up all week, and the exertion from our fight seemed to be exactly what I needed to release that stress, even as my whole body ached. Both of our faces were bleeding, and my fists were bruised. I sat on the floor with my back against the bed while Oliver lay flat on his back, breathing hard.

Addison lurked in the doorway, ready to lecture us. Her arms were crossed, her lips tight as her nostrils flared. "Did you guys get it out of your system?" she asked, stepping forward. "You're both assholes!" She knelt down in front of Oli first, checking him over as she continued to gripe at us.

Addison Arthur MD ripped into both of us as she checked our wounds, but Oli cut her off mid-sentence. "When did you know you loved him?"

She paused what she was doing. "What?" she asked breathlessly.

He sat up, turning to face me. "How long have you been in love with her?"

With his question, I felt the weight of my exhaustion. Not just from today, or this week, but the last eleven years. It all seemed to hit me at once, and I sighed. "I'm so tired of this bullshit. Oliver, you want to know the truth?"

He nodded, his voice steady. "That's what I'm asking for."

I blew out a breath and spoke my truth. "Since we were seventeen, and I had to walk the new girl to her first class where my best friend in the entire world, the one person I could always count on, asked her out. I tried for years to stop thinking about her, but she was always there. We were twenty before we realized we both had feelings for one another. Things spiraled from there."

His mouth gaped, and he looked frozen for a moment before tilting his head to Addison as if to confirm my story. The grief showed through her expression, and she closed her eyes and nodded.

Oli froze again before his head shook back and forth as if

he couldn't believe it. He blinked. "So, for the past eight years, you two have been—"

"No," Addison said, "We haven't been together since before our engagement."

I added, "When you told me you were going to propose, I knew it had to stop, and the only way for that to work was if we didn't see each other."

Realization seemed to hit Oliver. "That's why you took that job in Phoenix?"

I nodded.

He turned to Addison. "If you loved him, why didn't you break up with me?"

Her shoulders slumped. "Because I loved you too. We had a life together, Oli. I was really happy with you, but Travis had me all tied up when he was around. What I felt for Travis was separate from my feelings for you. I loved you both."

I had her all tied up? She was the one tying me in knots.

Oli said, "We've been engaged for almost two years, so that still means it was going on for six years."

I rolled my eyes. "It's not like we were fucking like rabbits. It only happened when we couldn't keep it from happening."

Oliver glared at me. "What does that mean? Oops, I tripped, and my penis slipped into your vagina again. I guess we just keep rubbing together until it's all better."

I wanted to laugh, but I knew that wasn't appropriate, so I said, "You're the one who asked for the truth."

"I'm still asking." He said in earnest. "What do you mean you couldn't keep it from happening?"

"Come on," I said, "Haven't you had a moment where it was physically painful not to touch someone. And it doesn't matter how close you get because it will never be enough, and you just lose control." I felt Addison looking at me, and maybe I shouldn't have been so blunt.

Oliver seemed to work that over in his head, and knowing his expressions, I saw the moment he got it. "See, you have."

"It was the woman from the hotel," Addison sounded a little breathy, and Oli looked guilty.

He said, "Her name is Willa. She doesn't trust many people, and in an effort to become friends, we promised we would only tell each other the truth," he paused, "even if it was ugly, even if it made us look bad."

Addison seemed perplexed why he was telling us this, and then she asked, "Are you asking if I want the ugly truth?"

Oli nodded. "Yes."

She sighed. "Yes, Oli, I want the ugly truth."

He swallowed and then began. "I think I would've been content to stay married to you if I hadn't met Willa, but she woke this part of me I didn't even know existed. I didn't know anything was missing until I felt them with her. I realized I need someone who will argue with me.

"I love you, Addison, but I got so wrapped up in fitting myself into your plan for the future, that I forgot how to live my own life. I wish I could go back in time and change that. I obviously haven't been tuned into what's happening around me, or I think I would've at least had some suspicion of you two."

"Are you going to go after her?" There was resolution in the way Addison said it.

Oli shrugged. "I think I'd have a better chance at regaining her trust once you and I are no longer married. But even then, I don't know where she lives. I don't even have her last name. I know her ex-husband's full name."

Addison and I exchanged a look, and I asked, "I thought you guys were totally honest with each other."

"We were, but we shared meaningful things, not our profile information. Actually, that's not true. She has all of my information, but I don't see her reaching out anytime soon."

"If she's what you want, then we need to figure out how to get divorced. Technically, we haven't consummated our marriage, so I don't even know if it counts."

"You could get an annulment, but I think it takes longer," I added, wondering how those words were coming out of my mouth not even ten hours after they said I do.

"We don't have to figure it out now, and there is a good chance she will never want to see or speak to me ever again."

Addison snorts. "You underestimate your appeal."

"Says the woman who cheated on me."

"Ouch!" she glared at him.

I looked between them. "This is fuckin' weird, you guys. I don't think I'm ready for this."

"No worries," Oli said, "You'll get to escape back to Phoenix in no time."

Addison sighed and left the room. I looked at Oli, having no idea where we stood. "Are we still friends?"

He shrugged. "I don't know. It seems like Addison's been your best friend this whole time."

"Yeah, but she's been a shitty best friend."

"Hey!" Addie cried, coming back into the room with ice packs in hand. "I mean, it's kinda true, but still." She handed Oliver one icepack and the other she gave to me.

Oliver put the icepack under his left eye and groaned. "I need some time to come to terms with everything that's happened this week. I'm still mad at both of you, but if you two hadn't fucked up, then I wouldn't have met Willa, and I never would've known that I was missing something. So, I don't hate either of you, but I don't like you either."

I held the ice over my jaw. "I'm sorry this is the way things went. I'm sorry I fucked up. I really tried to fight it. We both did. I still love you, man."

"I know. I believe you. Otherwise, you wouldn't have moved across the country, but it still sucks."

I used the bed frame to pull myself up to a stand. "You need time to work it out. I get it. I'll get out of your hair." As I walked out, I added. "Just don't go giving barbies to anyone else, thinking you can replace me."

His snort was nearly silent, but I'd heard it, and I smiled, remembering my jaw hurt and detoured into the half bath to see how bad I looked. I cleaned myself up, relieved to see my beard would disguise the nasty bruise that was sure to show on my jaw.

39

ADDISON

"He worked really hard to get us down that aisle," I said to Oliver once Travis left the room. "I tried to break up with you once, back when you and Travis lived together. I left you a note because I didn't know how to do it in person. I couldn't help how I felt about him, and I knew you deserved better. Travis found the note before you did. He confronted me, and I told him I'd rather lose both of you than for you to lose each other. He begged me not to break your heart because he didn't want you to end up as jaded as the rest of us. Forgive him, Oli. He made a mistake, but he loves you like a brother, and you are the only family he has left." I took a steadying breath and walked out of the room, closing the door behind me.

I caught up to Travis in the kitchen. He put his ice pack back in the freezer and leaned against the counter, studying me. I looked him over. He'd cleaned his face, but he still had blood on his collar. He didn't look too bad. Oliver was definitely in worse shape.

"You should leave the cold on for longer," I said.

"Nah. Oli will need it more than I do."

I scoffed. "You want to return to Deena all swollen and bruised?"

He rolled his eyes but walked back to the freezer to grab a pack of frozen peas. He wrapped it in a towel and pressed it against his jaw, going back to his same position against the counter. I'd always liked Oliver clean-shaven, but Travis made roughed up look good. His short beard was manly, and the stubble from the day only made him appear more rugged. I suppressed the urge to run my fingers through his messy hair and wondered if I would ever outgrow my crush on him. Is this how Oli feels about Willa?

"How did you do it?" I asked as I leaned into the kitchen island.

He lifted a brow in question. "Do what?"

"I can't help but compare myself to her. A woman he's known a few days made him second guess our entire relationship. How do I not compare myself to her? You watched Oli and me together for years. You must've compared yourself to him or wondered why I'd stay with him when I had feelings for both of you. That had to have messed with your head."

"It did, but you were with him first."

"But maybe Oli and I should've ended it a long time ago. You tried to tell me to be honest with him."

He stared at me. "It doesn't matter now. We can't change the past."

"It was selfish of me to stay with him."

"Then listen to my advice now. Are you actually okay with him pursuing a relationship with someone else when you're the one having his baby?"

I pushed back from the island counter. "I can't control who he loves."

"That's not what I mean. I'm saying be honest with him now. You're going through a life-altering breakup while pregnant. It's okay to feel uneasy about him dating someone. Especially so soon."

I trailed my fingers along the granite counter as I rounded the island. I leaned back against it, standing across from him. "Why are you always so good to me?"

A small grin curved his lips, and he stepped forward. He removed the ice pack from his jaw, and his free hand wrapped around the back of my head, pulling it forward. He pressed his lips to my forehead. As he spoke, his lips moved against my skin. "Because we're the same."

I pulled away so I could look at him. "How do you figure? You're an asshole, but you're also warm and kind. You're easy to love. I'm prickly and intimidating and don't even know how to make genuine friendships."

"We're both damaged. It's how I've always seen through your bullshit. You don't let people in, but I snuck through the bars of your fancy gilded cage a long time ago."

It was true. I stepped forward, fiddling with the buttons on his vest. I swallowed. "You've always known me, but I tried for years to let you go. To set us both free." My palms pressed flat against his chest.

He took a step back, abandoning the peas on the counter. He held my hands in his. "You did free me, and I went to Phoenix and found out who I was without you or Oli. I was free from the guilt I always carried, and I found out how easy relationships are when I'm not comparing everything I do to my best friend or lusting after his girl."

"Lust? Is that all?"

He tilted his head to the side. "You know what I mean."

I took a step away, pulling my hands from his. "Do you think Deena is the one?"

He nodded. "Yeah, I think so."

"Congratulations," I whispered, forcing myself to smile for him. He deserved all the happiness.

"Thanks. It doesn't mean I'll disappear. If you ever need anything, call me. I'm only a flight away, and I doubt we'll stay in Phoenix. It's too hot, and we both miss the seasons."

"What about your jobs?"

"I can work remotely, and Deena can consult in any big city."

"When will I see you again?"

Would I see him during the holidays? No one tied him to New York anymore. His parents were dead, and his adoptive family hinged on Oli. I was the only other person who tied him here, and though I desperately wanted his friendship, I couldn't escape the deeper feelings that lurked below the surface, especially after everything he'd done for me this week. We were a picture of dysfunction, but we loved each other too much to walk away. Didn't we?

"I don't know." He was inching his way toward the door. "I can come back anytime."

But he wouldn't. I knew that. They'd spend the holiday with Deena's family. But would he come when the baby was born? Or would he go off and live his happily ever after with Deena and never look back for fear of being sucked back in by this succubus? I was throwing another pity party, but I wasn't ready to let him go just yet. "What time is your flight?"

"I have to be at the airport by midnight."

I looked at the clock. "It's only ten. Do you have to go back to the hotel?"

"No, everything is packed up."

"Then where are you running off to?" I tried to hide my panic. "Stay for a while."

"You've gotta be exhausted. I can wait at the airport."

I looked him in the eye. "I have no idea when I'll see you again. Please, don't leave yet."

"Okay."

He walked toward the living room, and I followed. As soon as we sat down, Oliver entered the living room, coming from the bedrooms. He complained, "These ice packs don't stay cold for very long."

"Use the bag of peas on the counter," Travis said. "It'll stay cold longer."

Oliver nodded as he entered the kitchen. I worried my bottom lip. Travis was right. This was fucking weird. I blew out a breath and looked at Travis, who was already watching me.

Oliver walked back through the living room, stopping in front of the sectional. "So what does this mean for you two?"

I pulled my legs onto the couch. "What do you mean?"

Travis must've understood because he said, "We're friends."

Oli let out a huff. "You risked everything because you couldn't resist each other, and now you have the opportunity to be together, and you don't take it?"

Oh, that. "He's in love with Deena."

Oli looked at him. "Have you bought a ring?"

Travis gave one slow nod.

My chest tightened as my heart knocked against my rib cage, demanding to be heard. I placed a hand over it, trying to hush its protests, glad no one was looking at me.

Oliver asked, "Does she know about your history with Addison?"

Travis shook his head, and Oliver scoffed. "And you think she'll be okay with your friendship after you tell her?"

Travis swallowed.

Oliver's pointed stare remained on Travis. "You are going to tell her, right?"

He nodded in response. "I'm going to tell her everything when I get home."

"And what will you say when she tells you that you can no longer be friends with Addison?"

Travis's forehead wrinkled. "What makes you think she would?"

Oli shrugged. "Common sense, but I really don't know her well enough to know if she's a jealous person."

"She's not, and our relationship is solid."

"Good," he said frankly before turning toward the hall. "I'm going to bed. Have a safe flight. I'll see you when I see you."

"Goodnight, Oli," Travis said in return.

"Night," I added.

The silence lingered after Oli left the room. The totally impractical wall clock that was more for style than function ticked loudly in the interim between words. I was so tired. I pulled a throw blanket off the back of the couch and wrapped my body like a cocoon as I sat on the couch, going over everything Oli had said.

Travis interrupted my thoughts. "Addie, she's not going to demand we end our friendship."

I looked at the dark TV screen straight ahead of me, studying our reflections—me bundled up, using the blanket to protect me from him, and him sitting forward, watching me.

I leaned my face into the blanket. "I'm more tired than I realized."

The clock ticked away all the unspoken words between us. I wouldn't speak my fears or listen to his responding reassurances. I refused to dance in the same circle we had already spun through too many times. Just like the hands on the clock, we were going in circles, counting time, but getting nowhere. I refused to go through it again. I would rip that damn clock off the wall.

"I should go." He stood, and my chest tightened, my vendetta against the clock already forgotten. He was leaving. "It'll take me extra time to return my rental car."

I let go of the cocoon around me and stood from the couch, following him to the door.

He spun to face me, and I spoke before he could. "If she asks you not to speak to me again. Listen to her. She must be pretty special for you to have chosen her. Don't lose her over this."

I memorized his warm, honey-speckled eyes. He leaned forward to kiss my forehead, but I backed out of his reach, shaking my head. "Goodnight, Travis."

"You're saying goodbye, and I'm saying I'll see you later. Why are you acting like you've already lost me?"

"It's the opposite. I am setting you free to go live your happily ever after."

He narrowed his eyes. "I'll call in a few days to check-in. Call me if you need anything before then."

"I'll be fine. Thanks for everything, Travis."

He opened the door and was halfway through when he turned back to me. "I love you, Addie."

"I love you, Travis."

He stared for a second longer before walking out into the darkness. I wanted to claim him, but I had no right. I closed the door behind him, unwilling to watch him walk away.

TRAVIS WENT BACK HOME to Phoenix and never checked in like he'd promised. He had chosen Deena. Oliver chose Willa and he was planning to go after her as soon as we were divorced.

Both of the men I loved had picked me first, yet something inside me was broken, making me unchooseable. I wouldn't even choose me. But I wasn't fortunate enough to have a choice. It hurt to feel unchosen, but I guess I should want to choose myself before anyone else would want me. I would learn to love myself, and to do that, I had to let go of my possessiveness over Oli and Travis. My primary focus needed to be making the best life for myself and my baby. That meant I needed to figure out what self-love looked like.

I didn't know how much time I had left on this earth. My mother was only thirty-two when she suddenly died of an aneurysm. It's part of the reason I tried to stay as healthy as possible, and I was going to make the best of my time with my child, however long that might be.

40

TRAVIS

BY THE TIME I got off the plane and got my luggage, I was exhausted. I just wanted to go to sleep. I let Deena know I was on my way from the airport, taking an Uber so she wouldn't have to roll out of bed at five in the morning to come get me. The three-hour time difference always messed up my internal clock.

The Uber driver had to wake me as we pulled up in front of my condo. I was only half awake when I unlocked our door. It was six-thirty in the morning, so it surprised me to see Deena awake and dressed. She stood by our dining table with coffee in hand.

It felt so good to see her. Deena was a constant. I could always depend on her, and after the week I'd had, I was excited and relieved she was here, waiting for me to come home.

I dropped my bags just inside the door and went straight to her, enveloping her in a hug. My hands ran up her back, and I held her head as I demanded a kiss that quickly became more than just a kiss. I expected her to strip me down, but she pushed against my chest, breaking contact.

I let her pull away and stepped back, looking down at her. Was she upset, or was it my sleep-deprived mind conjuring issues that weren't there? "Babe?"

She said, "I've barely spoken to you. How was the wedding?"

"It's such a long story, and I'm too tired to go through it all. They're married but decided it was a mistake, and they're getting a dissolution."

Her face fell, and she nodded, looking sad.

"They're okay," I said, trying to comfort her. "It was messy, but I think they made the right decision."

"I don't get it. They seemed so happy. Why would she cheat on him?"

I shrugged. "Why does anyone cheat? In the week they separated, Oliver met someone else and fell in love."

"That's crazy! He's gonna leave Addison for someone he just met?"

I sighed. I just wanted to go to bed. I didn't want to have this conversation. "Can we talk about this later? I'm so tired."

"I have barely spoken to you in a week. And I tried to give you the time you needed, but I think I've waited long enough. I want to hear about your week." She crossed her arms and pressed her lips together. An eyebrow climbed up her forehead, daring me to argue.

"You're right. I'm sorry. I'm just not thinking."

"What I don't understand is why Oli didn't call you. His fiancée cheated on him, and he doesn't call his best friend. But Addison called repeatedly."

Fuck. I didn't really want to have this conversation. "Oliver wasn't ready to talk about it yet."

Deena pressed her lips together as she put more room between us. "Because it was you."

"What?"

"You slept with Addison."

It wasn't a question. This was a trap. It's then that I caught a glimpse of the suitcase she had tucked behind the table. My eyes flicked back to her face, my heart racing when I realized what was on the line. Knowing she'd see right through a lie, I wracked my brain for the best way to admit guilt. "It was years ago. Before we met."

"Then why didn't you tell me about it? I gave you almost an entire week to tell me, but you didn't. Did you cheat on me?"

"No. I didn't. I wouldn't!" I took a step toward her. My hand grazed her arm, and she jerked away from my touch.

She looked up at me with tears in her eyes. "You had an ongoing affair with Addison. Addison!"

"Babe?" I tried again, reaching for her.

She denied me, slapping my hand away. "You made me feel stupid for ever thinking there was anything between you two. And then she calls, and you drop everything, including me, to hop on an earlier flight so you can fix everything that you messed up. How could you do that to Oliver? He's always been there for you. Always! And you slept with his girlfriend, and then lied to me about it." She was shaking her head, not expecting an answer. "You're not the man I thought you were."

"Deena," I begged. "It was a mistake. A horrible mistake. Of course I didn't want to tell you. I didn't want you to leave me. I'm not still that same guy. I—"

"Are you in love with her?"

I let out a breath and let the truth spill out. "I was. Back then, I was."

"And now?"

"Now, I have you. I love you."

"So because you have me, you don't love her?"

"Not the way I love you."

"Are you in love with me? You know what. It doesn't matter. You're not going to cut her out of your life, and I can't trust you even if you do. You're turning me into a distrustful woman. I will always feel like the stand-in for Addison. I mean, she's single now. Shouldn't you be going after her?"

"She's pregnant with Oliver's baby."

Her eyes flared. "So you've thought about it!" she grabbed the handle of her suitcase. "Wrong fucking answer, Travis!"

"No! No, Deena," I reached for her, needing to stop her escape. She fought me, but I overpowered her, holding her body against me. "That's not what I meant. I don't want to go after her. I don't want her. I want you."

Eventually, she stopped fighting me and began sobbing. Her arms wrapped around me, her tears wetting my shirt.

"Fuck you, Travis," she sobbed against my chest. She jerked away, her tears turning angry as she screamed, "Fuck you for making me fall in love with you and then ruining it!"

There was nothing I could say to fix it. "You're right. I fucked up."

She wiped her tears and said, "I'm staying with my sister until I can find a place. I'll come get the rest of my stuff once I do."

She walked out, and I stayed frozen in place, hating the extra effort it took to breathe. The thought of us being over paralyzed me. I couldn't believe it. I wouldn't. I would find a way to fix it.

41

ADDISON

TWO WEEKS AFTER OUR WEDDING, Oliver and I pulled up to my parent's house. They had invited us to have dinner with them once we returned from the honeymoon they didn't know we had canceled.

Neither of us moved to get out of the car. I clasped my hands together in my lap as I stared up at the towering stone exterior. Travis had always referred to this place as a castle, and after seeing it that first time, he'd started calling me princess.

Well, this princess was about to fall from her throne, and I felt betrayed that Travis wasn't with me to help cushion the fall. He had promised to help me break the news to my father, but I hadn't heard from him since he left for Arizona.

Oliver's hand landed on my wrist, and he gave it a squeeze. "It's going to be okay. They might be upset, but they're reasonable people, and they love you."

Oliver had never experienced Judge Arthur's anger. It was my fault he didn't understand. Travis was the only person I'd ever told. It'd been years since my father had laid a hand on me, and I had to believe he wouldn't lose his temper if I brought Oliver with me.

"Thank you for coming," I said to Oli. I blew out a breath and reached to open the door, climbing out of the car.

Oliver got out and met me at the front door. "Ready?" he asked.

I nodded, and he rang the doorbell.

My mother welcomed us with hugs of excitement. She called, "Jonathon, the newlyweds have arrived."

I inwardly cringed. I wasn't wearing my ring, and I knew we had to break the news to them before we attempted to eat. I had tried to talk them into an earlier time, so if this went poorly, we wouldn't spoil a meal, but Jeanine Arthur wouldn't hear of it.

She led us into the sitting room where we sat, and she gushed over our wedding. I was relieved when my father stepped into the room because the prattling stopped. My father shook Oliver's hand and kissed my cheek, a shocking show of affection. I blinked back my surprise.

My father took his seat, and a conversation started around me. I finally had his approval, something I had always coveted. And if I didn't do this soon, I'd talk myself out of it.

I stood up and spoke over the polite conversation. "We have something we need to tell you both."

"Mind your manners, Addison," my father reprimanded.

Oliver's gaze swung to me. He hadn't expected me to be so forward. Neither had I.

Oliver stood beside me, and I hesitated, but I'd drawn everyone's undivided attention. "Actually, it's two things." I took a breath.

"Way to wind up the suspense, Addison," Jeanine chimed.

I blew out my breath and went for it. "We're pregnant. I'm keeping the baby, but Oliver and I are getting divorced. We didn't want to drag out our relationship and end up in a messy divorce, especially now that it involves a baby. So, we have ended things amicably. Things have not been right for a while, and though I deeply wish we could have come to this realization prior to our nuptials, I believe we are making the right decision for our child and us."

I felt Oli's arm at my back. A sign of solidarity.

Jeanine looked from us to my father and back. "Is this some kind of joke?"

I shook my head. "No. We knew on our wedding night that we had made a terrible mistake. We canceled our honeymoon and have spent the time sorting out our situation. The dissolution paperwork has been filed, and we put the house on the market this morning. Oliver has moved out, and I'm looking for a place."

Jeanine looked like someone had sucker-punched her. She leaned against the arm of her chair, placing both of her hands over her heart. "Oh no," she breathed.

My father stood. "If you're divorced, then what is he doing here?"

I glanced at Oliver. "I asked him to come with me to break the news. We are still friends, and we're both going to parent our child."

My father shook his head. I watched his anger rise, the red splotchy skin climbing his neck. "I have never been so disappointed in you, Addison. And Oliver, do you have an explanation why you would knock up my daughter and then leave her?"

Oli responded in a calm tone, as if the world weren't ending. "She and I are not in love."

My father barked a derisive laugh. "You think being in love has anything to do with marriage?"

"With all due respect, sir—"

My father held up a hand to stop him. "Respect? You've lost every ounce of my respect." His eyes turned to me. "Addison, you have completely lost the reigns over this relationship. You split up the night of your wedding, which means you conceived before getting married, and now your weak pregnancy addled mind is ruining your rationale." He looked at Oliver. "And you're letting her bulldoze you like always. Do you have no spine?"

He didn't give him a chance to speak. "Of course not, or you wouldn't have let that trash you call a friend steal your woman. Luckily for both of you, I have a backbone, and I'm saying no. Absolutely not. We'll void the paperwork. You can take your house off the market. My grandchild will not be a bastard."

I was speechless, but I shook my head until I could gather my words. "We aren't asking for your permission."

He let out a frustrated sigh. "You two gave up too easily. Perhaps you just got too comfortable and began looking for reasons to destroy your lives." He zeroed in on me. "How is your delicate female ego going to weather when you're a single mother? It will mess up your career, and no one will ever want you. A failure like that mars you for life."

In his eyes, I had failed. He would rather I stay unhappily married because divorce was a failure, being a single mother was a failure, and Arthurs didn't fail.

Oliver rubbed a hand over my back, whispering, "I'm sorry." Then he stepped forward, shaking his head. "I should've listened to my trashy friend because at least he saw you for what you are. A bully." He pointed at me. "She is your daughter, and she was terrified to face you today. Now I see why. You can disrespect me all you want, but your daughter needs your support, not a lecture."

I stood with my mouth gaped. It was the only time I'd ever seen Oliver angry with him.

"Get out." My father shouted.

"With pleasure," Oliver shot back, and with a look to Jeanine, he said, "I apologize for ruining the delicious meal I'm sure you already had prepared."

Jeanine nodded woodenly.

Oliver started for the door, but I wasn't ready yet. Seeing Oliver's anger validated my feelings—validated that my father was in the wrong—validated that I didn't deserve his scorn. I stared him down, watching the redness in his face and the bulging veins in his forehead. This was the man I had idolized growing up, and I couldn't remember why. I shook my head in disgust before walking away from my father. It's the first time I walked away feeling disappointed in him instead of myself.

How long had he twisted the truth? How long had I let him?

I caught up to Oliver in the foyer and had just opened the front door when my father stormed in, announcing, "You're setting your baby up to fail."

I spun to face him, my hand resting on the doorknob as I stared him in the eye. "You're one to talk, Father. The only child you raised got knocked up and divorced. Never mind that she's a doctor. Never mind that she's happy." I was shaking with trepidation and forced my voice to steady as I continued, "And you think you're disappointed in me. Imagine how I feel about you."

He'd always been a giant in my mind, but as I looked at

him then, my top lip curled in disgust. He was nothing but a self-important, overly critical, pudgy, old man in a power suit. When my gaze returned to his, I finished, "By your own measure, that makes you a failure. Guess we know where I get it from."

Arrogant men didn't like when their significance was called into question. His face was burgundy by the time I spun and walked out of the house. Oliver's wide-eyed stare told me I'd shocked him. I had shocked myself too, but I didn't let it show. My heart pounded so violently, it made me dizzy, but I clamped my mouth shut and walked to the car with my head held high.

I stayed brave until we were out of sight and then cried the whole way home. I think a part of me had always subconsciously hated my father. I definitely hadn't trusted him fully since he hit me that first time. So why did I long for his approval? It defied logic.

I knew walking away was the right thing to do, but sometimes the right thing hurt.

TRAVIS

I TOOK ANOTHER SWING, hitting the punching bag. I'd been avoiding my condo since Deena had moved all her shit out. Luckily, there was a gym next door, so here I was, beating the shit out of the bag. Working out is how I coped with stress, but it wasn't working.

"Back at it again, Travis?" Devon commented as he headed toward the free weights. He was the kind of guy who only came to the gym to post selfies for social media or for the multiple dating apps he was on. He was a douche, and he knew it. Unfortunately, we had sort of become friends.

I threw a few more punches. "Yep."

He leaned against the bag I was using, effectively halting my workout and pissing me off while he said, "A few of us are getting together to watch the UFC fight tonight. Wanna come?"

"Fuck, no!" I didn't want to go anywhere, especially not a fuckin' party, but it had been a month since Deena left me, and I couldn't stand being home without her.

Devon clung to the bag. "Great, so I'll see you at seven?"

"I'll be there at eight," I grumbled, so he'd get the fuck off my bag before I hit him.

"Any word from Deena?"

She had stopped answering my calls weeks ago. I had sent her flowers and chocolates, a fucking fruit basket, and a case of wine. But throwing gifts at her wasn't working. I hoped if I gave her time, she'd remember what we had and how good it had been. I needed her to come back.

Devon knew better than to ask about her. I took a swing, and he jumped back from the punching bag just before my fist made contact.

From a few steps away, he complained, "Shit, you're such a miserable bastard. There are plenty of fish in the sea that will make you forget all about the one that got away."

I tried to ignore him, going back to my workout, but when he didn't leave, I asked, "Don't you need to go pose for Instagram or something?"

He patted his thighs. "Yep. It's leg day, which means I might accidentally get dick bulge in the pictures, but I can't really be blamed for that."

It's then that I noticed the bulge in his grey sweats. I might be pissed if it weren't so funny. I barked out a laugh. "Did you stuff a sock in there or something?"

"It's all me," he crowed, looking proud.

"Did it fall off? Because it's halfway down your thigh, bro. No one's going to believe that shit."

Devon looked down and cursed, reaching in his pants to retrieve whatever he had stuffed in there.

I shook my head. "You have issues, man."

Devon shrugged. "I'm a grower, not a shower, but these chicks want grey sweats with dick outline." That's when he whipped a giant pink dildo out of his pants.

I retreated back, yelling, "What the fuck? Get that outta here. Why the fuck do you have a dildo?"

"It's a prop, duh. I got the extra veiny one, so it shows through the material. Looks more realistic that way."

I glared at him. "What is wrong with you? Put it away!"

He shoved it back inside his pants, positioning it by angling it down one thigh.

I rubbed a hand over my face. "Devon, nobody wants to see that."

"Hell, yeah they do," he argued, "Girls go crazy for this shit."

"Seems like a false advertisement to me. Do you take the dildo with you on your dates too?"

"No. I told you. I'm a grower, not a shower. I'm telling you. It works to catch those slutty fishies."

I let out a sigh. "Stop referring to women as fish."

He snorted. "You haven't gotten laid in over a month, and it shows, my friend."

I jumped at him like I was going to punch him, and he threw his arms up before rushing off, yelling, "Don't blame me. You know it's true."

Even after he left, I couldn't get the image of that stupid veiny dildo out of my head. What a fucking douchebag.

DEVON DIDN'T BRING his dildo to the UFC party. The gathering was in a condo just a few doors down from me. There were eight of us, but everyone seemed leery of me, probably worried they would say the wrong thing, and I'd beat the shit out of them. I had been building muscle, and I knew I looked intimidating.

They knew Deena left, and they knew I'd been in a shit mood since she left. Everyone avoided talking to me except Devon, who was swiping through dating apps. He sent his fake dick bulge picture to every woman who showed a hint of interest. And he felt the need to keep me up to date on his progress, oblivious to my obvious annoyance.

I cracked my knuckles and knew I was making some of the other guys nervous. They wanted to leave the fighting to the professionals on TV.

Devon swung his phone in front of me. "Oh, look at this one."

I shoved his phone back at him. "Jesus, can you stop?"

"Fine," he said. "Just trying to show you there are options."

"I don't give a fuck. I'm not dating," I replied.

"But, maybe it's time," another guy said.

That's when I realized everyone was looking at me with pity.

"What?" I demanded.

Devon offered, "They're all scared shitless to tell you, so I will. Deena's been dating for a couple of weeks. I keep seeing her on these apps, and Tod," he gestured to one of the guys I didn't know well, "said she has a date with his coworker tonight."

Rage pummeled me, but I kept a lid on my emotions. That's why they had all been extra cautious tonight. I glanced at Devon, giving him a nod of appreciation. He may carry around a fake cock, but at least he had the balls to tell me the truth.

I left without a word.

I KNEW DRIVING to Deena's new place was a bad idea. I knew I shouldn't even know where she lived. But it'd taken her a while to stop sharing her location with me, so I figured it out. She had turned me into a stalker. Great.

She wasn't home when I got there, which only seemed to confirm what I'd already been told. But I could almost convince myself that she was out doing something else at ten o'clock at night.

But when she pulled up in a car I didn't know, with a man I'd never met, I knew it was true. And it hurt. How could she be over me so quickly? After everything we had been through together, I couldn't wrap my mind around what I was seeing.

And she couldn't seem to wrap her mind around what she saw either as she walked toward me. "Travis, what the hell are you doing here?"

I stared at the guy she was with. He looked like the stereotypical man you would find working in IT—straight-laced, thin with a rounded gut, hipster glasses, and a receding hairline. I was offended, but hey, maybe he had an outstanding personality.

He glared at me. "Deena, who's this jagweed?"

Or maybe not.

He looked like he wanted to kick my ass, but at the same time, he stayed hidden behind Deena.

I gave Deena a questioning look. "Really, this guy?"

She crossed her arms. "You have five seconds to explain why you're here?"

"Or what?"

"Travis!"

"I was at a thing tonight and heard you were dating. You're not answering my calls, so I dropped by to see if it was true. Judging by the way this guy is looking at me, I'd say it is."

She shook her head. "You're so arrogant."

"Arrogant?"

"Yes. Arrogant, because no matter how many ways I tell you it's over, you can't seem to get it through that thick skull that someone would actually dump you. Because no one can resist your charm, right? Including Addison because nothing is off-limits to the great and powerful, Travis."

I glared at her, not recognizing this side of her. She stepped forward. "Sucks, doesn't it? Being on this side of heartbreak. Since you're not used to it, let me explain how things work. When someone breaks up with you, moves their stuff out of your condo, stops answering your calls, and doesn't respond to all the cheesy gifts you send them, they aren't playing hard to get. They honestly don't want you. Showing up at their apartment to discuss their relationship status a month later is fucking ignorant. I will date who I want and fuck who I want, but neither of those will ever be you. So, I kindly invite you to get the fuck out of my life."

I pressed my lips together and nodded. At least she made it crystal clear where she stood, and her bitchiness made it a little easier to leave. I took a breath. "Okay." I started walking away. I attempted to brush shoulders with her date, but he pivoted behind Deena. I almost let it slide but couldn't. I turned back to Deena, noting, "One tiny little observation. Just because your date is unattractive doesn't automatically make him a nice guy. I mean, he's been hiding behind you this whole time. At least he didn't run off, but I'm guessing that's only because he's hoping to get some."

She raised her brow. "He's not hoping. I told him on the way here all the things I was going to do to him. I'm not looking for a gentleman, Travis. I'm looking for a nice big cock to fill the void you left, and my date puts you to shame."

The way the guy's eyes widened, I knew she was lying, but I didn't call her on it. Instead, I nodded, saying, "Glad you're getting your needs fulfilled."

Her wince was barely noticeable, but seeing her bitterness made me hate myself. I said, "Be happy, Deena. Don't settle." I walked away before she could respond.

I thought that would be the end of it, but a week later, Deena drunk dialed me and broke my heart all over again. She called several times after that, and each conversation was worse than the last. Then the calls stopped altogether, and I hated the silence.

43

ADDISON

IT WAS EARLY AUGUST, and Oliver and I were staying in a hotel just south of Cincinnati, Ohio. We had finalized our divorce a couple of weeks ago, and in a weird twist, we were looking at moving states together.

We had separate hotel rooms and semi-separate agendas for being here. I was here to interview for a job, which went great, and they offered it to me.

Oliver was here to win Willa back with his grand gesture, but it hadn't gone as planned, and Willa had turned him down.

None of this change had been easy for me, but I felt I owed Oliver a happy ending, and I was determined to make that happen, even if it meant tracking Willa down myself. So when Oliver went out for a morning jog, I searched his hotel room for Willa's address. I was curious to meet the woman who stole his heart and then turned him down.

While I was in Oli's room, someone knocked on the door. I peeked through the peephole, finding a woman on the other side. Her dark wavy hair draped over her petite shoulders. She was beautiful in a way I could never be with her dark eyes, full lashes, and caramel skin. My skin burned when I looked at the sun, but she looked like she belonged on a beach. I had seen pictures of her, but it didn't seem real until this moment. I felt a stab of jealousy and pulled open the door before I lost my nerve. I watched her mouth open to speak, only for a small gasp to escape as her eyes widened. Her hopeful look disappeared the moment she saw me. I expected her to say something. Her mouth was still slightly ajar, and I could see the emotions working behind her eyes, but instead, she let out a breath and began walking away.

I stepped out into the hall. "Willa?"

She turned to me, her sharp eyes assessing my threat level. I knew how to exude confidence, even if I didn't feel it. And right now, I didn't feel it at all.

She intimidated me. This small curvy woman with hair I'd die for.

I had to stop comparing. We weren't in a competition. She wasn't my enemy. She was the only person who could lessen the damage I'd done to Oli, and I would do anything in my power to make it right. "He told me you turned him down."

She swallowed and nodded. "I did."

I stepped forward. "But you're having second thoughts?"

"Not anymore," she said, trying to run from me.

I closed the hotel door behind me and followed her, suggesting, "Let's get a drink in the lobby."

"Oh-kay." We walked to the elevator in silence.

I wasn't sure she wouldn't bolt when we got to the lobby, but I had the elevator ride to reason with her. "Oliver went for a run this morning. He runs more when he's upset.

You've turned him into a pretzel. He's all twisted up and doesn't know what to do with himself."

She was giving me the side-eye, but I knew she wanted to know more.

The doors opened, and we walked out into the lobby. I was relieved when she made a left into the lounge area with me. She got a coffee while I fixed a tea for myself. I took a seat at a table by the windows, and she joined me.

"I know this is probably strange for you," I said with a laugh, "It's strange for me too, but I'd like us to be friends because the truth is, I'm not going anywhere, Willa. I will always be a part of Oli's life. I'm having his child." My hand automatically went to the slight baby bump. "He has sacrificed so much for me. He's followed along with my life plan and made every transition so much easier for me. He took care of me in med school. When I was gone for long hours, he'd pack me a lunch, or fill my car with gas, or bring me meals. He would do all the random things I was too exhausted to do and never complained. That's who he is. That's what he's always done for me. If he loved me enough to do those things for me, I can only imagine what he will do for our daughter."

Her eyes widened. "It's a girl?"

"Yeah, we found out the other day." I couldn't help my smile, feeling wistful for a moment before pulling myself back to the matter at hand. "Oliver came here to see you. I came here to interview for jobs. Cincinnati is just over the river, and there are a lot of options for me. Oliver has made every move for me. It's time I made one for him. He wants to be closer to you. He's been scoping real estate while I've been interviewing."

She shook her head. "I don't understand."

I leaned on the table. "I knew he was in love with you before we said our vows. He went through with the wedding because he didn't want to hurt me. I love Oliver, but in all honesty, after we got engaged, things were never the same. Travis moved away, and I began to wonder how much of my staying with Oliver was because I felt guilty and trapped. It's like one morning I woke up and realized I was the villain of my own story, but by then, I had a little life growing inside of me. Maybe that's where my sudden conscience came from because that little voice is the reason I told Oliver about Travis and me. It's the reason he left and found you.

"You opened his eyes to all the twisted things I'd put him through, and in the meantime, all I could think about was how I didn't know how to do life without him. He was the one holding me together. Travis was there for me, but he doesn't treat me the way Oliver does, or at least the way Oliver used to treat me.

"I was unfair to him in so many ways, but when I saw how much it hurt him to leave you, I knew his love for me had changed."

Her spine straightened. "Are you still in love with him?"

I gave her a sad smile, admitting, "I was only in love with how much he loved me. I know how bad that makes me sound, but that's my honest truth. I didn't realize what I was doing to him until I saw the tears he cried for you during our wedding. That's when I knew I had to let him go."

Her face gave nothing away, but her words revealed her hand. "And what happens when you change your mind and realize you want him back? You have a child together. You have a history. I can't compete with those things."

I couldn't blame her for her skepticism. "There is no

competition," I reassured. "He wants you, and I won't change my mind. Oli and I have run our course."

She swallowed, fingering her cup of coffee. "He's going to be an amazing father."

I nodded, my smile warming.

But her comforting words were cut off by her curiosity. "Why were you in his room this morning?"

"I had a feeling you would come." Okay, that was a lie, but it sounded better than admitting to snooping in his room for her address. "And I wanted to meet you. I'm glad you came when you did."

"You really think we can be friends?" she asked.

I wanted to laugh because friendships were not something I excelled at, but I was turning over a new leaf. "I don't know, but I'd like to be."

She gave me a brief nod, looking as if she was still turning it over in her mind. "Do you know when he'll be back?"

I shrugged. "It might be a while. He left just before you came."

"Will you tell him to call me?" she asked, pulling out her phone as if he was going to call her just then.

"Of course," I said with a smile.

After she left, I went back upstairs and fell to pieces. It hurt to set Oliver up with someone else. I thought I could stay analytical about it, but I was more emotional lately, and this wasn't just anyone. It was Oliver, the father of my baby, the man I thought I'd spend my life with. I felt grief at the idea of losing him to someone else. The very notion that I'd be able to stay pragmatic and rational about this was laughable. But I would do my best to pretend. I would do what it took to help Oli because he deserved more than I could ever give him.

PART THREE

44

TRAVIS

THREE MONTHS HAD PASSED since the post-wedding breakup, which meant it had been three months since Deena had first broken my heart. We'd talked a few times, and each conversation felt more devastating. All the love I'd had for her was turning into bitter hatred, and I no longer knew who I hated more, her or myself. Finally, the calls ceased altogether, which should've been a relief. But I couldn't stop imagining how different things should've gone. I was going to propose to Deena, and now here I was, moving across the country to get away from her.

I'd thought to call Addison or Oliver a hundred times, but I hadn't. I didn't know where I stood with either of them. It wasn't unusual for us to go a month or two without talking, but I didn't like how we left things. I didn't want to be the one reaching out. But I missed them, especially with all of life's recent changes. Everything had shifted so quickly, and I hadn't recovered from the whiplash.

Columbus, Ohio, was never somewhere I had considered living. I thought Ohio was full of farms and hillbillies, but there was a city in the center of all those fields. I could've stayed at my previous job and worked remote from anywhere, but I was offered a higher paying position in Columbus.

After two weeks in my new high-rise apartment smack dab in the center of the city, I'd started settling in. Work was only a block away, and though I had a car, I opted to walk most of the time, leaving the car tucked away in the parking garage.

I walked home from work, enjoying September in Ohio. I preferred the milder weather to Phoenix's triple-digit temperatures. Filling my lungs with the late summer breeze, I thought about doing an outdoor run tonight. I stepped into the lobby of my high-rise apartment building and caught an elevator that someone just deserted. As it rose toward my apartment, my phone rang, and Oliver's face lit the screen.

"Hey," I answered, sounding a little too eager.

"I was going to text, but there's too much," Oli said, "Do you have a minute?"

"Yeah."

"Addison said you guys haven't spoken since you left."

The elevator opened, and I stepped off onto my floor. "No, my life's been kinda hectic."

He puffed out a breath in an almost laugh. "So has ours. We're divorced and moving to Kentucky."

"What?" I stopped at my front door. "Why?"

"It's where Willa lives."

"Addison's moving with you?" Unlocking the door, I pushed into my apartment.

"Yeah. Addison was offered a job in the city. She's renting an apartment close to the hospital. But she's looking to buy a house closer to Willa and me before the baby is born."

"That's generous of Addie."

"She says she's trying to make up for past mistakes." He sighed. "Addison is the reason Willa and me are together. She spoke to Willa and convinced her to give me a second chance."

I was glad he couldn't see my face because what the fuck? Who did that? Set their baby-daddy up with another woman while she was still pregnant. Not only that. She moved states so she could live nearby and witness their happiness. Talk about pouring salt into a wound. Addison probably felt she deserved to have her pain rubbed in her face. It was like the scalding water all over again. She was punishing herself.

I took a breath, frustrated that Oliver didn't see her sacrifice for what it was.

Oli said, "I'm worried about her." He let out an exasperated huff. "Our split disappointed her father, and I know she values his opinion of her. I'm worried their relationship is still suffering. She's been so positive, but I know she's holding back. It's not really my place to force her to talk about her feelings, but this can't be an easy move for her. I guess I want you to talk to her. Make sure she's okay."

Okay, so maybe he wasn't blind to her sacrifice. "Does this mean I'm forgiven?"

"Sure."

I was doubtful of that. "I'll call her, but I don't know if she'll talk to me."

"You always get the truth out of her."

I rubbed a hand across my forehead. "Yeah, but I told her I'd call and check in on her, and now it's been three months, and we still haven't spoken."

"Why? Did Deena ask you not to speak to her?" he asked.

"No, Deena left me. She figured out I lied to her about

Addison and ended things the day I got home from New York. I didn't even have a chance to explain." I exhaled a long breath. "You can say I told you so."

There was a pause before he said, "I'm sorry you lost her. Is there a chance of winning her back?"

"No."

"So, why haven't you called Addison?"

Saying that I blamed her for my fuck-up would only make me sound like an asshole, but I needed to own my mistakes. "I was going to propose to Deena at Christmas, but now she fucking hates me. I didn't know how to deal with it. Part of me blamed Addie because I didn't know how to bear all the blame myself."

After a pause, he said, "We're all going through some shit. Stop feeling sorry for yourself and call her."

It was so out of character for him to be so indelicate. I pulled my phone away to look at the screen. Sensitive Oli had grown a backbone. I laughed, saying. "I moved to Columbus, Ohio, two weeks ago. Where are you in Kentucky?"

"You moved to Ohio? Why?"

"I wanted to get the hell out of Phoenix, and I found a good job here."

"We're only a couple of hours from Columbus. Addison's apartment is in Cincinnati. Willa and I are just a little south. I'm taking Addison to look at houses tomorrow."

"Wow, that feels pretty permanent. Not tryin' to be a dick, but you're both rearranging your lives to fit Willa. Are you sure that's a good idea?"

"You are a dick," he said bluntly. "But you're not the only one to question me. It's not a mistake. Willa, Addie, and I are on the same page."

"Willa's it, then. Did you move in with her?"

"I have an apartment here, but I stay with her a lot. We don't want to move too fast, but we're not eighteen. We know what we want."

"I get it. That's what I thought I'd had with Deena."

"I'm sorry it didn't turn out the way you'd hoped."

I shrugged. "I guess I'm still trying to figure out how relationships are supposed to work."

Oliver cleared his throat, sounding uncomfortable as he asked, "Do you think you and Addie will ever be a thing now that you're both single?"

With a frown, I ran a hand over my head. "I don't know, man. I don't think that's likely."

"But do you want a relationship with her? You know, romantically?"

Fuck. How the hell did I answer that? I took a breath. "I love Addie. You know that, but I don't know. There's so much baggage there."

I didn't want to touch that baggage. I'd carefully packed it up, zipped it away, and the zipper bulged under the pressure of too much history. If I touched it now, it was likely to explode with years' worth of shrapnel, and Addie and I wouldn't be the only victims. The consequences would hurt everyone around us. It would be best left alone.

I continued, "I think it's best for everyone if we leave that door closed."

I tried not to read into Oliver's deep sigh. He asked, "But you'll still call her?"

"I'll always be her friend, Oli, even if I am a shitty one." I wanted to say more or ask what he thought of Addie and me in an actual relationship. But that felt too awkward, so I changed the subject to the first thing I could come up with.

"What are your new addresses? I wanna see how far you guys are from me."

"I'll text them to you. And before I forget, remember how I didn't know Willa's full name when I first met her?"

"Yeah."

"It's Rose. I couldn't believe it. It's no relation to you, but still, that's crazy, right?"

"So what you're saying is I'm no longer your favorite Rose?"

He laughed. "Sorry, man. Oh, Willa just walked in. I gotta go."

"K. Good to hear from you. Talk to you later, man"

We hung up, and I sat down on the edge of the couch, staring at my phone, my thumb hovering over Addison's name. I blew out a sigh and swallowed my nerves. I could do this. It was Addison. My thumb tapped the screen, and I held my breath as it rang.

45

ADDISON

MY PHONE VIBRATED on the side table, and I looked to see who was calling, shocked to find Travis's face pop up on the screen.

Why the hell was Travis calling me? Why now? Did he sense that I was about to crack and he was calling to push me over the edge?

As desperate as I was to hear his voice, I knew it would only hurt me when he told me how happy he and Deena were together. Everyone was so in love, and I didn't need any more of it rubbed in my face.

The call went to voicemail, and almost immediately, a text came through. I wanted to ignore it, but not reading it would drive me crazy. I looked at the message.

Travis: Sorry I've been a shitty friend. I miss you.

How was I supposed to respond to that? I decided not to. I had enough to do. I didn't need to worry about him, and he obviously hadn't been concerned about me. I looked around my apartment, piled high with boxes. The movers had come yesterday, and though the furniture had been set up, there were so many boxes I still needed to go through. Most of my things went to a storage unit. I would eventually only use this apartment for the nights I worked late or if I had several shifts in a row. My apartment was one big room that combined kitchen, dining, and living room in one open space with a wall separating the bedroom and through the bedroom was the only bathroom.

I was going with Oliver to look at houses tomorrow, which would suck up all of my energy. Forget the unpacking. The movers had hooked up my TV, and my couch was in place. I shoved the boxes against the wall, finding the one labeled *bedding*. I pulled a fuzzy blanket out of a box and curled up on the couch with it.

Being pregnant made me tired, and I would have plenty of time to be miserable tomorrow. Right now, I wanted to ignore my growing list of problems and binge-watch crap television.

THE NEXT MORNING I received another text from Travis.

Travis: Oli said you were going house hunting today.

I wondered why they were talking about me? I didn't like it.

Me: Stalker.

Travis: Watching you from the bushes right now.

I grinned at my phone.

Me: Nice try. No bushes here.

Travis: I want to come visit you.

What was with him all of a sudden? I hadn't heard from him in months, and now he acted as if nothing had happened. He had promised to call me, and I waited for his call. I should've known better.

Travis was a good friend when he was present, but he was a far cry from dependable. He was hot and cold. All in or totally uninterested. When we were together, it was hard not to hang onto his every word and believe he meant what he said. And then he was gone without so much as a peep for three months—three of the hardest months of my life. Travis wasn't stupid. He was intuitive and would've known how badly I needed him. There were so many times I wanted to call him, but he'd abandoned me, and we both knew it. So why reach out now?

Me: I think I'll be busy the day you visit.

Travis: Guess I'll come today!

Me: Funny guy!

Travis: I live in Columbus.

Travis: Oli gave me your address. I'm halfway there.

My eyes widened, and my heart raced. Had he really moved?

Me: No, you aren't. Liar.

Travis: It's not safe to text and drive. See you in an hour.

Fuck him and his head games. Why the fuck was he in Columbus? How long had he and Deena been there? Why hadn't he bothered to tell me?

Maybe he was coming to see me behind Deena's back. Asshole.

I pushed the texts out of my mind and got in the shower. I would not change my day for him. But by the time I got out of the shower, it was driving me crazy. I sent Oliver a text.

Me: Did you invite Travis to go with us today?

I had just finished drying my hair when my phone rang with a call from Oli.

I answered, and Oliver said, "I talked to Travis yesterday. I mentioned we were looking at houses today, but he said nothing about coming with us. He did say he wanted to visit sometime. He lives in Columbus, now, by the way. Did he tell you that?"

That was just awesome. "Yes, he just started texting me out of the blue, but I didn't know if he was serious about coming today or not. Did you give him my address?"

"Yeah. He said he wanted to see how far the trip was. I had no idea he was thinking of driving down today. Are you okay with him coming?"

"I don't know. I guess so. He said he was already halfway here."

"Huh." He paused. "Are you still meeting me at Willa's?"

I pinched the bridge of my nose. "Yeah. I'll be there." I took deep soothing breaths.

He added, "I have another reason for calling. I just emailed you a couple of new listings. I wanted to get your take on them. See if they were worth squeezing in today."

"Okay." I grabbed my laptop bag and unzipped it. "Let me pull them up on my computer."

While I was logging in, he said, "Are you sure he's coming today?"

"I don't know. His texts made it sound like he was. But it's Travis. I didn't even know they moved to Columbus."

"They?" he asked, then clarified, "It's just Travis. Deena broke up with him as soon as he got home from our wedding. It sounds like it was pretty rough."

"Wait," I said, staring unseeing at my computer screen. "They broke up?"

"Yep. She was waiting for him when he walked in the door."

The sting of betrayal just kept on stinging. If what Oliver was telling me was true, then Travis had been single for three months. I had assumed Deena was the reason Travis hadn't called. But if it wasn't Deena, then why hadn't he reached out? I'd felt bad before when I thought he chose Deena over me, but this felt worse. Deena hadn't made him cut me out of his life. He cut me out all on his own. Anger mixed with rejection, but I kept my tone calm, "Did you know he was moving?"

"Nope. I just found out yesterday when I talked to him."

At least Oliver sounded just as surprised as I did. I focused on my computer and opened my email, looking at the new listings. "I like the first one—the green house. It's cute. I don't like the blue one, though."

"Okay, I'll add the green one to the list," he said, "See you in an hour."

I looked at the clock, and sure enough, the morning had flown by. When I was off the phone, I busied myself by unpacking boxes while also attempting to untangle my jumbled thoughts about Travis and the emotions that surrounded them.

I kept coming up with reasons to peek out the windows that overlooked the parking lot, so I knew the moment he pulled in. I watched him walk toward the building.

My heart rate doubled, and I started looking around frantically, as if just now realizing what Travis would see when he walked in the door. I was barely put together, and my dinky loft apartment was a disaster. I wouldn't usually care, but I wanted to rub it in his face how well I was doing without him, but I wasn't doing well. I had moved from our large house with the heated in-ground pool to a tiny apartment. My pregnancy bump was more visible now, making me feel fat and uncomfortably bloated. And I had less of a pregnancy glow and more of an oily shine.

I started breathing hard. A sob caught in my throat, and I hated that I cared what he thought of me after he had already proven I wasn't worth caring about. I was an afterthought. Out of sight, out of mind. But he never left my mind. Maybe it had always been about the chase for him, and now that Oli no longer wanted me, neither did he. I hated him. I hated him for the things he made me feel about myself.

My phone chimed, and I jumped, startled and on edge. I glanced at the screen. It was only a shipping notification on a package I'd ordered, but it was enough to jerk me out of my downward spiraling thoughts.

I took deep breaths, working to calm my overzealous heart rate. I moved to the front door, expecting him to knock at any moment. I was only on the second floor. He didn't have that far to go.

When there was no knock, I looked through the peephole. He was standing there, just on the other side, but I hesitated to open the door, realizing something. This was the first time we would interact as single adults, and I had no idea how to act around him. I had always had to suppress my feelings for him, holding back. Now I didn't have to. But I would. Not because of Oliver, but because I valued myself too much to let Travis throw me away twice.

He seemed hesitant to knock, and I wondered what his hesitation was about. What was he feeling? I watched him, distorted through the peephole. His brows folded together, and he stared at the door for several moments. I started to get nervous that he knew I was watching. Could he see my shadow through the peephole? Or maybe he could hear me breathing as I pressed myself against the door.

This was stupid. I was so angry with him, but I had butterflies like I was fourteen. I pulled away and swung the door open, ripping the bandage off before I stewed about it a second longer. His surprise turned into a smile, and the butterflies turned to dragons, burning me from the inside. I hadn't realized how badly I missed him and how much I craved his touch until he was there, and I was throwing my arms around him. He caught me in a hug, and we held onto each other.

One thing I hadn't realized until after Oli and I broke up is how much I would miss physical touch. I'm not talking specifically about sex, but all physical contact. Physical touch was never something I had especially craved, but it had been so freely given. I used to feel annoyed by Oliver's constant affection, but now, I felt hollow without his touch—without anyone's touch. I'd resorted to cuddling with a pillow at night just to feel like I wasn't alone.

When I thought back to the times before Oliver, I realized it had been Jeanine offering those hugs and hand squeezes. Those little touches of affection. But I couldn't even go to her now. She was hundreds of miles away, and I wasn't welcome at their house anymore.

If I had girlfriends, this is when they would rally around me, and their encouragement and hugs would tide me over, making the adjustment easier. I wanted to belong to a group of women—to have a tribe. Here I was on the cusp of thirty, and I still hadn't learned how to make friends, but I'd been trying harder.

Sandra, Gracie's mom, was probably the closest thing I had to a girlfriend. She was ten years older than me and lived several states away, but after Oli and I split, I had some candid conversations with Sandra. Even after revealing my mistakes, she still considered me a friend.

Travis used to be my best friend. I wasn't sure what he was anymore, but my heart and body reacted to him like an old friend before my brain could catch up and pump the brakes. He held me tight, and it felt so good that tears leaked from my eyes. His chest rose and fell against mine, and I felt my anger slip, slip, slipping away.

"I thought you'd be mad at me," he said when we pulled apart.

"I'm furious with you," I said, my brain finally catching up. I turned, heading inside. "I didn't want you to come here today."

He followed me in, closing the door behind him. "I can tell by the way you greeted me. Such a cold, unwelcoming reception."

I ignored his sarcasm.

My apartment wasn't the best setup for having company, but I wasn't planning to entertain here. I leaned against the back of the couch, facing him. "You . . ." I wanted to say he rejected me, but instead, I said, "You abandon our friendship without warning, and I assumed it was because of Deena, but then Oliver informs me you guys broke up months ago. Why, Travis? Why wait until yesterday to reach out?"

He opened his mouth to say something and then closed it. He scrubbed a hand over his face. He'd shaved off his beard, and he had a tan from the summer. His brown hair was a tinge lighter, but his honey brown eyes were the same. He was dressed casually, and he looked more buff than he had three months ago. Had he been spending all his time at the gym, and that's why he couldn't be bothered to call me?

His sad brown eyes landed on me, and I knew there was a

mountain of rocky terrain ahead. I felt ill-equipped. If I didn't protect myself from him, I knew I would fall for all of his excuses.

"Addie, I'm sorry. I . . . I practiced what I was going to say the whole way here, and I still don't have the right words."

I kept my voice steady. "I tried to let you off the hook before you left New York, but you still promised you'd call."

"I know. It's . . . my life fell apart as soon as I got back to Phoenix, and I was angry and sad and struggling to get through each day. Then the days turned to weeks and then months. So much time had gone by, and I didn't know how to reach out anymore. "

"So why are you reaching out now?"

"Oliver called me. He briefly got me caught up on what's happened since June. I realized while I've been going through hell, you've been going through your own version. Setting your ex up with a woman while you're pregnant and then moving closer so you can experience their relationship firsthand. Why did you agree to that, Addie?"

I stepped back. "I shouldn't have to defend my choices to you. Oliver and Willa deserve to be happy, and I'm not sad to leave New York. Things didn't go well with my father, and I don't mind having some space between us. I found a good job here, and once I settle in, things will become easier."

He glanced at my belly, and I put my hand on it. "I'll be settled by the time she gets here."

"She?"

I nodded. "It's a girl. Her name is Emerson."

"You have her name picked out." He gave me a look filled with warmth. "How far along are you?"

"Almost five months."

"Wow! You're gonna be a mom." There was a light in his

eye as he said it and a softness that was dangerous for my heart.

I looked for a distraction, saying, "Your muscles look ridiculous."

I didn't phrase it as a compliment, but he smirked and said, "Thanks, I've been working out."

"Don't you have enough trouble finding clothes that fit? Why are you bulking up? Is it steroids?"

He grinned. "You know I don't do that shit. The gym helps calm me, and the harder I push myself, the better I sleep."

I wondered if he was sleeping alone, but it was not something I should care to know. "Careful you don't wear your body down."

"Thanks, mom," he teased.

I breathed in deep and spun toward my bedroom to hide my confusion. My emotions were all over the place, and I couldn't seem to reign them in or stick to one. I busied myself by picking imaginary lint from the couch.

"I was a personal trainer. I know what I'm doing with my workouts, Add."

I spun back, crossing my arms and asking, "Why are you here, T?"

He rubbed a hand back and forth over his jaw while his eyes ping-ponged around the room. "Because you and Oli are the only family I have left." His hand dropped, and his gaze zeroed in on me. "If you'll still have me."

I stiffened. "I thought I had already lost you."

He shook his head. "You didn't lose me."

I glared at him. "You never called."

"You could've called me."

Arching a brow, I let out a breath. "I took my cues from

you, Travis. I didn't want to do anything to threaten your relationship because I thought you were living your happily ever after with the woman of your dreams."

He tilted his head. "So if I had been off living my happily ever after with Deena, you're saying you would've been fine with me never calling you again?"

"Not fine, no, but I would understand it. I would respect it. But it was you who decided to ditch me, and that's not what friends do."

He closed his eyes. "When you told Oliver the truth, did you even consider giving me a heads up?"

I took a step back. "You're blaming me?"

He sighed. "It wasn't just your secret."

I backed another step.

He continued, "At first, I blamed you, but then I realized it was my fault. Deena once asked me if you and I had ever been involved. I could've told her the truth, but I lied. I denied anything had ever happened between us. My mom had just died, and I was sad. But it was also to protect you. I realize I chose you over Deena many times. Hell, sometimes I chose you over myself. When you called before your wedding, I dropped everything and came to help you. I could've stayed in Phoenix and told Deena the truth. I could've done a lot of things, but I was so focused on you that I fucked up my life. I'm not blaming you. It's just taken me time to come to terms with everything. I'm sorry I haven't been there for you the past three months. I could barely take care of me for a while."

I processed his words, feeling selfish. He made it sound like I was such a burden but . . . "I never asked you to drop everything to come fix my problems. I never asked you to drive me to Michigan. I'm sorry I didn't tell you before I told Oli. I didn't know if I could go through with telling him."

He shrugged. "It's okay."

But it wasn't okay. We had both hurt each other. Again. We had both messed up. Again. We were going around and around in this same vicious cycle. We had a history of saying hurtful things we didn't mean, but I'd rather argue with Travis than for him to leave my life again. His absence was worse than all of the terrible things we'd ever said. I step forward. "It's not okay. I'm so sorry you lost Deena."

He whispered, "She broke my heart, Addie."

I nodded. I had witnessed how much he loved her, and his words hit on my own pain. I confessed, "Part of the reason I agreed to move here is because I was afraid I'd lose Oli if I didn't. Oli and I might not have a normal relationship, but he's the closest thing I've ever had to family."

He moved closer as I spoke, and when I finished, he pulled me into his powerful arms.

"I hated losing you, T. But I thought you were at least happy."

He let out a breath. "I've been miserable."

I gave a hollow laugh. "Me too. My father disowned me when I told him I was pregnant and getting divorced. And you're right, it's painful seeing Oliver with Willa. FYI, get ready. That's where we're meeting him today."

"We're gonna have a conversation about your dad, but why are we meeting at Willa's house?"

46

TRAVIS

ADDISON WORE a fitted white t-shirt that showed off her baby bump. I hadn't prepared myself to see her pregnant, but she was definitely showing, and she had a glow like she had just walked off the beach. She was put together with classic simplicity. Her straight blonde hair was longer than I'd ever seen it, her strands reaching the middle of her back.

Looking at her, no one would guess what was going on inside her mind. But despite how well she was put together on the outside, she was a mess on the inside. Oliver was right to be worried.

She was strong-willed and determined, but she had clung to her perfect image. It's how she judged her worth. Now that it was gone, I wondered if she felt freedom or just disappointment.

"Do you want me to drive?" I offered.

She shook her head. "If you want to come with me, that's fine, but I'm driving." She gathered her phone and purse from the kitchen counter.

"Okay, then I'll ride with you," I said.

She opened the apartment door. "Fine."

I followed her out, and she led the way to her car. I climbed in and slid the passenger seat back to give room for my legs. When I looked over, she was tucking her seatbelt into some sort of hook between her legs.

"What the hell is that?"

"It holds the seatbelt, so the strap isn't across my abdomen."

"Is that why you wanted to take your car?"

"It's one of the reasons. Also, if I want to leave, I don't want to rely on anyone to take me home."

She wanted to maintain as much control as she could, and I didn't blame her. "I would take you home if you wanted to go."

She didn't respond right away, but eventually, she said, "This way, I don't have to ask for permission to leave."

Her eyes were on the road as she drove, and I had to hold myself back from touching her hair. I wanted to run my fingers through its length. I looked away before she sensed me staring.

I thought about what Oliver had asked me about a potential relationship between Addie and me. Did I want a relationship with her?

Her emotions seemed a little erratic today, but then again, mine did too. There were still sparks between us, but everything felt so delicate and new. It was like we were starting over, but not from the beginning. We couldn't erase the past twelve years, and neither of us were ready for a romantic relationship. But could we salvage our friendship?

∾

We pulled up to a cape cod style home, and Oliver popped out the side door as we pulled into the driveway.

I hopped out of the car, giving Oliver a brief hug like there had never been bad blood between us. I slid into the middle of the back seat while Oli sat in the front so he could give Addison directions.

"Ready?" Oli asked Addison, who nodded, looking far too morose for house hunting.

Oliver pretended not to notice, but shot a worried glance toward me. He then directed Addison to the first house on the list.

It was a quick *no* on the house, and we visited several other nos before finding the green ranch in the middle of town. It was a three-bedroom that had been recently updated with a new picket fence surrounding the moderately sized backyard. Addison had been quiet throughout the process, not giving much away. So when she said, "This is it. I want this one." Oliver and I exchanged a look.

Oli asked, "Are you sure? We still have others to look at."

"No, I want this one," she insisted. "It's close to you. There is a master bedroom and bath. The nursery can be across the hall, and I could use the third room as a guest room or play-room when the time comes. The living room and kitchen are open and airy with a great backyard."

"The garage is detached. Are you sure you're okay with that?"

"That's fine. The breezeway is nice."

"We can look at bigger houses too," he offered.

"I don't want a bigger house. I want this one."

While Addie and Oliver worked out the details of the offer, I wandered through the house. There was an unfin-ished basement with a laundry area. The basement was a decent size. If she ever were to finish it, she could gain a lot more space. There was a dinky workout bench in the corner, and I pictured what that corner would look like as a real gym with weights and a heavy bench. But Addison wouldn't want a weight bench. She would want a room to do yoga and pilates. I needed to stop rearranging her basement with myself in mind.

I climbed the stairs and looked through the rooms. I kept envisioning myself here with Addison. Maybe it was just that old habits were hard to kill.

I'd envisioned a life with Deena, and that had fallen apart. Maybe Addison was the one I was supposed to end up with. As she stood in the kitchen talking to Oliver, I wondered if she realized she was resting a palm against her belly.

Perhaps it was some sort of primal instinct that made me want to make a nest with her. But that wasn't my bun in her oven and she didn't seem to want anyone, most of all, me. Why did that make me so sad?

WE DROPPED Oliver back off at Willa's, and as soon as Oli got out of the car, Willa pulled into the driveway. She parked next to us and got out of her car. I recognized her from the hotel in Michigan. Oliver went to her, wrapping his arm around her shoulder. She was dark and curvy and so much smaller than him. She and Addison were both beautiful women, but that's where their similarities ended.

Willa stepped toward Addison's car window, and Addison rolled it down. There was no mistaking the change in Addie. Her melancholy mood seemed to disappear. She forced her shoulders back, and a smile appeared on her lips. And then she put on a show.

Willa's eyes flicked to me and back to Addie, asking, "How'd the house hunt go?"

"I put an offer in on one," Addison's voice rose with an excitement she hadn't shown all day.

"Really?" Willa sounded delighted, and it baffled me. Shouldn't she see Addison as a threat? Was it some kind of fake happy game they played for Oliver's sake?

I leaned across the console and waved. "Hi, I'm Travis."

Willa's smile disappeared as her dark, soulful eyes seemed to stare straight through me. "I know who you are."

Her instant and obvious dislike of me made me smile, and I clarified, "You know of me. That doesn't mean you know who I am."

"No, I'm pretty sure I have a good idea." She pressed her lips together as she arched her brow, daring me to argue. Oliver squeezed her shoulders, and she took a breath. Her inability to play nice said a lot about her. It told me she wasn't one to shy away from confrontation, which meant her attitude towards Addison was genuine. She didn't seem capable of fluff. She wasn't a cotton candy kind of girl. She reeked of substance, and I respected her for it.

Addison cut in with her cotton candy manners, sugaring up the air. "Oliver will show you the house. I'm starving, or I'd do it myself."

Oliver said, "I'll call you when I hear from the sellers."

As we drove away, Addison's aura shifted. Her shoulders slumped, and worry lines creased her forehead.

I noted, "That was quite a show you put on."

She made no indication that she'd heard me, and that's when I realized how bad things really were.

I added, "It must be exhausting, watching them and pretending to be okay."

She still didn't bite, and I felt like an asshole, so I stopped talking. It was a half-hour back to her apartment, and I prepared myself for a long silence when she said, "Oli—the man who divorced me—has been the only one who's been there for me these past few months. And Willa has every right to hate me, but she's kinder to me than I deserve. They both are. If they knew it hurt me to be around them, then I would lose them both, and I can't lose him."

I blinked. Had I heard her right? She didn't want to lose Oliver. Did she regret their breakup? She hadn't shown him any sort of affection today. They hadn't even touched.

She blew out a shaky breath. "I know we made the right decision by splitting up, but it still hurts."

I swallowed. "I'm—"

She interrupted, "I realized how little Oliver understood me when he compared me to a rose. He always bought me those damn purple roses." She sighed at the memory. "I made them our wedding flowers even though I've always hated roses and I don't even know why. And then Oli compares me to a beautiful precious rose." She glanced at me, reiterating, "I'm not a fucking rose. I'm not some delicate flower that needs to be cared for. I'm not a pretty accessory you throw away after a few days. You know our wedding roses started wilting the very next day. Three days later, they had all wilted and started falling apart. I shredded them. Cut them into tiny pieces and buried them in the backyard."

I stared ahead at the road as I listened to her story.

She went on, "I tried to burn them, but the petals were too wet, so I buried them. I dug a hole and had a little funeral for our wedding roses. A funeral for the person Oliver thought I was—for the person I pretended to be for all those years. I've never been weak. I'm a fighter. A fucking survivor. I don't need you to come here and feel sorry for me. I don't need you to treat me like I'm a scared little bird. I'm doing just fine."

I gawked at her. "I never doubted you, and I'm not trying to fix you. I can't. I'm more fucked up than you are."

She sniffed. "I don't need you to hold me together."

"Are you saying that to yourself or me?" I asked. "Because I can't save you. I can't even save me." I groaned. "I'm pretending the same as you. We're both putting on a show while we put our lives back together one piece at a time, but it won't always be this way."

She reached over and grabbed my hand, squeezing it. "I hate how much I've missed you," she confessed.

"Right back at you, princess." I held her hand, never wanting to let go as old feelings and a new possessiveness overwhelmed me, but she pulled her hand out of my grip and placed it back on the steering wheel. She might have missed me, but that didn't mean she would allow herself to let me back in. I had hurt her, and I knew it would take time to regain her trust.

We were both going through some significant life changes, and it wasn't the right time for us to get involved. However, I planned to be there with her when that day came. I'd be damned if I let her go this time. But I wouldn't rush her. She needed time to sort herself out.

47

ADDISON

TRAVIS and I talked or texted every day for the next two weeks. After him being gone for so long, it was nice to have his attention, but I was still worried he'd disappear again.

So far, he hadn't let me down and I was starting to warm up a bit. I even invited him to come down to celebrate the house inspection going well. My closing date was only a few weeks away, set for October twelfth.

I took him to my favorite restaurant in Cincinnati. We took advantage of the rooftop seating. This place had the best veggie burgers I had ever tasted, and even though Travis thought veggie burgers were "fucking disgusting," he still tried one after I talked them up so much.

The following week, I drove up to Columbus. The entire ride there, I wondered if I was doing the right thing. At first, I thought about surprising Travis for his thirtieth birthday, but decided it was safer to see if he was okay with me coming to celebrate with him. He'd sounded excited.

I had a gourmet cake boxed up in my passenger seat. It was from the same bakery that made Oliver's and my wedding cake. I loved it at our cake tasting but barely got to taste it on our wedding day. Travis had raved about it. I thought it would be a treat for both of us. I also had stuffed two obnoxiously bright foil balloons in my trunk. The balloons were in the shape of a three and zero. I smirked just thinking of his reaction.

He'd told me to call him when I arrived so he could walk down and get me. It was only seven, and I hadn't expected to make it for another hour. I was early, but he said he would be home. I called as I rounded the block, searching for a parking spot.

"Hey, Addie. Are you on your way?"

"I'm here. I got an earlier start than anticipated."

"Shit. Listen, there's been a minor change of plans. Some of my friends from Phoenix just dropped in unexpectedly."

There was shouting in the background, and Travis muffled the phone before yelling at them to shut up.

I felt ignorant for not realizing his other friends would want to see him for his birthday. He never mentioned other people, but I should've known. Travis collected friends easily. He attracted all kinds of people with his wit and charm. Even his gruffness didn't seem to turn people away.

I was ready to drive back home when Travis said, "I'll meet you in front of the building. I have a parking spot for you."

"Travis, I can come back another time."

"No. I invited you. I didn't invite these fucktards. They just showed up."

"Erm..."

"Please, Addie. I'm on my way down."

"Okay," I relented, pulling in front of the building in the no-parking zone.

We hung up, and a moment later, he was opening my passenger door. I watched him climb in, and everything about him overwhelmed me. The smell of his cologne flooded my senses with memories of him. His smile filled me with so much warmth, pushing out any lingering thoughts about leaving. He gently picked up the cake box and moved it into his lap as he sat down, his size filling the space.

My lips parted, and for a moment, I felt breathless. His smile turned to the cake. "Did you get this for me?"

I pulled myself from my stupor and smiled. "It's not a birthday without cake. It's the same kind from the wedding."

He moaned, and I bit my cheek to keep me from smiling too big.

He directed me where to go, and we ended up in a parking garage attached to his building. After we parked, he carried his cake while I grabbed the obnoxious balloons from the trunk.

I said, "I would've brought a bigger cake had I known other people would be here."

"I had no idea they were coming." His eyes widened when he saw the balloons. "Wow, are those my balloons?"

I smiled. "Yes." I stepped forward and handed them to him. He gave me the cake before taking the balloons. With a smile, he led the way to his apartment.

"So, who is it that surprised you?" I asked as we stepped onto an elevator.

"Two of them lived in my building in Phoenix, and the other is someone I met at the gym. I apologize in advance. They're all a bit much, especially Devon."

"And they all just hopped on a plane to fly across the country to see you."

"These guys make stupid money. I'm pretty sure Devon has a big enough trust fund that he doesn't need to work."

I smiled. "You've come a long way from wanting to take a cheese grater to your balls before spending time with rich assholes."

He shrugged. "I didn't do it on purpose."

"What? Become a rich asshole?"

He scowled at me.

I smiled. "You have a big important job now and make enough money to live in a historic tower apartment in the center of the city. Your new friends have trust funds. And judging by your temporary license plates, you just bought an expensive new car."

He tilted his head as we exited the elevator. "Just because I finally make a little money doesn't make me an asshole."

I smiled. "That's true. You've always been an asshole."

He laughed, wrapping his arm around me. He kissed my temple and broke away to open his apartment door. I could hear the beat from the music before the door opened. Travis said, "I'm gonna kill 'em." He turned the knob, adding, "By the way, they don't know who you are, and I haven't told them anything about you."

He swung the door open, and the music grew tenfold. I stepped in, and the three guys pouring shots at the kitchen counter turned toward me to stare.

Travis walked in behind me and immediately turned down the Bluetooth speakers. "Fucking assholes. It's like you want my neighbors to hate me."

The guys were still staring at me, giving me a once over. I'd tried to look nice tonight, doing my makeup and curling my hair. I wore dark skinny jeans with a loose-fitting tunic. Between its fit, geometric design, and asymmetric hem, the shirt did an excellent job camouflaging my baby bump. It's not that I wanted to hide it necessarily, but I hated strangers thinking it was okay to touch my belly.

When Travis had said nothing about my appearance, I thought maybe I didn't know how to look cute anymore. But based on how the guys looked at me, I thought perhaps I did an okay job.

Travis stepped directly in front of me, looking me in the eye as he took the cake box from my hand. "We're not sharing this with them. We'll eat it later."

I nodded, and he turned away, walking to his fridge. I wondered about introductions, just as Travis said, "Guys, this is Addison. She's an old friend and off-limits for you dipshits, so don't even try."

"Addie, this is Pete, Jordan, and Devon. Pete and Jordan were my neighbors in Phoenix. We met Devon at the gym next-door."

Devon stepped forward, "Addison, it's nice to meet you. How do you know Travis?"

I glanced at Travis, who looked curious, probably wondering what I'd say. "We've been friends since high school. I tutored him in calculus."

"And she does just mean tutoring," Travis clarified.

Devon said, "So, you're smart."

Travis answered for me. "She's a doctor—a pediatric oncologist."

Devon's brows shot up. "That's fucking hot. Do you wear those lab coats doctors wear?"

I shrugged. "Sometimes."

"Mmm. I have a partial just thinking about you in nothing but a lab coat."

I glanced at Travis, who had his face in his palm while he

shook his head. Travis was protective, and I found it odd he wasn't sticking up for me. I put my hands to my belly, pulling the shirt in. "I'm six months pregnant."

Devon smiled. "Well then, I can't knock you up, can I?"

Jordan and Pete were no longer looking at us. They were pouring more shots. Travis stepped forward, smacking Devon in the back of the head. To me, he said, "Devon has been known to stuff his boxers with large pink dildos to trick women into thinking he's packing more than he's got."

Devon spun towards him. "How's that any different from a girl wearing a padded bra? You take the bra off, and boom, boobs disappear."

I laughed. "I mean, I guess I can see your point, but the dildo seems extreme."

"You're a doctor. Why is it that some men are showers and others are growers?"

I tilted my head. He couldn't be serious. "That's not my area of expertise, and just because I'm a doctor doesn't mean I want to hear about your body parts."

TRAVIS'S FRIENDS talked us into going out to a bar. I offered to drive, but there was no need as everything was within walking distance.

"Are you okay walking?" Travis asked as we stepped out of the building. "There's a bar in the building we can go to instead."

I narrowed my gaze on him. "T, I'm fine. I walk an average of ten miles a day."

"Damn." Pete said, "Isn't that too much while you're . . . you know . . . in your condition?"

"I have a normal pregnancy. It's good for me to maintain a healthy level of activity, and now that the hyperemesis has passed, I feel pretty good."

Devon asked, "Hyper what now?"

"Constant barfing," Travis said to Devon. He looked at me. "I'm glad that part is over."

"Me too."

WE'D BEEN at the bar for about an hour, and conversation flowed around me. The guys brought out a different side of Travis than I was used to seeing. He seemed so carefree around his friends. Then again, he was the same way with Deena. So maybe I had it backwards. Perhaps it was Oli and me that made Travis feel on guard. It made sense, and I felt stupid for not realizing I put Travis on edge. Or at least I used to. Things felt different tonight.

I knew the real Travis, but observing him now, I second-guessed myself. I'd never seen him look so comfortable in his own skin. He wasn't trying to prove his worth or acting like a hardass. I hadn't realized how forced his confidence had been until I watched him now with his easy confidence and worry-free smile. He let things roll off his back in a way I had never witnessed before.

It seemed Travis had matured.

He was up playing pool when Devon leaned toward me, asking, "Is baby daddy in the picture?"

"He is, but we're not together."

He nodded. "So you like Travis?"

"We've been friends for twelve years," I said, staying diplomatic.

"Why haven't you ever dated?"

"Never the right time."

His gaze moved to Travis, and he confessed, "He was a miserable bastard after Deena. I'm glad he seems to be getting over her."

I turned toward him. "We're not a couple."

He glanced at me. "I know, but this is the first time I've seen him smile in months, so whatever you've got going on seems positive. I was worried he'd off himself. That's why we're here, but he seems like he's doing better now."

I seriously hoped he was being dramatic, and Travis wasn't doing so poorly. He'd seemed shaken but not suicidal. I looked over at Travis, who was lining up a shot.

Devon went on, "Travis is a chick magnet. I need to go take care of his overflow."

I kept observing Travis. So many women had approached him, and his friendliness came off as flirty. I'm not sure he even realized it, but ultimately, he turned everyone away. He also not so subtly invited his friends to stay at a hotel. The guys didn't seem to mind, and Travis and I left them at the bar a few hours after we arrived.

"You don't have to leave on my account," I told him as we walked out into the cool late September evening.

"I can't stop thinking about that cake you brought me." He rubbed his hands together in anticipation.

"I hope it's as good as we remember."

It was.

We sat at his kitchen bar, and I marveled at how far we had come from those seventeen-year-old kids who thought they had everything figured out. Now, at thirty, we realized how much we still had to learn.

"Thanks for coming for my birthday, Addie." There was a spark in his eye.

I nodded. "I wouldn't miss it."

His long gaze made me look elsewhere. I needed to leave before I did something stupid—like kiss him. I loved his attention far too much, especially since I knew how bad it felt when his attention disappeared.

48

TRAVIS

Two weeks after my birthday, Addison closed on her new house. That weekend, I agreed to drive down to help her move.

Addison had a movable storage unit, so all we had to do was pull it into the driveway and unpack it. Everything was labeled, and I would expect nothing less from Addie. She was over six months along, and Oliver didn't want her moving anything heavy. So Oliver and I did the heavy lifting while she directed us. We put all the boxes and furniture in their designated rooms.

As Oli and I were carrying in a couch, he said, "This reminds me of moving Addie into her New York apartment for med school."

I nodded. "Except this couch is heavier."

Oli grumbled, "It has a hide-a-bed."

"Somebody better sleep on this bed," I called, loud enough so Addie could hear.

"It's good to have just in case," she said.

Oli laughed. "That means she has no plans to use it."

"You better at least let Emerson use it when she's old enough. Unfold it and make a pillow-fort or something," I suggested.

Later in the afternoon, Willa came by, bringing lunch. She stayed to help unload boxes in the kitchen. By evening, we had most of the house unpacked. One bedroom was used as storage for holiday decorations and miscellaneous boxes. The nursery remained empty, awaiting the matching crib, rocker, and changing table Addison had ordered. Addison's bedroom furniture was in place, but we hadn't unpacked those boxes. She insisted on unpacking her room later, once everyone left.

In the evening, once Oliver and Willa were gone, I ordered a pizza for me and a salad for Addison. "Are you sure you're eating enough?"

"Yes. I snack all through the day," she said before taking another bite of her salad.

"Yeah, but are you getting enough protein?"

"Yes, T." She gave me an exhausted look, and I knew she had to be tired. I let go of the topic.

When Addison finished eating, she leaned back in her seat at the dining table and looked around the open floor plan. She sighed. "We accomplished a lot today. Thanks for helping, T."

I swallowed my bite and said, "I know you're using me for my muscle."

She laughed. "Duh." She looked down the hall toward her bedroom, looking wistful.

I said, "Why don't you go organize your room while I clean this up."

She stifled a yawn and nodded. "Thank you, T. I'm getting tired."

"I know. At least get your bed together so you can sleep comfortably tonight."

She pushed away from the table. "Good idea."

She walked down the hall and disappeared into the master bedroom. She was acting more and more comfortable with me being around. I counted each minor success. When I finished eating, I cleaned up the food and joined Addison in her bedroom. The bed was still unmade, and she was hastily pulling boxes open to search their contents.

"How's it going?" I asked from the doorway.

She ran her fingers through her hair and huffed, "I can't find the sheets."

I moved forward and started picking through boxes on the other side of the room. "This open one is labeled bedding."

Addison glanced over, saying, "It was just pillows. There should be another one labeled bedding, but I don't see it."

"This one says blankets."

"That's not it either."

"Let me see if we accidentally put them in the other room." I went into the spare room across the hall and began sorting through boxes.

"Travis!"

She sounded panicked. I rushed back to her room. "What?"

She was standing by the bed looking down at her hands on her belly.

I looked for blood. "Did you hurt yourself?"

She looked up with a smile, saying, "Come here."

As soon as I moved forward, she grabbed my hand and pressed it against her abdomen. I felt a little nudge against my palm—the baby. My eyes widened, and I jerked them to Addie's face. She wore a thoughtful smile.

"It's the baby," she confirmed.

"Have you felt her move before?"

"Yes, but not like this." She kept feeling her belly even after Emerson seemed to settle.

Her face fell, and she sniffed.

I put my hand on her cheek, lifting her chin. "Whoa, whoa, why're you crying?"

She took a steadying breath, saying, "I knew this was going to happen soon, and I'm . . . I'm happy I'm not alone. That I have someone here to experience this with me." She blew out a breath. "I know I'm being irrational."

I pulled her into a hug. "No, you aren't. This is a big deal, and I'm fortunate to get to share it with you. It's a special moment."

Over her shoulder, I noticed the closet door was cracked open, and inside was a stack of boxes. "Have you looked in the closet?" I asked when she pulled away.

She shook her head. "I thought it was empty."

She went to check and found the box she was looking for on top. She pulled it to the floor and opened it, finding multiple sheet sets inside vacuum-sealed bags.

I helped her make the bed, and once we finished, she laid on top. "I'm so tired."

She patted the other side of the queen bed.

I laid down and rolled to face her. She smiled at me while adjusting the pillow under her head.

I did the same, and when we settled, she whispered, "Hi."

"Hi."

"Are you still planning to drive home tonight?"

I shrugged. "I don't know. That pull-out sofa is looking pretty good right now."

She smiled. "You're welcome to stay. You can give the hide-a-bed a purpose." Her eyes closed. "You know where the sheets are."

"I'll let you sleep." I moved to get up, but she reached out, her hand capturing mine.

Her eyes opened to look at me. "Thank you for being here, T." Her eyelids seemed too heavy to keep open, but her hand held firm to mine.

"I'm glad you let me."

She sighed, and her breathing evened out, her hand going limp in my own as she fell asleep. I watched her sleep for a while, loving the way slumber wiped the worry from her face. Eventually, my own lids became too heavy to keep from closing.

I WOKE TO DARKNESS. Addison must have woken and turned off the lights. She tucked herself under her blankets, and she must have draped a soft blanket over me. I was a light sleeper. How had I not woken, and why hadn't she tried to wake me?

I hadn't meant to fall asleep in here. Did she want me in here with her? She had found a blanket to cover me so I wouldn't get cold. The simple act struck me as sweet. Maybe I was reading into it. It was probably something any decent human would do, but Addison had kept a certain porcupine-like behavior toward me since I had returned to her life. Whenever she felt we were getting too close, she would rattle her quills, becoming brash as a way of telling me to back off.

But tonight, she kept her quills down, and I didn't know what to make of it.

On my birthday, I feel like Addison got the impression I had my life together. From the outside, it did look that way, but my breakup with Deena haunted me. It left me feeling hollow and angry. Being around Addison seemed to soothe that anger. It didn't make sense. Addison hadn't been especially kind, but I needed her to be brash with me. I didn't want her sympathy. When I was with her, I didn't feel as sad, and I didn't want to talk about what happened with Deena.

I hadn't seen Deena coming and was blindsided. She swept me off my feet, taking my breath away. It was one of the most profound connections I had ever made. Part of me was still reeling from losing her, but I would never go back. There was no future there. Too many things had been said and done that we could never take back. I thought we were unbreakable, but we broke—shattered, and now I stared at Addison, wondering what I actually had to offer her—a broken heart? She already had one of those.

I still couldn't help but think about the future, wondering what it would be like to wake up next to Addison every day.

One day, our hearts would no longer feel so heavy. I wished I could skip forward to those days.

TO MY UTTER DISAPPOINTMENT, Addison was not cuddled up against me when I woke. She wasn't even in the room. She must have made her side of the bed and left. I rolled over and put my feet on the floor, getting myself tangled in the blanket she laid over me. I untangled myself and folded it on the bed before going to look for Addison.

I found her in the living room, lounging in an oversized upholstered chair, looking gorgeous with her bare face and messy hair. She had her legs tucked up on the chair under a blanket and a mug of something steaming between her palms.

"Good morning," she greeted.

"Good morning. Why didn't you kick me out of your bed? I didn't mean to fall asleep."

She shrugged. "You looked so comfortable. I didn't want to wake you. Do you want some breakfast?"

I rubbed at my eyes. "No. I should go. I have to get some work done before Monday, and I didn't bring my laptop. What's your schedule like this week?"

"Today is my last day off for a while. I'm going to do some more unpacking and enjoy the house while I can since I'll be at my apartment all week."

"You have your birthday off, don't you?"

She nodded. "I work that morning but then have the evening and next three days off."

"I'll be back for your birthday. Do you have anything planned?"

"No." There was a sadness that fell over her. It was the first year she didn't have something planned on her birthday, and it was her milestone thirtieth birthday.

"Now you do," I said with a smile. "I can take you out for veggie burgers and Shirley Temples."

She laughed and agreed.

And I couldn't wait.

49

TRAVIS

I SPENT MORE and more time with Addison. I could work from anywhere so visiting her usually wasn't an issue. When I couldn't make the trip to see her, we still spoke or texted nearly every day. I was beginning to forget my heartbreak, and she had kept her quills tucked neatly in place. By November, she was opening up to me about work—the good and the heartbreaking.

I promised myself a long time ago that if Addison and Oliver ever broke up, I wouldn't let Addie slip through my fingers. She'd be mine. I knew at least part of her loved me, but she was pregnant with Oliver's baby, and I didn't know how that would complicate her feelings.

My tongue should be bloody and raw from biting it so often. I made a concerted effort to keep from calling her beautiful or gorgeous, or telling her I wanted to wake up next to her every morning. It had only gotten harder to restrain myself, and I barely kept myself from kissing her on her birthday.

A week later, I drove down to see her again. I couldn't get

enough. We had just returned to her apartment from having dinner out to celebrate her patient's cancer-free diagnosis. She was lighter than I'd seen her in ages. She stripped out of her coat and hung it in the closet, along with mine. We usually met at her apartment since there were more things to do in the city, and it was a half-hour closer to me. I had slept on her couch a few times after I'd stayed too late to make the trek home, but we had kept things platonic.

She sat on the couch, and I joined her. "Gracie would be proud of you."

She smiled. "I hope you're right."

"When have I ever been wrong?"

She laughed softly, and the sound hit me in the chest. Her smile affected me in ways that didn't make sense. Her blue eyes sparkled in the dim light, and my grin melted as our eyes locked. This woman made my blood sing. I had to touch her, so I did. Her skin was silk as I ran my knuckles over her jaw.

Her smile waned as her lips parted. Her eyes closed. She lifted a hand to mine, holding it still while she pulled her face away from my touch. "T, we can't."

"Why?"

"I'm having Oliver's baby."

I leaned in, keeping my voice low. "So that means I can't touch you? I can't love you because you're pregnant with his baby."

She shook her head, avoiding eye contact. "It's not about Oliver. I don't want to get involved with anyone right now, especially you."

I jerked back. "Why, especially me?"

Her grief-stricken eyes met mine. "Because you're too important to me, Travis. You're my best friend. And because you're still heartbroken over Deena. I deserve more than being a consolation prize. Our mistakes have already cost us too much. Loving you is the reason Oli and I split."

My eyes narrowed. "Oliver is happy, so why can't you be happy?"

"I am happy."

I lifted her chin, whispering, "Addie, we could be—"

"I'm trying to do the right thing here, T. Please, don't force this." She was breathing hard.

"Why?" I asked, almost silent in my pleading.

"You won't like what I have to say."

"You don't have to say anything." I wrapped my hand around the back of her neck, feeling goosebumps spread across her skin as her nipples peaked. I loved the way her body responded to me.

She tried to pull away, but I just needed her to turn off the analytical part of her brain and just feel me. So instead of letting her go, I pulled her closer, demanding her attention. My mouth crushed hers, and immediately her lips moved against mine even as she pushed against me. She sighed into my mouth as her body reacted. I ran my hands down her back, feeling the tension release from her posture.

When I pulled back slowly. Her eyes remained closed. When they opened, she said, "Travis, you should leave."

"Why?"

She pulled further from me. "Because I can't be with you right now."

"Addie, we've spent the last two weeks together. I've come to visit you almost every day."

"Yeah, but not like this."

I sat back. "I don't get it. You say I'm your best friend, and you and I both know we have chemistry. Your body lights up like a fucking Christmas tree when I touch you. What is it you don't want?"

She huffed, "I told you. I don't want that kind of relationship right now."

"Seriously, Addie? We're already in *that* kind of relationship."

She shook her head in refusal, denying what was so obvious. "No, we're friends, and just because we slept together in the past doesn't mean that is what's happening this time. We're friends, T. That's all."

"Is that all you'll ever want from me, Addie? Because I gotta say, I want a lot more than that. I want all of it—all of you. You've already got me by my balls. You have for years."

Her lips parted in a gasp.

I pulled her toward me, burying my face in her hair. Lowering my lips to her neck, I kissed a line from her jaw to her shoulder. Against her skin, I whispered. "I can't turn it off, Addie. I've fucking tried."

"T . . ."

I sat back, seeing the regret in her expression, and feeling like my heart was clutched between her fingers. "Don't reject me, Addie."

She cradled her round stomach as she pulled back. "I have to do what's best for us. And right now, that means being alone. I'm sorry, T, but neither of us are ready. You know that's true."

I closed my eyes, exhaling defeat. My jaw worked as I held in my emotions, but it was too much. It was all too fucking much. I laughed. "I always thought Oliver was the reason we weren't together, but I never had a chance, did I?"

"Travis, that's not it. It's—"

I held out a hand to stop her, shaking my head. "It's simple, Addie. Either you want all of me or none of me. You don't get to pick and choose."

Her voice grew hard. "You're giving me an ultimatum?"

I ran a hand down my face. "Jesus, Addie, it shouldn't be that difficult. I'm fucking stupid in love with you. I have been for fucking ever. Do you feel even a fraction of that for me?"

A tear slid down her cheek as she shook her head. "Stop it, T. You know you're my best friend."

"Is that all I am? Your friend."

She held her breath for a long time before exhaling, "Yes." She swallowed. "Right now, yes."

I shook my head, determined to make her see. "You can deny it all you want, princess, but when I'm near, your pulse zings to life." I ran my fingers from her shoulder to her neck. "A chill of anticipation spreads over your skin, and your nipples peak." My palm grazed her cheek. "Your breath catches." My thumb ran over her parted lips. "You're desperate for a taste, which is why that wicked tongue of yours moistens those full lips before they part, desperate for me."

I stared her in the eye, challenging, "I'm no doctor, Addie, but that sounds like arousal to me. Part of you wants to slap me because you know I'm right, but mostly you're dying for me to taste the sweet pool between your thighs. Tell me I'm wrong."

She grabbed my hand and pulled it away from her face. "Just because you evoke a physical response from me doesn't mean I want sex from you. I'm not driven purely by my base desires, Travis. I'm an accomplished adult, and I didn't get here by pursuing every impulsive whim. My body doesn't rule all of my decisions."

I narrowed my gaze. "So which part of you decided to sleep with me while you and Oliver were together?"

Her eyes pinched. "I never said I didn't make mistakes, but my answer today is no."

"How can I hate you so much and still love you? Thank God you're a better doctor than you are a friend. And I hope your little girl takes after Oli."

That seemed to strike a nerve, and she jumped off the couch, fuming, "You're like a toddler lashing out because you didn't get what you want. Is that why Deena left? Are you always so mean when you lose an argument?"

I stood, too, defeat settling heavily on my heart. I sighed, "Don't fool yourself, princess. There are no winners here tonight."

I was a fucking idiot. I turned and walked for the door.

Addison cried out, "So that's it? Our friendship is over. Just like that?"

"You think that's painful," I snapped, looking over my shoulder. "Just imagine having blue balls for twelve fucking years." I gripped the door handle. It was important for me to get out before I talked myself into some fucked up compromise just to keep part of her.

50

ADDISON

A SHRILL RING WOKE ME, and I groaned. I was so tired and didn't want to go to the hospital. But wait, I wasn't on call tonight. I grabbed my phone and didn't recognize the number.

"Doctor Addison Arthur," I answered.

"You fucked up," the voice slurred.

I closed my eyes, rubbing at my face. "Travis?"

"Yeah, 'member me?"

I sat up. "Where are you?"

"I dunno," he slurred, and I heard panting.

"Travis . . ."

He groaned into the phone.

"Tra—" I was cut off by a woman's voice, demanding, "Faster baby, faster."

My breath caught and I felt a spike of ice stab at my heart. "Are you kidding me, Travis?"

"Someone thinks I'm good enough."

My shock and pain turned to anger. "Jesus, T. This is fucked up. Even for you."

"More fucked up than hearing you and Oli going at it for years."

A woman moaned long and loud. "Don't stop, baby."

Disgusted, I disconnected and threw my phone on the bed as I got up to pace my room. The intention of his call was to hurt me, and I wouldn't let myself cry over him. If anything, this just proved I had made the right decision.

Eventually I got back in bed and I tossed and turned, trying to get back to sleep.

An hour later, my phone rang with another unknown number.

My heart hammered in my chest as I answered, "Doctor Addison Arthur."

"Hey doctor Addison Arthur, this is bartender Mike," he said with a hint of teasing. "I have someone here claiming he belongs to you. Do you know Travis?"

"Yes."

"He dropped his phone in his drink, but he keeps trying to get ahold of you. If you don't come get him, then I'm calling the cops to pick him up. He's breaking shit."

"Of course he is," I groaned. "Doesn't he have a girl with him?"

"The girls seem to have left him here. He said you'd come pick him up. I can call the cops instead, but he begged me to call you."

I slid out of bed. "I'll be there, but do us all a favor and tell him he's acting like his father."

"Yeah, I'm not gonna do that. He's broken enough of my shit."

"Fine, I'll do it when I get there."

Travis shouted in the background. "Hi, Addie, 'member when we fuuucked."

"Jesus," I hissed, "Where are you calling from?"

"Mike's Bar and Grill on Main. But no one would blame you for letting me call the cops. I just kinda felt bad for him."

"No, it's fine. I'll be there in fifteen."

After the call I received an hour ago, I questioned my immediate response to go to his rescue. But I knew the Travis who called an hour ago wasn't the same Travis I had known for the last twelve years. He seemed more like the guy Devon had described at Travis's birthday. I was mad at him, but that didn't mean I wasn't also worried.

I threw on some clothes and drove to the bar. I found parking easy enough as most bars were closing. When I pulled the heavy door open, my hand went to my belly before I even realized it. I pulled it away and rolled my shoulders back as I entered.

The bar was almost empty, but the mess spoke of a much larger crowd. Behind the bar, a guy who looked to be in his mid-thirties asked, "You Addison?"

I nodded.

"I'm sorry, it's Doctor Addison, isn't it?" he said with a flirtatious grin.

I put my hand back to my belly, pulling the flowy shirt in to show off the baby bump. That usually stopped the flirtation. "Where is he?"

Mike's eyes dropped to my belly and his eyebrows rose. "That his baby?"

I glared at him. "Is that your business?" I snapped, then remembered he wasn't the cause of my anger, and apologized, "Sorry. No, it's not his baby."

"Sounds like he'd sure like it to be."

"Yeah, well, we have a complicated history." Why was I telling him this?

Travis was half on a stool, his upper half draped over the bar, trying to reach for a bottle that he wasn't even close to reaching.

"Come on, Travis," I clipped.

He spun toward me, and a lazy grin spread across his face. "Hey, Addie!" he slurred in excitement. His shirt was stained, and his fly was open. His hair stood up, disheveled, and he had a bruise on his cheek. His head swayed as he looked at me with unfocused eyes. My heart broke. He looked just like his father.

He grabbed his crotch with his cracked and bloody fist. "You come back for this dick?"

"You're being a dick, alright. Come on. I'm your ride."

"I'll ride you," he hiccupped and laughed at his joke.

I rolled my eyes. "Either you come with me or the cops are gonna come pick you up because you're making a complete ass out of yourself."

His smirk melted into such a sad frown. Tears came to his eyes as he grabbed my arm, pulling me forward with both hands so he could lean his head against me. "Why can't you love me? What's so wrong with me. I'd be so good ta you."

God, he was a disaster, and the pregnancy made me emotional, but I held in my emotions, saying, "Come on, T."

"Teeee," he repeated. "Tha's what ya call me when you like me, bu' you don'." He pulled away.

I looked up at Mike. "Why didn't you cut him off?"

"I did."

Travis grinned like the cat who ate the canary. "Shhh," he put his hand to his lips and loudly whisper-slurred, "Some girls were sharin' drinks wit' me. I'm a hot commodditiddy. conomidty, comididy, comm—you know that word. It's hard ta say."

"Come on, Travis." I held my hand out to him. "Can you stand?"

He nodded robotically, trying to appear more sober than he was. He pushed my hand away and stood, immediately falling to his knees.

His biggest fear in life was being like his father and now as I looked at him, I watched his biggest fear coming to life. I looked to the ceiling and took a calming breath.

While I was looking up, Travis scooted forward on his knees. He wrapped his arms around me, laying his head against my round belly. He lifted my shirt, so his face was against my skin as he kissed my stomach, mumbling, "Hey baby, Emmmerson. It's uncle T. You gotta li'l time ta cook, but I can't wait ta meet you. I'ma love you sooo much. I could'a been a good dad."

I put my hand on his head, smoothing his hair. Sweet Travis was my biggest weakness. I felt his tears against my skin. He was a train wreck, but he was my train wreck. I loved him, despite what he thought.

He continued to hold his arms around my legs. After a moment, I said, "Come on, T."

His hands glided up the back of my legs, sliding up to grip my ass.

"Come on, man," the bartender said, grabbing the back of his shirt to "help" him up. The bartender was a big guy, but Travis was bigger, and even with my help, the two of us struggled to get Travis to his feet.

The walk to the car was slow. Thank God Mike helped me. On the way out the door, Mike said, "I liked you a lot better the first time we met."

I realized he was talking to Travis. "Wait, you two know each other?"

Mike said, "We met at my buddy's barbecue a few months back. We started talking music. He seemed like a good dude, but shit, he's rough tonight."

"He's usually much more pleasant."

"You're an angel for picking him up. I kinda feel irresponsible sending him home with you."

I shrugged the shoulder that wasn't holding Travis up. "I've dealt with worse as a doctor."

Travis turned his head toward me and smiled. "I knew you'd come for me."

Once we got him buckled into the front seat, I thanked Mike and slipped him a hundred-dollar bill. Once Travis sobered up, I was going to send him back here to apologize and pay for any damages. I rounded to the driver's seat and climbed in behind the wheel.

As I buckled myself in, Travis's head lulled towards me from the passenger seat. "Those women didn't think I was defective. They let me kiss 'em. Both of 'em. They made me feel like a man. Not like you. You just turn me down even though I make you purr. You're like crystal, and they're like warm beer, but at least warm beer doesn't treat me like I don' matter. They love me more dan you."

"You think that's love?"

He shrugged. "What would I know? I left all the girls who could love me to be with a heartless bitch who can't love me back."

"You're a mean drunk."

"Ha. If only Papa could see me now. Wouldn't he be proud?"

He became silent. I wondered if he was reflecting on his life decisions, but as we stopped at a light, I peeked over and saw him roll back in his seat, his face looking a shade too light. The sheen across his forehead, along with the long breath he blew out, told me I didn't have long before he puked. I cracked his window, and he lifted his face toward the cold air, breathing it in.

"I'll pull over up here," I told him, rolling his window the rest of the way down.

He didn't give me any indication that he'd heard me, but I pulled to the side of the road, and as soon as we stopped, he leaned out the window, and dry heaved but didn't throw up.

I rubbed his back, and after a few moments, he sat back in his seat, and I pulled onto the road continuing to my apartment.

We got to my apartment, and I helped unload him out of the car. "You're gonna have to use your legs. I can't carry you."

He wrapped his arm around my shoulder, and somehow, he managed to keep himself upright all the way to the elevator, up the elevator, down the hall, and into my apartment.

He collapsed on the couch, leaning his head back to look up at the ceiling. I put water in the plastic sippy cup he gave me as a gag gift, and I grabbed a puke bucket for him.

I set it down in front of him, saying, "It's water."

He cracked a smile when he saw the cup, and then his heavy eyes lifted to me and his smile faded. "I don't deserve you," he slurred. "But you still take care've me." He held out his arm, gesturing for me to come forward.

I hesitated, stepping back to keep from caving.

He watched the movement, and his eyes closed as his head fell back again. "It hurts."

"What hurts?"

"Everything. I need the pain to go away." His body slumped to the side and he laid down on the couch.

"Next time, don't drink so much."

"Not that." He shook his head. "The other pain. The one that makes me sad. I'm so sad. What is all this suffering for, anyway? God's laughing at us. Laughing and laughing and laughing." He curled up on the couch as his voice grew softer. "Don't you hear it sometimes? The laughter?"

He sounded like a psych patient. I sat down next to his head, running my fingers through his hair.

He was crying. "Deena ruined me, Add. Nobody will ever want me."

"You're not ruined, T. You're going to be okay."

His hand brushed my knee, and then he was pushing himself up. He stood and stumbled to the bathroom where I heard him retching as he voided the contents of his stomach. I pushed off the couch and followed with his water.

I HAD BARELY GOTTEN four hours of sleep. I was afraid Travis would choke on his vomit, so I stayed up with him well into the night. He fell asleep on the bathroom floor, but at some point after five AM, he must have crawled into my bed with me. It was nine when I dragged myself out of bed, leaving him to sleep off the hangover that was sure to be a doozy.

Hours later, I heard signs of life. The toilet flushed and I heard running water. A few minutes later, Travis emerged from my bedroom. I stood in the kitchen, making my third cup of tea.

As a greeting, Travis said, "Where is my phone?"

I shrugged. "According to the bartender, you dropped it in your drink."

He shielded his eyes from the sun as he moved forward. "That sucks."

He sat on a stool at the kitchen counter where he folded his arms on the granite and dropped his forehead onto them, groaning, "I think . . . I think I fucked up last night. I don't remember the last time I drank that much."

"You were a mess."

"I think I got into a fistfight," he said to the counter.

"I can't confirm that, but I think you did too based on your face and knuckles."

He blew out a breath, admitting. "I think I might've had sex with someone."

"You did."

He lifted his head slowly.

I clarified, "You called me."

His eyebrows pinched with a look of horror. "Like to tell you about it afterwards?"

"No." I shook my head. "During."

He held his breath and lowered his head back onto his arms, his voice muffled as he asked, "Why did you pick me up?"

"Because if I didn't, you would've ended up in jail."

"You should've let me go to jail."

"I think what you meant to say is thank you for not letting me go to jail, Addison."

He groaned. "I'm so sorry, Addie."

I moved across from him, placing a hand on his shoulder. "For the record, I wasn't turning you down because I thought you weren't good enough. It isn't the right time for us, and everything that happened last night proved that. It isn't that I don't love you, Travis. I wouldn't have picked you up if I didn't love you. And I'm trying to react to your drunken hookup as a friend would. Not like a spiteful, angry girlfriend."

He blew out a breath.

I continued, "Last night, you told me that Deena ruined you. You begged me to take the pain away. I believe that you love me, but if there is ever hope for us in the future, you have to take care of yourself." I grabbed his hand. "I'm going to give you a hard truth that you won't want to hear."

He raised his face to me.

"You were acting like your father last night."

I tried to hold on, but he pulled his hand from mine and spun away.

I continued, "That's not who you are. I'll be your friend, but I won't be your crutch. And I won't end up heartbroken like your mom."

His eyes grew wide. "You've really mastered that whole kick 'em while they're down, haven't you?" He ran both hands over his scalp. "I'm gonna go." He stood, grabbing his jacket from the back of the couch. He pulled it on, feeling for his keys and wallet. I knew they were there because I had put them there myself. "Can I borrow your phone to call for a ride?"

"No," I said, grabbing my purse. "I promised Mike I'd bring you back myself."

"Who the fuck is Mike?"

I slipped into my coat, saying, "The bartender who called me instead of the cops. You owe him an apology."

"Oh, that Mike." He sighed. "Fuck."

We drove to the bar in silence. And when we arrived, he said, "I'll go in and make amends. Thanks for the ride and stuff." He glanced at me. "I'll see you around, Addie."

Then he was gone again.

51

TRAVIS

IT WAS only noon when I entered the bar. I remembered coming here last night, but I did not recognize the mess. The bartender was sweeping up broken bottles beneath a table.

Mike's Bar and Grill hadn't been random. I met Mike two months ago at a coworker's barbecue in Columbus. He told me if I was ever in Cincinnati to visit his bar. I bet he regretted that, now. Having a friend in common is probably the only reason he hadn't called the cops on me. That and I wasn't a fucking disaster the first time he met me.

He noticed me and paused his sweeping. "So that angel of a woman didn't murder you?"

"She did not. Thank you for calling her instead of the cops. I'm sorry I was out of control last night. I'll pay for any damages."

"I think you can do better than that," he said, setting down the broom and walking toward me. "Last night, when you were begging me not to call the cops, you said you could fix the sound system. Is that true?"

Apparently, I was feeling cocky or desperate because I had no idea if I could fix it. "I don't know. I can take a look."

"It's back here." He led me to a room for employees where security footage and the sound system controls sat side by side.

"You have a lot of cameras," I noted, seeing live footage on the surveillance grid.

"Yes, I do. It would cover my ass if anything were to happen. I have years' worth of footage, just in case." He hovered over a file dated yesterday. "You wanna see how big of a prick you were being? Just click on that file."

"I'd rather not."

He showed me the sound system, and I realized it wasn't the sound system that was the problem. It was more of a computer issue. I went to work, using the internet to learn the parts I didn't know. An hour and a migraine later, I was restarting the system. While I waited for it to reboot, I clicked on the footage from last night.

I fast-forwarded into the evening and hit play. On-screen, I watched myself stumble toward a table of women. I swayed and caught myself on the table. I swore I was watching my father. The way I moved and stumbled in my drunken state. I fast-forwarded through the part of me taking a woman to the bathroom with me. Then I was fighting, or more like getting my ass beat. No wonder I was sore. The fight broke up quickly, and I threw glass bottles at the wall. What the fuck was wrong with me? I didn't recognize myself, and the similarities to my father were unmistakable. I clicked out of the security feed and focused on the sound system.

Soon enough, I had music blasting from the speakers. I turned it down before my head exploded and met Mike by the bar. He had finished cleaning the space. Everything was back to normal, aside from the broken booth in the corner, a casualty to the fight I had started.

Mike smiled, "Hey, you fixed it!"

I nodded. "I'll pay for the booth I broke too."

"So you watched the footage?"

"Enough of it."

"You were having a bad night. It happens."

This guy seemed pretty unshakable, and I thought I'd at least try to get some information out of him. "You remember those girls I was with last night?"

He nodded. "Yeah. Two of them are regulars. The one you hooked up with left her panties and the used condom on the bathroom floor."

"Fuck." I ran a hand over my face. "I'm sorry. I can't remember the details."

"Her name's Mary. She's harmless, and you didn't knock her up. She had a hysterectomy a few years ago that she's very vocal about when she's had a few drinks."

I stared at him. "Well, aren't you a spring of information."

Mike shrugged. "Only on my regulars. Do you want something to eat? Soak up some of that hangover."

"Nah, I've gotta get home. How much do I owe you for the table?"

I paid him for the booth table and thanked him again for putting up with me. Then I was driving back to Columbus, set on avoiding Cincinnati for the rest of my life.

52

ADDISON

Thanksgiving was coming up, and I was relieved to work the holiday, so I didn't have to try to make plans or feel pathetic as I stayed home sulking. I would work with sick children on Thanksgiving, and if nothing else, that really brought perspective to my life.

The week before Thanksgiving, I called my stepmother, hoping she would answer my call. We had talked a few times, but I could tell she felt uneasy about our conversations. She didn't want to rock the boat by bringing up uncomfortable subjects, and she was so graceful in her avoidance, evading truths with eloquence. She didn't just tiptoe. She was a ballerina dancing en pointe around significant issues. We discussed frivolous topics, which made me roll my eyes and want to pull out my hair.

How had I ever considered that normal? Is that what my relationship with Emerson would become?

I could sense my mother was about to make an excuse to go, but I needed something more concrete. I tried to be delicate and bring it up casually, but I'm sure she found it loud and tacky, tap shoes stomping on her ballerina slippers. I didn't care. I needed something more. "I might be in New York around Christmas. Oliver's family invited me. They want to see me."

"That's wonderful, dear," she gushed. "I'm delighted you could maintain a friendly relationship with Oliver's family after all the difficulties over the summer."

Difficulties? I wanted to laugh.

"I thought since I was in the area . . ." I let the sentence dangle, hoping she would snap it up and invite me over, but she said nothing. "Could I come home to visit?"

I cringed at the desperation in my voice. I squeezed my eyes tight and swallowed, holding my breath as I awaited her response.

"Your father is still upset, Addison. He asked that you not visit this Christmas. I would love to meet with you separately if I could find the time to step away."

Sneak away is what she really meant.

I sighed. "No, no. I know your holiday schedule is quite hectic. We'll find another time. Perhaps once Emerson is born."

Her voice was soft but reluctant as she said, "This hasn't been easy on your father—this rift between the two of you. If you would apologize for your behavior and admit you made a mistake, then I'm sure he would forgive you."

I let out a breath of disappointment. Whenever I spoke to her, she made me doubt myself, but I would not feel ashamed of my behavior.

I queried, "You still volunteer at a battered women's shelter, yes?"

"Of course." She sounded unsure of where I was going.

"Do you ask those battered women to apologize for their behavior because it is hard on their abuser?"

"This is not the same thing," she snapped. "Your father has never mishandled you and implying such is despicable. You're better than this, Addison."

"And I thought you were better too. What a disappointment for us both."

"I will not continue this conversation. Do not call again until you've learned some respect." She hung up.

I looked down at my phone, feeling numb. I wandered around the house aimlessly, forgetting what I was doing before that disaster of a call. I ended up staring out my front window, watching the two kids across the street from my house. They were out playing in their front yard while their father was in the open garage working on something. He kept taking breaks to play with the kids, and it hurt to watch them.

My father was nothing like the man playing with his children. My father was distant and impersonal most of the time, but I lived for his rare moments of praise. I ate them up. I broke myself trying to impress him while the dad I watched now praised his daughter for trying and failing to shoot a basketball through the hoop. There was no way she could make it. Her tiny three-year-old arms lacked the strength to make a full-sized hoop.

Her older brother retrieved the ball and gave it back to her. When she went to shoot again, her dad lifted her, holding her right next to the hoop while she giggled and dropped the ball through it. He cheered for her, and she beamed as the three of them celebrated together. I smiled for her as tears spilled down my cheeks.

My dad had never praised me for trying. Only achieving.

Only winners were worth anything in his mind. I should've hated him for the love he withheld, but it only made me more desperate for his affection.

Even now, knowing he was a cold man, I still wanted his approval, and his rejection hit me somewhere deep.

In his eyes, I had failed. I would not apologize. Not this time. I wouldn't grovel for his love no matter how much I craved it. I was doing the right thing, but the right thing sometimes hurt, like refusing Travis. I loved what we had, and I knew we had grown closer, but it would have been irresponsible to jump into a relationship with him right then.

I was nearly two months from my due date. My focus needed to be on my daughter, not on Travis, and certainly not on my father.

AFTER FEELING restless most of the day, I decided to get to know my new neighborhood. I drove down to the main strip in town and walked the little row of shops.

The pet store on the corner had cats in the windows. The sign read that they were visiting from a nearby animal shelter. While most of the cats basked in the rays of sun coming through the window, a fluffy white cat was hiding in the corner of its cage, trying to camouflage itself behind its too small litter box. It looked so sad. According to the sign on the cage door, her name was Rozsa, and she had special needs. I wondered what special needs meant for a feline and went inside to ask.

It was relatively empty in the store, and I asked the clerk at the counter, "What special needs does that cat have?"

The man perked up. "The Persian? She's beautiful, isn't she?" He came around the counter to walk with me toward her cage. "She had one of her hind legs amputated a couple of months ago. Her owner didn't want her anymore, said she didn't act the same."

"Of course she didn't. She just had her leg amputated." I was angry and taking it personally. The guy looked at me with a raised brow, and I continued in a calmer tone. "Imagine how you'd feel if you'd just had a limb removed and then the only family you've ever known abandoned you."

He nodded, "They felt they couldn't take care of her anymore. A family adopted her a couple of weeks ago but brought her back, saying she wasn't a good fit."

"Is she mean?" I asked as I walked toward her cage.

He followed. "No, she's kind of mopey, and the vet believes she might be experiencing fantom limb pain, but that usually fades."

"Can I see her?"

"Of course."

He opened the cage door, and she desperately tried to hide, scurrying to the back. He started reaching in, but I grabbed his arm. "Stop."

He pulled back, reassuring me, "She's just nervous. It's okay."

"No," I insisted. "She's scared. I don't need to see her right now. I'd like to adopt her, and then I'll get to know her at home once she's comfortable."

He looked at me for a moment before saying, "We're being a bit picky about who she goes home with. We don't want her to have to go through another failed adoption."

"I won't fail her," I said, relating to the feline.

"There's an application you have to fill out and a seventy-five dollar adoption fee."

"That's fine. Can I take her with me today?"

"As long as the application looks okay. And are you aware pregnant women should not be in charge of changing the cat's litter? There are risks."

"I'm aware of toxoplasma, but it's preventable. I'll wear gloves when changing her litter box, and I'll change it frequently. Although it shouldn't be much of a risk since she's an indoor cat and won't be fed raw meat."

He nodded in surprise. "You certainly know your facts, but it's still better if your husband could change the litter."

I held in an eye roll and bit my tongue, trying to stay calm. "I'm aware of the risks, but honestly, I'm more likely to get toxoplasma by eating raw meat or gardening. I'm a doctor. I brushed up on my knowledge when I found out I was pregnant."

He seemed impressed that I was a doctor, which was the only reason I brought it up. He went to get an application for me.

As I filled out the paperwork, I saw I needed to list a vet I intended to use. I texted Willa, asking what vet she used for her Bella. That dog was like a baby to her, so I knew she would only use the best vet. She replied right away, and I continued with the extensive application. I wasn't sure he'd let me have the cat if he realized I lived alone, so I listed Oliver on the application, hoping they wouldn't call him. I handed in the application and sent Oliver a text.

Me: I'm adopting a cat. If they call, tell them you live with me.

Oliver: Should I be concerned?

Me: No.

A few minutes later, I got another text from Oli.

Oliver: HOLY SHIT! Are you sure it's a good idea to get a cat while you're pregnant? I just read about it.

I rolled my eyes.

Me: The internet is a crazy place where everything gets hyped up. Emerson and I will be fine.

Oliver: What if Emerson is allergic?

Me: Then I'll figure something out. But neither of us have allergies, so it's unlikely, and I'll keep the cat out of the nursery.

Oliver: I don't know…

I could feel myself getting hot.

Me: I'm not asking permission. I'm getting a cat. Tell them whatever you want. I'll steal it if I have to.

That was probably a lie. I was feeling a bit irrational, but I wouldn't go to jail over a cat. Probably. I walked over to Rozsa's cage and whispered in at her, "I know I was supposed to find you today." Her bright blue eyes, round and assessing, glared at me as she backed into the opposite corner. It wasn't the reaction I was looking for, but it's a reaction I could understand. She didn't trust anyone. People had let her down.

The man startled me with his soft-footed approach. "Good news! You're approved!" He called. "Being a doctor really helped your case."

He went over several things with me, and then I gathered the necessities—everything I would need to own a cat. I scattered some treats at the bottom of my brand-new cat carrier and held it open, waiting patiently for Rozsa to move independently.

The clerk fidgeted next to me. "I can just scoop her up and put her in."

"No, I want her to trust me."

"You might be here all night."

I looked at him. "If she doesn't get in the carrier by the time you close, then I'll let you put her in, but I want to give her the chance to do it herself."

"You're going to stand there for two hours?"

"If I have to, yes."

He shrugged. "Have at it. You're just as stubborn as the cat. We'll see who wins."

I pressed the carrier against the cage door, but my arms got tired after only a few minutes. I was regretting my big stand to let the cat go on her own. What if she didn't?

I called for her, clicking my tongue and making other ridiculous noises that respectable adults didn't make. I hated baby talk, and I was doing the equivalent. It wasn't working anyway, so I changed my tactics. "Listen, Rozsa. I know what you're feeling. My family rejected me too. And the man I always knew I'd marry decided I wasn't a good fit. I won't do that to you. Come home with me, and you'll have the run of the place. You don't want to stay here in this two-by-two cell with all these weird noises and smells."

I set the carrier on the floor and held a treat out to her. She lifted her nose, sniffing the air before taking a tentative step forward, then another. I felt her whiskers tickle my fingers, and then she snapped the treat and retreated, chomping and licking her lips.

She looked me in the eye and then looked back to my open palm. I put another treat on my palm, and the tedious process continued until she was at the edge of the cage. She purred and nudged her face into my hand. She let me pick her up and I petted her for a moment, but she seemed uncomfortable and frightened, and I realized it was the missing hind leg. Phantom limb pain was real, and Rozsa was in pain.

I got her in the carrier an hour before they closed. She was not too happy about it, but it was a quick trip home.

I let her out at home, and she immediately ran under the oversized chair. She crouched underneath it, and those bright blue eyes watched me. I set up her litter box and placed the food and water close to the chair so she wouldn't have to go far to get it. Then, I ignored her as I went about my evening.

I hoped she didn't pee on anything. I left her litter box out in the open so she could find it easily. Eventually, I'd move it to a more discrete location.

This may have been one of the most impulsive decisions I had ever made in my life, especially because I had two homes and spent full days at the hospital. But if I needed to come back to the house at night instead of the apartment, I would. Rozsa was damaged, but that didn't mean she didn't deserve a good life.

In the morning, I would make a vet appointment and lookup cat sitters in case I'd ever need to go anywhere or couldn't get home. I could always ask Oliver or Willa, but I would only use them as a backup.

I felt confident I had made the right decision even as I went to bed, and Rozsa remained glued to the same spot under the chair. It would take her time to warm up, but I knew how to be patient, or as the clerk said, stubborn.

I WOKE IN THE NIGHT. It was dark and silent, and I didn't know what woke me. Then I saw the shadow move across the bed. A fluffy tail leisurely waved as the cat moved across the bed. It settled right next to my head, curling herself into a ball only inches from me. I smiled, feeling triumphant. This happened a lot faster than I expected. I wanted to pet her, but her purr told me she was content, and I didn't want to upset her, so I left her alone. Baby steps. I fell asleep to the comforting hum of her purr.

53

———

TRAVIS

NOVEMBER SEEMED like a month that just wouldn't end. I missed Addison. Without her, I had nothing to distract me from my thoughts. I felt the loss of my mom all over again. When she died, her death felt like a mercy since she had been in so much pain at the end, but now I started to forget how sick she was. I remembered the fiery woman I'd grown up with, and her absence left me with a physical pain. I'd spent every Thanksgiving with her, even last year when she could barely swallow or open her eyes.

I buried myself in work and spent Thanksgiving doing a turkey 5k. I came home, showered, and ate dinner alone while staring at my mother's urn. I could handle silence, but the noise in my head seemed to drown out any kind of peace. I couldn't escape my self-doubt and loathing. I recognized the signs of depression, another sign that I was becoming my father. But I refused to give in to the sadness. I upped my workouts, hoping to increase my endorphins.

Oliver reached out, inviting me to his parent's for Christmas. With a miserable Thanksgiving so fresh in my mind, I accepted his invitation. I didn't think I could face another holiday alone. It wasn't until after we hung up that I realized I might be better off alone than surrounded by a family who would hate me if they knew I was the reason Addison and Oliver weren't together.

Oli had another reason for calling me. He asked me to help him find an obscure gift for Willa after failing to find it himself. I scoured the internet. I didn't need Willa to like me, but I thought it would work in my favor if I helped him find it. Also, I was happy Oliver had reached out. We'd hung out a few times, and things had become more comfortable. I was working on rebuilding his trust.

I dropped by to show him what I had tracked down for Willa, hoping it was correct. It was and I was relieved. It finally felt like I had done something right.

"Want to come in for a beer?" Oli asked.

I could've blown it off, but I needed to tell someone. "Nah, I, uh. I stopped drinking."

"What? Why?"

No one asked you why you drank. They only ask why once you stopped. I'd practiced this response, but man, I felt like a pussy. "I had too much to drink one night. Made some fucking stupid decisions. I saw myself on video the next day, and it fucked with my head. I swore I was watching my dad. It was disgusting. I always promised myself I'd never end up like him."

"You are nothing like your father. One night doesn't make you like him," he said.

"I know, but I didn't like what I saw, so I'm gonna lay off it for now."

Oliver nodded. "I respect that. Are you okay with people drinking around you? Or does it make it harder on you?"

"I don't expect others to stop drinking just because I do. I'm not an alcoholic." I cringed. Most people who said that phrase were, in fact, alcoholics in denial. So I explained, "I don't have withdrawal from not drinking, and it's not like I was drinking every day. I'm a social drinker, but I just . . . It scared me, man. I never wanna be like him."

"You aren't," he reiterated. "I don't know about that night, but I've never seen you act anything like him."

"Thanks, man."

"It's the truth."

Oliver sent Willa's gift with me so he wouldn't be tempted to give it to her before Christmas. I offered to bring it to New York with me, making it even more difficult to back out.

Addison and I hadn't spoken since the day I left her apartment, but she texted me the week before Christmas begging me to ride with her to New York. She said Oli and Willa offered for her to ride with them, but she had already told them she and I were going together. Addison was using me to get out of riding with them. I couldn't blame her. I agreed to go with her, knowing that if I bailed, at least I could send Willa's gift with Addison.

AT TEN-THIRTY AT night on December twenty-second, there was a knock at my apartment door. I rolled out of bed and went to see who it was. After a look through the peephole, I ran a hand through my hair before opening the door. "What are you doing here?"

Addison pushed past me. "Bathroom!" She rushed off.

I sat down on the couch, turning on some lights. It was

the first time we'd seen each other since the bar incident, and I wasn't prepared for her. I wasn't expecting her until the morning, and I had already planned to make an excuse not to go to New York. The more I thought of it, the less I wanted to spend Christmas with people who felt sorry for me or were happy and in love.

When Addison joined me in the living room, I said, "I wasn't expecting you until morning."

She put her hands on her hips and glared at me. "You're bailing on me, aren't you?"

"Why do you say that?"

"We're supposed to leave at six am, and Willa's gift is by the door, but you don't have a bag packed."

"How do you know I haven't packed?"

"Your hamper is overflowing with dirty laundry."

"So. That doesn't mean—"

"You were going to hand me Willa's gift and send me on my way."

Well, fuck. "No," I continued denying it, but she knew I was lying.

She sat down next to me on the sofa. "If you're not going, then I'm not." She reclined back, propping her feet on the ottoman.

I glanced at her. "I don't know why you'd want to go in the first place."

She shrugged. "My own parents didn't invite me home for Christmas, but Buck and Kim both want me there. It's good to feel wanted. Didn't it feel nice to receive an invitation?"

I thought about it and sighed. "They wouldn't want me there if they knew about us. And how does Willa feel about us going?"

"I don't know. She and Oli offered for me to ride with them, so I'm guessing fine. And Oli asked you to bring Willa's gift, so I think they're better with all of this than we are."

I stared at her. "I thought I could do this, but it doesn't feel right to me."

She sighed. "You think I want to spend the next few days watching Oli and Willa make googly eyes at each other? It's going to suck, but I also love Oli's family, and right now, they seem to be the only family accepting me. I don't want to throw that away. Do you?"

I shook my head.

"They're all expecting us," she breathed. "I can't do this without you, and if neither of us goes, Willa doesn't get her gift. Not to mention, the hotel rooms are already booked."

I looked at her. "Wait. What hotel rooms? What're you talking about?"

"I thought it'd be easier if we had a place to escape if we needed it. I booked us connecting rooms at a hotel halfway between Oli's parents."

I carefully asked, "Are you going to try to get together with your parents?"

She shook her head. "We're still not on speaking terms."

"Not even with Jeanine?"

Another head shake.

I sighed, resigning myself. "So, we're going to spend Christmas in a hotel while visiting family that isn't our own."

She stared at me. "You and Oliver are my family."

I dropped my head back against the back of the sofa. "Did you come tonight to talk me into going?"

"Yes. I know this Christmas might be rough without your mom and Deena. Don't shut the rest of your family out."

I lifted my head to look at her. "I hate the holidays."

"It'll get better. It has to."

I hoped she was right. As silence fell between us, I noticed the white hair all over Addison's black pants. "Is this dog hair?"

She looked down, brushing a pant leg. "I got a cat—a white Persian who loves to lay on my black pants. I have lint rollers everywhere now, but I still miss spots."

I gawked at her. "You got a cat?"

She nodded. "Her name is Rozsa. She recently had one of her hind legs amputated."

"Why?"

"A bookshelf fell on her, crushing it."

"Damn. And how'd you end up with her?"

She started picking at the hair left on her pants. "As it turns out, not many people are interested in a traumatized cat. Except me. I found someone to cat-sit while I'm gone."

"So you're like a bonafide cat lady now?"

She stopped picking at herself and smiled at me. "I think to qualify as a cat lady, I would need multiple cats."

"Give it time," I joked.

She glared at me. "Shouldn't you be doing laundry or something?"

5 4

ADDISON

We stayed up late, finishing Travis's laundry. Since we were up, we watched a movie, and I fell asleep on his couch.

We left at six in the morning, and the drive wasn't terrible. We were mostly quiet, lost in our own thoughts as we made our way to New York. I was worried things would feel weird between us, but we seemed to pick back up like his drunken night had never happened.

We pulled into Buck and Janet's driveway around noon. Buck and Oliver arrived just before us and were getting out of a truck while Travis and I unloaded from my car. Buck smiled when he saw us. He was still tall and handsome, but his dark hair was turning silver, and he had put on some weight over the years. He lumbered over to me, his smile a welcome balm on my scattered nerves.

"There's my girl," he said, pulling me into a bear hug. "Good to see you, princess. How're you doing?"

I melted into his hug, longing for the same kind of affection from my own father. "I'm well." I pulled away before I became emotional. "But I really need to use the ladies' room."

Coming up behind me, Travis complained, "We stopped every two hours."

"It's not my fault," I defended, "I tried to hold it, but Emerson loves to jump on my bladder."

While Buck and Travis hugged, I noticed Oliver looked worried. We all moved forward, Oli leading the way. I caught up to him, asking, "What's wrong with you?"

"I left for a quick errand while Willa was sleeping. It was a half-hour trip that ended up taking two hours."

I shrugged. "Things happen. Willa can handle herself."

He shook his head. "I promised I wouldn't leave her."

"Oh. Well, then why did you?"

He raised a shoulder. "Because I thought she'd sleep through it. I messed up."

Oli was the first one through the back door off the kitchen. The rest of us followed, finding the family had gathered around the kitchen island with mimosas in hand.

Oliver's mom, blonde and ageless, had a classic beauty and stunning eyes. They were sharp and intelligent, azure like the sky on a clear day. Oliver had inherited those same eyes. But where Oliver's were kind, Kim's were calculating. She was sweet as pie as long as you didn't rub her the wrong way. I had worked hard to stay in her good graces and was relieved she still accepted me as family.

Shelby stood next to her mom. She was a few years older than me and was beautiful like her mother, but Shelby looked like a mixture of her parents. She was tall with dark auburn curls and an attitude borne from years of getting her way. She was a spoiled child who grew into a spoiled adult. I always knew how to handle Shelby, that was, until her nasty divorce from the cheating asshole, Brad. She was pregnant with her daughter before the divorce, and sweet little

Cadence was the only good thing to come out of that disaster of a marriage. I couldn't believe she was already five-years-old. Her shoulder-length brown curls bobbed as she bounced on Kim's back, piggyback style.

"Auntie Addie, you got a big belly," Cadence announced.

Everyone laughed at that, and Shelby laid her hand on my belly, gushing, "Ohh, you make the most beautiful pregnant woman. Why couldn't I have looked that cute when I was pregnant?"

"Oh, hush," I cajoled. "You were gorgeous when pregnant, and I can only dream of bouncing back as quickly as you did."

"Willa, do you want kids?" Kim asked rather abruptly, and all eyes turned toward Willa. She looked stunned by the question, and I felt for her. I had always hated that question. As I looked at her with sympathy, I realized she looked a mess. Something brown was smeared over her cream sweater, and her leggings had holes in them.

Willa's voice was small as she said, "Someday."

Shelby butted in, "Well, better be sooner than later, or all your lady parts will shrivel up." I glanced at Shelby, shocked at her flagrant disregard for Willa's feelings. But she wasn't finished. "And you'd better start preparing because Oliver's going to be a dad in a few short months. If you're not ready for kids, then jump ship now."

Willa's eyes landed on me, and I felt terribly uncomfortable. I wanted to turn and walk out the door, while also wanting to hug Willa and tell her to ignore Shelby. I settled for giving her what I hoped was an encouraging smile.

She said, "I can't wait to meet baby, Emerson."

Oliver wrapped his arm around Willa and kissed the side of her head. I'd seen him do this before, but now it was in front of his entire family, and it hit home how much I didn't belong here anymore. I tried to keep my smile in place as I knew everyone was watching me.

Finally, Oliver broke the tense moment as he looked over Willa, "What happened to you?"

Willa looked down at herself and said, "Oh, yeah. I need to go change." She set down her mimosa and grabbed Oliver's hand, sweeping him out of the room.

I glanced at Travis, and he nodded as if he agreed we shouldn't have come.

Janet, Buck's wife, was a sweet woman with a calm presence. She moved forward to hug Travis and me, saying, "I'm so happy the two of you could make it."

Kim and Shelby began a conversation with Buck, and Janet quietly added, "Travis, I know how tough holidays can be after losing someone. The first year after my mom died, I was a mess. I'm here if you want to talk." She squeezed his arm, and Travis pulled her back in for another hug. I felt like I was intruding, so I escaped to the bathroom.

I gave myself a small pep talk in the mirror before rejoining the others. Harry came into the kitchen. He and Kim had been married for ten years, and I never could get a read on him. He dressed like an old school professor, despite having retired several years ago. He claimed his IQ was genius level, but he was not excellent in social situations. Even now, his eyes glanced right over me without a word and went to Kim. "Darling, it's time for us to go."

They said their goodbyes just as Oliver and Willa rejoined us. Willa had changed her outfit and looked as beautiful as ever. No wonder Oliver couldn't keep his hands off her. He wasn't groping her by any means, but I was very conscious of all the little touches I missed so much.

NEXT ON THE agenda was our Gingerbread house tradition. Janet baked the gingerbread in advance and had everything we needed spread across the island counter. Oliver and I had always been partners, but this year he had Willa, and Shelby claimed me as her partner.

Shelby had no desire to actually take part. She leaned back and began drinking heavily while I worked on our gingerbread house alone. Buck and Janet helped Cadence with her gingerbread, and even Travis participated this year.

I heard the playfulness between Oliver and Willa. The two of them laughed quietly, floating in their soap bubble of happiness. I focused on the project at hand. Extreme focus could get me through almost anything, but it didn't stop me from hearing them, disgustingly in love.

It put me on edge. I took a calming breath. I was fine. Everything was fine. I could do this. It was only the pregnancy hormones that filled me with a mountain of regrets and sadness. I tuned everything out and focused on making my house perfect.

While the others were doing simple one-story houses, mine was a three-level home, each level just a little smaller than the ones beneath. It gave it a whimsical flair. I etched intricate details with piped icing, drowning out everything else.

Travis's creation distracted me a bit toward the end, as he had constructed a very unfestive war zone prison of sorts. Maybe his thoughts were just as dark as mine.

We finished with the gingerbread houses, and while mine was the prettiest house, it was not a memory I would hold dear. It was a task I checked off of my to-do list. The other homes may have been second rate, but everyone else had prioritized building cherished memories over building the best house.

After Cadence's father came by to pick her up, ice skating was next on our agenda. I tried to think of a way to get out of going, so I wouldn't be forced to watch Willa and Oli canoodling as they skated laps.

Shelby suddenly announced, "We aren't all going to fit in one car?"

Oliver said, "We're driving separate. We have a few things we need to pick up from the store."

It was weird not to be included in that we.

Shelby said, "Okay, so that leaves Dad, Janet, me, Addison—"

"Um," I interrupted, "I think I'm going to sit this one out."

"What?" Shelby gasped, "No. Come on. You never miss this."

"Yeah, but I'm kinda tired, and I don't even know if my swollen feet will fit into ice skates."

"Addison, you're going," Shelby said, not accepting my excuses.

At least I had Travis to lean on for support so it wouldn't totally suck.

"Travis, are you going?" Shelby asked.

"Hell no! You know balancing on tiny blades isn't my strong suit."

If he wasn't going, then I sure as hell wasn't going. "See, I'll stay and keep Travis company."

"I'm actually leaving," Travis admitted, giving me a sheepish look. "I'm just not going ice skating."

I couldn't hide my surprise. He was abandoning me. We

were supposed to be in this together. And where the hell was he going? "Where are you going?"

Travis shrugged. "Meeting up with someone?"

"Ooh," Shelby singsonged, "Who's the lucky lady?"

"None of your business," he sang right back.

I didn't have time to question him as Shelby turned her attention back to me. "You love skating."

Willa spoke, offering a friendly smile as she said, "You should come."

I stared at her for a moment, desperately wanting to go back to the hotel alone, but I had to prove I could do this. I nodded. "Okay."

"Perfect," Shelby concluded before pinning Travis with an inquiring look. "So, Travis, who is it that you're meeting up with?"

"An old friend," he offered vaguely. "I figured I'd catch up with her while I was in town."

"Have fun catching up." Shelby giggled.

Travis turned to me. "Do you mind dropping me on the way? It's not too far, and I'll get a ride back, so you don't have to pick me up."

I swallowed. "Sure."

I DROVE AND TRAVIS NAVIGATED. He spoke to me more about how to get there than what he was going to do once I dropped him off. Why hadn't he mentioned this old friend before? Was it just an excuse to get away? Was she just a hook up like Shelby implied?

I almost asked him, but I didn't care who she was. I cared

that he was ditching me. "I can't believe you're making me go ice skating without you," I complained.

"You can back out," he said.

I shook my head. "I told them I'd be there."

"Can't pregnancy get you out of almost anything?"

"Maybe." I shrugged. "But they'll know I'm avoiding them, and I have to prove that Oli and I can still be friends. I need them to know I'm fine with Willa."

He looked bewildered. "Why?"

"You saw how rude they were to her."

He scoffed. "Willa can handle herself."

"You have a lot of faith for someone who doesn't even know her. Who are you meeting that's more important than me, anyway?"

"Yolanda. She's an old friend." He smiled as he said her name.

"Yolanda?" I questioned, "And why have I never heard of her?"

He shot me a look like I was crazy. "Like I know all your friends' names. Calm down."

I didn't have friends. I had colleagues. But that didn't seem important. I said, "I just can't believe I'm dropping you off to go hook up with some chick."

I felt his eyes on me and looked over. "Is that really what you think?" His glare made me want to recoil, and his words had the same affect. "I am capable of more than hookups. I do have female friends."

"Like who?" I challenged, never knowing when to back down, especially with Travis.

"Yolanda, for one. She's not some chick I'm hooking up with. I don't do that anymore."

"Really? Are you going to marry that girl from the bar last month? Is she the one?"

His brow raised as his voice dropped. "What do you care about my sex life in the first place, Miss Judgmental? Last I checked, you turned me down."

"Not this again." I rolled my eyes.

He pointed up ahead. "Up here on the right."

"What is this place?" I asked, pulling off the road.

"It's the Arts and Cultural Center."

People were milling around outside in groups, and I asked, "Is there some kind of event here or something?"

As soon as the car came to a stop at the curb, Travis opened his door. "Don't worry, you're not missing a charity gala or anything. Just a bunch of eligible women to hook up with." He shook his head at me. "Jesus, Addie." He got out of the car, and just before he closed the door, I heard, "See you later."

Travis went a whole five steps before a beautiful woman accosted him. She shouted his name, and a second later, their arms were around each other.

"You've gotta be kidding me." I narrowed my eyes, disappointed. Pulling back onto the road, I peeked in the rearview mirror and they were still embracing. "Who the fuck is she?"

JANET AND SHELBY were already skating when I arrived. It looked like Willa and Oli had gotten there just before me, and as usual, Buck was waiting until the last possible second to change into his ice skates.

Skates in hand, I caught up to Willa and Oli, saying, "Oh, good! I'm not too late."

Willa commented, "Those are nice skates."

"Thanks. My father has a cabin in Canada. There's a pond that freezes over every winter, so we all have ice skates." I realized Oli had rentals, and asked, "Oliver, you didn't bring yours?"

"No, I left them at home. I didn't think about ice skating. The rentals are fine, though."

Willa laughed. "I'm sure yours are better."

Oliver blew it off, and I wondered if he had left them at home on purpose. Maybe he didn't want to wear the skates he used when we were together. He wanted to match Willa, not me. I sat down on an available bench to change into my skates.

Willa and Oliver sat across from me with their rentals. I set my skates on the ground and bent down. Or tried anyway. My enormous belly was in the way. I knew I could get the skates on, but it would be awkward, and I didn't want anyone to witness me making a fool of myself. I planned to wait until Willa and Oli were out on the ice, but Oli squashed that idea. He had his skates almost all the way laced up when he noticed me. He gave me a questioning look.

"I'm going to sit this one out," I said.

His smile was endearing as he knelt in front of me. "Here, let me help."

I sucked in a breath at his chivalrous character. Why hadn't I fought harder to keep him? I rolled my eyes at my train of thought and complained, "I feel like an invalid."

"You're not an invalid," Janet said, having stepped off the ice. "You're carrying a miracle in your belly. Creating a life isn't easy."

"I'm just ready to have my body all to myself," I said with a sigh.

Janet patted my shoulder. "I know. Not too much longer, dear."

Oliver finished lacing my skates and helped me to my feet, asking, "How does that feel? Too tight? Too loose?"

"They're perfect. Thank you." I smiled to mask my regret. It was hard to be here with him in a place that held so many sweet memories.

Janet and Buck went out onto the ice with me, while Oliver stayed with Willa.

Shelby pulled me away from Buck and Janet. "Dish, girl. I wanna know what you really think of that little tramp that stole my brother."

I loved ice skating. It was peaceful, and I wanted Shelby to go away so I could sort my head. I knew the truth, but my emotions were playing tricks on me. "She's not a tramp. I like Willa. They're good together."

Shelby snorted. "You and Oli were good together and don't pretend to like her. Nobody likes the woman who stole their man away."

"She didn't steal him," I argued, "Oli and I weren't together when they met."

She scowled at me. "Nope. I don't believe it. She must've gotten her claws in both of you. There is no reason you should talk nice about that woman. Something weird is going on."

I sighed. "Give her a chance, Shelby. You've been so unwelcoming."

"Unwelcoming? It's called having your back. You're practically my sister."

I never expected Shelby to stick up for me, but she was all fired up as she spoke, "He knocked you up and left you. The brother, I know, wouldn't do that. No. Something is evil about that little bitch."

I blew out a breath, but didn't respond. I was touched she had my back, but she wasn't listening to me. This day had worn me out, and it was only five o'clock.

Shelby puffed out a long breath and grabbed my hand as she glided in front of me, bringing us to a stop. She looked me in the eye as she spoke heartfelt words. "Addison, it's hard being a single mom. I love Cady, but it's exhausting doing it all alone. Brad helps less and less. There is no time to date or have friends. Trust me. You do not want to do motherhood alone. I know Oliver is better than Brad, but what happens when he and Willa have babies of their own?"

My chest grew heavier with each sentence. As if she realized this, she shrugged, saying, "It's just something to think about." She slid back to my side without forcing me to respond.

I hadn't been letting myself think too far into the future for fear I would hate what I saw. I couldn't stop time. And look where my planning had gotten me so far. I just had to let life happen and deal with it as it came. But Shelby just touched on some of my biggest fears. Would I be alone forever? I put a hand on my belly. I would have Emerson, but she would eventually grow into her own life.

Oli wasn't mine to claim and years down the road when I found time to date, Travis would be claimed by some hot piece of ass who didn't come with stretch marks on her belly and a kid that wasn't his.

I looked over at Willa and Oliver. She put her hand on Oli's chest as she laughed. He wore a small grin, his eyes shining with adoration, and it hurt. Willa was everything I wasn't, from her cute little figure to her dark features.

I'd agonized over my diet, trying to maintain a feminine figure. I'd been applying wrinkle cream since I turned twenty. I had spent thousands on moisturizers, toners, and makeup—all the things to keep me looking my best. Without makeup, I looked sickly, but Willa didn't need any of it. I'd seen her fresh-faced and dirty hair, and she still looked beautiful. No wonder Oliver chose her over me.

Shelby kept talking to me, but I was momentarily distracted by my panic. I wasn't okay. None of this felt okay, and I worried nothing would ever be okay again.

I didn't realize Shelby was pulling me over to the happy couple until we were there, and I was face to face with their love. They laughed together at some inside joke, and I fought back against my panic.

I put my hand to my belly, remembering the life inside.

I was okay. I would be okay. I had to be.

TRAVIS

I WAS PISSED off when I got out of Addison's car. I didn't understand her. She acted jealous and judgmental, and it didn't seem to matter how much I had worked to better myself. She still saw me as a man whore unworthy of her. And, of course, she threw the evidence in my face. One regretful night and I had destroyed any progress I'd made with her. But I was done trying to prove I was good enough.

"See you later," I snapped, shutting the car door behind me.

"No freaking way!" My eyes followed the voice. I hadn't seen Jasmine in years, and the last time I had, she'd been barely old enough to drive. Now she had to be about twenty-three. "Travis!" she yelled as she threw herself at me. I returned her hug.

When she pulled back, I got a better look at her. She looked good, and I was relieved. I knew things could've gone very differently for her.

"How are you, Jazzy?"

"Oh my god, nobody's called me that in like five years."

She laughed, and a man came up behind her. She turned and put her hand on his chest. "This is my boyfriend, Jackson." To her boyfriend, she said, "I know Travis from the old days before Daddy died."

"He died?" I asked.

She looked back at me, and her face fell. "A few years ago —OD'd on heroin."

Jazzy had tried most of her life to prevent her father from overdosing. I hoped she didn't blame herself. "I'm so sorry. How's your mom and Ariel?"

"Mom's still drinking, but she's been able to hold a job for a year this time. So at least she's a somewhat functioning alcoholic. Ariel started using a couple years ago. She turned into a tweaker and got busted making crank. Now she's got another three years to go on her sentence."

Ariel was a happy child. She seemed oblivious to the chaos in their home, dancing around in her own little world, while her big sister got to clean up all the messes and make sure food was on the table.

"Fuck," I said, "That sucks. How old is she?"

"She was nineteen when they busted her. She's twenty now."

"I'm so sorry to hear that."

She shrugged. "She turned into a real bitch and sold my car for drug money. I know it's the addiction, but I'm really over it."

I nodded. "I'll bet. You look like you're doing well."

She smiled. "I am." She wrapped her arm around her boyfriend. "We're getting married." She flashed me her ring, and I was happy there was at least one happy ending for her family.

"Congratulations, Jazzy Jazz."

"I'd kick your ass for calling me that if you weren't so ginormous."

I laughed and changed the subject. "Do you guys always come together?"

Jasmine shook her head. "No, this is only his second time."

Her fiancé added, "Helps me understand what I'm marrying into."

Jazzy sighed. "He already struggles to understand why I put up with Mom."

I nodded. Oh, how I understood, and I knew there were more challenges to come for them. "Good luck. Do you know why there are so many people here tonight?"

"Some business had their Christmas party in the Arts center. It shouldn't affect the meeting, though. We're still downstairs."

I nodded. "Do you know if Yolanda's here yet?"

"Yeah, she's in the meeting room, setting up."

"Okay, I'll catch up with you more later. I wanna see her before the meeting starts."

She nodded, and I took off, taking the steps to the basement two at a time. I rounded the corner and stopped in the doorway. Yolanda was still in the process of lining up chairs.

"Hey, YoYo!" I called from the door.

Yolanda turned, and her eyes widened, her arms opening as she took me in. "My God, son, you got big!"

I stepped forward. "It hasn't been that many years."

"No, but you weren't so buff before." She patted my biceps.

I laughed, giving her a hug. When I pulled away, I said, "I work out when I'm stressed."

"Well, I supposed that's better than eating, which is what I do when I'm stressed."

I grinned. "I do that too."

She smiled. "So what brings you here?"

"I'm in town visiting for the holidays. Thought I'd come for a meeting."

"You visiting your momma?"

"No," I rubbed the back of my neck. "She actually passed away last year around this time."

Her face fell. "Oh, Travis, I'm so sorry to hear that. I wish I had known. I would've come to pay my respects."

"It was such a crazy time, and the memorial was small."

She tilted her head to the side. "So who'd you come to visit, other than me?"

"My friend Oli and his family."

"Oh, you mean your bonus family." She smirked.

"Exactly." I nodded. "So, how are your kids?"

"They aren't kids anymore." She pulled out her phone, pulling up pictures of her boys. "The twins just turned eighteen, and Joey is twenty-one. He's got a girlfriend he's really serious about." I took the phone, looking at a recent family photo. All three of her sons towered over her, and the oldest had a beautiful girl on his arm.

"They look happy."

She smiled wistfully, "My babies are happy. Thank the Lord for that!"

"What about Doug?" I asked, handing her back her phone.

She shook her head with a sigh, "Prison."

I winced.

She blew out a breath. "Good riddance. I'd say he fell, but I swear that man leapt off the sobriety wagon as soon as we turned our backs for a second."

"I'm sorry to hear that."

"That man and his addictions put us through hell. I'm glad he's not mine to take care of anymore."

"Are you still running both Al-Anon and Alateen meetings?"

"You know it!" She smiled and it lit up the room. She radiated joy. It was her way, like a magic aura that glowed around her. "I'll do these meetings for as long as I can. There are lots of families out there hurting because of the addictions of their loved ones. I know how that feels, and this place kept me sane through the worst of it, so, yep. I'll be here."

"Same ol' YoYo." I had missed her.

"You staying for the meeting?"

"That's the plan."

I had never told Addison or Oliver about the meetings I attended through my late teens and early twenties. They helped me get through my dad's death, and they felt like something personal. I knew Addie and Oli would've supported my decision to go, but I didn't want them asking about them, so I kept it to myself.

ADDISON

WILLA AND OLIVER skated hand in hand. They smiled at each other, then laughed as they glided along. I watched all the emotions play out. And then she was pinning him to a wall and about to kiss him. From my peripheral vision, I saw a kid gliding straight at me from the side. I tried to dodge them, going down on my knees at the last second, so I didn't plow into the kid.

The problem was I couldn't stand back up from my knees. My belly was too big, and the skates were too clunky. I slid down onto my butt. Suddenly Oliver was right in front of me, getting down on his knees. Just two seconds ago, he was on the other side of the rink. I wondered how the hell he had gotten to me so quickly.

His face was a mask of concern. "Are you okay? What happened? Are you hurt?"

"I'm fine." As I said the words, suddenly the family swarmed around me. Buck, Janet, and Shelby all crowded me, and a few seconds later, Willa arrived. Meanwhile,

Oliver was patting me down and checking for injuries, "Are you sure you're not hurt? Is the baby okay?"

I shoved his hands away, saying, "I fell to avoid plowing into the little kid who darted in front of me. Oliver, I'm fine." I pushed him back. "Give me some space."

"Are you sure you're okay," Oliver fussed.

I gave him a look of exasperation. "I'm sure I'd know if something was wrong. I landed on my knees, not my belly. The baby's fine. I'm fine. Everyone is fine. Now, will you please help me up? My butt is freezing."

Oliver stood and helped me to my feet, which was no easy feat as he lifted my dead weight. "Do you want to go get checked out just to be sure?"

"Oli!" I scolded.

"Oliver." Willa sounded just as irritated.

Janet said, "She's obviously fine, son. Let it go."

Buck put his arm over Oli's shoulder, leading him away, and I heard him say, "Oh, this is just the beginning. The baby hasn't even been born yet. Just wait until . . ." My stomach dropped when I saw the look on Willa's face. She was having second thoughts. This was a challenging situation, and I couldn't blame her for questioning it. I wanted to say something, but I was not the right person to talk to her right now.

Whether or not she liked it, this baby would be a part of Oli's life. And I wasn't going anywhere. I couldn't be the one to convince her to give him another chance. Not when part of me wanted him for myself. I'd already handed him to her on a silver platter, and I would not put myself through that again.

We all filed off the ice, and Oliver coddled me like I was a ninety-year-old fall risk. He helped me out of my skates while Willa sat on a bench alone. "Oliver, Willa is the one you need to worry about right now. Not me."

"Willa is fine. We've talked at length about our situation. She understands."

"Just because she understands doesn't mean it's easy," I said, and he nodded.

He went off, turning in his rental skates before finding Willa. The couple talked, and after a moment, Oli returned, asking if he could ride back with me. I glanced past him and looked at Willa, but as soon as our eyes connected, she spun and walked toward her car.

"Sure," I said. "Are things okay?"

"Yeah, she knew I was worried about you."

AFTER DINNER AT BUCK'S, I texted Travis to ask if he was going to see Christmas lights with us. He said he'd be out late, and I couldn't help but picture him with that pretty young woman who had thrown herself at him. I was in a terrible mood and wanted to go back to the hotel and wallow, but Buck sounded so excited to go see the Christmas lights as a family. He decided we were going to take their old van so we could all fit in one vehicle.

There was so much tension in the van that I irrationally worried it actually would affect the baby. Shelby told old stories about coming to the lights, while I tried to lighten the mood, but Oli and Willa seemed determined to stay perturbed.

Once we were out of the van, the frosty winds were wicked. I pulled my scarf up as we moved forward.

Shelby continued bringing up stories from the past, like

the year I had too much eggnog, and Oliver had to carry me to the car. I wanted Shelby to stop. She was only reminding me of what I was missing, and I knew her point was to get us back together, but she was only hurting us.

Eventually, Shelby said too many wrong things, and Willa snapped back at her. She pulled away from Oliver, saying, "I'll wait at the entrance."

I watched Willa walk away and looked at Oliver to see what he would do. He shook his head at his sister. "God, Shelby, you and your mouth." He turned and jogged after Willa.

Janet held her hand out, palm up. "Give me the van keys," she said to Buck, and he obliged, pulling them from his pocket and placing them in her palm. Janet began walking back toward the entrance.

Shelby took a step to follow, but Buck steered her away. "Best to give them time, Shell Bell. With the hot streak you're on, you'll just piss them off further. Come on, let's get hot chocolate."

I didn't know which direction to go, and I desperately wished I had driven separately. I moved toward the parking lot. That way, at least I'd be closer to getting out of here.

I spotted Oliver standing by himself in the middle of the cement path. Groups parted to walk around him as he stood frozen, looking lost.

I joined him in the middle of the path, and the foot traffic continued around us. I didn't know what to say to him, so I stood in silence.

Oli sighed. "When did life get so damn hard, Addie?"

I wanted to laugh, wondering when life had ever been easy. "It's always been hard. You simply have a sunny disposition and have lived with your head in the clouds."

He ran a gloved hand over his face. "It's so fucking cold out here."

. I nodded. "Yes. It was insane of us to think this was a good idea." All of it was a bad idea, but I'd address one thing at a time. "The lights, that is."

"Where's the rest of the group?"

I pulled my scarf up over my nose to block it from the wind. "Janet took the van keys and ran after Willa. Buck and Shelby are getting drinks, and we're just standing here in the freezing cold surrounded by lights none of us are paying any attention to. I wish I could go straight back to my hotel room and take a long hot shower, but now I have to ride back with this fun group."

His eyes shot to me, "Hotel?" he asked, "I thought you were staying with your parents."

I had led him to believe things were better between my parents and me than they actually were. At first, I was hopeful my parents would try to patch things up, but the chasm between us had only grown, so I told Oliver the truth. "My dad's still not talking to me." He didn't need to know I was estranged from Jeanine too, and I thought I could use it as an excuse to get a break from his family at some point. "I'm meeting with my stepmom while I'm here, but he told her I'm not welcome at the house."

"Addie," he wrapped his arms around me, pulling me in for a hug. "I'm so sorry. I didn't realize it was that bad."

My eyes closed. He smelled so familiar—so tempting, and a decade of memories flooded my mind, stirring inappropriate thoughts. But he wasn't mine. And he didn't want me. I pulled away, saying, "You probably shouldn't have your arms around me, Oli." I glanced around to make sure no one had seen us hugging.

He stepped back. "Willa's mad at me," he blurted, then winced.

Maybe I could win him back. I knew how to manipulate him, but I wouldn't. I wasn't that person anymore. So, I listened and tried to give good friendly advice, but from the moment he hugged me, I couldn't stop remembering him wonderfully naked. I missed the look of desire in his eyes, and the way his body moved with mine. It wasn't that I wanted him, but this whole trip had made it excruciatingly obvious just how much I missed him.

I felt truly alone.

57

TRAVIS

THE MEETING RAN LONGER than expected, and Addison had texted asking if I was going to the Christmas lights with them. I declined, opting to go to dinner with Yolanda and some other old friends.

Yolanda offered me a ride back to the hotel. I felt good after spending an evening with her. I felt loved. She had that way about her. Her kids were lucky. They may have a shit dad, but their mom was pure gold.

As we drove away from the restaurant, Yolanda said, "So what prompted you to come tonight?"

I sighed, confessing, "The past year has been tough. My mom died. My best friends split up. My girlfriend broke up with me—broke my heart. One night, I just couldn't deal anymore. It was too much. I lost control and got blackout drunk. I did some idiotic things. Things my father would've done. I hate that I look like him, but I can't stand to act like him."

"Then don't." She shook her head. "It's not a forgone

conclusion that you will become him. I think you need to forgive him."

My gaze narrowed. "Forgive him for what? I didn't hate him."

"But you hate that you might become him?"

"Well, Yeah."

"Son, you don't have a drinking problem. You've got a fear of turning into your father problem. If that keeps you from drinking, fine, but deal with the root of the problem. Your dad drank to forget. My husband drinks because he loves the feel of being drunk and wants to live his life there. Why do you drink? What caused you to get blackout drunk that night?"

I shook my head. "A lot of things."

"Those are things you need to work through. The healthy way. Don't work through your problems like your dad did because you know that doesn't work. It only multiplies your problems."

"Thanks, Yo."

"You know, grief is a powerful force. You might need some help sorting it out. Counseling has helped me work through a lot. Have you ever thought about going?"

I shrugged. "Kinda seems weird to sit and tell a stranger my problems."

"I used to be a stranger, and now look at us. You gotta start somewhere."

I nodded. "You have a point."

"I always do," she said as we pulled up in front of the hotel.

I smiled, and she noted, "You have a beautiful smile. Don't let anyone or anything steal that from you. You take care of yourself and don't be a stranger. You have my number."

"I'll keep in touch. Thanks for the ride and the advice." I opened the door, but before I got out, I swallowed and faced Yolanda. "I've met a few people in my lifetime who have changed me in a big way, making the biggest impact. For better or worse, they've shaped me into who I've become. I'm really grateful you're one of those people." I gave her a genuine smile and got out of the car.

I went into the lobby, and Addison had left my room key and her car keys at the counter for me. I went out to her car and grabbed my luggage, hauling it to my hotel room.

58

—————

ADDISON

I WAS LYING in bed when Travis texted that he was on his way to the hotel. I couldn't get Oliver out of my head and the stupid hug that started it. It wasn't Oliver I wanted, but I missed being in his arms. I missed feeling loved, adored—not discarded. I wanted to be wanted. I ached to feel like more than a vessel for this life growing inside. I wanted to feel like a woman—sexy and desired.

I had about driven myself mad by the time Travis entered his room. I'd left the door between our rooms cracked, and it sounded like he was alone. I sighed in relief and got to my feet.

I slowly pushed the door between our rooms wide open. He had his back to me, pulling things out of his suitcase. He didn't notice me right away, and I started to lose my nerve. I contemplated leaving, but I needed this. He could do this for me. He'd given it away for less. I didn't even care if he thought about someone else.

I was struggling not to cry. Of course, my emotions

457

would get to me now that he was back. I swallowed just as Travis turned and caught sight of me.

"Oh, how long have you been standing there? I didn't see —" His eyebrows drew together, and he stepped forward. "Whoa, whoa, what's wrong?"

His concern brought on the waterworks. I couldn't hold back the tears, especially not when he came forward to embrace me. He held me against him, stroking my hair as he hugged me.

I wrapped my arms around him, letting my hands slide over his back, feeling his solid form. It solidified my decision, even if it was off to a rough start. My hands slipped under his shirt, touching skin. His body stiffened, his hand ceasing its motion as he held his breath.

The feel of him beneath my fingertips only increased my desire, and I didn't want to deny myself the pleasure he promised. I continued to feel him, the ridges of his muscles and smooth skin. I breathed him in, filling my brain with memories linked to him. Naked memories. My tears dried up as a pool formed between my thighs, and I was grateful it had nothing to do with the baby. No, tonight I wasn't a vessel. I was a woman hot with desire.

Travis removed his arms from me and tried to step back, but I held on, afraid to look him in the eye in case he rejected me.

"Did you have sex tonight?" I asked, my voice coming out breathy.

"No."

My thighs squeezed together to hold off the need, but I was breathing too heavily.

"Addison, are you okay? What's going on?"

I forced myself to let him go, stepping back, my cheeks

burned with embarrassment and desire as I confessed, "Travis, I want you to have sex with me."

He gave me no sign that he'd heard me. He just stared, his mouth slightly ajar. Then he shook his head. "Why are you doing this?"

"Because I'm not just pregnant. I'm a woman with needs. And it's not like I can go to anyone and ask them to fuck me. I can't pick up strangers in a bar. It's not safe, and I'd end up with a weirdo with a pregnancy fetish. I trust you. I'm attracted to you. We've had great sex in the past. Please, Travis. I don't care if you want to turn on porn and think of someone else. I just need some relief. Someone to touch me and make me feel like I'm not huge and unwanted."

Tears shown in his eyes, confusing me. Was he about to turn me down? I clarified, "I know you were just out with someone. I'm not asking for commitment. This can just be a one-time thing."

He looked away and up toward the ceiling before his eyes fell back on me. "You're sure about this?"

I stepped forward. "Do you think I'd come in here and embarrass myself like this if I wasn't sure?"

He took a step toward me. Slowly his palm ran across my cheek, his thumb brushing my bottom lip. He leaned forward, and his lips replaced his thumb, his hand sliding back to the nape of my neck. He pulled me against him, and my mouth moved with his. I forgot how good he was at kissing. His tongue slid along mine, and I whimpered, pulling away long enough to ask, "Does that mean yes?"

He let out a puff of air in an almost laugh. "Yes, Addie."

I slid my fingers beneath the hem of his shirt and lifted it, feeling his skin. He pulled the shirt over his head and tossed it away. I did the same with mine.

I unhooked my bra and slid it off. My breasts had grown larger with pregnancy, so at least I had that going for me. He didn't look repulsed, and I rejoiced in that.

He pulled me back in to kiss me, but I paused, saying, "I know I'm as big as a house. If you need something to—"

"Shut up, Add." He took my hand in his as he devoured my mouth. He moved my hand to his dick, and I felt him, hard in his pants. I let out a breath of relief. He wanted me.

I teased him through his pants for only a second before he unfastened them, redirecting my hand inside. I felt the silky skin of his penis and ran my thumb over his velvety soft tip, feeling his pre-cum.

He wanted me. It made me feel powerful.

"On the bed," I commanded.

His brow raised, but he did as I said, slipping out of his pants and boxers. He pulled off his socks before relaxing back on the bed. He was a superb male specimen, and tonight he was mine. He watched me crawl onto the bed. My palm wrapped around his shaft. I ran my tongue over his tip, tasting him. Then I took him into my mouth, my lips skimming over his most sensitive skin.

His head fell back, and in a strained voice, he said, "I thought you wanted a release?"

I pulled away. "I do. I just love your dick."

He gave a throaty laugh, cut short as I took him back in my mouth. His hands reached for me, and his fingers skimmed my breast. I felt like he was going easy on me, waiting for me to tell him to stop, but I wouldn't. I pulled back and stood to slip out of my pajama pants. He sat up at the edge of the bed, grabbing me and pulling me closer. His tongue flicked over one nipple while his hand caressed the other. His other hand went to the sweet spot between my thighs.

I let out a long moan as his fingers dipped inside while his thumb rubbed circles over my clit. My fingers dug into his shoulders. "That feels . . . mmm."

"Addie, you're so wet."

"I've been thinking about you," I confessed. "I was hoping you weren't bringing someone back with you."

He paused his movements, and I let out a desperate whimper.

"Where do you want me, Addie?"

"Inside me."

"Right here, like this?" He moved his hand.

"I want more." I pulled away so I could think. "I want you behind me." I climbed on the bed on all fours, sticking my ass in the air.

He grinned and grabbed a condom from his condom case that he had set on the nightstand. He slid one on and a hand slid down my back while the other dipped inside me.

He leaned forward, his lips brushing my shoulder. Then his fingers left. He lifted his fingers to taste me.

"So fuckin' sweet." As he said it, his dick slipped through my wet folds. I spasmed around him, a quick mini orgasm, proving how long it'd been. I was desperate to be touched— to be desired.

"Jesus, Addison."

Once I stopped trembling, he began moving in deep strokes. "God, you're beautiful," he said.

"Mmm." I wasn't capable of words, only noises, but I soaked up his words, his movements, the feel of him. Travis was everything and everywhere. He made it believable, like he might mean the words he was saying. He made me believe he wanted me.

"Faster," I pleaded.

He obliged, his hand reaching around me to pinch my nipple. My orgasm pulsed through me, and the world faded away as ecstasy overwhelmed my senses.

"Oli," I moaned, then gasped, realizing what had just come out of my mouth. It was an accident. Oli wasn't even on my mind. Why had I said that?

Travis hadn't stopped moving. He kept thrusting fast and hard. Maybe he hadn't heard my slip.

He leaned forward, his breath on my shoulder. "Fuck you, Addison."

I sucked in a breath. I deserved that, and I expected him to stop, but he didn't. He only moved faster, harder.

"Travis, I didn't mean—"

"Shut up," he hissed.

His release came quickly, and he immediately pulled out, disappearing into his bathroom. A moment later, the shower turned on.

I slumped the rest of the way to the bed. My body was sated, but my head and my heart were a mess. I'd hurt my best friend again. I grabbed the shirt he'd discarded and pulled it on, soaking up the smell of him. I went to my bathroom to clean up, and when I came back, Travis was still in his bathroom. I laid on his bed to wait for him, hoping he'd speak to me.

My eyes felt so heavy. Too heavy. It had been an incredibly long day.

59

———————

TRAVIS

SHE THOUGHT I'd just come back from a date, and she asked me to fuck her. It broke my heart how little she thought of herself. But I didn't want her stooping so low as to fuck some rando on the street. I would've asked her to stay in my bed. I would've begged her to love me, but she said his name. She seemed so supportive of him and Willa that I thought she was over him. But of course she wasn't. And I would never be him.

I had already established that I would give her anything she wanted. She had to know I wouldn't turn her down.

Fuck.

I missed Deena. Everything was easy with her, and I didn't want to blow my goddamn brains out when I was with her. But she was smart to get out when she did. My crazy had already leaked over into her life. No wonder she wanted no part of me.

I knew Addison was using me tonight, but for so long, I had wanted to be inside her without feeling guilty or thinking of Oli. She allowed me to show her how great it could be. She wanted me behind her, which was a vulnerable position. I thought it showed trust, but it was not about trust. She didn't want to look me in the eye while she was thinking of him.

My pulse thrummed with anger. She knew she was hurting me and she didn't care. I came out of the bathroom, knowing I needed to leave. I would pay whatever it cost for a ride back to Columbus.

Walking to my suitcase, I stopped dead in my tracks. Addison was asleep on my bed wearing nothing but my t-shirt. Fuck. I had dreamt of this moment for so long. She was curled up, her arms wrapped around herself. When I moved closer, I noticed her tears had dotted the pillow beneath her head.

If I was still on the fence about going home, all plans to leave dissolved when I saw her tears.

I let out a sigh of defeat. Fuck.

ADDISON

I STARTLED awake as Travis lifted me from the bed. The night's events came back to me, and I twisted to face him, clinging to his neck as he held me.

"Wait. No." I didn't want him to remove me from his bed or his room. "No. I didn't mean it. I spent the whole day with Oliver and it was miserable. Horrible. I've had a terrible day. And I missed you. I wasn't thinking of him, Travis. I swear, I wasn't. I'm sorry. I'm so sorry."

He watched me with tired eyes. His chest was bare, and as he set me on my feet, I realized he was only wearing boxers. I couldn't tell what he was thinking.

He asked, "Are you sleeping in here or in your room?"

I didn't expect him to give me an option. "Wherever you are."

I didn't know if he'd let me, but he pulled the blankets back for me. Then he rounded the bed and got in on the other side. I slid beneath the blankets and did something I'd wanted to do forever. I cuddled with Travis. His body intertwined with mine and I fell asleep to the sound of his deep breaths.

I WOKE with pressure between my legs. It took me a second to remember where I was and reacquaint myself with the present. Travis was spooning me, and his very erect penis was pressing between my thighs. He was rougher with me than before as he slid inside me. He bit my shoulder and then kissed it and then bit again.

"Deena," he whimpered as he moved.

I wondered if he was even fully awake. Did he realize what was happening? His breath was hot on my neck as he wrapped his arms around me, nuzzling in closer. His breath caught, and I felt moisture against my shoulder. He was crying. What the hell was happening?

One of his hands pressed against my stomach as if feeling for the baby. This was too weird.

"Travis," I whispered.

He pulled away from me. "Fuck."

I lost him completely, feeling the cool air against my back as he moved to sit on the opposite edge of the bed. I rolled over and found his back to me, his feet planted on the floor, and his head cradled in his hands.

I sat up. "Travis?"

It took him a minute to respond. "Sorry, I . . . I'll pay for testing." He stood. "I didn't realize . . . I—"

"What testing? Travis!"

He looked at me. I didn't know what I expected to see, but it wasn't the hollowness. He looked lost, void. A boy with no family and no one to turn to, hanging onto the thread of friendship he had with Oliver—hanging onto me even though I was dead weight.

I stood, wearing only his t-shirt. "Oh, Travis." I walked around the bed, but he held out a hand to fend me off.

His red-rimmed eyes were on my belly as he claimed, "She was pregnant. Deena was pregnant."

He sat back down on the bed as if he needed the support. His eyes were on the floor, his voice hollow. "She didn't find out for weeks after our breakup, and by the time she called me to tell me about it, she'd already decided to get rid of it. She didn't want anything tying her to me. I tried to talk her out of it. I would've done anything for her, but she threw me away. And she threw our child away so she could pretend it never happened."

He paused to compose himself, rubbing a hand over his face, he said, "I told her I'd take the baby. I told her I would pay for everything, but it didn't matter. She'd already made her decision, and she said I deserved to know. She wanted to hurt me the way I'd hurt her."

My heart sank, and my hands instinctively went to my belly. "Why haven't you told me?"

He looked up at me. "I just did."

I went to him, gathering his hands in mine as I knelt on the floor in front of him. "No, Travis. You should've led with this when you showed up to my apartment in September." I realized with horror. "I made you go baby shopping with me. Why? Why didn't you tell me? God, Travis, I'm so sorry."

He swallowed. "I would've been better than my dad."

"Of course you would have. And you will. Your life's not over."

He pulled his hands from mine and wiped away his tears, showing the emotion his father always scolded him for having. He looked at me, and I watched the damn break. All the feelings I suspected he'd been holding inside flowed out in a rush of words. "Deena turned into someone else after our breakup. I don't understand it. I knew her, and then one day, I didn't."

He looked at the floor, continuing, "I know she had a right to be angry, but she wasn't angry. She was vengeful. I couldn't even get her to attempt to work things out with me."

He shook his head. "I don't get it. She helped me when my mom was dying. She handled the deep shit. She felt real, unshakeable. She was my person. Until she wasn't. And I don't understand how someone can go from who she was to who she is now." He lifted his gaze to me. "She turned on me. Did I do it to her? Is it my fault, or is that how people are? Did I break her?"

"No, Travis. It's not your fault. You didn't lie to be cruel. You didn't cheat on her, and you never meant to hurt her. I'm surprised she didn't want to work through it, but I guess people change. I know how much you loved her, and she's an idiot for letting you go. I'm sorry she broke your heart, and I'm sorry she didn't keep your baby."

My feet started feeling numb, so I moved to sit beside him on the bed. I ran my hand over his back, leaning into him. "I love you, Travis. I might not be your person, but I've always got your back."

He turned to me, staring at me for a moment before sliding back into bed and pulling me down with him. He spooned me, holding me against him with his hand over my heart. His breath fell against my neck, and chills spread across my skin. I was getting turned on, but I didn't think that's what he was going for. I held still in his arms and let him hug me, relishing the feel of him. His arms felt warm, and I felt safe and secure in their hold.

I wanted to spend every night locked in his arms, and he'd offered me that just over a month ago, but I'd turned him down. I promised I wouldn't get involved with anyone until after Emerson was born. And he was still heartbroken over his ex and the baby he'd lost.

His lips brushed my shoulder, my neck, and my jaw. My body moved against him, my hips moving back, and without discussing what was happening, we moved in a sensual rhythm. And then I felt him at my entrance, I tilted my hips, granting him easier access. I moaned as he buried his erection inside of me. His breath against my neck became unsteady as he moved with me and in me. He'd already been inside me without a condom, so I didn't see the point just then, and taking him bareback felt more intimate, more sensual. At that moment, we were one, and I never wanted to leave his arms. His name was a constant moan on my lips, and his scent surrounded me. I wanted him to brand me, and at the same time, I remembered all the reasons I couldn't allow it. But for tonight, we rocked together, slow and steady.

Hours later, Travis was fast asleep next to me, but I couldn't quiet my mind enough to find that same slumber. I thought about what I would've done in Deena's situation, but in a lot of ways, we were in the same boat. Except she didn't want her baby, and I couldn't imagine giving mine up. If I hated Oliver, would I feel the same way about Emerson?

It couldn't have been a simple decision for her, but my

concern was only for Travis. I knew one thing for sure. He didn't deserve any more bad shit.

THE NEXT MORNING we didn't discuss what happened in the night. We'd grown more intimate, and I couldn't keep my hands off him as we got ready for the day. We had a fifteen-minute make-out session before breakfast.

We were like hormonal teenagers who couldn't get enough, but I knew it couldn't last. Travis made me break all my rules but being with him was too risky. We were dynamite together, but dynamite explodes, and I had to put Emerson first. I would not fail her, and this thing between us couldn't last. I suspected he knew it couldn't last either, but neither of us wanted it to end. So, we avoided talking about it as we got ready to leave for Kim's house.

As we were leaving the hotel, Travis realized he forgot his dress shoes for tonight. I waited in the lobby while he ran back up to get them.

There was a family of four standing at the front desk. The two kids were both under five, and their parents looked exhausted. Then I overheard why. The man explained to the clerk, "But our house flooded. There has to be a room left. We'll take anything. Come on, it's Christmas Eve."

The clerk looked sympathetic as he explained, "I'm sorry, sir. We are fully booked. I have nothing to offer."

I watched the parent's shoulders slump and felt for them. The youngest of the kids stared at me with curious green eyes.

When Travis came back down with the shoes, I asked him. "Can I stay in your room tonight?"

He looked surprised by the question but nodded. "Great." I stepped toward the front desk. "Excuse me." The family turned to me. "I couldn't help but overhear. We have an extra room we aren't using." I looked at the clerk. "Can we switch our reservation so they can use the room?"

"Are you sure?" The clerk asked while the family looked at me with anxious eyes.

"Yes, of course. I just have to move some luggage, and the room is yours."

The woman said, "Oh, thank you. You have no idea how much this means."

"I'm happy I can help," I said.

Travis grabbed the room key from me before running back up to our rooms to move things, while the family continued to thank me profusely. They told me about the pipes bursting and water flooding their home while they were sleeping. They salvaged some of their children's gifts, but the house was uninhabitable until the water was extracted.

When we turned in our keys, I made sure the clerk kept my credit card on file to pay for the family's room. They had been through enough.

61

TRAVIS

EVERY YEAR we spent Christmas Eve's Eve with Oli's dad and stepmom, while we always spent Christmas Eve with Oli's mom and stepdad. It was another event-filled day that was off to a rocky start.

"Knock knock," I said as Addison and I walked in the back door of Kim's enormous house. Oli and Willa sat at the island breakfast nook, and Kim was standing opposite them.

Fluffy, Shelby's small goldendoodle, ran up to greet me with a shoe hanging from his mouth.

"You little bastard!" Shelby shouted, chasing him.

Before Shelby reached him, I told Fluffy to sit.

He did.

I commanded, "Drop it."

Fluffy dropped the shoe.

Shelby slid to a stop and threw her hand back in preparation to slap the dog, but I grabbed her wrist. I had to take a beat and remember Shelby had no intention of ever owning a dog. Cady's father bought the dog for Cady's birthday and then claimed the dog couldn't stay with him because of allergies. Cadence begged her mom not to get rid of the dog, and Shelby caved. She was trying to do right by her daughter, so I kept a grip on my anger.

My voice was calm but firm, "Acting hysterical isn't going to make your dog listen to you, and hitting him won't make him understand."

She gave me an evil, bitchy look. "What are you? The dog whisperer." Jerking her arm out of my grip, she reached down and grabbed the shoe, waving it an inch from my face. "These were twelve-hundred-dollar shoes!"

I snorted. "That's your fault for spending twelve-hundred dollars on shoes!"

She was shaking, her face turning red. She let out a frustrated shriek and stomped out of the room with the damaged shoe in hand.

I felt everyone's eyes on me, but I ignored them, bending down to scratch Fluffy's head.

Oliver's stepdad came into the room, and everyone turned their attention to him. He slid his wire-framed glasses off his face and said, "What's all the commotion?" He pulled a handkerchief out of his pocket and cleaned his glasses.

Kim sighed. "Shelby's having an unpleasant morning."

"Oh." He slid the glasses back on. "Addison, Travis, nice to see you." He nodded. "Oliver." His eyes slid over Willa like a big *fuck you* before leaving the room. I had never especially liked Harry. The only thing he seemed to care about was proving he was the smartest person in the room. I always felt like he was silently judging me, and once, he'd accused me of stealing cigars from him.

Oliver stood, grabbing his and Willa's bags. "I'm going to put these in my room."

"Okay, but be quiet," Kim warned. "Cady's sleeping in there."

"Nuh-uh!" Cady said from the kitchen entrance. She lurched forward. "Auntie Addie! Did you know Santa's not real?"

Addison knelt down to be the same height as the little girl. "Who told you that?"

"Daddy."

"Well, it sounds like Daddy's been on the naughty list one too many times," Addison said smoothly, "Of course, he doesn't believe in Santa. That doesn't mean Santa isn't real."

"But he said the elves and reindeer aren't real, either."

"Well, I've seen reindeer with my own eyes. I can tell you for a fact that they are real."

"Really?" Cady asked.

"Yep."

"So Santa might be real, too?" Cady asked. Her eyes looked up at me. "Do you know if Santa's real, uncle T?"

I crouched down. "Who else would've put me on the naughty list?"

Her eyes rounded. "You're on the naughty list?"

"Afraid so, munchkin." I tousled her hair.

She smiled and turned to Oliver. I stood and helped Addison up out of her crouch as Cady asked, "Uncle Oli, do you believe in Santa?"

He smiled. "Of course I do."

She looked at Willa. "And you?"

Willa nodded, and Cady said, "Mommy's right. Daddy is a bastard."

I snorted, and Oliver coughed to cover his laughter, choking out, "I gotta take these . . ." He left the room with their overnight bags, leaving Willa alone at the island.

Kim stepped toward Cady. "But remember, name-calling isn't nice. It can get you put on the naughty list."

Cady said, "Are you on the naughty list for calling Oliver's friend a gold-digging whore?" I glanced at Willa, who gave nothing away.

Kim froze, tentatively asking, "Uhh . . . where did you hear that?"

"I heard you and Grandpa Harry talking." Cady turned to Willa and walked toward her chair. "I wanna be a gold-digging whore. Do you get to keep the gold?"

I wanted to laugh but knew this had to be a blow for Willa. Addie was biting her lip with worry.

Willa opened her mouth and tilted her head to the side. With a mischievous grin and a raised brow, she said, "I get to keep all the gold."

Cady's eyes widened. "Really? Is it the kind of gold with chocolate inside?"

Willa's smile grew larger. "It sure is."

Cady climbed into Willa's lap, and Kim looked miffed.

Cady ran a hand across Willa's arm, asking, "Did you eat too much chocolate, and that's why your skin looks like chocolate milk?"

Willa laughed. "Not exactly. I was just born this color."

Cady looked up at her. "It's pretty. Do you think if I eat chocolate, my skin will be like yours?"

"I don't think so, but your skin is pretty just like it is."

She was unflappable. One of us should have stepped in, coming to her rescue in this fucked up situation, but Willa didn't need it. She rescued herself.

Kim reached out a hand, saying, "Cady, come with me. We need to get you ready to go." Cady hopped off Willa's lap, and she and Kim walked out of the room. Addison moved forward with the same worried expression on her face. She sat next to Willa, but Kim popped back in, asking, "Addison, would you help me get Cady ready?"

Addison stood up. "Sure."

Then it was just Willa and me. I peeked around the corner and saw Oliver talking to Harry in the other room. I sat next to Willa. I wasn't her favorite person, but someone should commend her for reacting the way she did. Without looking at her, I said, "Don't worry. I've been called worse things."

"You were never sleeping with their son," she said coolly.

"Nope." I shook my head. I only slept with their son's woman, and if they knew, they'd all hate me. "Not their son."

Willa's head jerked to me, and I shrugged.

She turned to look out the window. There was a flurry of tiny snowflakes that never seemed to touch the ground. She sighed. "I have thick skin."

I scoffed. "I never doubted that. I know you're tough."

I wasn't getting my point across, but before I could say more, she turned to glare at me. "We aren't the same."

I smirked. I liked her. She hated me, but I liked her. "Hallelujah for that, right?" I stood. "Welcome to the family." I grazed my knuckles over the counter, knocking twice before leaving the room.

CLASSY CHRISTMAS WAS by far my least favorite part of being with Oli's family. The catered dinner was always delicious and disgustingly expensive, not that I was supposed to know that part. But before we could eat, everyone had to dress in suits and gowns to pose for pictures, which took a minimum of an hour to get all the combinations Harry insisted upon.

For so many years, I fretted over what to wear and whether I could afford something nice enough. I didn't want to complain because it was nice that they included me in their family photos, but it almost didn't seem worth the mental anguish. I posed for five minutes, and then I had a front-row seat to watch Oli's beautiful family smile and pose together. It always reminded me that they might consider me *like family*, but I was the outsider. At least the meals were good.

I'd had some uncomfortable Classy Christmases in the past, but this day was fucking torture. And I was stone-cold sober. Why the fuck had I let them talk me into coming to New York? I leaned back in the chair, propping my ankle on my knee as I watched the family pose. I ran a hand down my beard, taming it. It didn't need taming. It had just become a nervous habit I'd picked up.

Addison looked gorgeous in her silky ice-blue gown. The color of her dress brought out the bright blue of her eyes. Cady kept calling her Elsa and insisted she was wearing her hair wrong. Addison had pulled her blonde strands up off her neck where Cady wanted them down in a braid like Elsa's.

Oliver's face pressed to Addison's stomach while she smiled like a mother in love. It made me miss my mom. I wish I hadn't sold her trailer. I could've gone back there just for something familiar. Familiar that didn't feel borrowed. I was only here because they felt sorry for me. Once again, I was borrowing Oliver's family, just like I'd borrowed his baby momma last night. I wanted to be up there pressing my face against her belly, but she had said his name last night. It was his baby, not the one I would never get to meet.

It made me miss Deena. The Deena from before. The one that never fucked with my heart. She was all in. Until she was out. Addison couldn't figure out whether she was in or out. She was like a fucking house cat that couldn't decide and just continuously pawed at the door from either side.

Oliver kissed Addison's belly, and jealousy spiked through me, hard and ugly. I wondered if his obvious love for Addie and their baby worried Willa. If I were her, I wouldn't be able to handle it. She sat across the room, also tossed aside after only a few photos. I glanced over at her, realizing she was watching me.

I pulled my hand away from my lips, realizing I'd been chewing at my nail beds. Her gaze didn't jerk away like most people would when caught staring. She looked at me like I was a puzzle. I approved of her blatant dislike of me. Unlike everyone else, she saw me for the parasite I was. I wondered how she would react if I told her Addison called out his name while I fucked her last night. Maybe Oliver called Addison's name too.

I looked away. Where had my mind gone? Fuck! I wanted out of here. I could go back to the hotel, buy some snacks from the hotel lobby.

That sounded pathetic. Maybe I needed to get a dog or something. Fluffy wasn't so bad once you got past the humping and eating everything. Or maybe a cat. But cats shit in a box, and I didn't want to clean that shit up or smell it all the fucking time. Maybe I'd be better suited for a goldfish. Fuck fish. I wanted a dog. I was going to get a dog if my apartment allowed them, and if not, I would move.

Willa suddenly left the room, and I thought that sounded

like a great fucking idea. I needed some fresh air. She went toward the bedrooms while I went out the back door. It had started snowing—only a dusting, but the crisp air felt refreshing compared to the oppressive heat inside.

Buck and Janet soon pulled into the driveway, and Cady came out to greet them. When Cady realized there was snow, she wanted to stay outside. I offered to stay with her so Buck and Janet could go inside. They were dressed nice for dinner, and I knew Janet had to be cold, but neither of them seemed in any hurry to go inside. From the outside, it would seem weird that they were here at all, and I wondered if they hated Classy Christmas too.

We were by the driveway when I spotted Willa rushing to her car. She held her dress hem with one hand and her coat with the other as she ran on the toes of her high heels. I exchanged a glance with Janet, and she said, "Go check. We'll keep Cady occupied."

I nodded and headed for the back door. I found Shelby, Kim, and Harry in the family room. They talked amongst themselves, but I wasn't about to ask them for details. Their dislike of Willa would taint their version of events.

I was about to search for Addison and Oli when Addison walked into the room with a drink in each hand. Her eyes found mine, and I gave her a questioning look with the tilt of my head. She nodded toward the family room. I took a seat on the corner of the sofa. Addison was about to join me, but Shelby addressed her, "Can you believe the nerve of that woman?"

Addison had her back to the others. I was the only one who saw the anger on her face, making it clear she was on team Willa. Addison handed me a glass of bourbon and set her water on the coffee table. She blew out a breath before spinning to them. "Willa's words were harsh, but haven't you been unkind towards her?"

I scoffed. "How diplomatic of you, Addie. I don't know what happened, but I doubt Willa called any of you gold-digging whores."

Kim shrugged. "She didn't deny it. Maybe because she couldn't."

I leaned forward, setting my glass next to Addison's. "Or maybe because she has more class than that." I knew I was on thin ice, but I would rather break the ice than to sit in silence and listen to them tear another person apart.

Kim said, "You didn't hear her tirade. She verbally assaulted Shelby. I don't know what Oliver sees in her."

Shelby whispered, "She's practically unhinged."

"It's better he sees it now than months down the road," Kim added, sounding sympathetic.

I was about to lay into them, but Oliver stepped around the corner, and the room fell silent. All heads turned to him. I had never seen him look so pissed.

"Finally," Addison said under her breath so only I could hear as she leaned against the side of the couch.

Oliver glared at his mom and Shelby, asking, "Is that what you think?"

They exchanged a glance while Harry looked disinterested. Buck walked into the room, but Janet was still out distracting Cady.

Oli stepped forward. "I begged her to come here with me and meet all of you because you're the most important people in my life." He shook his head. "I've never been more disappointed in my family."

"In us!" Shelby shrieked. "What about you?"

He spun to her. "What about me?"

"Come on, Oliver. Addison is having your baby. The two of you belong together. We figured if we could get you together, you would see that."

He opened his mouth to speak, but nothing came out.

Addison groaned. "This isn't a Hallmark movie, Shelby. Just because we're back in our hometown doesn't mean the magic of Christmas is going to bring us back together. We still care about one another, but we're adults, and together, Oli and I ended our relationship. The end."

"But your history—"

"Is just that," Oliver said, regaining his voice. "History."

"But she'd take you back," Kim said, looking to Addison. "Wouldn't you, Addie?"

Addison's eyes widened. "Oh, wow!" She pushed away from the sofa, saying, "No. I wouldn't."

There was a long period of quiet before Addison continued, "No, I won't take him back because I'm not in love with him, and he's crazy in love with Willa."

"You could get that love back," Shelby said. "Look, we all know I made a mistake with my douche of an ex-husband, but Oli is one of the good ones. And so are you."

Addison huffed in frustration and then shot Oliver an apologetic look before confessing, "I cheated on him." She took a breath. "He didn't want to tarnish my reputation or for anyone to blame me for our breakup, especially while I was pregnant with his child. But I cheated on him. He's forgiven me, mostly because if it hadn't happened, he wouldn't have found Willa. She's the person who helped put him back together after I blew up his life, so stop blaming her for anything. They belong together. Not us. Stop trying to put us back together."

I wondered how much of that she truly believed and how

much she was saying for everyone else's benefit. The quiet in the room was palpable after the confession. Everyone exchanged glances, and Addie seemed like she was barely breathing as the tension grew.

I leaned forward, grabbing Addison's glass of water from the coffee table. I raised it in a toast, saying, "Happy birthday, Jesus!"

As people thawed, there were a few small laughs, and people took long drinks of whatever alcohol they had nearby. I handed Addie her water, and she glanced at the untouched bourbon with curiosity.

Before she could inquire further, Shelby asked, "Why in the world would you cheat on him?"

Addison winced, turning away from me. "I don't know. I was stupid and reckless. It was years ago, and I was confused."

Addison and Oliver wouldn't throw me under the bus, and I almost wish that they would. I didn't want to go on wondering if these people would still care about me if they knew I was the main reason for the couple's split.

Shelby started, "But—"

Oliver stepped forward. "It's in the past. I've forgiven her."

Shelby turned to him. "You clearly haven't if you're no longer together. Not saying you should be together. But if it's between Addie and Willa, Willa doesn't seem like she even likes kids. She got all freaked out when Cady got her shirt dirty. Newsflash! Kids are gross."

Oliver was losing his patience. "She likes kids, Shelby. She's a teacher."

Shelby snorted, "Poor kids."

Oliver raised his voice, "Shelby, that's enough! I'm done with your attitude."

She sucked in a breath, gawking at him.

Oliver went on, "She wasn't upset Cady got her shirt dirty. She was upset—"

My phone vibrated in my pocket, pulling my attention from Oli as he continued to lay into his sister. I had a new text from Addie. I glanced over at her. She held her phone loose at her side while she watched Shelby and Oli going back and forth. I looked back at the text.

Addison: I'm sorry I talked you into coming to New York.

Me: You think I'd want to miss this shit show?

Addison glanced at her phone, smiled, and typed back.

Addison: Yes.

Addison: Very much so.

Addison: Sorry to make you go through all of this with me.

Me: I'm used to family drama. Reminds me of growing up. Only fancier.

She smiled at her phone but didn't text back.

I tuned back into Oli as he said, "—heartless to Willa. You owe her a huge apology." He turned to the rest of the group. "You all do. Don't worry. I plan to spend the rest of my life with her, so you'll have plenty of time to figure out your apologies."

I glanced at Addie to gauge her reaction to that news, but she wasn't giving anything away.

62

ADDISON

OLIVER PLANNED to spend his life with Willa. I already knew this, but to hear him say it so passionately left me with mixed emotions. Had he ever been that passionate about me? Did it matter?

Oliver left the room to call Willa, and after an ominous phone call, we all went out looking for her. Oliver was losing his mind for the hour it took us to find her. Her car had careened off the road and collided with a tree. Oliver wouldn't even let me look her over until we got back to Kim's. He held Willa, cradling her in his arms like she was his entire world.

I tried to convince Willa to get checked out at the hospital, but she refused. I bandaged her up at Kim's, and afterward, gave Oli and Willa some alone time.

When I reentered the family room after all the commotion, Oli's family had seemed to turn a corner. Maybe they realized their pettiness could've led to Willa dying, and they all witnessed Oli's reaction.

Before I could sit down, Travis pulled me into a side

room. Kim and Harry had a sauna installed in their mudroom a few years back. Even though the sauna wasn't on, warm light radiated from its glass doors. The muted light made me yearn for sleep.

Travis placed a hand on my arm. "Are you okay?"

I yawned, turning to him. "I'm just tired. I didn't get a lot of sleep last night, and it's been a stressful day."

His warm brown eyes looked darker in the dim light, and images from last night came to mind. He looked damn good in his suit, and even better now that he'd removed his jacket and tie. The top buttons on his shirt were undone, and my hands went to his collar. My fingers grazed down to the opening of his shirt as I stepped closer.

I avoided his eyes. I knew I shouldn't touch him, and I certainly knew I shouldn't touch him here. Not the way I wanted to anyway.

I leaned into him, resting my forehead against his shoulder. With him so close, his tantalizing scent filled me with so many emotions.

His fingers traced up and down my upper arms as he spoke in a low voice, "You look incredible tonight." Letting out a puff of breath, he said, "Who am I kidding. You're fucking gorgeous all the time, and I've never been allowed to tell you that, but I'm saying it now."

His face dipped to my ear, the scruff of his beard grazing my cheek. "You are beautiful, Addie. There has never been a time I wasn't attracted to you. Even the nights you showed up at the trailer, crying because of your father. I wanted to take you in my arms and tell you how amazing and beautiful you were. At my last birthday celebration, it fucking killed me not to say anything. Your wedding day—fuck."

The next time his hands ran up my arms, they didn't stop

at my bicep. They continued over my shoulders until his palms rested just below my jaw. He lifted my chin.

There were so many words burning in his eyes, but before he said more, I pressed my fingers to his lips. "Shhh." I shook my head. I couldn't let him say more, or I'd have to turn him down, and I didn't want that. I wanted to pretend a little longer.

I lifted my face, pressing my lips to his. His fingers gripped my face and held me while we kissed. It wasn't nearly long enough. I ached to lock the door and get undressed, but this was not the place, and we could do that at the hotel room later. The last thing I wanted was for someone to spot us in here together.

As I pulled away, Travis asked, "Will you ever not be ashamed of me?"

My mouth parted. "What?"

He didn't repeat it. He just stared at me, looking dejected.

I placed my hand on his face, running my fingers along his short beard. "I have never been ashamed of you. I'm ashamed of myself. I—"

The door opened, and I grabbed hold of Travis and pretended to sob. I didn't have to act very hard because these days, even fake crying made me actually cry. Damn pregnancy hormones. Add to that, Travis wrapping me in a hug, and the tears were pouring down my face. If it were Harry at the door, he'd leave at the sight of unpleasant emotion. If it were Kim, I'd tell her I missed my birth mother. Of course, it was Shelby who'd been the one to open the door, and I knew just how to get rid of her.

"What's happening in here?" she asked, flipping on the overhead light.

I had the words ready, but I choked on a real sob, unable to stop what I had started. Oh, hell.

Travis covered for me. "She just got a call from work."

Shelby threw her arms up in surrender. "Nope!" She backed away and closed the door, leaving us to ourselves. Nothing scared Shelby more than her child getting sick. It was to the point that she pretended children didn't get sick. Not hospital sick, anyway. Whenever I spoke about my job, Shelby would disappear or yell at me to stop. Travis must have picked up on this phobia of hers.

Travis snickered. "I was just going to tell her work wished you a Merry Christmas."

I grinned as I wiped away my tears.

He gawked at me. "Wow, you can really turn on the waterworks. I don't think I'll ever trust your tears again."

I laughed. "It's this damn pregnancy. But really, we should get out of here. We can talk at the hotel later."

He nodded and brushed a thumb under my eye. "Perfect," he whispered before turning to lead the way out of the sauna mudroom.

A WHILE LATER, I walked back toward Kim's master bathroom. I had been tasked with getting Oliver, and I still needed to change out of my gown. I almost ran right into him in the hall. He had an overnight bag in his hands.

He held it up, explaining, "Willa needed her undergarments."

I nodded. "Your dad asked me to come get you. I can take that to Willa."

He looked leery.

"I'm not going to bite her."

He handed me the bag. "Tell her I'll be right back."

I nodded. "I will."

We went separate directions, and I knocked at the bathroom door.

"Come in," she called.

I opened the door and slid inside, closing us in together. She clearly hadn't been expecting me, and she gripped her towel tighter.

"I told Oliver I'd bring this to you." I held out her bag. "His dad needed to talk to him. I hope you don't mind."

I turned my back to her, my nose practically to the door. "I won't look. You can change, but I need to say some things to you while I have you cornered."

I didn't hear any movement. I was guessing my audacity shocked her.

But she surprised me by saying, "I'm sorry that I looped you in with the rest of them earlier."

"Oh, I don't blame you. I love Oli's family, but they can make anyone crazy."

I heard her rifling through her bag and pressed forward, saying, "Oli is the sweetest man I've ever met, but also completely oblivious at times. His mom and sister can be vicious, and you were right. They were trying to put Oli and me back together, but we set things straight after you left. I told them I cheated and that you were the one to help Oliver pick up the pieces I'd left behind."

She was quiet, but I could hear her getting dressed. I continued, "Willa, I know this must be difficult for you. Honestly, it's not the easiest for any of us, but I think we're all adjusting and making compromises in order to make this work. I'm not trying to come between you two. And for what it's worth, I've never seen Oli stand up to his family the way he did tonight. He would fight to the end for you, and I think you should know that."

I heard her zip up her bag, saying, "You can turn around."

I spun to face her in her brand-new pajamas. I was jealous and couldn't wait to put mine on.

"I know Oliver loves me, but sharing him with you is hard." She looks so sincere, and I took a breath to respond, but she held up a hand to stop me. "I can't compete with you, Addison, and I really don't want to, but there are little things that nag at me. You have a history together. His family loves you. You're having his baby. I know how important you are to each other, and I'm not against your friendship. It's just hard not to be jealous of you sometimes. Especially of your connection."

I smiled, feeling a bit melancholy. "Oliver is special, and he doesn't know it. If he were anyone else, neither Travis nor I would be here for his family Christmas, and your life would be a lot simpler, but Oliver doesn't give up on people. T and I are essentially strays that followed Oli home from school one day, and once he invited us in, he's never been able to get rid of us. The three of us became a family, albeit a dysfunctional one, but we don't give up on one another." I wiped a tear. "Wow, pregnancy has made me soft."

"I think soft is a good thing," she replied, handing me a tissue.

I dabbed at my eyes. "I'd really like for us to be friends, Willa. Honestly, you're probably the closest thing I have to a girlfriend, which *is* as pathetic as it sounds."

She watched me for a moment before saying, "It doesn't appear that you're going anywhere, so we might as well become friends." She ended with a smirk.

I liked her, even though part of me rebelled at the idea of us being friends. I knew befriending her was the only way forward, and I didn't hate it. I sniffed, dabbing at my eyes again before peeking at myself in the mirror. I cleared my throat and looked back to Willa. "Come on, let's go join the others."

"Oh, I think I'm just going to bed. I can't go to a Classy Dinner like this." She gestured to her snowflake pajamas.

I rolled my eyes, though I couldn't blame her for being skeptical. I grabbed her wrist and pulled her along with me. "Don't worry about it."

We ran into Oliver in the hall, and I passed Willa to him, saying, "Oh good. She was going to hide in the bedroom." I handed her over and retreated down the hall, excited to change into something more comfortable.

63

———

TRAVIS

It was nearing ten o'clock by the time Addison and I drove back to our hotel room in our new flannel Christmas pajamas. Kim always bought us pajamas to wear on Christmas morning. This year we got to wear them earlier than expected.

It had been a long, tiring day, and I'd been looking forward to going back to our hotel room. I had plans for Addison when we got there. Before the hotel door closed, my arms were around her, and my tongue was in her mouth. I wanted to keep her forever, but I would settle for tonight.

After seeing how close Willa came to dying, I needed to show Addison what she meant to me. Life was short. Bad shit happened all the time, so I would take advantage of all the little positives while I could.

Addison pushed back, saying, "T, what are you doing?"

"You know what I'm doing," I breathed against her neck.

"But why?"

I kissed her neck. "Because I want you, and life is short."

She hesitated, so I started unbuttoning my way-too-hot

491

pajama top and let it fall to the floor. Her eyes roamed my chest, and I slipped out of the pants.

She whimpered as she looked me over, and that was a heady feeling. I began stripping her, and she helped me remove her clothes.

Our positions were slightly limited because of her pregnancy, but I wanted to watch her pleasure, and I wanted her to know it was me. I pulled her to the floor-length mirror and stood behind her.

She had a question in her eyes. "Travis, I really don't want to see myself."

"Then look at me." I guided her hands to the smooth glass so she could balance herself, and then my fingers grazed down her spine, and I pulled her ass out. I dipped my fingers between her thighs. It didn't take long to get her warmed up, and she was writhing against my palm.

I pulled my hand away, and she inhaled a sharp breath as my dick filled her. She let out a slow moan of approval. I guided her hips back for a better angle and kissed her shoulder, warning, "Hold on."

Her fingers stretched against the mirror, and her heavily lidded eyes were watching my reflection. I groaned as my teeth grazed her shoulder. "Watch what we do to each other, Add."

I removed my mouth and began thrusting my hips, watching her breasts bounce with the movement. I drew it out until we were both sweaty, and she was crying out for release.

My pace slowed as my hands roamed, one wrapped around her to cup her breast and pinch her nipple while the other ran downward until my fingers found that sensitive bundle of nerves. Her legs quivered as an orgasm gripped her. She clenched around me, pushing me over the edge.

We stood together, my arms wrapped around her while she held the mirror. The only sound was our breath as we fought against gravity. I never wanted to come back down. I wanted to stay in this post-orgasm bliss with Addison wrapped in my arms for eternity.

I found her eyes in the mirror and said, "Be with me."

Her body tensed, and her eyes looked fearful as she held my gaze. I watched an array of conflicting emotions cross her face before she breathed, "I can't."

"Why?"

She shook her head. "This isn't how we should have this conversation."

She tried to pull away, but I held tight to her, saying, "It never seems to be the right time to have this conversation."

She didn't like that. I saw the spark of heat in her eyes and tasted the bitterness as she said, "What about the woman you were with last night?"

I shook my head. "What about her?"

She tried again to get away, but I wasn't letting go. She looked down, avoiding my eyes. "T, it's a bad idea. I . . . I've been feeling vulnerable, but I don't want to give you the wrong impression." She glanced back up, looking afraid to see my reaction.

It seemed on my way down from blissful euphoria, I'd somehow bypassed earth and went straight to Hell.

I smiled a dead man's smile and said, "And what impression would that be, princess? Keep in mind, my dick is still inside of you."

She didn't appreciate my comment as she fought like hell

to get away from me. I let her go, and she rushed into the bathroom, slamming the door.

I wanted to punch something. I wanted to get drunk and forget. Self-destruction would only make things worse. I tried to remember Yolanda's words. Everything had made sense when I spoke to her, and now, I couldn't focus on anything but the roaring anger in my head. I dropped and did pushups, counting out fifty, and then another. After several sets, my arms were shaking, and the roaring anger was only a growl. It was manageable.

By the time she came out of the bathroom, I had put my pajamas back on, switching the flannel top for a t-shirt. Addison had wrapped herself in a robe. While my anger had decreased, hers had only grown, and she came out spitting fire. "First of all, how dare you hold me against my will. Travis, I care about you, but how can you ask me to be with you when you just went out to meet another woman last night? Does your dick make all of your decisions? How can I take you seriously when I know you're not over Deena? You're the only person I trust enough to come to like I did last night. I love you, Travis, but I can't be with you. And I may have slipped up and said Oli's name even though I wasn't thinking about him, but don't forget you called me Deena while you slid inside me bareback."

My eyebrows pinched. I had done that, but I hadn't meant to. I didn't even know what was happening until she called my name. My gaze dropped as shame flooded me. "I didn't mean to."

"I'm not Deena," she said, almost breathless.

I glared at her. "No shit."

She accused, "You still blame me, don't you?"

"Blame you for what?"

"If I had never confessed our infidelity to Oli, none of this would have happened, and you would be proposing to a very pregnant Deena instead of being stuck here with a very pregnant me." She took a shaky breath. "The only reason you called me in September is because Oliver made you feel bad for me. Then you projected Deena onto me because I'm pregnant, and all I really am is a charity case who begs you for sex. Oh my god! What is wrong with me? What's wrong with us? Why can't we stop hurting each other?"

"Because we don't know how to love one another without hurting ourselves."

She stumbled back, sitting at the end of the bed. Her face dropped into her hands. "What have we done, Travis? Here we are, thirty years old, and we've destroyed each other. And for what? Love?" A derisive laugh bellied out of her as she shook her head. "Love doesn't hurt this much."

I stepped forward. "Love always hurts. Loving my dad nearly killed my mom. Almost killed me too. Loving both of my parents and watching them die fucking hurt. Loving you and Oli has always hurt. The only time loving someone didn't hurt me, is when I was with Deena, but she ended up being the one who hurt me the most. So don't tell me love doesn't hurt. It always fucking does."

I ran a hand over my face, and when I looked at her again, she was watching me. She blinked, and a tear slipped from her eye. I watched it run down her cheek and drip onto her robe. She swiped at the moisture and stood, looking around the room, she said, "I don't want to stay here tonight. Let's go back to Kim's. They have extra bedrooms upstairs, so we don't have to share a bed or a room."

I nodded, and we packed up and left.

Halfway to Kim's, Addison asked, "So what are we?"

I arched an eyebrow. "Are we having a define the relationship conversation right now?"

"Don't make me feel small, Travis. I need you to tell me what we are?"

I shrugged. "I've already put all my cards on the table. But you don't trust me to give you anything more than a good fuck when you're in the mood. So, I'd say fucked up friends with benefits."

She shook her head. "I don't want that."

"Which part? The friendship? Because just last night you begged me to fuck you."

She looked out her window while I drove. The silence stretched, awkward and painful.

"You can be a real asshole," she finally said.

"Yep. And you can be a real bitch. It's why we get along so well."

She half laughed, half groaned.

It was midnight by the time we arrived back at Kim's. Shelby appeared to be the only one awake. We found out there was only one available bedroom upstairs since Shelby and Cady weren't sharing a room like they usually did.

Addison and I dumped our stuff in the guest room we'd be sharing. At least there was a bed and a pullout sofa, so we had separate beds. While I set the bed up, Addison went down for a midnight snack or just to avoid me. I wasn't sure.

When I finished setting up the pullout bed, I went to find Addison. I was just about to enter the kitchen when I heard my name and paused.

". . . interested in Travis?" Addison said, making my ears perk.

"Oh, I'm not interested in Travis," Shelby said, "But I still wouldn't mind stumbling into his bed in the middle of the night for some fun."

What the hell? I stepped into the kitchen, noticing Willa had joined Shelby and Addison. "Shelby, stop pretending anything has ever happened between us."

Shelby turned to me. "Oh, but you forget that we once kissed for seven minutes in heaven."

"And you slapped me when I tried to cop a feel."

"You were my little brother's friend. I wouldn't have even let you kiss me if it wasn't part of the game."

Willa cut in. "How old were you when this happened?"

I gestured to myself. "Uh, I was twelve. She was fourteen or fifteen."

"Shelby!" Addison said with mock outrage.

Shelby held up her finger. "First of all, fuck you guys! And second, he did not look like he was twelve, and I was definitely only fourteen."

"Is that the only time you two—"

"Yes," we said in unison.

Shelby said, "Oliver got weird about it."

"Weird, protective?" Willa asked.

"No, like he wanted us to get married so Travis would be part of the family," Shelby said.

Willa laughed. "That doesn't surprise me."

Shelby set a drink in front of Willa and turned to me with a flirtatious grin. "But we could always mess around without letting Oliver know."

"That sounds like an awful idea, Shel. Friends with benefits doesn't work." I said it for Addison, but I didn't dare look at her. Let that sink in, Princess.

Addison stood, and we all looked at her. Her eyes ran over my smug smile, and she said, "I swear, Emerson is using my bladder as a trampoline." We looked after her as she left the room.

Shelby offered, "Travis, would you like a drink?"

"Nah, I'm going to bed. Good night, ladies." I remembered Shelby's words and added, "Shelby, I better not wake up with you in my damn bed."

"Don't flatter yourself. I'm not actually that desperate."

I was already walking out when Willa said, "'Night."

Addison stood on the other side of the family room, in the mouth of the hall. She glared at me with her arms folded over her chest. "Do you always have women slip into your bed at night?"

With a humorless laugh, I said, "What difference does it make to you? Is it so you can judge me and feel more ashamed of me, or are you jealous?"

She rolled her eyes. "It's more likely you'd fuck me in your sleep again."

"That's if you don't beg me for it first. You wouldn't want to give me the wrong impression again. But I can't promise I won't attack you in my sleep again since my dick makes all my decisions."

She blew out a big breath. "Travis, let's just drop it, okay. Obviously, we're not getting anywhere. It's fine," Addison hissed.

I rolled my neck. "I fucking hate the holidays."

She snapped, "Just run off to go fuck one of your girlfriends then."

"Are you fucking serious, Addie?"

"Does this one know you're not over your ex?" she accused.

"Jesus, Addie, you're such a bitch."

"And you're a fucking dick," she said back.

I shook my head. "Let's just get through the next twenty-four hours, and we can be done with each other."

She sucked in a breath, and I saw the hurt in her eyes. She nodded slowly. "Probably for the best."

She turned and walked back to the kitchen. I dropped my face into my palm. I probably should've told her who I met with last night, but I was hurt that she assumed the worst.

I heard a noise and looked up. Willa was patting her legs as she walked through the room, trying way too hard to look casual. I wondered how much she had overheard. None of it was good, and she already hated me.

She attempted to look surprised when our eyes met, like she had just suddenly spotted me. She said, "I thought you were going to bed."

"And I thought you were having a drink in the kitchen."

"I need socks." She pointed at her bare feet as if to prove it.

She walked around me, and I clarified, "It's not what you think."

I didn't know what she thought exactly, but it couldn't be good.

She spun to face me, asking, "What isn't?"

I watched her trying to figure her out before realizing she was giving me an out. She was going to pretend she'd never seen anything. I shook my head. "Nothing."

She nodded. "'Night, Travis."

64

ADDISON

WHEN I MADE it to bed in the wee hours of the morning, Travis was asleep on the pullout mattress with Fluffy curled up next to him.

When I came into the room, the dog lifted his head but didn't move from his spot tucked next to Travis. I never really cared for Fluffy, but I had to admit watching them cuddled together was cute.

I pictured us curled up together like that just last night, and my tears came. I curled into my pillow. I didn't want to cry. I wanted to feel normal again, and I didn't want to share a room with a man I both loved and hated.

His voice startled me even though it was soft, barely above a whisper. "This is what happens when we have sex, Addison. We both end up hating ourselves. When will we learn?"

He must have heard me crying. I sniffled and wiped my face, but the tears only came harder.

His voice stayed quiet as he asked, "You wanna know where I was last night?"

He meant when I took him to meet that woman. "I know where you were."

"No, Addison, that's the problem. You only think you know."

I didn't want to play this game. "I dropped you off, T. I saw you with Yolanda. She practically attacked you."

He sighed. "No, you have that wrong. The woman you saw attack me, I call Jazzy. It drives her crazy, but she lets me get away with it because we've known each other since she was twelve. She's twenty-three now, and her fiancé was standing right next to her. Jazzy's mom is an alcoholic, her dad OD'd, and her little sister is in jail for making meth."

I stared at the wall, trying to figure out what he was trying to tell me, and I didn't know if it was because I was tired or pregnant, but I wasn't comprehending. "What?"

"Yolanda is the leader of an Al-Anon group I've gone to on and off for years. It's a support group for people whose lives have been affected by other's drinking. Yolanda is like an aunt or a big sister to me. I've never once thought about sleeping with her. The people in these groups understand how messy addiction is in a way you and Oli never could, and I guess it was something personal I never really felt you or Oli needed to know."

It took me a while to wrap my mind around that. "We would've supported you."

"Your support comes with judgment, Add."

I sat up. "When have I ever judged you?"

He propped his head on his fist. "When I tried to meet with a support group, you alluded that I was a man whore. But I haven't been that guy for years. I fucked up at the bar last month. I saw myself on video, and I looked just like him, just like my dad. I acted like him too. I haven't had any alcohol since."

"T, you're not an alcoholic. It was just a terrible night."

He stared at me. "One you probably won't ever let me live down."

That wasn't fair. "Travis, that night wasn't only hard on you. Two hours after professing your love for me and then declaring our friendship over, you called me while having sex with someone else. What was I supposed to think?" I sighed. "I'm sorry that I thought Yolanda was a hookup, but why didn't you correct me?"

"Because it fucking hurt. It pissed me off. You should know me better by now. You shouldn't just assume I only meet with women for sex. I shouldn't have to prove myself to you. The night you rejected me, I was at my worst, but you should know that's not where I live my life. The reason I slept with you is because I was afraid there would never be another chance. If I just wanted some action, there are a million other women less complicated than you. I hate how much I love you. Nobody can infuriate me like you do, and no one makes me feel more worthless."

I laid back down, trying to hide my emotion. "I'm sorry." I only had a month left before the baby came. I wanted him in my life, but it was selfish to hold on to him when I only caused him pain. I said, "Maybe it is better if we spend some time apart." Saying it terrified me.

"I think you're right," he agreed.

I blew out a breath. I missed him already.

WE SPENT Christmas morning with Oliver's family, and we both took naps in the afternoon before heading home. I dropped Travis at his apartment around ten and didn't get home until close to midnight. It felt good to be in my own bed, and Rozsa curled up next to me, her purr letting me know she approved of me being home.

PART FOUR

65

ADDISON

MY WATER DIDN'T SUDDENLY BREAK like they do in the movies. I woke at three AM with cramping. It subsided, and I thought little of it. I still had two more weeks of being humongous and miserably pregnant, but as soon as I fell back to sleep, I woke with another round of pain. I figured I was only having Braxton Hicks contractions, but the rhythm became slightly more frequent and intense.

I was scheduled to work that morning, so I figured I would swing by the Emergency Department before work, just so they could confirm that it wasn't real labor. But by the time I got out of the shower and got dressed, I could barely catch my breath. I crouched over the bed with a crippling pain in my lower back.

I sent a text to my colleague, a fellow pediatric oncologist, letting her know I was having cramping and needed to go to my OB when they opened. She asked about my symptoms, and when I told her, she said I was being stupid and told me to go to the hospital. I knew she was right, but suddenly, I wasn't ready. I was miserable and huge and didn't want to be pregnant anymore, but the next time I came home, I'd have a tiny, fragile human who relied on me for every single thing. My anxiety over all the things that could go terribly wrong grew exponentially more terrifying. I was a doctor. I knew too much.

I was hyperventilating. I hadn't prepared enough to be a mom. My life would never be the same. And what happened if Emerson got injured, or what if something went wrong during delivery? There were so many unknowns, and every kid I had ever treated flashed through my mind. What happened if my child ended up like Gracie?

I wasn't ready. I couldn't do this, but as another contraction rolled through my body, all of my doubts were momentarily wiped away by the pain.

When the worst of it passed, and I could think again, I grabbed my phone and called Oliver. If I were too far along, they wouldn't give me an epidural, and I wanted an epidural. I wanted all the things to make this process easier.

While I waited for Oliver to pick me up, I realized I needed to clean the house. It would be harder to clean when I had a baby with me. Rozsa sat on the back of the couch watching as I started mopping the kitchen floor because that seemed to be my highest priority. Better to focus on the kitchen tiles than think of all the terrible ailments that could afflict my child.

Oliver used his house key, rushing inside like a tornado had chased him. He spotted me and said, "I thought you'd be on the porch waiting for me." His eyes widened. "What are you doing? Why are you mopping?"

"The floor was dirty."

He let out a strangled laugh. "Good Lord, Addison!"

"I want my house to be clean when I bring the baby home," I reasoned as I continued.

"You have the cleanest house I've ever seen. I could eat off your floor. Now drop the mop and come on."

"I can't leave it like this. It's not finished."

He walked toward me, taking the mop from my hands. "I thought you were in pain?"

"I am, but I have to finish this." I grabbed for the mop, and he pulled it out of my reach.

"Willa will finish the floors. Come on. Get your coat. Where is the go bag?"

"I don't want Willa to finish the floors. She shouldn't have to do that for me."

He shook his head. "She'd be doing it for me, so I don't lose my mind. Come on!"

"I could've been finished by no—o—owww." I grabbed my lower belly with one hand while the other gripped the counter. The contraction reminded me who was really in charge, and it sure as hell wasn't me.

As soon as it passed, I looked up to Oliver, who looked as if he would kill me if I didn't get in the car. I nodded. "The go bag is by the door. My coat is in the closet."

I texted the cat sitter on my ride to the hospital. Then looked to Oli, saying, "If I die during delivery, I'm glad Emerson has you and Willa."

He looked over at me, his eyes wide. "Addison, you and Emerson are both going to be just fine."

"You don't know that."

"I'm going by the odds."

"Willa will be a good mom, and I don't think she'll treat Emerson any differently from her own children."

"You're right, and you'll get to see that for yourself."

"Okay, but if it comes down to me or the baby, choose the baby, okay? Oh my god, I should've made a will."

"Addie, please stop."

M Y LABOR WAS LONG ENOUGH that the doctor offered a cesarean. The baby was not in distress, so I just kept pushing even when I didn't think I could. I was in terrible shape and knew I was minutes away from a c-section even if I didn't want it.

I was not my best self. Despite the epidural doing its job, I still felt lots of pressure and cramping. It was hard to push something I could barely feel, like whistling after receiving a mouth full of Novocain. I couldn't tell how things were going. I had shouted at Oliver and sworn at the doctor and nurses. I was starving but only allowed to have ice chips. I was hangry, sleep-deprived, and weary. I had studied labor and all its parts, but I could never have prepared myself for the physical and emotional exhaustion.

At eleven PM, the pressure shifted, and I heard Emerson cry for the first time. It was as if time stood still when I heard her first little scream. I realized nothing else mattered but the body attached to that shriek. Tears of exhaustion and joy mixed with the beads of sweat dripping down my face.

A piece of my heart now lived outside of my body, and I needed it back. I reached for her, my eyes following the nurses. The doctor was talking to me, but I couldn't hear him. Not until Emerson, tiny and slippery, was in my arms. I cried tears of elation, forgetting all the pain it took to get us here.

I looked over to Oliver, whispering, "We did it."

∾

HOURS LATER, I was still marveling at her ten tiny fingers and ten adorable toes. Toes that I would paint pink in a few years. My perfect baby girl. I had never felt such an intense bond. I would kill to protect this tiny human. Hot tears streamed down my cheeks, continuing my crying streak.

"Oliver, look at her."

"I am," he said, so close I felt his breath on my bare shoulder.

I peeked up at him and pressed my lips together when I saw the moisture in his eyes. He stared at our daughter like she was the most precious thing in the world. She was, of course. I reached out and squeezed the hand he rested on the edge of the bed. I laughed through my tears. "We made this."

His eyes softened further, reminding me of his tender heart. He had been with me for the last twenty-four hours, and for many of those hours, I had been a monster, scream-ing, exhausted, and emotional. And through it all, he'd been there, holding my hand and encouraging me. It reminded me of how badly I'd messed up. Here we were, forever bonded by this beautiful bundle of genetics. Holding her with Oliver right next to me, it no longer made sense that we weren't a family.

His knuckle grazed her chubby cheek. "She has your nose." His eyes flicked to mine.

I couldn't breathe. "Oli." My lips trembled. "Did we make a mistake?"

He held my eyes as he started to understand what I was saying.

"Shouldn't we be a family?" I said softly.

He gave me a sad smile. "We are a family."

I put my hand on his cheek. "But I mean a proper family."

He put his hand over mine and turned to kiss my palm before pulling my hand away. "Addie, we made a lot of mistakes, but separating wasn't one of them."

I turned my head, wishing I could take the words back or leave the room. I could cradle Emerson like a football and charge out of the room, except my body hurt, and I was in no shape to run anywhere. So, I'd have to settle for looking out the window.

I felt Oliver's hand on my chin. He pulled my face toward him as his eyebrows pinched together. "Addie, you're not alone. I'm here. I'm part of this with you. Just because we're not together doesn't mean we aren't in this together."

I blinked, feeling beyond exhausted. "I need to sleep."

"Do you want me to take her to the nursery?"

My eyes shot open. "No." I squeezed her against my chest like he would attempt to rip her from my arms.

He held his hands up in surrender. "Okay. Sleep." He pointed at the chair next to the bed. "I'll be right here if you need anything."

"Don't you need to get back to Willa?"

He pretended not to notice the venom in my voice, saying, "She should be here soon. She stopped at your house to finish mopping the kitchen."

I rolled my eyes. "Well, isn't she just perfect?"

Oliver sat down. "Sleep, Addie. You'll feel better after you rest."

"Don't tell me what I'll feel. You have no idea what I'm feeling."

"Shhh, Addie." He leaned forward to stroke his finger across Emerson's fuzzy blonde head. "She's sleeping."

It was the most delicate way he could scold me without

actually scolding me. I didn't want Emerson to pay for my short-comings, and I never wanted her to hear us arguing. I kissed her head and ran my hand over her back until I fell asleep.

WHEN I WOKE, my arms went to Emerson only to realize she wasn't there. My eyes flew open, and I sat up in a panic. "Where is she? Where is my baby?"

The room was empty. I knew I was thinking irrationally, but I needed to know she was okay. I needed to find someone and make them take me to her. I swung my feet off the bed, my body aching with the tremendous effort it took to move. Then I remembered where I was and grabbed the call light.

A nurse came into the room. "Addison, did you need something?"

"Where's my baby?"

"She's with her father just outside the nursery. He wanted you to be able to rest."

"Well, I'm awake now. Will you please ask him to bring her back?"

She nodded. "Of course."

"Thank you."

I looked around the room. It was noon, so at least I had slept for a few hours, but I wasn't ready to be away from my baby. Plus, she was probably hungry.

A moment later, I heard a small knock at the door. At first, I figured it was Oliver, but as the door slowly opened, I heard Travis call, "Addie?"

"Yeah, come in."

The door opened fully, and in walked Travis with an obnoxious bouquet of pink pacifier balloons anchored to a gift wrapped in pink packaging with frilly ribbons and bows.

Unexpected tears interrupted my laugh. Damn it. I was so emotional. I hadn't seen him since Christmas, and I wasn't expecting him to come. But I was glad he was there.

"It's great to see you." I wiped my eyes and said, "Sorry, I'm a little emotional."

"I think that's to be expected."

I smiled through my tears as he set the gift down on the side table and leaned in to hug me.

"Shh, don't cry," he said, holding me, which only prompted more tears. I felt his lips graze my temple as he held me.

"I missed you," I confessed.

"I missed you too." He pulled back just as the room door opened again.

66

TRAVIS

Oli came into Addison's hospital room holding their baby. She looked so tiny in his arms.

"That's her?" I asked, sounding like an idiot.

Oli looked down at her. "Nah, it's just one I found."

"Shut up." I stepped forward to get a better look at her. "She's so tiny."

"Six pounds, eleven ounces. Twenty-one inches long," Oli bragged.

"I don't really know if that's good or not, but she seems perfect to me."

She started fussing, and Addison said, "She's probably hungry."

Oli moved toward the bed. "Do you want to nurse her? If not, the nurse offered to get a bottle."

Addie shook her head, looking offended. "No, I can nurse her."

Oli nodded. "Do you want the lactation—"

"No. I can do it," she insisted.

He handed her the baby. "Okay, but if not, call the nurse."

She nodded, cooing at the baby. Oliver started moving toward the door, and Addie asked, "Where are you going?"

"I'm gonna head home for a shower. I'll be back in a couple of hours. Call me if you need me sooner. Do you want me to pick up some food for you?"

"Yes!"

Oli grinned. "What would you like?"

"Pasta and orange juice and chocolate," she said.

I made a face of disgust, hoping she wasn't eating them together, but Oli looked like it was a totally normal request. "Is that all?" he asked.

She hesitated. "Yes."

"Are you sure?"

"Yes." She nodded. "Thank you."

"No problem. I'll text you when I'm on my way back. Let me know if you think of anything else."

"Thanks, Oliver. Is Willa coming back with you?"

He looked uncomfortable. "Depends on how you're feeling."

She rolled her eyes with a sigh. "I'm fine."

Emerson started fussing, and Oli moved toward me, patting my shoulder. "Hey, Travis. Walk me out."

I turned, joking, "I didn't realize we were dating? Do you want me to carry your books? Should we stop by your locker?"

Oliver rolled his eyes. "Come on. Give her some privacy to nurse Emerson."

I nodded and to Addie said, "Just text me when it's safe to come back."

"Okay, but it might take a little while."

"I don't mind. I still want to hold the little peanut."

She grinned and nodded. "I'll text you."

Once we were out in the hall, Oli said, "Thanks for coming."

I nodded as we headed out of the maternity ward. "I was always planning on coming to meet the baby. What's going on? What was all the weirdness in there?"

He raked a hand through his hair. "Her emotions are kind of unreliable. I mean, she suggested we should never have broken up."

I shrugged. "She's vulnerable right now. I'm sure she's exhausted, and her hormones have to be all fucked up. She had a traumatic day, and you've been there with her through it all."

"Will you stay with her until I get back?"

"I already told you I would over the phone."

"Thanks."

Oliver left the hospital, and I waited around until Addison texted me.

When I went back in, she held a sleeping Emerson in her arms. She was so tiny. "Addie, she's perfect."

"I know. I can't stop staring at her."

I ran my hand over her shoulder. "How are you feeling?"

"Tired. Sore. Hungry. Emotional. And so in love." She stared at Emerson for a while longer before looking up at me. "Do you want to hold her?"

I swallowed. "She looks really breakable."

Addie laughed. "She is breakable, but you won't hurt her." She lifted her to me, and I held her in my hands. I could fit her whole body in my two palms. She opened her blue eyes— eyes just like her parents. Her little lips made a little O before morphing into a yawn.

"Are you tired?" I asked the baby. She frowned, and her

little lips trembled before opening for the most heart-breaking cry I'd ever heard. I held her out to Addison.

Addie shook her head, refusing to take her. "You're holding her like you're about to sacrifice her to the gods or something. Hold her closer."

I pulled her against my chest, readjusting and tucking her into the crook of my arm. Her crying stopped. And she rubbed her face against my chest. "I don't have any milk."

Addie said, "See, you're a natural." She gave me a warm smile. "You'll be her favorite uncle."

Emerson looked up at me as her swollen eyelids grew heavy, and after a moment, she fell asleep in my arms. I felt a deep primal protectiveness. This little girl was cherished beyond measure by her mom, her dad, me, and I knew Willa would feel the same. My eyes grew moist, and I knew I had to give Emerson back before I lost control of my feelings.

Addison gladly took her back, and we sat in comfortable silence for a while. Her stomach growled, and I asked, "Do you want me to get you something to eat? Don't they serve food?"

"They do. I ate something this morning, but Oli should be back soon with my food. You know what sounds really good is a giant chocolate cake from that vegan bakery. But that's so far out of the way. I couldn't ask Oli to go there. He already thinks I'm a nutcase."

"He knows you aren't a nutcase."

"Yeah right. Why else would he ask you to come stay with me?"

Busted.

I tried to play it off. "I always planned to come visit when Emmy got here."

She was momentarily distracted as she looked down at

her sleeping baby. "You hear that, Emmy. Uncle T gave you your first nickname."

I pulled out my phone and texted Addison's chocolate cake order to Oliver. It would be good to earn bonus points now that she knew she was being babysat.

"I don't need a sitter," she said to me.

I hit send on the text and looked at Addie.

"He didn't want you to be alone. And I had to restrain myself from coming yesterday when I got news you were in labor. You can be pissed that I'm here, or you can enjoy my company and use me as your servant. Either way, you're stuck with me."

After a moment, she said, "I'm still happy you're here. It just feels tainted now. With you, I never know how much you do out of love and what you do out of loyalty. Today I'm going to pretend you're here because you want to be, and I won't feel bad for wanting you here."

I wanted to be there with her more than she knew, but twelve hours after delivering a baby wasn't the right time to delve into deeper feelings.

6 7

ADDISON

ONCE EMERSON WAS asleep in the bassinet, Travis made me open his gift, which was a box filled with baby girl clothes.

Travis gave a self-deprecating laugh. "Everything was so cute and girlie. I couldn't stop myself. And those shoes. Completely pointless, I know, but she'll be the best-dressed baby in the neighborhood."

I laughed. "I can honestly say I wasn't expecting this from you."

I folded the baby clothes back into the box when someone knocked at the door.

"Come in," I called when the door remained closed.

Travis went over and opened it. He peeked out into the hall before stepping back and opening the door wider to let Willa inside.

She came into the room and glanced at me. In a soft voice, she asked, "Travis, will you give us a minute?"

Travis glanced at me, and I nodded.

As he left, he said, "I'll be just outside if you need anything."

The door closed, and Willa looked nervous. She stepped forward and blew out a breath. "Oliver told me to wait for him, but he doesn't understand women sometimes. He told me what you said to him, and I have to know, did you change your mind?"

I had expected him to tell her, but I hadn't expected her to confront me. I stumbled over my words before regaining my balance. "I—I didn't—I couldn't have prepared myself for all the emotions I've had in the past thirty-six hours. I was sleep-deprived and overwhelmed when I suggested Oli and I should be together. I didn't mean it and immediately regretted it. I'm sorry."

She came forward as I spoke until she was right next to the bed. "I don't want you to be sorry. I want you to be honest. You told me before that you wouldn't change your mind, but if you have, or even if you think you have—"

"I haven't." Shame flooded me as I bit my lip and shook my head. "I promise I haven't. I just got lost in the moment."

Willa nodded, peeking into the bassinet, holding in tears of her own. Her voice shook. "Can I admit something to you?"

I nodded, observing her.

"Hospitals bring up terrible memories for me." A tear slid down her cheek, and she wiped it away. "It scared me to come here. I was afraid I'd resent you and have some aversion to Emerson."

"Do you?"

Willa shook her head. "No," she cried. "Can I hold her?"

"Of course."

Willa scooped her up, a natural mom. The lingering bitterness I'd been feeling toward her was washed away by her candor and obvious adoration for my daughter. She rocked Emmy, and I wondered when it'd be her turn.

Oliver arrived without knocking. He swept into the room in a panic, but as he took us in, his expression relaxed, and he held up a pastry box, saying my three favorite words. "I've got cake."

~

THE HOSPITAL DISCHARGED Emerson and me late the next morning. Oliver drove us to my house, and as we pulled into the driveway, I saw we had unexpected company. My father and Jeanine stood outside while Willa stood sentry in the doorway.

"Did you know they were coming?" Oli said as we parked.

I stared at my dad as he turned and headed for Oli's car. "I had no idea."

Oliver offered, "I'll get Emerson and meet you inside."

I nodded, getting out of the car, feeling timid about facing my father again after so many months of rejection. Had he changed his mind? Was he here to make amends and restore our relationship?

I met him on the sidewalk at the front of the house. "What are you doing here?"

His head jerked back. "Is that any way to greet your father? I drove seven hours to visit my daughter and her new baby, and this woman won't let me in the house." He waved a hand at Willa. "It makes me wonder if we made a mistake in coming."

I blinked, taking a breath of the cold air as I pulled my coat closer. "I didn't—what are—I wasn't expecting you. It's a surprise. I'm surprised, is all." I looked at Willa. "It's okay. Please let them in."

Willa glared at my father before moving out of the way. She had come to my house early to clean the litter box and do some last-minute things before we arrived home with Emmy.

We all filed into the house, Oliver in the rear with the baby carrier. He set Emerson down while he shut the door and removed his coat.

My father was still in a huff. "Is there a reason you didn't tell us you gave birth to our granddaughter? Do you know how humiliating it was for Jeanine to hear about it from Oliver's parents? We couldn't believe you'd do that to us. We had to come see for ourselves, because surely our daughter wouldn't keep our granddaughter hidden from us."

I blinked. They hadn't even looked at the baby carrier.

My father glanced around, his eyes falling on Willa. "Addison, is this woman your housekeeper? If so, you should fire her. This house is filthy. Look at these floors. Do you want a baby crawling on these?" His lips curled in distaste when he spotted Rozsa. "Is that a cat?"

My father had always emphasized how dirty animals were. He couldn't understand the appeal of having an indoor pet. I turned to him, watching as he continued appraising the space. I reasoned, "Emerson won't be crawling for months. Willa is not my housekeeper, and I haven't been able to clean the last few days because I was in the hospital."

He returned his gaze on Willa. "If she's not your house-keeper, who is she?"

Oliver had finished getting Emerson out of her carrier and moved to stand next to Willa. "She's my girlfriend."

The redness started creeping up my father's neck and

continued to climb as he stepped toward Oliver and pointed at Emerson. "But that's not her baby! You're going to knock up my daughter and leave her for this woman?" He sneered. "I expected more from a man like you."

"Dad," I begged.

Willa stepped in front of Oli, looking ready for battle. "Does it look like he just left her?"

Oliver pulled Willa back with his free hand before addressing my father. "It might seem unconventional to you, but we all love Emerson. Willa is here to help. I'd appreciate it if you'd lower your voice. Emmy and Addison just got home from the hospital, and none of us need you in here criticizing everything."

My father's cheeks turned burgundy, and I worried about his blood pressure. "Addison doesn't know what she needs. She's never known what's best for her! Without my direction, she never would have become a doctor or finished the top of her class. She wouldn't be the success she is today without my guidance. And the only thing you and your mistress are doing is derailing her life."

I took a calming breath, keeping my voice even. "I'm grateful for my education, and I'm lucky to have a father who could financially support me as a student. I've been fortunate, and I don't take it for granted, but you don't get to take credit for all of my successes. Those accomplishments are mine, and I did them despite your constant criticism and demeaning remarks. I'm not a child anymore. I make my own decisions. Also, you haven't spoken to me in months and now you just drop in without notice the day I get home from the hospital. That is incredibly thoughtless of you, and I would like for you to leave."

There was a beat of silence before my father scoffed. "Get

control of your hormones, Addison! For God sakes, you disrespectful—"

"Get out!" I shouted, my body shaking.

My father shook his head, stepping towards me. "You don't tell me what to do."

I leaned against the couch. Everything hurt. My heart, my body, my spirit. I sighed, looking up at my father. "For Emerson's sake, I have to ask you, father, to get the hell out of my house."

He backhanded me. Hard.

Jeanine gasped.

My hand covered the stinging in my cheek as pain reverberated in my jaw. I looked at him in disbelief.

Oliver darted forward, getting between my father and me, while Jeanine pulled on my father's arm, scolding, "Jonathon!"

I heard Emerson cry and searched for her, finding her safe in Willa's arms. Oliver pulled my face toward him, gently cupping my cheeks. His eyes were wide and searching.

"I'm okay," I said, feeling detached from the situation. These were the moments I had always run to Travis, so it made sense that my mind conjured him when I closed my eyes. I pictured being safe in his arms. He would've killed my father had he actually been there.

Even Oli, the least violent man I knew, looked like he was ready for blood. He spun toward my dad, taking a step, but I caught his hand. "Leave it, Oli. He's just a sad old man lashing out because he didn't get his way. Will you see him out? I need to lie down."

He nodded, and I turned away.

"You are not the daughter I raised," my father called after me. "Come on, Jeanine. We're leaving."

"I'll meet you at the car," she said.

I went into my room and got into bed, leaving the door open to hear if Emerson needed me. Her crying had stopped, and I knew she was safe with Willa. Before I could close my eyes, Jeanine entered my bedroom. She watched me with a sorrowful expression. Placing her soft hand against my cheek, she said, "Tell me that's the first time."

Jeanine's eyes roamed my face, and I said, "You know it's not."

She shook her head. "Why would you say that? He's tough on you, but he's never laid a hand on you before."

I nodded. "Whatever you say." She didn't want the truth even as it stared her in the face.

Her eyebrows knit together. "I would've known if he hit you. I would've seen it. You would've come to me, right?"

As she watched my face, her expression fell. Maybe she did want the truth.

"Oh, Addison," she breathed as tears filled her eyes.

TRAVIS

I TEXTED Addison when I pulled up in front of her house to let her know I was there. She'd only been home from the hospital for a week, and I knew enough to know you shouldn't pop in on a new mom, but this was by-the-book, Addison. I figured she had it down to a science at this point. Oliver said she was killing it as a new mom. Jeanine had offered to stay to help, but Addison said she had everything under control. Oliver and Willa lived just down the street, and he said they had been over every day to see Emerson.

Addison: Come on in.

When I walked in, everything looked standard—clean, together, untouched by the chaos of a baby.

I found Addison in the kitchen. She held the baby against her chest, bouncing while she stirred the pot of yellow noodles.

"Are you eating mac and cheese?" I looked from her to the pot. "With hotdogs?"

She pinned me with a glare, pointing the spoon at me. "If you tell anyone, I'll kill you!"

"Do you want me to take her?" I offered.

"No, I think she's finally sleeping. I need to put her in the swing. I know that's not what you're supposed to do, but it's the only place she will actually sleep." She left the stove to lay Emerson in a cradle, then she hit a button, and it started rocking slowly.

Addison rushed back to the stove, took the pot off, and then proceeded to eat straight out of the pot, using the wooden spoon to shovel the processed cheesy noodles and meat into her mouth. Her eyes closed with a moan. Her shirt was stained, and her hair looked greaser than I had ever seen it.

She didn't seem to notice me gawking at her. "Ehh, you doing okay, Add?"

She looked pissed that I'd interrupted her. She swallowed her mouthful and complained, "My boobs hurt. My nipples are leaking. My clothes are stained with breastmilk and spit up. I don't remember the last time I washed my hair. I'm sooo hungry. I still feel like a cow, but also kinda like I could eat a cow. My vagina hurts, and I'm worried it's never gonna be the same. And I'm so, so tired."

I stared at her, afraid to say anything.

"Don't look at me like that!" She shoved another heaping spoonful of mac and cheese in her mouth.

I shifted my eyes to look elsewhere, but everything else seemed in order other than her behavior and appearance. Was she cleaning instead of sleeping?

I offered, "Aren't you supposed to sleep when the baby sleeps, or something?"

She gave a laugh that sounded half demonic. I spun back to her so I could see if she was about to attack. "You're a funny guy, Travis. I still have to cook and clean, go grocery shopping, do laundry, and another dozen or so things. And I have to do them all while she's sleeping because when she's awake, she is sucking the perkiness out of my breasts."

"Have you told Oli you need help?"

She groaned long and loud before snapping, "I'm her mother! I'm the one she needs, and I should be able to do this by myself. I don't want Oli's help, and I don't need Willa proving she's better at all of this than I am."

"Why did you send your mom home?"

"My father wanted her home, and the last thing I need is for my father to be more upset with me. This is my mess. I shouldn't call it a mess. Emerson is a miracle. She's absolutely worth it. She deserves the best, and I'm failing her."

"Why don't you go shower and take a nap? I'll watch Emerson this afternoon."

"I will not let you babysit because you feel bad for me."

"It's not because I feel bad for you. It's because I feel bad for her having to smell you like that. You need a shower."

She glared at me. "You know nothing about babies."

"I know enough to keep her alive for an afternoon."

"Do you?"

"I mean, I've never changed a baby's diaper before, but I took care of my dad when he was incontinent. I feel like if I could handle that, a baby would be easy."

She nodded. "I forgot you did that."

"I'll be fine, Addie. Will she take formula, or are you only breastfeeding? Is she on some kind of feeding schedule?"

"She'll take a bottle. I breastfeed most of the time, but I'm not sure how much I'm producing, so I still give her a few bottles of formula. She eats about every hour or two, but then she sometimes goes four hours."

"Okay, I'll feed every one to four hours. How much?"

She walked me through how to mix formula and how to warm up a bottle. When she finished, she stepped back. "Are you sure about this?"

"Yes. Go."

She walked backward toward her bedroom, eyeing Emerson. She glanced back at me, nodded, and then went to her room.

I heard the shower running and relaxed back on the couch, pulling up YouTube tutorials on how to change a baby's diaper.

ADDISON

I WOKE IN A PANIC. Where was Emerson? What if she had stopped breathing, and I slept through it?

These terrible scenarios played through my mind more often than I'd like. I knew it was normal to have anxieties, but mine were bordering on Shelby's level. I had seen too many bad things when I worked in the emergency department. I knew too much. But I also knew I couldn't be everywhere at once, and no matter how careful I was, accidents happened. Not everything was preventable, and I just had to have faith that she would be okay, or I'd drive myself crazy.

I walked out into the living room, and my heart came to a standstill. My footsteps faltered, and I fell in love with the picture before me. Travis held Emerson against his chest. She looked so tiny in his big, powerful arms.

Travis looked up and smiled at me. "She survived."

I had to catch my breath. "I see that. How'd it go?"

"Nothing I couldn't handle. She does love to spit up, doesn't she?"

"Oh, yes. And it always seems to miss the burp cloth. She has a talent. I can take her."

"Nah, she's comfy here. Let her sleep. She'll probably be up soon, anyway."

I leaned against the oversized chair. "When did she eat last?"

"An hour ago, and I burped her and changed her before she fell asleep."

"Thank you, Travis."

"Addison, I'm happy to help, but you need to let Oli do some of this. He wants to spend time with his daughter, but he doesn't want to step on your toes. I know your emotions are a little wonky, and it's probably hard to ask for his help when part of you still loves him, but tell him what you need. If that means for him to take Emerson for the night, let him. If that means for him to leave Willa at home, then—"

"I'm not in love with Oli." I closed my eyes, inhaling through my humiliation. "That was a momentary lapse in judgment. It's just that this can feel pretty lonely, and then Willa comes by and makes everything look so easy. I like her, but I'm already feeling insecure, and she's everything I'm not. My dad only made me feel worse."

His brow perked. "What about your dad?"

"He dropped in the day we got home from the hospital."

He sat up straighter. "Your dad was here?"

I nodded. "He backhanded me and really made an ass out of himself in front of everyone. Jeanine's offer to stay was her way of making up for not being there in the past. She was shocked that he hit me. She never knew he laid a hand on me. I couldn't give her all the details. It would only make her feel worse. She would've been staying here out of guilt and to avoid my father. Their marriage is in trouble, and I don't want to make things worse for them." I sighed.

He looked livid. "Did Oliver see it?"

I nodded.

"Did he hit him back?"

Shaking my head, I said, "No, and I didn't want a fight. I just wanted him to leave. Oli made sure he left our house. I could tell Oli wanted to hit him if it makes you feel better. For a second, I thought Willa might go after him, but she was holding Emmy. I know you would've murdered him."

"Damn straight. Did you tell Oli it's happened before?"

I shook my head.

"You have to be honest with him, Addison. If not about your father, then at least about when you need help with Emerson. You have unrealistic expectations for yourself, and it's only going to hurt you and Emerson. We all care about you, and every single one of us would do anything for this little girl."

I was suddenly envious of my baby wrapped up in his arms. I wanted to be in his arms with her. I wanted him to look at me with that same adoration. I'd made a lot of mistakes, but even if I'd done nothing else right in my life, at least I did this one good thing. If I died young like my mother, my daughter would be surrounded by people who adored her.

The love I felt for Emerson was immeasurable. My heart gushed with it, overflowing. It didn't matter what she did with her life. She would be loved for more than her achievements. She would never wonder if she was good enough or feel she had to prove her worth.

I sunk down onto the chair, realizing how ridiculous it sounded. My father's love had always been conditional.

Why? Why wasn't I enough? Travis, who held no blood relation to Emerson, was looking at her with more affection than my father had ever spared me. The thought hollowed me out. Where did the fault lie?

Was I unlovable in the eyes of my father, or was he just incapable of showing the love I'd been seeking my entire life? Why did his opinion of me even matter? And hadn't I already worked through this before. It was a wound that never seemed to heal, even years later.

"You okay?"

My eyes snapped to Travis, and I nodded, giving him a forced smile.

"Come here," he beckoned me, putting an arm out on the back of the sofa.

I took the seat next to him, and he wrapped his arm around my shoulder, drawing me into him. He kissed the side of my head before asking, "Where'd you go?"

"What?"

"Your thoughts. You seemed lost for a minute."

"Oh, yeah, just thinking."

"About."

"How Emerson has so many people who love her, and she's only a week old."

"It helps that she has an incredible momma."

"I don't know about that. I've been eating so much crap this week."

Travis laughed, and I glared up at him.

His laughter stopped. "Oh my god, you're serious. A week of mac and cheese won't kill you."

I watched Emerson's chest rise and fall. "My mom died at thirty-two. I should do everything I can to stay healthy for Emerson's sake."

"Addison, look at me."

When I looked up at him, he continued, "Is that why you went vegan? Because you're afraid you're gonna die young like your mom?"

I shrugged.

"Addie, you're in great health. Maybe a bit tightly wound, but your mom died of an aneurysm, right? Is that genetic?"

When I shook my head, he said, "None of us know when it's our time, but you're not gonna die because you ate mac and cheese. You've gotta learn to relax a little."

"It's never a good idea to tell a hormonal woman to relax," I warned.

"I say it with love," he said, kissing the side of my head to soften the blow.

Something about the easy way he held me and showed me affection choked me up. I tried to swallow it down, but suddenly everything felt so overwhelming, and to my sheer embarrassment, I couldn't contain my tears. He'd seen me cry before, but there had been reasons. This time, out of nowhere, I was an emotional mess.

He pushed the hair away from my face. "Why are you crying?"

"I don't deserve you," I cried. "You've seen me at my worst, and yet you still come back. You lo—love—you love Emerson, and you don't even have to." I was all out blubbering.

When I peeked up at him, he smirked. "You have no idea how hard it is to get rid of me. And if you're trying to scare me away by acting all crazy, you'll have to remember who I grew up with. My mom could outcrazy just about anyone."

I grabbed tissues from the side table and blew my nose. "Thank you, Travis. For being my friend. For loving my daughter. For continuously looking out for me. You mean so much to me." I was dangerously close to confessing all my feelings for him, but some rational part of my brain must have been working well enough to tell me it was not the time.

He was giving me a warm look, but suddenly his eyes glanced down, and with a brief grin, he said, "Uh, you're leaking."

I looked down, and sure enough, I was leaking breast-milk. "Damn it. Of course." I stood and went to change my clothes, remembering to put the nipple pads in my bra this time. Nipple pads might not be sexy, but nothing said sexy like leaking nipples. Dear Lord, women had to be insane to put their bodies through this shit over and over again.

70

ADDISON

IT TOOK a few weeks to get the hang of being a new mom, and I still had areas to improve. My jealousy of Willa was the first thing that had to go. I sucked up my pride and asked her to come over.

We sat in the living room while Emmy napped. After making brief small talk, I opened up about why I asked her to come.

Just like Willa had done in the hospital room, I laid out my feelings. I sat forward on the couch. "Willa, you make everything look so easy. I'm killing myself trying to keep up with you. You're faster at diaper changes and making bottles. You're better at dealing with the nonstop crying. And you look like that." I waved a hand at her. "I'm jealous. I mean, you aren't covered in spit up, your boobs aren't leaking, and you don't have a sagging stomach that's impossible to hide. And I'm a doctor who specializes in pediatrics. I already feel like I should be better at this than I am. But I feel like a failure."

My parents raised me to hold in my emotions and dance

light-footed around ugly truths. So admitting something that painted me less than perfect felt terribly inappropriate and fantastically liberating.

Willa didn't laugh or shame me. She looked befuddled and took a moment to gather her words. Shaking her head, she leaned forward in her chair. "I honestly can't believe you're feeling that way. Addison, you are an amazing mom. I'm not better than you at any of those things. I'm just well rested because I'm not up every two to four hours through the night. I have time to get myself together in the morning, and I have more patience with a crying baby because I'm not sleep-deprived. I'm also a teacher so I'm used to whining and crying. You're right, I don't have the leaky boobs or loose skin on my stomach, but those are things I would kill for if it meant coming home to my baby every day. In my eyes, those are things you should be proud of, and for what it's worth, you still look incredible."

She continued after a moment. "Oliver and I haven't wanted to step on your toes, but why don't you let us help more? I know nursing makes it difficult for us to keep her overnight, but why don't you let us stay here for a few nights a week. Oli and I can even take turns. Whatever makes you the most comfortable. If you'd rather only have Oliver here, that's fine."

I gawked at her. "You'd be okay with Oliver spending the night at my house?"

She nodded. "Yes. I trust you guys."

I stared at her. "Even with our history? Didn't your ex cheat on you? How can you trust anyone?"

"It's not always easy, but I trust Oliver. And you've proven to be honest with me. I appreciate your sincerity."

"You have a really good heart, Willa. I'm glad Oliver chose you."

~

WE WENT on to work out a schedule that worked for the three of us. I took four months of maternity leave, and as much as I loved Emerson, I was itching to get back to work. Willa watched Emerson over the summer and offered to take the year off teaching to stay home with her full-time. It made me wonder if I should have had a desire to stay home with her, but as much as I loved my daughter, I'd been going stir crazy at home. Work kept me sane. It was my passion, and I was much better at saving lives than I was at being a stay-at-home mom. Really, Willa's offer was perfect because I didn't trust most people to watch my child, but Willa was amazing with Emerson.

Travis visited a few times a month while I was on maternity leave, but once I went back to work, I went months without seeing him. In fact, I barely heard from him, but I was so busy that I didn't realize how much time was slipping by. I worked through the day and spent my evenings with Emerson. It's when we bonded, and I cherished that time with her. Every once in a while, when I needed a good night's sleep, Willa and Oliver took her overnight.

Willa and Oli sent me pictures of Emerson almost every day while I was at work. They sent them to Travis too. Oli said Travis got upset when he didn't get enough pictures, and Travis's obvious love for Emerson warmed my heart and filled my mind with wistful thoughts.

Travis seemed to pop into my mind at the least convenient times, and I wrote out so many texts that I never sent. I wanted to tell him how I felt about him, but it didn't seem fair. What could I really offer him? Travis deserved to be someone's priority, but between Emerson and work, I had no time and nothing concrete to offer him. I wanted him in my life, but I didn't have the time to put into a relationship.

When Oliver let it slip that Travis had been dating, I felt like maybe it was a sign that I needed to let him go. So I kept my feelings to myself and let the months pass without speaking to him, but it didn't keep me from thinking of him all the time.

Mid-August, I was picking Emerson up from Willa's. I stood with Willa in her kitchen while she told me about her and Emmy's day. Emerson was fast asleep in my arms when Willa abruptly changed the topic.

"Have you spoken to Travis lately?"

I shook my head. "No. Why? Is he okay?"

She narrowed her eyes. "Are you two avoiding each other?"

I shrugged. "No. I've just been busy with work and Emerson."

"So busy that you haven't spoken to your best friend?" she questioned.

I huffed, "He could reach out to me too."

She tilted her head. "I will never understand you two."

I looked down at my sleeping daughter. "I'm the one with a baby. He should be reaching out to me. Unless maybe he doesn't want to talk to me."

She stared at me for a long moment.

"What?" I asked.

She hesitated. "Are you in love with him?"

Never did I expect her to be so bold. I shook my head. "I

don't know, and it doesn't matter. Emerson needs me right now."

She bit her cheek, looking at me quizzically. "Do you think maybe you're using Emerson as an excuse?"

I rolled my eyes. "Emerson has to be my number one—"

"Priority. I know. You say it all the time. But why does it have to be all or nothing? There is such a thing as balance, and Oli and I can keep Emerson if you need some extra time. You're allowed to have a night off."

I blinked. "I'm confused. Are you saying you want me to be with Travis? You don't even like him."

She shrugged. "I've seen changes in Travis over the last few months, and I feel like you're hiding from him."

"I'm not hiding." I started bouncing Emerson. It was a habit to soothe her, and now I was bouncing for myself. I stilled my movement. "I'm right here. He knows where to find me."

"It's a two-way street," she offered, "When's the last time you reached out to him?"

I sighed as I thought, unable to come up with a definitive answer. "I don't know. But maybe I shouldn't reach out. I don't want to interrupt the positive changes you've seen, especially because I have nothing to offer him. I know he's dating, and that's good he's healed from his breakup with Deena."

She watched me for a moment before turning away, shaking her head. She grabbed Emerson's diaper bag from the table. "Do you need help out to the car?"

"I feel your judgment," I stated.

She laughed. "I'm not judging. I'm only trying to understand."

I took the diaper bag from her. "Thanks for watching her. I'll see you tomorrow."

I left, feeling a clashing of emotions that I couldn't work out. I wanted Travis to be the one, and in a way, he always had been, but I didn't feel worthy of him.

After an hour of stewing, I picked up my phone and called Willa.

"Addison, is everything okay?" she answered. I never called, only texted, so I understood her worry.

"I am in love with him, which is why I haven't reached out," I confessed. "If our track record tells you anything, it's that we've done nothing but hurt each other. He deserves to be happy, and if he can find that love elsewhere, it's probably for the best. I can't promise we won't hurt each other, and I don't know how to survive losing him again."

"Uhh," she hummed. I'd taken her off guard, but she soon regained her words. "I understand your hesitance, but if you've decided he's not worth the risk, haven't you already lost him?"

I swallowed, closing my eyes. "We've hurt each other so many times."

"I know, and if you can't get past the hurt, then maybe it's healthy to let him go."

Everything inside me revolted after hearing my own thoughts spoken back to me.

71

TRAVIS

THE AUGUST EVENING was perfect weather to sit on a restaurant patio. A beautiful woman sat across from me, and I stared at her pouty lips. They couldn't be real. It looked like she was having an allergic reaction, and I wondered if she had an EpiPen. I struggled to concentrate on the words coming out of her mouth as those plump balloon animal lips bounced off each other. She was blabbing on and on about how she just entered her five-year-old daughter in a beauty pageant.

My counselor had recommended for me to date women who were not Addison. He didn't say it that way, but he said our relationship had toxic traits. I couldn't even argue after telling him all the shit we had put each other through.

I still believed we could be more. We just had to get our shit together. I was working on mine, and I hoped she was working on hers. He made a point that I was always making sacrifices, so now I was waiting for her to reciprocate. I don't think that's what my counselor meant, but it's how I interpreted it.

I had stopped going down to Cincinnati to visit her, and the dozen times I picked up my phone to text her, I remembered not to. I hadn't spoken to her since June, and I needed her to make a move soon.

In March, about the same time I started counseling, I also started visiting animal shelters to look for the perfect dog. Nothing quite fit. And again, my apartment did not allow dogs. I rationalized that I should keep my apartment because it was nice being so close to work. Even though I could work from anywhere, I still preferred to go in, probably because it was the only consistent interaction I had with people.

While visiting an animal shelter, they asked if I wanted to volunteer, and since I had no life, I decided that was probably a great idea. I had to go through classes before volunteering, and when I finished those, I began working with the dog trainers. By June, I was working with the problematic dogs. The dogs that had been mishandled or just never handled at all.

I got my dog fix by working with the most stubborn and temperamental dogs at the shelter. It took patience I didn't realize I possessed. Somehow watching the transformation in these dogs steadied me. I learned from them and they slowly replaced my counseling sessions. My counselor agreed it had helped me, and I could feel myself changing with every dog I helped.

I kept in touch with Oli, and he always sent me videos of Emmy—Emmy crawling, sleeping, eating her first baby foods. Emmy's belly laughs were my all-time favorite. I missed my friends. I wanted to move to Cincinnati, but that felt desperate and would go against my counselor's advice.

So here I was in August, sitting across from this beautiful woman who seemed great on her dating profile but mentioned nothing about her love of children's pageantry. That wasn't my world, and her lips looked painful. She was leaning back in her chair, talking animatedly. Her volume had gotten increasingly louder, and she didn't seem to give two shits that I wasn't interested.

My phone vibrated on the table. It was rude to look, so I left it, but after a few more minutes without getting a word in, I looked at my phone. It was a text from Addison.

Addison: I'm thinking about bringing Emmy up to the Columbus Zoo. She loves our zoo so much, and I wanted her to see the baby polar bear.

Me: Do seven-month-olds like the zoo?

Addison: She does. Her whole face lights up at the aquarium. They have manatees there, right?

Me: What makes you think I've been to the zoo?

Addison: You're just the kind of person who screams zoo. I'm surprised you didn't know that.

I stifled a smile.

"Are you even listening to me?" my date asked.

Shit. I looked up and thought about giving her an excuse, but she deserved the truth. "No, sorry. You seem like a great woman, but I'm not into pageant stuff, and you've been talking for—" I checked the time on my phone. "Eight minutes straight without letting me get a word in or caring that I have no interest in what glitter spray is used for. I don't mean to be rude, but our bill is paid, and I think I'm gonna go."

While she was still speechless, I left, getting out before she ranted in run-on sentences at me. I was so relieved we drove separately.

As soon as I got to my car, I texted Addison back, elated that she reached out. She had even drawn up an elaborate plan to see me. I was lucky she couldn't see my excitement as we made plans to go to the zoo.

IT WAS A WARM SEPTEMBER DAY, perfect for walking around outdoors. I waited just inside the zoo entrance gate, so I spotted Addison immediately as she came through. The sight of her had me smiling. She looked like the hottest zoo guide I'd ever seen as she walked toward me with her stroller. Her hair hung an inch above her shoulders. I always loved her long hair, but that's because I had never seen it short before. It showed off her slim shoulders and the curve of her neck. I had the instant urge to run my fingers up into its short lengths.

She had a lot of leg showing between her brown sandals and green safari-like shorts. She wore a pastel tank top that had a brown elephant on the front. In the stroller, eight-month-old, Emmy, wore a pastel elephant romper.

"I see you coordinated your outfits," I laughed.

She shrugged. "It felt like appropriate zoo attire."

"I didn't know there was a dress code," I teased.

She opened her arms for a hug, and I snapped her up, lifting her off the ground. She let out a squeak that turned into a laugh. It was music to my ears. Once I set her down, I freed Emmy from her straps and lifted her from the stroller.

"There's the cutest girl in the world," I said to her, not giving a shit that Emmy had turned me into a baby-talking grown man. She had a power over me, and I couldn't resist. Her chubby hands went straight for my beard, giving it a painful tug.

"She's getting stronger," I noted, untwining her fingers from my beard.

"Yes, no one is safe."

"Is that why you cut your hair?"

Her fingers latched onto a short strand as if verifying its length. "Yeah, and I was ready for something different."

"I really like it," I said, tugging at it playfully.

Her lips quirked. "Thanks."

I motioned toward the path ahead. "Shall we?"

"Lead the way."

We began walking, her pushing an empty stroller while I held Emerson. She was a squirmy little thing, more active than the last time I had seen her.

I glanced at Addie, who was watching us. "So what have you been up to, Add?"

She shrugged. "Life's been busy, and I don't know, I guess time just got away from me. I'm back at work. Two of my patients have gone into remission since I've been back, so that's a reason to celebrate. What about you? What have you been doing?"

"I've started working with dogs at a local shelter, mainly the dogs with behavior difficulties. Usually, it's the ones who were abused that need the most work. It stretches my patience sometimes, but it's pretty rewarding."

"Do you think you'll adopt one? I know you mentioned it before."

"My apartment doesn't allow them, and I think the kind of dog I want deserves a yard. Even if I took it for walks, it would still need space to run. I like athletic dogs, something like a Vizsla or a German Shepherd, or maybe a Boxer or a Doberman."

"So you're not into cute fluffy dogs."

I laughed. "I like all dogs, and I've worked with some great fluffy dogs, but no, they are usually not my type. I have thought about moving. I'm jealous of your backyard. It'd be perfect for a dog."

She cringed. "I've treated too many children with dog bites. I think I'll stick with Rozsa."

"If you teach children how to act around dogs and vice versa, and monitor them, it shouldn't be a problem. I mean, Emmy is around Willa's dog all the time."

"I know you're right, but I really don't need another thing added to my plate."

"I'm not telling you to get a dog. Just saying your yard would be perfect for one."

"I know, but I could see getting one down the road. Like when Emmy is old enough to take on some responsibility."

We walked through North America, making our way to the polar bears. Emmy didn't seem to care so much about the baby bear. She was just mesmerized by the giant bears swimming underwater.

Eventually, Emmy started getting fussy, and we took a break after seeing the Polar bears. We stopped at a shaded picnic table, and I put Emerson in her stroller. She reluctantly took a bottle, but her eyes lit up when she saw the baby food Addison pulled out of a stroller pocket. Addison snapped a baby food tray on the front of the stroller to work as a highchair.

I laughed, and Addison smiled. "She really likes to eat, and so far, she hasn't been picky."

"I can relate," I said to Emerson.

Addison asked, "Do you want to feed her?"

"What? She doesn't know how to do that yet? I guess I'll have to teach her myself."

Addison handed me her baby food. "Sure, go ahead."

Emmy's eyes were razor-focused on the food. She was already opening her mouth, expecting a bite before I even had it ready. I got a spoonful and zoomed it like an airplane. I didn't know a baby could scowl so well, but Emmy scowled at me.

"You're taking too long," Addison noted.

The spoon hit Emmy's mouth, and her scowl disappeared. I got another spoonful ready and continued to feed her. "She's pretty intense about her food. Should we slow down or stop to burp her or something?"

"She'll eat the whole thing first."

Emmy kept opening her mouth for more, even after it was gone. I tried to tell her there was no more, and she slammed her hand against the stroller, demanding more. I tried not to laugh, but she was adorable.

Addison pulled baby puffs out of another pocket and spread a few across the tray.

"That will keep her happy for a bit. There's a cheetah run in a few minutes. I don't think it's very far from here."

EMERSON HAD FALLEN ASLEEP, so Addison and I found a place to eat lunch. We settled at a picnic table with our food and it was nice to see that Addison had relaxed her strict diet. As she ate another bite of her corndog, she said. "I don't usually eat this poorly, but I started getting insane cravings while I was nursing Emerson. If I didn't eat enough, I would get dizzy. So, I learned to give a little with my diet. Still, corndogs are unusual for me."

"I'm proud of you." I said, taking a bite of my greasy

cheeseburger. "And are you still doubting yourself as a mom?"

Addison laughed. "Only at every turn. I feel bad about wanting to keep my career, and I second guess every decision. It's exhausting, but I never learned how to be okay with failure. Perfection was expected of me, and if I couldn't be perfect, then I was taught to fake it. But I can't fake it when I know it's not what's best for Emerson. I mean, what would I be teaching her? It's better for her to see my failures than to pretend, right?"

It was a rhetorical question, but I nodded anyway to show my support for what she'd said.

"I don't want to teach my daughter to numb all of her emotions until she's dead inside." She sounded resolute.

"I never liked robot Addison. I always preferred to see the ugly emotions."

"I'm serious," she reiterated.

"So am I."

She swallowed. "So, enough about me. I hear you're dating."

"Yeah. It's awful. Some of these women seem okay from their profiles, but none of them are what I'm looking for."

"Are you going to keep at it?"

"I don't know. My counselor encouraged me to get out there, but . . ." I sighed. "I don't really want to. What about you? Are you ready to get back out there?"

"God, no! All those dating apps sound terrible, and I feel like it's scarier for women. Men seem to have expectations. My friend Rachel has told me so many horror stories about her dating life."

"Rachel?" I beamed. "Look at you making new friends."

"Yeah, I'm finally learning how to build genuine friendships. It's uncomfortable and feels a little like dating. I keep expecting the worst, but so far, I'm finding that most women are pretty amazing."

"You and I must be meeting different women."

She smiled. "I'm sure we are. I still don't know if I would date any of these women. I mean, if I was into women romantically."

I closed my eyes. "Mmm."

She shoved me. "Grow up! What I mean is my friend Rachel is eccentric and a little looney, but she's an incredibly fun friend. I imagine it would not be as fun if I were to date her, but I know there has to be someone to match her crazy."

I gave her a questioning look. "What's that?"

"Most people complain that they can't find anyone normal, but normal doesn't exist. We're all crazy in our own way. So what people are really looking for is someone to match their crazy."

My damn cheeks hurt from smiling, but I couldn't help it. She made me happy.

Once we finished eating, we walked and talked, getting caught up. We saw a few more exhibits along the way, and once Emmy woke, we went into the aquarium.

I walked Addison and Emmy to their car when we left. I kissed Emmy's cheek before Addison strapped her into her car seat. Addison and I exchanged a long hug, longer than was probably appropriate, but I didn't want her to leave. I didn't know when I would see her again.

When she stepped back, she said, "I'd really like to get together again."

I nodded. "I'm around. My schedule is flexible. You just tell me what you want."

She nodded. "Let me check my schedule and get back to you."

LATER, after she got home, she texted to let me know she wasn't sure when she could get together again. She was still trying to make up for the time she lost while out on maternity leave, and she was in the middle of writing an article for a medical journal.

The next week, I went down to Cincinnati to visit Oli, Emerson, and Willa. Willa had started warming to me a little. I lingered at their house, waiting to run into Addie when she came to pick up Emerson.

"Shouldn't Addison be here to pick up Emmy by now?" I asked conversationally as I looked at the clock on the wall.

"She's not picking her up tonight. She's out with Ryan again. A guy she met at work. She said she'd be out late so she'll just stay at her apartment. So we get Emmy overnight."

Was I too late? No. It had to be a misunderstanding.

"Is it a date?" I asked.

Oli had sympathy in his eyes. "I think so. She has been out with him a few times, but this is the first time she's asked us to keep Emmy overnight. I thought you were both dating other people."

"Yeah." I nodded. "Yeah, I guess we are. She just said she wasn't ready to date."

Oli hissed. "I'm sorry, man."

I tried to shrug it off, but on the drive home, I stopped by Addison's apartment. She wasn't there. I thought about staying, but that felt like something a possessive stalker would do, so I sent her a text, giving her a chance to explain.

Me: I'm driving through Cincy. You home?

It looked like she was typing a reply and then she stopped, only to begin typing a moment later. This happened several times before I finally received a response.

Addison: No. I'm having dinner with a friend. Sorry I missed you.

I sighed, disappointed.

Me: Me too.

Maybe it wasn't what it sounded like. I guess I would just wait for her to reach out.

But she didn't. I didn't hear from Addison for two more months when she asked if I was going to New York for Christmas.

72

TRAVIS

I DIDN'T SPEND Christmas with Addison, Oli, or his family this year. Instead, I flew to Maui and stayed at a friend's timeshare. I had mailed a Christmas gift to Emmy, and Oliver sent me the video he recorded of her opening it. The kid seemed more excited about the wrapping paper than the toy. I could've just wrapped an empty box. I never knew I could feel so attached to someone else's kid, but Emmy had a special place in my heart.

The trip was only supposed to be a week, but I extended it to two, so I could hike more of the scenic trails all over the island. It was a great place to do some soul searching. On the last night of my trip, I watched the sun set over the ocean and knew exactly what it was I wanted for my life.

It was the same thing I had always wanted. I wanted a family I could call my own. I wanted to marry the love of my life. And I wanted to prove I was a better father than my old man.

I'd been on a few more dates, but there were no sparks. I deleted my profiles, doubting they would ever work for me because I already knew who I wanted and no one would measure up to her. I didn't know if she was still dating that guy. I didn't ask about him, and no one ever offered me any information. Regardless, I needed to be straightforward with Addison.

EMERSON'S first birthday quickly approached, and I couldn't wait to see her. By the time I got to Willa and Oli's house, Willa's parents were there, as well as all four of Oliver's parents and stepparents. A few close friends arrived shortly after me, but Addison and her mom hadn't made it yet.

Bella was the first to greet me, giving me puppy dog kisses. I rubbed her head for a minute before finding the birthday girl. I kissed Emmy's cheek, and she giggled, showing off her big cheeks as she reached for me. I picked her up, and her hands went straight to my facial hair. We were going to work on that. I handed her back to Willa after a moment so she could change Emmy into her pink sparkly party dress.

I said hello to the people I knew and introduced myself to the people I didn't. The doorbell rang and Willa's mom, who I just met for the first time, answered the door. Jeanine stood in the doorway, looking like a deer ready to bolt. I made my way to her and watched her shoulders relax when she saw me. I gave her a hug and showed her where Oli's parents were. She and Kim got along well, and I stood back listening to the many conversations throughout the living room and into the kitchen. It was a small space for so many people.

"Hi. I'm Jodi." I heard and turned to the petite woman. "I'm Willa's best friend. I've heard stories about you."

I could only imagine what Willa had told her about me. "I guess I don't need to introduce myself then."

She looked contemplative, saying, "I hear you work with dogs."

That wasn't what I expected her to say. "I do. I volunteer at a shelter."

"Did you know Willa used to volunteer at a shelter?"

I shook my head. "No. I did not."

"Yeah, that's where Bella came from. Have you adopted any dogs yet?"

"No. I can't have them in my apartment."

"But doesn't it kill you when your favorites are adopted out?" Jodi asked.

"Not really, no. Most of the ones I work with have come from awful situations, so we give them a second chance at life—a better life. I'm excited when they get adopted. There is a pregnant dog that came in a few months ago. I've been working with her. Her puppies are seven weeks old now, and I think they'll be the hardest to see go."

Her face perked. "What kind of dogs?"

"Mom is a boxer mix, and we think dad was a Rottweiler."

"Oh, big dogs," Jodi noted.

I nodded.

"Did you get to name them?"

I laughed. "No, the woman who runs the shelter named them. She named mom, Sunshine. So when sunshine had six puppies, they named the girls Mercury, Venus, and Saturn. The boys are Jupiter, Neptune, and the runt of the litter is Pluto."

"What? No Uranus?" Jodi laughed at her own joke and said, "So if I were to decide to get one, which would you recommend?"

"It depends on how serious you are. Puppies are a lot of work."

"Yeah, but my oldest won't shut up about getting one, so I've considered it."

"If you're not sure, then I'd say don't get one of these pups. They're very high energy, and unless you can dedicate some time, it's probably not a good fit. There are other puppies that aren't as much work."

"Are you talking about getting a dog again?" Addison said, coming out of the kitchen with Emerson in her arms. She took my breath away. I hadn't seen her arrive, and it'd been months since we last spoke, but the affect she had on me was instant and profound.

What were we talking about? What had she asked me? I force myself to answer. "I was just telling Jodi that I can't adopt a dog right now."

Jodi glanced at Addison and back to me. "So, who is your favorite?"

"Favorite?"

She gave a sly grin, "Puppy."

Oh, shit. My brain had stalled. Focus on the dogs. Nothing but the dogs. "Neptune is my buddy. He follows me around and bites at my shoes when I walk. He'll be a challenge to whoever gets him, but he's also very smart. He'll be a very loyal, loving dog. I'll make sure he goes to the right home, but none of them are available for adoption for a few more weeks."

Addison said, "Of course you love the high energy dog that bites at your feet and requires a lot of time."

I avoided her eyes by making a face at Emerson. The little girl giggled, gripping onto Addison tighter. With my sights on Emmy, I said, "But eventually, all that time and energy pays off." I glanced at Addison, getting pulled in and lost in her eyes. I forgot how to look away, but as her lips parted, my eyes dropped. Fuck. I blinked hard, pulling in a sharp inhale. I forced another breath. "Did you see your mom?" I pointed in Jeanine's direction.

She diverted her gaze, looking where I pointed. "No," she said, "I need to say hi." She bolted with Emmy in her arms, tugging at her short hair. I watched them join Jeanine before remembering Jodi.

Jodi fanned herself with her hand.

"You okay?" I looked around, coming up with a game plan in case she was about to pass out.

She blew out a breath. "Yeah, I just didn't know if I'd survive that heat between you two."

I raised an eyebrow. "Huh?"

In a breathy voice, she said, "All that time and energy pays off."

I gawked at her.

She snorted. "Don't pretend you didn't feel the sparks between you two."

"I was talking about dogs," I defended.

She laughed. "Uh-huh. I'm sure she came to that same conclusion." She rolled her eyes.

I narrowed my gaze just as a little girl ran up to Jodi, whining, "Mommy, Max won't give it back."

Jodi glanced at me. "If you'll excuse me, I have to go wrangle my human pups."

She left, and I went into the kitchen, but Oliver and Willa were wrapped up in a loving embrace. I backed away. They were getting married in a few weeks, and their affectionate displays only seemed to grow.

Addison sat next to her mother. Emmy was wiggling to

get out of her lap. The seat next to her was open, so I took it, playing with Emmy while Addie caught up with her mom. I knew it hurt Addison not having her father here, but the bastard hadn't apologized. I was proud that Addison was finally brave enough that she wasn't backing down.

I was unsuccessfully teaching Emerson to fist bump when she climbed into my lap. Her chubby little hands grabbed my beard and yanked.

EMERSON DIDN'T SEEM to care about the number of gifts she received. She had no idea what was going on or why we kept taking her wrapping paper away. She was way more excited by her cake, and as soon as she got the chance, she dove for it, mouth first. The pink and purple icing went everywhere, and Bella helped clean the floor beneath Emmy's mess. Addison ended up stripping Emmy down and rinsing her off before putting her in her jammies.

The party dwindled. Oliver's parents were staying at a nearby hotel while Jeanine insisted upon driving straight home. Most grandmas would want to stay and visit with their granddaughter, but Jeanine didn't seem overly affectionate toward Emmy. I realized it had nothing to do with Emmy. She just wasn't particularly fond of babies.

I was one of the last to leave, and I helped Oliver and Addison sort the gifts. Some were staying at Oliver's, but several items were going to Addison's. I helped her pack up her tiny car.

"Addie, these aren't going to fit. Why do you have such a compact car?"

"I drive a lot. And the car isn't that small. Babies just come with so much stuff."

I looked at the awkward box that wouldn't fit. "This play castle seems unnecessary."

"I didn't say we needed it all, but Emmy will love it."

I grinned. "She's so spoiled."

"And so loved," she said in defense. "I seem to remember you getting her that damn ball pit for Christmas. You think that's necessary?"

"I bought that for me, so I could play with it when I come over."

She laughed. "You got my daughter an obnoxious toy just so you could live vicariously through her. It might be big, but you won't fit."

"Was that a fat joke?"

She patted my stomach. "You won't always be able to maintain a six-pack with your second helpings of cake."

In a whisper, I said, "Remember, I know about the mac and cheese."

She laughed, covering her face. "Oh, I don't even want to know what you must have thought of me."

I stepped closer. "I thought it's about time she indulged a little."

"Ha! Right." She looked back to her packed car. "I guess I'll come back for the rest of it tomorrow."

I took the boxes that didn't fit. "I'll put them in my car and bring them over. That way, I can unpack both cars while you get Emerson ready for bed."

"You don't have to."

"No shit. I offered. Let me do something nice."

She pulled her coat tighter. "Fine. If you've got those, then I'm going back inside. It's too cold out here."

I put the rest of the gifts in my car and returned inside to say goodbye to Oliver and Willa.

Oliver held a sleepy Emerson. "Are you sure you're okay to take her tonight? I know you've been working a lot."

"Oli, I'm fine. I miss my baby. I have her tonight and tomorrow. I'll bring her back Sunday evening."

"Okay. I'll carry her out to the car. Do you need help unpacking the gifts at your house?"

"No, Travis said he would help. He has to come anyway because the gifts wouldn't all fit in my car."

Oliver gave her a look. "I told you, you need a bigger car."

"My car is fine. It's not like I'm usually stuffing a mountain of gifts inside."

Willa came from the kitchen, wrapping an arm around Oliver's back and leaning in to kiss Emerson on her chubby cheek. "She's going to be out by the time you get home."

"It's been a lot of excitement," Addie said, picking up the diaper bag.

"I'll carry her out," Oli offered.

Addison was blocking me in the driveway, so I was in no hurry to go outside. The door closed behind Addison and Oliver, and it was just me with Willa and her dog.

I turned to Willa. "Thank you for throwing this party."

She looked surprised. "It wasn't—"

"You did most of the work, and now you and Oli have the cleanup. Thank you."

She gave a hesitant smile. "I don't need credit. I was happy to do it."

I wanted to say a lot of things to her, but she was still not completely comfortable with me. She wasn't as forgiving as Oliver. Most people weren't. But I had to say something. "You've been good for them. For Oli, Emerson, and even

Addie. You make all their lives better. I know you were reluctant to step into such a complicated situation, but I'm really happy you did."

She appraised me, looking so petite and calm, but I knew better than to underestimate her. She might look delicate, but under that small frame, she was brave and powerful. She was a soft presence, but one that would fuck you up if you hurt someone she loved. I smiled as I realized who it was she reminded me of. "You're a lot like Oliver's Gran."

When she gave me a strange look, I clarified, "I mean that in the best way possible. She was one of my favorite people in the world. I'm pretty sure she saved my life."

She bit the inside of her cheek, her eyes narrowing. "I still haven't figured you out," she said. "You betrayed Oliver to be with Addison. It's obvious you love her, so why aren't you together?"

I shrugged, feigning neutrality. "I think we've hurt each other too many times. She made it clear that we're better as friends, and a man can only take so much rejection."

"I think you gave up too easily."

My anger was swift, her words hitting a sore spot. "You have no idea what you're talking about."

She smiled at my anger. "What would Gran say?"

Checkmate. "Damn, you go straight for the kill."

She shrugged. "I like to see my friends happy."

I smiled, feeling her words in my chest. "Aww, am I your friend now?"

"Don't make me regret it." She shoved me forward. "Now, get out of my house."

I opened the door, stepping out onto the porch. Oliver was heading back toward the house. He looked between me and the open door with curiosity.

"Willa called me her friend," I bragged to Oliver. Addison was already pulling out of the driveway.

Oli smiled as he stepped toward me. "The honey badger has finally accepted you. Congratulations."

I'd heard him refer to Willa as a honey badger before and wondered, "Is that a sexual thing I don't know about?"

"No, honey badgers are badasses. Willa's mom was the first to compare her to a honey badger. But it fits."

"What kind of animal would I be?"

His answer was immediate, "A jackass."

I laughed. "Stubborn and protective. You might be onto something."

He smiled and took a step toward the door. "Thanks for taking that stuff over for her."

"No problem."

It was a quick drive to Addison's. She was getting Emerson out of her car seat when I pulled in. Emerson was sleeping as she carried her inside. While she put her to bed, I unpacked both cars. By the time I finished, Addison was in the kitchen, wearing pajama pants and a baggy sweatshirt. Her blonde hair was short enough that I could see the back of her neck as she washed Emerson's plastic dishes in the sink. I leaned against the kitchen doorframe, watching her.

I thought of Willa's words. Addison and I had been through so much. Maybe it just hadn't ever been the right time before. Emerson was a year old now, and Addison seemed to finally find her equilibrium, learning how to be a mom, and making time for her career. She and Oliver had redefined their relationship. She and Willa had even become real friends. She might still be dating someone, but if it were serious, he would've been there tonight.

Addison was facing the darkened window overlooking

the backyard, so she noticed my reflection as I moved forward.

"Did you get everything out of the cars?" she asked.

I stepped behind her, placing my hands on the counter, on either side of her. "I did," I said softly in her ear, watching as goosebumps spread down her exposed neck. Her body stiffened, and I peeked over her shoulder to gauge her expression in the window.

"What are you doing?" she sounded breathless.

I pushed in closer, my chest pressing against her back. When she didn't push me away, I kissed the exposed skin of her neck. Her quick intake of breath only encouraged me. The running water ceased, and Addison moved her head to the side, giving me better access.

"Are you sure about this, T?"

I groaned. "Uh-huh."

"Wait, what is this?" she spun in my arms, her face mere inches away while her ass rested against the counter.

I knew she said something, but my focus was split. I pressed in closer, my hands abandoning the counter to wrap around her, seeking out her skin. They slid under her baggy sweatshirt, finding her warm, smooth skin. My palms slid up the curve of her back.

She seemed to melt a little, her lips inching closer, but she was holding back until I answered her question. Shit, what was it? She wanted to know my intentions.

"I want to make love to you, Addison, for the rest of my life. Only you. It's always been you."

She inhaled sharply, her eyes wide.

Her hands met at the nape of my neck, and she pulled me down to meet her lips. The sparks between us had always been intense, but this was something else. There was a thrumming of energy just below the surface.

She pulled away, gasping, "T, you sure this is what you want?"

"It's what I've always wanted. You're the one who keeps pushing me away."

She pulled me back in, her hands cradling my face. Her tongue slid into my mouth, and I tried to slow things down. I didn't want this to be quick and desperate. I wanted unhurried and sweet—something that spoke of more. I needed to show her it was more than just passion.

It reminded me of the last time we had sex, and I pulled away. "I'm not going to sleep with you tonight."

Her eyebrows drew together. "What? Why?"

"Because I don't want a piece of you. I want it all. If you aren't ready, I understand, but I'm all in. I'll give you time to think about it. I know you've been dating—"

She made a face. "No I haven't."

"What about Ryan?"

She gawked at me. "What *about* Ryan?"

We stared at each other for a moment and her eyes narrowed. "Ryan is a woman. She's my friend."

"But Oliver—"

She tilted her head. "Why didn't you just ask me?"

"I thought you weren't telling me on purpose. I thought you weren't ready for me."

"That's why you started acting distant this fall." She shook her head. "I won't lie to you, Travis. Next time, you have a question, just ask me."

"I'm asking you now. Be with me. Marry me. Spend the rest of your life with me."

She let out a long breath, "Have you thought about this,

Travis? Like really thought about it? I have Emerson, and my life is hectic. Explaining our relationship to Oli's family and everyone we know in New York might be awkward."

I shook my head. "Getting to spend time with Emerson is a perk, not a complication. And I don't give a fuck what Oli's family thinks. I care what you think."

"And what about your job? Your life is in Columbus."

"My life is standing right in front of me. I can work from anywhere."

She blinked, and moisture filled her eyes. I leaned in, pressing my lips to hers. She kissed me back, but I kept it chaste, pulling away despite the burning desire to do more.

I cleared my throat. "Take some time and think about it. I'll love you either way, but then at least we know how to move forward."

IT'D BEEN a week and a half, and I'd heard nothing but agonizing silence. Maybe I should've given her a timeframe. I was in a piss poor mood and kept snapping at people at work. I spent extra time at the gym this morning, hoping that would curb my frustration. It had not.

My phone vibrated with a text. It was Kristen from the animal shelter.

Kristen: I know you wanted approval over who adopted Neptune, but I can assure you, he went to a good home.

Fucking fabulous. What a great fucking day.

I couldn't restrain any longer. I sent a text to Addison.

Me: How are you?

Addison: Busy. I'll get back to you later.

Well. Fuck.

A little while later, my office phone rang. It was Amanda, the office's receptionist. "Hey, Travis, you have a visitor."

I looked around. She usually just sent people up to me.

I asked, "Did you send them up?"

Through the phone, I heard a commotion. "No. I couldn't even get her name. Her dog keeps barking. She has a volunteer shirt on from an animal shelter."

"Hmm, okay, I'll be right there."

Kristen from the shelter had a little crush on me, but that was innocent flirting. She was happily married. Fuck. I hoped. I got up and walked toward the lobby. The balcony from our office on the third floor overlooked the entrance, and there I saw a woman in the unmistakable neon orange volunteer shirt trying to wrangle a crazy dog. Not just any crazy dog. It was Neptune.

What the hell?

73

ADDISON

I should've known it was a bad omen when the balloon I had custom ordered popped as soon as I put it in the car. Instead, I brushed it off. I could do without the balloon.

I had spoken to Kristen, who ran the animal shelter in Columbus. I had explained everything over the phone, and she knew to expect me, but the roads were slick. My drive to Columbus took an hour longer than usual, and I almost missed her.

When I got there, Kristen directed me back to the puppies, raving about Travis the whole way. The puppies looked much bigger in person. They had to be close to twenty pounds at nine weeks old. I liked animals, and puppies were so cute they were hard not to love, but I had never been a dog person. So when Kristen placed Neptune right in my arms, and he licked my face, I tried not to outwardly cringe.

Kristen asked, "Do you want to take him for a little walk around the building? He probably has to go potty."

I nodded. I didn't necessarily want to go out into the misty freezing rain, but I did it with a smile as the dog chased my shoes as I walked. After several minutes, the puppy still hadn't peed. He was too busy playing. I met back up with Kristen to fill out some paperwork, and as soon as everything was finished, I picked up Neptune. Kristen scratched at his furry head. His tail took off wagging, and his butt wiggled with it. I smiled at the cuteness, but my smile was short-lived as I felt something warm run down the front of me. I held the puppy away from my chest, watching him continue to pee all over the place.

Oh dear god. What had I done?

My outfit was ruined. My hair was wet and frizzy from the useless dog walk. Feeling sympathy for me, Kristen gave me one of their volunteer shirts.

I thanked her profusely and left the shelter, placing Neptune inside the crate I had prepared in my backseat. I got in the car, flipping down my visor mirror to attempt to fix my hair. With a sigh, I flipped it back up. It was useless. I wanted to postpone my plans, but the puppy cried in the back seat, reminding me I had no idea how to handle a puppy. There was no other option than to move forward. So I drove through Columbus in the bad weather. On the way, my phone chimed with a message. I had my car read it to me.

Travis: How are you?

I had my car respond.

Me: Busy. I'll get back to you later.

I was frazzled. I had planned to do everything outside of Travis's office, but the rainy mixture made that impossible. After I found a place to park three blocks away, I realized I couldn't hold the dog and the umbrella. I wanted to cry.

In romance novels and movies, there was always a grand

gesture, and I knew Travis deserved something spectacular. I had planned the perfect surprise. It was a go big or go home kind of gesture, and the way things had gone so far, I was more than ready to go home. I just needed Travis to go with me, so I had to continue with my unraveling grand plan.

Leaving the umbrella, I ran to the building, holding Neptune under my jacket. He wiggled around so much that I had to set him down, and he jogged next to me for the last block.

We stepped into the lobby, both soaking wet, the puppy chewing on his leash, while I pushed the damp hair from my face. Something black dripped onto my fingers, and I realized my mascara had run down my face. I didn't think it could get much worse. Then Neptune began barking.

Travis had talked about his colleagues bringing their dogs to work, so I knew it was a dog-friendly place, but I doubted barking was appreciated. I bent down to shut the dog up. He stopped for a moment, and I wiped at the mascara running down my face. I reached in my coat to text Travis.

My heart dropped, and I closed my eyes, willing away this nightmare. I realized in my hurry, I had left the phone in my car. I tried not to cry, but this isn't how it was supposed to go. I'd never done something so sloppy in my entire life.

I botched it.

My coat dripped on the floor, leaving a puddle around us. I took it off, draping it over an arm. I squared my shoulders, picked up the dog, and walked to the front desk.

"Hi, I'm here for Travis Rose."

She nodded and said something, but I couldn't hear because Neptune barked furiously at something across the lobby.

I tried to calm him down, but it wasn't working. I gave

the receptionist an apologetic glance and set Neptune on the floor. I knelt in front of him, blocking everything from view. "Listen here, you little jerk, you're my ace. I need you to behave."

He whined and jumped around me to bark some more. Everyone was looking at us. I was mortified.

"Why does he even like you?" I whisper shouted at the puppy. "You're just as much of a mess as I am." And then realization hit me. I sat on the floor, staring at the puppy who had finally stopped barking. Travis didn't love me because I was perfect. He loved me with of all my imperfections. He loved me even when I was a mess, and somehow me coming to him like this seemed appropriate.

I don't know how he found me, but a moment later, Travis knelt down in front of me. "Hi."

Neptune jumped and stumbled around in little circles, wagging his tail as he peed all over the floor. I didn't know how he had anything left to pee. Travis just laughed.

I looked up at him as I wiped the tears from my face. "I didn't mean to embarrass you at your job."

He wore a grin that made me feel like maybe everything would be okay. "Do I look embarrassed?"

I shook my head.

He lifted my chin, and in a gentle voice, said, "You're a mess."

I winced. "I know."

His smile grew. "You did all this for me?"

"All of what? Nothing went as planned."

He cupped my cheeks, saying, "God, I love you."

I smiled through my tears, and he leaned in and kissed me. It was a quick kiss, and when he pulled back, he wiped his thumbs over my cheeks to clean them, saying, "Even when you're a mess, you're still gorgeous."

He took the leash from me and stood, reaching a hand out to help me up. He leaned over to the receptionist, asking, "Rachel, can you call maintenance?"

"They're already on their way," she said.

Neptune started barking again, and Travis poked him, making an "Eh" noise that effectively quieted the yapping dog.

I couldn't believe it. "You're going to have to teach me how to do that."

He nodded and asked, "Rachel, can you watch Neptune for a moment."

"Of course." She came around the desk and took the puppy. In high pitched baby talk, she asked, "Who's the cutest boy? You are."

Travis pulled me away from the front desk. When he turned to look at me, he pushed my hair away from my face. "You know I can't have this dog at my apartment."

I nodded. "He'll stay at my house, and I'm hoping you will too." It felt ridiculous to say it out loud. I wasn't just asking him to move in with me. I was asking him to uproot his entire life and move in with me today. I swallowed, realizing it was way too much at once, but I continued, giving him my reasoning. "I know. Maybe I got a little ahead of myself, but I needed to do something to prove that I'm all in. I want to wake up next to you every morning and for you to be the last thing I see when I close my eyes at night. I have loved you for a long, long time."

His expression hadn't changed, and I shut up, feeling overly exposed and self-conscious. I needed him to say something.

"Go on," he prompted with a cocky grin.

He didn't expect me to continue, but I remembered more that I wanted to say. "When Emerson was a week old, you came to visit me. I was an absolute mess, and you watched her while I showered and slept. When I woke up and found you holding her on the couch, I wanted to beg you never to leave me." I swallowed. "But I knew you wouldn't believe me, not after what I'd said to Oli at the hospital. I love Oli, but he never had all of me. Not the way you do. Not the way you have for the last thirteen years."

His smile disappeared as his honey brown eyes glistened. "Why wait so long?"

I shrugged. "You started going on dates, and I thought I didn't have anything to offer you. But I have everything to offer. I'm scared I'm going to mess this up, but I want to try. We owe it to ourselves to try. So here I am, offering you a family, a home, a backyard for your dog. Uproot your life and come move in with me—with us. Be an official part of our family."

He continued to stare at me, and his pause made my anxiety grow.

"What do you say, T?"

His grin grew. "I say fuck yeah." He swooped in for a kiss, our arms wrapping around each other. He lifted me from the floor, and my hands clung to him as our kiss lingered.

I could breathe again. He was my everything.

When he set me down, he said, "You know everything is going to be harder with a puppy, right?"

"I learned that quickly after meeting the hellion of a dog, but I'm up for the challenge if it makes you happy."

He whispered, "How's Rozsa going to feel about that?"

"Oh, I'm sure she'll be pissed at first, but I'm counting on you to train Neptune."

He laced his fingers through mine. "Let's go get our dog and go home."

74

TRAVIS

THERE WAS AN ADJUSTMENT PERIOD. The first thing we did was go to Willa and Oliver to explain that we were together. Willa's dog loved Neptune, and the two wore each other out while we talked. Neptune nipped as most puppies did, and I was nervous about him and Emmy together, but he was gentle with her. I still never left them alone together.

I worked with Neptune every day, and he quickly picked up new commands. It took Rozsa a few weeks to warm up to him, but Emmy loved the puppy immediately.

Six months flew by in a euphoric blur. I had never been happier. My relationship with Addison was easy. It was all the years of fighting love that made our relationship so difficult. I loved living with Addison, and Emmy rolled with the changes as if Neptune and I had always been there.

It was great living so close to Oliver again. I think he was relieved that Addison and I were together. He told me that at least I hadn't betrayed him for nothing.

My apartment's lease wasn't up for a few months, and

before moving everything to the house, Addison and I decided to have the basement finished. It was large enough for a bedroom, bathroom, office, play area, and gym. The contractors had already drawn up plans for us to approve, and Addison and I were in the basement discussing them. Willa had Emerson at her house, and Neptune was entertaining himself by chasing his tail.

Addison's phone rang upstairs, and she ran to get it. I heard her talking to someone as I continued looking over the plans.

A few minutes later, Addison came back down the stairs, practically floating.

I grinned. I loved seeing her happy. "Who called?"

She took a breath. "I feel like everything is finally going right. I mean, we're together, the construction starts on the basement soon, and my dad just called me out of the blue. He sounded pleasant and asked me to come for a visit. He still hasn't actually met Emmy, and he sounded truly excited on the phone."

"Are you thinking of going?" I asked, trying to keep my jaw from hitting the concrete floor.

"Of course. He wants to see his granddaughter."

I blinked, speechless.

She sighed. "I know you've never liked him, but I want you to be excited for me. I miss him."

I rubbed at the back of my neck. "You do?"

"Of course I do. You know it's been hard not having a relationship with him for the past two years."

"So you're going to take Emmy on a seven-hour car ride there and back to meet the man who hit you the last time you saw him?"

She blew out a breath. "He's her grandpa, Travis."

"Even serial killers can have grandchildren. Do you think their parents encourage them to visit Grandpa McMurder in prison? I doubt it."

Judging by her face, it was the wrong thing to say. "How dare you put my father on the same level as a serial killer!"

"You seemed fine without your father, and now all of a sudden, you're bending over backward to make him happy again. How do you think Emmy will do for seven hours in a car?"

She shook her head. "I came to you excited. I wanted to share the good news, and you just started attacking me out of nowhere. At least attempt to act civil. You're a grown man!"

I took a breath, then another, but it didn't help. I was seething. I reminded myself that I loved her, but this wasn't her. This was how the judge twisted her mind.

I needed to find the right words, and once I thought I had them, I spoke evenly, desperate for her to understand. "Please try to understand why I can't believe you want to take her to see him. What if he breaks her down the same way he broke you? What happens if he disapproves of her the way he disapproved of you?" My anger broke through my resolve, and my voice grew. "What happens when she comes back with bruises all over her body and tells you that she deserved it for not being fucking perfect? What then, Addie?"

She turned like she was about to walk away but spun back. "Fuck you, Travis! How dare you throw that in my face!"

I threw my arms out. "I'm trying to make you see reason!"

Neptune disapproved of our arguing and ran upstairs.

Addison said, "My father would never lay a hand on my daughter."

I shook my head. "She's not just your daughter."

"Yeah, well, it's not your decision, is it?" she seethed.

I barked a laugh. "That's a shit thing to say, and you know it. I'm not Jeanine. This isn't your parent's house where the biological parent makes all the decisions. You invited me into Emmy's life, and I will fight like hell to keep her safe. That means keeping her from the bastard who abused you your entire life. And if that's not enough, I'll go have a conversation with her other biological parent."

We heard the creak in the bottom step, and both looked toward the stairs.

Willa stood there, eyes wide, face ashen. In a soft voice, she said, "Sorry, I was calling your name. I brought Emerson. She's upstairs. I—we could hear you, and I didn't think you heard me."

Addison pinched the bridge of her nose while her other hand rested on her hip. She took a calming breath.

"Does Oli know?" Willa asked.

I had to hand it to her. The woman had guts. She didn't even shrink back at Addison's glare. Instead, she stepped forward and clarified, "About your dad and the abuse?"

Addison shot a look toward me. If looks could kill, I'd be dead a hundred times over.

Addison said, "Travis is making it sound worse than it was."

Willa didn't look like she bought it.

"No, Oliver doesn't know," I said to Willa.

"Travis!" Addison shouted.

I glared at Addie. "I kept your secret for thirteen fucking years, Addison, and look what good it did! It's not just about you anymore, and she's Oliver's daughter, too. He should know what you're exposing her to."

She made a noise of annoyance in the back of her throat. "I would never let him touch her!"

"Even if he never lays a hand on either of you, don't for a second think he won't belittle you in front of your bastard child. Isn't that what he calls her? Him walking out of your life is the best thing that's ever happened to you aside from Emerson. I don't understand your need to get back in his good graces."

"He's not evil, Travis. I shouldn't have to defend him to you. Oliver knows he's a not a bad man."

"Oliver never knew him!" I roared, noticing Willa's absence.

Addison's next words were quiet. "Dammit, Travis. What is it to you? It's not like she's your child!" Her words were a slap in the face.

I took a menacing step forward, my voice low. "You talk to your father for five minutes, and you're already acting like him. You know how much I love that little girl. She might not be my blood, but that doesn't make me love her any less. You always hit below the belt when it comes to the judge."

She shook her head. "Travis, you are way overstepping."

I scoffed. "It's what I should've done years ago, Addison. I let you down before. I'm not gonna let her down too."

Addison glared at me for a moment longer before turning away. "I have to go see my daughter."

I took a moment to calm down before following her upstairs. I found her standing alone at the kitchen sink. She was looking out the back window, watching as Willa pushed Emerson on the baby swing. Oliver stood close to Willa, his eyes fixed on the kitchen window. I'd never seen Oliver look so broken before.

Oliver walked in, closing the door behind him. "Willa

took Emerson outside to play while you had your shouting match." He directed his gaze to Addison. There were so many unspoken words between them. I watched Addison swallow her emotions, barely containing her tears.

Oli shook his head. "How could I not see it? He back-handed you in front of me, and I was angry, but I thought it was the first time. I never imagined you would keep something so important from me. If I knew . . ." He continued shaking his head. "I should've known. I should've recognized it, but I failed you."

Addison lowered her face. "No. No, Oliver. You never failed."

He looked at me. "That's why you've always hated him. It makes sense now. Everything makes a lot more sense." He directed his gaze between us. "How could you keep it from me?"

I said, "I tried to tell you, but you knew I hated him, so you never listened."

He winced. He knew it was true. I never hid my revulsion of the man.

"I should've trusted your instincts, but I was caught up on the good things he'd done." He exchanged a look with Addison, and I felt like I was missing something.

"He's not that man anymore," Addison said, making me see red.

"Bullshit," Oli said. "Just eighteen months ago, he struck you. He backhanded you minutes after you got home from the hospital. He turned us away at Christmas, and he wouldn't come to Emerson's first birthday. If he wants to make amends, he's going to put in the effort. Not the other way around. You're not taking our daughter for a seven-hour car ride to see a man who has physically and verbally assaulted you your entire life. Fuck him, Addison!"

She was all out crying now. I wrapped my arm around her and tried to push Oliver away, but his anger had caught up with him.

"I can't believe you! It makes me question your parenting skills. You wouldn't let your patients go home with an abusive parent, but when it comes to your own daughter, you're fine with putting her in harm's way."

"Of course not, but—"

"There is no but, Addie!" Oliver shouted, then quieted himself. "I can't tell you what to do with your own life, but you're not taking Emmy."

Addison took a deep breath, her anger simmering, and I was waiting for it to explode again.

In a soft voice, I said, "The last time you saw him, you kicked him out of your house. You know we're right. Why are you holding onto a relationship that has only hurt you?"

She looked up at me, and I watched her emotions shift. "The same reason you helped your dad who treated you like shit. He's my father."

I pulled her into my chest, holding her close. In that moment we had an understanding, but Oliver was still seething. "I don't care who he is."

She didn't let go of me as she spoke to Oliver, "Your parents are too good for you to understand."

Oli scoffed, "I don't know what that means."

Addison held onto me for a long time, mumbling, "I know you're right. I won't go."

Oliver still looked angry. When he opened his mouth to speak, I shook my head. Now was not the time to delve into all of the details of Addison's past. We could do that once tempers had cooled and emotions had calmed.

When she finally let go of me, she said, "Why do I still care what he thinks of me?"

I kissed her forehead. "Because you love him even though he doesn't deserve it."

75

ADDISON

IT HAD BEEN A HOT DAY, and even as the sun dipped below the horizon, the evening still felt warm. After work, I went out to dinner with a friend in the city. The evening had finally cooled by the time we left the restaurant. I was still getting used to having girlfriends. It was nice, and I was glad Travis forced me to go out even though so many nights I couldn't wait to get home to him and Emmy. He knew how important it was for me, and I loved that I finally had a couple of friends. After going so many years without true girlfriends, I didn't take friendship for granted.

It was dark by the time I got home. Pulling into the driveway, I noticed the candlelit path to the front door.

"What in the world?"

I got out of my car, walking to the sidewalk that led to the front porch. It was lined with electric votive candles, and blocking the way was a little table with a single purple rose and a card sitting next to it. I picked up the card, flipping it open to see a note.

Follow the trail of purple roses.
    -T

That's when I realized the path wasn't only lined with candles, but dozens of purple long-stemmed roses. Why would Travis get me purple roses?

I walked the path, careful not to step on any roses. I found another note taped to the front door.

Beautiful and delicate, but they wilt and die. Come on in.
    -T

I opened the door carefully, unsure of what to expect. The path of votives continued through the entryway and into the living room. The dim light showed what I thought were rose pedals at first glance, but they were roses that had been cut to pieces, stems and all. They were shredded, just like I had done to my wedding flowers. Rozsa was batting part of a rose around the living room.

There was another table and another card.

It's the path you walked to become the strong independent woman you are today, and I love every piece of you with every fiber of my being. Please join me outside.
    -T

The curtains were drawn over the sliding glass door that led to the backyard. I slid the curtain aside and saw the candlelit path continued outside. There was a note taped to the glass door. A window vase was suctioned to the door with a single crystal rose sitting inside. It shimmered in the light, and I removed it from its vase before reading the note.

Not every rose is delicate or easily broken. They come in all shapes and sizes. Some last a lifetime, and then some.
  -Travis Rose

I slid the door open and found Travis standing at the edge of the patio. My fingers went to my lips, overwhelmed with emotions.

Lights were strung above, and a line of candles led me to him. My lips trembled as I walked forward, feeling like I was in a dream. He wore a dark suit, looking unbelievably handsome. I noticed the shimmering of crystals and stones along the pathway, and then he was there, just in front of me.

"You've never been a delicate rose. In fact, you've never been a Rose at all, but would you like to be? You're an accomplished doctor, so you may not want to change your last name, but I want to spend the rest of my life with you."

He pulled a ring out of his pocket and took my hand in his before kneeling. "Doctor Addison Marie Arthur, will you marry me?"

I nodded, crouching down to take his face between my palms. I kissed him, wrapping my arms around him and never wanting to let go.

But I pulled back. "Yes. One thousand times, yes."

"Thank God." His brown eyes glowed in the flickering lights as he slid the ring onto my finger.

I went to kiss him again, but I heard, "Momma!"

I turned around, and Emerson came running at me with Neptune close behind. Willa and Oliver were slower in their approach.

We were still kneeling, and we wrapped Emerson into our hug, while Neptune licked at our faces.

"Congratulations," Willa said, moving forward.

Oliver frowned. "Have you always hated purple roses?"

I grimaced.

Willa turned to him, wrapping her arm around him. "That's a yes, dear. You need to get over it."

"You like the wildflowers, though, right?" he asked Willa.

"I love them and everything they stand for," she said.

He grinned at her, and I turned back to my little family. Emmy didn't know what was happening, but her excitement fit the event.

"It's not fair," I said to Travis. "You're grand gesture was way more successful than mine."

He laughed. "Thank God for that!"

"I still would've said yes. Even if I came home and the house was on fire. I still would've said yes." I leaned forward and kissed him. "But this was perfect. Now we can begin our happily ever after."

76

TRAVIS

A WEEK after Addison and I got engaged, I went on a little road trip. I didn't tell Addison where I was going. I didn't lie to her, but I may have alluded that I was going into the Columbus office. Instead, I drove to New York to have a sit-down talk with Judge Arthur.

He knew I was coming. He only agreed to it because he thought I was bringing Emerson. If he actually believed I would bring her behind Addison's back, he was a bigger moron than I realized.

They hadn't moved in all the years I knew Addison, and their home still looked very much like a castle. I rang the doorbell and waited. And waited.

Finally, the door opened.

"Where is Emerson?"

Fucking moron. "Oh, gee, how forgetful of me. I forgot to bring her." I couldn't help it. This man brought out the juvenile prick inside me.

He started closing the door, but I put my hand out, stopping him from shutting me out. I was much stronger than him and could take him by force, but I was here to have a civil conversation.

"I'd like to talk with you, man to man."

He looked over my shoulder. "I believe I'm the only man here."

"Addison and I are getting married."

His face went slack, and he gave up on shutting the door. "Over my dead body."

That could be arranged. "May I come in?"

He eyed me a moment longer before stepping back and inviting me in. "When did this development take place?"

"You had to know this was coming. We've been living together for six months."

He spun on me. "You're shacking up with my daughter?"

"Shacking up? Is that what you called it when she lived with Oliver?"

"I thought at least Oliver would treat her with respect, but we all know how that ended."

He led me into his office and shut the door. He motioned to a chair in front of his desk while he went around and sat in the gaudiest throne-looking chair I had ever seen in my life. Its gold embellishment with red upholstery gave off a very royal vibe.

"Nice chair."

"It's an antique worth more than your car."

"Sounds comfortable."

"It's not meant to be comfortable. It's meant to remind anyone across from me who is in charge."

"Why don't you just whip your dick out onto the desk while you're at it." I whistled. "Or is that a touchy subject? Will it not reach?"

"Trash," he sneered.

"Oh shit. My bad, I forgot who was in charge for a second. It's good you have that hideous throne to remind me. I'll be on my best behavior."

Judge Arthur glared at me. "You'll never be able to provide for her, you know."

I scoffed. "What makes you think someone needs to provide for her? Have you met the woman? She's intelligent and independent and stubborn. Oh, and a doctor. She makes her own money in a career she loves. I don't need to provide financially if that's what you mean. But I will be her partner, her best friend, and she has always been the love of my life, but I think you know that. I'd do anything for her. She chose me too. I'm not coming to you for permission because, in my eyes, you gave that up the moment you started demeaning and mistreating your daughter. I want nothing from you. I'm here to make a few things clear. One, I am going to marry Addison. Two, you will not object. Three, if you want to make things right with your daughter, you apologize. If you don't, then stop toying with her and dragging her down the way you always have."

He cleared his throat. "I would think you'd have more respect after I squashed that case against your mother."

"My mom?"

"They arrested her for assault. She spent the night in prison and had a hearing the next day. I dismissed the case because Addison and Oliver found out and begged me to drop it, knowing you would've been on your own at seventeen."

He let those words resonate, knowing he was dealing a big blow. He wanted to knock me off my feet to gain the upper hand.

I tried to keep my face neutral, hiding my confusion. How had I not known anything about this? Unless he was lying.

He leaned forward onto the desk. "I did it from the goodness of my heart, but then I met you and wished I had never helped your mother. You would've been sent to foster care. You would have been a blip in my daughter's life, and she would be in a much better place."

I wanted to believe he was lying, but it explained so much. This was why Oliver had built a blind loyalty to the judge. Fuck. How had I not known? I hated the idea that I may have been part of the reason Addison kept giving her father more credit than he deserved.

I shook my head and stood, towering over him. "You're wrong. At seventeen, I worked a full-time job and maintained a passing GPA. I would've filed for emancipation, which they would've granted me. I don't know what case you're talking about, but I bet my life on my mom's innocence. She may have been a little hot-tempered, but she wouldn't assault someone unless they deserved it. What happened to the person who filed charges?"

"How the hell would I know? You think I remember every name that crosses my desk?"

"You're a piece of shit. Did you even listen to my mom's side of the story?"

The motherfucker grinned, knowing he had gotten under my skin.

"You fucking egomaniac!" I knocked over the chair I'd vacated and watched him flinch. "Is Addison the only woman you beat up to feel powerful, or are there other people out there?"

"I don't beat women. Addison is a drama queen who lets

her emotions rule her. Her mother would be so disappointed—"

I pounded my fist on his desk. "Don't you dare talk about her mother!"

He sat back, glaring at me. "Addison is the reason her mother died, you know. She could've gotten treatment in time."

"What the fuck are you talking about?"

"She had a terrible headache but had promised to take Addison for ice cream. She should've gone to the doctor instead of out for dessert. They may have caught it in time, but she indulged our child and died shortly after."

"If Addison wasn't with her, do you really think she would've gone to the hospital, and even if she did, do you think they would've caught it?"

"We'll never know, will we?"

I looked at him with disgust. "You're a monster. You know what Addison remembers about her mother? She remembers that you always bought her mom lilies. She remembers that her mom would stick up for her. That she would fight on Addison's behalf, against you, her father, because you have always been a bully."

I moved to leave, but stopped in the door, warning, "If you have any sense, you won't fight our engagement. If you make her cry one more time, I will destroy you."

He stood from his throne and walked around his desk. "Allow me to walk you out since you'll soon be my son-in-law. What do you say, son?"

I glared at him. "Don't ever fucking call me that."

"Such a well-spoken man. I heard you received an education, but even the degree can't change your garbage genetics."

As we stepped out into the daylight, Jeanine pulled into

the driveway, and instead of going to the garage, she joined us outside my car.

"Travis! What a pleasant surprise. Is Addison with you?"

We exchanged a brief hug. "No, Addison is working today. It's just a solo trip."

From behind me, the judge said, "Did you know about Addison and Travis's engagement?"

Jeanine looked shocked, and discomfort crossed her features before she tucked it away and smiled as she tiptoed around the subject. "Love is always something to celebrate. I'm happy for you two."

"Thanks, Jeanine. I've gotta get going. It's a long drive back."

"Come back soon," Jeanine called as I slipped into my driver's seat. The judge had already walked back to the door with no desire to see me off. I pulled away and began my trek back home, anxious to see my fiancée.

FOR ONCE, I wasn't speeding. Maybe Oliver had rubbed off on me, or perhaps I drove more carefully now because I had so much to live for. I double-checked my speed as the cop's flashing lights came on behind me. I moved lanes to let the emergency vehicle pass. They merged, too, staying right behind me. I pulled to the shoulder and stopped my car. The lights flashed brightly behind while another patrol car slid into place in front of my car.

What the hell?

I didn't know what he did or how he did it, but the judge was a sadistic motherfucker. I pulled out my phone and sent Addison a quick text.

Me: I'm sorry. I'm in New York and I think I'm about to get arrested.

Addison: What!?! Is this a joke?

Me: No. I don't know how, but it's your father.

My phone rang, and I silenced it, turning it off as the officers flanked my car.

Fuck!

I was compliant as the officers surrounded my vehicle and peeked inside. I answered their questions and did my best to stay calm and respectful. Little did I know the evidence was in plain sight right behind my driver's seat. A diamond ring, sterling cufflinks, and a pearl necklace that the judge claimed I had stolen.

I didn't resist arrest. I had no criminal record, and it was the first and hopefully the last time I would ever be taken into custody.

I reluctantly chose Addison for my phone call. She was understandably angry.

I said, "Remember the time your grand gesture went terribly wrong, but I found it endearing. I hope you look at this in the same light."

Her voice was sharp. "I didn't end up in jail, Travis. This isn't the same."

"You know I didn't do it, right? My windows were cracked. He must have slipped the items into my car while Jeanine distracted me. I wouldn't steal anything from them, and if I had for some reason, I wouldn't leave it out in the open. That doesn't make any sense."

"You're accusing my family of setting you up." Her voice was void of emotion.

"I know Jeanine didn't have anything to do with this."

"You're accusing my father, and my father is accusing you. That's just great."

I worried she wouldn't forgive me for coming to New York behind her back. "I'm sorry, Addie," I breathed. "I'm so sorry. I never should've come here."

"No, you shouldn't have," she rebuked.

All I had accomplished was to put her in a terrible position between her father and myself. I fucking hated that man, and I prayed she could finally see his true colors. "I'll fix this. Don't worry about it. I'll figure this out. I love you."

There was a long pause, and I hung up before I begged her to choose me over her father.

77

ADDISON

My nude high-heels clicked on the marble floors of the courthouse. My white jumpsuit was a strategic move. The light, flowy fabric gave me a carefree look while accentuating my imposing height and strong shoulders. Yet, I retained my femininity with the cinched waist that emphasized my delicate curves. The suit was innocuous or threatening depending on my motive, and I intended to use it to my advantage.

The mid-morning sun glared through the giant arched windows at the front of the courthouse, but I soon lost the natural light as I wove my way through the halls.

The guard outside my father's chambers perked at my approach and blocked the door.

I gave him a pleasant smile. "Hi, Kirt, how are the kids?"

He softened his stance when he realized it was me. "Well, if you aren't a sight for sore eyes. The kids aren't so much kids anymore as they are pain-in-the-ass teenagers."

"Ugh, teenagers. It's just a phase. They'll grow out of it," I said lightly, and he laughed with me. "Is he in?" I asked, gesturing to the door.

"He is, but he asked not to be disturbed."

I rolled my eyes. "Of course he did. He works too hard." I gave him my best version of puppy dog eyes. "Will you make an exception for me?"

He hesitated.

"Please, Kirt. I'll tell him I bribed you or gave you the slip."

He reluctantly stepped aside, saying, "Okay, Addison. I always had a soft spot for you."

"Thanks, Kirt. Give Veronica my best," I said, turning the handle and stepping in, sure to close the door with a click behind me. With my back to my father, I took a calming breath. When I felt steady, I turned around.

He was on the other side of the room, glaring at me from his seat at his desk. "You must have laid it on thick to get past Kirt."

I kept my expression blank as my heels clicked across the room. "Arthurs have a way of getting what they want. Don't we, Daddy?"

He narrowed his gaze. "I suspect you're here about that piece of garbage you're dating."

"You mean, my fiancé. The one you put in jail." I gave a hollow laugh. "My happiness never was a priority to you. I assume you pulled some strings—had him arrested on the evidence I'm sure you planted."

He scoffed. "I'm sure his past just caught up to him."

I raised my brow. "If by past, you mean you, then you're correct."

He stood. "That piece of trash thought he could threaten me. I let it slide once. Never again, Addison."

I had to refrain from screaming, but I would not let him rattle me. "Do you know how many times he begged me to cut you out of my life? Do you know how many times I've defended you? Do you even care? Of course not. You cut me out of your life the moment I made you look bad."

He looked bored. "Is there a point to all of this?"

I pulled the folder out of my shoulder-bag. Tapping it, I said, "I should've listened to Travis a long time ago, but I didn't, at least not about cutting you out of my life." I set the folder on the desk and slid it over to him. "I always wanted to believe that you loved me. I wanted my daughter to meet you. I wanted to hold on to the only family I had, but in the back of my mind, I think I knew that was a fantasy."

I could tell he was dying to open the folder, but he didn't want to look like he cared.

"So, Father, I didn't cut you out of my life, but I started to doubt you. And I started keeping records."

His curiosity or fear got the best of him, and he opened the folder. His brows nit together as he looked at the images.

I rested my fingertips on his desk to keep them from trembling. "Photos of the bruises and cuts you left. The dates, a brief description of the events that led to the abuse."

He was flipping through photos, insisting, "This wasn't me."

I tapped the photo of my cheek. "That imprint is especially damning," I said, the cut matching the insignia of the ring on his finger. He looked at his ring and then back to the photos, his face a mask of horror.

I swallowed. "I can stop by your house and speak to Jeanine. I have copies of all of these. She knew you were hard on me, but she still doesn't know how hard. I never gave her all the details, but she watched you backhand me, which almost led to divorce. After seeing these, she will not only divorce you. She will corroborate my story, as will Travis."

He was quiet.

I leaned onto my steepled fingers, warning, "You will undo this. You will have Travis cleared and released immediately!"

His face still zeroed in on the photos spread across his desk.

I slapped my hand on top of the photos to grab his attention. He startled, looking up at me with frightened eyes.

"You can't undo this," I said, tapping the photos. "That damage is done, but you have until the end of the day to fix what you've done to Travis, or else everything you see will be used against you in a court of law and leaked to the media. I will destroy you. Your reputation, your career, your marriage. It will all be over."

I stood up straight, giving him one last look before turning on my heels and walking for the door.

"Addison," he called when I was across the room.

I paused, glancing back.

Regret was written across his face, tears in his eyes. "I . . . I didn't realize I was . . . so hard on you. I will get Travis out, but these . . . I didn't know I ever left a mark."

I took a step toward him. "That doesn't make it okay. You knew you were hitting me, shoving me, laying your hands on me. And those are just bruises. The worst of it, you can't see. What would Mom think of you now?"

I spun to the door. "Goodbye, Judge Arthur."

I walked out of his office, giving Kirt a friendly smile and thanks. I left the courthouse, going back the way I came in. My heels barely made a sound across the parking lot as I nearly ran to my car. As soon as I was inside, my shoulders slumped, and I had to catch my breath. I wanted to feel like I had won, like I was a badass, but nothing about this felt like winning.

Pulling myself together, I drove to the police station where they were holding Travis. I only hoped he would forgive me.

TRAVIS

Addison came for me. Standing stock-still in the waiting room, she looked intimidating and powerful, but also like a goddess in her white jumpsuit. She drew a lot of attention to herself, though she seemed not to notice. She was lost in thought, wearing a mask of calm, but I knew she must have a flurry of emotions under her calm exterior.

Did she believe her father? Or would she listen to my side?

I ran a hand through my hair, taming it the best I could after spending the night in jail. I walked toward Addison, taking a deep breath. She was the love of my life, but if she couldn't trust me now, after everything we had been through, I would walk away for good. I shouldn't doubt her, but she'd always twisted things and lied to herself when it came to her father.

It took her a moment to notice me, but when she did, she took a deep breath and stepped forward. She looked me over, and I still couldn't tell where we stood. Would I plead with her to believe me?

She closed the gap between us, placing her hand on my jaw with a deep sadness in her eyes. "I'm so sorry, Travis. You shouldn't have come here behind my back, but I understand why you did. This never would've happened if I'd stood up to my father sooner. This is my fault."

The tension drained out of my shoulders, and I cupped her face between my palms. "It's my fault for thinking I could make it better. I only wanted to make it easier for you."

She pulled me forward for a kiss, her arms twining around me. I didn't deserve her.

When she pulled away, she promised, "It will never happen again. I made sure of it."

"What does that mean exactly?"

She glanced around. "Let's get out of here, and we can talk."

I nodded, and we headed for the car.

As soon as she pulled out of the parking lot, she said, "I recognized the pattern in my father. Even as much as I tried to stay optimistic, I knew him hitting me wasn't right. I kept records and photographic proof every time my father lost his temper. I hoped I would never need it, but today I showed my father all the evidence. I doubt it would hold up in court, but it is enough to destroy his reputation and his marriage."

I gawked at her, shocked to hear how far she'd gone and that she had all the evidence. Even after she'd been in denial all these years, a part of her must have known. I was speechless.

She glanced over. "We have to pick up your car from the impound lot."

I nodded.

She sighed. "The saddest part is, I don't think he realized he was hurting me. He was so wrapped up in himself that he didn't see the bruises he left in his wake. Just like I couldn't see how often he twisted the truth and manipulated me."

"But you finally do. You see it?" I probed.

She nodded. "I see it."

I threw my head back. "Fucking finally!"

She looked at me. "He's still my father, but what he did to you was the final straw. I won't make excuses for him anymore."

"Speaking of excuses. Is the stuff about my mom true? Did she get arrested for assault?"

She instantly looked guilty, and I knew we had a lot more to talk about.

SHE DROPPED me at my car, and we both drove to the diner where my mom worked most of her life.

We sat at the counter, and the owner, Bo, greeted us with a friendly smile. "Well, if it ain't Travis and Addison. What the hell are you kids doing here? I thought you both moved far away."

"We did," I said, "But we're back visiting the area."

Addison snickered at that.

He looked me in the eye and said, "We sure miss your momma."

"I do too."

"So what can I get ya?"

We ordered, and while we were waiting, I asked Bo if he knew anything about my mom's alleged assault.

He took a step back. "Your mom made me promise never to talk to you about that."

"So it's true? She assaulted someone?"

On a long sigh, he said, "Well, I might as well tell you now. That was ugly business. That prick turned the tables on her. She was going out to her car after her shift one night, and this guy tried to grab her. She fought him off, broke his nose with her elbow, and the next day he had her arrested for assault. I got his picture on the board in the back. He's on our do not serve list."

"Can I see?"

He nodded. "Sure, let me grab it."

As he disappeared, I peeked at Addison. Her eyes were downcast, and she shook her head. "I should've known it wasn't true. I should've realized it, but I didn't know your mom well at the time."

I placed my palm over her hand on the counter. "It's not your fault, Addison. You still tried to help her."

When Bo came back out, he set a grainy printed photo on the counter. A name was written underneath.

"What is this?" I asked, pointing to the name.

"That's the asshole's name. We got it when he pressed charges."

I didn't recognize him from the picture, but I pulled out my phone to do a quick search of his name. I found out a lot about him in under thirty seconds. His mugshot attached to a news article headlined—*Serial Rapist Sentenced to Life in Prison*—pretty much said it all. I flipped through the story and felt sick to my stomach. I wanted to murder him, but they had locked him up for life.

My mother had successfully defended herself. They should've given her a medal. Instead, the victim was blamed for defending herself. The judge shouldn't have dismissed the case. He should've looked at it and heard my mom's side of the story. He may have prevented this man from hurting anyone else.

"I would like to have another chat with the judge," I said.

I expected Addison to talk me down, but she replied, "I'm going with you."

We forced ourselves to eat, though our appetites had vanished.

WE DROVE to her parent's house separately, and Addison still knew the code to get in. It was clear her parents weren't home yet, but they would be soon enough, so we waited.

She looked around as we wandered through the rooms. "It looks even more like a museum than it used to. He's collected more items since I was here last."

"Maybe buying shit makes him feel like he has a purpose."

She shrugged and led me into the library. She ran her fingers over the table where she used to tutor me. "You know, this has always been my favorite room in this house. I loved the big picture windows, because it's a beautiful view and because it overlooked the driveway, so I always knew to prepare myself when my father came home. The wall of books is my favorite." She spun back to me. "After I would tutor you, your cologne lingered, and it smelled like you in here."

"Damn, was my cologne that strong?"

"No, I was just tuned-in to your scent." She walked to me, wrapping her arms around my waist. "Can I tell you a secret?"

"Always."

She whispered, "I wanted to kiss you so many times in

here. I had all these crazy fantasies where you'd swipe all the books off the table and throw me on it."

I pulled her closer, whispering in her ear, "I had those same fantasies. I always dreamt you'd drop your pencil, and when you were down on the floor picking it up, you'd spot the massive erection I was constantly hiding. Then you would demand to see it and touch it and—you know."

I could feel her smile. She pushed away, walking toward the door. It closed with a loud click, and she turned back to me with a wicked smile. She moved forward, her hand going to the zipper hidden in the side seam of her jumpsuit.

I watched, enraptured, as the white fabric pooled around her ankles. She stood in only a thong and heels, and then she was peeling herself out of her thong.

"Fuck." I bit my knuckles.

"Yes, that's what I had in mind."

"We can't do this here."

She sat on the edge of the table and spread her legs wide, revealing her glistening center. "Can't we?"

I groaned. "What about your parents?"

She lifted her chin toward the window. "We'll be able to see them coming. And it feels right, doesn't it." She put her arms out. "This is where it all started."

Her naked body called to me with her peaked nipples and glistening pussy. I moved forward, wrapping my arms around her. "I'm glad we finally got it right."

"Fucking finally!" she called, as she helped me undress.

I slid inside of her, watching her eyes rolled back, and we went to work, satisfying all of the positions we had fantasized about over the years.

∽

WE HAD ALREADY BEGUN GETTING DRESSED by the time we saw the judge pulling into their long driveway. By the time he came inside, Addison and I were waiting for him in his office.

He had to have spotted our cars out front, but he still looked shocked to find us in his office. We sat in the two seats opposite his desk.

"What is this? Why are you here?" he asked.

Addison gestured to his throne. "Have a seat."

He looked leery but did what she said, watching Addison the whole time. He looked . . . sad. It took some wind out of my sails. I had never seen him look anything other than self-righteous, but the way he eyed Addison now showed grief I didn't think he was capable of.

He finally tore his eyes off Addison long enough to see the article we had pulled up on his glowing computer screen.

"What is this?" he asked.

"This is the man who accused my mother of assault. It was self-defense, and if you had listened to her, you would know that. You didn't help my mom or me. You let a rapist go free."

He sighed, leaning back in his seat and rubbing the bridge of his nose, looking subdued.

I leaned forward. "You've held this like leverage, waiting for the right moment, but it backfired. Just like framing me backfired."

It was less satisfying to throw the truth in his face when he showed some signs of remorse.

Addison stood. "We said what we came to say. Let's go, Travis."

"Not yet." I sat at the edge of my seat. "That ring you accused me of stealing. Where did that come from?"

His eyes met mine. "It belonged to Addison's mother."

Addison looked at her father. "You said you got rid of Mom's things."

He looked at her with a sliver of hope in his expression. "I kept a few items."

"Can I see?" she asked.

He nodded and pulled out a desk drawer. From the drawer, he lifted a lockbox. He unlocked it and spun it toward Addison. Addison leaned over the desk to get a closer look at the items. It was mostly jewelry and a few pictures. Addison looked through the pictures and picked up a necklace. It had a locket, and she opened the delicate clasp.

She sucked in a breath and covered her mouth. I stood behind her, peering over her shoulder. Inside the locket was a picture of mother and daughter. I felt like I was looking at Addison and Emmy's picture, but I knew it was Addison with her mother. Addison looked just like her. On the other side of the locket, it read: *Bloom Little Rosebud.*

Addison was struggling to hold back her tears. I placed a hand on her shoulder, so she knew she wasn't alone.

"Take it," her father said. "It was always meant for you. I just couldn't part with it."

Addison's fingers curled around it possessively. I didn't know whether she would scream or cry, but I knew I needed to get her out of there.

I leaned into her ear. "Come on, Addie. Let's go home."

She glared at her father but nodded to me. As soon as she turned to come with me, he spoke.

"For what it's worth, I am sorry. I didn't realize I . . . I was so hard on you. You're right. Your mom would be very disappointed in me."

She squeezed her eyes shut, and her breath stuttered. I

wrapped an arm around her shoulder and led her out of the room.

We didn't stop until we were outside. I wished we didn't have two vehicles. I didn't want to leave her like this, but we couldn't leave a car here.

"Are you okay to drive?"

She nodded. "Yeah. It will give me some time to think."

"Are you sure?"

She placed her palm over my heart. "I love you. I'm sure. I just can't wait to be at home together."

I nodded, and she got in her car. I closed her door and stepped back, going to my car while she pulled out. I quickly lost sight of her, but I knew where she was going. I got in my car and drove to the cemetery.

I found Addison kneeling next to her mother's grave. I gave her a few minutes of privacy before joining her.

Without looking up, she said, "How'd you know I'd come here?"

"I know you."

She sniffled. "Did you bring the bat in case my zombified mother talks back?"

I laughed. "You know it."

Her shoulders rose and fell. Blowing out a breath, she said, "She used to call me her little rosebud. I completely forgot. I loved it until she died, and then I decided I hated roses. I never let anyone call me a rosebud ever again, but she must've known I was always destined to become a Rose." She gave me a teary smile.

I knelt down next to her. "And we'll live happily ever after."

ADDISON

I HADN'T REALIZED how much of a mistake it was to marry Oliver until I married Travis. The day was a perfect mess. It poured the entire day, so outdoor pictures were a bust, and everyone complained about frizzy hair. The florist had gotten into a minor car accident on the way to deliver our flowers. She was okay. Our flowers were not. They looked as if they'd been tossed around. It was so far from perfect, and I didn't care.

I'd had a picture-perfect wedding, and it remained one of the worst days of my life. But marrying Travis was all I cared about, so frizzy hair and messy flowers didn't matter.

Emerson looked adorable in her flower girl dress, but she'd turned into a very shy two-and-a-half-year-old and was too afraid to walk down the aisle by herself. So we walked together, hand in hand, until she saw all the people. She got scared, and I swooped her up before she could cry and carried her on my hip down the aisle.

Travis smiled at me as I walked toward him. He looked so happy and handsome. I handed Emerson to Oliver, who was

Travis's best man. I knew people gossiped about the dynamic there, but I didn't care what they said. I was happy. I had never been so happy in my life.

We chose to have small wedding parties. Willa was my matron of honor, and Shelby had somehow talked her way into being a bridesmaid. We had grown closer, and I wanted to include her, but Travis had to choose another groomsman once we added her. When he decided on Devon, I questioned it, but I had learned that Devon wasn't a complete tool. He had a softer side to him.

I had a handful of amazing new friends to invite, and I had maintained some of my old friendships too. I was excited that Gracie's mom and sister, Sandra and Marley could make it. Gracie still felt like an angel watching over my shoulder, helping me on the hard days at work.

Oliver's family was there. Willa's parents had come too. I had gone back and forth on whether to send my father an invitation, but he had tried to make amends. In the end Travis and I invited him and Jeanine, and I was happy they were there to witness our happiness. I made it clear my father was not walking me down the aisle. I didn't need anyone to give me away. I was an independent woman, and I was the one giving my heart to the love of my life.

"We finally got it right," Travis whispered in my ear as we danced together.

I nodded. "We finally did."

"And now we have forever."

"Or until death parts us."

He pulled me in closer. "Nah. I'll find you in the afterlife. Now that I have you, I'm never letting you go."

From across the room, I heard a commotion, and Shelby yelled, "Pervert!"

Devon laughed at her disgust. I rolled my eyes. "They've been arguing all day."

Travis spun me away, saying, "Not our problem. Remember, we're in our happily ever after."

I laughed. "Fucking finally!"

EPILOGUE

TRAVIS

IT WAS LATE when I heard Addison come home. I was already in bed, and Neptune perked up from his bed in the corner of the room.

She had been working on another study for a medical journal, which kept her long hours. She usually made her rounds to the kids' rooms and then came to bed. I waited a while, but when she didn't come to bed, I looked at Neptune. "Looks like it's one of those nights, bud."

I climbed out of bed and walked down the hall. Micah was fast asleep in his crib, so I went to Emerson's room. There was Addison, lying next to Emerson in her tiny twin bed. A purring Rozsa cracked an eye to squint at me from her spot at the foot of the bed. I leaned against the doorframe and listened to Emerson tell Addison about her day at school. She was loving kindergarten. Meanwhile, Addison stroked Emmy's hair, looking at her like she was the most precious thing in the world.

Emmy spotted me. "Hey Pops, momma's home." Oliver

would always be Dad to Emmy, but she'd bumped me up to Pops somewhere between two and three years old.

Addison turned to look at me, knowing I busted her.

"I think it's way past both of your bedtimes," I said.

"Aww," Emmy griped.

"He's right," Addison said. "You have to rest up for school tomorrow."

Emmy perked up at that. "And you have to save some fucking lives."

Addison shot me a glare before saying, "That's right, but we don't use the F word. Especially not like that."

"Pops does."

"Pops is an old man. When you're that old, you can say it all you want."

"Fine."

Addison nuzzled Emmy's cheek for a moment before reluctantly leaving her bed. I wrapped my arm around her shoulders and led her to our bedroom.

As she pulled away from me to start changing clothes, she said, "I told you the F-word would come back to bite you in the ass."

"I told her to use it only in special circumstances."

She let out a huff. "She's five!"

"I know. I'll talk to her again."

Suddenly she turned to me with a look of worry. "Our kids are healthy and happy, right?"

I nodded, stepping forward. "Yes. Did you have a rough day?"

"I'm just extra emotional and can't help but worry about them."

"Did you lose someone today?"

She shook her head. "We've gained someone." Her hand went to her belly.

My eyes widened. "Are you pregnant?"

She nodded. "I've done it. I've become one of those crazy women who decided to do the whole pregnancy thing more than once."

I squinted at her. "Addie, you've already done it more than once."

"I know," she cried. "I should know better by now. I know I'll be miserable, but I just love them so much."

I kissed her forehead. "You're an amazing mom, and third times a charm," I said, pulling her into my lap. "I'll be there every step of the way."

She nodded. "And we'll all live happily ever after?"

My arms tightened around her. "Exactly."

ACKNOWLEDGMENTS

Thank you to all my readers for taking the time to read my long-ass book!

Writing acknowledgments never feels like enough. I have the best group of people surrounding me and feel my words never fully express the extent of my gratitude. This book felt especially daunting, and I am incredibly grateful for the fantastic people who helped improve this story. You all deserve sky-written thank-you notes!

To my mom, who was the first to read this book, and of course, you thought it was amazing because you think I'm amazing. I'm so blessed to have your very biased and unconditional support. Thanks for giving me a bighead.

Melissa Di Rienzo, thank you for talking me through the times I wanted to give up. You helped me get over the humps and through the overwhelming spirals. You are a true friend, and without you, I'm not sure I would still be writing. These really are "our" books.

Heather Mackenzie, thanks for diving into this book. Your advice and critiques made a world of difference. You helped to shape this story, and because of you, this book is so much better.

Leah Anastasakis, your feedback was invaluable to this book. I am so grateful our mutual love of Colleen Hoover brought us together. You always awe me with your meticulous assessments and observations. Thank you for helping me make this story the best it could be.

Tim Rezes, I say it every time. Thank you so much. Your support means a ton, and you are a wizard at finding the little mistakes I breeze right over.

Heather Coates, thank you for taking the time to improve my work while simultaneously stroking my ego.

Jenn Redenshek, I'm so glad we roped you into reading the books out of order. Every person offers a fresh perspective, and I am so grateful for your feedback.

Mary Catherine Kline, I still hear your voice in my head. I think of you often and feel lucky to have known you. Cancer is a thief that stole you away from us way too soon. Fuck Cancer!

And of course, I have to thank my husband, who puts up with me when I write for hours on end. Thanks for encouraging me and supporting me even though sometimes I act like a crazy person, and other days (or weeks) we barely see each other because I'm locked away in my writing room. You are my favorite person, and I don't know what I'd do without you.

ABOUT THE AUTHOR

For more from Anna Rezes visit:
www.annarezes.com
www.instagram.com/anna_rezes
www.facebook.com/annarezesauthor
amazon.com/author/annarezes
goodreads.com/author/show/19051292.Anna_Rezes